Susan

THE WHEEL

by Susan Howatch

Howatch

OF FORTUNE

SIMON AND SCHUSTER • NEW YORK

In memory of my uncle, Jack Watney, 1916–1983

Library of Congress Cataloging in Publication Data

Howatch, Susan.
The wheel of fortune.

I. Title.
PS3558.0884W5   1984   813'.54   84-5357
ISBN 0-671-49989-0

The author is grateful for permission to reprint lyrics from "Walk Right
Back" by Sonny Curtis, copyright © 1960 by Warner-Tamerlane Publishing
Corp. All rights reserved.

Contents

PART ONE

ROBERT

1913

---

*I know the many disguises of that monster, Fortune,
and the extent to which she seduces with friendship the
very people she is striving to cheat, until she overwhelms
them with unbearable grief at the suddenness of her
desertion....*

—Boethius
The Consolation of Philosophy

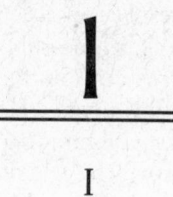

I

How SEDUCTIVE are the memories of one's youth! My cousin Ginevra once said she would never forget dancing with me beneath the chandeliers at Oxmoon while the orchestra played "The Blue Danube." Women are such incurable romantics. I was a romantic myself once but I recovered. A rational disposition must necessarily preclude a romantic outlook on life, and only the failures of this world can afford to dispense with a rational disposition.

No one could have called me a failure. I have always recoiled from the second-rate; whenever I compete I have to come first, and every time I come first I take another step away from that disaster I can never forget, that catastrophe which followed my dance with Ginevra, my own Ginette, beneath the chandeliers at Oxmoon while the orchestra played "The Blue Danube."

However as a rational man I could hardly mourn an adolescent tragedy like a lovesick swain sighing for some lost Arcadia. I admit I still had my maudlin moments, but they seldom survived sunrise, breakfast and the leading article in *The Times.* Recovering from an ill-starred romance is, after all, to anyone of sufficient willpower and self-respect, purely an attitude of mind.

I reminded myself of this proven fact when I opened *The Times* on that May morning in 1913, perused the leading article on the Marconi scandal and then found I could not remember a word I had read. To skim uncomprehendingly through an article on financial machinations is pardonable; nothing can be more boring than high finance at its most convoluted. But to skim uncomprehendingly through an article on the idiotic financial machinations of Isaacs and Lloyd George suggested an absence of mind amounting almost to derangement. I was involved in politics, particularly in Liberal politics. I greatly admired Asquith, the Prime Minister, but Lloyd George, his Chancellor of the Exchequer, was the Welshman in whom I felt a special interest. To find my attention now wandering from the latest headlines in his history was disturbing in the extreme, and after making a mental note to find a new mistress without delay I applied myself to reading the article again. A prolonged abstinence from carnal satisfaction—never a desirable state of affairs—had evidently resulted in a depression which was affecting my powers of concentration, and remedial measures had to be taken without delay.

At this point my man Bennett glided into the room with the morning's post. I sighed with relief. Now I could postpone asking myself why I had lost interest in carnal matters; now I could avoid examining the shining surface of my well-ordered private life for blemishes which logic dictated could not and should not exist. With alacrity I cast aside *The Times*, picked up the paper knife and slit open the envelopes which lay waiting to divert me.

I divided the contents into four piles; invitations, personal notes, bills and rubbish; all business correspondence was delivered to my chambers downstairs. The invitations were wearisome but most of them would have to be accepted. A rising young barrister with unlimited ambition must seize every opportunity to meet the people who matter, but how much more entertaining life would be if the people who mattered had more to recommend them! However, boredom on social occasions is an inescapable hazard for the overeducated, and for the over-ambitious it must be endured with what my mother would no doubt have called Christian resignation.

So much for the invitations. The personal letters included a typically dreary offering from my mother herself—my mother was a good woman but with a provincial cast of mind—an obsequious scrawl from one of my numerous tiresome siblings, but still nothing from my father. That was a pity but evidently he was too busy to escape to London for one of his "little sprees." The remainder of my correspondence, I saw as I unfolded writing paper of varying degrees of opulence, consisted of *billets-doux*. If I had been vain I would have found such attentions flattering but I knew well enough that these society women saw me only as a myth in my barrister's wig and gown. No woman had ever seen me as I really was, no woman except my cousin Ginevra long ago in that lost paradise we had shared at Oxmoon.

So much for the personal letters. I turned to the bills and found them unpleasant but not unreasonable. I was not given to wild extravagances which I considered to be the mark of an inferior intellect. I neither gambled nor showered overpriced gems on music-hall girls. Even when I was not living like a monk I never kept a mistress; my mistresses were kept, usually in great style, by their complaisant husbands. Soon, I knew, I would have to marry in order to further the political career I intended to have, but since I naturally intended to marry money my bank account would hardly suffer when I made the required trip to the altar. I intended to marry into the aristocracy too, but not the impoverished aristocracy, no matter how charming its feminine representatives might be. Man cannot live on charm alone, and an ambitious man cannot live on anything less than wealth, good social connections and substantial political influence. One must be rational about such matters, and being rational need not mean being cold. I had every intention of being fond of my future wife, whoever she might be, and I had every confidence that we would do tolerably well together. Marrying for love might be romantic but I considered it the hallmark of an undisciplined private life. Romance is the opiate of the dissatisfied; it anesthetizes them from the pain of their disordered second-rate lives. I was neither disordered nor second-rate and so I had no need of opiates, just as I no longer had any need of my cousin Ginevra, my own Ginette, now fifteen years married and still living happily ever after in New York.

So much for the bills. Turning to the rubbish I discovered not only circulars and begging letters but also passionate outpourings from disturbed females who apparently thought I wanted to wreck my future political career by making a speech in favor of women's suffrage. I consigned all these effusions to the wastepaper basket, filed the invitations, bills and personal letters in the appropriate pigeonholes of my desk and took a deep breath. My day was about to begin. My life was in perfect order. I was healthy, wealthy and supremely successful and if I were not happy I was a fool.

I was not a fool, therefore I had to be happy.

I *was* happy. Life was exciting, glittering, a perpetually coruscating challenge. First I had to go downstairs to consult my clerk, talk to my fellow attorneys, glance through the new briefs that had arrived. Then I would take a cab to the Old Bailey where I was in the midst of defending a most charming woman who had promised me tearfully that it had been sheer coincidence that she had bought arsenic three days before her husband had died such an unpleasant death; I could not believe this but the jury would—by the time I had finished with them. Later I would dine out. The McKennas were giving a political dinner party and I had heard Lloyd George was to be present; my young hostess Pamela would make much of me and to repay her I would be debonair and charming, stifling my yawns as the ladies rattled on interminably about the wedding of Princess Victoria Louise. But after the ladies had withdrawn and the port was circulating the real business of the evening would begin.

We would talk of politics; I would keep respectfully silent as Lloyd George discussed Welsh Disestablishment—but if he were to ask me for my opinion I would, of course, have a few well-chosen words prepared. Then no doubt someone would say what a bore the suffragettes were and someone else would say what a bore most women were anyway, and Lloyd George and I would look at each other, two Welshmen in the land of our masters, and wonder how English gentlemen ever summoned the effort to reproduce themselves.

Then the port would go round again and we would talk of Turkey and Bulgaria and the Kaiser and the Dreadnoughts until propriety forced us to join the ladies in the drawing room and talk of Caruso, Melba and the rising price of pre-Raphaelite paintings. However I would escape before eleven; someone was sure to invite me to Brooks's or some other club, but I would have to retire to my chambers and burn the midnight oil in order to ensure that I won my case on the morrow. By the time I went to bed I would be exhausted, too exhausted to lie awake and think maudlin thoughts, but when I awoke at six another enthralling day would be waiting for me—for I was so lucky, always fortune's favorite, and I had everything I had ever wanted, everything but the life I longed to lead with

11

the woman I could never have, but what did such sentimental aspirations matter when I was so happy, success personified, forever coming first and winning all the way along the line?

I told myself I could not be unhappy because it was logically impossible. But then I remembered those Greek philosophers, all eminently sane and rational, arguing with inexorable logic towards a truth which turned out to be not a truth but an absurdity. Zeno had proved everything in the world was fixed and unchanging, Heraclitus had proved everything in the world was changing continuously, and both men had provided impeccable arguments to support their points of view. But reality, as Democritus had later tried to show, had all the time lain elsewhere.

I saw a chaotic world of infinite complexity where reason was impotent, and instinctively I recoiled from it. I had long since decided that a successful life was like a well-ordered game governed, as all games were, by rules. One grew up, learned the rules, played one's chosen game and won. That was what life was all about. Any fool knew that.

But what was the nature of my chosen game? And how had I wound up in this particular game in the first place? And suppose it was the wrong game? And if it was the wrong game then what was the point of winning it? And if winning was meaningless what was my life all about? And if I had no idea what my life was all about, did this mean my life was in a mess and if my life was in a mess did this mean I was a failure? And what exactly had I failed to do and how could I repair the omission when I had no idea what I had left undone?

The telephone rang in the hall.

"I'm not in!" I shouted to Bennett as he emerged from the pantry.

The ringing ceased as Bennett addressed himself to the instrument. Presently I heard him say, "One moment, Mr. Godwin, I thought he'd left but it's possible—"

I sprang to my feet and sped to the hall.

"Papa?" I said into the mouthpiece as Bennett yielded his place to me. "Is something wrong?" There was no telephone at Oxmoon, and I thought such an unexpected communication might herald news of a family disaster, but I was worrying unnecessarily. My father's letter telling me of his imminent visit to London for a "little spree" had gone astray; he had arrived late on the previous evening at his club, and finding no note from me awaiting him there he was now telephoning to ask when we could meet.

"—and I've got the most extraordinary news, Robert—"

For one aghast moment I wondered if my mother was pregnant. My parents had an obsession with reproducing themselves and were the only couple I knew who had celebrated their silver wedding anniversary with such undisciplined zest that an infant had arrived nine months later to mark the occasion.

"—and I wonder if I should tell you over the telephone or whether I should wait till I see you—"

"My God, it's not Mama, is it?"

"What? Oh no, she's fine, in capital form, sent you her love and so on—"

"Then what is it? What's happened?"

"Well, it's about Ginevra. She—hullo? Robert?"

"Yes, I'm still here. Go on."

"What?"

"What's the news about Ginette?"

"Well, there's no need to shout, Robert! I may be on the wrong side of fifty now but I'm not deaf!"

"God Almighty, I swear I shall go mad in a moment. My dear Papa, could you kindly tell me with as much speed as possible—"

"It's Ginevra's husband. He's dead, Robert. She's coming home."

II

In my dreams I always said to her, "Take me back to Oxmoon, the Oxmoon of our childhood. Take me back to Oxmoon and make it live again."

How seductive indeed were the memories of my youth, and the older I grew the more alluring they became to me until they assumed the gilded quality of myth. If romance is the opiate of the dissatisfied, then surely nostalgia is the opiate of the disillusioned, for those who see all their dreams come true and find themselves living in a nightmare. The present may be ungovernable, crammed with questions that have no answers, and the future may be unimaginable, obscured by doubt and bewilderment, but the past thrives with increasing clarity, not dead at all but running parallel to the present and often seeming, in my memory, more real than the reality of my daily life in 1913.

At the beginning of my life there were my parents, who were hardly more than children themselves, and at Oxmoon with my parents was this grubby little girl who talked to me, pinched me, played with me, slapped me, helped me to walk and generally made herself useful. She was somewhat stout and vain as a peacock; she was always standing on tiptoe to examine her ringlets in the looking glass. For the first few years of my life I found her full name impossible to pronounce, but she was gracious and permitted me to use an abbreviation, a favor that was never granted to anyone else.

I seem always to have known she was not my sister. "You're not my sister, are you?" I said to her once, just to make sure, and she exclaimed, "Heavens, no— what an idea!" and was most offended. She knew I disliked sisters. Later she explained to me, "I'm Bobby's cousin," although when I asked her how that could be possible when my father was so much older than she was, she snapped, "Ask no questions and you'll be told no lies," which meant she had no idea.

I thought that if this story was true she should call my father "Cousin Bobby" but in truth my father, still resurrecting his bankrupt estate from the grave, hardly had the time to concern himself with a minor detail of family etiquette. Later when my mother had recovered from the nightmare of her first years at Oxmoon she became more strict about what she called "doing the done thing," but even then Ginette usually forgot to address her guardian as "Cousin" so the exact nature of the relationship between us was never stressed.

Eventually I discovered that her father and my grandfather had been half-brothers; her father, the child of a second marriage, had been the younger by twenty years, a circumstance that meant he belonged more to the generation of his nephew, my father, than to the generation of his half-brother, my grandfather. He had spent his early childhood at Oxmoon and in later life long after he had removed to the English Midlands, he and my father had remained good friends. My father had even borrowed money from him when the reconstruction of the Oxmoon estate was begun, so presumably the ties of affection which united them had remained strong; that those ties survived unimpaired despite the borrowing of money was demonstrated when my great-uncle drew up a will in which he named my father the guardian of the infant Ginevra. Within a month he had died of typhoid, and his young widow, who must have been a tiresome creature, went into a decline and eventually managed to starve herself to death on the nearest picturesque chaise longue.

I was nine months old when Ginette came to live with us, and Oxmoon was barely habitable at the time. My parents pretended to occupy the entire house but in fact lived in three rooms on the ground floor. However despite my parents' straitened circumstances it never crossed their minds that they might make some other provision for Ginette and they always treated her as if she were their daughter. No doubt my father's affection for her father made any other course of action unthinkable to him, while my mother too would have felt bound by an absolute moral duty.

"Poor little me!" said Ginette later when she reflected on her predicament. "But never mind, all the best heroines are beautiful orphans, abandoned to their fate, and the one thing that's certain about my situation is that I'm going to be a heroine when I grow up."

"Can I be a hero?"

"Well, I suppose you can try. But you'll have to try very hard."

I can remember that moment clearly. My parents had by that time reoccupied the whole house, but we had left the nurseries to escape from the smell of boiled milk and wet nappies and were heading for the kitchen garden to rifle the strawberry beds. Ginette wore a white pinafore with an egg stain on it, and there were holes in both her stockings. She must have been about eight years old.

"I don't think you're at all likely to be a heroine," I said, aggrieved by her pessimism on the subject of my heroic potential.

"Why, what impertinence! Here I am, being constantly noble by devoting all my time to you even though you're two years younger and a boy and do nothing but drive me wild! The truth is that if I wasn't a heroine I wouldn't do it. I think I'm wonderful."

We gorged ourselves on the strawberries in silence, but eventually I said, "Heroes have to marry heroines, don't they."

"Of course. But actually I don't believe I'll marry anyone. Think of all the nasty smelly babies one would have to have!"

14

We shuddered.

"Friendship's best," I said, "and friendship's forever because no baby can come along to spoil it." And when I grabbed her hand she laughed and we ran off down the path together to our secret camp in the woods.

We had decided while my sister Celia was an infant that babies were undesirable. Unfortunately in our family a new baby arrived every eighteen months but to our relief they all, apart from Celia, failed to survive. Charlotte lived a year but succumbed to measles. William breathed his last within a week of his birth and Pamela faded away at the age of six months. Only Celia flourished like a weed, whining around our ankles and trying to follow us everywhere, but I took no notice of her. I was the male firstborn and I came first. That was a fact of nursery life, as immutable as a law of nature.

"First is best, isn't it?" I said to my father as we walked hand in hand through the woods past the ruined Norman tower, and he smiled as he answered, "Sometimes!"—which, as I knew very well at the age of eight, meant "Yes, always."

"First is best, isn't it?" I said to my mother in the housekeeper's room after my eighth birthday when she decided to increase my pocket money by a ha'penny a week. In the affable atmosphere generated by this gesture I had decided the time was ripe to seek reaffirmation of my privileged status.

"What, dear?"

"I said first is best, isn't it?"

"Well, that depends," said my mother. "I was the second in my family and I always thought *I* was the best—but then my father spoiled me abominably and gave me ideas quite above my station. In fact I think that for a time I was a very horrid little girl indeed."

That was when I first realized the most disconcerting difference between my parents: my father told me what I wanted to hear and my mother told me what she felt I ought to hear. Resentment simmered. I sulked. When Lion was born a month later I knew straight away that I was outraged.

I waited for him to die but soon I realized that this was not the kind of baby who would oblige me by fading away into the churchyard at Penhale. I tried to ignore him but found he was not the kind of baby, like Celia, who could be ignored. He was huge and imperious. He roared for everyone's attention and got it. My mother began in my opinion to behave very foolishly indeed. I felt more outraged than ever.

"Robert dearest," said my mother after overhearing my declaration to Olwen the nursemaid that I had no intention of attending the christening, "I think it's time you and I had a little talk together."

My mother was famous for her "little talks." Her little talks with servants were conducted in the housekeeper's room and her little talks with children were conducted upstairs in the large bedroom that belonged by tradition to the master and mistress of the house. My mother had a table there where she did her sewing, but when she had an arduous interview to conduct she always sat at her dressing table and pretended to busy herself with rearranging the pots, jars and boxes lined up below the triple looking glass. My mother seldom glanced directly at her victims

15

while she spoke, but watched them constantly in the cunningly angled reflections.

"Now, Robert dearest," she said, emptying a jar of pins and beginning to stick them with mathematical precision into a new pincushion, "I know quite well you think of yourself as a little prince in a fairy tale, but because I love you and want the best for you"—a quick glance in the mirror—"I think it's time someone told you a few home truths. The first truth is that you're not a prince, and the second truth," said my mother, turning to look at me directly, "is that this is no fairy tale, Robert."

She paused to let me digest this. I contented myself with assuming my most mutinous expression but I took care to remain silent.

"I thought life was a fairy tale once," said my mother, resuming her transformation of the pincushion. "I thought that until I was sixteen and came to Oxmoon—and then, when I found myself face to face with what really went on in the world, I felt angry with my parents for failing to prepare me for it. However," said my mother, glancing into the far mirror, "now is hardly the time for me to talk to you about the ordeal your father and I endured at the hands of his mother and Mr. Bryn-Davies. You're too young. Suffice it to say that the world is a very wicked place and that one has to be very resolute to lead a decent orderly life— and you do want to lead a decent orderly life, don't you, Robert? People who have no self-discipline, who are perpetual slaves to all their weaknesses, are inevitably very unhappy indeed. In fact I would go so far as to say," said my mother, pinning away busily, "that tragedy inevitably lies waiting for Those Who Fail to Draw the Line."

"Yes, Mama." It took a great deal to cow me but I was cowed—not by this familiar reference to drawing the moral line but by the mention of the Great Unmentionable, my grandmother and Mr. Bryn-Davies. Even though I was only eight years old I knew that Oxmoon had not always been a pastoral paradise where little children wandered happily around the kitchen garden and feasted at the strawberry beds.

"So we must always reject morally unacceptable behavior," said my mother, tipping the rest of the pins from the jar and aligning them between two scent bottles, "and one kind of behavior that is morally unacceptable, Robert, is jealousy. Jealousy is a very wicked emotion. It destroys people. And I won't have it, not in this house—because *here I have my standards*," said my mother, facing me again, "*and here I Draw the Line.*"

I opened my mouth to say, "I'm not jealous!" but no words came out. I stared down at my shoes.

"There, there!" said my mother kindly, seeing I had fully absorbed her homily. "I know you're a good intelligent boy and I now have every confidence that you'll behave well towards Lionel—and towards Celia—in the future."

I retired in a rage. When I found my father I said, "Mama's been very rude to me, and if you please, sir, I'd be obliged if you'd tell her not to be so horrid in future." But my father said abruptly, "I won't hear one word against your mother. Pull yourself together and stop behaving like a spoiled child."

I ran away and hid in a basket in the wet laundry. I realized that my father,

16

who normally never said a cross word to me, had been suborned into sternness by my mother, while my mother, normally affectionate enough, had been rendered hostile by her irrational desire to place the infant on an equal footing with me. I felt I was being subjected to a monstrous injustice. Vengeance should be mine; I decided to repay.

Leaving the wet laundry, I prowled around the house to the terrace and found two of the estate laborers installing a new pane of glass in the dining-room window. The previous pane had been cracked when a sea gull had flown into it in an indecent haste to return to the coast which lay a mile away beyond Rhossili Downs. When the laborers had retired I remained, eying the new pane meditatively. Then I extracted a croquet ball from the summerhouse, returned to the terrace and took a quick look around. No one appeared to be in sight but unfortunately the new pane was reflecting the light so that I could not see the maid who was setting the table in the room beyond. When the croquet ball crashed through the window she dropped six plates and ran screaming to my mother.

My mother went to my father and my father lost his temper. This was a great shock to me because I had not realized he had a temper to lose. Then he beat me. That was an even greater shock because he had never laid a finger on me before; he always said he had a horror of violence. Finally he summoned my mother and when he told her it was high time I was sent away to school, my mother agreed with him.

I cried. I said they wanted to get rid of me so that Lion could be first and best. I told them they were making a very big mistake and that they would both live to regret it.

"What rubbish!" said my father, still in a towering rage, but my mother, whom I had thought so implacable, knelt beside me and said, "There, there! You always knew you'd be going off to Briarwood when you were eight—you can't pretend now that you're being sent away to make room for Lion!"

But I recoiled from her. She was responsible for Lion and Lion was responsible for my humiliation. I turned to my father, and then miraculously the violent stranger vanished as he swung me off my feet into his arms. All he said was, "Don't you worry about Lion," and that was when I knew first was still best in his eyes despite all my iniquity; that was when I knew nothing mattered except coming first and staying first, over and over again.

"I'll be the best pupil Briarwood's ever had," I said to him, "and you'll be prouder of me than you could ever be of anyone else"—and thus I was committed to the compulsive pursuit of excellence and set squarely on the road to disaster.

III

"It's Ginevra's husband. He's dead, Robert. She's coming home," said my father twenty-three years later, and my immediate reaction was This time I shall come first. This time I'm going to win.

"What an amazing piece of information! Well, I daresay it'll be rather amusing to see the old girl again." I was almost unconscious with emotion. I had to lean against the wall to ensure that I remained upright. "When does she arrive?"

"I don't know. I'll show you her wire when we meet tonight. . . ." My father went on talking but I barely heard him. I was only just aware that I was arranging to meet him at the Savile after my dinner party. When the conversation ended silence descended on the hall, but in my memory I could hear the orchestra playing in the ballroom at Oxmoon and see the candles shimmering on the chandeliers.

I thought of my mother saying long ago, "This is no fairy tale, Robert." But who was to say now that my own private fairy tale could never come true? If I got what I wanted—and I usually did—then I would go home at last to Oxmoon, the Oxmoon of my childhood, and Ginette would share my life once more in that lost paradise of my dreams.

The prospect stimulated such a powerful wave of euphoria that I almost wondered if I should become a romantic again, but fortunately my common sense intervened and I restrained myself. This was a situation that called for care, calculation and a cool head. The jilted hero who still yearned passionately for his lost love might possibly seem attractive in a French farce but it was quite definitely a role which I had no wish to play in public.

Thinking of roles reminded me of the living I had to earn, and an hour later, masked by my barrister's wig and gown, I had slipped back into my familiar role as the hero of the Old Bailey.

But all the time I was thinking of Ginette.

IV

I survived a day that would normally have reduced me to exhaustion and arrived, clear-eyed and fresh, at my father's club soon after eleven that night. The idea of a widowed Ginette was a powerful stimulant. I felt taut with nostalgia, prurient curiosity, sexual desire and impatience. It was a lethal mixture, and as I drifted through the rooms in search of my father I half-feared that I might be vibrating with excitement like some wayward electrical device, but fortunately all my acquaintances who accosted me assumed I was merely excited by the result of the trial.

When I finally reached the corner where my father was waiting I found he had

18

Lion with him. I assumed a benign expression and prayed for tolerance.

"I hear you won your case, Robert!" my father was saying with enthusiasm. "Very many congratulations!"

"Thank you. Hullo, Lion."

"Hullo, Robert—I can't tell you how proud I am to be related to you! Why, I'm famous at the bank just because I'm your brother!" He sighed with childlike admiration, a huge brainless good-natured youth towards whom I occasionally contrived to feel a mild affection. It seemed preposterous to think that I could ever have wasted energy being jealous of him. Graciously I held out my hand so that he could shake it.

"Well, Lion," said my father mildly when further banalities had been exchanged, "I won't detain you—as you tell me you have such trouble getting to work on time in the mornings I'm sure you'll want to be in bed before midnight."

But Lion wanted to hear more about the trial and ten minutes passed before he consented to being dispatched.

"Stunning news about Ginevra, isn't it!" he remembered to add over his shoulder as he ambled off. "Won't it be wonderful to see her again!"

I smiled politely and refrained from comment, but seconds later I was saying to my father in the most casual voice I could muster, "Let's see this wire she sent."

The missive was almost criminally verbose. I have come to believe women should be banned from sending cables; they are constitutionally incapable of being succinct in a situation that demands austerity.

DARLINGS, gushed this deplorable communication, SOMETHING TOO DREADFUL HAS HAPPENED I HARDLY KNOW HOW TO PUT IT INTO WORDS BUT CONOR IS DEAD I STILL CAN'T BELIEVE IT ALTHOUGH I SAW IT HAPPEN HE MUST BE BURIED IN IRELAND SO I AM TAKING HIM THERE AT ONCE I CAN'T STAY HERE ANYWAY IT'S NOT POSSIBLE I'LL WRITE FROM DUBLIN ALL I WANT IS TO COME HOME TO OXMOON LONGING TO SEE YOU ALL DEEPEST LOVE GINEVRA.

"Typical," I said. "She squanders a fortune on a wire but still manages to omit all the relevant details of her predicament. She seems to assume we'll know by telepathic intuition when she plans to arrive in Wales."

"My dear Robert, don't be so severe! The poor girl's obviously distraught!"

"To be distracted is pardonable. To be incoherent is simply unobliging. However I suppose in due course we'll get a letter. What was Mama's response to the news?"

"Well, naturally," said my father, "her first thought—and mine—was for you."

I took a sip from my glass of brandy before saying in what I hoped was my most charming voice, "I assume my mother sent you to London to find out exactly what was going on in my mind. Perhaps when you return you could be so kind as to remind her that I'm thirty-one years old and I take a poor view of my mother trespassing on my privacy."

My father stiffened. I immediately regretted what I had said but he gave me no chance to retract those words spoken in self-defense. With a courtesy that put me to shame, he said, "I'm sorry you should find our concern for you offensive,

Robert. I'm sure neither of us would wish to pry into your private life."

"Forgive me—I expressed myself badly—I've had such an exhausting day—"

"Bearing the past in mind we can't help but be concerned. And of course, as you must know, we've been increasingly anxious about you for some time."

"My dear Papa, just because I'm taking my time about marrying and settling down—"

"I wasn't criticizing you, Robert. I wish you wouldn't be so ready to take offense."

"I'm not taking offense! But the thought of you and Mama worrying about me when I'm having this dazzling career and enjoying life to the full is somehow more than I can tolerate with equanimity!"

"Your mother and I both feel that if only you could come back to Oxmoon—"

"Please—I know this is a painful subject—"

"It's as if you've got lost. Sometimes I think it don't do for a man to be too educated—or too successful. It cuts him off from his roots."

"I'm not cut off. Oxmoon's my home and always will be, but for the moment I must be in London. I have my living to earn at the bar and soon I'll have a political career to pursue—and it was you, don't forget, who wanted me to go into politics!"

"I just wanted you to be the local M.P. More fool me. I should have listened to Margaret when she said you'd never be satisfied until you'd wound up as Prime Minister."

"What's wrong with being Prime Minister?"

"Success on that scale don't make for happiness. Look at Asquith. Why does he drink? I wouldn't want you to end up a drunkard like that."

"Asquith's not a drunkard. He's a heavy drinker. There's a difference."

"Not to me," said my father, looking at his untouched glass of brandy, "and not to your mother either."

We were silent. There was nothing I could say. My father was the son of a drunkard and had endured a horrifying childhood about which he could never bring himself to speak. No rational debate on drink was possible for him.

At last I said neutrally, "We seem to have wandered rather far from the subject of Ginette."

"No, it's all one, we're still discussing your obsessions. Robert," said my father urgently, leaning forward in his chair, "you mustn't think that I don't understand what it is to be haunted by the past, but you must fight to overcome it, just as I've fought to overcome the memory of my parents and Owain Bryn-Davies—"

"Quite, but aren't we wandering from the point again? Let me try and end this Welsh circumlocution by exhibiting a little Anglo-Saxon bluntness! You and Mama, it seems, are worried in case I now resurrect my adolescent passion for Ginette and embark on some romantic course which you can only regard as disastrous. Very well. Then let me set your mind at rest by assuring you that I'm not planning to conquer Ginette as soon as she sets foot again on Welsh soil."

"And afterwards?"

"Papa, I'm not a prophet, I'm a lawyer. I don't waste time speculating about the future on the basis of insufficient evidence."

"Of course not, but—"

"The one inescapable fact here is that Ginette is now a stranger to me. Who knows what I shall think of her when we meet again? Nobody knows, it's unknowable, and so in my opinion any attempt to answer such a question can only be futile."

"That's true. But all the same—"

"Go home and tell Mama," I said, "that I no longer believe in fairy tales—and tell her too," I concluded strongly, "that despite the somewhat dramatic nature of these circumstances I have every intention of behaving like a mature and intelligent man."

Yet all the while I was speaking in this commendably sensible manner I was listening to the voice in my mind whispering to Ginette as it had whispered so often in my dreams: "Take me back to Oxmoon, the Oxmoon of our childhood. Take me back to Oxmoon and make it live again."

V

"Friendship's forever!" said the child Ginette in that lost paradise of Oxmoon when I had no rival for her affections. "I wonder if you can possibly realize how lucky you are to have a friend like me?"

I did realize. During my first term at school I had spent many a homesick night imagining her playing with Gwen de Bracy or Angela Stourham and forgetting my existence. When one is eight and has a friend of ten one is perpetually worrying for fear one may be dismissed in favor of more sophisticated contemporaries.

"No matter how long I'm away at school I'll always come first with you, won't I?" I said, anxious to quash any lingering insecurity generated by my absence.

"Always. Here, lend me a penny, would you? I want to buy some of those boiled sweets."

We were in the village of Penhale, two miles from Oxmoon, and enjoying one of our regular excursions to the village shop. I remember thinking as I stood in the dark cozy interior and gazed at the tall jars of sweets that perfect happiness consisted of returning home from school and finding everything unchanged, Ginette still with the holes in her stockings and the stains on her pinafore, the jars in the village shop still waiting to gratify our greed.

"I wish it could be like this forever," I said as we walked home munching our purchases.

"I don't. I'm becoming partial to the idea of growing up and getting married, like Bobby and Margaret. They're always laughing and behaving as if marriage was rather a lark."

"But think of all the babies!"

"Maybe they'd be rather a lark too."

I was silent. My dislike of infants had remained unchanged, although I now took care to conceal this from my parents. I was aloof but polite to Celia. I feigned an Olympian interest in Lion. But I was still quite unable to imagine myself responding to a sibling with genuine enthusiasm.

Then, two years after Lion was born, John arrived in the world.

Lion was livid. That automatically pleased me, and from the beginning I patted John's head when I made my regular visits to the nursery to inspect him. This delighted my mother but Lion was enraged and tried to block my path to the cradle by flailing his little fists at my knees. My mother became cross with him. Their discord was most gratifying.

Finally, much to my surprise, I realized I was becoming genuinely interested in the infant. He was acute. He talked at an early age, a fact that made communication less of an effort. Although we lived in an English-speaking area of Wales Welsh was my father's first language, and because he wanted his children to grow up bilingual my mother had followed a policy of employing Welsh-speaking nursemaids. However for some reason although we all grew up with a rudimentary knowledge of Welsh colloquialisms, John was the only one who became bilingual. This impressed me. After Celia and Lion, who were both stupid, I had not anticipated the advent of an intelligent brother. Later, as an intellectual experiment, I taught him a letter or two and found him keen to learn, but before we could advance further into the world of literacy I was obliged to depart for my first term at public school and the lessons fell into abeyance. However when I returned from Harrow for the Christmas holidays, there was John, waiting for me on the doorstep, eyes shining with hero worship.

Here was someone who had realized, even at a tender age, that first was best. My private opinion of siblings underwent a small but telling revision.

"I think that child might turn out reasonably well," I remarked to Ginette as he waited on us hand and foot in the holidays.

"Isn't he a poppet? So different from ghastly Lion. Honestly, I can't think what Margaret sees in that monster. If ever I give birth to something so plain and stupid, I hope I'd have the sense to drown it."

She was fifteen. I was thirteen. The gap in our ages was widening but I was unaware of it. As far as I was concerned she was still my own Ginette and paradise was still coming home to Oxmoon and finding her waiting to welcome me back; paradise was still riding with her over the Downs or walking to the sea or scrambling across the tidal causeway called the Shipway where long ago Mr. Owain Bryn-Davies had drowned and my grandmother had gone mad and my father had witnessed all manner of horrors which were now enshrined in local myth; paradise was laughing over such distant melodrama and saying how droll it was that dotty old Grandmama should ever have played the role of the tragic heroine. We laughed, how we laughed, and paradise was laughing with Ginette at Oxmoon while we played croquet on the lawn and paradise was suppressing laughter in church as I tried to make her giggle at the wrong moment and paradise was laughing at her latest three-decker novel which she found so romantic and laughing as she tried to box my ears and laughing as we rode to hounds with the West Gower hunt, laughing, laughing, laughing from Llangennith to Porteynon, from

22

Penrice to Oxwich, from Penhale to Rhossili, from Llanmodoc Hill to Cefn Bryn, and paradise was the Gower Peninsula, sixteen miles of heaven on earth stretching westwards into the sea beyond the industrial wasteland of Swansea, and the glory of Gower was Oxmoon and the glory of Oxmoon was Ginette.

It remained so clear in my mind, that paradise lost, the blue skies, the corn stubble, the lush stillness of the bluebell woods, the purple of the heather on the Downs, the brilliant sea, the shimmering sands. I remember even the golden shade of the lichen on the dry-stone walls and the streaks of pink in the rocks on the summit of Rhossili Downs and the coarseness of the grass in the sand burrows of Llangennith. I remember the cattle being driven to market along the dusty white roads and the sheep being herded across the Downs; I can hear the larks singing and the Penhale church clock celebrating a cloudless high noon. It all seemed so immutable. I thought nothing would ever change. And then in the June of 1896, shortly after I had celebrated my fourteenth birthday, my father wrote to me at Harrow.

My dear Robert, I read, *this is just a quick line to let you know we've had a spot of trouble with Ginevra. To put the matter in a nutshell, I can only tell you that she tried to elope with a cousin of the Kinsellas but he's gone away now and Ginevra's staying with the Applebys while she recovers. I'm afraid she's cross with us at the moment, but I'm sure it won't last so don't distress yourself—it was really just a little storm in a teacup and no harm's been done. I remain as always your very affectionate father,* R.G.

At first I was so stunned by this communication that I was incapable of action. I merely sat and stared at the letter. I had, of course, been aware that Ginette was growing up in various ways which were all too visible but I had long since decided it would be kindest to take no notice; I felt genuinely sorry for anyone who had to grow up into a woman. But the thought that she might now be old enough to take a carnal interest in the opposite sex had never occurred to me. I found the notion both horrifying and repellent, but far more horrifying and repellent was the knowledge that she could have cared deeply about someone other than myself. I had thought myself safe till she was eighteen and put her hair up—by which time I would be sixteen and, puberty permitting, fit to present myself as a future husband without arousing either her laughter or her incredulity. But now I was so young that I could hardly stake a claim without looking ridiculous. My voice had not finished breaking. I was too lanky. None of my clothes seemed to fit me. I had decided that surviving adolescence was purely an attitude of mind but now when I contemplated the utterly unfinished nature of my physique I was in despair. How could I ever compete with a full-grown male who displayed predatory intentions? The entire future had become a nightmare.

In agony I reread the letter in the vain hope that I had misinterpreted it, and this time the news seemed so preposterous that I seriously wondered if my father had gone mad. The theory seemed all too plausible. I remembered my grandmother, locked up in a Swansea lunatic asylum and allowed home only once a year, and the next moment before I could stop myself I was writing urgently to my mother for reassurance.

My dearest Mama, I began, determined to conceal my panic behind a civil, rational epistolary style, *I have just had the most extraordinary letter from Papa. In it he appears to state that Ginette has left Oxmoon and is staying at All-Hallows Court. Is there perhaps some misunderstanding here? Ginette thinks Sir William Appleby an old bore and Lady Appleby dry as dust, and as for that lily-livered Timothy, Ginette and I both agree that you could put him through a mangle and wring out enough water to fill a well. How can she choose to live with such people? I suspect someone is not being quite honest with me about this.*

Have you and Papa thrown her out of Oxmoon because you suspect she's lost her virtue? If so please accept my respectful assurance that you must be mistaken: she would never lose it. The heroines of those dreary novels she reads always preserve themselves most conscientiously, and Ginette is well aware that Fallen Women are inevitably doomed to a tragic fate. (Please excuse any indelicacy here and kindly attribute any unwitting coarseness to my inexperience in writing on such subjects.) Anyway, how could any cousin of the Kinsellas' be less than sixty years old? I didn't even know they had any relatives except for some bizarre Irish connection which they do their best to conceal.

Dearest Mama, please believe me: even if Ginette were partial to gross behavior, for her to lose her virtue to a man over sixty must surely be physically impossible, and for her to lose her virtue to an Irishman of any age is mentally inconceivable. Please, I beseech you, write and tell me what's really going on. Ever your affectionate and devoted son, ROBERT.

I then wrote Ginette a fevered note in which I begged her to solve the mystery at once, but it was my mother who answered by return of post; Ginette failed to reply. My mother wrote with calm fluency: *My dearest Robert, I am so sorry that you should have been so distressed. I know that was the last thing your father desired when he wrote to you, but your father, though acting with the best will in the world, finds it hard to adopt a blunt, or one might almost say an Anglo-Saxon, approach to unpalatable facts. This is neither a fault nor a virtue but merely a racial difference which one must recognize and accept. However let me do what I can to clarify the situation.*

First of all let me assure you that nothing bizarre has occurred. Alas, I fear such incidents happen only too frequently when a young girl is as beautiful as Ginevra and is heiress to a fortune of thirty thousand pounds. Second, let me quash your notion that the elopement was some extraordinary fiction. The man was, as you surmised, one of the Kinsellas' Irish connections, but you were wrong in assuming he had to be over sixty. He was twenty-four, tall, dark and handsome, but having said that I must add that he was quite definitely not a gentleman by English standards, and I have no doubt that he had only one purpose in coming to our obscure corner of Wales and paying his respects to these aging, distant but wealthy relatives of his. He had the mark of the adventurer upon him, and of course it wouldn't have taken him long, in our small community, to find out that Ginevra is an heiress.

We met him at the Mowbrays' house, but if it hadn't been there it would have been somewhere else—indeed even Lady de Bracy might have received him at

24

Penhale Manor out of courtesy to his relatives who are so thoroughly blameless and respectable. When we met him I could see Ginevra was charmed at once, just as I could see that the young man was, as my dear papa used to say, "a wrong 'un." I said afterwards to your father: "That's one young man we don't invite to Oxmoon," and your father agreed with me.

Shortly after this meeting with young Mr. Kinsella a most unfortunate episode occurred. I had to go away—you will remember how I wrote to you recently from Staffordshire after poor Aunt May's baby died. Of course it's most unusual for me to be away as I hate leaving home, but May wrote me such a pathetic letter that I felt I would be failing in my sisterly duty if I refused to visit her for a few days. I should have taken Ginevra with me but I knew May would want no visitors other than myself and besides I thought Miss Sale would be able to supervise Ginevra without trouble. Miss Sale might have had her shortcomings as a governess, but she had always been a conscientious chaperone and I had complete confidence in her.

What can I say except that my confidence was misplaced? There were clandestine meetings on the Downs. I don't blame Ginevra entirely. Young Conor Kinsella is the kind of man who would lead even the devoutest nun astray, but of course when I came back and found out—as I inevitably did—what was going on I was very angry and so was your father. (Being greatly preoccupied with the estate he too had been all too ready to put his trust in Miss Sale's competence.)

Your father and I told Ginevra that we could not permit her to see Mr. Kinsella again, and this edict, I regret to say, led to some most unfortunate words being exchanged between the three of us. This was the night on which Ginevra slipped out of the house and rode all the way to Porteynon to the Kinsellas' house where she proceeded to throw stones against a window which she supposed to belong to her beloved. It belonged, however, to Miss Bridget. More distasteful scenes ensued. It is quite unnecessary for me to chronicle them in detail, so I shall simply say that Ginevra was left feeling so humiliated and miserable that it seemed kindest to suggest she stayed elsewhere for a while. When she received the suggestion gratefully I appealed to Maud Appleby and Ginevra's removal to All-Hallows Court was then arranged with the utmost speed.

Why should she go and live with such people, you ask with such regrettable rudeness. I shall tell you. Looking after Ginevra is going to be an increasingly arduous responsibility and I did not feel Bobby and I had the right to ask for help in any other quarter. As Sir William is her godfather, it is nothing less than his moral duty to help us surmount such a crisis.

Your father saw Mr. Kinsella in order to buy him off, but much to our surprise Mr. Kinsella refused to take a penny. We might have been impressed by this if he hadn't sworn he had never at any time behaved with any impropriety. Of course he was trying to save his skin—no doubt he thought that if he accepted money from us it would rank as a confession of guilt in the eyes of his wealthy relatives— but I fear poor Ginevra must have been quite crushed when she heard he had denied his advances to her. All we can do now is hope and pray she has learned from the *experience and will be a little wiser when the next fortune hunter makes his inevitable approach.*

So much for Mr. Kinsella. The gossips of Gower, needless to say, are having a fine time exercising their tongues, but believe nothing you hear which does not accord with the above account.

You were perfectly correct in your assumptions regarding Ginevra's virtue; you may be distressed that her reputation has suffered, as it inevitably has, but you may rest assured that she has not been sullied beyond redemption by this squalid but by no means catastrophic experience. (Your remarks on the subject were somewhat singular but I realize you were trying to express yourself with propriety and on the whole, considering your youth, I think you did well. In future, however, you should not allude to the carnal capacities of gentlemen in any letter you may write to a female. This is most definitely not The Done Thing.)

And now I must close this letter. I do hope I have to some extent alleviated any anxiety you may have suffered through being ill-informed, but should there be any further questions you wish to ask about this unfortunate incident, please do write to me at once so that I can set your mind at rest. Meanwhile I send all my love and in adding that I long to see you again I remain, dearest Robert, your most affectionate and devoted MAMA.

VI

I became obsessed with the name Conor Kinsella. I remember writing it down and as I stared at it I thought what a sinister name it was, so foreign, so different, so smooth yet so aggressive, the stress falling on the first syllable of each word so that the hard C and the hard K seemed doubly emphasized, twin bullets of sound followed by the soft ripple of easy consonants and vowels. The Porteynon Kinsellas, an elderly celibate trio of a brother and two sisters, were descended from an Irish pirate, sole survivor of an eighteenth-century shipwreck in Rhossili Bay, and the wild lawless Gower Peninsula of a hundred years ago had been just the place for a wild lawless Irishman to settle down and feel at home.

Remembering the past I at once saw Conor Kinsella as an Irish pirate, invading my home and capturing what was mine by right. Scraping the barrel of my unsophisticated vocabulary I thought of him as a cad and a blackguard, a rip, a rake and a rotter, but all the while I was reducing him to cardboard in this fashion I was aware that somewhere in the world was a flesh-and-blood man ten years my senior who ate and drank and slept and breathed and shaved and cursed and counted his pennies with anxiety and probably gave flowers to his mother on her birthday and perhaps even helped little old ladies over the road on his way to church.

The truth was that I knew nothing of Conor Kinsella. Yet when I finally saw him, I recognized him at once, not merely because he fitted my mother's chilling description but because I sensed he was like Ginette, and in knowing her I knew him.

I am uncertain how I knew that he was going to come back into her life. Perhaps it was because in the beginning she herself was so sure of it.

"He swore he'd come back for me," she said. "He told me he'd go to America and make some money and then he'd come back and sweep me off on horseback into the sunset and we'd get married and live happily ever after."

"I didn't know men ever talked such rot. You didn't believe him, did you?"

"Yes, I did. He meant it."

We were at All-Hallows Court, the Applebys' home, which stood three miles from Oxmoon on the parish boundary of Penhale and Llangennith. The house, which was considerably smaller than Oxmoon, was what we in South Wales call a squarsonage, meaning that it was a cross between the home of a parson and the residence of a country squire, and the unlikely name was said (erroneously no doubt) to be a corruption of "Hail Mary," the last words of a group of Catholics slaughtered during the Reformation by a faction group of Gower wreckers dead drunk on contraband brandy. The Applebys were smugglers and wreckers themselves at one time but later they became respectable and produced several vicars of Penhale; that meant they still smuggled, but they gave up wrecking. Probably, as my mother would have said, they felt they had to draw the line somewhere.

"I just don't understand," I said to Ginette. "How could you possibly have behaved in such an appalling fashion?"

She began to cry. I was aghast. I was not unaccustomed to seeing her in tears for she had always cherished the tiresome belief that weeping was a necessary adjunct of a heroine's passionate nature, but these tears were far removed from her usual histrionic displays of emotion. They filled her eyes and trickled down her cheeks in silence, and as I watched she bowed her head in despair.

"Ah Ginette, Ginette . . ." I did not know what to do. We never embraced. I was being educated in a culture that judged it very sloppy for a boy to make a spontaneous gesture of affection. In the end I merely sat down beside her on the window seat and suggested the only possible panacea. "Come home to Oxmoon."

"I can't. There was a dreadful quarrel. Didn't they tell you?"

"But they've forgiven you!"

"I haven't forgiven them. They were horrid about Conor, they said he wasn't what he seemed to be but that was the whole point: he was. He was real. But nothing else was. I'd been living in a fairy tale." She blew her nose on a grubby handkerchief before adding unsteadily, "I don't want to live in a fairy tale anymore."

"You're living in a fairy tale if you believe that villain will ever come back for you!"

"No. I'm going to marry him."

"But you can't! What about me? You can't just throw me over as if I no longer exist!"

She gazed at me helplessly. "I'm sorry, it's as if we don't even talk the same language anymore."

"But you swore I came first with you!"

"And so you did," she said. "You were there in the beginning, you were part of the magic of Oxmoon, and you'll be with me always in my memory, always to the very end of my life." She broke down again. I tried to grab her hand, as if I could lead her back to the strawberry beds, symbol of our paradise lost, but she jumped up and ran sobbing from the room.

I was alone.

VII

She did go back to Oxmoon but only for an occasional visit with Lady Appleby and the Applebys' son, Timothy, who had recently come down from Cambridge. The presence of Timothy annoyed me for I thought him a poor fish, and I became even more annoyed when Ginette, who had once described him as the lamppost the lamplighter forgot, never failed to giggle at his idiotic jokes.

"You don't care for Timothy, do you?" I said to her once on a rare occasion when we were alone together.

"Good heavens, no!" she said. "But he's very amusing, and it's nice to have an older friend who's been out and about in the world."

In the autumn she was sent to Germany to spend six months at a finishing school, but she had barely arrived home from Germany in the March of 1898 when she and Timothy announced their engagement. I was at Harrow but my father wrote, my mother wrote and this time even Ginette herself wrote to break the news. Her letter arrived first.

Darling Robert, she began. Advancing years had taught her how to be effusive, and I knew very well that the more nervous she was the more effusive she became. *Something simply too divine has happened and I'm engaged to be married!!! To Timothy!!! I'm so excited I can hardly put pen to paper but of course I had to tell you at once because after all you're so special to me and always will be, quite the best first-cousin-once-removed that anyone ever had, and I'm sure that when you marry I shall be madly jealous and gnash my teeth and long to be an absolute* CAT *to her!*

Now Robert, don't be too livid with me—a girl really does have to get married, you know, and Uncle William and Aunt Maud were having second thoughts about giving me a season because Timothy was so passionate about me and they thought it would be rather heavenly if I married him and I suppose they didn't like the idea of me meeting heaps of luscious gentlemen in London, and quite honestly I didn't care for the idea much either, I decided I'd already had more than enough of luscious gentlemen who promised to love me forever and then disappeared without trace.

Bobby and Margaret are thrilled, in fact they're both being simply wonderful, and darling Bobby says he's going to give a ball for me at Oxmoon on my eighteenth birthday next month, so hurry home from Harrow, my dear (what *a collection of breathless aspirants!*) *because I simply can't wait to see you! Undying love, yours through all eternity,* GINETTE.

I had barely recovered from this sickening effusion when my father's letter arrived. After breaking the news of the engagement, he wrote, *I myself am convinced that this is the best possible solution for Ginevra and when you come home we'll have a talk and I'll explain why. Meanwhile behave like a gentleman and do nothing that would make me ashamed of you—but I have every confidence that your conduct, as always, will be exemplary. Ever your affectionate and devoted father,* R.G.

This elliptical letter seemed curiously empty. I read it and reread it and felt more despairing than ever. I wanted immediate comfort; the promise of future explanations coupled with exhortations to behave like a gentleman merely increased my baffled misery. I wanted someone to say, "Yes, you must be appalled," and suggest if not a remedy, at least a road to resignation.

My mother's letter arrived two days later.

My dearest Robert, she wrote, *Of course you will be appalled by the news of Ginevra's engagement. But try to be patient. It is a difficult situation but there are arguments in favor of the engagement which I must leave to your father to explain. It is not a mother's provenance to talk of the Ways of the World to her sons.*

No doubt you will be feeling frustrated that your father hasn't written at length, but when considering the Ways of the World an oral discussion is more efficacious than an exchange of letters. Also your father is subject to uneasiness when he has to write long letters in English. Remember that he has not had the benefit of your first-class education, and try to understand how sensitive he feels on the subject. It was terrible for him to be sent home from school at the age of thirteen because his father would not or could not pay the bills, terrible for him later when no tutor would stay in a house so impregnated with immorality and corruption. Again, be patient. And have courage. Remember, everything passes, even the most unspeakable horrors. Believe me. I know. I send my best love, dearest Robert, and remain now and always your most affectionate and devoted MAMA.

VIII

I returned to Oxmoon two weeks later for the Easter holidays, and on the morning after my arrival my father asked me to accompany him to the library, a long tousled room dominated by the leather-bound collection of books ordered for Oxmoon by my eighteenth-century ancestor Robert Godwin the Renovator. My father, who used the library as an estate office, read only magazines when he was at leisure; he never opened a book. My mother read *Mrs. Beeton's Book of Household Management* and, occasionally, moral tracts which she felt might be suitable for the servants' hall. My parents, in other words, were a perfect example of how to succeed in life without benefit of a worthwhile education.

"Sit down, Robert," said my father, motioning me to the chair by his writing table, but he himself remained standing by the fireplace.

My father was a tall man, over six feet in height, and he looked like the hero he was. I cannot remember a time when I did not know he was a hero, saving his ruined inheritance, overcoming all manner of adversity, winning a reputation throughout the length and breadth of the Gower Peninsula as a just landlord, a hardworking farmer and a devoted family man. At that time, when I was two months short of my sixteenth birthday, he was still only thirty-six, three years older than my mother, but as he stood facing me in the library I thought neither of his youth nor of his hero's looks, which were so familiar that I took them for granted, but of his lack of education which my mother had recently underlined to me.

My father was a gentleman, a member of an Anglo-Welsh family which had survived in Gower for many hundreds of years, but at that moment I suddenly saw him through the English eyes I was busy acquiring at Harrow and I realized for the first time how hard it would be to place him within the conventional framework of the English class system. His casual country clothes were in impeccable English taste but there was something foreign about the way he wore them; Englishmen are prone to be shabbily, not elegantly, informal. Then his hands were wrong; they hinted at past manual labor, not gentlemanly pursuits. But his voice was the most marked anomaly of his gentleman's appearance, even more marked than the unfashionable beard which any English gentleman would have been tempted to shave off years before. He had a country accent. In the eighteenth century this would have been unremarkable in a provincial gentleman who seldom went to London, but here we were, almost in the twentieth century, and my father did not speak English as it should be spoken. His accent, the curious hybrid of Gower in which Devon meets and conquers Wales, was not marked, no more than a steady Welsh inflection mingled with Devonian vowels, but it was sufficient to label him an oddity in a society where every man is immediately placed as soon as he opens his mouth. My father was a Welshman living in a little corner of England which history and geography had combined to maroon behind the Welsh frontier, and in his English Welshness Oxmoon stood reflected, English yet not English, Welsh yet not Welsh, a cultural and racial conundrum endowed with an idiosyncratic charm and grace.

"Well, Robert," said my father, so charming, so graceful, so anxious to help me in any way he could, "let me explain why I approve of this engagement which you find so detestable. It's like this: a girl such as Ginevra, a beautiful girl, an heiress, lives in constant danger as soon as she's old enough to go out and about— and even before she's old enough; I don't have to remind you of what happened with Conor Kinsella. Now, an early marriage to a suitable young man is the best thing that could happen to a girl like Ginevra, particularly a girl who's already got herself talked about in an unfavorable way."

"Yes, but—"

"Believe me, Ginevra could do worse—much worse. This is a good match. Socially the Applebys are beyond reproach, and I've no doubt Ginevra would enjoy the future Timothy has to offer—an amusing sociable sort of life divided between London and Gower. Also the two of them have plenty of friends and acquaintances in common and no one denies marriage is easier when the partners share a similar background. Besides, they find each other good company. I don't see why they shouldn't do tolerably well together, indeed I don't."

"I can see the truth of what you're saying, but—"

"I know what you're thinking. You're wondering how she could be happy with a plain boy who wears spectacles and likes collecting butterflies instead of playing cricket. Well, there's more than one kind of happiness, Robert. He'll make her happy because he'll give her a secure respectable status as a married woman. And if she wants a more exciting sort of happiness she'll be eligible to look elsewhere later."

I stared at him. "I don't understand."

"No. Well, that's the way of the world, Robert. A girl like Ginevra is certain to favor the kind of life that in our society only married women are allowed to lead."

I went on staring. "But surely when women are married they still have to play the game and stick to the rules!"

"I'm not talking about God's rules—we all know what they are. I'm talking about society's rules, and there are rules governing carnal behavior just as there are rules governing how to eat at table. The difference is that passion's more important than table manners, and if you break the rules of passion you can be smashed to pulp." He was still staring into the grate. Then abandoning the fire he moved to the window. As he slipped his hands into his pockets I saw that his fists were clenched.

"Passion... carnal desire..." He seemed to be working his way towards some vulgar colloquialism but in the end as usual he eschewed all Anglo-Saxon bluntness and when he next spoke I realized he had fallen back on the elliptical but time-honored phrase that had been sanctified by the Bible. He was entrapped not only by his Welshness but by the verbal restraint of his generation. "Acquiring carnal knowledge is like swimming in the sea," he said carefully at last. "The sea's so beautiful to look at, so wonderful to swim in, but you must never bathe unless it's safe. People so often drown in the sea and some coasts are so very dangerous... like the coast of Gower."

Drifting back to the writing table he paused to look down at the ink-stained blotter. "As you know," he said, "I saw a man drown once. I saw a man drown and a woman go mad. And one day, Robert," said my father, slowly raising his eyes to mine, "one day I'm going to have to talk to you about my mother and Owain Bryn-Davies."

I respected him far too much to ask what connection there could possibly be between this hoary old skeleton in the family cupboard and Ginette's disastrous engagement, and presently—as usual—he backed away from the subject without imparting further information.

"So you be careful of that shining sea," he said, and as he spoke I thought how Welsh he was, wrapping the truths of life in metaphors and serving them up to me on a salver of myth. "Be careful as I was—and as I am." He paused. His very blue eyes seemed unnaturally clear and when he looked straight at me again I found it was impossible to look away. "A good wife's the only answer," he said. "Anything else isn't worth the risk of drowning. You'll notice I don't just say marriage is the answer, because if you choose the wrong wife it's no answer at all. There's no hell on earth like a bad marriage. My parents...yes, I must tell you about them someday when you've seen a little more of the world. They didn't stick to the rules, you see—neither God's rules nor the rules of society—and in breaking the rules they were both destroyed."

There was a pause in which nothing moved in the room but the flames of the fire in the grate.

"So," said my father, suddenly altering the mood by giving me his most charming smile, "I'm sure you can understand now how dangerous life could be for Ginevra and how we must do everything in our power to ensure her safety by encouraging her to make a satisfactory marriage."

"Yes, of course she's got to have a husband to look after her, I quite understand that, but as far as I'm concerned there's only one possible solution: I must marry her myself. Now, I do realize I'm a little young at present, but—"

"I concede," said my father, "that I married at nineteen and it turned out to be quite the most fortunate thing that's ever happened to me, but I'm afraid I could never consent to you marrying while you're still in your teens."

"But this is an emergency!"

"I think not. I recognize that you feel a very deep affection for Ginevra, but you in your turn should now recognize that it's fraternal."

"Oh no, it isn't!"

"I'm sorry. I know you're jealous. I know you've been unhappy since she left Oxmoon. I know this is all a nightmare for you, but you must try to be grown up, try to be sensible, try to accept that this is something you can't change."

This maddened me beyond endurance. "I'd like to kill him!" I shouted in a paroxysm of rage. "That would change things soon enough!"

The next moment my father was slamming me face down across the writing table and the scene had dissolved with terrifying speed into violence.

IX

He never did it. He never beat me. I cried out in shock and the cry paralyzed him. For five seconds he held me in an iron grip but then with a short painful intake of breath he released my arm which he had doubled behind my back. As he walked away from me he said, "Never, never say such a thing again." He spoke in Welsh but as it was a simple sentence I understood it. However a moment later, realizing he had used the wrong language, he repeated the order in English. The English was broken, a foreigner's attempt at an unfamiliar tongue. He sounded like a stranger. I was terrified.

"We don't talk of murder at Oxmoon," said my father.

"Forgive me, I didn't mean what I said—"

"You ought to be ashamed of yourself, behaving like a spoiled child all over again—and to think you have the insolence to talk of marriage! It'll be a long time before *you're* fit for marriage, indeed it will—all you're fit for at the moment is the nursery!"

"I'm sorry but I'm just so damnably unhappy—"

"*Unhappy!* Don't talk to me of unhappiness, you don't even know what the word means! My God, when I was your age—"

"I'm sorry, I'm sorry, please don't be angry with me anymore, please—"

"Then sit down at that table and stop whining like a pampered puppy! That's better. Now take a sheet of notepaper and write as follows." My father hesitated before continuing with appropriate pauses: "'My dear Ginette, I must apologize for not writing earlier to send my best wishes to you on your engagement, but I'm very much looking forward to celebrating the news with you at your birthday ball at Oxmoon. After all, I'd be a poor sort of friend if I couldn't share your happiness! I shall be writing separately to Timothy to congratulate him but meanwhile please do give him my warmest regards. I hope you will both be very happy. Yours affectionately'—or however you close your letters to her—'Robert.'"

I finished writing. My father read the letter over my shoulder and said, "Yes, that'll do," but on an impulse I scrawled beneath the signature: *P.S. Make sure you save a waltz for me at the ball!* I wanted a waltz not because it would give me the opportunity to hold her in my arms but because I knew she liked waltzes best and I wanted my dance with her to be a dance she would remember.

"Well, I don't care," I said as I watched my father seal the letter. "Let her marry whom she likes. My friendship with her will outlast any marriage."

My father said tersely, "Even if you'd been older your mother and I could never have approved of you marrying her. She's too alluring and you're too jealous. She'd make you very miserable."

But I was miserable enough already and my misery had hardly begun.

X

The ball to celebrate both Ginette's engagement and her eighteenth birthday was held on the twenty-third of April, 1898. That was when my life finally began. The previous fifteen years and ten months had been merely a rehearsal.

All Gower came to Oxmoon for by that time my parents were famous for their lavish hospitality. It was their weakness. Everyone, after all, must occasionally have a holiday from hard work, self-help, drawing the line and doing the done

33

thing, and my parents were in many ways a very ordinary Victorian young couple. My mother specialized in what she called "little dinner parties for twenty-four," but her English talent for wielding power with implacable attention to detail was only truly satisfied by giving balls for a hundred. My father, displaying an inborn Welsh inclination to hospitality, seized the chance to abandon the austerity which he had been compelled to practice for so much of his life, and glide down the glittering road of extravagance. The result of their combined efforts to entertain their neighbors was unbridled sybaritic luxury served up with a shattering military precision.

At first I had no intention of making more than a brief appearance; I not only loathed the prospect of seeing Ginette with her fiancé but in my misery I knew another of those moments when I was overwhelmed with the drearier aspects of adolescence. Once again I was undergoing a bout of rapid growth; I looked ridiculous in my evening clothes, and as I stood before the looking glass I thought I had never seen a youth who looked more unappealing. There was even a spot on my chin. I never normally had spots. I did not believe in them. But now I found myself obliged to believe, and the next moment I was noticing what a distasteful color my hair was. In childhood it had been pale yellow and attractive. Now it was mud-brown and repellent. My eyes were blue but not bright blue like my father's; they were light blue, unendurably anemic. It suddenly occurred to me that my looks were second-rate. I would never be classically handsome. A sense of failure overpowered me. I was in despair.

Then my mother looked in to see how far I had progressed with my preparations and when she saw me she said briskly, "This won't do, will it?" and hustled me along to her room where my father, golden-haired, classically handsome and every inch a hero was somehow contriving to look elegant in his braces.

He lent me some evening clothes and life began to seem fractionally less hopeless. Finally I ventured downstairs. The house seemed to be throbbing with a powerful emotion and so strong was the aura of glamour that I did not at first realize that this powerful emotion lay within me and was not some mysterious miasma emanating from the walls. All the main rooms were adorned with flowers from the garden and the hothouses. In the ballroom the scent of lilies, very pure and clear, drifted faintly toward me from the bank of flowers around the dais where the gentlemen of the orchestra were busy tuning their instruments. No amateur trio scraped out the music whenever all Gower danced at Oxmoon; my parents imported a dozen first-class musicians from London. I glanced up at the chandeliers. Every crystal had been washed, every candle replaced. The room was mirrored. Perhaps Regency Robert Godwin had dreamed of Versailles, and as I stood in what I later realized was such a quaint provincial little ballroom I saw reflected in those mirrors the fairy-tale prince of my personal myth.

The guests began to arrive. The music began to play. The room began to hum with conversation and still I remained where I was, saying her name again and again in my mind as if I could will her back from the brink of her great catastrophe and deliver us both to the happy ending of a traditional nursery fairy tale.

I was in the hall when she arrived at last with the Applebys. Through the open front door I saw their carriage coming up the drive and although I wanted to retreat to the ballroom in order to pretend I was barely interested in her arrival, my feet carried me inexorably past the staircase, through the doorway and out into the porch.

I saw her and for the first time in my life I found myself old enough to recognize feminine perfection. I was reminded of the silver cups which I regularly collected at school in my compulsive quest for excellence. She was a prize. She was waiting to be awarded to the man who came first, and when I finally realized this I knew I had to have her; I knew I had to win.

True to the conventions of the fairy tale I was instantly changed. The long tedious journey through adolescence was terminated as abruptly as if my fairy godmother had waved a magic wand, and at that moment childhood lay forever behind me and only manhood was real.

"Robert! My dear, isn't this thrilling! *What* a birthday treat..." She swept on, radiantly oblivious of my transformation, and disappeared into the ballroom. Presently I found I had to sit down. Then I found I could not sit down but had to stand up. I was beside myself. All the famous love poetry which I had previously dismissed as "soppy" and "wet" now streamed through my brain until even the rhythm of the iambic pentameters seemed impregnated with a mystical significance. Like the author of the Book of Revelation I was conscious of a new heaven and a new earth. I stumbled forward, broke into a run and hared after her into the ballroom.

"Ginette, Ginette—"

She heard me. I saw her turn her head idly and give me a languid wave with her fan. "Don't worry, I haven't forgotten!" she called. "I've saved the first waltz after supper for you!" And she began to dance away from me in Sir William Appleby's arms.

Some sort of interval passed which I can only presume I spent dancing with the girls I was supposed to dance with and behaving as I was supposed to behave. I must have shown some semblance of normality for no one inquired anxiously after my health. Did I eat any supper? Possibly. I have a dim memory of sipping a glass of champagne but giving up halfway through because I was afraid I might go mad with euphoria.

"Oh good, this is your waltz, isn't it, Robert? Thank goodness, now I can relax! I never before realized how exhausting it must have been for Cinderella having to be radiant to everyone in sight.... Lord, I'm in such a state, Robert, does it show? I feel so excited I don't see how I can possibly survive—in fact maybe I'm already dead and this is what it's like in heaven.... Oh, listen—Johann Strauss—yes, that proves it, I *am* in heaven! Come on, Robert, what's the matter with you? Let's dance!"

And that was the moment when we danced together beneath the chandeliers at Oxmoon as the orchestra played "The Blue Danube."

"Oh, this is such paradise!" exclaimed Ginette, echoing my thoughts word for word but glancing restlessly past me to the doors of the ballroom as if she could hardly wait to escape. "I'll remember this moment forever and ever!"

35

"I'll remember it till the day I die. Listen, Ginette, wait for me, you've got to wait—"

"What? I can't hear you!" The orchestra was blazing into a new coda and as we whirled by the dais I saw her again look past my shoulder at the open doors in the distance.

"I said you've got to wait for me because—"

She left me. The orchestra was still playing "The Blue Danube" but as she ran the full length of the ballroom all the couples stopped dancing to stare at her. She ran swiftly and gracefully, her feet seeming barely to touch the ground, and suddenly there was a flash of diamonds as she pulled off her ring, tossed it aside and carelessly consigned her engagement to oblivion.

He was waiting for her in the doorway. As I have already mentioned, I had no trouble recognizing Conor Kinsella. He was smiling that charming Irish smile of his and as she flung herself into his arms he kissed her with appalling intimacy on the mouth.

The music stopped. No one moved. A great silence fell upon the ballroom and then in my mind's eye I saw the mirrored walls darken, the chandeliers grow dim and my fairy tale turn to ashes to foul the perfumed festering air.

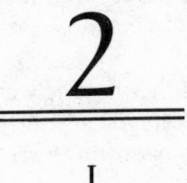

2

I

So much for romance. Later I considered it fortunate that this early experience had granted me immunity, and I was never troubled by such irrational behavior again.

After the ball life went on. I admit I did wonder at the time how it could but it did, and presently the natural human instinct for self-preservation nudged its way to the forefront of my mind. I suddenly saw that no one must know how I felt. Sweat broke out on my forehead at the thought of people pitying me. Horrifying visions smote me of a future in which my unrequited love made me an object of derision throughout Gower, and in panic I realized that my only hope of avoiding such humiliation lay in exercising an iron will and concealing my feelings behind the facade of my quasi-fraternal friendship. If I followed this course I could permit myself a certain amount of fractious moping because it would be expected of me, but I had at all costs to beware of extremes; I had to keep eating, talk to people, go about my daily business. Eventually I would have to pretend to recover and this would be a formidable challenge, but sheer pride alone made it imperative that I should succeed.

I began to rehearse a series of appropriate remarks which I could use later to deceive my parents. "Ginette? Oh yes, I suppose I was a trifle possessive, wasn't I—rather amusing to look back on that now...." Endless scenes in this endless charade of indifference slipped in and out of my mind. My inventive powers impressed me but unfortunately they were unable to relieve my misery whenever I thought of Ginette with Kinsella. My imagination, never normally intrusive, was now a torment to me. So was my sexuality. Together the two demons destroyed my sleep, gave me a consumptive look and did their best to destroy the grand illusion of resignation which I was trying so hard to propagate.

Meanwhile, as I floundered in the toils of my adolescent's nightmare, Kinsella had taken advantage of everyone's paralyzed stupefaction to sweep Ginette off on horseback to Swansea, our nearest large town, and bear her away by rail to Scotland where the lax matrimonial laws had long been God's gift to clandestine lovers. There he had married her despite the fact that she had been made a ward of court, and afterwards they had evaded legal retribution by slipping into Ireland on a ferry from Stranraer to Larne. They had sailed to America from Cork a week later.

There was much talk about what could be done to preserve Ginette's fortune but the debate soon lapsed as her well-wishers acknowledged their impotence to alter her fate. Before long general opinion favored treating the disaster as a *fait accompli* and making the best of it. No one knew how Kinsella was earning his daily bread, but later, when the lines of communication had been renewed, Ginette's letters indicated a life of affluence with no sign of an apocalyptic retribution hovering in the wings.

Timothy Appleby was dispatched on a world cruise to recover from the catastrophe and had all manner of adventures before meeting a rich widow in Cape Town and settling down in Rhodesia to make a study of the butterflies of Africa. Ginette's defection was undoubtedly the best fate that could have overtaken him, but the more I heard people remarking on his lucky escape the more I wondered how Ginette could have treated him so badly. The situation had no doubt been abnormal but her deliberate entanglement with a man who meant nothing to her continued to puzzle me and when we had drifted into a faultlessly platonic correspondence I asked her outright for an explanation. In reply I received a typical letter, full of romantic hyperbole and feminine flutter, which I knew meant she was still struggling with her guilt and remorse:...*yes, I know I behaved like a serpent, and believe me I'll have poor Tim on my conscience till my dying day, but the truth is quite simply that I was mad. Aunt Maud drove me mad, intercepting my letters from Conor and lecturing me about chastity and sending me to that ghastly place in Germany which was just like a prison—or worse still a convent—so in the end I saw clearly that my only hope of escaping her was to marry and the only man (or so I thought) who wanted to marry me was Timothy. I knew I'd still have to spend part of the year at All-Hallows but at least I would have been my own mistress instead of Aunt Maud's prisoner and at least I would have been able to spend most of the year in London where I would have met all sorts of exciting people and had a simply heavenly time.*

So that was why I decided to marry Tim. I had no way of communicating with Conor and (thanks to Aunt Maud) I'd given up all hope of hearing from him.

And then—just after my engagement had been announced—Conor finally managed to outwit my jailer! He sent over from Ireland the most extraordinary gentleman called Mr. O'Flaherty who posed as a jobbing gardener and managed to smuggle a letter to me by seducing the second housemaid—my dear, I can't tell you how romantic it was and the housemaid had a thrilling time too—and then I told Mr. O'Flaherty about the ball at Oxmoon and Conor sent word that I was to leave a packed bag beforehand with the second housemaid who would take it to Mr. O'Flaherty who would be waiting in the grounds of All-Hallows by the ruined oratory—my dear, I was simply ravished by excitement, in fact when the orchestra was playing "The Blue Danube" and I saw Conor had finally arrived I'm only surprised I didn't swoon in your arms! At least when I die I'll be able to say: well, never mind, I've lived. Oh, but what a nightmare it was before Conor came, thank God I've escaped, thank God the ghastly old past can't touch me anymore. . . .

Years afterwards when she and Kinsella paid their first and last visit to England I said to her, "If All-Hallows was such hell, why didn't you come back to Oxmoon?"

"But my dear!" she exclaimed as if astonished that I could be so obtuse. "Margaret would have been just as bad as Aunt Maud! Can't you imagine all the homilies on drawing the line and doing the done thing?" And we laughed together, just two platonic friends, just first cousins once removed, just two strangers who had been childhood playmates long ago in a little Welsh country house in the back of beyond, but I wanted her then as strongly as I had ever wanted her and although I concealed my feelings I knew that they had remained unchanged. It was as if they had been frozen in time by the shock of her sudden desertion; it was as if, so far as my deepest emotions were concerned, I was still dancing beneath the chandeliers at Oxmoon while the orchestra played "The Blue Danube."

This should have been romantic. However in reality—the reality I had to master when I was sixteen—it was both inconvenient and bewildering. I had read enough novels by that time to know that a hero in my position had to yearn for his lost love in impeccable chastity and perhaps hunt big game in Africa to relieve his feelings, but I had no interest in game hunting and no interest, as I presently discovered to my horror, in being chaste.

It took me a few months to realize this, but when I returned home for the summer holidays I found I finally had to face the prospect of Ginette's permanent absence. In other words, for the first time in my life I had to live with the concept of losing.

I did not know where to begin. Then I gradually became aware that I wanted to conquer this new world of carnality and prove I was still capable of coming first. At that point I should have confided in my father but two factors inhibited me. The first was that I was so obsessed with acting my charade of indifference towards Ginette that I shied away from any conversation which would have betrayed my true feelings, and the second was that I could so clearly remember my father talking of the dangerous sea of carnality and telling me a good marriage was the only answer.

I struggled on in silence, utterly confused, utterly miserable, but then one morning I got up early and on wandering downstairs I found a very junior house-maid polishing the floor of the drawing room. Immediately I recalled my recent letter from Ginette on the subject of the erring housemaid at All-Hallows, and immediately I saw what possibilities had confronted the mysterious Mr. O'Flaherty. One thing led, as I fear it so often does, to another until at last, to put a turgid episode in the shortest, most salutary sentence, she stooped, I conquered and we both fell from grace. I was back at school by the time my father was obliged to make a financial provision for her and I was still at school when to the relief of all concerned she miscarried and emigrated to Australia, but when I returned home for the Christmas holidays I found a most unpleasant reception awaiting me.

It was my mother who had found out. Her chilling expression was bad enough but the worst part of the affair was that my father was entirely at a loss. He was stricken. His expression of bewilderment, his painful halting attempt to reprimand me, his air of misery all formed more of a punishment than any violent dem-onstration of rage, and in an agony of shame I begged his forgiveness.

"I'll turn over a new leaf, sir, I swear I will," I added desperately, and on this edifying note of repentance the conversation ended, but I knew, as soon as I had left him, that my problems remained unsolved. I was just wondering in despair if I could secretly ask the local doctor for a drug that would suppress my carnal inclinations and was just trying to imagine the celibate future studded with cold baths that lay ahead of me to the grave—for of course I could never marry if I could not marry Ginette—when Lion banged on the door and shouted that my mother wanted to see me.

She was making a blouse for Celia and her worktable was littered with various pieces of material, but my mother herself was, as I had anticipated, sitting at her dressing table in front of the triple looking glass. Her box of assorted buttons was open before her and she was sifting through the collection in search of a suitable set for the blouse.

"Sit down, dear," she said, not looking up. "I've just been talking to your father."

I sat down. The chair was cunningly angled so that I was reflected in all three mirrors, and as I noticed this unnerving multiplication of my guilty image I felt a queasiness form in the pit of my stomach.

"Your father," said my mother, poking away busily among the buttons, "is capable of considerable eloquence, but when a conversation is of a painful nature he often finds it difficult to be as explicit as he would wish. I have spoken of this to you before and attributed this characteristic to his Welsh temperament but we must also never forget that he was not brought up to speak English by his Welsh mother and his Welsh nursemaids and that in times of stress he thinks more easily in their language than in ours."

Poke-poke-poke among the buttons. A swift glance into the far mirror.

"So I thought," resumed my mother tranquilly, "that I should see you for a moment to...clarify your father's statements in the unlikely event that you might be feeling a trifle bewildered or confused." She paused, glanced into all three mirrors and then returned to the buttons before adding: "Now, I want to talk to you briefly about your grandmother and Mr. Bryn-Davies—your father has not, I think, yet broached the subject with you in any detail."

I was so startled that it took me a moment to answer, "No, Mama."

"Well, that's as it should be. Your father is the best judge of when you should hear the whole story, but I think a word or two from me now wouldn't come amiss, especially as the case seems strangely...pertinent to what I have to say." She toyed with a large red button. Then putting it aside she continued with the same tranquil fluency: "Let me start with your grandmother. Now, you may be surprised to hear that I do not entirely condemn poor Grandmama for her liaison with Mr. Bryn-Davies. She loved him. Her husband had treated her vilely. She certainly deserved a little happiness. Of course her conduct was immoral and wrong, that goes without saying, but," said my mother, deciding to look at me directly, "everyone in this world is subject to temptation and since very few people are saints, most people cannot always succeed in living as they know they should live. So Grandmama's lapse was, in that sense, pardonable; she was guilty primarily of human frailty. However," said my mother, finding two more red buttons, "where Grandmama made her cardinal error was that she abandoned all attempt to keep up appearances. A secret liaison conducted with discretion would have been socially acceptable. A public performance as a harlot destroyed her. Remember that, Robert. Discretion is everything. And it has nothing to do with morality. It's a question of good taste, common sense and consideration for those you love and who love you. Have I made myself entirely clear?"

"I—"

"There are standards of immorality as well as standards of morality, Robert. Make sure yours are high. You may not end up a saint—I'm not at all sure I would want a son who was a saint—but at least you'll end up with an ordered civilized private life. Oh, and of course—though it's hardly necessary for me to add this—an ordered civilized private life doesn't include seducing family servants and causing extreme embarrassment to the parents who love you. There are to be no more seductions beneath this roof, Robert. I draw the line. What you do elsewhere is entirely your own affair and I neither expect nor desire to know anything about it—you should ask your father for further advice on the subject, and when you do you must *insist* that he's explicit with you. It is not a mother's provenance," said my mother, "to advise her son on subjects of a carnal nature."

After a pause I said, "No, of course not, Mama."

We looked at each other for one brief telling second in the triple glass. Finally I managed to add, "Thank you."

"Oh, there's no need to thank me," said my mother. "I'm merely clarifying what your father said—or what he would have said if he hadn't been subject to linguistic difficulties when distressed."

The interview was concluded. At first I was conscious merely of an overpowering gratitude towards her for reprieving me from a lifetime of cold baths, but later my attitude became more ambivalent. I was aware that in some nameless competition which I could not begin to define she had come a highly commendable first while my father had come a most ineffectual second, and this truth which instinct urged me to deny but which my intellect forced me to acknowledge ran contrary to my most deeply entrenched beliefs not only about my parents but about the male and female sexes. In the world in which I felt most comfortable men were always first and best, heroes were always more important than heroines and the father who idolized me could do no wrong. But my mother had unwittingly opened a window onto another world, the world which Ginette had shown me when she had eloped with Kinsella, the real world which I secretly knew I had yet to master and which I secretly feared I might never master to my satisfaction. In my dread of coming second there I resented that world and above all I resented the women who had shown it to me. I still loved Ginette—but there were moments when I hated her too. I loved my mother—but there were times when I resented her so much that I could barely keep a civil tongue in my head when I addressed her.

My mother's understanding should have brought me closer to her but in adult life I found we were estranged. We were each faultlessly polite whenever we met but nothing of importance was ever uttered between us, and later when my considerable success had deluded me into believing I had mastered the real world, my attitude mellowed from resentment into an affectionate contempt. Poor Mama, I would think, so plain, so dumpy, so unfashionable, so provincial—what did she know of life when she had barely ventured from her rural backwater since the age of sixteen? The only crisis she had had to surmount had been her mother-in-law's determination to live in sin with a sheep farmer, and even that droll little inconvenience had been smoothed aside by my father who had played the hero and visited his mother regularly in her Swansea asylum.

My father never did tell me the whole story about his mother and Owain Bryn-Davies, but the older and more sophisticated I became the less curious I was to hear about this amusing slice of Victorian melodrama which I felt sure by Edwardian standards would be judged tame. In my late twenties when I became involved with defending criminals of the worst type I quickly reached a state of mind in which no human behavior could shock me, least of all a little indiscreet adultery in South Wales in the Eighties, and when my father said after my grandmother's funeral that my mother had been urging him to talk to me of the past, it was all I could do to suppress a yawn and assume a look of courteous sympathy.

"It must be exactly as you wish, Papa," I said. "If you want to talk then I'm willing to listen, but you shouldn't let Mama dragoon you into a course of action which at heart you've no wish to pursue."

"Your mother thinks you could be a comfort to me," said my father. "I feel so tormented sometimes by my memories."

We were strolling together across the heather to the summit of Rhossili Downs. It was a clouded winter day not conducive to walking, but after the ordeal of my grandmother's funeral we had both felt in need of fresh air. I was twenty-eight but considered myself worldly enough to look older; my father was forty-eight but considered himself lucky enough to look younger; we had reached the stage when we were occasionally mistaken for brothers.

"Yes, I must tell you," said my father. "I must."

We paced on across the heather in silence. I waited, but when nothing happened I automatically fell into my professional role of playing midwife to the truth.

"What were they like?" I said, throwing him a bland question to help him along.

"What were they like?" repeated my father as if I had astonished him. "Oh, they were charming, all of them—my mother, my father, Bryn-Davies... Yes, they were all the most charming and delightful people." He stopped to stare at the skyline and as I watched the color fade from his face he said in a low voice, "That was the horror, of course. It wasn't like a melodrama when you can recognize the villains as soon as they step on the stage. It wasn't like that at all."

"They were just three ordinary people?"

"Yes, they were just three ordinary people," said my father, "who failed to draw the line."

I suppressed a sigh at this fresh evidence of my mother's middle-class Victorian influence over him. It was only the middle classes—and in particular the *nouveaux-riches* middle classes—who made a professional occupation of doing the done thing and drawing moral lines. Anyone of any genuine breeding did the done thing without thinking twice about it and left drawing lines to clergymen who were trained as moral draftsmen.

"It was all a tragedy," my father was saying. "My poor mother, she was so beautiful. My father wasn't very kind to her."

"Because he was a drunkard?"

"He was the most splendid fellow," said my father exactly as if I had never spoken, "and so fond of children. I was the apple of his eye. Bryn-Davies was very civil to me too. Interesting chap, Bryn-Davies. Strong personality. Just calling him a sheep farmer gives no clear impression of him."

"But surely," I said, deciding to risk a little Anglo-Saxon bluntness, "you must have resented Bryn-Davies when he took over Oxmoon after your father died of drink. Surely it became an outrage when he lived openly with your mother and kept you from your inheritance."

"It was all a tragedy," repeated my father. "A tragedy."

I gave up. We walked on across the Downs.

"And afterwards," said my father, "after Bryn-Davies had had his little accident with the tide tables and drowned on the Shipway, it was all so difficult with my mother but Margaret was wonderful, such a tower of strength, and she found out all about the Home of the Assumption where the nuns were so kind to the insane. Sometimes I wondered if my mother should come home more often but Margaret said no, only at Christmas. Margaret drew the line and of course she was right— because terrible things happen," said my father, his face bleached, his lips bloodless, his eyes seeing scenes I could not begin to imagine, "when people fail to draw the line."

I said nothing. The silence that followed lasted some time, but at last he thanked me for listening so patiently and said he was so glad he had talked to me.

But as he and I both knew perfectly well, he had still told me nothing whatsoever.

II

When I related this incident to Ginette in my Christmas letter she wrote in reply: *Poor Bobby, but what defeats me is why he and Margaret make this big mystery out of the past when it's quite obvious to anyone of our sophistication, my dear, what was going on: the drunken husband developed a penchant for beating the wife, the wife dived into a grand passion in sheer self-defense and the lover, being both naughty and greedy, grabbed not only the wife but all the money he could lay his hands on when the husband obligingly died of liver failure. Heavens, such sordid goings-on happen all the time everywhere—and as always in such frightfulness, the people who suffer most are the poor innocent children. Really, it's a wonder some of them survive at all and if they do survive they're lucky if they're not scarred for life by their experiences!*

And it was then, as I read this passage in her letter, that it first occurred to me to suspect that my father was not a flawless hero but a deeply damaged man.

III

I was damaged myself although at that time I did not admit it. I had enjoyed so much worldly success that the prospect of private failure was inconceivable; it never even crossed my mind that anything could be amiss.

It would be immodest for me to record my achievements at Harrow so I need only say that it was taken for granted that I would achieve a first when I went up to Oxford to read Greats. This made life a little dull; success loses its power to charm if insufficient effort is involved in its acquisition and after I had demonstrated to my contemporaries, my tutors and the various females of my acquaintance that whatever I saw I conquered, I acknowledged my boredom by looking around for a new challenge that would make life more amusing. I had just finished my second year at Balliol when a friend invited me to stay with him in Scotland and for the first time in my life I saw the mountains.

There are plenty of mountains in Wales, but the spectacular ones are in the north, and since my parents never took holidays I knew little of Wales beyond the Gower Peninsula and little of England beyond Central London, Oxford and Harrow. There are no mountains in Gower, only the smooth rolling humps of the Downs, and although I had long been attracted to the spectacular cliffs by the sea, these were so dangerous that my father had always forbidden me to climb them.

However I was now presented with a challenge that no one had forbidden me to accept, and I knew I had to climb those mountains. I had to get to the top. I had to win. I was enslaved.

During the next few months I drove my parents to despair, nearly ruined my career at Oxford and almost killed myself. That was when I first realized something had gone wrong with my life; it occurred to me that when my desire to win had been channeled into academic excellence the compulsion had formed a benign growth on my personality, but when that desire had been channeled into mountaineering it had formed a cancer. I did recover but not before the cancer had been cut out of my life. I gave up mountaineering.

"I shall never come back here," I said to the doctor who attended me in the hospital at Fort William when I lay recuperating from the accident that had killed my three best friends. "I shall never go climbing again."

"They all say that," said the doctor, "and they all come back in the end."

But I was certain I could stay away; there was a void in my life but I thought I could see how to fill it. I had to fight the opponent I had discovered on the mountains, the one opponent who consistently mesmerized me. It was Death. Death had won my three friends; Death had almost won me. But now I was the one who was going to win—and I was going to win by outwitting Death over and over again.

I then had to decide on the arena best suited for my battles. I toyed with the idea of becoming a doctor but decided it would involve me in the study of too many subjects which I found tedious. I was interested in death, not disease. Then I considered the law, and the law, I saw at once, had considerable advantages. It not only blended with my classical education but it was a profession that could ease my way into public life, and since I knew my father dreamed that I might enter Parliament I thought I could see how both our ambitions might be satisfied.

As the eldest son I was heir to Oxmoon but my father's youth and the likelihood of him living until I myself was far advanced in middle age made it imperative that I had some occupation while I waited for my inheritance. I also had a very natural desire to be financially independent, and no one denied there was money at the bar for a young man who was determined to reach the summit of the profession.

I won my double first at Oxford in Greats and Law and was called to the bar of the Middle Temple in 1906. To my family I pretended it was sheer chance that I became involved with criminal law; I did not disclose how I had engineered a meeting with a famous K.C. and more or less hypnotized him into engaging me as his "devil"; I did not disclose that I had selected him as my master because a number of his clients ran the risk, in the formal words of the death sentence, of being hanged by the neck until they were dead. While I deviled for him I met the important solicitors and soon I was acquiring a few briefs of my own. Unlike many barristers I did not have to endure briefless years at the bar. I grabbed every

44

opportunity I could and when there was no opportunity I created one. My career began to gather in momentum.

Of course I said it was pure coincidence that I ended up defending murderers who had no hope of acquittal, but the truth was I deliberately sought out the hopeless cases because there was more pleasure in winning a hard victory over Death than an easy one. I pretended to be nonchalant, claiming murder trials were somewhat tedious, but in my heart I loved every minute I spent fighting in court. I loved the excitement and the drama and the perpetual shadow of the gallows; I loved the jousts with Death; I loved the victory of saving people who would have died but for my skill. To compete with Death, as I had discovered on the mountains, was to know one was alive.

It made no difference that sometimes, inevitably, Death won. Some of my clients died on the gallows just as my three friends had died on the mountain, but that only made the next battle fiercer and enhanced my satisfaction when the lucky clients were saved.

My work became an obsession. Although I tried to deny it to myself I was suffering from cancer of the personality again, and gradually I became aware of the familiar symptoms appearing: the fanatical dedication, the withdrawal from other pursuits, the loss of interest in carnal pleasure, the isolation of the soul. I even found myself postponing my entry into politics. Westminster was not the Old Bailey. There was no shadow of the gallows there.

Then one day I saved a client whom I loathed and believed to be guilty, and suddenly I not only asked myself what I was doing but saw the answer all too clearly: I was wasting my life in order to satisfy obsessions I could not master. The cancer was upon me again and I knew I had to cut it out to survive.

That was when I discovered that some cancers spread so deep that no surgery can remove them. My cancer now had such a hold on me that I did not see how I could remove it and retain my sanity; I felt as if I were on the edge of some mental breakdown, but as I struggled to imagine a life in which winning no longer mattered I saw, far away and unattainable, across the abyss of the past and beyond the walls of the present which imprisoned me, the world where I knew I could be at peace. I saw the road to Oxmoon, the lost Oxmoon of my childhood, and Ginette was with me once more in her grubby pinafore as we ate strawberries together in the kitchen garden. I saw a world where winning and losing had no power to drive me because with Ginette's hand in mine I was always content, and when I saw that world I knew that she alone could cure my cancer because she alone could take me back to Oxmoon and resurrect that lost paradise of my dreams.

But Ginette still wrote regularly of married bliss with Conor Kinsella. Fifteen years after we had danced to "The Blue Danube" she was still living happily ever after in New York, and although time and again I asked myself how I could win her back I knew there was nothing I could do. I was powerless, and as I acknowledged my absolute failure to change my life I felt I must surely be condemned to live unhappily ever after in London, a man rich, famous and successful—yet losing, lost and alone.

IV

I awoke very suddenly in the middle of the night, and my first conscious thought was: She's coming home.

Using one of Cicero's favorite metaphors I told myself that the Wheel of Fortune of Conor Kinsella had finally spun him into extinction and now my own Wheel of Fortune was spinning me back into life.

I lit the gas and immediately my cold austere masculine bedroom was bathed in a warm sensuous glow. I drew aside the curtain. Below me the formal lawns below King's Bench Walk were bathed in a powerful white moonlight and far away beyond the Embankment the river glittered beneath the stars. I stood there, transfixed by this vision of an erotic enchanted London, and as I listened to the night I heard the bells of St. Clement Dane's chime a distant half-hour.

Letting the curtain fall I turned abruptly from the window and decided to take a long cool rational look at the immediate future. Tomorrow—which was in fact today—I would go down to Oxmoon for a protracted weekend. On the following day Ginette would arrive in Swansea on the Irish steamer for an indefinite stay in the Gower Peninsula. We would meet, possibly enjoy one or two quiet passionless talks on our own and then part; I had another important case pending and it was necessary for me to return to London to prepare for it. During the next twelve months further meetings would doubtless occur and, all being well, our platonic relationship would be comfortably reestablished. After that I would have to wait and see what my prospects were, but the one strikingly obvious aspect of the situation was that I could not now descend upon Oxmoon like some overheated knight of medieval legend, fling myself at the feet of the lady I loved and beg her to marry me immediately. I could think of nothing that would irritate Ginette more, particularly a bereaved Ginette who had lost her husband in unexplained but apparently tragic circumstances.

As promised in her wire she had written to my parents but still she had not clarified the mystery of Kinsella's death; indeed she had begged them not to inquire about it. Having wound up her New York life with extraordinary haste she had sailed to Ireland with her two sons within a week of Kinsella's death, and after the funeral she had resolved to leave her sons temporarily in the care of her husband's family while she visited Wales. She did not explain this decision in her letter to my parents. Perhaps she felt it would be better for the boys to remain with their father's family instead of being swept off into a milieu where their father had been disliked; perhaps she had simply wanted to be alone for a while; perhaps her decision represented a combination of these reasons, but whatever her motives the fact remained that she was due to arrive alone in Swansea on the morning of Friday, the twentieth of June, and that she had begged that no one, absolutely no one, was to meet her at the docks except my father's coachman with the family motorcar.

I want to fulfill a dream, she wrote to me in response to the brief formal letter of sympathy I had sent to her in Dublin. *I dreamt I was coming home to Oxmoon and all the family were lined up on the porch steps—it was like an old-fashioned photograph, I could even see the sepia tints! So don't be at the docks to meet me. Be at Oxmoon with the others and make my dream come true.*

I found her letter and turned up the gas to reread it.

So Ginette too had her dreams of returning to Oxmoon.

The bells of St. Clement's sang faintly again on the night air and beyond the window the sky was lightening but I could not sleep. Cicero's metaphor of the Wheel of Fortune had captivated my imagination, and moving to the bookshelves I found the volume written by that later philosopher who had restated the ancient metaphor for the men of the Middle Ages who had known little of Cicero. From King Alfred to Chaucer, from Dante to a host of other Continental writers, all medieval Europe had been mesmerized by Boethius, writing in *The Consolation of Philosophy* about the sinister Wheel of Fortune:

> I know the many disguises of that monster, Fortune, and the extent to which she seduces with friendship the very people she is striving to cheat, until she overwhelms them with unbearable grief at the suddenness of her desertion. . . .

I thought of Ginette abandoning me for Kinsella in the ballroom at Oxmoon. But now Fortune herself was speaking; the monster was making her classic statement about her notorious wheel:

> I was inclined to favor you . . . now I have withdrawn my hand. . . . Inconstancy is my very essence; it is the game I never cease to play as I turn my wheel in its ever-changing circle, filled with joy as I bring the top to the bottom and the bottom to the top. Yes, rise up on my wheel if you like, but don't count it an injury when by the same token you begin to fall as the rules of the game will require. . . .

I saw myself facing a new opponent in the game of life. Death had been replaced by Fortune. I was riding upwards on her wheel at last but this time when I got to the top I was going to stay there. I was going to beat that Wheel of Fortune and bend Fortune herself to my will.

A variety of erotic images teemed in my mind. Then, thinking how appropriate it was that Fortune should be represented as a woman, I returned to bed and dreamed of conquest.

V

I left Bennett at my chambers in London, just as I always did when I went home. It would have been pretentious to take a valet to Oxmoon where under my mother's regime shirts seemed to wash, iron and starch themselves and where my father's man was always on hand to attend to any detail that defied the laundress or my mother's omnipresent needle. Bennett, who was a Cockney, never minded being left in London. No doubt he enjoyed the respite from ironing *The Times* and performing all the other minor rites which must have made life with me so tedious. As he handed me a perfectly packed bag to take to Oxmoon I made a mental note to give him an increase in wages.

My brother Lion had threatened to accompany me on the train journey to Swansea, but fortunately he had been dismissed that week from the bank where he had been pretending to earn a living and had already bounded back to Gower to resume his favorite occupation: the pursuit of idleness in pleasant surroundings. Justice compels me to add that Lion was not vicious, merely a young man of twenty-three with a limited intellect and an ingenuous disposition. In my opinion such people are much better suited to life in the country and should leave places like London well alone.

However despite Lion's absence I did not travel on my own to Swansea that day. My favorite brother John was at Paddington Station to meet me; he had recently taken his finals at Oxford and had been spending a few days with friends in London to recuperate. Term had ended, his rooms had been vacated, his possessions had been dispatched to Gower. He was, in short, in that pleasant limbo when one successful phase of life has ended and another is yet to begin, and he looked as if he had been finding the hiatus enjoyable. Having made some aristocratic friends up at Oxford he was fresh from sampling the pleasures of the London season from a base in Belgrave Square.

"How's the decadent aristocracy?" I said as we met on the platform.

"You sound like an anarchist!" He laughed to show he was redeemed from priggishness by a sense of humor but I suspected he was mildly shocked. John would not have approved of anarchists. Nor would he have approved of any decadence among the members of the aristocracy, for in our family John represented the final triumph of my mother's *nouveau-riche* middle-class values. With an apparently inexhaustible virtue he dedicated his life to drawing lines and doing the done thing.

He was twenty-one, ten years my junior, better-looking than I was but not so tall. Neither was he so gifted athletically and academically. This meant that jealousy would have been quite uncalled for on my part, and indeed I had never seen any reason why I should be other than benign towards this intelligent sibling who always behaved so respectfully in my presence, but occasionally—perhaps once every two or three years—I did wonder how he avoided being jealous of me. Lion did not compete. Neither did Edmund, my third brother, who was two years younger than John and a mere lackluster version of Lion. My fourth brother

Thomas was at present too juvenile to take seriously but showed every sign of growing up stupid. But John had brains, and John, I knew, was ambitious, and John was just the kind of young man who might resent an older brother who always came first. However, he had apparently found some solution to this dilemma because I could tell he still hero-worshiped me. Perhaps he merely told himself that jealousy was not the done thing.

"It's so good to see you again, Robert! It seems ages since we last met—of course I know you've been uncommonly busy—"

"I should never be too busy to deny myself the opportunity for civilized conversation," I said at once. I felt guilty that although he had been in London for some days I had been too preoccupied with my obsessions to see him. "It's the fools, not the intelligent men, whom I find impossible to suffer gladly."

John relaxed. "Talking of fools, I suppose you know Lion's been sacked? I saw him at a ball last weekend and he told me how thrilled he was. He was rather squiffy and trying to teach some married woman the Paris tango."

"I trust you gave him a wide berth."

"The widest, yes. I spent an hour discussing the Marconi scandal with three elderly bores and praying that no one would ask me if Lionel Godwin was a relation of mine...."

We found an empty first-class compartment, paid off the porters and settled ourselves opposite each other while John talked earnestly of the Marconi scandal and the absolute necessity for a strict morality in politics.

"Quite," I said, and to steer him away from the subject of morality which so entranced him I added, "So much for politics. Tell me about yourself. Met any interesting girls lately?"

John liked girls. For some years I had waited for him to ask my advice on the vital subject of premarital carnal satisfaction, but evidently my father had improved on his discourse on the shining sea of carnality because the appeal for useful information had never come.

"Well, I met this most fascinating suffragist at a tea dance—"

"Oh my God!"

"—and she knew the woman who threw herself under the King's horse at Epsom the other day—"

"If you ask me *The Times'* leader put the entire matter in a nutshell by saying the woman showed a thorough lack of consideration for the jockey."

"—and did you realize, Robert, that the woman had actually won a first at Oxford?"

"Then that woman's suicide is the best argument I've yet heard against higher education for women. All women should be educated at home by a governess—as Ginette was."

The name was out. I, who prided myself on my immaculate self-control, was apparently reduced to dragging in the name of my beloved at every conceivable opportunity as if I were some addlepated schoolboy who had fallen in love for the first time.

"I say!" said John, so young, so innocent, so utterly unaware of my chaotic thoughts. "Isn't it splendid to think that Ginevra's coming home! How long is it since we last saw her? Four years?"

"Five." The train lurched forward at last and my heart lurched with it as the station began to recede before my eyes.

"It was a shame she only managed to visit us once during her marriage but I don't think Kinsella liked us much, do you? Robert, now that he's dead, do tell me—what was your final opinion of Conor Kinsella?"

"I've been educated as an Englishman. The English don't have opinions about the Irish. They have prejudices," I said, determined to repel all memory of Conor Kinsella, but the next moment the view from the train window had faded and in my mind I was once more drinking port with him five years ago at Brooks's, once more longing to smash my glass against the nearest wall.

VI

"I'm clean overpowered by the honor you're doing me!" said the villain. "Dining in a famous London club with a true English gentleman! I never thought I'd ever rise so high—or sink so low, depending on which side of the Irish Sea you're standing!"

"I'm a Welshman."

"To be sure you are—a Welshman with one of the most famous Saxon names of all time! Wasn't it Earl Godwin's son who fought William at Hastings?"

How does one talk to such people? If they somehow avoid talking about religion then they talk of race, and all the time they drag in history by its hind legs as if the past were a recalcitrant hero who obstinately refused to die.

Of course I had been obliged to ask him to dine. I had wanted above all to perpetuate the myth that I no longer cared about Ginette's marriage so I knew I had to make some demonstration to convince her husband that I wished him well. But beyond my compulsion to shore up my pride with such a charade I was aware of a terrible curiosity to examine my successful rival at close quarters. I think I hoped I could write him off as a failure, someone who was patently inferior to me despite his achievement in winning Ginette.

During our dinner I tried to size him up but this was difficult. I found myself increasingly aware that he came from a part of the British Isles that I had never visited, and because it was such an alien part I found it impossible to place him against any background that was familiar to me. The Welsh may be Celts as the Irish are but they are a different kind of Celt. To know the Welsh well was no passport to understanding that mysterious race which lay on the other side of the St. George's Channel.

To make matters still more confusing I sensed that the life he now lived in New York had little connection with the life he had led in Ireland. Ginette had told me his father had been the manager of a small shipping firm in Dublin, a

50

fact which implied that Kinsella had come from a respectable middle-class home, and she had also told me that Kinsella himself had received a Catholic education, whatever that meant, in a reputable Dublin school, but as I faced him across the table at Brooks's that night it seemed to me that he had discarded both his religion and his respectability a very long time ago. Despite the fact that he dressed well and knew how to behave I sensed that he was a criminal. He had the kind of soft dark eyes which I often found among my clients, eyes that could watch iniquity with indifference. He drank too much without any noticeable effect. And in his well-kept hands and in the occasional turn of phrase I saw the cardsharper and heard the gambler speaking.

"Cards on the table!" he exclaimed at last after the waiter had brought us our port. He had a variable accent which in one sentence could range from Dublin to New York and back again. "We've been watching each other like hawks throughout the meal—why don't we now strip off the mask of courtesy and exchange our true opinions of each other?"

I had no objection. Far from it. I seized the chance to annihilate him with my perspicacity. All I said was, "Who goes first?"

"We'll toss for it!" said the gambler and flicked a florin in the air.

I called heads and won. With a smile I said, "I'm to be entirely frank in giving my opinion of you?"

"Altogether and entirely—with no offense given or taken on either side!"

"Very well." I lit a cigar. "I think you're the black sheep of your respectable Dublin family. You say you own two restaurants in Manhattan but I think your money comes not from the dining rooms but from the gambling hells—and worse—upstairs. Perhaps you have other interests too which are equally dubious because I think you've got the nerve and the flair and the sheer amoral greed to sail dangerously close to the wind in your business ventures and emerge unscathed. Some men are born criminals. I believe you're one of them. Crime really does pay for men like you. You have the well-oiled veneer of a man who's constantly on the receiving end of glittering dividends."

He roared with laughter and drank a glass of port straight off. "Oh, for shame!" he said. "And me an innocent man who goes to Mass every Sunday!" Then he poured himself some more port and leaned forward with his forearms on the table. He was still smiling. "And now," he said, "we come to you."

I was unperturbed. What could he say? I was impregnable behind the massive walls of my success, and it was inconceivable that he could reduce them to ruins.

"I look at you," said this gambler, this criminal, this personification of all my misery, "and what do I see? I see a tough customer who's made a career of grabbing what he wants and profiting out of it. You have as much amoral greed as I have but you cover it up by masquerading as an English gentleman—ah yes, you may be Welsh by birth, Robert Godwin, but it's an Englishman you are through and through and like all Englishmen you think you should be top dog. And being top dog means getting what you believe is owing to you—money, power, fame, fortune... and women. But you don't think of women as women, do you? You see them as prizes—glittering dividends, if I may quote your own phrase against you—but the prize you've always wanted, Robert Godwin, is the prize you can never win, and that's why you're sitting there, God help you, hating my guts and wishing I was dead. Ah, to be sure it's a terrible tragedy you've suffered! To lose your best prize to another man would be enough to break your heart—but to lose your best prize to an *Irishman* must be enough to destroy your English soul entirely! How can you dine with me and feign friendship? I swear I'd find your pride contemptible if I didn't already find it so pathetic!"

I drank a little port and eyed the glowing tip of my cigar. When I was sure I had myself in control I said, "An inaccurate survey of my private thoughts—but an amusing one."

"Are you denying you still want her?"

"There are other women in the world."

"Women who can match that childhood sweetheart?"

"Playmate," I said, "would be a more appropriate word to use, I think."

"Little girls don't stay playmates. Little girls become big girls and big girls become sweethearts."

"I was only fourteen when she left home to live at All-Hallows Court."

"I started doing all manner of things when I was fourteen," said Conor Kinsella.

There was a pause. I said nothing.

"In fact if I'd had a sweetheart like Ginevra when I was fourteen I sure wouldn't have let the grass grow under my feet."

"I happen to be exceedingly partial to grass. What the devil are you trying to say to me, Kinsella?"

"You had her, didn't you?"

I got up and walked out.

He followed me to the cloakroom.

"So I was right," he said. "Well, cynic that I am, I've always found it hard to believe in platonic friendship!"

"You're wrong," I said, "and to hell with your bloody cynicism."

"Oh, don't misunderstand!" he said after only the most fractional pause. "Of course when I married her she was as virginal as three nuns knocking at the gates of heaven—lucky man that I was!—but one can travel far, can't one, without meddling with virginity, and you can't blame me for wondering in the circumstances if the two of you had been in the habit of taking long journeys together."

I returned to the dining room, signed for the meal, stubbed out my cigar and left the club. He was just putting on his top hat as I emerged into the street. It was raining. I remember the cabs splashing mud and a motorcar sidling along like a noisy crab while nearby a bunch of inebriated young sprigs were trying to sing "Hullo Dolly Gray."

"Not a word of this to Ginevra," said Kinsella, very much the sophisticated older man telling his junior how to behave. "The poor woman wants to think we're bosom friends—ah, such a romantic she is!—and loving her as we do we've no choice but to humor her, have we? But I'll not bring her back here in a hurry—I wouldn't trust you not to try and win her when my back was turned. Oh, I know you English gentlemen! You'd lay waste the world to get what you wanted and afterwards you'd claim it was the will of God!"

And off he sauntered along St. James's Street on his way back to Claridges and his wife.

VII

It was late in the afternoon when the train approached Swansea on that June day in 1913 and John offered a paraphrase of William Blake:

"Here come the dark satanic mills."

The familiar bizarre landscape once more met my eyes. As the full curve of Swansea Bay came into sight we could dimly perceive through the pall of smoke the blue expanse of the sea and the masts of the many ships which crowded those shining, polluted waters. John hastily pulled up the window to keep the smell out as we passed through the copper-smelting area, and we both averted our eyes automatically from the scars of coal mining that marked the industrial wasteland on the ruined east side of the city.

Yet beyond the east side in the central district lay the Swansea which had provided us with our first experience of urban life, a teeming, tousled town flung against the steep hills overlooking the bay like some Naples of the North. The main streets had English names but Swansea always seemed to me as Welsh as its male choirs. Welsh dynamism pulsed through the busy streets and throbbed daily in the vast market; the Welsh lust for culture was on exhibition at the great library which was one of the city's finest buildings; the Welsh addiction to music continually floated in some form or another upon the Welsh air where the tang of the sea persisted in mingling with the reek of the smoke. Swansea might have been raped by the industrial revolution but she had survived with her vitality, if not her beauty, intact.

"I feel such a foreigner in England sometimes," said my brother John, gazing out of the window at our native land. "I feel so torn between one culture and another."

"Well, stitch yourself together again because here comes the station." I always felt John exaggerated the conundrum of belonging to two countries. Wales was home but England was the center of the world and if one wanted to get on in life one moved freely between the two without making a fuss.

To our surprise and pleasure we found that my father had dispensed with the services of his coachman and had motored himself to Swansea to bid us welcome.

"It's not often you come home nowadays, Robert," he said as we shook hands, "so I felt this was a special occasion." Scrupulously fair to John he then added: "And you deserve a royal welcome too after three such successful years up at Oxford!" I might be my father's favorite, but my father was always most conscientious about not neglecting his other children.

We retired to my father's motorcar which, though new, looked elderly because it was covered with white dust from the Gower lanes. My father loved his motorcar with a passion which John shared. The two of them spent much time discussing the merits of this new soulless brute, which was called a Talbot, while I yawned and thought what a bore the subject of mechanics was. A passion for horses I can understand; a horse is an aesthetically pleasing animal with an honorable history of service to mankind, but a passion for a few scraps of metal slapped on four wheels seems to me not only irrational but also indicative of an unintellectual, possibly even of a working-class, cast of mind.

With my father at the wheel we were soon careering through central Swansea. We roared past the ruined Norman castle, blazed past Ben Evans, the largest store, and swept by the grandest hotel, the Metropole. Other motors hooted in friendly admiration, the carriages and carts jostled to escape and the pedestrians dived for cover. While my father and John laughed, I amused myself by planning how I would defend my father against a charge of manslaughter by motor but presently I was diverted as we ascended the hill out of the city and our pace became funereal. John offered to push but my father said that would be an admission of defeat. We toiled on.

With the summit of the hill behind us we soon found ourselves on the outskirts of the city, and then with that suddenness which always took my breath away we entered a different world. A wild moorland wilderness stretched before us. Mysterious hills shimmered in the distance. We had crossed the threshold into Gower.

"Swansea's secret—the Gower Peninsula!" said my father in Welsh with a smile, and John, exhibiting somewhat showily his parrotlike trick of bilingualism, made a swift response which I failed to comprehend.

We drove on into an England beyond Wales, into a hidden land, pastoral and idyllic, which basked innocently in the summer sun. Beyond the moorland stretch which bounded the outskirts of Swansea, fields drowsed between English hedgerows and little lanes twisted through the countryside to villages which looked as if they had been transplanted from far beyond the Welsh border. We might have been a thousand miles now from teeming Swansea and a thousand years from that industrial wasteland on the bay.

"How peaceful it looks!" said John to me, but as soon as he said that I thought of Gower's lawless past. This was a land where the King's writ had so often failed to run, a land soaked in the crimes of smuggling, wrecking and piracy, robbery, murder and rape. I have always thought it an irony that we have become so civilized that we can now regard places such as Gower as "romantic" and "colorful." Personally I can think of nothing more terrifying than to live in a land where law and order have no meaning and violence is the rule of the day.

On and on we traveled through South Gower, that ancient Norman stronghold, and now on our right Cefn Bryn, the backbone of Gower, rose to form a long treeless line of land beneath the blue sky. To our left the sea at Oxwich Bay flashed far away, sometimes hidden, sometimes revealed by the gates set in the hedges. And ahead of us at last, shimmering with promise and seemingly beckoning us on into a mythical kingdom, the hump of Rhossili Downs marked the end of the Peninsula and a view that I believed no land in Europe could surpass.

We turned off before the Downs. The motor picked up speed as we roared into the parish of Penhale. Moors dotted with wild ponies stretched before us again, but we could see the trees of Oxmoon now, and presently the high wall of the grounds bordered the lane on our right.

"Hurrah!" cried John as we reached the gates.

Oxmoon lay ahead of us, droll little Oxmoon, an eighteenth-century parody of the classical architecture made famous by Robert Adam. We had arrived. My father halted the motor with a triumphant jerk and as the noise of the engine died I at once felt in a better humor. We had been traveling with the roof closed and all the windows shut in order to keep the dust out, so when we flung open the doors the fresh air came as the most exquisite luxury. I got out, stretched my long legs which had not been designed to suffer gladly fifteen-mile journeys in motorcars, and took a deep breath. The air was fragrant with the scent of new-mown grass mingled with lavender. I could hear the larks singing and suddenly, for one precious moment, I was back in my childhood with Ginette so that when I turned to face my home again I saw not the provincial little country house of reality but the fairy-tale palace of my dreams.

My mother opened the front door.

Instantly the past was wiped out and I was left with all my most ambivalent emotions in a highly uncertain present. Assuming an impregnable mask of filial respect I exclaimed with warmth, "My dear Mama, how splendid to see you again!" and moved swiftly up the steps to embrace her.

"Dearest Robert," said my mother, regarding me tranquilly with those pale eyes which saw far too far and much too much, "welcome home."

VIII

I was at Oxmoon waiting for Ginette. It was seven o'clock on the evening of my arrival and I was dressing for dinner. Fifteen hours to go.

When I had finished I paused to survey my oldest possessions which, arranged around me on shelves, created a powerful atmosphere of nostalgia. Here were the silver cups I had acquired during the course of my academic and athletic career as a schoolboy. Here were the favorite books of my boyhood, the dog-eared collection of Robert Louis Stevenson's work, the battered copy of *Eric*, the haggard edition of *The Prisoner of Zenda*. Here were my school photographs hanging at regular intervals on the wall above my bed to record my progress from stony-faced small boy to supercilious young man. Why had I kept this amazing collection of trivia? I could only suppose that despite my well-ordered mind I had fallen victim to one of Oxmoon's most exasperating traditions: everything was hoarded; nothing was thrown away.

Tucked discreetly behind a cushion on the window seat I even found the toy dog which I had been given in infancy, his white woolly coat worn threadbare and his ears sagging with age. To my astonishment I saw that his tail had recently been repaired. This seemed to indicate either the presence in the house of a demented housemaid or a tension so profound in my mother that she had been obliged to scour the bedrooms for something to sew. I was just picking up the dog tenderly by the front paws and remembering how I had screamed when Ginette had once tried to annex him, when the door of my room was flung open without warning to reveal a small intruder in a nightshirt.

"You're wanted," said my youngest brother Thomas, and seeing the toy in my arms he added, "I want that dog. I took him last week but Papa said I had to ask you if you minded. We had a tug-of-war over it actually and his tail came off. The dog's, I mean, not Papa's. Well, Papa doesn't have a tail. Anyway it didn't matter because Mama sewed it on again. Can I have him?"

"No. Who wants me?"

"Mama. She's in her room. Why can't I have Dodo?"

"Because you haven't said Please and you didn't knock before you came in. Run away and learn how to behave."

"Yah!" said the infant, sticking out his tongue at me, and stumped off angrily to the nurseries.

In a large family it is not uncommon to find a sting in the tail and the sting is usually referred to as an "afterthought." This afterthought, far from being ignored as befits the youngest and least significant member of a tribe, is often most foolishly pampered until he has ideas far above his station. Thomas was six and his ideas of his own importance were so elevated that they probably, like the occupants of the recent record-breaking balloon, needed oxygen to survive.

How he had come to enter the world was a mystery to me, and not a pleasant mystery, either. In fact I had been much disturbed when in my mid-twenties I was informed that my mother was expecting another child. My feelings arose not because I felt it was in poor taste for my mother to indulge in parturition at an advanced age; at that time she was still only forty-two, a curious but by no means preposterous age at which to embark on pregnancy. The truth was that I was disturbed by the news because it seemed my father had lied to me about his private life.

I was twenty when I found out he was unfaithful to my mother. There was no dramatic scene. The dénouement arose from my observation that he had formed the regular habit of going up to town once a month and staying three or four days at his club. My mother said this was a good idea because he tended to work too hard at home and now that he was older she felt it was important that he should go away to relax occasionally. I thought no more about this reasonable explanation for his absences, but one day during the long vacation when he and I were out riding together I said casually, "What do you do with yourself when you're up in town, Papa?" and he had answered with regret but without hesitation: "I knew you'd ask me that one day and I made up my mind that when you did I'd be honest with you."

He then told me he kept a woman in Maida Vale.

"Of course," he said, "your natural reaction will be to think me a hypocrite after all I've said to you on the subject of reserving that sort of pleasure for marriage but in fact my views haven't changed. I don't like what I'm doing and I don't ask you to condone it. All I ask is that you should try to understand and not judge me too harshly."

He said the intimate side of marriage had become repugnant to my mother and added that this was hardly surprising after so many pregnancies.

". . . certainly I don't blame her, how could I, she's the most wonderful wife in the world and I'm the luckiest man on earth and I love her with all my heart, as you know. But . . . well, on religious grounds your mother don't hold with anticonception, and as for chastity that's a gift I don't possess, not at the age of forty after twenty-one years of perfect married life."

He revealed that my mother herself had suggested that he kept a mistress.

"She said she wouldn't mind so long as it was a business arrangement conducted a long way from home—she said it would even be a relief to her because the last thing she wanted was to make me unhappy. So . . . well, we thought London would be best. I didn't want to go into Swansea. In fact I couldn't. You see, my father used to go into Swansea and . . ." He stopped. As usual he could never bring himself to talk about his father but this time I saw to my horror that he was about to break down altogether. There were tears in his eyes. Hastily I gave him my word that I quite understood his predicament and thought none the worse of him for his solution.

The conversation then closed and I never raised the subject again until he told me Thomas had been conceived.

"But my dear Papa, I thought you told me that side of your marriage had ceased!"

He laughed and said quickly, "It was the night of our silver wedding—just an isolated occasion."

"But you said my mother—"

"Oh, now that she's had a rest from childbearing she's anxious for one final pregnancy."

I was a trained lawyer by that time but an inexperienced one; it was not until later that my professional instincts told me my father had had something to hide. This fact by itself, however, was neither remarkable nor a cause for alarm for there was no reason why my father should have told me every salient detail of his private life, particularly as any marriage is a very private affair. But what troubled me was that I sensed my father had brought off a *tour de force* which I could only regard as sinister: I suspected he had blended fact and fiction with the skill of an uncommonly gifted liar.

As soon as I had formed this judgment I dismissed it as ridiculous, but Thomas always reminded me of it and I knew I was more abrupt with the child than I should have been. Making a mental note to bestow the toy dog on him with my blessing I remembered the message he had brought me. It was time for battle again at Oxmoon. Smoothing my hair I looked in the glass to ensure that my appearance was immaculate, and then I set off to wage war with my mother.

IX

"Hullo, dear," said my mother, barely glancing up as I entered the room. She was seated at the dressing table and sifting through one of her jewel boxes for a suitable adornment for her dowdy evening gown. As I closed the door she retrieved a dreary trinket studded with jet and began to pin it on her ample bosom. "Do sit down," she added as an afterthought, nodding at the customary victim's chair nearby.

I moved the chair back against the wall so that it stood facing her but out of reach of the triple looking glass. Then I manifested nonchalance by sitting down and crossing one leg over the other but immediately she readjusted the far mirror until against all the odds my reflection was recaptured. Embarking on a study of the ceiling I prayed for patience and heartily wished myself elsewhere.

I wondered not for the first time if she really had told my father to take a mistress or whether my father had invented this magnanimous gesture in order to gloss over the wifely failings that had driven him elsewhere. Anger pierced me suddenly. I sensed she had made my father unhappy, and if she had rejected him I felt I could only find her attitude repellent.

It also occurred to me, as I continued to observe her, that her rejection showed a lack not only of charity but of gratitude. A plain middle-aged woman should surely be so thankful to have a handsome successful devoted husband that she should make every effort to accommodate him. I remembered how my father never uttered one word of complaint about her *nouveau-riche* background and her appalling relations in Staffordshire. He had married beneath him when he had married her, and although her Midlands accent had long since disappeared and her more unfortunate social attributes had been ironed away by a formidable air of refinement, she could never be his equal in rank. The marriage had been arranged to save Oxmoon from bankruptcy. If my father had been older and if his mother and Owain Bryn-Davies had been less desperate for money, I had no doubt that my father would have looked elsewhere for a wife.

However the marriage had been successful enough in its own way and my mother did have many virtues. Reminding myself how fond I was of her I made renewed efforts to be charitable.

"What did you wish to speak to me about, Mama?" I said, knowing perfectly well that she had diagnosed the state of my heart with unerring accuracy and had resolved to advise me against marrying Ginette.

"Well, dear," said my mother, poking around in her jewel box, "I just thought we might have a little chat before Ginevra arrives tomorrow. Your father told me of the conversation he had recently with you in London."

"Ah yes," I said; "I did wonder if you'd think his report needed clarification." We exchanged smiles.

"Oh no, dear," said my mother. "You told your father, I believe, that you had every intention of behaving like a mature intelligent man. What sentiment could be more clearly expressed? I simply wished to reassure you that like your father all I want is your happiness, Robert. I wanted to reassure you of that in case you were harboring some suspicion that I had every intention of making you miserable."

"Far be it from me, Mama, to suspect you of such an unworthy aim."

We laughed politely together. There was a pause. I waited.

"I do so disapprove," said my mother, extricating a pair of jet earrings from the jewel box, "of mothers who meddle in the lives of their grown-up children, so you need have no fear that I'm going to meddle. After all, why should I? You're a man of the world. You don't need your mother to remind you of the hazards of marrying a widow of thirty-three with two growing sons and a somewhat... unusual past. Nor do you need your mother to tell you how much better you could do for yourself. Nor need I point out to you the danger of relying on illusions which bear no relation to reality—naturally you're well aware of the dangers of carrying an adolescent infatuation forward into adult life. So all in all, Robert—bearing in mind that you're a supremely rational man and thoroughly experienced in the Ways of the World—I have decided to say nothing whatsoever on the subject and to hold my peace in order to display my utmost confidence in the ultimate triumph of your good sense."

There was another pause. When I was sure I had my temper in control, I said, "Mama, it's hard to believe you've never studied Cicero. One of his favorite oratorical tricks was to declare, 'I shall say nothing about this' and then to say everything in the most excruciating detail." Standing up abruptly, I moved beyond the range of the triple looking glass before saying, "You seem to be implying I'm a complete fool."

"It's a sad fact of life, dear, that not even men of a brilliant intellectual caliber are incapable of making a mistake where affairs of the heart are concerned. Indeed quite the contrary, I've always thought."

"I'm not interested in your opinion of some idiotic state of mind which as far as I'm concerned exists only in the pages of romantic fiction."

"Oh my dear Robert—"

"I'm sorry, Mama, but really this skirmishing is exhausting my patience!"

"Then let me be direct." Leaving her dressing table, she moved swiftly to my side, gripped my shoulders and spun me to face her. "Let me speak straight from the heart. Your father believes you when you imply you've recovered from Ginevra, but you haven't recovered, have you, Robert? I think you're bound to see Ginevra's bereavement as an opportunity for you to rewrite the past and wipe out the memory of that time when you were humiliated. You're such a very clever man, but very clever men can be capable of such disastrous emotional naivety!"

"Why are you so against Ginette?"

"When she visited Oxmoon five years ago, I had the chance to sum her up and I saw exactly what kind of a woman she had become."

"A beautiful woman necessarily finds it hard to win the approbation of her own sex—"

"Oh, don't misunderstand me! I don't disapprove of her because she's the sort of woman who wouldn't think twice about being unfaithful to her husband—

such women often manage to sustain successful marriages. No, I disapprove of her as a wife for you because I think she's a complex woman with all kinds of problems you couldn't begin to solve."

"Mama—"

"You see, I know you, Robert. I know you better than you know yourself. You're like me. At heart your emotional tastes are really very simple."

"I'll be the best judge, thank you, Mama, about what my emotional tastes really are. And if you think I'm like you then all I can say is that I can't see the resemblance."

There was a silence. For a moment we stood there, inches apart, and stared at each other. Then she covered her face with her hands and turned away.

"Mama . . ." I was immediately appalled by my cruelty. "Forgive me, I—"

"It was my fault," she said levelly, letting her hands fall and moving back to the dressing table. "I shouldn't have meddled."

"I do have the greatest respect and regard for you, Mama—"

"Oh yes," she said flatly. "Respect and regard. How nice." She found a garnet ring, shoved it onto her finger and snapped shut the box.

"I have always entertained the very deepest affection—"

"Quite." She made no effort to respond as I stooped to touch her cheek with my lips. I had a fleeting impression of eau de cologne and anger. Her plump cheek was cold. When she said abruptly, "Hadn't we better go downstairs?" I made no effort to detain her, and after opening the door in a formal gesture of courtesy I followed her in silence from the room.

X

Unable to sleep that night I lay awake remembering the aspersions which my mother had cast on Ginette's capacity for marital fidelity.

In the old days Ginette had been conspicuous for her loyalty. I could remember her standing shoulder to shoulder with me in the nursery, writing to me at school every week without fail and even after her marriage keeping in touch with me when a less faithful friend would have permitted the relationship to become moribund.

Yet although I did not question her capacity for loyal friendship I knew well enough that sexual fidelity was a game played to different rules. Friendship might be forever but people fell in and out of love, and marriage was far from immune to this well-known ebbing and flowing of desire. Would I blame Ginette for being unfaithful to Kinsella? No, of course not. A man like Kinsella deserved an unfaithful wife. But I wasn't Conor Kinsella and my marriage would be played to different rules.

Not only would I give Ginette no cause for infidelity, but I would make it clear to her from the beginning that she was to behave as a wife should. Like servants, women need to be told what to do; they like firm guidance, and that is why I am so unalterably opposed to votes for women. In reality it would not mean independence for females. It would mean that all the masterful husbands, lovers, fathers and brothers would have two votes instead of one. A woman's talents are limited to managing a home and bringing up children. One can no more expect a woman to show independence of mind by casting an intelligent vote than one can expect a woman to debate an important issue in the House of Commons with implacable oratorical skill.

I thought of my mother reminding me of Cicero, the greatest orator of all time.

But that proved my point. All my mother had ever wanted to do was to manage a home and bring up children. My mother was a clever woman, possibly the cleverest woman I had ever met, and she had no interest whatsoever in women's suffrage.

When I finally fell asleep it was well after midnight but by six o'clock I was already awake and picturing Ginette asleep in her cabin on the steamer that had been carrying her overnight from Dublin to Swansea. Would she be nervous? She had been nervous when she had returned for her visit five years before, although she had tried to hide her feelings behind a mask of exuberance.

"Robert darling, how heavenly to see you again—give me a divine platonic kiss to celebrate our eternal friendship!"

I shuddered at the memory and wondered how I was going to survive the inevitable sexual frustration which lay in store for me. She herself would be safe, locked up in her role of the bereaved widow, but what on earth was going to happen to me as she dabbed her eyes with a black lace handkerchief and succeeded in looking seductively haggard?

I groaned, and then gritting my teeth I began to plan a debonair speech to welcome her home.

XI

Four hours later I was awaiting her imminent arrival. I had made some excuse to escape from the mob milling in the hall and was standing motionless at the landing window which faced the drive. As I nervously embarked on smoking a cigarette I wondered what to do with the ash, but in the end I was in such a state that I merely let it drop to the floor.

Various inane remarks floated up the stairs.

"Let's all pose for a photograph!" Celia was calling breathlessly.

"Celia, give me your camera!" That was the infant, being obstreperous as usual.

"No, Thomas—no, Thomas—oh, Mama, do stop him—"

"Edmund," said John, intelligent enough to remain urbane amidst all this hysteria, "what about a quick game of billiards? I bet the steamer's been delayed."

"But supposing it hasn't?" Edmund, even though he was now nineteen, suffered from a constitutional inability to make up his mind.

"I think she'll be arriving at any minute," said Lion, "and if you go off to the billiard room you'll be fools. Lord, isn't this a thrill? I keep visualizing this splendid creature swathed in black and looking unutterably sumptuous—"

"Shhh! Here comes Mama."

"Boys, have you seen Robert anywhere?"

"No, he's gone off to be wonderful somewhere else, thank God," said Lion, revealing that he was less than respectful when my back was turned.

"That will do, Lionel. No, Thomas, you *cannot* have Celia's camera. Edmund—"

"Here's the car!"

"She's coming!"

"Quick, quick, quick—"

"Papa—quickly, Papa, the motor's here!"

"Out to the porch, everyone—"

"Come on, Celia—"

"Come on, Edmund—"

"Come on, everyone!"

There was a stampede of feet below me. Meanwhile I had dropped my cigarette and was making the most intolerable mess. Having unforgivably ground the butt beneath my heel I drew back for cover behind the curtain as my father's Talbot bore the bereaved widow at an appropriately funereal pace up the drive to the steps of the porch.

"Hurray!"

"Welcome home!"

"Welcome back, Ginevra!"

"Shhh, boys, a little less noise and a little more decorum, if you please— remember she's in mourning."

My brothers fell obediently silent but as soon as the motor halted they rushed forward to catch a glimpse of the passenger. It was impossible for me and probably difficult for them to perceive her with any degree of clarity. The white dust from the Gower roads had once more laid a pale mask upon the windows.

"Ginevra!" cried Lion, beaming from ear to ear as he flung wide the door of the motor, and then the next moment his mouth dropped open in astonishment. Everyone gasped. My father was suddenly motionless. My mother appeared to be rooted to the ground.

Evidently our visitor was making some shattering impact but since I could see only the roof of the motor I still had no idea what was happening. In a fever of curiosity I flung up the window as far as it would go so that I could lean out over the sill, and it was at that exact moment that she began to descend from the motor. Then I understood. As soon as I saw her I too gasped, for she was not wearing mourning. The image of the widow swathed in black was at a stroke smashed to smithereens.

"Darlings!" cried Ginette, gorgeously clad in a brilliant turquoise traveling costume and sporting a corsage of orchids. "How simply and utterly divine to see you all again!" And as everyone continued to stare at her in stupefaction she glanced carelessly upwards and saw me framed in the window above.

A great stillness descended on her face but a second later she was blowing me a kiss with a smile. "Heavens, darling!" she called richly. "Just like Romeo and Juliet in reverse—all you need is a balcony! What are you doing up there?"

"I was on my way to the kitchen garden to pick you some strawberries!" I said laughing, and at once saw the past recaptured in her dark and brilliant eyes.

3

I

WE DRANK CHAMPAGNE in the drawing room, a spacious room which Robert Godwin the Renovator had called a saloon and filled with eighteenth-century furniture. Unfortunately this elegant collection now lay under dust sheets in the attics, for my parents, whose aesthetic tastes could most kindly be described as eclectic, had long since decided to cram the Oxmoon reception rooms with overstuffed chairs, obese sofas and a bewildering jungle of bric-à-brac.

Oxmoon was famous for its ready supply of champagne to complement important occasions. It was the only alcoholic beverage which my father permitted himself to enjoy; he would take two glasses and, very occasionally, a third. Now that I was older I admired his abstemiousness the more because his cronies among the Gower gentry were a hard-drinking bunch, and I knew from experience how difficult it was not to drink to excess when in the company of men determined to be inebriated.

On this current momentous family occasion my father permitted himself a third glass of champagne. My mother, according to a custom which she never varied, took two glasses with enjoyment and declined another drop. Lion seized the opportunity to join my father in a third glass, John followed my mother's example to show how good he was at drawing the line, and Edmund, as usual, could not make up his mind whether to continue drinking or to abstain. Celia, who had a weak head, was still conscientiously nursing her first glass while I, who could normally take my drink as well as the next man, was keeping pace with her. It is one of the idiosyncrasies of my constitution that under great stress my emotions are not soothed by the consumption of alcohol but exacerbated by it.

Meanwhile in the midst of this studied moderation Ginette was drinking the champagne as if it were lemonade. As the celebration progressed we all stole uneasy glances at my mother to see how she was tolerating this further manifestation of conduct unbecoming to a widow, and although my mother continued to smile serenely the tension steadily increased. I was just wondering how I could abort this sinister emotional momentum when Ginette tossed off the remains of her fourth glass of champagne and said rapidly to my mother, "Margaret, you must be quite horrified, do forgive me, but I'm simply overwhelmed by the desire to rebel against the way I was treated in Ireland—everyone behaved as if my life was finished, and suddenly I couldn't bear it any longer, as soon as I reached the steamer I wanted to throw all my mourning clothes into the sea . . ." She stopped. She was on the verge of breaking down.

"Even your hats?" I said promptly.

"Oh my dear, you know what I'm like about hats!" she said, laughing through her tears. "Even the black ones are much too gorgeous to throw overboard!"

"You'd make any hat look gorgeous!" said Lion roguishly.

"Darling Lion, how adorable you are!"

"Where did you get those incredibly vulgar orchids?" I said to put an end to this cloying exchange of compliments.

"I forced poor Williams to drive up and down the main streets of Swansea until we finally found that very grand florist near the Metropole. No wonder I was late getting here!" She had recovered her equilibrium. Her hand moved automatically back to her glass.

"Orchids and champagne!" said my father who became subtly more carefree under the influence of alcohol. "Good friends—amusing company—laughter—happiness! Yes, that's the remedy I'd prescribe to anyone recovering from terrible times—and we know all about recovering from terrible times, don't we, Margaret?"

"Yes, dear," said my mother.

"Ginevra," said my father, "I insist that you permit me to write a prescription for you: I propose a little dinner party for twenty-four as soon as possible!"

Celia protested amidst the ensuing cheers: "But Papa, I don't suppose Ginevra wants to see anyone outside the family just yet!" She glanced nervously at my mother.

"And what would all the neighbors think?" said John, so driven by his desire to do the done thing that he failed to shrink from exhibiting a lamentably bourgeois cast of mind.

"Oh, damn the neighbors!" exclaimed Ginette, and in the absolute silence that followed I was acutely aware of my mother straightening the garnet ring on her right hand.

Ginette blushed, and in the panic-stricken glance she sent me I read a desperate appeal for help but I was already speaking. Moving to her side I said casually, "I expect women say 'damn' all the time in New York, don't they? *Autre pays, autres moeurs.*"

"What a rotten French accent you've got, Robert," said John, valiantly collaborating with me in helping the conversation along, but Ginette proved quite unable to permit us to gloss over the disaster.

"Margaret, I'm so sorry—please do excuse me—awful vulgarity—frightful taste—" She was in agony.

Ignoring her my mother said serenely to my father, "I think a little dinner party would be acceptable, dearest, provided we have only our oldest friends. But it must be quiet. No champagne; I think champagne would look too eccentric in the circumstances."

"I agree," said my father obediently. "A good claret—perhaps a touch of hock somewhere—but no champagne."

"And of course," said my mother to Celia, "you and I must wear dark gowns, dear, to acknowledge the fact that there's been a tragedy in the family."

"Yes, Mama," said Celia.

"Dearest Ginevra," said my mother, smiling to conceal how implacably she was wielding her power, "you must think us so provincial and old-fashioned in our ways, but we're so far removed here from a modern city like New York! I do hope you understand."

"Yes, Margaret," said Ginette. "Of course." She was clutching her glass so hard that I thought the stem would snap.

"Naturally," pursued my mother, "I wouldn't dream of dictating to you on the subject of dress. I have every confidence, dearest, that you'll contrive to look dignified as well as fetching on any occasion when people outside the family are to be present."

"Yes, Margaret." Her hand shook as she put down her glass. She stood up clumsily. "I must go upstairs and unpack—all my black gowns will need ironing— I wonder if perhaps your maid—"

"I'll send her to you at once," said my mother, clinching her victory with a single succinct sentence.

"I'll come and help you, Ginevra," said Celia, and we all rose to our feet. Lion, John and Edmund all tried to open the door in an orgy of chivalry, and there was much laughter as they bumped into one another. The women departed. My father said, "Who's going to volunteer to deliver the dinner invitations? Time's short as Robert's going back to London on Monday, so we'll have to give this party tomorrow night."

An argument began about how quickly the invitations could be delivered but I did not stay to listen to it. Opening the garden door I slipped out onto the terrace and the next moment I was escaping across the lawn.

II

Cutting a straight line past the freshly painted croquet hoops I circled the lawn tennis court and paused on the edge of the woods by the summerhouse, a two-roomed frivolity built at the whim of my grandfather Robert Godwin the Drunkard in the days before his unfortunate habits had driven his wife to seek consolation with her sheep farmer, Owain Bryn-Davies. In the open doorway I turned to look back at the inheritance his son had resurrected from the grave.

Oxmoon's original name had been Oxton-de-Mohun, which in a loose translation of the three conquerors' languages involved meant "the settlement by water belonging to Humphrey de Mohun." Of the three aggressive races who had battered the Peninsula the Vikings, prowling the coasts in their longships, had probably had the least effect; the Saxons, trading continuously from North Devon, had steadily insinuated their influence among the indigenous Celts, and the Normans had blasted their way into the seat of power with their usual brutal efficiency.

Humphrey de Mohun had been a twelfth-century Norman warlord who had delegated the running of his Gower estate to a Saxon mercenary called Godwin of Hartland. Hartland is the Devonian peninsula that lies south of Gower across the Bristol Channel, and in English-speaking South Gower—called "The Englishry" to distinguish it from "The Welshery" of the Welsh-speaking northeast—Devon is reflected like a mirror image, a little distorted but plainly recognizable, the result of centuries of communication between Wales and England across the busy waters of the Channel.

Godwin set the seal on a successful career when he married de Mohun's younger daughter. When de Mohun died, the elder daughter received her father's vast estates in the Welsh Marches but the younger inherited the fiefdom in Gower which included the fortified tower in the woods below Penhale Down. Financially, socially and territorially Godwin had arrived, and giving his son the Norman name of Robert he settled down to become more Norman than the Normans.

The Norman tower remained the home of the Godwin family until Tudor times when fifteenth-century Robert Godwin tried to celebrate the Battle of Bosworth by building a moated manor, but after this architectural innovation had been razed by a faction from Llangennith he retired to the Norman castle of his ancestors. In the seventeenth century the master of Oxmoon attempted to build a Jacobean mansion on the site of the Tudor manor, but he abandoned the attempt when it became obvious that the result would be a disaster. However the founder of modern Oxmoon, Robert Godwin the Renovator, decided that this uncompleted monstrosity could be finished and given a new look. He had met Robert Adam in Italy during a typical eighteenth-century tour of Europe, and later he became acquainted with the architects of the Wyatt family. Inspiration inevitably followed, and in the library we have one of his letters declaring his intention of making Oxmoon the grandest house in Wales.

A highly idiosyncratic vision of classical architecture was thus initiated, a rustic rendering of a magnificent dream. The portico was rather too large, the windows a fraction too narrow, pediments and chimneys appeared in unexpected places. But if not the grandest house in Wales it must have been one of the most unusual; in South Wales particularly such places are few and far between.

That was the end of the rebuilding of Oxmoon although various additions to the house and grounds occurred later. Robert Godwin the Regency Rake added the ballroom after a visit to Bath, and experimented with an orangerie which collapsed. My grandfather Robert Godwin the Drunkard later restored it before turning his hand to designing the summerhouse.

The results of these centuries of idealistic efforts to bring civilization to this formerly remote and lawless land lay now before my eyes. Despite the small failures of design, which were less noticeable at a distance, the house was at least passably proportioned. It had no basement, two floors and an attic. Virginia creeper, clinging to walls that should have been left bare, gave it an unorthodox look of shaggy coziness, and this unorthodoxy was enhanced by the presence of the ballroom, a startling excrescence upon the Georgian symmetry which looked as if the architect had been reading too many of the Gothic novels of Mrs. Radclyffe during a fatal visit to Brighton Pavilion. However the balance in favor of the conventional was somewhat restored on the other side of the house where the kitchen wing meandered into courtyards which embraced the servants' quarters, the stable block, the farmyard, the timberyard, the kitchen garden and the blighted orangerie where nothing would grow except stunted grapes. Provincial and relaxed, sunlit and cherished, twentieth-century Oxmoon faced its future master across the manicured lawn of the eighteenth-century "pleasure garden" and shimmered beguilingly in the hot noon light.

I felt at peace.

Yet the very peace, which was so unfamiliar, served to remind me of my intractable problems. Rising to my feet to shut them from my mind I sought refuge in the soothing shadows of the woods but at the ruined Norman tower I turned back. Another path led me out of the trees on the far side of the tennis lawn, and strolling down the lavender walk I found myself heading into the walled rectangle of the kitchen garden.

Most of the fruit lay at the far end where an ancient orchard flourished, but nearby I was aware of the strawberry beds exuding their old seductive fragrance. I paused. My senses sharpened. I felt that nothing had changed—despite the fact that everything had changed. I felt time had stood still—and yet I knew it had moved inexorably on. Stooping impulsively I plucked a strawberry from beneath the leaves, and then as the past repeated itself by sliding ahead of the present I knew immediately, without looking up, that Ginette was once more moving down the path to my side.

III

"Robert."

She had changed into a plain black skirt and an elaborate black blouse which opened at the neck to reveal a string of pearls. She had looked striking in turquoise and orchids but in stark black with chaste jewelry she was alluring beyond description. I found myself smiling as I realized how effortlessly—and no doubt unconsciously—my mother's veiled demand for seemliness had been outwitted.

"You shouldn't have let my mother dictate to you in the matter of dress," I said abruptly, offering her the strawberry in my hand.

"My dear, whenever Margaret opens her mouth and says 'dearest Ginevra' I'm immediately reduced to a mindless mass quivering with terror! Heavens, how delicious this strawberry is. Do you remember—"

"Vividly."

"—how we overate and were sick and Margaret put us on bread and water as a punishment—"

"Are all children so mindlessly preoccupied with food, I wonder?"

"Of course! Eating's the first of the great sensual pleasures of life—although of course children don't believe heroes and heroines should be sensual at all. Do you remember how you said you wanted to be a hero?"

"I remember expressing considerable doubt that you'd ever be a heroine."

"I suppose it all depends how you define heroes and heroines, doesn't it? I've come to the conclusion they're unheroic people who flounder around, stagger in and out of awful messes and somehow manage to survive without going mad. Oh, I became a heroine, Robert! But the big question is . . . what became of you? Who are you now? Are you still there?"

I knew at once what she meant. "Yes," I said. "I'm still here."

"Thank God. You terrified me when I arrived. All I could see was this formidable stranger encased in glamour." She stooped to pick another strawberry. "Darling, for heaven's sake take me away from here before I make a complete pig of myself."

We smiled at each other. Our hands clasped. We said no more but walked away without hurrying, and around us past and present kept shifting and interlocking like a constantly shaken kaleidoscope. Bees hummed lazily along the lavender walk and as we drew nearer the tennis lawn the scent of lavender once more gave way to the scent of new-mown grass, drifting towards us on the limpid summer air.

"I can hear the larks singing," said Ginette suddenly.

"Oxmoon Redux."

"What does that mean?"

"The past recaptured."

We reached the summerhouse and turned in unison to look back across the lawn.

"Oxmoon!" said Ginette, and as the tears filled her eyes she said in a shaking voice, "I've done it. I've come home."

I gave her my handkerchief and helped her sit down on one of the wicker chairs. As I sat down besides her she whispered, "I did love him."

"Yes." I watched the curve of her neck below her auburn hair. "I saw that when you were eighteen and I saw it five years ago when you were twenty-eight. Why should I start disbelieving in your love now?"

"Because I'm behaving as if I'm mad with relief. But I'm mad with pain and grief too—it's hard to explain, I'm in such a muddle, oh Robert, Robert, why do I always end up in these ghastly messes?"

"You need someone who can train you to be orderly. Let me offer my services by attempting to dissipate this air of mystery which is clinging to you like a fog—no one can hope to be orderly while they're wallowing in mystery. How did he die?"

"He was shot."

"What! How?"

"With a gun."

"Oh, don't be so stupid, Ginette! I meant how did it happen?"

"Oh, that sort of thing happens quite often in New York. It's that sort of place. I hated it at the end but I loved it in the beginning. It was the city of my youth, the place where all my dreams came true—"

"Never mind that sentimental twaddle for the moment. Let's keep this a well-ordered narrative. Just tell me why he was shot."

"Oh God, I don't know, how should I know, I suppose he got on the wrong side of the Sicilians over his gambling debts, certainly his Irish friends said it would be safer if I left town as soon as possible—"

"But this is barbarous! Are you trying to tell me—"

"Oh yes, it was barbarous, it was hell, it was ghastly beyond belief, God knows why I'm not dead with shock and horror—"

"Tell me exactly what happened."

"He was shot dead on the sidewalk outside our apartment block. We'd been to the theater. He died in my arms." She was sitting on the edge of her chair, my handkerchief clenched in her hands. "That sounds romantic, doesn't it, but it wasn't. It wasn't romantic at all." Tears streamed down her face again. "He screamed in pain and choked on his blood," she said, her voice trembling, "and his last word was an obscenity. 'Shit,' he said. That was all. 'Shit.' Then more blood came out of his mouth and he died." She covered her face with her hands, and although by this time instinct was telling me that her married happiness had not been unflawed, she sobbed with a grief which I had no choice but to acknowledge was genuine.

I took her hand in mine again. No further words were necessary. She knew I sympathized, she knew I understood the horror she had endured, she knew I was there to stand beside her and give her all the help I could, and gradually her tears ceased. She was just turning towards me in gratitude at last when we were interrupted. Far away across the lawn the garden door was flung wide as Lion, John and Edmund bounded out onto the terrace.

"Oh God," I said. "Let me go and fend them off."

"No—no, it doesn't matter, I'm all right now. . . . Oh, look at them, how adorable they are, so fresh and new and unspoiled—"

"Spare me the sentimentality. They're noisy, tiresome and ignorant, and at present they're no use to you at all. Now look here, Ginette. This is what you must do—"

"Robert, I must see you on your own again before you go back to London, I simply must."

"Don't interrupt. Just pay attention to me for a moment before those three boys get within earshot. Are you listening? Very well, now summon all your energy to survive luncheon. Then retire to your room and *rest* for the remainder of the day—you're obviously worn out. But we'll meet tomorrow. In the morning I have to go out with Papa to see the estate but in the afternoon I'll borrow the motor and we'll escape."

"But Robert, what will Margaret think?"

"My dear Ginette, I don't care what she thinks and neither should you! Why this slavish preoccupation with my mother?"

"Because she's the only mother I can remember, and daughters who are so hopeless at doing the done thing and sticking to the rules are automatically paralyzed with guilt whenever they come within fifty yards of a mother like Margaret."

"But it's irrational to be so intimidated! After all, who is she? Just an ordinary little woman with a provincial mind and conservative tastes! For God's sake, take no notice of her if she implies you should behave like Queen Victoria after Prince Albert died!"

Our conversation was at that point terminated by my brothers who were halfway across the lawn.

"Coo-ee!" called Lion idiotically. "What are you two up to? Reciting all your old nursery rhymes?"

"Darling Lion!" murmured Ginette, incorrigibly sentimental. "Who would have thought that monster of a baby would turn out to be so amusing? I'm passionate about his *joie de vivre!*"

I could think of more rewarding objects for her passion but I kept my mouth shut and contented myself with repossessing her hand.

All things considered I felt my prospects were not unfavorable.

IV

"Murdered!" exclaimed my father. He reined in his horse and stared at me.

"She herself doesn't want to talk about it, but she asked me yesterday to tell the rest of the family so I thought you should be the first to know."

We were riding down one of the narrow country lanes that crisscrossed the Oxmoon estate in the center of Gower. Penhale Down towered on our right, Harding's Down shimmered ahead and the lie of the land beyond the Oxmoon woods prevented us from seeing the long high line of Rhossili Downs which protected the inland plain from the sea. We were on our way to Martinscombe, the only one of my father's four major farms that specialized in upland sheep. I could see the sheep now, dotted over Penhale Down, but we were still half a mile from the farmhouse.

I was feeling very hot. I rode often enough in London for exercise so I could not complain I was unaccustomed to the exertion, but the weather was unusually warm and my mind was in an uncharacteristically overheated state. As the conversation turned towards Ginette I felt the sweat break out afresh on my back.

"But how appalling for Ginevra," said my father, "to see her husband killed before her eyes!"

"Appalling, yes." Following his example I too reined in my horse and we faced each other in the lane.

"How did it happen?"

I told him and added, "Obviously New York is the most barbarous and uncivilized place."

"As Gower used to be." My father stared at the tranquil rural landscape that surrounded us. "Barbarity's everywhere, that's the truth of it. Absolutely anyone is capable of absolutely anything."

"My dear Papa, I had no idea you were such a cynic!"

"That's not cynicism, that's honesty—as you well know, dealing with criminals as you do, seeing the human race continually at its worst."

"My profession has only underlined to me the importance of civilized behavior—a civilizing influence can be a powerful deterrent to iniquity....But you're thinking of Bryn-Davies, aren't you? Some people, I agree, are certainly capable of anything." As I spoke it suddenly occurred to me that I had been living with the mystery of his past for over quarter of a century and that now was the time to solve it, analyze it and file it away once and for all. "What exactly did Bryn-Davies get up to, Papa?" I said, adopting the tone of mild interest that I used with nervous witnesses. "I know he seduced your mother and plundered your estate, but was that the limit of his crimes?"

My father said nothing.

"Did my grandfather really die of drink?" I said, and started counting. A bad liar will let a silence of several seconds elapse while he tries to frame a reply. A good liar will play for time while he keeps the silence at bay.

"Your grandfather died of something-or-other of the liver," said my father without a second's hesitation. "The doctor wrote it down for me but the word looked so uncommonly odd that I could never work out how to pronounce it, but of course you'll know the word I mean; I believe the disease is very common among drunkards." He paused. He had now worked out what he considered to be the perfect reply. Smiling at me he said, "You mustn't start seeing murder in every death, Robert! I'm sure you'd never have thought of asking that question if you hadn't been working in a world where murder is commonplace."

That was a valid criticism, and smiling back I made a gesture to acknowledge it. We said no more on the subject. As we rode on my father began to talk of the Martinscombe sheep and soon he was recalling Bryn-Davies' famous dictum that Penhale Down might have been designed by God to produce strong ewes and twin lambs.

My father managed all four of the major farms on the estate himself and his four foremen answered directly to him instead of to a bailiff. He always said a bailiff would be guaranteed to annoy the laborers and make the wrong decisions, but no doubt he had been influenced by the memory of his father who had made a disastrous habit of hiring the wrong men for the post.

My father was also in a position, exceptional among his fellow squires, of having experienced the practical side of farming in his impoverished early years. The men in his employment knew he was no idle landowner who kept his hands clean and talked through his hat. They knew *he* knew what it was to shovel manure, rise before dawn to milk cows, bore himself into a stupor with hoeing and generally endure all that is most tedious in agricultural life.

"...and then I had this chance to buy into a closed herd..."

We had left Martinscombe after drinking tea with the foreman and his wife, and as we wound our way across the valley to Daxworth my father began to talk of the cows that awaited us there. Of the three other major farms beyond Martinscombe, Daxworth and Cherryvale were concerned with cattle breeding, while the task of the Home Farm was to supply a wide variety of food to the main house.

"...so taking it from a financial point of view, Robert, it works out like this...."

I tried not to yawn and succeeded but the truth was that I had no fundamental interest in farming. I loved Oxmoon; I enjoyed every leisure hour spent roaming around the countryside; I savored the peace and permanence of a home where my family had lived for generations, but whenever my father embarked on a cattle-breeding panegyric I felt my brain begin to atrophy.

"...and the cost of feeding a cow through the winter works out at..."

As my mind wandered I recalled Cicero's rhapsodies about the glory of farming. But of course his life had been centered on Rome. If he had lived all the year round in the country his views might have been less romantic.

My life was and would be centered on London but I saw no conflict in the future; there was nothing to stop me maintaining a successful parliamentary career while I kept Oxmoon as my country house. I would have to employ a bailiff but because I had mastered the necessary agricultural theories in order to please my father, I would be capable of the appropriate supervision, and I saw no reason why such an arrangement should not be a success. Certainly I judged myself more than adequately prepared to take the minimum interest required to pass on a prosperous estate to the next generation.

But the thought of my parliamentary career, which so far existed only in my mind, brought me once more back to my problems and I was acutely aware of not knowing what I really wanted from life. For a second I yearned for the mountains, but told myself I was only longing for the cancer that would kill me.

"...and Emrys Llewellyn tried to sell me this bull; you never saw such an animal, looked as if it would run a mile at the sight of a cow..."

My ill-fated grandmother had been a Llewellyn. The Llewellyns were one of the few Welsh-speaking families in The Englishry of southern and central Gower and were unusual in owning their own land in the parish of Penhale. My father was estranged from his Welsh cousins. He had never forgiven them for refusing to receive his mother when she had tried to leave her drunken husband.

"Is Emrys still referring to Grandmama as 'Aunt Gwyneth the Harlot'?" I inquired idly. I was becoming unable to sustain an intelligent interest in cows and bulls.

"We don't mention her nowadays. I've no patience with Emrys. Whatever I do he don't like it. It's all jealousy, of course. He'd like to be a squire with two thousand acres and an entry in *Burke's Landed Gentry* instead of a yeoman with two hundred acres and a pedigree which goes back to Hywel Da—and we all know that's a fable. I'm willing to treat him as an equal, I'm no snob, but it makes it worse when I'm friendly to him, he'd far rather I was breathing fire and making a nuisance of myself."

"I think it'll be a long time before the Llewellyns intermarry again with the Godwins!"

"Yes, thank God you've no desire to marry your cousin Dilys."

There was a silence as we remembered the other cousin who was now only too eligible to be my wife.

My father suddenly reined in his horse again. "How do you find Ginevra?" he said abruptly.

"In a state of shock and grief."

"No, I meant..." He hesitated, sifting through his English vocabulary but finding only an obsolete phrase which could express the nuance of the Welsh question in his head. "Will you pay court to her, do you think?"

"How quaint that sounds! Papa, I intend to be what she needs most at this time: a good friend."

"Is that possible? I saw the expression in your eyes when you were refilling her glass of champagne yesterday morning."

"What expression?"

"Oh, your mother and I both noticed it. Robert, I want you to promise me something. If you're going to pay your addresses to Ginevra, will you please not do so at Oxmoon? Your mother's never forgiven her for causing such a scandal, engaging herself to one man, eloping with another, and you can hardly now expect Margaret to welcome any signs that you still want Ginevra to be your wife."

"All I expect from my mother," I said, "is that she should mind her own business."

"And all I expect from you," said my father, "is that you should keep a civil tongue in your head and do as you're told in a house which don't yet belong to you."

There was a pause. Our horses fidgeted restlessly but we ourselves were very still. I was aware of a cow lowing far away by the river and a gull soaring overhead and a faint breeze swaying the poppies by the wayside but most of all I was aware of shock. It had been many years since my father had spoken to me so roughly. Too late I realized he was deeply distressed.

"I'm sorry," I said at last. "Yes, of course I'll behave as you wish—I regret if I've given you cause for concern."

We rode on but it was as if a cloud had passed over the sun and it was not until later as we were leaving Daxworth on our way to Cherryvale that I summoned the nerve to say to him, "Papa, I'm afraid your edict about Ginette puts me in an awkward position." And I told him how I had promised to take her out in the motor that afternoon. "I assure you my behavior towards her will be entirely fraternal—"

"Of course. Yes, by all means make the excursion—I'm sure it would do her good," said my father, obviously anxious to avoid a quarrel, and with mutual relief we exchanged smiles and rode on to Cherryvale.

V

"The sea! The sea!" exclaimed Ginette with a sigh of pleasure as I halted the car on top of the cliffs.

"That," I said, "is the most famous line in Xenophon's *Anabasis*."

"Of course," she said, teasing me. "What else?" And we laughed.

We were at the extreme western end of the Gower Peninsula and before us lay the matchless curve of Rhossili Bay. On our right Rhossili Downs rose from the vast empty golden sands which were marred only by the blackened timber of shipwrecks. Beyond the little village that slumbered beside us on the cliff top there was no sign of human habitation except for one house, built above the beach at the foot of the Downs.

Ginette was still wearing black but she had exchanged her flimsy shoes for a pair of walking boots and had donned a large hat with a suitable motoring veil. Now that the motor was stationary she was setting aside the veil and adjusting her hat.

"Thank God this brute of a machine behaved itself," I said, carefully ascertaining that the brake was in the correct position. Only an imbecile could fail to master such a simple skill as driving a motor but I was never at my ease with machinery, particularly as I would have been helpless in the event of a breakdown.

"Let's go and look at the Worm," said Ginette.

The Worm's Head is Gower's most striking claim to fame. It is an extension of the south arm of the bay; the cliffs beyond the village of Rhossili slope steeply to sea level and there, across the tidal causeway of rocks known as the Shipway, a long narrow spur of land arches its way far out into the sea. It has all the allure of a semi-island and all the glamour of a myth. "Worm" is an old word for dragon, and with a little imagination one can look at this unusual land formation and see a monster thrashing its way into the Bristol Channel.

The Mansel Talbots of Penrice who owned the land kept sheep on the Worm's Head, and it had been on his way to inspect this flock that Owain Bryn-Davies had met his death in the tidal trap of the Shipway. Bryn-Davies, born and bred in The Welshery of northeast Gower, had misjudged the dangers awaiting those unfamiliar with the landscape in the southwest.

"You're thinking what I'm thinking, aren't you," said Ginette suddenly. "Robert, did Bobby ever tell you—"

"The whole story? No, of course not, but what intrigues me is why my mother

74

should keep so resolutely silent. It's as if she feels the story must come from him because she herself doesn't have the right to tell it."

There was a pause. We stood there on the exposed headland and stared out across the silver-blue sea towards the coast of Devon which was hidden in a heat haze. The powerful light played tricks with the seascape and created optical illusions. The Shipway seemed a narrow strip of rocks instead of a curving swath of land many yards wide. The Inner Head, the first of the Worm's three humps, seemed close at hand and not half an hour's hard scramble away. On our right the shimmering sands seemed as remote as some beautiful mirage, and on our left the cliffs stretched away towards Porteynon into another haze. At that moment I was conscious of the shifting quality of reality, of the elusiveness of truth, and as my thoughts returned to the tragedies of my father's past I heard Ginette say, "Why would Margaret feel she hadn't the right to tell the story?"

"Because I believe," I said, "that my father connived at concealing a murder and she would think it to be her duty to protect him, not to confess to his children on his behalf."

"Good God! Are you trying to say—"

"Yes, I believe the lover poisoned the husband and that the wife knew of it but convinced the authorities he died of cirrhosis. I think Papa guessed but as he was only a child then, no more than fourteen, he was too frightened to do anything but keep quiet."

"Heavens!" She was staring at me wide-eyed. At least I had temporarily diverted her from her own tragedy. "But what makes you think this?"

"Well, first of all I don't believe the disintegration of a bad marriage is sufficient by itself to explain Papa's paralyzed reticence on the subject of his parents and Bryn-Davies. For a long time I've suspected there was more to the story than that, and this morning I finally subjected Papa to a cross-examination."

"Poor Bobby!"

"Not at all. He stood up to it well although he made the fatal mistake of assuming, without any open declaration from me, that murder was the subject under discussion. Of course he lied, but the really interesting question is Why did he bother? I gave him the perfect opening to make a clean breast of this story which I know he's wanted to tell me for a very long time. So why on earth didn't he take advantage of it?"

"Perhaps he simply felt it was the wrong time to launch himself upon a confession."

"But in that case when *will* be the right time? The whole thing's most odd."

We discussed my theory further during the journey down the cliff path to the Shipway, but presently the conversation drifted towards nostalgia again.

"Do you remember that picnic at Rhossili beach when you found a starfish and I helped you smuggle it home?"

"Ah, those picnics at Rhossili beach!"

"And at the Worm. Do you remember when we asked Bobby why Margaret would never go there? That was the first time we heard that Bryn-Davies had drowned on the Shipway."

I was conscious that we were back with Bryn-Davies again and Ginette was conscious of it too for the next moment she was saying, "How strange it is that the happy home Bobby and Margaret created for us was always permeated by that old tragedy. . . . Those ghastly Christmases when your grandmother was brought home from her asylum! How could we have laughed at the time and regarded poor old Aunt Gwyneth as a figure of fun? In retrospect it all seems unspeakably sinister and tragic."

"Tragedy and comedy often go hand in hand. Think of Shakespeare."

"Oh darling, must I? Let's go and look at the rock pools."

We had reached the foot of the cliffs and were standing on the grassy bank that lay on the brink of the Shipway. The ensuing scramble over the rocks was too arduous to permit conversation but when we had paused on the brink of a large pellucid pool Ginette murmured, "Oh Robert!" and heaved a sigh of pleasure.

"Yes?" I said neutrally, wondering how much longer I could repress the urge to embrace her.

"I was just thinking how wonderful it is to reminisce with someone who shares one's memories—and how even more wonderful it is to be with a man who simply treats one as a friend! To tell the truth, darling"—another sigh, another misty-eyed gaze into the rock pool—"I've absolutely exhausted the possibilities of grand passion."

"Ah," I said. "Yes. Well, I've always suspected grand passions were grossly overrated. Shall we go on?"

We began to flounder at a snail's pace across the rocks to the next pool but Ginette soon stopped to gaze out to sea. The entire seascape was, as I now realized, disastrously romantic. If we had been in a Swansea back street I was sure I would have had perfect control over my emotions but as it was I felt I was walking a tightrope suspended between two steadily sinking poles.

"I want to talk about the present," said Ginette. "I want to ask you all about your career and your London life. But I can't. All I can do is talk about the past. How do I escape from it? Sometimes I don't believe there's a present or a future; there's just the past going on and on."

I saw my chance. The poles supporting my emotional tightrope promptly collapsed as all reason and common sense slumped into abeyance, and putting my future at the stake I gambled, playing to win.

"No, Ginette," I said. "The past is over. The past is done. You may not be in a frame of mind to admit that at the moment, but later when you're more recovered from your husband's death, I'll help you see that a very different future is possible for you."

She looked at me. Then she turned away and stared again past the rocks to the alluring serenity of the sea.

I waited, outwardly calm yet inwardly furious with myself for disclosing my true feelings at such a premature stage of our reunion. Yet I failed to see what else I could have done for the truth was I was on the horns of a dilemma. So relieved had I been that Ginette and I should have slipped back with ease into our old friendship that I had not at first realized I could be setting out on the same road to failure by inviting the past to repeat itself, but now I could visualize a future in which I nursed Ginette back to emotional health only to see her turn to someone else when a platonic friendship no longer satisfied her.

The vision horrified me. I knew I must somehow re-form our relationship immediately in order to avoid such a disaster, but since she had just made it clear she wanted nothing from me but friendship, any change seemed doomed to repel her. I was thus in the uneviable position that whatever I did I lost. I was losing now as I sensed her emotional withdrawal. I would have lost ultimately if I had persisted in keeping my hopes for the future to myself. In despair I groped for the words to put matters right but the words—if they existed—continued to elude me. All I could say was "I'm sorry. I didn't mean to disclose my true feelings."

She turned in surprise to face me. "Disclose your true feelings? But my dear Robert, I've always known exactly how you felt!"

I was stunned. "But you couldn't. Not possibly."

"Oh, I agree you've acted superbly! But a woman always knows when a man's in love with her." She moved restlessly back to the first pool and it was not until she was standing by the water's edge that she added, "Has there been no one else?"

"Well..."

"Oh, of course you've had mistresses, I understand all that, but—"

"You're the only woman I've ever loved and you're the only woman I'll ever want and that's that. However I quite understand that this kind of sentimental twaddle is the last thing you want to hear at this particular moment, so—"

"I adore sentimental twaddle!" She was smiling at me. Then she said suddenly, "What a gloriously simple man you must be. Oh God, that sounds insulting, doesn't it, but what I meant was—"

"I know what you meant. Yes, I suppose single-mindeness is a form of simplicity."

"It's very attractive." As she moved forward again, I heard her say, "I'm so sick of complexity, so sick of mess and muddle and unhappiness."

"You were unhappy?"

"Yes, but saying I was unhappy is meaningless, it's too simple, it describes nothing here." She turned impulsively to face me. "I loved Conor," she said, "and he loved me, but it wasn't a restful sort of love. Quite the contrary."

I said nothing. I knew better than to interrupt anyone bent on confession but when she spoke again I sensed she was already retreating into generalities. "We were too alike, that was the trouble," she said idly. "When a marriage runs into difficulty it's always supposed to be because the couple grow apart. Nobody ever tells you how difficult it is when the couple grow too alike. To live with one's own faults is hard enough. To live with one's own faults mirrored in someone else is like looking into a glass and watching oneself grow ugly.... But sometimes even ugliness can exert its own irresistible fascination." She laughed briefly and I heard her murmur, "But we couldn't have parted. We were too attracted physically. That brought us together in the beginning and it kept us together at the end.... Odd, wasn't it?" she demanded unexpectedly, her voice crisp. "Most affairs of that kind fall apart after six months. Oh, what a white-hot muddle it all was! And then suddenly one bullet...a rush of blood...and after fifteen years of perpetual clamor—silence. I still can't get used to it. I wake in the middle of the night and the silence goes on and on."

"Naturally it'll take you a long time to recover."

"You keep making these wonderfully simple remarks which have nothing to do with reality. Recover, you say? How do I recover? Do I suddenly discover a talent for leading an orderly, peaceful life? I've never had a talent for that—I barely know what peace and order mean! Yet I long for them....Yes, I long to be safe...and protected...with someone I can trust, someone loyal who won't let me down....Oh God, what on earth's going to happen to me when I get to London? I'm so frightened, Robert, so frightened of all the predatory men, so frightened of getting into yet another appalling mess, sometimes I think I can't face London at all, but where else am I to go? I can't stay indefinitely at Oxmoon— oh, all thought of the future paralyzes me, I don't know how I shall ever survive—"

"I give you my word of honor that I shall come riding up on my white horse to slay every London dragon who breathes fire at you!"

"Oh Robert! Dear, *dear* Robert! How romantic!"

We were laughing together, just as I had intended. Meanwhile I had moved closer to her and the next moment I was aware of nothing save the muffled boom of the surf on the other side of the Shipway and the throb of the blood beneath my skin. The expression in her eyes changed. Unable to stop myself I held out my arms.

"Ginette—"

But she interrupted me. "Come to my room tonight," she said in a low voice. "After the dinner party. I'll be waiting for you."

The scene froze. It was as if the violins had once more stopped playing "The Blue Danube."

I was appalled.

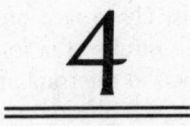

4

I

MY FEELINGS must have been clearly written on my face. I saw her turn so white that I was seized with the melodramatic notion that she might faint, but the moment of crisis passed and instead of fainting she managed to say carelessly, "Sorry! Wrong move. I stole your lines, didn't I? What a *faux pas!*"

I drew breath to speak but she forestalled me.

"If a man says to a woman, 'May I come to your room tonight?' they both think he's a very fine fellow," she said in a shaking voice, "but if a woman issues a similar invitation—even to a man she loves—the man automatically classes her as a whore."

"I could never think—"

"You thought it. I saw you. Well, maybe you're right. Maybe, according to your book of rules, I *am* a whore. But who wrote that book of rules, I'd like to know? Men! *Damned men!* They make the rules and have all the fun of breaking them while we women have to stay locked up in our straitjackets!"

"I absolutely deny—"

"Oh, don't bother!"

"But—"

"I've talked like a whore and now I'm behaving like some ghastly suffragette and I know perfectly well you're wondering how you could ever have loved me and oh God, I've done it again, I've made a mess of everything and I hate myself so much that I don't know how to bear it!"

She burst into tears. For one long moment I was transfixed by this harrowing display of feminine emotion but finally I recovered my wits and pursued the only intelligent course of action that remained to me.

She was still weeping. "Oh Robert, forgive me—please forgive me—"

"My dearest Ginette," I said, and took her in my arms.

II

There followed a somewhat predictable interval in which I lost the capacity for rational thought and made a number of declarations which sounded as if they had been invented by the worst kind of nineteenth-century poet. However most of the time I had the good sense to keep my mouth shut—or at least, to be accurate, to keep my nineteenth-century maunderings to myself; my mouth was busy proving the maxim that actions speak louder than words.

This extraordinary scene was interrupted all too soon by a party of jolly strangers on an excursion. The secluded beauties of the Gower Peninsula have never been entirely unspoiled since Baedeker wrote of them, but at that moment I felt I could resign myself to any intrusion, even the advent of four noisy fiends with Lancashire accents who sang "Rule, Britannia" as they strode down the cliff path.

"Maybe they'll drown on the Shipway!" murmured Ginette.

"Not a chance—the tide's barely past low water!"

We smiled into each other's eyes.

"Oh Robert..."

"Ah Ginette, Ginette..."

And so on and so on. I was not surprised when the strangers boggled in response to our polite "Good afternoon." They probably felt the landscape was quite romantic enough without two starry-eyed lovers cluttering up their path to the Worm.

"Darling, what time is it?"

"There is no time," I said, "only eternity." Of course I was still thoroughly demented.

"Darling, that's simply lovely and I'd adore to stay here in eternity with you forever, but unfortunately I promised Margaret that we'd be back for tea."

Eternity was terminated. "Why on earth did you do that?" I said annoyed.

"Because Margaret said to me before we left, 'Dearest Ginevra, have a lovely time and don't forget that there'll be a special tea waiting when you come back— you will be back for tea, won't you?' and I said, 'Dearest Margaret, yes, of course.'"

"I despair of you both."

"Oh Robert, she doesn't trust us an inch!"

"Yes, we'll have to reassure her by acting a charade of unblemished chastity among the teacups and the cucumber sandwiches."

We laughed. Then I said again, "My dearest Ginette!" and we paused for one last lingering luscious kiss before toiling back up the cliff path to Rhossili.

III

It took half an hour to reach the motor, and the interval proved salutary. By the time I was helping Ginette into the passenger seat I had recovered my capacity for rational thought, and although I was still in a fever of happiness I had at least emerged from my delirium. Thus when the engine stalled I made no attempt to restart it. I remained motionless, my hands gripping the wheel, my eyes watching the white lines of the breakers sweeping the beach far below.

"Ginette."

She turned to me. Her dark eyes were brilliant beneath their long black curling lashes. Her flawless skin was flushed from her walk. Her wide full-lipped mouth was irresistible and again I made no effort to resist. I kissed it.

"What's the matter?" she said when I released her.

"I can't come to your room tonight." I paused before adding levelly: "There are reasons—good reasons—why it's not possible."

All she said was "Go on."

I bent all my concentration towards translating confusion into clarity. "In my opinion you shouldn't go to bed with anyone at the moment," I said frankly. "The truth is your husband's been dead less than a month, you're in a thoroughly unstable state and if I took advantage of you now I think you might come to resent me later—I think I might become just another of those 'damned men' who you implied take what they want at the woman's expense. And I don't want you ever to think of me in that way, Ginette. I want you to think of me as a man who cares enough for you to postpone winning what he wants most."

Still she looked at me steadily. And again she said, "Go on."

"I also have to consider my parents. I promised my father this morning that my attitude towards you would stay fraternal while I remained at Oxmoon, and we both know why he extracted that promise from me; we both know my mother not only disapproves of the idea of any intimacy between us but is absolutely opposed to any irregular behavior beneath her roof. And annoying though I find my mother at present, I have to concede that I have a duty not to offend her in this respect."

"Yes, I understand. Go on."

"Well," I said, finally disconcerted by this continuing request to proceed, "that's it. All things considered I sincerely believe—"

"Are you sure there's no other reason? Can you promise me you're not acting out of anger?"

"Anger!" I was astonished. "But why should I be angry?"

"Because I was the one who took the initiative in suggesting that we meet tonight."

"What an extraordinary notion! No, of course I'm not angry with you because of that!"

"Then are you worried about Conor?"

"Worried about... my dear Ginette, what in God's name are you talking about?"

"Nothing. I'm sorry." She leaned forward to kiss me. "Shouldn't we be going?"

But after that kiss I was conscious only of my physical arousal. I said abruptly, "How soon can you come up to London?"

"I don't know. It depends what I do about the boys."

"Well, never mind, we can discuss that later." The thought of her two sons was not a stimulating one.

She was drawing on her gloves and as I watched Kinsella's rings disappearing from sight I was aware for the first time of complex emotions which I could not begin to analyze. I thrust them aside. Then with my confusion safely buried at the back of my mind, I got out of the car and made renewed efforts to start the engine.

Twenty minutes later we were motoring hell-for-leather up the drive to Oxmoon and praying we were not too late for tea.

IV

The special tea which my mother had promised Ginette consisted of a sumptuous repast on the lawn below the terrace. There were three different kinds of sandwiches, four cakes, a batch of scones, a heap of currant buns, assorted biscuits and, to add the final touch of luxury, strawberries and cream. When Ginette and I emerged from the house we found the meal had already started. Lion, John, Edmund and my father had all been playing lawn tennis; they were wearing whites, my father looking just as lean and strong as any of his sons. Celia had been sketching; her drawing board and pencils were tucked beneath her deck chair and she had a hot flustered look as if she had just beaten back Thomas's efforts to purloin them. Thomas himself, looking like a sulky cherub in his white sailor suit, was busy pouring his glass of milk over my father's dog. Meanwhile Bayliss and Ifor were circulating with the large plates of sandwiches, and beneath a striped umbrella which shaded the wrought-iron table my mother presided over the silver teapot. I was acutely aware of her watching us as we descended the stone steps to the lawn.

"No, no, Thomas," my father was saying mildly to the child. "Glendower doesn't like being christened with milk. Perhaps cold water, as it's such a hot day."

"Here come the childhood sweethearts!" caroled that idiot Lion.

"Where did you go?" called John cheerfully.

"Rhossili!" exclaimed Ginette. "My dear, that Worm's Head! Too divine! We toiled all the way down to the Shipway—imagine! I feel exhausted!"

"Have my chair, Ginevra—"

"No, have mine—"

"Mine's the best—"

"Darlings," said Ginette, reclining gracefully upon the nearest proffered deck chair, "how heavenly you all are!"

"I'm sorry we're late, Mama," I said, sitting down next to my father.

"That's quite all right, Robert. I hope you had a pleasant outing." She turned to the footman. "Ifor, we're going to need more hot water."

"So sorry we're late, Margaret!" said Ginette, accepting a cucumber sandwich from the butler. "I'm afraid it's my fault—Robert didn't realize that I'd promised we'd be home for tea."

"That's quite all right, Ginevra. Milk or lemon?"

"Oh, lemon would be delicious, as the weather's so hot! In America, you know, they have iced tea—it sounds horrid but actually when the weather's absolutely steaming..."

Settling down to join her in a bravura performance of our grand charade I began to discuss the merits of the motorcar with my father.

V

The next ordeal on the agenda was my parents' "little dinner party for twenty-four" which, since not all the invited guests were able to come at such short notice, had turned out to be a little dinner party for eighteen. The Mowbrays were up in town and the Bryn-Davieses had a previous engagement in Swansea, but the de Bracys, the Stourhams and the Applebys all professed themselves eager to welcome Ginette home.

I was sorry the Bryn-Davieses were to be absent. My father had long ago befriended Owain Bryn-Davies the Younger, and with admirable determination had persisted in demonstrating his belief that the sins of my grandmother's lover should not be blamed upon the next generation of the family. Owain the Younger had also suffered as the result of the debacle in the Eighties; his father had walked out on a wife and five children when he had gone to live at Oxmoon with his mistress. However later, well educated on the money his father had plundered from the Oxmoon estate, Owain the Younger had made an excellent marriage to the daughter of a Swansea coal-mine owner, and now he lived in immaculate middle-class respectability on the outskirts of Swansea. His only son Alun, a contemporary of mine at Harrow, was so grand that he barely knew one end of a sheep from the other.

"By the way," said Lion after tea when the conversation turned to the approaching dinner party, "there's something I want to ask." He glanced around to make sure Ginette and the servants had retired indoors. "Do we admit Kinsella was murdered?"

"Absolutely not!" said my mother, effortlessly drawing the line. "We say he had an accident with a gun and of course everyone will be much too well-bred to make further inquiries."

"Oh Mama, I don't really have to wear black, do I?" begged Celia querulously. "I'll look such a fright!"

"Well, I think navy blue *would* be permissible for you in the circumstances, dear. After all, Mr. Kinsella was not a blood relation and indeed was barely known to us. I of course shall wear black, but I see no reason why you shouldn't allow yourself a little latitude so long as the color of your gown remains discreet."

"My dear Celia," I said later as we found ourselves going upstairs to change, "you're twenty-nine years old! Can't you make your own decisions about what to wear for a dinner party?"

"Oh, leave me alone, Robert—you're always so beastly to me! Do you think I like being reminded that I'm nearly thirty and still living at home?"

For some reason which I failed to understand, conversations with my sister always sank to this fractious level. Celia seemed to think I despised her but I thought her worthy enough despite her plain looks and lack of intelligence. She occupied herself a great deal with charity work and was famous for her volumes of pressed wild flowers.

In my room while I waited for hot water to be brought to me I thought what a very different life Ginette had lived far away in unknown barbaric New York, and the next moment before I could stop myself I was seeing Kinsella's rings on her finger and hearing her talk of her marital intimacy. "It brought us together in the beginning and it kept us together at the end...." That disturbed me. I began to pace up and down. Finally I even shuddered, and when the hot water arrived it was all I could do not to cut myself as I shaved. I knew from my experience in criminal law that women, even good women, can become as addicted to carnal pleasure as many men, and it seemed to me that Ginette now sought not me at all but an opiate which would shut out her fear of the future.

I told myself firmly that I had reached the right decision on top of the cliffs at

Rhossili that afternoon. I did not want to be treated as a soothing medicine contained in a bottle marked TAKE REGULARLY AT BEDTIME. Nor—and this was an even more horrific possibility—did I want to be treated as a substitute for Kinsella. I wanted to be wanted because I was myself, because I was the best man in the world for her, and bearing this in mind I had no alternative but to wait until she could give me the response I deserved. Any other solution was quite unacceptable.

I felt better, and congratulating myself that my thoughts on this most complicated subject were now in order, I set off briskly downstairs to the drawing room.

VI

She entered the room and my well-ordered mind fell apart into chaos. She wore a rich black satin gown, very décolleté and trimmed with yards of erotic black lace. A diamond pendant, sparkling against her creamy skin, pointed downwards like an arrow as if to emphasize her breasts, and her thick glowing auburn hair, piled high, was secured with a diamond clasp.

"How very fetching you look, Ginevra," said my mother in a studiedly neutral voice.

"I'll have to keep you away from Oswald," said my father lightly, "or he'll be so overcome he'll swallow his soup spoon!"

Oswald Stourham, a great crony of my father's, lived in an ugly modern house at Llangennith with his wife, his unmarried sister and his daughter. The daughter was too young to attend the dinner party, but his wife and sister accompanied him to Oxmoon that evening and when they all arrived Stourham, who looked like a *Punch* cartoon of an English gentleman and talked like an old-fashioned masher, predictably dropped his monocle as soon as he saw Ginette. He was a good-natured, brainless fellow who had thoroughly deserved to inherit the fortune of his father, a Birmingham manufacturer who had patented an interesting form of hip bath.

His unmarried sister Angela, a woman of about thirty-five who had once shared a governess with Ginette, was just giving her old friend a warm welcome when Bayliss announced the arrival of the de Bracys with their daughter and two sons. The evening was gathering momentum. Taking care not to look in Ginette's direction I did my best to resume my grand charade.

Sir Gervase de Bracy, a gouty old roué who had seen better days, was already heading purposefully in my direction, jowls quivering with excitement.

"Robert, my boy—delighted to see you—heartiest congratulations on all your recent successes—"

Little Mrs. Stourham swooped down on me. "Why, Robert, how well you look—isn't Robert looking distinguished, Sir Gervase! I declare those photographs in the newspapers don't do him justice! Have you see the photographs of Robert in the newspapers, Lady de Bracy?"

"I only read *The Times*, Mrs. Stourham."

Meanwhile Oswald Stourham had cornered me. "I say, Robert, uncommon clever of you to win that latest acquittal, don't you know—I didn't like to think of a pretty little thing like that ending up on the gallows—"

"But what I want to know," interrupted the de Bracys' daughter Gwen, "is how she got hold of the arsenic! I never quite understood—"

"Gwen dear, murder's so vulgar. Must you?"

Ginette and I were facing each other across the room. Hastily glancing in the opposite direction I found myself looking straight at my mother, and my mother, I was unnerved to discover, was looking straight at me.

"—yes, yes, I *know* she was acquitted but that was entirely owing to Robert's brilliance—"

Meanwhile Oswald Stourham had turned aside to gossip with his crony. "... and how the deuce did poor Ginevra's husband die, Bobby?"

"Oh," I heard my father say easily, "it was just a little accident with a firearm."

"Margaret"—Mrs. Stourham darted between me and my mother—"I hardly expected to see Ginevra looking so *thriving!*"

"Dearest Ginevra," said my mother, "has great recuperative powers."

At that moment Bayliss announced the arrival of Sir William and Lady Appleby, and out of the corner of my eye I saw Ginette steel herself for new horrors.

"Dear Ginevra, you must have been quite prostrated..."

The Applebys, who had long since decided to thank God that Kinsella had saved their son from a disastrous fate, were now more than willing to inundate Ginette with benign platitudes to conceal how much they disliked her.

"Dear Aunt Maud," said Ginette, kissing Lady Appleby on both cheeks, "how kind you are! Yes, I'm sure it'll take me simply years to recover—"

"Are you all right, Robert?" said John at my elbow.

"No. I think I've got a touch of sunstroke."

"Lord, how awkward! Tell Mama."

"No, I'll struggle on."

I struggled. Gallantly I took Lady Appleby in to dinner. Valiantly I labored through watercress soup, vanquished my lobster and feinted an attack on my roast duck. Doggedly I toiled in the coils of some formidably forgettable conversation. And all the while across the table Ginette glittered in her satin and diamonds and made a mockery of my charade of indifference.

"Robert, you're shifting around on your chair as if it were a bed of nails!" protested Gwen de Bracy on my left.

"I'm so sorry, I thought I was showing matchless stoicism in the face of dis-comfort."

I was indeed in discomfort but the discomfort was of a nature inconceivable to an unmarried woman.

"Do tell us more about London, Robert!" urged Mrs. Stourham across the table. "I suppose you go absolutely everywhere—what's it like at Number Ten?"

I duly trotted out my Margot Asquith stories and before I could be asked how much her husband drank I deflected the conversation towards his eldest son Raymond whom I had known up at Oxford; like myself he was a Balliol man.

Somehow I survived the introduction of pudding, cheese and dessert and sustained the illusion that I was still eating. My glass of claret remained untouched, an impressive monument to my sobriety, but in contrast all the other guests had become very merry indeed and I had to spend a considerable amount of energy trying to pretend I was equally carefree.

Finally to my unutterable relief the ladies retired and the cloth was drawn. I hardly dared stand up as the ladies left the room, but managed to do so with a subtle flourish of my napkin. Sinking back into my chair as the door closed I then allowed myself to hope that my physical condition would be eased now that Ginette was no longer shimmering before my eyes, but I was to have no respite. Oswald Stourham embarked on some long story about a friend of his who knew someone who knew someone else who had slept with Lillie Langtry, and the very thought of a man fortunate enough to go to bed with any woman, even an aging Lillie Langtry, was enough to make me start shifting again in my chair.

My father had by this time noticed that something was amiss. "Robert, are you quite well?"

"I think if you'll excuse me, sir, I'll retire to the cloakroom for a moment."

More sleight of hand with my napkin followed, but everyone was much too busy talking of Mrs. Langtry to pay any attention.

I was just washing my hands some minutes later when my father knocked at the cloakroom door and called my name.

I drew back the bolt to let him in. "I'm afraid I've just been sick," I said, dredging up my remaining strength to lie convincingly. "I must have caught a touch of the sun this afternoon at the Worm. Would you and Mama think it very bad form if I excused myself and went upstairs?"

Five minutes later I was sitting on the edge of my bed and wondering, amidst the ruins of my well-ordered mind, what the devil I was going to do.

VII

Although I was by no means sexually inexperienced I had never before been rendered irrational by physical desire. Periodically I had felt the need to have sexual intercourse and periodically I had done so. I had always tried to behave well; I had not consorted with prostitutes; I had not made trouble with husbands; I had never had more than one mistress at a time; I had always terminated the affair as painlessly as possible when it bored me; I had done my best to be courteous, honest and kind. However it had never occurred to me before that this splendidly civilized behavior had only been possible because my deepest emotions had remained unengaged.

This uncomplicated private life had suited me well, perhaps better than I had realized at the time. I actually have very simple emotional tastes. (Someone else had commented on that recently but I could not quite remember who it was.) My prime concern when I embark on a liaison is that there should be no fuss and no mess. Naturally I expect to do what I want in bed but there again my tastes are straightforward and no woman has yet appeared to find them tiresome. Sexual athletics require skill, of course; I have no wish to imply that Burton's translation of the *Kama Sutra* escaped me at Oxford, but in my opinion the skill is easily mastered and although I enjoy the game there are other sports I enjoy as much and more. I would put it below mountaineering, on a par with rugger and slightly above cricket in any list of sports in which a gentleman should wish to excel.

Yet as I sat on the edge of the bed that evening I found that mountaineering was a distant memory, while rugger and cricket seemed as irrelevant as a couple of Stone Age tribal rites. I even felt that my entire previous life was not only remote but fantastic, a bloodless dance by a machine to a barrel organ that played only one tune. I supposed I was very much in love. This fact, I knew, was worthy of euphoria and I was indeed euphoric, but I was also alarmed. The unknown is often alarming and to be deeply in love was for me an unknown experience. Before that day my love for Ginette had been little more than a romantic myth but now it was a reality, and I felt confused, nervous, ecstatic, appalled, irrational and dangerous. I knew I should remain in my room but the next moment I was padding to the head of the stairs to see if the guests were on the brink of departure.

They were. In the hall all was noise and confusion, laced with fond farewells and fatuous remarks. I retreated to my room to think. It came as a relief to me to find I was still capable of thinking, but unfortunately I was thinking reckless thoughts of nocturnal expeditions; I was realizing the impossibility of running around Oxmoon in my nightclothes. I had to be able to say to anyone I met unexpectedly, "Oh, I'm feeling so much better that I thought I'd go out for a breath of air before I turn in." I felt like a murderer plotting his crime. Stripping off my evening clothes I pulled on a pair of white flannels, thoughtfully packed by Bennett in anticipation of lawn tennis, and found the accompanying shirt. White socks and white canvas shoes completed the picture of a gentleman in quest of sport, and after a quick glance at my transformed reflection in the glass I opened the door again to gauge the advisability of a further reconnaissance.

The guests had gone. Everyone was drifting upstairs to bed. I decided to remain where I was.

A seemingly vast span of time elapsed which was probably no more than half an hour. At last, taking no candle, I risked another reconnaissance but all the lights were out in the hall and everyone seemed to be safely stowed out of sight.

Returning to my room I waited for sleep to vanquish even the most active brains, and another eon passed. I finished the last cigarette in my case but fortunately perfect Bennett had included an additional packet in my bag. I mentally awarded him yet another increase in wages.

When the clock on my bedside table told me it was one o'clock I decided that to prolong the suspense would be more than my beleaguered flesh and blood could stand. I put out the candle. Darkness descended, rich and sensuous as the black satin of Ginette's evening gown. I felt intense sexual excitement, and beyond it the old hypnotic vision of winning was beating its familiar drum to lure me on to the end of my dreams.

Leaving my room I moved swiftly and soundlessly down the corridor, tiptoed across the landing past the door of my parents' room and glided down the passage into the other wing.

Time warped in the darkness around me and bent back in a great curve before running forward once more in a straight line. I was the child Robert again, tiptoeing through the night for a midnight feast with a bag of boiled sweets in his hand, and the child Ginette was waiting with licorice hidden beneath the eiderdown of her bed. Then I remembered that Ginette was no longer in her old room. My mother had put her in Foxglove, the best spare room, as if a line had to be drawn beneath the past.

When I reached the spare rooms I found the darkness unbroken. Foxglove, still named after its former wallpaper, was now only six feet away but there was no light visible beneath the door.

I knocked lightly on the panels and at once I heard a match flare in response. The bed creaked as she left it, and seconds later she was opening the door.

We looked at each other for one long exquisite moment in the candlelight, and after that there was no need for explanations. All I said in the end was, "I've changed my mind."

VIII

As I stepped past her she closed the door behind me and moved into my arms. We kissed. I drew her hard against me both to gratify myself and to prove to her how unmistakable my need was, and she laughed softly and yielded her pliant mouth to mine.

"Come to bed."

I smiled, recognizing her desire, and withdrew my hands from hers to strip off my clothes.

My fingers grazed her rings.

My fingers grazed the rings that Kinsella had given her.

My fingers—her hand—Kinsella's rings—and suddenly I was in a nightmare, the most horrific nightmare of my life, half-dressed, wholly paralyzed and absolutely and unquestionably impotent.

I was on the Shipway again and Ginette was saying, "It brought us together in the beginning and it kept us together at the end." I was in the dining room at Brooks's and Kinsella was saying, "The prize you've always wanted is the prize you can never win." Having come second to an Irishman in the past I was now coming second to an Irishman again, and the prospect of defeat was dancing before my eyes like a demon. I was failing, I was losing, I was lost, unable to do anything but stare at the floor as the sweat trickled down my naked spine, unable to be rational by telling myself I was a better man than Kinsella, unable to summon the willpower which would convince me that I could outshine him in the most important contest of my life. Panic beat around my brain like a demented hammer. I had a hellish glimpse into an unutterably complex world that was far beyond either my comprehension or my control.

"Robert." She slipped her arms around my neck and stroked my hair. "It's all right, I understand—I understood this afternoon—oh, I shouldn't have told you so much about my marriage, but I was so consumed with the desire to put Conor behind us forever—"

"Forever?" I said, hearing the one phrase I could understand and grabbing it.

"Oh darling, I long to set him aside—wasn't that obvious when I invited you here?"

"But you implied that physically, despite all your troubles—"

"Yes, but the marriage was so ghastly, such a nightmare, and now I just want someone utterly different—I want you, Robert, you, you, you—"

"Yes, but—"

"There's no competition. He's dead and you're different and you're going to win, Robert. You're going to win because there's no one now, *no one*, who can possibly stand in your way."

She took off her rings. She tugged them from her finger in a single impulsive gesture and the next moment she was flinging them into the farthest corner of the room. The past merged again with the present. In my memory I saw her throw away Timothy Appleby's ring as she moved into Kinsella's arms, and now as she threw aside Kinsella's rings I saw her moving into mine.

I held her tightly. "I'll always come first with you now, won't I," I said, "no matter what happens next."

"Always!" Her eyes were brilliant with love.

"And you really love me?"

"Yes. Best of all. Always."

"Promise?"

"Cross my heart and hope to die!" she said laughing, echoing our old nursery oath.

She lived.

We went to bed.

I had not been in bed for more than a few seconds before I realized that the pleasure awaiting me there far exceeded even my most imaginative expectations, but I was in such a state by that time that the word pleasure seemed to bear little relation to what was going on. Despite all she had said I found myself consumed with worry. This was another new experience for me. In the past I had assumed that if one possessed physical fitness, the necessary desire and the required modicum of knowledge biology would do the rest, but now I found that although I was physically fit, beside myself with desire and well-nigh gasping to put my knowledge into practice, I was obsessed with the fear that biology would let me down. Fortunately impotence was now the least of my worries but other disastrous possibilities were jostling for pride of place in my fevered imagination. Caught between trying to remember the *Kama Sutra* on the one hand and my fear of an early ejaculation on the other, I was soon floundering around like a virgin schoolboy.

Then she put everything right. She whispered, "Darling, I'm sure you don't want me to speak but I can't help it, I've simply got to tell you what heaven this is," and suddenly I forgot my fears and started thinking about heaven instead. This was a much more profitable exercise, and presently I found that no further ordeal divided me from the pleasure which exceeded all my dreams.

Afterwards for some time I was much too happy to speak but when she too remained silent I found I needed to hear her voice. Tightening my arms around her I asked if everything was well.

"Darling!" She gave me a radiant smile. "What a question!"

I felt compelled to say, "I'll be better next time. The truth is I'm out of practice. I've been on my own too long."

"Robert, I despair of you! No sooner have I convinced you that you're not in competition with anyone than I find you're still in competition with yourself!"

We laughed and kissed. I felt so much better that I even thought how pleasant it would be to smoke.

"I wish I'd brought my cigarettes with me."

"Do you want one?" Opening the drawer of her bedside table she produced a packet. "So do I."

"I shall never again disapprove of women smoking!"

We smoked pleasurably and intimately for a time. I was just about to tell her that I had never been so happy in my entire life when she asked idly, "Why has it been so long since the last occasion?"

"Oh . . ." I could hardly bore her with an explanation which involved disclosing the more convoluted aspects of my personality. "I've been working too hard. There's been no time for pleasure."

"What a mistake!"

I smiled. "But everything will be different now I have you," I said, and it occurred to me that I would no longer even miss my mountaineering. We kissed. I extinguished our cigarettes and it was then, just as I was preparing to caress her again, that we both heard the soft footfall in the corridor.

X

We stared wide-eyed at each other. Then we both sat bolt upright and held our breath.

The footsteps halted. There was a long pause, followed by a tentative tap on the door.

Too late I remembered that in the drama of my arrival we had failed to turn the key in the lock.

"Who is it?" called Ginette unsteadily.

"Bobby. Ginevra, do forgive me but I'm so worried about Robert and when I was outside just now for a breath of air and saw a light was still burning in your room—" As we watched, both paralyzed with horror, the door began to open. "—I wondered if I could possibly talk to you—just for the briefest moment, of course; I'm sure you must be very tired after the dinner party..."

His voice stopped. There was a short terrible silence. Then he began to back away.

"So sorry...unpardonable intrusion...should have waited for permission to enter...very remiss...just so worried...forgive me—it never occurred to me...forgive me."

He left. The door closed behind him but before his footsteps had faded into the distance Ginette had jumped out of bed and was fighting her way into her dressing gown as she ran across the room.

"Bobby—" She opened the door and rushed out into the corridor. "Bobby, please—come back."

I was pulling on my white flannels. My shaking fingers slipped futilely among the buttonholes of my fly as my father with great reluctance returned to the room.

"Bobby," said Ginevra in a shaking voice, "you mustn't betray us to Margaret. *Please*, Bobby, promise me you won't."

"Of course he won't!" I said abruptly. I drew her aside so that I could face him. "I'm sorry, sir—you've every right to be very angry. I'm also sorry that you've been so worried about me, but I assure you I'm going to settle down now, I'm going to be happy at last and I'm going to live my life very differently in future."

My father said nothing. He looked at me, he looked at her, he looked at me again but he was quite unable to speak. The silence seemed to last a long time. Then he said simply, "Please excuse me," and once more he left the room.

XI

We sank down on the bed. Ginette was trembling so I put my arm around her and kept it there until she was calmer. Then I said, "Never mind my mother. Never mind my father. Never mind either of them. I've apologized for my bad manners in flouting their rules and as far as I'm concerned that's that." I waited again before adding firmly, "Of course you'll marry me."

"Darling Robert!" she said and burst into tears.

An emotional interval followed during which she clung to me and swore weeping that she wanted to marry me more than anything else in the world but she was so frightened, frightened, frightened in case the marriage never happened and she lost me and wound up in a mess for the rest of her life.

"My dearest Ginette! How can you lose me? Friendship's forever! Don't you remember how we used to tell each other that?"

The memory calmed her. She said tearfully, "Nothing can ever destroy that shared past, can it?" and I answered, "Nothing."

After we had embraced she whispered, "Don't go back to your room, sleep here, I don't want to be alone."

I locked the door, returned to bed and, thoroughly exhausted by this time, slept almost as soon as I had pulled her into my arms.

XII

My last conscious thought was that I had to wake no later than five; my mother always rose early to supervise the start of a new day in her household, and I had no wish to encounter her as I slipped discreetly back to my room.

When I opened my eyes again the hands of the clock on the chimneypiece told me five o'clock was still ten minutes away so I stayed where I was, savoring my good fortune and struggling with my guilt. Shuddering at the memory of my father's intrusion and blotting it from my mind before it could mar my happiness, I drew Ginette closer to me and wondered if there were any joy on earth that could compare with the joy of waking up for the first time beside a woman one has single-mindedly desired for more than fifteen years.

She awoke, clung to me, pulled my mouth down to hers. Yet I knew further intimacy was impossible at that time and in that place. My guilt that I had broken my word to my father seemed to lie physically on my body like a lead weight, and in my mind I could hear my mother saying as she had said so often in the past, "Here I have my standards, and here I draw the line."

After one last kiss I left the bed and pulled on my clothes.

"It's much too early to announce our plans," I said as I smoothed my hair into place. "If we did we'd simply shock everyone to the core and estrange ourselves from those we most respect. We'll have to go on with the charade for a while. No choice."

"None. Oh God, Robert, I'm so frightened—"

"Don't be. I can manage this—I've always been able to manage my father. I'll see him in private directly after breakfast and make a clean breast of the situation so that he can help me tame my mother—he won't turn his back on me once he realizes my happiness is at stake, I know he won't." I kissed her. "Courage!" I said smiling. "Be brave!" And I kissed her again before slipping out of the room.

I met no one. On the landing I could hear the housemaids beginning work downstairs, but the door of my parents' room was still shut and there was no sound behind the panels. I skimmed past, silent as a ghost, but by the time I reached the sanctuary of my room I was breathing hard not, I realized with contempt, because of the sudden exertion but because I was overcome with nervousness about my mother. After rumpling my bed to give an impression it had been occupied, I drew back the curtains to reveal another brilliant midsummer's day. Then just as I was turning aside I glanced across the garden and saw a figure moving on the far side of the lawn.

It was my father. He was still wearing the casual clothes he had donned for his nocturnal walk, and as I recognized the old tweed jacket it occurred to me that he might have spent all night wandering around the garden to ease his insomnia. I stared. There was an aimless quality in his strolling which hinted at some profound disorganization. He paced around the tennis court in a semicircle, doubled back, headed for the summerhouse, doubled back again. My bewilderment sharpened. Kneeling on the window seat I leaned out over the sill.

He had his dog with him, the latest in a line of golden Labradors all called Glendower, but just as I was wondering what the dog was thinking of his master's erratic movements, my father sat down on the bench by the tennis court and drew the animal close to him as if for comfort. This strange childlike gesture disturbed me still further. Leaving the room I headed abruptly downstairs to the garden.

As he saw me coming across the lawn he rose to his feet. The dog looked up, tail wagging, but my father ignored him. My father had eyes only for me.

"Robert."

"Papa?" I was unsure why I made a question of the word. Perhaps it was because he seemed so unlike himself; perhaps I used an interrogative to imply I wanted to know what was wrong; or perhaps I sensed I was finally in the presence of the stranger who had always kept himself hidden from me.

We paused. We were some six feet apart. Above us the sky was very pale, very clear, and the sun was already hot. The lawn was sparkling with dew.

"Papa?" I heard myself repeat at last.

"Oh Robert," he said, the words tumbling from his mouth, "the moment's finally come—I can't put it off any longer. I've got to tell you, Robert. I've got to tell you about my parents and Owain Bryn-Davies."

5

I

PAST EXPERIENCE with clients had taught me that people in trouble often make confessions which at first appear irrelevant but which in fact have a profound bearing on a truth not easy to approach. So when my father made his statement about his parents and Owain Bryn-Davies I did not say, "What on earth's that got to do with last night's disaster which has obviously upset you so much?" I said instead, "Let's go into the summerhouse and sit down."

"No," said my father. "Not the summerhouse. That's where my mother used to meet Bryn-Davies before my father died. I saw them once and Bryn-Davies caught me and said he'd kill me if I told anyone. I was so frightened I couldn't speak. I didn't think my mother would let him kill me but I wasn't sure. She let him do what he wanted. He was a powerful violent man.

"Yet after my father died—of course I knew they'd murdered him—Bryn-Davies was kind to me, took trouble, I knew he was just doing it to please my mother but I liked him for it, it made life easier. But I was always frightened of him, I was always frightened of her and I thought they might kill me one day because I knew of the murder and they knew that I knew—my mother had confessed to me. After my father died I said to her, 'It was the arsenic, wasn't it, the arsenic you got for the rats,' and she broke down, she said she'd be hanged if the authorities found out, she said if I made trouble Bryn-Davies would kill me and she wouldn't be able to stop him. She was weeping, she was terrified and I was terrified to see her in such a state—I was just a child, only fourteen and I was so frightened. I was so frightened that I couldn't sleep at night, I used to go and hide in the stable loft and cover myself with straw before I could sleep without fear of being killed.

"I didn't ask why she'd murdered my father, I knew how unhappy he'd made her, but Bryn-Davies was afraid I might take my father's side and hate my mother so he spared me nothing, he told me everything, oh God I can't tell you, I was so appalled, so frightened, I was just a child, only fourteen, God Almighty, I used to think I'd die of the terror.

"So I took my mother's side and said I forgave her for the murder, my poor mother, she'd suffered so much, my father had been so cruel to her. I used to wonder why they had ever married. It was an odd sort of match, he from the gentry, she the daughter of a Welsh farmer, but as you know the Llewellyns are such an old family, and when Henry Tudor granted them their land after Bosworth

94

that set them apart from all the tenant farmers in Gower. . . . But even so to marry a Godwin was a social triumph for my mother, yes, I can see why she married him. And he would have married her because she was so beautiful and he prized beautiful things, I suppose he thought that if he married anyone he might as well marry someone beautiful, and he had to marry because of Oxmoon, he loved Oxmoon so he had to have a son. . . . But he shouldn't have married. He shouldn't have married anyone.

"In the beginning I think he drank to suppress his vice and in the end I think he drank because he'd given way to it. You wouldn't believe how he drank. I loved him but he frightened me. He frightened her. He'd start drinking brandy after breakfast and he'd be dead drunk by noon. Then he'd get violent and start shouting at her. He used to beat her . . . and worse. I'd run out of the house and hide in the woods because I couldn't bear to hear her screams. . . . She left him in the end, it was when he started bringing boys home from Swansea, she ran away back to her father and took me with her, but her father was a religious man and said he wouldn't have a deserting wife in the house. So she had to go back, and when she did Bryn-Davies escorted her. He was visiting the Llewellyns' farm at the time to sell her father a ewe, and it was then, when she was rejected by the family who should have helped her, that she came to know him well. They already knew each other slightly because although he was born in The Welshery his farm was nearer, he used to graze his sheep on Llanmadoc Hill. My poor mother, how absolutely she fell in love with him . . . but it was all my father's fault. It was his wickedness that drove her to adultery, it was his wickedness that drove her to murder and it was because his wickedness had driven her to such evil that I myself was driven to . . ."

He stopped.

His face was white, beaded with sweat, but his voice had remained level throughout this shattering monologue. He was looking across the lawn at Oxmoon, and as I watched he clenched his trembling hands and shoved them deep into his pockets in a pathetic attempt at self-control.

"Sit down, Papa. Sit down again on the bench here."

We both sat down on the bench by the tennis court, and the dog Glendower, resting his long nose on his master's knee, gazed up at him with devotion. My father stroked the golden coat, kneading the fur with strong repetitive movements of his fingers.

"But you do see, Robert, don't you," he said. "It was the vice that lay at the root of the disaster, it was the perversion. I couldn't forget that. I can't forget it. That knowledge came to dominate my whole life, and you have to understand that in order to understand me—oh God, I was so frightened, Robert, always so terrified that I'd inherited the vice and would grow up like my father.

"I didn't look much like my father but I had his build, I kept growing taller and taller, and I thought if I had his build that might mean . . . Oh God, how it horrified me, I thought I'd go mad with the horror, but meanwhile other horrifying things were happening—Bryn-Davies taking control of Oxmoon—my mother living with him openly—the estate going to ruin—the rats infesting the house . . . For

95

a while I just went my own way and tried not to notice but in the end I wasn't allowed to be passive, in the end I had to act. Well, it couldn't go on, could it? He was stealing my inheritance, robbing me blind, shaming my mother, ruining us all... Oh yes, I knew it couldn't go on.

"But I was afraid of my mother ending up on the gallows. I was afraid that if I once embarked on revelations to the law there was no knowing where those revelations might end. And above all I was afraid of Bryn-Davies. But of course the situation couldn't go on, and after you were born, I looked around, I saw the world I'd brought you into, and I knew I couldn't tolerate it anymore. I had to change it for you. I had to cleanse it and put it right. I did it for you, Robert; I did it for you and for Margaret. You gave me the courage to act.

"I talked it over with Margaret and decided the best plan was to arrange a meeting with Bryn-Davies at the Worm's Head. This was a favorite spot of mine, I often took your mother there to escape from Oxmoon, even after you were born we used to take the pony trap to Rhossili and walk out to the Worm and you'd be strapped in a little pack on my back. I knew the Worm like the back of my hand. But Bryn-Davies didn't. He'd never been there but he talked of going because the sheep there were legendary, wonderful quality, and he was interested in buying into the flock.

"But on the day he died he didn't go out to the Worm to see the sheep. That was just what we told everyone later. He went out to see me. I wrote him a note saying I'd meet him there to discuss my father's murder and the future of Oxmoon, and then I left immediately for Rhossili—with you and your mother, of course. I didn't dare let either of you out of my sight.

"Well... We got to Rhossili and... and I realized I'd made a little mistake with the tide tables... silly of me.... I saw at once, as soon as I looked down at the Shipway, that it would be going under in half an hour.

"Well... I settled you and Margaret in a secluded spot farther along the cliffs and then I went back... but he'd already started out. The Shipway's so deceptive, it looks safe long after it's begun to be dangerous. He was caught in the middle. And he didn't have a chance.

"You know what happened next. My mother arrived. She'd found the note and realized... well, no doubt she was worried about what might happen. She came and I was there and there was nothing we could do but watch him drown.

"It drove her mad. It wasn't just that he died before her eyes, it was because she thought I'd killed him. I told her over and over again it was... well, just a little accident with the tide tables, but she refused to believe me. And she went mad. But I was glad of this because it gave me an excuse to lock her up. She had to be locked up, you see, because she was a murderess, she'd poisoned my father— and besides, I wanted Oxmoon purged, I couldn't have had her there, polluting the house with her memories of adultery and murder.... No, she had to be locked up. As Margaret always said, in the circumstances what else could I possibly have done?

"And so we come to Margaret. We come to your mother. You think she's so commonplace, I know you do, but my God, you've no idea, Robert. You've no idea at all.

"She got me through all this. I couldn't have survived without her. And I don't just mean she stood by me before and after Bryn-Davies died. She gave me the will to pull Oxmoon back from the grave. I stood in the ruined hall with her and said, 'I can't manage, I don't know where to begin.' I felt so helpless because I knew nothing about the estate, but she said, 'I *know* you can manage,' and suggested searching the library for papers that might help me. We found nothing but later she said, 'Let's take one last look,' so we went back and there in the library the most enormous rat was sitting on the table and chewing a candle. It was a vile moment. Beautiful Oxmoon, ruined, infested, decayed... Margaret screamed and I grabbed the nearest book and flung it at the rat and killed it. And then when I replaced the book I found there were papers stuffed behind it—the journals of my grandfather in which he'd described in detail exactly how he'd managed the estate.... Margaret just said, 'Where there's a will there's a way.'

"But it was her will. And her way. She made everything come right, you see, even when we were first married. I was so terrified that I might be like my father, but Margaret proved I wasn't. And you proved I wasn't. That was why I wanted a lot of children because every time a child was born it proved how different I was from my father, who, so Bryn-Davies told me, only consummated his marriage twice in the normal way. So every time I was in bed with my wife...being normal...do you see what I'm trying to say? It was like an erasure, like a victory over memory, until in the end bed became not just a way of forgetting my father but a way of forgetting everything I couldn't bear to remember. And gradually... as time went on... I found..."

He stopped again. I waited but when he clearly found it impossible to continue, I said in the neutral voice I used to clients when I was playing midwife at the birth of some terrible truth, "As time went on you found Margaret alone couldn't help you forget." I used my mother's Christian name deliberately to foster the illusion that I was a mere lawyer who bore no personal connection to my client or anyone he knew.

"Yes," said my father. He had stopped caressing the dog and now he closed his eyes as if the truth were a physical presence which he could not bear to see. "But I'm afraid I haven't been very honest with you about that, Robert. I'm afraid I lied to you about the past. You see—" He opened his eyes again but he could not look at me. "—I wanted you to go on thinking of me as a hero. I couldn't endure to think you might be disillusioned."

"I understand. But now—"

"Yes, now I must tell you—I *must*—that it wasn't your mother's fault that I was driven to adultery. I lied when I implied it was. I know your mother's a stickler for convention but as a matter of fact she's very down-to-earth about marital intimacy, I always thanked God I didn't marry some well-bred lady who hated it. Your mother and I always got on well in that respect and she wanted children just as much as I did so there was no conflict. Actually I liked her being pregnant and she liked it too so that never created any difficulties either—rather the reverse, if anything. But then . . . I couldn't help it . . . I just had to go elsewhere as well—"

"Did you really discuss the problem with Margaret? Or did you lie when you told me you did?"

"Oh God, of course I discussed it with her, how could I avoid it? I was beside myself with horror, I couldn't face what I'd done, she helped me get through it all, she saved our marriage—"

"You mean when it all began?"

"Yes," said my father, "when it all began." He paused before saying, "My infidelity had begun a long time before you found out about it." And after another pause he said, "You were fourteen and away at Harrow when it all began."

"I see," said the lawyer, a model of neutrality and detachment. "I was fourteen, you were thirty-four, Margaret was thirty-one—"

"—and Ginevra was sixteen," said my father, and covered his face with his hands.

II

"Of course," he said at once, letting his hands fall as he swiveled to face me, "I didn't seduce her, never, never think I could be capable of such wickedness, but . . . I was foolish. And the direct result of that foolishness was that I went to London and committed adultery for the first time with a woman I met there."

Several seconds passed. When I could finally trust myself to speak I said, "This . . . this incident with—"

"Incident, yes, that's all it was—utterly appalling, utterly wrong, but just a little incident in the music room—"

"How did it happen?"

My father seemed to relax. I had seen criminals relax like that when they thought they were past the most harrowing section of their story. He started to knead Glendower's golden coat again.

"I was out riding one day with Oswald Stourham," he said conversationally, "and we were just chatting about women as we so often did when Oswald said to me, 'By Jove, Bobby, that little cousin of yours is turning into quite a peach!' and I said, 'Oh yes? I can't say I've noticed'—which was true because I still thought of Ginevra as a child—and as a daughter. Well, Oswald laughed so hard he nearly fell out of his saddle. 'By Jove, Bobby!' he says again in that hearty voice of his. 'A man would have to be a second Oscar Wilde not to appreciate the charms of your little cousin Ginevra!'

"I said nothing but I couldn't forget that gibe about Wilde. Then a disastrous thing happened: Margaret had to visit her sister and once she was gone I found I was thinking continually about Ginevra . . . I suppose it became an obsession. Anyway, to cut a long story short, I kissed Ginevra one afternoon when she was practicing her piano in the music room. She was upset and, I saw at once, very frightened. I tried to reassure her, swore I wouldn't do it again, but I suppose she felt she couldn't trust me and that was why soon afterwards she rode to Porteynon and tried to elope with Kinsella—she wanted to run away from Oxmoon . . . and from me. . . . But her action took me wholly by surprise. I didn't know she'd been having clandestine meetings with him ever since Margaret had left.

"Well, I was in a terrible state but as soon as I'd confessed to Margaret she sorted everything out. She sent me to London to get me out of the way for a while, and then using Kinsella as her excuse she arranged for Ginevra to go to the Applebys'. . . . Oh God, Robert, if only you knew how wretched and ashamed I felt—"

"You went to London."

"Yes. For two weeks."

"And there you committed adultery for the first time, you said."

"Yes. I was in an appalling state and kept remembering all I didn't want to remember—my father—Bryn-Davies—the little accident with the tide tables—my mother raving—Oswald talking about Oscar Wilde, it was all jumbled up together, I couldn't sleep, I couldn't eat, I tried drinking but I was so frightened of getting drunk, I thought that too would mean I was ending up like my father—"

"So you found a woman and managed to forget. When did Margaret find out?"

"Oh, I told her as soon as I got back," said my father. "Of course."

I suddenly found I was on my feet.

He looked up. His very blue eyes were bright with fear. He had to struggle to stand.

"Oh God, Robert, forgive me—oh my God, my God, what a retribution this is—"

"You told my mother," I said, "and what did my mother say?"

"She said she could understand but no one else would so it had to be kept absolutely secret. She said I must do what I apparently had to do but it must always be done in London."

"So she sanctioned the adultery. And eventually, I suppose, she took you back."

"Oh, we were never estranged. We always shared a bed."

"You mean . . . I'm sorry, I think I must have misunderstood. You're surely not trying to tell me—"

"Yes. She never rejected me. She knew I'd have gone to pieces utterly if she'd done that."

After a moment I managed to say, "I see. So everyone, it seems, then lives happily ever after—until Ginette comes home and you and Mama realize that I'm still dead set on a marriage which you can only regard with horror. No wonder you were driven to approach Ginette last night when you saw the light was still burning in her room! You were under a compulsion to find out how far I'd gone with her!"

"No, you misunderstand. By that time your feelings were no mystery but what I *had* to find out was how Ginevra felt. If she just wants to be your mistress then

I don't think Margaret will interfere, but if she wants to be your wife—" He covered his face with his hands again.

"Quite." I looked across the sparkling dew-drenched lawn to Oxmoon, shining in the morning light. The maids had now drawn back all the curtains on the ground floor.

"But at least now I've spoken to you," said my father. "At least now I can tell Margaret you know everything and that there's no need for her to tell you herself. And perhaps eventually . . . after you've thought over all I've said about my parents and Bryn-Davies . . . you might find it in your heart to understand . . . and make allowances . . . and possibly one day forgive me for . . . Oh Robert, if only you knew how much I regret that past foolishness with Ginevra—"

"Quite," I said again.

He was crying. My clients, both male and female, usually cried at the end. The birth of truth can be so painful. I was well accustomed to witnessing such ordeals, so accustomed that the sight of the emotional aftermath had long since lost its power to move me.

"I must thank you for confiding in me, sir," I said. "Please don't think I'm unaware of the considerable strain such confidences have imposed upon you. And now I have only one question left to ask: did you tell my mother that you found me in bed with Ginette last night?"

He simply looked at me. The tears were still streaming down his face. I shrugged, turned my back on him and walked away.

III

Sodomy, adultery and murder; robbery, madness and lust. The Greeks would no doubt have considered this catalogue standard fare at the table of life. I thought— I tried to think—of *The Oresteia*. I felt that if I could reduce my father's story to the remote status of Greek tragedy, I would somehow transform it into a saga I could contemplate with equanimity—or if not equanimity, at least with an ordered mind, the mind which I had applied at Harrow to translating Aeschylus. But my nerve failed me as I remembered my father's appalling understatements.

Just a little accident with the tide tables. Just a little incident in the music room. The phrases rasped across my consciousness, and as I recalled that voice speaking of the unspeakable I knew I had no defenses against the horrors he had revealed.

I was in the woods by Humphrey de Mohun's ruined tower. I was in the woods thinking of sodomy, adultery, murder, robbery, madness and lust but I dared not think of guardians who abused a position of trust. There my courage failed me. I thought only of the evil which existed in the realms of Greek literature—although such evil was more commonplace than civilized people dared believe; I knew that well enough. Had I not always seen the Gower Peninsula not as the pretty playground eulogized in the guidebooks but as the lawless land soaked in blood where the King's writ had so often failed to run? It was the peace and order of my parents' Oxmoon that were unusual; the nightmare of the Eighties had merely represented Gower running true to form.

I now fully understood my parents' obsession with setting standards and drawing moral lines. Having been to hell and back their central preoccupation lay in keeping hell at bay, and as far as they were concerned they believed that observing the conventions was the best way to stop hell encroaching. Within the fortress of their self-imposed morality they could feel they were safe, but after their experiences neither of them could doubt that beyond the fortress walls lay violence and madness, perpetually hovering to destroy all those who failed to draw the line.

I thought of my parents fighting from their moral fortress but not, as I had always supposed, winning the battle against the forces which besieged them. I saw now that they were slowly but inexorably losing as my father, my desperate damaged father, sank ever deeper into the mire of his guilt and his shame.

Trying at last to consider my father's disastrous weakness rationally, I told myself that he was a victim and that any civilized man could only regard him with compassion.

I waited for compassion to come but nothing happened. Then into the void which compassion should have filled I felt the darker emotions streaming, emotions which I knew I had to reject. But I could not reject them. I was too upset. In fact I was very upset, very very upset indeed, more upset than I had ever been in my life, and my thoughts were spiraling downwards into chaos.

"Just a little incident in the music room..."

I was trembling. I gripped the ivy that clung to the walls of the ruined tower, and above me the jackdaws beat their sinister wings and cawed as if in mockery of my collapse.

I was thinking of Ginette at last. I tried not to, but I could no longer stop myself. I knew she should have told me but I knew too that it would have been impossible for her to confess. I decided I could not blame her. There was only one person I could blame and that was my father.

I went on gripping the ivy as first rage and then hatred overpowered me. That kiss in the music room had set Ginette on the road to Conor Kinsella, the road which had led to the destruction of my adolescent dreams and the blighting of my adult life. How farcical to think that during all those years I had continued to regard my father as a hero! As I could see now with blinding clarity he was no hero; he was a lecher, a cheat and a fool.

I vomited. Afterwards I still felt ill but I was mentally calmer, as if my mind had rebelled against the violence of my emotions and forced my body to make a gesture of expulsion. As a rational man I knew I had to forgive my father, that victim of past tragedy, and I did indeed believe I would eventually forgive him— but not yet. And perhaps not for a long while.

Washing my face in the stream I tried to pull myself together by considering the immediate future, and at once I saw how imperative it was that no one should know I was so distressed. In other words, my father was now not my immediate difficulty; I could deal—or try to deal—with him later. My immediate difficulty lay in summoning the strength to return to the house, change into a suit, appear at breakfast and later go to church with the rest of the family as if nothing out of the ordinary had occurred.

I vomited again. Then, disgusted by such an exhibition of weakness and humiliated by my loss of control over my emotions, I forced myself to leave the woods, return to the house and face the full horror of my new grand charade.

IV

Breakfast was not until nine on Sundays so I had plenty of time to prepare for my ordeal. I wondered whether my father would ask my mother to read the customary prayers before the meal, but I came to the conclusion that this was unlikely. He too would be bent on hiding his distress by keeping up appearances; he too would have decided, just as I had, that no other course of action was available to him.

I thought of us both saying to ourselves: No one must ever know. No one must ever guess.

I found myself quite unable to think of Ginette now. I knew that at some time in the future I would have to talk to her about my father, but that future was apparently beyond my power to imagine at that moment. In my room as I washed and changed I told myself I could cope with only one ordeal at a time, and my first ordeal without doubt was surviving the family breakfast in the dining room.

I set off downstairs to the hall.

When I arrived at the foot of the stairs I found to my dismay that my watch was five minutes slower than the grandfather clock which traditionally marked the correct time at Oxmoon. That meant I was late. That also meant a bad start to my charade, and I was still staring at the clock in futile disbelief when far away in the distance I heard the dining-room door open.

A second later my mother was bustling into the hall.

"Ah, there you are!" she said with satisfaction. "Come along, we're all waiting—you mustn't miss prayers!"

But I was transfixed. I looked at her and could not speak for suddenly I was seeing her not as the woman who was so familiar to me but as the unknown girl of sixteen, brought up in a cheerful moneyed home and catapulted into the moral and financial bankruptcy of a terrifying alien world. I thought of her standing by my father in the beginning when a lesser woman might have run sobbing home to her parents; I thought of her sticking by him through thick and thin; I thought of her mastering crises that most women would have found not only insuperable but unimaginable. And I thought how I had misjudged her, dismissing her as narrow and limited when in truth the narrowness and limitation had been all on

102

my side. I saw her helping me at that crucial moment in my adolescence when she realized my father had failed me; I saw her trying to talk to me although I had always been too proud to listen; I saw her understanding me far too well for my own conceited contemptible comfort, understanding me as my father never had and never could. In my memory I heard her say, "You're like me—you really have very simple emotional tastes," and for the first time I realized what she must have suffered from that complex man she had married and whom she had apparently loved, as single-mindedly as I had loved Ginette, from the age of sixteen.

"Come along!" she was repeating briskly. "You mustn't keep your father waiting!" But hardly had she finished speaking when I was stepping forward to take her in my arms.

For a brief interval she was silent. Then she patted my back and said kindly, "There, there. We'll sort it all out later. Now come along and let's do what we're supposed to do."

Still mute I followed her to the dining room.

V

I noticed at once that Ginette was absent. That disturbed me. By this time I was so obsessed with the desire to pretend that everything was as it should be that any small deviation from the normal was unnerving.

"Are you feeling better, Robert?" inquired John when the prayers were finished.

"Better?" I said blankly.

"Your sunstroke, dear," said my mother. "I nearly sent a tray up to your room this morning, but then your father told me you were quite recovered. I'm so glad."

"Mama decided to spoil Ginevra instead!" Lion informed me. "And incidentally, Mama, how tired do I have to be before I'm allowed to miss family prayers and have breakfast in bed?"

After the laughter had subsided I accepted coffee, fried eggs, bacon, sausages and toast and sat toying with my knife and fork. My father chose bacon alone and managed to slip it slice by slice to Glendower. At the other end of the table my mother had cunningly ordered a boiled egg, and since no one could see through the shell no one could tell how much of it she ate. She drank two cups of tea and looked tranquil.

Meanwhile an animated postmortem on the dinner party was being conducted. I had forgotten what a noise large families make but although I winced periodically I was glad of the opportunity to remain silent.

"Well," said my father, making a great business of pulling out his watch, "there are one or two things I have to do before church, so if you'll all excuse me—"

The door of the dining room opened and in walked Ginette.

"Ginevra!" chorused my brothers in delight.

"Darlings!" said Ginette radiantly to them. "I simply couldn't stay in bed, it made me feel too guilty!" She looked down the table at my mother. "Margaret, it was so kind of you to send up a tray but I really did feel I wanted to join the family for breakfast. I'm sorry I missed prayers."

She was wearing a plain black day frock with no jewelry. She had not replaced Kinsella's rings and in my fevered state I thought this omission a disastrous error, but when I glanced around the table I soon realized that no one had noticed such a minor detail of her appearance. I willed myself to keep calm.

"Good morning, Robert!" she was saying as Ifor drew out the chair next to mine. "How's your sunstroke?"

"He's decided to live!" said Lion promptly. "We're all mortified!"

"Well, I really mustn't linger," murmured my father, and to my envy he finally managed to escape.

But I knew I had to stay at the table. I could hardly abandon Ginette now that she had flung caution to the winds by walking into the lion's den, and as I glanced at her tense smiling face I recognized a pattern of behavior with which I was not unfamiliar: the prisoner became so exhausted by the strain of waiting in his cell that he could barely be restrained from rushing into court to confront the judge and learn his fate.

"Papa looks awful, Mama," John was saying with concern. "Is anything wrong?"

"No, dear, just a little touch of insomnia as the result of last night's lobster."

"Mama," said Celia, preparing to leave the table, "how are we all traveling to church? Will there be room for me in the motor or are Robert and Ginevra accompanying you and Papa?"

"Oh, there'll be room for you, dear," said my mother. "Robert and Ginevra won't be going to church."

Everyone looked at her in astonishment.

"But it's the rule!" shrilled Thomas scandalized.

"No doubt they'll go to Evensong, dear, but this morning they have an important matter to discuss."

"What's that?" said Lion automatically.

"Lion dearest," said my mother, "it's a personal and private matter connected with Ginevra's recent sad loss, and I think it would be indelicate of you to inquire further. A widow," said my mother, sipping her tea, "naturally has many legal and financial problems which require the attention of someone experienced in such matters."

"Oh, I see." Lion subsided into a puzzled silence.

"Shall I eat this third rasher or not?" mused Edmund, who was still pondering over his breakfast. "I can't make up my mind."

"Leave it," said John, standing up so suddenly that I knew he had sensed the tension in the room. "Come on, fellows, time to play hunt-the-prayer-book."

"Can I get down, please?" said Thomas perfunctorily. He was already moving to the door with his mouth full.

"Very well, Thomas. Edmund, make sure you change your tie before church. You've got an egg stain on it."

"Oh, Lord, so I have! Thank you for telling me, Mama."

"That will do, Bayliss," said my mother to the butler. "I shall ring later when I want you to clear."

"Very good, ma'am." Bayliss left with Ifor at his heels. Thomas and John were already in the hall and as I watched both Lion and Edmund followed them.

"I wonder which hat to choose," mused Celia. "I think I'll wear the one with rosebuds."

She drifted away. The door finally closed. My mother remained at one end of the long table and Ginette and I remained side by side some distance away on her right. In the silence that followed I felt Ginette's hand groping unsteadily for mine.

"I'm sorry you saw fit to come down, Ginevra," said my mother pleasantly at last, replacing her teacup in its saucer. "I intended to say what has to be said in the privacy of your room. I didn't want to embarrass you in front of Robert." She paused before adding: "Perhaps you'd prefer Robert to leave now?" Her voice was solicitous. She made it sound as if she had only our welfare in mind.

I pulled Ginette's hand above the table so that my mother could see our fingers were interlocked. "I'm staying," I said.

"Oh, I don't think you want to stay, Robert," said my mother. "Not really. I think you'd be much happier if you let me have a little talk with Ginevra on her own."

I put my arm around Ginette's shoulders. She was trembling. Holding her tightly I repeated, "I'm staying."

"Very well." My mother paused to reorganize her thoughts. Finally she said, "Ginevra, I must tell you that Bobby had a long talk with Robert this morning, and Robert is now aware that you haven't been honest with him."

I both heard and felt Ginette's horrified gasp but I said with lightning speed as if she were a client in great danger, "Don't say a word."

Ginette was rigid with fear. I was painfully aware of the color suffusing her face but still I kept my arm around her and we remained silent.

"Now, Ginevra," said my mother, suddenly becoming very businesslike, "I think that if you intend to marry Robert you really should be honest. You may well be content to deceive him but in my opinion such a deception would be quite wrong and I could not possibly condone it. But perhaps I'm mistaken and you have no intention of marriage? If you merely intend to continue as his mistress then of course Robert must take you as he finds you and I'll say no more."

I said, "We're getting married."

"Ah," said my mother, "then I fear I have no alternative." She stood up, a small neat square figure in gray, and we stood up too, Ginette leaning against me, barely breathing, fingers frantically clutching my free hand.

"I am now going to church," said my mother. "While I'm gone, you, Ginevra, are going to tell Robert exactly what happened at Oxmoon when you were sixteen, and when I come back I shall discuss the situation further with him. If I find you haven't told him the truth, then believe me I most certainly shall."

I intercepted her. "Ginette can tell me nothing," I said, "that I don't already know."

She looked at me steadily. Her pale eyes seemed darker than usual as they reflected the somber shade of her dress. She had a wide plain broad-nosed face with a mouth that could harden in a second to express implacable resolution. It hardened now. As I instinctively recoiled from her, I heard myself say—and to my horror my voice was unsteady—"I know what you're trying to tell me but I don't believe it. I don't, I won't and I can't. You're just acting out of spite and revenge."

She turned abruptly to Ginette. "We must put him out of his misery at once. Are you going to tell him or shall I?"

"Oh Margaret, no—*no*—"

"My dear, you can't fool him indefinitely. He's much too clever and he deals daily with criminals and liars—look at him, he already knows although he refuses to believe it—"

"*I can't tell him!*" screamed Ginette. "I can't, I can't, I can't!"

"Very well," said my mother. "Perhaps I was expecting too much. Perhaps I should have made greater allowances for you considering all you've been through." Then she turned to me and said kindly, with a complete lack of all the emotion to which she was entitled, "I'm sorry, Robert, but your father didn't tell you the whole story. It's not his fault, it's just that he's emotionally incapable of it. The truth is simply this: he seduced her. She slept with him. And it nearly destroyed us all."

PART
TWO

GINEVRA
1913-1919

---

*But you are wrong if you think Fortune has changed
towards you. Change is her normal behavior, her true
nature. In the very act of changing she has preserved
her own particular kind of constancy towards you. She
was exactly the same when she was flattering you and
luring you on with enticements of a false kind of happiness. You have discovered the changing faces of the
random goddess. To others she still veils herself, but to
you she has revealed herself to the full....*
—Boethius
The Consolation of Philosophy

"AND IT NEARLY destroyed us all," said Margaret.
I fainted.

No, that's not right. That's fantasy and in this journal I must be concerned with reality. I'm like one of those wretched women who suffer from some disorder of the womb yet lie to their doctors because they fear having their private parts examined. If you don't tell the truth to your doctor how can you expect to get better? And if I don't tell the truth to my journal how can I hope to extricate myself from the messy lies of my ghastly private life?

So no more lies, not here. No more writing, "I fainted" as if I were the virginal heroine of a romantic novel. (Oh, how divine it would be to be a virginal heroine! I wouldn't even mind pressing all those frightful wild flowers.) What I have to do is to record in the past tense what, to the best of my recollection, seemed to be happening, and then to comment in the present tense on what was—and is— really going on. Then perhaps I'll master reality and avoid the horror of a future based on illusion.

So bearing all this in mind, I must be brave, resolute and blindingly honest (all the things that I'm not). Cross out "I fainted." And start again.

"The truth is simply this," said Margaret, rather as if she were discussing some troublesome dinner-party menu with Cook. "He seduced her, she slept with him and it nearly destroyed us all."

I thought: Well, that's that. All over. And I sank down on the nearest chair. I was conscious of nothing but relief that disaster, long anticipated, had finally struck. I thought of my childhood heroine, Mary Queen of Scots, finally being obliged to put her head on the block. What bliss! What relief! Nothing else to do but wait for the ax.

So I sat at the dining-room table in a passive stupor amidst the ruins of breakfast while nearby a very tall man was facing a very small woman who was saying in a passionless voice, "I shall now go to church. However, should either of you wish to resume this conversation with me later, I shall be only too willing to help in any way that I can."

Neat little footsteps tip-tapped past me, and after the dining-room door had closed neat little footsteps tip-tapped away to the hall. I went on waiting for the axe but when nothing happened I eventually nerved myself to look at my executioner. He was staring at the dirty plates on the table, the crumpled napkins, the sordidness, the disorder, the mess. Then he said in an abrupt voice, "Go and wait for me in the music room." He might have been marshaling a tiresome solicitor out of his chambers; I almost expected him to advise seeing his clerk for a further appointment.

He held the door open for me as I left the room but I did not dare look at him and I suspected he did not dare look at me. Stumbling down the corridor I prayed I wouldn't meet anyone and I didn't. (Why is it that God so often answers trivial prayers but not the prayers that really matter?) The little music room, where I had spent so many hours thumping out those boring scales, lay off the passage that led to the ballroom, and there by the window stood the same table where long ago I had teased my ineffectual governess Miss Sale by drawing grossly sensual treble clefs.

I went to the piano.

"How well you play!" said Bobby in my mind, the Bobby I could bear to remember, the man who was always so kind and good with children. Another Bobby had existed but he could be allowed no place in my memory. Sometimes he tried to slip in—he was trying to slip in now—but fear made me strong and I shut him out. The road to remembrance was guarded by a terrible coldness and as soon as I shivered I thought, I won't think of that. Yet I was always terrified I would. I was terrified now. I knew I was going to have to remember that other Bobby but I did not see how I could speak of him and remain conscious. I thought I would die of the shame.

To distract myself I began to play "The Blue Danube," but I was in such an agony of terror that all the notes came out wrong, and I had just broken off in despair when the inevitable happened; footsteps echoed in the corridor and Robert walked into the room.

I struggled to my feet. He was expressionless but exuding a businesslike efficiency. My terror deepened.

"Sit down, please," he said, gesturing to the table.

We sat down opposite each other by the window. There was a pile of sheet music between us, and as I stared at the treble clefs they became meaningless, mere recurring symbols between those recurring parallel lines.

"Now," said Robert briskly, "this is what we're going to do. You're going to tell me the truth, the whole truth and nothing but the truth. Then once the truth is established beyond all reasonable doubt I shall reduce it to order so that we can conduct a rational survey of our dilemma. However before I begin... Are you listening?"

I whispered that I was.

"Then look at me."

I somehow raised my eyes to the level of his watch chain.

"That's better. Now before we begin there are two points I wish you to understand. One: don't lie to me because I'm on my guard now and I'll be able to spot a lie almost before it's spoken. I'm trained to recognize lies, and in fact although I shut my mind against the knowledge I knew earlier that my father hadn't told me the whole truth; he was very plausible but I noticed how he relaxed in relief when he thought his big lie had been safely delivered.... So you see, you must always tell me the truth because if you don't I'll know and that'll mean the end."

"Yes." I heard the word "end" and realized dimly that he spoke of it not as if it were in the present but as if it were in the future, and not just in the future but in a future that was not necessarily inevitable. I was apparently being granted some fearful stay of execution. I thought of the rack and disembowelment and began to see the advantages of a simple beheading. Perhaps Mary Queen of Scots had been luckier than I had ever realized.

"Very well, that's the first point I want to make," said Robert, "and the second point is this: whatever the truth is don't be frightened of confessing it to me because I can't possibly be shocked—I'll have heard it all before. May I remind you that I don't just defend murderers at the Old Bailey. I go out on circuit, and at the assizes I defend people accused of robbery, assault, rape, sodomy, bestiality, incest and any other criminal offense you care to name. You do see what I'm trying to say, don't you? You do see what an enormous advantage my profession gives us here?"

I managed to nod but I still couldn't imagine how I was ever going to speak of the unspeakable. However Robert saw my difficulty and tried again.

"If you can help me by doing as I ask," he said, "then I can help you. Regard it as a new charade to play: I shall think of you as my client, someone in great trouble who requires all my professional skill, and you must think of me as your lawyer, the only person on earth who has a hope of getting you out of this mess."

I suddenly understood not only his proposal but the logic that lay behind it. He was trying to distance us from the horror by making it impersonal. We were no longer lovers. We were lawyer and client. I was in ghastly trouble but he could help, he had seen it all before; he was calm, he was professional, he could cope. All I had to do to survive was to trust him.

"This sort of case is in fact not uncommon," said Robert, shoring up my confidence. "You may be surprised to hear that there's even sometimes on the part of the child a degree of acquiescence which can amount to encouragement. I say that not to imply that this was true in your case but to reassure you that I'm wholly familiar with such incidents. Now... shall we begin?"

I nodded but was immediately plunged into panic again. As far as I could see no beginning was possible.

"Ginevra." That snapped me out of my panic as abruptly as a slap in the face for he never called me Ginevra as everyone else did. "You must trust me," he said, and when I looked into his eyes I found I could not look away. "You must."

"Yes... I will... I do... but I can't see where to begin."

He smiled. Like so many juries I had surrendered my mind to his and the first hurdle had been overcome. I was so relieved to see him smile that tears came to my eyes, and when he offered me a cigarette (a noble gesture from a man who hated women smoking) I nearly wept with gratitude.

When our cigarettes were alight he said, "The first matter I want to clarify is the chronology. This case is all mixed up with your first encounter with Kinsella, isn't it? What I'd like to establish is whether the two incidents were related or whether they were merely running concurrently. Let's start with Kinsella. You met him at the Mowbrays', didn't you, in the May of 1896, shortly after your sixteenth birthday?"

"Yes." This was easy. I thought of Conor and how divinely glamorous he had looked at twenty-four, a fascinating rough diamond in a pearls-and-primness setting. "It was a grown-up dinner party," I said. "I wasn't 'out,' of course, but it didn't matter because it was just a gathering of old friends. The Porteynon Kinsellas came with Conor, and the Bryn-Davieses were there as well. I remember saying to Conor, 'Mr. Bryn-Davies's father and my cousin Bobby's mother were involved in a simply scorching grand passion!' and Conor was very entertained, but Margaret overheard and was livid with me afterwards."

"What was Bobby's attitude to you at this time?"

"Normal." I was grateful to him for using Bobby's first name instead of any word that would have underlined their relationship.

"Very well. What happened after this dinner party when you created such a deep impression on Kinsella?"

"Nothing. There was no deep impression. You see, I was so young, I still wore my hair in plaits—I hadn't a hope of winning any serious attention from a sophisticated man of twenty-four. Besides, he was after his cousins' money—the money that went to that wretched dogs' home in the end—and so he had to be on his best behavior. He couldn't afford any unwise flirtations."

"But he did like you."

"Oh yes, I think he found me amusing but I soon realized nothing was going to come of it. Margaret hadn't cared for him at all so I knew he'd never be invited to Oxmoon."

"Very discouraging for you. What happened next?"

"I mooned around at home, shed a few tears of frustration and decided my life had finished at the age of sixteen."

"All very normal behavior, in fact, for a young girl in the throes of calf love."

"Oh yes, everything was absolutely normal. But then..."

"Just take it in strict chronological sequence. There you were, you say, shedding tears like a lovesick heroine—"

"—in the summerhouse, yes, I was just weeping over my volume of Browning when...when Bobby t irned up with Glendower—or at least the Glendower of seventeen years ago. He asked me what the matter was and when I poured out my heart to him he was so kind and understanding." This was the Bobby I could allow myself to remember. I was able to speak the words without difficulty.

"Was there any manifestation of an abnormal interest at this stage?"

"No, but after that he became nicer and nicer to me, and I kept meeting him by accident at odd moments—only of course the meetings were no accident—"

"I'm sorry, I've lost track of the time here. Is this still May or are we in June?"

"It must have been still in May. I met Conor at the beginning of the month, and I don't think this unusual interest from Bobby went on for more than a fortnight or so—three weeks at the most."

"But there was still no hint of impropriety?"

"No, I knew his interest was unprecedented but I just thought he was making an extra effort to cheer me up."

"He didn't kiss you here in the music room, for instance, when no one was around?"

"No, never. But it's odd you should mention the music room because he did come here more than once when I was practicing the piano." I tried to recall the incidents. I had spent so many years trying to forget that my memory had become shadowy, but I now found as a matter of pride that I wanted to dispel the shadows in order to impress Robert with my courage. "Wait a moment," I said to him. "I must try and get this right."

"Take your time."

I went on thinking. I now felt no pain, no fear, just a consuming desire to confess as accurately as possible, and as I sat there in silence the past seemed no longer an emotional nightmare but an intellectual puzzle which I felt morally bound to solve.

At last I said slowly, "I think the truth is probably this: Bobby may well have wanted to kiss me—or hold my hand—or something—by that time, and I think if I'd been older I'd have realized that he was thinking of me sexually, but I didn't realize and he didn't actually do anything."

"Very well, I accept that."

"You see, when it did happen it was as if I'd had no warning..." My voice shook and I had to stop.

"Yes, I understand but don't jump ahead—keep to the sequence. Margaret went away at about this time, I think."

"Yes, to Staffordshire to see Aunt May whose baby had died. Poor Aunt May, she was so nice—trust awful old Aunt Ethel to be the sister who survived—"

"A tragedy, I agree, but don't let's be diverted by Aunt Ethel's indisputable awfulness; let's concentrate on the May of 1896. Now: Margaret was away in Staffordshire and Kinsella, presumably, was still at Porteynon. How did you manage to see him after Margaret left?"

"I didn't. I never saw him. That story of the clandestine meetings was invented by Margaret later to hush up what had happened."

"I see. Very well. So there you were at Oxmoon, but you certainly weren't alone with Bobby. You had your governess and Celia bobbing around you whenever you weren't being pestered by the babies in the nursery, so Bobby must have had to choose the moment for the seduction very carefully."

"Yes. He did."

"If I were Bobby I'd have gone to your room at night."

"Yes," I said again. "He did." As I crushed out my cigarette I heard myself say rapidly, "That was what was so awful, Robert, about last night when Bobby interrupted us. Of course I knew perfectly well he only wanted to find out how likely I was to marry you—I knew he had no sinister purpose in mind—but when he came in it was as if the past was repeating itself—oh God, I can't tell you what a nightmare last night was—"

"It was a nightmare for all three of us. But let's return to the nightmare of '96."

"That's why Margaret didn't put me in my old room this time. She knew—she understood—"

"Never mind 1913. We're in 1896 and Bobby's come to your room to show he can no longer think of you as a daughter."

"Yes, he... he kissed me and... I'm sorry, I *will* be able to go on in a moment—but you'll have to ask me another question; I can't see where to go next—"

"Did he seduce you then or did he merely set the scene for a later seduction?"

"Oh God, the answer's both yes and no. I'm sorry, I know that sounds ludicrous, but—"

"Not at all. He seems to be conforming to a well-known pattern. What you're saying is that he did seduce you but he didn't—he left you a virgin physically but not mentally and emotionally."

"Yes, it was all so... oh, so indescribably awful, *awful* because... because... well, you did say just now, didn't you, that in such cases the child sometimes acquiesces to the point of encouragement... and I did acquiesce, it was because he frightened me. I knew it was wrong, but what shattered me was that I could see *he* knew it was wrong yet he couldn't stop himself—and when I saw him like that, a changed man, a stranger—oh God, it was so terrifying, all I wanted was to put things right.... He said he was unhappy, you see, so I thought that if only I could make him happy he'd become the Bobby I knew again—"

"Did he explain why he was unhappy?"

"He said that with Margaret away he was afraid to sleep alone because he knew he'd have nightmares, and he asked if he could sleep with me for a little while to keep the nightmares at bay. And the awful thing was, Robert—"

"He was telling the truth. He was genuinely desperate and of course you longed to help him—oh yes, the really consummate liars of this world always use the truth as far as they possibly can! Very well, so the truth gave him the excuse he needed to get into bed with you, and you were much too terrified by this revelation of the unbalanced side of his personality to do anything but consent. I accept all that. Now—"

"He did say he wouldn't do anything I didn't want him to do, but the trouble

114

was... well, I didn't really know what he meant, I'd never discussed passion with anyone—'sex' as Mr. H. G. Wells calls it—well, you just thought it was soppy, didn't you, and Margaret had only said she'd have a little talk with me later before I had my first dance—of course I had inklings of what went on because of all the animals, but I was still so ignorant—"

"I understand. Now, what was Bobby's reaction afterwards? Did he immediately ask if he could return the next night?"

"Oh no—no, quite the reverse! Robert, he was horrified, absolutely appalled—and of course that made me more terrified than ever because at that point he seemed irrevocably transformed into someone wicked who did terrible things. He sat on the edge of the bed and said, 'I've done a terrible thing and no one must ever know about it'—oh, God, how he frightened me! Then he got in a state about the sheet because... well, I said I'd sponge it off but he didn't trust me, he had to do it himself. He was in a panic. He said, 'You mustn't worry, you're still a virgin, I haven't harmed you,' but when he looked at my expression he saw how he had harmed me, and he said, 'Oh God forgive me,' and I thought he was going to break down but he didn't, he just repeated he'd never do such a thing again, and then he left."

"But he came back—"

"The next night, yes."

"—and completed the seduction."

"Yes. I couldn't bear to see him so distressed, and when he broke his word I was almost relieved. I thought: Now I'll be able to put matters right. But—"

"How many times did full sexual intercourse take place?"

"There were two more occasions but I didn't mind, I was just so relieved to make him happy because afterwards the stranger disappeared and he was himself again."

"And after the final occasion—"

"Margaret came home and the horrors began." I closed my eyes for a moment and when I reopened them I found myself again staring at the sheet music on the table. "He told her straightaway," I said. "I think that shocked me more than anything that had happened previously. I knew by that time that he couldn't be trusted to keep his word, but he'd sworn he'd never tell her and he'd made me swear too... all for nothing. It destroyed him for me when he did that. I hated him. I felt betrayed. It was vile. I felt so filthy, so unclean, so absolutely *defiled*—"

"What did Margaret do?"

"She was very fierce and very ruthless. 'I'm not going to let my home and family be destroyed by this,' she said to us. 'I've been through too much in the past and I'm damned if it's all going to be for nothing.' Then she said, 'Let me think about what has to be done and then we'll meet again in the morning.' It was late at night by that time. I went to bed but I was so wretched, so overcome with shame and guilt and grief, that I knew I couldn't bear to stay in the house. It was Margaret, you see... I knew I'd lost her love forever... the only mother I could remember... I didn't know how I was going to bear it."

"Yes." He paused before asking, "What happened next?"

"I ran away. I thought the least I could do to make amends to her was to run away so that she would never have to see me again. And of course I was frightened of Bobby still, frightened that he would come to my room in spite of everything. I knew I could never live at Oxmoon again—it was all destroyed, the Oxmoon I loved, the Oxmoon of our childhood—the fairy tale had come to this terrible end and I had to escape somehow into the real world outside."

"So you turned to Kinsella."

"It was the only solution I could think of. I was so desperate—naturally I'd never have dared to approach him under normal circumstances, but I thought he might help me start afresh in Dublin—I thought he was the sort of unconventional man who might possibly be bold enough to come to my rescue. Well... you know what happened next. I rode to Porteynon, roused the whole household by mistake and wound up making a complete mess of everything. More horrors. Scandal. Ghastliness. The only gleam of light in the ink-black landscape was that I finally succeeded in capturing Conor's imagination—that was when he realized that I was just the sort of woman he wanted.... But I didn't tell him the truth. I just said I was unhappy at home. I never told him the truth, never, he tried to make me when he found out two years later that I wasn't a virgin, but I said I'd had an accident riding and I stuck to that story through thick and thin. You see, I couldn't talk about it, even to him. It belonged to the horrible evil fairy tale I'd left behind; I felt that if I once talked about it to anyone afterwards it would become part of the real world and I didn't see how I could possibly live with it.... Oh God, I was so frightened that he'd find out but luckily although he never quite believed in the riding accident, he always thought the lover was you— and he never suspected Bobby at all."

There was a pause. Presently when I was more composed I said, "There's not much more to tell you. Soon everyone believed I'd had a row with Bobby and Margaret about Conor and that I was being sent to live with my godparents because I'd behaved so disgracefully. I didn't mind by then what people thought. I was just so glad to escape to the Applebys."

"And Kinsella? How had you left matters with him?"

"In all the uproar we barely had thirty seconds alone together but he told me I was magnificent and that I was to wait for him while he went to America to make some money. He swore he'd never forget me and that when he came back we'd be married."

"And you believed that."

"Oh yes, I was much too young and romantic to do anything else. But in fact, as even a cynic would have to admit, his attitude was credible enough. I did have thirty thousand pounds. I was, as Margaret would say, 'fetching.' Conor was proud, too proud to marry when he was penniless, but once he had a little money behind him it wasn't so surprising that he thought it worthwhile to return to Europe to collect me."

"True. But you lost faith in him, didn't you? Otherwise you wouldn't have become engaged to Timothy."

116

"I never entirely lost faith in him, but Robert, as time went by I began to see another horrible prospect drifting towards me and I knew I simply had to marry to escape it. I didn't dare wait for Conor any longer."

"Oxmoon?"

"Exactly. I was terrified that in the end I'd have to go back. You see, once Margaret became confident that she had Bobby in control she was quite shrewd enough to realize how odd it would look if they didn't offer to have me back; they couldn't go on exiling me indefinitely because of my mad behavior with Conor."

"Margaret discussed this with you, I assume."

"Yes, she was very kind to me. She guaranteed Bobby's good behavior and said I was never to think she wouldn't welcome me back to Oxmoon whenever I chose to come. Oh Robert... I cried when she said that. I was old enough then to see how absolutely she'd saved us all... but of course I knew I couldn't go back. I couldn't trust Bobby, you see, no matter what she said. I knew I could never trust him again."

"No, of course you couldn't. So, in conclusion, you became engaged, disengaged and—finally—married."

"Yes—out of the frying pan into the fire as usual. But that's another story," I said, and when I managed to look at him I saw he was smiling at me.

"Oh Robert..." I began to cry. I sniffed and snorted and huge tears streamed down my cheeks and I'm sure I looked a perfect fright. I've never had any patience with those romantic heroines who weep beautifully into dainty pieces of lace while the strong silent hero tells himself she's A Woman Sorely Wronged.

"Why the devil is it," said Robert exasperated, "that you never have a handkerchief? Here you are, take mine and start mopping."

"Oh Robert, you do believe me, don't you? I've told you the whole truth, I swear I have—"

"Yes, I realize that. Have another cigarette."

I started weeping again because he was being so nice to me. I was in far too emotional a state to wonder how genuine his mood was and what it all meant. I was simply living minute by minute, second by second, and marveling that I should still be conscious after such an ordeal. I now thought of the ordeal as "over." Where it left us I had no idea but I was for the present too relieved to care. At that point, I told myself, matters could only improve. Now that Robert had all the information at his fingertips he could sort it out, file it away, erase all trace of the mess and tell me how to live happily ever after.

Looking back I can see I was positively unhinged by my relief. In fact I was almost on the point of hallucination; as Robert lit my second cigarette I had no trouble seeing him as the hero who would forgive me everything and swear never again to mention my past.

"Very well," he said, extinguishing not only the match but my sentimental delusions. "So much for 1896. Now let's turn to your marriage. How often were you unfaithful to Kinsella?"

That shocked me out of my tears fast enough. It also brought me face to face with reality. My ordeal wasn't over. On the contrary it had just begun, because

117

although Robert had got what he wanted as usual—the truth—he couldn't cope with it. Unable to bear the thought of me with his father he was now ricocheting in self-defense toward the murky waters of my subsequent sexual experience.

I knew very well that he had loathed Conor. In fact I was almost tempted to confess that Conor had been unable to keep me to himself, but fortunately despite my panic I still had the sense to see that any pleasure Robert might derive from this information would be utterly outweighed by his horror that I had given myself to other men. Robert was deeply jealous and very possessive. (This was now part of his attraction for me; in his jealousy and possessiveness I saw the shield that would protect me against predators.) However although I was willing to tolerate and even embrace this side of his personality, I did clearly see that a little jealousy could go a very long way.

Discretion was obviously called for.

"What makes you think I was unfaithful?" I said to play for time while I decided what to say.

"Ah come, Ginette, you may as well tell me about your marriage—why not? What could be worse than what you've already told me this morning?"

He had called me Ginette again. My spirits soared. Whatever happened I now had to avoid the disaster of falling at the final fence.

"But I was never unfaithful to Conor," I said, assuming my most candid expression. "I loved him too much to look at anyone else."

Robert gave me one long contemptuous look. Then he stood up and walked out.

"Oh my God." I'd fallen at the final fence. Rushing after him I caught him up in the hall. "Robert, wait—Robert, *please*—"

"I can't talk to you anymore." He began to hurry up the stairs. "I can't listen to lies."

"All right, I'll tell you the truth, I swear I will, I swear it, I'll do anything you want..."

He took no notice. He never even looked back.

I hitched up my skirts and tried to race after him but I nearly fell flat on my face. Sometimes I think women's fashions should be abolished by act of Parliament. I was wearing not only a hobble skirt but a vile corset, currently much in vogue, which reached almost to my knees in order to ensure that the skirt fell in the right lines.

I was still teetering absurdly up the stairs when I heard the door of his bedroom slam in the distance but I never faltered, and seconds later I was bursting across the threshold. "Robert," I panted, "Robert, *listen*—"

I had grabbed his arm but he wrenched it away. "No hysterics. I can't stand hysterics. I won't tolerate them."

"All right, I'll be calm, look how calm I am, I'm so calm I'm virtually dead. Robert, I admit I wasn't faithful to Conor, but I only lied to you because I couldn't bear the thought that I'd make you even more upset—"

"*Upset!* That word's so shattering in its banality that I hardly know how to respond!" It was now obvious that he had lost his grip on the situation. He could

118

no longer pretend he was my lawyer; our new sexual intimacy precluded him from assuming his familiar role of platonic friend and my revelations had turned his role of lover into a nightmare. He was beside himself. He had nowhere to go. His only escape lay into rage.

"You've consistently lied to me." He could hardly speak. "You've tricked me, you've deceived me, you've—"

"Every word that I spoke about Bobby was the truth!"

"Oh yes! Just now! When you knew you had no choice! But last night—when I came to your room—"

Amidst all my terror I knew that my one hope of saving us both lay in forcing him to face reality.

"Oh, for God's sake, Robert!" I burst out. "How on earth could I have embarked on the truth last night? Don't be so absurd! A woman doesn't say to a man who's obviously got nothing but copulation on his mind: 'Oh darling, I'm so sorry but I slept with your father when I was sixteen and I was just the tiniest bit unfaithful to my husband later on!' God Almighty! Wake up! This is no dream, this is—"

"Reality. Quite. That's precisely why I want to know how many men you've slept with."

"Very well, I'll tell you," I said. "I'll tell you exactly how many men have slept with me just as soon as you've told me exactly how many women have slept with you."

He stared at me. In the baffled silence that followed I had a glimpse of that curious naivety which lay beyond his intellect at the hidden core of his personality.

"But I don't understand," he said, too astonished to sustain his anger. "What have my mistresses got to do with you?"

"Absolutely nothing, Robert. And my lovers and my husband have absolutely nothing to do with you either."

He was floored. And he hated it. He could never bear anyone to get the better of him, and as his injured pride streamed to his rescue I saw him once more go white with rage.

But I stood my ground. I was convinced now I had nothing left to lose and in my sheer soul-splitting misery I wasn't afraid of his rage and I no longer cared how much I shocked him as I used the truth in my defense. I heard him shout, "A man has a right to know the past of a woman he's promised to marry—" but I cut him off.

"Shut up!" I screamed. "Don't talk as if my past is a closed book to you when you've just put me through hell by forcing me to recall every damned minute of it! My lovers meant no more to me than your mistresses meant to you, so what the hell do they matter now? The past is over, it's finished, it's done!"

"But I was a bachelor—you were married! You had duties, obligations—"

"We're not talking about marriage; we're talking about copulation!"

"No, we're not, we're talking about marriage—*your* marriage—and what I want to know is—"

"All right, just you listen to me! You're a criminal lawyer, you say, you've heard it all before, you say, very well, just you listen to this and see if you can

119

make head or tail of it, because I don't think you've heard it all before at all! It's no good trying to give you an orderly rational explanation of my marriage because there isn't one. Conor and I were the victims of what's popularly known as a grand passion except that grand passions aren't as they're described in story books, in real life they're quite different, you hurtle around between heaven and hell until you want to commit murder—or at the very least a dramatic suicide—my God, no wonder all the famous lovers in history killed themselves, I'm not surprised, that sort of passion's enough to drive anyone round the bend!"

"You mean—"

"I mean Conor and I fought and screamed and yelled and laughed and loved and were passionately happy and utterly miserable and he wasn't faithful to me and I wasn't faithful to him and he was a bastard and I was a bitch and we each got the partner we deserved and we were wild about each other and it was all awful and wonderful and chaotic and appalling—and thank God it's over because I couldn't have stood it much longer, and if you understand all that mess and muddle better than I do, then you really *are* brilliant and not just a man with a first-class brain which you've trained to go through legal hoops!"

"But—"

"The trouble with you, Robert, is that you know nothing about life. Oh, you know it all in theory—my dear, those criminal cases! Do tell me about the bestiality sometime!—but you're always on the sidelines looking at other people, you've no idea what it's like to be so damned involved that you can't see the sidelines for dust. So don't you pass judgment on me—you're not in court now and anyway you're not a judge. If you want to go back on your offer to marry me, then go back on it—God knows you're entitled to revoke it utterly after all you've heard this morning and I certainly shan't blame you if you do. But don't start losing your temper with me just because I'm not the fairy-tale princess of your dreams—lose your temper instead with yourself for being romantic and foolish enough to propose marriage after a few hours' reacquaintance and a passing victory between the sheets!"

I stopped speaking. He was ashen. Nothing happened, but I knew I now had the upper hand and must ram my advantage home. A magnificent exit was called for so I swept out of the room across the landing, I swept halfway down the stairs— I was traveling on a tidal wave of emotion, but tidal waves don't last forever and on the half-landing I found myself beached in the most intolerable shallows. I stopped. I knew I had to flounder out of the shallows but I knew too that I couldn't go on.

Drying my eyes I crept back and listened at the door.

There was no sound.

I went on listening and suddenly I could endure his silent grief no longer. What was unendurable was not that I'd made my lover miserable; all's fair in love and war, and love can be as brutal in its own way as war can be. What was unendurable was that I'd made my friend unhappy. No one could have wished for a more loyal and devoted friend than Robert. I remembered how pleased he had always been to see me when he returned from school, I remembered his precocious letters sprinkled maddeningly first with Latin and then with Greek, I remembered him spending his pocket money on gifts for me when I was ill, I remembered the midnight feasts and the secret picnics and the illicit raids on the strawberry beds... And then I saw the road to Oxmoon, the lost Oxmoon of our childhood—and I knew that only Robert could lead me back there to the peace I so longed to find.

I thought: Well, I may have been a disastrous mistress and of course I'll never now be his wife, but at least I can still be a good friend and comfort him when he's so unhappy.

I tapped softly on the door and peeped in. He was sitting on the bed with his head in his hands.

"Darling Robert," I said as he kept his eyes shaded. "How unkind I was to you, I'm so sorry. Isn't this crisis a nightmare? I do so wish we could go off and plunder the strawberry beds and forget all about it."

He gave a short awkward laugh and let his hands fall. Of course his eyes were tearless. "If you can apologize to me," he said in his best rational voice, "then I can apologize to you. You weren't the only one who was unkind." Then, movingly, he covered his eyes with his hands again and whispered in despair, "I feel so confused."

"Oh darling..." I put my arms around him and when he made no attempt to push me away I saw he had reached the end of his resources and had no idea what to do next. I saw too more clearly than ever that salvation was turning out to be a double-sided ordeal. He had saved me by playing the role of the detached attorney and eliminating all falsehood between us, and now I had to save him not only by insisting that he faced reality but by unraveling the complex emotional aftermath which he was far too proud to admit he couldn't master.

"Listen," I said gently, taking his hand in mine, "I know the situation couldn't be more confusing, but think of all the things that haven't changed. I'm still your friend and whether we marry or not I'll still need someone loyal who'll stand by me in the future."

"Yes, but—"

"No, never mind marriage for the moment. Marriage is complicated. Let's keep this situation very, very simple. We'll be friends. We're very good at being friends; I think we've got a unique gift for it—perhaps it's because we're like brother and sister without all the bore of being confined in a close blood relationship."

"True, but—"

"No, don't worry about bed. That's not important at the moment either. If later on you find you do want to sleep with me now and then, well, that would be heaven because I thought we got on rather well in that direction, but meanwhile you probably feel that having me as a mistress would be too complicated for you, and don't worry, I quite understand, we'll just wait till the way ahead seems clearer."

"What makes you think the way ahead will get clearer?"

"Well, it usually does, you know. One crashes around in a fog but eventually one does see a gleam of light in the distance—"

"I never crash around in a fog."

"That's the point, darling—that's why you must trust me about this business: because I'm so much more used to crashing around in fogs than you are."

We smiled at each other. His hand tightened on mine. After a long silence he said unsteadily, "I love you," and started kissing me. When he paused for breath he added more to himself than to me, "I've got to have you, I swore I'd have you, I've got to win."

"Well, that's certainly what I want, darling, and don't think for one moment it isn't, but—"

"Marry me."

"Of course I'll marry you, but don't you think it would be better if . . . Oh heavens, how difficult it is to know how to say this! Listen, Robert, I don't want you turning on me later and accusing me of taking advantage of you while you were too confused to make the right decision. You've had some dreadful shocks this morning—and I don't think you should marry me until you've recovered from them."

"Very well, I'll wait six months. But not a day longer. We'll marry at Christmas."

"Well, that would be wonderful, darling—wonderful . . . but only if you're absolutely certain—"

"I know what I want and by God I'm going to get it." He got up, locked the door and began to unbutton his trousers.

"Heavens, do we have time?" I couldn't help saying nervously. "They'll all be coming home from church soon!"

"I don't give a damn."

"Well, now you come to mention it," I said, realizing that he needed a display of enthusiasm to shore up his confidence, "neither do I."

The next few minutes weren't pleasant, but I wasn't so naive as to expect rapture from a man who has been seriously hurt emotionally and who is far more angry than he can admit either to himself or to anyone else. As I forced myself to go limp I thought, Everything passes, even this, and sure enough it passed and afterwards his violent feelings were sufficiently purged to enable him to whisper a plea for forgiveness as he buried his face guiltily in my hair.

I automatically reassured him, but as I spoke my thoughts were elsewhere. I had just realized that emotionally he was color-blind. I saw human relationships as a great glorious splodgy painting where every color in the spectrum was represented in unending ever-changing patterns. Robert saw human relationships as a black-and-white geometrical design which, being fixed, was always orderly and subject to rational interpretation. This meant that whenever he encountered a piece that was neither black nor white he was lost. He had no way of placing it in his design; he had no way of creating a new pattern that made sense.

"You do love me, don't you, Ginette?"

"Darling, you know I do. Very, very much."

"Then nothing else matters," said Robert, resolutely sweeping aside all the messy garish colors from his design and masterfully calling his black-and-white

122

world to order. "I'll go and see Mama just as soon as she arrives home from church."

Very well, that was reality as I remember it. But now for the gloss on reality; now let me write about what was—and is—really going on; now let me try and pin down the chaotic thoughts in my head.

What do I truthfully think of Robert? Oh yes, we all know he's six feet two and divinely glamorous, but what do I really *think*? How attractive do I actually find him? Robert said gloomily to me once that he would never be classically handsome and he was right, but nevertheless he *is* good-looking and far better-looking now than when he was a fierce lanky spotted adolescent. I like that tough mouth of his. How does it ever manage to relax into such a charming smile? A mystery. Yes, I'm wild about that, and as for his eyes . . . Who would have thought that eyes the color of dishwater could be so alluring? Remarkable. Oh yes, he's very attractive but not in an obvious way and I like that; I'm getting to an age when I can appreciate the more subtle forms of masculine appeal. Robert may not radiate sexual charm as Conor did, but do I really want a man who's carnal knowledge personified? No. Not now. A brilliant good-looking man like Robert will suit me very well, thank you, and I shall adore living in London and basking in all the reflected glory of his inevitably dazzling political career. (Can't wait to meet the Asquiths!)

However . . . beyond all the divine glamour . . . oh, let's be honest, I've no doubt he can be very tricky. There are bound to be times when I shall find him willful, selfish and thoroughly pigheaded, but so what? I shall only be faced with that extraordinary emotional simplicity—I'll just need a bit of guile when he's difficult, but that's not a problem because I'm an old hand at the art of being beguiling. There's something curiously endearing about that simplicity. It attracts me. Heavens, what a contrast to Conor he is! Conor's emotions were as volatile as my own, and my God, that's saying something. How restful it'll be to live with someone so simple and straightforward! I feel quite entranced by the prospect.

Am I madly in love with Robert? No. But that must be good. I've had enough of being madly in love, and besides, my feelings for Robert are far more stable than that. There's our shared past, that old, old friendship which nothing can destroy, and that must surely be a good basis for marriage, far better than that lethal sexual affinity I shared with Conor.

Yes, that's the truth. That's reality. Oh yes, I must marry him, I must! It's the wisest decision I could possibly make. . . .

"All's well," said Robert half an hour later when he returned to the bedroom. He embraced me with a smile. "She's resigned herself to the inevitable and says she's prepared to give us her blessing."

Clever, *clever* Margaret. I tried to imagine the depth of her horror and rage but my imagination failed me. I felt weak. In my overpowering relief that Robert

123

still wanted to marry me my mind had neatly glided around the problem of how we were going to face his parents. Whenever I have a severe problem in my private life (which is most of the time) I always say, "I'll cross that bridge later," and put the problem out of my mind. So when Robert and I had been conducting our long crucial harrowing conversation earlier I hadn't once thought, even at the end: My God, what are we going to do about Bobby and Margaret? I had remained acutely aware of the problem, just as one would be continually aware of a vast wardrobe in an underfurnished room, but I had classified it as a bridge to be crossed later. And now "later," to my absolute terror, had without doubt arrived.

"I'll give you a blow-by-blow description presently," said Robert, who was looking naively pleased with himself. Endearing emotionally simple Robert didn't quite see the problem as I did, of course. He probably thought he had mastered the entire situation after a ten-minute chat with his mother. "But meanwhile Mama would like to see you on your own for a moment. She's waiting in her room."

"Oh *God.*" I now felt so weak that I even swayed in his arms but Robert merely laughed, patting me kindly as if I were a lapdog, and told me to stop being so melodramatic. I would have slapped him but I was too weak with fright. Instead I looked in the glass, smoothed my skirt and made sure that every hair on my head was in place before I sallied forth at a funereal pace to meet my future mother-in-law.

The bedroom which by tradition belonged to the master and mistress of the house was a high wide sunny chamber which Bobby and Margaret, purging it after its occupancy by Gwyneth Godwin and Owain Bryn-Davies, had filled with their usual junk-shop furniture. At least, the furniture had been purchased new from a respectable Swansea store but it still looked as if it had been acquired in a junk shop because each piece was in such execrable mid-Victorian taste. Possibly Margaret's *nouveau-riche* background among the Potteries of Staffordshire had given her a penchant for vulgar grandeur, but Bobby also had a weakness for oversprung comfort, and between the two of them they had accumulated a collection of objects, all of overwhelming ghastliness and all displayed against the background of a garish flock wallpaper. When I eventually became mistress of Oxmoon...but that was far in the future and meanwhile I had this dreadful bridge that had to be crossed. I knocked on the door, Margaret tranquilly bade me enter and somehow I found the strength to creep into her presence.

Margaret was only fifteen years my senior but she looked older, partly because her clothes were always ten years out of date and partly because her hairstyle (which she never altered) had gone out of fashion at least ten years before she was born; her dull straight brown hair was parted in the center and drawn back into a bun at the nape of her neck. In spite of her lack of interest in fashion she was a feminine woman in appearance. She was very round, very curvy—but in a maternal, not a seductive way. Of course plenty of men like that overweight, motherly, comfortable look; although Margaret wasn't in the least pretty I could see she did have her attractions. She had the most exquisite skin, flawless and velvet-smooth, and a mild benign expression, which she no doubt believed to be the essence of seemly femininity, but unfortunately this mildness was marred by that straight tough mouth which I found so attractive on Robert. It looked very odd indeed on a woman—and particularly odd on a woman like Margaret who in every other respect looked so cozy and conventional.

When I entered the room she was seated at her dressing table and engaged in a favorite occupation of hers, poking around in one of the several large jewel boxes which were all full of worthless trinkets. She disliked precious stones. I think she had read somewhere once that *nouveau-riche* women had a vulgar habit of wearing too much flashy jewelry. As I edged reluctantly towards her I saw she was lining up her mourning brooches (sordid little squares filled with dreadful swatches of faded hair) and piling her jet brooches into a pyramid.

"Oh, do sit down, Ginevra," she said casually, nodding towards the nearest chair. "How good of you to come so promptly. Thank you."

As I sat down speechlessly I was aware of a terrible desire to burst into tears.

"Well, we mustn't be emotional about this, must we," said Margaret, idly arranging four mourning brooches into a quadrangle. "There's no room in this situation for petty little displays of hysterics."

"No, Margaret." I realized at once that she was handling me in the cleverest possible way. I need to be handled firmly when I'm quite beside myself with guilt and terror.

"So," said Margaret, surveying her quadrangle of brooches before glancing at me in the glass to make sure I had myself in control, "Robert still wants to marry you. Very well. If you two now decide to marry in spite of what you've been through this morning, all I can say is that you've certainly earned the right to do so. However—"

I had never realized until that moment that "however" could be quite one of the most sinister words in the English language.

"However," repeated Margaret, suddenly abandoning the quadrangle and turning to look directly into my eyes, "I think this marriage, if it ever takes place, would be a very big mistake. Robert's marrying you for all the wrong reasons. He's marrying out of pride; he's marrying because he's invested so much emotional energy in you that he feels he can't change his mind without looking a fool and suffering a fatal loss of self-respect. And as for you—" She turned aside and taking another brooch she converted her quadrangle into a pentagon. "—well, I won't embarrass you by saying what I think is going on in your mind, but I'll say this: you shouldn't marry anyone until your husband's been dead a year—and I'm not just talking about the proprieties when I say that; I'm talking about the dangers of marrying on the rebound."

She paused. Then she took me by surprise. As I braced myself for her next verbal assault she stretched out her hands to mine which were clasped in agony in my lap, and when she next spoke her gentle voice reminded me of days long ago when she had looked after me with as much love and care as if I had been her own child. "Ginevra...my dear, don't think I don't understand. I of all people know why you're so afraid to be alone and unprotected—I of all people will never forget what happened to you once when I left you defenseless and alone. Do you think I can ever forgive myself for not realizing what was going on in Bobby's mind during that dreadful summer of '96? I shall always feel guilty about you, and I shall feel even guiltier if you now make the wrong decision as the result of that past tragedy."

I began to cry. I tried to find Robert's handkerchief but I'd lost it. I tried to blink back my tears and failed.

"You're a very beautiful woman," said Margaret in her most passionless voice as she efficiently passed me a lavender-scented handkerchief from the top drawer of her dressing table, "and as such, as you well know, you're the prey of unscrupulous men. Of course you feel you need a strong man like Robert to protect you and keep you safe—that's quite natural and I utterly understand it. But my dear, you don't have to *marry* Robert to ensure the love and security you need. He'll look after you whether you're married or not, so why not simply continue as his mistress? I'm sure that would suit you both far better and be much more in keeping with your old friendship."

After that there was an interval of some minutes because I broke down and could do nothing but weep. Margaret was very kind and very patient and even passed me a second lavender-scented handkerchief. I hardly knew how to bear it.

Eventually I controlled myself sufficiently to whisper, "But Margaret...why wouldn't marriage be in keeping with our old friendship too?"

"Oh, friends find it very difficult to live together," said Margaret. "Haven't you noticed? In fact it always seems to me that the quickest way to end a friendship is for the parties to try to live in harmony beneath the same roof. But if you're Robert's mistress you'll both have your own establishments, and then the dangers of too much proximity won't arise."

"But Margaret—"

"Just think it over," she said. "You do at least have six months to reflect on the situation before you journey to the altar—I only wish Robert would wait longer, but never mind, the gossip caused by a hasty marriage is the least of our problems. Ginevra—" She was now crisp and businesslike again; I watched her cram all the mourning brooches but one back into the jewel box and snap shut the lid "—this may come as a surprise to you, but I think the real difficulty in this situation lies not between you and me. I think we'll both try hard and manage tolerably well. No, the real problem for the future lies between Robert and Bobby—and that, I confess, is worrying me almost to death. Will you help me?"

"Oh, Margaret, you know I'd do *anything*—"

"Then don't cut Robert off from Oxmoon. It would break Bobby's heart if Robert withdrew utterly to London."

"Well, of course I give you my word I wouldn't persuade Robert to do such a thing, but surely Robert himself would never—"

"Robert will try to give you the life you want, and you like the glitter, don't you, Ginevra, you like the glamour and the fame. You want a smart London life with a thoroughly successful husband, and Robert's going to see that you get it."

"But surely that's what Robert himself wants!"

"I don't think Robert knows what he wants," said Margaret, "but he'll use you to clarify the confusion in his mind." She began to pin on her selected mourning brooch. "You don't know Robert very well, do you?" she added casually. "But then how could you? You've lived apart for so long. A great deal can happen in fifteen years—and that reminds me: have you discussed your boys with him?"

"Well, actually . . . no. No, there hasn't been time."

"Has he asked about them?"

"No, not exactly. I mean, no, he hasn't. But you see, what with one thing and another—"

"Quite. Well, never mind. I don't need to remind you, do I, how much Robert has always disliked children. I'm sure you can remember that all too clearly." She stood up to terminate the interview. "You'll have a great many problems to sort out between you," she said, "and all I can do is wish you well. But do remember what I've said. Marriage is very different from a love affair and very, very different from a romantic fraternal friendship, no matter how powerful that friendship may be."

"Yes, Margaret."

"Oh, and Ginevra—"

"Yes?"

"I should be greatly obliged if you and Robert would observe the proprieties while you're under this roof. What you do elsewhere is of course entirely your own concern, but here I have my standards—and here I draw the line."

"Yes, Margaret. Of course. I'm so sorry, please forgive us," I stammered, and somehow managed to escape from her in an agony of guilt and shame.

Now that I've calmed down, what do I think of Margaret's advice? Not much. I've got to be married. Otherwise I shan't feel safe. Besides, how could I manage on my own in London with the boys? (That was a very nasty gibe of Margaret's about Robert and my boys and at some time I'll have to consider it, but not just yet; I'll cross that bridge later.)

No, I've got to be married—and so has Robert. He's reached the age now when he really has to have a wife, particularly as he's about to enter politics. We simply can't settle for a smart little love affair; it wouldn't work. If I were unmarried I'd flirt with other men, I know I would, and then I'd be sure to end up in a ghastly mess, whereas if Robert were my husband, watching over me and frightening away all the predators, I know I'd never be lured into naughtiness. The trouble is that although I'm terrified of men in some ways I adore them in others; men are my great weakness but at least I'm terrified enough to want to fight it by vowing to be utterly faithful to darling Robert.

My God, what a muddle my emotions are. Can Robert cope? Yes. Robert will slip the wedding ring on my finger, iron out my problems and then take whatever steps prove necessary to ensure that we live happily ever.

I'm going to marry him.

· · ·

I'm in London and it seems so gray and dispirited, so different from shining Manhattan with its glittering vistas and gaudy crowds and rowdy celebration of life. I loved New York once and now that I'm away from it I have this terrible suspicion I love it still. But I mustn't start thinking of New York. If I do I'll start thinking of Conor and then I'll feel so unhappy, and God knows there's quite enough muddle going on at the moment without me deciding to play the part of the grieving widow.

But I miss New York and all my friends there. They all promised faithfully to write, but they won't. Once or twice perhaps but no more. Do I mind? No, not really. I need to make a fresh start. I don't want to be reminded of that life I shared with Conor.

I find London intimidatingly grand. Life in the raw exists here, just as it does in New York, but the British have drawn the line as usual and the rawness has sunk obediently out of sight behind it. There's the East End and there's the West End and ne'er the twain do meet. Was any city so absolutely divided between the acceptable and the unspeakable? Of course the West End too has its unspeakable side but it's all veiled discreetly by the twin gods of Tradition and Propriety which have to be ceaselessly appeased in order to keep the real world, the chaotic world, under control. No race knows better than a conquering race how anarchic the real world can be, and no race knows better than the British how to master reality by subjugating it, by setting those chilling standards and drawing those brutal lines.

Yet after all isn't this exactly what I want? There's comfort in convention, security in being ruled by the rules. Don't think of gorgeous free-and-easy vital New York which made you feel so intoxicatingly liberated. Liberation has to be paid for, just like any other social amenity, and the price I paid was chaos, the chaos symbolized by Conor's violent terrible end. No. No more New York, no more violence, no more chaos. Welcome to London, welcome to Robert's well-ordered world.

Robert has taken a short lease on a furnished apartment in Kensington. The English call it a "mansion flat," which means it's spacious and comfortable, and downstairs in the reception hall a porter in Ruritanian uniform presides over acres of red carpet. My apartment is on the second floor—which the English call the first—and faces south over a pastoral square. I adore it and when I wake up in the morning I rush to the window and fling back the curtains and feel lyrical. Robert's chambers near Temple Bar are some way away, but fortunately the underground railway is very accommodating in London and it doesn't take him too long to reach me. Meanwhile I'm only two minutes (on foot) from Kensington Gardens and five minutes (in a cab) from divine Harrods, which is just as good as any store in New York and where I know I shall be perpetually lured to spend too much money.

I'm rather naughty about money, I know I am, but I'm going to reform. How lucky it was that although Conor spent all the money that became mine outright on my marriage (he was *very* naughty about money and he *never* reformed), ten thousand was locked up on trust to me for life with the remainder to my children, and this meant he could never get his hands on the capital. Heavens, what rows we used to have about the income—and about money in general—but I won't have to go through all that ghastliness with Robert. Robert's bound to have his financial affairs under iron control, and anyway he must surely earn thousands so I daresay he won't mind if I'm a little bit naughty with money now and then.

Robert is paying for this heavenly mansion flat, but we haven't actually talked about money yet. I've been too busy settling down in London and recovering from the ordeal of my visit to Oxmoon. It was dreadful that I couldn't stay on there for more than a week after Robert left. I wanted to. I know it must have looked so odd to come home after many years and then rush off to London ten days later, but I couldn't bear to stay. I'm still trying to work out why. Bobby and Margaret were faultless and the boys were adorable, but. . . it was ghastly. I suppose my guilt must have been responsible for the fiasco. Or Bobby's guilt. Or—oh God—maybe even Margaret's guilt. How *dreadful* I feel when I think of Margaret feeling guilty; but I must blot that out of my mind and think instead of how exciting it was to move from Oxmoon into this gorgeous apartment in London.

It has a drawing room, a dining room, a bathroom, a very elegant water closet, a kitchen with a scullery, four bedrooms and a sort of cupboard beyond the kitchen where a half-witted maid sleeps; a cook-housekeeper arrives daily to provide rudimentary intelligence and food. One of the large bedrooms has been set aside for housing the luggage, the other large bedroom I sleep in and the two remaining bedrooms, which are smaller but still comfortable, will be allotted to darling Declan and darling Rory when they arrive from Ireland. I think they'll be able to manage there without too many fights. That reminds me: I must write to Dervla and Seamus to say I'm now ready for the boys to join me. But before I do that I simply must raise the subject of the boys with Robert and make sure he understands that I can't bear to be parted from them any longer.

Perhaps if I were to show him the letters that arrived this morning. . .

Dear Ma, wrote Declan. *Thank you for your letter. We were glad to hear you are not in a decline but remembering how prostrate you were all the way across the Atlantic, not to mention how you nearly fainted into the grave at the funeral, I don't think you should be on your own any longer. It's not safe. You might kill yourself in a fit of passion and then regret it afterwards. You know what you're like. So all in all I think it would be best if we came over and collected you and brought you back here where I can keep an eye on you. I know you have the apartment in London, but I'm afraid I can't live in England, it would be quite contrary to Pa's wishes, so I'm making inquiries through Uncle Seamus about the possibility of renting a place in Dublin. The sooner you get here the better, in my opinion, because I'm becoming worn out with worrying about what might be happening to you. With fondest love from your respectful and anxious son,* DECLAN KINSELLA.

That letter touched me but made me feel very nervous. Rory's letter simply touched me. The little love wrote: *Dear Ma, I miss you, I can't sleep at night for crying for Pa and wishing you were here, please come and get us, to be sure if you don't we'll die of grief altogether completely, and you'll be left with nothing to do but sob on our grave. Love,* RORY.

My darling boys! I spent the whole morning feeling so sentimental that I forgot to dwell upon all the problems they represented, but long before Robert arrived that evening with his customary bottle of champagne I was asking myself in absolute panic how I could tell my darlings that I was already planning to remarry.

"Darling," I said to Robert after we had made love, "I'm rather anxious about Declan and Rory. Please could we talk about them for a moment?"

We were lying languidly in bed, and far away at the other end of the flat the half-witted maid who always retired early was safe in her cupboard. It was half-past ten. We had dined out as usual and as usual we had not lingered at the restaurant because we had been so anxious to spend as much time as possible alone together. Robert never stayed the whole night, not merely because he had no wish to enthrall the morning porter downstairs but because he worked hard at hours when less successful men were asleep. Sometimes I wondered if he worked a little too hard, but I put this down to his bachelor life. Bachelors do tend to keep irregular hours, but I was sure his habits would be quite different once he was married.

"You see, darling, it's like this..." I took a deep breath, delivered what I had planned as a calm unemotional statement of the problem and finally, when I had sunk into incoherence, thrust the boys' letters mutely into his hands.

"Hmm," said Robert, pale cool eyes seeming to become paler and cooler as he skimmed through the pages. "Very un-English." He handed the letters back to me.

"Well, darling," I said nervously, "they're *not* English, you know. They're two American boys who have been brought up to think of themselves as Irish to the core."

"I agree that's unfortunate but never mind, it needn't necessarily be fatal." He smiled at me. "I assume you're telling me you want to pay a visit to Ireland."

"I—"

"I'm glad the subject's come up," said Robert, and at once I knew I was being manipulated around an uncomfortable truth as if I were some peculiarly awkward witness, "because although I guessed the situation had become as obvious to you as it's become to me I was naturally reluctant to broach the matter myself. I thought it better if the suggestion came from you."

"What suggestion?"

"The suggestion you've just made—that you should visit them in Ireland."

"I didn't make that suggestion, Robert."

"Yes, you did—you said you wanted to see them again as soon as possible, and it must be as obvious to you as it is to me that it would be better if they didn't come to London until after we're married."

"But Robert—"

"To be honest I never thought much of the idea in the first place. You've got quite enough to do, settling down here, looking for a house and preparing for the wedding, and if those boys come you'll soon be utterly worn out. Besides, how are we ever going to have any premarital privacy when you're perpetually chaperoned by two boys on the threshold of adolescence?"

This indeed was the question which I had always been unable to answer.

"But what shall I do?" I said in despair. "I must see them soon, I simply must—look at Rory's letter! The poor little love's crying every night because he's missing me so much!"

"Yes, it's disgraceful that a boy of his age shouldn't be able to control his emotions better. A boy crying for his mother at the age of twelve! I've never heard such nonsense, and anyway I don't believe a word of it. He's just saying that to tug at your heartstrings."

This also had occurred to me. Darling Rory did so enjoy exaggeration.

"Go to Ireland for a fortnight," said Robert, "and see them. I absolutely understand that a visit is necessary and of course I shan't stand in your way."

"But Robert, I can't leave them in Ireland for the next five months!"

"Why not? If you explain to them carefully that this is a temporary situation which has arisen because you're in the process of setting up a new home for them, I'm sure they'll accept it. Of course they'll miss you, but I'd be prepared to wager a large sum of money that their father's relatives are at this moment lavishing affection on them and making sure they're having a splendid time."

I was in despair not because he was wrong but because he was right. What he said was logical, sensible and true. The only trouble was that this superbly rational approach to the problem took no account of my emotional muddle.

"Darling..." I took another deep breath, made a new great effort. "There are two difficulties. One is that I hate the thought of going to Ireland for regular visits because I feel I can't face Conor's family. They'll...well, they'll remind me of Conor and I can't cope with Conor's memory at the moment—"

Robert began to shift restlessly against the pillows.

"—and the second difficulty," I said frantically, "is that I love my boys so much and I want to make sure they know it. They've just lost their father, and if I tell them I don't want them in England at present they're going to be terribly hurt and upset."

"It sounds to me as if you spoil those children abominably. Good God, boys of their age shouldn't expect to have their mother in constant attendance and drooling over them daily! Very well, have them here for the summer if you must, but I think it's a very big mistake and I'm quite sure you'll soon be regretting it. If you want my opinion—"

"No, I don't!" I cried. "You don't understand anything—*anything!*" And I burst into tears.

Robert sighed. I could almost feel him praying for patience. "There, there!"

he said kindly, taking me in his arms. "It's not the end of the world."

"It feels like it." I felt horribly upset, not only because he seemed to be incapable of understanding my point of view but because I was apparently incapable of explaining it to him. And suddenly I thought: Conor would have understood. But I pushed that truth from my mind.

"This is simply a problem which requires a solution," Robert was saying with that superb confidence which was so very hard to resist, "and of course we're going to find the solution and overcome the difficulty."

"Are we?"

"What an extraordinary question! Why the doubt? Solving awkward problems simply requires the right attitude of mind. Now listen to me, Ginette. Please don't think I'm hostile to those boys. They're your children and I'm more than prepared to treat them as if they were my own. But you must realize that I can see this situation more clearly than you can at present because as usual you're wandering around in one of your emotional fogs. Now, do you or do you not want order in your life?"

"I do."

"And do you or do you not want someone to look after you and stop you getting into a mess?"

"I do."

"Then kindly oblige me by taking my advice and desisting from feminine tantrums."

"I'm sorry but I'm in such a state that I've forgotten what your advice was."

"Leave the boys in Ireland until we're married and content yourself with regular visits to see them. You'll just have to grit your teeth about facing your husband's family. Be honest—in the long run it'll be easier to grit your teeth than to enter into a situation which is likely to reduce you to a state of exhaustion."

"True." I was still in despair but by that time I was so hypnotized by the power of his personality that I no longer had the energy to resist. "I'm sorry, darling; I know I'm being hopelessly emotional as usual."

"Never mind, after thirty-one years I'm used to your vagaries. Now for God's sake let's put all that emotional energy to better use," said Robert sensibly, and seconds later all was well but for a moment I couldn't help comparing this down-to-earth invitation of his with Conor's imaginative and outrageous seductions in similar circumstances.

"Ginette... what are you thinking about?"

Of course I couldn't tell him. I just said, "I was wondering how on earth I'm going to break the news to Declan and Rory that I'm planning to remarry."

"My God, don't let's start arguing about those boys again! Give the subject a rest, there's a good girl—the whole problem's bound to seem less harrowing in the morning..."

• • •

Robert was wrong. It's more harrowing than ever. I'm in a terrible state because although I know that rationally Robert's right, I know too that I can't leave my darling boys in Ireland. If they're so far away from me they'll be unhappy, and if they're unhappy I'll be a failure as a mother, and if I'm a failure as a mother I'll be unable to live with my guilt. I know this is emotional stupidity, I know it is, but I can't help it. It's what being a parent is all about, but Robert's never been a parent and so he doesn't understand.

I'm in such a state that I can't look at houses today. I go to Harrods instead and buy three enormous picture hats, all costing twenty and a half guineas, all lavishly decorated with flowers and feathers and all looking exactly what they are—the last word in foolish extravagance. But I always feel better when I buy things.

This sinful shopping expedition has helped me get through the morning, but now it's afternoon and I still can't relax so I think I'll go out again and buy some cream cakes for tea—terribly naughty, and I can almost hear my corset groan in anticipation, but I simply can't rest until I've sunk my teeth into a divine mille-feuilles... or perhaps an éclair... or—oh God—an utterly sumptuous meringue...

"There's a gentleman waiting to see you, ma'am," said Edna the half-witted maid when I returned later with the wickedest assortment of cream cakes I could find. It was my cook-housekeeper's afternoon off and Edna, in sole charge, had scurried out to meet me as soon as I had opened the door.

At first I wasn't sure that I had understood her. Her cleft palate made even the simplest words enigmatic.

"Is it Mr. Godwin?" I was surprised because I hardly expected to see Robert before half-past six.

"Yes, ma'am, but—" Incomprehensible syllables followed.

"Very well, make tea, would you, Edna, and put these cakes on a plate."

I walked into the drawing room and there I found not Robert but Bobby, looking very formal and very embarrassed, and as soon as I saw him I knew that familiar coldness which always assailed me on the rare occasions when he and I found ourselves alone together.

"Bobby, what a lovely surprise!" I said.

"Good afternoon, Ginevra," he said, remaining rooted to his spot on the far side of the room. "I spoke to Robert on the telephone this morning and he suggested that I met him here, but I'm afraid I'm a little early. Perhaps I'll go for a walk. I don't want to distract you when you must have so many things to do."

Of course I wanted to get him out of the flat and of course I knew I couldn't. He was going to be my father-in-law and we were both morally bound to pretend the past had never happened.

"Don't be so silly, Bobby," I said. "Sit down and have some tea. Excuse me, I'll just make sure the maid brings two cups—she's rather a half-wit."

I escaped. When I was sufficiently composed I reminded Edna about the cup, steeled myself against the inevitable repulsion and returned to the drawing room.

"I'm only up here for a couple of days," he said as I came in. "I wasn't even going to bother Robert, but Margaret said it would be wrong not to telephone so I had a word with him and he was uncommonly civil, said his case had been postponed and that he'd meet me here at teatime—of course, I won't stay long—"

I couldn't bear his horrible humility. "How's everyone at Oxmoon?" I interrupted, sitting down some distance away from him and praying Robert wouldn't be delayed.

"Oh, everyone's very well, thank you, in capital form. . . . But how are you, Ginevra? You look a little tired. I hope nothing's wrong."

And suddenly I saw not the sad and pathetic stranger who angered me but my cousin Bobby, so kind, so gentle, so understanding.

"Oh Bobby!" I exclaimed in despair, and the next moment I was pouring out my troubles to him. I talked and talked and Edna brought the tea and Bobby said, "By Jove, look at those meringues!" and I answered laughing through my tears, "Aren't they wonderful?" and at last I began to feel better.

"But my dear," said Bobby when I gave him the chance to respond to my dilemma, "the answer's very simple: I'll have the boys at Oxmoon and then you can visit them as often as you like. It's such an easy journey to Swansea nowadays, far easier than that long exhausting journey to Dublin."

I was so grateful I could hardly speak. "Oh, but it never occurred to me to think of Oxmoon—all the awkwardness—"

"Never mind about that. Ginevra, at last I have the opportunity to help you and Robert. Don't deprive me of it—and don't worry about those boys either. I'll make sure they're as happy as larks."

I knew he would. Bobby had brought up four sons and was still bringing up a fifth. He understood boys and had a gift for managing children.

"Bobby, I can't tell you how grateful I am—"

"Would you like me to go to Ireland to fetch them for you? I'd enjoy that."

I stopped weeping with relief by embarking on an éclair. "No," I said. "I wish you could but I really must go myself. I have to tell them I'm going to remarry."

"Do that at Oxmoon. The last place you want to disclose your future plans is in the bosom of your husband's family."

Here was advice far removed indeed from Robert's rational but useless conclusions. Here was sound, sane, utterly realistic common sense.

"My God, that's true!" I said. "But . . . oh Bobby, how on earth do I break the news to those boys?"

"Well, tell them the truth, my dear, why not? After all Declan's fourteen. Tell them that no matter how much you loved their father you can't be alone in the world without a strong man to look after you, and Robert's the strongest man you could ever hope to find. I think you'll find Declan at least is at an age when he can understand your difficulty. You needn't stress the romance, of course. Just say you've no choice but to be practical about the future—for their good as well as yours."

I felt a new woman. I was even able to abandon my éclair.

"In fact," added Bobby, "if you have difficulty explaining I'll help you out. So even if Robert don't accompany you when you visit the boys, you won't have to face the difficulty on your own."

"Robert...yes. Bobby, I'm a little worried..." But I stopped. In the vastness of my relief I had gone too far. The one thing I could never do was discuss Robert with his father.

"A capital fellow, Robert," said Bobby as he saw my difficulty. "There's no challenge he can't master if he has a strong motive for succeeding so you can wager he'll manage those boys well enough when the time comes. Look how good he was with John."

"So he was!" I said, much cheered. I had a memory of dear little Johnny, chattering away in Welsh and English, bright as a button and delectably naughty. It was sad to think he had turned into such a boring priggish young man. "But what strong motive did Robert have for succeeding with Johnny?"

"He wanted to kill two birds with one stone—please Margaret and make Lion jealous."

We laughed—but then the next moment the smiles were wiped off our faces as we heard Robert enter the hall.

I feel much better about Bobby now, and not just because we managed to share something that resembled a normal conversation. I feel better because I can see how desperately anxious he is to put our relationship on a tolerable footing so that we don't inevitably go through hell whenever we see each other. He's realized—and so have I—that my boys can provide us with a common ground upon which we can meet as two normal people instead of two people perpetually crucified by guilt. I know I shall never be fully at ease with him and I'm sure he'll never be fully at ease with me, but at least our compulsory charade can now become more of an automatic reflex and less of a harrowing effort, and that must surely rank as an improvement.

I'm beginning to think Margaret was right when she said that the problem in future will be the relationship between Bobby and Robert. Look what happened today. Robert sailed in, shook hands with his father and was impeccably courteous throughout the remainder of Bobby's visit, yet although no one could have faulted his behavior, the atmosphere was nonetheless subtly cold, indefinably wrong. Sometime in the future—after we're married and can relax sufficiently to iron out all our problems—I'm going to have to talk to Robert about Bobby because I've come to realize that it's much better if horrid subjects can be aired instead of being buried to fester at leisure. The one subject which I could never discuss, Bobby's seduction, has been a terrible burden to me in the past, and the reason why I can now see this so clearly is because I feel the burden's been eased by my confession. I shall never, never be able to recall the incident with indifference but at least now I don't have to say to myself, "I can't talk of that or I'll go mad." I can say instead, "I talked about it to Robert and stayed sane."

135

Robert needs to talk to someone about that morning last month when he heard in shattering detail exactly what kind of man his father was, but the trouble is that if I suggest as much to him he'll simply say, "Why?" Robert, I suspect, is in the deepest possible muddle over this, but that's not the main problem. The main problem is that he doesn't know it, and even if he does he won't acknowledge it. Emotionally color-blind Robert has made up his mind that so long as he can adopt certain attitudes (courtesy to his father, passion to me), the past can be tied up in pink ribbon, like a legal brief, and locked safely away forever in the vault of his mind. But I'm not color-blind like Robert and I don't think the answer to his difficulty is that simple. In fact I don't think it's any answer at all.

"Ginette, what the devil are these three new hats doing on your bed?"

"Oh darling, yes—well, you see—"

"I gave you fifty pounds last week to spend on essentials, not to descend on Harrods like Attila the Hun!"

"Oh, I know, darling, but it's all right—I've hardly spent any of your fifty pounds yet! I saw the most charming man in the Harrods credit department—"

"Are you trying to tell me you bought these hats on credit?"

"Yes, isn't it wonderful! I took along the letter from my bank manager to say that my trust money had been safely transferred from New York, and—"

"But you told me you'd already spent your income for the rest of this quarter!"

"True, but I didn't think that mattered, as you were being so divinely generous—"

"Sit down, Ginette," said Robert, "and listen to me. I think it's time you and I had a serious talk together."

We've had the most horrible row about money, quite different from any row I ever had with Conor. At least Conor never made me feel a fool and we always ended up going to bed together. Robert merely made me feel a half-wit and then he walked out and didn't come back.

Well, maybe I deserved his anger. Maybe I *was* a fool to lose my temper and call him a cold-blooded bastard, but what else can you call a man who has just told you he now believes more firmly than ever that the law is right when it classifies married women with lunatics and children? How dare he behave as if I'm incapable of adult behavior, how dare he!

Very well, I *am* naughty about money. But I'm not stupid. In fact when I have to be clever with money I can be brilliant (think of that time when I had to pay for the boys' clothes out of my housekeeping money because Conor had had a disaster at poker). So I don't like being treated as an imbecile who's not responsible for her actions. It's not my fault I had no education. I regret it but Margaret always said the last thing any future wife and mother needed was instruction in academic subjects, so my brain was allowed to atrophy at Oxmoon with a stupid governess.

The trouble with Margaret is that she married at sixteen and coping with the resurrection of Oxmoon, the raising of a large family and the rigors of an unreliable husband has absorbed every ounce of her energy throughout her adult life. That's why she's never been able to imagine that an intelligent woman might like the idea of acquiring an education before she acquires a husband and children; Margaret sees education as irrelevant—as in her case indeed it was. Well, I've certainly never had any wish to be a bluestocking, but when Robert slings a Greek quotation at me and translates it by Tennyson's line "Woman is the lesser man," I'd love to be able to sling back a quotation in Latin to the effect that practice makes perfect and although God did create Adam he was more accomplished when the time came for him to create Eve.

Is Robert one of those male monsters who pride themselves on being thoroughly patronizing on the subject of masculine superiority? That's a chilling thought, but no, brilliant, rational Robert could surely never be guilty of such stupid irrational opinions. He just wanted to show me how vexed he was by my behavior.

Yes, Robert takes what he's pleased to call my "feminine foolishness" very, very seriously but never mind, now that I know how he feels about money I'll be scrupulously careful, and I've no doubt that when we're married we'll never have another cross word on the subject.

We've just had the most divine reconciliation. On the morning after our quarrel telegrams of repentance arrived, and the florist's boy staggered upstairs to my front door with a lavish bouquet of flowers. Fortnum's delivered the champagne after lunch. Finally at eight Robert swept me off to dinner and a most successful evening later culminated in a most memorable night in the bedroom. It really is remarkable how much can be achieved with the aid of orchids, champagne and a heavenly dinner at the Ritz.

And now . . . is this the moment when I can finally compare Robert with Conor and dispose of the problem of comparisons once and for all? Yes, I think it is, because at last I feel I've got that particular difficulty solved. What bliss! At least there's one bridge I've managed to cross before the wedding.

In that brief but nerve-racking crisis which blew up immediately before Robert and I went to bed together for the first time, I told him glibly that there could be no competition between him and Conor in the bedroom, but I said this (a) because it was obvious his confidence needed boosting and (b) because I knew that if he had crowned his romantic dreams by being impotent our affair would have been finished before it had begun.

However the awful truth remained that Robert *was* a competitor in a nightmarish trial of sexual prowess, and although Robert's mind might have been in an uncharacteristic fog at the time my mind was (for once) as clear as crystal because I knew without a shadow of a doubt that I was going to compare him with Conor. How could I have avoided it? The situation, in short, could easily have dissolved into disaster, but to my relief the gods decided to smile on us because Robert *was* very different from Conor in bed, and although I did make a comparison or two, I soon realized that comparisons were more meaningless in the circumstances than I'd dared to hope they might be. To compare Conor and Robert was like trying to compare "The Blue Danube" with the latest Paris tango; both compositions rank as musical entertainment but they appeal to the audience in completely different ways.

Despite Robert's Welsh background he's an Englishman by education and temperament, and he's very much the Englishman in bed (contrary to what scornful foreigners think, this needn't necessarily be a disaster). For Robert passion is a sport, like cricket or rugby football, and being Robert he's bent his will to ensure he knows how to produce a first-class performance. If Oxford University awarded blues for passion, as it does for cricket and rugger, then Robert would undoubtedly have won his blue at passion. And because passion is a sport for him and because he's an Englishman he obeys the rules and would never dream of breaking them. Breaking the rules wouldn't be playing the game; only damned foreigners and cads break the rules, every Englishman knows that.

Conor was a damned foreigner and a cad. He made up all the rules as he went along and then had the most glorious time breaking every one of them in the most amusing way his limitless imagination could conceive. Robert would be appalled by such wildly disordered antics, but interestingly this doesn't damn Robert for me. I think I enjoy him as he is first because he really is very competent and second because this rational well-ordered sportsmanship is such a novelty that I find it erotic.

This leads me inevitably to myself. What do I truly think about physical love? I've been truthful about my two men and now I must put myself alongside them to complete an honest picture of my private life.

I think I would like to record once and for all that I enjoy passion not because I was seduced at sixteen, but in spite of it. Men have such odd ideas about early seductions and seem to assume such an episode automatically converts a woman into a furnace of sexuality, but the truth is that I wasn't in the least keen about passion at first. It raised too many appalling memories for me, and the chief among those memories was fear. I'll never forget how much Bobby frightened me by turning into someone else. I've always thought the tale of Dr. Jekyll and Mr. Hyde is quite the most beastly story ever invented.

I don't believe I exaggerate my situation if I write that Conor saved me. I was very frightened when I first went to bed with him because I thought he too might turn into an evil stranger but he didn't; he merely became more gorgeous than ever. That was the major hurdle overcome, and eventually my cure was completed (and it was by no means an overnight miracle) because Conor cared enough about me to be patient and I cared enough about him to respond to his patience. I was so lucky not just because (as I now realize) I was born with a considerable capacity to enjoy myself in bed but because at that crucial moment of my life fate presented me with a man who was able to free that capacity from its burden of fear.

I've been naughty about passion in the past. I can't deny that, but all I can say

138

in my own defense is that I'm not by nature promiscuous. When I was unfaithful to Conor it was for a variety of reasons but never because I merely fancied an exciting roll in the hay. I was unfaithful because he was unfaithful to me and I wanted to get even with him, or because it seemed an escape from problems I couldn't face, or because I was so depressed that it seemed easier to say yes than to say no. The fact is I don't think I *would* have been unfaithful to Conor if life with him had been less racked by ghastly crises. Conor satisfied me sexually. So does Robert. I want, I long, I yearn to be faithful to Robert. The rock-bottom truth is that I can't stand infidelity. Such a mess, such a muddle, such hell.

Hell makes me think of Bobby again. Do I now write down what Bobby was like in bed? Or is that aspect of the subject still absolutely *verboten* despite my confession to Robert? I always thought it would remain *verboten* for the rest of my life or at the very least until I was eighty and past passion altogether (or will I ever be past it? Horrid thought!) but maybe writing down my opinion will help, just as talking to Robert of the seduction helped. But perhaps all I need say is that after I'd first been to bed with Robert I thought, Thank God he'll never remind me of his father. Yes, that was certainly a moment for heaving a sigh of relief. Disciplined, competent Robert... Perhaps that was when I first consciously formed the judgment that Bobby was no good in bed, although of course I had always felt that the experience with him was one which I never wished to repeat. However perhaps with other women Bobby's different; perhaps he was too disturbed when he was with me to give an adequate performance, but one thing I know for certain: sex wasn't a sport for him. What it was exactly God only knows, but it wasn't a game at all.

Enough. No more Bobby. No more Conor. I've just had the most wonderful night with the man I'm going to marry, and all that's left for me to say is thank God we're never likely to have a row about sex...

We've just had the most ghastly row about sex. At least, that's what Robert thinks the row was about. Actually although he refused to admit it we were having a row about my previous sexual experience. The stupid thing is that Robert would hate it if I were still the miserable timid woman whom Conor acquired when he married me; Robert can't stand the incompetent or the second-rate, and he enjoys me exactly as I am. What he doesn't enjoy—and what he can't face at all—is the thought of how I acquired my competence.

When I realized what the problem was I tried to allay his fears that my past adultery meant I was hopelessly promiscuous, but he cut me off. He couldn't bear to hear me talk of other men, he couldn't bear to hear me talk of Conor, he couldn't bear to be reminded that I had ever loved someone else.

He couldn't admit that, of course. That was why the whole row took place on another subject: my bedroom manners. He had the nerve to say that "a woman who plays an assertive role in bed isn't very womanly." Honestly, if I hadn't been so upset I would have laughed. Anyone would think from that statement that I was some fierce suffragette who bellowed orders at the top of her voice! The truth is that I'm sensitive and considerate in bed, and although I never lose sight of my own pleasure, I do my imaginative best to give a man what he wants. And the last thing Robert wants is some female who does no more than lie on her back with her legs apart—he'd be bored to death.

This time I didn't lose my temper and indulge in what he would have described as "a feminine tantrum." I said politely but firmly that he might not think much of my bedroom manners but I thought still less of his if he treated an intelligent, devoted partner as if she ought to be a mere mindless receptacle for male seed—at which point *he* threw a tantrum by yelling, "Bloody women, bloody sex, bloody hell!" and retiring in a rage to the lavatory. I know men and women are utterly different but sometimes the little similarities of behavior make one wonder if the differences are as great as everyone says they are.

We were soon reconciled but afterwards it hardly seemed the right moment to insist that he faced the reality of my marriage to Conor, and what now worries me is whether the right moment will ever come. It's obvious that Conor represents a serious problem for us, but it's equally obvious that Robert's decided to solve the problem by locking it up at the back of his mind and refusing to speak of it. Is this a solution? No. It's merely another example of Robert's curious emotional naivety; he simply can't see that before we can hope to resolve the difficulty we have to discuss it frankly together.

The trouble with this particular difficulty is that I'm not very good at facing Conor's memory myself at the moment. I'm too afraid that if I start thinking of him my bereavement will overwhelm me, just as it did at the funeral in Ireland, and then I shall have a nervous collapse which Robert would find an awful bore. The only way I can cope with my life at present is to keep going steadily towards my goal—marriage with Robert—and not look back. If I lose my nerve, disaster will be sure to follow, and then chaos will descend again.

Perhaps I should be optimistic. After all, it's a fact of life that all second marriages somehow have to adjust to the idea that previous partners existed, and in the majority at least an adjustment is made. The truth is that time will distance us both from Conor and so eventually he's bound to seem less important.

Yes, I'm sure that after our marriage we'll find that darling Conor will simply fade away. . . .

"*Marriage!*" shouted my darling Declan, looking at me as if I were the original serpent in the Garden of Eden.

"And Pa not yet cold in his grave!" shrilled my darling Rory, who adores being dramatic and emotional.

"Oh darlings, *please* don't be upset—"

We were at Oxmoon a week later. After a joyous reunion I had lured them up to my bedroom to give them two new watches (bought on credit from divine Harrods), and as soon as I was sure both boys were delighted I embarked on my confession. I had spent hours rehearsing my speech, and by that time I was so nervous that I could delay no longer. I was afraid sheer terror would drive me into forgetting my lines.

"I'm sorry, Ma," interrupted Declan, "but I can't allow this."

Declan was taller than I was and already an expert in the art of intimidation; he had walked up to me and was glaring into my eyes. Amidst all my fright I was aware of thinking what an attractive young man he would be when he grew up. He had a great look of Conor, particularly around the eyes and mouth.

"Darling, just listen!" I pleaded weakly, backing away until I could subside onto the edge of the bed. "I'm doing this for all of us!"

"Then you'd best go on strike and do no more!"

"She must be mad, Declan—look at her, destroyed with grief, just like Aunt Dervla said—"

"That's enough!" I screamed. "Be quiet, both of you!"

"Now Ma, there's no need to be hysterical—"

"None at all," said Rory, sitting down close to me on the bed and grabbing my hand for comfort.

I put my arm around him and planted a kiss on his red hair. I felt racked by guilt, driven by the need to lavish affection on them to compensate for my behavior and beside myself with terror for the future. In short I was in my usual mess.

"Look, Ma," said Declan briskly, "I know you need looking after, Pa always said you did, but *you don't have to get married to be looked after.* I'll do it. I'll make it my permanent occupation."

"Oh darling, that's heavenly of you, but—"

"Now that I'm fourteen, I don't need to go to school anymore, I know all there is to know and anyway as I can use a gun and play poker I'm sure I'll have no difficulty taking Pa's place."

"But Declan—"

"No, don't worry about anything, Ma; I'll organize your life now. We'll have a swell apartment in Dublin, and you can turn over your income check to me every month and I'll give you the money for housekeeping just as Pa did, and I'll be so soft-hearted I'll even let you smoke in the parlor. And when I eventually get married, you can come and live with us, I'll take special care to find a girl you can get along with—"

"Oh Declan—darling—"

"But Ma, you can't get married, not again, not ever, it would be so disrespectful to Pa, so disloyal—in fact how could you even think of such infidelity to the man you always swore was the Love of Your Life? No, no, you've got to dedicate yourself to chastity and wear black forever—and maybe now at last you can turn to the Church, just as every decent widow should, you know it was the tragedy of Pa's life that you stayed a Protestant—"

"Darling, please," I said, "not religion. Not now. My nerves can't stand it."

"But Ma—"

"No, my love, you've been simply adorable and I'm deeply moved but now I'm afraid you must listen to me. Listen, pet, I did love Pa. You know I did. And he was without doubt the Grand Passion of My Life, just as I've always told you

141

he was. But there are different kinds of love, and the man I love now I love in quite a different way. Robert's my friend. He's like a brother to me. I'm terribly lucky that he wants to look after me because he's a fine man, brilliantly clever and successful, and he wants to do his very best for all of us, not just for me but for you too."

"I'm not living in England," said Declan, "and I'm not living with an Englishman. It would be contrary to my principles as an Irish patriot and an insult to Pa's memory."

"Robert's a Welshman, Declan—and before you make any more of those dreadful anti-British remarks please remember that before I went to live at Oxmoon I was born in Warwickshire and that makes me English. I know darling Pa always preferred to gloss over that, but—"

"All right, if you insist on living here I guess I'll have to live here too to look after you, but I'm not receiving an English education. Rory, you wouldn't go to an English school, would you?"

"I wouldn't mind so long as I saw Ma every day," said Rory, "although of course I couldn't approve."

"Darling Rory!" I hugged him lavishly again. "Declan, there are some very, very good Catholic schools in England, places where even Pa would have been proud to be educated. Robert's been making inquiries at Downside which is a very famous Catholic public school—a private school, as we would say in America—"

"I'm not letting Robert organize my life," said Declan, "and hell, Ma, I'm not letting him organize yours either. Maybe Robert hasn't realized I could keep you in the lap of luxury by playing poker and working for Irish republicanism—in fact maybe he's just offered to marry you out of kindness because he thinks there's no better fate awaiting you, but don't worry, I'll talk to Robert, I'll set him straight, you just leave it all to me."

Are there any two people on earth doomed to clash as disastrously as Robert and Declan? I can see the clash coming—I've seen it coming from the beginning, although I was too frightened to dwell upon it—and now I'm well-nigh gibbering with terror.

I have four days to devise some master plot that will solve the insoluble, four days before Robert arrives here for the weekend and Declan tries to sabotage our future. Can I confide in Bobby who's being a tower of strength, winning the boys' liking and respect and giving them exactly the kind of cheerful, friendly, sympathetic attention that they need? No, I really can't start hatching schemes with Bobby. Robert might think we were conspiring against him and that would lead to some new frightfulness. And the awful thing is I don't need to confide in either Bobby or Margaret because it must be as plain to them as it is to me that Robert's not going to be able to cope with Declan.

No, that's not true. Robert will cope with Declan. Robert can cope with anyone.

But I won't be able to cope with the way he copes with Declan, and Declan won't be able to cope with it either.

Horrors.

There's only one thing to do: warn Robert that this is a situation which will require all his professional skill. That will appeal to his vanity in addition to putting him on his guard. And while I'm about it I may as well stop talking of "Darling Declan" and start talking about "Difficult Declan" instead.

Oh God, how on earth are we all going to survive...

...and so, darling, I wrote, scribbling away feverishly as I sat at the desk in the morning room, *although the last thing I want to do is mention Conor I really think that you'll understand Declan better if I tell you just a little more than you already know about the background of my marriage. The truth is Conor wasn't exactly a restaurant owner. He was a professional gambler who had a financial stake in what he used to call a "cabaret," meaning a drinking place where they have low entertainment downstairs and even lower entertainment upstairs—a sort of brothel-pub. Of course he kept his family well apart from all this, in fact I never even saw the cabaret (well, actually there were several of them) and neither did the boys, but they've grown up thinking it's the height of manhood to play poker, so you see they're not exactly very English in that respect...*

I paused. I was wondering if I could avoid the subject of Irish patriotism, but I knew that if I didn't mention the Brotherhood, Declan most certainly would.

I gulped some air and bent over my pen again.

...and I'm afraid they're not very English either, darling, when it comes to discussing Ireland, but that doesn't matter, does it, because I know you've always held the most advanced Liberal views on the subject of Home Rule. All the same, I think you ought to know that Conor was involved with some rather rabid patriots, and I'm afraid boys of Declan's age do think that sort of thing is very glamorous. I was never happy with the situation, but what could I do? I felt it wasn't my place to criticize Conor when he entertained these people—although I did feel so nervous when they started talking about the beastly English, but Conor just told them I was Welsh and they used to say, "Ah yes, another race crushed beneath the Saxon heel!" and quite honestly, darling, it somehow seemed so very much safer just to say, "Oh yes, those beastly Saxons, such a bore." However, never mind, I'm sure the boys will soon realize that being rabidly anti-British simply isn't the done thing at all...

I paused for another deep breath. Now I had to turn to the subject of the boys' education but I had trouble phrasing my next sentence. Those boys had to go to boarding school. I accepted that not only because British upper-class boys always went to boarding school but because I knew Robert wouldn't settle for anything less. However I wasn't being entirely feeble here, meekly letting Robert dispose of my children for two-thirds of the year. Although I adored my boys, I was still sensible enough to see that they needed both the discipline and, after the great upheaval, the stability of a good school that could provide them with a familiar

Catholic atmosphere. I also honestly believed that the massed company of British boys of their own age would help them make the difficult adjustment to another culture and another way of life. But although Robert was in favor of packing them off to Downside as soon as the term began in September, I was now convinced that they needed more time before they were sent away to school. Conor's death had been a dreadful shock to them.

. . . and talking of doing the done thing, darling, that reminds me of our decision to send the boys to Downside in September. Bearing in mind how very un-English they are, don't you think it might be better if we postponed boarding school till the new year? I'm not saying they should be with me in London—I do accept that this solution of Oxmoon is ideal, but if Bobby and Margaret consent perhaps we could engage a tutor to spend the autumn here with the boys . . .

I wondered what Robert would think of this suggestion. It seemed reasonable enough, but when I read through what I'd written I thought, He's not going to like me making regular visits to Oxmoon for the next five months. He's not going to like it at all.

"I don't like the idea of you making repeated sorties to Oxmoon during the next few months," said Robert four days later. "That may be pleasant for the boys, but I think you're going to wind up exhausted. Why, look at you now—you're worn out! No, I'm afraid it won't do. You're in a muddle as usual, and you must let me sort you out."

My heart felt as if it had plummeted straight to my boots, but I was aware to my interest that I wasn't angry with him. What Robert said was true. I was indeed worn out, and repeated visits to Oxmoon would indeed put me under severe emotional strain.

"Those boys now have six weeks to recuperate from their bereavement in eminently suitable surroundings," pursued Robert, "but by September they'll be ready for school and to school they must go. If they loaf around any longer they'll get into mischief; in my opinion they'd mince a tutor in no time and eat him with bacon for breakfast."

I knew he was right. That, I was beginning to discover, was the great difficulty in dealing with Robert. Rationally he was always right. But not all situations can be mastered by reason alone.

I said fearfully, "Declan will argue with you."

"Good," said Robert. "Let him try."

I suddenly found I had to sit down.

It was after dinner at Oxmoon on the evening of Robert's arrival, and at Bobby's suggestion Lion and Johnny had taken the boys off to the billiard room so that Robert and I could snatch a little time alone together. We had wandered across the lawn to the summerhouse, and now as the twilight deepened over the woods I sank down on one of the wicker chairs and found myself once more struggling against my tears.

144

"Don't be too severe with Declan, Robert. He's not nearly so grown up as he pretends to be."

"I've no intention of being severe with Declan. Nor, I must tell you, do I intend to be sentimental. I intend to be a stepfather whom he can respect."

"Oh God, I'm in such a muddle over this—"

"Obviously, but do try and be calm. The situation is in fact very simple: we're discussing what kind of stepfather you want for those boys—or in other words, whether you want me to be active or passive. Now, if I'm active I treat those boys as if they were mine, and that means that they've got to recognize that I, as the Boers say, am the boss. If I'm passive I simply stand by and let them run wild while you undermine all discipline by your misplaced maternal indulgence—no, don't interpret that as a criticism! You can't help being overemotional, and anyway, the truth is that no woman's fit to cope single-handed with two boys verging on adolescence."

"Yes, darling. But—"

"Ginette, if I adopt a passive role here I think those boys will wreck our engagement in no time. After all, that's what Declan wants, isn't it? So now you have to decide what *you* want. Do you want our engagement wrecked or don't you?"

"I don't. I couldn't bear it—"

"Very well. That means you authorize me to be an active stepfather. Thank you. I shall now take whatever steps I deem necessary to preserve our future—in other words I'm going to have order, discipline and respect, and I'm going to have them now, right from the beginning. In my opinion children are like wives and servants: you've got to start as you mean to go on."

Children are *nothing* like wives and servants. And anyway wives aren't like servants—or they shouldn't be. I can't say that to Robert, though, because I'm too afraid of another ghastly quarrel. It was bad enough quarreling about money and sex, but if we quarrel over the boys I shall have a nervous collapse and then Robert will decide he'd do better not to marry me after all and oh God, what would I do, how would I manage, no, *I must stave off* a nervous collapse and I can start by making up my mind that whatever happens we must avoid quarreling over the boys.

I can also help myself by acknowledging that once again Robert's right—in theory. He's got to be an active stepfather in order to win the boys' respect, but the trouble is that Robert's idea of being an active stepfather is certain to embrace behavior I shall hardly know how to endure.

And yet... Let's be honest; the truth is there's a dreadful secret relief in letting Robert try to annihilate this problem. I can't control those boys, never could. Conor was good with them but he was out at work most of the time, and I was the one who had to try to keep them in order while the nursemaids gave notice and the cook had hysterics and the apartment began to look like a lunatic asylum.

Yet now Robert's going to reduce chaos to order with his usual skill, and of

145

course he's going to succeed; he's going to win. But what about me? I think I'm going to lose. I'm going to end up being forced to side with Robert against the boys and Declan will never forgive me. He'll think I'm betraying them just as I've betrayed his father. Rory's sufficiently young and frightened and lost to forgive me anything, but Declan has a hard fanatical streak, like Conor, and he'll violently oppose anyone he believes has wronged him.

I can see horror approaching, no, not just horror but HORROR in capital letters. But what can I do to avoid it? Nothing. If I don't let Robert win here I'll lose him and if I lose Robert I'll collapse, I'll be driven mad by predatory men, I'll be wrecked and ruined in no time at all. No, I can't stand alone, how can I, I'm too vulnerable, *too frightened*—and that means I've got to marry Robert, got to protect myself, got to, got to, got to, and besides . . .

If only we can get these frightful problems sorted out before the wedding I'm sure our marriage will be blissfully happy.

"If you think I'm going to be locked up for two-thirds of the year in an English prison, you'd better think again!"

"Declan, Downside isn't a prison—it's a very fine school run by monks—"

"Holy shit! I don't want to live in a monastery!"

"Declan, how dare you use such language to me!"

"Why not? Pa did! But you wouldn't remember that, would you—all you can think about is that English bastard Robert!"

"Declan, *I will not have you behaving like this*—"

"*Who's going to stop me?*"

"I was wondering when you were going to ask that question," said Robert blandly from the doorway.

At his request I left them alone together in my room. I managed to walk away steadily down the corridor but on the landing the tears overwhelmed me and I rushed up the stairs to the attics. The Oxmoon attics were not set aside for the servants, who were housed in the kitchen wing which overlooked the stable yard, and the long chain of rooms was filled with junk and rejected heirlooms. Nothing was ever thrown away at Oxmoon, and as I blundered around among the memorabilia I came across the well-remembered portrait of my aunt Gwyneth, Robert's grandmother, who had gone mad as the result of her love affair with the sheep farmer Owain Bryn-Davies.

Feeling on the brink of madness myself I sat down by her picture and wondered if she too had ever felt divided beyond endurance between her lover and her son. Poor Aunt Gwyneth, I could remember those bright blue eyes of hers so clearly, the eyes Bobby had inherited. Johnny too had inherited those eyes, and as I looked at the portrait of Aunt Gwyneth in her prime I was struck by the fact that Johnny was far more like her than Bobby was. Johnny was the only one in the family who had her dark hair.

I tried to go on thinking of Johnny in order to avoid thinking of Declan. Why had Johnny, once an adorable little boy, bright as a button and delectably naughty, turned into this prim dreary young man of twenty-one? This was a mystery that could occupy me for some time but no, I was unable to concentrate on it, and the next moment I could think only of Declan.

Burying my face in my hands, I once more abandoned myself to despair.

Margaret and Bobby are being immaculate as usual at keeping up appearances; they're behaving as if nothing's happened, but Robert's brothers are less expert at concealing their feelings. Johnny manages well but Lion keeps glancing at us in fascination while Edmund is too embarrassed to look at us at all. Celia is being kind (she thinks) and has offered to show me her pressed wild flowers, but I've muttered some excuse and escaped to my room for an early night. I want Robert but I know he won't come to me. We must observe the proprieties at Oxmoon, no choice, so I'm alone and weeping, I shouldn't weep, I know I shouldn't, but I can't help myself.

I haven't seen Declan since the ghastliness began. Robert's locked him in his room and forbidden me to go near him, and of course I daren't disobey. It's not that I'm frightened of Robert (although I am—petrified); I just feel that if I'm to support Robert I must support him utterly and then perhaps the horrors will finish sooner. If Declan once believes I could be won over to his side he'll go on and on and on in the hope that I'll give way.

But I won't. Everything's at stake, Robert, my marriage, my future, my entire life, and I've now reached the stage where I can't go back. I've come so far, salvation is in sight and whatever happens I've got to go on.

"If you don't want me anymore I'll go and live in Ireland with Uncle Seamus and Aunt Dervla."

"Oh Declan darling, you *know* I want you, you know it . . ."

It was the next morning, a Sunday, and Robert had given me permission to see Declan so that I could take him to Mass with Rory at the Catholic church in Swansea. Declan was white and there were dark shadows under his eyes and he was trying so hard to be brave but when I put my arms around him he began to cry. As I had told Robert, Declan was still so young even though he wanted so much to be grown up, and Conor's death had been very terrible to him.

"I want Pa. . . . Why did he have to get killed like that . . . I don't believe in God anymore. I don't want to go to Mass. . . . I want Pa, I don't want that bastard Robert. . . ."

"Declan, I can't hear a word against Robert, I'm sorry."

"But he hurt me, *he hurt me*—"

"He won't hurt you if you behave well, Declan."

"But Pa never hurt me, he never laid a finger on me!"

"Pa's dead. It's terrible, it's tragic but it's true and you must try to accept that I've no choice but to give Robert permission to treat you and Rory as if you were his sons."

147

"But in New York—"

"We're not in New York, Declan, not anymore. Here Robert sets the standards, and here he draws the line."

"Don't worry about the boys—I'll cheer them up, I promise," murmured Bobby to me when the time came for me to return to London with Robert, but Margaret merely remarked with chilling truth, "They'll be well enough once no one's here to upset them."

I had wanted to stay on at Oxmoon with the boys but this was impossible, not only because Robert would have been angry but because we had social engagements to fulfill and cancellation would have caused considerable awkwardness. Rory shed a tear to see me go but Declan was dry-eyed and withdrew into the house without bothering to watch the motor drive away.

When we arrived in London some hours later Robert escorted me to the flat, sent the housekeeper home early, dispatched the maid on an errand to Kensington High Street and then to my extreme distaste drew me into the bedroom to make amends for the nights at Oxmoon when we had been obliged to conform to Margaret's standards. By that time I was feeling so ill with distress that all I wanted was to be alone, but of course I couldn't have told him that. Instead I tried to display enthusiasm, but when we were in bed together I found that competent sportsmanship of his no longer seemed so erotic, and at once the effort of acting a charade was almost more than I could bear.

Robert withdrew from me. At first I thought with relief that his desire had died but I was mistaken. He was merely pausing to clear up the muddle.

"Are you angry with me?"

"No. You're right to want to be an active stepfather, and I'd be a fool if I stopped you. But"—I prayed for courage—"I'm afraid I *am* upset. Please try not to mind. It's just that I'm a mother and I can't bear to think of my children being unhappy."

He considered this carefully. He applied the full force of his formidable intellect to the problem. At last he said with touching simplicity, "I thought this would make you feel better."

It was a logical assumption to make. The only trouble was that it was quite wrong.

We went on lying there, unjoined, Robert propped up on his elbow, I lying inert on my back, but when I saw his anxiety increasing I couldn't bear it. He was so concerned and loved me so much. A powerful affection for him overwhelmed me. I heard myself say, "Time to raid the strawberry beds again!" and then I pulled him back once more into my arms.

I can't stop thinking of those boys. They're going to hate boarding school. Downside may be the finest school on earth but they'll loathe it. I'm a mother who can't bear to think of her children being unhappy, and I know they're going

148

to be unhappier. But what can I do? Nothing. Robert must have me to himself for two-thirds of the year, and if he can find some way of decimating that final third he'll do it.

Robert doesn't like sharing me. He never did. I remember how furious he became when I spent time playing with Lion—darling Lion, what a huge gorgeous captivating baby he was! But in the end I had to call Lion a monster and say I hated him; I had to pretend to hate all babies otherwise Robert would be upset.

What on earth is he going to be like when we have a child of our own?

No, I must stop. It's pointless worrying about the distant future at the moment, and anyway I'm sure that as soon as we're married and living happily ever after, that sort of problem will turn out to belong to the very distant past . . .

"We've been invited to the Wharf!"

"Robert, how exciting!"

The law courts were about to close for the long vacation and the invitation to the Asquiths' country house on the Thames was only one of a number of important invitations that Robert had received from various well-wishers in Society. Because of my bereavement we had not announced our engagement formally, but word of our proposed marriage had soon circulated with the result that the invitations had been extended to include me.

This was very gratifying, and now I had my first delicious glimpse of the affluent political world that would be waiting for me on the far side of the altar. As I immediately blossomed in bliss I found that the shady glamour of my New York life seemed—thank God—more than a million miles away, and in fact I was so captivated by the change in my fortunes that I bought rather too many smart clothes in celebration. But I told myself how important it was for Robert's sake that I should make a suitably fashionable impression.

We did not mingle much with the aristocracy for the Liberal Party had alienated this section of Society during the constitutional crisis of 1911, but nonetheless there were a number of lords and ladies who had succeeded in advancing from the nineteenth to the twentieth century by embracing the Liberal creed, while the Asquiths themselves, commoners and self-made, generated a frenetic and somewhat eccentric social life of their own. Oddly enough I was more intimidated at first by the Asquiths than by the aristocrats, but fortunately Margot Asquith chose to regard me kindly and showed her benign interest by bestowing on me one of her outrageous remarks. ("At last Mr. Godwin's found someone who hasn't had to poison her husband to win his attention, Mrs. Kinsella—or did you perhaps poison your husband after all?")

Wherever we went that summer I found that my bedroom was always next to Robert's, and this escape from the standards set at Oxmoon also added to my enjoyment. In fact I was in ecstasy—or so I told myself. Probably it would be closer to the truth to say I was feverishly trying to divert myself from the ghastliness to come. At some stage during all this hedonism I had ordered two sets of school uniform, and at the beginning of September I returned to the flat to start sewing on name tapes. Bobby brought the boys up to town a day later, but although Rory was willing to see the sights of London Declan shut himself in his room and refused to go out. I was terrified he would also refuse to go to school when the time came, but Bobby had persuaded him to give Downside a try, and after a tense miserable week I think Declan was willing to go anywhere to escape from Robert.

Robert visited us every day and took trouble to be pleasant to both boys, but Declan could hardly bear to be in the same room with him. However Robert's behavior continued to be immaculate. He escorted the boys himself to Downside; he made sure that a watchful eye would be kept on them; he did everything possible to lessen the ordeal of beginning a new life. That was why he was so angry and I was in such despair when three weeks later Declan ran away. Robert was quite justified in feeling he himself had done all he could to avoid such a disaster.

To make matters worse Declan didn't run away to Oxmoon, where he would have been assured of a nonviolent, if disapproving reception. Anxious for money which would take him to Ireland he came to London to see me, and arriving late at night he found me with Robert.

A hideous scene followed.

After Declan had been locked in his room Robert stayed the rest of the night at the flat to ensure that I exhibited no criminal weakness, and then he took Declan straight back to school the next morning. I didn't think Declan would go but he did. He knew Robert would beat him again if he refused. I tried to kiss him goodbye but he spat at me, and although I at once cried out, "No, Robert—" Robert only exclaimed, "You don't think I'm going to let him get away with that, do you?" and more horrors ensued.

Returning from Somerset soon after six, Robert reported that the school authorities had been most understanding and had told him he had done entirely the right thing. This failed to surprise me. Robert always did the right thing. However at least this time he was expecting me to be upset so I didn't have to pretend that everything in the garden was lovely once the two of us were alone together again. He made no attempt to lead me to bed but sat on the sofa and put his arm around me as he held my hand.

"You're being a great comfort, Robert," I finally managed to tell him when my tears were under control.

"I'd be a poor sort of friend if I wasn't!" he said surprised, and when I thought of all those times he had stood by me in the past I dimly saw, far away in the distance, a gleam of happiness.

"Oh Robert!" I exclaimed passionately, aching for reassurance. "We'll be all right, won't we?"

"How can we possibly fail?"

That settled that. Robert had decided our marriage was going to be a huge success. In exhausted relief I surrendered all my fears, all my anxieties and all my battered emotions to his irresistible self-confidence, and told myself that everything was bound to come right in the end.

Let me see, it must be three months since I wrote anything in this journal. Why did I stop? Because having finally made up my mind that everything was under control, I no longer had an urgent need to set down my conflicting emotions in an effort to understand what was really going on. I was also diverted by the fact that after the crisis with Declan I had to spend much time house hunting and preparing for married life (and spending too much money but I won't think about that just yet). However now is the time to pick up my pen again because here I am in Gower on the nineteenth of December, 1913, and tomorrow at five o'clock in the afternoon I shall be marrying my formidable second husband in Penhale parish church.

I'm in such a muddle about this bloody wedding that it almost beggars description. (Oh, what a relief to write that down in black-and-white!) What I really wanted was to marry Robert quietly in London in the briefest of ceremonies and then leave immediately for some destination like Timbuktu where the past would seem a thousand years away. But what I wanted was impossible. Margaret made that clear to us well before we had embarked on our wedding arrangements, and I knew I could not possibly oppose her.

Robert's attitude to his mother has changed from a patronizing filial courtesy to a profound filial respect. We've never discussed this but I know it's connected with his discoveries about his father (that's why we don't discuss it). Very well, I don't mind him respecting Margaret. God knows she's earned his respect, and God knows I respect her myself. But when iron-willed Robert, who normally stands no interference from anyone, least of all from a woman, prepares to listen in meek obedience as his mother tells him how he should get married, I want to scream with exasperation.

Margaret declared—in a long sinister highly Victorian letter liberally sprinkled with the words "Ginevra dearest" and "dearest Robert"—that we had to be married at Penhale and endure a reception at Oxmoon afterwards because from the point of view of keeping up appearances this was the right thing—indeed, said Margaret, the only thing—to do. All Gower would expect the wedding of the heir to Oxmoon to be a big occasion, and all Gower could not be disappointed. Otherwise there might be unfortunate comment that the marriage was unpopular and this, Margaret explained serenely, would be "tiresome." The church ceremony must necessarily be austere, since I was marrying within months of being widowed, but this "little awkwardness" could be glossed over with the help of a magnificent reception at Oxmoon. A ball and supper would "suit admirably" and she looked forward to conferring with us further as soon as possible.

Robert said he really didn't care what happened so long as he danced with me to "The Blue Danube," and I then discovered to my absolute horror that he had every intention of making this waltz our special tune.

"For me it symbolizes the moment when my life really began," said Robert, "the moment at your ball in 1898 when I held you in my arms beneath the chandeliers at Oxmoon and knew I'd never be content until I'd married you—

and that's why when we do marry I'm going to dance with you there again to 'The Blue Danube' and then the past will be rewritten, all my unhappiness will be cancelled and that tune will become a symbol of the greatest triumph of my life."

"Oh darling, how romantic!" I said, heart sinking, because of course for me "The Blue Danube" belonged to Conor. It symbolized that moment when he had appeared in the ballroom to save me; it symbolized the end of the horrors at Oxmoon and the beginning of a new life. How was I ever going to cope with a second marriage haunted by the strains of "The Blue Danube"? I had no idea then and I have no idea now.

What a prospect! Can Robert honestly fail to realize how awful this wedding at Oxmoon is going to be for me? No. Emotionally color-blind Robert has simply shut out all the aspects of the situation that might interfere with the celebration of his mighty victory but meanwhile, half-blinded by the gory colors of my own emotional spectrum, I can't help but visualize ghastliness at every turn.

Anyway here I am, staying at Penhale Manor with the de Bracys in order to fulfill the traditional requirement that the bride and groom shouldn't meet on the night before their wedding. It's very kind of Sir Gervase and Lady de Bracy to offer hospitality because they probably think it's dreadful of me to rush to the altar before my first husband's been dead a year, but Gwen's such an old friend of mine and no doubt she's been campaigning vigorously on my behalf. This evening the whole family has nearly driven me mad by telling me how romantic it is that I'm marrying my childhood sweetheart. When Gwen said cheerily, "Now all you have to do is live happily ever after!" I had a hard time suppressing the retort "Never mind living happily ever after—the main question is whether I can survive the next twenty-four hours."

I wonder if my boys are all right. Dearest Bobby said he would take special care of them. He *is* kind. How bizarre it is to think that someone as decent as Bobby should ever be capable of doing what he did to me. How sinister life is, how frightening. I remember Robert saying once that some of the murderers he had met had been quite charming. Ugh! A vile thought. Well, at least poor Bobby's not a murderer.

I wonder if Declan really will come to the wedding. He's promised Bobby he will, although how Bobby extracted that promise I can't imagine. But Bobby's such a magician with children. He doesn't have to beat them to get his way. I think Declan will be there but only to please Bobby. He won't want Bobby to be disappointed in him.

Let me cheer myself up by thinking how simply stunning I'll look in my pale green velvet wedding gown with those luscious dark green trimmings and that sumptuous matching shallow hat with the gossamer-thin veil (twenty-five guineas from divine Harrods). I hope to God naughty little Thomas doesn't throw a tantrum at the wrong moment. I didn't want a page but Margaret said Thomas would enjoy it so that was that. However at least I've had the brains to recruit little Eleanor Stourham as a bridesmaid so that Thomas has an eleven-year-old partner to keep him in check. Maybe they'll fight. Oh God, I wish the whole nightmare were over....

But I must stop groaning and be for one moment, as Robert would say, rational. How do Robert and I stand as we prepare to sally forth upon our greatest adventure of all? I think our position is favorable but I can look back now and see how far I was deceiving myself when I hoped we'd have our problems solved before the wedding. We've got them under control but nothing's been solved. We don't talk about Bobby, we don't talk about Conor, we don't talk about what's going to happen to those boys—and these three areas of silence represent three huge bridges to be crossed. But we don't have any other problems, do we? And I'm sure everything will come right in the end.

So am I ready to promise to love, cherish and obey Robert till death us do part? Yes. Absolutely. But how stern that marriage service is, how forbidding. Till death us do part...

I hate death. I hate all thought of death. I want to live and love and have a wonderful time...and that's exactly what I'm going to do.

Darling Robert, what a dear little boy he was, offering me his boiled sweets and saying he wanted to be a hero when he grew up.... Yes, Gwen's right after all. It *is* romantic that Robert and I are finally getting married, it's a fairy-tale happy ending, it's a dream come true and I'm *passionate* about it. Forget Conor. Forget the rows and the lies and the cheating and the adultery and the tears and the rages and the misery and the sheer soul-destroying awfulness of disillusioned love. Down with reality, long live romance! I'm marrying the man I *really* love at last and nothing on earth can now stand in my way.

"I Ginevra take thee Robert..."

We were married.

It was gorgeously romantic, the ceremony taking place on that dark winter afternoon in Penhale's old candlelit church which had already been decked for Christmas with holly and evergreens. But all through the service I could not forget that I was due to be the belle of the ball again at Oxmoon and that Bobby would be waiting to kiss me under the mistletoe.

Oh, the horror, the horror...

"Dearest Ginevra—welcome home again!" I was there. I was at Oxmoon. And Margaret was holding out her arms to embrace me.

Ghastly. God help me. Please don't let me break down.

"This is the happiest day of my life!" exclaimed Robert to the guests.

Don't think of the past. Don't think, don't think, *don't think*—

"Are you happy, Ginette?"

"Darling, how can you ask? This is the happiest day of my life too!"

"Truthfully?"

"Truthfully—cross my heart and hope to die!"

And may the Lord have mercy on my soul.

But I had to lie. I had to survive. Was I going to survive? Could I? Yes, of course I was but—

"Ginette, Ginette!"

—but I was in the ballroom at Oxmoon and the past was about to repeat itself.

The ballroom was dazzling, a glittering dream glowing with winter flowers, and all the mirrors reflected a glamorous celebration of life as the gentlemen of the orchestra raised their bows to their violins.

"The waltz, Ginette! The first waltz this time!"

I looked back over my shoulder to the ballroom doors and all I saw was the emptiness where Conor had stood fifteen years before. He wasn't there. He would never be there again, and as I realized that I realized I was alone among the radiant crowds at Oxmoon, alone and bereaved and longing for the dead man I still loved.

The music began.

"Isn't this romantic, Ginette?"

"Darling," I said, "it's sheer unadulterated heaven!"

And then we danced again beneath the chandeliers at Oxmoon as the orchestra played "The Blue Danube."

It was hell.

I'm rather horrified that I experienced quite such an overwhelming sense of my bereavement at a time when I should have been thinking only of Robert, but I suspect the explanation lies in the fact that for the past few months I've been resolutely refusing to contemplate Conor as I struggled towards the blessed security of my new marriage; I've been suppressing my grief and that was probably unwise, but the truth is that my feelings for him are so deep and complex that I was afraid to dwell upon them in case they diverted me from my goal. However all will be well now that I'm safe with Robert. I'll have the courage to grieve secretly every now and then, and soon the awful pang of bereavement will be dulled until finally I shall have Conor securely locked up in the past where he now belongs.

Meanwhile perhaps I should start savoring the fact that I've survived the wedding, God knows how, and here I am, strolling with Robert down the Champs-Élysées just as a quarter of a century ago we used to pitter-patter hand in hand along the lane to the village shop at Penhale. We're enjoying ourselves hugely, rushing off on exciting expeditions as if we were children again, only this time, as Robert points out amused, nobody's going to be cross with us if we turn up late for tea. Yes, I think I'm recovering from that ghastly wedding—and certainly a heavenly honeymoon is a useful start to the rigors of married bliss. . . .

What a wonderful honeymoon! Darling Robert's spent money like water and this proves he's quite capable of being generous when it suits him. He did make one edgy remark about my weakness for lavish spending but I pretended not to hear, and anyway I'm absolutely determined to reform. (Yes, I really am. I *must*.)

We're now back in London again at our heavenly little house in Ebury Street and everything in the garden couldn't be lovelier—except that Declan and Rory are due to arrive from Oxmoon tomorrow, and new horrors are without doubt about to begin.

The boys have gone back to school after four frightful days and Robert has told me frankly how pleased he is to have me to himself again. To do Robert justice I have to admit he has good reason to be pleased; when the boys are with us I'm in such a state of excruciating tension that I'm very poor company and a most inadequate wife. I'll have to pull myself together but it's hard to be serene when Declan calls me a whore and encourages Rory to be as disobedient as possible. I daren't tell Robert who's fortunately out of the house most of the time. If Robert knew what I was going through there would be more beatings and I couldn't stand the strain.

However now they've gone so I have a breathing space for eleven weeks— although I shall visit them next month at the school. But I don't have to think about that yet. All I have to think about now is my delicious new social life as Mrs. Robert Godwin. For a day or two I had this frightful worry that I might be pregnant, but thank goodness it was a false alarm. As I told Robert at the beginning of our affair when he finally roused himself from his passion to consider the potential consequences, I've never had an unwanted pregnancy, although I've certainly had some bad scares in my time.

I do want another baby, of course—I'd like two more, a boy and a girl—but not just yet. Robert would be livid if he couldn't have me entirely to himself once the boys were out of the way, so I must be careful—and in being careful I'm being realistic. Some marriages can take the strain of an early pregnancy, some can't. Ours couldn't, and it's much better to face this truth and acknowledge it. In a year or two it'll be different—after all, Robert's told me he wants a son and I believe him—but at this particular moment little unborn Robert Godwin would most definitely not be welcome.

I hate to admit it but I'm uneasy. Having acknowledged that our marriage isn't yet stable enough to welcome a child, I now have to acknowledge that our unsolved problems are assuming a sinister clarity of outline. I can't keep saying to myself, Oh, everything will come right after we're married. This statement may well be true—my God, it's got to be true!—but here we are, married, and we now have to grit our teeth and solve these problems. Or, to be accurate, I've got to solve them, since Robert won't admit there are problems to be solved.

Heavens, how worrying it all is! In fact I'm so worried I can't even begin to think of divine Harrods and their slightly overwhelming blizzard of bills. . . .

"Ginette, I'd like a word with you, if you please."
"Yes, darling, of course. What about?"
"Money."

I inwardly quailed but somehow managed to give him a brilliant smile.

We were browsing through the Sunday papers on a snowy day at the end of January. Outside in our little walled garden which stretched to the mews, the morning light was bleak but in our drawing room the fire was burning in the grate and all was warmth and coziness.

I was very pleased with our house in Ebury Street. I would have preferred something bigger and more positively Belgravia, but I recognized that there was no sense in thinking in those terms without a substantial private income, so I had done my best to find an attractive house and make it as charming as possible. I had succeeded, but sad to say, such a success could hardly have been achieved without generous expenditure.

Robert had approved the cost of the renovations to the main reception rooms but had urged economy on redecorating the rest of the house, so I had made up my mind to skimp wherever possible. But of course the hall and stairs had to look well, to match the standard of the drawing room and dining room, and of course some alterations were essential in the kitchens, which were positively medieval, and of course I couldn't skimp on the boys' rooms because I did so long for Declan and Rory to be happy in their new home. I was sure Robert would understand the need for this additional expenditure so I didn't ask his permission beforehand, and anyway I planned to pay for the boys' rooms out of my own income—but something seemed to have happened to my quarterly payment (could I really have spent it all in advance?), and then I had some bills from Harrods which I thought I would be wise not to open, so I hid the unopened envelopes at the back of my desk and said to myself, "I'll think of all that later."

However I kept thinking of those unopened bills, so to divert my mind from this little awkwardness I took a stroll along the Brompton Road, and I was just drifting past Harrods—of course I never intended to buy a thing—when I saw in the window this dressing table which was quite exquisite and I couldn't help thinking how ravishing it would look in our bedroom where I'd skimped and saved until it looked no better than a monk's cell. Frankly, I'm not too keen on monk's cells. Anyway I bought the dressing table but then I found I couldn't rest until I'd bought one or two other items to go with it. Well, three or four. Or five or six. What does it matter, the point was that our bedroom suddenly became divinely exciting and I adored it. I knew I'd been naughty but in my opinion the result made my liberality (what a much nicer word that is than extravagance!) worthwhile.

"Don't worry, darling," I said glibly to Robert in the hope of forestalling his complaints. "I'm going to reform."

Robert tossed aside his newspaper, stood up and moved to the window to watch the falling snow. He looked very tall, very authoritative and very menacing. Then turning to face me he said, "I had a letter from Harrods yesterday and I've decided it would be better for our marriage if I have complete control over our financial affairs. Otherwise quarrels over money will be a recurring feature of our married life."

"You mean—"

"I want your credit account terminated and the income from your trust fund assigned directly to me."

Silence.

"Let me reassure you," said Robert, pleasant but implacable, "that I intend to be generous in the amount I shall give you to cover the cost of housekeeping and your general expenses."

Another silence.

"So you'll have no cause for complaint," said Robert, still speaking in a pleasant voice, "and in fact I'm sure you'll find such an arrangement will make life much easier for you. The truth is it's no good expecting a woman to balance a checkbook. The feminine mind is quite unsuited to even the lower forms of financial management."

I at once thought of Conor telling me how clever I was as I eked out the housekeeping money to cover his disaster at poker.

"You were always hopeless with money," said Robert, slicing through my memories. "Right from the beginning you were always borrowing the odd penny from me to buy extra humbugs and then forgetting to pay me back."

"Licorice. I never liked humbugs. And I always paid you back!"

"No, you didn't! Oh, I admit you gave me the occasional boiled sweet, but—"

"I borrowed money from Celia to pay you back!"

"Exactly. You borrowed from Peter to pay Paul, as the saying goes, and you're doing exactly the same thing now with appalling results. I'm sorry, Ginette, but my mind's made up. I'm your husband and I can't allow this situation to continue."

"But Robert—"

"You want order in your life, don't you?"

"Yes, but—"

"Well, this is it. This is order; this is freedom from chaos. Now run along like a good girl and fetch your bills so that I can see the exact dimensions of your latest mess."

"How dare you talk to me like that!"

"What do you mean? I'm your husband, aren't I?"

"That doesn't give you the right to talk to me as if I were a mentally deficient schoolgirl!"

"And being my wife doesn't give you the right to behave like one! Now pull yourself together and face reality. We're married now, the rules of the game have changed and it's my absolute moral duty—"

"Oh my God."

"—to look after you in as kind, as considerate and as generous a way as possible, and it's your absolute moral duty to be loyal and obedient and to do as I say in all matters regarding the welfare of our marriage. I know perfectly well you have an inclination to be strong-willed and independent, but I'm going to be the boss of this marriage, and I think the time has come—"

"If you talk of drawing lines I shall scream."

"—to make it clear exactly what I will and won't tolerate. Now, I know this is difficult for you. Our old friendship gets in the way here because you can still look at me and see the small boy two years your junior whom you used to order around, but—"

"What! I never ordered you around! You were ordering me around as soon as you could talk! 'Ginette, do this, Ginette, do that'—all the time, every day, God knows how I ever stood it—"

"I'm sorry, I realize women can seldom resist the urge to digress but I must recall you to the subject under discussion. As your husband, I—"

"Oh, be quiet! You're not behaving like a husband, you're behaving like a jailer! Oh, how dare you treat me like this, how dare you—"

"I'll tell you exactly why I dare. Because you're no good with money. Because I'm ultimately responsible for your debts. Because you asked me to stop you getting into messes. Because I care about our marriage and rows such as this are something we have to avoid in the future at all costs."

"If you care about our marriage you'll treat me as an adult woman ought to be treated!"

"I am," said Robert.

I stormed out and slammed the door.

I've married a male monster. Is this a fatal mistake? Not necessarily. Male monsters can often be absolute pets. I've flirted with a number of delicious ones in the past and I've adored feeling that I'm the only chink in their antifemale armor, but I've always thought what a bore they would be as husbands and my God, now I know I was right.

However I'm not a feminist. I'm enjoying myself much too much being a first-rate woman to want to be a second-rate man, and I've no quarrel with the way the world's arranged. I don't care whether I have the vote or not. Certainly I would never bother to chain myself to the railings of Number Ten Downing Street; I'm much too busy wondering when I'm going to be invited to dine there. But despite my indifference to feminism there's one belief I hold very strongly and no one can talk me out of it: women are not born inferior to men. They're born different, but not inferior. And I resent, *deeply* resent being treated as if I were something less than a normal human being.

Why did I never realize Robert could be like this? Because he was playing the game according to the rules and making no attempt to be a male monster until he became my husband and acquired (he thinks) the right to be one. He did give me inklings, though; I can remember him saying the law was right to class married women with lunatics and children, but I just wrote that off as male arrogance, something to be taken with a pinch of salt. However I can't take the loss of my income with a pinch of salt. I'll need a huge indigestion pill to enable me to absorb an outrage like that, but for lack of alternative I'd better start swallowing one.

Is there really no choice but to acquiesce? I must try to be dispassionate; I must ask myself what the truth of this situation is, and the truth is that Robert *is* my husband. He can cancel my credit account and if I refuse to assign the income of my trust fund, my life soon won't be worth living.

Let me now try digesting that very unpalatable verdict. Well, the first fact which stands out like a sore thumb is that rationally Robert's right—as usual. I've been very naughty and very extravagant. No more using that delightful word "liberality" now; I must confront my problem. I'm not incapable of handling money but I can't blame Robert for deducing that I am. I should also admit that Robert's not taking an unusual line here; plenty of husbands refuse to let their wives buy goods on credit, and plenty of husbands refuse to let their wives have checkbooks, and this may even be good for their marriages, particularly if their wives have the brains of a cotton reel.

Yet the fact remains that although Robert's logically right he's emotionally wrong. That trust money is mine. It was left to me—*me*—by my father. I may be only Mrs. Robert Godwin in the eyes of the world, but to my bank manager I'm still an individual, not merely an extension of my husband—I'm the recipient of those funds, a human being who deserves to be treated with respect, not an idiot wife who can expect no better fate than to be the target of remarks like "the feminine mind is quite unsuited to even the lower forms of financial management." I have this horrid feeling that if I assign the income from my trust fund there won't be any *me* anymore, and I'll be diminished in some way quite impossible to describe to someone like Robert.

I feel wretched about this, and not merely because I'm furious with myself for not anticipating the severity of Robert's reaction. I feel wretched because I know our marriage now has another problem. I can manage; I can cope with a male monster if I have to, but the fact that Robert and I have different notions of what marriage should be like is hardly going to make life easier. I believe marriage should be a partnership aided by a reasonable amount of give-and-take and based on mutual respect and trust. Robert apparently regards it as a variation of a master-servant or parent-child relationship. Why on earth didn't I realize this before? How can one sleep with a man for six months without discovering this fundamental difference of opinion?

I blame the old friendship. I assumed we'd jog along on more or less the same lines after we were married. How spine-chilling it was just now when Robert said the rules of the game had changed! He would put it that way, of course. Typical.

Yes, I'm horrified but never mind, the first year of marriage is notorious for unwelcome revelations, and most partners manage to adjust to the unpleasant home truths in the end. Meanwhile it's certainly no good prolonging the quarrel. Robert won't behave as Conor did, seducing me whenever he wanted to get his hands on my money. If Robert doesn't get what he wants he'll withdraw from me emotionally, and I couldn't stand it; I want a loving Robert at my side, not a monster labeled HUSBAND; I want *my friend*, my companion at the strawberry beds and the loyal confederate who lent me the extra pennies to buy that mouth-watering licorice long ago in Penhale. . . .

I really should have given him more boiled sweets in compensation. I might have known that little mistake would catch up with me in the end.

"I'm sorry I lost my temper, Robert."

"I'm sorry if I upset you."

"Well, I do realize I've been very stupid and I do concede you have the right to cancel my credit account. But the trust fund... Robert, that fund is special to me, it comes from my father, and I'm sorry but I really do think a wife shouldn't be utterly dependent on her husband for money—"

"And I think she should be."

Another fundamental difference of opinion. I tried not to panic. "I can't think why," I said evenly, "we didn't discuss all this before we were married."

"We did. I made it very clear what I thought of your extravagance."

"You never said you thought I should be utterly dependent on you financially!"

"Naturally I had to give you the chance to manage your affairs. I did want to be fair."

"If you could give me just one more chance—"

"No. It would only lead to another scene like this, and I won't have it. We're not going to quarrel all over again, are we, Ginette?"

I shook my head, went to my desk and extracted the hidden bills from Harrods. Then at his dictation I wrote a letter to my bank manager to say that I wished the quarterly income from my trust fund to be paid directly into my husband's account.

"Thank you," said Robert. "Now we need never again have a row about money."

I stared in silence at the blotter. I could not bring myself to ask how much he intended to give me each week. I only prayed it would be sufficient and that I wouldn't have to beg for more.

Robert was glancing at his watch. "It'll take me a day or two to survey our expenditure and decide how much you need," he said, "so we'll conclude this discussion later. And now if you'll excuse me I must go to my study and work. I've got a lot to do." And with my checkbook in his pocket he left me on my own in my beautiful but extravagant drawing room.

Robert's working much too hard. I had no idea he could be so obsessed with his work. How could I possibly sleep with a man for six months and not realize... But I mustn't start saying that again. The brutal truth is that a love affair puts the partners on their best behavior. It takes marriage to ensure that all the unpalatable truths come sidling out of the woodwork of the happy home.

Robert is now rushing off to his chambers in the Temple at six in the morning so that he can work in peace before all the other barristers and clerks arrive to distract him. At first he used to leave without having breakfast but I put a stop to that by conspiring with Bennett.

Bennett used to be Robert's man before our marriage, and he's now our butler, wielding authority with great skill over Cook, the kitchenmaid and the parlormaid. I don't have a personal maid; they're usually an awful bore and anyway I learned how to live without one in New York. The trick is not to economize on a laundress and to track down a retired lady's maid who is willing to come in now and then to attend to the more difficult aspects of hairdressing. I'm good at sewing, thanks to Margaret, so mending presents no problems. When Robert becomes very grand I dare say I shall acquire a maid but meanwhile I manage well enough without one.

Bennett and I get on well, which is fortunate because valets often lapse into paroxysms of jealousy when their masters acquire wives, and when I told him how worried I was by Robert's increasingly eccentric working hours, he was sympathetic. Eventually we agreed that he would provide an early breakfast and I would coax Robert to eat it, but the trouble is that since this conversation of mine with Bennett, Robert has lost all interest in food and is eating the early breakfast only in order to keep me quiet.

Food isn't the only subject that no longer interests him. After our social engagements have been fulfilled he retires to his study to work into the early hours of the morning, and when he finally comes to bed he sinks instantly into unconsciousness while I'm left lying awake in the dark and wondering what happened to that lover who won his blue at passion.

Last night I said, "Darling, how long is this peculiar behavior of yours likely to go on?"

This embarrassed Robert but I'm sure I was right to signal to him that in my opinion he's carrying professional dedication too far. The entire trouble is this wretched murder case which he jokingly told me he took on in order to pay for the honeymoon. His client is accused of murdering his wife, chopping up the body and distributing it in bags deposited at various left-luggage offices all over London. Robert won't discuss the case with me so I have no idea whether he thinks his client is innocent or not, but I find the whole affair repulsive and can't imagine why Robert should find it so all-absorbing—not that he spends all his working hours on this case; he doesn't. He works so hard in order to keep up with his other cases, but I'm beginning to think that the murder alone is responsible for this sinister aura of fanaticism. It's the first murder case he's accepted since I came back into his life from America, and he seems to be turning into someone else altogether.

Nothing could frighten me more.

"No, no—stay away from me, *stay away!*" shouted Robert, and I awoke to find him in the middle of a nightmare.

"Darling, it's only a dream—"

"He was there again, he was coming towards me across the snow—"

"Who?"

"Death." He slumped back exhausted on the pillows.

I thought: What a vile nightmare. But I judged it tactful to remain silent so after switching on the light I merely slipped my hand into his to comfort him.

He clasped my fingers tightly and seemed grateful for both the light and the silence, but at last he said, "I seem to be in a mess again but I don't understand why. I thought I'd be cured once I had you."

I was astonished, "Cured of what, Robert?"

"I've got this bloody awful obsession; it's like a cancer of the personality."

"Cancer!"

"Don't be idiotic; I'm speaking metaphorically—oh God, I forgot you were terrified of illness—"

"But what on earth is this obsession of yours?"

"I'm obsessed with death."

There was a pause. We lay there, our hands clasped, and listened to the silence. I tried to speak but nothing happened. I was too revolted.

"It's all mixed up with this other obsession—"

"Other obsession?"

"Winning. I have to compete, I have to win, I can't stop myself. Now I thought this was all the result of my third obsession—"

"*Third obsession?*"

"Yes. You. It was a terrible thing when I lost you, Ginette; it was as if my whole life was dislocated—I kept trying to push it back into position by winning everything in sight. So I won and won and won until the easy victories no longer satisfied me, and then finally I found the challenge I needed, I found a competitor who would give me the most enthralling game of all—"

"And who was that?"

"Death."

My hand went limp in his but he didn't notice. He was too absorbed in his explanations.

"I thought," he said, "that once I had you back, I wouldn't feel the need to compete anymore. I thought I'd be able to go home again to Oxmoon—"

"*What?*"

"Oh, not literally! I was thinking of the lost Oxmoon of our childhood—I was seeing Oxmoon as a state of mind, a symbol of happiness."

"Oh, I see. For one moment I thought you meant—well, never mind, go on."

"But I'm still looking for the road back to Oxmoon, I'm still locked up in a way of life which is fundamentally meaningless to me—"

"Oh come, Robert, don't exaggerate! You love the glamour and the fame of your life at the bar!"

"No, I've come to hate all that. Glamour and fame have become symbols of my imprisonment. I'd give up the bar but—"

"*Give it up?*"

"—but I can't now that I have a wife and family to support, and besides if I'm to go into politics I must have a lucrative career. But do I really want to go into politics? Won't Westminster ultimately be just another cage like the Old Bailey? Oh God, how muddled I feel sometimes, how confused—"

"But my dear Robert, surely you don't doubt that you're cut out for great political success?"

"But what does that mean?" said Robert. "What's the point of pursuing a career

162

which has nothing to do with what one's life should really signify?"

"But what do you think your life should signify?"

"That's the conundrum. I don't know. All I know is that I'm not at peace. I ought to be; I've won you, I've cancelled out my loss and now I can be happy—except that I can't. It's almost as if I hadn't won you after all—oh God, what a mystery it is; how bewildered I feel, how despairing, how utterly tormented by the irrationality of it all—"

"Darling." I finally managed to pull myself together. "The first thing you must do is to stop talking of 'winning' me as if I were one of those ghastly silver cups which clutter up your bedroom at Oxmoon. One doesn't win people—they're not inanimate objects. The fact is that you've married me, which has more to do with existing and surviving than with winning or losing, but never mind, that's not a disaster, that's good, because of course I'm going to do my best to help you, just as a good friend should, and I'm sure that together we'll be able to sort out these horrid problems of yours. But to be quite honest, darling, I think you're suffering from nervous exhaustion brought on by overwork."

"You've understood nothing." He got out of bed and groped for his dressing gown.

"I understand that you need a thorough rest!"

"But I can't rest. That's the point."

"Yes, but once this murder case is finished—"

He walked out. I stared after him. Then I jumped out of bed and pulled on my kimono. By the time I reached the dining room he was drinking brandy by the sideboard.

"Robert, I do want to help—you're not being very fair to me—"

"I'm sorry. That's true. I haven't told you the whole story, that's the trouble. But perhaps I should." He looked down at the brandy in his glass. Then he said slowly, "This reminds me of the morning when my father talked to me about you. He didn't start by saying he wanted to talk about you, of course. He said, 'I want to tell you about my parents and Owain Bryn-Davies.' It was because he knew that only by talking of his adolescence could he explain why he did what he did to you, and I now feel that only by talking of the mountaineering can I attempt to show you why I feel my present life has very little connection with the kind of man I really am.... Or should I keep my mouth shut? You're looking appalled. I'm sorry, I didn't mean to upset you by mentioning my father."

I gave him the only possible response. "Pour me some brandy too, please, and let's sit down at the table."

Robert poured me some brandy. We sat down. And then the horrors really began.

"All my life," said Robert, "I've been made to understand that I'm unusually gifted. This has been my father's attitude to me ever since I can remember. This was the attitude of my teachers at school. And finally at Oxford the tutors at Balliol confirmed that I could have an outstanding career in law and politics, the road to the highest offices in the land—and of course I had no quarrel with this vision. It all seemed so attractive that I accepted it unquestioningly. But I didn't think, Ginette. Until I saw the mountains I never applied my so-called exceptional intellect to asking the simplest and most important of questions: what did I really want to do with my life? And then I saw the mountains and I knew. I just wanted to climb. Nothing else mattered.

"Afterwards—after it was all over—I told myself I'd undergone a form of insanity which had resembled a cancer on my personality. So I cut out the cancer: I abandoned mountaineering. But now I feel dead. And lately I've come to ask myself, Which was the real cancer? The academic life followed by fame and fortune at the bar? Or the climber's life which I rejected? And I have this terrible suspicion that it's the life I now lead which is killing me, strangling my personality and blighting my soul.

"Why did I actually give up mountaineering? I'd had a shock, of course. I was stunned not only with grief but with a rage against death—the rage which ultimately led me to the Old Bailey; I found I had to fight death in order to come to terms with the loss of my friends, but I found too that I couldn't fight death anymore on the mountains, I had to find another theater of war.

"But I know now that I didn't give up mountaineering just because I'd had a shock. I gave it up because I was a coward—yes, I gave it up because I was afraid, that was the truth of it, afraid of death. And I'm still afraid. Dying is losing. To die is to fail—and to fail utterly because once one's dead there can be no second chances; one can never go winning again.

"So I turned back to the academic life where there was no risk of dying. I'd been on the brink of wrecking my university career but at that point I realized I could still save it, I could still emerge a winner ready to master this brilliant future which had been forecast for me. So I did it—coward that I was, I did it: I took the easy way out. Back I went up to Oxford to conform, to crucify myself and to win.

"But I can see those mountains so clearly in my mind's eye. Oh Christ, how I loved those mountains.... When one's climbing one exists in a very simple world from which all the trivialities and irrelevancies have been cauterized. It's all so beautiful, so exciting—and best of all there's the unique comradeship with one's fellow climbers and the satisfaction of being a man among men—"

I could keep silent no longer. "And what consolation was that to you," I said, "when your three friends were killed?"

"You don't understand. Well, you're a woman, I suppose you can't. It doesn't matter."

"Of course it matters and it's possible—just possible—that I'm capable of understanding this peculiarity better than you yourself do. You seem to be describing some sort of compulsion to escape from the realities of life. I believe it's very common among young people growing up—they can't face adult life so they retreat into a fairy-tale world of their own creation—"

"What nonsense! Mountaineering *was* my reality!"

"Then tell me more about it so that I can understand. Tell me exactly what happened on this last climb of yours."

"You'll never understand."

"Why not? Think of me as an asinine juror who has to be conquered!"

This challenge proved too tempting for him to resist. Pouring himself some more brandy he said, "Very well, try and imagine a January day in Scotland—we'd reached the stage, you see, when we found winter climbing more exciting. It had snowed but the snow was crisp and conditions were good. We set off from Fort William, my friends and I, and I was so happy, I remember how happy I was—I suppose when all's said and done I prefer the company of men, and if it wasn't for sex I wouldn't bother with women at all—apart from you. My dearest Ginette! Putting the bedroom aside for a moment, I can honestly say that you're the only woman I've ever met who can be good company just like a man.

"Well, there we were, heading for Ben Nevis, and both women and bedrooms were far away, thank God, so we were able to concentrate on our...is 'calling' too strong a word? The term 'obsession' describes nothing here. It omits the spirituality. That morning I felt at one with God—in whom I didn't believe—and at one with the universe; I felt as if I were playing an allotted part in the scheme of things; I felt intensely happy and completely fulfilled—and *this* for me was real life. Everything else was makeshift and make-believe."

"Yes, but...No, I'm sorry. Go on."

"We decided on an easy climb up the Tower Ridge. The main difficulties lie in the first three hundred feet, but we overcame those easily enough and we then decided for fun to take the last stretch as a diagonal climb to make the expedition more of a challenge." He paused as if he expected me to make some disparaging remark, but when I said nothing he continued: "There was a very high wind, and this had two results which were crucial. The first was that it meant a large amount of new snow had accumulated, and the second was that we didn't notice when the temperature suddenly began to rise. We were all roped together. I was the last man. We were skirting an overhanging rock as we moved around the corner of the mountainside. The other three had completed the stretch successfully and were out of sight when my rope snagged and I had to stop. The only thing to do was to untie the rope from my waist so that I could unhook myself, and I was just flicking the rope free when the end came.

"There was a tremendous roar. It was like the end of the world. I flung myself under the overhang and saw the loose rope whipped from my fingers. Then at last the silence fell. I can't begin to describe my emotions. Eventually when I managed to get around the corner for a look, I saw that the whole face of the mountain had moved—a huge block of snow had broken free and slid a thousand feet or more towards the valley. There was no sign of my friends.

"I tried to go back but it was impossible without a rope and *then* I was frightened because I knew that if I had to spend a night on that mountain I could die of exposure. So I willed myself to keep warm. All through that night I fought to live but I knew Death wanted me, I could feel him there, and when the dawn came I saw him coming to claim me as he walked across the snow.

165

"He wore red—yes, red, not black—and he had a white face with no features.

"Of course I was hallucinating. The dawn light was playing tricks with the snow. But to me at that moment he was intensely real. 'Stay away from me!' I shouted, and I was so terrified because I thought he was going to win. But he didn't. He receded and vanished as the sun came up. The rescue party reached me soon afterwards. The doctor at Fort William was surprised not only that I was alive but that I wasn't suffering from frostbite. 'You'll survive unmarked!' he said, but he was wrong. There are some marks no doctors can see.

"I was marked by the guilt that I was alive while my three friends were dead. I was marked by my need to atone for my guilt by fighting death in revenge. And worst of all I was marked by my fear of death, because I had now seen so clearly that to die is to fail once and for all.

"As I've already said, I couldn't face that knowledge. I found I couldn't go back to the mountains because I was too afraid that next time I confronted death I'd lose—and yet... I was wrong, wasn't I? Death's everywhere, that's the truth of it. You can't hide from him, he'll come and get you when he wants you no matter where you are. So in that case the way to outwit him, in the limited time available, isn't to retreat into a way of life which is alien to you; the way to outwit him is to live the life you were put on this earth to lead. It's wrong to waste yourself in work that means nothing to you. It's not only a waste of talent. It's a prostitution of the soul.

"I've begun to think I'm wasting my life but I can't bear to think of that so I don't, and when I'm working like a demon I don't have to think of anything but the case in hand. But I want to go back to the mountains, and if I inherited a suitable fortune I'd abandon my London life without a backward glance and... I'm sorry, you obviously think I'm talking like a maniac so I must stop. Perhaps I was a fool to have said so much."

"Don't be absurd! It's vital that you should be absolutely frank with me—how else am I to understand your dilemma? But darling, I still think this huge pessimism of yours is largely due to the fact that you're worn out. Come back to bed and let's discuss it further later."

"I've horrified you, haven't I?"

"No, of course not, darling; don't be so silly. I'm just deeply concerned about your health."

"My God, if you start wishing you'd never married me—"

"Now you really are talking like a maniac!" I said, laughing, and at last I succeeded in coaxing him back to bed.

He's right. I'm horrified. Who would ever have thought Robert could be so convoluted and disordered? I mean, *I'm* the one who's supposed to be perpetually in a mess. One of the most important reasons why I married him was because I thought he could sort out my problems but now I find I have to sort out his. Well, I wouldn't mind doing that, but they're so bizarre and I'm not sure I can. Can Robert be on the brink of losing his mind altogether as the result of this case? But it seems he's been secretly like this for years. *Why did I never guess? Why did I never know?* I feel so shattered by the entire episode that I can hardly nerve myself to dwell on it, but I suppose I must try.

Robert is in love with mountaineering. Well, we all have our little peculiarities, but why can't he see this "calling" of his (honestly, what romantic exaggeration!) as just an undergraduate hobby which went disastrously wrong? And why does he have to talk like a demented disciple of muscular Christianity—all that rubbish about being a man among men (and to think men say women have the monopoly on sentimentality!) and all that rot about how women and sex pale in comparison with platonic masculine comradeship. Laying aside all sexual prejudice the rock-bottom truth of life is that women and sex mean the perpetuation of the human race and that platonic masculine comradeship is, as the Americans say, a dead-end street. Well, I mean, sex *is* life, isn't it? So how can Robert possibly argue that his obsession with mountaineering is in some way superior? And let's be honest: Robert likes sex as much as anyone, and he's absolutely normal there, thank God, and he'd be the first to object if he were condemned to perpetual chastity on a mountain with a bunch of male chums. I admit he's temporarily lost interest in sex but that's just the strain of this appalling case.

As for him saying he'd give up the law and London tomorrow if he had the means, that's just laughable. Robert would be *miserable* without his glamour and his fame, and he'd die of boredom if he were deprived of his life here for more than a month! He's a brilliant man and he enjoys worldly success. That's natural. To turn his back on it would be most unnatural and he'd soon be racked with regret.

Yes, I understand him better than he himself does. Poor Robert, what a state he was in; I did feel so sorry for him . . . But how simple Conor seems in retrospect! He knew what he wanted from life well enough, no muddled agonizing for him. "I want to have one hell of a good time!" I can hear him say it now—I can even hear him laughing. No obsession with death ever clouded his mind. All he cared about was life and that was all I cared about too.

Oh, I keep thinking the grief will fade, but it doesn't; it's still there and I miss him, I miss him dreadfully, I miss him and want him to come back. . . .

I nearly scratched out the above maudlin paragraph because I'm so ashamed of it, but I'll let it stand as a monument to the shock I felt at the time. I don't miss Conor as much as that; I only think I do when I'm feeling depressed. I'm so happy with Robert, and anyway he's better now because the case is over.

He lost. I was most apprehensive when I heard the news but Robert took his defeat better than I'd dared hope, although he was very quiet as he went off to see his client for the last time. However that's understandable. What on earth does one say to someone whose next appointment is with the gallows? Presumably Robert has a formula but nevertheless it must be a harrowing experience. However afterwards he went for a ride in the park and came back saying '*Mens sana in corpore sano*,' so presumably he now believes himself to be on the road to recovery.

167

Even *I* know what that Latin tag means. It means Robert's no longer sound asleep while I'm lying awake frustrated in the dark. It means I'm no longer seized by the urge to ransack Harrods to take my mind off my troubles. It means Robert is dining tonight with his friend Raymond Asquith, the Prime Minister's son, in an attempt to explore the future with someone who can give him sound advice.

Robert has a special respect for Raymond because Raymond's about the only person in London who's cleverer than he is; Raymond, with his numerous Oxford prizes and multiple academic honors, leaves even Robert, with his double first, outclassed. A gap of four years separates them in age but because of their Balliol background they have all manner of interests and acquaintances in common so I can well imagine them chatting away happily to each other, both thrilled to dine with someone of their own intellectual caliber for a change. Robert told me once that one of the worst things about being brilliant is that one finds most people dreadfully dull. Well, at least that'll never be one of my problems. I find people endlessly fascinating, and I like Raymond who, not content with being an intellectual phenomenon, is good-looking and charming, just like Robert, and normal enough to have a wife and two children as well as a successful career at the bar. If Raymond can apparently manage his life so happily and adroitly, then surely Robert can too.

But someone mentioned to me the other day that Raymond's problem was that he was without ambition. Perhaps Raymond too is convoluted and disordered beneath the shining surface of his life. How little we know even of those who are closest to us. How can we hope to know those with whom we're barely acquainted?

I'm becoming pessimistic again, so I must stop. But I can't help it, I'm still very worried indeed...

All's well. Thank God. Robert's decided to give up criminal law, since it undoubtedly feeds his obsession with death, and move to chancery chambers specializing in trusts. However that will take time to achieve, and while this rearrangement is taking place he'll start pursuing a political career in earnest. He's dining again this week with Raymond, and with them will be two successful Liberals of their own age, "Bluey" Baker and Edwin Montagu. At least Robert has first-class political connections, and I'm sure it won't be long before he's adopted as the prospective Liberal candidate for some promising constituency.

I couldn't be more pleased by this evidence that Robert's recovered his equilibrium. Really, I can't think why I let myself get so upset! I might have known that brilliant rational Robert would be able to sort out his problems efficiently in the end...

Robert's just told me he wants to give everything up—the law, London, any hope of a political career—and live cheaply in the country so that he can afford to return to mountaineering.

I realize at once that this is some form of delayed nervous breakdown so I don't have hysterics. I keep very calm and ask him what we're going to do about money, because even the smallest gentleman's residence in the country can hardly be run on a shoestring.

He tells me there's only one solution. We must live at Oxmoon—not in the main house, he hastens to add (no doubt I looked as if I were about to faint), but on the estate. He can ask his father for a portion in advance of his inheritance, and if Bobby cedes him one of the major farms, then the farmhouse itself can be improved and extended into a residence suitable for a gentleman; Bobby would probably even offer to pay the cost of the alterations because he would be so pleased to have Robert back in Gower. Then we could rent the house in Ebury Street to boost our income, and it would certainly need boosting even though Robert thinks he might be able to earn the odd sum here and there by writing, first about his famous trials and later about his mountaineering. However he has a little capital, I have the income from my trust fund and we would both have the small income from our future farm, so, as Robert himself points out, we wouldn't starve; he would be able to return to the mountains, and whenever he came home I would be waiting for him at Oxmoon, just as I'd been waiting in the old days, and then the Oxmoon of our childhood would finally be recaptured and we would live happily ever after encased in a glowing aura of romantic nostalgia.

I've asked for time to consider this ridiculous fantasy—I really can't dignify it by calling it a plan—and Robert has said yes, of course I must have time, and of course he realizes what a shock he must have given me, and he's very, very sorry but he can no longer go on living a meaningless life.

Quite.

Oddly enough now that I've stopped burying my head in the sand and telling myself that everything in the garden's lovely, I do feel much better. This is because I'm no longer worrying about what might happen; I'm worrying about what *has* happened and can concentrate on solving a specific problem. For of course I can't let him make this catastrophic mistake. I've got to stop him, and as far as I can see my only hope of doing so lies in presenting him with the brutal truths he's apparently unable to face.

We've been married eight weeks today. What a mess. Never mind, once we're over this crisis, matters must surely improve. God knows they could hardly get any worse.

"Robert, before I start I want to apologize for what I'm going to say. I'd never be so brutal unless I honestly felt I had no alternative."

"Go on."

"I can't live on your parents' doorstep. But that's not my major objection to your plan. My main objection is that I don't believe you could live on their doorstep either."

There was a silence. We had cancelled our evening engagement and were alone after dinner in the drawing room. Robert was standing by the fireplace, his eyes watching the flames flickering in the grate, but as the silence lengthened he turned to face me, one hand remaining on the mantelshelf as if he felt the need to steady himself. I was sitting on the edge of the sofa. We were some eight feet apart.

"It's no good you pretending that we can ever have a normal relationship with your parents," I said, "because we can't. It's impossible."

He said evenly, "I've forgiven my father. He's a deeply damaged man. I must forgive him."

"I was damaged too. And he damaged me."

"That's all in the past now."

"That's exactly where you're wrong, Robert. We may all pretend everything's forgiven and forgotten, but that's just to keep ourselves sane. The reality is much more appalling than you've ever allowed yourself to acknowledge but if we were to move to Gower you'd have to face that reality every day, and quite frankly I don't think you could do it."

"I—"

"The truth is that every time I see Bobby and Margaret I remember—we all remember—all that past horror lives again in our minds. I admit you're a late-comer to this horror, but no matter what you say you can't persuade me you're unaffected by it. I think you're very affected by it, but you've managed to gloss over the problem in your mind because we're two hundred miles from Oxmoon and living a life in which your parents have no part to play. You forgive your father, you say. That's admirable. But is it true? You're a jealous possessive man and I don't believe you could ever tolerate for long the company of a man who you knew had gone to bed with me. I suppose you think that with sufficient willpower anything's possible, but I think this is the kind of situation, Robert, that could break your will in two, put us all through hell and wreck our marriage."

He made no effort to dispute this. After a protracted pause he said with distressing awkwardness, "You don't think that if we were both back at Oxmoon we could recapture the magic of the lost Oxmoon where we were so happy?"

"No," I said. "That's a romantic and sentimental notion which has nothing to do with reality. I can't take you back to that magic Oxmoon, Robert, because the magic was destroyed and can never now be recaptured. I'm sorry but I can't work that particular miracle for you."

"Yet sometimes," he said, "in your company, I see those days live again."

"Well, you certainly wouldn't if we removed now to Oxmoon. All you'd see in your mind would be your father crawling into bed with me and pulling up his nightshirt."

He flinched and turned away. Jumping up I ran to him. "Darling, forgive me, I'm being so cruel, I know I am, but I've got to make you see—"

"Won't you ever want to go back?"

"Yes," I said. "When Bobby's dead and Margaret's pensioned off somewhere and you're Prime Minister, I shall be delighted to spend part of the year there. We can make it into a weekend retreat for all the most famous people of the day!"

He gave a small painful smile and said nothing.

"Darling..." I put my arms around him. "Don't think I'm unsympathetic about the mountaineering—I do understand how much it means to you; but treat it as a hobby. To devote your life to it would be to give way to an obsession—it would be most unhealthy. Why don't you at least give politics a try? I can't understand why you've recoiled from it like this."

"Raymond was talking the other day of the futility of it all."

"But he's been adopted as the prospective candidate for Derby!" I was now definitely having second thoughts about Raymond Asquith. I wondered what *his* wife had to go through whenever he suffered a bout of nihilism.

"Raymond's feelings are very complex," said Robert. "But it can't be easy to be the son of the Prime Minister."

"Well, at least you're spared that problem! Maybe you should see less of Raymond and more of someone like Edwin Montagu, who's so brilliant and so ambitious and thinks politics is the only life for a man."

Robert said nothing.

"Darling..." I kissed him. "Please—for my sake—do nothing rash. Do nothing you might regret later."

He nodded, still mute. I kissed him again and suggested we went to bed, but he said he wanted to think a little more so I went upstairs alone. Naturally I was too nervous to sleep. I lay awake and at last, well after midnight, he joined me.

"Do you love me?" he said as we lay beside each other in the dark.

"Darling, you know I do."

"Then all's well," said Robert. "I'd give up everything for you, even mountaineering."

"But I'm not asking you to give up mountaineering!"

"I couldn't treat it as a hobby. Either I devote my life to it or I don't, but so long as you love me I don't much care about anything else. Anyway, if we can't go back to Oxmoon I can't afford a removal to the country, and if we can't live cheaply in the country I can't go back to mountaineering. Problem solved."

He began to make love to me with his usual efficiency but the performance went wrong, and afterwards I had to hug him tightly to show I didn't mind. Conor would have said, "Holy shit!" and hugged me back before falling asleep, but Robert was silent and tense in my arms, and I knew he was racked by a sense of failure.

"Darling, *don't* worry, please don't—I know ten seconds isn't such fun as ten minutes—or longer—but no one can be perfect in bed all the time!"

"What about Kinsella?"

I knew a moment of horrified panic but I somehow managed to answer briskly, "Good heavens, Robert, surely you know hard drinkers aren't always perfect in the bedroom!"

That satisfied him. He went to sleep but I continued to lie awake, and despite the renewal of his decision to enter politics, I knew our marriage was still in very great trouble indeed.

· · ·

171

I'm praying that was rock-bottom. Surely after this matters can only improve. If only Robert doesn't have to wait too long for the opportunity to enter Parliament! I'm sure that once he reaches Westminster he'll be thoroughly happy and then our worst problems will be at an end—or at the very least considerably eased.

Meanwhile his career at the bar is still worrying him. He's decided he would be a fool to leave his common-law chambers, since it would inevitably entail a drop in income while he built up a new reputation for himself as a chancery lawyer, and anyway he thinks he'd be bored to tears with trusts or tax. In his opinion he would be better off staying with the criminal cases and trying to specialize in nonviolent crimes such as fraud, but I do wish he could get right away from crime. However in a few years' time it won't matter because he'll be in the Cabinet with a substantial salary and then he can retire from the law altogether.

But first of all he must get into Parliament. Since the Prime Minister's taking such a benign interest in him I doubt if he'll have to wait long, but any wait is tiresome, particularly in these nerve-racking circumstances, so I've made up my mind to do all I can to make life smooth for Robert at home.

I'm counting not only the pennies but the ha'pennies and farthings in the generous allowance he gives me, and I'm drawing up elaborate accounts so that he can see how clever I can be with money when I put my mind to it. I'm also refusing to go anywhere near Harrods. In fact I'm at the point where all I need is polish for my halo, but it's such hard work being parsimonious that I've barely had the strength to tackle the problem of the boys.

Nevertheless I managed to dredge up sufficient nerve to tell Declan that if he could survive till the end of term without being expelled I'd let him spend the Easter holidays in Ireland. So now he's in Dublin. It was the only answer, as my marriage couldn't have stood another onslaught from Declan at the moment. However Rory I summoned to London, and now here he is, good as gold without Declan and enjoying his outings with me to galleries, museums and picture theaters. I must say, I feel rather dashing going to picture theaters—so amusingly *déclassée!* Robert doesn't approve of me going to a darkened room frequented by the lower classes, but he quite understands that darling Rory would punch any man who tried to be uppish with me when the film broke down.

I'm much happier about Rory, and I really think he'll survive this chaotic year intact. He does moan that he hates school, but I'm not going to be upset by that (a) because I can't afford to be and (b) because Rory's gregarious and I honestly think that once he's thoroughly settled he'll enjoy school very much. He's not as clever as Declan but he's good at games, and in an English public school this is a guarantee of happiness; the poor little love said they stopped calling him Yankee scum when they realized he was good at rugger.

I did say I was willing to spend Easter at Oxmoon but Robert just said, "No, that's not necessary," so I think my speech about the ever-present nature of the past horrors must have sunk in. We'll have to go down for Christmas, of course— there's no way out of that obligation, but I've told Robert I accept this and that he's not to worry about me when December comes. What a relief to have that situation clearly defined! I can face Oxmoon once a year. Just.

Bobby visits London regularly, but although Robert conscientiously sees him, I don't. I must say, I do admire Robert for maintaining the trappings of a normal relationship with his father. I'd love to know what he says in his weekly letters to his mother but Margaret in her elaborate replies gives little clue. After transforming the task of saying nothing into a high art, she always sends her love to me and she never, never reproaches either of us for avoiding Oxmoon. This makes me feel so guilty that I try not to think of her, but even this coward's course isn't available to me at the moment because she's just written to ask if we can have Lion to stay. He's got a new post in a City bank, and he needs a roof over his head while he finds himself some bachelor chambers.

Lion is traditionally accepted as being Margaret's favorite, and this, of course, is why she writes to me with her request and not to Robert. She knows Robert would make some excuse not to have Lion, just as she knows I can't possibly refuse her, but nonetheless Lion's arrival will create an awkward situation because Robert is very possessive at the moment; it's as if he has to be constantly reassured that I love him, and this means I have to give him my undivided attention whenever he comes home. He won't want me to be distracted by any visitor, least of all Lion. Personally I adore Lion and I can quite see why Margaret turns to him in relief after struggling with the more tortuous-minded members of her family, for Lion's nature is so simple and open. He's always cheerful, always bursting with high spirits, always exactly what he appears to be—ingenuous, naughty and, beneath the bombastic manners, as gentle and kind as Edmund. Yes, darling Lion is blissfully straightforward and darling Lion must definitely come to stay, but to keep the peace I'll need every ounce of diplomatic skill I possess.

Was there ever a first year of marriage like this one? Honestly, I think if I survive to celebrate the first anniversary I ought to be given a gold medal—or perhaps one of those ghastly silver cups awarded to Robert during the course of his morbid and sinister career as a winner...

Darling Lion has confided in me. He *is* a pet. He says he doesn't think he was designed by nature to earn his living, so he's had a brilliant idea: he's going to marry an heiress. He tells me this as if no penniless young man had ever thought of it before, and adds quickly that his only requirement is that he must be passionately in love.

"However," says sunny-natured Lion, beaming at me from ear to ear, "that's no difficulty because I fall in love all the time, nothing to it, easiest thing in the world. I'm sure I can very easily fall in love with a girl who's rich if I put my mind to it."

Robert tells me Lion's being ridiculous because no rich girl in her right mind would dream of marrying him.

But I'm not so sure. Lion may be plain and he may be brainless, but he's six feet five in his stockinged feet and he has a splendid physique to complement his engaging personality, and I think there might well be an heiress who'll find him irresistible.

Anyway I've promised to do all I can to help. It'll take my mind off my marital problems, and besides... poor darling brainless penniless Lion really does need all the help he can get.

Life has been transformed—salvation is at hand! A Labour M.P. has dropped dead in South Wales, and Robert has been adopted by the Liberal Party as their candidate in the inevitable bye-election! The only trouble is that although Wales is a Liberal stronghold, this constituency of Pwlldu beyond the Rhondda Valley is so impoverished that the dreaded Labour Party has gained a grip on its voting population. The area is so scarred with coal mining that it looks like a fouled desert, the long bleak streets are lined with terrace-house slums, the children are barefoot, the women are old at thirty and the men are wizened and choking with coal-dust disease.

What can Harrow-and-Balliol Robert, one of Britain's charmed elite, say to such people? The new Labour candidate is a man of the working classes, a Welsh-speaking demagogue who wants people like Robert exterminated and the nation's wealth redistributed. I shudder but Robert is greatly stimulated. What a challenge! He can't resist it. Soon he's forgotten all his problems. He's too busy perfecting his rusty Welsh by hiring a tutor to converse with him, too busy planning strategy, too busy going respectfully to Mr. Lloyd George for tactical advice.

Mr. Lloyd George has always been friendly towards Robert, though in a detached way because Robert is an Asquith protégé, but now Mr. Lloyd George is beginning, like a baby, to "sit up and take notice." Mr. Lloyd George, naughty man, is certainly taking notice of *me* but luckily I find him absolutely resistible: too old, too crooked, too full of empty charm.

For the coming election I've ordered some new clothes, absolutely plain, all black and navy, no trimmings, and I'm cultivating a serious austere air so that no one will want to murder me for being a Society woman with a penchant for raiding divine Harrods. I've also been practicing "You *will* vote for my husband, won't you?" in Welsh in front of the looking glass. I can't remember much of the Welsh that we all picked up in a haphazard fashion from the Welsh-speaking nursemaids whom Margaret employed, but at least I can brush up a few choice phrases, and Mr. Lloyd George tells me my accent is superb.

Robert laughs admiringly as I trot out my Welsh phrases, and when he laughs I laugh too so that suddenly, miraculously, we're happy once more, no longer an ill-assorted husband and wife but *friends*, rushing off hand in hand into a thrilling new adventure.

"My dearest Ginette!" says Robert shining-eyed, and as he kisses me I know he doesn't mind anymore about his absurd plan to withdraw from London, just as I know that he's grateful to me for standing by him in his hour of need, just as a friend should, to stop him making such a terrible mistake.

"I love you," I say, and I do. I'm deeply connected to him by some unique emotion which has nothing to do with any conventional idea of passion—and suddenly as I realize this I know that in our minds we're back at Oxmoon, the lost Oxmoon of our childhood, and I can see the strawberries ripening beneath the powerful summer sun.

Life is still absolutely stunning—oh, I *am* enjoying myself! Robert has just made his last speech before the election, every word in Welsh, and his audience has cheered him to the echo. How did he do it? He's told his listeners that he's a Welshman but because he's had an English education he has a unique insight into those English minds at Westminster, and therefore he, unlike his opponent, is qualified to play the English at their own game with lasting benefit for Pwlldu. This is all nonsense, of course, but by playing on their nationalism he avoids the issue of class on which his opponent had hoped to impale him. And then, thrill of thrills, triumph of triumphs, Mr. Lloyd George, the greatest Welsh statesman since Owen Glendower, appears on the platform to endorse Robert's views and the audience go wild.

Victory is still touch-and-go, but if Robert does win tomorrow it will be a tremendous triumph not only for him but for the Liberal Party, which has lost too many seats to the Unionists in various bye-elections since the second general election of 1910. In fact the Unionists now have more seats in the House than the Liberals, and although at present the Labour Party backs Mr. Asquith, such support might prove unreliable in shifting circumstances, and obviously the Liberals would prefer to have their own man representing Pwlldu rather than a Labour ally who might or might not be loyal in the days to come.

I've been modest and retiring, loyal and admiring, bold and courageous, meek and mild, depending on which performance each occasion has required. I've been asked regularly for my views on the suffragettes, but I just say, "I love my husband and I think a woman's place is in the home." However I'm beginning to think I'd rather like to be a Member of Parliament. All that glamour, that excitement, that intrigue, that power—delicious! I can see myself wearing trousers and smoking a cigar, like George Sand, and briskly calling the Cabinet to order.

Enough! No more idle fantasy. I'll never have the vote and I'll never have a seat in the House and I'll certainly never be Prime Minister. But I really do think darling Robert's going to be a huge political success, and that, when all's said and done, will be quite enough for me.

He did it. He won. He had a majority of over a thousand votes, and when the result was announced the waiting crowd began to sing "Land of Our Fathers." I cried. The party organizers cried. Robert wanted to cry but his English stiff upper lip was too much for him and he couldn't bring himself to do it. But he was very moved and very thrilled and afterwards, long afterwards when we were finally alone together, he thanked me for pushing him into politics and said he realized now that I had been absolutely right and he had been absolutely wrong on the subject of our withdrawal from London.

There's nothing mean about Robert. He's warm and honest and generous to his friends. We'll live in amity now, I'm sure of it, and all those horrid marital quarrels will belong entirely to the past as I continue to share his new career. Am I really being too optimistic if I write that I feel our long-delayed marital happiness is finally about to begin?

I wasn't being too optimistic. Our long-delayed marital happiness has begun, and please God may it go on forever. We've swept back to London in triumph and now everyone, but *everyone*, is panting to know us and we've been scooped into a frenetic social whirl.

I'm now passionate about London. All the trees are lush and green, all the flowers are glowing in the parks, a brilliant sun is blazing from cloudless skies. High noon in the capital of the world, high summer in ravishing glorious 1914 and there's no limit to the glamour and the gorgeousness—it's like the finale of some stupendous symphony except that unlike any other symphonic finale this one is set to stream on indefinitely with no end in sight. How lucky I am to be moderately young, moderately rich, vastly fortunate and vastly happy in such a place and at such a time! I feel now that nothing can stop all my dreams coming true.

Robert says we're riding the Wheel of Fortune; we've been at the bottom and now we're being carried right to the breathtaking top. What an alluring picture that conjures up! Robert says it's not an original metaphor of his as it was made famous by some old pet called Boethius who lived in the year dot. Darling Robert, always so intellectual! However I must confess that at the moment my thoughts tend to center on more prosaic matters, such as how I can acquire the evening gowns I need without propelling Robert into bankruptcy.

However Robert is perfect when I confess to him that I'm worried about my wardrobe, and he quite understands how important it is for me to be well dressed. In and out of all the famous houses we go—from Taplow to Panshanger, from Alderley to Avon Tyrrell, from Mells to the Wharf—we eat, we drink, we dance, we patronize the theater, the opera, Ascot and Henley—life's one long sumptuous party but like all parties it's hard work. One needs plenty of stamina. But I feel so full of *joie de vivre* that I barely notice any weariness, and Robert, still working hard at the bar, somehow manages to look radiant on four or five hours' sleep a night. He wants to accumulate as much money as possible this summer so that he can give his full attention to politics after the coming recess.

I simply doted on Number Ten when we were invited to dine there. I know they say Mr. Asquith drinks too much (When? Where? I've never seen any sign of it), but he's *such* a pet and I think he's just as keen on women as Mr. Lloyd George is although no doubt he's kept in check by the terrifying Margot. Or is he? I heard someone say... But no, I will *not* let this entry degenerate into vulgar tittle-tattle, no matter how much I adore finding out what *really* goes on behind the scenes! I always feel sorry for men having to pretend to be above gossip. So dreary for them, poor dears.

Anyway I'm in such a whirl I can hardly fit my appointments with my dressmaker into my crowded calendar, but I haven't forgotten Lion, who's busily bounding around looking for an heiress, and he has an open invitation to call at our house whenever he likes. I thought he might share chambers with Johnny, who's also working in town now, but they preferred to go their separate ways. In order to be fair, though, I've also given Johnny an open invitation to our house so now here I am with these two eligible young men on my hands, and I'm beginning to feel like Mrs. Bennet in *Pride and Prejudice,* a woman unable to think of anything except matrimony for her loved ones. Actually Johnny's too young for marriage; he's only twenty-two, whereas Lion's twenty-four, but Johnny is looking for a wife, I can sense that just as I can sense that he too is after money. But he doesn't confide in me. I used to think he confided in Robert, whom he hero-worships, but I now realize they talk only of intellectual matters.

Enigmatic Johnny, Bobby and Margaret's male replica of Bobby's beautiful, doomed, passionate mother—but unfortunately this romantic resemblance is only skin-deep. Johnny may be beautiful in his masculine way but he'll never wind up doomed; he's much too clever and ambitious, and he hasn't a scrap of passion in his prim puritanical little mind.

However I feel mean criticizing this paragon because he's pleasant and courteous and he really is doing very well. Having won a first in modern languages at Oxford he passed third out of four hundred entrants in the Foreign Office examinations and is now settling down to be a success as a diplomat. Obviously he's toiling away trying to follow in Robert's brilliant footsteps, but this must be an unrewarding occupation, because Robert is so exceptional that Johnny, despite his considerable achievements, is always going to end up coming second. A first but no double first for Johnny at Oxford, no blues at cricket or rugger although he's good at games, no glamour and fame at his worthy but possibly dull position at the F.O. In fact if I were Johnny I'd loathe Robert but he doesn't. Johnny doesn't loathe anyone because that wouldn't be the Done Thing, and Doing the Done Thing is Johnny's prime delight in life. He's such a single-minded prig that I even wonder if he's a virgin but no, he can't be, he's much too good-looking, although his personality is so aseptic that I don't find him sexually attractive. That's just as well because no doubt Johnny would think that being sexually attractive isn't the Done Thing at all.

"Ginevra," he said to me the other day, "would you mind not calling me Johnny? I'm not in the nursery now and I find the name somewhat undignified."

I find it the only available antidote to his dreariness. Poor Johnny! So dull.

However Johnny can look after himself without my help. Lion can't. We toil away together hatching elaborate schemes as we plot the downfall of every heiress in sight, and whenever he wants to give up in despair I harangue him until he's feeling more cheerful. We usually end up giggling together. Robert hates this so we have to be careful not to giggle in his presence. Lion's terrified of Robert, and although he resents Robert's coldness he would secretly love to be friends so that he wouldn't have to be terrified anymore. He has a deep admiration of Robert's achievements and speaks reverently of Robert's intellect. I find this touching and tell Robert so.

"I'm getting very tired of Lion perpetually occupying my drawing room" is all Robert can say in reply. "Can you make it clear that I'd prefer him to call less often?"

Back we are in the nursery again. Robert isn't sexually jealous of Lion, of course, but he just can't bear not being the center of my attention. It reminds me of those dreadful scenes he made after Lion was born when he realized there was another little boy who had a claim on Margaret's time.

I somehow conceal my impatience and resentment but I'm determined not to abandon Lion. Without my constant encouragement he'd drift away brokenhearted to Oxmoon, but in my opinion he deserves a rich wife. After all, these rich girls have to marry, and think what ghastly men they constantly choose! Lion's not ghastly. He's affectionate and lovable, and he'll be so pleased to be saved from the dreariness of earning a living that he's bound to adore his savior. I think she'll be a very lucky girl . . . if we can find her.

Luckily Robert's been diverted from Lion by politics because he's now absorbed with the ordeal of making his maiden speech in the House. As a woman I was brought up to be uninterested in political issues. Margaret said all I needed to know was that the Liberals were for change and freedom while the Tories (as they were called when I was young) were wicked enough to want everything to stay exactly the same, even the poverty and suffering. The Godwins were a Whig family in the eighteenth century, and in the nineteenth they drifted along with the Liberal tide. Bobby is actually quite radical, despite his place in that established order which the Unionists seek to preserve unchanged. Bobby said to me once that anyone who had known impoverishment could never vote for the Unionists.

When Robert entered politics I wondered whether to study the big political issues such as Free Trade and Home Rule, but Robert said the last thing he wanted was a wife who held forth on politics, so I didn't bother. However I'm beginning to be interested in the major issues of the day and I do wish Robert would speak on Ireland. Declan would be impressed by his advanced views, but Robert is shying away from that graveyard of political reputations and says he intends to speak on foreign affairs. Such a pity, because what could be more dreary than foreign affairs at this time? Something's going on in the Balkans as usual but honestly, who cares? Something's always going on in the Balkans; it's a standing joke, just like that hoary old warning regularly issued by the Job's Comforters that we're on the brink of war. I've been hearing that for years and I'll believe it when it happens. Meanwhile the Balkans are a big bore as usual. Let the Balkanese get on with it, I say, and good luck to them. I've got more important things to worry about.

What am I going to wear when Robert makes his maiden speech?

• • •

What a stunning success we both were yesterday! I wore royal blue, the skirt of the costume so narrow at the ankle that I could barely glide, and the material draped and swathed in gorgeous curvy lines over my hips and legs. A new corset and three days' rigorous banting had ensured a slim waist, and all the surplus flesh above was pushed upwards so that my bosom, discreetly swathed beneath pale blue trimmings, was guaranteed to rivet the male eye. I also wore a sumptuous new hat decorated with osprey feathers (thirty guineas at divine Harrods), and when I entered the gallery even the male monsters on the benches below dropped their eyeglasses and gaped. Sometimes I do think the suffragettes are very stupid. They shouldn't go around wrecking everything in sight. All they need to do to get the vote is wear splendid hats and look lavish.

Darling Robert made a wonderful speech about the boring old Balkans and was warmly congratulated. Later so was I—in fact we were both positively weighed down with "dewdrops" and the evening finished in a haze of champagne. What heaven! I adored every minute of it, and in the midst of so much euphoria I quite forgot Lion but lo and behold, today he's appeared again, madly in love, and says this is *it* and please could I help him and he's utterly desperate because he knows his whole future happiness is at stake.

She's perfect for him. Her name is Daphne Wynter-Hamilton, and her father, Sir Cuthbert, has a house in Belgravia and thousands of acres in Scotland complete with castle and grouse moor. Daphne is an only child. Her father dotes on her— and her wretched mother, of course, wants her to marry someone with a title and ten thousand a year.

But this is a nice, sensible girl, not pretty but very jolly, and she doesn't mind Lion having no money. She's passionate about him and he's passionate about her and whenever they're not giggling together they're sighing into each other's eyes. Yes, they must certainly marry but how are we going to overcome the cold-eyed mother who thinks a penniless younger son of an untitled Welsh squire is about as low as one can go without sinking into the middle classes?

I'm going to ask Robert if he can cultivate Sir Cuthbert.

"Good God, certainly not!" said Robert. "Let Lion fight his own battles! Ginette, you'll oblige me, if you please, by doing as I say and terminating this consuming interest you have in Lion's affairs. I'm not prepared to tolerate it any longer, and for the good of our marriage I'm now drawing the line."

I'm back with my husband again. My friend has vanished. I'm back with this ghastly male monster who says that for the good of our marriage I should obey him unquestioningly—even when he's being unreasonable and wrong.

Of course we've just had the most appalling row. I felt so angry with Robert after our clash this afternoon that this evening I flirted with a charming American

179

at a reception in Grosvenor Square. I knew at the time that it was a stupid thing to do, but I wanted Robert to know how livid I was with him.

I'll never do it again, though, because just now, when we were shouting at each other in the bedroom, I felt genuinely frightened. Violence always frightens me and Robert is potentially a violent man. Curiously enough Conor, who was certainly a violent man in some ways, was never violent with me; when he wanted to hurt me he just slept with someone else or perhaps extorted my money to lose at poker. But that's not Robert's style. Robert's style is first to slap me so hard across the mouth that I fall backwards across the bed and second to assert himself in the most obvious way available. It's not rape exactly because I'm sensible enough to give in without a fight, but whatever it is, it's vile. All I could think in the bathroom afterwards was: Conor would never have done that, never, never, never. And to my horror I found myself grieving for Conor all over again.

Robert apologized afterwards but spoiled the apology by adding: "Nevertheless I'm your husband and I'm entitled to make a strong demonstration of my marital rights if you appear to need reminding of your marital duties." Anyone would think I'd been guilty of the grossest infidelity, yet all I had done was flutter my eyelashes at this inoffensive diplomat over a glass of champagne.

However with great self-restraint I made no comment on Robert's monstrous statement and presently in bed in the dark, he slipped his hand into mine to show he wanted to be friends. What's my final verdict? Oh, I daresay we shall be friends again in a day or two. I don't mind Robert when he's trying to be a friend. It's when he's trying to be a husband that he's so absolutely bloody impossible.

I now feel quite exhausted with getting Lion off my hands, almost too exhausted to consider the problem of the school holidays. Declan is determined to go to Ireland again and Rory is determined to go too, but although I'm not keen on this I feel I can't cope with them here while Robert's being even more possessive than usual. With reluctance I shall tell them that they can spend the first month of the holidays with Dervla and Seamus but the second month must be spent with me—and yet I'm sure now, if I drum up the courage to be honest with myself, that this time when Declan goes to Ireland he'll have no intention of ever coming back.

How did the war creep on me like this? One moment I was thinking of Lion battling for Daphne and worrying what in God's name I was going to do about Declan, and the next moment the ultimatum was expiring and the Germans were on the rampage. I know a great many people felt they had been taken by surprise but I thought I should have been more aware of what was going on.

"Why didn't you tell me how crucial matters had become, Robert?"

"I thought all you cared about was getting Lion married."

Robert's still being thoroughly impossible. I know I should put matters right by being especially warm and loving to him, but frankly I can't be bothered. I want someone to be warm and loving to *me*. I'm desperately upset about Declan, and I'll never forget that dreadful scene two weeks ago on the eve of his departure for Ireland. . . .

"Declan, you're not coming back, are you?"

"No, I'm sorry, Ma, but it's impossible. I promised Cousin Bobby I'd stick it for a year to see if things got better, but they haven't. I loathe that school. I loathe England. I loathe Robert."

"Do you loathe me?"

"Yes, sometimes. But generally I just feel you're no use to me and I'd be better off on my own. Are you going to raise hell if I don't come back?"

"There's no point, is there?"

We were silent for a time. We were in his room, which only so recently I had planned for him with such care. It still looked new and unused, a symbol of his hatred of the house and everyone in it. Declan looked older than fifteen because he was tall. His dark hair grew exactly like Conor's and even waved in the same places. His dark eyes, also exactly like Conor's, regarded me with gravity. A lump formed in my throat. I turned away.

"Will you remember," I said to him, "that this separation's not of my choosing? Will you remember that whatever happens I love you and will always want you to come back?"

"I couldn't come back so long as you're married to Robert, Ma. So it's no use wanting the impossible."

"But you'll write to me?"

"No. I don't want any correspondence. I want to start again without having to read your letters telling me how miserable I've made you."

"I wouldn't reproach you, I swear it—"

"The very letters would be a reproach. I'll send news regularly to Aunt Dervla, and if you want to know what's happening you can write to her."

"Oh Declan—"

"No, it's no use crying, Ma. You've brought all this on yourself, behaving like a whore, betraying Pa's memory, smashing all my faith in you by marrying a bastard like Robert—"

I left him, and the next day he left me. I managed to control myself at the station but when I arrived home I shut myself in my darkened room and cried as I had not cried since Conor's death fourteen months before.

"I'm sorry," said Robert. "Very sorry. I know how you must feel. But it may all be for the best."

My nerve snapped. I flew at him, hit him, screamed that I wished we'd never married. Then I burst into tears again and flung myself down upon the bed.

I felt him sit beside me but he said nothing, and when at last I felt compelled to look at him I saw his face was stricken with grief. His pain was obviously so genuine that I couldn't bear it. One can be driven to be cruel to a husband, but no matter how adverse the circumstances one should never be cruel to a friend.

Struggling upright I pushed my tangled hair away from my face and put my arms around him. After I had apologized I said, "You did your best, you tried so hard, this failure isn't your fault. Some problems really are insoluble and Declan's one of them. There's nothing we can do but let him go."

He seemed not to hear. He whispered, "Do you really wish you'd never married me?"

"Darling, I wish no such thing, and I don't hate you either, but do try to understand. I've just lost my son. I'm demented with grief—"

"Of course. Yes. Forgive me—oh God, what a fool I am sometimes," said my poor friend, pathetically acknowledging how baffling such a complex situation was to his simple emotional nature. He put his arms around me and we hugged each other. Finally he said in a low voice, "I'm beginning to think I've been a most obtuse and unhelpful husband. I must try and put matters right. You mean everything to me, Ginette, everything in the world, so...what can I do? Tell me how I can help you get over this tragedy."

I kissed him to show how precious he was to me. Then when I was calm enough to speak, I said, "I want to have a baby."

Robert's response is perfect. He says it's the best possible idea and he's only sorry he didn't think of it himself because he wants a child just as much as I do.

No more douches of vinegar. No more sordid little chunks of sponge tied with flesh-colored thread. The dreary side of physical love will be eliminated for nine blissful months, and at the end of it all will be another adorable bundle in a shawl, a new little Robert Godwin for Oxmoon—or perhaps a little Ginevra for myself. I've always longed for a daughter. What a pity it was that my first marriage was so arduous that I never had the strength to embark on a third pregnancy, but at least now I can make up for lost time. Conor wanted a daughter. I'll never forget the rows we had after Rory was born and I, encouraged by a sophisticated friend, started to conspire against pregnancy with the aid of vinegar and sponges. I can so clearly remember Conor shouting that it was contrary to his religious principles and he wanted me to have a baby every year.

"And who's going to look after them?" I screamed, demented with motherhood as I struggled to survive two small boys with the aid of incompetent nursemaids. "And who's going to pay for them?"

Sulks. Then a smile. Then a laugh. And finally acquiesence, laced with the charm that made me forgive him everything. "Suit yourself, sweetheart, but say nothing more. Then I'll lie more easily in the confessional."

What a villain he was, but how we laughed! And we did so enjoy my pregnancies, our times in bed became better than ever—and of course that was why he wanted me to be constantly pregnant, the rogue; it had nothing to do with his religion at all.

I understood him and he understood me but now Robert finally understands me too so all's well. Oh, I simply can't wait to conceive....

This war is really rather alarming. At first, reassured by Harrods' notice that business would be as usual, I thought the squabble would be a nine-day wonder, but ghastly things have been happening in Belgium and someone's now invited me to a charity bridge afternoon to raise money for the refugees. I don't play bridge but I'm going to learn. The Asquiths are mad about it. However I can't learn just yet because there's no time. Darling Lion, triumphantly engaged to be married at last, is busy telling me I'm the best sister-in-law a man ever had and I'm just wholeheartedly agreeing with him when we hear that our joint victory has been eclipsed by his younger brother. Johnny has announced his engagement to the beauty of the season, Blanche Lankester. How typical! Lion huffs and puffs, I moan and groan, we both end up in a stupor of exhaustion securing a nice plain little girl who apart from her money is nothing out of the ordinary, and then Johnny, without any apparent effort, walks off with the catch that richer and more blue-blooded men than he have been fighting for since the season began.

"How did you do it?" gasps poor Lion, overcome with admiration. "You're just as penniless as I am!"

"True," says Johnny, who I'm beginning to think is a very cool customer indeed, "but my prospects at the F.O. are excellent, and Mr. Lankester is convinced that I have a first-class diplomatic career ahead of me."

The benign Mr. Lankester has a large estate in Herefordshire, a house in Connaught Square and a private fortune which Margaret might describe as "useful." Like Daphne, Blanche is an only child. I would love to write that she's a spoiled bitch of an heiress certain to make her smooth-tongued Lothario unhappy, but honesty compels me to admit the child is perfect. She's eighteen, charming, lovely, modest and accomplished. In fact she's the kind of girl who makes a married woman like me feel like a garish old war-horse. I'm probably jealous of her youth. Let me combat my jealousy by saying how lucky Johnny is. I feel her musical talent, which is considerable, is quite wasted on him, since he's one of those people who only recognize "God Save the King" because people stand up.

I still say he's too young to get married, but if Mr. Lankester's happy with his daughter's fate, who am I to criticize? I think Bobby and Margaret are perturbed, though, for Bobby's been dispatched to London to size up the situation, but Bobby is charmed by Blanche and confesses himself unable to object to the match.

Silly Lion's talking of enlisting. I tell him it's pointless as the war will be over by Christmas, but he thinks being a soldier would be a terrific lark. Apparently down at Oxmoon Edmund thinks so too. Men *are* odd. I can't see the point of enduring all sorts of tedious discomforts like poor food and primitive lavatories unless there really is a chance that the war will last, but Sir John French will soon mop up the Germans and everyone will be on their way home again before Lion can emerge from some dreary training camp. Thank God I'm a woman and can sit at home and knit Balaclava helmets. Who in their right mind would want to do anything else?

Silly Lion.

I can't conceive. At least I'm sure I can, but I haven't yet. I tell myself it's because I'm still so upset about Declan, and that's true; I am. But Rory was so nice to me when he came back from Ireland, and I'm sure he'll be less difficult now that Declan's gone. I wonder what he'll think when I have the baby. Declan would have hated it but I suspect Rory will be generous. He's more forgiving and has such an easygoing nature.

Oh, I do hope I conceive soon! Perhaps this time next year I'll be preparing for the christening. . . .

Excitement about the war is rising to fever pitch and all we need now, as Robert says sardonically, is a panegyric from Kipling. However Robert takes a bleak view which is quite out of step with all this raging Jingoism. He says he knows death too well to be deceived; he says death often appears brilliantly attired in the theater of life, but once that mesmerizing figure starts to move downstage the gorgeous garments dissolve to reveal the horrors beneath. What a revolting image. I thought Robert had finally set aside that morbid obsession with death, but it would take a morbid mind to imagine that death could ever seem glamorous. It's war that's glamorous, not death. It's death that makes war vile. I know war is vile, of course I do, but nevertheless unlike Robert I do see the glamour of this great European convulsion. It's jolted everyone out of their ruts, sent a thrill of excitement crackling through all the ranks of society and united our unstable problem-racked country in an electrifying comradeship against the common foe.

However as usual I have Lion to divert me because it now looks as if he'll be sent to France in the new year and he wants to marry before he goes. (I thought the war would be over by Christmas but it seems everyone's got bogged down in France. Such a bore.) I told Lion to press for an early wedding day, and to my surprise the Wynter-Hamiltons have now given way. But no doubt they feel that our fighting men have to be humored wherever possible, and certainly everyone's rushing to the altar at the moment. Even Johnny's taking advantage of the current rage for the quick marriage, although there's no obligation on him to rush into uniform; his position at the Foreign Office would exempt him from military service even if military service were compulsory—which it isn't. However I can see Johnny's becoming muddled about his position because although he wants to do the Done Thing as usual, he can't work out what the Done Thing is. Should he resign and enlist? Or should he stay where he is? Robert tells him in no uncertain terms that anyone can enlist but not everyone can do Johnny's work at the F.O., and that as the Home Front will ultimately be as important as the Front Line, Johnny has an absolute moral duty to stay where he is. That settles it. He stays.

Robert sets Johnny an example, thank God, by deciding from the start to stay at Westminster, and he says he's determined to stick to that decision no matter how long we're bogged down in France. Of course being a Member of Parliament is more important than being a Foreign Office clerk, but Robert says the principle is the same: he can be of more service to the nation at home than overseas. And now this truth has just been confirmed by Mr. Asquith himself who has dropped a hint that Robert will be given an Under-Secretaryship at the earliest opportunity. Robert can hardly flout the Prime Minister's plans for him so there's nothing he can do now but remain in London—unlike his friend Raymond, who isn't yet a Member of Parliament and will probably enlist. But perhaps Raymond, like Lion and Edmund, is keen to be a soldier. At least it'll give him a respite from the legal and political worlds for which he apparently has so little enthusiasm.

"You're not secretly longing to escape into uniform, are you, Robert?" I say nervously, just to make sure.

"Good God, no," says Robert. "I wouldn't want to compete with death when the odds are stacked against me."

That chills me. It chills him too—but we're chilled for different reasons. Robert's chilled because he's afraid I'll think him a coward, but I don't, I just think he's appallingly rational; I could never doubt Robert's courage after hearing the details of that fearful climbing accident. No, I'm chilled because he's implied how badly the war's going and because he probably has secret information about the current situation in France.

"Asquith's got us into the war," says Robert, "and now he thinks all he has to do is let the generals get on with it. But I don't share Asquith's touching faith in generals. God knows where it'll all end."

I say, "Don't let's talk about it anymore." Honestly, I'd rather not face such pessimism, and Robert, seeing he's distressed me, falls silent.

I'm not worried about Lion. Lion will bounce in and out of danger with his usual insouciance and regale us all later with amusing stories about how he won the war. But it's Edmund's fate that terrifies me—twenty-year-old mild gentle Edmund who loves gardening and whose biggest problem has always been how many rashers of bacon to have for breakfast. Could anyone be less suited to a military life? Yet he says he wants to do his bit to ensure that the Huns are kept out of Oxmoon. Edmund loves Oxmoon. Since he left school he's been pottering around there, officially helping Bobby on the estate, but I think he spends most of his time growing roses. Bobby and Margaret, who are both so insistent that Lion should be employed in London, are far more lax with Edmund because they accept how unworldly Edmund is, how unsuited to earning a living in a city. How can he ever survive this nightmare waiting for him in France?

I can't bear to dwell on that so I won't.

I'll think of Celia instead. Poor Celia has been staying with us for a few days, and I've been drumming up eligible men for her to meet, but alas! I know she hasn't a hope of suiting them. She's thirty now and yearns to be married but has never had anyone in love with her. What can it be like to be a virgin of thirty, six feet tall with mousy hair, protuberant eyes and a flat bosom? I think I'd cut my throat and pray for reincarnation in a more tolerable form. How unfair it is that women's entire lives depend on their physical appearance! I honestly do feel very sorry for Celia, and so although she drives me to distraction with her boring conversation, I make every effort to be nice to her.

Robert just treats her as an imbecile, of course, but then Robert would. It's men like Robert who make life hell for women like Celia.

Anyway poor Celia's rather a strain, and then on top of that I now have a fearful servant problem because perfect Bennett, butler and valet *par excellence*, has regretfully decided that it's his patriotic duty to enlist. Really, it's small wonder I'm not pregnant. I've got much too much on my mind.

Lion looks gorgeous in his uniform. He says he adored his training camp and can't wait to get to France. Poor Daphne looks up at him with shining eyes. Can it really be two weeks since they were married? It seems like yesterday. Johnny marries Blanche tomorrow at St. James's Piccadilly, and Robert, who's to be the best man, has taken him out tonight to celebrate his last evening as a bachelor. Not that Johnny's interested in getting drunk and having a good time; he'll go home early and be tucked up in bed by midnight.

But Robert will come home and I'll seduce him. Oh, how I wish I could get this baby started. . . .

Christmas at Oxmoon. Bobby and Margaret utter not one word of reproach that we haven't visited them since our wedding a year ago, but I talk too much out of guilt about how frantically busy we've been. Margaret asks me in private if all's well, and I say yes, simply divine and I'm trying to have a baby. I shouldn't have mentioned the baby before it's been conceived—not the Done Thing—but I had to find some way of convincing her that Robert and I are in the seventh heaven of marital bliss.

Margaret says, "That's nice, dear; I'm so glad" and rearranges her mourning brooches into an octagon.

Robert seems closer to his mother than ever, and now I notice that his feelings go beyond mere filial respect. Neither of them shows emotion to the other; they're much too English for that, but in a crowded room he seeks her out as if she's the only person worth talking to, and in his company she seems to relax her grip on that relentless air of refinement and become blunter, pithier and wittier. She doesn't quite slip back into her Staffordshire accent, which I can dimly remember, but I can now look at her and see that tough energetic forthright little girl in her teens who looked after me so conscientiously during my earliest years long ago.

To my horror I find that I'm jealous of her close alliance with Robert. He treats her as an equal. He treats her as if she's capable of balancing a checkbook. He treats her as a friend.

I don't get treated as a friend anymore. That thrilling campaign at Pwlldu was just a romantic interlude. I've now been permanently converted into an object labeled WIFE, and I hate it, I hate being treated as if I'm an inferior being incapable

186

of understanding a subject like politics. I know much more about politics now and I would certainly vote sensibly if I were given the chance.... Heavens, I'm beginning to sound like a suffragette! I must stop before I succumb to the urge to chain myself to the nearest railing.

The truth is it's no good grumbling about Robert. He has his tiresome side, just as we all do, and I've no choice but to resign myself to it until we can embark on our joint venture, parenthood. Once I'm pregnant matters are bound to improve because of course the baby will draw us together.

Or will it?

Yes, of course the baby will draw us together. I was feeling drenched in pessimism when I wrote that last sentence because the most ghastly things have been happening in France. But I won't think of them. Robert's become convinced that the country can't continue in wartime with a one-party government, and he talks privately of coalition and reorganization. I now actively enjoy Robert's reports from Westminster not only because I'm becoming increasingly interested in politics but because it stops me thinking about what might be happening in France.

Lion's left now and Edmund's also due to leave soon. They're in different regiments, which I think is a good thing because one hears frightful stories of multiple fraternal casualties sustained during a single offensive.

London seems full of men in uniform now and the whole atmosphere of the city has changed. People say the tough new liquor laws are at the bottom of the new sobriety, but it's not as simple as that. Everyone I know is still drinking like a fish—more so than ever, in fact, and the social life goes on at a hysterical pace as if to compensate for the abnormal times we live in, but London is darker, mentally darker; mentally London is now gunmetal-gray, and the symbol of this bleakness is DORA, the Defence of the Realm Acts, which give the government dictatorial powers to keep us all in order. Nobody talks about "Business As Usual" now. The talk is all of DORA and the servant crisis and whether so-and-so really is a Swiss and not a German who ought to be locked up.

But perhaps London seems so bleak to me because today I had the most depressing consultation with a gynecologist who told me I may have damaged myself by indulging in what Mrs. Sanger has described so neatly as "birth control." It's the only explanation he can offer for my failure to conceive. I hated him, although I'm not sure why. I hated him for being the bearer of gloomy tidings but perhaps there was another reason too for my deep antipathy. He made me feel like an imbecile. He was Robert in a different guise.

Damn it, why shouldn't a woman practice birth control if she wants? It's her body and no man has the right to dictate to her what she should do with it.

Oh, I feel so angry sometimes, so *angry*...

"Ginevra!"

"Julie? Is it—can it be Julie?"

It was indeed Julie Harrington, who had been at boarding school with my old friend Gwen de Bracy. Gwen and I had for some years shared a governess with Angela Stourham, but at the age of fourteen Gwen had been sent to finish her education at Eastbourne and later Julie, her new friend, had spent more than one holiday with her at Penhale Manor.

"Ginevra, it's been years! How are you?"

"My dear, quite overcome that we should bump into each other like this in the middle of Piccadilly—do you have time to pop into the divine Ritz for a cup of coffee?"

Julie is thirty-four, a few months younger than I am, but unlike me she's not married and she has a job. Why, I ask her (I know she doesn't have to work for a living). She says she does it because she likes it. She has a good job. She's not just an office clerk working for a pittance. She's an editor on that dreary magazine A *Woman's Place* which instructs its readers how to embroider tablecloths, but Julie's trying to broaden the magazine's outlook by including articles on modern life. It sounds interesting. *She's* interesting. I'm so puzzled about why she's never married (obviously she must have had her chances) that in the end I ask her directly. She says she's never fancied it. How peculiar. Can she be a Lesbian, I wonder? How exciting! I've never met a Lesbian before and have always longed to find out what they actually *do*.

Julie lives *all alone* in a little flat in Bloomsbury and *she has a checkbook*. I saw it when she opened her smart leather handbag. (How did we all manage without handbags a few years ago?) Naturally I suspect her of being a suffragette but somehow I can't quite see her attempting to strip Mr. Asquith naked on a golf course. She's far too busy enjoying her independent life.

I wouldn't like a life like that, of course, but I admire her for having the courage to live it, and we get on very well—so well that finally I tell her what a beastly visit I've had to the gynecologist and how horrid doctors can be to women sometimes.

"Why not go to a doctor who's a woman?" says Julie carelessly. "I do."

A woman doctor! Heavens, how daring. But I like the idea, and when I tell Julie so, we arrange to meet again. I won't tell Robert, though. He'd just say women are temperamentally unsuited for the upper reaches of the medical profession, and besides... I don't think he'd care at all for Julie Harrington.

"How do you do, Mrs. Godwin. I'm Dr. Drysdale—do sit down."

The lady doctor was tweedy and foursquare but so kind and she quite understood why I'd spent so much time cutting up sponges into little chunks and drenching myself in oceans of vinegar. She also assured me that it was most unlikely that I'd done myself any harm because she could see no evidence of scarring or infection.

"However," she added honestly, "I do think this: if you've managed to avoid pregnancy for thirteen years with only douches and sponges to help you, you

188

might well be less fertile than the average woman." But she added to encourage me: "Even so, that's no reason why you shouldn't have a baby eventually."

She then asked me about Robert. "He's anxious for this baby, is he?"

"Oh yes! He's been so understanding about it!"

"Excellent," said Dr. Drysdale satisfied. "I only ask because sometimes when all isn't well between husband and wife, the wife becomes too tense to conceive."

"Oh, that couldn't apply to me at all," I said glibly, but as soon as the words were spoken I began to wonder.

"Robert, you remember Julie, of course."

"Indeed I do—how are you, Miss Harrington—but I don't think we ever had much to do with each other in the old days, did we? You two girls went off with Gwen while I went off with Gwen's brothers and the two sets seldom met. . . ."

Julie had telephoned me earlier to ask if she could interview me for an article she was writing on the servant problem, so I had invited her to tea and soon after her arrival she had asked me if I had ever thought of writing professionally. Would I be interested, for instance, in writing a thousand words about life in New York?

"How long's a thousand words?"

"A lengthy letter to your best friend."

I had been excited by this idea because I knew it would take my mind off the subject of pregnancy. I had told Julie I would try, and then just as our delightful tea party was concluding Robert arrived home from his chambers in the Temple, and having no alternative I had reintroduced him to her.

For a time all went well. They chatted about the old days at Penhale Manor and discussed the de Bracys. In fact I was just thinking with relief that I had been wrong in assuming they would detest each other when the conversation started heading for disaster.

"But you would agree, surely," said Robert to Julie in response to a remark of hers about working women, "that most women find fulfillment in the home."

"Yes," said Julie, "I think I would agree with that. A canary shut up in a cage will find fulfillment by singing. Otherwise it would die of melancholy."

"Darling," I said quickly to Robert, "shall I ring for more tea or are you in a rush to get to the House?"

"No—no tea, thanks. Am I to take it then, Miss Harrington," said Robert, settling down to annihilate her with his usual forensic skill, "that you don't believe women find their greatest happiness in being wives and mothers?"

"Not being a wife or mother, I wouldn't know."

"Exactly. In other words—"

"All I know is," said Julie, "that I'm very happy exactly as I am."

"But you don't pretend to speak for the majority."

"No, I speak for myself. I don't pretend to speak for all women—how could I? All women are different."

"But nevertheless, despite the minor differences, you must surely concede that all women want at heart to be wives and mothers."

"No. They don't. *I* don't. I disprove that entire thesis simply by my happy existence."

"Robert darling," I said in a rush, "we really mustn't delay you if you're on your way to the House."

"But Miss Harrington, don't you find your solitary life very lonely?"

"Why should you assume my life is solitary?"

"No doubt you have a wide circle of friends, but when you're at home don't you miss the companionship of a husband?"

"Good God, no!" said Julie amused. "I see my lover two or three times a week and that's quite enough for me, thank you!"

I was stunned. I realized I had just seen Robert outtalked, outwitted and out-maneuvered in a debate—I had just seen Robert *defeated—and by a woman!* Amidst my horror that the meeting should have ended in disaster, a small voice at the back of my mind whispered: "Good—and about time too."

"My dears!" I said, somehow finding my tongue, "what an enthralling dialogue! But now I must ask you to excuse Robert, Julie, because he really does have to rush off to Westminster—"

"—and besides," said Robert, recouping his losses with professional smoothness, "no matter how enthralling the dialogue I feel too handicapped by my upbringing as a gentleman to bring the argument to any rational conclusion. Chivalry insists, Miss Harrington, that I allow you to have the last word."

"How charming of you," said Julie smiling at him, "but isn't this supposed to be the twentieth century? We're not in the Middle Ages now, you know!"

Robert somehow restrained himself from slamming the door as he walked out.

"Darling, how lovely—you're back early!"

He arrived home soon after eight but not before I had prepared my defenses. I was going to say "Heavens, these feminists—such a bore!" but when Robert immediately announced, "I trust you won't ask that woman here again—I don't want you associating with anyone who talks like Rebecca West in *The Clarion*," I suddenly found my patience was exhausted.

"It's heavenly of you to be so concerned for me, darling," I said, "but I think I might be allowed to choose my own friends."

"Any woman who leads a Bohemian way of life and who is almost certainly a suffragist, if not a demented suffragette, is certainly not fit company for any wife of mine!"

"Oh, what absolute—" I paused to choose between the New York obscenity and the raw English slang but (no doubt fortunately) he did not allow me to finish.

"I'm sorry, Ginette, but I refuse to allow you to associate with a woman who despises marriage—she'll introduce you to the wrong people, she'll encourage you to take a lover—"

"You don't seriously think I'd take a lover, do you?"

"Well, why not?" he said. "You've done it before."

I felt as if I had been assaulted, not merely slapped in the face but slammed in the stomach. Turning my back on him I groped my way to the *secrétaire* and sat down abruptly on the chair beside it. I wanted to remind him that I was trying to have his child and that other men had never seemed less important, but all speech was impossible.

"I'm sorry," said Robert at last. I thought he was going to embark on some conciliatory speech but when he could only repeat in misery "I'm sorry," I saw he had shocked himself as much as he had shocked me. Eventually he added: "I suppose I'm uneasy because I know you're restless and dissatisfied."

"Only because I haven't been able to conceive! And you don't make life any easier when you refuse to let me choose my friends and refuse to allow me any control over my money—"

"Oh God, not that old quarrel again!"

"It may seem nothing to you!" I shouted. "But it means a very great deal to me! I hate having nothing of my own—God, no wonder I want a baby, what else do I have that's even partly mine? Everything is yours—yours, yours, yours! It's *your* house, *your* money, *your* career and *your* friends whose wives I have to cultivate—boring silly women though most of them are! And then on top of that I find I have no individuality anymore, I'm just *your* wife, someone who can be treated with contempt!"

"Christ Almighty, how dare you say that!" He was white with rage. "I've made all manner of sacrifices to give you what you want! I love you more than anyone else in the world and yet you spend your whole time being discontented, nagging me because I've finally reduced *your* life to the order *you* wanted and offered you a world which is compatible with *your* idea of happiness! Very well, just what the devil is it you want from me—and from life? I'm beginning to think you're just a spoiled pampered Society woman who can think only of herself!"

I did not reply immediately. I could only stare down at the sloping surface of the desk but at last I said in despair, "Perhaps that's true. I don't know. I just know I'm upset at the moment because I'm still not pregnant. I'd no idea before how awful it is to want a baby and not be able to start one."

"Well, I want a child as much as you do," said Robert, "but if this is what happens when you attempt maternity I'd rather we remained a childless couple."

"Oh yes," I said drearily, too exhausted to do more than retreat into passive acquiesence, "I daresay I've been difficult lately. But you see," I added, somehow dredging up the strength to make one final effort to clarify my feelings, "that's why I've so enjoyed meeting Julie again. She's helped to take my mind off the awful problem of pregnancy—she's suggested that I write an article for her magazine—"

"Oh, I couldn't permit that," said Robert.

"But I want to!"

"I'm sorry, I hate having to repeat myself, but I can't have you associating with that woman."

"Robert." I rose to my feet, dashed away the tears that had collected in my eyes and walked straight up to him. "Robert, you mustn't go on treating me like this.

It's disastrous. You're acting as if you're so uncertain of my love that you have to resort to tyranny to feel secure!"

"What nonsense! I'm just trying to be a good husband!"

"In that case could you possibly try not to be such a good husband? You used to behave so differently when we were merely friends—"

"Of course I did—before we were married we were two independent people! But marriage isn't about independence, Ginette, it's about dependence. It's a mutually beneficial arrangement, guarded by a web of rights and duties, to encompass the biological fact of life that women are weak and need to be looked after while men are strong and seek to protect them."

"Yes, of course, but—"

"You wish to be unmarried and independent, perhaps?"

"No—oh, God, no, I'd hate to live Julie's kind of life—well, how could I, all those awful men battering away at my defenses, I'd be half-dead with terror in no time, no, I must have someone to look after me, I absolutely must—"

"Then I fail to see how you can criticize me as a husband."

I gave up. I was miserable, baffled and in utter despair. As usual I knew that rationally he was right—and as usual I sensed that in some way beyond my powers of definition he was absolutely wrong.

Robert is as thoroughly upset by this conversation as I am, but he won't give in and eventually, to make life more bearable, I let him think that he's achieved a reconciliation. How chilling that competence in bed seems now. I lie awake in the dark and think so longingly of Conor that when I fall asleep I dream of him and know all the pleasure that Robert's failed to give me. I wake up full of joy but then I remember. Conor's dead. The man next to me in the dark is Robert. This is 1915 and Conor's been dead nearly two years.

I don't suppose I'll have the baby now. I'll always be too upset to conceive. Maybe it doesn't matter but yes, it does, it matters terribly. Both Daphne and Blanche have confided to me that their husbands didn't spend their honeymoons in idleness, but although I'm trying so hard to be happy for the girls I can't help feeling twinges of jealousy. I must beat them back before I start to share Robert's belief that I'm just a spoiled selfish Society woman. Am I so spoiled and selfish? I don't mean to be, I honestly don't, I do try not to want the baby but it's no good, I have such an urgent need to fill the gap that Declan's left in my life and I find I'm longing for the baby more than ever.

I shall divert myself by thinking of that article on New York. For of course I'm going to write it. And of course I'm going to see Julie again.

Oh, I've had such fun! I wrote a very racy article and Julie says it's mesmerizing. The only piece she's cut is the anecdote about the preacher and his three wives—she's kept my description of cabarets and she's even kept my explanation of why streetwalkers are called streetwalkers! (But she says her senior editor may strike this out.) I feel very proud and very happy and for hours and hours I haven't thought of the baby at all.

I'm to be paid ten guineas. I daren't ask for the sum in cash; that would give rise to the suspicion that I was working behind my husband's back. But what do I do with the check? Would the bank hand over the money to me without telling Robert? Whatever happens Robert mustn't hear about this. I think the only answer is to endorse the check to the Red Cross and look upon my writing as war work. That'll help alleviate my guilt, and nowadays I'm not just guilty that I'm deceiving Robert; I'm guilty because I haven't been knitting socks or visiting maimed young men or canteening or organizing a bridge afternoon to raise money for war orphans. One longs to do *something*, but I loathe hospitals, and I tend to shy away from the bossy worthy souls who flourish in charitable organizations.

I've stopped trying not to think of the war. It's impossible not to think of it. One can hardly believe that a year ago there was cricket at Lords and racing at Ascot and everyone was chattering away about what they were going to wear at Cowes. Now there's no formal sport at all and everyone's talking of the Zeppelins whenever they're not whispering about the report of the Royal Commission on Venereal Diseases. They've even revived that awful old play *Damaged Goods* which Robert says he doesn't have the time to see, but I wouldn't mind seeing even a play about venereal disease—I'd welcome anything that would take my mind off the ghastly events in the Gallipoli Peninsula which have followed the disaster in the Dardanelles. I thank God daily that both Lion and Edmund are embroiled in the stalemate in France, although God knows there's little to choose between one hell and the other.

It's such a relief to turn from the news of the overseas horrors to my personal reports from Robert on the Home Front. Robert says a coalition is now certain but he's sure Asquith has the power to come out on top. Churchill will have to be dropped, though, after the Dardanelles debacle, and how many other Liberals will have to be butchered to make room for the leading Unionists? To my astonishment I find I'm becoming quite obsessed with politics, but better to be obsessed with what might or might not be happening at Westminster than to be obsessed with what might or might not be happening in France.

Darling Lion writes that he's at last found the life that suits him: eating, sleeping and gossiping in an amusing little billet behind the lines. He's somewhere near Neuve Chapelle where the British recently pierced the German lines, but Edmund is nearer the front than Lion. Edmund is at Ypres. How frightened I feel when I remember Edmund but he sent me a placid little letter recently saying what a bore it was to have to cart around a gas mask.

Men have been gassed during this second battle of Ypres. They say the results of gassing are—no, I mustn't think of such things, I *mustn't*.

I'll think instead of Mrs. Pankhurst proclaiming the suffragists' desire to help in the war effort. Even Robert is impressed by this desire of the suffragists to put patriotism before their cause, and yesterday he asked me idly if Julie had voiced an opinion on the subject. I said I had no idea as I hadn't seen her.

I meet Julie regularly at The Gondolier, a cozy little restaurant which serves light luncheons and heavy teas to ladies who shop in Kensington High Street. It's so middle-class that I know I'm safe; no one Robert knows will ever see me there. Since Julie wouldn't normally patronize such a conservative backwater either I've had to confide in her to explain why it's such an ideal meeting place, but she was sympathetic, offering no criticism of Robert but merely accepting that he was a man who would drive his wife to hide behind steak-and-kidney pie with two vegetables in a middle-class coffin like The Gondolier.

Julie wants me to write another article, this time on transatlantic travel. Apparently the readers of A Woman's Place are now in retreat from articles on war work and yearn to be reminded of the more glamorous aspects of peacetime. I say I'll do my best but do I or do I not disclose what goes on in the lifeboats when everyone's awash with champagne?

"Oh, toss it in!" says Julie. "Sex is all the rage now that everyone's either racing to the altar or wailing about the illegitimate issue of our gallant soldiers or rushing around pretending V.D.'s just been invented."

We laugh. Full of ideas for my new article I rush home and there I find a lovely surprise: a letter from Daphne to say that Lion's coming home on leave.

"I'm immensely flattered!" said Lion impudently. "I'd no idea the Huns thought I was so important—I leave the Front for a little peace and quiet and what happens? I'm pursued by Zeppelins in London!"

Only Lion could have had the nerve to joke about the Zeppelins. As I laughed I felt nearly overcome with emotion; I could hardly believe he was back in my drawing room, a thinner, paler Lion but still just as full of bounce and charm. On the sofa Daphne was looking radiant, her plain little face transformed with happiness. They were staying at the Wynter-Hamiltons' London house for the duration of his brief leave, and both Bobby and Margaret had come up to London to visit them there.

"Darling Lion, how wonderful to see you again—and looking so well! One hears such ghastly rumors—"

"Oh, I never believe rumors," said Lion breezily. "The truth's always so much more entertaining. I'm enjoying this war hugely—never had such a good time in my life! Of course it's a bit muddy in the trenches but one meets such fascinating people..." And he embarked on a series of amusing reminiscences before his new daughter woke up and began to cry. Daphne, who had been holding the baby, immediately panicked and begged Lion to call for the nanny, but in an effort to beat back my jealousy by being helpful I exclaimed, "No, let me hold her for a moment!" and I took little Elizabeth in my arms. She was plain and bald, just as most new babies are, but when she luckily stopped crying, I said warmly how angelic she was and Daphne blushed with pleasure.

"I'm glad it's a girl," said Lion later. "I don't want a baby who might one day wind up in even the most entertaining of trenches. I wonder what John and Blanche will produce. I suppose a cherub with a halo is the least they can hope for."

We all giggled. Johnny and Blanche, who had established themselves as the perfect couple, were without doubt destined to be the perfect parents of an intolerably perfect child.

I could feel the jealousy creeping over me again so I said firmly, "Lion, you're being *very* naughty!" But Lion just exclaimed outrageously, "That's what makes life such fun!" and burst into peals of laughter.

The casualty lists are so appalling that I feel numb now whenever I hear someone I know has been killed. I say, "How dreadful!" and I know it *is* dreadful, but the full dreadfulness has somehow become impossible to absorb. I felt overwhelming terror when Lion left, but I've recovered from that now and I still believe he'll go on bouncing his way to safety. Meanwhile my worry about Edmund has eased. He's had dysentery and is being sent to a convalescent home in Surrey to recuperate.

I shall conquer my horror of medical institutions and go to see him just as soon as I can.

"Ginevra!"

Edmund was looking so ill, so waxen and gaunt, that I found it hard to believe he was going to live, but the sister in charge of the ward said he was much better and well on the road to recovery.

"Poor Edmund!" I said, forcing myself to kiss him despite my irrational desire to shy away from someone who had been so sick. "What an awful time you've been through."

He looked vague. His mild blue eyes were untroubled. All he said was "It doesn't matter."

"But of course it matters!"

"No, nothing matters. Chap I knew wrote a poem about that. I rather liked it. Wish I could write poetry."

"Does he write much?"

"Oh, not now, no; he's dead."

"I'm so sorry, I—"

"It doesn't matter, one gets used to everyone being blown to bits. In the end it's the little things one minds most, like the rats and the lice."

"Oh my God—"

"Sorry, bad form, should be saying it's all tremendous fun. . . . Poor Ginevra, don't be upset—I've been so lucky! I'm not dead, I'm not blind or mutilated, I'm soon going to be fit as a fiddle again! Now . . . tell me all about your life in London."

What could I say? The chasm between the Home Front and the Front Line suddenly seemed not only bottomless but obscene. Gripping my handbag tightly I willed myself to be calm, and in an effort to convince us both that London had

195

not been entirely untouched by the horrors he had survived, I began to talk in a steady voice about the Zeppelins.

Christmas at Oxmoon, and everyone's thrilled because Edmund's been judged fit enough to complete his convalescence at home. This is probably the first time in his life that Edmund's been the center of his family's attention but he seems not to notice; he's eerily placid and I find his monosyllabic responses soon become unnerving.

Lion is in France and Daphne and little Elizabeth are with the Wynter-Hamiltons in Scotland, but Johnny and Blanche are at Oxmoon for three days before joining Blanche's father in Herefordshire. With them is their new daughter Marian and everyone is busy saying with truth what a perfect baby she is. However Blanche really is a dear child and I hate myself for being catty enough to think she's much too good to be true. Meanwhile Johnny's as priggish as ever and looks at me as if I'm a Soho trollop just because I have a divine new evening gown that's a trifle décolleté. Well, at least I'm not married to Johnny. Thank God for small mercies.

Robert and I are rubbing along somehow and I'm determined not to complain— things could be worse so a complaint would be hard to justify. We're pleasant and affectionate to each other, and as I never mention my longing for a baby there's never a cross word spoken on either side. Margaret eyes my figure but says nothing. I immediately find I have to tell her how blissfully happy Robert and I are. Margaret says she's so pleased. Robert gives her special attention as usual and I keep coming across them chatting privately in corners. I hate it, I hate being here, I hate Oxmoon, *hate* it. Oh, I can't wait to escape to London again. . . .

I feel so depressed, so absolutely cut off from Robert by our mutual pretense that we have an untroubled marriage, that I'd like to take a lover. But I won't— and not just because I'm terrified of what would happen when Robert found out. (Of course there'd inevitably be someone only too willing to tell him.) I won't have an affair because I proved conclusively to myself during my first marriage that adultery solves nothing when it stems from despair. It may temporarily alleviate one's misery but one's problems remain not only unsolved but exacerbated by guilt.

I do think a case can be made for adultery but only when the misery of the partners reaches huge proportions: if the husband is impotent, for example, or the wife hopelessly revolted by the sexual act—or if venereal disease, habitual drunkenness, perversion and cruelty persist in raising their vile heads to blight the matrimonial landscape. But my marriage is far removed from such a marital hell and I've no right to behave as if it isn't.

The truth is I have a husband who loves me. The way he expresses that love may not be particularly acceptable to me, but I must at least try to love him loyally in return. I daresay our marriage will jog along well enough in the end. Certainly

I feel better able to tolerate it since I started writing magazine articles and meeting Julie for luncheon at The Gondolier.

Julie has suggested that I might like to answer the readers' problem letters in the new year. What an irony if I end up advising women on their marital difficulties! But at least no one can complain that I'm inexperienced. . . .

Edmund's gone back to France. I really must stop crying and telling myself I shall never see him again.

I keep thinking the war can't get any worse but it does. Robert says there'll shortly be a handbook issued which advises on the correct behavior in the event of an occupation. Everyone assumes an occupation can never happen, but can it? *Can it?* The inconceivable has a nasty habit of coming true these days. Everyone said gold sovereigns would go on circulating but they've stopped. Everyone said there'd never be compulsory blackout but it's coming. Even the public clocks are shortly going to cease to chime. We're no longer mentally gunmetal-gray; we're slate-gray edging towards black but nobody can stand that thought so everyone's rushing to the overflowing theaters and dancing themselves into a frenzy in the Soho nightclubs and drinking and drugging themselves into a stupor.

Yes, I've heard some very unsavory stories recently about girls with a yearning for morphia, but here, handed to me by Julie, are some very different though in their own way equally hair-raising stories. I know just what goes on among the rich, but now I'm about to find out how the other ninety-five percent of the country live.

"Dear Nurse—" The magazine pretends its problem-letter page is in the charge of a nurse because this is supposed to stimulate the readers' desire to confess their most intimate troubles. "—I am twenty-five years old and am not sure what is meant when gentlemen 'take liberties' but I met a soldier on leave last week who said it was my patriotic duty to. . ."

"Dear Nurse, I have three children under four with twins expected next month and my husband is in France and I don't know how I can go on. . ."

"Dear Nurse, I have allowed a sailor to kiss me on the lips. When will I have the baby?"

"Dear Nurse, My husband has just run off with a land girl and I have no money and nowhere to turn. . ."

"Dear Nurse, My husband has been wounded. . ."

"Dear Nurse, My husband has been blinded. . ."

"Dear Nurse, My husband has been castrated. . ."

"Dear Nurse, I'm a war widow and feel I have nothing left to live for. . ."

I stop. The well of undiluted misery and ignorance is so appalling that I feel as if God has reached out, seized me by the scruff of the neck and given me a violent shake. Here are hundreds of women, all far, far worse off than I am. Yes, pull yourself together, Ginevra Godwin. Robert was right—as usual—and it's time you stopped behaving like a rich spoiled bitch. This is your chance to do some worthwhile war work at last and alleviate the suffering on the Home Front.

Roll up your sleeves, stop thinking of yourself and make a big effort to help those who are so much less fortunate than you are.

I like the effect of the new summer-time act. It means the evenings are so light that I can sit at my *secrétaire* after dinner and draft my answers to the problem letters while the sun's still shining in the summer sky. Robert's at the House so much at the moment and I always seize the chance to work when I'm on my own.

I was glad to be alone this evening because I have a horrible letter to answer— not a letter from a reader of *A Woman's Place*, but a letter from France. It's from Lion. I shrink from reading it again but I can't delay my answer so I must somehow drum up all my courage and confront that terrible message for the second time. . . .

My dearest Ginevra, Lion had written, *things are busy here for a change, although I haven't mentioned this to Daphne as I didn't want her to worry about me. Ginevra, if anything happens please will you always keep in touch with her? She's frightened of Mama and she thinks Celia's a bore and she finds Blanche maddeningly pi, but you she genuinely likes. You were so nice to us when I had my leave after Elizabeth was born. What a wonderful sister you've always been to me, it seems strange to think you're really just a cousin. God bless you, and my love always,* LION.

I read the letter a third time but found myself unable to write a word in reply. I merely sat with my pen poised over the blank paper as the sun finally set and the darkness began to fall.

Later I tried to think of Edmund, who so clearly had the mark of death on him, but I found I couldn't worry about Edmund anymore. Edmund, I knew, was safe behind the lines, whereas Lion . . . well, obviously Lion was right at the front.

Robert came in at ten, and after kissing me he asked in concern if I felt well. I assured him I did. Then I heard myself say in a calm voice, "Robert, there's a big show brewing, isn't there?" and he answered after only the briefest hesitation: "Yes. The British Army's lining up along the Somme."

Nobody knows what's happening. It's July the first, 1916, and nobody knows what's going on. Robert says this will be the greatest action of the war so far, an action by a British army of continental size. Robert is optimistic. Lloyd George believes Haig is about to win the war, and Robert is Lloyd George's man at heart now even though they both still claim allegiance to Asquith. But the war's proving too much for Asquith. The war's proving too much for us all.

I'm thinking of Lion all the time, I'm praying and praying to my nice kind Church of England God, the God whom I first met long ago during my magic childhood with Robert and whom, like Robert, I've always been unable to abandon. During my marriage to Conor I nearly turned Catholic three times but I always balked at the last minute; I felt the Roman Catholic God would be too demanding and we'd be forever having rows which would leave me a nervous wreck. My Church of England God doesn't mind if I go to church only at Christmas and Easter; he sits up in heaven quiet as a mouse but if I ever want him he's always there to listen even though he can seldom be bothered to reply. But perhaps out of sheer horror he'll now intervene and look after Lion for me. It's only as I pray that I wonder if God really is benign. Perhaps he's evil. Or indifferent. Or simply not there at all.

"Any news?" I keep saying, but there never is. The Somme. What a vile name. It reminds me in shape of the word "tomb." But that's an unspeakable thought which I must erase at once. I must think of the name as a clean-cut shining syllable, sharp as the edge of some invincible sword; I must picture the word as it will appear in future history books. "The Great War, which began in 1914, was triumphantly concluded in July, 1916, by the mighty victory of the British Army on the Somme. . . ." Yes, I can see it all: the battle that will go down in history as the battle that won us the war, the greatest British battle since Waterloo, the last huge battle of the twentieth century—

THE BATTLE OF THE SOMME.

They say there are nineteen thousand dead. They say there are nearly sixty thousand casualties and nineteen thousand dead—in a single day. And nobody's winning. The battle's just going on and on and on.

How does a nation survive such a hemorrhage? I feel like a damaged nerve in a body that is fatally ill.

Nineteen thousand dead. And that's just the beginning.

I can't eat. I can't sleep. I can't work. I can't do anything. I just sit and wait for the telegram from Oxmoon to arrive. The official telegram will go to Scotland, where Daphne's retreated with her parents, but the Wynter-Hamiltons will wire Bobby and then Margaret will wire us.

Nineteen thousand dead, and all over the country the telegrams are starting to arrive; all over the country there are people like me, sitting, waiting, listening for the ring of the doorbell—but no, there's no ring of the doorbell for me, only Robert returning home at eleven o'clock in the morning. I look out of the window and see him paying off the cab, and the instant I see his face I know all there is to know.

"I'm afraid . . ."

"Yes." I turned away and went upstairs to our bedroom. I was trying to remember how many clean shirts Robert had. With Bennett gone it was so easy to lose sight of what was happening in Robert's wardrobe. When I reached the bedroom I moved to the tallboy and started counting shirts. I wondered how long we would be at Oxmoon and decided a minimum of three days would be required. Putting down the shirts on the table I stood looking at them. I remember the sun shining.

199

I can see the sun shining on those shirts. They were achingly white.

"Robert—"

But he was there, and as he took me in his arms I knew I had my loyal friend back again. It seemed like a miracle. I had feared my grief might irritate him but now that I had my loyal friend restored to me I knew there was no need to suppress my feelings. For he was grieving too, grieving for the life that had been lost, and beyond the grief lay his old rage against death which now set fire to our emotions with the violence of a torch thrust into a tinderbox.

We were embracing but without passion. We were merely two friends locked for comfort in each other's arms, but as I sensed that rage exploding in Robert's mind we felt the sexuality vibrate between us and the next moment we were overpowered by a force which neither of us attempted to resist. Robert locked the door. I pulled the curtains. We shed our clothes, fell on the bed and copulated. It had no connection with any conventional notion of passion. What I chiefly remember is that it seemed the obvious natural thing to do, and the act was strangely functional, as if all sensuality had been cauterized by grief. It was our violent protest against the war, our savage litany for the men who had died on the Somme, our unyielding determination to defy death by celebrating life. Lion was dead. His joyous life had been brutally laid waste but we were still alive to rebel against his end.

Later, much later, when I had resumed sorting our clothes for the visit to Wales, I began to cry, but Robert was there still, my beloved Robert, the best friend anyone could wish for. Robert took me in his arms and when he said, "My dearest Ginette," it was as if by some miracle we were back at Oxmoon, the lost Oxmoon of our childhood, and in our shared memories we saw it live again.

Oxmoon's in a shambles because Margaret's withdrawn to her room and Celia is distractedly trying to manage a household in which the servants seem as mindless as lost sheep. I'm shattered by this new evidence that without Margaret Oxmoon falls apart; against my will I'm reminded of that time when she visited her sister in Staffordshire and my childhood came to such a horrific end.

However I try not to think of that. I do my best to be strong and capable, but that's not so easy because the most unnerving aspect of this unnerving situation is that Bobby's useless. With a glass of champagne in his hand he drifts around talking of wartime farming and how splendid all the land girls are, and at regular intervals he pauses to pronounce that all will be well once Margaret's recovered— as if Margaret will miraculously iron out the tragedy by bringing Lion back to life.

Robert soon loses patience with his father and yells at him to be quiet but Johnny's with us, thank God, and—yes, I have to conquer my antipathy and admit it—Johnny's a tower of strength, not only soothing poor Bobby but coping with little Thomas, who's obviously so disturbed by Margaret's withdrawal that he's seizing every opportunity to create havoc.

I'm not sure at first how I should approach Margaret but in the end I send in

200

a little note of sympathy to indicate that she needn't see me if she doesn't want to. However she decides I have to be seen, so we have a short interview during which she thanks me for coming to Oxmoon to help. She's not in bed. She's sitting by the window in a shabby old dressing gown and looking much older than her age, which must now, I suppose, be fifty-one. Her eyes are tearless but she frowns when she says how special Lion was to her, a baby so miraculously full of life after the three babies who had died.

"Yes, he was lovely, Margaret. I can remember him so clearly in the nursery."

And I can. I want to cry but Margaret stops me when she starts to speak again in that low passionless voice.

"I don't know whom Lion resembled but I loved him the better for not reminding me of anyone. It's so difficult when a child, poor innocent little thing, reminds one of someone one loathed, but I never had that difficulty with Lion. I can see why people thought he was my favorite. If one could choose one's favorites I would indeed have chosen him, but one isn't allowed to choose, is one? There's always one child for whom one cares so much that his existence becomes almost an ordeal, but that sort of relationship has nothing to do with choice; it exists whether one likes it or not. I tried to explain that to Robert yesterday and I think he understood. Now that Lion's dead it's finally possible to have a rational conversation with Robert about him."

I nod to show her I understand, but all the time I'm thinking neither of Lion nor of Robert but of the child who reminds her of someone she loathed. She's thinking of Johnny reminding her of her mother-in-law, I know she is, but she and Johnny get on so well together and Johnny's the most devoted son. If only Robert could have got on equally well with Declan, who must have continually reminded him of Conor, but Declan was hardly his own flesh and blood, just a little Irish-American second cousin who came from a world Robert was unable to comprehend.

Thank God Declan's survived the Easter Rising in Dublin. I hope he can escape to America—but oh God, supposing his ship's sunk by U-boats! I worry about Declan all the time still so I know what Margaret means when she says one can care so much for a child that his existence becomes an ordeal. I love Rory because he's so cheerful and uncomplicated—like Lion—but Declan is to me as Robert is to Margaret, and I know he'll always be the son who's closest to my heart.

I seem to have missed this month, but I'm sure I can't be pregnant so I suppose this is a physical reaction to the shock of Lion's death. I'm trying to arrange a visit to Scotland to see Daphne, but Robert refuses to go, despite the fact that it's August and many of our friends will be in Scotland too. But the Wynter-Hamiltons' castle is a stone's throw from Fort William and you can see Ben Nevis from nearly every window, and this must surely be why Robert shuns a visit; he can't bear to be reminded of his climbing days and the dreadful accident which scarred his mind.

However I must see Daphne so I've nerved myself to go without him, and at least I have Rory to look after me on the long train journey. As soon as I leave Robert will go down to Pwlldu to deal with various constituency problems, and then he'll journey south into Gower to make sure Bobby's pulled himself together.

Thank God that for once I have a genuine excuse not to accompany him to Oxmoon.

I seem to have missed again, but of course I can't be pregnant; this is the product of nervous strain resulting from my visit to Daphne. I found it a great ordeal. I could have borne it better if she'd been distraught but she was so brave that I felt I was the one in constant danger of breaking down. However I know she was glad to see me, so I did the right thing by forcing myself to undertake the visit. Little Elizabeth is nearly a year old now. She's fat and happy and has Lion's impudent blue eyes, and as I cuddle her I can't help longing again for the baby I know I'm never going to have.

"Raymond's dead."

"Oh Robert, no—not Raymond—"

"He's dead. The army's dying. It's the biggest graveyard the world's ever seen."

It was my turn now to comfort him, but what could I say? I thought I had become immune to the full horror of the casualty lists but now that someone like Raymond had died I felt the horror batter me afresh. Someone like Raymond... But there was no one quite like Raymond Asquith. So much brilliance, so much charm, so much wit—and all obliterated one September day by a German bullet in a French hell. Although to me Raymond had been no more than a delightful acquaintance I knew he had meant far more than that to Robert who could so readily associate Raymond's image of brilliance with his own, and as I sensed Robert thinking, There but for the grace of God go I, I suddenly had an intuition of what was to come.

"Christ, what a bloody coward I am," whispered Robert, and covered his face with his hands.

"Rubbish," I said at once. "It takes great courage to stay on the Home Front when both the new law and public opinion push men to enlist."

"I deserve to be thought a coward. I *am* a coward. I'm just so bloody afraid of dying—of losing—"

"Anyone in their right mind should be afraid of dying. That doesn't mean you're a coward."

"I ought to enlist, I know I ought to enlist—"

"How can you? You've been ordered by the people who are running this war to stay where you are!"

"Raymond was told to stick to his staff job. But he had the courage to go back to his men—"

"You're not Raymond, Robert. Not only is your position quite different as an Under-Secretary in the Commons, but I suspect your personalities are more different than you've ever realized. The truth is we don't know much about Raymond, but I'll say this: if he was so keen to go back and dice with death in very adverse circumstances then I suspect he was a far more complicated man than you are. You're a simple man with complex problems. Raymond seems to have been a complex man with complex problems. There's a difference."

"But—"

"To put it bluntly, Robert, if you rushed off to enlist now you wouldn't prove you were courageous, you'd simply prove you were suicidal. Don't be ruled by guilt! Be ruled by reason—and *that*, in the circumstances, will require just as much courage as the courage displayed by most men in uniform."

He made no attempt to argue. Some time passed while I held him close but finally he said in a low voice, "This'll knock the heart out of Asquith. Lloyd George will disembowel him now." And then he began to talk of Raymond's intellectual glamour, of his own golden days up at Oxford and of a vanished world that had been blasted beyond recall.

Today I've been shopping, partly to distract myself, partly to recuperate from the ordeal of writing to Raymond's wife and partly because I thought I might buy some charming but inexpensive cuff links for Rory in the Burlington Arcade. I always like to take him a little present when I visit the school at half-term. However I couldn't find what I wanted at the right price so I abandoned the Arcade, and I was just wandering idly through Fortnum's, as one so often does when one's marooned in Piccadilly a long way from divine Harrods, when I saw the most sumptuous blackberries. Good fruit is hopelessly expensive nowadays but I was seized with the urge to pamper myself so I went wild. I bought six oranges, six peaches and two pounds of blackberries, and the price I paid was almost enough to buy off the German blockades.

I can't help but think now how curious that impulse was, just as I can't help but remember my passion for fruit, particularly oranges, when I was pregnant with both Declan and Rory. The craving would strike in the early months and last several weeks. Conor used to say it was like living in a Florida orange grove, and we had such fun peeling the skins off and chasing the pips around the sheets.

I don't dare hope too much for fear I might be disappointed but a visit to my kind Dr. Drysdale would surely settle the question in no time....

"Are you sure?" said Robert.

"Darling, *yes!* Isn't it wonderful!"

"Wonderful, yes, but how extraordinary! I wonder when—"

"Lion's death. It's the only date that makes sense."

"That's more extraordinary than ever! The occasion was so bizarre that the question of reproduction never even crossed my mind!"

"Yes, that was absolutely the last thing I was thinking about too, but oh Robert, isn't it thrilling! I'm in ecstasy—let's have some champagne!"

We drank some champagne.

"What a relief it is to see you happy again!" said Robert, smiling at me.

"Oh darling, I'm sorry I've been so difficult over the last eighteen months, but our married life will be utterly changed now, I promise you!"

"Splendid!"

I waited for him to say, as Conor would have said, "Let's go to bed and celebrate!" although why I should have thought Robert would choose that moment to display a belated resemblance to Conor I have no idea.

"Well, I must be off," said Robert presently, glancing at his watch. "Don't wait up for me because tonight's debate may be a long one."

Then he kissed me. He turned his back on me. And he left me on my own.

I suppose I know what's going to happen but I can't face it, so I'm turning the problem into a bridge we can cross later. The only trouble is that Robert and I aren't good at crossing bridges. Crossing bridges has become for me a synonym for marital hell.

To divert myself from the crisis that I know is now approaching, I start to read the political news again in *The Times* and soon I realize that Robert has a genuine excuse to avoid me by immersing himself in affairs at Westminster.

They've got rid of Asquith at last. Lloyd George has made his bid for power and this puts Robert in a cruel dilemma. He wants to be loyal to Asquith, his original patron, and with Raymond's memory still in the forefront of his mind his natural inclination is to stand by Raymond's father, but there's no room for such sentiment in politics and now Lloyd George is beckoning; the Welsh wizard is weaving his divisive spells. Lloyd George has had his eye on Robert for a long time, and now he's offering him the prospect of a major role in a glittering future. Robert's seduced. He's going to leave the Asquith camp and back the new leader who has emerged from the dramatic *coup d'état*.

Nothing can stop Robert's career now, nothing—except possibly a failed marriage and a session in the divorce court.

But that's a future I refuse to accept. How could I even think of such a disaster! Pregnancy must be making me unbalanced so I must recover my equilibrium without delay. Perhaps I'll just fly off to Fortnum's and buy some more fruit....

"Robert, are you awake?"

"Barely. What is it?"

"Robert, I know this'll make you angry because you always like to take the lead in such matters, but *please* don't be cross—"

"At the moment I'm merely exasperated. Would you mind coming to the point?"

"Yes, well... Robert, are you leaving me alone at night because you think you might harm the baby? If so you needn't worry—now that the beginning of the pregnancy is over it's safe until the seventh month."

"Yes, I did know that."

"Oh. Well, in that case why—"

"Oh for God's sake, Ginette! Go to sleep and stop nagging me! Why is it you're never satisfied? I've made you pregnant—isn't that enough for the time being?"

A long, long time passed while I lay on my side and pretended I was asleep. I made no noise but my pillow was soon sodden. Even though the rejection was not entirely unexpected I still found it very hard to bear.

Then he made a fatal mistake. He too was pretending to be asleep but when I failed to stifle a sob he shouted in a paroxysm of guilt, "I suppose Kinsella wanted it all through your pregnancies!" and I screamed back, "Yes, he did—he wasn't an overgrown spoiled child who hated babies!"

Our peaceful interlude of friendship was brutally terminated and once more the marital horrors began.

I blundered out of bed, I blundered across the landing, I blundered into Declan's room. It was a desperate flight through the dark, and when I sank onto the bed I burrowed under the eiderdown as if all thought of light terrified me.

"Ginette." I heard the click of the switch by the door and felt him sit down on the bed, but when he tried to pull aside the eiderdown I clung to it so fiercely that he abandoned the struggle. As the silence lengthened I knew he was frantically groping for the emotional subtlety that would have reduced the scene to order.

But Robert was capable only of emotional simplicity. He said touchingly but uselessly, "This is our child, yours and mine, and I want it and it has nothing to do, so far as I'm concerned, with those babies I found so tedious at Oxmoon long ago."

I thought: Yes. That's the situation as it should be. That's the situation that you, emotionally color-blind Robert, believe it to be. But that's not the situation as it really is.

I felt so cold then that I burrowed more deeply beneath the eiderdown than ever to ward off the chill of that terrible truth.

"But the trouble is," persisted Robert, struggling on, never for one moment allowing himself to believe that any problem could be incapable of a rational solution, "that I don't find pregnant women desirable. Some men do, some men don't. I don't. I don't know why."

I said nothing. Pregnancy to Robert meant not being the center of attention. Not being the center of attention meant not winning. And not winning to Robert meant a failure he couldn't endure.

I knew him so well that I could see so clearly each contorted fold in that powerful mind which his reason was powerless to iron smooth. I was powerless too. I was seeing truths he was too emotionally simple to recognize. I was seeing a gory pattern which had no place in his rational black-and-white world.

"So the truth is this," said Robert, moving from one statement to another with matchless but impotent logic, "I love you, I want the child but for the moment I can't express these feelings in bed. Of course," he added carefully, "all will be well again after the child's born."

I no longer had the strength to cling to the eiderdown and he was able to ease it away.

"I'm sorry," he said rapidly when he saw my face, "but I had no idea beforehand that this would happen."

I merely waited for him to go but he lingered, fidgeting with the cord of his dressing gown and twisting it continuously between his fingers. At last he said humbly, "Won't you come back to bed? Despite everything I don't want to sleep on my own."

"Don't you?" I said. "I'm afraid I do. Indeed I'm afraid I must. I can't go on sleeping chastely with you night after night like this; it's driving me mad."

He was too shattered to speak.

"I accept that I can't change you," I said, "and I accept that all will be well after the baby's born, but meanwhile you must let me choose my own way to survive this horrible crisis as best I can."

He managed to stammer, "But you've no right to reject me like that!"

"Why not? You've rejected me!"

He crept away without another word.

Robert comes back at dawn in a terrible state and says he's been quite unable to sleep because he now realizes he's being a bad husband, failing in his marital duty to make me happy. He says he's sorry, desperately sorry, he knows he's deserved every ounce of my anger but please, please could I forgive him because he so much wants to make amends.

But I see only that he's locked into the most disastrous competition with a dead man and that he can't rest while he feels he's coming second.

I beg him to leave it for a night or two. I say I do want him, but we're both tired and upset and it would be far better to postpone our reunion.

But he can't listen to me. He daren't. He's got to prove himself, he's got to win, so he gets into the single bed with me and then, inevitably, the worst happens, probably one of the worst things that could ever happen to a man like Robert, and we wind up in a far worse mess than before.

"I don't understand, I simply don't understand—"

"Darling, listen for a moment, *listen*. There's only one thing to do with a nightmare like this and that's to come to terms with it. We've got to accept that our marriage has been dislocated and that the dislocation will last until next spring. That's ghastly, I agree, but it's not permanent and fatal, it's transitory and curable, so we must both make up our minds to endure the present in the knowledge that we can look forward to the future."

"But why am I failing like this? I just can't understand it—"

"Well, it's no vast mystery, Robert! You said frankly earlier that you didn't find me desirable."

"Yes, but I want to! I'm willing myself to! So why can't I succeed?"

"Robert," I said, "there are certain situations in life which aren't subject to the power of your will, and very unfortunately this seems to be one of them. Let it be, I beg of you. Let it rest."

"Was Conor ever like this?"

With horror I noticed the change of name. My first husband was no longer "Kinsella" to Robert, no longer a cipher who belonged to a past which could be conveniently forgotten. He was a rival. He was present. And he was winning.

"Oh Robert, *please*—"

"I can't help it, I've got to know. Did Conor ever fail you as completely as this?"

"Oh God, yes, lots of times!"

"You're lying, I don't believe you."

"Robert, he drank! He drank too much too often! He was often far from perfect in bed—why, I told you that before; I distinctly remember telling you—"

"But was he ever actually—"

"Oh, of course he was impotent occasionally! He wasn't a machine, he was a man!"

"But what did he do when he suffered from impotence?"

"He usually said 'Holy shit' and went to sleep."

"And at other times? What did he do then?"

"I think you'd call it breaking the rules."

"You mean—"

"No, Robert, I absolutely refuse to say any more—"

"I don't mind breaking the rules. I'd never normally suggest such a course to my wife, but if you don't mind then I don't care."

"I do mind—I don't want to do with you what I did with Conor!"

"Why not?"

"Well, because... because Conor had this knack of making forbidden things come right, but they weren't the sort of things I'd normally—"

"You mean he was better in bed than I am."

"No! Oh God, no, no, no—"

"You loved him so much that you didn't care what he did, but you don't love me so much so you do care!"

"No! No, no, no!"

"You love him—you still love him—you'll always love him—and you love him better than you'll ever love me!"

I screamed and screamed in denial but he had already stumbled from the room like someone maimed.

Horrors. Robert's wrecked, I'm wrecked, the marriage is wrecked, and all the time the little baby is growing millimeter by millimeter, fluttering every now and then to remind me how joyous I should feel.

Of course we're keeping up appearances, but I'm now in such a state that I'm quite incapable of answering my problem letters, so I telephone Julie with the excuse that my doctor's advised me to take life at a more leisurely pace until the spring. Julie says never mind, I can always come back to the work later, and how lovely it is to think of someone having a *wanted* pregnancy for a change.

I immediately start weeping into the telephone. Julie says, "Meet me at The Gondolier at one," and as soon as I've controlled my tears I rush off to Kensington High Street.

"What shall I do, Julie? What on earth shall I do?"

"Take a deep breath and calm down. I agree the situation's awful but you're going to get out of it."

I had been weeping all over my steak-and-kidney-pie-with-two-vegetables but when Julie gave me this hope for the future I managed to control my tears again. I knew then that she was the best woman friend I would ever have. Every woman needs a special friend of her own sex with whom she can "have a haircombing" about everything from menstruation to male monsters, and Julie had become that kind of special friend. It made no difference that she had never been married. She was a woman of the world and she had an intuitive sympathy that was almost telepathic in its grasp of a situation. I hadn't had to regale her with every detail of my horrors; I'd merely sketched the outline and she'd penciled in the rest.

"For a start," she was saying, "forget about the truth, whatever the truth is. It doesn't matter which of those two men you love best. All that matters is that Robert should believe it's him."

"But what can I say to convince him?"

"Anything. You've got to mount a propaganda campaign in his favor. Forget about bed—obviously you can do nothing there at the moment—but treat him as if he's God and be passionate about him."

"But won't he be suspicious and skeptical?"

"Don't be silly—he'll be weak with relief and only too willing to believe every word you say!"

"But supposing he drags up the subject of Conor again?"

"I agree Conor's ghost will have to be exorcised. But Robert's not going to try—he'll be much too scared. You're the one who'll have to perform the exorcism."

"Oh God, Julie—"

"No, don't panic. All you have to do is to convince him that it's a compliment, not an insult, that you don't want to do with him what you did with Conor. Tell him you never liked what Conor did when he was drunk, although you wanted to believe out of sheer wifely loyalty that anything he did was right. Then say you simply couldn't bear the thought of Robert the Greek god feeling driven to descend to Conor's pagan Irish level. What explanation could be more rational and comforting?"

Hope now succeeded despair and overwhelmed me. Once more I began to weep into my steak-and-kidney pie, but afterwards I felt so encouraged by this conversation that I even had the energy to walk to Harrods to buy a present for Johnny and Blanche's second baby. It was due to arrive at any moment, and I told myself it would never do if I were so preoccupied by my troubles that I failed to have a gift waiting to welcome the baby into the world.

More ghastliness. Blanche had a little boy but he only lived a few hours. The clergyman came as soon as it was realized that death was inevitable and the baby was christened John before dying in Blanche's arms. I feel very, very upset and condemn myself utterly for my past cattiness about Johnny and Blanche when I mocked them for being a couple who were much too good to be true. I was just jealous because the marriage is so blissfully happy—and there's no charade going on there either; they're both far too young and innocent to fool a cynical old hag like me.

The tragedy has made me nervous about my own baby although Dr. Drysdale assures me that all is well. Certainly the baby feels healthy enough. I'm always so excited when the baby becomes active, and despite my troubles I'm excited this time too. I can picture the baby gritting his toothless little gums and flailing away with his little legs and wondering where on earth he is. Why do we think of the womb as cozy? I think it must be terrifying, a dark padded cell. Poor little baby. But never mind, he'll be free soon, and once he's free Robert and I can begin to emerge from this nightmare which has overtaken us.

It's quite a challenge trying to treat Robert as if he were God, display endless loving solicitude and still keep the charade reassuringly sexless, but I'm battling on. Julie was right when she said that Robert would be relieved. He is. No doubt he imagined he would be burdened with a frustrated sulky lump for the remainder of the pregnancy, so in his gratitude he's sending me flowers every day and giving me extra money to spend at Harrods to ensure that I keep smiling.

Of course he feels guilty because he's made me miserable, and of course I feel guilty because... Well, I made him miserable too, didn't I, but I didn't mean to, it was an accident, I got in a panic and said the wrong thing, that's all. Darling Robert, what a dear little boy he was; I can see us picking those strawberries in the kitchen garden, I can hear him saying, "I'll always come first with you, won't I?"—oh yes, I love Robert so much, he *does* come first, and Conor's just a skeleton in the closet who periodically rattles his bones too loudly.

That's the truth. That's reality... or is it? Yes, of course it is, and I shall now prove it by conducting the conversation that will triumphantly exorcise Conor's ghost once and for all. . . .

"...and I can't believe any decent woman would approve of such behavior, but because he was my husband... well, it was my duty as his wife to obey him, wasn't it, and he did have the right to do what he liked in bed..."

Would Conor have recognized this description of our marriage? No. He would have burst into incredulous laughter, but I couldn't stop to think of that. I didn't dare.

I struggled on.

"...and that's why I was so horrified when you suggested...well, you do understand, darling, don't you? I didn't want our marriage dragged down to that level, and I didn't want *you* dragged down to that level because I think of you as a much finer person than Conor, far more civilized, far more...well, to be frank, far more the sort of man I want to be married to."

I paused. I decided it was time I gave him an honest look so I dredged up my courage and gave him one. We were sitting side by side on the sofa in the drawing room before dinner. I had had to conduct the interview before dinner because otherwise I would have been unable to eat.

Robert's eyes were steady. "I see," he said. "Yes. Thank you."

I almost collapsed with relief. The hard part of the story was over. All I now had to do was to add the finishing touches.

"I love you better than I ever loved Conor," I said, and added in a rush: "Oh darling, you do believe that, don't you?"

"Oh yes," said Robert. "Of course." And as soon as he spoke I knew how deeply I'd lied—and what was far, far worse, I knew *he* knew how deeply I'd lied. For one terrible second we were back in the music room at Oxmoon in 1913. I could hear him saying brutally, "Always tell me the truth because if you don't I'll know and that'll mean the end."

To my horror I started to cry. "I've told you the truth," I whispered. "You've got to believe it's the truth, you've got to—"

But he stopped me from betraying myself further. His mouth closed protectively on mine for three seconds, and when he withdrew I found myself beyond speech. I could only listen as he said with perfect calmness, "We'll both accept that what you've said is true, shall we? And I think we should also accept that although we've been distressed we've discussed the matter satisfactorily, with the result that we can now put it behind us once and for all."

I nodded dumbly, still weeping. He passed me his handkerchief.

"Oh Robert..." I felt my tears flow faster than ever.

"My dearest, think of the baby, calm down and be sensible. I love you just as much as I ever did, and I'm sure everything will come right in the end."

It's a lie. The entire conversation was a lie. He knows it, I know it, but because we love each other we've invented this charade which will enable us to go on. I can't ask myself how long we can go on or where the charade is going to end. I can't ask because I can't face the answers. I can't even confide in Julie. I'll just tell her all's well—and so it is, in a way. Robert's affectionate and considerate; I'm loving and cheerful, but it's all an act, it's false through and through, and beneath the falsehood I can feel our marriage disintegrating.

. . .

I must be very near my time because I've joined in my housemaid's spring cleaning. I can't sit still, I'm turning out my wardrobe, I have to be constantly busy. Conor said I was like a bird who had suddenly realized at the last moment that it had forgotten to feather its nest. Now I'm rushing around feathering it.

I do wish the baby could be a girl, but Robert would never love a daughter, not a hope, he'd simply regard a daughter as a failure to have a son, so it's got to be a boy and I must reconcile myself to the fact that I'm destined to be the mother of sons.

Stop. I feel the first twinge. Oh God, how thrilling this is, and how sad, how very very sad that Robert can't share my joy.

"Is it a boy?" I gasped, and when I heard it was I fainted not from the ordeal of giving birth but from relief. However panic returned the instant I recovered consciousness. "Is he normal?" I said wildly. "Is he deformed? A cretin? An imbecile?"

My kind Dr. Drysdale hastened to end these agonized inquiries, and while she was speaking the midwife placed the baby in my arms.

He was washed, shining, serene.

"Oh!" I was speechless.

"Isn't he lovely?" said the midwife pleased. "I don't see them like that every day, I can tell you!"

I felt confused still after the gas and I had the dreadful desire to hide the baby from Robert as he entered the room a few minutes later, but I soon stopped feeling terrified. After he had kissed me he gazed down at our immaculate pink-and-white infant, so different from the messy red-faced babies who had cluttered up the nurseries at Oxmoon, and to my joy I realized he was stupefied with delight.

"What a *tour de force!*" he exclaimed with complete sincerity, and as I wept with joy I thought, If we can survive this we can survive anything. Yet despite all my euphoria I knew the fate of our marriage was still very far from being resolved.

I'm taking infinite trouble. I've decided (with reluctance) not to breast-feed because I sense Robert would find this repellent. I've bought a new brassière—how on earth did we manage before with those awful camisoles?—and I'm lacing myself daily into a fiendish corset so that I can regain my figure as quickly as possible. I've bought a gorgeous nightgown, wickedly décolleté, for the coming seduction. I'm reading the parliamentary reports from end to end so that I can be an interesting companion. I display unflagging absorption in the news of all Robert's activities, I hang on his every word, I pet him, cosset him and utterly exhaust myself with the effort of being the perfect wife.

It's such a relief to be with the baby because then I don't have to be perfect, I can just be myself. Dear little baby, he's quite adorable, and we've decided to call him Robin. He'll be christened Robert Charles after his father and grandfather, but to address him as Robert would be too confusing and of course there's no question of calling him Bobby. Robert did say that "Robin Godwin" sounded odd and the baby might well object to it in later life, but I said we'd cross that bridge later.

Why worry about the future? There's quite enough to worry about in the present because although Edmund's safe in hospital again, this time with an attack of typhoid, Declan's still on the run in Ireland, and meanwhile the war gets worse and worse. The food shortages have now begun in earnest. I'm bribing both the butcher and the grocer so I've had to ask Robert to increase the housekeeping money, but this was inevitable anyway because food prices have soared out of sight. There's some demented Food Controller at the Food Ministry at Grosvenor House who's covered up the Rubens murals to protect the virgin typists from corruption and is issuing a stream of orders forbidding the consumption of crumpets. It gives a new mad dimension to a life of rushing into the Underground stations to escape from the latest air raids, skimming through the casualty lists and writing the mechanical sympathy letters. To conform to the new regulations, The Gondolier can now only serve a two-course meal in the middle of the day, but I don't mind because I'm banting.

America will come into the war soon after her three sunlit years of sitting on the fence. Her soldiers will saunter across the Atlantic to save us, and how surprised they'll be when we regard them with anger and resentment! They won't realize that they've waited too long and that we're now beyond their naive notion of saving; we've bled too much, and the wounds are too deep. We may survive to live again, but it'll be a very different kind of living from the life we knew before.

Meanwhile we still haven't won and the war's going as badly as ever, and I know I'm going to start worrying about Edmund again as soon as he returns to France....

Wonderful news! Dervla writes to say that the authorities have dropped the charges against Declan: they accept that he didn't shoot the British soldiers after all. Thank God. Dervla tells me Declan's come out of hiding and plans to join Michael Collins, the famous Irish leader, so this is only a brief respite for me. But at least I know Declan's not in immediate danger of execution.

I've written a note to tell him about Robin but I know I'll have no reply. Yet I think one day there might be a letter. I shall never give up hope of a reconciliation, never, but meanwhile I can only console myself by looking at my old photographs of Conor and remembering those happy days we all shared in New York.

I've just survived the christening at Oxmoon. Everyone adored the baby and said how wonderful it was to see that Robert and I were so happy. Margaret was so relieved that she even confessed to me how worried she had been in case Robert had disliked the baby on sight, but fortunately I only needed to smile in reply because Robert is in fact behaving very well. It helps that the baby is greatly admired; Robert can consider his venture into fatherhood a huge success and regard himself once more as a winner.

That was the right moment to stage the seduction so I staged it. We were pathetically out of practice but I'm not worried; we achieved what we wanted to achieve and so logically, rationally, it should only be a matter of time before our private life returns to normal.

And yet...

There's something going on here, but I'm not sure what it is. Robert seems as interested in sex as ever, but... No, I really don't know what I'm trying to say.

I won't think about it.

Another wonderful piece of news—Edmund's been wounded at Passchendaele! And he wasn't permanently maimed—he just suffered a severe leg wound which has rendered him unfit for further service! It's so wonderful that I want to cry when I think of it. Edmund's coming home. He's won, he's safe, he's going to live....

Thank God Edmund was invalided home because if he'd remained he'd be dead by now. The past seems to be bizarrely repeating itself as if the war were completing some macabre circle. The old names are recurring again; we're on the Somme, we're at Ypres, we're on the Aisne and now at last, in the June of 1918, we're back once more along the Marne. The same few miles of mud, the same terrible suffering, and only the names of the dead have changed.

I suddenly long to turn my back on it all by accepting Daphne's invitation to spend August with her in Scotland. It would suit Robert too because he's been working much too hard and his doctor has recommended a holiday, but I know very well I'd have to go on my own....

"I'll come with you," said Robert.

I was both amazed and delighted. "Darling!" I exclaimed, kissing him warmly. "Nothing could please me more, and I'm sure it would do you good, but... well, don't think I wouldn't understand if you refused to come. I know why you always shy away from the thought of returning to the country around Ben Nevis."

"I shall be all right." He made no other comment and I made no attempt to pursue the matter, but of course, as I realized later, I had no understanding whatsoever of his aversion to the sight of Ben Nevis. I merely thought he was reluctant to be reminded of a past tragedy but the truth was I was like a wife who had offered her drunkard of a husband a bottle of brandy—and, what was worse, just poured it into the largest glass she could find.

"But you swore you'd never go climbing again!"

"I'll only go once. Just once."

He went back to mountaineering. At first he had merely contented himself with long walks in the company of one of the ghillies from the Wynter-Hamiltons' estate, but soon he had gone riding into Fort William to buy climbing equipment and renew his acquaintance with the mountain guides.

"Just once," he said. "Just once." But he could no more satisfy himself with one expedition than a drunkard could satisfy himself with a single glass of brandy. He went climbing once but he didn't stop. He couldn't. He went out every day. He cut all the social engagements the Wynter-Hamiltons had arranged and he even ignored the start of the grouse season. I was deeply embarrassed by this rudeness to our hosts, but my embarrassment, as I was finally coming to realize, was the least of my problems. After so much physical activity during the day he would sleep as soon as his head touched the pillow at night—and that, I realized as the truth slowly dawned on me, was exactly what he wanted.

"Today I climbed that same stretch where my friends were killed," he said later. "It looks so different in summer."

I could think of nothing to say except "Did you reach the top?"

"Oh yes," said Robert, and I knew he was thinking: I won.

I understood then the exact nature of his obsession. In the black-and-white world of mountaineering, a climber either won or he lost; he either reached the summit or for some reason he turned back and waited till he could try again. There were no grays there, no shadows where one appeared to succeed yet ended in failing, no hellish competition with a dead man who somehow still managed to be alive. Mountaineering was the sport in which Robert knew he could always come first but he had come to believe that sex was the sport where he would always come second.

I saw now the depth of his humiliation when he had failed to consummate our marriage during my pregnancy, and I knew that even though he was no longer impotent he was unable to forget the memory of that failure to live up to Conor Kinsella. No doubt he had wanted to forget. No doubt he had struggled to come to terms with the memory, but when all was said and done this had proved impossible for him, so impossible that in his confused despair, mountaineering had represented the only escape from emotional problems he knew he could never solve.

As the end of the holiday drew near he told me he intended to go to the Inner Hebrides and would join me later in London.

"I want to go to Mallaig," he said, much as a devout Moslem might have expressed the yearning to go to Mecca. "I want to get the boat to the islands. I want to experience again that magic moment beyond the Isle of Eigg when one can look across the glittering sea to those mystical Coolins of Rhum."

I looked at him. He was in a dream. I saw then what a hopeless romantic he was, talking of glittering seas and mystical mountains, conjuring up a fantasy

214

world like Valhalla where happiness was always endless, winning was always guaranteed and everyone lived forever in a haze of glory and masculine comradeship. I was a realist who adored romance. Robert was a romantic who adored realism. We might have been two people inhabiting different planets.

"What about your work?" I said, not exactly trying to drag him down to earth but at least trying to ease him back as painlessly as possible. "What about Mr. Lloyd George?"

"He can wait."

That was when I formally acknowledged to myself that we stood on the brink of disaster.

We were in our room at the castle, and one of the Wynter-Hamiltons' maids was helping me pack. Beyond the long window the rain was gusting across the loch and the mountains were half-hidden in mist. Turning my back on the view I dismissed the maid, waited till the door was closed and then said in the firmest voice I could manage, "Robert, the cancer's growing again on your personality and you must cut it out to survive."

"No," he said. "This is my personality as it should be. This is the man I really am."

I was too appalled to speak. The silence lengthened. Then he said, "I'm such a bloody coward that it's taken me years to face up to this, but now I'm determined to have the courage to live my life as it should be lived."

"But Robert—"

"Life's short. Life's precious. I can't go on wasting my time like this in London; it's not only wrong, it's obscene. During the war I've lived while others—men like Raymond, better men than I—have died. That's a terrible truth to have to live with, and I can only live with it by leading the kind of life I was put on this earth to lead. Then I shall feel that my survival, unmerited though it is, has some point."

So he was using his guilt about the war, not the failure of our marriage, to explain his behavior, and I knew then that he would never realize he was running away from problems he couldn't solve. His nature was too simple, his emotional understanding too limited.

We stared at each other and the void of our estrangement yawned between us.

At last he said, "So long as the war lasts I must stay at Westminster. That's my duty. But as soon as the war's over I'm giving up London and I'm giving up politics."

No longer able to look at him I turned away towards the half-packed trunks. The clock told me it was four o'clock. I dimly remembered my promise to Nanny to look in at the nursery for tea.

"I'm sorry," said Robert, not unkindly, "but perhaps I can save us both from emotional scenes if I tell you that my decision is unalterable. I gave in to you once on this subject and regretted it. I'm not giving in to you again."

That settled that. Over. Finished. Done.

"We'll go back to Gower," said Robert, "just as I originally planned."

I whispered, "What about Bobby and Margaret?"

215

"Oh, I don't care about that difficulty anymore—and anyway that's your problem to solve, not mine, because I'll be away climbing most of the year. Time's short. I'm thirty-six and that's old for mountaineering. I must go to train in the Alps if I'm ever to tackle the Himalayas, and I must go as soon as possible before I'm forty."

I sat down on the bed. "If you still loved me, you wouldn't condemn me to Gower."

"I do still love you but I can't go on pandering to this abnormal sensitivity about something that happened over twenty years ago."

"But surely we could stay in London—I wouldn't mind if we had to move to a small flat—"

"I can't afford London."

"Then perhaps I could earn a little—find employment—"

"*Find employment?* Good God, no, I don't want my wife earning a living! I want her looking after my home and child wherever I choose to live, and I don't choose to live in London, I choose to live in the parish of Penhale—and not merely for financial reasons, either. I want Robin to grow up in Gower as we did."

"But—"

"I'm sorry, but I'll stand no argument. I've given you what you want for damn nearly five years, and now it's my turn to have what I want—and that, I'm afraid, Ginette, is really all I have to say."

I have but one thought, and that is I mustn't quarrel with him. If Robert and I part I'm bound to take a lover eventually, and then unforgiving, implacable Robert will take me straight to the divorce court and wind up with custody of Robin. But that's never going to happen. *Never.*

I've got to struggle on somehow. At present I can face only one day at a time. Better not to think of Bobby and Margaret just yet. I'll cross that bridge later.

One day at a time. A little sex would help. I don't want Robert but without sex I eat and drink too much, and I feel quite miserable enough already without feeling miserable because I'm fat.

But supposing he can't be bothered to make love to me again?

Oh God, what shall I do, what shall I do, what shall I do...

He's made love to me again, though I found I was too bitter to enjoy it. I might have known he'd stick to the rules and do his marital duty in the bedroom, just as he's now doing his patriotic duty by attending sessions in the House.

But the war's coming to an end. I do believe it's almost finished, and now I can see the bridge called New Life looming ahead of me, the bridge which represents the final crisis in a marriage wrecked quite beyond repair.

· · ·

The war's ended today. I know I should feel joy, so after I've stopped grieving for Lion I try to drink champagne with a smile. But the joy's a charade. I feel the word "joy" can never be the same again, and suddenly I see that golden summer of 1913, the summer I returned to Oxmoon; I see us all laughing and lounging on the lawn while little Thomas pours milk over Glendower and Margaret presides over the silver teapot and Robert and I are in an ecstasy of romantic excitement. All gone now. A lost world utterly vanished. I'm alive in a grim drab postwar London and enduring a grim drab marital reality for which I can see neither amelioration nor cure.

They say Parliament is to be dissolved and the election held at once, so my days of respite are coming to an end. Robert won't change his mind about his career so I shall soon have to tell our friends that we're about to sink without trace into Wales. I've decided I shall be quite brazen about it and pretend to be thrilled—it's the only way of concealing my horror, but what our friends will think God only knows. Most of them will drop us immediately. It's at times like this that one discovers who one's friends really are.

Julie will stay my friend. I think I would have gone mad by now without my lunches with Julie at The Gondolier. I even go to her flat sometimes when Robert's at the House, and she's introduced me to the most delicious drink based on gin. Of course it would be dreadfully common before the war for a woman to drink gin but this is after the war and everyone's much too busy trying to keep sane to worry about being common. "Bugger being common!" says Julie, who as a socialist believes not only that we'll all be common one day but that we'll all absolutely love it.

I absolutely love gin so I suppose my next problem will be chronic drunkenness. What a bore, but oh God, what *am* I going to do, how can I stop Robert living in Gower, never mind the mountaineering, let him climb every mountain in sight, but I've got to stop us winding up on the doorstep of Oxmoon.

I haven't told Julie about Bobby. That's *verboten*, but she sees clearly that I can't bear the thought of living near my parents-in-law and that this has now become my major nightmare.

"Ginevra, why not try to enlist his mother's help? I can't believe any mother in her right mind would welcome her brilliant son wrecking his career in order to pursue an undergraduate hobby, and if he sticks to his career he'll have to stay in London, won't he?"

This strikes me as shrewd advice. I don't honestly believe that anyone can now stop Robert climbing, but if anyone can it's Margaret.

I decide to act on the principle Nothing venture, nothing gain.

We're going down to Oxmoon for Christmas as usual, and Robert's talking of advancing the date of our departure because he's so anxious to discuss the future with his father. This means that I'll soon see Margaret, but nevertheless I think it would pay me to write a little letter warning her that everything in the marital garden is rather less lovely than it appears to be...

• • •

"Here you are, Robin my angel, have some of Mummy's heavenly licorice."

Nanny said strongly, "It'll all end in tears, Mrs. Godwin, if you don't mind me saying so. Little children weren't designed by the Almighty to digest licorice on trains."

"I want it!" said dear little Robin, reminding me of Robert, and grabbed the licorice from my hand.

"Say Thank you, my pet," I said dotingly, but Robin was too busy cramming the licorice down what Nanny called "the little red lane."

It was early in December and Rory was still at school when we all left London. We had a first-class compartment on the train to ourselves, but Robin, who was twenty months old and very active, kept Nanny busy by rushing up and down the corridor at high speed. Nanny was right about the licorice. My fatal indulgence did end in tears but darling Robin was so adorable that I couldn't resist spoiling him. Fair-haired, blue-eyed, rosy-cheeked, sunny-natured and divinely intelligent, he was the one ray of sunshine in my dark private life, and although I detested mothers who doted excessively on their offspring, I was quite unable to stop myself being detestable. As Robert sat in his corner of the carriage with *The Times* and tried to pretend he had no connection with two distracted women and a child who was screaming of nausea, I ignored him and lavished all my attention on poor sickly little Robin instead.

Poor sickly little Robin was eventually borne off by Nanny to the lavatory to vomit. I was just heaving a sigh of guilty relief when Robert suddenly put down *The Times* and covered his eyes with his hand.

"That's uncommonly odd." He let his hand fall, squeezed his eyes shut, shook his head violently and opened them again. "I'm seeing double. Reminds me of the time when I was hit on the head by a cricket ball."

I was most alarmed. "Oh God, Robert, do you think it's a recurrence of the injury? One hears such extraordinary stories about head wounds."

"I'll probably be all right in a minute."

But at Swansea his condition was unchanged. As we left the train he said to me, "Don't mention this at Oxmoon. I'll see a doctor tomorrow if I'm not better."

I was concerned but he seemed only mildly troubled, so I did my best not to think of damaged retinas and concentrated instead on the task of greeting Bobby who had come to Swansea to meet the train.

The great ordeal of the 1918 Christmas was finally about to begin.

We're not the only ones in a mess apparently—what a relief it is to hear that other people too have their troubles! Poor Celia, who's more spinsterly than ever now that she's in her mid-thirties, has fallen madly in love with a German P.O.W. whom she met while she was doing V.A.D. work at the Cottage Hospital. The P.O.W. was removed from his camp in order to have an appendix operation and Celia nursed him back to health. She says he's a chemist from Heidelberg and she shows me a photograph of a cherubic youth who must be at least ten years her junior.

"My dear—a younger man—how do you do it!" I say to cheer her up, because of course Bobby and Margaret are livid and Bobby swears that even now the war's over he won't have "that damned Hun" in the house. Well, I'm not mad on the idea of her marrying a German either, but the boy looks rather a pet, and anyway if I were nearly thirty-five and had never been to bed with a man I'm sure I'd be capable of marrying anyone, even a damned Hun.

Ironically it's Edmund, the one who's suffered most from the Germans, who says, "The Huns are no different from us. They bleed and die just as we do."

Edmund's looking a little better but not much. Apparently he had a bad bout of shell shock, complete with rigor, while he was recuperating from the leg wound, and he's still odd at times, odd enough to spend several days without talking, but he seems reasonably normal at the moment although he still limps as the result of his wound. He looks at least ten years older than twenty-four.

However I've no time to meditate on Edmund's suffering because Celia's demanding all my attention. She asks what on earth should she do because Dieter is bound to be repatriated soon and this is her One Chance and if she ignores it she'll have nothing to do but press wild flowers for the rest of her life, and she can't bear it, she simply can't, and she's tried to explain to dearest Mama and dearest Papa, but they refuse to listen.

There's only one answer to give, and as one woman to another I give it.

"Celia: your dearest Mama and Papa married when they were in their teens. Obviously they haven't the remotest idea what it's like to be a spinster approaching thirty-five. I agree with you; this is your one chance; grab it and to hell with them."

This sort of advice is hardly likely to endear me to my mother-in-law, the one person whose help I so desperately need, but I'm safe for the moment because Celia can't elope with her cherubic Hun while he's still in his prison camp.

I must plan my interview with Margaret. If I were still religious, now would be the moment to pray.

"Yes, come in, Ginevra," said Margaret. "I thought it might be suitable if we had our little talk before dinner. Do sit down."

As usual we were in her room, and as usual she was sitting at her dressing table, and as usual the jewel boxes were open before her, but as I slowly crossed the room she piled the stray jewelry back into the boxes and shut the lids with ruthless movements of her fingers. I felt exactly as if I were watching a boxer hang up his gloves and prepare to fight with his bare hands.

"You mentioned a little trouble in your letter," said my mother-in-law politely. "I'm so glad you've seen fit to confide in me. Do please go on." And she set her straight mouth in its hardest, most implacable line.

I stammered away, repeating myself, contradicting myself, making the worst possible mess of my prepared speech. When I finally ground to a halt in misery all she said was "You don't seriously think I'm going to side with you against my son, do you?"

I was annihilated in a single contemptuous sentence. Amidst all my chaotic emotions I was shattered by the revelation of how much I was disliked. I wanted to cry but I was too appalled, and I was still groping futilely for words when she said, "You broke your promise to me. You said you wouldn't keep Robert from Oxmoon but you did. And you've made him very miserable, haven't you? Well, that's no surprise, not to me, I never thought you'd make him anything else, but thank God all that London nonsense is going to stop now, and if you've a grain of sense in that frivolous selfish head of yours you'll pull yourself together as fast as you damned well can and be a good wife to him for Robin's sake."

The word "damned," coming from Margaret, was more shocking than any common obscenity. I found I could barely speak. "I—I just thought the moun-taineering... not what you would want—"

"I want Robert to be happy. If climbing mountains and setting up a home in Gower will make him happy, then I want him to climb mountains and set up a home in Gower—and what's more that's what you should want too if you've got any conception at all of what a decent marriage should mean. Of course it would be hard to imagine a woman less suited to a country life than you are, but now that Robert's made his decision you have an absolute moral duty to make the best of it. Life can't always be one long dance to 'The Blue Danube,' Ginevra. There comes a time when the music stops and life—real life—has to begin."

There was a long, long silence. I felt there was so much I could say to her but I knew that whatever I said she would never understand. She saw the world in black-and-white. Like Robert she was emotionally color-blind, and for the first time in my life I caught a glimpse of her marriage from Bobby's point of view.

When she next spoke I realized she was retreating again behind her mask of refinement. Her mouth softened; she assumed a milder expression, and as I watched she became once more the Margaret who was so familiar to me, the placid, provincial little woman who emanated that subtle sinister air of authority, the self-made Victorian lady who pursed her lips in disapproval if a word like "damned" was uttered in her presence.

"Dearest Ginevra," I heard her say as she idly opened her favorite jewel box again, "don't think I'm entirely unsympathetic. Marriage can be very difficult, can't it? But then it's only the fools who think it should be a bed of roses." She stretched out her plump little hand to examine the rings on her wedding finger. "However," she said presently, "I believe even a difficult marriage has its rewards, and I'm sure that when you remember your sons you'll agree with me—in fact there's no reason, as far as I can see, why even the most arduous marriages shouldn't in the end prove happy and successful. Happy and successful marriages," said Margaret, looking me straight in the eyes, "can be sustained simply by the right attitude of mind. One needs willpower, courage and an invincible determination to keep up appearances."

I said nothing. Having drawn the line against marital failure Margaret seemed to think my problems had been resolved—or at least reduced to manageable proportions. But as far as I was concerned she had offered me no solutions; she had simply restated my dilemma, and this dilemma had become even more intractable since she had refused to help me.

I could see why she had refused. I realized she had hated Robert being swallowed up by London just as I had hated Declan being swallowed up by Ireland. I realized that although she had been proud of his achievements, she had also resented them because they had served to cut Robert off from his family. Margaret wasn't about to shed a tear because Robert was abandoning his chances in the world of politics. All she cared about was having him back in the world of Oxmoon where he would see more of his family and make Bobby happy.

So much for Margaret. So much for my hope of an ally.

Somehow finding the words to excuse myself I crept away and began to cry.

Robert's double vision has disappeared overnight but I've sent him off to see Dr. Warburton anyway. I like Gavin Warburton. He's in his mid-thirties, just as we are, and I met him during our visit to Oxmoon two years ago when I was pregnant and the Boxing Day goose had disagreed with me. When he paid his call I could see he didn't think, Here's a silly woman who's made a hog of herself and deserves to be sick. He was cheerful and sympathetic and prescribed me some delicious medicine which made me feel better.

Yes, he's a good man, someone who reminds me that not all male doctors are horrid. I wonder what he'll say to Robert.

I know I ought to consider the future again, but I can't face it at present. Margaret upset me too much and if I start remembering that interview I'll only cry, and that would be disastrous as someone might notice my eyes were suspiciously red.

Must keep up appearances.

Mustn't let anyone know.

Warburton says the double vision could be the result of the old injury but he doesn't believe it is. He thinks it's more likely to be a form of eyestrain, and he recommends that Robert has his eyes tested as soon as he returns to London. What a relief! At least, amidst all the current horrors, I don't have to worry about Robert's health.

Bobby's thrilled that Robert wants to settle on the Oxmoon estate, and the two of them have gone off this morning to inspect Martinscombe Farm which is situated below Penhale Down a mile away. I expect he minds, just as Margaret obviously does, that I'm being brought back into their lives but they're both so glad to have Robert home again that I've assumed the status of a tiresome inconvenience. They'll adapt to my presence in the end. Margaret will say, "Tolerating dearest Ginevra is simply an attitude of mind," and that'll be that. After all, anyone who can deal with the kind of problems posed by Aunt Gwyneth and Owain Bryn-Davies would find me child's play in comparison.

How brutal they were to Aunt Gwyneth, keeping her locked up year after year and only letting her visit her home at Christmas! Poor Aunt Gwyneth, now that I'm older I don't think she was mad at all, just vilely unhappy—as I shall be, shipwrecked at Martinscombe, sipping gin from dawn till dusk and trying not to seduce every shepherd in sight.

Enough. No more suicidal pessimism. I must face the problem squarely and try to work out what I can do.

As far as I can see—after prolonged and painful thought—there's one most unpalatable truth here which I have to acknowledge. If I want to save my marriage (and in order to keep Robin I've no choice but to try), then I must throw all my energy into creating an attractive home which will periodically lure Robert away from his mountains and console him when he's too old to climb seriously anymore. The prospect of embracing with enthusiasm a permanent country life on my in-laws' doorstep is repellent indeed, but at present it seems I've no choice but to admit this is the only course I can take. The one question that remains is Am I capable of taking it?

It's tempting just to answer "no," but I must try to be constructive. I think the answer could be "yes"—but only in the context of a marriage that is very, very different from this current nightmare. If I knew I could visit London regularly, if I had an interest like my journalism which I could develop without fear of Robert's disapproval, if I could keep in touch with my loyal friends like Julie, if I could even discreetly take a lover now and then to make up for the fact that Robert no longer genuinely wants me in bed—*then* I could say, Yes, very well, I love the Gower Peninsula, it's a wonderful place for Robin to be while he's growing up and I'm content with my lot. It wouldn't be the ideal life, it would certainly require some sacrifices on my part, but as Margaret said, life can't always be one long dance to "The Blue Danube." However the major difficulty about launching myself on an unconventional marriage is that Robert's never, never going to consent to the suggestion that I become an unconventional wife.

However he's bound to feel guilty if he goes away climbing for months at a time. He might make concessions later, and besides there's always the possibility that he'll wind up bored stiff, decide he's made a mistake and move back to London.

No, I mustn't despair. I must live in hope, dredge up all my strength—and somehow summon the nerve to go on.

Christmas is only a day away now, and Johnny and Blanche, that perfect couple, have joined us with their perfect child little Marian, who's now three and very pretty and wonderfully well behaved. Blanche is expecting another baby soon and is radiant. Johnny's bright-eyed with happiness. There was a point in 1917 when we all thought he would have to go to France; the authorities had a "combing-out" at the Foreign Office to sweep the less useful members of that gilded fraternity into the army, but perfect Johnny was deemed essential so he was ordered to stay where he was. He was also promoted. However, as I know from my experience with Robert, those who served on the Home Front have wound up half-dead with guilt, so I've no doubt there are some complex thoughts churning away behind Johnny's immaculate facade.

But we don't talk of the war now and we certainly don't talk of politics and the "coupon" election. It's a relentlessly merry Christmas and Robert's as merry as anyone, laughing and joking and acting as if he hasn't a problem left to solve. Without bothering to consult me first he's declared that we'll stay at Oxmoon while the Martinscombe farmhouse is prepared for us. The house is structurally sound and by no means a hovel, but it will need to be substantially extended and refurbished before it can be classed as a gentleman's residence. Bobby says he knows an architect in Swansea, a charming fellow, who would be delighted to help us, and I say, What fun, I can't wait to consult him.

I drink more champagne than usual and Robert makes Margaret livid by breaking another glass from her best set. That's the second champagne glass he's dropped recently and the shattered fragments seem horribly symbolic of our marriage.

However at least his double vision hasn't recurred.

What a Christmas.

We've seen the architect and I've displayed boundless enthusiasm for his schemes. Much good that did. Robert says he intends to spend the rest of January in Scotland, and would I mind putting the Ebury Street house on the market while he's away. We only have a short leasehold interest in the property, but Robert's decided on reflection that it would be more prudent and less wearying to dispose of it and invest the proceeds than to let the house to tenants who might prove unreliable.

He almost forgot to make love to me before he rushed off to make love to his mountains, but luckily his training as a gentleman reasserted itself and he resigned himself to playing the marital game for ten minutes. After all, if one had a wife one had to copulate with her now and then. That was the Done Thing, a ritual which had to be performed to keep up appearances.

What a farce.

Robert's returned to London from Scotland after only three days. I was most surprised but apparently he's worried about the hand that dropped the glasses; his fingers seem to be liable to occasional muscular spasms, and since this makes him a danger on the mountains, both to himself and to his companions, he's going off this morning to consult our family doctor.

Tiresome for him.

Good news for a change. Celia's eloped to Heidelberg with her pet of a damned Hun, and meanwhile here in London Blanche has had her baby, another boy, but in contrast to the poor baby who died, this infant is strong and noisy and is clearly going to thrive.

A worrying thing happened when we went to drink champagne at Johnny's house to celebrate Harry's arrival. Robert dropped his glass yet again as he suffered another muscular spasm in his hand. We'd both thought he had recovered. On the doctor's advice he had been wearing his arm in a sling, and after a few days Robert had been convinced the rest had cured the trouble.

He's so upset that I can't help feeling sorry for him.

"Let's go and dine at the Ritz."

"Robert! What a heavenly idea—but can we afford it?"

"No, but let's go anyway."

I could not make up my mind whether he was issuing the invitation to divert himself from his worry about his physical fitness or to alleviate his guilt that he had been neglecting me, but whatever his motives I was delighted. I decided to treat the offer as a gesture of friendship, and indeed once we reached the Ritz we slipped easily into our role of old friends, chatting away about amusing trivialities until I sensed we were more relaxed in each other's company than we had been for months.

"Darling Robert!" I said afterwards as we held hands in the cab that drove us home. "I know you think I'm loathing everything you do at present, and up to a point I am, but I'm truly glad if you're so much happier."

"And I'm truly sorry if I'm making you so miserable," he said, and I knew, in one of those moments of comradeship which had become so rare between us, that he was just as sincere as I was.

Our concern for each other still survived, and as I saw our old friendship, bruised, battered but apparently unbeaten, still shining amidst the ruins of our marriage, I heard myself say strongly, "Friends must stick together. I shall be all right."

"Friendship's forever?" said Robert, smiling at me.

"Apparently!"

We laughed, kissed and were happy, but after we had arrived home he said with a yawn, "I'm afraid I'm hopelessly sleepy—too much claret, I suppose," and I knew I had been rejected again. It was as if a curtain had descended abruptly on our friendship and I was alone once more in our unhappy marriage.

He sensed my feelings and immediately the marital tension began to grind between us.

"Well, never mind the claret," he said. "Perhaps I can wake up after all."

As soon as he said that, I wanted to snap back: "Oh, please don't bother—I really couldn't care less." It was so obvious that he was only doing his duty as a husband, and I felt both humiliated and repulsed. However I knew it would be fatal to refuse him. If I did that he might not offer again, and besides I spent so much time resenting his lack of desire for me that I could hardly fly into a sulk on one of the rare occasions when he felt obliged to make amends.

We undressed in our room. Drearily I trailed to the bathroom, drearily I performed my dreary rites with the vinegar and sponge and drearily I returned to bed. He performed some more dreary rites to ensure that his body did what he wanted it to do, and since there was no serious impediment, like my pregnancy, which prevented his body from obeying instructions, copulation drearily ensued for precisely sixteen seconds. I was counting for lack of anything better to do while I waited for it to be over.

"Sorry about that," said Robert, acting the perfect gentleman. "I'm afraid the claret told after all."

"Never mind," I said, and in fact neither of us minded in the least. Trailing to the bathroom I prepared for more tedium, but was awoken from my stupor of distaste by finding that the little flesh-colored thread had become detached from the sponge while the sponge itself had been shoved beyond the reach of my longest finger.

I sighed, prayed for contortionist skills and returned to the fray but in the end I gave up. I spent some time debating whether I should use the douche again, just as I always did, but in the end I was too nervous. Supposing I washed the sponge so far up that I had to have an operation to remove it? I shuddered. I was unsure what went on in the nether reaches of the feminine anatomy, but I pictured some unspeakable nastiness taking place among the ovaries. Wholly repelled I abandoned all thought of douching and toiled exhausted back to bed.

Men have no idea what women have to go through sometimes, no idea at all.

The lost sponge has finally turned up. Thank God. Really, that sort of incident is enough to put anyone off sex for life.

Robert's having his hand X-rayed, although what good that will do I don't know. Robert now tells me he's been unable to move the middle finger of his right hand for three days, and with a shock I suddenly realize how sinister this is. Could he be suffering from a series of minor strokes? It seems unlikely but this recurring weakness—we don't call it paralysis—must surely mean there's something wrong with the part of the brain that controls the muscles. Or does it? I don't know. Robert doesn't know. The doctor doesn't know.

It's all very worrying.

We've found someone who wants the house but I can't think of that at the moment. I'm too worried about Robert. He's recovered the full use of his hand but the specialist says he must have a thorough examination, and as I'm terrified of illness I'm now in a great state.

No wonder I've missed this month. Supposing Robert has a brain tumor? Supposing he only has three months to live? Supposing he drops dead tomorrow? I could do without my husband but how could I manage without my friend? Even if we eventually separate once Robin's grown up, I must have Robert in my life. Who else would stand by me through thick and thin? Who else would always be there when I needed him?

I panic. I'm demented with anxiety. In fact I'm in such a state of hysteria that

I even go to Brompton Oratory, where I used to take the boys to Mass, and make a feverish attempt to pray.

Robert's all right. Oh God, the relief! The exhaustive examination found nothing—no brain tumor, no stroke, no diabolical illness. Very strange about his hand, but I suppose it was just one of those inexplicable physical vagaries like the double vision.

Odd how these little ailments come and go. . . .

"Oh my God!"
"Robert—what is it?"
"I've got that double vision again. Damn it, *damn* it—I thought I'd finished with those bloody doctors. . . ."

He's seeing another specialist. Oddly enough I'm not so worried this time. After all, the double vision can hardly be connected with the trouble in his hand.

Or can it?

I'm suddenly so frightened that I can't even get to Brompton Oratory to pray.

I did go to the Oratory later but I couldn't feel God listening so I walked down the road to Harrods instead. There was a fruit stall on the corner of the Brompton Road and I automatically bought two pounds of oranges. Then I came home.

Five minutes ago I finished eating my third orange and now I want to eat a fourth.

I know what that means. It means I made the wrong decision when I failed to reapply the douche after that dinner at the Ritz. It means that sixteen seconds of unwanted copulation has had a very unwanted result. It means . . . but no, I simply can't face what it means.

I'll think about it later.

"Ginette, I'm afraid I wasn't entirely honest with you when I came home from Harley Street just now."

We were in the drawing room having tea and I was eating a slice of gingerbread. My hand paused halfway to my mouth. "What do you mean?"

"The specialist wasn't encouraging."

I put the gingerbread down on my plate. On my right the fire was burning, warding off the chill of a dank April day, but all the warmth seemed to have vanished from the flames.

"What did he say?"

"He thinks I have some obscure illness, but there's no method of proving the diagnosis. We can only follow an Asquith policy of 'Wait and See.'"

"Oh."

Robert continued to drink his tea. His vision had returned to normal before he had seen this second specialist, and his hand was once more unimpaired. He looked fit and strong, glowing with good health.

"But why didn't this specialist believe as the other one did that the trouble was caused by mental strain?" I said baffled at last.

"He didn't rule out that possibility. He merely said this odd combination of disorders in the eyes and hand suggested that a specific illness was responsible."

I finished my tea. "What is this illness?" I said as I put down my cup.

"He didn't go into detail. He said it involved paralysis but apparently remissions are common and people can suffer the disease yet have few symptoms."

"That doesn't sound too bad, does it," I said relieved. "How long does one take to recover?"

"Oh," said Robert, "one doesn't recover. But one needn't die prematurely either. He said the moderate cases could experience a normal life-span."

I looked at my empty teacup. I looked at the spring flowers on the sill. I looked at the pale afternoon light beyond the window. And I felt Death lay his finger on us gently, very lightly, from a long, long way away.

"There are three possibilities here," said Robert, summing up the situation with unperturbed logic. "One: this diagnosis is wrong and my physical troubles are resulting from a stress which will ease once we remove to Gower. Two: the diagnosis is right but I experience a continuation of the remission I'm enjoying at the moment. And three: the diagnosis is right but my remission isn't sustained. This uncertainty is without a doubt most tedious but one fact at least is crystal-clear: if I do have this illness I can never go climbing again. Even if I were temporarily capable of doing so it would be too dangerous because I could be stricken with paralysis at any time."

My mind was in such chaos that I hardly knew how to reply but I managed to stammer: "I'm sorry. I know how much climbing means to you—"

"Yes, well, don't let's wallow in sympathy just yet. I may not have this illness. I may recover completely, and meanwhile it seems to me all we can do is continue with our plan to remove to Gower."

I struggled to match his calmness. "You still won't consider staying in London?"

"That would be no more possible financially if I were ill than it would be if I spent my time mountaineering."

"No, I suppose not. I'm sorry, I wasn't trying to nag you again about London—"

"Besides, I want to go home. If I can't climb at least I can still go back to Oxmoon and give my son the kind of life I had when I was young."

"I understand." I thought of him still yearning for that lost Oxmoon and my throat began to ache. I knew no mere physical removal to Gower could recapture it, nothing could recapture it, it was lost and gone forever.

Robert finished his tea. "There are two matters of immediate importance," he said briskly as if he suspected I could barely contain my emotions. "The first is that I don't want anyone to know about this or else I'll have everyone staring at me as if I'm an animal at the zoo. And the second is that we must stop the builders at Martinscombe. We must have new plans drawn up in order to provide for every eventuality."

I was struggling so hard for self-control that I could only say, "What kind of plans?"

"I think it would be better to abandon the farmhouse and build a bungalow nearby. A single-story dwelling would be easier for a wheelchair."

In the grate the fire now seemed to be raging. I was so overwhelmed by the heat that I thought I would faint.

"I'll open a window," said Robert as I put my hand to my forehead.

He flung wide the casement and as he paused beside it I was able to say, "You think you do have this illness, don't you. What's it called?"

"Oh, it has some hopelessly long-winded medical name which for the life of me I can't remember."

I knew what that meant. It meant he didn't want me to look it up in the medical dictionary. It meant he himself had looked it up and been appalled.

Panic overwhelmed me.

"Darling..." I hardly knew what I was saying. "Forgive me, obviously we must talk more about this, but I'm afraid I simply must go and lie down for a while; I'm feeling thoroughly worn out."

He said he was so sorry and of course I must rest and he did hope I would soon feel better.

I escaped.

I'm much too frightened to think about the future, my mind shies away from it, so I ponder instead about whether God intends me to find some deep meaning in the fact that I'm pregnant while my husband is incurably ill.

For of course I know Robert's ill, just as I know I'm pregnant. I know it, feel it, I don't have to wait for a diagnosis.

After prolonged meditation I've come to the conclusion that there's no deep meaning in this situation and almost certainly no God. I haven't truly believed in God anyway since the Battle of the Somme, but if God does exist and has some purpose in mind for this baby, I'd very much like to know what that purpose is. As far as I can see, this pregnancy is quite the most pointless thing that's ever happened to me; I've got to endure the removal to Gower and Robert's illness and I just can't face any additional ordeal; I can't bear it. But I've got to bear it, haven't I? Can't face an abortion, too squeamish; couldn't. Other women can do as they like, I don't mind, let them get on with it, they should be able to do just what they like with their own bodies, but I know what I can do with mine without going mad with guilt.

I could arrange to erase this embryo physically but I could never erase it mentally. I'd remember it every year on the anniversary of the day it was never born—or perhaps on the anniversary of that dinner at the Ritz—and I'd picture it, as adorable as Robin, holding out its arms to me and asking to be loved. Yes, that thought's hideously emotional and hideously sentimental but it also happens to be hideously true. It's what would happen. I know myself, I know the kind of woman I am and I know I can't get rid of this child, I've got to endure it.

Can I endure Robert taking years and years to die of this unnamable paralytic disease? That question reminds me of the time I asked myself if I could endure a country life on his parents' doorstep. The obvious answer is "no" but one has to try to be constructive.

Perhaps I could survive with someone who was hopelessly ill, but my state of mind would have to be so radically different from its present state that I can't begin to imagine it. How does a woman who loathes illness stick with a sick estranged husband who insists that she remain a conventional wife? A brave woman would stick it. A religious woman would stick it. A strong woman like Margaret would stick it. But I'm neither brave nor religious nor strong. I'm cowardly, agnostic and feeble. I'm not cut out to be a heroine. All I'm cut out to be is a broken reed and a mess.

"I'm going to be a heroine when I grow up!"

"I want to be a hero!"

Dear little Robert, what fun we had...

"Friendship's forever!"

How sad to think of us saying that. For of course friendship's not forever. Friendship can be destroyed by adverse circumstances just as Robert's body can be destroyed by this illness. Nothing's forever, nothing—except the memory of Oxmoon, that lost Oxmoon of our childhood, the memory that no adverse circumstances have ever been able to destroy.

I think I'm on the brink of imagining the unimaginable, but wait; I must beware of sentimentality; I must deal only with what is real and true.

Robert asked me once if we could recapture the magic of Oxmoon and I just said brutally, "I can't work that particular miracle for you."

But that in fact is what I now have to do. I somehow have to lead us back into the world we knew as children because that's the one world which no tragedy will ever be able to annihilate.

How do I do it? We'll go back to Gower, but as I've already realized, that removal by itself means nothing. I have to re-create something intangible, a world that exists only in our heads but a world that is as real to us as Mount Everest is to a mountaineer.

It's all a question of friendship in the end, isn't it? The marriage can't help us. That's dead, and our present friendship is such a maimed pathetic affair that it's small wonder I've been tempted to discount it. But we gave friendship a unique meaning at Oxmoon, that lost Oxmoon of our childhood, and if that old bond's recaptured we'll go home again at last.

"Are you asleep?"

"No, come in, darling, I'm about to get up. I must have a word with Cook about dinner." As he entered the room I rose from the bed and drew back the

229

curtains. It had turned into a beautiful evening and below us in the courtyard the daffodils were blooming in the jardinière.

"Are you better?"

"Yes. Sorry I collapsed like some feeble Victorian heroine."

"Unlike a feeble Victorian heroine you had good reason to swoon. Ginette, can we have just one honest conversation before we go on?"

"Why not? Life's so awful at the moment that the prospect of an honest conversation doesn't even send a shiver down my spine." I straightened the bed and we sat down on it. "Where do we begin?"

"Where we left off. With the illness. Ginette, I do think I've got it. What's more, I suspect this is going to be a far worse experience than anything we can begin to imagine, so what we should do now is try to work out how we're going to face it."

All I said was "Go on."

"You loathe illness; it repulses you. You enjoy physical love; the prospect of you being tied to a cripple is ludicrous. You love London; the thought of a country life appalls you. To sum up, I can't believe you want to continue with this marriage and therefore I think it's only right that I should offer to release you from it."

"Robert—"

"Wait. I haven't finished. You must hear me to the end. Our marriage has been a failure. You know that—I know that. We've both been very unhappy, but at least I still love you enough to do all I can to put matters right. I can't drag you through this ordeal that lies ahead of me—well, to be frank, I don't think you could stand it, so if we're going to part it's far better that we should do so now. We'll forget about Martinscombe. I'll live at Oxmoon with my parents and that'll mean I'll have sufficient funds to maintain you in London—in a flat, though, I'm afraid, I couldn't afford a house. As for Robin, he must be with you while he's young although I do hope you can bring him to visit me. I wouldn't dream of asking you to come often, as I know how you hate seeing my parents, but the occasional visit would mean so much to me, and—"

"Darling—"

"No, you must let me finish, I'm sorry but you must let me have my say. The occasional visit would mean so much to me, and I would find it easier to bear the divorce if I knew I wasn't going to be entirely cut off from you both. Now, it'll be awkward about the divorce, because neither of us have any grounds, and even if I manufacture some infidelity you can't divorce me on the ground of adultery alone, but once we've lived apart for two years you could claim both adultery and desertion and then you'd be entitled—"

"No," I said.

He stared at me. "No what?"

"No divorce."

"But surely—"

"No divorce, Robert."

"Well, I admit it would be far less messy if we merely entered into a legal separation, but—"

230

"No. No legal separation."

He was dumbfounded. "No legal separation either? Oh, but I think you should consider it for your own sake. It's best to tie these things up formally—you should see a solicitor, have the legal situation explained to you."

"That's unnecessary. I want to remain married to you."

"For Robin's sake, you mean? But... how could we sustain a normal marriage?"

I said nothing. We went on sitting on the bed, he looking at me, I staring at the rings on my wedding finger.

"It would be impossible for me to be a conventional husband to you," said Robert. He paused to consider the logical deductions which could be drawn from this fact. Then he said with his characteristic simplicity, "Therefore I couldn't expect you to be a conventional wife. That wouldn't be fair at all. That wouldn't be playing the game." And as he paused again, frowning as he tried to imagine the complex relationship which lay far beyond the bounds of the marital game as he perceived it, I covered his hand reassuringly with mine.

"There are all kinds of marriages, Robert. Ours will simply be a little different from most marriages, that's all."

"Yes, but... well, it wouldn't be a marriage at all, would it, because it would be absolutely essential to me that you lived entirely as you wished—"

"It would still be a marriage, Robert."

"—because, you see, I couldn't bear it if you came to hate me for blighting your life—"

"I understand."

"—and that's why I shan't mind if you can't bring yourself to visit me much— I couldn't bear you to look at me with loathing—or repulsion—or worst of all pity—I'd rather set you free altogether, no matter how much I came to miss you—"

"Very well. Set me free. But set me free within the bounds of our marriage."

He still did not understand. He looked at me trustfully, waiting for an explanation, and when I saw that trust I knew time was completing its circle at last and we were moving back to where it had all begun.

I thought: Nearly there now, nearly home. And as I clasped his hand in mine I could see in the distance the strawberry beds and the mellow walls and the sunlight streaming down upon the kitchen garden long ago.

"But are you sure," said Robert when I remained silent, "that you'll wish to stay married once you're living apart from me in London?"

"I'm not staying in London," I said. "I'm coming with you to Gower."

I saw the trust in his eyes eclipsed by the blackest despair. He said in a shaking voice, "That's just sentimentality! You're being stupid, emotional and unrealistic! You're embarking on a charade you'll never be able to sustain!"

But I could see the strawberries, large and juicy among their thick leaves. I could feel the sun blazing down upon us, and at that moment the circle was completed, time was displaced and *we were there*, side by side in the kitchen garden at Oxmoon with the magic past recaptured and the strawberries in our hands.

"No, Robert," I said. "This is no charade, no illusion and no lie. There's one absolute truth in this situation, and it's the truth I intend to prove to you till the day you die."

"But for God's sake, what truth can that possibly be?"

Speaking in a voice that never faltered I completed the reformation of our marriage which he himself had had the courage to begin. "Robert," I said simply, "I could always walk out on a husband. But I could never turn my back on a friend."

PART THREE

JOHN
1921-1928

Why then do you mortal men seek after happiness outside yourselves, when it lies within you? You are led astray by error and ignorance. I will briefly show you what complete happiness hinges upon. If I ask you whether there is anything more precious to you than your own self, you will say no. So if you are in possession of yourself you will possess something you would never wish to lose and something Fortune could never take away....

—Boethius
The Consolation of Philosophy

1

I

"SHE SAID, 'I could always walk out on a husband, but I could never turn my back on a friend.'"

"What an extraordinary remark."

"She's an extraordinary woman."

"Quite."

I moved restlessly to the window. The spring sun, shining on Ginevra's chaotic garden, emphasized herbaceous borders crammed with a variety of unsuitable shrubs, most of which had failed to survive the winter. A group of vulgar stone cherubs, part of a dismantled fountain acquired at an auction, were grouped beyond the swing where Robin was playing, and his nanny was staring at them as if she were wishing she had a supply of fig leaves. A wail from a nearby rug indicated that the baby was as usual oppressed with his peculiarly vocal variety of unhappiness.

"Shut the window, would you, John? I can't stand the way that child cries all the time. It gets on my nerves."

It was not one of Robert's better days. He was sitting in his favorite armchair by the hideous modern fireplace and fidgeting with his crutches as if he longed to break them in two. Ginevra had gone to London for a week, but when I had ventured to suggest that a wife's recurring absences from home could hardly be in the best interests of her husband, he had become angry. In vain I had tried to explain that I merely wished to sympathize with him in his depression; that had made him angrier than ever. He had said he loathed sympathy. Again I had tried to apologize and again I had been shouted down. Grudgingly conceding that my intentions had been good, he had said he had no alternative but to show me that my sympathy was misplaced, and the next moment, to my embarrassment, he had launched himself upon an explanation of his relationship with his wife.

I had always accepted that despite their recent adversity Robert and Ginevra had the happiest and most perfect of marriages, so it came as a considerable shock to me to hear that the marriage had been highly unorthodox for over two years.

I did not care for unorthodoxy. When Robert told me he had not pursued his marital rights since the onset of his illness, I was uncomfortable enough to rise to my feet; when he added that Ginevra was the kind of woman who would find intimacy with a diseased man repulsive, I hardly knew where to look and when he told me neither of them cared anyway that this aspect of their marriage had ceased, I found myself moving aimlessly around the room to cover my extreme distaste for the conversation. Robert completed this Bohemian marital portrait by declaring that he had no idea what Ginevra did in London, but he hoped she drank plenty of champagne, visited Harrods every day and had at least three lovers.

"... because if that's the price I have to pay for having a good friend at my side, then by God I'm more than willing to pay it," he concluded truculently.

My diplomatic training ensured that I answered: "Quite so. I entirely understand," but I was appalled. I did not blame Robert. Obviously for the children's sake he had no choice but to be a complaisant husband, but I felt that Ginevra, never noted for either her decorum or her good taste, had sunk even lower than I had always feared was possible.

"I must make a move," said Robert. "Ring the bell, would you?"

I did not offer to assist him to the cloakroom. His man Bennett had been a hospital orderly during the war and was more adroit than I was at giving the help necessary when Robert was finding his crutches a trial. As Bennett entered the room I said, "I'll just say hullo to the children," and then I escaped through the French windows into the bungalow's untidy garden.

Robin came running to meet me as I crossed the lawn. He had recently celebrated his fourth birthday and was tall for his age. Since neither Robert nor Ginevra had any talent for parenthood he had been abominably spoiled, but he was a good-looking intelligent little fellow who with luck would survive his upbringing. Meanwhile he was merely precocious and tyrannical.

"Hullo, Uncle John! Mummy sent me a postcard from London!" And pulling a crumpled picture of Buckingham Palace from his pocket, he read the message in order to show off his formidable reading ability.

I knew people thought Blanche and I were old-fashioned, but we still preferred the dignity of "Mama" and "Papa" to the mediocrity of "Mummy" and "Daddy." However as usual Ginevra had no taste in such matters. Her Kinsella sons actually called her "Ma" although allowances had to be made for their New York background.

I inspected the picture, commented admiringly on the gushing message and paused to bid the nanny good afternoon before turning my attention to the baby, who was sitting moodily on his rug. He was eighteen months old but backward, disinclined to walk or talk. His pale blue eyes looked up at me fearfully; his large nose quivered; he was very plain.

"Silly Kester!" said Robin, trying to tug me away.

The baby had been named Christopher after the patron saint of travelers because

236

Robert and Ginevra had felt they had such a difficult journey ahead of them, but although I liked the name it was never used. Ginevra had adopted this coy rustic abbreviation because she claimed to find it "romantic," and Robert was too indifferent to the child to object.

To divert Robin, I gave him my watch and asked him if he could tell the time. Then I knelt on the rug and tried to encourage the baby to take a few steps. He managed three and fell down. Howls ensued. "Pernicious infant," said Robin, showing off the vocabulary that Robert taught him as a jest, and handed me back my watch. "It's quarter past four. Are you staying to tea?"

But I had planned to be home for tea. Extricating myself from a situation that threatened to become increasingly noisy, I patted both children on the head and retreated to the drawing room. I was very much aware that I had not yet disclosed to Robert the main purpose of my call at the bungalow that afternoon.

Bennett was helping Robert into his chair again as I closed the French windows.

"Will you be staying to tea, Mr. John?" said Bennett as he prepared to leave the room.

I glanced at Robert but he said nothing. I knew he was too proud to ask for fear I might think he was begging for company.

"Yes, I will," I said abruptly, "but could you telephone my wife, please, Bennett, and say I'm staying on?"

As soon as Bennett had left the room Robert said, "John, I hope you didn't abandon a promising career at the Foreign Office because you thought you had some repellent moral duty to be my unpaid companion."

"Don't be absurd! I hated the F.O. and was only too pleased to begin a new life in Gower for reasons which had nothing to do with my moral duty!"

"I still find your decision surprising—and to some extent hard to explain. Why did you really come back here? You're a dark horse, John! I sometimes wonder if even you yourself have any idea of what's really going on in your head!"

"Good heavens, how very sinister you make me sound! I assure you I'm just an ordinary, simple sort of chap—"

"A touching description—but I suspect hardly a truthful one. Never mind, let it pass. Personally I'm only too glad that when Papa's senile and I'm a vegetable there'll be someone in Gower who's capable of ruling the Godwin roost—and now you're going to fling up your hands in diplomatic horror! My God, is it really so impossible to have an honest conversation with you?"

"Damn you, I *am* being honest! As you well know, I came back here because I was unhappy in London. Naturally I was influenced in my decision by the fact that Papa isn't getting any younger and your health isn't what it should be, but—"

"A truly magnificent euphemism. Go on. I can hardly wait to hear what you're going to come out with next."

"—but above and beyond my moral duty to give my father and brother any assistance which may become necessary in the future, I was concerned primarily with my family's happiness and welfare—which I feel will be better served if I live the life of a country gentleman in Gower than if I pursue a life of ambition in a career which means nothing to me."

"It all sounds most implausible," said Robert mildly, lighting a cigarette, "but since I benefit so profoundly, why should I start worrying that you've gone off your head? Very well, I accept what you say. You're a saint who yearns for the simple life. Very nice. I congratulate you."

I was silent. This was evidently one of Robert's more difficult days not only physically but emotionally as well, and I had no wish to continue a conversation which could so easily become acrimonious. I too lit a cigarette in order to provide an excuse for my continuing silence, but I was still wondering how I could turn the conversation towards the subject I wished to discuss when Robert said, "Forgive me. I know you genuinely believe in what you say and that means I've no right to treat you as a *poseur*. I suppose I'm cynical about your decision because I know you enjoyed the glitter and glamour of London far more than I ever did, but I must say you've given no indication that you miss your old life—and that in turn, as I said to Papa the other day, makes me wonder how well I ever knew you in the first place."

I saw my chance. "Talking of Papa, Robert," I said swiftly, "I've reached the stage where I can no longer condone his disgraceful situation—in fact I feel so embarrassed by him nowadays that I hardly like to take my family to Oxmoon every Sunday. Something's got to be done. His conduct is absolutely beyond the pale."

"I agree it's regrettable. However—"

"Regrettable! What an odious understatement! For Papa to keep a mistress in London is one thing; for him to keep a mistress in Gower is quite another—and for him to keep a former Oxmoon parlormaid in a tied cottage in Penhale is simply beyond the bounds of all permissible behavior."

"I do see it must be awkward for you and Blanche. But if Mama can tolerate the situation then I think you should too."

"I'm afraid I'm finding that old argument of yours increasingly unsatisfactory. Obviously Mama can no longer cope. She needs active assistance, not tactful silence."

"When Mama wants assistance she'll ask for it."

"Obviously she's too proud to do so. Robert, in my opinion it's your moral duty as the eldest son to tell Papa—"

"Any reprimand from me would be futile because unfortunately a man as troubled as Papa can rarely be cured by censure."

"But how dare he break all the rules like this!"

"I agree it's tragic. But try to remember the mitigating circumstances."

"What mitigating circumstances?"

"His sufferings in adolescence."

"How can they be mitigating circumstances? They should have taught him that the wages of sin are death!"

Robert sighed as if praying for patience.

"Well, look what happened to Owain Bryn-Davies!" I shouted, maddened by his obtuseness.

"Ah yes," said Robert blandly. "Mr. Owain Bryn-Davies and his little accident with the tide tables."

I looked away but not quickly enough and Robert saw the expression in my eyes. I heard his quick intake of breath. Then he said, "So you know. How the devil did you find out?"

"I haven't the slightest idea what you're talking about."

"My dear John—"

"I know nothing, absolutely nothing."

"Then why don't you demand that I explain myself? For someone who's asserting ignorance of the past you show the most remarkable lack of curiosity!"

There was a silence. I tried to speak but nothing happened, and at last Robert said mildly, coaxingly, as if I were some peculiarly difficult witness, "You've known for some time, have you? Who told you? And why did you never confide in me? It's the devil of a shock for a man, as I well know, to discover that his father's committed—"

I found my tongue just in time. Before he could utter the unutterable I said with all the force I could muster, "I'm sorry, Robert, but this is a matter which I refuse to discuss either now or on any later occasion. I also refuse to be diverted from the subject of Papa's present behavior, so let me now ask the vital question again: Do you or do you not intend to tell him he must pull himself together and mend his ways?"

"I most certainly do not. It would only exacerbate a situation which is already quite painful enough."

"Very well." I rose to my feet. "Then if you won't tell him, I shall."

"Oh for God's sake, John, don't be such a bloody fool!"

"I hate to contradict you, Robert, but I absolutely deny being a fool, bloody or otherwise. I'm a man intelligent enough to have high standards—and here I draw the line."

II

"What an odd boy you are," said my father. "Impertinent too."

"I'm not a boy, sir. I'm a man of twenty-nine."

"Then behave like one."

We were in the billiard room at Oxmoon shortly after six o'clock that evening. I had found my father and Edmund between games, and when I had asked for a word in private, Edmund had drifted away before my father could suggest we withdrew to the library, the room where he usually chose to conduct private conversations.

There was a superficial physical resemblance between us but this was muted by a difference in manner. My father, unmarked by the stamp of an English education, concealed his Welsh shrewdness behind an informal, almost indolent charm. So appealing was this charm that one tended to underestimate his strength, which was considerable. He was not a weak man. He had strong feelings, strong opinions and a strong inclination to be stubborn in the face of opposition. Although gentle and affectionate with his children he was capable of violence if his temper was roused, and the moment I finished speaking I knew I had roused it.

I was already nervous but now I became more nervous than ever. I did love my father but the love was confined in a straitjacket of fear because whenever I looked at him I could never forget that I was seeing a man who had committed murder and got away with it. I knew that the murder had been justified. I knew he was a good man. But always I was aware that he was capable of anything, and that was why I felt it was so important that he stuck to the rules of a civilized society when conducting his private life.

"Sir, please believe me when I say I speak only out of respect and concern—"

"I don't know what the devil you're speaking out of, but I doubt if respect and concern have much to do with it." He turned away from me, flung open the door and shouted, "Margaret!"

I was horrified. "Papa, for God's sake—you can't drag Mama into this conversation!"

My father lost his temper. As I backed away, automatically keeping the table between us, he shouted, "How dare you try to tell me what I can or can't do! How dare you have the insolence to preach to me in this hypocritical fashion!"

"I'm no hypocrite. I'm just doing what I honestly believe to be right."

"Your trouble is that you'd like a mistress in Penhale yourself but you know your wife would be a lot less understanding than mine!"

I was so angry that I forgot my fear of his violence and walked right up to him. "That's a bloody lie!" I shouted. "*You* may have no more morals than your bloody mother, but at least *I* have the bloody decency not to follow in your footsteps!"

A plump little hand closed on my arm. My mother said in a voice cold with fury, "That's a disgraceful thing to say to your father. Apologize this instant," and her manner shocked me into composure.

I said, "I'm sorry. I'm very sorry, I—" but even before I could finish speaking my father was addressing my mother.

"Margaret, I can't manage this boy, I can't talk to him, he makes me too angry."

"Yes, don't worry, dear," said my mother, "I'll straighten out this little difficulty for you."

He kissed her and left the room. My mother's hand was still gripping my arm, but as his footsteps receded she released me, stepped back a pace so that she could more easily look me in the eyes and then said with a coarseness which shocked me to the core, "You damned fool—why in God's name couldn't you come to me if you wanted to complain about Mrs. Straker? For an intelligent man you seem to have behaved with the most unforgivable stupidity."

240

III

I had anticipated neither my mother's anger nor her attitude to my father's behavior, and for a moment I was too distressed to marshal my defenses. I was very fond of my mother. Lion was supposed to have been her favorite, but it seemed to me I had been favored too because I sensed she made special efforts to be loving towards me. In early childhood I had taken this warmth for granted but later when I was all too aware that my resemblance to my grandmother might make me repulsive in my parents' eyes, I had gratefully interpreted my mother's marked affection as a sign that I was not to be condemned to a low place in her esteem.

But this resolute determination of hers to be just was characteristic behavior. What I admired most about my mother was her infinite capacity for rejecting wrongdoing, and whenever she said, "I draw the line," I felt an overwhelming relief and gratitude. My mother was the bastion against madness, chaos and catastrophe. In a world where I had known from childhood that absolutely anyone was capable of absolutely anything, my mother offered an infallible recipe for normality: one set oneself high moral standards, one drew the line against what was wrong—and one survived with one's sanity intact. My fear of my father had long been ameliorated by the knowledge that my mother would always stop him if ever he began to breach his own rules too flagrantly.

I thought she would stop him now.

"Mama, please do forgive me but I came here this evening with the very best intentions—"

"Your father is not to be upset like this! He needs compassion and understanding, not pigheaded intolerance!"

"Well, all I can say is I think it's time *he* showed some compassion and understanding! What about us? What about his family? I can't stand Blanche being exposed to scandal like this—"

"Have you told her?"

"What about?"

"The past."

"What past?"

"Oh, for God's sake, John! Sometimes I think this Welsh evasiveness will drive me mad!"

"I'm not Welsh, not at all, I'm English by education, inclination and temperament."

"Good. Then perhaps you'll now practice the Anglo-Saxon virtue of calling a spade a spade. Have you or have you not told Blanche that your father was driven to kill his mother's lover and shut his mother up in an asylum for the rest of her life?"

"Good God, no! Of course I've never told Blanche that!"

"Then may I suggest that you should? Quite apart from the fact that she's your devoted wife and deserves your confidence, she's also a compassionate intelligent girl, and I think if she knew the full tragedy of your father's past she would be willing to forgive him now for putting you both in such a difficult position."

"I'm sorry," I said, making a great effort to remain calm, "we're ostensibly conversing with each other but I'm beginning to think no communication's taking place. Are you trying to tell me that you're refusing to draw the line against Papa's immorality despite the fact that this is an occasion when the firmest possible line should be drawn?"

"I do draw the line," said my mother. "I draw the line against your un-Christian, uncharitable and unforgivably priggish behavior. I find it repellent."

"But it's his behavior that's repellent! How can you tolerate him keeping Mrs. Straker in Penhale—Straker the parlormaid whom you had to dismiss from Oxmoon because he couldn't keep his hands off her! I think the entire episode's disgraceful, and how you can stand there and criticize me when all I'm trying to do is prevent innocent people from suffering as the result of his despicable conduct—"

My mother slapped me across the mouth. As I gasped, I saw not only the rage but the dislike blaze in her eyes.

The world went dark. The past began to suppurate. Chaos had come again.

"I don't pretend to understand you," said my mother. "I never have. I've always made a special effort not to be prejudiced, but really it's very hard not to be prejudiced when I see Bobby upset like this. I know just what's going on in his mind—he used to lecture his mother about her immorality and now he must feel as if her ghost has crawled out of the grave to lecture him in return!"

"But I had no idea I'd remind him of—"

"Oh, be quiet! Can't you see how you're tormenting Bobby by treating him as if he's in danger of ending up like his mother?"

"I just want him to live up to his own high standards—"

"He would if he could but he can't. That's the truth of it. Your father's haunted by the past. He thinks it'll drive him mad unless he uses every means he can to control it, and I think he's right; it'll drive him mad if he can't live with the memory of what happened. Women help him live with it. I don't know why. He doesn't know why. It doesn't matter why. What matters is that women keep him sane. I don't care about the mistresses. I did once, but not anymore; I don't give a damn. I'm the one he loves and that's all that counts—and as for Milly Straker, I tell you frankly that she's the best thing that's happened to Bobby for a very long time. I concede it's unfortunate that he has to keep her in Penhale, but now that he's getting older it's no use expecting him to travel up to London or even as far as Swansea in order to get what he must have. I accept that she has to live in Penhale, but that's all right; that's a concession I'm prepared to make because Mrs. Straker, provided she's paid well, won't cause trouble; quite the reverse. She's clever and discreet, and if he has to have a whore at least I have the satisfaction of knowing he has a whore who has high standards and sticks to them. I can respect someone like that, no matter how common and vulgar she is, and besides I'm sufficiently practical to understand that there are worse fates for an elderly lecher than Mrs. Straker. Gervase de Bracy died of syphilis. Oswald Stourham's taken to drink. In contrast Bobby's healthy and reasonably happy—whenever

242

you're not making him miserable by reminding him of his mother. Now go home, talk the whole matter over sensibly with your wife and never, never let me find you making such a scene here again."

She left the room. For a long time I stayed by the billiard table, my forefinger tracing meaningless patterns on the green baize, but at last I slipped furtively out of the house and drove home in misery to my family.

IV

"Hullo, darling! There you are, Marian, didn't I tell you Papa would be back in time to say good night? Let me see if Harry's finished his bath. . . . John, is anything the matter?"

"No, everything's fine," I said. "Couldn't be better."

"Papa, I've chosen my bedtime story," said Marian, who was going to be six in the autumn.

I read a fairy tale about a handsome prince who fell in love with a ravishing peasant girl. After interminable vicissitudes they succeeded in getting married and living happily ever after.

"That's like you and Mama, isn't it, Papa?"

"Well, Mama was hardly a peasant girl, Marian, but yes, we did get married and live happily ever after."

Blanche returned to the night nursery with Harry in her arms.

He was two years old. He looked very clean after his bath and very fresh in a newly laundered little nightshirt. A faint scent of talcum powder drifted towards me. His dark hair, much darker than mine, had been neatly parted and brushed.

"Kiss Harry, darling," said Blanche to Marian as Nanny hovered in the background with the customary approving expression on her face, "and then Papa will hear you say your prayers."

Harry yawned again. His small head drooped against my chest to betray how tired he was after yet another stimulating day. Then, conscious that I was smiling at him, he looked up and smiled brilliantly back at me.

I thought of spoiled little Robin and tedious little Kester and knew a moment of intense pity for Robert, but a second later I had recognized this pity as an ambivalent emotion and was suppressing it rigorously. It would never do to enjoy Robert's misfortune, and it would certainly never do to savor the notion that my life was turning out to be more satisfactory than his. These were contemptible thoughts indeed, suggesting hidden jealousies which could not be permitted to exist.

Chaos as always was waiting. And as always I drew the line.

"Darling," said Blanche uneasily several hours later when we were in bed. "I know something's wrong, and I do wish you'd tell me what it is. I must be a poor sort of wife if you feel you can't confide in me."

"Don't be absurd; you're a perfect wife, you know you are!"

"In that case—"

"I'm worried about my father, but I don't want to talk about him."

"Ah." I heard her sigh in the dark. "I wish there was something I could do when you're troubled," she said, laying her cheek gently against my shoulder. "I hate feeling I'm incapable of helping you."

I knew at once how she could help me but I spent a great deal of my married life trying not to exploit her love by giving vent to selfish inconsiderate behavior, and I now shrank from taking advantage of her. She had been exceptionally generous to me only the night before.

"I wouldn't dream of—"

"It doesn't matter."

There was a silence while I tried to work out what was the right thing to do. No decent husband imposed himself on his wife on two consecutive nights. On the other hand if the wife expressed willingness this could be held to exonerate him, although if she was merely expressing willingness in order to be a good wife, then the consent failed to be genuine and restraint was called for.

"Darling..." She pressed closer to me. To my humiliation I was conquered, and despising myself I embarked on the most pleasurable way I had yet discovered of forgetting what I had no wish to remember. The exquisiteness of that pleasure never failed to appall me, and that night after Blanche had fallen asleep I found myself struggling afresh with memories that not even the most exquisite pleasure could annul. I knew all too well what could happen to those who became addicted to carnal pleasure—and the next moment I was back in the past again while my grandmother screamed for mercy, my mother struck her to control the hysterics and my father shouted at me in Welsh at the top of his voice that insanity and ruin lay waiting for all those who failed to draw the line.

V

I had no respite when I fell asleep because that night she invaded my dreams, just as she always did when I was seriously upset. My grandmother had died in 1910 but for me in 1921 she was still alive. The straight line of time bent so that 1903 kept recurring interminably in my mind, the Christmas of 1903 when I had been eleven years old.

My grandmother had been sixty-two. She had not aged well. She was thin and haggard. She had bony hands which she twisted together continually. Her glance darted furtively hither and thither among her grandchildren, as if she were trying to pin us all in her mind so that she could savor us during her lonely months in the asylum where we never visited her. We all thought her both pathetic and a bore, a perpetual blight on our otherwise exuberant family Christmas, a cross which we had to undertake in the name of Christian charity. Grandmama was

244

mad and not normally a fit subject for discussion, but once a year her portrait had to be brought down from the attics and hung in the dining room, and once a year for a few hours we had to endure her presence. We sighed and groaned and yawned but every Christmas submitted ourselves to the tedium of the inevitable.

The Christmas of 1903 began in unremarkable fashion. On Christmas Eve my father fetched my grandmother from the Home of the Assumption. On Christmas morning we all racketed around in our noisy fashion, pulling all the gifts out of our stockings, eating a huge breakfast and setting off for church. The presents under the tree were never unwrapped until after dinner which at Christmas, in order to spare the servants, was taken in the middle of the day. When we all returned from church my mother went to the kitchens to see how the dinner preparations were progressing and my father remained in the drawing room to keep an eye on my grandmother. It had only recently occurred to me that my parents never left my grandmother alone with their children.

Robert, always aloof, had wandered off somewhere in search of solitude. Ginevra was absent in America. Celia and Lion were playing an acrimonious game of cribbage while Edmund looked on. I was reading a book, *Kidnapped* by Stevenson it was, I remember it well, just as I remember glancing up from the page and seeing my grandmother watching me from her position by the hearth.

My father was talking to her casually in Welsh about his plans to redesign the kitchen garden. He was just saying, "And I've a good mind to double the asparagus beds" when Ifor the footman rushed pell-mell into the room and gasped that the head parlormaid was having what he described as a "pepper-leptic" fit in the dining room.

"Good God!" said my father, and hurried out.

"Heavens!" said Celia, and rushed after him.

"This sounds too good to miss!" said Lion outrageously, and bounded away with Edmund, the constant shadow, pounding at his heels.

I was just setting aside my book after making the obvious decision to follow them when my grandmother said suddenly, "Johnny."

I was called Johnny in those days. I had always thought the name John very dull, redolent of John Bull and English stuffiness, and I had long been envious of Lion's racy evocative first name.

"Yes, Grandmama?" I said politely in Welsh.

She beckoned me. Trying to disguise my impatience, I drew closer and thought, Poor mad old crone.

"I want to give you a little present," she said, "a special present, every year I've brought it to Oxmoon to give to you and every year I've never had the chance to see you on your own." She looked nervously at the half-open door. Her eyes were bright with fear. "Take me somewhere private, Johnny, where they won't find us."

I thought this was possibly some new manifestation of madness, but I was intrigued by the thought of a special present and she seemed harmless enough.

"Very well," I said politely, helping her to her feet. "We'll go to the music room. We'll be quite private there."

We set off, she clutching my arm in an agony of nervousness, I feeling gratified that I had been singled out for special attention. Bayliss the butler was passing through the hall when we left the drawing room, but he was too busy to do more than cast us a passing glance, and a minute later we had reached our sanctuary. I was just saying kindly, "There! You're quite private now!" when to my horror my grandmother embraced me amidst floods of tears.

"Forgive me." She saw how alarmed I was and at once she withdrew, but the tears continued to stream down her cheeks. "I couldn't help myself," she whispered, "I've loved you so much for so long, such a fine boy you are, the finest in the family and so special to me, but of course I never dared say so in front of Margaret because that would make her angry and then she might not let me come home anymore, and if that happened I'd never see you and that would break my heart because I love you so much, so much love I have and no one to give it to, not anymore, but just for a little while at Christmas I can look at you and love you without Margaret knowing about it—oh, how frightened I am of Margaret, turning my son against me, keeping me from my grandchildren, so hard your mother is, Johnny, so cruel and unforgiving, but never mind that now, all that matters is that I have you on my own at last and I mustn't waste any time."

She produced a carefully folded handkerchief and held it out to me.

"Here, take this, take it, it's something to remember me by, something that will always remind you I love you better than anyone else does, better than your parents do, such a large family they have, so many claims on their affection, but never mind, you come first with me always although you mustn't tell Margaret or she won't let me see you anymore. Yes, unfold the handkerchief, I used my best handkerchief specially for you, yes, it's a ring, a man's signet ring, it'll be too big for you now but you can wear it later in memory of me. It belonged to the man I loved. They took it from his corpse after he was drowned. I asked Bobby for the ring and he saw that I got it but I don't know if he ever told Margaret. Margaret wouldn't have wanted me to have it, oh I'm so frightened of Margaret, and that's why you must hide the ring from her, Johnny, hide it until you're grown up, because if Margaret ever finds out that I've given you the ring which belonged to—"

She stopped. Her eyes dilated in terror. Spinning round I found that my mother had soundlessly opened the door.

"So there you are," said my mother, very composed. "Bayliss said he saw you disappearing together down the corridor to the music room." Stepping back into the passage she called, "All's well, Bobby. I've found her."

My grandmother began to tremble. She had backed away against the wall. As I watched, paralyzed by the guilt and fear that emanated from her, I saw the tears flow down her cheeks again.

My mother stepped back into the room. "Dearest Grandmama," she said kindly, "how generous of you to give Johnny one of your little mementos. Mr. Bryn-Davies's ring, isn't it? Yes, I thought I recognized it. However I'm afraid Johnny

246

couldn't possibly accept such a gift. It wouldn't be fitting."

She spoke as always in English. I had never heard my mother speak a word of Welsh and yet I suspected she understood more than she would admit. I had no idea how much of my grandmother's speech she had overheard but I could see that my grandmother feared the worst and was petrified.

"Johnny dear, give Grandmama back the ring, please."

"Mama, please don't be cross with poor Grandmama—"

"Give her back the ring."

"What ring?" said my father from the doorway.

My grandmother covered her face with her hands and began to sob.

"Dearest Grandmama, Bobby," said her daughter-in-law, "has decided to single out Johnny for special attention by giving him the ring which belonged to Mr. Bryn-Davies."

"My God," said my father to his mother, "you bloody whore."

"Bobby, no—Margaret, please—Margaret, stop him—"

He slammed the door and seized me by the scruff of the neck. I was terrified. As my relaxed cheerful familiar father dissolved into a taut violent stranger, I felt as if I were witnessing a shining surface cracking apart to reveal unspeakable horrors beneath. Certainty, security, safety, peace—all the cherished attributes of a happy childhood—all were blasted from my life in seconds. I had been catapulted into a chaotic darkness. I knew instinctively that we were each one of us in hell.

He snatched the ring, shoved me aside and shook his mother by the shoulders. "You filthy, disgusting old woman, how dare you ask any son of mine to wear a ring which belonged to that thief, that blackguard, *that bloody villain Bryn-Davies* who ruined you and robbed me blind and soaked us all in evil—"

"I'll take the child out, Bobby," said my mother crisply. "This isn't good for him."

"Oh no!" shouted my father. "He stays where he is! He's going to find out all about this vile old woman who's singled him out for special attention!" And he began to talk in Welsh in graphic detail about how she had poisoned her husband in order to live a life of debauchery with her lover.

My grandmother went down on her knees and begged him to stop. He hit her and went on. Then she went down on her knees to my mother.

"Send Johnny away, Margaret—spare him—please—"

"No, it must be as my husband wishes," said my mother without expression, and stood by unmoved as my father hit my grandmother again until she cowered sobbing at his feet.

"...and it was her wickedness which drove me to evil..." He never stopped talking, even when he was hitting her. He was talking all the time. "...and I killed Bryn-Davies, yes, I killed him—I trapped him and drowned him on the Shipway so that Oxmoon could be purged and we could all be saved—"

My grandmother saw my expression and could bear the torture no longer. She began to scream for mercy.

My mother stepped forward. "She's hysterical, Bobby. You'll have to hit her again."

"I daren't. I might kill her."

The door opened. Celia was revealed on the threshold.

"Mama, what on earth—"

"Celia, leave us at once and keep the little ones out of the way. Very well, Bobby, I'll deal with this."

My mother walked up to my grandmother and slapped her firmly twice, once on each cheek. That ended the hysterics, but not the scene. My father, sweat streaming down his face, then took advantage of the silence to shake me as if I were a bunch of rags and shout, "Look at her! Go on, look at her! She picked you out because she thinks you're like her, but if ever you're tempted to depravity just you remember this vile filthy old woman, utterly ruined, hated by those she loves, damned through all eternity—yes, just you remember her and never forget— *never forget for one moment*—that insanity and ruin lie waiting for those who fail to draw the line!"

He released me. My mother said to him, "Lock her up in one of the attics. She's not fit to dine. She'll have to go back to the asylum this afternoon."

My grandmother whimpered but was too terrified to speak.

"If you behave now," said my mother to her, "we might let you come back next year. I'll have to think about it. But if you do come back, you are never, never, *never* to address another word to any of my children. You're to keep silent and speak only when you're spoken to. Very well, Bobby, take her away."

My father removed the object. I could not think of her as a human being anymore. She had become evil personified, a threatening force which had to be perpetually kept at bay. Overpowered by fear I hid my face from her and hurtled blindly into my mother's arms.

"There, there," said my mother soothingly as I tried without success to cry. "You're quite safe, Mama's here and I'm going to tell you what you're going to do in order to feel better. First of all, you're never going to mention this scene to anyone—we'll draw a line neatly underneath it and then it'll belong to the past where it can no longer trouble us. Then afterwards you're going to be a specially good boy so that your poor papa is never reminded of his mother's wickedness."

I finally managed to cry.

"There, there," said my mother again. "Papa's a good, brave, thoroughly decent man and you must never think otherwise. He was just driven to wickedness by that evil woman, but that's all over now and I'm in control and there's no more wickedness at Oxmoon, not anymore—because *here I have my standards*," said my mother, uttering the magic incantation that warded off all evil, *"and here I draw the line."*

My grandmother paid six more visits to Oxmoon before her death, but she never spoke to any of her grandchildren again. She was too frightened, and whenever I saw her I was frightened too, terrified by the sinister possibilities of heredity. I had changed myself as far as possible, rejecting my Welshness, calling

248

myself John and devoting myself to an austere life, but there remained the physical likeness which was beyond alteration, and so often when I saw my face in the looking glass I would fear there might be other inherited traits, now dormant, that might one day burgeon beyond control.

I was frightened of the uncontrollable. I was frightened of myself. As I passed from adolescence into adult life I realized that for my own peace of mind I had to keep my life in perfect order. Nothing, I told myself, must flaw the perfection and any drift towards chaos must be immediately checked. I knew I was jealous of Robert, but I saw how I could master that by pursuing a brilliant career in the one field in which I knew I could outshine him: modern languages. I knew I resented the fact that as a younger son I was unlikely to inherit my family home, but I resolved to do so well in life that I would wind up with a far finer home than Oxmoon—which, after all, was merely a pleasant Welsh country house of no great architectural merit. I knew I had to make some arrangement to neutralize the potential dangers of my sexuality, so I married young. I knew that in order to realize my ambition I had to surmount the handicap of being penniless, so I married money. I had overcome problem after problem, defused danger after danger, and now here I was, twenty-nine years old, with a perfect wife, a perfect home, two perfect children and a perfect life as a gentleman farmer.

It had been difficult to leave the Foreign Office, even though I had hated working there. How could I continue to equal Robert, I had asked myself in despair, if I abandoned all thought of the diplomatic service? But then Robert, fortunately, had abandoned his own career and soon afterwards his illness had ended our competition forever. I no longer had to be jealous of Robert. I had been set free to love him as I should, and in the relief of this liberation I had found I was also set free to do as I wished with my life.

I knew then what my real ambition was. I wanted—in the most tactful sympathetic way imaginable—and of course for the best possible motives—to take Robert's place. I knew my father had been greatly upset by Robert's illness. He had been looking forward to the prospect of Robert following in his own footsteps in Gower, but now Robert was following in no one's footsteps. Neither was Lion. Edmund was shell-shocked and ineffectual. Thomas was troublesome and appeared unintelligent. That left me, and I...

I was going to be the son my father had always wanted. No more coming second for me, not now. I was going to come first with my father at last; I was going to redeem myself wholly for my unfortunate resemblance to his mother, and we were all going to live happily ever after. I would be the prop of my father's old age and a pillar of strength to Robert, and by being indispensable I would wipe out the guilty memory of how much I had resented my father for idolizing Robert and how jealous I had been of Robert for being idolized. No more resentment! No more jealousy! My life would be in perfect order at last, and I could relax in the knowledge that I was permanently safe from a moral catastrophe. It was the most attractive and alluring prospect.

I might even inherit Oxmoon in the end. If my father outlived Robert he would certainly turn to Robin, but supposing Robin were to turn out badly, as spoiled children so often do? Nobody took any notice of Kester, so I could discount him. As the next son in line I thought my prospects were promising, but I kept my imagination in tight control because it was safer to believe I would never have Oxmoon than to envisage some possibly chaotic future in which the title deeds fell into my lap.

Oxmoon was the joker in the Godwin family pack, and the joker was circulating as we all played our cards. So far it had not appeared in my hand but I sensed it was coming nearer, and meanwhile I was bunching my cards closer together to leave a gap where the joker could slip in.

Naturally I could not acknowledge my hopes in regard to Oxmoon. That would have been a breach of taste while Robert lived and quite definitely not the done thing at all. Nor could I actively pursue my ambition to be master of the estate. That would hardly have been the done thing either. But I saw no reason why I shouldn't be a good son and a good brother and secretly hope a little. That appeared to be well within the bounds of civilized behavior, and it was of course unthinkable that I might ever step beyond those bounds. That way chaos lay.

I drew the line.

2

I

IT TOOK ME some time to recover my equilibrium after the disastrous scene with my parents in the billiard room at Oxmoon, but I concealed my distress from Blanche. I felt better after I had written my parents letters of apology. To my father I regretted behavior which he had justifiably regarded as lacking in filial respect, and to my mother I wrote that although I could not condone my father's conduct, I was willing to keep up an appearance of amity by continuing to bring my family to Oxmoon on Sundays for tea.

My father wrote back by return of post: *My dear John, Least said soonest mended. I remain always your affectionate father, R.G.*

My mother did not reply.

That upset me. It made me remember that dislike in her eyes; it made me remember my grandmother saying how hard my mother was and how unforgiving. I had suffered many nightmares about my grandmother but the one that never failed to horrify me was the nightmare in which the traditional roles were reversed. Supposing my grandmother were the tragic heroine of the story and my parents were the villains of the piece? This was a horrific thought indeed. I could not endure to think that my grandmother had loved me but that I had repudiated her as a vile and loathsome object in order to please my parents. Neither could I bear to think that my parents were villains, unjustified in their cruelty to a pathetic old woman, because if this were the truth then their high standards were a mockery and chaos had remained unconquered. These ambiguities tormented me, and after my quarrel with my mother I found the torment deepening. I felt my mother had to approve of me in order to put the situation in order and be the mother I needed her to be. If she continued to dislike me I might feel driven to turn for consolation to the memory of my grandmother, who had loved me so much, and once I started to embrace this symbol of evil, God only knew what might happen.

When I next saw my mother after church the following Sunday I said, "I trust your failure to reply to my letter doesn't mean we're estranged," but she merely replied, "If any estrangement exists, John, it's entirely of your own creation," and then my father joined us so that further opportunities for private conversation were curtailed.

I spent some time analyzing my mother's reply but I could not make up my mind what to think of it, and finally I was in such confusion that I appealed to Robert for help. I found him unsympathetic about my continuing moral stand against Mrs. Straker but he was willing enough to help with my mother, and presently I received a note which ran: *Dearest John, Robert tells me you're quite tormented by our little difference of opinion. I'm sorry. I would not wish any of my children to be tormented. Our best course would seem to be to consider the matter entirely closed, but I am sad to find you still so lacking in humanity in regard to your father's predicament. Never doubt that I remain always your most devoted mother,* MARGARET GODWIN.

I disliked this note so intensely that I burned it on the spot. Then I began to feel angry, an unacceptable emotion for a devoted son to feel towards a devoted mother. I finally controlled myself to the point where I was able to behave in her presence as if nothing were wrong, but I felt I had suffered some profound injury. I longed to confide in someone, but Robert, echoing my mother's sentiments with monotonous regularity, was clearly unsuitable, and naturally I would never have burdened Blanche with my complex resentment. In my misery it became more important to me than ever that no hint of trouble marred the perfection of my home, for at least when I was with my family I could pick up the script of my life, which I had worked out so painstakingly in my teens, and resume my familiar, comfortingly unflawed role of the perfect husband and father.

Fortunately several matters at this time conspired to divert my attention from my mother. The most obvious was the state of the nation, which was dire. We had survived the miners' strike and the threat of a general strike, but as far as I could see revolution was only a stone's throw away and the class war was about to begin. I had always leaned towards the conservative in politics. While wishing to alleviate the sufferings of the working classes I believed that the only way to keep Britain well ordered was for it to remain exactly as it was. God only knew what would happen if the Labour Party came to power but I had no doubt chaos would immediately ensue.

This air of political crisis was diverting enough but I was diverted still further by the problems of my new estate which I had acquired a year ago, soon after Robert and Ginevra had established their own home in Gower.

It was now the May of 1921, two years since Robert's illness had been diagnosed and seventeen months since the Christmas of 1919, when he had awoken at Oxmoon to find his right leg was paralyzed. Before that the illness had been a secret between him and his wife; after that no concealment had been possible.

They had been making their plans for some time. My father had already given Robert Martinscombe, the sheep farm below Penhale Down, but the farmhouse was now let once more to a foreman, and a bungalow, specially designed for the future wheelchair, had been built a quarter of a mile away. As the result of Ginevra's dubious taste, this most eccentric new home consisted of a single-story block sandwiched between two towers, and had been nicknamed "Little Oxmoon" by the baffled villagers of Penhale. Pursuing a course of unflagging diplomatic tact whenever my opinion was sought on the structure's aesthetic qualities, I made every effort to ensure that Robert never guessed how sorry I was for him having to live there.

I was much more fortunate. My father-in-law died in the influenza epidemic of 1919, and although he could not leave me his country home, an ugly Jacobean mansion entailed on an heir in Canada, he did leave me his three thousand acres of Herefordshire farmland and his house in Connaught Square. To be accurate, I should record that he left them to Blanche, but naturally Blanche wanted to share her inheritance with me, and after I had made my decision to leave the F.O. I think she hoped we might settle in Herefordshire. However when I explained that it was my moral duty to return to Gower to help my father and Robert she was most understanding, and after engaging a manager to run the Herefordshire farms for me, I sold the town house in Connaught Square and began to cast around for a suitable property in Gower.

Fate stepped in with admirable neatness. Early in 1920 Sir Gervase de Bracy died, his widow and unmarried daughter removed for reasons of health to Bournemouth and the Penhale Manor estate found its way to the auction block. Both the de Bracy boys had been killed in the war.

I was the highest bidder. I had never ceased to thank God I had had a respite from financial worry since my wedding day, and I felt sorry for Robert, who must often have been obliged to wrestle with money troubles. He had written two books, one a memoir on Lloyd George and the other a dissertation on his famous trials, and both books had been well received, but, as everyone knows, there's no money in writing. He had some money saved, but Ginevra was an expensive wife and I suspected her extravagance was hard to control. I was appalled when I saw how much she must have spent on furnishing the bungalow to reflect her vulgar taste. Penhale Manor also needed refurbishment, but Blanche had exquisite taste and never made any purchase without my permission, so we managed to achieve beauty without profligate expenditure and elegance without vulgarity.

My one item of extravagance was a new grand piano which I bought for Blanche to thank her for her loyal support when I had left both the Foreign Office and our smart life in London. Blanche's great passion was music, and she was wonderfully accomplished. I myself am not musical; my talent for languages means that I have the most acute ear for sound, but the only instrument my ear can master is the human voice engaged in phonetic patterns. However because of my musical shortcomings I doubly admired Blanche's talent, and indeed I often felt sorry for Robert having a wife whose only talent lay in dressing in a manner which recalled the Edwardian *demi-monde*. I would not have permitted my wife to dress as Ginevra dressed. I constantly marveled that Robert allowed her such latitude, but it was not my place to criticize, so I took care never to make any inappropriate remarks.

Blanche always looked matchlessly beautiful. She was dark and slender and had a pale creamy skin. Naturally she dressed to perfection. I never had to worry about Blanche looking raffish and hinting at an unfortunate past. I was very, very lucky to have such a flawless wife, and when we removed to Penhale Manor I knew I was very, very lucky to have such a potentially flawless home. As soon as I was settled, I applied myself conscientiously to the estate to iron out the remaining flaws.

Judicious expenditure might have been sufficient to make the house charming, but the estate required both brains and hard work to master and I spent long hours pondering on the problems it represented. It was not a large estate. There were less than three hundred acres attached to the Home Farm, which lay a mile from the house, but the land had been indifferently farmed by a succession of inadequate bailiffs, with the result that when I took over the farm it was little better than derelict. Much capital investment was required, but that raised no difficulty; I had only to sell off some land in Herefordshire to finance my schemes. Meanwhile I had resolved to manage the land myself with the help of a foreman whom I would install at the Home Farmhouse, and my father, much pleased by this decision, offered to inspect the land with me in order to determine what should be done.

Having grown up on a thriving estate I had a good general idea of what farming involved, but I had no practical experience of farm management so I knew it was crucial that I found the right foreman. Delighted as I was that my father should be interested in my plans, I thought his enthusiasm would pall if I kept running to him for help when things went wrong, and I was just wondering how I could find the agricultural sage that I needed when my father, who must have feared my inexperience as much as I did, offered me the services of his foreman at Daxworth; apparently the man was ambitious enough to fancy the idea of transferring to a semiderelict farm which would test his skills to the utmost, and certainly I was willing enough to consider him. He was a Welshman from Carmarthen called Meredith, and he was two years my senior. We met, liked each other, shook hands—and in that brief commonplace gesture I sealed his fate, and although neither of us guessed it, he sealed mine.

However when we first met we did not think in melodramatic terms such as fate because we were much too busy considering my decision to gamble on the new opportunities offered by motor transport. The remoteness of Gower before the war meant that cattle breeding was the type of farming favored and that crops were grown primarily for winter feeding, but with improved communications other avenues of farming could now be explored.

I decided to continue with the cattle breeding but expand the growth of crops so that the farm would produce a surplus which could be transported by motor lorry to Swansea for sale. Endless cogitation then ensued about which crops would be best to grow, not only for sale but to feed the cattle during the winter. Did I or did I not grow mangolds? How profitable were swedes? What were the pros and cons of potatoes? How much clover should be grown? I became so absorbed with these vital questions that I could hardly tear myself away to inspect my new lorry, but soon my father and I were indulging our passion for mechanics as we examined the lorry's huge engine together. My father enjoyed himself immensely. He told me more than once how happy he was that I had returned to Gower, and I assured him how delighted I was to be back. After each meeting we parted in a haze of gratification.

Meanwhile Blanche was settling down well and involving herself in village life. She kept saying how kind my mother was to her and how lucky she was to have such a helpful affectionate mother-in-law. I was deeply pleased. I knew my mother had always approved of Blanche but it was very satisfactory to learn that she also found her so congenial. My mother had never cared for Ginevra and I knew my parents had been disappointed by Robert's marriage.

"I think we're doing well, sir," said my foreman, Huw Meredith, in the spring of 1921, and I answered, thinking not only of the farm but of my place in my parents' affections, "Yes, we certainly are."

That was before the quarrel and immediately afterwards I was besieged with problems, as if fate had decided to dent my pardonable complacency. First of all we had a problem with a stockman who drank too much and had to be dismissed. Then I had a row with my cousin Emrys Llewellyn, whose sheep had trampled across one of my fields with disastrous results for the crop; he claimed that de Bracy had granted him a right-of-way over the field in the Nineties, but when I asked for the legal evidence of the easement I was informed that none existed. My cousin told me he had merely taken the word of a gentleman although, he added sourly as he looked me up and down, in his opinion all gentlemen farmers, particularly English gentlemen farmers, ought to be abolished and their land redistributed.

Until that moment the conversation had been conducted in English, for now-adays, apart from the occasional remark in Welsh to my father, this was the only language I permitted myself to speak, but Llewellyn's gibe made me forget that any betrayal of my Welshness was like a declaration of kinship with my grand-mother. I told him in his own language that I was just as Welsh as he was and that he spoke out of jealousy because he secretly wished he himself had been brought up at Oxmoon instead of in his commonplace rural hovel. His jaw sagged at my command of Welsh but he recovered, and for some time we shouted at each other in a thoroughly un-English fashion until he called my grandfather a drunken bastard and I called his grandfather a bloody peasant and we almost came to blows. Fortunately he then started talking about "Aunt Gwyneth the Harlot," and this reminder of my grandmother pulled me to my senses. I told him in English to keep his sheep off my land and said that if he failed to do so I would sue him. Then I retired, still in a towering rage, to the Home Farm to consult Huw Meredith.

The hour had come. It was eleven o'clock on the morning of July the eighteenth, 1921, and my perfect life with my perfect family in my perfect world was finally about to unravel.

II

The farmhouse was about two hundred years old, a square little building of faded brick with a slate roof. There was no garden in the English manner, merely a vegetable patch on one side of the house and some grass shaded by an oak tree in the front. The farmyard lay at the back, and as I halted my Sunbeam abruptly, I saw two children peeping out of the hayloft above the stables. This surprised me. Meredith was married but childless. I remembered that the new stockman had progeny but could think of no reason why they should be playing at the farm.

As usual I entered the house by the back door. In the kitchen Mrs. Meredith was scolding the local servant girl, but when I came in she broke off with a smile and told me her husband had just departed for Standing-Stone Field, where Llewellyn's sheep had been running riot. I said I would go and catch him up. As I turned back to the door I added, "Who are your visitors?"

"My sister's here from Cardiff with her children. Ah, here she is! Bronwen, this is Mr. Godwin, whom we talk so much about! Mr. Godwin, this is my sister, Mrs. Morgan."

I glanced over my shoulder at the woman who had entered the room, and instantly I knew I had to make a crucial decision: either she was ugly or she was beautiful. I decided that she was ugly. She was pale and thin, with garish red hair which was scraped back from her face into a bun.

"How do you do, Mrs. Morgan."

She murmured something which ended in "sir" and bobbed a brief awkward curtsy, which indicated she had been in service. Her voice was heavily accented like her sister's but gruffer, somewhat harsh. I thought it most unattractive and found it hard to believe that dark, plump, loquacious Mrs. Meredith, whose vivacity made her pretty, could have such a pallid unprepossessing sister.

Excusing myself I retreated to the farmyard. The children were no longer visible in the hayloft but I could hear their laughter in the distance, and as I paused for no reason except that I could not remember why I had wanted to see Meredith so urgently, Mrs. Meredith's voice drifted towards me through the open kitchen window nearby.

She came from a Welsh-speaking area of South Wales, and now she had reverted to her native tongue.

255

"Yes, he's such a handsome gentleman, isn't he, and he has this beautiful wife, such a lovely lady, so sweet and kind and unaffected…"

I walked away.

Three minutes later I had caught up with Meredith in Willow Lane and was giving myself the pleasure of railing against Emrys Llewellyn to a thoroughly sympathetic audience.

Meredith was the best kind of Welshman, quick, industrious and with cultural tastes that would have put an Englishman of a similar class to shame. In truth they even put me to shame, for although I myself was by no means uninterested in intellectual subjects I was still suffering from a reaction to my exhausting labors at Oxford, and nowadays I seldom opened a book more demanding than an Edgar Wallace thriller. Naturally I did not disclose these Philistine's tastes to Meredith. He believed an Oxford education represented a passport to a perpetual intellectual Elysium, and I had no intention of disillusioning him.

"Emrys Llewellyn's reminding me of Pip's sister in *Great Expectations*," he commented brightly. "Always on the rampage."

I racked my brains to cap this reference and managed to say, "Well, he's made a mistake if he thinks I'm going to be as passive as Joe Gargery." I hastened to divert him from literature. "And talking of sisters, is Mrs. Morgan staying long with you?"

"Till her husband gets back from the sea. He didn't leave her enough money and the poor girl's been turned out of her rooms."

"How very unpleasant for her."

I dismissed Mrs. Morgan from my mind but three days later I saw her in Penhale. I was driving back from Llangennith where Oswald Stourham, an old crony of my father's, had been trying unsuccessfully to sell me a horse, and as I passed through Penhale I saw Mrs. Morgan and her children leaving the village stores. She was carrying two full baskets and looked paler than ever.

I was a gentleman. Though disinclined to burden myself with the company of an inarticulate working-class woman, I drew up the car and offered her a lift.

She reddened in embarrassment. Indeed she was so overcome with confusion that she was unable to open the door, so suppressing a sigh of impatience I got out to help her. Her little boy shot into the back seat with great excitement but the little girl lingered shyly by her mother.

"What's your name?" I said to the child when they were all settled in the back seat.

"Rhiannon."

"Rhiannon!" I remembered the fairy tales spun by a succession of Welsh nurse-maids long ago. "After the heroine in the *Mabinogion*?"

"No, after my grandmother in Cardiff."

I laughed. Mrs. Morgan smiled. I noticed that although she had the true Celtic skin, so white that it was almost translucent, the bridge of her nose was peppered with freckles. Reminding myself that I had always found freckles unattractive, I returned to the driving seat.

"And what's your name?" I said to the little boy as I drove off, but he failed to reply.

"Dafydd doesn't speak much English yet," said Mrs. Morgan. "He's only four and hasn't started school."

"Ah, I see. Do you like motors, Dafydd?" I said in Welsh, and glancing in the driver's mirror I saw the woman stir in surprise as she realized I spoke her language.

The little boy said yes, he loved motors but he had never ridden in one before, he had only ridden on a motorbus in Cardiff and on a train to Swansea and in a wagonette to Penhale. I asked him if he had enjoyed the train journey, but before he could reply the little girl said to me, "You speak English like an Englishman and yet you speak Welsh just like we do."

"I'm somewhat like a parrot. When I hear strange sounds I find it easy to copy them."

"You don't look like a parrot," said Dafydd.

We all laughed. I noticed that Mrs. Morgan had very white, very even teeth. I wondered if they were false. The dental condition of the working classes was notorious.

Passing the gateway of the Manor we traveled another hundred yards down the lane before swinging off onto the cart track that led to the farm.

"And how old are you, Rhiannon?"

"Six."

"Say 'sir,'" whispered her mother. "He's a gentleman."

"My daughter's nearly six," I said. "Perhaps you can come to tea in the nursery someday and meet her."

Mrs. Morgan said in a rush, "That's very kind of you, Mr. Godwin, indeed it is, but of course we couldn't presume—"

"Nonsense, Marian's always complaining that she has no little girls to play with." I felt irritated by her humility but at the same time I realized that I would have been even more irritated if she had failed to be humble.

We reached the farmyard. As soon as I opened the door of the back seat the children scampered away, the little girl thanking me in a very well-mannered way for the ride, and I was able to lean into the car to draw out the heavy shopping baskets. Mrs. Morgan then emerged awkwardly onto the running board; setting down the baskets, I turned to offer her assistance.

"Thank you, sir." Her hand grated against mine. The palm was clammy. It was a hot day, and I was conscious of the heat as we stood there in the sun. Mrs. Morgan was wearing a straw hat which concealed her ugly red hair and shadowed her pallid face as she glanced down at the baskets. "Thank you," she murmured again, and when she looked up at me the sun shone in her eyes.

They were bright green in the brilliant light. I was reminded of the color of the sea by the Rhossili cliffs on a midsummer day. It was an extraordinary color, most unnatural.

I found I was still holding her hand.

I dropped it.

"Good day, Mrs. Morgan."

"Good day, Mr. Godwin." As she turned aside, her face immediately fell into shadow and I could see again how nondescript she was. I returned once more to the driver's seat. She was already walking away with the baskets, but as I drove off I saw in the mirror that she had paused to stare after me. For a second her slim solitary figure remained silhouetted not against the farm buildings but, mysteriously, against some uncharted landscape in my mind, but the second passed and the next moment I told myself it had been forgotten. Treading hard on the accelerator I drove at a breakneck speed down the cart track and hurtled up the lane to the comforting familiarity of my home.

III

"We had such a nice nursery tea today," said Blanche a week later as she put on her diamond earrings. She was wearing a white satin gown and her dark hair was coiled into an elaborate knot on the top of her head. That night we were due to dine at Oxmoon to celebrate Edmund's twenty-seventh birthday.

"Nursery tea?" I said vaguely as I wandered in from my dressing room.

"Mrs. Morgan came with her children—what a good idea of yours that was! Marian enjoyed herself so much, and Nanny said afterwards how very well behaved Rhiannon was for a little girl of her class—and you know how discriminating Nanny is! But I wasn't surprised the children were well behaved because Mrs. Morgan is a most superior girl, as my dear Mama used to say, so quiet and dignified and polite."

"I'm glad the visit was a success. I must say, I did have second thoughts after I'd issued the invitation."

"Oh, I don't think these social differences matter much when children are young, darling. . . . There! I'm ready and we must go. Do you have Edmund's present?"

I retrieved the book on rose growing, which had been beautifully wrapped by Blanche in lemon-colored paper, and five minutes later we set off for Oxmoon. It was a dull summer evening, murky and cool, and Oxmoon had a moody look as I turned the car into the drive. Though built to conform to the classical conventions of architecture popular in the eighteenth century, it somehow contrived to hint that a wild unorthodox streak lurked behind its severe well-disciplined facade, and as I stared at it I thought again, as I had thought so often before: Oxmoon the enigma, the joker in the pack. Then suddenly in a bizarre moment of self-knowledge I realized I was seeing not the house but my own reflection in stone and glass. I was the enigma, the joker in the Godwin pack, and beneath my conventional English manners lay the Welsh stranger I was too afraid to know.

Edmund came out of the house to greet us. He was looking a trifle more animated than usual but still less than half alive, and once more I was acutely aware that the war had divided me from him, just as it had severed me forever from Lion. I had been becalmed on the Home Front while Edmund had been brutalized in the Front Line, and now an abyss of chaotic emotion lay scrupulously concealed between us; our conversations represented the nadir of social banality.

"Hullo, old chap. Happy birthday and all that rot."

"Thanks. I say, what a beautiful parcel! Almost too good to open!"

Edmund had a square face with pale blue slightly protuberant eyes and pale brown thinning hair. He had put on weight since he had been invalided home in 1918 but although his limp was now barely perceptible and his general health had improved, he made no effort to leave home. Mild, vague and chronically indecisive, he drifted from one bout of melancholy to the next, so I was particularly relieved to find that evening that he seemed to be in good spirits. Whenever I saw how damaged Edmund was, I hardly knew how to endure my guilt as a noncombatant. Egged on by Robert, who had never known a day's uncertainty over his decision to remain on the Home Front, I had allowed myself to be persuaded that it was my duty to stay in my exempt position at the Foreign Office, but I had spent the war in such a miserable muddle that several times I had found myself wishing I could have died on the Somme with Lion. My guilt was one of the reasons why the Foreign Office had become intolerable to me; I had felt so debilitated by my self-disgust that I had wanted only to make a fresh start in a world where no one would look at me askance.

"Daphne wrote to wish me many happy returns," Edmund was saying, uncannily mentioning our sister-in-law as if he knew I was remembering Lion dying on the Somme. "She's coming to stay here next month with Elizabeth."

"How lovely!" exclaimed Blanche. "Marian will be thrilled! Isn't that good news, John?"

I agreed, although in fact I did not care for Daphne, who was one of those bouncy gushing Society girls dedicated to a vacuous life. I had heard from friends in London that she had become rather fast, but I had taken care not to mention this to Blanche.

"I'm surprised old Daffers hasn't remarried," said Edmund as he led the way up the steps into the house. "I know she's plain but she's tremendous fun. I like girls like that. Dash it, if I had a bean I'd marry her myself! Or is one forbidden to marry one's brother's widow? I bet one is. All the really amusing things in life are forbidden, aren't they . . . But oh Lord, I didn't come out here to talk of amusing things, quite the contrary, I came to tell you something awful: Robert's worse. He's in a wheelchair. Mama sent me out to warn you so that you'd be prepared."

My youngest brother Thomas chose that moment to come slouching down the stairs. Fourteen is a difficult age, and Thomas, who enjoyed being difficult, was making the most of his new capacity for obstreperousness. Spoiled by doting parents who should have known better, he seemed perpetually outraged that his much older siblings and beyond them the world in general paid him such scant attention. However he behaved well to my parents, and I had come to suspect that his pose of *enfant terrible* had been adopted to counter his fear of being overlooked as the last and least important member of a large family.

He had a square face not unlike Edmund's and a wide full-lipped mouth which he kept tucked down neatly at the corners. His golden hair and blue eyes gave a misleading impression of a cherubic nature.

"Hullo," I said to him, and added in an attempt to demonstrate a friendly interest, "When did you get back from school?"

"Why do you want to know?"

I sighed, gave up and followed the others into the drawing room, where my parents, having yielded to postwar social change, had authorized that cocktails as well as wine might be served before dinner. This was characteristic of them. My mother disapproved of spirits and my father drank little else except champagne, but when they entertained guests they were lavish in their hospitality and no one could have accused them of being either mean or old-fashioned.

I saw the wheelchair as soon as I entered the room, and at once I was grateful to my mother for having had the presence of mind to send Edmund to warn us. The wheels with their long spokes seemed symbolic of a medieval ordeal. I felt cold with pity for Robert, then sick with relief that I myself was healthy and finally rigid with guilt that my life should be so perfect while his should be so infused with suffering.

"Johnny darling!" cried Ginevra, who was clearly far beyond her first glass of champagne. "Come and admire the chariot! Robert now rattles around at a terrific pace!"

I said the first thing that came into my head. "Ginevra, I do wish you'd stop calling me Johnny as if I were some Edwardian rake who spent his time throwing roses to chorus girls."

"But darling"—Ginevra had acquired in America the vulgar habit of calling everyone darling much too often—"think how perfectly thrilling it would be if you were an Edwardian rake tossing roses to chorus girls!"

"Oh shut up!" said Robert, who often behaved towards his wife as if they were both back in the nursery. "Well, John? What do you think of this latest innovation?"

I thanked God for my diplomatic training. "My dear Robert, I'm sure it's a king among wheelchairs—forgive my lack of alacrity in making an immediate obeisance, but I wasn't prepared to encounter royalty when I arrived here tonight! Is it easy to maneuver?"

He was satisfied. All pity and sentimentality had been avoided and he could relax.

Robert's illness was erratic, striking severely and at random but then receding either wholly or in part. The temporary improvements tended to divert attention from the steady progress of the paralysis. His right leg was immobile, his left was now weak; I noticed he had slight difficulty turning his head, although his facial muscles were untouched and he had had no visual problems for two years. He looked closer to fifty than to forty. His muscles had run to fat, but the power of his intellect, sharpened rather than dimmed by his physical weakness, was kept ruthlessly honed by his incessant reading, and he was even talking of engaging a companion, one of his old Oxford friends, who could converse with him on the classics; he knew well enough that I had closed my mind against intellectual matters after my drudgery at Oxford.

My father offered me a glass of champagne, and I accepted it with relief. I was feeling in a nervous unreliable frame of mind for reasons which were ostensibly connected with the appearance of the wheelchair but which I sensed also derived from other sources beyond analysis. I was aware of sinister changes, of a fixed world trying to slide stealthily out of control.

"I say, I'm reading *The Mysterious Affair at Styles*," said Edmund, providing me with a welcome diversion. "You read it recently, didn't you, John? Do tell me—who's the murderer? I simply can't work it out at all!"

"Edmund, you don't ask who did the murder! You read to the end and find out!"

"I think it might be that attractive girl with the red hair..."

But I did not want to think about attractive girls with red hair. Evading him I moved over to my father, but my mother intercepted me.

"Robert looks a little better, don't you think?" she said. "I think the unexpected mobility of the wheelchair has put him in better spirits."

We both glanced across at Robert, and out of the corner of my eye I saw my father drain his glass of champagne and reach automatically for a refill. He too was watching Robert, and suddenly I knew all three of us were united by a grief beyond description. I had an absurd longing to say to them, "I'm here—I'll make it up to you," but of course the words could not be spoken, and my parents, as usual when Robert was dominating their thoughts, were oblivious of me. My old jealousy which I had thought dead now rose from the grave to sour my compassion for the brother I admired so much, and I was horrified. Chaos was approaching. At once I drew the line—and as always I felt safe and secure behind it. Consigning my vile jealousy once more to the grave, I too drained my glass and turned to the bottle of champagne for further sustenance.

The bottle was empty. My father had clearly been helping himself for some time.

"Open another bottle, John," he said idly as he saw my plight but my mother said in a voice of steel, "I think not," and turned her back on him.

My father, who had been lounging in his usual debonair fashion against the chimneypiece, stood up ramrod-straight and went white. At once I said, "It's all right, I don't think I want another glass after all."

"Have mine," said my father, thrusting his glass at me, and stumbled after my mother. "Margaret—"

My mother was ringing the bell to signal to the servants that we were ready for dinner.

"—only wanted to be hospitable—special occasion—Edmund's birthday—"

"Quite."

"...and my dear!" Ginevra was exclaiming to Edmund. "I hear from London that all women are now to look like boys and pretend to have no bosom and no hips! What on earth am I to do?"

261

As Edmund guffawed with laughter I was aware of the wheelchair spinning across the room towards us.

Robert said, "Mama, are you all right?"

"Yes, dearest, just a little worried about the soufflé after last week's disaster with the Stourhams."

Robert looked skeptical. My father looked painfully anxious. Deciding it was high time I exerted my diplomatic talents to save the situation, I speculated whether Oswald Stourham had yet recovered from his disastrous second marriage to an errant platinum blonde.

IV

Despite the underlying tension, dinner passed off better than I had dared hope, first because a failed dinner party was unknown at Oxmoon, second because my parents were superb at keeping up appearances and third because we all drank steadily from my father's hoard of prewar wine—all, that is, except Thomas, who was too young, and my father, who having consumed far more champagne than normal before the meal now behaved like a man who had taken the pledge. I drank, I knew, far too much and this was most uncharacteristic of me. Indeed my father, whose drinking habits were normally so moderate, had always made it clear to his sons that drinking was not an essential adjunct of masculinity, and certainly I had always shied away from the more dangerous consequences of too much wine, the fatal sense of well-being, the risky loosening of the tongue and the sinister relaxation of the will to behave as one should. I had also shied away from the aftermath of alcoholic excess, the depression, the restlessness and above all the inexplicable frustration which made me feel as if I were a dog endlessly chained up in a backyard and endlessly obsessed with the longing to be free.

However that night, disturbed by my impression of a clear-cut world slipping inexorably out of focus, I drank to maintain the illusion that nothing had changed, and soon I found I could look at Ginevra's décolletage without being embarrassed and at my father without remembering Mrs. Straker and at my mother without resenting the fact that she found it hard to love me as she should. I could even look at Robert and not feel ashamed because I found it so much easier to be devoted to him now that he was sick and helpless; I could even look at Robert and pity him because he would probably die before he could inherit Oxmoon.

"... and of course there's no denying we farmers have done well out of the war," my father was saying after the women had retired and the cloth had been drawn, "but times are changing so rapidly now, and sometimes I worry about the future of this place."

"Oh, Oxmoon's all right," I said, finishing my glass of port. "A large estate can always survive, given good management, Oxmoon's all right. I could run Oxmoon and run it bloody well, changing times or no changing times, although of course

I don't want Oxmoon, wouldn't touch it with a barge pole, it all goes to Robert, everyone knows that. However if I ever did wind up with Oxmoon—"

"You never will," said my father, "so that's that. You're still going to outlive me, aren't you, Robert?"

Robert, who was smoking a cigar, said sardonically, "John evidently has his doubts."

"Oh, for Christ's sake!" I exclaimed, half knocking over my glass. "Just because you're in a bloody wheelchair you needn't act as if you're in a bloody coffin!"

"Steady on, old chap," said Edmund.

"You're not going to die just yet, are you, Robert?" said Thomas, who had somehow reached the age of fourteen without mastering the art of being tactful. He had just sneaked and wolfed a glass of port from the decanter while my father had been busy lighting a cigar.

"Unfortunately not," said Robert drily. "Sorry to disappoint you."

I spun round on Thomas. "What the hell are you doing swigging port on the sly and asking bloody stupid questions?"

"My God, you *are* bad-tempered!" exclaimed Thomas, livid that I had called attention to his stolen drink. "And don't think we can't all guess why! You're fed up because you have to make do with measly old Penhale Manor when you think you're so bloody perfect and so bloody wonderful that you ought to be ruling the roost at Oxmoon!"

I leaped to my feet with such violence that my chair was flung over behind me, but my father shouted, "Enough!" and my fury was checked. Then as I remained motionless, he said in a level voice to Thomas, "Did I give you permission to drink port?"

"No. But I didn't think you'd mind—as it's a special occasion—"

"Nobody drinks port in this house before they're eighteen, special occasion or no special occasion. Very well, that's the end of your evening. Excuse yourself to the ladies in the drawing room and go to bed." He waited until Thomas had slouched off in a fury before adding, "Robert, will you please oblige me by going with Edmund to join the ladies. I want a word with John on his own."

"I'm afraid I provoked John, sir," said Robert. "I must ask you not to hold him responsible for this debacle."

My father said nothing. Robert then apologized to me but I shook my head to indicate that no apology was necessary. Retrieving my fallen chair I stood stiffly by it as Edmund and Robert left the room.

"You've drunk too much," said my father to me as soon as the door closed.

"I know. Unpardonable. I'm very sorry."

"Why did you do it? What's the matter with you?"

"Nothing. Everything's fine. Couldn't be better."

"So it would seem, certainly. You've got well over two thousand acres in Herefordshire, haven't you?"

"Yes, sir."

"And you have nearly three hundred acres here together with one of the finest old manor houses in Gower?"

"Yes, sir."

"And you have money on top of all that, haven't you, and good health and good looks and a devoted wife and two fine children?"

"Yes, sir."

"You've everything a man could wish for, in fact?"

"Yes, sir."

"Then let's have no more nonsense about Oxmoon. It goes to Robert and if Robert dies before I do it goes to Robin and that's my last word on the subject."

"I absolutely accept that, sir, and what's more, I always have accepted it. I can't think why you should be taking Thomas's idiotic remark so seriously."

"A man's private feelings aren't so private when he starts to drink, and God knows I can recognize avarice when I see it. I remember how Owain Bryn-Davies used to covet Oxmoon while my father was still alive."

"I'm not Owain Bryn-Davies! And how dare you compare me to such a bastard, why are you always so bloody unfair to me, it's unjust and I resent it, *I resent it*, it's not my fault I look like—"

"Be quiet! That's enough! Take yourself home at once and don't show yourself here again until you're sober!"

"I'm not drunk!"

The door opened, interrupting me, and swinging around I saw my mother had returned. "Please," she said, not to me but to my father, "could you go to the drawing room and deal with Thomas. He's making a fuss and I can't cope. I'm afraid everything's quite beyond me this evening."

"Of course," said my father, greatly agitated by this unprecedented confession of defeat, and left the room.

My mother sank down on the nearest chair.

"Mama..." Shock sobered me. When I stooped over her in anxiety I found she was crying. "Mama!" I was appalled. I had never seen my mother cry, not even after Lion died. I drew up another chair and sat down beside her. "Mama, what is it?"

But she was already controlling herself. "Nothing. But I live under such strain and sometimes I hardly know how to bear it."

I was deeply distressed. "What can I do? I'm so sorry, I had no idea, tell me how I can help."

"Oh, you can't help," she said flatly. "You have too many problems of your own."

"What problems?"

"My God," she said, "how's that poor child Blanche ever going to cope?"

"Mama, I think you're a little overwrought—"

"Overwrought? Oh yes, I daresay. Lion dead, Robert dying, Edmund shell-shocked, Thomas impossible, Celia cut off in Heidelberg, you cut off in some dangerous world of make-believe—"

"My dear Mama—"

"—and Bobby," wept my mother, "Bobby no longer strong enough to live as he longs to live...a decent life...free of scandal...It's so terrible to see a good man, someone one loves, slip deeper and deeper into degradation—"

"There must be something we can do to stop it, there must be!"

"No. There's nothing." She wiped her eyes clumsily with the back of her hand before adding: "This is retribution. People pay for the wrong they do, and then hell exists not in the hereafter but *now*, right here on earth—and here we are, 1921, thirty-nine years after that terrible summer, and I'm in hell, Bobby's in hell and that man's still drowning on the Shipway and that woman's still being destroyed in her asylum." She wiped her eyes again and managed to say in a calmer voice, "Sometimes I ask God to remember how young we were. Young people are capable of such brutality but it's because they know nothing of life. All they understand is the instinct driving them to survive, but sometimes the price they have to pay for survival is so very terrible."

There was a silence. I did not know what to say. I was consumed with the longing to terminate this morbid stream of quasi-religious reflection which I found both tasteless and embarrassing, yet at the same time I was moved by my mother's grief and I desperately wanted to help her. I racked my brains for a consoling diplomatic response, but when it continued to elude me I realized that this was because it did not exist; no words were appropriate and she was inconsolable. In bewilderment, not knowing what else to do, I put my arms around her and kissed her gently on the cheek.

This was evidently the right approach. Her fingers clutched mine. She looked up at me with gratitude. "Dear John," she said, "how very good and kind you really are." Then she said with more than a hint of her old self, "You must have too much to drink more often!" and she smiled as she kissed me in return.

"Forgive me—I'm afraid I've just had an appalling row with Papa—"

"It doesn't matter. I'll put it right. So much has gone wrong tonight that I'm almost past caring. It's just so sad about Robert," said my mother, weeping again. "I couldn't bear to see him in his wheelchair."

If I had been sober I would have murmured a platitude. As it was I said painfully, "I couldn't bear it either, but you shouldn't retreat into religion, Mama, in order to make sense of the suffering—you shouldn't start flagellating yourself with concepts like retribution. You're the heroine of this story, not the villainess." And when she covered her face with her hands, I put my arm around her again and said, "I don't care what you did in the past. You're a wonderful woman—a magnificent woman—and we all love and respect you so much. If you're suffering now it's unmerited, I know it is—it can have nothing whatsoever to do with that vile summer back in the Eighties."

My mother let her hands fall. She stared at me. Her eyes shone with tears. "Oh God forgive me," she whispered. "To think that *you* should be the one who loves me enough to say that."

The door opened as my father reentered the room. "Margaret—"

"I'm all right now," said my mother. "I'm better. And so's John. I'm sure he's willing to drink a lot of black coffee, and so there's no need for him to leave yet." She rose to her feet, she squared her shoulders, she set her mouth in its familiar determined line. "We must all go to the drawing room," she said, "and we must all keep up appearances. Whatever happens that's always the right thing—indeed the only thing—to do."

V

"Are you all right, darling?" said Blanche, in our bedroom later. "When Thomas returned to the drawing room he mentioned something about a quarrel."

"Oh, that was nothing, just a little difference of opinion."

I was so anxious to put an end to these questions and so overwhelmed by my desire to forget, for a few precious minutes, the hellish evening I had just endured that I started to claim my marital rights while the light was still burning. Blanche never complained about anything I did but this time she did whisper, "Darling— the candle," and I had the grace to mutter, "Oh, God, I'm sorry" before I clumsily extinguished the flame.

I had once heard up at Oxford that a surfeit of alcohol damages a man's performance in bed, but all I can say is that exactly the opposite now happened to me. Under cover of darkness I stripped off my pajamas and almost asked Blanche to remove her nightdress, but fortunately I had not drunk four cups of black coffee in vain, and I somehow managed to restrain myself. Then I found I was obsessed by the desire to prolong the episode beyond five minutes. Usually I tried to restrict myself to three or four. I also had other desires which are without doubt better left unrecorded. I was appalled by myself but at the same time hopelessly engulfed in pleasure. Blanche tolerated it all like a saint, God knows how. I loved her so much for her tolerance that I finally, after an interval which I fear was at least ten minutes, managed to conclude the episode and spare her further embarrassment. Pleasure ended. Self-hatred and guilt began. I begged her to forgive me, but she said she loved me so nothing mattered. At that point my alcoholic excesses caught up with me and I sank mercifully into unconsciousness.

I dreamed I was a dog chained up in a backyard but someone was calling to me from a long way away and suddenly I longed to be free. Slipping my collar I sprang over the wall of the yard, and there ahead of me was a vast space where Edmund's voice echoed, "I think it's that attractive girl with the red hair."

Then a rope encircled me and began hauling me back to my kennel. An anxious little voice kept saying, "John! John!" but I took no notice because John was no longer my name. I was Johnny again, Welsh-speaking Johnny who got into scrapes with Lion and lived adventurously at Oxmoon. I could see Oxmoon clearly now and it was Welsh, all of it, every brick beneath the creeper, every slate upon the roof.

"John, wake up! Darling, it's three o'clock in the morning and the telephone's going on and on and on—"

I scrambled back over the wall, pounded to my kennel, dragged the collar of my Englishness over my head and woke up. Pain immediately shot through my head and made me gasp. My mouth was desert-dry. Far away in the hall the telephone was shrilling like a demon.

"Good God, who the hell can that be?" I woke up further, apologized for my language and crawled out of bed. To my horror I realized that I was stark naked. I groped frantically for my pajamas as Blanche lit the candle.

"I'll go," Blanche said, seeing that I was hopelessly befuddled, and slipped out of bed.

"Lord, I'm sorry." I struggled into my discarded pajama trousers and plunged next door for my dressing gown. I was then delayed because I thought I was going to vomit. A stream of embarrassing memories threatened to overwhelm me but I shut them out, and when vomiting proved impossible I raced to the head of the stairs just as the demonic bell ceased to ring in the hall.

"Penhale three," said Blanche anxiously. "Who is it, please?"

I hurried down the stairs. During the pause that followed I saw her become rigid with shock. "Oh, Edmund," I heard her whisper. "Edmund . . ."

I was beside her. The phone was cold as I seized it from her hands.

". . . and there's no doubt about it," said Edmund's frantic voice at the other end of the wire. "She's dead, Blanche, Mama's dead—oh Christ Almighty, what in God's name will happen to us all now?"

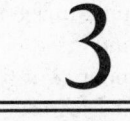

3

I

OXMOON WAS in darkness. My headlamps raked the opaqueness of the night and shone on the black windows. When I emerged from the car the darkness seemed suffocating. There was no moon and the distant woods formed a sinister mass beneath the sky.

The front door opened. Edmund stumbled down the steps.

"Johnny—" The old nursery name trembled on his lips, and I did not need to see his face to know that the semblance of normality which he had assumed for the dinner party had been destroyed.

"Where's Papa?"

"Upstairs—with her." He began to sob.

"Tell me exactly what happened." I grabbed the lamp from his hand and led the way into the house.

"Papa woke me. He'd just come back from Mrs. Straker. He asked me to telephone Warburton because he thought Mama was ill. He was so odd that I went with him to their room, and of course as soon as I saw her I realized—"

"Yes. Very well, telephone Warburton. Telephone Robert. Wake Bayliss. Get dressed." I headed for the stairs.

"I can't," whispered Edmund. "I can't." He was crying again. "Oh Johnny, I did so want to make it up to her, and now I never shall—"

"Make what up to her?"

"The fact that I survived instead of Lion."

I recoiled from him. Then I said savagely, "Don't talk such rubbish. I'm sure she was only too glad you weren't both killed," and I rushed up the stairs to escape. On the landing I looked back and saw that he had sunk down on the bottom step and was weeping helplessly, a pathetic figure in his faded dressing gown. Guilt gnawed me. I wanted to console him but I knew my father must come first.

I reached my parents' room and tried the handle but the door was locked, and although I banged on the panels there was no response. Visions of suicide gripped me. Lighting one of the candles arrayed on the landing table, I stumbled down the corridor to the door of my father's dressing room. It opened. With lightning speed I moved to the door that led into the main chamber.

"Papa!" The childish name which even in adult life none of us had had any inclination to change suddenly sounded ridiculous. I thought of my contemporaries who referred to their fathers with antipathy as "the governor," but my father had never been a mere figurehead at the top of the family dining table. I saw him as he had appeared to me in the early years of my childhood, tall and tranquil, gentle yet authoritative, a golden double image of father and hero.

"Papa!" I shouted. "It's John! Let me in!"

The key clicked in the lock. The door swung wide. The old memory disintegrated as I faced the complex stranger I feared.

He was fully dressed and unmarked by grief. His eyes were a brilliant empty blue.

"Not so much noise," he whispered disapprovingly. "Your mother's asleep."

I groped for my diplomatic skills. "I heard Mama was unwell," I said, obediently keeping my voice low. "Perhaps I could see her for a moment."

"Did Edmund telephone Warburton?"

A reassuring affirmative seemed necessary. "Yes," I said, and edged my way into the room. All the candles had been lit, and I could clearly see my mother in bed, her head tilted to one side, her hair gray against the pillows.

"I found her like that," said my father, "when I came home. After all the guests had gone, I walked to Penhale and visited Milly. Have you met Mrs. Straker, John? I can't remember."

"No. I was in London during that brief time she was employed at Oxmoon." My mother's face was pulled down on one side. I knew she was dead but to make sure I carefully reached for her wrist. There was no pulse.

"Milly's husband was killed at Jutland," said my father. "He came from these parts and he met Milly in London—a wartime romance—they didn't have long together. After he was killed she had no money so she came down to Swansea to

268

stay with his sister and she worked in a munitions factory, awful it must have been, I don't know how these modern women do it. But after the war she went back into service. A wonderfully efficient parlormaid she was—Margaret said she was the best we'd ever had. 'Straker's got the brains to be a housekeeper,' she said; I can clearly remember her saying that. Margaret was sorry she had to dismiss her after only three months, but there we are. Got to stick to the rules. Terrible things happen to people who fail to stick to the rules."

On the dressing table lay the jet brooch which my mother had worn that evening. Opening the jewel box, I put the brooch away.

"I closed her eyes," whispered my father. "I didn't think it was right that she should sleep with her eyes open, like a sleepwalker."

I took a deep breath. "Papa..." I began but it was no use. Speech was too difficult. I waited, then tried again. "Papa, I'm afraid there's nothing Warburton can do."

"Nonsense, he's a very clever doctor and so good with Robert. Make sure you tell him how cold she is. I held her in my arms to warm her up but it was no use so she'll have to have an injection."

I waited again before saying, "Come downstairs with me and I'll fetch you some brandy."

"Oh, I never drink brandy," said my father firmly, but allowing himself to be led from the room. "Never. My father used to start drinking brandy after breakfast and he'd be dead drunk by noon. But when he was sober he was the most charming fellow, I wish Margaret could have met him, but of course he died before I knew her. She met Bryn-Davies. He was nice to her, much nicer than my mother was. My mother wasn't kind to Margaret, such a mistake, Margaret never forgot. I was very fond of my mother, though, devoted to her, and Bryn-Davies was the most remarkable fellow in his way. A pity about Bryn-Davies, but I made amends by befriending his son and helping him marry that heiress, although luckily Owain the Younger's not in the least like his father, and anyway he was a victim just as I was so it was easy to be friends with him. Of course he never knew the truth. I just told him it was a little accident with the tide tables."

We were on the landing. Down in the hall, Edmund dragged himself to his feet and looked up at us. His face was blotched with weeping.

"Yes," said my father meditatively, "Margaret was the one who thought of the tide tables, but as soon as she mentioned them I saw it was the right thing—the only thing—to do. Margaret always knows what the right thing to do is. That's why I couldn't possibly live without her. You do see that, don't you, John? I couldn't live without Margaret. Impossible. You must explain that to Warburton, but doctors are so clever nowadays and Warburton's such a delightful chap and I'm sure he'll know just what to do."

"Edmund," I said, "take Papa to the library and sit with him while I make the telephone calls. I'll wake Bayliss and ask him to make tea."

"Oh, I don't want tea," said my father. "I want champagne. Ask Bayliss to bring a bottle from the cellar."

I could see that Edmund was about to lapse into hysteria, so I said crisply,

"Very well" and led them to the library. My father at once began to tell Edmund the well-worn family legend of how he had found the means of saving Oxmoon as the result of encountering a rat chewing a candle on the library table.

"...and I flung book after book at the bloody rat before I succeeded in killing him, and then when I went to the space on the shelves where the books had been I found my grandfather's records showing exactly how he had managed the estate..."

Returning to the hall I unhooked the telephone and began the lengthy task of recalling the postmistress to the village switchboard.

II

Ginevra answered the telephone at Little Oxmoon. I wanted to tell her that my father was demented, but since I knew the postmistress was eavesdropping with an excitement that just failed to be breathless, I confined myself to the fact of my mother's death. I had expected Ginevra to become hysterical, but to my surprise although she was shocked she remained calm. She said she and Robert would be at Oxmoon within half an hour.

With relief I then summoned Warburton, but afterwards I found I was too exhausted to wake Bayliss. Taking the cellar key from the board in the butler's pantry I retrieved a bottle of champagne and headed for the dining room where the glasses were kept in the sideboard. While there I helped myself to a double brandy from the decanter. I remembered hearing at Oxford that the best cure for a hangover was another drink, but this was the first time I had been obliged to put this repellent piece of folklore to the test.

In the library I found my father telling Edmund all about his courtship of my mother.

"...and her father was a wonderful old tyrant, no manners or breeding but a great personality, called a spade a spade and stood no nonsense. He'd built that pottery business up from nothing, and he was in Swansea because he wanted to explore the possibility of shipping china clay across the Bristol Channel from Cornwall. All the copper ore used to come that way in the old days to be smelted. Anyway he was out drinking somewhere and feeling fed up with the Welsh when he ran across Bryn-Davies, who had just sold some sheep at the market for a great price and was celebrating in his usual way. Well, they got on like a house on fire and Bryn-Davies invited him to Oxmoon—Bryn-Davies was master by that time— and as soon as Mr. Stubbs saw Oxmoon he realized he had an opportunity to marry one of his daughters into the gentry—"

"Do you want some champagne, Edmund?"

Edmund said, "No. Whisky," and disappeared in search of it.

"—and of course he thought Ethel would do, she was the eldest, but I didn't fancy her, she was stuck-up, pretentious, I knew she'd be a bore. The younger

270

girl May was only fourteen so she didn't count. That left your mother but that was all right because she was down-to-earth and sensible and I liked the way she laughed. Afterwards, after Bryn-Davies had drowned and my mother was in the asylum, Margaret and I stood in the ruined hall at Oxmoon and I said, 'I want to hear you laugh.' She said, 'My God, what a thing to say at a time like this!' and sure enough we both laughed. And later I said, 'In the future we're going to laugh all the time, I'm going to make you happy even if it's the last thing I ever do,' and years later when we held our first ball at Oxmoon I gave her a red rose and we drank champagne, just as we'd promised ourselves we would, and then we opened the first dance beneath all those glittering chandeliers while the orchestra played 'The Blue Danube.'"

"Here's your champagne, Papa."

"Thank you, John. Delightful! Yes... I can remember Ginevra dancing to that tune years later, how terrible it was about Ginevra, but Margaret says we mustn't talk of that anymore. Dear me, John, you don't look at all well! Here—take this glass you brought for Edmund and have a little champagne—yes, I insist! Do you good. There you are. Now, where was I? Oh yes, Ginevra. Yes, it was terrible when Robert married her, terrible how he cut himself off from us, but I accepted it, it was retribution. Margaret didn't accept it, though, Margaret hated it, blamed Ginevra, but poor Ginevra, I didn't blame her, Margaret's so hard sometimes, but never mind, Robert's always uncommon civil to me, he makes such an effort that I think perhaps he might still be a little fond of me after all... Sorry, did you say something?"

"I said, 'You're not making sense.'"

"Am I upsetting you? Well, we won't talk about it. We must never talk of things that upset us—I said that to Oswald Stourham after that tart of a second wife of his had run off with the American sailor. All he could do was sob 'Belinda' into his brandy, but I told him to stop thinking about her, wipe her clean out of his mind and then he'd be all right. He shouldn't have remarried so soon after his first wife's death—and of course he shouldn't have married a girl young enough to be his daughter, silly old chap, a platinum blonde, I knew it would never do. Margaret didn't even want to receive her but I said Oswald was one of my oldest friends and I had to stand by him... Where are you going?"

"I must just see what's happened to Edmund," I said, and escaped.

In the dining room Edmund had emptied the whisky decanter and was seated sobbing at the table.

"Edmund, you've got to pull yourself together—"

"Fuck you, why the bleeding hell can't you leave me bleeding fucking alone?" bawled Edmund in the language of the trenches, and tried to hit me.

I retreated, paced up and down the hall, looked in on my father, listened to some more disconnected monologue and then escaped again to the front doorstep, where I spent some time peering into the dark. At last I heard the sound of a motor. Robert or Warburton? I waited, straining my eyes to pierce the gloom, and finally recognized the old Talbot which my father had ceded to Ginevra after buying his new Bentley. Leaving the front door open, I returned to the library.

"Papa, Robert's here."

"Robert! But what a wonderful surprise!" He sprang to his feet. "Get another glass from the dining room!"

"Papa, you mustn't—you can't go on pretending like this—"

"Don't argue—if Robert's come all the way from London he must certainly be offered champagne!"

My nerve snapped. I pushed past him into the hall just as Ginevra, white and tired in a black coat, hurried through the open front door.

"Johnny—can you give Bennett a hand with the chair...Bobby—darling— I'm so very sorry—"

I ran outside. Bennett had helped Robert into the chair and was standing beside him at the foot of the steps.

"Robert, thank God you've come—Papa's demented—the situation's quite beyond me—"

"So I see," said Robert. "Very well, help Bennett lift this bloody thing up the steps. Where's Warburton?"

"He's not here yet. I told him I thought she'd had a stroke. Oh God, Robert, I can't begin to tell you—"

"Then don't."

We reached the top of the steps. I was just moving aside to allow Bennett room to maneuver the chair over the threshold when Ginevra rushed out to join us. She looked gray enough to faint.

"Robert, he mustn't see you in that chair, he's forgotten the illness, he'll have such a shock—oh Johnny, help me, don't let Bobby see—"

But she was too late.

"Where's Robert?" demanded my father, opening the front door wide, and the next moment he was confronted by the invalid in the wheelchair.

He stopped. Then he said confused, "I want Robert" and added, "I want Margaret." He looked around in panic. For a second we were all transfixed, but when Ginevra and I darted forward instinctively to protect him, he shouted, "Margaret! Margaret!" in a terrified voice before keeling forward into unconsciousness.

III

"He'll be all right," said Warburton, closing his black medical bag. "He'll sleep through the rest of the night and wake around noon."

We were in the bedroom which had belonged to Lion and which after his death my mother had ruthlessly refurbished for the use of guests. My father lay asleep in Lion's old bed, his hand finally limp in mine.

"When he does wake," Warburton was saying, "don't force the reality of the death upon him but on the other hand don't join in any fantasy. I think with any luck he'll be normal—that's to say, he'll be deeply upset. I'll come back after lunch and see how he is, but if there's any trouble telephone me and I'll come at once."

Warburton was forty, a dark neat slender man who kept a boat at Porteynon and liked to sail and fish in his spare time. He was a distant cousin of Lady Appleby's and had become enamored of the Gower Peninsula during summer holidays spent at All-Hallows Court. He came originally from Surrey where he had attended Epsom College. Before the war my sister Celia had fancied herself in love with him, but he had married a London girl and although she was now dead he had shown no inclination to remarry.

"Warburton, now that you've dealt with my father I wonder if you could take a look at Edmund. I'm afraid he's in a bad way."

We found Edmund still in the dining room, his head pillowed in his arms as he lay sprawled across the table. Both the whisky and the brandy decanters stood empty beside him, and with horror I noticed he had even started on the sherry.

"Not much I can do there," said Warburton, "except give you a hand to carry him out."

We lugged Edmund into the morning room and arranged him on the sofa with a cushion beneath his head. He showed no sign of waking.

"And now," said Warburton, "we come to you."

"Oh, I'm all right, absolutely fine, no need to worry about me at all."

"Nonsense, you've had a bad shock!"

"I'm all right now Robert's here."

"He won't be here for much longer. It's essential that he should go home to rest."

But Robert had other ideas. Warburton and I both tried to argue with him, but he flatly refused to listen. "I've got to be there when my father wakes," he said to Warburton, "and that's that. Ginette, tell Bayliss to make up a bed for me on the morning-room sofa."

I explained that the sofa was already occupied.

"Ridiculous!" said Robert. "Turn Edmund out and tell him that he's bloody well got to pull himself together. No one else goes to pieces in this house, not while I'm here; I won't have it!"

Warburton and I were just glancing at each other in despair when there was an interruption. The door opened and in walked Thomas in his pajamas, his eyes puffy with sleep.

"What's going on?" he demanded. "Why's everyone rushing around in a frenzy at four in the morning?"

"John," said Robert, "you're good with children—take the boy away and deal with him. Ginette, organize Edmund's removal. Warburton, you can go. Thank you for your help. We'll telephone if we need further assistance. Well, don't just stand there gaping, all of you! *For Christ's sake do as I say!*"

We all gave in, collapsing in exhaustion beneath the power of his personality. Piloting Thomas away to the far corner of the room, I broke the news to him as gently as possible.

He looked livid as if his mother had offered him an unforgivable insult. Then his mouth became softer and his eyes brighter. He glanced away.

"I want Papa."

"He's sedated," said Robert, who had begun to draft a cable to Celia. "He won't wake till noon. John, how does this sound? 'Prepare shock regret Mama dead you essential Dieter prohibited Erika optional'—do you think that makes it sufficiently clear to a woman of Celia's limited intellect that although she can bring the baby with her she's on no account to bring the damned Hun?"

Watching Thomas I saw a tear drop pathetically into the cup of tea I had just given him, and a lump at once hardened in my throat. Grief is very contagious.

"I'm sorry, Robert, I can't—quite—"

"Conjugate Latin verbs—that's always an infallible recipe for keeping a grip on oneself. Now pay attention, please, while I read the message again. 'Prepare shock—'"

"He doesn't care," said Thomas to me in a shaking voice. "I hate him."

"For Christ's sake!" yelled Robert in a fury, and with his stronger arm hurled both pencil and paper at the wall.

When I had retrieved them and promised to send the wire, all he said was "I've got to rest," and I knew he was worn out. "Bloody hell," he said, raging against the illness that impaired him, but he was so weak he could hardly speak above a whisper. I wheeled him into the morning room. Edmund had been carried out. A bed was being prepared on the sofa. Bennett and Ginevra were both there. "John, give me your word you'll wake me in time to deal with Papa."

I gave him my word and hurried back to look after Thomas.

IV

"What a pretty blue paint Margaret chose for the walls," said my father, waking to find he was in Lion's refurbished room, and his eyes filled with tears.

We waited, I by the window, Robert in his chair by the bed, and eventually my father, wiping his eyes on the sheet, whispered, "I want to see her."

"Now or later?" said Robert with a bluntness which I could never have emulated.

"Now. I always think one ought to see the body. Otherwise one wonders whether the person's really dead. Better to make sure."

"Quite right," said Robert as I inwardly shuddered. "Very sensible."

"Such a relief it was," murmured my father as I helped him into his dressing gown, "when Bryn-Davies was washed up. I had nightmares that he'd somehow survived and swum ashore." He said no more at that moment, but when we all reached my parents' room he went without hesitation to the bed and looked down at the lifeless figure. "Yes," he said, "there's nothing there now. Just the shell." He covered the face again with the sheet, withdrew to the window and paused. Then at last he said, "I shall think of after-the-funeral later. Now all I shall think

274

about is the funeral itself, and of course it must be a perfect funeral, everything done properly, nothing omitted, not a rule broken. I shall be all right, you see, absolutely all right so long as I stick to the rules."

We promised to help him organize a perfect funeral.

"And no atheism," said my father sternly. "I don't hold with it. Atheism's not the done thing at all."

We assured him we would behave as correctly as the devoutest members of the Church. He was satisfied. Methodically his thoughts turned elsewhere. "And now I must take care of the children," he said. "Let me see. You two are here, Lion's dead, Thomas... where's Thomas? Who's looking after him? Find him, John, I want to see him at once. And where's Edmund? He's got to be looked after too. And what's happening about Celia?"

"John's sent the wire. I'm sure she'll come at once."

"I won't have that damned Hun in the house!"

"Don't worry, I made that very clear."

We returned to Lion's room, but to my relief we did not have to coax my father back to bed; he was still affected by the drug Warburton had administered, and for another hour he was too groggy to consider getting dressed. Later Warburton said to me, "He's better than I thought he would be, but I'm worried about how well he'll be able to stand the coming stress. I suppose there's no chance of the funeral being a quiet one?"

"None whatsoever," I said levelly, and we found ourselves once more regarding each other in despair.

V

My father then proceeded to astonish us all by giving a bravura performance as an indomitable *paterfamilias*. He relieved me of the responsibility of looking after Thomas, he attended to Edmund with such success that Edmund became capable of conducting a rational conversation, he addressed the weeping servants with such skill that they pulled themselves together, he gave calm audiences to the vicar and the undertaker, he chose hymns and flowers with meticulous care, he even redrafted Robert's notices for *The Times* and the *Morning Post*. Afterwards Robert was finally sent home to rest, Ginevra's emotional but clearly reluctant offer to stay on to manage the household was refused and I myself to my great relief was dispatched to Penhale Manor. Now, I thought, I would at last be free to grieve in peace.

Yet when I arrived home I felt as if the mechanism for grief had jammed in my consciousness. I told myself how devoted I had been to my mother and how much I was going to miss her, but the words echoed emptily in my mind until I realized with horror that I was unable to connect them with a genuine emotion. Genuine emotion lay elsewhere, and suddenly I was aware of an anger which represented forbidden thoughts such as She should have loved me better, She didn't understand me, I doubt if I'll miss her much once the shock's worn off.

This reaction, which was so far outside any conventional idea of grief, shocked me so much that I hardly knew what to do with myself. Blanche was kind, as gentle a wife as any bereaved man could wish for, but her attitude only made it more impossible that I should confide in her. Amidst all my deplorable emotions the sheer perfection of her response seemed almost more than I could endure.

Blanche told the children their grandmother was dead. We were both present but she was the one who spoke. Marian shed a tear but was consoled by the thought of Granny happily ensconced among the angels in heaven. Harry was uninterested and obviously did not understand, but Blanche thought it better not to stress the death by further explanations, and I had no doubt she was right.

The funeral was perfect. It was everything my father wished. People came from all over Gower and South Wales to attend. Every villager in Penhale was crammed into the churchyard. My father had some antique notion that motorcars were unsuitable for transporting coffins, so the traditional black hearse drawn by black horses was used. Edmund, Thomas and I joined the undertaker's men in shouldering the coffin. Aunt Ethel, my mother's surviving sister, tried to tell Thomas he was too young but since he was as tall as Edmund and considerably more robust, we had all supported his wish to participate. Aunt Ethel, a massive figure in black veils, was proving a great trial to us all, but my father was so charming to her that her natural inclination to be frightful was temporarily muted. In fact my father was quite faultless, faultlessly dressed, faultlessly tearless, faultlessly demonstrating how a genuine grief could be displayed with dignity and good taste. I had never admired him more.

However unfortunately not everyone could follow his example. My sister Celia, a foolish but kindhearted woman of whom I was moderately fond, sat beside Edmund, her favorite brother, and snuffled and sniffled until I thought I would lose my patience entirely. Edmund himself wept without ceasing but then, as I reminded myself, allowances had to be made for Edmund. Ginevra sobbed in a most vulgar manner, but what else could one expect? Ginevra had never been renowned for either lack of emotion or good taste. Robert, who ignored her, looked bored as if the whole occasion were beneath his notice, and once even glanced at his watch. That horrified me. I too could hardly wait for the agonizing ceremony to be concluded, but I knew I could never have manifested open impatience.

Afterwards in the churchyard the only people with dry eyes were my father, Robert and I myself. I wondered vaguely what was on the menu for luncheon.

Luncheon, served that day at two tables joined in a T, turned out to be a five-course banquet for thirty-three, the food plain but perfectly cooked and accompanied by no more than a light hock, just as my mother would have deemed appropriate. Those present consisted of my father, my sister, my brothers, Ginevra, Blanche and me; Aunt Ethel with her three unmarried daughters, Dora, Rosa and Clara; her son Montague, who ran the family pottery business, and his wife; dead Aunt May's daughter Evadne and her husband Frank; Lion's widow Daphne with her parents, Sir Cuthbert and Lady Wynter-Hamilton; Ginevra's son Rory Kinsella; Oswald Stourham with his sister Angela and his daughter Eleanor; Owain Bryn-Davies the Younger with his wife and his son Alun; Sir William and Lady Appleby; Lady de Bracy and her daughter Gwen; the vicar, his wife and Gavin Warburton. The conversation was universally appalling. Sandwiched between my cousins Dora and Clara, both keen feminists, I came to the conclusion that postfuneral lunches should be banned by law.

"My dears!" exclaimed Ginevra, who was seated opposite us. "What fun you girls are! Johnny, why did we always write off the Staffordshire crowd as a dead loss in the old days?" It was obvious she had had too much hock.

"Dead loss?" said Aunt Ethel, who had the kind of hearing that would have permitted her to eavesdrop at fifty paces. She turned to my father. "Bobby, did you hear that?"

"Well, as a matter of fact," said my father with great courtesy, "I didn't." He suddenly looked very tired. Pushing away his glass of hock, he turned to the butler. "Bayliss, bring me a glass of champagne."

"*Champagne?*" said Aunt Ethel. Unlike my mother, she had never fully conquered her Staffordshire accent. "Bobby, I don't know how you can think of drinking champagne when my poor dear sister has been laid to rest only an hour ago, but all I can say is—"

"John," said Robert at once, but I was already on my feet. We had long since worked out a plan of action in case Aunt Ethel's frightfulness assumed intolerable proportions.

"Papa," I said, moving swiftly towards him, "let me take you into the library for a quiet cigarette."

"But I can't abandon my guests," said my father. "That wouldn't be the done thing at all."

"Oh, don't mind me!" said Aunt Ethel. "I know I'm only here on sufferance to keep up appearances! I realized long ago I wasn't considered good enough for Oxmoon!"

I looked at Cousin Montague for help. He had been educated at some minor public school and I thought he might have the decency to keep his mother's vulgarity in check, but evidently he shared her grudge against my family, for he merely toyed with his fruit knife and said nothing. Meanwhile silence had fallen with lightning speed over the table, and into that silence Robert suddenly unleashed his fury.

"You stupid woman!" he shouted at Aunt Ethel. "How can you have the insolence to talk of your 'poor dear sister' when we all know you were so jealous of her that you could hardly ever bear to visit this house! I've had enough of you simulating grief in the most vulgar way imaginable—just you leave my father to grieve in peace!"

"Well!" said Aunt Ethel, puce with rage. "*Well!* Never in all my life have I been so—"

"Papa," I said, stooping over him, "you can leave your guests now—the meal's over. Edmund—Celia..."

Edmund, Celia and Thomas all rushed to the rescue.

"Poor dearest Papa," said Celia, "you've been so brave—don't take any notice of that horrible woman—"

"Montague," said Aunt Ethel, "are you going to let your mother be insulted like this?"

Cousin Montague said, "I must say I find this behavior most uncalled for and quite definitely not the done thing at all."

"You are, of course," said Robert, "referring to your mother's conduct. In which case I utterly agree with you."

"How dare you!" shouted Aunt Ethel.

"And how dare you," shouted Robert, "degrade my father's hospitality like this!" He turned to Ginevra. "Take me out of here; get me out."

"—never been so insulted in all my—"

"Please!" My father was on his feet. Silence fell. His children stepped back a pace as if allowing him room to speak. He was ashen. "I must apologize," he said to his guests, "for this unforgivable scene. Ethel, I apologize in particular to you because I know my children's insults are the last thing Margaret would have wanted you to suffer. And now, if you please, I must beg you all to excuse me." Exquisitely polite, shaming us by the very perfection of his manners, he walked out of the room.

Edmund, Thomas, Celia and I all looked at one another and then turned as one to follow him.

He was waiting for us in the hall. "Margaret will be very angry when she hears about this," he said severely. "Very angry indeed."

As we stared at him in appalled silence, Ginevra wheeled Robert into the hall, and in panic I swung to face them. "Robert, Papa's unwell again—"

"I'm not surprised!" Robert was still shaking with rage. "I'm only surprised that we're not all raving lunatics after this bloody unspeakable charade!"

We all gasped. My father was suddenly very white, very still, and the next moment Robert was turning on him with a horrifying brutality.

"Why couldn't you bury her quietly?" he shouted. "She was English and she deserved an English funeral—why did you have to give her this Welsh circus? You talk so much of doing the done thing and sticking to the rules, but all you're capable of is vile pageantry and bloody hypocrisy!" And covering his face with his hands, he began to shudder with inaudible sobs.

We were all staring appalled at him but no one was more appalled than my father. At last he whispered humbly, "I'm so sorry if I've offended you, Robert. Please forgive me," and blundered away towards the library. Thomas ran after him, but my father said, "I'm sorry, I must be alone. John will look after you till I'm better."

The library door closed. Robert let his hands fall. His bold strong striking face was battered with grief. I saw him reach for his wife's hand and saw too that it was waiting for him.

"Robert's right," said Ginevra. "I don't know why we're not all raving." She turned the chair and began to wheel him away from us. Over her shoulder she added: "We're off to the kitchen garden to raid the strawberry beds."

"The season's over!" called Edmund the gardener automatically, but Ginevra did not stop, and the next moment he was seizing the chance to escape by dashing after them to help her maneuver the chair into the garden.

Celia and I looked at each other.

"I'll deal with the other guests," she said, "if you can cope with Aunt Ethel."

I glanced at Thomas. "Will you be all right?" I said. "Celia and I have to go back, no choice, but you can stay here if you want to."

"I'm staying."

I could hardly blame him. Celia said with admirable resignation, "I'm afraid it's a case of 'Onward Christian Soldiers,' John," and seconds later we were reentering the dining room.

VI

I had already received the hint that some deep fissure existed between Robert and my father. In his dementia following my mother's death my father had referred to it obliquely, but in my distress I had discounted his words as the rambling nonsense of a sick man. Yet now, having witnessed Robert's unprecedented hostility to him, I began to wonder anew and to try to recall what had been said. My father had talked of Robert's marriage. That much I could clearly remember. But had he in fact disclosed anything which I did not already know?

We were all aware that my parents had opposed Robert's marriage to Ginevra, even though they had ultimately given in with good grace. As Celia had said in one of her more acid moments, "Who in their right mind would want their son to marry a woman who acts like a courtesan and was married to an Irish-American brigand?" However Ginevra was certainly a lady, despite her raffish manners; a broken engagement and an elopement may rank as deplorable incidents, but they hardly turn a woman into a courtesan. Yet what kind of a lady was she? She had a foreign air, no doubt acquired in America where all women, so I had heard, were bossy and independent, unmarked by the virtues of English tradition, and even though I had no evidence that she had been unfaithful to either of her husbands, I thought her untrustworthy; there was a shadiness about her which hinted at all manner of private eccentricities, and although Robert was devoted to her, I had been far from surprised when my parents looked askance at the match.

What now surprised me was that their disapproval had apparently deepened. I thought they had accepted the marriage. I had been well aware that Robert and Ginevra visited Oxmoon only at Christmas—how could I have been unaware of it when I was so meticulous in visiting my parents far more often?—but I had not imagined that this could have led to bitterness. I had done well at the Foreign Office, but I had been no more than a clerk promoted later to a personal assistant;

279

Robert, on the other hand, had been maintaining a brilliantly successful career, and I had fully understood that unlike me he had found it almost impossible to find the time to visit Oxmoon. However my parents had evidently found understanding not so easy. Why had my mother blamed Ginevra, who had always seemed to bend over backwards to please her? And what had my father meant when he had called the separation from Robert retribution?

I was too busy salvaging the shreds of the luncheon party to indulge in speculation beyond this point, but to my relief the guests now showed signs of departing. Presently the de Bracys, who were staying at All-Hallows Court, left with the Applebys; the Bryn-Davieses left in the company of Warburton; the Stourhams gave the vicar and his wife a lift to Penhale on their way to Llangennith; Daphne and her parents swept away in their chauffeur-driven Rolls-Royce to the Metropole Hotel in Swansea while Rory Kinsella, now a volatile undergraduate of twenty, slipped off through the grounds to his mother's bungalow at Martinscombe.

That left the crowd from Staffordshire. They were all staying at Oxmoon but not, Aunt Ethel assured me, for a day longer than was necessary; she said it was against her principles to remain in a house where she had been so grievously insulted, and were it not for the fact that she was about to be prostrated by a migraine brought on by mourning for her poor dear sister, she would have left immediately. Her daughters somehow coaxed her to bed and then departed with Montague and his wife for a very long walk. Aunt May's daughter Evadne said she was exhausted and she hoped we wouldn't mind if she and her husband retired to rest. Somehow we restrained ourselves from saying we were delighted. After they had disappeared upstairs, Celia and I, who had by this time perfected our act as host and hostess, thanked Bayliss and the servants for making the luncheon such a success, and then we withdrew to the hall to decide what to do next.

My father had not emerged from the library, but Blanche, who had been playing the piano quietly in the music room, appeared to ask what she could do to help. She volunteered to stay on at Oxmoon, but I did not want to worry about her any longer; I considered she had been exposed to quite enough distress, so I asked my father's chauffeur to drive her home to the Manor, and as soon as the motor had departed I said to Celia, "I think we should have a family conference to plan how we're going to survive the rest of the day."

Celia agreed, and collecting Thomas from the hall, we retired to the drawing room where a glance from the windows revealed that Ginevra and Robert were sitting by the summerhouse on the far side of the lawn. After separating Edmund from his whisky in one of the greenhouses, I hid the decanter under a large flowerpot and shepherded my flock out of the kitchen garden.

Robert and Ginevra saw us coming as we moved down the lavender walk, and suddenly I experienced a longing for Lion. I could almost hear him saying, "Let's draw lots for who murders Aunt Ethel!" and I thought how he would have bounced out of his deep grief for my mother to raise our spirits with his vitality. The sight of Robert and Ginevra too heightened my longing for a past that had been lost. In my earliest memories I could remember the two of them in the summerhouse, Robert wearing his first pair of long trousers and looking immeasurably grand,

Ginevra a remote goddess with thick plaits, a white frock and holes in both her stockings. "Here come the babies," I had so often heard her say as Lion, Edmund and I advanced to invade their privacy, and now in an eerie echo of the past I heard those same words repeated.

"Here come the babies," she said idly to Robert as we crossed the tennis lawn to the wheelchair.

"You've come at the right time," said Robert to us. "I'm feeling too hot out here—lift the chair into the summerhouse, would you?"

He seemed composed again. In the summerhouse, I did say, "Robert, if you want to go home now, I shan't blame you in the least," but he answered at once, "Don't be ridiculous—how can I leave without apologizing to Papa for that monstrous scene I created with Aunt Ethel?" and various sympathetic comments were made about Aunt Ethel's frightfulness before I called the meeting to order. I then declared that we should plan the rest of the day like a military operation in order to avoid further ghastliness.

"An idea which is none the less brilliant for being obvious," said Robert. "Continue."

Thus encouraged, I launched myself on a forecast of the next stage of the nightmare. "With any luck," I began, "Aunt Ethel won't emerge from her room again today, but if she does, leave her to me. I think I can just manage to survive her."

"John should never have abandoned a diplomatic career," said Celia to the others. "He's been quite wonderful."

"Well, you were wonderful too, Celia—"

"Enough of this mutual admiration," said Robert, "or I shall start to remember how I allowed Aunt Ethel to reduce me to her own appalling level of vulgarity. Go on, John."

"I suggest we divide the entire tribe between us and swamp each section with charm and good manners."

"What a revolting prospect," said Edmund.

"I think it's all rather heavenly," said Ginevra. "Shall I take on Dora, Rosa and Clara? I simply adore it when they talk about Emmeline and Christabel!"

Robert groaned. More comment on our frightful relations followed, but eventually I divided them as equitably as possible between Edmund, Thomas, Celia and Ginevra.

"And what do you and I do, John," said Robert, "while our siblings struggle with these repulsive duties you've assigned them?"

"We cope with Papa."

We all looked at each other.

Edmund said unexpectedly, "I think he'll crack now. I saw it happen in the trenches. When the brave ones cracked they cracked utterly. One just can't keep up that kind of performance forever."

Robert said to me, "He's right. This is where our troubles really begin," and I thought again of that moment in the hall earlier when my father had started talking of my mother in the present tense.

"I don't understand," said Thomas truculently, trying to keep the panic from his voice. "What do you mean when you say he'll crack?"

"Break down and cry," said Celia soothingly before anyone could mention the words "go mad."

"He's postponed his grief by organizing that appalling luncheon," said Robert acidly. "What a mistake! We should have forced him from the start to face reality."

"I'm sorry, Robert," I said, "but with all due respect, I couldn't disagree with you more. This *is* Papa's way of facing reality. It may not be your way but that doesn't mean it isn't equally justifiable. He had to go through this charade. It was essential to him to make a ritual of her death so that he could believe in it."

"Do you understand any of this, Edmund?" said Celia.

"Not a word, old girl, no."

"I do," said Ginevra unexpectedly, "but I'm not at all sure who's right."

"I am," I said. "I think he's done the right thing so far, although I do concede that another breakdown is now a real danger. He's finished being the perfect mourner at the perfect funeral, and what we now have to do is to help him over the interim that must inevitably exist before he can start playing the perfect widower at perfect Oxmoon."

They all stared at me as if I were talking some esoteric Welsh dialect.

"Well, isn't that what life's all about?" I said, exasperated. "You write the script, pick your role and then play that role for all it's worth! Papa's between roles at the moment, that's all."

"What's he talking about?" said Thomas to the others.

"He seems to be saying," said Robert, "that one must never on any account face reality—either the reality of one's true self or the reality of one's true circumstances. I've never heard such a recipe for unhappiness in all my life."

"But what is reality?" demanded Edmund moodily before I could launch myself on a heated protest. "Who knows?"

"Well, I agree," said Robert, getting into his stride, "that Kant says it's virtually impossible to know reality. However—"

"Oh darling, surely everyone knows what reality is!" protested Ginevra. "Why do intellectuals always tie themselves into such absurd knots? Reality is—"

"Reality is—" began Celia and I in unison.

"Reality," said Thomas, "is that Papa's walking across the lawn towards us at this very minute—what on earth do we do now?"

VII

My father had changed into a black lounge suit and was strolling idly across the lawn in the company of his golden Labrador Glendower. A light breeze ruffled his hair and emphasized his casual grace of movement. Behind him Oxmoon, shimmering in the July sun, heightened the impression of mirage and illusion.

I was unnerved, and a quick glance at the others told me that my tension was shared. This, we had agreed, was going to be the moment when my father broke down again, yet never had he seemed more composed.

"Still living in his fantasy," muttered Robert.

"No," I said suddenly, "it's all right, Robert—he's playing his old self. This is the interim role."

Robert looked scandalized, but when he refrained from arguing, I realized he was reluctantly coming to accept my point of view. Meanwhile my father had raised his arm in greeting and we were all waving back much too heartily.

"Shouldn't we be talking?" whispered Ginevra, and added in a normal voice: "It's a new Glendower, Celia—did you guess? Old Glendower died last Christmas—hardpad, poor darling. We were all devastated."

"How simply too frightful," said Celia with nauseous brightness. "Hullo, Papa, how lovely to see you again!"

Ignoring this drivel Robert said crisply, "I do apologize, sir, for my behavior earlier—I'm afraid I chose quite the wrong moment to give way to my grief. And of course I do apologize too for my remarks about the funeral. I'm sure everything was exactly as Mama would have wished."

My father was by this time on the threshold of the summerhouse. "That's all right, Robert," he said with an easy smile. "Least said soonest mended." His smile broadened as he glanced at the rest of us. Then he said with his most winning charm, "I'll wager you've all been on your knees thanking God I didn't marry Ethel forty years ago!"

We laughed vigorously. In the deadly pause that followed, my father stooped over the dog. "Sit, Glendower, sit...that's it. Good boy." He gave the dog a pat and added without looking at us, "I've been thinking things over. Just thought I'd like to say a few words." Still fondling the dog, he glanced up at Robert as if waiting for encouragement.

"Yes, of course," said Robert in the mild neutral voice I had heard him use in court to soothe frightened witnesses, and at once looked immensely sympathetic.

"Well," said my father, duly encouraged and straightening his back as he faced us all, "I just thought I'd like to say thank you to everyone for being so good to me during these past few days. I've got a wonderful family. Don't know what I'd have done without you. Luckiest man in the world. Especially glad to see you again, Celia," he added suddenly. "Bury the hatchet and all that. I've missed you since you've been away."

"Darling Papa!" cried Celia, much moved.

I wondered what all this was leading up to. Sweat began to prickle beneath my collar.

"And I just wanted to reassure you all," resumed my father, his mild casual manner masking his unknown but clearly implacable purpose, "that I shall be all right now—I've had a little think in the library and I've worked everything out." He moved forward to slip his arm around Thomas's shoulder. "Sorry I closed the door on you like that, old fellow," he said, "but I knew it was very important that I should have my little think."

"And what did you decide, Papa," said Robert with extreme delicacy, "as the result of your little think?"

My father moved on from Thomas and drifted to the far side of the room before turning to face us once more. "Well, I can tell you this for a certainty," he said: "I shall never marry again. I shall be loyal to Margaret till the day I die. No one could ever take her place as my wife." He stood up straight and looked both proud and dignified. "You won't find *me* following in Oswald Stourham's footsteps and marrying a platinum blonde young enough to be my daughter!" he said. "I wouldn't dream of embarrassing my children and shaming myself before my friends in that fashion. I shall keep up appearances and live exactly as a widower ought to live. Although of course," said my father, stooping to pat Glendower, "I shall have to have a housekeeper. But that's not the same thing at all."

"Of course not, Papa!" cried Celia, blinded by sentimentality.

I was transfixed. I saw Robert dart me a warning glance, but I ignored him. My voice demanded roughly: "What exactly are you trying to say?"

"Shut up, John," said Robert. "Leave this to me."

"Celia my dear," said my father with his most exquisite courtesy. "Ginevra— please would you be so good as to excuse us? I'd prefer to be alone with my boys for a moment."

"Of course, Bobby," said Ginevra. "Come on, Celia, let's go and organize tea. Thomas, why don't you come with us?"

"Why should I?" said Thomas rudely, and moved closer to my father.

Ginevra looked at Robert, who said pleasantly, "Are you sure you want Thomas to be present at this conversation, Papa?"

"Certainly," said my father. "You can't treat a fourteen-year-old boy as if he were fit only for the nursery. That would be quite wrong."

Thomas, who was still very much a child despite his strapping physique, looked smug.

"Nevertheless—" I began.

"No," said my father, suddenly showing the tough side of his personality. "No 'nevertheless.' That's my decision and you'll oblige me by accepting it."

Robert shot me another warning glance. I kept my mouth shut. The two women began to walk away across the lawn.

When they were out of earshot my father said in a low but level voice, "Now I must speak frankly. I don't think that you boys have faced the—" He fumbled for the right English word. "—the *reality* of your mother's death. Your mother's death is, of course, a tragedy—a tragedy," he repeated, as if greatly relieved he had been able to file the episode away under some comprehensive heading which needed no further explanation. "I know all about tragedies. I'm good at them— sorry, that sounds absurd, wrong phrase. I mean I'm good at surviving them. Done it before. Do it again. Quite simple—just obey a few elementary rules. Rule one: don't dwell on the tragedy, don't think about it. Rule two: take stock of what's left and work out what you need to go on. Rule three: get what you need. Rule four: go on. Well, I've spent the afternoon taking stock and I know what I need—I need the best possible woman to manage the house, and it just so happens I know the best possible woman for the job." He hesitated to drum up the nerve to complete his speech but the pause was minimal. "This evening," he said, "I shall go to Penhale and offer Mrs. Straker the post of housekeeper. Then—once I have my house in order—I know I shall have the strength to go on."

He finally stopped speaking. Edmund, Thomas and I all turned automatically to face the wheelchair.

"Thank you so much, Papa," said Robert with a courtesy that not even my father could have bettered. "I'm sure we're all most grateful to you for explaining the position and advising us of your plans before you consult Mrs. Straker. I needn't remind you, of course, how devoted we all are to you and how deeply concerned we are for your welfare at this most crucial and difficult time. May I venture to hope that bearing our concern in mind, you'll permit me to make one or two observations which I cannot help but feel are pertinent to the situation?"

After a moment my father said, "Very well."

"I think we're all a little troubled," said Robert, "by the effect of any immediate visit of yours to Mrs. Straker. While we perfectly understand that you should wish to see her, we can't help but wonder what people will think when they find out, as they inevitably will, that you visited your mistress on the day of your wife's funeral. Would it not be possible for you to postpone the visit for a day or two?"

My father considered this carefully and said, "No."

"My God!"

"John, *you must leave this to me.* Now, Papa: is it possible for you to explain to us why you have to see Mrs. Straker tonight?"

My father brooded on this but finally said, "I'm afraid I'll go mad if I have to spend another night utterly alone. If I see Milly tonight then perhaps she can move to Oxmoon tomorrow."

"Jesus bleeding Christ!" said Edmund, and sank down on the nearest chair.

"He's out of his mind," I said rapidly to Robert. "This is it—he's lost his mind."

"Just a minute." Robert was still calm. "Papa, don't listen to them, just listen to me. I understand every word you've said but now you must try and understand me because I'm going to tell you a very simple but very vital truth: you cannot bring your mistress into this house, in no matter what capacity, within a week of your wife's death. That wouldn't be sticking to the rules, you see, and terrible things happen, as you well know, to people who fail to stick to the rules."

"I've drawn up some new rules," said my father. "I've spent all afternoon drawing them up. I won't marry her. Nor will she be just a nominal housekeeper. She'll occupy a genuine position in the household, with her own room in the servants' wing, and she'll call me Mr. Godwin and I'll call her Mrs. Straker whenever we're not alone together."

"But my dear Papa—"

My father suddenly shouted with great violence, "Margaret would have understood!"

That silenced even Robert.

I had to speak. It was beyond all my powers of endurance to keep quiet a second longer. "How dare you say such a thing!" I cried in fury. "How can you conceivably think she would forgive such an insult to her memory! What you propose to do is absolutely unforgivable!"

"I agree," said Edmund, scarlet with emotion as he struggled to his feet. Until that moment I would have judged him incapable of opposing my father, and his blast of rage stunned us all. "I don't give a damn whom you sleep with, Papa, I don't believe in God or religion anymore and I can't stand people who preach about morality, but John's right for once, this is vile, this is the worst possible insult to my mother—on the very day of her funeral..." His voice broke. He turned away.

"You bloody fools, both of you!" said Robert angrily. "It's no good being emotional here—that's the worst course you can possibly take!"

"Robert," said my father, "just explain to them that I can't be alone. If I'm alone I'll have to drink to stop myself remembering the past, and if I drink I'll end up like my father—yes, tell them how frightened I am, Robert, always so frightened that I'll turn into a drunkard and start seducing boys as my father did—"

"Oh, my God—"

"Christ Almighty—"

"Get that child out of here—"

"Thomas, leave us at once—"

"*Quiet!*" shouted Robert. "Good God, there's no need for two grown men to throw a fit of hysterics just because they've found out their grandfather's hobby was seducing boys! Pull yourselves together! Now Papa, let's just try to be rational for a moment. Your father may well have been a drunken pederast who made a mess of his life, but he's been dead for well over forty years and in the meantime you've proved *beyond dispute* that you're a very successful man who's sustained a very successful marriage and shown himself to be a very successful father to six children. You never touch alcohol except on social occasions, when you spend the entire evening imbibing half a bottle of champagne, and bearing all that in mind, I can only say that if you see any similarity whatsoever between yourself and your father I'd very much like to hear about it."

"I don't want to talk about him," whispered my father. "I can't think of the past, I daren't, and that's why I've got to have Milly here as soon as possible."

"But that's irrational, can't you see?" cried Robert in despair. "It's quite irrational!"

"Of course it's irrational," I said violently. "He's mad." I swung round on my father. "Sir, if you bring that woman into this house either now or at any other time, neither I nor my family will ever cross your threshold again. And if you're depraved enough to sleep with your mistress on the night following your wife's funeral, all I can say is that I'll never forgive you. I feel thoroughly revolted by your behavior and I condemn it from the very bottom of my heart."

"So do I," said Edmund.

I turned to him. "You'll come and stay with me at the Manor, of course."

"Thank you. Yes, I couldn't possibly condone such an insult to Mama's memory by staying here."

"Thomas," I said, "you must live with me too. Papa's not fit to look after you anymore."

Thomas stared at me. His face had a white pinched expression. He looked very young and very frightened.

"There, there, Thomas," said my father, putting his arm around him again. "It's all right. They can't take you away from me. Don't let them upset you."

"I find it hard to believe, sir," said Robert, "that you—a man who's always taken such care in the upbringing of his sons—can be blind to the effect of your conduct on Thomas."

"Don't talk such bloody rubbish," said my father. "What do you know about bringing up children? A fine mess you made of those stepsons of yours!"

"And a fine mess you'll make of Thomas!" I shouted.

"Be quiet!" my father shouted back. "Thomas has just lost his mother, but he's not going to lose his father too! Children need love, not damned preaching! Now get out, the whole bloody lot of you, and leave me and Thomas alone!"

"That's the first sensible suggestion you've made for some time," said Robert, "and I'm sure we'll all be delighted to oblige you, but before we go I'd just like to say this: I shan't cut myself off from you because frankly I don't think you're fit to struggle on with only the support of Thomas and Mrs. Straker, but you should understand that I find your conduct very hard to condone and I certainly deplore the way you've deepened our bereavement by making a painful situation well-nigh intolerable. John—Edmund—"

We lifted the wheelchair from the floor of the summerhouse and carried it down the step to the lawn. Edmund began to push the chair away, but I found I had to make one last attempt to talk to Thomas.

"If you change your mind," I said to him, "don't forget you can always have a bed at the Manor."

"Go away!" yelled Thomas, his face streaked with tears. "I'm staying with my father!"

Glendower barked as if to underline the statement, and as my father exclaimed, "Damn you, leave the boy alone!" something snapped inside me.

"Your father's a filthy disgusting old man!" I shouted to Thomas. "And the sooner you realize that the better!"

My rage carried me all the way across the lawn in my brothers' wake, but by the time I reached the house I was gripped by my next all-consuming problem: I was wondering how on earth I was going to break the news to Blanche.

4

I

I TOLD BLANCHE as soon as I returned to Penhale Manor. We were in the long drawing room which with the dining room next door had once formed the old medieval hall; it faced south over what had once been a moat and was now a rose garden. All the mullioned windows were open, and as I stood with Blanche beside her grand piano I could feel the warmth of the late-afternoon sun and hear the buzzing of the bees in the shrubs that clustered against the ancient stone walls of the house. Blanche had been arranging some white roses in one of the French crystal vases that had been given to us as a wedding present. No matter what time of year it was the drawing room never seemed to be without flowers.

"I hardly know how to tell you this," I said. "If there was any way of keeping it from you I would, but unfortunately the scandal will soon be notorious."

"Scandal?" said Blanche, pausing with a white rose in her hands. Her dark eyes, which slanted above her high cheekbones, were disturbed but trustful as she waited for me to continue. Naturally she knew that any incipient scandal could not possibly relate to me.

Rigid with embarrassment I told her that my father was planning to keep Mrs. Straker at Oxmoon. I could not tell her he proposed to sleep with his mistress on the night of his wife's funeral. I was too ashamed, too angry. As it was I had a hard time keeping my voice unemotional.

"...and so we shan't be calling at Oxmoon once that woman's there. I refuse to condone such immorality."

"Of course," said Blanche. She fell silent, her face grave as she considered the situation. She was still holding the white rose. "How very sad it is," she said at last, and added more to herself than to me: "Your poor father."

I was shocked. "I really think sympathy's uncalled for, Blanche!"

"But obviously he's unhinged by your mother's death."

"That's no excuse! He has an absolute moral duty to his family not to degrade himself in this fashion!"

"Oh, I agree the immorality's dreadful," said Blanche rapidly as if she feared she had given me offense. "You mustn't think I'm arguing with you, darling. But my dear Mama used to say that it was easy to condemn sin but hard to be compassionate—to be Christian. I'd like to think I'd always try to be compassionate, even if the fault were very hard to understand."

"Well, no understanding's possible in this case," I said, "and I've used up all

288

my compassion." But I kissed her to show how much I admired her goodness, and dropping her white rose on the top of the piano, she put her arms around me comfortingly.

"You look so tired, John—I do wish you'd rest."

"No, I'm too upset. I'm going for a walk."

"If there's anything I can do—"

"No, there's nothing," I said. "Nothing." And before I could break down and distress her with every detail of the sordid scene in the summerhouse I left her, a slender oddly forlorn figure beside her bowl of perfect roses.

II

I walked down the drive to the gates. The Manor stood on the edge of Penhale village, less than a quarter of a mile from the church but more than a mile from Oxmoon, which lay farther south along the road to Rhossili.

I headed into the village. It was a typical settlement of the Gower Englishry, complete with cottages grouped in traditional English fashion around a green, but it had a tousled casual air which an English visitor would have found alien. There was the usual village shop, which also served as the post office, and beyond the green lay the forge which still refused to cater for the motorcar. The church had been built on the orders of the two medieval warlords, Gilbert de Bracy and Humphrey de Mohun, and was resolutely Norman in design; the square tower was not a common feature among the churches of Gower. In contrast the interior was a monument to the excruciating taste of the Victorian de Bracys who had conducted renovations while my grandfather Robert Godwin the Drunkard had been too preoccupied with his troubles to care what was going on. The church had caused endless rows between the two families in previous centuries, for although the de Bracys had treated it as an extension of Penhale Manor, the living of the parish had been in Godwin hands. The poor vicars must have had a hard time surviving in the cross fire.

I hesitated in the shadow of the lych-gate. Then I walked around the tower, sat down on an iron bench and stared at the dying flowers on my mother's grave.

I wanted to forget my father by grieving for my mother, but again conventional grief eluded me, and rising to my feet in an agony of restlessness I began to walk in a clockwise direction around the Godwin tombstones. Then I turned and completed a circle anticlockwise. After that I realized I was beside myself not with grief but with a chaotic mess of emotion which I could not begin to subjugate, so I sat down again, put my head in my hands and gave way to uncontrolled despair; my father had failed to draw the line and beyond that line, as I knew so well, lay misery, madness and death.

I saw him following inexorably in my grandmother's footsteps, and at once I found myself wondering if some hereditary weakness could exist which might condemn a man to moral degradation against his will and his better judgment. That was a terrifying thought. I recalled my own sexuality and shuddered. At least I had it in tight control. But perhaps my father too had had his sexuality in control at the age of twenty-nine.

I rubbed my hand across my eyes as if I could wipe out my vision of intolerable possibilities, and suddenly I missed my mother. I wanted to hear her say, "Here I have my standards—and here I draw the line." But my mother's voice had been silenced, and although I was repeating her words the magic had gone from the incantation which warded off all evil, and now no one was listening to them.

I moved to the grave, stooped over the wreath of white roses which Blanche had made and pulled out the card which I myself had written. *In loving and devoted memory*, I read, *John, Blanche, Marian and Harry*. I spoke the words "loving and devoted" aloud, and at last I recognized an emotion that resembled conventional grief. Slipping the card into my breast pocket, I immediately felt better. I was now thinking not of whether my mother had loved me but of how much I had loved her for continually keeping hell at bay. I had been loving and devoted, just as the card had said. That was real, that was true. Then I remembered at last how my mother had embraced me on the night of her death and said, "Dear John, how good and kind you really are," and I knew those words had been spoken from the heart. "To think that *you* should be the one who loves me enough to say that," she had said, overcome with remorse for her past omissions when I had praised her, and suddenly I felt that whatever had been wrong had been put right. I too had spoken from the heart, and after years of dutiful formality we had at the end achieved an honest conversation during which love had undoubtedly been present.

I sank down on the bench again, shed a tear, stole a furtive glance around the churchyard to make sure I was unobserved and then cried for thirty shameful seconds. That cured me. I felt I had arranged my memory of my mother into an acceptable pattern which could be fitted into the script of my life; I felt I could now be, without difficulty, the devoted son of a loving mother.

That night I was so exhausted that I thought I would sleep as soon as my head touched the pillow, but I was wrong. Obsessed by the thought of my father sleeping with his mistress on the night of his wife's funeral, I tossed and turned in misery until dawn.

III

"I saw Mrs. Morgan today," said Blanche a week later.

"Oh, yes?" I said. I had just had a row with Edmund and was feeling distracted. "Which Mrs. Morgan?" Morgan is a very commonly encountered name in Wales.

"Mrs. Meredith's sister. I asked her if Rhiannon would like to play here again, but unfortunately they're all returning to Cardiff. It seems Mr. Morgan has returned from the sea and secured new accommodation for them."

"Oh yes?" I said again. "Well, I daresay that's for the best—we don't really want Marian becoming too friendly with a working-class child, do we. Darling, listen, I've just had the most appalling row with Edmund..."

In the week that had elapsed since my mother's funeral Mrs. Straker had been installed as housekeeper directly after the departure from Oxmoon of Aunt Ethel and her tribe. The entire parish of Penhale was now throbbing with a prurient delight, lightly masked as scandalized horror, and I was aware of the villagers observing me compassionately as if I were suffering from some monstrous affliction. From Llangennith and Llanmadoc in the north to Porteynon and Penrice in the south, from Rhossili in the west to Swansea in the east, the gossip was reverberating through Gower, and I was just telling myself that matters could hardly be worse when Edmund, who had been staying at Penhale Manor, announced his intention to return to Oxmoon to condone my father's conduct.

Edmund's argument—which was Robert's; Edmund was incapable of developing such a closely reasoned approach—was that if we were all to behave as if everything were aboveboard the gossiping tongues would at least be handicapped, if not silenced.

"That may be true," I said, "but I refuse to compromise my moral principles by condoning Papa's conduct."

"Oh, don't be so bloody pigheaded, John! Why don't you be sensible and give in for the sake of all concerned?"

"I might have known you'd take the line of least resistance!"

"I beg your pardon," said Edmund, "but it wasn't I who stayed safely in London throughout the war."

We did not speak again before he returned to Oxmoon, but when I next called on Robert he was very severe and said I had made Edmund utterly miserable.

"Well, what the devil does he think he's made me?"

Further protracted argument followed about the situation at Oxmoon.

"Intellectually what you say is right, Robert. But morally you're dead wrong, and I'm sticking to my principles. I draw the line."

"Well, I'm all for drawing lines," said Robert. "God knows nothing would be more boring than a world of unbridled excess where nobody bothered to draw any lines at all—sin would quite lose its power to charm. But has it never occurred to you that you might be drawing your lines in the wrong places?"

"Don't be ridiculous!"

"You're the one who's being ridiculous, drawing this brutal line between yourself and Edmund, who's actually showing great courage in a very difficult situation."

I was too guilty when I remembered the war to hold out for long against a reconciliation with Edmund, and on the following Sunday after church I offered him the olive branch of peace. My father had not returned to the church since my mother's funeral but had asked Edmund to take Thomas to Sunday Matins.

Edmund was pathetically pleased by my suggestion that we should end the estrangement. "If you knew how much I've regretted that bloody awful remark about—"

"Quite," I said, "but let's forget it. Least said soonest mended and all that rot."

The next night he came to dine at Penhale Manor, and after Blanche had left us alone with our port I asked him how he was getting on at Oxmoon.

"Well," said Edmund, welcoming the opportunity to confide and lowering his voice cozily, "it's not as bad as I thought it would be. The best part was that Papa was so pleased when I come back—honestly, I don't know how we each managed to maintain a stiff upper lip—"

"Spare me the sentimental drivel about how you and he almost sobbed in each other's arms. What about Straker?"

"My God, John, she's amazing! All the servants gave notice and sat back waiting for her to beg them to stay, but not a bit of it. 'All right, out you go!' she says, and brings in a gaggle of girls from Swansea, all terrified of her. She rules 'em with a rod of iron and the house runs like clockwork. Incredible."

"But surely not all the servants were dismissed?"

"No, Papa exercised clemency in a few cases. Bayliss is still there, white as a sheet and absolutely cowed—"

"All right, never mind the servants. How's Thomas?"

"Oh, fine! Actually he and Milly get on rather well."

"My God, Edmund, you don't call her Milly, do you?"

"Not before the servants—no, of course not," said Edmund blushing.

I was appalled.

After he had departed I said to Blanche, "If I were Edmund I'd leave Oxmoon and seek a position in London but of course he won't. It's a pity. I think his lack of ambition condemns him to great unhappiness."

"Perhaps," said Blanche, "but my dear Mama used to say that unambitious people often have a greater capacity for happiness than those people who yearn for worldly success."

I was becoming a little tired of hearing Blanche's Dear Mama quoted against me, but I said nothing because with our holiday fast approaching I wanted no cross word to mar our happiness.

I took my family each year to the Isle of Wight in August, not only because it was a delightful spot for the children but because the yachting at Cowes gave us the chance to keep up with our London acquaintances. I intended eventually to lease a flat in town but at present we seldom went to London. Blanche's aunt had a house near Knightsbridge and we occasionally stayed there, but I did not care for Aunt Charlotte, who thought her niece could have done better for herself than to marry the younger son of a Welsh squire. However Blanche was devoted to her aunt, the only sister of her Dear Mama, so I had to employ much diplomatic tact to avoid awkwardness in that direction.

Marriage is full of such trying little pitfalls. In fact I was not surprised that some couples were driven into regular quarrels. Blanche and I never quarreled, but now and then I did feel that we came dangerously close to a tiff. However I always labored diligently to suppress any cross word, and my reward for our unsullied marital happiness was our annual holiday when I could play with my children in the day, enjoy smart dinners in the evening and at night make love to my wife with a greater frequency than unselfishness usually permitted.

We had not been at Cowes more than a week when I realized that Blanche was hoping to conceive again. Nothing was said between us but then there was nothing to say. Certainly I was not about to object because my wife became subtly more gentle and loving than usual, but sometimes as we walked across the sands together I found our silence oppressive, as if we were divided by some gulf I did not understand, and then I thought I did not want another baby to divide us further. Yet that made no sense. How could it make sense when I wanted a large family and considered my marriage idyllic? Classifying such thoughts as morbid, I dismissed them firmly from my mind.

We were away a month, just as we always were, and returned home at the end of August. Still nothing had been said between us on the subject of pregnancy, but the fact that Blanche had been spared her monthly affliction had not passed unnoticed by me. Normally, when I pursued my marital rights once or at the most twice a week, it was possible for her to suffer her affliction without me knowing about it, but I had indulged myself at Cowes and I knew her health had been unimpaired.

I wondered when the symptoms would begin. Blanche spent a large part of her pregnancies lying either in bed or on a sofa to counter her general feeling of malaise, and to my distress I found this ill health annoying. I was not repelled by pregnancy itself but by the joylessness and lassitude that accompanied her infirmity. I did not want to be repelled. I was most upset that Blanche should be unwell, particularly when she never complained, but nevertheless I found her pregnancies dreary and knew they were made even drearier by my conscientious removal to a separate bedroom. Naturally I could not have forced myself on her at such a time. Only a savage would have been so inconsiderate.

"How nice it is to be home!" said Blanche as we reached the Manor. "Oh look, darling, the roses are lovelier than ever! Aren't they beautiful?"

"Beautiful," I agreed mechanically, and indeed my home did seem ravishing to the eyes, the garden glowing with flowers, the old house encircling us with its mellow charm, and beyond the Manor walls Gower too was ravishing, the Downs shimmering in the summer light, the earth of my lands a terra-cotta red, the cattle grazing peacefully in the water meadows.

Yet no sooner had I returned than I found that everything was going wrong. It had been one of the driest summers in living memory, too dry for the comfort of the cattle, and a freakish cold spell in June had laid a deathly hand not only on my new acres of crops but on the vegetables in our kitchen garden. Then just as I was wondering how in God's name I was going to water my cattle if the river ran dry, I heard that damned Llewellyn had been marching his sheep over my land again. I was so furious that I immediately drove into Swansea to see my solicitor, but he merely regaled me with legal obscurities till I lost patience. After telling him that he was to get me an injunction even if he were struck off the rolls in the attempt, I retired exhausted to Penhale.

The first person I saw when I entered the hall of the Manor was little Rhiannon

Morgan. She was doubled up with laughter at the foot of the stairs as Marian slid down the banisters.

I stopped dead.

"Marian!" exclaimed Blanche, emerging from the drawing room in response to the squeals of laughter. There was no sign of Nanny. "Off those banisters at once!" She turned to greet me. "Hullo, darling—how did you get on in Swansea?"

I said blankly, "That's Rhiannon Morgan."

"Yes, isn't that nice! I saw Mrs. Morgan in the village this morning so I asked her to bring Rhiannon to play."

"But she returned to Cardiff."

"Oh, she arrived back at the farm last night for another little holiday! However I think she must have taken the Merediths by surprise, because when I saw them yesterday they didn't mention—ah, here she is! You'll stay to nursery tea, won't you, Mrs. Morgan?" she called. "Nanny assumed you would."

Mrs. Morgan had emerged from the kitchens. She wore a pale limp green cotton dress that needed ironing, and cheap white sandals. Her garish hair was scraped back from her face as usual and lay in a lump on her long neck. She looked tired.

"Thank you, Mrs. Godwin," she said awkwardly, and added to me with an even greater embarrassment, "Good afternoon, sir."

"Good afternoon, Mrs. Morgan," I said, and walked away into the drawing room.

"Papa!" cried Marian, rushing after me. "Come and have tea with us!"

"I'd love to, Marian, but I'm afraid today I've too much to do." I looked around the drawing room in search of some all-consuming occupation, but fortunately Marian took no for an answer and dashed away again into the hall.

"Dafydd's playing with a friend in the village," said Blanche, following me into the drawing room. "He's too young for the girls and too old for Harry—oh and darling, talking of Harry, I must tell you what he did today! He ran in here and played 'God Save the King' on the piano—with both hands and not a note wrong..."

There was a fresh bowl of white roses on the piano. While she was talking I stooped to smell them, but found they had no scent. They were perfectly formed, perfectly arranged, but they had no scent. I stared at them, and the more I stared the less real they seemed to me until finally it was as if they were made of wax, bleached of color, devoid of life.

"Darling, I don't think you've been listening to a single word I've been saying!"

"Sorry, I was thinking of wretched Llewellyn and his sheep."

After tea I retired to my study and tried to write some business letters, but I was unable to concentrate. I kept thinking of those white roses. Then I started thinking of color—the brilliant sea-green of the water by the Worm's Head and the flaming sunsets over Rhossili Bay. I remembered the white roses on my mother's grave, a symbol of death, but for one split second beyond them I glimpsed the fire of life, red-hot, all-consuming, terrifying.

I decided my Welsh blood was making me fanciful. Mixing myself a whisky-

and-soda, I abandoned my correspondence, settled down in my favorite armchair and escaped into the very English world of John Buchan as I reread his famous shocker *The Thirty-nine Steps*.

IV

I remember every detail of that evening clearly. Blanche wore an evening gown of a most ethereal shade of yellow, paler than primrose, barely darker than cream, and with the gown she wore the amethyst pendant I had given her for her eighteenth birthday after our engagement had been announced. At dinner we discussed the possibility of inviting Daphne and little Elizabeth to stay in the autumn, as it was now out of the question that they should stay at Oxmoon, and soon afterwards I began to reminisce about Lion. I tried to explain how awful he had been and how wonderful he had been and how although I had expected to miss him less and less I found myself missing him more and more.

"He had more spunk than Edmund," I said, "and so much more warmth than Robert, and he was never sullen like Thomas—he was always so jolly and such fun. God, how we used to laugh when we were young! Yes, we had good times... but later we drifted apart, and at the end of our teens he called me a prig and I called him a rake and that was that. But I always remained fond of him. He was—" I hesitated before finding the right word. "—he was a very *real* person. There was no illusion there—he never played any roles, and he had such vitality—he was *so alive*." I stopped to reflect on what I had said before adding in wonder: "How strange it is that I should say all that now, five years after his death! I thought I'd finished grieving for him long ago." And when I saw that Blanche was moved, either by my reminiscence or by the fact that Lion was dead, I said abruptly, "Well, we won't talk of him anymore. I'm sorry—I was being morbid. Will you play me some music instead?"

We retired to the drawing room and she sat down at the piano, her pale yellow gown shimmering in the light from the candle sconces; the fresh white roses, perfect as ever, in the same crystal vase nearby.

She began to play. The music meant nothing to me, but I enjoyed watching her and thinking how beautiful and talented she was. Then I started worrying about Harry, playing "God Save the King" perfectly before he was three years old. A musical inclination was no use to a boy at all.

I was just wondering if I could find a miniature cricket bat to give him for Christmas when Blanche suddenly stopped playing.

"Are you all right?" I said, springing to my feet as she put her hand to her forehead.

"No—I'm sorry, darling, but I've got the most beastly headache. It's come on very suddenly. Will you excuse me if I go up to bed?"

"Of course," I said sympathetically, and thought with a sinking heart: Pregnancy.

To conceal this inexcusable antipathy I said quickly, "Shall I telephone the doctor?"

"No, don't worry, darling—it's only a migraine."

"I'll sleep in the dressing room so that I don't disturb you."

"No." She looked wretched. "I know you hate that."

"Don't be absurd! When you're not well I don't mind in the least!"

"You do," she said, and to my horror she began to cry.

"Well, we won't talk about that now," I said hastily, but she only wept harder and whispered, "We never talk, never, and there's so much I want to say."

"But my dear Blanche . . . what do you mean? We're always talking! We get on so well!"

"I feel so lonely."

"*Lonely?*"

"I'm frightened in case you don't love me."

"But I adore you! How can you possibly say—"

"I'm frightened in case I can't be the sort of wife you want me to be, I'm frightened that I won't be able to cope with our marriage much longer, I'm frightened that you don't confide in me, I'm frightened because I don't know what your silence means—"

"My darling, you must stop this nonsense—yes, I insist that you stop! You're simply tired and overwrought. I love you and you're the best wife in the world and—"

"Then why do you never talk to me?"

"I do and I will—but not now when you've got a bad headache. Come on, I'll take you upstairs."

"No," she said desolately. "I'll say good night here." She dried her eyes, gave me a chaste little kiss which I dutifully returned and vanished upstairs into the dark.

I felt very, very disturbed. I closed the piano and saw the roses shiver on their long stems. Then I shut all the windows. I felt as if I were battening down the hatches—but against what? I had no idea. Retreating to the study I mixed myself another whisky-and-soda and prepared to escape again into the world of John Buchan, but now Richard Hannay too was fleeing from forces that terrified him and in his flight I saw my own flight reflected.

Moving outside into the moonlit garden, I wandered down the path to the potting shed. An owl hooted above me, and as I remembered similar nocturnal expeditions with Lion long ago at Oxmoon I suddenly knew I wanted to be Johnny again, safe in an uncomplicated past.

But I was in a complicated present, and my wife was unhappy—except, as I well knew, this was impossible because she had no reason to be other than contented. What had happened? What had gone wrong? I had no idea.

I thought of Blanche weeping, "I'm frightened that I won't be able to cope with our marriage much longer," and at once I heard my mother saying in despair, "How's that poor child Blanche ever going to cope?" That was the moment when I knew it was all my fault. I had no idea what "it" was, but I was going to find out. Glancing up at the dark window of our bedroom, I wondered if Blanche was still awake, and I hesitated, torn between my reluctance to disturb her and my compulsion to solve the problem. Naturally, I never doubted that the problem—"it"—could be solved.

"It" won. I hurried indoors, lit a candle and padded up the staircase. At the bedroom door I paused to listen, but all was quiet. I tapped lightly on the door.

"Blanche?"

There was no answer. Opening the door, I looked in.

"Darling, I hate to disturb you—"

But she was awake. Although she was lying in bed, her eyes were open.

"—oh, you're awake. Thank goodness. Blanche, I really must talk to you further about all this—"

I stopped.

She had not moved. Her eyes did not see me. She was looking at some point beyond my left shoulder. "Blanche?" I said sharply, but there was no reply. It was almost as if she were dead, but that I knew was impossible. Healthy young women of twenty-five did not die without warning in their beds. Setting down the candle, I touched her cheek with my hand.

It was cold.

I found it extraordinarily difficult to know what to do next, but since it seemed that some mysterious drop in her temperature had caused her to lose consciousness, I pulled off my shoes and got into bed beside her to warm her up. While I waited I tried to imagine what "it" could be. What had I done? I loved her, she loved me and we were happy. Except that we weren't. At least, I was. Or was I?

"Blanche?"

She was wearing a white nightgown, white as the white roses. Vile white roses. Odorless. Listless. Dead.

I got out of bed, pulled on my shoes again, picked up the candle and went downstairs to the telephone.

"Dr. Warburton, please," I said to the postmistress when she responded to my call.

I was now no longer baffled but incredulous. In fact I was outraged. How *could* she have been unhappy? I had done everything possible to ensure a successful marriage. I had told her lie after lie in order to protect her from my troubles. I had restrained my baser physical inclinations endlessly in order not to give her offense. I had toiled year after year at the task of behaving perfectly towards her— and as I thought of this, I could hear my mother's voice again. She was holding me in her arms in the remote past and telling me how I could feel safe and happy. "You're going to be an extra-specially good boy so that your poor papa is never reminded of his mother's wickedness..."

My mind suddenly plunged into chaos as past and present collided. Instinctively I squeezed my eyes shut in a futile attempt to blot out the Christmas of 1903.

"Hullo? Warburton speaking."

"Warburton, it's John Godwin." I was so acutely aware of time being dislocated that I could not pin myself to the present. I said, "It's all to do with my grand-

297

mother, my grandmother and Owain Bryn-Davies," and then I hung up so that I could concentrate on the task of staying sane. Something seemed to be happening to my mind. I felt as if my capacity for producing rational interlinked thoughts were being savagely dismembered.

The telephone rang. I answered it. One always answered telephones when they rang. That was normal.

"Godwin, you need help, don't you?"

It was Gavin Warburton calling back, nailing me firmly to the September of 1921. The past receded. I was back, shattered but sane, in a horrifying present.

"My wife's dead," I said, "except that she can't be dead because she's only twenty-five and there was nothing wrong with her."

Warburton said he was on his way.

V

"I'm sorry," said Warburton, "but I'm afraid there'll have to be an autopsy. Of course there's no question of death from unnatural causes, but when a young person dies suddenly the cause of death must be conclusively established."

"You're saying she's dead."

"I'm saying she's dead. I'm very, very sorry. It could have been a heart attack," said Warburton, persistently talking in order to underline the truth which I was still trying to reject, "but it might have been a cerebral hemorrhage. Did she complain of a headache?"

I stared at him.

Warburton started talking again, but this time I could not hear everything he said. His voice seemed close to me at one moment, far away the next. "Possibly born with a weakness in one of the blood vessels of the brain...could have happened at any time...or perhaps a blood clot...sometimes when a young woman is pregnant...very tragic...so much admired...deepest sympathy...My dear Godwin, I think you'd better tell me where you keep your brandy."

The next thing I knew I was drinking brandy in my study while Warburton telephoned for an ambulance. When he rejoined me I said, "I don't understand. This shouldn't be happening. It's as if my script's been torn up, it's as if someone's rung down the curtain in the wrong place and now I've got no lines, no part, nothing, I don't know what to do next, I don't even know who I am anymore."

Warburton waited a moment. Then he said, "Shall I telephone your father and ask him to come over? I think he'd understand what you're going through."

"Good God, no!" I said, shocked at last out of my wretched loss of nerve. I pulled myself together. "But I'll talk to Robert. He'll know what to do. I'll telephone him straightaway."

Warburton began to speak but checked himself. I looked at him coldly. "You needn't worry," I said. "I haven't forgotten he's an invalid. I'm not going to behave like my father, throwing a hysterical fit and mixing up past and present." I was going to say more but those last five words paralyzed me; I was too frightened to go on. I ran to the telephone but found I did not know what to do with it. I said, "This is September, 1921. Robert's in a wheelchair. My mother's been dead for two months. I'm twenty-nine years old. My grandmother's been dead since 1910, eleven years she's been dead, and this is now 1921."

"I'll talk to your brother," said Warburton. "Come and sit down again while I make the call."

He poured me some more brandy. I drank it. And gradually I began to be calmer.

VI

"I must establish straightaway," I said to Robert and Ginevra, "that I'm now on an even keel following my initial shock. No more dementia; we've had quite enough demented behavior in this family, thank you very much, so if you think I'm going to go to pieces like Papa, you'd better bloody well think again. Sorry, Ginevra, please excuse my language, I'm afraid I'm still a trifle upset."

"That's all right, darling," said Ginevra.

"Of course it's tempting to go to pieces because that would prove how much I loved Blanche, and I did love her, no doubt about that, although it wasn't a grand passion because I don't believe in grand passions, they're much too dangerous, think of Grandmama and Bryn-Davies—chaos, anarchy, madness and death. Awful. Stick to the script is the answer and don't deviate from it. Hold fast, stand firm and soldier on, as John Buchan might have said, although actually I don't think he ever did."

"Yes, darling," said Ginevra.

"Have a sedative, John," said Robert, "and go to bed."

"No, I'm going to sit by Blanche and grieve for her."

"They've taken her away to the mortuary, John, you know they have. You saw the body being taken out."

"Steady, Robert," said Warburton.

"I know I saw it," I said, "but I forgot for a moment, that's all, it was just a little slip of the memory, there's no need to treat me as if I'm a bloody lunatic. Sorry, Ginevra, please do excuse my language, I'm not quite myself yet."

"It doesn't matter, darling," said Ginevra.

I suddenly realized she was humoring me. "I'm not mad!" I shouted. "I'm not! I absolutely refuse to be mad! I draw the line!"

"It's all right," said Warburton, gripping me. "Don't panic; it's the shock, it's normal, you don't have to worry about madness. Now, if you can sit down and take off your jacket... Ginevra, can you roll up his sleeve?"

"My poor grandmother," I said, "it was retribution. But then the wheel turned a full circle and Papa and Mama knew retribution themselves. The wheel . . . Robert, you used to talk about that wheel—"

"All right, Godwin—just clench your fist and count to five."

"And to think it was *she* who thought of the tide tables—he did it but she thought of it—oh, the horror, I can't bear it, can't face it, blot it out, blot it out, blot it out—"

The needle found the vein. I started counting in Welsh and within seconds was fathoms deep in oblivion.

VII

I woke at six. Evidently Warburton had reduced the dose he had given to my father—or perhaps because I was younger and stronger the drug had had less effect—for I had no inclination to sleep till noon. I felt dull-witted but not ill. I did have one moment of bewilderment when I found myself lying semidressed beneath a blanket on the drawing-room sofa, but my brain was functioning normally again, and although I shied away from the memory that Blanche was dead, I could recall the fact without confusion. My main preoccupation was with Robert and Ginevra. I was just shuddering at the memory of the scene I had created in their presence when I was mercifully diverted by the sight of a note propped on the nearby table.

Darling, I read, *ring me as soon as you wake up and I'll come over to hold the fort. I've spoken to Nanny and she'll tell the children. All the servants know. Gavin will be returning to see you at nine. Much love,* GINEVRA.

My mind fastened on the word "children." I knew I had to tell them myself. That was the right thing to do. A glimmer of a new script presented itself. I had to be the perfect widower, and the first act consisted of surviving the funeral with decency and good taste. I had no idea what the second act would be about, but I could think of after-the-funeral later. Meanwhile I had to look after my children and behave properly.

Leaving the wings I began to move to the center of my new stage.

VIII

"Mama's gone to heaven?" repeated Marian dazed and burst into tears.

"When will she be back?" said Harry mystified. I saw that this second death in the family, coming so soon after his grandmother's, had made him feel death was a subject he wanted to understand.

"She's dead, you stupid baby, she's dead!" wept Marian before I could choose the right words for him. "And dead people never come back, never!"

"Shhh...Marian..." As I held her tightly, I saw Harry's dark eyes fill with tears.

"But that's not fair," he said.

There was no answer to that. Leaning forward, one arm still around Marian, I drew him to me as he started to cry.

IX

"My wife's aunt will of course be coming down for the funeral, Nanny, but she's suggested that you take the children now to her house in London for a few days." Ginevra had offered to have the children to stay, but Robin was always aggressive towards anyone who tried to share his nursery, and I thought Harry and Marian would be better off under Aunt Charlotte's roof.

"Oh, that would suit very well, sir—much better for the poor little lambs to be far away from here while the funeral's going on.... Oh sir, I can hardly believe it...such a *lady* she was, always so thoughtful to others, always so sympathetic and understanding..."

But I could not stop to think about Blanche. There was no time. My new script called for an audience with the vicar, and soon I was hurrying into Penhale on cue.

X

"I want the shortest possible service," I said to Anstey, who was a Swansea man about five years my senior. He did not have Gavin Warburton's County connections but my father, always conscious of his own lack of education, liked him the better for not having attended a public school. Anstey preached a brisk twenty-minute sermon, kept his services free of Romish tendencies and could be relied upon to discuss the weather intelligently. In my opinion no parish could ask more of its parson than that.

"But you'll have music, of course," he said to me. "Everyone will remember your wife's gift for music—although she was always so modest and unassuming—really, she was such an exceptional person, wasn't she, so sensitive to the welfare of others, such a very Christian lady—"

"But she's dead," I said, "and funerals are for the living to endure. I want no music, no hymns, nothing. This is to be a short plain private English funeral, and I'll have no Welsh circuses here."

XI

My butler was making an emotional speech telling me that all my servants offered their deepest sympathy.

"...the best lady we ever worked for...always so ready to help...nothing was ever too much trouble or beneath her notice..."

I thanked all the servants for their sympathy and loyal support. Then I retired to my study to draft the notices for the newspapers.

XII

My father wrote me a note.

My dear John, I'm so very sorry. How seldom one meets someone who is beautiful and good and nice. It makes the tragedy worse. Tragedies hurt. I don't like to think of you in pain. Please come and stay for a while at Oxmoon. I want so much to help. Always your loving and devoted father, R.G.

I tore up the note. I burned the shredded paper. And I scattered the ashes from the nearest window.

Then, because I had a break between scenes, I started to think. That was a mistake because my thoughts were not in accordance with my script. I was aware that a portrait was inexorably emerging of someone I did not recognize, someone who listened to people's problems, someone who was deeply involved in caring for others, someone to whom people talked and who talked to them in return. My fragile exquisite wife whom I had preserved so conscientiously beneath the glass case of my love now seemed to be disintegrating in my memory while into her place moved a stranger I had never cared to know.

The world was grinding out of focus but I ground it back. I told myself I would think of all that, whatever "all that" was, after the funeral. Then I drove to Little Oxmoon to embark on the next scene in my script.

XIII

"Ginette and I feel we must talk to you," said Robert at Little Oxmoon on the night before the funeral.

I had gone there to dine with Aunt Charlotte, who had arrived that afternoon. Since I had temporarily dismissed all my servants from the Manor by giving them a week's holiday with pay, this meant—to my relief—that I was unable to invite

Aunt Charlotte to stay, but although I had expected her to go to the Metropole Hotel in Swansea, Ginevra had compassionately offered her hospitality instead.

Dinner had now finished; Aunt Charlotte had retired, pleading exhaustion, and as soon as the drawing-room door had closed Robert was launching himself into the attack.

"We want to talk to you about your decision to spend a week entirely alone without servants after the funeral tomorrow."

"Darling," said Ginevra, taking the lead in a rush, "you *can't* be all alone in that house for a week! I know it's madly romantic to want to entomb yourself with your memories, and of course I'm simply passionate about romance, but—"

"Who's going to iron your shirts and wash your underwear?" said Robert with his usual brutal common sense. "Who's going to provide heated water for your shave?"

Ignoring him I said simply to Ginevra, "I know it must seem odd but I've got to be there."

"But darling, why?"

I thought carefully. It was hard to know how to express my complex emotional instincts in words, but at last I said, "I have to arrange my memories." I thought how much better I had felt after I had sorted out my muddled feelings towards my mother. "I have to arrange my memories into the right order before I can draw a line below the past and make plans for the future," I said. "And to do that I have to be alone in the house where Blanche lived."

They were silent but it was not a comfortable silence. I felt I could guess what they were thinking.

"Don't worry," I said, "I'm not about to go mad. I've rejected the grand folly of an elaborate funeral followed by a smart luncheon party. I'm quite in touch with reality, I assure you."

"I can think of nothing less in touch with reality," said Robert, "than shutting yourself up for a week in a manor house with no servants."

"Well, if I don't like it," I said, "I can always leave. What are you two getting so flustered about?"

They looked at me. They looked at each other. But they both decided there was nothing more they could say.

XIV

The air reeked of flowers, and all the flowers seemed to be white in remembrance of her French name. The servants' children had even offered wild white daisies from the hedgerows in little bunches tied with white ribbon. The September morning was warm but overcast; the sky seemed to reflect a burning white light which accentuated the aching glare of the white flowers. I had ordered a wreath of white roses and had instructed that the card should read: *In loving and devoted memory, John, Marian and Harry*. Later I planned to return to the churchyard, just as I had after my mother died, and put that card in my breast pocket. I was very mindful of how that small gesture had meant so much to me.

I had asked for the funeral to be private so the mourners in the church were restricted to the family, but outside all the village had gathered. Ginevra cried at the graveside. I knew she was prone to tears at emotional moments but nevertheless I was touched. I thought how kind she had been to me during the past few days, and I even wondered if I had judged her too harshly in the past. I resolved to be less censorious in future.

My father was there. He had tried to speak to me before the service but I had cut him dead. Edmund had been shocked. I thought, Silly old Edmund, and I started missing Lion again.

At last the service ended. I shook hands with Anstey and thanked him for conducting the service. I thanked Robert and Ginevra for being so kind. I thanked Aunt Charlotte for what I described as her understanding and patience in a time of great trial. Vaguely appalled by my diplomatic glibness, I excused myself from Blanche's Herefordshire cousins and promised to visit them later when I had recovered from what I described as "this sad and difficult occasion." I cut my father again, nodded to Edmund, said, "Thank you for coming, Thomas—that was good of you" and headed for the lych-gate. The silent crowds parted before me. My car was waiting. I drove off and two minutes later was halting the car outside the door of my home.

Now, finally, I could be alone to grieve. Taking a deep breath I expelled it with the most profound relief and then ran willingly, without a second's hesitation, into the nightmare that lay waiting for me beyond.

XV

The grandfather clock in the hall was striking noon. All through that day I remember the clocks chiming the passing hours and reminding me that time was moving on for those who were left alive. Only the dead were beyond time, and Blanche was most certainly dead—"gone to heaven," as I had told the children when I repeated the phrase that Blanche herself had used to break the news of my mother's death. I shuddered. "Heaven" in that context conjured up an image of a celestial concert hall, complete with harps and massed choirs, and since I had no ear for music I found this vision more hellish than heavenly.

Occupied with these comfortingly vacuous thoughts I drifted into the dining room, mixed myself a whisky-and-soda and sat down at the table to reflect further on life after death and other fables. Time filtered idly but not unpleasantly by until I found myself meditating on the meaning of life which I knew was a desperate subject for a man who had insufficient courage to believe in either atheism or God. I decided I had to pull myself together. Mixing myself a second whisky-

and-soda, I set aside all metaphysical speculation and said aloud, "Now I shall grieve." I waited. Nothing happened, but that, as I realized, was because I was in the wrong room. I went into the drawing room and opened the lid of the piano so that I could more easily picture Blanche playing her music. Still nothing happened, but that, as I told myself, was because I needed time to unwind after the ordeal of the funeral.

The clock on the chimneypiece struck one, the fine French china clock that Blanche's ancestor had smuggled out of Paris during the French Revolution. I had always thought this episode in the clock's history was most improbable, but I had to concede that improbable things did happen. It was improbable that Blanche should have died yet she was undeniably dead and here was I, undeniably alone as I waited to grieve, just as every good widower should, for the wife I had so greatly loved and admired.

I debated whether to have another whisky but decided against it. Instead I began to wander around the house as I waited for the grief to come. I decided my trouble was that I had so many precious memories that I could not immediately decide how they should all be arranged, and suspecting I would think more clearly if I had something to eat, I entered the kitchens just as the clock in the servants' hall chimed two. Nosing around in the larder, I found a piece of cheese and ate it. "'Appley Dapply, a little brown mouse, goes to the cupboard in somebody's house'!" Lion had chanted long ago. I could not accurately recall the rest of Beatrix Potter's rhyme, but I knew that Appley Dapply had been charmed by cheese. However I was less than charmed by the piece I ate, and closing the larder door I began wandering again.

Upstairs in our bedroom the little hand of the clock on the bedside table pointed to three, and when I opened the window I heard the church clock in the village boom the hour. Penhale church was as unusual in its possession of a clock as it was in its possession of a square tower. The previous Lady de Bracy, an English-woman who had found Wales distressingly unregulated, had installed the clock to encourage the villagers to lead more ordered lives, but nobody had paid it the slightest attention. Enraged by the continuing unpunctuality, Lady de Bracy had ordered that the chimes be made louder, and from that day onwards the clock of Penhale church had been famous for the manner in which it thundered the hour.

I stood by the window listening to it. I liked the thought of the clocks all chiming away, all doing what they were supposed to do, but that only reminded me that my own behavior was leaving much to be desired, so I embarked on my most serious effort so far to arrange my memories. My first task obviously was to picture Blanche with the maximum of clarity in order to conjure up the appropriate emotions, so turning aside from the window I examined the silver-framed wedding photograph that stood on top of the chest of drawers nearby.

I continued to stare at the handsome young couple in the picture but after a while they began to seem like an illustration from some old-fashioned book of homilies. I could imagine the text: "This is how you should look on your wedding day. This is how you must appear as you prepare to live happily ever after." Then it occurred to me that the photograph was just a pattern of black-and-white shapes.

It had no reality, it was just a prop in my script, and when I looked at Blanche I could not see the Blanche I wanted to remember.

I shoved the frame face down on the chest of drawers and opened the wardrobe so that I could touch her clothes. Here was reality. Now I could visualize her clearly in the clothes she had worn. I saw her smooth, shining hair, so dark that it was almost black, the pale, creamy skin, the slender waist, the delicate breasts, the lovely line of her neck, her—but no, I could not see her face. In my memory, my glance traveled upwards from her neck and found a void beneath the cloud of dark hair.

I was unnerved. I had to see her face. I looked at the wedding photograph again but that was useless; her face was like a death mask. I had to see her being normal, laughing with the children, being the wife I remembered.

The grandfather clock in the hall struck four as I raced downstairs to the drawing room, but in panic I discovered that the photograph albums had vanished from the cupboard below the bookcase. This was bizarre indeed; it was almost as if Blanche had never existed, as if she had been a mere figment of my imagination, yet another prop in my script, but I knew I could not cope with a mad thought like that so I thrust it aside and dashed into the study. There was a photograph of Blanche on my desk, a studio portrait taken after she had recovered from the loss of our first son, who had died within hours of his birth. I stared at the new arrangement of black-and-white shapes. She looked like some actress who had been miscast in Shakespearian tragedy; I saw her as Ophelia, or perhaps as the poor queen in *Richard II*, someone struggling with adversity on a cold bleak stage, someone wearing a mask not of her own making, someone toiling in the wrong part assigned to her by some blockheaded producer who had entirely failed to understand her talents.

Reality began to grind into focus again, and this time I could not grind it back. I told myself I had to find those photograph albums. They were my last chance. Without the photograph albums I would be unable to visualize the Blanche I had loved, and if I could not remember her properly how could I arrange my memories? I started to ransack the house from top to bottom.

I ended up in the nursery just as the cuckoo clock on the wall was hiccuping five. It had occurred to me that Nanny had removed the albums from the drawing room and forgotten to replace them; no doubt the children too had wanted to see the photographs as part of the ritual of grief. I hunted among the toys, but at last ran the albums to earth on the bedside table in Marian's room. Sinking down on the bed I began to turn the pages.

I looked for a long time and in the end I even took the collection downstairs to the study where I could examine the pictures with the aid of a magnifying glass.

More time elapsed and on the chimneypiece the carriage clock struck six.

I glanced up at those two hands pointing in opposite directions. I was in my study at Penhale Manor, the room the de Bracys had called the library. That, I knew, was true. That was real. But nothing else was. All the albums showed me was my script. In a variety of charming scenes the perfect mother played and laughed with her perfect children; the perfect wife smiled adoringly at her perfect husband. But there was no sign of the other Blanche, the real Blanche who had wept and said we never talked to each other, the Blanche who had been so frightened and alone. I had never known the real Blanche. It had not suited me to know her. I had been too busy acting out my script in which I outshone Robert and secured my parents' approbation by making the perfect marriage. I had not cared for Blanche. The only person I had cared for had been myself. I had had this wonderful wife, who everyone now told me had been so exceptional, and yet I had never loved her enough to bother to become more than formally acquainted with her. And what was worse, I had made her desperately unhappy.

This was a different situation indeed from my mother's death. There I had been able to console myself that matters had been put right between us before she died, but Blanche had died when I was estranged from her; she had died alone and unloved.

The truth stood revealed in its full horror. I had been a bad husband. My marriage had been a failure. My life had been false. "I want to arrange my memories," I had said grandly. What memories? I had no memories of anything except lies, and now, I realized to my horror, I was going to have to live with them. But how did one live with such guilt and such shame? I had no idea. I felt I couldn't cope, couldn't manage, couldn't think how I was going to go on. I had never before experienced such a horrifying consciousness. The pain was excruciating. How did one live with such pain and stay sane?

The Victorian clock in the dining room thudded seven as I uncorked the bottle of champagne. I drank the first glass straight off and poured myself another, but seconds later the glass was empty again. I went on drinking, and gradually as the familiar lassitude stole over me I managed to control my panic. I knew I had been fond of Blanche. That was real, that was true, and I thought that if I could now grieve for her, not as a husband should grieve for his wife but as a man mourning the loss of someone precious, I would find my disastrous failure easier to accept. But my guilt defeated me; although I waited and waited and waited, the grief still refused to come.

I stopped drinking. I knew I should eat to avoid becoming ill but I had drunk too much, and in the kitchens all I could do was vomit into the sink. I returned to the hall, and as I entered the drawing room the silence came to meet me, the silence of those white piano keys, the silence of the white roses, the silence of reproach and estrangement. The room was utterly silent, utterly still, unbearably silent, unbearably still, and suddenly I was overpowered by the silence, choked and racked by it, and I knew I had no choice but to escape.

I burst into the garden. The evening air was clear but the rose garden was an intolerable blur of white light, and the next moment I had started to run.

I ran to the front of the house, I ran down the drive, I ran past the gates into the lane. I ran towards the village but even before I saw the church I knew what I wanted to do. I wanted to take the card from the wreath. I wanted to see those words *loving and devoted* and tell myself they did bear some relation, no matter how distorted, to reality. I thought that once that card was in my breast pocket next to my heart, I would finally be able to grieve as I had grieved for my mother.

I reached the lych-gate. I passed the porch. I turned the corner of the tower to confront the grave on the far side of the churchyard.

Some yards away in front of an ancient yew tree the white flowers, symbol of death, were heaped on the dark earth. But beyond them was color, a flash of shimmering red, the fire of life coruscating in the pale evening light.

I stopped.

A woman was seated casually on the ground by the grave. She was plucking the short grass nearby and throwing it aside in hypnotic rhythmic movements of her hand. Her brilliant red hair was very long, stretching all the way to her waist, and it waved over her shoulders like burning liquid gliding over molten rocks.

She went on tearing the grass, her head bent in deep, concentrated thought, but at last she became aware that she was being watched and her fingers were still.

She looked up. She saw me. She leaped to her feet. For a long moment we stood there, both of us transfixed with shock, and then above us, far above us in the belfrey, the church clock began to thunder the hour.

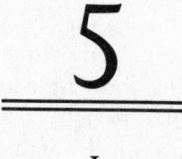

I

SHE BEGAN to walk towards me. The evening sun, slanting across her face, lit those light eyes to a deep glowing sea-green. With a quick movement of her hand she pushed back her long fiery hair but again it slid forward to frame her face, and as the church tower cast its shadow across her translucent skin I knew, as indeed I had always known at heart, that she was ravishing. The clock, hammering her extraordinary beauty deep into my consciousness, struck again and again and again.

The last stroke died away. It was eight o'clock on the day of my wife's funeral and I was alone with Bronwen Morgan in the churchyard at Penhale.

"Mr. Godwin," she said rapidly in her low heavily accented voice, "forgive me for intruding. You want to be alone with your grief and I'll leave you at once."

I stopped her by raising my hand. "Why are you here?" I said. My voice was puzzled, confused.

"I couldn't be in the churchyard this morning with the rest of the village because Dafydd was sick, but I did so want to pay my respects...Mrs. Godwin was such a very lovely lady and so kind to me."

I had a brief poignant glimpse of Blanche being kind, and in that glimpse I saw both the familiar Blanche and the Blanche I had never known. The horror of my estrangement from my wife overwhelmed me afresh, and I leaned dumbly against the wall of the tower.

"Mr. Godwin, you're not well. Come and sit down, sir, you really should sit down, indeed you should."

I was too overcome by misery to protest. "I've done a very foolish thing," I said as we reached the iron bench by the yew tree. "I've dismissed my servants because I wanted to be alone to grieve, but solitude's proved too . . . difficult, and I don't know what to do next. I can't think clearly at all."

"Have you had anything to eat?"

I discounted the cheese and shuddered at the memory of the champagne. "No."

"Then if you like, sir," she said, "I'll make you some tea and a sandwich. You mustn't have too much but you should have something, and tea's so clear, so cool, you'll be able to think more clearly once you've had some tea."

I could at once picture the tea, fragrant and steaming, in one of the white Coalport cups. "That's very good of you, Mrs. Morgan," I said. "Thank you."

Leaving the churchyard, we crossed the green and walked down the lane to the Manor. No one was about. I supposed everyone was either at home or in the pub or at a meeting that was in progress in the church hall. In the lane the hedgerow glowed with wild flowers and the summer air was fragrant. Neither of us spoke. When we reached the house I led the way into the hall.

"I know where the kitchens are, sir," she said. "You go to the parlor—the room with the piano—and rest. I shan't be long."

"I'm afraid the fire in the range is out—"

"Then I'll light it," she said tranquilly, and disappeared beyond the green baize door.

Returning to the drawing room, I sat and waited. The room grew darker, and I was just rising to my feet to light a lamp when I heard her footsteps recrossing the hall.

She was carrying a tray. On it stood a teapot with a milk jug and sugar bowl, a plate bearing a cheese sandwich, and an apple. There was only one cup and saucer.

"I hope the bread's not too stale, sir."

"It doesn't matter. Mrs. Morgan, you've only brought one cup. Don't you want any tea?"

"I have a cup waiting in the kitchen."

"Then please bring it in here. I've been alone too much in this room today."

She retrieved her tea, and when she returned she brought not only more hot water but a second sandwich. The tea tasted exquisite. I ate and drank with single-minded concentration until finally I felt strong enough to look back over my shoulder at the piano, but although the image of Blanche returned to me I was still unable to see her face.

I said suddenly, "I can't grieve. I want to but I can't. I've set this time aside to grieve but now the grief won't come and I don't know how to summon it."

"There is no timetable for grief," said Bronwen Morgan. "Grief isn't a train which you catch at the station. Grief has its own time, and grief's time is beyond

309

time, and time itself... isn't very important. It's the English who think time is a straight line which can be divided up and labeled and parceled out in an orderly fashion, but time isn't like that, time is a circle, time goes round and round like a wheel, and that's why one hears echoes of the past continually—it's because the past is present; you don't have to look back down the straight line, you just look across the circle, and there are the echoes of the past and the vision of the future, and they're all present, all now, all forever."

I looked at her and saw far beyond her into the remote comforting mysticism of Celtic legend. She leaned forward, putting her elbows on her knees and cradling her chin in her hands, and as her hair streamed over her shoulders to frame her face again, I felt the magic of that other culture beckoning me away from the down-to-earth brutality of the Anglo-Saxon tradition in which I had been educated. And then it seemed to me that the culture which had been hammered into me at school was not only inferior to hers but less in touch with the real truths of life, and I felt my familiar world shift on its axis as if pulled by some gravitational force far beyond my control.

"Tell me about the echoes of the past," I said. "Tell me how I can look across the circle and hear my wife's echo in time."

She said, "It may be tomorrow, it may not be for years, but you'll hear it. Perhaps the children will sound the first note, the first chord in time; perhaps one day Master Harry will go to the piano and when he plays you'll see her there and you'll think, Yes, it's sad I shall never hear her play again, and you'll grieve. Or perhaps you'll think, Yes, it's sad, but there was happiness before the sadness, and then although you'll still grieve you'll be grateful for the memory, and the memory will echo on in time. And later perhaps you'll hear one of her favorite tunes played by someone else and you'll remember again, perhaps less painfully, perhaps even with pleasure that the memory should bring her close to you again, and the echo may be fainter but still very clear, so clear that you'll tell your children about it, and then it'll be part of their memory too, and so it'll go on echoing again and again in time, and that time is beyond time, time out of mind."

She paused. She was still looking at the unlit fireplace, and behind her the soft light from the lamp made her hair blaze against her uncanny skin.

"When I was two," she said, "my father died in the Boer War. I have no memory of him. I thought later, How sad I can't remember him, can't grieve as I should—for of course to me he wasn't a hero, he was just someone who'd gone away and left us, and I resented him for being killed and then I felt guilty that I resented him, and what with all the resentment and the guilt I never thought the grief would come, I thought I'd never hear his echo in time, and indeed I forgot all about grieving, but gradually, as I grew up, other people would talk to me about him, and I thought, Why do they do this, what makes them speak now after so many years, and then suddenly I realized it was because of me, because I *was the echo* for those people, and for them the past wasn't lost far away down the straight line after all but coming back towards them in a curve. It was as if he was still alive, for when they looked at me they saw him, and when I understood

310

this, when I understood he was present in me, then I knew him, then he became real to me, then the resentment died and the guilt fell away and at last, years after his death, I was able to grieve." She stood up and stacked her own cup and saucer with mine on the tray. "I'll take these to the kitchen and wash them up. Please excuse me, sir, for talking so much."

After a moment I followed her. She looked up startled as I entered the scullery.

"Thank you," I said. "I feel much better now." I was trying to decide how I could best express my gratitude to her. Obviously I could not offer her money but I felt some tangible gesture of thanks should undoubtedly be made, and after careful thought I said, "I must go through my wife's possessions soon. Perhaps you would accept something in memory of her."

"Oh, but I wouldn't presume—"

"Nonsense. She liked you, spoke well of you."

She was speechless. She set down the newly dried teapot as if she feared it might shatter to pieces in her hands.

"Perhaps you'd like some of her clothes," I said suddenly. "They're no good to her maid, she's the wrong shape."

"Oh, but I couldn't possibly accept—"

"I don't see why not. Why don't you at least have a look at them and see what you think?"

"Well, I... it's very, very kind of you.... When?"

"Now?"

"Oh! Oh yes—yes, indeed—if you wish." She hastily dried the last plate and hung up the cloth.

The twilight was heavy by this time but although the hall was in gloom it was not in darkness. Carrying a candle more out of courtesy than necessity, I led the way upstairs. We were both silent. I had fixed my mind on the subject of Blanche's clothes and was debating whether to donate them to the Red Cross or to the Salvation Army after Mrs. Morgan had made her selection.

In the bedroom I walked to the wardrobe and opened the doors.

"These are the clothes she usually wore," I said over my shoulder as I held up the candle to illuminate them. "But there's another wardrobe in the bedroom across the passage where she kept the clothes she wore less frequently."

Mrs. Morgan cast one glance at the contents of the wardrobe and said, "I'm afraid I couldn't possibly take any of them, sir. They're much too good for me."

In the pause that followed I was acutely aware of my hand setting down the candle. Then before I could stop myself I said, "You're too modest, Mrs. Morgan. You're far, far too modest."

Everything changed. I had never before realized that a mere inflection of the voice could destroy a world forever, but as I spoke I saw that Anglo-Saxon world in which I had always secretly been such a misfit keel over and begin to fall soundlessly, endlessly into the void.

The other world moved closer. I saw the open spaces, the timeless light, the freedom beyond imagination, and suddenly in a moment of absolute certainty I

311

knew that this was the way, the truth, the life I longed to lead.

The chained dog finally slipped his collar. I rushed forward, she stumbled towards me and a second later we were in each other's arms.

II

I kissed her exactly as I wanted to kiss her. There was no question of worrying in case I offended delicate sensibilities, because I knew that she too was exercising no restraint. Her arms were so strong that they seemed almost as strong as mine, and her mouth was strong too, very free and supple, and her fingers were strong but sensitive as she caressed the back of my neck. Our tongues were silent together. I knew a moment of intense intimacy followed by such a violence of desire that I would have swayed on my feet if she had not been holding me so strongly, and in her strength I saw a reflection of my own.

I was aware of Blanche's bed behind her, and beyond the awareness lay the knowledge that whatever happened next could never happen there. I hesitated, and into the mental space created by my hesitation streamed the training and self-discipline of decades, no longer tormenting me with the image of imprisonment but offering me the only possible escape from the terror of my new freedom.

In panic I released her. I backed away, covering my face with my hands as my voice, the voice of an English gentleman, said with absolute correctness, "I'm so sorry; I do apologize. Obviously I'm unhinged by my grief."

There was a flurry of movement. Slim, strong fingers gripped my wrists and pulled my hands from my face. Great green eyes, fierce with the most desperate emotion, blazed into mine.

"Don't you lie to me!" she shouted in Welsh. "Never lie to me! *I don't deal in lies!*" And bursting into tears she rushed from the room.

I tore after her, and suddenly I was overwhelmed by the sheer reality of my emotion. I was blistered and bludgeoned by it, my old ways shattered, my past blown to bits and all my defenses incinerated by a white-hot heat. It was as though every mask I had ever worn, every lie I had ever told were being blasted from the face of my personality until at last, at the very bottom of my consciousness, my true self began to stir again in its long-forgotten, long-abandoned grave.

I caught her on the landing and grabbed her back from the head of the stairs. We were a long way now from the bedroom I had shared with Blanche, and nearby us a door led into one of the spare rooms which had never been used.

I remember how I noticed that door.

I opened it. The room contained only a narrow single bed with a shabby mattress but that didn't matter. Nothing mattered now except the door. It was the door I always remembered so clearly afterwards, the door leading from one world into another, the door which connected past and present and opened onto the future.

I remember flinging the door wide, I remember shoving the door shut, I remember the door slamming with utter finality behind us—yes, it's the door I'll always remember, the door, the door, the door . . .

III

The miracle was the absolute cessation of pain. At one moment I was in such pain that I was incapable of imagining life without it and the next moment there was no pain, only a deep all-powerful forgetting, not a peace, for peace implies stillness, and not oblivion, for oblivion implies unconsciousness, but a freedom to sever myself temporarily from the unbearable sources of my distress.

We were together for a long time. Then the episode was concluded but within minutes, mysteriously, our strength was renewed. I use the word "our" deliberately because she was as exhausted as I was. I had never before witnessed feminine exhaustion of that nature, although I had known it could exist; I had heard stories about such phenomena, but I had thought only prostitutes could be so untroubled by reticence. However, I passed no judgment, registered neither astonishment nor disbelief; I was beyond such banal emotions. I was deep in my forgetting, only thankful that she wanted me again without constraint, so we went on and the new strength brought with it a gathering ease, but again I neither registered astonishment nor marveled in disbelief. I was wholly absorbed in the miracle of my painlessness and wishing only that it could last forever.

But passing time and the inevitably finite nature of all that one might wish to be infinite eventually conquered us. Exhaustion came again, and although we later achieved yet another renewal, it was short-lived. Unaccustomed to such excess my body had become sore, and I sensed she was sore too for the same reason. Her fingers hardened on my back; I felt our release uniting us for a few more precious seconds, but although I tried to sustain myself afterwards I failed. The force was spent and a moment later we had fallen asleep in each other's arms.

IV

When I awoke it was sometime in the dead of night but the moon had risen and the room was brighter. I was at first aware only of the body pressed to mine but presently I observed that the window was curtainless, the mattress was lumpy and the air was cool upon our nakedness. I shivered and she woke up.

"Bronwen." I sighed and kissed her and sighed again. I had never been face to face with a naked woman before. My knowledge of the feminine anatomy had

313

been derived first from classical statues and later from tactful explorations of Blanche's body under cover of darkness.

After some time I said, "May I ask you something outrageous?" I was still existing entirely in the present. There was no past and no future. I was by a miracle suspended in time.

"Outrageous!" She laughed at the prospect. "You'd better ask in Welsh or I mightn't understand!"

I laughed too. Then I touched her below her narrow waist and beneath the curve of her hip. "Is your hair there," I said, "the same color as your hair here?" And I kissed the shining strands which, dark in the moonlight, streamed past her cheek to fall across her breast.

"Of course!" She started laughing again, and so did I. "Why should my hair be red in one place but not in another?"

"My brothers, who are all much fairer than I am, have hair that's darker on their bodies than on their heads," I said, and thought, What an extraordinary conversation! I began to laugh again. It amazed me that I should want to laugh with a woman in such very intimate circumstances.

"I know nothing about fair-haired men," she said simply. "My husband's dark and there's been no one else."

"I've had no one else but my wife. But that wasn't because I'm virtuous, as you undoubtedly are. It was because I felt I had to pretend to be perfect."

"But no one's perfect except in a fairy tale!"

After a pause I said, "Blanche was."

"No, she wasn't! That was why she was such a lovely lady—she wasn't cold and faultless like a stone angel in a churchyard; she was warm and human and real."

"But when I think how she slaved and slaved to be the perfect wife I so selfishly wanted her to be—"

"Ah, that reminds me of myself. I slaved and slaved to be a perfect wife to Gareth, but that wasn't because I was a saint. It was because I was afraid he'd fall out of love with me and leave me for someone else. I was weak and timid and dishonest. I wasn't a heroine at all."

"And did he leave you?"

"Yes—for the sea and the bottle. We still share a bed when he's home, but I don't bother to pretend to be a saint anymore, and now I'm much happier. Better to live in the truth, however terrible, than to murder your true self by living a lie."

I stared at her. Then I tried to imagine Blanche as weak and timid, perhaps even a little dishonest, not a saint but a flesh-and-blood woman who had loved me not perfectly but well enough to accept the burden of trying to be the wife I wanted. At last I said, "I never knew her. And she never knew me either. She only knew the English side of me; she only knew me as John. But in the old days I was Johnny and I was Welsh."

"What happened to Johnny?"

"I murdered him. I murdered my true self in order to live a lie." Pulling her closer I buried my face in her streaming hair.

"But he's come back, hasn't he?" she said. "Can't you see the curve of time? You didn't murder him after all. He's still alive."

V

Soon after four she said in English, "I must go. Myfanwy will be up before sunrise to bake the bread."

In alarm I asked if her sister would have waited up for her but she shook her head. "No, I always go to bed later than either Myfanwy or Huw. I don't have to be awake so early." She slipped out of bed. "I must wash," she said abruptly. "I'll go down to the scullery."

"What's wrong with the bathroom?"

"I'm not sure what to do there."

"What on earth do you mean?"

"Could you come with me?"

We removed to the bathroom which she had apparently visited during the night after using the lavatory next door.

"There are two taps," she said, "and I didn't know which one to use. The second sink in the scullery just has one tap so I knew I wouldn't have to worry there."

"Ah, I see." I stared at the bath and basin, two humdrum objects which I had taken for granted for as long as I could remember, and tried to imagine the background of someone to whom they represented a worrying challenge. "Yes," I said, pulling myself together. "Well, you can use either tap at the moment— it won't make any difference because the boiler's out and there's no hot water."

"Oh, I see. Yes, I wondered if the H on the tap stood for Hot but I wasn't sure. It's better to ask, isn't it, if one's not sure."

"Much better."

"I was afraid it might be some special drinking water which mustn't be used for washing. When I was in service there was no bathroom—river water came out of the pump in the yard and drinking water came from the well, and when the gentry wanted hot water it was heated in copper vats and carried upstairs to their bedrooms in jugs."

"Oxmoon used to be like that when my parents were first married. I daresay many country houses in remote areas took time to acquire modern plumbing and bathrooms."

"I've never seen a bathroom before," said Bronwen simply. Then she smiled and said with a trace of her old awkwardness, "I'll be all right now."

I kissed her and departed to my dressing room to put on some informal clothes. On my return to the spare room I said, "When's your husband coming home?"

315

"I don't know. It depends whether it's the Lisbon or the Naples run."

"Didn't you ask him which it would be?"

"No, I was too angry because he was leaving me with hardly any money and I knew we'd have to go back and live on Huw's charity again."

"Why couldn't he leave you more?"

"He'd drunk it."

We went downstairs in silence. I tried to imagine her life in cheap rented rooms in Cardiff but it was beyond me, so I thought instead of Disraeli, thundering three-quarters of a century ago about the two nations of Britain, the rich and the poor. Instinctively I recoiled from this vision; I reached out my hand as if I could bridge the unbridgeable, but as I looked across the void that separated her nation from mine I saw the glittering bayonets of the class system waiting to impale all those who fell into the abyss below.

"What are you thinking about?" she said suddenly as I opened the front door.

"Nothing."

She stopped. I saw her face and said, "Class. I shall never take it for granted again."

"What else can one do but take it for granted? It's the way of the world." She paused on the doorstep. "I want to say goodbye here."

"Can't I walk up the lane with you?"

"I'd rather say goodbye to you here, where you belong."

"But of course we'll meet again!"

"Where?" she said. "How?"

"But—"

"It doesn't matter," she said rapidly. "You needn't pretend that there could be more between us, you needn't try not to hurt my feelings. I accept that there's no future but I don't mind because I've had my one perfect night, the night I thought I could never have, and now on the dark days when life seems very hard I'll be able to look across the circle and hear your echo in time."

I could only say "I must see you again."

"How?" she repeated, and added: "Black is black and white is white and gray isn't allowed."

"Except in the bedroom."

"Oh yes! If the woman's a whore." She began to walk away.

"For God's sake, I didn't mean—"

"No, I know you didn't. But that's the truth, isn't it? And that's why I can't see you again."

We stood motionless facing each other. The sky was lightening in the east, and across the dew-soaked lawn in the opaque woods the birds had started to sing. I took her in my arms. After a long time, I said stubbornly, "I know we'll meet again, I know it," but she shook her head, said, "Goodbye, Johnny" and walked off down the drive to the gates.

316

VI

I sank down exhausted on the drawing-room sofa. My last conscious thought before sleep intervened was: Johnny. And in my dreams Lion was laughing once more at my side.

When I awoke I saw that the French clock had stopped. Outside in the broad daylight it was raining, but I barely noticed because memory was slamming through my mind with the force of a tidal wave and I was rushing out into the hall.

The grandfather clock, still ticking somnolently in its corner, told me that the time was twenty minutes past seven. I toyed with this fact, wondered what to do with it, but it meant nothing. All I knew was that there was still no past and no future and that I was still suspended in time.

I wandered around the hall, rubbed my face absentmindedly and remembered that I had to shave. The quest for hot water occupied me satisfactorily for quarter of an hour, but at last I was heading upstairs with a steaming kettle. I was enjoying the timelessness, savoring my detachment from the world, luxuriating in a mild but most delectable euphoria. Johnny! Not even Lazarus, raised from the dead, could have been so blissfully unconscious of everything save the fact that he was once more alive.

In the dressing room I poured the water into the basin, picked up the razor and glanced at my reflection in the glass.

I hesitated. I was wearing a blue shirt, and this performed the usual sartorial trick of making my eyes, never pale, seem bluer than ever. I looked into those eyes and saw my father looking back at me. And beyond my father, I saw my grandmother Gwyneth Llewellyn.

I dropped the razor. I got my back to the glass. Some time passed during which I stood leaning against the basin and gripping the edge to steady myself. I could think of nothing but madness. It filled my entire mind. Even if I had fought in the war I believe I could hardly have known such all-consuming terror. I had broken the rules and gone mad. Or had I? In my panic a thought so terrible occurred to me that I began to tremble from head to toe. I was wondering if my night with Bronwen had been the fantasy of a sick bereaved mind. I was wondering if my madness was even more profound than I had imagined.

I stumbled down the corridor, burst into the little spare room and rushed to the bed but I was safe because the mattress was stained. I touched the stains to make sure they were new and found them stiff. Colossal relief streamed through me. I was sane. It had all happened. It was all real, all true. The words formed a litany in my brain. All real, all true; all real, all true—

I was trembling again. I had just realized that I could not allow what had happened to be all real, all true.

I ran to the bathroom, found a cloth, soaked it, ran back and began to scrub the mattress. I scrubbed till my arm ached. Then I fetched the pumice stone and scrubbed all over again. The stains had long since vanished, but this made no difference because I could not believe the mattress was clean. I wondered how I could fumigate it. Finally I took it downstairs to air in the backyard but I had forgotten the rain and was obliged to leave my burden in the laundry room. In the hall I wrote *Replace mattress* on the note pad by the telephone, and as I wrote I became aware that the hall seemed unnaturally quiet. Then I realized that the grandfather clock had stopped.

I blundered into the study, but found that the carriage clock had stopped before six. The clocks were stopping, all of them; the wheel of time was standing still so that I could crawl aboard again and suddenly I knew that was what I wanted; I wanted to scramble back into Anglo-Saxon time so that I could shelter behind my Anglo-Saxon mask and feel safe.

But when I went into the drawing room I found the white roses were wilting on the piano, and the next moment Blanche was moving to meet me in my memory. I saw her clearly, very very clearly. I saw her standing by the white roses on the evening of my mother's funeral. I heard her talking about my father.

"I'd like to think I'd always try to be compassionate, even if the fault were very hard to understand..."

The memory became unendurable. I heard John Godwin, hard and selfish, smug and insufferable, commenting rudely: "No understanding's possible in this case and I've used up all my compassion."

I thought, I cannot be that man anymore.

The truth caught up with me then, but I found there was nothing I could do but face it because this particular truth could not be erased like a semen stain with soap and water and a pumice stone. I had betrayed my wife on the very day of her funeral, and now, as my mind turned back towards her, my one memory was of her talking of forgiveness.

Sinking down on the piano stool I bowed my head over the silent keys, and at last I was able to grieve.

VII

The car responded to my first attempt to start it. The rain had stopped. It was a cool morning, and I felt not only cool too as I drove down the lane but curiously older, as if I had grown up overnight instead of aging from adolescence to maturity over the conventional period of years.

As I headed south I drove into open country where stone walls intermingled with the hedgerows to enclose the fields of the valley. The road curved, the moorland drew closer and above the long line of the ridge that marked the summit of Rhossili Downs I could see huge white clouds billowing in from the sea.

The high wall of the grounds had already begun on my left. A moment later I was turning in at the gates, and there before me Oxmoon lay in an enigmatic challenge, goading me on to the end of my now inevitable mission.

It was seven weeks since my mother's funeral but I felt as if I had been away seven years or longer. As I parked the car I wondered if my nerve would fail me but I was conscious only of a fanatical determination to do what had to be done.

I rang the bell.

A new parlormaid, young and crisp in a spotless uniform, opened the door and said, "Good morning, sir" with a little bob of respect, but when she showed no sign of recognition I realized she was a stranger to the district, one of the untrained girls who had been recruited from Swansea.

"Good morning," I said. "I'm John Godwin and I've come to see my father."

The parlormaid displayed her inexperience by looking flustered. To spare her I stepped across the threshold without waiting for the invitation to enter, and as I paused in the hall a woman emerged from the passage at the far end. I took off my hat, she moved forward with a smile and the next moment I found myself face to face at last with my father's mistress Milly Straker.

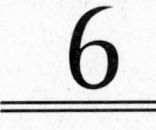

6

I

I HAD SEEN her once or twice in Penhale but never at close quarters, so although I could recognize her, the details of her appearance had remained unknown to me. I controlled my immediate antipathy by telling myself that I of all people had no right to rush to judgment.

"It's Mr. John, isn't it?" she said courteously in a limpid voice. It was the voice of a Londoner, but not of a Cockney born within the sound of Bow Bells. I heard the inflections of the London suburbs—Wandsworth, perhaps, or Clapham— where drab little villas lined "respectable" streets, their windows festooned with lace, their parlors filled with obese furniture, and suddenly I felt I had stepped back fifty years into some erotic Victorian world where forbidden rites were enacted in secret rooms in which heavy blinds were perpetually drawn. Mrs. Straker was wearing a plain black dress with a cameo brooch pinned to her flat bosom. Below the severely parted black hair I saw a sallow face, sharp eyes and a foxy look. She gave the impression that she had seen a lot, done more, and what she had neither seen nor done she could intimately describe with the help of a bottomless imagination.

"This *is* a surprise, sir!" she said, still speaking in a well-modulated voice. "May I take the liberty of introducing myself? I'm Mrs. Straker." Dismissing the fascinated parlormaid, she added tranquilly: "Mr. Godwin's breakfasting in his room, but I'm sure he'll be ever so pleased to see you. If you'd care to follow me, sir, I'll take you up to him myself."

I wanted to tell her I could find my own way upstairs, but I knew I could hardly burst in on my father unannounced. In fact I would hardly have been surprised if Mrs. Straker had asked me to wait in the morning room while she found out whether or not my father wished to receive me. I decided I had no right to quibble about an escort.

"Thank you, Mrs. Straker," I said.

She led the way upstairs. She was thin, with narrow unfeminine hips, but her ankles were good. She moved well too, neither elegantly nor seductively but with a smooth unhurried self-confidence. It was impossible to guess her age but I doubted if she was younger than thirty.

"An unexpected visitor for you, Mr. Godwin!" she called mellifluously as she knocked on the door of my parents' bedroom.

"Come in!" was my father's cheerful response.

She opened the door. I heard her say "It's Mr. John," and the next moment I was moving past her into the room. Then she left us, and as the door closed behind her I found myself alone once more with my father.

He was sitting at the table by the window with the remains of his breakfast in front of him, and in his hands was a copy of *Country Life*. He was wearing the spectacles he used for reading, but when he saw me he pulled them off as if he feared they were deceiving him.

"John?" He struggled to his feet. His cup rattled in its saucer as he knocked it accidentally. The magazine fell to the floor.

"Good morning, sir," I said formally, but found myself so paralyzed with emotion that I was unable to embark on my prepared speech.

"But what a wonderful surprise!" said my father in a rush. "Please—sit down." He gestured towards the chair opposite him and nearly knocked over his cup again.

I managed to do as I was told but before I could make another attempt to speak my father said anxiously, "How are you? I've been so worried, I hardly slept a wink last night. Have you had breakfast? No, I don't suppose you have, you wouldn't feel like eating, but you must eat, that's important." He raised the lid of the silver dish in front of him and peered inside. "Yes, there's plenty here and it's still hot. I'll ring for an extra plate and some cutlery and a fresh pot of tea."

I somehow declined food and drink. I still could not remember my prepared speech, but now I no longer cared. "Papa," I said, "I've come to apologize. I was very cruel to you after Mama died. I don't expect you to forgive me straightaway, but perhaps in time..." I could say no more but it did not matter, for as soon as I stopped he began to talk to me in Welsh.

"My dear John," he said, "if only I had had just one-half of that courage which has brought you here this morning." He stooped, picked up the magazine from the floor and began to smooth the cover with his fingers. "I was just as cruel to my mother," he said, "but I never had the courage—or the humanity—to say later I was sorry. And after she was dead I regretted it."

I said, "You're giving me praise I don't deserve. I'm not showing nobility of character, just a shamefully belated understanding of what you must have suffered."

"Understanding's one thing. Having the courage to display it is quite another."

"But you don't realize—you don't know what I did last night—"

"Oh, I think I do," said my father, and when I looked at him I knew there was nothing else I needed to say.

After a while he said, "Your wife was a dear little girl but perhaps not entirely right for you. I daresay you feel guilty now that you weren't able to love her as she deserved. Guilt is a very terrible thing," said my father, staring at the rain which was falling again on the tranquil garden. "Believe me, I know all about guilt and how it can torture you when you're alone."

My fingers were interlocked on the table in front of me. Reaching out he covered them with his hand.

"It's strange," said my father presently, removing his hand and pouring himself some more tea, "how Margaret's absence has enabled me to see my children more clearly. I suppose it's because I keep looking for her in you all. Robert's the one who's most like her, of course, but do you know, I don't believe I ever really conceded that until Margaret was dead. I had a great need to idealize Robert always—to see him as myself, the self I would like to have been. It was all mixed with the fact that his birth gave me the courage to deal with Bryn-Davies and build a better world at Oxmoon. Robert was my justification, you see, and the more brilliant and splendid he was the more I felt justifed in what I'd done—in fact I do believe that even if he hadn't been brilliant and splendid I'd have made myself believe he was. It was necessary to me. Very wrong, though," he added severely as he sipped his tea. "It did Robert no good to spoil him, and it was hard on you other fellows—and particularly hard on you. But you see, I didn't want to look at you and be reminded of myself. I only wanted to look at Robert and be reminded of the man I fancied myself to be. Very silly," said my father, watching the rain again. "But there we are. No parent's perfect. We all make mistakes. The great trick is to recognize them and put them right. Not always possible, of course. But one can try."

There was a silence as he continued to sip his tea.

"Yes," he said as if he had at last completed a satisfactory meditation on some particularly convoluted subject, "I was afraid, that was the trouble—afraid that you might be like me—and my mother—but now I can see how foolish my fears were. I don't care what brought you here this morning—all I know is that long ago I couldn't bring myself to do what you've done today. So the truth is, isn't it, that the likeness isn't all-important. What's all-important is that even if two men are dealt similar hands of cards they'll always play those cards in different ways." He smiled at me. "You'll play your cards far better than I ever have," he said. "I know you will. I know it."

I could not speak but we were at peace with each other. Indeed I thought perhaps I was at peace for the first time in my adult life. And then, before I could begin to absorb the full meaning of this new freedom, the door opened and in walked Mrs. Straker.

"Well, dears," she said as soon as the door was closed, "had a nice little chat? I've brought some extra dishes in case John was faint with exhaustion and longing

321

for food—God knows, staging a reconciliation at breakfast is enough to beat anyone to their knees, but look at you both, dry-eyed and poker-faced, I don't know how you gentlemen do it, I really don't! Here, move your hands, John, and I'll set your place."

I kept my hands exactly where they were on the table and said, "Thank you, Mrs. Straker, but I don't require breakfast."

"Call me Milly, dear, all your brothers do except Robert but of course I don't see much of him, poor man. What ghastly things happen to people in this world, which reminds me, dear, let me offer you my condolences—you won't want them, but I'll offer them anyway for what they're worth. Well, there's no subject that kills a conversation like death, is there, so let's talk of something else. Bobby, is that all you've eaten? What's left in this silver dish? Oh, look at that, you've hardly touched it, you *are* naughty! Eat up at once before I get cross!"

"Well, as a matter of fact," said my father, smiling at her, "I do feel hungrier now."

I stood up abruptly. "I must be on my way."

"Oh, but you can't go back to that empty house!" exclaimed my father in distress. "Stay here!"

"That's very kind of you, Papa, but I've realized I must join the children in London."

This was a decision he could accept. "Very well, but when you come back—"

"I'll call on you," I said, "naturally. No, Mrs. Straker, you needn't see me out. Good day."

"And good day to you, John!" she said pertly, giving me a tough shrewd look with her amoral black eyes.

Somehow keeping my face devoid of expression I left the room and retired, profoundly shaken, to my car.

II

I was too disturbed to return home immediately. Instead I drove to Rhossili, parked the motor on top of the cliffs and stared through the rain at the windswept sands far below. Long lines of surf ceaselessly battered the black stumps of the shipwrecks. A mist hid both the Worm's Head on the left and the top of the Downs on the right, and above the three-mile beach in the fields of the rectory the sheep seemed pinned to the grass by the gale.

I realized, as I smoked several cigarettes, that I was trying to recover—and not merely from my rage, which was considerable. I was trying to recover from my shock that the scene at Oxmoon, in one respect more satisfying than I had dared hope, had evolved into a nightmare which I had no idea how to assimilate. How did one deal with someone like Milly Straker? As far as I knew, no book of rules had yet been written on the subject of how a gentleman could coexist in amity with his father's mistress, but I doubted if any book of rules could have solved the dilemma in which I now found myself. It looked to me as if I were going to be cut off from my father at the exact moment when we had finally come to understand each other.

I knew very well that my shock sprang from my naivety; I had had some sentimental notion that in forgiving my father I would automatically discover that Mrs. Straker was the most charming and delightful woman who would be only too willing to help us all live happily ever after. Because of this I had gone to Oxmoon prepared to bend over backwards to be civil to her; indeed I had felt almost under a moral obligation to like her, and so when she had revealed herself in her true colors I had been even more appalled than I would have been if I had arrived at Oxmoon expecting to meet a monster.

Once more I reviewed those true colors. Of course she was common, but I had been prepared for that. Of course she was vulgar, but even her intolerable familiarity, nauseous as it was, I could somehow have overlooked for my father's sake. But what I could not overlook was the unmistakable sign that Mrs. Straker was addicted to power. My years at the Foreign Office had taught me a good deal about power and the manipulation that inevitably accompanies it, and I recognized in Mrs. Straker a clever, ambitious, thoroughly unscrupulous woman. Her vulgarity had not been the artless chatter of a woman who knew no better; it had been carefully staged, and every word she had spoken in that bedroom had been designed to underline to me her influence over my father. Desiring above all else to avoid a new quarrel with him I had kept quiet, but nevertheless I had been horrified.

I could see exactly how the situation would appear to her. My father was fatally dependent on her company, Robert was a cripple, Celia was in Heidelberg, Lion was dead, Edmund was ineffectual and Thomas was a child. She was safe from all opposition there. That left me, and I was the one potential enemy. She must have long since realized that if anyone threatened her rule at Oxmoon it would be "Mr. John," and that was why she had staked out her territory so forcefully the moment I had recrossed my father's threshold.

Oxmoon was no stranger to predators. It had survived Owain Bryn-Davies, and I supposed it would survive Milly Straker, but nonetheless the prospect of an avaricious woman exercising her power there without restraint was chilling indeed. The only conclusion I could reach was that whatever happened I had to avoid quarreling again with my father.

It seemed a daunting challenge, and after grinding out my cigarette in despair I drove to Little Oxmoon to consult Robert.

III

"This is one of those nerve-racking situations," said Robert, "when one yearns for the gift of clairvoyance. Our main problem here is that we have insufficient information."

"I don't understand."

"Well, you're taking a dim view of the future on the grounds that Straker's a clever scheming woman, but on the other hand it's quite possible that he may have tired of her by Christmas. How long do Papa's mistresses last, I wonder? If he's like most men his affairs probably run a predictable course over a predictable period of time."

"She has an appalling air of permanence."

We were in the dining room where I had just finished an excellent breakfast. Ginevra had gone to Swansea with Robin and his nanny to see Aunt Charlotte off on the train to London. Kester was howling somewhere as usual in the company of his nursemaid. Outside it was still raining.

"I simply can't understand what he sees in her, Robert. She's neither good-looking nor particularly young. It's a complete mystery."

"My dear John, it's the commonest of all fallacies that sex can only flourish in an atmosphere of youth and beauty. I had the most extraordinary case once involving a man of forty, a woman of sixty-five and a youth of eighteen with a harelip..."

Robert talked on but I barely heard him. I had begun to remember another most extraordinary case of sexual attraction, the case of a gentleman of twenty-nine who had become obsessed overnight with a working-class girl six years his junior. I was thinking of their two separate worlds, coexisting in time yet unlinked by any bridge but the bedroom.

"Robert," I said, interrupting his saga of the homicidal youth with the harelip, "have you ever slept with a working-class woman?"

He naturally assumed I was still trying to make sense of my father's affair with Mrs. Straker. "Of course. Why?"

"Did you find the experience exceptional? I mean...did you find you could talk to such a woman more easily?"

"Talk! What about? How can one even attempt a serious conversation with such a person? There's no common ground. Anyway one hardly goes to bed with a working-class woman with a view to conducting a *conversazione* between the sheets!"

"No," I said, "I suppose one doesn't.... Robert, have you ever known a fellow who actually married a working-class woman?"

"One does, of course, hear of the occasional blockhead like Oswald Stourham who becomes besotted with a platinum-blond chorus girl, but fortunately such disasters are fairly rare. Don't worry, John, I believe Papa when he swears he'll never marry this woman. He's not a complete lunatic."

I was silent.

"The last thing he'd want is to commit social suicide," said Robert soothingly. "Even if he could face being ostracized by his friends, how could he ever face being humiliated before his children? No, he'll stay away from the altar, don't you worry—he'll draw the line there."

"Draw the line," I said. "Yes." I stood up to go.

"Well, John," said Robert, preparing to say goodbye, "I'm sorry you spent all last night being racked by loneliness, but if that's resulted in a better understanding of Papa then maybe you haven't suffered in vain. Now promise me you'll come back here tonight instead of incarcerating yourself all over again in that bloody Manor. There's nothing heroic, I assure you, about preferring suffering to comfort."

But I needed more time to consider my plans, and after promising to telephone him later I returned once more to Penhale.

IV

Back at the Manor I gradually began to realize that my situation had become intolerable for at least three reasons, and that once more my life required a radical change.

The first reason involved my father. If I remained in Gower, I doubted if I would be able to avoid clashing with him eventually over the subject of Mrs. Straker—and a clash would be just what my enemy wanted; in fact she would probably do all she could to promote it in order to drive a wedge between me and my father and keep me out of Oxmoon. My best hope of outwitting her undoubtedly lay in being a dutiful, affectionate but distant son until he came to his senses.

The second hard truth that I had to accept was that despite Bronwen's understanding words, Blanche's memory was intolerably painful to me and likely to remain so for some time. I did realize intellectually that my feelings about Blanche would become more quiescent as time passed, and I did think it likely that one day in different circumstances, I might well wish to live again in the house that was so conveniently close to Oxmoon, but at present I could see nothing but the piano and the white roses and know only that I had not loved my wife as I should.

The third reason which made a departure imperative concerned the woman I did love. If I stayed on in Penhale I would inevitably meet Bronwen again, and then I knew we would be drawn into an affair which she had made it very clear she did not want. It was useless for me to be foolish and romantic, dreaming of establishing her in a neat little terrace house in Swansea. Even if she were willing, such a scheme would be out of the question because the deserted husband would be sure to make trouble, and in the resulting scandal all the children, both hers and mine, would be certain to suffer.

I had a vision of chaos and shied away from it. I thought of my mother and of how horrified she would have been by the scandal. I thought of my father

325

deciding I had played my cards disastrously after all. And finally, when there was no one else left to think about, I thought of my grandmother and Owain Bryn-Davies.

At once I made up my mind that I could never see Bronwen again.

Insanity threatened.

Destruction was imminent.

I drew the line.

V

I met Harley Armstrong three weeks later at a reception given by my former chief at the Foreign Office, and nineteen months afterwards Armstrong was introducing me to his daughter Constance. I had known for some time that he wanted me to marry her.

I have often examined this part of my life with scrupulous care, but I have come to the conclusion that in the worst possible way I was destined for Constance. I told Robert later that it was as if a *deus ex machina* were operating, and Robert promptly embarked upon a dissertation on the Greek concept of fate which incorporated the so-called "madness of doom," the hell where men rushed to destruction because they were driven by forces beyond their control. However at the time I thought I was being supremely sane and Robert thought I was being commendably rational. Never were two intelligent men more deceived.

To have avoided Constance, I would have been obliged to avoid London for even if I had somehow managed to elude Armstrong in 1921, I would certainly have met Constance and her sister in 1923 when they were moving in Society. But I did not avoid London. I embraced it as a solution to my problems in Gower. I could have retreated to my lands in Herefordshire, but I recognized that I was going through an interim period of my life, and it seemed to me that such an interim could be most profitably passed in the capital. There I could slip back more easily into a social life which would help me recover from my bereavement, my children were bound to benefit from a stimulating environment and I would, if I were lucky, find some occupation far more congenial to me than my former dull routine at the Foreign Office.

I was unsure how long my self-imposed exile from Gower would last, but I suspected five years would see the conclusion of my problems. At the end of that time my father would surely have tired of Mrs. Straker, Blanche would be no more than a poignant memory and Bronwen would have faded into a Welsh myth. Then I would be safe.

Having arrived this far in the new script of my life, I looked around for someone who would lead me to the center of the stage, and immediately I was collared by Harley Armstrong.

Armstrong was an American of uncertain origins who had made and lost two fortunes on the New York Stock Exchange before the war, recouped his losses afterwards by profiteering in first canned food and then army surplus stock and was now in what he was pleased to call "Europe" to continue his profiteering in the new industries that had been developing fast since the war. He had acquired interests in petroleum, plastics and gramophone records, but his steady income came from his canning corporation, which was based in New York State. However Armstrong was bored with tinned food, and although he had opened a European subsidiary with a factory in Birmingham and occasionally toyed with the idea of launching a chain of grocery stores, his heart was now in plastics. I did wonder why he had abandoned America, but later he told me he regarded New York as an unlucky city for him, the scene of his two earlier lost fortunes, and he was one of those Americans who believe that if one cannot live in New York one might as well conquer Europe for lack of anything better to do.

During the period of his first fortune, he had contrived to marry a lady who independent sources assured me was far more respectable than he was, but she had not accompanied him to London, and later I learned that they had parted by mutual consent. Mrs. Armstrong lived with her two daughters in her native Boston. When I asked Armstrong what Boston was like, he said, "Even worse than Philadelphia" and shuddered. However he was very fond of his two daughters and dictated long, sentimental letters to them every week. Mrs. Armstrong was apparently interested in the idea that they should enjoy a season in London, and as soon as this possibility had dawned on the horizon, Armstrong was drawing up plans to crash his way into London Society.

"I've got to be in a position to launch my little girls in style," he explained to me, and at once I knew that at the back of his mind lurked the delicious notion that his "little girls" might marry Englishmen and settle down forever within a mile of his doorstep.

I thought at first he was equating himself with Vanderbilt, whose daughter Consuelo had married the Duke of Marlborough, but in fact Armstrong had the kind of vitality which ensured that he would find the upper reaches of the English aristocracy repellently effete. As a self-made man he also possessed what Constance told me later was called an inferiority complex. Shrewd enough to know he was vulgar and ambitious enough for his daughters' sake to want to do something about it, Armstrong decided towards the end of 1921 that what he needed was a well-bred, well-educated British private secretary—no one too grand, and certainly no one who had a title, but someone diplomatic and resourceful who could teach him how to behave in public.

He offered me the job on the morning after we had met.

My automatic inclination was to turn him down but then I thought, Why not accept? I had spent years loathing the stultifying English formality of life at the Foreign Office, and now here was an extraordinary opportunity to work for an unconventional bombastic foreigner. Whatever happened in his employment I was unlikely to be bored and I might even be greatly entertained. It would certainly divert me from the recent past. I therefore decided to accept his offer; the die was cast, and immediately I was whirled into the maelstrom of Armstrong's private life.

Within six months I had extricated him from his lavish but unsuitable nine-bedroom flat at the wrong end of Westminster and had installed him in a house with a first-class ballroom at Eaton Walk off Eaton Square. I gave Harrods *carte blanche* with the interior decoration and the acquisition of the necessary antiques. It seemed safer to trust the leading department store in London than to rely on some fashionable decorator, particularly as very peculiar things were happening at that time in the world of interior decoration.

Once the house had been decorated I engaged the staff and ensured that the housekeeper and butler reported directly to me. I paid the wages. I organized regular and successful "little dinner parties for twenty-four" to show that I was a true son of my hospitable parents. I reconstituted Armstrong's wardrobe and told him very firmly what ties he could never wear. I somehow got him accepted as a member of Brooks's and Boodles. I bought him a suitable country estate in Kent for weekend entertaining and an equally suitable villa in St. John's Wood for his mistress, a young French tart who had advertised herself as a governess. She had greedy tendencies but I enjoyed haggling with her in French over her allowance.

In fact I enjoyed every aspect of my new life, and the triumphant finale of my first months in Armstrong's employment came when I bought him a Rolls-Royce. I could not remember when I had last enjoyed myself so much. John Godwin would have hated the life, but my old self, my true self, was amused by these wrestling bouts with unbridled vulgarity. I kept thinking how Lion would have exclaimed, "What a lark!" and burst out laughing. I laughed too, frequently and spontaneously, and thought how many entertaining memories I would have when I finally retired to Gower.

Those were the innocent days. They came before that evening in 1922 when he invited me to dine with him to celebrate the first year of our association. We dined in great style. Then over brandy and cigars he told me I was the son he had always longed for and that he wanted me to become involved with his business empire.

I was staggered. I had never taken the slightest interest in his business empire; my heart was in neither plastics, nor petroleum, nor tinned food. I was also appalled, in the way that only a man educated at an English public school can be appalled, by this naked display of emotion. But above all else I was touched. Armstrong might be fifty, foreign, florid and frightful; he might periodically infuriate me with his tantrums and his pigheadedness; but there was an element both pathetic and endearing in his gratitude for rescuing him from loneliness in the country of his adoption.

However I knew I needed to be very careful, and after telling him in all sincerity that I was moved and flattered, I asked for time to consider his offer and retired to my little house in Kensington to analyze my new script.

To put it bluntly, in the smallest possible nutshell, I was being offered the chance to become a millionaire. I was also being offered the chance to exceed Robert's success, because with that kind of money behind me there was nothing

I could not achieve. Oxmoon would finally cease to matter. I would be able to acquire a bigger and better home for myself than a quaint little Georgian conundrum set squarely on the road to nowhere, and all my old jealousies would be extinguished once and for all.

Yet if I accepted Armstrong's offer I would inevitably be cut off from my family, for I would be too busy to journey regularly to Gower. What had happened to those moral obligations about which John Godwin had once talked so loudly, particularly the obligation to be a pillar of strength to his father and brother in their declining years? I shuddered as the depth of my hypocrisy now stood revealed to me. I could see that although I had genuinely wanted to help my father and Robert, I had been concerned first and foremost with myself. I had wanted to take advantage of Robert's illness by ingratiating myself with my father and becoming the favorite son—a triumph which would have represented a final victory over Robert and which in turn would have been symbolized by my acquisition of Oxmoon.

For one long clear-eyed moment I thought of Oxmoon, that seductive focus of all my past discontent. I knew I still wanted it. Probably I would always want it. But at least now I was not obliged to regard it as the only panacea for my private unhappiness. Besides, the truth—the truth which I had always been too muddled and unhappy to accept—was that I was never going to inherit that place. If Robert outlived my father, nothing would stop Robin inheriting. If Robert failed to outlive my father, Robin would still inherit—as the favorite grandson. My father had made that perfectly clear, and no matter how strong his new affection for me I could not see him disinheriting the elder son of his eldest son when Robin was a child of such exceptional promise. I was already well provided for. My father could not be blamed for thinking his moral obligations lay elsewhere.

The only sane conclusion I could draw from all these clear-eyed deliberations was that I was not destined for a life in Gower; in fact, as I could now see so well, I would be a fool not to realize that my fortune lay elsewhere and an even worse fool to turn my back on the dazzling new script I was being offered by Armstrong.

Yet I was wary of dazzling scripts.

In the end I told Armstrong that I liked the idea but felt I needed another year to prove to us both that I had the necessary talents to master the world he was offering me, and Armstrong, impressed by the fact that I was making no immediate attempt to grab every penny in sight, suggested that I took charge of his two new charities to find out if I enjoyed wielding power from an office desk.

I enjoyed it. I also excelled at it. The Armstrong Home for Wayward Boys was in Battersea and the Armstrong Home for Distressed Gentlefolk was in Putney, and within six months I had organized them into formidable charitable machines. Throughout my labors I took care to ensure that Armstrong's name as a philanthropist was much quoted in the press, for by now it was 1923 and it was time for me to put the finishing touches to the American gentleman I had created out of the New York gangster I had met eighteen months before. Far away in Boston Mrs. Armstrong was preparing to launch her daughters across the Atlantic for their London season, and their social success was heavily dependent on my skill in promoting their father as a respectable generous benefactor who could be welcomed at even the highest levels of society.

"You'll like my daughter Constance," said Armstrong as the day of the girls' arrival drew nearer. "She's intelligent and well educated, just like you."

I knew an order when I heard one. My role in the script was being amended so that I could play Prince Charming as well as Heir Apparent, but although I expressed diplomatic enthusiasm, I knew I was still in no hurry to remarry. By that time I was well aware that my decision to marry at the absurdly young age of twenty-two had been prompted in part by the belief that sexual satisfaction could be safely obtained only within the framework of marriage, but now I knew that other frameworks were available. Naturally the idea of consorting with prostitutes was repugnant to me, and naturally I shied away from the loose-living Society women whom I met in increasing numbers, but eventually I encountered a gentle, unaffected young widow who was a seamstress. She visited my house regularly to attend to Marian's clothes, and one afternoon when I was on my way to the Boys' Home in Battersea I gave her a lift in my car to her room in Pimlico. Later I paid the rent on a flat for her near the Fulham Road, and when I realized how lucky I was to have found someone so pleasant, so grateful even for the smallest kindness and so anxious never to be demanding I started paying her a small income. Needless to say I spent much time worrying in case this arrangement marked the beginning of an inexorable decline into profligacy, but as the months passed I finally dared to admit to myself that I was doing the right thing. At least it guaranteed I did not rush into marriage a second time out of sheer sexual frustration.

Another reason why I had no wish to rush into marriage was because I was so aware how important it was that I should find the right woman to be my wife. I knew my father had been correct in saying that Blanche had not been entirely suited to me. I still wanted someone who could be gentle but paradoxically I now felt that what I needed most in a partner was strength. I had spent so much of my life in an emotional muddle that I longed for someone who could be guaranteed to see life clearly whenever I became bogged down in confusion, and for the first time it occurred to me how attractive my mother's personality must have been to my father. I had no desire to marry someone exactly like my mother, but her unflinching ability to discern the truth of a given situation and deal with it efficiently, no matter how horrific the truth might be, now struck me as a priceless asset.

The picture of my future wife began to form more clearly in my mind. I wanted someone strong, though the strength had to be entirely feminine; I wanted someone intelligent, like Blanche, but less musical and with more eclectic interests; I wanted someone not necessarily beautiful but certainly someone whom I found sexually attractive. I decided that although I could not contemplate a divorced woman, I might consider a widow. Virginity struck me as being overrated. I felt I had had enough bashfulness in my sexual history to last me for the rest of my life, and I decided it was high time I conquered those emotional constraints which I later discovered from Constance were called inhibitions.

By the time Constance arrived from America in the April of 1923, the portrait of my second wife had crystallized in my mind. I was now looking for a woman who was smart, sophisticated, good-looking, intelligent, efficient, sensible, sexually satisfying, popular with her contemporaries, admired by the world in general, affectionate towards Harry and Marian, devoted to me and altogether a paragon of womanhood. However as this extraordinary combination of feminine virtues not surprisingly proved elusive, it had slowly dawned on me that I might have to lower my impossibly high standards. I decided that I might after all marry a virgin if she showed unmistakable signs of sensuality. I also decided that I might marry a foreigner provided she could adapt herself without difficulty to my world. Armstrong's enthusiastic descriptions had made me suspicious, but when I met Constance I could see that he had by no means fabricated her attractions.

We were introduced at his house on Eaton Walk on the day of her arrival in London. Mrs. Armstrong never traveled anywhere on account of what were described as her "nerves," so her daughters had been chaperoned across the Atlantic by family friends who were heading for a grand tour of Europe.

Constance was nineteen. Dressed with severe smartness in a beaded black gown accompanied by a diamond necklace and earrings, she appeared more self-assured than her English contemporaries. Not a wisp of her fashionably bobbed hair was out of place. Her unobtrusive American accent gave her speech a formal tone, but beyond her apparent poise I sensed she was nervous in case she failed to appear suitably *soignée*. With the aid of my most polished manners I did my best to put her at ease.

"John!" Armstrong was surging towards me with his younger daughter bobbing saucily at his side. "Meet Theodora! Teddy my dear—Mr. John Godwin." And he gave her a doting look, a perfect example of a normally sensible man in the grip of a paternal sloppiness. Yet I knew Teddy was not to my taste. As soon as I saw her round blue eyes, bee-sting mouth and conscientiously "naughty" expression, I realized she would be a chaperone's nightmare, thoroughly unsuitable for me. However I took another look at Constance and decided she had possibilities.

Exerting the full force of my diplomatic charm I slipped casually and disastrously into the role of Prince Charming.

VI

At this point I needed someone to shout at me, "Don't you deal in lies!" and shake me till my teeth rattled but unfortunately no one performed these useful offices and I continued to think that I was behaving in a rational manner. Having made up my mind that it would be wonderfully fortunate if Constance turned out to be the kind of woman I wanted to marry, I now saw with striking clarity how wonderfully fortunate it would be if I decided to marry her. It would save me from disappointing Armstrong, who was offering me this wonderfully fortunate future which so neatly solved all my problems, and whenever I remembered those problems I became increasingly convinced that I did not care for the idea of disappointing Armstrong. I felt that Armstrong's disappointment was a prospect on which it was safer not to dwell.

However I did not forget my past experience with Blanche. Prince Charming, in other words, was a role I had played before with results that had been dubious in the extreme, and armed with this knowledge, I now decided the time had come to analyze my feelings for Constance with scrupulous honesty.

She apparently had everything to commend her. I found her sexually attractive; with her slim neat figure and her dark hair and eyes, she belonged to a physical type that I had always strongly admired, although despite this surface resemblance she was very different from Blanche. The most striking difference was that she was well educated enough to discuss French literature with me, an accomplishment which I regarded at first with antipathy but later with a reluctant fascination. It was by this time ten years since I had come down from Oxford, and I was ripe to recover from the anti-intellectual reaction I had suffered after so much exhausting academic toil. Deciding I would start to read novels in French again, I took Constance with me to Hatchard's where she bought all the novels that I bought so that we could embark on our literary journeys together. This joint venture resulted in some enthralling discussions, and I had to admit to myself that the prospect of a well-educated wife opened up vistas of hitherto unexplored intellectual pleasures.

Better still, Constance was no mere bluestocking but a well-informed articulate young woman who even read the reports of the political debates in *The Times*. The political state of the nation had been in turmoil for some time, with the Conservatives marching and countermarching, the Liberals continuing to hack themselves to pieces and the Labour Party waiting breathlessly in the wings as the Coalition fell apart. I found it all of absorbing interest, particularly since I had begun to doubt that the country would disintegrate if a Labour government came to power. Constance and I spent long hours debating the possibility of class war, revolution fermented by Bolsheviks and the elimination of all that was most inequitable in British society. In the election I voted Conservative out of loyalty to my class, but through the newspapers Constance and I followed Ramsay MacDonald with rapt attention as he inched his way closer to power. Constance said she found it so moving that he was illegitimate, and although I smiled, I knew what she meant. He proved that the socially unacceptable could still win their way to the top; he represented those who were discriminated against because of circumstances which they could not avoid; he stood for the victims of social prejudice, for all those in that unknown world where people did not know what H meant on a basin tap and were turned out of their rooms because their husbands had drunk the rent money.

"Nevertheless," said Constance, "I'm glad the Conservatives were elected. What would happen to the stock exchange if Labour came to power? *The Times* says today..."

To my amazement she started to quote from the City pages. As usual, she had read all the newspapers and knew everything. I began to wonder how she ever found the time.

She did play the piano, but it was a mere technical accomplishment and she preferred to listen to her gramophone or her crystal set. So did I. I bought her many records—classics, popular songs, dance tunes—and found she could comment intelligently on them all. Then we transferred our attention to painting, a subject about which I knew nothing, and Constance explained modern art to me. I still considered it was rubbish, but I thought it was wonderful how well she talked about it.

In addition to this exhausting intellectual activity, we somehow found the time to expend some energy on more mindless pursuits. I danced with her at numerous balls, dined with her at uncounted parties, escorted her to Ascot, to Henley and to Wimbledon, wrote my name against the most important dance in her program when Armstrong gave the coming-out ball for his daughters at Eaton Walk. Armstrong was now confidently expecting me to propose at the end of the season. So were Constance and Teddy. So was London Society. So was I. The only trouble was that I found it hard to imagine myself ever doing it.

Something was wrong, and because I admired Constance so much and longed so intensely for the happy ending to which I felt entitled after so much sadness and muddle, I made a new attempt to analyze my situation so that I could define the problem and put it right.

I knew she was a little too serious, but I liked that. The modern girl who constantly erupted with gaiety like an overshaken cocktail I found noisy, tiresome and unsympathetic. I did wonder if Constance's seriousness would affect her behavior in bed, but I came to the conclusion that this was unlikely, first because she struck me as an intense girl who would be capable of the most passionate emotion, and second because she was so competent in everything she undertook that I could not imagine her failing to master the basic pleasures of sex.

I had no doubt either that she would make an exemplary stepmother. "The subject of raising children is just so fascinating," she confided in me one day. "I've been reading the latest book on the subject of child psychology."

I had never even heard of the subject of child psychology. Gazing at her in unstinted admiration I thought yet again what a remarkable girl she was, and I was just telling myself I was a complete fool not to rush immediately to Bond Street to buy a ring when my brother Edmund arrived to stay with me and announced that he was looking for a wife.

"Between you and me and the bedpost, old chap," said Edmund as we smoked our cigars after dinner on the evening of his arrival, "I'm getting too old to turn out on a winter's night and drive all the way to Llangennith whenever I want a good you-know-what, and now that I'm almost twenty-nine I can see that marriage does have a lot to offer."

"I understand exactly," I said, remembering uncomfortable winter journeys down the Fulham Road.

I had become closer to Edmund since my reconciliation with my father two years ago. Whenever I returned to Gower we had plenty of opportunity for long talks together, because I had installed him at Penhale Manor to look after my house and estate for me. At first it had seemed merely a neat solution to an awkward problem, but to my surprise and gratification, it had turned out to be the best offer to Edmund that I could possibly have made. The opportunity to lead an independent life and the salaried responsibility of the position not only had diverted him from the chronic melancholy he had suffered since the war but had given him the confidence he had always lacked. All my father's children had known what it was to be overshadowed by Robert, but only Edmund had known the horror of being overshadowed by everyone.

I realized belatedly that he had grown up convinced he was useless, an opinion my parents had unwittingly reinforced when they had allowed him to live at home without earning a living, and it was only when I had offered him work that he had begun to believe he was not compelled to go through life as a failure who lived on his parents' charity.

His position was not arduous, since Huw Meredith was a first-class manager, but Edmund took his responsibilities seriously and applied himself with enthusiasm to the estate. However his chief interest remained horticulture, and at my request he had embarked on the task of removing all the scentless white roses from Blanche's garden.

"My one insuperable problem," said Edmund after he had revealed his decision to contemplate matrimony, "is money. I know you and Lion each brought off the fantastic feat of marrying an heiress, but you yourself are so obviously cut out to be a huge success in life, and even old Lion was cut out to be a huge success as a bounder, while I'm not cut out to be a huge success at anything."

I recognized the plea for reassurance. "Stop talking drivel—you're earning your living, you've been to the right school, you're thoroughly respectable and you're a jolly nice chap. What more can any girl want?"

"Money for diamond hatpins."

"Edmund, girls don't go to bed with diamond hatpins. They go to bed with men."

This put us on safer ground. Edmund had overcome his conviction that no woman could possibly look twice at him; at least his experiences in wartime France had not all been hellish, and when he returned home he had embarked on a long affair with a land girl called Joan who worked at Stourham Hall. Unfortunately Joan, having decided that no wedding ring was ever going to be forthcoming from Edmund, had now announced her plans to marry a Swansea bank clerk, and it was this catastrophe, rather than his advancing years, which had led Edmund to consider that matrimony might have more to offer than a love affair.

"I was so upset," he confided in me, "that I damned nearly proposed to Joan myself, but Papa talked me out of it and I know he was right. It's simply no good marrying out of one's class, is it? Of course he and Mama did, but he was *déclassé* and she was exceptional and the circumstances were so peculiar that it didn't matter. But normally... well, you know what happens. The marriage winds up in a social mess, and it's always such hell for the children."

"True. I tried to explain to Armstrong once that to marry out of one's class here is like marrying someone of a different-colored skin. That's the only parallel that an American can understand."

"You don't think I'm being a bloody snob?"

"No, just bloody sensible."

Edmund visibly blossomed as I praised his good sense, but was still anxious enough to say, "All the same my position isn't easy. Do you by any chance know of a gorgeous young heiress who's simply panting to marry a man whose only talent lies in being a jolly nice chap?"

"Possibly—but what kind of a girl are you looking for? I suppose you'd like a sweet shy English-rose type of person who's fond of gardening."

"Good God, no!" said Edmund horrified. "What use would that be? Isn't it bad enough that *I'm* a sweet shy English-rose type of person who's fond of gardening? No thank you, I want someone utterly different! I want one of those marvelous modern girls who says outrageous things and laughs all the time, someone who smokes like a chimney and drinks like a fish and thinks sex is jolly good fun!"

"Say no more, Edmund. Let me introduce you to Teddy Armstrong."

VIII

I had spoken with the rashness that so often follows a pleasant dinner and half a bottle of claret, and when I awoke the next morning I was at once uneasy about my role of matchmaker. However I told myself it was most unlikely that Edmund and Teddy would discover a mutual passion which would drive them pell-mell to the altar.

Never was I more mistaken. Edmund was quickly reduced to a shining-eyed wraith who could neither eat nor sleep, and Teddy was quickly driven to confide that he was "every right-minded girl's dream come true." I noted the word "right-minded" as I acknowledged her determination to be besotted with him, and realized that Teddy had frightened herself by her fast behavior that season. After ricocheting in and out of love with a fine display of emotional pyrotechnics, she had lost her heart to a former army captain who had turned out to be not only a professional gambler but a married man. Her hired chaperone had washed her hands of her. Even the doting Armstrong had been shocked enough to talk of sending her back to America, but I had convinced him that his best chance of avoiding scandal lay in keeping her at his side.

"Of course nothing actually *happened*," confided Edmund to me. "She's told me all about it."

I thought it kindest to maintain a diplomatic silence. It was certainly possible that Teddy's virginity was intact but on the other hand hired chaperones seldom return their fees unless racked by the most profound sense of failure.

"Poor little Teddy's been awfully misunderstood," said Edmund. "She says all she really wants is to get married and live happily ever after near her father. She doesn't get on too well with that mother of hers in Boston."

That sealed Edmund's fate, and his fate made it well-nigh impossible for me to break with Armstrong even if I had wished to do so. If I now refused to marry Constance, I knew he would intervene in revenge to prevent his other daughter marrying my brother. I did wonder if he would object to the match, but I soon realized the bizarre truth that Edmund was even more of an ideal son-in-law for Armstrong than I was. Armstrong wanted to control his favorite daughter's life; this meant he needed a docile son-in-law whom he could manipulate, and in this respect Edmund posed no threat to him. He must have hoped that Teddy would do better for herself but after the scandal he was willing to concede that she could do very much worse, and as always he was keenly aware that if she failed to marry she would have to return to her mother in the autumn.

Deciding to approve of Edmund, Armstrong then asked me when I was going to propose to Constance.

"On her birthday," I said without a second's hesitation. The date was two weeks away.

"No, let's sew this up right now," said Armstrong, unable to resist pushing to conclude the deal that would scoop both his daughters away from his wife. "Constance isn't eating or sleeping properly, and I want her put out of her agony. Take the day off tomorrow, buy the ring and fix the date."

I said I would. Despite my anger that I had been the victim of an exercise in power, I was also conscious of relief that the decision had been taken out of my hands. Constance had not been the only one enduring an agony of uncertainty, and I went home convinced that proposing to her was the right thing—indeed, the only thing—to do.

I had just entered the house when my father telephoned. My nephew Robin, six years old and his parents' pride and joy, had fallen to his death from one of the tower windows at Little Oxmoon, and Robert wanted me to return to Gower at once to organize the funeral.

IX

"Have you ever noticed," said Edmund the next morning as our train thundered towards Wales, "how tragedy so often strikes at people who already have a surfeit of tragedy in their lives? I saw it happen again and again in the war. Men would have their balls blown off and then the next day they'd get a letter saying their wives had run away or their mothers had dropped dead or their children had died of diphtheria."

I said nothing. I was too busy thinking how I would feel if Harry's life had been cut short, and alongside my grief for Robert lay the memory of Robin, spoiled and precocious but still a child of exceptional promise and charm.

We were alone in our first-class compartment. I had thought Rory Kinsella would be accompanying us, but he was on holiday with his Dublin relations and would be approaching Wales from Ireland. Two years ago he had been sent down from Cambridge for incorrigible idleness, but Robert had somehow obtained a position for him in a well-known firm of stockbrokers and Rory had promised to turn over a new leaf. I was skeptical. Both those Kinsella boys had turned out badly, although since the formation of the Irish Republic, Declan was no longer in danger of being shot by the British.

"Of course it would be the best of the bunch that gets killed," Edmund was saying. "That always seemed to happen in the war too. Poor Ginevra! She hardly deserves yet another catastrophe."

I suddenly could not endure to hear him talking so calmly of such brutal chaos. "There's got to be some meaning in it all," I said in despair. "I just can't accept that life can be so disordered."

"Accept it, old chap," said Edmund placidly, "or you'll go mad. I found that out in the trenches."

"Oh, shut up about the bloody war!" Any talk of madness always had an adverse effect on me.

The rest of the journey passed in silence but as the train entered the industrial wasteland on the eastern side of Swansea I did apologize to him. Edmund promptly apologized in his turn for upsetting me, and with an uneasy peace established between us we steeled ourselves for the ordeal of our father's welcome.

He was waiting by the ticket barrier, and for once he looked his age. He was sixty-one, thirty years my senior. I noticed that he was stooping slightly and that his hair, which had once been a dark gold, was now a pale silvery yellow.

After I had embraced him I said, "This must have been a terrible shock for you."

"It was a tragedy," said my father so firmly that I knew he was incapable of discussing the subject. "Why, Edmund, how well you look! Tell me all about this nice little American girl you've met in London."

Edmund promptly began to chatter about Teddy, but when we reached the motor my father asked him to sit in front with the chauffeur and the paean was curtailed.

Somewhere beyond the Penrice Home Farm my father said to me, "He was such a game little fellow."

"Yes. I expect he reminded you of Robert, didn't he?"

"Just like him. It was a miracle. It made up for Robert being ill. Well, at least Margaret was spared this. No more little replacement, no more little miracle... and do you know, I can't face Robert, not yet, I'm too upset... that awful bungalow—the wheelchair—Ginevra—"

"Don't worry, Papa, I'll explain everything to Robert. I'll make sure he understands, just as I do."

My father wiped his eyes and said, "Oh, I'm so glad to see you, John! If only you knew how often I wish you weren't so far away in London..."

And that was when I first allowed myself to acknowledge how much I now wanted to come home.

X

"Oh, there you are," said Robert. "I heard you were rushing down from London, but to be frank I don't want to see you. I'd much rather be left alone."

"I'm sorry. Well, in that case—"

"However since you're here you may as well sit down, have a drink and drum up the strength to face the whole bloody mess. Ginette's gone to pieces, of course, constant hysterics and no use to anyone, I'm fed up with her. Oh, for Christ's sake don't look like that! If I had any bloody strength I'd bloody hit you. Get me some whisky. I'm not supposed to have any at the moment but God knows I could hardly be worse than I am now. No, that's not true: I could be infinitely worse. I could be blind, incontinent and only able to breathe in gasps. That's all to come, of course. What a bloody bore. Why don't I kill myself? Too much of a coward. I still want to shit whenever I think of death. God, how I despise myself. I think up wonderful excuses why I should live, though—my best one was that I wanted to see what Robin would be like when he grew up but that's no good now, so I'll have to dream up something new, but what excuse can I conceivably produce for putting Ginette through hell like this? Sheer bloody-mindedness liberally seasoned with sadism is now the only explanation I can offer—unless I confess my cowardice, but we can't admit to cowardice, can we, it's not the fucking done thing."

"You'll be better in a week or two, Robert. Warburton said this would just be a temporary setback."

"Oh yes—better! Back in the bloody chair! Fuck being better! Still, I agree it's an improvement on being bedridden like this. Christ, I always thought only overemotional women talked about being 'prostrated with grief,' but look at me, I'm literally prostrated. Ah, the whisky. Thanks. You'll have to get me a straw and prop me up... that's it. Now ease me back a bit. That's right. ... God, that's a strong drink you've given me! Take it back and add some more water. No, on second thoughts don't bother. What does it bloody matter, nothing matters. We'd better talk about the funeral. The first thing you've got to understand is that neither Ginette nor I will be there. And for God's sake tell Papa not to go either—the last thing we want is him going round the bend again, that really would be the final straw. I want no fuss. Put the child in a box and bury him with the minimum of drama. He's dead and that's that. God, this whisky tastes good! Give me some more."

As I refilled his glass I said, "Is Ginevra seeing visitors at the moment?"

"God knows. I don't. We had a row and shouted at each other and I haven't seen her since. She's probably drunk. Look, John, if you really want to help here, get hold of Warburton, point a gun at his head and say that woman's got to be carted off somewhere for a few days. She's got some idiotic notion that she can't leave me, but I can't stand the thought of her turning herself into a martyr, it's enough to make me stop shitting with fright at the thought of death and fucking well cut my throat. I told her straight out that she was being a selfish bitch and driving me to suicide, but that did no good—she just had hysterics all over again and rushed off to get drunk—and she's been drinking much too much for some time, I know she has, my spy Bennett keeps an eye on the gin bottle and anyway I can see the results for myself. She's got too fat and she looks blowsy as a tart and damn it, she's in a mess, that's all there is to say, a bloody mess, and *she's got to be helped out of it*. Robin's dead. No one can do anything for him now, but Ginette's alive and *someone's got to do something about her*. I'm frantic, I can't think of anything else, I'm beside myself, she's now the only thing that makes my life bearable, and I've *got to save her*—"

"Don't worry, Robert. I understand. I'll go and talk to her straightaway."

XI

"I'll quite understand if you don't want to see me, Ginevra, but Robert's rather worried about you, and—"

"Don't mention bloody Robert to me! Just because he can't show grief he thinks it's bad taste whenever anyone else does! God, how I hate him sometimes, I hate him, I wish he'd bloody well hurry up and die—"

"Ginevra—"

"Oh, *shut up!* What do you understand about all this? You just have no idea, no idea at all! There you stand so bloody perfect and so bloody lucky— you've never been in a situation where all you can do is scream with pain—"

"I do at least know what it's like to hold one's dead child in one's arms. Ginevra, I'm going to phone Warburton. Will you promise me you'll do as he says?"

"Do what you like, I don't care what happens to me now, I don't care, I don't care, I don't care—"

"Well, *I* care," I said with a finality that I hoped would conclude the conversation, and the next moment she had collapsed sobbing in my arms.

XII

"It's all right, Robert, she's agreed to go. Warburton's sent for an ambulance, and he's arranged for a bed at the Home of the Assumption. Apparently it's more of a rest home than a lunatic asylum nowadays."

"Thank God. Now I shall feel better. Are you off to see the vicar about the funeral?"

"No, I think my next task is to attend to Kester. Where is he?"

"No idea. Ginette sacked both the nanny and the nursemaid on the spot after the disaster and they packed their bags and left immediately."

"But who's looking after the child?"

"Don't ask me. Cook, probably. He knows his way to the kitchens. God, imagine us being left with that little freak! But maybe he'll turn out to be passable in the end. I don't *think* he's mentally defective. What's so bloody awful is that he looks just like a girl."

"I agree his looks are . . . unusual—but maybe he'll be striking later."

"Rubbish. The only way he could be striking would be as a transvestite. Christ, I sometimes feel like making sure he really does have a penis. It's all Ginette's fault for wanting a daughter. My God, if you only knew the fights I've had with her to keep his hair cut and his wardrobe free of Little Lord Fauntleroy blouses—"

"I can't believe Ginevra would deliberately—"

"Poor little devil, what a wretched life he's had, and I've contributed to that wretchedness by my indifference, I know I have, but never mind, I'll make it up to him now and that'll give Robin's death meaning, the death will make sense if I think of it as a punishment and show I've learned my lesson—"

"My dear Robert, I hardly think—"

"Shut up. I don't care what you think. I know you don't believe in God. I don't either. But this is a punishment whichever way you look at it, and if I have my way some good's going to emerge from this disaster to benefit that wretched child."

"In that case there's all the more reason why I should now—"

"Yes, find out where the hell the little bugger is and then tell me what the devil you think I should do with him."

340

XIII

"Hullo, Kester," I said, "I was wondering where you were! Are you all right?"

"Don't be frightened!" said Cook to him kindly. "It's your Uncle John!" She turned to me and whispered, "Poor little boy, he doesn't know what's happening, but don't you worry, Mr. John—Betty and I have been looking after him."

Betty was Watson, the parlormaid. Both servants were local women who had always been employed on the Oxmoon estate, and I knew they were reliable. Feeling matters could have been worse, I advanced on Kester. He was sitting at the kitchen table in front of a plate of sausages and mashed potatoes, but as he looked up at me the spoon trembled in his hand and he abandoned the attempt to eat. His pale eyes filled with tears. As I put out my hand to reassure him, I noticed with distaste that his thick reddish-brown hair waved to his shoulders.

"I expect you miss your nanny and nursemaid, don't you, Kester," I said. "Do you know why they had to go away?"

He shook his head. Two huge tears trickled down his cheeks. So no one had bothered to offer him an explanation.

"We told him Master Robin had gone on a visit to the angels," said Cook, who was a well-meaning soul, "but we didn't know whether Madam wanted us to say any more. Poor little mite, he's not four yet, is he? He wouldn't understand about D-E-A-T-H."

I picked Kester up, sat down with him on my knee and embarked on the necessary explanations.

XIV

"He's all right, Robert, but I don't think he should stay here with only the cook and the parlormaid to keep an eye on him. I've just telephoned Angela Stourham and she's very kindly said he can stay with her until Ginevra's better. Eleanor's driving over straightaway to collect him."

As far as I could remember, Stourham Hall, where the unmarried Angela Stourham kept house for her brother Oswald, was the nearest place where a nanny was still on active duty in the nursery. Eleanor, daughter of Stourham's first marriage, was now a young woman of twenty-one, but the fruit of his disastrous second marriage to the platinum blonde was only a child of three.

"That's very good of Angela," said Robert. "Can you convey my thanks to Eleanor when she arrives? I don't want to see anyone."

"I think you should see Kester before he goes."

"What for?"

"Because you're his father, Robert, and it's the sort of thing a father ought to do."

"Very well, what do I say?"

"Tell him you're sorry that everything's been such a muddle but you do hope he enjoys his little holiday with Belinda. I've told him what's happening so there's no need for you to embark on explanations."

Kester was summoned. As he was obviously nervous, I kept his hand clasped in mine after drawing him to the bedside.

"Well, Kester," said Robert abruptly, "I—good God, John, look at the length of his hair! Quick, get some scissors and chop it off before Eleanor arrives!"

Kester immediately began to cry. Startled I bent over him. "What is it, Kester? What's the matter?"

"Oh, don't take any notice," said Robert impatiently. "He's just terrified of scissors."

"But in that case how idiotic of you to suggest a haircut!"

"I'm not letting that child leave this house looking like a bloody girl!"

Kester howled. Robert cursed. I wished myself a thousand miles away.

XV

Order was eventually restored. Ginevra, heavily sedated by Warburton, was borne away in an ambulance to the Home of the Assumption, the Gothic mansion on the outskirts of Swansea where my grandmother had spent her final years. Robert's man Bennett managed to trim Kester's hair while I held the child in my arms and constantly assured him that he was safe. Later, after he had been collected by Eleanor Stourham, I interviewed the servants to make sure they knew what they were doing and then, leaving Robert to rest, I retreated to the night nursery, where Robin's pathetic little broken body lay beneath a sheet.

I wanted to say a prayer, but it was no use. The words refused to come and the faith I longed for remained absent. Chaos had broken into an ordered world but this time no drawn line could have stopped it, and although I tried again to make sense of the tragedy the pattern was too savage to comprehend. All I could think was that blind chance was on the rampage again, the same blind chance which had killed Lion and left Edmund alive, but then I wondered if the blindness lay not in chance but in the human beings who looked upon it. I could remember Robert saying in 1921 during our discussion of Milly Straker, "One yearns for the gift of clairvoyance . . . we have insufficient information." Perhaps chance was merely another name for a preordained future which had been conceived on such a vast scale that it was beyond the human understanding—but no, I found that a repugnant thought. I recoiled from the idea of a preordained future. I had to believe human beings could choose the way they played their cards; I had to believe they could be saved from suffering by drawing those lines to keep evil at bay. The alternative—a hopeless, helpless submission to uncontrollable, incomprehensible forces—seemed to me to be a vision of hell, a road that led straight to despair.

I stopped. I normally had no time for metaphysical speculation which had always seemed to me to be the enemy of a well-ordered mind, and I found my chaotic thoughts unnerving. A need to escape from the bungalow overwhelmed me. Leaving the nurseries in the west tower, I ran downstairs and seconds later was setting off at a brisk pace down the drive.

I decided a walk would help me relax after the harrowing scenes I had endured, but I did not take the path up to Penhale Down, where Robert's sheep now grazed among the megalithic stones. I headed straight on down the bridle path past Martinscombe towards Penhale village, and when the church spire came into sight among the trees, I turned away up the ancient track to Harding's Down.

The two hills, Penhale Down and Harding's Down, lay inland from the sea but parallel to the long ridge of Rhossili Downs which rose sharply from Rhossili beach. In the valley between this long ridge and those twin hills lay the parish of Penhale, and from the summits of all the Downs it was possible to see not merely Penhale but most of the Gower Peninsula, from Llanmadoc and Llangennith in the north to Oxwich Bay in the south, from the sea in the west to Cefn Bryn, the backbone of Gower, which stretched east towards Swansea. Harding's Down was a favorite retreat of mine; I could remember making secret camps long ago with Lion beneath the ramparts which crowned the summit. This hill fort, built by tribesmen hundreds of years before, was now no more than a vast ring enclosing a sloping wilderness of bracken, but it was still a powerful sight, and as I reached the grassy ditch and scrambled up onto the ramparts I knew again the exhilaration I had known as a child.

It was by this time early evening. The haziness of the warm July day had receded in the changing light, and the view stretched with eerie clarity before my eyes as I stood on the southern edge of the circle. I looked beyond Llangennith to the north arm of Rhossili Bay; I looked past Llanmadoc Hill to the bright water of the Loughor Estuary; I looked beyond the rolling farmland to the village of Reynoldston on the spine of Cefn Bryn. So deceptive was the extraordinary light that Penhale seemed barely a stone's throw away in the valley below, and as the sea wind hummed in my ears I heard the chime of the church clock and remembered how I had once listened to it thundering the hour.

I spun round. I was standing on the highest point of the wall so that the entire summit of the Down lay before me, and as I turned I saw that on the other side of the fort far below a slim figure in a pale green dress had scrambled up onto the ramparts. The wind hummed again across the ancient lonely landscape, and the evening sun shone fiercely on that unmistakable fiery hair.

She did not see me immediately but I made no effort to escape. I merely stood motionless, overwhelmed by all the memories I had tried so sensibly to forget, and then at last as she looked up across the circle I knew we both heard the same echo in time.

7

I

SHE WORE her hair up but the wind had whipped it into untidiness; shining strands blew about her face and her long lovely neck. Freckles still peppered the bridge of her nose before fading into that very pale, very clear skin. She wore with her old faded green dress white sandals and no stockings. Her eyes shone with joy.

Taking her in my arms I kissed her first on the cheek, as a valued friend who had helped me survive a past crisis, and then, before I could stop myself, on the mouth as a lover.

"How strange it is," I said at last, "that death keeps bringing us together."

"Ah no," she said, smiling at me. "It's life that keeps bringing us together. Death's only a part of life, isn't it?"

"God knows what it is. I don't understand any of it. All I do understand is that life's so precious and one wastes so much time doing things one doesn't want to do."

We looked at each other and both knew exactly what we wanted to do. The clasp of our hands tightened. Descending from the ramparts into the shelter of the embankment, we moved once more into each other's arms.

II

"Did your husband leave you penniless again?"

"Yes—for the last time. He died last month in a waterfront brawl in Marseilles."

We were lying in a little grassy hollow framed by gorse bushes which protected us from the sea wind. Around us the bracken grew waist-high, and we could see the fronds rippling in the breeze like a wheat field. It was quiet. When a lark burst into song above us we both jumped, but by the time we looked up he had gone and only two sea gulls were drifting across the sky.

"Myfanwy and Huw say I can stay on at the farm," said Bronwen, "but I can't live on their charity so I shall go back to Cardiff, rent a room from my in-laws and get work."

"What work?"

"Housework. I did it last year so that we wouldn't be turned out of our rooms again."

"It must be very dreary."

"No, it's all right if you find a nice lady. I like polishing all the beautiful furniture while I daydream."

"What do you dream about?"

"I dream I have a house with six bedrooms, like my last lady, with a lovely bathroom all tiled in blue and a big kitchen with a refrigerator in it and a garden with flowers, and I dream I have several teapots, I do so love teapots, they're such a pretty shape, and I dream I have a book once a week—a magazine, ladies call it—with a nice love story in it where the beautiful heroine marries the handsome hero and lives happily ever after." She laughed, showing her perfect teeth. "Life's not much like that, is it?" she said. "But that's why it's so important to dream a little."

"I like to dream too," I said, "but I dream all the wrong dreams." And I told her about Constance.

When I had finished she said, "What will you do?"

"I can't imagine. All I know is that I'm in a frightful mess—as usual—and I'd rather not think about it. Will you come away with me for a while?"

She considered this carefully. "Would it make things better if I did?" she said at last. "Or would it make things worse?"

"I don't know and I don't care. To be frank I wouldn't care if all life on earth ceased so long as I'd had a couple of weeks alone with you first."

She smiled. Then she said, "Where shall we go?"

When I had finished making love to her again, I lay on my back and pondered on this question. Finally I said, "Have you ever been to Cornwall?"

"I've never been out of Wales."

"I've never been to Cornwall either but they say it's like Wales' first cousin. I think we'd feel at home there."

As we dressed we made our plans. I told her I could leave directly after Robin's funeral. She said she could leave at any time; she knew her sister would be willing to look after the children.

"But I'll have to be honest with her," she added. "I'll have to tell her the truth."

I paused in the act of buttoning my waistcoat. "Must you?"

"You needn't worry, she'll hold her tongue."

"But won't she be very shocked?"

"Yes, but I think she'll be forgiving. She knows what a terrible time I had with Gareth."

"She'll certainly be angry with me."

"Why? Everyone knows gentlemen do this sort of thing. She'll probably think you do it all the time." She looked at me with a smile and said, "Maybe you do!"

"No." But I told her about my mistress in Fulham.

"Does she love you?"

"I think she's fond of me. I'm fond of her. But the fondness merely stems from a mutual convenience." I slipped my arms around her waist again. "You're the one I love."

She said nothing.

"Don't you believe me?"

"I don't know." She looked up at me steadily. "And I don't think you know either," she said. "Not really."

"Bronwen—"

"But I love you," she interrupted, "and all I want is to spend a few precious days alone with you. Isn't that all that matters for the moment?"

Two days later we were on our way to Cornwall.

III

I told Robert and my father that I had to return to London, but I wired Armstrong that I had to remain in Wales for a further two weeks. As for Edmund, rushing back to London directly after the funeral, he was far too preoccupied with thoughts of Teddy to query my statement that Robert needed me until Ginevra returned from the nursing home.

On the morning after the funeral my father's chauffeur drove me into Swansea, supposedly to catch the train up to town, and my disappearance began. First of all I entrusted my leather bags to the station's left-luggage office. Then I bought a cardboard suitcase, filled it with cheap off-the-peg clothes and finally, much stimulated by my escape from my upper-class identity, I retired to the men's lavatory at the station to change. In my new blue suit I certainly looked *déclassé*, but I was aware too that I looked foreign, un-British, a man outside the confines of the English class system. I knew my accent, that inexorable bondage, would give me away as soon as I opened my mouth but even that would cease to matter in Bronwen's company since we always spoke to each other in Welsh.

I felt liberated. I walked out of the station as if I had been reborn.

Bronwen was due to arrive at ten o'clock on the motorbus from Penhale, and as I walked to meet her I methodically reviewed my list of new possessions to confirm that I had forgotten nothing. Outside a chemist's shop I stopped. I knew what I ought to buy there, but I hesitated, thinking how ridiculous it was that I had reached the age of thirty-one without attaining more than the dimmest grasp of a subject which was of vital practical importance. An eighteen-year-old soldier issued with regulation French letters in the trenches would have known more than I did. After several miscarriages with her husband, my mistress in Fulham had had an operation to ensure that pregnancy never recurred, so the question of prevention had not arisen in her company. I had never bought contraceptives in my life. What did one ask for? Armstrong had at least stopped short of asking me to buy his French letters for him, and besides he had never bothered unless he went to a brothel and needed protection against disease. I shuddered. "The women I like can look after themselves," he had said, referring to his more respectable exploits. I wondered if Bronwen could look after herself. Dafydd was now six. I remembered her admission that she had shared a bed with her husband whenever he came home from the sea, but even though he had presumably been anxious to make up for lost time, she had not conceived again. I decided that indicated a knowledge of contraception. Or did it? I paced up and down outside the chemist's shop.

Finally, despising myself for my cowardice, I went in but there were women present so I left. The answer, as I knew, was to ask for the trade name but trade names had never cropped up in any discussion on the subject with Armstrong, and I had always shied away from mentioning the matter to anyone else. How *could* I have permitted myself to remain in such a state of ignorance? I mentally cursed John Godwin for keeping me a priggish adolescent until the age of twenty-nine.

In the end I decided to postpone the problem. Bronwen was a practical woman whenever she wasn't dreaming of blue-tiled bathrooms, and if she was worried I judged her sensible enough to say so. If she did, I would at once take action, but meanwhile it was undoubtedly pleasanter to go on loving her without any sordid impediment. Again I thought of Armstrong protecting himself against disease, and again I shuddered in revulsion.

Abandoning the chemist, I hurried on down the street to the bus station.

IV

In the train I took off the wedding ring Morgan had given her and slipped on her finger the plain gold band that I had bought before I had embarked on my quest for cheap clothes. Hours later in Penzance when I wrote *Mr. and Mrs. John Godwin* in the hotel register I felt as if I had been married to her for years but had somehow mislaid all memory of the wedding. The hotel was small and quiet, and from our attic room when we awoke next morning we could see over the rooftops to the sparkling sea beyond the promenade.

After breakfast we went out. We found our way down the hill past the harbor, and when we reached the esplanade we paused to gaze across the bay to the fairy-tale castle of St. Michael's Mount.

"It hardly seems real," I said, but it was. We bought a guidebook, and the next day we went across to the Mount and it was all real, all true. The fairy tale had become reality, and reality exceeded all our dreams.

Later our guidebook led us to Mousehole and Lamorna and Logan's Rock, to St. Mawes and the Lizard and Kynance Cove. The weather deteriorated but we hardly noticed. We were too busy sitting in country buses and missing much romantic scenery by kissing at the wrong moment.

At first we were muddled about meals, since Bronwen was unaccustomed to

347

dining at eight, but I had no wish for such formality so apart from our breakfast at the hotel we ate in cafés or at small, casual harbor inns where we could order fresh seafood. Bronwen had never eaten lobster before. I had never eaten baked beans on toast. We laughed and laughed as we saw each other's expressions after the first taste. In the café where I tried tomato sauce on my fried potatoes, we both laughed so much that the good-natured proprietor, thinking us mad foreigners, gave us a free pot of tea and asked where we came from.

"We're from Wales," I said in English, and when I saw his astonished face as he heard my accent I began to laugh all over again.

We talked endlessly. She told me about the little village above the Rhondda Valley where she had been born and where her parents had worked as cook and gardener for the local vicar. After her father's death her mother had stayed on at the vicarage, but when she too had died Bronwen had traveled south to join Myfanwy, who was in service at a rectory near Cardiff.

". . . and then very luckily there was a vacancy for a kitchen maid at the Big House and I went to work there, but it was horrible, I hated it, the housekeeper was cruel and the other girls laughed at me because my English wasn't good and the footman tried to manhandle me and then finally, thank God, Gareth became one of the undergardeners and he began to take notice of me and I thought if I married him I'd be safe and live happily ever after. I was only sixteen and Myfanwy wasn't in the neighborhood anymore because she'd married Huw so there was no one for me to talk to—oh, I was so weak and silly, but sometimes I think one has to suffer a little in order to grow up strong."

I told her about Oxmoon. I talked about how awful it had been to have this great god Robert whom we had all had to live up to and how wonderful it had been when the great god had singled me out for special attention. I talked about Lion. I talked about school and what fun it had been once I conquered my homesickness.

"Poor little boy!" said Bronwen. "How cruel the upper classes are, getting rid of their children by shutting them up for two-thirds of the year in institutions!"

"But I loved it! At school no one compared me with Robert—the masters remembered him, of course, but even so, it was easier to escape from him there."

"Poor little boy!" said Bronwen again.

"No, no, I had this wonderful childhood—I was so happy! And then . . . when I was eleven . . ."

"Yes?"

"Something happened but I'll tell you about it later."

Later she said, "In Penhale they still talk of your grandmother and Mr. Owain Bryn-Davies. What was your grandmother like? Do you remember her well?"

And then I told her everything.

V

After some days we moved on to North Cornwall. The Cornish moors reminded us of the Gower Downs; even the mining territory around St. Just seemed to echo the industrial wilderness east of Swansea, and as we gazed at the ruined engine houses silhouetted against the sea, Bronwen said the coast must be almost as fine as the coast between Rhossili and Porteynon. But we agreed Gower was unsurpassable. Our bus crawled on along the coast road, through the hamlets of Morvah and Zennor until finally we reached the crest of a ridge, and there before us in a brilliant panorama of sea and sky lay the curve of a vast bay and the famous fishing town of St. Ives.

The town sparkled in a hot, bright foreign light, and beyond the beaches the sea was a rich glowing Mediterranean blue. We found a guesthouse in a cobbled alley in the heart of the town, and having shed our luggage we wandered through the narrow twisting streets to the harbor.

"I think the weather will stay fine now," I said rashly, and despite this tempting of fate, the sun continued to shine. We became idle, heading every morning for the beach and returning every afternoon to the seclusion of our room. From our window we could watch the gulls swooping among the crooked chimney pots as the fishing boats returned to the harbor, and in the evenings when the town became bathed in its golden southern light, we would wander to the summit of the hill behind the town and watch the sun sink into the sea.

"We're like pilgrims in a legend," I said to her once, and we talked of Welsh legends and read about Cornish legends in our dog-eared guidebook. I told her about French legends too, and described my visits to France before the war when I had been studying modern languages up at Oxford. She asked about Oxford but could not quite imagine it. I told her about Paris. She could not conceive of such a place, but was enthralled. We never mentioned London.

"I'd like to travel one day," she said. "I'd always accepted that I'd never leave Wales, but now that I have...oh, I must read books about travel, real books with hard covers; I shall talk to the lady of the traveling library and ask her advice, and then I shall read and read and read so that when I talk to you in the future—"

We looked at each other. She blushed painfully, but I pulled her to me. I did not want her hating herself for mentioning a future neither of us dared imagine.

When I had kissed her I said, "Of course I could never marry Constance now."

She made no effort to disguise her relief, and in her honesty I saw how vulnerable she was. But still she had the courage to say: "You must do as you must. I don't want you blaming me later and saying I ruined your life by spoiling all your fine prospects in London."

"I don't care about London anymore. I'm going back to Gower." We were watching the sun set again. The sun was a brilliant red, the blue sky was streaked with gold and the sea was a glowing mass of fiery light. It was the most alluring prospect, the kind of prospect that would tempt even an unimaginative man to see visions of paradise, and I was by no means an unimaginative man.

"Now that poor child's dead Oxmoon will come to me eventually," I said at last. "My father may promise Robert out of kindness that Kester will be the heir, but that promise will die with Robert. My father prefers Harry to Kester, and besides... I know very well that my father feels closer to me now than he does to his other sons."

After a pause Bronwen said, "But do you think you're suited to a country life at Oxmoon?"

I was startled. "Why should you think I'm not?"

"I remember Huw saying after your wife died that he wasn't surprised by your decision to go to London. He said he thought you'd become bored with being a gentleman farmer at Penhale Manor."

"Being a gentleman farmer at Penhale Manor is one thing; being master of Oxmoon is quite another and would certainly provide me with the challenges I need to stave off boredom." I tried not to sound annoyed. "That's a jaundiced judgment from your brother-in-law!"

"Oh, you mustn't think that," she said quickly. "He admires you so much. But he finds you a puzzle—and so do most people, if you really want to know. 'Mr. John's a dark horse,' they say. 'Doesn't seem to know what he wants. Up to London, back to Gower, up to London again—rushing around like an inklemaker in a drangway,' as they say in their funny Gower English—"

"I admit I've been confused in the past. But if I knew I had Oxmoon coming to me, all confusion would be at an end."

"Why? It's only a house. How can stone and slate solve muddle and unhappiness?"

I made a great effort to express my complex feelings simply so that she could understand. "I feel I need a reward," I said. "I want compensation for all those years I came second to Robert. I want compensation for all those years when I murdered my true self in a futile effort to please my parents as much as Robert did. I feel it's only fair that I should get Oxmoon; I feel it's owing to me."

"What's owing to you," said Bronwen, "is love, but you won't get that from Oxmoon. Nor can Oxmoon change the past. Forgiving your parents, not inheriting Oxmoon, is the only way you can stop the past from haunting you."

I stared at her and as she stared back I was aware, not for the first time, of the extreme clarity of her mind. It was as if she saw a spectrum of reality that was entirely beyond my field of vision.

"But of course I forgive my parents," I heard myself say. "I'm a good son, I always have been, so how can I not forgive them? To bear a grudge would imply I disliked and resented them—and how could I dislike and resent them, why, I'd despise myself, such feelings would be quite incompatible with being a good son."

Bronwen said nothing.

"My parents were innocent victims," I said strongly. "My grandmother's the one to blame. *She's* the one I loathe and resent as the source of all my unhappiness."

Bronwen kissed me and said, "Forgive her."

"How can I? If I don't blame her for what went wrong I must blame my parents

350

and I can't—yet I've got to blame someone, I must, I've suffered, I went through hell, it distorted my whole life—"

"Yes," said Bronwen, "it was dreadful. But you must break free, you mustn't let it go on distorting your life, and the road to freedom isn't the road to Oxmoon. You won't be happy in a world where you think you need compensation, because the compensation will only chain you to the past."

There was a silence. The sun continued to sink into the sea and we continued to watch it, but finally I turned aside and said, "My father may well live another twenty years, so Oxmoon's not important now. What's important is that I should return to Gower so that we can have a life together there."

I saw her fear as clearly as I saw her joy.

"Of course," I said, "we'd be married."

She looked more fearful than ever. "But how would I manage?"

I kissed her. "We'll both manage very well." I kissed her again and began to sort through my pockets for coins. "Let's find a telephone so that I can discover what's been going on. I think I've got the courage now to return to the world we left behind."

As we set off through the cobbled streets I heard a clock chiming far away by the harbor, and when Bronwen's hand tightened in mine I knew she was aware of my thoughts. Anglo-Saxon time was waiting for us, and in that world of weeks, days and hours lay a crisis of catastrophic dimensions. I had realized, as I sent my last batch of postcards to my children, that I had been away for far longer than I had intended.

VI

"What the hell have you been doing?" shouted Robert. "Where are you? What's going on? That bloody American of yours has been persecuting us for information and saying you're supposed to be in London proposing to his daughter!"

"I've no intention of proposing to his daughter. I'm in Cornwall with the woman I love."

"You're *what?*" His voice receded; he had evidently turned aside to confide in his wife. "John's gone completely off the rails." He readdressed the telephone. "For God's sake, what woman?"

"Her name's Bronwen Morgan, and she's Huw Meredith's sister-in-law. Robert, are you better? And how's Ginevra? Do please forgive me for not telephoning you earlier—"

"Oh, don't worry about us," said Robert. "We're now the least of your problems. Tell me, is there any chance of seeing you in the immediate future, or do you intend to ramble around Cornwall in a romantic haze indefinitely?"

"I'm returning to Gower tomorrow. I have to take Bronwen back to Penhale before I go up to London."

"Good. I'll have the straitjacket waiting," said Robert, and hung up.

"Of course you must realize," said Robert kindly, "that you're quite insane, but fortunately it's nothing to worry about; this form of insanity is very common, and there's no doubt you'll recover—probably sooner rather than later. Now, the most important thing is that you should start to come gently down to earth. Take your children to the zoo or something. Give those appalling off-the-peg clothes to the nearest branch of the Salvation Army. Read a newspaper. Have a haircut. Do all those boring little everyday things which remind one constantly of how drab life really is. And above all, my dear John, abandon this romantic pose of the Celtic Twilight Visionary—set aside this nauseous Celtic mysticism and try to see the situation not with Anglo-Saxon clarity—I don't ask the impossible—but at least with true Welsh hardheadedness and good sense. It's only the English who think the Welsh spend all their time wandering around singing at a perpetual Eisteddfod, so if you must see yourself as a Welshman, for God's sake see yourself as an intelligent one and don't wreck your life while you're not responsible for your actions."

It was early evening, and we were alone in the drawing room at Little Oxmoon. Ginevra had tactfully left after giving me a brief embrace; I was relieved to see she was looking better. So was Robert. He was no longer bedridden and had returned to his wheelchair.

"Robert, you don't understand. This is the way, the truth, the life I long to lead—"

"What way? What truth? And for God's sake, what life? John, have you really no idea how absurd you sound? Look, I'm going to get to the bottom of this. Contrary to the romantic poets, I don't believe falling in love is a random phenomenon—in my opinion it's always the symptom of some underlying disorder of the personality."

"If you think that," I said, "then obviously you've never been in love."

"It's precisely because I've been in love that I know what I'm talking about. Sex should be a sport, not a destructive obsession."

"You don't seriously regard sex as a mere sport, do you?"

Robert stared at me. "Well, how do you regard it?"

"Sex is life—real life. Sport is just a way of keeping real life at bay—it's just a poor substitute for what life's really all about."

"What an extraordinary remark! It's hard to believe you ever went to Harrow. Have you by any chance come under the influence of that turgid little writer D. H. Lawrence?"

"My knowledge of modern English literature stops with John Buchan. Anyway why are we talking about sex? I'm talking about love!"

"Oh yes, yes, yes, of course you are—people who can think of nothing but sex always ennoble their emotion by calling it love, but don't worry, I refuse to let myself be defeated by this problem. You're my favorite brother and I'm very fond of you and I'm going to save you from yourself even if it's the last thing I ever do."

Robert was at his most formidable. He was carefully dressed in a black suit with his Old Harrovian tie, and although his right side was too weak to permit him to sit entirely straight in his chair, he still gave the impression of being bolt upright. His thinning hair, neatly cut and severely parted, was the color of iron. His deep-set, somewhat hypnotic eyes were steel-blue. Even his useless right hand, curled inwards like a claw, seemed to express aggression, and I had to make a considerable effort not to be mentally pulverized by the full force of his personality in top gear.

"There's obviously some lack in your life," he was saying, "which has driven you to compensate yourself by escaping into this addle-brained Celtic sloppiness. Now, let me see. What is it that's lacking? You're rich, healthy and good-looking. You enjoy your work. You have two attractive children to whom you're devoted. You have loyal servants and a wide circle of admiring friends—you even have a saintly mistress tucked away in Fulham who apparently never gives you a moment's anxiety—and on top of all this quite extraordinary good fortune, you have an American millionaire who thinks you're God's gift to a middle-aged buccaneer with a paternity obsession, and you have a good-looking, cultivated girl who can't wait to make you a matchlessly competent wife. Yet are you satisfied with this Elysium you've created for yourself? No, you're not. You rush off to Cornwall with a cleaning woman from Cardiff, gaze into golden sunsets and talk twaddle about ways and truths and lives you long to lead. Very well, I give up, you tell me: what's wrong with your London life? What's missing?"

"Bronwen."

"That's no answer. That just restates the conundrum. Christ, give me some more whisky! It's hard work providing a rational explanation for such thoroughly irrational behavior."

There was a pause while I removed our glasses to the decanter and refilled them. It was not until I was adding the water that Robert said slowly, "But perhaps I'm entirely wrong. Perhaps there's no lack in your life—quite the reverse. Perhaps there's a superfluity. Perhaps you've simply decided you don't need London anymore, and perhaps this raging love affair with a Welsh peasant is your peculiar way of celebrating your liberation. . . . But why would you feel you no longer need London?"

"All I care about is living with Bronwen in Gower."

"You couldn't conceivably be quite such a fool."

"Robert—"

"You wouldn't give up all for love—you're much too ambitious. You'd only give up your present Elysium if you thought you saw another more attractive one on the horizon—and so the big question is, isn't it, what's more attractive to you than a million pounds and all the worldly success you've ever wanted?"

"Oh, for God's sake! Listen, Robert—"

"No, I'm sorry, John, but you're going to have to listen to me, because I'm now quite beside myself with horror. I can see that your whole behavior has been the result of a most disastrous miscalculation."

"What the devil do you mean?"

"You're not going to get Oxmoon, John. Not now. Not ever. Drink up that scotch. Pour yourself some brandy. And I'll explain."

VIII

He said he was going to make sure Kester was the heir.

"Well, of course you are," I said without a second's hesitation. "I'd do the same for my own son if I were in your shoes." I took what I thought would be a sip of whisky and found myself draining the glass.

"You know what I told you after Robin died: Kester's going to benefit. It'll make sense of Robin's death."

"Yes, don't worry, Robert, I absolutely understand." I revolved the empty glass in my hands to give the impression it was still half full.

"No, I'm afraid you don't understand, not yet, but I'm equally afraid that I'm going to have to make sure you do. It may result in us being permanently estranged, but I can't help that. I've got to save you from messing up your life as the result of a misapprehension about the future of Oxmoon."

"Whatever you say we couldn't wind up permanently estranged."

"I wonder. Very well, listen to this. You think everything will still come right for you because I don't have a mild case of this illness and with any luck I'll be dead in ten years."

"My dear Robert—"

"Shut up. You think Papa's bound to outlive me and that once I'm out of the way he won't hesitate to make you his heir—but you see, John, that's where you make your big mistake. I'm going to tell Papa that he has to make Kester his heir and Papa's going to do what I say. There's no question about it. I've got him by the balls."

I stood up, took a clean glass from the salver and poured myself some brandy. "How?"

"He did something once that was so bloody frightful that it had a profoundly adverse effect on my life. He's been racked by guilt ever since, and he'll see my blackmail as a chance to cancel his guilt and finally be at peace with himself."

"I see." I drank some of the brandy. "I knew something had gone wrong between you," I said, "but I didn't realize it was so catastrophic. What happened?"

"It's not necessary that you should know that. All that's necessary is that you should believe that Oxmoon will never be yours."

I was silent.

"I'm sorry," said Robert, "but all I can say in my own defense is that I don't believe the loss of Oxmoon will ultimately matter to you. In my opinion you're not suited to the life of a country gentleman. You're like Ginette. You're drawn to the city lights and the glamour of worldly success; you enjoy money and power and smart women and smart cars. Your recent past with Armstrong proves that to the hilt. Have you ever enjoyed life more than during these last eighteen months in his employment?"

I drank some more brandy and said, "My recent past shows the worst side of me. But I do have a better side."

"There's nothing bad about thriving on a smart London life, John. You're in the company of numerous charming and talented people. It's nothing to be ashamed of."

"You make me sound contemptible."

"Not at all. You're only saying that because you want to deny your true self; but let me reintroduce you to your true self, John, the true self I've been watching so intently from this wheelchair since 1921. Why did you really go to London after Blanche died? 'To build a new life away from my tragic memories,' you say, but I say you went because you knew you'd made a mistake trying to play the country squire and after the novelty had worn off you were bored, restless and frustrated. In fact I think you ran to London gasping with relief, and what happened when you got there? 'I'll find some quiet civilized sort of work,' you say with charming modesty, but within a month you're hobnobbing with Harley Armstrong. 'I can't bear Americans!' you used to say at the F.O., but in fact Americans excel at being successful on a vast glittering seductive scale, and of course you now allow yourself to be seduced. Are you horrified by your new employment? No, you're thrilled and stimulated. You look well, sound cheerful and everyone remarks how splendidly you've recovered from your bereavement. 'I couldn't consider remarrying for at least five years!' you say earnestly at regular intervals, but when Armstrong plays the matchmaker do you laugh and tell him to go to hell? No, you most certainly do not. You—I'm sorry, do you want to comment?"

"No. Go on." I set down my empty glass.

"You start seeing a good deal of this girl and you even decide to marry her— and why? Because she's the symbol, isn't she, John, the flesh-and-blood symbol of your way, your truth and the life which you not only long to lead but which quite frankly I don't think you can do without. Forget Oxmoon, John. You'd only find it was an unnecessary and tedious drain on your increasingly valuable time. And forget Mrs. Morgan too—or if you can't forget her at the moment, then make some sensible provision for her until you've exhausted her possibilities. But what you mustn't under any circumstances forget is the life you deserve, the life that's owing to you and the life which can satisfy you as no other life can. Now go up to London, make your peace with Armstrong and slam that ring on his daughter's finger, because believe me, any other solution to your present crisis can only end in misery."

There was a long silence. I walked to the window and looked out at the garden. Then I began to roam around the room until I stopped by the brandy decanter. Removing the stopper, I poured myself another measure.

"Everything you say is absolutely right," I said at last, "and yet everything you say is absolutely wrong."

"But you must surely concede that I'm presenting a rational argument!"

"There's more to life than being rational."

"Not much more."

"I disagree. All the most profound mysteries of life are inexplicable in rational terms."

"My dear John, I hope you're not going to dive from Celtic mysticism into full-blooded Neo-Platonism!"

"God knows what I'm going to do." I drank my brandy and headed for the door. "I'll telephone you from London."

"We're parting friends?"

I had opened the door, but I abandoned it and moved back to his chair. "Yes. Friends. Always," I said, taking his hands in mine, and saw his poignant look of gratitude before he masked his feelings with a smile.

Utterly confused, thoroughly miserable and well-nigh beside myself with jealousy and rage I left him and drove to Oxmoon.

IX

"It's Mr. John, sir," said Bayliss, showing me into the library where my father was writing letters. To my relief there was no sign of Mrs. Straker.

My father looked up startled. Then he rose to greet me and we shook hands as Bayliss withdrew.

"Would you like a drink?" said my father, hospitable as ever, but he seemed relieved when I declined. No doubt I reeked of brandy.

Making a great effort to appear stone-cold sober, I said in a neutral voice, "I'm in a spot of trouble, Papa, and I've come to you for help."

"Delightful county, Cornwall, I believe," said my father, closing the blotter on his unfinished letter. "Wish I'd traveled more when I was younger, but Margaret never fancied it and we were always so busy at home."

"So Robert's been keeping you informed."

"No," said my father. "Mr. Armstrong telephoned to inquire where you were, and afterwards I telephoned your house and spoke to the children to make sure they were well. Marian said they were so pleased with all your postcards."

Unsure what to say next I sat down opposite him, and we faced each other across the writing table. My father, behaving like a model parent, made no attempt to pry or criticize but merely waited for me to confide.

"I'm supposed to be proposing to Armstrong's daughter," I said, "but after three weeks in Cornwall with another woman I don't see how I can."

"When in doubt, don't," said my father with what Robert would have described as Welsh hardheadedness and good sense.

"Yes. Quite." I was silent.

"Suppose that would put you in difficulties with Armstrong," said my father at last, helping me along.

"Not only me. Edmund."

"Edmund's old enough to fend for himself. And as far as Armstrong's concerned—"

"He's offering me such extraordinary prospects."

"Well, I've no doubt you can live with the prospects, John. But can you live with the woman?"

"Oh, she'd be a perfect wife, I'm certain of that."

"But if that's true then what were you doing in Cornwall with someone else?"

I was unable to reply. My father suddenly leaned across the table. "What good are extraordinary prospects if you can only get them by making yourself miserable?"

"I'm afraid I'd be even more miserable without them." Out of his sight, below the surface of the writing table, my fists were clenching. I stared down at them and said, "I'd give up my prospects in London tomorrow if I knew I had prospects here. But Robert tells me I have none." I raised my eyes to his. "I've come to find out whether that's true. I've got to find out, I must know—"

"I don't understand."

"Robert says he's going to use your old quarrel with him, whatever that was, to insist you leave Oxmoon to Kester. Is that true? Or is it just a story Robert's invented because he feels it's his duty to drive me back to London?"

My father's face was at once painfully fine-drawn. Several seconds passed before he was able to say: "Robert's said nothing to me."

"But would you make Kester your heir?"

"Ought to. Tradition. Eldest son to eldest son." He was now so white that his face had a grayish tinge.

"But that's rubbish. There's no entail. And there's not even a strict tradition of primogeniture. What about the eighteenth century when Robert Godwin the Renovator took over from the cousin who turned out to be an imbecile? You're under no obligation at all to leave Oxmoon to Kester!"

"But if that's what Robert wants," said my father, "then that's what Robert must have. That's only fair."

"*Not to me!*" I shouted, springing to my feet. Somehow I managed to get a grip on myself. Sinking down in my chair again I said in a level voice, "I'm sorry. Please do forgive me but the main reason I'm so distressed is because I find this quite impossible to understand. If you could only tell me what happened between you and Robert—"

"I can't," whispered my father. "I would if I could, but there are other people involved besides me and Robert, people I can't possibly betray."

I waited till I was sure I had myself well in control. Then I said, "Very well, I'll say no more." And leaving him abruptly I returned in desperation to Little Oxmoon.

357

X

"Do you understand, Robert?"

"Yes."

"Will you tell me?"

Silence.

"If I know," I said, "I'll be all right."

Another silence.

"You've got to tell me, Robert. You must. You owe it to me. Please—I beg of you—"

"Yes. Very well. Sit down."

I obeyed him. I was rigid with tension and so was he, but his face was expressionless and his voice was unemotional. When I was seated he said, "It concerns Ginevra," and the name he never used made his statement sound flat and impersonal. "He seduced her when she was sixteen."

Some seconds passed. I began to wonder if in my disturbed state I was hallucinating. "I'm sorry, Robert, but obviously you can't mean what you seem to be meaning. Perhaps if you could be a little more specific—"

"He fucked her."

That was certainly specific. Several more seconds trickled by. Finally I said, "I don't believe it."

"I found out in 1913 when I wanted to marry her. Naturally Mama made sure I knew the truth."

"My God. Oh my God, my God—"

"He wrecked Ginette's adolescence and in wrecking hers he wrecked mine. Of course after the seduction she was prepared to do anything to stay away from home, and so I lost her because of him—and even later when I got her back the past...soured everything. I wanted to forgive and forget but I never could. I used to look at him and hate him. Sometimes I still do. I came back to Gower because it suited me financially to do so, because I wanted Robin to grow up on the estate and because if one's going to spend a long time dying one may as well do it in the place one loves best, but that father of ours has been a continuing blight on the landscape. Fortunately he doesn't come here too often. He knows I prefer him to stay away."

"But Robert..." I searched for the words to express my revulsion, and when they eluded me I could only say in despair: "How *could* he have done such a thing?"

"Oh, he's so bloody muddled up he's capable of anything! Christ, what Mama must have suffered!"

"Don't." I covered my face with my hands. Then I said, "Right. That solves that. Of course there's nothing else that can possibly be said on the subject. Oxmoon goes to Kester to atone for what Papa did to Ginevra—and to you." I stood up to go.

"Promise me," said Robert, "promise me—"

"Oh, of course I'll never tell a soul. That goes without saying."

"—promise me you won't think any the worse of Ginette."

"How could I? For the first time I feel I've come within a thousand miles of understanding her." I stooped to cover his hands with mine and said, "I'm very grateful to you, Robert, for telling me. Forgive me for being such a bloody nuisance and putting you through hell."

All Robert said was "Make it up to me by proposing to Constance as soon as you arrive in London."

But I could not reply.

XI

I was in the library of Armstrong's house on Eaton Walk. Armstrong was shouting at me. He was a heavy man of medium height with silver hair, which gave him a look of spurious distinction, and a mouth like a steel trap. The scene was such a nightmare that I had ceased to be upset and was regarding him with detachment, as if he were a stranger who was determined to embarrass me by making an unpleasant exhibition of his bad manners.

"... and sure I always knew you'd be the kind of guy who'd keep some woman or other on the side, but Jesus, what a way to behave, leading Constance on, leading me on and then vanishing without trace for three weeks in order to get an ex-mistress out of your system..."

I let him rant away for a while. When he finally paused for breath I said, "Look, sir, I still admire Constance very much but I'm in a great muddle and I speak with her best interests at heart when I say that I must have more time to consider whether or not I want to marry her."

"Your time's expired, sonny! Marry or quit! What kind of a man do you think I am? I don't let any man on earth mess me around like this and get away with it!"

"But—"

"You want more time? Okay, I'll give you more time. I'll give you ten minutes— ten minutes to remind yourself just what a mess you're proposing to make of your life if you don't wise up right away. I've got friends in this town now. I'll spread it around that you're not to be trusted, and then you'll never get another job that isn't a dead-end street. As far as Edmund goes, forget it. I can smash up that little romance if I put my mind to it, and Teddy will soon recover and fall in love with someone else. But Constance won't. Constance is a single-minded, serious girl who's one hundred percent devoted to you, and that's why if you jilt her now I'm going to blast you off the map—and don't think I'd be weak and sentimental just because I've been thinking of you as a son! The truth is I can only go on thinking of you as a son now if you marry my daughter, so make up your mind: do you want to be a success in the only way that matters a damn in this world or do you want to be washed up and plowed under before the year's out? Okay, let me leave you to think about that." He took out his watch, synchronized it with the clock on the chimneypiece and said, "You've got ten minutes starting from now."

XII

"Here I have my standards," said my mother, "and here I draw the line."

I thought: I'll be all right if I draw the line.

But I wasn't sure what line I was supposed to draw or where I was supposed to draw it. My head was throbbing. It was hard to think coherently. I felt as if I were on the brink of madness—but of course I wouldn't go mad, couldn't, because I'd draw the line and keep myself sane.

"You'll play your cards better than I ever have," said my father. "I know you will. I know it."

I shuddered as I remembered how my father had played his cards. No drawn lines there. I thought of him seducing Ginevra—I thought of blighted lives, of good people suffering—and suddenly as I heard my grandmother screaming and my father shouting about the wages of sin, the past smashed its way into the present again and tore my mind apart with glimpse after glimpse into hell.

Chaos, anarchy, madness and death—looking down at the cards in my hand I asked myself only how I could play them and survive.

Oxmoon had gone, I saw that at once. Oxmoon, Wales, a country life—all those cards had been wiped from the pack, and when I looked at the cards which remained I saw LONDON written on them all. Then I tried to imagine Bronwen in London but the possibility was unimaginable. She would be like a lark penned up in a cage. I pictured her cut off from her country, severed from her culture, blaming me for her misery, wishing we had never met. And was I seriously proposing to keep her in London as my mistress while I married Constance to secure my future? Not only was the idea ludicrous—Bronwen would never have debased herself in such a fashion—but it was also unworkable. If I had Bronwen in my life there would be no room for Constance. The marriage would be a sham which I would never be able to sustain.

Bronwen and Constance were both present in the hand of cards that I had been dealt and one of them would have to be discarded, I could see that, just as I could see that I favored discarding Constance, but if I discarded Constance I discarded London and this was a move I knew I could no longer make. I had to retain London. How else could I compensate myself for what had happened? Robert had said the life Armstrong was offering was the life that was owing to me, and now of course, having lost Oxmoon forever, I could so clearly see that he was right.

It was time to be honest with myself. To marry out of one's class was one of the quickest roads to marital misery available. I could instead keep Bronwen discreetly as my mistress, but what sort of life would that be for her? The truth was that I would crucify her if I did marry her and crucify her if I didn't—and whether or not we were married, I'd crucify myself by terminating all my prospects in London. Bronwen was the most exceptional woman and I loved her but how could I choose any course of action that would ruin us both? To pursue a grand passion without regard for the consequences was the road to self-destruction and catastrophe, that was the truth of it—and that was the truth my grandmother had never been able to face.

But I was facing it. I was on the rack but I was facing it. I felt as if I were being beaten and brutalized, but I was facing it.

I drew the line.

XIII

That night I wrote to Bronwen. My final draft was completed at dawn.

I spent a long time trying to decide how to begin the letter. Any endearment, Welsh or English, seemed too cruel in view of what I had to say so in the end I merely plunged into the first sentence without addressing her. I wrote in English: *I can't think how to begin this except to tell you that I love you, but that will only seem a mockery when I tell you also, as I must, that I can't see you again. I know this will make you unhappy but all I can say is that if I continued to see you I would make you very much unhappier. I'm deeply sorry and wish I could undo all the unhappiness. I see now I was wrong to take you to Cornwall, wrong to treat you so selfishly and wrong to pretend we could have any kind of future together. I loved you so much I couldn't help myself. But it was wrong.*

I'm now doing what I believe is right and committing myself to my life in London. You'll realize what this means, so I shan't explain further. I don't ask you to understand and I certainly don't expect you to forgive me, so there's no need for you to reply to this letter, but I had to tell you my decision before you heard of it from someone else. I shouldn't close by telling you I love you but in fact that's all I have left to say.

I signed the letter JOHN to match both the English words on the paper and my decision to be an Englishman, and posted the letter at once before I could change my mind.

I did wonder if she would reply, despite my assurance that no reply was necessary, but she never wrote. Later when word reached me that she had returned to Cardiff I sent a check to the Home Farm to be forwarded, but the check found its way back, torn in two, and there was no covering letter.

My father wrote to me as soon as the engagement was announced. He usually wrote brief colloquial letters which said nothing of importance, but this time he had taken trouble. When I pictured him laboring over several drafts, as he undoubtedly had, and looking up every trying example of English spelling in the dictionary, I was touched—or at least in other circumstances I would have been touched. However after Robert's revelations I felt so angry that I could barely bring myself to open the envelope.

My dear John, my father had written. *Allow me to congratulate you on your engagement. I am delighted that you should be on the threshold of yet another match which by worldly standards must undoubtedly be judged as splendid. I have heard nothing but good of Miss Armstrong and I hope it will not be long before I can come up to town and have the honor of meeting her.*

However, mindful of your recent confidences to me on the subject of your future, I feel I must add that I have been very worried about you and that my worries are by no means allayed by your good news. I trust you are quite certain that you wish to marry this girl, because if you have any remaining doubts I would most strongly counsel you against marriage. It is the greatest possible mistake to marry in pursuit of worldly ambition alone—as my mother did. Perhaps you might be comforting yourself with the thought that I too married for worldly reasons, and indeed I did marry for money, but I liked your mother so much even before I began to love her. She was so jolly and sensible and I liked the way she made me laugh. Do you like Miss Armstrong? Love can come later but liking won't. And does she make you laugh? Marriage is often so difficult that one needs to laugh every now and then.

Please do not take offense at this letter. I am well aware that you are a mature man of thirty-one, and if you have no doubts about your decision I have absolute confidence that it is the right one. I remain ever your most devoted and affectionate father, R.G.

I thought of him putting my mother through hell by his abuse of Ginevra and setting in motion the chain of events that had deprived me of Oxmoon. In my opinion he was quite unfit to lecture anyone on the necessary ingredients of a happy marriage, and I tore up his letter without rereading it.

Just before the wedding Robert said uneasily, "Are you still in touch with Mrs. Morgan?"

"Good God, no," I said. "That's all over and I'm completely recovered."

I knew as I spoke that the words formed the biggest lie of my life, but I knew too that it was quite impossible for me to acknowledge it. My future, the future I had to have in order to be at peace with myself, depended on my ability to forget Bronwen, so I fought against her memory with every ounce of willpower I possessed and day by day, as I battled successfully against the truth, I moved deeper and deeper into my disastrous lie.

XIV

Armstrong gave his daughters a sumptuous double wedding on a mild sunny day in December at St. George's, Hanover Square. It was one of the biggest Society weddings of the year, and after the service the reception for five hundred at Claridges set the seal on the day's perfection. Guest after guest said what a romantic occasion it was, two ideal weddings between two ideal young couples with all parties blissfully in love.

"This is the most wonderful thing that's ever happened to me," confided Edmund misty-eyed over the champagne, and he was right: it was. I shook his hand and said how happy I was for him. Overshadowed by his brothers, brutalized by the war, bludgeoned for so many sad years by his melancholy, Edmund at the age of twenty-nine had emerged into the light of a dazzling good fortune. Falling in love had made him vivacious. He sparkled. He made Lion-like "naughty" remarks. Straight-backed, bright-eyed, glowing with health and happiness, he told me I was the best brother a man ever had and he would never forget all I had done for him.

"... and I'll be grateful to you till my dying day, and I only hope you'll be as happy with Constance as I shall be with my wonderful, my divine, my celestial—"

"Isn't he gorgeous?" demanded Teddy, appearing from nowhere to gaze up at him in adoration.

I looked around for Constance but she was on the other side of the room. I felt tired. Acting is an exhausting profession and that day had required a gala performance. It was then that I realized how tired I was going to be in the future. I had told myself that everything would be well after the wedding; I had argued that once the deed was done and no further possibility of escape existed I would be able to relax, accept my situation and enjoy married life for I had become fond of Constance, fond enough to convince myself that I would love her once the strain of the engagement had given way to the relief of matrimony. But now at the reception it occurred to me that matrimony was not going to bring relief. The ordeal was going to go on but with the difference that escape was no longer possible. A door had been locked and I was trapped irrevocably behind it.

"Is everything all right, darling?" said Constance as we set off on our honeymoon to Paris and the Riviera.

"Everything's wonderful!" I said, kissing her warmly.

This was easier. This was a familiar role. I had traveled this road before. In fact so strong was the impression of the past repeating itself that it gave me a shock whenever Constance reminded me how different she was from Blanche. The reminders came with increasing frequency.

"Now, John, I don't want to be like some boring Victorian maiden—I want to be modern and enlightened, because I believe sex is healthy and right and I want to enjoy it and make you happy..."

The curious part was that as our lavish glamorous honeymoon progressed, I thought more and more of Blanche on our quiet little wartime honeymoon in

Suffolk. Constance and I stayed at the most luxurious French hotels, but in my memory I was at the little inn in medieval Lavenham and Blanche was once more at my side.

On our first morning in Monte Carlo we breakfasted in our suite, and afterwards when the obligatory two dozen red roses had arrived in response to my order, Constance spent some time attending to them with her usual meticulous skill. She was full of theories about how flowers should look, but as I watched her I thought of Blanche, arranging flowers not with mathematical precision but with spontaneity and an unfailing eye for beauty.

"Darling, this is so romantic!" said Constance as the champagne arrived at noon, but in my memory Blanche and I were lunching at our country inn and Blanche was saying how fond she was of a glass of stone-ginger.

"Oh, they're playing 'The Blue Danube' again!" said Constance carelessly as we drank tea in the early evening. "What a bore—I think Strauss is so hackneyed!" And at once in my mind Blanche was playing "The Blue Danube" for Robert and Ginevra. It was their special tune.

"Darling, is anything the matter? You seem a little quiet."

"I'm merely savoring the glamour and the romance!" I said smiling, and suddenly I longed for someone gentle who never pestered me with questions, someone who knew when to be silent, someone who was sensitive and undemanding.

"You do love me, don't you, John?"

"You know I do!" I protested, and thought: I would have loved Blanche better now. Then I had a moment of sadness so deep that I feared Constance would notice, so to divert her I suggested we went shopping on the morrow. Constance loved shopping. The next morning I bought her a gold bracelet and the purchase made us both feel better; she stopped asking me if I loved her, and in the effort of pleasing her I stopped thinking about Blanche.

Later when we were back in England I was surprised to remember how Blanche had haunted me, but I knew why I had retreated into my first marriage. It was less painful to remember Blanche at Lavenham than Bronwen in Cornwall. In fact, I was unable to think of Bronwen. I was too frightened of where my thoughts might lead.

When we arrived home at the end of January, my father-in-law handed us the title deeds of our new mansion in Surrey, and presently we went down to Dorking to see it again. Built in the eighteenth century it was an architecturally superior Anglo-Saxon version of Oxmoon, and Constance declared with enthusiasm that after the necessary renovations by the right interior decorators it would be perfect for house parties. I walked through the empty rooms, which were devoid of all the memories that made Oxmoon precious to me, and said what a wonderful wedding present it was and how fortunate we were.

Constance had decided that my Kensington house was not smart enough for the home she had in mind, so we began our married life at a much larger house in Chester Square, not far from Eaton Walk. My father-in-law liked this because it meant he could call on us all the time, and Constance, who loved her father and perhaps loved him the more because she had never been the favorite daughter, basked in this constant paternal attention. I kept my thoughts on the subject to myself, but I found that Armstrong's brash personality, which I had once judged so refreshing, was becoming increasingly abrasive once it began to flood my private life. Fortunately we had a respite whenever he took himself off to visit Edmund and Teddy in their *pied-à-terre* in Chester Mews, but Edmund and Teddy were often absent from town. Shrewdly gauging Edmund's capabilities Armstrong had appointed him to run his estate in Kent, but as there was a manager in charge of the farms Edmund was not overworked. Armstrong himself used the Queen Anne mansion on weekends, but Edmund and Teddy were allocated the Regency dower house with its fine views over the Weald, and as far as Edmund was concerned he had been allocated paradise. I became weary of him telling me what bliss he was experiencing, and wearier still when Constance's demanding exuberance continued unabated.

"John, we must plan our trip to the States—Mother says she'll make sure we have a wonderful time. . . ."

Mrs. Armstrong, somehow conquering her nervous disorders, had crossed the Atlantic for her daughters' wedding and had spent much time being hysterical because they were settling down three thousand miles away from her. I had found her so tedious that I now searched for an excuse to postpone my American visit, but as matters turned out I hardly had to search hard. The excuse soon presented itself.

"Darling, there's something I want to tell you. . . . Oh, sweetheart, I think— I'm almost sure . . ."

She was pregnant. So was Teddy. Edmund was demented with delight. I managed to find the appropriate words to express pleasure and pride, but I barely heard myself utter them; I was too busy listening to the slam of the steel door as I found myself locked up in my new windowless cell.

"John, you *are* pleased, aren't you?"

Still I had to endure this quest for reassurance.

"John, you do love me, don't you?"

Still the futile questions droned on and on.

"John, I've asked the doctor and he says we can go on having sex for the time being . . ."

Constance liked sex and, just as I had anticipated, she was good at it. In fact my original estimate of her had proved accurate in every respect. She was an excellent wife. Although she was young she had just the right degree of authority with the servants; she was a first-class hostess, a splendid organizer of our social calendar and a superb administrator of my home. She took a conscientious and devoted interest in my children, and I had no doubt she would make a conscientious and devoted mother. She was already studying the subject of babies and working out how the perfect infant could be, as she put it in her American fashion, "raised."

". . . and the husband mustn't be overlooked—all the books say how important that is, darling, so you mustn't think I shall ever neglect you."

"My dear, after your ceaseless attentions during the past months I'm sure I could survive a little benign neglect!"

"What do you mean?" She was at once deeply wounded.

"Nothing. It was a joke, Constance, just a joke."

"I don't see it."

"No." I had married a girl who had no sense of humor. I could not imagine how I had once regarded her lack of humor as a charming seriousness, and in a terrible moment of truth I saw that although I respected her many excellent qualities, I was never going to love her and would often dislike her very much. That was when I first asked myself not how difficult it would be for me to sustain my marriage but how much longer I could continue with it. At first I thought marital breakdown would begin in the bedroom but ironically that was the one place where the marriage continued to flourish, the one place where Constance could be guaranteed to keep her mouth shut and I could be guaranteed the opportunity to do exactly as I liked. In the end the bedroom offered me my only compensation for my disastrous mistake but even there, as the months passed, my time ran out. Constance's pregnancy began to show. She was in good health but naturally I had to be careful, and this small attempt at restraint proved almost too much for me to bear. I found too that the visible signs of her pregnancy made me feel guilty. I felt guilty that I had fathered a child I did not want, guilty that I could not give Constance the love any pregnant woman needs and deserves, and guilty above all that I had wronged her by marrying her, by dragging her out onto the stage with me as I acted out my lies.

My marriage ended in the May of 1924, five months after our wedding day. I was breakfasting with Constance by the window of our bedroom, and outside the spring sunlight was shining on the new leaves of the trees in the square. My chauffeur was not due to bring the Rolls to the front door for another ten minutes, and I was just studying *The Times* before going to the nursery to have a word with the children. I remember that I had finished the cricket report and was steeling myself to face the parliamentary columns. The new Labour government had been horrifying and enthralling the country ever since they had failed to wear court dress at Buckingham Palace.

The butler entered the room and handed the morning's post to Constance.

She was wearing an emerald-green negligée which looked striking with her dark hair, and she had been reading the latest copy of *The Tatler*. On the table between us amidst the Royal Worcester breakfast set, two orchids wilted languidly in an exquisite silver vase.

"Here's a letter from Oxmoon," said Constance, sifting diligently through the post as usual in order that I might not be bothered by correspondence which would unnecessarily consume my time. She passed me the envelope bearing my father's handwriting. "We ought to go down there again soon, John—shall I arrange for the Manor to be prepared for us at the end of the month? I think we could fit in a weekend there before the Derby."

But I had now reached the stage where I was afraid to see those closest to me for fear I might break down and tell them the truth. Abandoning my newspaper

I rose to my feet to make my escape and murmured, "But I have to go to Birmingham at the end of the month." Since my marriage I had been thrust deep into the dreariness of the Armstrong Canning Corporation.

"You surely don't have to go on a weekend, darling! Now, let me see: is there anything else here that you should look at before you go? Bills, receipts, invitations... oh, and what's this? Swansea postmark, cheap paper, probably a begging letter... Oh, my! It's in Welsh! Here, darling, for once I can't cope—over to you."

I had been halfway to the door. I looked back. Always I can remember looking back at the orchids dying in their siver vase while the spring sun shone beyond them on the brilliant green leaves of the square.

Returning to the table, I took the letter from her without a word.

Dear Mr. Godwin, Myfanwy Meredith had written on lined paper in a clear script. *I think you should do something about my sister. She'll never ask for help so I must. I write not to make trouble but because I believe you wouldn't want her to suffer. Please may I see you to explain?*

An hour later I was aboard the train to Swansea.

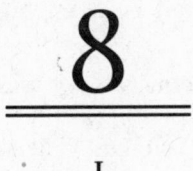

8

I

I saw the pram immediately. It was parked in the shade of the tree that stood in front of the farmhouse. I had walked the short distance from the Manor but now I broke into a run. The sun shone sporadically from a sky dotted with small white clouds, and beyond the cart track the front meadow was gay with buttercups and clover.

The perambulator was little better than a wooden crate on wheels, but it had been painted a smart navy-blue and cleverly lined inside with white cotton. Beneath a blanket embroidered with yellow ducks the baby lay fast asleep. It had some fairish down on top of its head and very small, very new features. When I lifted the blanket, I found that the nappy was damp. Pulling the cloth to one side, I saw I had a son.

A light breeze fanned the delicate skin I had exposed, and he awoke. I rearranged him beneath the blanket, but he was inconsolable, and hardly knowing what I was doing, I picked him up. He whimpered against my chest. Twenty yards away the front door of the house slammed. As I looked up, rigid with misery, Bronwen stopped, rigid with anger, and we stared dumbly at each other for one long moment of all-consuming despair.

The baby began to cry again.

"Hush, Evan." She rushed forward, scooped him out of my arms and hugged him tightly. "Who told you?" she demanded, not looking at me. Her voice shook as she turned away. "Was it Huw? Was it Myfanwy? Was it some old gossip in the village? I thought no one doubted he was Gareth's—I didn't think anyone remembered exactly when Gareth died—" She broke off as the baby, sensing her distress, began to cry more loudly. "Shhh... there's a good boy... shhh." Her hair was loose, and as she bent her head over him, a long strand tickled his cheek. He stopped crying and peered at her. He was too young to smile, but I saw him focus his eyes as he gazed upward. Hugging him again she rocked him gently in her arms.

"Your sister wrote."

"How dare she! I'll never forgive her, never!"

"But why didn't you want me to be told?"

"Because I knew," she said, tears streaming down her face, "that we ought never to meet again."

We stood there side by side. Eventually she wiped her eyes with the back of her hand and said in a flat voice, "He's very wet. I must take him indoors to be changed."

Automatically I followed her but she turned on me in a rage. "Go away! I don't want your pity or your charity! Go back to your wife!"

"Never."

That silenced her. It silenced me. As her eyes filled with tears, I took her in my arms.

After a time she whispered, "You mustn't lie to me anymore. It's cruel. When you wrote and said Cornwall was wrong and marrying a girl you didn't love was right—"

"I'll get a divorce."

"Oh, damn you, what good would that do!" she shouted. "You'd only leave me later when you found another woman of your own class who suits you better than I ever could!"

"I'm never leaving you again."

That settled that. My arms tightened around her, she raised her tear-stained face to mine and the poor baby had to endure being crushed so hard between us that he screamed with rage. In consternation we sprang apart, and then as the sun blazed down upon us all our misery dissolved and once more we were smiling into each other's eyes.

II

It was late in the afternoon. The children were home from the village school but out playing somewhere in the fields. From the kitchen came the sound of Myfanwy's voice as she talked to a visiting neighbor, but after entering the house through the front door we avoided them by going straight upstairs to the room that Bronwen shared with the baby.

"I can't be with you yet," said Bronwen simply. "It's too soon after the birth."

"I understand. When was he born?"

We began to talk. I sat on the bed as she changed the nappy, and then she lay on the bed in my arms while she fed him. She told me that when she returned to Cardiff she had found domestic work again but had been dismissed by her employer when the pregnancy became obvious, and although she had tried to go on working she had begun to suffer from anemia, a misfortune that had made her afraid for the baby's health. Finally, unable to pay anything to her in-laws for her room and board, she had been obliged to return to the Merediths. Both of them had been horrified by her condition but had taken her in without hesitation.

"But I knew I couldn't go on living on their charity," said Bronwen, "and besides I was too afraid of you finding out, so I told Myfanwy I'd emigrate to Vancouver where we have cousins who would have lent me the fare. I suppose that was what drove her to write to you. She wanted you to pay for me to stay in Wales."

I told her that at some remote time in the future when we had been married so long that we had nothing better to do, I would take her on a visit to her Canadian cousins, and we laughed together. Meanwhile the baby had finished his feed and had to be held up and patted and encouraged to perform the rituals of digestion. As I stroked the down on the top of his head, I said abruptly, "You should have said something in Cornwall about the possibility of this happening. I assumed you couldn't have any more children."

"Why?"

I explained.

"Oh, I see," she said. "But Gareth was too drunk most of the time to be a husband to me." She wiped the baby's mouth carefully and smiled at him as if to negate the unhappy memories. Then a thought struck her. She looked up frightened. "Are you angry about the baby?"

"Of course I'm angry—but not with you or with him. I'm angry with myself for ignoring my responsibilities in Cornwall and leaving you alone to pay the price."

"That's silly," she said. "It takes two to make a baby. If I hadn't wanted him I would have said something."

I was interested to discover that I had not after all underestimated her practical streak. We discussed contraception idly for a time. Among the working classes, I learned, birth control consisted of *coitus interruptus*, sodomy and old wives' tales, although since the war French letters had provided a welcome relief for those who could afford them. Bronwen referred to sodomy as "what they did in the Bible," and as I laughed at this contraceptive vision which would have appalled all fundamentalists, she laughed with me. I tried to remember when I had last felt so happy and that was when I realized how miserable I had been ever since our holiday in Cornwall.

"But we'll both be happy again now," I said. "We'll live very quietly at the Manor—I'll engage a housekeeper so that you won't have to deal with the servants, and we needn't entertain so you won't have to meet a stream of people who would make you feel shy."

"I don't want to cut you off from—"

"I want to be cut off. My life requires surgery on the grand scale."

"But what about your father? Supposing he becomes angry and decides not to leave you Oxmoon?"

"Ah," I said. "It turned out that I wasn't destined for Oxmoon after all. But I don't care. Not anymore."

"You mean—"

"You were right. Love's the compensation I've always needed, and so long as I have you I know I can escape from the past and be free."

III

"But he's not free!" said Myfanwy to her sister. She was so stupefied by our news that she spoke in Welsh, forgetting I could understand her.

"He's going to get divorced."

"But you can't possibly marry him!" She was appalled. Her plump friendly little face was white and hostile. "How would you manage? He can't mean it! He's just making another of his false promises!"

"Oh no I'm not," I said.

Her hands flew to her mouth in the classic gesture of dismay. "Forgive me, sir, I quite forgot you'd know what I was saying—"

"I promise you I'll look after Bronwen now."

"But your wife..." She swung back to face her sister. "You can't have forgotten what's being said in the village. Both those American ladies are having babies in the autumn, both of them. How could you think of taking a man away from his pregnant wife? How could you think of building your happiness on someone else's misery?"

"Well, what about *my* misery?" screamed Bronwen, losing her temper. "And what about *my* baby?"

"You're not his wife, are you! You're just the girl who's fool enough to give him what he wants when he wants it!"

"I'm the girl who loves him and I'm the girl he loves and all else is falseness and wrong—for him, for me and for the American lady too! I shan't feel sorry for her having a deserting husband, indeed I shan't, no, not one bit, he'll be doing her a kindness by divorcing her—oh, I know all about the torture of being married to a husband who doesn't care so how dare you say he should stay chained to a loveless marriage for her sake, how dare you!"

There was a silence while Myfanwy passed the back of her hand across her forehead and leaned for support against the kitchen table, but at last she said unsteadily, "I'm sorry, Mr. Godwin, I mean no disrespect, but I'm just so worried about my sister."

"I understand. But I swear I'll put everything right."

"How can you?" she said in despair. "She'll never fit into your world—how can you bring her anything but misery?" And sinking down on the nearest chair, she covered her face with her hands and began to weep.

IV

"Well, John," said Robert, "what can I say? I've never before suffered from speechlessness, but this time I confess that the hitherto unimaginable has occurred and I'm at a loss for words. Let me try and collect my shattered thoughts. What should one brother say to another in such a truly catastrophic situation?"

"'Good luck' would be a useful start."

"*Good luck?* My dear John, you're going to need far more than that to guarantee your survival! You're going to need the heroism of St. George, the hide of an elephant and the constitution of an ox—oh, and how about your fairy godmother, complete with magic wand? Since we're dealing with fantasy we may as well admit a little magical support to keep your dreams bowling merrily along, but may I be unbearably prosaic and ask how you're going to break the news to Papa? That would seem to be your most immediate problem."

"I was hoping you'd help me."

"My worst fears are now confirmed. Go on."

"I've been in rather a muddle about Papa for some time, and I'm afraid that if I break the news to him we'll generate some emotional scene which will only make the muddle worse. But you're so cool and levelheaded, Robert, and—"

"You want me to reduce Papa to order for you. John, you must surely realize you're asking the impossible; a raging love affair with a Welsh peasant is not a subject on which we can expect our father to be rational."

"But if you stress I'm going to marry her—"

"He'll be appalled, just like everyone else. The only way he could ever accept Mrs. Morgan's presence in your life would be if you were to keep her tucked discreetly away in Swansea."

"But if you could explain to him that Bronwen's good, decent and honest—and utterly different from that bloody villain Bryn-Davies—"

"Has it ever occurred to you," said Robert, "that we've only heard one highly prejudiced version of that story? It's quite possible that Grandmama too saw her lover as someone who was good, decent and honest."

"Oh, bloody hell, let's forget all that, I don't care about those horrors anymore, I've escaped from the past—"

"We never escape from the past," said Robert. "It's the biggest jail of all time. Very well, I'll tell Papa that although you're behaving like a lunatic, you're not automatically destined for incarceration in the Home of the Assumption. What else can I possibly say? Ah, here's Ginette. Come in, my dear, and mix yourself a very large pink gin. What do you think's happened? No, don't even try and guess—I'll tell you. John's leaving Constance and going to live at Penhale Manor with Mrs. Morgan and their new illegitimate infant. Intriguing, isn't it? Maybe country life's not so dull after all! Oh, and by the way, I nearly forgot to tell you—he's going to marry her once he can get his hands on a divorce."

Ginevra, who was wearing a tubelike navy dress with a very short skirt, stopped dead to gape at me. Her full feminine figure was so unsuited to the boyish style of her clothes that she was looking not only raffish but bizarre. I remembered the nightmare of her adolescence and tried to make allowances for her, but I was on the defensive by that time, and all my old antipathy towards her was rising to the surface of my mind. I knew she had never liked me. I knew she still privately judged me a prig, and I thought how entertained she would be to see me fall from grace. I pictured her savoring my discomfort behind my back and gossiping about me in amusement with her smart friends in London.

"Robert, you're joking. I don't believe a word of it."

"Don't worry," I said abruptly before Robert could reply. "I'm fully expecting you to share his view that this is a disaster of the highest order."

"Disaster?" said Ginevra. Then she laughed and cried, "Rubbish! I think it's absolutely wonderful and quite the most romantic thing I've ever heard in my life!" And she stretched out her hands to me—Ginevra whom I had always distrusted, Ginevra whom I had never liked—and as she kissed me on both cheeks she exclaimed with a sincerity I never forgot, "Darling Johnny, I didn't know you had it in you! Congratulations—well done—I'm with you all the way!"

V

"You're insane," said Constance dry-eyed, and set her mouth in a hard unyielding line.

"I'm sorry. I know this is an appalling shock for you, but I can't go on with this lie any longer."

"But you love me—you like me in bed, I know you do!"

"Constance—"

"What does she do that I don't? Whatever it is I can learn it."

"Constance, this has nothing to do with sex."

372

"What! *Nothing to do with sex?* Who do you think you're fooling!"

"Look, I know this is terrible for you. I know it is. And don't think it isn't terrible for me too. I feel riddled with guilt just standing here talking to you—guilty that I married you, guilty that I let you get pregnant, guilty, guilty guilty, but I can't help it, Constance, I've got to leave and I think that once you've recovered from the shock you'll be glad—you'll realize, once I'm gone, that I could never have made you happy."

"You could. You have."

"But I've been acting, can't you see? I've been acting all the time—you've never known me as I really am! You're in love with someone who doesn't exist!"

"Sure you exist. You're tall, dark and handsome and wonderful in bed."

"What the devil's that got to do with what I'm talking about? A man's soul isn't located in his genitals!"

"Well, as far as you're concerned it's obviously no more than an inch away! Anyway, Freud says—"

"No, don't let's start on Freud. Freud's the biggest piece of intellectual claptrap you've ever bored me with, and my God, that's saying something!"

"Okay, I'll stick to the point. I love you. I want you to stay with me."

"Well, I suppose it's only natural that you should say that now when you're so shocked, but later the situation is bound to seem different to you. You'll meet someone else. You're clever and attractive, and I'm quite sure that in no time at all you'll have at least half a dozen suitors."

"I'm not interested in anyone else but you."

"All right. You're not interested. Not now. But later, when you've got the divorce—"

"What divorce?" said Constance, annihilating me.

VI

"Take it easy, sweetheart," said Armstrong as Constance finally broke down and wept against his chest. "That's my brave little girl— no divorce, no surrender. I'm very, very proud of you. Okay, now just you leave this to me. Run along to your room and dry your eyes and I'll be up to see you shortly."

Constance, who had indeed been very brave, now proved her courage afresh by controlling her tears and walking out of the room with her head held high. By this time I was feeling ill.

"You goddamned bastard," said Armstrong as soon as the door closed. "I'll see you goddamned ruined unless you pull yourself together in double-quick time."

"Go ahead. I don't give a damn."

Much shouting and abuse followed. Finally I tried to walk out but he grabbed me by the arm and shouted, "Okay, just you tell me this: how the fucking hell are you going to live with your conscience?"

"How the fucking hell are you going to live with yours? You flogged me into this mess! I accept that I've played the major role in the disaster, but don't try and pretend you haven't led a full supporting cast!"

He tried to hit me but I sidestepped him. He was just a fat stupid man on the far side of middle age. I walked out of the room but he blundered after me, and as I left the house I heard him shouting at the top of his voice that I was a cheater, a four-flusher and a goddamned son of a bitch.

VII

"Daphne?" I said rapidly to Lion's widow from the telephone kiosk at my nearest club. "Thank God, I wasn't sure whether you were in town. Has Ginevra been in touch with you?"

"Rather!" said Daphne, who was by no means as ingenuous as her hearty manner suggested. "My dear, I'm simply reeling! What can I do to help? Ginevra said you were worried stiff about the children."

I explained that Penhale Manor had been running on a skeleton staff since Edmund's departure for Kent, and this meant that I was unable to retire there immediately with two children, a nanny and a governess.

"...and so I was wondering if—"

"Say no more. Toss them all over here to Cadogan Place—Elizabeth'll be thrilled! How soon can they come?"

I felt ready to collapse with relief. "Tomorrow morning?"

"Bring them tonight, if you like."

"No, that's very good of you, Daphne, and I can't thank you enough, but... well, I have to prepare the children for this and I'll need a little time to explain..."

VIII

"But Papa," said Marian, "how can you marry someone who's not a lady? In fact is such a thing even allowed? I seem to remember Nanny saying there's a law against it."

"No, there's no law against it, Marian. Mrs. Morgan's the woman I love, and love matters more than class."

"That's not what Nanny thinks," said Marian. "Nanny thinks nothing matters more than class, and I'll tell you this, Papa: Nanny will be *most put out* if we have to leave London, because how am I ever going to mix with girls of my own class in a provincial place like Wales? Nanny," said Marian, regarding me with baleful blue eyes, "will say it doesn't suit."

374

Nanny would have to go. A long vista of domestic difficulties stretched in front of me but I kept my face impassive. "I'll have a word with Nanny, Marian," I said.

"Yes, I think you'd better. And I warn you, Papa, she'll be terribly shocked that you and Mrs. Morgan have had a baby without being married, because Nanny believes babies don't happen unless there's a wedding first. By the way, will the baby be common like Mrs. Morgan or will he be a gentleman like you?"

Before I could reply to this question, which only a sociologist would have welcomed, Harry looked up from dismantling his best toy train and said sharply, "I don't think I want a brother, thank you very much."

"But brothers are fun, Harry! And think what fun it'll be to live at the Manor again!"

I saw his dark eyes, so like his mother's, glow with the animation her eyes had always lacked. Forgetting the engine in his hands he gazed enthralled at me. "Is there still a piano in the drawing room?"

"Silly baby," said Marian, "why should he have sold it since we were last there for a visit? Papa, I'm still worried about this. I realize you and Constance have to get unmarried and I don't mind that much, but I do wish you didn't have to marry Mrs. Morgan. Will there be any risk of me growing up common now? Because if there is—"

"The commonest thing you can do, Marian," I said strongly, "is to continue to talk in this vulgar fashion. Class is something true ladies never discuss."

Marian burst into tears and the next moment Nanny herself was bustling into the room to the rescue.

"There, there, my precious, my angel—"

Marian hurtled sobbing into her arms. "Oh Nanny, Papa's leaving Constance and marrying Mrs. Morgan and they already have a new baby even though they're not married and I'm so afraid of growing up common and Papa doesn't understand and he's being simply horrid to me..."

More terrible vistas opened up into the future. As Nanny became scarlet in the face with startling rapidity, I dredged up the dregs of my strength and once more prepared for battle.

IX

"What beats me," said Edmund that evening at Brooks's, "is how you can do this to your children—and I don't just mean Harry and Marian, although God knows how they'll turn out if you live openly with your working-class mistress. What about Constance's child? How are you going to face it in future when you walked out on it before it was born? No, I'm sorry but I think this decision of yours is absolutely disgusting and your behavior makes me sick."

"Edmund—"

"How could you be such a fool? I mean, I'm a jolly broad-minded chap, and God knows if I had your looks I'd be rolling in the hay with everything in sight, but at least even *I'd* have the brains to keep that sort of woman in the hay where she belongs. Why the devil can't you just keep her quietly somewhere and visit her now and then like any other decent civilized fellow?"

"Edmund, I don't want to quarrel. I know that in the circumstances this couldn't be more awkward for you, but please try and accept that there's nothing else I can do."

"No, I bloody well can't accept it! Can't you at least stay with poor Constance until after the baby's born?"

"It would be pointless. What sort of an atmosphere do you think there'd be if I stayed on now? It would be unendurable for us both, you must see that!"

"Well, don't expect me to stay on speaking terms with you. I've got my own wife to think about, and I don't want her to be more upset than she is already."

"I understand. But I hope later you'll feel differently."

"Good God, you don't think Teddy or I would ever receive that woman, do you?"

"I certainly hope that when she's my wife—"

"She'll never be your wife, John! I don't know why you keep behaving as if Constance doesn't mean what she says about a divorce!"

"She means it at the moment. But she's bound to change her mind."

"Don't you believe it! Hell hath no fury and all that. She'll hang on. And meanwhile you'll be in the biggest possible mess. Christ, how can you conceivably explain to those two children that you plan to live in sin with a woman who's barely fit to be their nursemaid?"

"That needn't concern you," I said, and walked out on him without another word.

X

"I told Papa," said Robert when I telephoned him later.

"What was the reaction?"

"Unmitigated horror. You'd better come down here first thing tomorrow morning, John."

"I can't! The children are safe with Daphne but I've got appointments with accountants and lawyers and bank managers—"

"They can wait. Papa can't. I mean that, John. I can't say any more on the telephone, but get that train tomorrow because I've got to talk to you without delay."

The next morning I caught the earliest train to South Wales, and some hours later I was traveling around the great curve of Swansea Bay. The industrial approaches to the city seemed as grotesque as ever, but a stillness had fallen since the war on that ravaged landscape and the numbness of despair was paralyzing its people. Mining was a depressed industry. Brave buoyant Welsh Swansea, bunched on its hills above the sea, was limp with the dole queues and sodden with the misery of the unemployed.

I stepped off the train in my Savile Row suit, a visitor from a world those unemployed millions would never know, and found my caretaker waiting, his cap respectfully in his hand as if to exacerbate my guilt that I should be privileged. To negate it I reminded myself of the world I was rejecting, and as we drove beyond the outskirts of the city I thought of all the moneyed people I knew, dancing and drinking themselves to distraction to distance themselves from the war and its aftermath—and then it seemed to me that their lives were so far removed from reality that I wondered how I could ever have shared their futile illusions created by the two-faced glamour of affluence. We drove on into Gower, and when I saw the sunlit fields and the secret valleys and the sparkling sea flashing in the distance, I felt as if I were recovering from some illness which had nearly proved fatal.

At Little Oxmoon, I told my caretaker to drive on to the Manor with my luggage and then I joined Robert in the drawing room.

"Do you want a drink?" said Robert. "Or some food? There's a cold buffet laid out in the dining room."

"I don't think I could eat and I'm quite sure I shouldn't drink. Tell me the worst."

"I went to see him yesterday morning and said my piece, but he couldn't take it in—or, to be accurate, he took it in but couldn't face up to it. He became disconnected with reality again."

"Oh *God*. Robert, I think I will have a drink after all."

"A wise decision. Help yourself. You haven't heard the worst part yet. When it became obvious that I wasn't going to get a word of sense out of him, I yielded to the inevitable and summoned Straker. She was so competent that my suspicions were aroused. I thought to myself, Hullo, she's been here before, so after she'd led him off to rest I summoned Bayliss and cross-questioned him till he broke down, poor loyal old man, and confessed that the only reason why he was continuing to endure Straker's dictatorship was because he was so worried about 'The Master' that he couldn't bear to leave him. He hadn't planned to confide in me, since I was ill, but he had planned to write to you if things got worse—which they now have. In other words, John—"

"Papa's been deteriorating for some time but Straker's hushed it up."

"Exactly. And you can see why. If Papa has a complete mental breakdown we have a legitimate excuse to interfere in his affairs, and naturally the last thing

Straker wants is an intervention which curtails her power."

I swallowed some whisky and said, "What do we do?"

"First we must help him over this present crisis. You must give him the re-assurance he so obviously needs, and with luck that will restore his equilibrium."

"But what the devil's going on, Robert? Why's he like this? What's at the bottom of this instability?"

"That leads me on to what I was going to say next. As soon as he's rational we must coax him to see Gavin Warburton. We can't let him drift on like this without seeking medical help."

"But do you think—"

"No, I don't. There's no need for you to look as if we're all in the middle of your recurring nightmare. I'm convinced we're not dealing with hereditary mad-ness here."

"What makes you so sure?"

"I'm sure because I don't think Grandmama was mad—at least, not in any sense that would be accepted today. It was Ginette who gave me that idea. She was mad as a hatter after Robin died, but that was just a temporary nervous breakdown and now she's her old self again."

I swallowed some more whisky. After a while, I heard myself say, "I can't cope with this crisis, Robert; I just can't face it, it's too much for me."

"That's exactly why I'm trying to drill it into your head that Papa's derangement, such as it is, has nothing whatsoever to do with Grandmama. I know perfectly well that you've got a bee in your bonnet about Grandmama, insanity and the Home of the Assumption."

"I can't talk about that." I got up and began to pace around the room. "I've nothing to say."

"Maybe not," said Robert, "but I have. It seems to me—after much speculation on the subject of this peculiarity of yours—that you've translated the past into some Gothic nightmare which has very little to do with reality." He paused to let that sink in before adding in his most soothing voice: "After all, what actually happened? Mama had an unusually awkward problem with her mother-in-law. With Papa's consent she took advantage of Grandmama's nervous breakdown to install her at the Home of the Assumption, a reputable asylum, where Grandmama was apparently well treated. Grandmama then submitted—perhaps out of some desire to be punished—to our parents' decision that she should remain there. The situation was tragic, I admit, but hardly worthy of a horrific poem by Poe."

"What can be more horrific than shutting up a sane woman in a lunatic asylum? No, I refuse to believe our parents would do anything so fiendish!"

"Those parents of ours were capable of anything."

"No!" I shouted. "Grandmama was insane and they were the innocent victims of her evil!"

"There you go again, translating a mere melancholy ditty into a raging grand opera! My dear John, you can't divide these unfortunate people neatly into heroes and villains—it's simply not that kind of story!"

"Oh yes it is," I said. "It's got to be. I've got to have it quite clear in my mind

378

whom to hate and whom to love or the ambiguity will tear me apart and I'll go mad. In fact I feel I'm going mad now, just talking about it. I can't face it, can't cope, can't see Papa, can't be reminded of the past—"

"You've got to see him. There's no one else. Now look here, John. You're an intelligent man. It's inconceivable that you can go on being irrational about this—"

"Oh, shut up, you don't understand—"

But this was exactly the response Robert wanted. "Very well, then explain your feelings to me."

I made a great effort. At last I managed to say: "All I know is that I can't dismiss the past lightly as you can. I've suffered too much. I can't forgive and I can't forget, and because of this I have to blame someone for what I've had to endure, and I can't blame my parents because it was always so important that they should love me, and anyway I've always loved them—although God knows, when you told me about Papa and Ginevra—Christ, that was terrible, *terrible*, I was so shocked—and *so angry* too, angry with him for not behaving as I needed him to behave, it reminded me of how I used to feel as a child—I used to feel so *angry* with him... and with Mama... for being prejudiced against me just because... but I couldn't feel angry, of course I couldn't, not really, well, I mean how could I when I loved them and I knew they loved me, I knew they did, of course they did, but oh God, how upset I was when you told me about Papa and Ginevra... But there I was, being a hypocritical prig again. I've now treated Bronwen and Constance just as badly as he ever treated my mother, and I've no right to be angry with him anymore. I'm just as bad as he is, I'm just like him, and if he now goes mad—as Grandmama went mad—two people who committed murder—all that evil—hereditary madness—oh God, I'm so frightened, *so bloody frightened*, you don't know how frightened I am whenever I think what could happen to me in the future..." I had to stop. I could no longer go on. I rubbed my eyes furtively with the back of my hand and tried to drink some scotch.

Robert waited a moment before saying in his calmest voice: "I never used that word 'evil' when I was defending so-called evil people. It usually seemed more accurate to describe them as pathetic or unlucky or stupid. They weren't fiends in human guise. They tended to be almost boringly ordinary."

"What are you trying to say?"

"I'm suggesting that you should think of our parents—and of Grandmama and Bryn-Davies—as ordinary people trapped in a situation which was quite beyond them. I think that's a lot closer to the truth than your Gothic melodrama."

I was unable to speak.

"And try to see Grandmama," persisted Robert, "not as a fiend lapsing into a hereditary madness for her sins, but as a sexy woman who got in a mess and in consequence had a most understandable nervous breakdown."

I tried to consider this. A knot of tension seemed to be expanding in the pit of my stomach. "But if I see Grandmama as—as—"

"Forgivable," said Robert.

"—how do I see our parents?"

"As two children in their teens who had to grow up fast with disastrous results. They can be forgivable too, John."

"But if I forgive everyone, whom do I blame?"

"'That Monster Fortune,' to quote Boethius. We're all locked to the Wheel of Fortune, John, and some of us have a rougher ride than others."

I thought about this. Then I said, "Are you saying we have no control over our fate?"

"No. I believe Fortune gives us choices and we have to choose. But think how hard it is, John, when one has choices, to draw the right lines in the right places."

There was no answer to that. I thought of the wrong line I had drawn when I had rejected Bronwen, and suddenly for one brief powerful moment I saw my grandmother as a pathetic old woman, cut off from those she loved by the wrong decisions which had ruined her.

I said, "If only I could believe there was no hereditary madness involved. But if Papa's now suffering from a severe mental disturbance again—"

"That need only indicate that he too is having some form of temporary mental collapse, but as far as I know nervous breakdowns aren't hereditary. I'm sorry, John, to deprive you of your melodrama, but the truth is real life just isn't grand opera. It's much more in the nature of *opéra bouffe*."

I looked at him, a man afflicted by tragedy, and at once despised myself for my cowardice. "Hold fast," I said aloud to myself. "Stand firm. Soldier on." And those phrases, so reminiscent of the simple world of John Buchan where the heroes never had any trouble being as brave as lions, were comforting to me as I struggled with the complexity of my emotions. "How weak I've been," I said ashamed to Robert, "and how very unheroic."

"Ah," said Robert, "but the real heroes of this world aren't the men who preen themselves on how well they're doing their moral duty. The real heroes are the men who somehow nerve themselves to face a crisis even when they want to shit with fright at the thought of where it's all going to end."

I took a deep breath. Then I said, "I shall be all right now," and I set off on the road to Oxmoon on the first stage of my journey into hell.

XII

"Good afternoon, Mr. John," said my enemy, emerging briskly into the hall as I was handing Bayliss my hat. "Would you care to come into the drawing room, sir?"

Thanking her with equal civility, I allowed myself to be led across the hall. Mrs. Straker was immaculate in dove-gray, not a hair out of place on her sleek head. Her black eyes were inscrutable.

We entered the drawing room. The door closed. We stripped off our masks.

"I understand my father's not well."

"Well, that's just it, dear, I'm afraid he's not well enough to see anyone at present."

"He'll see me. Go upstairs, please, and tell him I'm here."

"As a matter of fact, dear, he's not upstairs—I've coaxed him out into the garden to see if any of the strawberries are ripe yet. They won't be, but at least he'll have a breath of fresh air. He's been shut up in his room talking of you-know-who until I'm ready to scream.... By the way, you look a little peaky yourself, dear, you really do—would you like a whisky?"

"No, an explanation. When you say 'you-know-who'—"

"That mother of his, dear, and her ruddy lover. Why those two couldn't have managed their affair better I can't think. Pure selfishness, if you ask me. In fact she must have been a very stupid woman, letting her lover get out of hand like that—and why kill the poor old homo husband? Most homos are ever so sweet when you get to know them, and he probably only drank because she treated him like dirt. Still, never mind me, I'm prejudiced—I've never had any patience with women who do everything wrong from start to finish. Now, what are we going to do about you? Frankly I think if you see him you'll make him worse."

"Nevertheless—"

"You *have* put the cat among the pigeons, haven't you, dear! Not that I blame you. That girl's got something all right—I admire your taste, and I wouldn't say no to hers either! I'm sure you make very tuneful music together, and I hear there's ever such a lovely baby!"

"Mrs. Straker—"

"All right, I suppose it's no use hoping you'll take yourself off, but don't say I didn't warn you. Christ, there he is! Now, what's he doing by the summerhouse? He's supposed to be in the kitchen garden. Well, dear, do we toss for it? Who goes to the rescue, you or me?"

I made no reply but opened the door and stepped out onto the terrace. "Has Dr. Warburton been consulted?" I demanded over my shoulder.

"Don't be daft. Bobby's tough as old boots when it comes to keeping doctors at arm's length—he's too afraid of being carted off to the loony bin."

I closed the door in her face, crossed the terrace and ran down the steps to the lawn. My father, dressed casually in gray flannels and a tweed jacket, was standing motionless in front of the summerhouse with his back to me. I went on walking. Eventually Glendower saw me and gave a bark to warn my father of my approach, but my father, apparently absorbed in some private meditation, took no notice. Sweat prickled on my back. I was seized by the nightmarish fear that when I saw his face I would find it changed beyond recognition, and in an automatic attempt to steady my nerves, I called a greeting and broke into a run to cover the last yards which separated us.

My father glanced idly over his shoulder. To my profound relief he appeared to be normal.

"Hullo, John," he said. "I was just thinking that the summerhouse should be repainted. Looks a bit shabby."

He held out his hand. Controlling my rapid breathing I took the hand and shook it. We smiled at each other, and that was the moment when I realized his behavior was abnormal. He ought to have been distressed and angry. His casual affability indicated a mind that had deliberately disconnected itself from pain.

The sweat began to trickle down my spine. "How are you, Papa?"

"Wonderfully well," said my father. "I admit Robert did upset me yesterday, but I've quite recovered from that now."

"I'm sorry Robert upset you. It was I, in fact, who asked him to call."

"Robert's very cruel sometimes," said my father. "Like Margaret. They mean well—when they interfere, they call it 'sorting things out' and 'setting things straight'—but they don't understand how muddled life is, how confusing."

"I'm sure Robert didn't mean to be cruel, Papa. He just wanted to explain—"

"Don't worry, I didn't believe a word he said; I knew it wasn't true. You wouldn't do what he said you were going to do. You're a good decent boy. You'd draw the line."

"Ah. I can see he gave you a wrong impression." I wiped the sweat from my forehead and shoved back my hair in a quick movement of my hand. "Why don't we go and sit in the summerhouse? I'd like to talk to you and explain everything."

"Oh no," said my father, "not the summerhouse. Quite definitely not the summerhouse. They meet in the back room."

"Met. They're dead."

"Yes, I know. But everything's come a full circle and now it's all happening again."

"No, Papa, the past never happens twice. People play their cards differently, don't you remember?"

My father turned away and began to wander towards the bench by the tennis court. "My mother and Owain Bryn-Davies," he said, "used to meet in the back room of the summerhouse but that was a long time ago, and now we keep the tennis net there during the winter."

"That's right."

"Thomas will put up the tennis net," said my father, "when he comes home from school in July. Thomas plays tennis with the Bryn-Davies boys." He paused to survey the tennis lawn before adding carefully: "The Bryn-Davies boys are called Owen and Peter. Owen is spelled the English way, which I think is a pity, but their mother's English so what can you expect? Their father is Alun, who was at Harrow with Robert, and Alun's father is my friend Owain the Younger, and *his* father was my mother's lover who drowned on the Shipway at the Worm's Head. A little accident with the tide tables. Have you ever taken Harry and Marian out to the Worm for a picnic, John? It's such a beautiful spot. Blanche would enjoy it too."

We seated ourselves on the bench, and my father, crossing one leg over the other, whistled for Glendower.

"Papa," I said, "Blanche is dead. I'm married to Constance now, but it was all the most appalling mistake, and I've decided—"

"Did I say Blanche? Stupid of me! Old age. Awful. I'm sixty-two—no, wait a minute—am I? Yes. It's 1924, isn't it?"

382

"Yes, I've been married to Constance for five months. However I now realize—"

"Wonderful wedding that was, had the time of my life. Wonderful champagne too—Veuve Clicquot, wasn't it? I'm always very partial to Veuve Clicquot."

"Papa, I'm in love with this Welsh girl Bronwen Morgan, and I intend to marry her once I have my divorce from Constance. There's no question of living in sin indefinitely. Bronwen's an honest respectable woman, and I intend that she should remain so."

"Honest respectable women don't have bastards." He stood up again and moved restlessly back towards the summerhouse. "My mother had two miscarriages when she was living with Bryn-Davies," he said. "It was disgusting. She was quite without shame. I was humiliated. She broke all the rules—and terrible things happen," said my father, tears suddenly streaming down his face, "as I well know, to people who fail to stick to the rules."

Far away Mrs. Straker had emerged from the house and was descending the steps of the terrace. The sight of her seemed to come as a relief to my father. He tried to wipe his eyes on the cuff of his jacket. "Ah, here's Milly—expect she wants to know if you're dining tonight. Wonderful woman, Milly, quite remarkable, don't know what I'd do without her. She wants to marry me, of course, but I won't because it's not the done thing for a man in my position to marry someone like that. Got to stick to the rules, you see—and then nothing very terrible can happen."

But it had happened. He saw my expression, knew I was thinking of my mother replaced by a whore and shouted, "You've no right to judge me!"

"And you've no right to judge *me!*" I shouted back before I could stop myself.

"I'll have to ask your mother to talk to you," said my father to me in despair. "Margaret will have to deal with it." He turned his back on me only to be confronted by the figure of Mrs. Straker, representing an intolerable present. He turned towards the summerhouse only to be confronted once more by the intolerable past. He rubbed his eyes and looked dazed. "Sorry," he muttered. "Not well."

Pity mingled with my guilt and drove me to make a final effort to communicate with him.

"Papa, you're under strain and I think you should see Warburton. There are modern drugs—"

"No!" said my father fiercely. "I'm not seeing a doctor!"

"But you've just admitted you're unwell!"

"Old age. Not so young as I used to be."

"But—"

"*Nobody's going to shut me up anywhere!*"

"That's all right, Bobby," said Mrs. Straker, covering the last few yards of lawn with the speed of lightning. "That's all right, my pet. Nobody gets shut up just because they get a bit upset now and then. The idea of it! If that were true we'd all be locked up, wouldn't we, John?"

Ignoring her I took my father's hands in mine. "Papa, I give you my word that

I'll never let anyone take you to the Home of the Assumption—or indeed, to any other institution of that kind."

His eyes filled with tears once more. He whispered, "You're such a good kind boy, John—and that's why I can't bear to see you destroying yourself like this."

"Oh, come off it, Bobby!" said Mrs. Straker at once. "This one's not going to destroy himself in a hurry—just look at him! Smart as paint, smooth as glass and clever as the Indian rope trick! You mark my words, a man like that could keep a bloody harem in a church if he put his mind to it! Now, don't you worry, my poppet. You run along and look at those strawberry beds, just as you said you would, and John and I'll work out how he can live happily ever after at the Manor. He's not stupid and he's not interested in destroying himself and I'm sure we'll have everything settled in no time at all. Oh, and watch that dog in the kitchen garden. I hear he's a terror for digging holes in all the wrong places."

This demonstration of crude street-corner sanity was evidently just what my father needed. He wiped away his tears, kissed her briefly and trailed away across the lawn with Glendower at his heels. I watched him for some time but even before I had nerved myself to face Mrs. Straker, I knew she was poised to move in for the kill.

"Well, *Mr.* John!" she said with heavy irony. "Don't you think you should come down off your high horse before you fall flat on your face? Let's go and sit in that bloody love nest of a summerhouse for a moment. I think it's time you and I had a cozy little chat together."

XIII

Robert had implied that we might one day have to go to war with Mrs. Straker about her position at Oxmoon, but neither he nor I had anticipated that she might now seek to go to war with us. Horrified by my father's condition, I was no match for her at that moment. I could only follow her into the summerhouse, and when she sat down on one of the wicker chairs I saw no alternative but to sit down opposite her.

She had crossed her legs primly as if she were drinking tea in her native London suburb, and when she began to speak this illusion of respectability only made her words the more bizarre.

"I was thinking of having a word with you, Mr. Casanova," she said, "even before this trouble blew up over your gorgeous redhead. I'd decided it was time you and your brother Robert realized how bloody indispensable I am here nowadays. You're hoping, aren't you, that this little trouble of your father's will give you the excuse to step in and get rid of me. Well, think again, my friend! Just you think again! You can't afford to wipe me off the slate, and if you can somehow manage to keep that handsome mouth of yours shut for a moment, I'll tell you the way things really are at Oxmoon.

384

"That's better. I can see I've got your full attention. I knew you weren't stupid. Now just you listen to me.

"There are two sides to my job here, and I do each of them damn well. Let's take the formal side first. I run that house like God runs heaven—perfectly. And unlike God I don't have a lot of angels to help me, and from a domestic point of view Oxmoon's a long way from heaven. It's old-fashioned, inconvenient and hell to keep organized. How your mother stood it I don't know, but of course she had a full prewar indoor staff of ten, whereas I now count myself lucky if I can get five servants living in and a couple of dailies from the village—your father won't pay for anything more. Never mind, I manage. I rule with a rod of iron and stand no nonsense, and fortunately the unemployment situation helps— people want to hang on to their jobs so they'll stand for a lot, and my God, I make them stand for it. Yes, I hold this place together all right. But remove me and it would fall apart at the seams.

"All right, so that's one potent argument in favor of keeping me: I do the formal side of my job damn well. But it's on the informal side that I'm bloody well indispensable. You might replace me as a housekeeper—if you were lucky—but you'd never find anyone willing to replace me for long in your father's bed. Nor are you going to find anyone who can control him in the way I can. You think my control over him's a bad thing, don't you? Well, this is the moment when you change your mind, my friend, because neither you nor your brothers have any idea what would go on at Oxmoon if I packed my bags and walked out. Shall I continue? Or shall I give you a moment to digest that? You look as if you could do with a cigarette. That's right, take out your case. I'll have one too—here, give me the matches and I'll do the lighting. That's right. Ah . . . that's better, isn't it? Nothing like a good puff to steady the nerves, and my God, your nerves are going to need steadying when you hear what I'm going to say next."

She leaned forward in her chair. Her sharp pointed face was close to me, and I could see the mole on her chin and the powder in the pores of her sallow skin and the hard lines running from her nose to the corners of her mouth.

"Your father," she said, "isn't the man he used to be. The present deterioration set in after Robin died, but if you ask me he's never been right since his wife's death, and now it's got to the stage where it doesn't take much to upset him and trigger him off. The only reason why this incident is different from other more recent ones is that this time he has a genuine excuse for being upset. However let's leave Mrs. Morgan for the moment—we'll get to her later.

"The truth you've now got to face is that although your father still spends a lot of time being sound as a bell, he's getting to the point where he needs a keeper, because whenever he's upset like this his one remedy is sex. So long as I'm here he's not going to go around doing God-knows-what to the nearest scullery maid, but once I'm gone he'll do it and, what's worse, he won't even remember afterwards that he's done it, he'll shut it clean out of his mind. Now, I know what to do with him. I can keep him satisfied, but he's got some weird tastes, and while I don't mind that—the weirder the better, as far as I'm concerned—there aren't many women who'd stand for that kind of behavior. Except prostitutes, of course.

And do you really want your father bringing the lowest form of street life into Oxmoon and turning the place into some kind of cross between a brothel and a lunatic asylum? Of course you don't. So look at me and be grateful because so long as I'm around you don't have to worry.

"Well, now that we've got all that straightened out, let's talk about the facts of life, otherwise known as pounds, shillings and pence. I'm worth my weight in gold, but Bobby only pays me a pittance as housekeeper. I filch a bit here and there, of course—why the hell shouldn't I, after all I do?—but Bobby's mean about money, and although he's a bit potty sometimes, he's still capable of being all too lucid when the subject of money comes up for discussion. The truth is he's so dependent on me that he gets a thrill out of saying no when I ask for things; it makes him feel more the master of his own home. Now I could go on filching—nothing easier—but why the hell should I have to scrape around like that? You're a rich man and it's in your best interests to pay me what I'm worth."

She stopped talking. I stubbed out my cigarette and stood up. Beyond the doorway, far away across the lawn, Oxmoon lay pallidly in the sunlight. I noticed that the creeper was beginning to die on the walls.

"I'll have to talk to my brother."

"Yes, I thought you'd say that, but think again, dear. For instance, why don't you and I come to a very private agreement, an agreement which will suit you as well as it'll suit me?"

"What do you mean?"

"Well, dear, before Bobby's really certifiable, why don't I whisper a little word in his ear about the will?"

"What will?"

"Oh, don't pretend you don't know about it! The will where he leaves everything to that little ninny Kester just because he wants to be kind to poor old Robert! What a lot of sentimental old balls—but don't you worry about it, my friend, because if you guarantee me five hundred a year, starting from now, I'll guarantee you Oxmoon when Bobby drops dead."

I knew it was vital that I never hesitated so the instant she stopped speaking I said, "I'll not cheat my dying brother. I draw the line." The most appalling part of this heroic statement was that I found myself wondering whether it was true.

"What's the matter, dear?" said the woman at my side. "Worried in case you wouldn't get away with it? But I'd keep my mouth shut, and anyway people can get away with anything if they put their minds to it. Look at your father! He got away with murder."

I turned to face her. "Did he?" I said.

We were silent. I thought of my ruined father, locked up in his private hell and shamed before the children he loved, but the thought was unendurable. Turning my back on the woman I walked out of the summerhouse.

"My God," said Milly Straker, "the man's incorruptible. That's the sexiest act I've seen in a month of Sundays." She followed me to the edge of the tennis lawn. "All right, dear, suit yourself, but let me know if you change your mind. And now—while we're still talking about sex—I think we'd better have a quick word about the luscious Mrs. Morgan. No, don't take offense! This is just a friendly word from a well-wisher. All I want to say, dear, is Don't live with her openly. I don't know whether you really intend to install her immediately in Penhale Manor as your mistress, but take it from me it just won't do."

"Mrs. Straker—"

"Oh, don't misunderstand! I'm not like your father— I'm not worried about *you*, I'm worried about *her*! You love her, don't you? All right, then if you're as decent as you've almost convinced me you are, take time off from your romantic dreams and imagine what hell life's going to be for her if you put her on public display nailed to a cross with a placard inscribed MISTRESS around her neck! If you've got to keep her at the Manor, let her call herself a housekeeper or a nanny or a tweeny or something—give her a title to hide behind when the inevitable happens and everyone realizes what's going on. Believe me, you'll have to fight tooth and nail to preserve that girl, and don't think I don't know what I'm talking about. My God, I've seen some crucifixions in my time! The bloody men get off scot-free and the girls end up in the bath with their wrists slashed—oh, I've seen it all! So take my advice for her sake and stop being so bloody selfish and naive."

After a pause I managed to say: "As I intend to marry Mrs. Morgan, I hardly think your advice is applicable."

"Why, yes, of course you intend to marry her, dear. A gentleman always intends to marry the girl at first, doesn't he? After all, he wouldn't be a gentleman if he didn't." She stepped past me and began to walk away across the lawn. "But Mrs. Morgan's a lucky girl," she added over her shoulder. "I can see that now. And maybe you really will be fool enough to marry her—if, of course, that new pregnant wife of yours is ever fool enough to agree to a divorce."

I watched her till she had disappeared from sight. Then I stumbled back into the summerhouse, sank down on the nearest chair and covered my face with my hands.

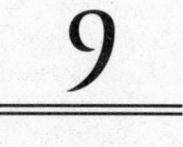

9

I

"SHE THEN SAID she would guarantee me Oxmoon if I guaranteed her an income," I said to Robert.

"How intriguing. What did you say?"

"I said I refused to cheat you."

"Oh, she'll never believe that," said Robert. "You should have reminded her instead that undue influence and unsoundness of mind can invalidate a will."

"No doubt I should. But I'm afraid I wasn't thinking too clearly at that stage."

"At that stage I'd have been dead of apoplexy.... Is that a car I hear outside?"

It was. Ginevra had arrived home from one of Esther Mowbray's smart bridge parties, and was looking overdressed in a shiny afternoon frock, an absurd hat like a semidestroyed Balaclava and a very, very long bead necklace.

"Are you going to tell her, Robert?"

"Of course. I always tell her everything."

This surprised me for Robert and Ginevra never gave an impression of marital intimacy and I had long since decided that their separate lives were linked by an enduring, genuine but not close affection. However when Robert now began to talk to her in the frankest possible manner, I found myself automatically trying to assess their marriage afresh. But it did not lend itself easily to assessment. The asexuality of the relationship struck odd notes; he made no effort to be charming or deferential to her, but was bossy and didactic as if she were a school chum who needed firm handling, while she in her turn made no effort to demonstrate her considerable feminine wiles but said exactly what she liked with varying degrees of rudeness. This meant they bickered frequently and energetically, but I had schooled myself to take no notice; I had realized that their two personalities, his so austere, hers so emotional, were locked in the harmony of opposites from which neither of them wished to escape.

When Robert finished speaking, she said to me, "How absolutely vile for you, Johnny," and suddenly as I realized she was genuinely upset I saw beyond her affectations to the sensitive woman I hardly knew.

She turned back to Robert. "What do we do?"

"I'm beginning to wonder. I'm afraid this is all much more hair-raising than I thought it was. How far did you believe Straker, John?"

"I hate to admit it but I believed every word."

Neither of them attempted to disagree with this verdict. Ginevra said, "So we daren't get rid of Straker. And he won't see a doctor. Is he legally certifiable, Robert?"

"Nowhere near. We've no evidence that he's not running the estate properly. Even Straker admits he spends most of the time being as sound as a bell."

"But he's deteriorating," I said. "He's going mad, Robert. This isn't just a nervous breakdown, it's hereditary insanity, I know it is, I know it—"

"Shut up. Pull yourself together. Christ, isn't it enough that Papa's sinking into this unspeakably sordid dotage? If you go round the bend as well I'll bloody well never forgive you!"

But Ginevra's hand slipped into mine and Ginevra's voice said gently, "Take no notice of him. He's only being awful because he's so upset."

"You bloody fool, stop pandering to him!" shouted Robert. "If he persists in clinging to this ridiculous obsession of his, he doesn't need kindness—he needs to be shaken till his bloody teeth rattle!"

Ginevra was furious. "My God, you are a bastard sometimes!"

"Oh, stop carping at me like a stupid bitch!"

"Shut up!" she screamed at him. "Just because you yourself can't stand any bloody emotion—"

"What I can't stand is everyone going to bloody pieces!"

"I'm sorry," I said hastily, jolted out of my fears by this searing marital squabble. "You're right to shout at me, I know I'm being useless—"

"Darling," said Ginevra, "after that scene at Oxmoon the miracle is that you're still conscious." She swung back to face Robert. "Since you're so bloody clever, you bastard," she said, "just you answer me this: if Bobby isn't going stark staring mad—and I agree with Johnny, I think he is—just what the hell do you think's going on?"

"I think the entire trouble's emotional. I suspect he's racked with shame because he's unable to stop himself sliding deeper and deeper into this appalling private life."

"My God, that's plausible," I said in spite of myself. "I hadn't thought of that."

"But why's he compelled to lead this ghastly private life in the first place?" demanded Ginevra. "Isn't that in itself evidence of derangement?"

"Possibly. But not necessarily. He told me once he regarded sex as an escape from facts he couldn't face. Straker now confirms this by saying he resorts to sex when he's upset. This nauseating private life may be evidence that he's disturbed, but it's not, repeat *not*, evidence of hereditary insanity."

"I think it is," I said.

"So do I," said Ginevra.

"If I don't quash this hereditary-insanity nonsense very soon," said Robert, "I swear I'll bloody well go mad myself. For God's sake let's get hold of Gavin Warburton and ask him for a rational, detached, qualified medical opinion on the subject. I think it's time we laid Grandmama's ghost once and for all."

II

"Without examining the patient," said Warburton, "it's impossible for me to give an opinion."

"All right, Gavin," said Robert. "We accept that's your official statement. Now let's talk unofficially. Could this mental disturbance result from a physical degeneration?"

"Yes, but I'd say that was unlikely. It's three years since I attended him after your mother died, but he struck me then as being in first-class health for a man of his age. He doesn't eat, drink or smoke to excess. He's not overweight. He moves well and there's nothing lifeless about his facial muscles so I think we can rule out a premature onset of senility—"

"What about syphilis?" said Robert as I shuddered in my chair.

"Most unlikely. There'd have been other symptoms, and besides the onset of syphilitic madness is somewhat different. There's usually a sort of—"

"Ginette, get John some brandy."

"I'm all right," I said. "I'm all right."

"Are you sure?" said Warburton in concern.

"Take no notice of him," said Robert. "He's merely incorrigibly squeamish about mental illness. Now, to return to my father—could he possibly be suffering from schizophrenia?"

"That's very hard to say," said Warburton evasively.

"Is that hereditary?" I said at once.

"No one knows."

"It's John's theory," said Robert to Warburton, "that my grandmother suffered from a form of hereditary madness with the result that all her descendants are doomed to be locked up one by one."

"Ah, I see." Warburton immediately looked more relaxed. "Well, that's much easier to ascertain. The Home of the Assumption would, of course, have a record of her medical history. I'll talk to de Vestris—he's the doctor in charge there, John—and arrange to see her file. What was your grandmother's first name, when did she go there and when did she die?"

I was unable to speak. Robert said: "Gwyneth. 1882. 1910."

Warburton wrote this information on a prescription pad and the conversation continued, but I did not hear it. I was still holding my glass of brandy but I could no longer drink. I sat motionless on the edge of my chair.

"Johnny?" said Ginevra suddenly.

"I'm all right," I said again. "I'm all right."

"John would like to see this doctor, Gavin," said Robert. "Can you make an appointment?"

"Yes, of course. When?"

"Now, if he's available."

"Let's find out," said Warburton, and headed for the telephone in the hall.

III

I listened to Warburton's side of the telephone call. I think I had some nightmarish fear that he and Dr. de Vestris would conspire to conceal the truth from me, but Warburton merely said the matter was of extreme urgency and asked if we could see him within the hour. De Vestris consented. Warburton then terminated the call, said to me, "Shall we go?" and drove me the fourteen miles to the Home of the Assumption at a brisk pace.

I had never been inside the gates. Only my father had ever visited my grandmother there, and when Ginevra had her nervous breakdown I had been with Bronwen in Cornwall. I had imagined hideous scenes being enacted daily behind that sinister Victorian facade, but as we were admitted by a cheerful nun I found the atmosphere was peaceful. I was hardly in a mood to perceive my surroundings

390

clearly, but there was a not unpleasant smell of furniture polish emanating from the glowing wooden banisters of the staircase, and a tortoiseshell cat was washing its paws absentmindedly in a corner of the hall.

"Here I am again, Sister!" said Warburton. "No peace for the wicked!"

"Oh, Dr. Warburton, the things you say!"

This extraordinarily normal conversation was conducted in cheerful tones and even followed by laughter. I could not quite believe I was listening to it, and when the nun took us down the corridor to Dr. de Vestris' office I could not quite believe either that I was where I was.

I found a little old man with white hair in a pleasant civilized room overlooking a formal garden high above Swansea Bay. He had in his hand several sheets of paper, and he glanced now and then at the fine copperplate writing on the top page as Warburton talked briefly about a family crisis that had made a full knowledge of my grandmother's condition imperative.

"Quite so, quite so," said de Vestris soothingly. He had the air of a benign schoolmaster. "Do sit down, both of you. Yes, I looked up our records as soon as we'd finished speaking, Warburton, although of course I remember the case. Such a nice old lady she was, and always so devoted to her family."

"What was the original diagnosis?" said Warburton.

"An initial derangement caused by an acute nervous crisis followed by periodic bouts of melancholy."

Warburton turned to me. "Nowadays we would call that a nervous breakdown followed by recurring bouts of depression." He added to de Vestris: "Did you have any occasion to amend that diagnosis, sir?"

"Yes, I thought there was no real need for her to remain here. She was one of our very mildest cases, always a little inclined to melancholy, but such a normal old lady on her good days."

"Godwin feared her disorder might be hereditary."

"Good heavens, no!" said de Vestris. He seemed scandalized by the idea. "There was never any question of that."

Warburton stood up and said to me, "I'm going to leave you with Dr. de Vestris because I know you'd like to have a few words with him on your own. I'll be waiting outside in the motor."

I nodded, tried to thank him and failed. The door closed. I was alone with my bridge to the past in that tranquil room high above the bay.

"This is very singular," mused de Vestris, filling a pipe. "The relatives usually prefer to forget—what a pleasant change to find one who wants to remember! You should be encouraged! Now, let me see. I know you're one of the grandchildren, but which one? I can't recall all their names now, but I know there were a lot of them, and Mrs. Godwin liked to show me their photographs. She had a favorite—a very nice-looking little fellow—damn it, what was his name—something quite ordinary—oh yes, Johnny, that was it. He was the one who grew up speaking fluent Welsh. I remember she said none of the others had an ear for it. Yes, little Johnny was a great joy to her, but she swore me to secrecy because she didn't want her daughter-in-law to find out. That was one of her eccentricities, you understand. She was abnormally frightened of her daughter-in-law. One often finds these irrational streaks lingering on in a patient who might otherwise be considered fully recovered.

"When I first came here in 1901 I did suggest that Mrs. Godwin was fit enough to live at home with a nurse to look after her, but Mrs. Godwin at once became so terrified that I realized this wouldn't do, and unfortunately there were no other relatives willing to take her in. I had a conference with her son and daughter-in-law, but they both agreed that it was much better for Mrs. Godwin to remain where she was. They were the most charming couple, I remember, and the young Mrs. Godwin was such a pleasant motherly little figure and spoke so kindly of her mother-in-law that I saw at once how deeply irrational the older Mrs. Godwin was about her. And the son was such a delightful man—and most generous in his donations to the Order which runs the Home—yes, he was a devoted son; he came to see her regularly and always, every Christmas Eve, he would arrive to take her back to Oxmoon.

"Yet there was something odd about their relationship. I tried to coax Mrs. Godwin to talk to me about him because there was no doubt he used to disturb her—although since she always longed to see him and since he always behaved kindly to her when they met, I came to believe she was disturbed not by his visits themselves but by the fact that they reminded her of the past.

"When the melancholy was upon her she used to retreat into the past. She would tell me how happy she had been with—good God, I've forgotten his name—oh yes, Bryn-Davies, and sometimes she'd seem to forget he was dead—she'd talk of him as if he were still alive—but I don't think she really forgot. It was just part of a deliberate effort to blot out the pain-filled present by re-creating a past which was bearable. No matter how difficult the past might have been, it was at least finite and, in a peculiar way, safe. She knew where she was there; she couldn't get lost. But in contrast the present overwhelmed her with its potential for suffering; another of her little eccentricities, you see, was that she feared her daughter-in-law would cut her off entirely from her grandchildren and stop her son's visits. She was so afraid, poor woman, always so afraid of the younger Mrs. Godwin.

"I tried hard to get to the bottom of her trouble, but I'm afraid I never did. What I did find out, however, was that some huge guilt was constantly present in her mind—but the guilt, strangely enough, didn't center around Bryn-Davies. It centered around the husband. Yes, it was the guilt which had driven her beyond the edge of sanity, I'm sure of it, although the exact nature of her guilt was never disclosed to me; she took her secrets with her to the grave, and all I can tell you is that she seemed to believe she was responsible for her husband's death. She said her adultery had driven him to drink and ruined his health, but that couldn't have been the whole story because when I spoke to her son he said his father had been a drunkard long before the advent of Bryn-Davies. 'I was a bad wife,' she used to say, weeping and weeping, poor woman—I can see her now—'I was wicked,' she would say, 'I yielded to evil, I could have stopped but I went on and now I'm paying and paying forever.' She was very Welsh, you know, very emo-

392

tional.... But of course, I was forgetting, you knew her, you're one of the grand-sons.

"In the end I decided that the best way to exorcise this guilt over the adultery was to enlist the aid of her son—such a delightful fellow he was!—and I suggested that it might help her if he were to tell her clearly that he forgave her for her past wrongs. 'Yes, of course,' he said, charming as ever, but do you know, he never did. That was when I realized what a strange relationship they had. There was unquestionably love on both sides, but it was crippled by a mutual revulsion. I suspect he must have turned against Bryn-Davies in the end... and of course it's always the children who suffer, isn't it, when the parents go off the rails.

"Well, I must stop rambling but the case interested me and stuck in my memory. After all, she was Mrs. Godwin of Oxmoon, wasn't she, and even though the great scandal took place twenty years before I met her, people still talked of it in Gower—well, look at us, talking of it today! The past doesn't die so easily some-times, does it, and I can see your grandmother as if it were yesterday, such a nice ordinary old lady; I see her sticking those photographs of her grandchildren in her album and turning page after page after page.... Yes, she loved those grand-children—but I keep forgetting, you're one of them, aren't you? Now, which one would you be? And exactly what can I tell you that will be of help?"

IV

It was almost ten by the time I reached Little Oxmoon again, but although Robert was in bed he was not asleep. Ginevra was sitting with him as they waited for me to return.

"It's all right," I said as I entered the room.

"Thank God," said Robert. "What did I tell you? I always knew it was rubbish to assume they were suffering from the same malaise!"

"You were wrong. The malaise was the same."

Both he and Ginevra boggled at me. I drew up a chair and sank down on it. I felt exhausted.

"But for God's sake!" said Robert, outraged by the possibility that he had drawn the wrong deductions from the facts. "What's the malaise?"

"Guilt."

They boggled at me again. "What the devil do you mean?" demanded Robert, but I saw that Ginevra had understood. I had noticed by that time that Robert's broad knowledge of human nature was essentially academic, whereas Ginevra's intuitive sensitivity gave her the power to comprehend complex emotional truths which lay beyond the reach of his rational analysis. Robert was capable of per-ceiving intellectually that I was unbalanced on the subject of my grandmother and that I had to be weaned from my melodramatic vision in order to be cured.

393

But it was Ginevra who had the intuition to perceive the exact dimensions of my cure when it came.

"Guilt," she said. "Of course. They both committed murder."

Robert was still outraged by this solution which he saw as irrational. "But none of the murderers I ever knew ever went round the bend years after the event!"

"Darling," said Ginevra, "the murderers you knew were either hanged or locked up or allowed to vanish into the blue. You've had absolutely no experience of what happens to people when they've been carrying a huge burden of guilt for years."

"Obviously not all murderers react in this way, Robert," I said to pacify him. "But the point is that this mother and this son, who were no doubt emotionally similar, appear to break down in the same way when under stress."

"Exactly," said Ginevra. "It's not murder itself that's important here, Robert— any serious wrongdoing would have the same effect. It's the guilt they can't endure."

"So the thesis is that the malaise is guilt and that Papa inherited his mother's emotional inability to survive it—and now I suppose you'll say the madness is hereditary after all!" said Robert, more outraged than ever.

"I could say that, certainly," I said, "but the point is that this particular madness doesn't have to be inherited, Robert. What I have to do to ensure my sanity is to avoid the bad decisions which would later drive me out of my mind with guilt— and that means the choice between sanity and insanity will always be mine; it means I'm not at the mercy of an uncontrollable heredity, I'm not strapped to the Wheel of Fortune with no possibility of escape—"

"May I interrupt this emotional monologue," said Robert, "to inquire if our parents and our grandmother can now be regarded as forgivable?"

I looked at my grand opera but found the stage was in darkness.

"No more fiends?" said Robert. "No more villains busily generating evil?"

"No." I found myself looking at a different stage. "It's not that kind of story. You were right at least about that, Robert." I thought with love and pity of my sad lonely grandmother turning the pages of her photograph albums. I thought with love and pity of my young parents struggling to survive that tragedy which had haunted them. And I knew that the need to blame someone for my past unhappiness was no more. One could blame evil people for evil deeds but not tortured people for tragic decisions; tortured people deserved only compassion, and the compassion, long witheld, was now streaming through my mind. The weight of my old terror was lifted; the burden of my anger was destroyed, and it was at that moment, as I triumphed at last over the past which had so often and so fatally triumphed over me, that I was able to say simply in judgment: "They were just three ordinary people who failed to draw the line."

V

Later, after we had left Robert to sleep, I said, "Ginevra, there's something I want to ask you. Straker gave me some advice today and I have a terrible feeling that it may be sound; she says that while I'm waiting for my divorce I should pretend Bronwen's in my employment—for Bronwen's sake, of course, not for mine. She's right, isn't she?"

"Ghastly Straker!" said Ginevra. "I'm afraid she is. How mortifying!"

"I'm going to have to get rid of Nanny. I suppose I could say that Bronwen's taken her place."

"Oh, darling, what a good idea! That's the perfect solution!"

"Bronwen's not going to like it."

"Why not?"

"It's a lie. And we want to live in the truth."

"But darling, it won't be a lie! She'll be there at Penhale Manor looking after your children, just as a nanny should!"

"Yes," I said, "and Straker's there at Oxmoon, managing the house just as a housekeeper should."

"But that situation's utterly different!"

"Yes," I said, "of course. But it's the same lie, isn't it?" And leaving the hall, I went out into the night.

VI

"I'd rather live with you without pretense," said Bronwen.

"Yes. That's what I want too. But there are cogent reasons against it."

"The children?"

"The children, certainly. But my main concern is for you. I don't know how long it'll take to get this divorce. Obviously nothing can be done until after the child is born, but even then . . . Constance may be stubborn."

She looked away.

It was after midnight, and we were sitting in the little front parlor of the Home Farm on a small uncomfortable sofa. Bronwen's hair was loose. As I caressed her it shone fierily in the candlelight.

"Then there's my father," I said. "He's literally ill with worry. If he knew I was going to keep up appearances and behave according to his rules he'd feel better. I do want to live in the truth, you must believe that, but I don't want to hurt people."

She made up her mind. "No. Neither do I. Hurting people can never be right." She pushed back her hair and turned to face me again. "But we must be truthful with each other in private," she said. "You must never lie to me again."

I promised I never would. She was satisfied, and blowing out the candle I took her in my arms.

VII

"He's very poorly indeed today, dear," said Mrs. Straker. "He's searching the attics, although God knows what he's looking for. What did Robert say about my salary—or did you have second thoughts and decide to take advantage of my offer about the will?"

"I told him. We'll pay you. But I'll discuss that later," I said, detesting her, and headed for the attics in search of my father.

The top floor of Oxmoon consisted of a chain of rooms crammed with Godwin possessions which ranged from family treasures to junk. Early poverty had encouraged my parents to hoard anything of value, but the tradition of accumulation had preceded my father's rule and there were even tin trunks marked R. CLIFFORD, which had been the name of Robert Godwin the Renovator before he had prised his way into the inheritance of his cousin the imbecile. But my father was not wandering among the relics of the eighteenth century. I found him seated by a collection of old books in the room where my grandmother's portrait was kept under a dust sheet. When he saw me he rubbed his eyes as if making a desperate attempt to concentrate.

"Are you looking for something, Papa? Can I help you?"

He shook his head. I saw then that he was too afraid to speak in case he mixed up past and present, and I found his awareness of his condition far more terrible than any ignorance would have been. My last doubts about the pretense of employing Bronwen dissolved. Putting him out of his agony, I promised I would stick to his rules.

After he had shed a tear or two of relief he said, "Thank God you've come to your senses. I really thought you might marry her, and of course that would never do."

I was silent. The last thing I wanted was to upset him all over again. I told myself there would be time enough to face that crisis when I had my divorce.

My father began to stack the books nearby into a neat pile, and as he worked I saw they were not books at all but old photograph albums. I thought of my grandmother, and suddenly before I could stop myself, I pulled the dust sheet from her portrait.

"I suppose she called Bryn-Davies the bailiff," I said, "when he moved to Oxmoon."

"No, she never bothered. Awful. I was so ashamed."

I thought of Dr. de Vestris saying, "It's always the children who suffer, isn't it, when the parents go off the rails."

A coldness gripped me. Covering the portrait I turned away once more from my grandmother and in my mind drew the line which would separate me from her.

But the line seemed very fragile.

"Hope you won't be too bored living at the Manor," said my father unexpectedly, providing a more than welcome diversion, and when I faced him I saw that although he still looked ill with exhaustion, the lines of strain seemed less pronounced. His voice was normal. Sanity had apparently been regained.

"I shall be all right."

"Nothing much for you to do there." My father had been keeping an eye on the estate for me since Edmund's marriage. "It would be a full-time occupation for Edmund, of course, but not for someone like you."

"I'm not ambitious, not anymore."

My father gave a short laugh and said, "That's because all you can think about at the moment is the woman. But you'll feel differently later."

"Perhaps. But I do have my lands in Herefordshire. I'm sure I can keep myself busy."

"I can't change my mind about Oxmoon, John."

"I know. But I'm not interested in Oxmoon anymore. I just want to live quietly with Bronwen at Penhale Manor."

"The pond's too small, John. You're a big fish."

"Then I'll have to find a bigger pond eventually, won't I?"

"That's what I'm afraid of," said my father.

At once I turned to face him. "There's no need to treat me as a fanatic who would stop at nothing."

"No? You're behaving like one—walking out on your pregnant wife, smashing up your home, stopping at nothing to get that woman—"

"That's different."

"Is it? I don't see much difference. If you stop at nothing to get a woman, why shouldn't you stop at nothing to get an estate?"

"Because you stopped at nothing to get an estate, Papa, and I've seen what that's done to you. No, thank you! I'm not playing my cards as you played yours!"

He broke down again. There was a long and distressing interval during which he clung to my hand and said how glad he would be to have me living nearby but how frightened he was in case he became old and feeble and allowed me to persuade him to cheat Robert.

"...and then I'll be damned utterly," he said, crying again. "This is my one chance for redemption, my one chance to right a terrible wrong."

"I understand. But you're safe, Papa—I'd never interfere with your affairs—I'd draw the line."

Or would I?

Yes, of course I would. I'd draw the line to stop myself ending up like my grandmother. But supposing...supposing I drew the line but the line became...eroded by circumstances beyond my control? Or supposing I drew the line but it became my moral duty to rub it out?

397

The nightmares burgeoned.

Chaos multiplied.

In terror I blotted the entire subject from my mind.

VIII

Meanwhile the chaos was streaming into my life as the result of the wrong line I had drawn when I had married Constance.

The moment I returned to London to resume the ordeal of winding up my life there, Marian's governess gave notice, and although I made no attempt to detain her, I was becoming very worried about Marian who had now lost her stepmother, her nanny and her governess in rapid succession. Nanny too had given notice as a gesture of protest, but she had expected me to beg her to stay, and my immediate acceptance coupled with the necessary glowing reference had shocked her to the core.

"How jolly awkward!" said Daphne unsurprised when I told her of the governess's decision. "Simply too diffy for words, my dear." She then told me that if Bronwen were to be the new nanny I would never find a governess who would stay. "Governesses can't bear being upstaged by nannies, John. It's one of the horrid facts of nursery life."

When I remained silent, forcing myself to face this unpalatable truth, Daphne said impulsively, "John, do let Marian stay here with Elizabeth! Harry'll be all right—he can share Kester's tutor, and so long as he has you perhaps he won't need a mother so much as Marian does, but Marian...Darling, don't be livid with me, you know I'm on your side, but what *is* it going to be like for Marian with your working-class mistress at Penhale Manor? Marian's nearly nine now, and she needs—"

"What Marian needs," I said, "is her father, working-class mistress or no working-class mistress, and I'm not going to abandon her by palming her off on you. She's coming to Penhale and that's my last word on the subject."

"I doubt if it'll be Marian's," said Daphne drily, and she was right. Marian, who was great friends with Elizabeth and who liked her cousin's nanny and governess, took a poor view of yet another upheaval in her small world and stormy scenes inevitably followed. These were exacerbated by the fact that Daphne, the nanny and the governess all secretly sympathized with Marian and thought I was behaving irresponsibly. At that point I knew Marian had to be removed as soon as possible, so after Ginevra had engaged the domestic staff I made a rapid visit to the Manor to install Bronwen and her children and then returned to London to tackle the nightmare of collecting my children from a home neither of them wanted to leave.

Marian became hysterical. Elizabeth became hysterical. Daphne was no use at all. I suddenly decided I disliked Daphne very much and could not imagine why Lion had married her. In my distress I needed someone to blame for this harrowing episode, and Daphne filled the role of scapegoat to perfection.

I had always thought with what I now classified as ignorant conceit that I was a good father, but at this point I found out that parenthood involved rather more than reading bedtime stories, patting little heads and distributing pocket money on Saturday mornings. I was alone with my children on the train to Swansea. There was neither a nanny nor a governess to cushion me from the realities of nursery life. Marian sobbed and screamed and sulked. Harry spent his time either picking fights with her or else misbehaving in some other way in order to gain my attention. Twice I restrained myself from spanking him but on the third occasion I did not, and afterwards I was as miserable as he was. I felt a complete failure as a parent.

My caretaker Willis, now restored to his former position as head gardener, met us in the car at Swansea, but at once the children were fighting again, this time for the honor of sitting on my lap. More tears and screams ensued. Willis looked shocked. I was exhausted. I had begun to think the journey would never end but at last we reached the Manor and Bronwen came out into the drive to meet us.

To this day I cannot recall what she said. But I can see the children looking at her, looking and remembering, and I knew she was reminding them of that other time when their mother had been alive. Their tearstained grubby little faces became smooth and still. Rhiannon and Dafydd were in the hall but I did not wait to see the reunion; I thought Bronwen could manage better without me, so I retired to my study and mixed myself a very dark whisky-and-soda.

A week later, just as I was thinking with relief that my home life was stable enough to permit me at least to attempt to find a new governess, I returned from a visit to Swansea to find that all my new domestic staff wanted to give notice.

IX

I made no effort to detain them. Employers do themselves no favor when they cringe and crawl before their servants, and I knew the only answer was to start afresh. The worst part of the disaster, however, was not the dislocation of life at the Manor but Bronwen's deep distress.

"It was because we shared the bedroom openly," she said. She was trying not to cry. "I overheard some remarks about it. I should have had my own room by the nurseries."

I had known that to preserve the proprieties fully, Bronwen should have had her own room, but the prospect of her position at the Manor being an exact mirror image of Milly Straker's position at Oxmoon was so repulsive to me that I had found this final hypocrisy intolerable. Now I realized that I had been stupid but at the same time I found myself unable to make more than a minor compromise.

"We'll set aside the room," I said, "but I'm damned if you're ever going to use it. We'll go to bed together in my room and wake up together in my room, just as if we were married, and I won't tolerate anything else."

"But no staff will stay—how will we manage..." She was crying, saying how frightened she was in case I already regretted my decision to live with her.

I stopped her tears. Then when I was sure she was convinced I had no regrets I told her not to worry, swallowed every ounce of my very considerable pride and went begging to Milly Straker.

X

She was very good about it. It would have been so easy for her to be smug, savoring my humiliation, but she was brisk and businesslike.

"Yes, I thought Mrs. Robert was making a mistake engaging good-quality servants," she said flatly. "I'm surprised they even stayed as long as a week. Never mind, dear, I'll talk to the agency I use in Swansea and get you a cook and a couple of maids—but what you really need is the right housekeeper, someone who'll flog everyone into shape and turn a blind eye to your sleeping arrangements. Let me telephone my friends in London and see what's going in the waifs-and-strays department. Whoever they suggest won't have references, but I'll make sure she's dead straight about money."

"I..." It was hard to find the right words. "She must be a decent woman. I couldn't possibly consider employing anyone who wasn't."

"Don't worry, dear, the victims of this world are usually a lot more decent than those who play their cards right. I'll see if I can find some able respectable woman whose employer asked her to be a bed warmer and then ended up with cold feet. After a dismissal with no references and a visit to the nearest back-street abortionist, a woman like that would think Penhale Manor was paradise and you were the Angel Gabriel."

I remained very worried but when Mrs. Wells arrived for her interview I found my worries were at an end. Good-looking but meticulously refined in her manner she had for the past five years been employed in a home where the wife was an invalid, and Mrs. Wells, having enjoyed a large amount of autonomy in consequence, was more than capable of taking sole charge of the household. This was exactly what I wanted. I engaged her.

"What did she do?" I said afterwards to Mrs. Straker. I despised myself for my curiosity, but I felt I ought to find out. "Was it the employer?"

"No, dear: his seventeen-year-old son, but keep Mabel away from hotheaded young men and you'll have no trouble at all; quite the reverse. I'm sure she'll suit very well."

For the next two weeks Mrs. Straker called daily at the Manor to make sure the new staff were behaving themselves. Bronwen said the servants used to tremble in their shoes, but I noticed the standard of my domestic comfort was rising. Mrs.

Wells, established in her authority by Mrs. Straker, proved both capable and pleasant, treating Bronwen and me exactly as if we were married. Mrs. Straker had ruled that any servant who was rude to Bronwen was to be dismissed on the spot. Bronwen thought she was wonderful.

"She's been very kind to me, Johnny."

"She mistakenly thinks you need her compassion." I found I loathed Mrs. Straker all the more now that I was so absolutely in her debt, and I did not like being thwarted in my loathing by evidence that she could be kind.

However our bizarre alliance continued and was even strengthened when Thomas arrived home for the summer holidays and declared he had no intention of returning to Harrow in the autumn. This led to rows at Oxmoon, but my father, who always prided himself on his ability to manage children, evidently found himself unable to ask me for help. It was Mrs. Straker who cornered me during one of my visits and told me what was going on.

"Bobby's getting upset again," she said. "It's no good expecting him to cope with a boy of seventeen, he's too old and he hasn't the stamina to solve the problem—and Thomas *is* a problem, make no mistake about that. He might have a nice nature, but who can tell? He spends all his time being bloody-minded. I'm fed up with him."

I felt the last thing I needed at that moment in my life was a bloody-minded adolescent, but I said I would do what I could. Thomas was out at that time but I left a note asking him to call, and rather to my surprise he rode over to the Manor that same evening and tramped truculently into my study for his audience.

XI

"Of course I know why you want to see me," said Thomas, flinging himself down in the best armchair and swinging his feet insolently onto my desk. "You've heard I'm refusing to go back for a final year at that bloody school and you want to give me some bloody lecture about the glories of education."

"Oh? Then let me set your mind at rest; I don't give lectures, bloody or otherwise. I say, would you mind very much if you took your feet off my desk? Try the fender; it's a far more comfortable height. . . . Thanks."

"I've had enough of school. I think education's a load of balls."

"I'm sure many people would agree with you. Too bad Papa isn't one of them. Cigarette?"

He grabbed the cigarette with such alacrity that he nearly pulled the case out of my hand. With compassion, I realized he was nervous, and in the knowledge that he was vulnerable I looked at him more closely. He was as tall as I was by that time but built differently. He was broader, heavier, more like my mother's side of the family than my father's, and he had a square, mulish jaw which reminded me suddenly of frightful Aunt Ethel in Staffordshire.

"Well," I said when our cigarettes were alight, "what do you plan to do now?"

"Raise hell, get drunk and fuck every woman in sight."

"Oh yes? Well, I agree that takes care of the nights. But what are you going to do during the day?"

Thomas immediately assumed his most belligerent expression. "Why do you want to know?"

"Sheer mindless curiosity."

"What are you after?"

"Why do I have to be 'after' anything?"

"Most people are," said Thomas, and I heard an echo of Milly Straker's cynicism in his pathetic attempt to appear worldly.

"I'm not most people, I'm your brother and I'm sorry that you and Papa should be at loggerheads. Is there anything I can do to help?"

"How about minding your own bloody business?"

"Certainly—if that's what you really want."

There was a silence while we smoked and eyed each other. Then in a gust of embarrassment Thomas stubbed out his cigarette. "Well, if that's all you want to say I'll be off. Unless you intend to offer me a drink."

"No. Just help."

"But what do you get out of helping me?"

"Abuse and bad language, apparently." I stood up and opened the door of the study. "Goodbye, Thomas."

He hesitated. He looked very young, and suddenly I was reminded of the scene in the summerhouse after my mother's death when he had been a frightened fourteen-year-old whose world had collapsed overnight.

I closed the door again. "What's it really like at Oxmoon," I said abruptly, "with Papa and Milly Straker? And how do you think you'll get on living there all the year round in their company?"

"Mind your own bloody business," said Thomas, and elbowed his way past me into the hall.

"Well, when you're ready to talk," I shouted after him, "remember that I'm always ready to listen!"

But the front door slammed in my face.

XII

Ten weeks later in October I received a letter from Constance, and as I ripped open the envelope at the breakfast table I found myself praying that after the news I expected, I would find the promise of a divorce.

My darling John, Constance had written, *our daughter was born yesterday at six o'clock in the morning and weighs exactly seven pounds. As we agreed earlier, she will be called Francesca Constance unless I hear from you to the contrary.*

Of course you may see her whenever you wish. Indeed you may see me whenever

you wish, and perhaps when you see the baby, who is so lovely and so perfect, you
will realize that divorce is not the answer for us, either now or at any other time.

Ever your loving and devoted wife, CONSTANCE.

I looked up. At the other end of the table, Bronwen was watching me. Around us the children were chattering, Marian and Rhiannon on one side, Harry and Dafydd on the other and the baby in his little portable cot by the window. It was a Saturday morning and the children, free from lessons, were in good spirits.

"...and turtles live to be three hundred years old..."

"...and it's called a six-shooter because..."

"...although as I said to my governess, how do they know turtles live for •hundreds of years when no one can live long enough to watch them?...What's the matter, Papa?"

Dafydd and Harry paused in their discussion of guns. All eyes were turned in my direction.

"Nothing," I said. I left the room. A second later I realized this had been the wrong thing to do, but I could not make myself go back. I was still hesitating when Bronwen slipped out of the room to join me.

"Is the baby all right?" she said rapidly.

"Yes." I handed her the letter. As she read it the color faded from her face until the freckles stood out starkly on the bridge of her nose. Handing the letter back she said, "Would you like me to tell the children?"

"No. I must."

We went back into the room. Bronwen picked up the baby, said briskly, "Rhiannon—Dafydd—I want to talk to you" and led the way out again into the hall.

Her children trooped obediently after her, but although Marian tried to follow I held out my hand.

"Wait, Marian, I want to tell you about the baby."

"What baby? Oh, that one. Did it come?"

"Yes. It's a girl. She's going to be called Francesca."

"What a perfectly frightful name," said Marian, "but never mind; I shan't see her so what does it matter?"

She shook off my hand and headed for the door.

"Marian—"

The door slammed. I was reminded of Thomas. I thought again of Dr. de Vestris saying what happened when parents went off the rails, and for a second my blood ran cold.

"The baby won't make any difference, will it?" said Harry suspiciously. "I don't want to go back to London and live with Constance. I want to stay here with Bronwen and the piano." The thought of the piano cheered him. He wriggled off his chair and ran to the door. "I'm going to have my practice now," he said over his shoulder, and disappeared. I smiled, mercifully diverted from the memory of Dr. de Vestris, but then sighed at the thought of the music. Urged on by Bronwen I now allowed Harry to play the piano daily, though for no more than half an hour; I had no wish to spoil his fun but without a time limit he would have wasted all day at the keys.

I thought briefly of Blanche playing the piano, but Blanche seemed to have existed so long ago that I could not connect her with my present life. I thought of Constance and shuddered, though whether with rage, guilt, grief or shame I hardly knew. Leaving the table I went upstairs to Marian's room. Bronwen looked up as I came in.

"I was promising that of course you'll take her to visit Constance and the baby," she said, "but she tells me she doesn't want to go."

"I just want to forget it all," wept Marian as I sat down on the bed and put my arm around her. "If I remember it'll only make me miserable, and I can't bear being miserable anymore. . . ." Sobs overwhelmed her, and when I pressed her closer she clung to me. Bronwen began to tiptoe towards the door, but I motioned her to stay. "I want Mama," whispered Marian. "Every night I ask God to make her come back to life, like Lazarus, but He doesn't listen, I pray and pray but nothing happens."

"Marian. . ." I tried and failed to frame a response, but Bronwen said in the heavily accented English which sounded so soothing, "I was wondering if you thought of her often now that you're back in the house where she used to be. I think of her often too. She may not be here herself anymore, but the memory's here, isn't it, and memories are so precious, such a comfort, because no one can take them away from you, and although she's dead yet in a way she's still alive, alive in your mind, and that's how God can bring her back for you. And although that's not as good as having her here alive and well, it helps to look across at the past, doesn't it, to look at her and know that she'll be there always in your memory to be a comfort to you when you want to remember."

Marian rubbed her eyes and gave several little gasps as if the sobbing had left her out of breath. I found a handkerchief for her, and at last she whispered to Bronwen, "Do you really think of her?"

"Oh yes, she was such a lovely lady, and so kind to me. When she was alive I wished that there was something I could do to repay her for her kindness, and that's why I was so pleased when Papa suggested I should look after you and Harry. It was something I could do for her, a payment of the debt, and that made me happy."

Marian thought about this.

"We must talk about her," said Bronwen. "It's such a waste to shut away precious memories and never speak of them. We'll talk about her and by talking we'll bring her back to you and then you'll feel better."

Marian gave another little gasp and blew her nose before turning to me. "Is Bronwen here forever? Or might you fall in love with someone else, do you think, and leave her as you left Constance?"

"No, I could never leave Bronwen. Impossible. Out of the question."

I felt her relax in my arms. "I don't want anyone else going away," she whispered to me.

I kissed her and said, "Everything's going to be all right." But as I spoke I thought of Constance, alone with her stubborn pride in London, and I knew the happy ending I was promising Marian was still far beyond my reach.

XIII

Three days later I journeyed to London and bought a toy rabbit at Selfridges. At the Carlton Club I consumed a whisky-and-soda before telephoning Constance.

"It was thoughtful of you to call," she said, "but there's no need for you ever to make an appointment to come here. This is your home and you can come and go entirely as you please."

I consumed a second whisky, this time without soda, and took a taxi to Chester Square.

Constance should no doubt still have been in bed but she had put on the emerald-green negligée which she knew I liked and had arranged herself not unattractively on the drawing-room sofa. I found that this pathetic attempt to look her best made me feel angry. I was too angry to analyze the anger, but I hated myself for giving way to it. Sheer misery overwhelmed me. I felt as if my consciousness were being hacked to pieces with a hatchet.

Giving her the carnations which I had forced myself to buy, I inquired formally after her health.

"I'm better now," she said, "but it was rough. I hope Teddy has an easier time."

"How is she?"

"Fine. But longing for it to be over." She sniffed the carnations. "Will you ring the bell? These ought to be put in water right away."

I did as she asked before departing for the nurseries.

It seemed a long way there but that was because I had to pause on the landing until I felt calmer. When I arrived the new nanny gave me a hostile stare but I got rid of her and moved to the cot.

The baby was so new that it still had a red face. Swathed in clouds of white linen and lace, it lay sound asleep, oblivious to luxury, in its expensive little resting place. Touching its small bald head with my index finger, I remembered Evan as I had first seen him in his wooden box on wheels, and I thought of my new daughter growing up to envy him. No money could ease emotional poverty. No material comfort could provide a substitute for an absent father.

I undid the toy rabbit from its gay wrapping, tucked it into the cot and turned away, but I was in such a state of grief and shame that I could not remember where I was. But when I looked back at the cot memory returned to me. I was on the far side of the line I had failed to draw when I had married Constance in the pursuit of avarice and ambition. I had wronged Bronwen, wronged Constance, and now I was wronging my child but there was no way back. The line could not be recrossed even in the event of a divorce. Constance and the child would still exist, and nothing could fully make amends to them for what I had done.

After a long while I reentered the drawing room and found Constance was still busy with the carnations; the arrangement was looking glacially formal.

"Isn't she lovely?"

405

I nodded. Constance offered me a drink but I declined. "I'm afraid I must be on my way."

"But you'll come again soon? Do bring Harry and Marian—I'd love to see them!"

"I'll have to write to you about it."

"Remember," she said, "that everything will always be waiting for you here. You can come back at any time."

"It's never going to happen, Constance."

"'Never' is a long time, isn't it? I'm going to go on hoping."

There was nothing left to say.

I walked out.

XIV

"Was it awful?" said Bronwen.

"Yes. Bloody awful. I just want to go to bed and forget about it."

We went to bed and for a while I did forget, but even when I was physically exhausted I was unable to sleep. Eventually Bronwen lit a candle and said, "Talk to me."

"I can't."

"You must. You know what happens when you can't talk. You get all muddled and lie to yourself and end up doing something which makes you and everyone else miserable."

This was such an accurate description of my talent for making a mess of my life that I could only groan and bury my face in the pillow, but finally I managed to say, "I despise myself, how could I have married that woman, how could I have turned my back on you, how could I have fathered that child, I feel as if I'm split in two, half of me wants to lead a good decent life but the other half does these terrible things, and supposing the other half wins? It's not impossible. I've known from childhood, ever since I found out the truth about my grandmother and my parents, that absolutely anyone is capable of absolutely anything—"

"Yes," said Bronwen. "Absolutely anyone is capable of absolutely anything. *But not everyone has to do it.*"

"I know, I know, one draws the line, but supposing I draw the wrong line again, supposing I get in a muddle about what's right—I'm so weak, so contemptible, I've done such terrible things, how I can trust myself, I don't, I can't—"

"I trust you. I agree you've done dreadful things, but now you're trying to do what's right, you're being honest and truthful and brave, and so long as you're honest and truthful you can't get in a mess by living a lie, and so long as you're brave you can't despise yourself for cowardice, and so long as you're all those things you'll be strong enough to draw those lines, as the English say so strangely when all they mean is choosing the right circle to live in, and once the lines are drawn you'll be the man you want to be and the man I know you are, and you'll be safe."

I wanted to make love to her again, but I was too exhausted and I collapsed into her arms. After a long time I heard myself say, "My father thinks I still want Oxmoon. Probably Robert thinks I still want Oxmoon. Sometimes even *I* think I still want Oxmoon—oh, God, I'm in such a muddle still; I don't want Oxmoon anymore, I truly don't, I'm fully satisfied just to live here with you, but sometimes I can help thinking—"

"Of course you covet it now and then. That's human. You covet it like I used to covet my lady in Cardiff's best teapot. But I wouldn't have stolen it. That would have been wrong."

"But supposing Robert thinks—"

"You don't lie to him, do you?"

"No, I told him how Straker tried to bribe me."

"Then you're safe. *Don't start lying to Robert.* So long as you're truthful with him you'll be safe."

"How can you be so sure?"

"Distrust grows out of lies. Wrongdoing grows out of distrust. Tragedy grows out of wrongdoing. But out of honesty grows love and love's so powerful, it'll be like a suit of armor, protecting Robert, protecting you."

"That ought to be true, but *is* it true? It all sounds vaguely religious but I can't believe in God, not after the war—"

"I never believed in God so long as I thought of Him as a person," said Bronwen. "To me He was like my father who'd gone away and couldn't help me. But then I stopped saying 'He' and said 'It,' and suddenly everything seemed simple. God's magic, that's all. It's all the things we can't see or explain. It's the rhythm of life. It's the circle of time."

"That reminds me of Robert talking about Boethius and the Wheel of Fortune," I said, and I began to tell her about that ancient theory of life which had become so popular in the Middle Ages. "I never studied Boethius," I said, "but when I was reading French and German up at Oxford I came across the work of Peter von Kastl and Jean de Meung who were both influenced by him..." And as I talked on about the Wheel of Fortune revolving in its endless cycle, I began at last to feel calmer.

"But that sounds as if people have no power to leave the wheel," said Bronwen, "and I think they have. I think there are many wheels, and if you have the will you can move from one to another."

"That's what I need to believe too but supposing free will is an illusion? For instance, take Robert's view: he says that although we're all strapped to the Wheel of Fortune, Fortune herself offers us choices to determine our fate. Now, that sounds fine but supposing those choices themselves are predetermined by forces beyond our control?"

"That's a horrible idea!"

"Horrible, yes—I've always detested and feared the concept of predestination.

However I have a feeling Boethius solved the problem, although I can't remember how he did it."

This time I did manage to make love to her again. Then having proved that renewal could follow exhaustion on our own private wheel of fortune, I found my courage returning and knew I could discard my despair and struggle on.

XV

I had no respite. The chaos continued but by this time I had realized that a section of my life would be in chaos indefinitely, so I was becoming resigned to the hard core of misery in my mind. My father telephoned with the news that Edmund had a son. Letters started to arrive from Constance about the possibility of a double christening. The long aftermath of my disastrous marriage seemed about to overwhelm me again, but before I could give way a second time to despair I was diverted by a crisis at Oxmoon.

It was by that time early November, and when the news of the crisis reached me I had just returned from fetching Marian from her private school in Swansea. Once Daphne's opinion that no respectable governess would remain long at the Manor had been confirmed, I had had no difficulty convincing myself that it would be good for Marian to go to school, but as Bronwen had refused my offer that her children too should be privately educated, Rhiannon and Dafydd continued to attend school in the village. Marian, not unnaturally, wanted to go there too, and when I refused I found myself involved in inevitably distasteful explanations. There was no row, since Marian quickly accepted the fact that ladies never attended the village primary school, but I foresaw the class system pushing its long cruel bayonets deep into my home and in time impaling us all.

"We must give all the children the same education," I said to Bronwen stubbornly, but she was equally stubborn in disagreeing.

"I don't want my children given airs and graces and being taught to look down on their own class," she said. "It wouldn't make them happy. Dafydd wants to be a motor mechanic, not a gentleman, and if Rhiannon gets a lady's education she'll end up too good for the boys of her own class and not good enough for the boys who are better."

There was undoubtedly much truth in this observation, but I foresaw the situation deteriorating as the children became aware of their differences. Marian was too aware of them already. I had that very afternoon in the car been obliged to reprove her for making a snobbish criticism of Rhiannon.

On our arrival home Marian dashed off to the dining room where everyone was having tea and I went to the cloakroom to hang up my coat and hat. I had just returned to the hall when I was startled by a thunderous battering on the front door.

It was Thomas, wearing his best livid expression. I knew at once he was very upset.

"Hullo," I said swiftly. "What's the trouble?"

"It's the old bugger."

I steered him into my study, but just as I was opening my mouth to reprove him for referring to our father so disrespectfully he collapsed into the nearest armchair as if it were a sanctuary and I realized a reproof would be inappropriate. His mouth was trembling. He managed to tuck it down at the corners as usual, but when he spoke his voice was unsteady.

"Got a gasper, old boy?"

I gave him a cigarette. "What's happened?"

Thomas inhaled deeply and managed to say in a casual voice: "The old bugger's gone crazy. Well, of course he's been gaga off and on for ages, we all know that, but this is worse, this is the last straw, this is absolutely bloody..." He faltered to a halt.

"What happened?"

"We had a row about the estate. The old bugger won't let me do anything. Well, I didn't mind loafing around for a time while I recovered from bloody school, but I'm bored now and I want to do something so I asked him a month ago if he could teach me how to run the estate, and he said no, I was too young and I ought to be at school. So we had a row and I went off to Daxworth and learned about cows instead, but I got a bit bored because I don't think they're really my kind of animal, so I thought I'd get interested in estate management again, and this afternoon when Papa was out I sneaked into the library and had a look at the books—"

"—and he caught you red-handed."

"Yes. Christ, he was bloody angry."

"Well, I suppose he had a right to be angry since you were prying among his private papers, but on the other hand I'm surprised he wasn't glad to see how keen you are to learn." I tried to stop myself wondering why my father should be so abnormally sensitive about anyone seeing the accounts. "What happened next?"

Thomas did not answer immediately. His blue eyes reflected complex emotions; anger and resentment were mingling with some deep distress, and as I watched I saw the distress become uppermost in his mind.

"Out with it, Thomas. You'll feel better once you've told me."

But still he was silent, struggling with his feelings. At last he muttered, "Don't want to be disloyal."

I was touched by this because I saw how fond he was of his father, but I was also disturbed and to my dismay I realized I was in the middle of an interview that was far more crucial than I desired.

"There's no question of disloyalty, Thomas," I said quickly. "He's my father as well as yours and I know very well he's subject to mental disturbances. What did he do? Did he hit you?"

"No. God, I wish he had. I wouldn't have minded that. But he didn't. He yelled at me and then—suddenly—he went to pieces. He said, 'I can't manage you anymore,' and he went out into the hall and shouted for Mama."

There was a silence. Thomas bit his lip, pouted but finally tucked his mouth down at the corners again. "Silly old bugger," he muttered fiercely. "I felt so ashamed for him."

"I'd have been both shocked and frightened," I said at once, implying that shock and fear were permissible emotions in the circumstances. "What did you do next?"

"Nothing. I was too... well, I just stayed where I was. Then Milly came, but he said he wanted his wife, not the parlormaid."

"Christ. How did Milly cope?"

"She said, 'Very well, Mr. Godwin, but why don't you sit down for a minute while I fetch you a little glass of champagne.' Then there was an awful silence, and just when I thought I was going to be sick, Papa said, 'Milly' and burst into tears. Oh God, John, it was so absolutely *bloody*—"

"Bloody, yes. Did you manage to escape then?"

"No, Milly told me to help her take him upstairs. He was shaking and crying and could hardly stand, but we got him up to his room somehow without the servants seeing. Then Milly said to me, 'Go out of the house for an hour—*go right out.*' She was very fierce about it so I went downstairs but I was sick in the cloakroom and the vomit got over my shirt so I went upstairs to change and then I heard noises going on in the bedroom, awful noises, I couldn't stand it, I felt sick again—"

"Yes, all right, Thomas, you don't have to say anymore."

"It was hearing the noises—he was sort of screaming—"

"Sit down again and I'll get you some brandy."

Retrieving the decanter and two glasses from the dining room, I poured us each a stiff measure. Thomas drank his too fast and choked. Afterwards he whispered, "I don't want to go back there just yet."

"No, of course not, I wouldn't dream of suggesting it. You can stay here for as long as you like. I'll go over to Oxmoon, have a word with Milly and sort everything out."

Thomas was too overcome to speak but not too overcome to grab the decanter and pour himself another measure. When he had gulped it down he said, "You're the only one of all those bloody brothers that's ever cared more than a pail of pigshit for me. I'm sorry I was so bloody awful to you in the past. I suppose I was jealous. I didn't like it when the old bugger fawned over you, but I don't suppose you'd ever understand."

I began to tell him how jealous I had been of Robert when I had been his age, but he was too upset to listen.

"I hate Robert," he said interrupting me. "I hate everyone and everything except you—the world, the weather, women, politics, Ramsay MacDonald, Stanley Baldwin, Bolsheviks, the Prince of Wales, Harrow, the English, the Germans, clergymen, God, the Devil and bloody sex. I hate them all and I only like animals and you—animals are better than humans because they don't let you down, and you're as good as an animal. You're the only decent human being I know, and I don't care who you sleep with."

I casually removed the brandy decanter as his hand wavered towards it, but my feelings were very far from casual. I was thinking of Thomas pitchforked from the secure loving innocent world my mother had created for him into the world of Milly Straker, and I had a long chilling view of my father's moral debacle. Then suddenly I was contrasting Marian, racked by sobs, with the happy little girl who had said her prayers in the nursery with Blanche, and once more I had a glimpse of a wheel which terrified me.

I closed my mind against it. Struggling to my feet I said abruptly to Thomas, "I'll ask Mrs. Wells to prepare a room for you and I'll tell Bronwen you've come to stay."

An hour later, when Thomas had been safely settled at the Manor, I found myself once more on the road to Oxmoon at the beginning of a new journey into hell.

XVI

"Much better for Thomas to be with you, dear," said Milly. "I'll go and pack a couple of bags for him straightaway. As for your father, I put him in the library because he's always happy pottering around there with his papers, but don't be surprised if he's not entirely twenty shillings to the pound."

My father looked better than I had anticipated but not at all pleased to see me. He was seated at the library table in front of the estate books, and as I entered the room he looked up at me suspiciously over his spectacles.

I asked his permission to look after Thomas for a while. "I think he could be useful to me at the farm," I said, "and I'd enjoy his company."

"Yes, very well, you take care of him. I can't manage him anymore; he's too difficult."

I thought of the strong capable father of my early memories. When I could speak again I said, "Papa, there's a question I'd like to ask but if it upsets you too much then naturally I shan't expect an answer. Do you want Thomas out of the house because he's difficult or because you're afraid of his interest in the estate books?"

"I don't know what you mean," he said instantly, but he did. He looked furious.

Once again I had to pause before I could nerve myself to continue. "I was wondering if the estate's getting too much for you now that—by your own admission—you're not quite so young as you used to be. If I can be of any help—"

"Absolutely not," said my father. "You've got to be kept out."

There was another silence. I remember thinking, in the detached manner that sometimes accompanies harrowing circumstances, that an outsider would have thought our conversation bizarrely disjointed.

411

"Will you talk to Robert?" I said at last. "Perhaps he could arrange for a first-class agent to help you."

"I can manage. Go away and stop trying to interfere in my affairs."

But I stood my ground as I tried to work out how I could say what had to be said next, and finally I replied, "I quite understand why you don't wish me to be involved in the estate and of course I completely accept your decision. But can I help you at all with your private income? I could perhaps attend to the correspondence with your stockbrokers, your accountants, the Inland Revenue—"

"I don't use accountants. Waste of money. I'm good with money, always was. Head for figures."

"I know that. But I thought perhaps I might help you during those times when you're not well."

"No need. I've got Milly. She's got a head for figures too, wonderfully clever she is, thinks just like a man."

The conversation shattered into silence again. During the interval that followed I framed my next sentence several times in my head before I found the version that satisfied me.

"How fortunate," I said. "I didn't realize you'd given her a power of attorney."

My father immediately flew into a rage. "What power of attorney? I'm not giving anyone a power of attorney! How dare you imply I'm incapable of signing my name!"

"Oh, I see. Milly just prepares the checks."

"I refuse to be subjected to this cross-examination any longer! Go away and leave me in peace!"

I went away. Upstairs in Thomas's bedroom I found Milly completing the packing of his clothes.

"I want to warn you," I said, "that I know you've involved yourself in my father's financial affairs and that I'll go to court if I find any evidence—any evidence at all—that you're abusing your position here."

"Abusing my position, dear? But I do nothing without his written authorization! What kind of a fool do you think I am?"

"Written authorizations are meaningless when someone's not competent to conduct his own affairs."

"Well really, dear, what a nasty mind you've got! I'm quite shocked! Now look here, my friend. If you don't think your father's fit to conduct his affairs, then go to court and get an order but don't come whining to me about undue influence when he's not certified, not legally incompetent and still has a right to manage his affairs as he pleases!"

"I just wanted you to know that I don't intend to tolerate larceny."

"The day I go to jail for larceny, John Godwin, is the day you retire to a monastery and become a monk. Oh, don't be so silly, dear, really, I feel quite put out! I thought we were friends nowadays?"

I picked up the packed bags and walked out without another word.

XVII

I arrived at Little Oxmoon to find a marital row of earsplitting violence was being concluded, and although I had schooled myself to take no notice of these searing verbal battles, I found it hard this time to look the other way.

"Just another little disagreement, sir," said Bennett soothingly as he admitted me to the hall. I had jumped at the sound of breaking glass. The next moment Ginevra was screaming, "All right, die—and the sooner the better!" and there was another crash before she rushed sobbing into the hall. She saw me, screamed, "Hit him, kill him, I don't care!" and stumbled, weaving, down the passage to her bedroom. As Bennett and I approached the drawing room we were almost overcome with the reek of gin, and on crossing the threshold we found she had smashed both her glass and the bottle against the wall.

"Oh hullo, John," said Robert, unperturbed. "What's this? Two visits in one day? Don't start flagellating yourself again in the name of moral duty; my nerves couldn't stand it. Bennett, get me out of here before I die of alcohol fumes."

We retired to Robert's bedroom. As soon as Bennett had left I said in a voice that I hoped was laconic, "Has she been drinking too much again?"

"Yes, but it's nothing to be excited about, just another of her bouts. They come and go like the Cheshire Cat's smile."

"What happened to upset her?"

"I was bloody ill this morning. My sense of balance went haywire and my vision was affected. Gavin thought rest would help and gave me a sedative and sure enough when I awoke I was better."

"Thank God."

"No, don't waste your time. I've now made up my mind that I must die as soon as possible."

"But you may not suffer that sort of attack again for years—"

"I can tolerate a simple inconvenience like incontinence, but the thought of being blind and possibly deaf and dumb—"

"But surely—"

"Oh, *shut up!* I want to die and I'm going to will myself to do it. People will themselves to live, don't they? I know I did, on Ben Nevis after the accident. Well, now I'm going to will myself to die. Death wants me to continue for another twenty years as a vegetable, but I'm going to outwit him; I'm going to win."

Since speech was impossible, I busied myself in drawing up a chair.

"Think of the way I was, John. You wouldn't want me to live as a vegetable, would you?"

I shook my head. But I whispered, "I'll be so alone."

"We're all alone," said Robert. "We're born alone, we live alone and we die alone. Any companionship is transitory and for the most part meaningless. The human condition is essentially tragic. Ask anyone over eighty who's seen all their friends die one by one."

Unwilling to upset him by arguing I said nothing, and eventually he asked why I had returned to see him.

"Bad news," I said. "But it can wait."

"Don't be a fool, can't you see that any bad news would rank as light relief after all I've been through? Get hold of Ginette at once and bring her in here."

I was most reluctant to disturb Ginevra but when he insisted I went to fetch her. She was calm but looked exhausted and disheveled in a dirty dressing gown.

"Robert thought you might like to join us—there's another crisis at Oxmoon, and—"

"Oh good," said Ginevra. "How simply heavenly, I can't wait to hear all the divine details."

We returned to Robert.

"I hated to think of you missing the fun," he said to her.

"Sweet of you, darling, it's made my day. God knows it needed making." She sat down beside him and covered his hand with hers.

Marveling at their endurance, I began to talk about my father.

XVIII

"What can we do, Robert?"

"I'm afraid the answer's still damn all."

"But there must be something!" exclaimed Ginevra.

"So long as he's insisting that he's fine, we'd have a hard time proving in court that he's not. Can't you picture the judge, who would probably be over seventy, saying, 'There, there, Mr. Godwin, I suffer from a poor memory myself now and then, it happens to us all!' No, Papa would have to have a full breakdown before we could successfully claim he was incapable of managing his affairs."

"But I'm quite sure," I said, "that his financial affairs are getting in a mess."

"That may well be so," said Robert, "but it's not a crime under English law for a man to make a mess of his financial affairs and it's not evidence of insanity if he voluntarily signs checks prepared by his mistress."

"So we just stand by, do we," said Ginevra, "while Oxmoon goes down the drain?"

"We have to stand by at present, certainly, but if Oxmoon starts to go down the drain on a grand scale, I think we should be the first to know about it. Let's get in league with the lawyers."

We agreed that I would seek an interview with my father's solicitor Freddy Fairfax. Then I offered to call at the major farms and talk casually to the foremen to see if there was any imminent possibility of catastrophe.

"Although it's my guess," said Robert, "that the estate can muddle on well enough for some time. He'll probably delegate more and more responsibility to the foremen and that would be a good thing. At least Straker doesn't know enough about estate management to queer that particular pitch."

"And his private fortune?"

"Oh, hopeless! She'll get her paws on that all right—and legally, too. He'll simply give it away."

"If only he could break down now—"

"No such luck. Life isn't so tidy."

The three of us were silent, considering the untidiness of life.

"I can't quite see the bottom of the wheel of his fortune," said Robert, "but I'm beginning to think it's a very long way down."

"That reminds me, Robert: how did Boethius circumvent the horror of predestination?"

"Darling," said Ginevra, "what a frightful question! How you could!" She stood up, caught sight of herself in the glass and winced. "God, I look eighty! Johnny, come and have some coffee. Robert, you should be back in bed."

"The horror of a preordained future," said Robert, embracing the diversion with relief, "is circumvented by saying there *is* no future. God is outside time and therefore as far as God and his preordained plans are concerned, past, present and future are all happening simultaneously. This permits the exercise of the individual will and yet still permits God to remain omnipotent."

"Good heavens!"

"I agree it's weak," said Robert apologetically, "but the postclassical mind often left much to be desired."

"I think it's all rather heaven," said Ginevra idly, ringing for Bennett, and drifted away to the drawing room.

When I joined her later, she was drinking black coffee and reading the label on the bottle of aspirin in her hand. Pouring myself some coffee, I sat down beside her.

"Just warding off the inevitable hangover," she said, putting the bottle aside. "Sorry we were so awful when you arrived but this morning was a bad shock."

"Does he mean what he says about dying?"

"He does and he doesn't. He'll be all right so long as he can sit in a wheelchair and read and talk to people. He can accept that. But beyond that point... yes, he'd be better dead, and he knows it. I know it too, but I couldn't kill him; I've made that quite clear. I think Gavin might if things got quite beyond the pale, but of course doctors have to be so careful. Especially Gavin." She had been watching her cigarette as she spoke, but now she looked directly at me. "Has there been any gossip," she said, "about Gavin and me?"

"None."

"Good. Robert was worried in case Gavin couldn't cope and wound up being struck off the register, but Gavin can handle a dangerous situation without losing his head. He's tough—and I'm careful." She smoked thoughtfully for a time. "Gavin understands how I feel about Robert," she said at last. "None of the other men ever did. Gavin understands Robert too, and Robert likes him—Robert's glad I have someone he can trust and approve of, so you see, we're all very close, it's... but what word can possibly describe it? It's comforting—yes, that's it.

Comforting—and not just for me but for all of us. We all benefit."

"I'm glad." I waited while she poured me some more coffee. Then I added: "I hadn't guessed. I suppose I've been far too preoccupied with my own affairs."

"Well, God knows they must be a full-time preoccupation, but all the same even though you don't have much time at present I do wish poor Bobby would let you help him with Oxmoon. Why won't he, do you think?"

I thought of Bronwen urging me to be truthful. "He doesn't trust me not to play the villain and cheat Robert."

"Don't be silly, darling, you mean he doesn't trust himself not to give Oxmoon to you and promptly die of remorse!" She smiled at me but her eyes were wary. "And that wouldn't be such a tragedy for you, would it?"

"Possibly not." I kept thinking of Bronwen. "I covet Oxmoon sometimes," I said. "Of course I do. But I couldn't take it by fraud or duress. I could only take it if I felt that was what Papa and Robert both wanted." I smiled at her suddenly and said, "I have to do what's right if I want to avoid the Home of the Assumption!"

"Darling Johnny!" said Ginevra, kissing me. "How thrilled your poor old grandmother would be if she knew what a fortifying influence she'd become!"

I was believed. As I held her hands I was aware of her trust. It made me want to believe too.

She escorted me outside to my car and when we opened the front door we saw that although there was no moon the stars were shining. It was cold.

"Thank you for telling me about Gavin," I said.

"I thought you might be worrying in case someone got hurt."

We embraced again.

"My God," said Ginevra, "what a life."

"What a life. Never mind. Hold fast, stand firm and soldier on."

"Darling, how divine—just like a poem by Kipling! It almost gives me the courage to say bugger Boethius and his ghastly Wheel!"

We laughed, drawing strength from each other. Then I left her, got into my car and drove on once more into the dark.

10

I

IT TOOK four years to complete my father's disintegration and all the while Bronwen and I moved deeper into a gathering chaos. Some of our early troubles were resolved: our domestic difficulties were eased after the advent of Mrs. Wells; Marian recovered from her initial misery; the children settled down tolerably well together. Most important of all Bronwen and I knew a deep personal contentment which created a happy atmosphere in the house, and by the end of 1924 it seemed we had evolved a pattern of life that transcended the differences between us.

That was the honeymoon. After that life became increasingly less easy.

At first Bronwen found life at the Manor so intimidating that she spent much time secluding herself in the nurseries and evading the servants, but gradually she adjusted to life in what was for her a large house, and she became less self-conscious. To help her I modified my own mundane daily habits; we did not dine at eight and on our own, as I would have done with Constance or Blanche, but instead ate an informal meal with all the children at seven o'clock. This was far past Harry's bedtime, but Bronwen's children seemed to stay up later without ill effect, so to my children's delight they found their day extended. By the time they were all in bed the evening was far advanced, but Bronwen and I were disinclined to spend much time on our own in Blanche's drawing room and we would retire to our bedroom, which had soon acquired armchairs and a table. It was here that Bronwen, shying away from the intimidating elegance of the down-stairs receptions rooms, was able to relax and soon I too was drawn to the room's attractive informality. Needless to say it was not the bedroom I had shared with Blanche. There was another bedroom, equally large, on the other side of the house, and Blanche's room was now set aside for the guests who never came.

But I was at peace with Blanche. Bronwen, as she had proved to Marian, was not afraid of Blanche's memory and in her mystical acceptance of Blanche's past presence in the house I found my own release from past guilt. Once I did say to Bronwen, "You're sure you're not oppressed by her?" but she merely answered in surprise, "How could I be? She was a good person. All the memories are benign." And in these simple statements she brought harmony to a situation that might well have been too complex to endure with ease.

Unfortunately the atmosphere of harmony at the Manor did not extend to the world beyond the gates. No one cut me dead but I was aware that no one was rushing to invite me to dinner, and soon it became clear that I was being treated as a traitor to my class. This by itself did not disturb me since I was more than willing to embrace such treachery, but I was determined out of pride that I was not going to remain a social pariah, and after careful thought I joined a golf club in Swansea.

I then realized that what everyone had been craving was some sign that I could still be treated as a normal person, and when I played golf with modest competence and stood drinks in the bar afterwards people were soon prepared to turn a blind eye to my private life. I now realized how wise I had been not to live with Bronwen openly. Probably I would have been refused membership of the club in those circumstances, but as a man separated from his wife and keeping up appearances as he lived quietly with his children in Penhale I was, with an effort of will and a little imagination, acceptable.

I began to be invited out to dine. Later I even gave a dinner party at the Manor and asked Ginevra to act as hostess. Bronwen, who wholeheartedly approved of my determination not to be a social pariah, kept thankfully upstairs. In fact so pleased was I by my success in overcoming the disapproval of my own class that it took me some time to realize how absolutely Bronwen was overwhelmed by the disapproval of hers.

However as usual when Bronwen's welfare was at stake, her sister was only too ready to enlighten me once she judged that the time had come to take action. I was told that Bronwen was now so afraid to leave the Manor for fear of unpleasantness that Myfanwy herself had to escort her on her visits to the Home Farm. There had also been anonymous letters pointing out that Evan had been born eleven months after Gareth Morgan's death. The minister at the chapel was thundering regularly about the wages of sin, and even Anstey the vicar had abandoned his cozy comments on the weather and retreated into monosyllabism.

"Why the devil didn't you say something to me?" I said angrily to Bronwen. "I thought you prided yourself on being honest!"

"I didn't think I had to say anything. I thought you knew what it was like," she said flatly, and added in defiance: "I don't care."

But she cared when life became difficult for Rhiannon and Dafydd at the village school, and soon we were arguing painfully about education again.

"I'm not having them educated above their station!"

"But can't you see that's the kind of view which perpetuates the class system? If all children were educated in the same way—"

"All right, send *your* children to the village school! Why do my children have to be the ones to change?"

"Because private education is better."

"Not for them! Anyway you can't iron out class by treating everyone the same, everyone's not the same and never will be and to say otherwise is just dangerous socialist rubbish, giving people expectations which haven't a hope of coming true. I'm all for improving people's lot in life as Mr. Lloyd George did with his welfare schemes, but I'm not going to ruin my children's lives by making them misfits!"

"Well, what do we do about Evan? If you think—"

"Oh, I know I haven't a hope of doing what I want with Evan, I know he'll be sent to boarding school when he's eight even though I think it's wicked and cruel—"

"Jesus Christ!"

The quarrel deepened. The controversy raged. We stood on either side of the abyss of class which divided us and shouted at each other until finally I said, "Class is evil, evil, *evil*—I hope there's a bloody revolution to abolish it," and I went off to play golf. I had work to do on the estate but I felt a retreat was necessary into my own class, and when I returned I found that Bronwen had gone to see her sister as if she too had felt such a withdrawal was needed.

We made up the quarrel, but soon the problem reached its climax when Rhiannon became hysterical at the prospect of going to school and Dafydd was stoned in the playground. At that point I arranged for the children to be transferred to a primary school in the nearest suburb of Swansea. There was no difficulty about transport because either Willis or I had to drive Marian into Swansea each day to her private school.

Bronwen wept with relief; the children, continuing their working-class education, soon settled down, but I knew their dilemma had merely been alleviated. At home they led a solitary life, unable to mix with the hostile local children and uninvited to the houses where Harry and Marian regularly went to play and have tea.

"Dear me, it's all so diffy for them, isn't it?" confided Marian to me. "Almost as diffy as it is for me not being able to invite any of my school friends here."

"I don't see your difficulty, Marian. Just say Bronwen's the nanny and that Rhiannon and Dafydd are her children."

"But how could I explain why they take their meals with us? They're both so common and it all looks so odd—"

"I'm sorry you should feel that's so important."

"Well, of course it's important!" stormed Marian, abandoning her precocious sophistication and becoming a tearful little girl of ten. "It's absolutely beastly, and I wish I could live with Aunt Daphne!"

Later I said to Bronwen, "That damned Daphne's a bad influence on Marian. I know she thinks it's monstrous that Marian should be brought up in these circumstances."

"Well, you can't stop Marian's visits to her. That would be disastrous."

"Everything I do with Marian's disastrous," I said. "Everything."

"It'll sort itself out once we're married."

"Ah yes. Of course," I said, but I knew that since Daphne would judge the marriage a hopeless *mésalliance*, Marian's embarrassment would continue.

Amidst all these difficulties I found it a welcome relief to teach Thomas as much as I could about estate management. I was in fact having a difficult time with my estate, and if my other troubles had not been so numerous I might well have become depressed by its ailing fortunes. My original plan to grow a surplus of cereals for sale with the aid of a motor lorry was sound enough, but a series of wet summers in the early Twenties had wreaked havoc with my adventurous schemes, and in addition the price of wheat had fallen from its postwar level of seventy-two and eleven a quarter to forty-nine and three in 1924, a year that turned out to be one of the wettest on record. I was considering a complete return to cattle breeding and growing cereals only for winter feed, but in the end I decided to wait, reasoning that both the weather and the price of wheat could only improve.

Meanwhile I thought I might try raising pigs. Thomas was keen on pigs and it occurred to me that the best way of keeping him out of mischief was to encourage an interest that gave him the chance to prove himself. Accordingly, to the Merediths' horror, I sanctioned the idea of a piggery and soothed them by promising to build it with an eye to the prevailing wind. Thomas was very excited, and as I listened to him expounding on the best methods of porcine castration I realized he was more of a farmer than I would ever be: I was interested not in farming for farming's sake but in farming as a business, and although I knew enough about farming to realize it could not be conducted in the same way as a manufacturing concern, I still tended to regard my estate solely from an accounting point of view. When my profits fell for reasons beyond my power to control I found myself growing impatient and restless, but I knew that a true farmer, while being equally disappointed, would have been able to console himself with the fact that he was still leading a life that satisfied him. No such consolation was available to me. I knew I was once more discontented with my career as a minor squire, and I began to wonder if I could carve out some business opportunities for myself in Swansea which as a large industrial port no doubt contained many attractive boardrooms. I resolved to cultivate the magnates of my acquaintance at the golf club.

However although I was privately dissatisfied with my situation Thomas was happy with his pigs, and fired by his enthusiasm I even began to share his interest in the brutes. They had a quick turnover. They bred frequently and in quantity. As far as I could see they stood a chance of being steadily profitable. I was intrigued.

I was also relieved that Thomas was enjoying his life at Penhale Manor. I gave him a certain freedom, as much as any young man of his age had a right to expect, but I drew up a set of rules which I insisted he should obey: he was to be civil to Bronwen; he was not to use bad language in front of the children; he was to be punctual at mealtimes; he was to drink wine or beer but on no account to touch spirits, and he was to report to my study for work at nine o'clock each morning. In exchange for obeying this elementary code of civilized behavior he received the instruction he wanted, a roof over his head and stability. This did not transform him instantly into an angel but he did improve.

I was interested to discover that he was by no means stupid despite his aversion to school, and although his strong opinionated humorless personality was not to everyone's taste, there was a childlike streak in him which I found touching. His devotion to me, once he had decided to bestow it, was so fierce that I sometimes felt in his presence as if I were accompanied by a large dog whose heart of gold lay beyond bared teeth. Bronwen, who was a little alarmed by him at first, soon found it easy to be friendly.

"I suppose you were sleeping with beautiful girls like that since you were younger than me," said Thomas gloomily, and recognizing this remark as a plea for guidance I said, "Not exactly" and told him of my protracted virginity, which had resulted in my rush to the altar while I was still emotionally immature. Thomas, who was obviously bothered by the subject of women, was so much cheered by this account of my youthful chastity that I took the opportunity to give him some useful information about sex. He was enthralled and gratified.

"I think you ought to be canonized as the patron saint of chaps my age," he said, and seemed surprised when I remarked drily that most people would consider me quite unfit to bring up an adolescent boy.

"Most people? I hate most people," said Thomas, closing the argument in his usual belligerent fashion, but although he talked truculently out of habit I never worried that he might get into trouble as the result of any violent behavior. I might have had acute anxieties in my private life, but they never centered around Thomas.

The anxieties deepened as time passed and Constance refused to change her mind about a divorce. In the end I gave up calling on her to discuss the situation. She made me too furious and Francesca made me feel too guilty. Photographs of Francesca arrived regularly but I could not bear to look at them and locked them away at once. Bronwen suggested it might be better if we looked at them together, but I found it impossible to agree and when she realized there was nothing she could do to help me the subject continued to lie between us like a lead weight.

Edmund sent me the occasional photograph of his children. His first son was followed by a second; he was blissfully happy. As he had soon regretted his decision not to remain on speaking terms with me, we did meet for a drink on my rare visits to town but he always made excuses not to visit Gower. No doubt Teddy found my father's domestic arrangements as objectionable as mine and had ruled that both Oxmoon and Penhale Manor were beyond the pale.

At first I thought that my father would be hurt by Edmund's desertion, but later I realized he was glad not to be obliged to entertain him. He had become more of a recluse. I suspected this was because he had come to distrust his ability to conduct a normal conversation, for Oswald Stourham, one of the few of his old friends who still saw him regularly, reported to me that "poor Bobby wasn't the man he used to be," and I realized he had been shocked by some new evidence of my father's decline. When I called at Oxmoon my father seemed pleased to see me, but he would not come to the Manor. He appeared to be withdrawing deeper and deeper into his home, and the house seemed to be withdrawing too, sinking in upon itself, the paint worn from the window frames, the walls stripped of the dead creeper, a slate or two missing from the roof. Once I had spoken to my father about the need for repairs, but he had only become angry so I learned to keep my conversations with him colorless. During my visits with my family he was always courteous to Bronwen but he never discussed her with me, and always, treating her as the nanny, he addressed her as Mrs. Morgan. With a cruelty that both enraged and staggered me, he took no notice of Evan at all.

"It's probably easier for him to pretend Evan isn't yours," said Bronwen, but I knew she was hurt. By that time Evan had fair hair, green eyes and a bright, intelligent little face. I thought any man would have been proud to have such a grandson, and I felt bitter.

When Evan was two, Bronwen said for the first time that she felt worried because he had no one to play with.

"He'll go to nursery school when he's older," I said.

"Yes—where everyone will know he's your bastard!" she cried and burst into tears.

The days were long since past when we could say to each other, "Everything will come right once we're married." I did start to say I would talk to Constance again, but Bronwen shouted, "You know bloody well that's useless!" and rushed upstairs to our room.

A very difficult conversation followed during which Bronwen admitted her unhappiness and said she thought I was unhappy too. I said I was unhappy only when I knew she was unhappy, and I offered to leave Gower to set up a home elsewhere.

"No, that would be disastrous." She spoke so promptly that I knew she had

421

been dwelling on the idea for some time. "If we left it would mean that I'd cut you off entirely from your family and friends."

I no longer assured her that I wanted to be cut off. I merely said with truth: "I doubt that we can solve this problem by moving away because wherever we go people would eventually find out we weren't married, and then the trouble would begin all over again."

She said nothing. The silence deepened and suddenly I was so afraid that I could bear it no longer. Grabbing her to me so fiercely that she cried out with shock I shouted, "You mustn't go away, you mustn't leave, I won't let you go, I won't!"

She burst into tears again and said she couldn't. For a while we were silent, embracing each other, but still, as we both knew, nothing had been solved.

At last I said, "Tell me what I can do to make life more bearable for you. I'll do anything, anything at all."

"Do you truly mean that?"

"You know I do. I swear it."

She whispered, "I want another baby."

Conversation ceased again. As I released her and turned away, the silence was broken only by the rain drumming on the windowpane and the fire crackling in the grate.

"I wouldn't mind all the difficulties then," said Bronwen at last. "I'd have someone for Evan to play with, someone who would be there later when . . . when Evan goes away to school. Rhiannon and Dafydd will leave just as soon as they can, I know that now. They hate it here. I'm so worried about Dafydd that I'm even thinking of asking Gareth's family if he could board with them and finish his schooling in Cardiff. It would be better. He doesn't like you, he resents you because of the life we have to lead. . . . It's all so upsetting . . ." She paused but managed to check her tears. Presently she added: "Myfanwy's offered to have Rhiannon at the farm, and that might be better too. I'd hate it but I'd still see her every day and Rhiannon would be happier. . . . It's Marian, you see. Marian isn't always very kind."

"Oh, Marian's quite impossible," I said. "I'm well aware of that." I began to move around the room.

"You won't want another child, of course," she said, sensing my thoughts. "Why should you? You don't need one. You have your work, your friends, your weekends at the golf club. You're not lonely, you're not isolated, you're not forced to watch your children growing away from you."

"No," I said, "I'm not. But if we have another baby that means we live openly together, and if you think we have difficulties now, all I can say is that they're nothing in comparison with the difficulties we'll have then."

"I shan't mind. If I have another baby I shan't mind anything, and anyway things couldn't be worse than they are now."

But I thought of Harry and Marian, no longer able to shelter behind the convention that Bronwen was their nanny. "I disagree," I said.

Bronwen lost her temper. A terrible interlude followed during which the full range of her misery and despair was finally revealed. She even said that although she was unable to imagine living without me, she was again tempted to emigrate to her cousins in Vancouver.

"Be quiet!" I shouted, overpowered by panic again as my worst suspicions were confirmed. "Don't you threaten me like that!"

"Then let me have a baby!"

"Oh, stop being so bloody selfish!"

We were a very long way now from those golden sunsets in St. Ives.

"You're the one who's being bloody selfish—all you can think of is what people will say if we live openly together—you're just a bloody upper-class snob after all!"

"Don't you talk of class to me and don't you call me a snob either! Have I ever complained that I can't dine at a civilized hour? Have I ever complained because you won't use the reception rooms and we have to spend all our time in this bloody bedroom which has come to look just like a bloody working-class parlor?"

She hit me. Then she screamed that she hated me.

I sank down on the bed. I was blind with pain but eventually I realized that she was sobbing, clinging to me, begging me to forgive her.

"For what? I'm the one to blame for your misery. It's all my fault." I opened the drawer of the bedside table, removed the contraceptives I kept there and walked to the door.

"Where are you going?" she said fearfully.

"To flush these down the lavatory."

Our second son was conceived less than a month later.

II

The hardest part to bear was the reaction of my family.

"Good God!" said Robert in disgust. "Is it too late for an abortion?"

I assume you don't want any congratulations, scrawled Edmund in reply to my letter, *so I won't offer any.*

Edmund tells me some truly appalling news, scribbled Celia from Heidelberg. *I am sorry—heavens above, just* think *what dearest Mama would have said....*

"Well, we won't talk of it," said my father. "The less said the better. You'll be quite ruined now, of course, but we'll pretend I know nothing about it. I don't want to see Mrs. Morgan or her children anymore. Come to see me as usual on Sundays but only bring Harry and Marian with you."

"Christ, John," said Thomas, "imagine an old hand like you being caught out! What happened? Did the French letter break?"

There was only one answer I could make to all these comments and I made it. I said, "We wanted the child. It's not our fault we can't be married and now we've decided to live together without resorting to subterfuge."

After that my family somehow managed to preserve a tactful silence but Milly said to me, "You'll crucify that girl yet, dear. I'm surprised at you. I thought you had more sense."

I was so depressed by this comment that although Ginevra had just returned from a visit to London, I avoided Little Oxmoon because I felt unable to face yet another adverse reaction to the news of Bronwen's pregnancy. But the next morning Ginevra arrived to see us, her arms full of flowers, and Ginevra, brave Ginevra living always with death, cried radiantly, "Darlings—so exciting—another life coming into the world, I adore it!" and after she had kissed us both she looked me straight in the eyes and said, "Let me go back to London as soon as I can to talk to Constance. Let me see if there's anything I can do."

III

It was by that time the spring of 1927, and London was beginning to seem as remote to me as the moon. I no longer bothered myself with the parliamentary reports in *The Times*. I had lost interest after the General Strike the previous May. When that fizzled out I knew Britain would never change in my lifetime. There would be no revolution; class would be perpetuated—and this was obviously what the British wanted. People get the government they deserve, and now the Conservatives were firmly back in power.

I was a divided man again, "cleft in twain," visiting my estates in Herefordshire, playing the gentleman farmer restlessly at Penhale, writing to my stockbrokers about my investment portfolio—and living like a radical freethinker, defying the society in which I lived and hating its cruel conventions. Driven by the subtle but searing pressures of my divided life, I began to read as I had not read since leaving Oxford: voraciously and compulsively. To escape from the baffling and intractable nature of my problems, I trekked through history, I dabbled in philosophy, I even meddled futilely with religion, but all the time I knew there were no answers, and when Ginevra did go to London to see Constance I knew she had no hope of bringing unity to the two halves of my troubled life.

"That's an impossible woman, darling, truly awful," she said when she returned. "So dreary, no sense of humor and now she's gone all religious, saying God will punish you for breaking your sacred vows. Then she had the nerve to say: 'You're such a loyal and devoted wife—surely you must be on my side!' How I curbed my hysteria I can't imagine, but I did manage to point out soberly that loyalty and devotion can't flourish when the marriage is a prison, and when marriage is a prison it's no marriage at all. However that cut no ice, of course, and she just said it was her moral duty to be faithful to you until death. Julie says Constance is wallowing in religion in order to sublimate her sex drive—isn't that fun! Darling Freud, how did we all live without him in the old days…"

424

I thanked her for trying to help and then realized that she had more news, although she was uncertain how to impart it. "I saw Francesca—such a poppet though not much like either of you yet," she said tentatively at last. "But you should see Edmund's Richard! Such a look of Lion, really quite extraordinary... oh, and talking of Lion, darling, that reminds me: I saw Daphne in London."

"Oh yes?" I said, trying not to sound hostile. I knew Ginevra was fond of Daphne, and at once I could picture them having tea at the Ritz, discussing my situation and trying to work out what on earth could be done to save Marian.

"I told her," said Ginevra carefully, "that Harry would stop doing lessons with Kester and go off to prep school this autumn now that he's eight, and Daphne said she was going to send Elizabeth away this autumn too—to St. Astrith's in Surrey. Apparently it's such a good school and the girls have such a jolly time there and Daphne's sure Elizabeth will adore it—like me Daphne herself hated being educated at home with a governess, so she's just as keen as I am on boarding school for girls, and... well, suddenly, darling, we had this very exciting idea: why doesn't Marian go with Elizabeth to St. Astrith's? You know what friends they are, and it would be such fun for them... and let's be honest, Johnny, wouldn't it be better from your point of view as well as Marian's? I remember how I felt about Declan and Rory when I was first married to Robert. I adored them but whenever they appeared on the scene Robert and I were quite wrecked. I know school was a disaster for Declan, but Rory loved it in the end and it really was the best solution—for everyone."

"Yes," I said. I found I could say nothing else.

"You're in favor?"

"Yes."

"Shall I have a word with Marian for you?"

But I knew I had to tell Marian myself. I thought she might make a fuss, but after allowing herself one grand tantrum during which I was accused of wanting to get rid of her in order to wipe out her mother's memory, she was prepared to believe I did have her welfare in mind.

"How nice it'll be to mix with girls of my own sort at last!" she said satisfied. "All the girls I know at school at the moment are really rather middle-class, you know, Papa, but I'm sure things will be quite different at a lovely posh boarding school. I wonder how many titled girls there'll be in my form?"

"Probably none. They'll all be at home with their governesses."

"Divine for them," said Marian, borrowing as effortlessly from Ginevra's speech mannerisms as she did from Daphne's. "But then I don't suppose they come from homes where the nanny and the master of the house sleep in the same bedroom and have babies without being married."

She stood there, not yet twelve years old, blond, blue-eyed and outwardly the picture of innocence. My one thought, as I fought back the desire to strike her, was how horrified Blanche would have been if she could have seen us.

"I'm afraid I can't allow you to pass that sort of remark, Marian," I said politely at last, "and I'm only surprised that you should have seen fit to make it. I would have expected you to shun such vulgarity."

"Aunt Daphne thinks it's a wonder I'm not more vulgar, considering the example I've been set."

I did not seriously believe that Daphne had passed such a remark in Marian's presence, but I had no doubt I was hearing an accurate reflection of her sentiments.

"Marian, is it really your intention to make me very angry?" I said, but I knew it was. Marian was angry herself and wanted the chance to scream and shout at me. However it was not until the baby was born that she egged me into losing my temper.

The baby was healthy and good-looking for a newborn infant, pink-and-white with dark hair and a soft bloom on his cheeks. We both wanted a Welsh name so Bronwen chose Geraint. Marian said the name was quite ghastly and very common (that was when I lost my temper with her), and Harry said he hated it and would call the baby Gerry instead. We tried to persuade him to retain the hard Welsh G but he refused, and soon we found that our English-speaking acquaintances were following his example.

"Well, at least he won't be christened Gerry," said Bronwen. That was before she realized there would be no christening. Anstey the vicar had christened Evan without a murmur because he had believed him to be Gareth Morgan's son, but I knew he could not condone my union with Bronwen by christening its patently illegitimate offspring. I did talk to him but Anstey had a stubborn streak beneath his inoffensive manners, and he pointed out that if he were to perform the ceremony the entire population of Penhale would be outraged.

"Well, if that's Mr. Anstey's attitude," blazed Bronwen, "I don't want the baby christened at all!"

"Neither do I," I said strongly, but I knew she was upset, just as I knew that more upsetting events were sure to follow.

A stream of abusive anonymous letters was followed by an act of vandalism; someone daubed in red paint on the wall by the gates: BROTHEL—WHORES AND BASTARDS ONLY. Because of my private life I had not volunteered to be a magistrate, but I made sure the bench handed out a stiff sentence when the village constable and I succeeded in tracking down the vandals responsible for the outrage.

Two maids had to be sacked for insolence but Mrs. Wells stood by us and prevented a collapse within the household. Eventually the village quietened down but by this time the scandal had traveled to the far end of Gower and when I next entered the golf-club bar all conversation abruptly ceased.

I had become a pariah again. This made me feel particularly bitter because I had been on the point of being offered a directorship in a shipping firm and I knew now the offer would never be made. It made me realize too how much I had been looking forward to returning to the world of commerce. 1927 had turned into another disastrously wet year, and to make matters worse the spring months had been abnormally cold. I saw the ruin of my cereal crop again and I was thoroughly disillusioned with farming.

In an effort to divert myself from the knowledge that I was trapped in a way of life which was failing to satisfy me, I embarked on a restless search for occupations that would fill my hours of spare time. I arranged for electricity to be installed in the house. Then I studied the subject of electricity so that I would know what to do if the power failed. I read more voraciously than ever. But despite these diversions the time that meant most to me was the time I spent with Robert. I had always called on him every day but now I found myself staying longer because he alone could assuage the loneliness which for Bronwen's sake I struggled to keep concealed.

"I despise myself for caring what people think of me," I said when I told him I had become a pariah again, "but what I care about is not so much being cut off from the company of my own sort but being cut off from any hope of leading a more interesting life in my working hours."

"I'll have a word with Alun," said Robert. Alun Bryn-Davies had been a contemporary of his at Harrow. "He's on the board of Suez Petro-Chemicals as well as the Madog Collieries. Maybe he can help."

So I lunched with Bryn-Davies at the new Claremont Hotel, and after I had made sure the luncheon was a success, he asked me to play golf with him. Following the game we adjourned to the bar and this time no one cut me; in fact when Bryn-Davies bought me a drink the members realized it was still possible to treat me as normal, and later, when I was offered a directorship of Aswan Products, which was a subsidiary of Suez Petro-Chemicals, they even accepted that I was employable. Yet the directorship was modest, demanding my presence only on one afternoon a week at the company's headquarters in Swansea, and I still found myself wrestling too often with boredom and frustration.

"How naive I was," I said to Robert one day as I spooned up his food for him, "to imagine that Bronwen could solve all my problems. I'm beginning to realize my major problem is that I've never found my true *métier*."

"Your *métier*," said Robert, "is organization and making executive decisions. It probably doesn't matter much what business you wind up in so long as it's large and challenging."

In acknowledgment of the shrewdness of this observation I said depressed, "Well, you always said I was unsuited to a rural backwater, and how right you were."

"You're certainly unsuited for confinement in a rural backwater but that's not necessarily the same thing as saying you're unsuited to country life. Ideally, I suspect, you should be able to fuse your country background with your talent for executive management—maybe your true *métier* is indeed to be a farm manager, but on a large twentieth-century scale."

"You mean I should have about ten small estates and roam around supervising them all?"

"Ten small estates," said Robert, "or one big one."

We fell silent as the image of Oxmoon slipped between us. Food dribbled from his mouth but I quickly mopped it up with a napkin. When I had finished he said, "Can't you combine managing Penhale Manor with a more active management of your farms in Herefordshire?"

"Not without leaving Bronwen on her own frequently, and as things stand at present that's quite impossible." I tried to change the subject. "But don't let's talk of the present," I said. "Let's go back into the past." For we spent much time now talking of the times that were gone, not the near past of the war but the extreme past, the golden past, the fairy-tale past of Edwardian Oxmoon. We talked of the dances in the ballroom and the tennis parties on the lawn and the expeditions to the Downs and the sea and the village shop in Penhale, and although in the past the ten years' difference in our ages had separated us, we now found that time had encircled us so that his experiences could fuse with mine.

"'In my beginning is my end,'" said Robert.

"Who said that?"

"It was the motto of Mary Queen of Scots. My motto would be to reverse those words and say, 'In my end is my beginning.' I feel so strongly that when there's no more future the present fades away and only the past is real."

We were silent, both thinking of Oxmoon again, and suddenly I knew that he was as aware as I was of that terrible ambiguity in my mind. I turned to him; I turned not merely to my brother but to my guide, my mentor and above all else my friend; I turned to him and I opened my mouth and I tried to say "Help me," but the words refused to be spoken. My ambiguity was so terrible to me that I feared I might never overcome it once I had formally acknowledged it in speech.

So I said nothing. But he knew. He could no longer reach out to take my hand in his, but I felt his mind flowing powerfully into mine.

After a moment he said, "In the beginning—my beginning—there was Oxmoon and it was a magic house. I tried to tell Kester that the other day. 'You're going to get this magic house,' I said, 'and you've got to put the magic back into it.' All my life I've wanted to do that, John, and now I never shall, but I can live with that knowledge—die with that knowledge—if I believe Kester will do it instead of me."

"I understand."

"I don't believe in a life after death," said Robert. "I don't believe human beings are capable of resurrection. But if Kester puts the magic back into my magic house then Oxmoon will *rise again* on the Wheel of Fortune, and *that* will be my resurrection; it'll be my redemption too because Kester will be so grateful to me for securing his inheritance for him and all my past neglect of him will be wiped out—and that means everything to me now, John, everything, I'm no longer extorting Oxmoon from Papa in revenge for the past, I'm extorting it to pass Kester the future which has been denied me and to give meaning to my death."

Robert was normally neither an emotional nor an imaginative man. Nor was he in the habit of baring his soul. Suddenly I realized that in an effort to demolish my ambiguity he had thrust the whole weight of his trust upon me, and I was dumb; I could only grope for his crippled hands to show that I wanted what he wanted, and for a moment his vision of Oxmoon united us, an Oxmoon radiant and restored, triumphing over the ravages of time.

"Well, so much for that," said Robert briskly with an alteration of mood so abrupt that I jumped. "Man cannot live on romantic sentimentality alone—thank God—and now that I've had my wallow I think I'd better get down to business. My dear John, how strong are you feeling? The truth is I'm in the devil of a mess and I'm afraid I'm going to have to ask you to rescue me."

428

IV

When I had recovered my equilibrium I said in great alarm, "What in God's name are you talking about? What kind of a mess?"

"A legal mess, naturally. Lawyers are notorious for making a cock-up of their legal affairs."

"But what on earth have you done?"

"It's not what I've done, it's what I've failed to do." Robert paused. Speech was no longer easy for him and the impairment, which gave his words a distorted staccato ring, was becoming more pronounced. I found myself leaning forward in my chair to make sure I heard him properly. "John, when Papa gave me Martinscombe back in 1919 there was no deed of gift. There were two reasons. First, it seemed unnecessary, since although I knew I was ill I had every intention of outliving Papa and inheriting Martinscombe along with the rest of Oxmoon when he died. And second, Papa was in a peculiar tax position at the time and needed Martinscombe for a year or two to set himself straight. So our arrangement was informal—always a fatal mistake."

"Fatal. But didn't you try to put matters right later?"

"Yes, but can't you imagine what happened? He couldn't face the increasingly obvious fact that I was going to die before he was, and he started talking about how he'd have to discuss the situation with Margaret. Having a pardonable horror of seeing him demented I then shied off. Time drifted by. However, goaded on quite rightly by Ginette, I nerved myself last month to dictate a letter to him on the subject. Back came a polite reply to the effect that he preferred to keep the estate together and that as Kester was the heir anyway, why not leave matters as they were. But you see the problem, don't you?"

"All too clearly. When you die Ginevra and Kester will have no legal right to remain here, and Papa may well be more unreliable than ever."

"Exactly. I detect the hand of Straker in this polite but profoundly unsatisfactory letter from Papa. She may not want the bungalow for her old age, but I can quite see her fancying the idea of letting it and pocketing the income."

"So can I. Very well, what's to be done?"

"Land Registration's been in force since the Act of '25. I want Martinscombe registered in my name, and I'll give you a power of attorney so that you can deal with the Land Registry on my behalf. Ginette's power of attorney is no use here; the Land Registry might look too closely at the matter if they knew they were dealing with a woman."

"Well, I'll certainly do all I can to help you, Robert, but how can you register something that's not legally yours?"

"That's the difficulty," said Robert, and beyond his speech impairment I heard the echo of a lawyer who was gliding with consummate skill around some very awkward facts. "We have two choices here. Either we involve Papa or we don't. If we involve him he'd have to sign a letter of authorization—at the very least; the Land Registry might well insist on seeing a formal deed of gift. However as

Papa won't discuss the estate with you and has proved himself highly evasive with me, this doesn't seem to be a feasible course of action."

"What's the alternative?"

"We take matters into our own hands."

"I'm not sure I'm too keen on this, Robert."

"My dear John, to quote one of Mama's most notorious phrases, it's the right thing—indeed the only thing—to do. How else can I protect my wife and son from a predator like Straker?"

"All right, go on."

"I think I can see a solution based on the fact that Papa and I have the same name. We'll approach the Land Registry and ask for Martinscombe Farm to be registered in the name of Robert Charles Godwin. That'll include the bungalow, which is still legally on the Martinscombe lands."

"Yes, but—"

"I'll engage a London firm of solicitors whom I've never used before and ask them to attend to the formalities of the registration—the documents, fees and so on. Then when the Registry issues a certificate I can lodge it with my normal solicitors in Lincoln's Inn. Once that's done I ostensibly have a title which I can devise by will, and if I behave as if I'm the legal owner of Martinscombe by remaking my will to include it, no one in London will question the ownership when I die. My new will will be granted probate, the title will be reregistered and there's no reason why either Papa or Fairfax's firm in Swansea should ever find out about it—unless Papa goes completely insane, Straker tries to evict Ginette and the deed has to surface to prove Kester's title. And all that may never happen. This is purely a defensive measure, not an act of aggrandizement."

"If Papa does go completely insane, surely Ginevra would have a legal remedy?"

"His sanity would still be a debatable issue. No, I'm taking no chances—if there's even the faintest possibility that Ginette might lose her case in court, I don't want her involved with the law at all."

"Fair enough, but I still don't see how you're going to get around this without involving Papa. Surely the Land Registry will want proof of title?"

"That's not a problem. I'll simply ask Fairfax, who as the Oxmoon solicitor has the Oxmoon deeds in his safekeeping, to lend me the Martinscombe abstract of title—or whatever documents the Land Registry needs. I'll say there's a point I want to establish in relation to my son's inheritance, and Fairfax isn't going to refuse me. In fact I may even improve on that story in order to keep the deeds in my possession. I'm sure that's well within my capabilities."

I ignored this chilling reference to the potential acrobatics of a legally trained mind. "And meanwhile," I said, working the scheme out, "the abstract of title will say the farm belongs to Robert Charles Godwin—"

"—and the Land Registry will innocently assume that's me and not Papa. Don't worry, John, this is nothing serious. It's just a little muddle over a name."

In such a manner might my mother have suggested my father's fatal juggling with the tide tables.

"My dear Robert, you appall me."

"I appall myself. But you answer me this: what the devil else can I do?"

I had no idea. I was silent, trying to consider the morality of the situation clearly. At last I said, "In my opinion it's unarguable that you have a moral right to that property—Papa intended in 1919 that it should be yours."

"Exactly. To square your conscience you can think of this as legalizing Papa's wishes."

"And since the estate will go to Kester anyway," I pursued, plowing doggedly on, "it doesn't matter whether he inherits Martinscombe from you soon or from Papa later. No one's being defrauded."

Robert hesitated. I looked at him sharply, but decided he was having trouble with his speech. His facial muscles were paralyzed so there was no expression for me to read. In the end he just said, "People will get what they deserve. Justice will be done."

"'Fiat justitia!'" I quoted, smiling at him, but he was too exhausted to reply. Ringing the bell for Bennett I said, "Don't worry. I'll arrange everything" and heard him whisper back, "You're the best brother a man ever had."

I only hoped I could live up to his opinion of me. I had no doubt that I was doing the right thing by helping Robert protect Ginevra and Kester, but once I started manipulating the legal ownership of property I felt I was on dangerous ground indeed.

V

"That stupid sissyish baby Kester said such a silly thing to me today," said Harry, wandering up as I tinkered with the engine of my motor to distract myself from my worries. "He says he's going to inherit Oxmoon! Imagine!" And he laughed with scorn and took a large bite out of the apple in his hand.

I straightened my back to look at him. He was within days of his ninth birthday, and although he took after his mother in looks, he had a bold adventurous personality which reminded me of myself when I had been Johnny long ago, living dangerously with Lion at Oxmoon. After my own experiences as a child I strongly disapproved of parents who had favorites but secretly, in my unguarded moments, I felt Harry was quite perfect. He was very good-looking, very clever, very athletic, very well mannered and very personable, and I often felt sad that Blanche was not alive to share my joy in him.

"I told Kester quite frankly," he was saying as he munched his apple, "that he hadn't a hope of inheriting. 'Tough luck, old chap,' I said, not wanting to be too beastly, 'but that's one yarn you simply can't spin.' And do you know what he did, Papa? He laughed! He said 'I know something you don't know!' and he stuck out his tongue at me. Of course, never having been away to school he's just pampered and spoiled, and he can't help behaving like an idiot, I realize that. But all the same... I thought it was pretty peculiar behavior. Everyone knows

431

Uncle Robert's dying, and everyone knows that when Uncle Robert's dead you'll be Grandfather's eldest surviving son. So that means you'll get Oxmoon eventually, doesn't it? And then I'll get it after you."

I glanced down at the complicated engine of my motor. I glanced at the damp cobbles of the stable yard, at the newly painted water butt, at the oil stains on my hands. I glanced everywhere except at Harry, shining perfect Harry who deserved everything a devoted father could give him. Several seconds ticked by. Then I picked up a nearby rag, wiped my hands and said, "Oxmoon passes from eldest son to eldest son, Harry, so Kester will inherit from Uncle Robert even though Uncle Robert may die before Grandfather."

Silence.

"You mean that's the done thing?" said Harry at last.

"Yes," I said. "It's the done thing. Grandfather has an absolute moral duty to leave Oxmoon to Kester."

"Oh, I see," said Harry. "I didn't realize." He stood looking at the apple in his hand. Then he threw the core away, said carelessly, "Well, never mind, I like the Manor much better than Oxmoon anyway" and skipped off across the cobbles.

I remember thinking with enormous relief that at least I had one child who never gave me a moment's anxiety.

VI

Christmas had become a bad time of the year for my father, and the Christmas of 1927 was no exception. When I arrived on Christmas afternoon with Thomas, Harry and Marian to pay our traditional call, we found he was in bed and seeing no one.

Against Milly's advice, I went up to his room.

"I'm not receiving you while you live openly with that woman and father bastards," he said when he saw me. "I don't suppose my disapproval will bring you to your senses, but I've made up my mind I must try and save you. I can't stand by passively while you ruin yourself."

Ironically this view reflected my own sentiments about him, but as there was no way the conversation could be prolonged I was obliged to leave.

In the new year Warburton said, "John, I think you ought to know I've been hearing rumors that your father's insane. Apparently there's a lot of discontent on the estate."

I had heard similar stories from Thomas, who mixed more with the local population than I could, but Warburton's words carried more weight with me. "I'll talk to Robert," I said automatically. "I'll see what he thinks I should do."

"No," said Warburton. "He mustn't be worried by your father's situation anymore—he's too ill. I'm sorry, John, but the moment's finally come: you're on your own."

The Wheel had become a rack, Fortune was tightening the screws and amidst all my grief I was aware of an overpowering fear that my courage would be insufficient to meet the ordeal that I could now so clearly see ahead.

But I had to conquer that fear. I could not allow myself to be defeated because too many people depended on me.

I struggled on.

VII

Again I saw Freddy Fairfax, the senior partner in the firm of Swansea solicitors who handled the Oxmoon estate. When I had seen him previously he had assured me he would let me know if ever he thought my father showed signs of being legally incompetent, but since then I had heard nothing from him.

Fairfax was in his late forties, a smooth sleek able and not unpleasant individual with whom I played golf occasionally at weekends. His reputation was good. Certainly I had never heard any story that reflected on either his honesty or his competence, and although he might have shunned me during my days as a pariah this was no reason why I should have distrusted his professional judgment.

"I'm worried about my father again," I said after we had exchanged preliminary greetings in his office. "Have you seen him lately?"

"I was over at Oxmoon the other day, old boy. Couple of new tenancy agreements needed. He seemed very much in the pink. Not quite the man he used to be, of course, but old age gets to us all in the end, what?"

"Have you heard rumors of trouble on the estate?"

"Rumors, old boy?"

"Well, you are the estate's solicitor, Fairfax! I assume you have your ear close to the ground!"

"Old boy, I hate to say this because I know you're well intentioned, but I really don't think I can discuss my client's affairs with you."

I persisted but got nowhere and eventually, profoundly skeptical, I left him and drove to Oxmoon.

VIII

"I won't receive you," said my father. "Please leave at once."

"I only want to help."

"I don't want your help. You're not to be trusted—you broke your word to me. You swore you wouldn't live openly with her."

"Surely despite my private life you can accept that my affection for you is genuine?"

"What if it is? My mother's affection for me was genuine too, but my God, what hell she put me through! Her spirit's possessed you, I can see that clearly now; you're her, you've come back to torment me, you've got to be kept out—"

"Papa—"

"*Stay away from me!*"

I left.

IX

"What can I do, Ginevra? Fairfax swears he's normal. He won't see Warburton, won't talk to me. Obviously he's mentally ill but how the devil do I get him certified?"

"My dear, what horrors, but I can't cope. I've got a mountain of horrors of my own."

"Oh, God, forgive me, I'm so sorry—"

"He can't bear being blind, he simply can't bear it. . . ."

She broke down, I took her in my arms and the darkness seemed to close over us as if we had been walled up alive in a tomb.

X

Five days later on Lady Day a band of tenants from the Oxmoon estate marched to see Robert to protest at the new steep increases in their rents. Treating my father as incompetent they had turned to his heir for justice, and when they found Robert was too ill to see anyone they refused to disperse. The telephone call came from Ginevra just as I returned to the Manor from the Home Farm, and taking Thomas with me I drove immediately to Little Oxmoon.

We found about thirty men encamped before the bungalow. They appeared peaceful enough at first glance, but as I halted the car they surged forward to surround it and I saw their mood was ugly.

"Keep your mouth shut," I said to Thomas, "and leave this entirely to me."

I noticed that the majority of the men were farm laborers who lived in my father's Penhale cottages, but when I saw that my father's foremen too were present, I knew the rise in rent was merely the straw which had broken the camel's back. Clearly this was the climax of years of increasing maladministration.

I got out of the car. The hostility seemed to thicken. I experienced a moment of acute uneasiness, but told myself their hostility could not be directed against me personally.

The next moment I was disillusioned.

"Here comes the adulterer!" said someone, and that was followed by the comment "We finally managed to get him out of bed!" There was contemptuous laughter. Someone spat at me. Flicking the spittle aside I pushed my way through the crowd, reached the doorstep and turned to address them. Cold sweat was inching down my spine.

"Good afternoon," I said strongly, projecting my voice to override the hostile mutterings. My mind, sharpened by shock, was darting in a dozen different directions at once. I was remembering the bullies at school and the necessity of displaying no fear which would heighten their pleasure, but I felt shattered, vulnerable and, most ambivalent of all, enraged that I should be judged in this fashion by men who should have been doffing their caps to me with respect. A second later, however, I saw that the class system could work in my favor and that this time all the bayonets would be on my side.

"If you want the justice you deserve," I said, "you'll treat me with the respect to which I'm entitled. I'm well intentioned but I refuse to negotiate with a rabble."

They stared at me. I saw their faces, young and old, still hostile but recognizing an age-old authority which the twentieth century had so far been unable to destroy. Mentally congratulating myself on this successful assertion of my strength, I thought with a bitter humor, That's the spirit that built the Empire! And I was still savoring my restored confidence when someone threw a clod of mud which hit me in the chest.

That was undoubtedly the spirit which had led to the General Strike. It occurred to me that the age-old authority was wearing thin after all.

"Very well," I said calmly, heart thudding like a sledgehammer. "If you're determined to be a rabble I can't help you. Good day." I stepped down from the doorstep and tried to walk away, but Thornton, the foreman at Cherryvale, intervened.

"Wait, Mr. John." He turned to the others. "We must deal with him; there's no one else." And he thrust a list of grievances into my hand.

Immediately a confused babble broke out, during which I heard the words "extortion," "bare-faced robbery" and "that witch Milly Straker."

"We mean no disrespect to your father, Mr. John," said Thornton hurriedly, "but the old gentleman's well known now to be at the mercy of others, and One Other in particular."

I returned to the doorstep, and when everyone was quiet I said, "My brother's dying. I must ask you to leave him in peace. But if you can elect three men to come to Oxmoon at sunset, I'll examine these grievances one by one and see what can be done."

They were satisfied. Thornton, who was evidently one of nature's diplomats, pulled off his cap and thanked me with a humility which both appeased and nauseated me. Someone in the crowd said, "How's the wife in London?" but a dozen other voices said furiously, "Shhh!" and I pretended not to hear.

Seconds later I was driving away.

"My God, you were wonderful, John!" said Thomas, who was enjoying himself immensely. "As good as Jesus Christ!"

I said nothing. I was suffering from a nervous reaction, and I had to grip the wheel hard to stop my hands trembling. Nausea churned spasmodically in the pit of my stomach.

As soon as we reached Oxmoon I knew something was wrong, and when I saw the stigmata of violence I found I was bathed in a cold sweat again. Evidently the loutish sons of the disgruntled tenants had not been idle. The windows of the library had been smashed and a slogan had been daubed on the wall by the front door.

"'WORKERS OF THE WORLD UNITE,'" mused Thomas. "Haven't I heard that before somewhere?"

I told myself that I had wanted class war and now I was getting it. In a detached manner which sprang from shock I realized that my primary emotion was again rage. I wanted to shoot every socialist in sight. So much for my intellectual radicalism. Apparently in a crisis reason and humanity counted for nothing and man's instinct was to return to the pack that had bred him. I knew then that at heart I was never going to change. I was what my class had made me; I was the victim of my education, the prisoner of my privileged life; all else was illusion and self-deception.

"My God!" cried Thomas, who had just seen the broken windows. "Look at that! Wait till I get my hands on whoever did it; I'll smash the bastards to pulp!"

I thought how pleasant it must be to have such a simple outlook, untroubled by any intellectual doubts or emotional complexities.

"Calm down, Thomas. We've got enough bulls in this particular china shop without you trying to join them." I was wondering if the mob was inside, wrecking everything in sight, but as we jumped out of the car the front door was opened by the village constable

"Oh Mr. John, thank God you've come—"

"Where's my father?"

"I don't know, sir; he seems to have disappeared, but Mr. Bayliss summoned me half an hour ago when the windows were smashed—"

"Where is Bayliss?"

"He came over poorly, sir, and had to lie down. All the other servants have locked themselves in the kitchens and won't come out."

"And Mrs. Straker?"

"They say she's gone, sir—slipped out at first light. Maybe she knew there'd be trouble, sir, today being the quarter day and people so upset with the new rents."

"Very well, go with my brother, search the grounds and make sure all the vandals have gone."

I went into the house. The servants, cowering in the scullery, unlocked the door when they heard my voice. I asked if anyone had seen my father. No one had.

"Very well." I turned to the cook. "Make some tea." I swung round on the footman. "See how Bayliss is and if necessary telephone for Dr. Warburton." I faced the parlormaid. "Send word to the glazier. I want those windows replaced immediately." My glance fell on the daily housemaids. "Clear up the mess in the library at once." At the door I stopped to look back. "I authorize a finger of brandy for everyone," I said, "and once that's been taken and the tea drunk, I shall expect everyone to go about their business as usual."

Leaving them all bobbing and curtsying, I returned to the hall and ran upstairs. The bedrooms were all empty but as I reached the back stairs I suddenly knew where he was.

The attics were musty and still. I called, "Papa!" and waited but there was no answer. I walked down the corridor, my footsteps echoing on the floorboards, and found him where I had found him before. He was sitting by the covered portrait of his mother and this time the photograph albums were open in his hands.

He was crying quietly to himself. He barely looked up as I entered the room.

"Papa," I said, stooping to put an arm around his shoulders, "it's all right now, I'm here."

But my father only went on turning the pages of the first album, and in that flickering kaleidoscope of black-and-white I saw the past recaptured, the happy laughing children of long ago, the wife he had loved and the magic house he had resurrected from the grave.

"Papa..." As I slid my hand over his, the pages of the album stopped turning and he looked up at me at last. But his watery eyes remained bewildered and all he could say was "Who are you?"

I

"I'LL TELEPHONE the Home of the Assumption," said Warburton.

"No. Absolutely not."

"But my dear John, it's the very best home in the district for mental cases—"

"He's never going to set foot in it."

"But what are you going to do with him?"

The district nurse arrived. I left her with Warburton and my father in the attics and ran downstairs to telephone Bronwen. By that time Thomas had returned from searching the grounds, so I sent him away in my car to fetch her.

When I returned to the attics I found the district nurse looking flushed and Warburton more troubled than ever.

"He won't budge, John, and I'm afraid he might be violent if I try to give him an injection."

"Wait." I bent over my father to coax him to his feet, but he behaved as if he were stone-deaf. I tried to take the album away from him, but he pushed me off savagely and hugged it to his chest.

"John, I know this is very upsetting for you, but—"

"Shut up."

I went on trying unsuccessfully to communicate with my father, and I was still trying when Bronwen walked in. I noticed that the district nurse immediately pursed her lips in disapproval, but Warburton said, "Mrs. Morgan, can you please convince John that his father must be taken to a place where he can receive the proper medical care?"

Bronwen said in English, "We're going to look after him at home." Then she said in Welsh to my father, "You can't understand what they say, can you?"

He looked up at her. She knelt beside him and pointed to the album. "Please can I see your photographs?" she said. "Please will you come with me so that we can look at them together?"

He went on gazing at her in wonder, but very slowly his wrinkled trembling old hand slid into hers. I helped him to his feet and while Warburton and the nurse looked on with incredulity we led him downstairs and took him home.

II

"That arch-cunt Straker!" said Thomas. "How could she have walked out on him like that?"

We were back at Oxmoon an hour later. My father, still trustfully holding Bronwen's hand in Blanche's old room at the Manor, had allowed Warburton to administer a sedative. A day nurse and a night nurse had been requested from the Swansea agency that was providing additional nursing for Robert. Mrs. Wells had risen to the occasion with her usual aplomb and even the vicar had called with a dutiful futility; I was aware of Penhale vibrating with excitement as gossip and rumor reached fever pitch.

At Oxmoon the constable reported that the servants had named the vandals, and as he bicycled away to make his arrests I realized with a sinking heart that I now had no further excuse for delaying my investigation of Milly Straker's reign.

"Bloody bitch," said Thomas, kicking his heel into the carpet to relieve his feelings. "I hate all women."

"Well, fortunately for us men not all women are like Milly Straker."

"Sez you. Personally I'd rather fuck sheep."

This remark, very typical of Thomas at his most disturbed, was not intended to be taken seriously so I merely said in a mild voice, "Really? I don't think I'd care for all the wool," and headed towards the green baize door.

"Where are we going?"

"We're going to make a preliminary survey of what I'm very much afraid is a catastrophe. I shouldn't think for one moment that woman's left any incriminating evidence of embezzlement behind, but we must make sure."

The housekeeper's room, Milly's office on the ground floor of the servants' quarters, proved unremarkable except for the number of unpaid bills piled beneath three large paperweights. We went upstairs to her official bedroom but it had an unused musty air. As I noted the disappearance of all her possessions, I realized she had been planning her escape for some weeks; she had gauged the hour of disaster with precision and when the train had approached the edge of the cliff she had nimbly jumped clear. Rage swept over me again but I controlled it. Rage was a luxury I could not afford. There was no time. "Thomas, I'm going to have to search Papa's room before the servants start poking around and discovering God-knows-what. Do you want to come with me or would you prefer to wait downstairs?"

"I'll come with you," said my watchdog, and beyond the fierce exterior I glimpsed a shocked and frightened youth who was not yet twenty-one.

We left the servants' wing by a door that connected with the back stairs, and moved in silence down the long passage to the other end of the house.

"The place is in a bad way, isn't it?" said Thomas suddenly, looking at the peeling wallpaper. "Maybe there are even rats in the library, just as there were when Oxmoon went to pieces under Bryn-Davies."

"I don't think we've sunk that low this time," I said, but a search of the bedroom soon changed my mind. I knew then that there were more repulsive symbols than rats of degeneration and decay.

"Jesus Christ!" said my innocent little brother, blithely opening a wardrobe. "What's all this?" And we found ourselves confronted, just as I had feared, by an unspeakable collection of erotic impedimenta.

I was by that time nearly thirty-six, and the days were long since past when I had denied my sexual inclinations by adopting priggish poses, but even so I was appalled. For a moment I wished I were as ignorant as Thomas, but both before and after my second marriage I had read a great deal about sex in an effort to place my sexuality in perspective, and the result was that I knew too much to misunderstand what I now saw. My sexual relationship with Bronwen, the natural result of the extraordinary harmony of our personalities, had always been so satisfying that I had never felt the need to resort to books to learn how I might enhance the experience, but in my efforts to compensate myself for my second marriage I had felt driven to set out down many unexplored avenues, and Constance, strongly sexed herself and quite humorless enough to reduce sex to a suitable subject for research, had egged me on. However, even with Constance I had drawn certain lines. My father, in his frantic efforts to divert himself from intolerable truths, had evidently drawn no lines at all.

In a moment of revelation I saw at last why he had been unable to remain faithful to my mother. He could never have asked her to share in such perversions. He had loved her too much and would have wanted above all to protect her from such sordidness, although I thought my mother must have guessed the truth in time; her knowledge would explain her remarkable and courageous resignation which could have come only through some profound understanding of my father's dilemma.

I then experienced a second moment of revelation as I at last perceived the conflict that had driven him inexorably toward breakdown. My father, fundamentally a good and decent man, would never have been able to forgive himself for the secret compulsions that had driven him not merely to be unfaithful to the woman he loved but to install Milly Straker at Oxmoon, a move that had ultimately led to the dissolution of his family life and the ruin of everything that had been precious to him.

Thomas was still demanding explanations but I merely ordered him to light the fire.

"But we can't burn all that stuff, John—the rubber'll make the most awful stink!"

"We'll bury what we can't burn."

Thomas set alight the housemaid's arrangement of twigs and coal in the grate and then tried to look at the pornography, but when I saw his expression I told him sharply to stop. "Spoilsport!" he muttered, but I knew he was thankful that he could abandon his perusal without a loss of face. More time passed. We toiled on.

"Get the pillowcases, would you? We'll use them to cart away the stuff we can't burn." I went on stoking the fire.

"John, you've got to tell me what all this is about, you've got to, or else I'll start imagining things, and imagining things is worse than knowing them—"

I knew he was right. I made a great effort to control myself but it was hard to find the right words and harder still to adopt the right unemotional manner. Shoving the last pictures of defecation into the flames, I straightened my back and said, "This is all connected with punishment. He seems to have welcomed physical humiliation."

"Christ! Why?"

"Guilt."

"Guilt? Oh, you mean all that mess about locking up Grandmama in the loony bin—he was always saying how guilty he felt about that. But how peculiar! Do you mean the bitch just punished him all the time with the whips and this other fantastic rubbish? Didn't sex come into it at all?"

"The greater the punishment, the greater the sexual gratification."

"Christ! But if he was so gratified why did he need that false cock over there?"

"Maybe it wasn't he who needed it."

"Christ!"

"Stop saying 'Christ' and give me a hand with the pillowcases."

We began to stow away our unspeakable booty.

"Hope the material's strong enough, John. The chains are bloody heavy."

But the pillowcases stood the strain. When they were full I poked around in

440

the grate to make sure all the pornography had been destroyed, and then we left the room to conduct the next stage of the operation.

We buried our haul in the shadow of Humphrey de Mohun's ruined tower, covered the grave with dead leaves and retreated to the house to drink brandy. The parlormaid told me Bayliss had been taken to hospital. The glaziers were at work on the library windows. The house seemed to be slowly returning to order but the sun was now setting on the bleak landscape, and as I drank my brandy I saw the three representatives from the band of tenants trudging dourly up the drive in pursuit of justice.

So as usual there was to be no respite. Downing the rest of my brandy I told the parlormaid to show my visitors into the morning room and prepared to face still more evidence of my father's disastrous decline.

III

After promising to review all the rents I sanctioned a delay in payment until my investigations had been completed and promised I would undertake a complete investigation of the estate so that I could straighten out the muddle which had arisen from maladministration. After the men had expressed their gratitude I told them I would see every tenant to hear each grievance, and I asked them if they knew of anyone suffering hardship that required immediate alleviation.

I was told of three old women who had no fuel and of a widow with five children who lived on bread and dripping. Noting their names, I gave an assurance that their plight would be terminated at once.

"So you'll be master of Oxmoon now, Mr. John?" said Thornton of Cherryvale.

"My father's master while he lives," I said, "but I shall now be managing the estate on his behalf."

They all said they were glad, and I saw then that they were no different from the men at the golf club; once they had realized that I could still be treated as a normal person, they no longer felt they had no alternative but to treat me as a wicked adulterer, and their moral obligation to be hostile evaporated. Taking their leave of me courteously they retired in satisfaction to Penhale.

I was still standing in the hall, still contemplating the hair-raising but stimulating challenge of managing a large rundown estate, still straining my eyes to peer into the convoluted machinery of my wheel of fortune, when Thomas emerged from the library to say he was unable to make head or tail of the estate books.

"All right, leave them, take the car, go back to the Manor, tell Mrs. Wells I want her to take charge temporarily here and then bring her back with her luggage. Oh, and bring a bag for yourself. You're going to be the Godwin in residence while we sort out this mess. Big houses run better if at least one member of the family is present to give the servants an incentive to behave well."

"But aren't you going to move in here yourself?"

"Papa wouldn't like it."

"Damn it, you've saved the old bugger from the loony bin, haven't you? What right's he got to complain!"

"The best right in the world—the right of an owner. Now off you go, there's a good chap, and stop making idiotic suggestions."

I got rid of him.

Then I went to the library, where a fire had now been lit, and sat thinking for a long time. After a while I found myself remembering Robert talking of putting the magic back into Oxmoon, and a very sensible, very rational, very persuasive voice in my head said: "But *I'm* the only one who can do that."

"...and Oxmoon will *rise again* on the Wheel of Fortune..."

I could hear Robert's voice so clearly. But then I could also so clearly hear him say, "You're the best brother a man ever had."

Blotting the future from my mind I sat down at the library table, opened the estate books and once more began to wrestle with the problems of the present.

IV

I was too exhausted to make more than a cursory examination of my father's papers, but I found his checkbook in a drawer of the table and soon discovered that every stub recorded a payment to Milly. I did stumble across correspondence from Fairfax urging financial prudence, but I stopped being grateful to him when I saw the size of his bills. I also stopped feeling grateful to my father's accommodating bank manager, Lloyd-Thomas, when I saw the profitable size of the overdraft and discovered the existence of a mortgage.

"We'll make a serious start on the mess tomorrow, Thomas," I said when he arrived back with Mrs. Wells. "I'm too tired to do more now."

"Did Milly do anything illegal?"

"I doubt it. No need. He just gave her whatever money she wanted, but by God, I'm going to fire Fairfax and remove the Oxmoon account from Lloyd-Thomas's bank! They should have given me warning long ago."

"Have they been negligent?"

"Not in a legal sense, as far as I can see. Just stupid. But I suppose they'll say in their defense that Papa's reputation as an excellent manager with a good financial brain drove them to assume, in the absence of any glaring evidence to the contrary, that he was competent—and don't forget Papa was very fierce in tolerating no interference in his affairs. Yes, I can see Fairfax and Lloyd-Thomas being intimidated by him, but nevertheless that's no excuse for their failure to confide in me."

"I'd like to flog and hang everyone in sight," said Thomas predictably.

I patted him gently on the shoulder and returned to Penhale.

V

Harrowing days followed. I obtained the necessary power of attorney, fired Fairfax, engaged a new firm of solicitors and also a firm of accountants, renegotiated the mortgage at a new bank and waded steadily through the mire of my father's accounts. Although my father had juggled the books, often most ingeniously, to present a false impression of the estate's finances, a stark picture soon emerged of disappearing money, capital depreciation and expenditure for which no receipts could be found.

"Is he bankrupt?" said Ginevra when I knew enough to report the full extent of the disaster to her.

"No—thank God he broke down when he did. Better late than never. And thank God too he had a private fortune to draw on in addition to the estate, but nevertheless it'll take Oxmoon years to recover."

"And to think he always prided himself on being so shrewd with money!"

"No doubt he became increasingly afraid she'd leave him and he was prepared to do anything to keep her."

"But how *could* he have been so infatuated! That awful thieving tart—"

"I'm afraid the entire catastrophe only proves to the hilt Robert's belief that love isn't always accompanied by youth and beauty and a full orchestra playing 'The Blue Danube.'"

"'The Blue Danube'—oh God, that reminds me. Let's have another drink, Johnny. There's something I must tell you about Robert."

We were in the drawing room at Little Oxmoon. I had paid my daily call on Robert, but I had stayed no more than five minutes and I had not mentioned the disaster at Oxmoon. At that stage it would not have interested him. He had said goodbye to my father a long time ago and now the outside world held no meaning for him. It was too remote. Lying lifelessly in his quiet shadowed room he had wanted only to listen to me talking of the past.

"He seemed a bit brighter today," I said to Ginevra.

"That's because he's decided when to die."

After a moment I said, "Do you mean—"

"No, I'm not talking about euthanasia. Gavin says that when people are very, very ill they sometimes seem able to choose when to let go. He told Robert and said the power to choose was related to the power of the will. Robert was tremendously excited and at once started making plans."

I drank half my pink gin and said, "Which day has he chosen?"

"My birthday. April the twenty-third."

"But why on earth—"

"He always said that was the day on which he first began to live. On my eighteenth birthday in 1898 Robert fell in love with me. We danced together beneath the chandeliers at Oxmoon while the orchestra played 'The Blue Danube.'"

I was unable to break the silence that followed. I sat motionless, staring into the fire, but after a while the flames seemed too bright. I looked away.

"He wants to end in the beginning," said Ginevra. She did not cry, and when I glanced at her I realized she was far back in the remote past, just as I was, listening to the violins playing that waltz which refused to die.

I said, "I was there."

She was amazed. "Were you? But how extraordinary! You couldn't have been more than six!"

"Special occasion. Lion and I stayed up late."

"Did you see us dancing?"

"Yes," I said. "I remember."

"Oh Johnny, you must tell him! When the end comes—"

"Yes, of course. I'll be there."

We were silent again. It was not until my drink was finished that I was able to say, "I hope Robert won't be disappointed."

"Don't worry. Gavin and I are determined that he won't be."

"Thank God."

The flames went on flickering in the grate. The firelight was kind to Ginevra, smoothing away the lines on her face and emphasizing her elegant legs, clad as usual in the sheerest of silk stockings. The only lamp in the room stood behind her, and suddenly I glimpsed again the radiant young girl who had danced long ago in the ballroom at Oxmoon when Robert's adult life had begun.

"Well," she said abruptly, "it's no use sitting around here swilling pink gin and chatting about death. I must go upstairs to Kester and you must go home to Bronwen.... No change in Bobby's condition, I suppose?"

"None," I said, but when I arrived home I had a surprise. After three mute weeks of recognizing no one, my father had begun to improve. Bronwen came rushing down the staircase as soon as I entered the hall.

"Johnny, wonderful news! He's asking for you!"

I agreed with genuine enthusiasm that this was wonderful but nevertheless I was conscious of ambivalence. During the past weeks I had often looked at the mindless shell which housed my father and thought that death would be a merciful release—and not only for him; once he was dead Oxmoon would pass to Kester and I would finally be beyond the torment of temptation.

Bronwen was talking rapidly as she led the way upstairs. She told me she had looked in to see my father half an hour before in order to relieve the night nurse, who had gone downstairs to make herself some tea, and as soon as the night nurse had left my father had spoken in Welsh.

"...and he said, 'I know you but I've forgotten your name. You're the pretty girl with the baby,' and when I said yes, I was Bronwen, he said, 'You belong to John,' and then he asked where you were and when I said you were at Oxmoon he suddenly realized he wasn't at home and he said, 'Am I in the Home of the Assumption?' and when I said no, you wouldn't let him be sent there, I thought he was going to cry but he didn't, and then Nurse brought the tea and he drank a cup and all the while he kept asking and asking for you..."

I entered Blanche's room. My father was propped up on his pillows. His silver

444

hair with its faint golden sheen had been carefully parted and brushed. His eyes filled with tears as he recognized me.

"Well, here he is at last!" said the nurse cozily. "Isn't that nice!"

I got rid of her. Bronwen had already retreated. Pulling up a chair I sat down at the bedside.

"My dear Papa," I said, "how very glad I am to see you better." I realized with relief as I spoke that despite my past ambivalence this statement was true. It was easy to wish him dead when he was no better than a vegetable, but quite impossible not to wish him a full recovery once he was showing signs of life.

"They say I'm at Penhale Manor," he whispered.

"That's right. Thomas and I are looking after Oxmoon until you're well enough to go back."

My father looked pitifully frightened. "You mustn't look at the books."

"It's all right, I've sorted everything out. All's well now."

Trembling fingers wrapped themselves around my hand in gratitude, and when I saw him trying to screw up the courage to ask the inevitable question I said as gently as I could, "I'm afraid I don't know where Milly is, Papa. She left without leaving an address."

"But Mrs. Wells would know where to send a letter. . . . They had mutual friends. . . ." The quavering voice trailed away.

I said evenly, "I'm afraid Milly made a great deal of trouble for you, Papa. I'm afraid she wasn't a good friend to you in the end."

My father nodded as if he perfectly accepted this judgment. Then a tear began to trickle down his cheek.

"Papa, believe me, I do understand how much she means to you, but—"

"I do so want Milly," said my father, the tears rolling down his cheeks. "I know you never liked her but she was so kind to me and so cheerful, always knowing how to make me laugh. I expect you thought she was only after my money, but I understood her, I knew how frightened she was of being old and alone and ending up in a workhouse as her mother did. She had a terrible childhood too, just as terrible as mine, oh, I understood it all, she used to say I was the only man who'd ever understood her and the only man she'd ever really liked. I won't give her any more money. You can continue to manage my affairs, but please, please write to Milly and ask her to come back."

"Papa—"

"You've been so good and kind, saving me from that place, I'm sorry I was so cold and unforgiving but I'll make all that up to you now, I swear I will, I'll do anything you want—alter my will—leave you all my money—why, I'll even leave you—"

I was on my feet. I heard myself saying firmly, "You can't make a will while you're still unwell, Papa. Don't worry about that now. Your first task is to get better."

"But if you could get Milly back—"

"If I do, it would only be because I know how terrible it is to be deprived of

445

someone you love. It wouldn't be because I'm looking for repayment."

"But you'll do it? You'll get her back?"

"I'll try."

VI

"You can't!"

"You're mad—she'll never come!"

The reactions of Thomas and Ginevra were predictable but they were wrong. She came. I met her at the station two weeks later. She wore a smart black coat with fox furs, and a little hat with a prim veil. She was accompanied by a mountain of very expensive leather luggage.

"Well, dear," she said, "life's full of surprises, isn't it? I'm sure we never thought *we'd* meet again! Never mind, I've had a lovely holiday and invested some money for my old age and now I feel ready for anything. I did meet a man who offered me a little house in Putney but neither he nor the house appealed—Oxmoon's ruined me, that's my trouble, Oxmoon and Bobby. Nothing but the best will do for *me* now, thanks very much! I wish I hadn't grabbed so much before I left, I know I was naughty, but when you're a woman old age is always just around the corner and if you've got no money you may as well cut your throat and be done with it. God, it's bloody hell being a woman, always at the mercy of men who treat you like horseshit—pardon my French—but that was what was so special about Bobby, always so charming, always such a gentleman, he *never* treated me like horseshit—no, nothing was too good for me where Bobby was concerned, nothing at all.

"I'm sorry he's been so bad. Mabel Wells wrote to me via Lily in Wandsworth to tell me what was going on, and I kept thinking of him. Of course you all probably thought I was drinking champagne in Monte Carlo and not giving a damn, but you were wrong. I thought of him. Poor old Bobby. Yes, I've missed him, and my God, I've missed that awful inconvenient old house too—oh, how I loved the *power* of being in charge there—God, I could give up food, drink and sex and just live on power alone, really I could. In fact if ever I'm reincarnated I'm going to ask God to let me come back as master of Oxmoon—not mistress, mind you, but master. Of course no one in their right mind would want to be reincarnated as a woman."

We traveled out of Swansea and headed through the narrow lanes into the heart of Gower. A gust of rain buffeted the car but it was only a spring shower and the next moment the sun was shining on the walls of Penrice as we passed the turning to the sea.

"How's that nice girl of yours? Not pregnant again, I hope? People get such funny ideas about having babies, it beats me, I've never been able to see the attraction myself. And talking of babies, how's little Thomas? Has he managed to get together with Mabel Wells since the two of them have been on their own at Oxmoon? Mabel was so coy about him in her letter that my hopes were raised— it would be so nice for her, wouldn't it, and the best possible thing for him. There's something a bit off-color there, but nothing Mabel can't cure. Funny how Mabel likes young men. I've never been able to understand it myself, all that noisy thrashing around and then behaving afterwards as if they've achieved some sort of miracle. Give me an older man any day, I say. They may still be just as self-centered—what man isn't?—but at least you've got some chance of uncovering a bit of sophistication..."

We reached the hamlet of Middleton and turned off along the road to Penhale. Another squall hit the car as we approached Oxmoon, and to our left on the Downs the wild ponies huddled together against the wind which was hurtling across the heather from the invisible sea.

"Ah, there's Oxmoon, nasty great brute of a house—oh, how I love it! No, I really shouldn't have been happy at all in that cheap little villa in Putney..."

We arrived at the Manor but I was too relieved that the journey was over to do more than take her straight upstairs to my father's room.

"*Milly!*" shouted my father as she walked in, and for a brief moment he was young again, ablaze with vitality, his face radiant with happiness. That was when I knew he would recover sufficiently to be capable of making a new valid will in my favor. "Oh, Milly, how wonderful to see you! Milly, I want to go home but the doctor says I must live quietly here for a time and there's a nurse who treats me as if I'm a baby, and I can't quite work out how I'm ever going to escape—"

"Don't you worry, my poppet," said Milly, giving him an affectionate kiss. "You just leave it all to me."

VII

My dilemma finally overwhelmed me.

Retreating to my room, I asked myself how I, a weak, divided and thoroughly unheroic man who seemed to spend most of his time in a state of moral confusion, could even attempt to play the hero's role that fate was so obviously trying to assign to me. How did I resist accepting Oxmoon? Of course my father was still of unsound mind and might feel less generous when he was fully recovered, but in fact had he not been irrationally guilty about that seduction which had happened over thirty years before? And had I perhaps yielded my most cherished ambition not out of logic but for emotional reasons which had become increasingly irrelevant as time went on? I had been shocked and revolted when I heard of my father's behavior with Ginevra; it was natural that I should have responded by insisting that my father expiated his crime by giving Robert what Robert wanted. But hadn't my father now suffered enough for his past wrongs? And was it right that the

447

present and future welfare of Oxmoon should be sacrificed because of a past incident which was best forgotten?

Oxmoon was the challenge I needed. Oxmoon could satisfy my ambition. I was tailor-made for Oxmoon, and now Oxmoon was surely waiting for me, waiting for the man who alone of all the family had the brains and the ability to restore its ailing fortunes.

Robert would never know of my betrayal, of course. He would die happy, convinced I would stand by his idealistic, moving but fundamentally impracticable dying wish that he could pass to his son his magic house and the life that might have been. Ginevra would be angry at first but I thought it unlikely that she would mind much in the end; she would be certain to return to London once Robert was dead, so why should she want to be saddled with Oxmoon? And as for Kester . . . well, Kester would undoubtedly be much happier in London with his mother. Naturally some sort of financial reparation would have to be made— and it went without saying that I'd bend over backwards to be generous—but I saw no reason why Kester should miss Oxmoon. How could he? He had never lived there. It hadn't been bred into his soul as it had been bred into mine.

I thought of soft, girlish little Kester. Without doubt he would be a disaster for Oxmoon. I thought of my bold adventurous Harry, following in my footsteps with ease.

The truth was that for Harry's sake—and for the sake of Oxmoon—I really had to accept my father's wishes if he decided—when he decided—to change his will. It was my moral duty. My father would understand that, of course, if— when—I explained it to him. Yes, he would see just as clearly as I now saw that he had to make me his heir; as my mother would have said, it was the right thing—indeed, the only thing—to do. . . .

VIII

"It would be wrong," said Bronwen.

"I know." I covered my face with my hands. "It would mean cheating Robert, cheating Ginevra, cheating Kester, but oh God, how do I draw the line and stand by it, I'm so terrified I won't be strong enough—"

"I think you will be."

"But I'm so weak, you know how weak I am—"

"I think that in the end you'll be strong."

"But Bronwen—"

"Don't despair. Go on loving Robert and being truthful with him. Then when he dies I think the pattern of love and truth will alter and re-form in an automatic act of magic and you'll be safe."

"I—simply—can't—imagine—"

"I can. And you must. Have faith. Be truthful. And love him right up to the end."

IX

A few days later on the twenty-third of April, 1928, my father was still alive, thriving at Oxmoon, and Robert finally reached the end of the terrible road he had been traveling since the war.

I went to Little Oxmoon after breakfast and found Ginevra waiting for me. She was wearing green, a color that suited her, and had taken immense trouble with her appearance. Accustomed to her taste for unsuitable clothes I was surprised by her plain dress devoid of ornament. She looked tired but tranquil.

"How is he?"

"I think he'll be all right. Gavin's coming at ten."

We went into Robert's room. There was a vase of daffodils by the window, but the only scent came from the lavender bags that disguised the atmosphere of the sickroom. Outside the sun was shining.

"Robert," said Ginevra, "it's John." She turned to me. "He can still whisper but come very close."

"Don't try to speak unless you want to, Robert," I said. "I just wanted you to know I was here."

He blinked in acknowledgment. He looked so old, so gaunt, so waxen, so different from all my memories of him. It was hard to believe that within that wasted unrecognizable body lay the hero of my childhood in that lost world of long ago.

"Shall I talk about—" I murmured to Ginevra, but she said, "No. Not yet. Wait till he wants to speak. Then he'll be ready," so we sat in silence with him for a while. Later Warburton arrived and it was soon after he had withdrawn to the living room to wait that Robert tried to speak.

"Yes, I'm here, darling," said Ginevra, "and John's with us too, just as he was on my eighteenth birthday. Do you remember him being there? I don't. It's extraordinary, isn't it? It really makes it seem as if we've arrived at the beginning again.... Johnny, tell Robert what you remember—tell us what you saw that night."

"I saw it all," I said. "It was such a special occasion and so exciting. Lion was eight and I was not quite six. Edmund was four and too young to stay up, but Mama said Lion and I could wear our sailor suits and watch. I remember it so clearly, Robert—yes, I was there—I was there in the ballroom when the orchestra played 'The Blue Danube,' I was there when you danced with Ginevra. If I close my eyes I can see you as if it were yesterday—I can look across the circle, as Bronwen would say, and hear your echo in time. It's an echo I'll hear all my life, Robert, and all my life whenever I hear that music I'll think of you and remember."

"Thirty years, darling!" said Ginevra to him. "It doesn't seem possible, does it? When I was young I used to think thirty years was an eternity, but now it seems no time at all—and even time itself looks different to me...Yes, what is it, darling? John? Yes, of course."

I leaned over the bed. "I'm here, Robert."

At first I thought he was going to be unable to speak but then I heard the word he wanted to say. It was his son's name.

"Yes, it's all right," I said. "I understand." And in that moment the past was forgotten and the future was irrelevant. All I knew was that at that single moment I wanted him to have what he wanted most. I knew he would never choose to die until he was at peace and I knew I was now the only person who could give him the gift of that chosen death.

"I promise you," I said, "that I'll look after him as if he were my own son, and I promise you," I said in my clearest voice, "that so long as I live I'll see he stays master of Oxmoon." I still had no idea how I was going to be strong enough to live up to my promises, but that for the moment was unimportant. All that mattered was that I loved him enough to speak what at that instant was the truth.

He whispered something, and I had a flash of panic because I could not understand him and I was terrified he was saying he did not believe me.

"Ginevra, I can't hear what he's saying—"

"He's saying you're the best brother a man ever had."

I could not speak but at last I realized he was whispering her name and I knew there was nothing more for me to do except say goodbye. I kissed him briefly, touched his hand for the last time and then I left the room so that Ginevra, with him alone at the beginning of his life, should be with him alone at the end.

X

Warburton left the drawing room when I entered it. I mixed myself a drink but when I found it was impossible to swallow I went to the window and watched the daffodils nodding in the spring breeze.

Warburton did not return but an hour later Ginevra came in search of me. She was calm and when I stood up she smiled.

"It was all right," she said.

"Did Gavin—"

"No. He had filled the hypodermic but then Robert's breathing changed and he lost consciousness. So Gavin said he'd rather wait and I said yes and we waited, and then the breathing changed again and some more time went by, but finally everything stopped and it was over." She sat down suddenly in a chair. "Gavin's just left," she added. "Another of his patients is dying—God, what a life these doctors lead!—but he'll be back as soon as possible."

"Good. Let me get you a brandy."

"Oh no, darling, I always think brandy's just like medicine. Could you mix me a very hefty pink gin?"

When I handed her the glass, she smiled radiantly at me again. "Thanks—oh,

Johnny, do forgive me for not bursting into tears, but the truth is I'm mad with relief and joy."

"I understand."

"It's extraordinary what happens to the survivor when a partner takes a long time to die—in the end, after one's used up every conceivable emotion, one's just consumed with a ghastly impatience that the dying should be taking so long. How demented that sounds, doesn't it, but perhaps after years of fighting a grinding battle to keep sane one does go a little mad at the end."

"I just don't know how you endured it."

"He was my friend," she said. She spoke as if this were not only the definitive description of her relationship with Robert but the one explanation of her endurance. Then with a laugh she exclaimed, "Oh, I'm so happy! I'd like to celebrate by getting drunk and having a divine nervous breakdown!"

"Sorry," I said, "not possible. I've had it with nervous breakdowns at the moment."

She laughed again and kissed me. As she tossed off her drink she said idly, "It's so strange how life turns out—of all Bobby and Margaret's children you were the one I liked the least, and yet during the past years I've often wondered what I should have done without you. I've never thanked you, have I, for being such a tower of strength? What an awful old bitch I am!"

"I'm not sure," I said, "that I would describe myself as a tower of strength."

But she was not listening. She was musing again on the strangeness of life. "I'm not religious anymore," she was saying, "but in the beginning when I did have a few hysterical bouts of praying for strength I always assumed that the strength would come—if it came at all—from my friends in London. But in the end it came from the direction I least expected and from a man I'd never liked. I suppose religious people would say God moves in mysterious ways."

She wandered to the gramophone. "It's odd too about 'The Blue Danube,'" she said, winding the handle. "I came to hate it so much—you see, I didn't fall in love with Robert when he fell in love with me; I fell in love with Conor, and later when Robert made it our special tune I always felt it was such a mockery that I wanted to scream whenever I heard it. But now you've put that right. I shan't mind hearing 'The Blue Danube' in the future. Whenever I hear it I shall remember you having the courage to make those promises which Robert had absolutely no doubt you'd keep—I shall remember you having the humanity which enabled him to die in peace. And whenever I hear it I shall think of Robert whispering that you were the best brother a man ever had." She put the record on the turntable and set the needle in the groove. "You'll remember it too, won't you?" she said, looking back at me, and as the music started to play she smiled at me with a trust I knew I could never break.

So in the end it was Ginevra who gave me the strength which never afterwards wavered, and "The Blue Danube" which saved me once and for all from the temptation that had tormented me for so long. I tried to imagine how I would feel whenever I heard that tune if I knew I had cheated the brother who had trusted me and embittered the woman who had already suffered so much, but of course I could not imagine it. It was unimaginable. I could only recognize it as the road to hell and slam the gates shut on it forever. I could only say to myself: "This far but no farther," and draw the final, the ineradicable line.

The sound of violins filled the drawing room and outside the daffodils were still dancing in the spring breeze.

When the record was over Ginevra said simply, "Yes. I don't hate it anymore now" and closed the lid of the gramophone. Then she exclaimed, "Oh, Lord, I've forgotten Kester! Darling, could you come up with me to break the news? I cancelled his lessons today so he's probably got his nose buried in *The Prisoner of Zenda*. He's developed rather precocious literary tastes, and he's simply mad on Ruritania at the moment."

Setting down my glass in obedience I went with her to take my first long hard resigned look at the child who was going to usurp me.

XI

Kester's room was in one of the towers attached to the bungalow, and its most noticeable features were the bars that had been placed on the windows after Robin's accident. The room was no tidier than Harry's room at the Manor, but it had a different atmosphere. Harry's room was filled with his toy trains, his bricks, his building set, his so-called scientific experiments, his fossil collection, his cricket bat and all the other paraphernalia essential to the life of a normal nine-year-old boy. Kester, still seven months short of his ninth birthday, appeared to care only for soft toys, watercolors and books. When we entered the room we found him lounging on his bed amidst his collection of Teddy bears and greedily reading a handsome edition of Anthony Hope's classic romance. Putting the memory of Harry carefully from my mind, I bent my entire will towards being benign to the child I had promised to treat as a son.

As we came into the room he put aside his book with reluctance and stood up. He was tall for an eight-year-old, rather willowy. As usual his thick curling auburn hair needed cutting, and I thought again, as I had thought so often before, how out of place Robert's pale eyes looked below the rich tints of that hair inherited from Ginevra, and how strange her wide, full-lipped mouth looked when set above the ascetic fine-drawn line of Robert's jaw. His large nose, which he had apparently inherited from no one, gave him an elfin look. He gave the impression that he might dress up in green tights at any minute and vanish under the nearest toadstool.

"Hullo, Mum," he said. "Is he dead?"

"Yes, darling."

"Gosh, that's good, isn't it?"

"Yes, wonderful!" There was a pause in this extraordinary dialogue while she hugged him.

"You're awfully ginny, Mum. Are you drunk?"

"No, pet, just well buffed. Say hullo to your heroic Uncle John. I don't know what I would have done without him—he's been absolutely top-hole."

"Hullo, heroic Uncle John," said Kester, very pert.

"I simply must go to the lavatory," said Ginevra, "or I'll burst. Excuse me for a moment, Johnny. Kester pet, tell Uncle John how far you've got with *The Prisoner of Zenda*."

"Well," said Kester, preparing to enjoy himself, "you see, it's really the story of two cousins. One of them's King of Ruritania but he's no good. However he's got this cousin who's just an untitled Englishman, but he's a hero and absolutely first-rate, just as all heroes are, and he decides to take his cousin's place on the throne—for the best possible reasons, of course—"

"Yes, I do remember the story. Has Rudolph been crowned yet?"

"Yes, pages ago—I loved it when Black Michael was so livid!" Unable to resist the lure of the story any longer, he inclined his long nose towards the pages again.

After a moment I sat down beside him and said tentatively, "Kester, I'm so sorry about your father, but I thought you'd just like to know that at the end he—"

"No, thanks," said Kester. "I don't want to know at all. I'm sick of people dying all over the place."

It was seldom that I felt nonplused by a child, but I now found I had no idea what to do next. I felt he should know about my promise to Robert, but faced with Kester's complete lack of interest I appeared to have no chance to demonstrate my paternal concern. In the end, convinced that something should be said but unable to conjure up an attractive speech, I merely murmured: "I promised your father I'd look after you for him."

"Oh, don't bother," said Kester, turning a page of his book. "Actually I think fathers should be abolished." His pale eyes skimmed over the print. "I say!" he said excited. "I do like the villains in this book! The hero's really rather a bore, always keeping a stiff upper lip and doing the done thing, but I'm just wild about Black Michael and Rupert of Hentzau!"

I stood up abruptly and moved to the barred window. I was remembering Ginevra's remark, "I suppose religious people would say God moves in mysterious ways," and as I looked back at the profoundly unattractive child for whom I was now responsible, I decided God was evidently plumbing new depths of convoluted intrigue. However as far as I could see there was nothing to be done to ease the burden. All I could do was my inadequate best, like the miscast hero that I was; all I could do, once again, was hold fast, stand firm—and soldier on.

PART FOUR

KESTER

1928-1939

Inconstancy is my very essence; it is the game I never cease to play as I turn my wheel in its ever changing circle, filled with joy as I bring the top to the bottom and the bottom to the top. Yes, rise up on my wheel if you like, but don't count it an injury when by the same token you begin to fall, as the rules of the game will require....

—Boethius
The Consolation of Philosophy

1

I

"I'M WILD about those two villains Black Michael and Rupert of Hentzau!" I said wittily, unable to resist the temptation to shock stuffy old Uncle John to the core, and Uncle John looked at me as if I ought to be in a home for wayward boys. What irked him most was that I wasn't "doing the done thing." A boy of eight who has tragically lost his papa is supposed to fight back his tears like a brave little fellow and whisper humbly to his sainted uncle who has just made all manner of rash deathbed promises: "Oh, sir, will you be my father now? Oh please, sir, please!" What he is *not* supposed to do is say something like "Whoopee! Daddy's dead!" and launch into a eulogy of two villains. Uncle John clearly thought this was very low behavior, and I could see he was racking his brains wondering how the devil he was going to make a decent Godwin out of me.

Oh, heaven preserve me from my family!

At the age of eight I already knew I was the black sheep. Long before my father died in the spring of 1928, I had become aware of my family regarding me with baffled incredulity, and as I grew older I realized why they were so flabbergasted. I was the Godwin who ought to be written quietly out of the family tree but by a malign twist of fate I was also the Godwin destined to be permanently on display as master of Oxmoon. Oh, my poor family! My Uncle Thomas used to look at me as if he had already gnashed his teeth to the bone and was busy grinding the stumps. My grandfather could never remember who on earth I was. Uncle Edmund used to muse occasionally, "Funny to think he's Robert's son, isn't it?"—which, since my father was universally acknowledged to be a hero, was quite the most beastly comment Uncle Edmund could have made. In fact he was outdone in beastliness only by my brutal half-brother Rory Kinsella, eighteen years my senior, who used to say, "Sure Robert must have been half asleep when little Kessie was conceived!" Only stuffy old Uncle John—my "heroic" Uncle John, as my mother called him—had the sheer nobility of soul to keep his inevitable opinion of me to himself, but that was out of loyalty to my father. However my father's opinion of me had been equally low.

"That wretched child looks like a shrinking violet—cut his hair this minute, Ginette, and *stop treating him like a girl!*"

"Shut up, you bloody tyrant, shut up, *shut up!*"

My parents' marriage—if such a word can ever describe such a desperate pain-racked association—was so far from the romantic ideal of what a marriage should be that I came to understand early in life how great a gulf could exist between fantasy and reality—and fantasy, I soon decided, was infinitely the more attractive of the two. I loved fairy tales, particularly the ones where the prince and princess fell blissfully in love and lived happily ever after in the palace of their dreams, and spurred on by my desire to escape from my parents' bizarre relationship, I learned to read as soon as I could. Then whenever daily life at Little Oxmoon became too frightful I would dive onto my bed and lose myself thankfully between the pages of the most riveting story available.

I was not alone in this flight from reality. Gradually I came to understand that not only the whole household but all my parents' friends and relations had joined together in a conspiracy to weave a web of fantasy around the situation at Little Oxmoon. The brutal truth was that my father was dying by inches and that my mother had to spend nine years watching him die, and that truth was so ghastly that those who knew them had to wrap it up in fantasy in order to make my parents bearable people who could be visited or discussed in a normal way. Thus my father became the dying hero of legend, accepting his disaster with a stiff upper lip and unlimited courage, while my mother was transformed into a cross between Florence Nightingale and a Fallen Woman Redeemed by Suffering.

"What a wonderful marriage! So devoted! Such heroism!" breathed the world in unstinted awe as people locked themselves up in this myth to prevent the full horror of my parents' ordeal impinging on their sunlit daily lives, but I knew better. I was there, and with the special sensitivity of a child I absorbed every facet of the nightmare, the constant rows, my father's rages born of frustration and despair, my mother's drinking and hysteria, the awful nurses who pitter-pattered in and out and gossiped in corners, the wheelchair, the commode, the stench of decay—all the ghastly trappings of that more than ghastly illness. People not only had no idea how much my parents suffered; they did not want to have any idea. Neither did I, but I had no choice. My father became ill soon after I was conceived, and so the moment I was born I was pitched into this atmosphere of inexorable disintegration.

Yet now, as I look back, I can see that at the heart of this black reality lay the genesis of the legend which people found credible enough to accept. The real truth was that my parents were indeed courageous but their courage lay not in being saintly in the face of adversity (as the world yearned to believe) but in simply struggling on, day after day, and somehow keeping sane. Their devotion to each other, which the world blithely took for granted and which I as a child decided was nonexistent, was in fact, as I now see, very real. It was just that like their courage it was not obviously recognizable. They did not behave as a husband and wife, radiating the traditional marital virtues, but like a brother and sister who were forced to share a nursery under exceptionally trying circumstances, and later I realized that when tragedy had confronted them they had turned for strength not to their marriage, which was of comparatively recent origin, but to the childhood they had shared as cousins at Oxmoon.

However it took me years to reach this final judgment, and on the day my father died I was merely a child who knew his parents were desperately unhappy and who had prayed night after night for the death which could only be regarded as a liberation. By that time I had no strong feelings about my father. In the past I had dutifully attempted hero worship, but such devotion is hard to sustain unaided and my father gave me no help. At the end of his life he obviously did think more about me but even then his interest was detached, as if I were merely an unexpectedly useful pawn on his private chessboard. He was not interested in *me* at all; he never made any genuine attempt to find out what sort of person I was, but although I did go through a period of misery when I hated him for his indifference, my mother helped me over that. In fact when I look back on my childhood I can see so clearly how much ghastlier it would have been if I had been deprived of that racy, strong-willed buccaneer of a mother of mine.

"Oh Lord, pet!" she said briskly when I wept how I hated my father. "Do turn off the waterworks and brace up! Daddy does love you but unfortunately he doesn't know how to show it because he's hopeless with children. It's like you being hopeless at cricket—you try hard but when you keep missing the ball you get cross and lose interest. It's a question of having the knack, isn't it? Well, Daddy doesn't have the knack with you but he can't help it, it's just the way he's made, so you mustn't mind too much."

My mother had the knack.

My mother was very fat with an enormous bosom and she had flashing brown eyes and a rich purring voice and a come-hither look. Later I decided she looked like the vamp in those marvelous Hollywood Westerns, the lady who goes hipping-and-thighing through the saloon to make all the cowboys drool at the bar. I could picture her with a glass in one hand and a cigarette in the other as she declaimed Mae West's immortal line "It's not the men in my life I like—it's the life in my men!"

She didn't love me half as much as I loved her, but I could see there was some sort of love there, and this was a great consolation to me. When she was in a bad mood I used to hate her as much as I hated my father, but if my mother ever forgot herself so far as to let me know that she considered her unwanted fourth son to be a constant source of irritation, she never failed, once Robin was dead, to make some attempt to compensate me afterwards.

"Kester, what a *beautiful* picture you've drawn! Darling, what a *clever* little boy you are and how *lucky* I am to have you..." All rather exaggerated perhaps, but I was easily appeased and I loved being loved—and God knows, at the start of my life there had been little love circulating in my direction; ever since I could remember the waters of affection in the parental reservoir had been channeled into the canals of adulation that surrounded my brother Robin.

I have often wondered in retrospect what Robin was really like, but suppose the answer must always be that he died too young to permit any useful analysis of his character. I thought he was a cruel beastly villain, but I was prejudiced. He used to beat me up regularly while Nanny turned a blind eye; how I survived infancy I have no idea, but I was probably assisted by my nursemaid Daisy who let me hide under her bed. No doubt the prosaic truth was that Robin, worshiped by a doting world, was very jealous of me and quite unable to adjust to my arrival in the nursery. There was considerable evidence that he was an infant phenomenon. He could read fluently by the time he was three (this nauseating achievement was regularly drummed into me during my struggles with THE CAT SAT ON THE MAT at the age of four), and if he had lived he would probably have excelled at games as well as academic pursuits. I can remember him skillfully wielding a cricket bat like the perfect little Godwin that he was, but when he was six and I was three and a half, he fell out of a window and, as Cook put it, "sped off to heaven to sit as an angel on the right hand of God."

Poor God, I thought with genuine compassion, but I was delighted to have the nursery all to myself and felt sure I would now receive all the doting admiration that had been lavished on Robin. Never had I been more disappointed. I was ignored by everyone except Cook, who was a kindly soul, and my Uncle John, who, anxious to "do the done thing" as usual, arrived to rescue me from the kitchens where I had retreated after the dismissal of Nanny and Daisy. I had shed no tears for Nanny but I had been sorry to lose Daisy and now I did not want to be parted from Cook, but my parents were prostrated and Uncle John thought it best that I should be sent to Stourham Hall at Llangennith. There was a ghastly child there called Belinda, but she had a splendid Nanny who actually kissed me every night before I went to sleep. I was so impressed by this display of affection that in the end I was almost reluctant to leave Stourham Hall.

My return home was even worse than I had anticipated because my parents behaved as if they could hardly bear the sight of me. This was standard behavior for my father but I was horrified by my mother's undisguised aversion, and retreating to the kitchens I clambered onto Cook's lap and wept copiously against her bosom.

"Poor little soul!" cried Cook, and added knowingly to Watson the parlormaid: "I expect Madam's wishing it was him that went to heaven and not Master Robin."

I stowed this terrible information far away in the remotest region of my mind, but not long afterwards I concluded some childish tantrum by screaming at my mother: "You hate me because I didn't get killed—you wish I was the one in heaven instead of Robin!"

My mother went white. Then she sank down on the nearest chair and burst into tears.

Naturally I burst into tears as well. I was hysterical with cataclysmic misery. "I'll go and jump out of the window too!" I sobbed, heading for the window seat. "And when I get to heaven I'll tell God I've come in exchange for Robin, and then you can have Robin back and you need never see me again!"

My mother gasped, screamed, snatched me back, yanked me into her arms and crushed me so hard against her that I yelped. "You stupid little nincompoop!" she yelled at me. "Killing yourself's a wicked sin— you'll end up in hell—you'll never get to heaven at all!"

"But at least I'd be dead! Oh, how I wish I was dead!" I cried, but floods of tears overcame me as I visualized myself being roasted by the Devil while Robin went on sitting among the angels, and the next moment my mother too was in floods of tears again and I heard her sobbing, "Oh, God, what a frightful mother I've been, oh God forgive me, God help me—" Yet all the while this litany of despair was going on I was snuggling into her arms and feeling much happier because I could see she did care about me even though I fell so far short of the perfection achieved by little Saint Robin.

After that my mother was so often in my nursery that I almost got sick of the sight of her. However the main result of this incident lay not in her new theatrical displays of affection but in the understanding that developed between us, the understanding that was later manifested in a series of important conversations. My mother not only explained my father's coldness to me in such a way that my potentially self-destructive hatred was neutralized; she promised me that there was more to life than playing cricket and being a perfect Godwin; she assured me that there was nothing wrong with liking fairy tales or painting pictures or even playing with my secret collection of dolls, which were kept hidden in a box under my bed far from my father's presence and Uncle John's conscientiously prying eyes. It was my mother, no slave to convention herself, who helped me believe I was not necessarily doomed to disaster merely because I was the black sheep of the family.

"Although all the same, Kester," said my mother just before my father died, "you're really getting a bit old for dolls now. I won't take them to the jumble sale just yet, but see if you can't say goodbye to them nobly, one by one. It would be awfully brave if you could, and I'd admire you enormously."

"Oh Mum!" I said, much moved by her patience and tact, "I know I'll never be as good as Robin, but I promise to make it up to you one day!"

My mother was greatly irritated. "Lord, Kester, I do wish you wouldn't dramatize yourself the whole time and make these stupid remarks which always make me want to slap you! You're just as good as Robin was, but you're different, that's all—and that's good, I'm delighted. I don't want a second-rate Robin—I want a first-rate Kester, and for once in my life I've got what I want!"

"Oh Mum, that's so nice of you, so kind; but—"

"My God, what is it now?"

"Am I. . . am I a changeling?"

"A *what*?"

"A changeling. Like in fairy stories and history books. You know—the queen has a baby and it dies and she can't face the king with the news so her lady-in-waiting gets hold of another baby and smuggles it into the palace in a warming pan—"

"You read too much," said my mother. "That's your trouble. And your imagination's even more lurid than mine—and that's saying something! No, pet, don't be so idiotic! Of course you're not a changeling! You came out of my tummy and the midwife washed you and wrapped you in a blanket and gave you to me and I said, 'Very nice indeed! Blue eyes just like his father's and a little bit of auburn hair just like mine! Thank you, Nurse,' I said proudly, 'this will suit *very well.*' And then your father came in and he said, 'Oh, good! A boy for Robin to play with—thank goodness it wasn't a girl...'"

She went on spinning this fantasy for some time. God only knows what the reality was, but I didn't care. My mother loved me enough to invent this splendid taradiddle for my benefit, and that was all I needed to know.

"But Mum," I said at last when she paused to give her fertile imagination a rest, "if I'm not a changeling, why aren't I a true Godwin? Why am I so second-rate?"

My mother's bosom heaved, her dark eyes flashed and her fury was terrible to behold. *"Who says you're second-rate?"*

Greatly excited by this magnificent display of maternal loyalty, my mind zoomed past frightful Uncle Thomas, beastly Uncle Edmund and brutal brother Rory, zigzagged around stuffy old Uncle John and closed in upon the cousin who had taken Robin's place at the top of my list of most-hated people.

"Harry," I said—not entirely accurately, for Harry had never used the words "second-rate," but I felt a little inaccuracy was excusable in the circumstances. During our last quarrel he had called me a subhuman idiot who deserved to be laundered, shrunk and kept in a matchbox.

"Well, you just tell your cousin Harry," said my mother fiercely, "that you're twice the Godwin he'll ever be because both your parents were Godwins—you're the Godwinest Godwin of them all, and that automatically makes you incapable of being second-rate! You stand up for yourself and don't be intimidated by that boy just because he thinks going to prep school has given him a license to be bossy and boorish! It's not his fault he's such a little troublemaker, of course," she added hastily, as if she feared she had gone too far by voicing this delectable criticism. "The upbringing's really been quite impossible, but—well, we won't go into that. I'm very fond of Bronwen and I won't hear one word against Johnny and those children will probably turn out all right in the end, but meanwhile there's certainly room for improvement. Why, I wouldn't change you for a hundred Harrys! Second-rate indeed! How monstrous!"

"Oh Mum, you're so wonderful!" I exclaimed, tears in my eyes.

"Oh Lord, here we go again!" said my mother exasperated. "Kester, you really must stop being so emotional!"

"But you're emotional, Mum! Daddy's always saying how emotional you are!"

"Yes, pet, but I'm a woman—women are supposed to be emotional! Men are supposed to be... well, like your father. At least... oh, I do wish you could remember Daddy before he was ill! You're at a disadvantage there. Well, men are supposed to be like your Uncle John—yes, model yourself on Uncle John, darling. Uncle John's magnificent, so strong and tough, yet so very humane and

462

understanding, and he never cries at funerals and he always does the done thing—
well, almost always does the done thing—"

"But Mum," I said, driven by the acuteness of my anxiety to interrupt this
paean, "the trouble with Uncle John is that he just wants me to be like Harry."

"Oh, bother Harry!" said my mother. "Well, I don't know, Kester, I confess
it's a problem but I'm sure there's a way you can be perfectly masculine without
turning yourself into a replica of Harry."

"A replica of Harry—ugh!" I groaned, and then unable to resist wallowing in
all the emotion I was supposed to suppress I added: "Oh, Mum, if only you knew
how much I loathe that rat—that snake—that *villain* Harry Godwin..."

II

Even if Robin had lived he would have had a hard time outshining Cousin
Harry, slinky, slithery, slippery Cousin Harry, glossy in his perfection, the model
Godwin. He didn't look like a Godwin for he was dark, his smooth straight hair
ink-black, his narrow nasty eyes velvet-brown, but no one, least of all me, ever
doubted that he would grow up to be just as tall and handsome as any self-
respecting Godwin had a right to be. I was neither dark nor fair but a mediocre
mixture of the two, burdened by springy thick reddish-brown hair which was well-
nigh impossible to control, and humiliated by a lily-white skin which gave me
the look of a consumptive Victorian heroine. My overall appearance resembled
a mutated chrysanthemum. My enormous nose (where on earth had it come
from?) I considered little short of a deformity. My one hope was that I would
grow up to be tall—not taller than Cousin Harry; that would have been too much
to expect but by the time I was eight I had begun to believe I wasn't doomed to
be a dwarf and the thought was comforting to me.

Perfect Cousin Harry, superbly athletic, excelled at games. From football and
cricket to Ping-Pong and croquet, all sport was easy for him. He glittered, he
coruscated, he luxuriated in battles which always ended in victory. To make
matters worse he had been brought up by Uncle John to display good sportsmanship
at all times, so I was even unable to accuse him of arrogance. When he won at
Ping-Pong he would always make some gracious remark like "Thanks, old chap.
Jolly good game. Bad luck you lost," but his velvet-brown eyes would harden in
contempt before he allowed his thick black lashes to fall like a curtain to conceal
his private feelings. Harry and I might fight and quarrel, but never as the result
of a game. "Because after all, old chap," said suave Cousin Harry, "that wouldn't
be sporting, would it? That wouldn't be the done thing at all."

Self-confident Cousin Harry, matchlessly mastering the art of maintaining a
stiff upper lip, swept off to boarding school at the age of eight without a tear or
a backward glance and returned in triumph at the end of his first term with a
new air of sophistication and a new contempt for those who still did their lessons

at home. Of course he had a glowing report. Uncle John, who had the reputation of being good with children (God alone knew how that myth ever got started), was actually very sloppy about Harry and read the report aloud to my parents before it occurred to him that he was being tactless.

Stunning Cousin Harry, the mathematical genius who could do complicated arithmetic in his head while I was struggling unsuccessfully to do the sum on paper, excelled in all subjects but showed a scientific curiosity which left me cold. He kept tadpoles and white mice and made notes of their habits. He examined worms under his toy microscope, cut them in half and examined them again. He hoarded the most extraordinary things in test tubes. He lurked in the kitchens and drew anatomical diagrams whenever Cook skinned a rabbit or plucked a chicken. "If it were the done thing," said Cousin Harry, "I'd like to be an animal scientist when I grow up, but if it's common to be an animal scientist I'll have a big estate and keep lots of animals instead. Being a landed gentleman of a big estate like Oxmoon," said Cousin Harry, "is very much the done thing indeed."

"I thought you wanted to be a concert pianist?"

"Oh Lord, no—that wouldn't be the done thing at all! Playing the piano's very sissyish actually, and strictly for girls who have nothing better to do."

Musical Cousin Harry, who was capable of listening to an hour-long Bach concert on the wireless without one single yawn, could play the piano by ear. When I sat down at the piano at Penhale Manor I could just manage to pick out "God Save the King" with one finger, but Harry could play a two-handed version of any tune that took his fancy. It was an astonishing gift, and one I deeply envied.

"That boy of Johnny's is really very musical," said my mother to my father once.

"Much good that'll do him—John's quite right to discourage it," said my father, whose intellectual tastes were purely literary, and I thought how typical it was of Cousin Harry that he should so effortlessly succeed in extinguishing any awkward un-Godwin-like trait from his personality as he glided along the road to his (no doubt) golden adolescence.

In stark contrast to all this raging glamour, I was tucked shyly away at Little Oxmoon—not exactly kept out of sight, but hardly put on open exhibition. I had a kind clever tutor of whom I was very fond, but apart from Simon Maxwell no one else seemed to think I had much potential. Simon had been a contemporary of my father's at Oxford; severely injured in the war he found walking arduous, and so Little Oxmoon, designed for my father's wheelchair, suited him well. Although he enjoyed teaching me I knew his chief pleasure lay in acting as a companion to my father, and their favorite hobby was writing Greek verse together. It must have been sad for Simon when he discovered I was never going to be a Classical scholar, but he was so pleased by my precocious interest in English literature that he promised not to betray my Latin failures to my father. However, my father, trained long ago in the art of cross-examination, soon discovered my defects for himself and was enraged by my stupidity.

"Your cousin Harry could conjugate the verb *amare* in every tense by the time he was your age!"

Infant prodigy Cousin Harry became the complete monster when he turned out to be a born Classicist. It was too much for me. My temper was at boiling point. What had I ever done to deserve these ghastly paragons in my life? First Robin, now Harry. Such persecution seemed more than flesh-and-blood could stand.

"I shall explode entirely soon!" I said to my mother. "Oh Mum, is it always going to be like this? Is Harry always going to outshine me at absolutely everything?"

"Oh no, quite the reverse, darling!" said my mother complacently. "You're going to end up outshining Harry."

"But how? How, *how*, HOW?"

"Well, one day," said my mother, "you're going to be master of Oxmoon."

III

So one day fantasy was going to triumph and all my fairy tales would come true. The neglected little ugly duckling whom everyone despised would be transformed into the gorgeous prince, and I would live happily ever after in my beautiful palace with the ravishing princess who would inevitably accompany such good fortune.

"Gosh, Mum, are you sure?"

"Positive, pet. Daddy's arranged it with Grandfather. I know you find Daddy difficult, Kester, but never forget he's fought tooth and nail to get the best for you."

This was very satisfying. "So he really does love me after all?" I said, preparing to enjoy a wallow in Victorian sentiment (I was in the middle of a novel by Charlotte M. Yonge).

"Darling, he's devoted to you, I've always said so!"

I was still not at all sure whether I believed this, but I was prepared to concede that if my father had fought to win me Oxmoon, he was very far from being the dead loss he had always seemed to be.

Shortly after that I had my first and last meaningful conversation with my father. It was not easy to follow his words because his speech was impaired, but my mother acted as an interpreter when necessary.

"When I was a child," said my father, "Oxmoon was a magic place. I grew up there with your mother and we were like the prince and princess in a fairy tale. And then we parted and went away to lead other lives for years, but always I dreamed of coming home and putting the magic back into Oxmoon so that my fairy tale could live again. I shan't do that now but you're going to do it instead of me. You're going to put the magic back into Oxmoon and live the life I should have had."

I was so enrapt that for once I forgot to be frightened of him. I said simply: "I shall make it the best magic house in the world and I shall grow up to be a hero, just like you, and I shall marry a heroine, just like Mummy, and we'll live happily ever after, just as you would have done if you hadn't fallen ill, and then you'll look down from heaven and see your dream come true and be very, very pleased with me."

My father could not smile because his facial muscles were paralyzed but he gave a short laugh and my mother said warmly "Darling!" and gathered me to her bosom for one of her generous maternal hugs.

Later I said to her, "Was it really like a fairy tale when you were children? When did Daddy first realize he was in love with you?"

"Oh, that was the climax of the whole fairy tale, darling. There was a great ball at Oxmoon to celebrate my eighteenth birthday and Daddy and I danced to 'The Blue Danube' and that was when he fell in love with me. He was two months short of his sixteenth birthday."

Instantly in my imagination I saw it all: the glittering chandeliers, the glowing flowers, the glamorous guests, the gorgeous sweep of the violins, my ravishing parents plunged into passionate love, the drama, the romance and the sheer fairy-tale splendor of that magic paradise they had shared long ago. I felt then that the ugly reality of my father's illness could no longer touch me because I could see beyond it to what I unerringly recognized as Beauty and Truth. Beauty and Truth (spelled always in my mind with capital letters) made up in general for life being so absolutely awful. Truth spelled with a capital T was not in this case a synonym for reality; far from it. It stood for the way things ought to be, not the way things really were. My father might be dying and my mother might drink too much and they might continually quarrel with each other, but the Truth lay not in that reality but beyond it; the Truth, which utterly redeemed all the horrors of the present, was that they had fallen passionately in love with each other in the ballroom at Oxmoon while the orchestra played "The Blue Danube," and that their lives would undoubtedly have continued in this romantic vein if vile reality had not so catastrophically intervened.

However an unpleasant thought cast a temporary shadow over this gilded vision. "But Mum," I said, "after all that why did you go off and marry someone else?"

"Oh that," said my mother. "Well, pet, I was in rather a muddle at the time. You see, in those days a girl had to get engaged as soon as possible but Daddy was two years younger than I was so of course he wasn't old enough to propose. Then Timothy Appleby asked and he was so sweet that I said yes but later I regretted it and got in a panic so it seemed best to elope with Conor."

"But you did love Daddy all the time?"

"Robert was always very special to me," said my mother, "and I was always very special to him."

"And you did have your happy ending after all," I said satisfied, "when you finally married him."

My mother smiled faintly but could not speak. Obviously she was too moved by the memory of her fairy-tale romance, just as I was now moved by the thought of my fairy-tale inheritance.

I was particularly thrilled to hear I was to inherit Oxmoon because I had thought

466

it inconceivable that I could ever do so. It was a family myth that Oxmoon had passed from eldest son to eldest son (all mythically named Robert) since the Norman invasion of Gower, but any casual perusal of the family tree revealed that this was far from being the case. Eldest sons had died; younger sons (Geoffrey, Raymond, Piers, Alfred, Arthur, Edward) had periodically inherited; the occasional cousin in the female line had once or twice scooped the pool and graciously changed his name to Godwin to satisfy his childless benefactor. One or two eldest sons had been disinherited, one or two had been lunatics, one or two had disappeared in the Colonies. The truth was that as far as the Godwin family was concerned primogeniture was a guideline but not a strict rule, and my grandfather was under no obligation to leave Oxmoon to me. The general opinion among the servants was that it would go to Uncle John, and when Harry spoke of being a landed gentleman I knew he had every reason to believe that Oxmoon would one day drop neatly into his lap. Quite apart from being the son of the probable heir he was a great favorite with my dotty old grandfather, far more so than I was. Harry used to get tipped five shillings now and then on visits to Oxmoon. I never got more than half a crown.

"You're quite sure," I said uncertainly to my mother after she had broken the news of my great expectations, "that Grandfather won't leave Oxmoon to Uncle John and Harry?"

"Positive, darling. Daddy's the heir, you see, so he must have the final say in whom the heir's going to be once he's dead. That's only fair and Grandfather knows it."

"Gosh!" I finally allowed myself to believe in my good fortune. "I say!" I gazed out of the window at a world that had been miraculously transformed. "Gosh!" I said again, overcome with awe at the magnificence of my fate, but then suffered one last pang of anxiety. "But Mum," I said uneasily, "what does Uncle John think?"

"Your heroic Uncle John," said my mother, "wants your father to have his way about this. He thinks it would be the done thing."

"How absolutely ripping!" I said with enthusiasm, and finally abandoned myself to the most ravishing daydreams. I saw myself as grown up, very tall (could I possibly be taller than Cousin Harry?) and miraculously handsome. At my grandfather's funeral my upper lip would be stiff as a board, and afterwards in the dining room at Oxmoon before the assembled guests I would walk slowly and majestically to the great carved chair that stood at the head of the table. At that point Uncle John, speaking on behalf of all the family, would beg me to forgive them for their past behavior towards me, and after considering this request I would help Uncle Thomas to rise from his knees (he had of course been groveling at my feet) and graciously pronounce a general pardon before taking my place in my grandfather's chair.

This vision of the future was so delectable that after my father's death I said hopefully to my mother, "Do you think Grandfather might die soon?"

"I don't know, pet," said my mother. "He's a bit dotty but physically he's as fit as a fiddle and might live forever. Don't start counting your chickens before they're hatched."

Counting chickens! Ever since she had told me my fate I had been counting rooms, furniture, paintings, *objets d'art* and every piece of silver that I could remember. In my mind I had even arranged my books in the library. I found myself quite unable to stop dwelling on my great expectations, and once my father died and Oxmoon moved closer to me I dwelled on them more passionately than ever.

My father was cremated in Swansea, and by his own wish there was no religious service, only readings from the works of his favorite authors. Simon showed me these readings afterwards. There was a rather sinister passage from a philosophical work by a Late Latin gentleman called Boethius, a cheerful paragraph from Cicero on death (obviously written when he had felt in the pink of health), an excerpt from Plato's *Phaedo* which hinted that my father might not have been so much of an atheist as he wished to be, a casual salute to Shakespeare ("O God! that one might read the book of fate..."), Horace's advice *"Carpe diem"* (to add a cheerful note) and finally a stunning choice of a poem by Emily Brontë, stunning because my father had always appeared to believe English literature had been composed entirely by men, stunning because its strongly mystical streak seemed alien to my father's personality and stunning simply because the poem itself was stunning. I was only eight years old and too young, despite my literary precocity, to have embarked on the work of the Brontë family, but here in clear, brave simple language was a poem that spoke to me as it must have spoken to my father. "No coward soul is mine," I read. "No trembler in the world's storm-troubled sphere: I see Heaven's glories shine, And faith shines equal, arming me from fear."

"That was Emily Brontë's last poem," Simon said to me. "Robert couldn't quite share her faith but he admired her courage in facing death."

Simon had been very affected by my father's death, but my mother had arrived home after the funeral in great spirits and got tight on pink gin with Uncle John. Uncle John never got tight but after a pink gin or two he became human. Dr. Warburton, who had been diverted by an emergency call, joined them later and stayed on for an hour or two after Uncle John had left. Apart from Uncle John no one had been closer to my parents during their ordeal than Dr. Warburton. He was a thin energetic bright-eyed man in his mid-forties with a canine look. With only the slightest effort of my vivid imagination I could picture him on all fours, wagging a tail and careering headlong after a fox. He lived a bachelor life in a smart new house that had been built in the grounds of All-Hallows Court, and everyone wondered why he had never remarried, but his housekeeper told the village with relish that he was still in mourning for his young wife who had died at the end of the war.

"Darling Gavin," said my mother, kissing him warmly as she finally showed him off the premises (my mother was always calling people darling and kissing them warmly), "do let me know how Bobby is and tell me if you think I ought to call."

For after my father's death my grandfather had become ill, just as he always did when something upset him, and for some days he had remained isolated, attended only by Dr. Warburton and Mrs. Straker. Mrs. Straker, popularly supposed to be a witch, was reported to be curing him with herbal brews and black magic.

"Champagne and bloody bed more likely," said my disgusting Uncle Thomas, but Uncle John saw me sitting quietly in the corner with my ears twitching and he told Thomas in no uncertain terms to moderate both his conversation and his language. By this time I was staying at Penhale Manor. Uncle John had insisted that my mother went away for a month's rest after the ordeal of my father's last days, and she had decided to go to Ireland with Rory; after my father's death was announced in *The Times*, her long-lost eldest son, my unknown brother Declan, had written to ask her to visit him.

"Darling Declan!" said my mother shining-eyed, although why she should have wanted to speak of him with affection after the disgraceful way he had treated her I had no idea. Detesting her marriage to my father he had walked out on her long before I was born and had refused to answer any of the letters she had sent to his aunt's address in Dublin. I knew little about him—my mother had built a wall around her private grief by never mentioning his name—and such facts as I did know I had acquired by eavesdropping when Rory talked of him occasionally to other members of the family.

However now it seemed I was to hear of him *ad nauseam*. I learned that he was twenty-nine years old, had fought for the IRA and was now a respectable member of the parliament in Dublin. He was married. His wife had some unspellable Irish name. There was even a baby six weeks old. My mother, tears in her eyes, rushed off to Ben Evans, the famous store in Swansea, and bought rattles and baby frocks. Rory came down from town with a bottle of champagne to celebrate both her coming reunion with Declan and the arrival of her first grandchild, but although my mother radiantly offered me a little sip from her glass, I declined. I was feeling most put out. I had become so accustomed since Robin's death to my status as an only child that I had unconsciously formed the opinion that my half-brothers were of no consequence, the product of a marriage undertaken when my mother was too young to know better. Apart from telling me that she had eloped while in a muddle, my mother had never spoken of it; the general opinion in the family was that Conor Kinsella had been an Irish bounder and that her marriage had been a hopeless *mésalliance*; I had always thought it quite irrelevant to me. Yet now I saw how mistaken I had been to assume it was unimportant. Once my father was dead, Conor Kinsella seemed to return to life. Rory, who had an awful reputation and whom my mother had been happy to keep at arm's length in London, now started behaving very possessively towards her, and to make matters worse my mother loved it. She kept saying how lovely it was to be going to Ireland with him, and when I saw her hugging this redheaded stranger, I suddenly realized that this man was not just a bore who had to be tolerated at Christmas but *my brother*. I felt that my small secure world in which I had been the center of my mother's attention had slipped alarmingly out of focus, but although I was cross, frightened, baffled and resentful,

469

my mother remained blissfully unaware of my distress.

"Imagine darling Declan being an M.P.!" she exclaimed to Rory. "Except that he's a T.D., he says, because the Irish don't have M.P.s, and I must call the Irish parliament the Doyle, not the Dayle, even though it's spelled D-A-I-L. How like Conor he is, so proud of being Irish—oh Rory, let's look at all my old photographs of your father!"

Rory thought this was a wonderful idea. Trailing after them with incredulous horror, I stood by in silence while the excavated photographs revealed a shady-looking individual who boasted sly eyes and a smirk. I found my mother's inevitable rhapsodies the height of impropriety.

"Well, what's the matter with you, little Kessikins?" demanded Rory, catching sight of my expression and laughing heartily. "You look as if you're about to say, 'For shame, you wicked woman—and my father not yet cold in his grave!'"

That remark both pulled my mother to her senses and underlined to me how brainless my half-brother really was. He was supposed to have charm but I could never see it. In my opinion that carrot-topped nonentity with his beer drinker's paunch had about as much charm as a lump of lard.

"That'll do, Rory," said my mother. She put aside the album and gathered me in her arms. I feigned reluctance but was secretly overcome with relief, and tears sprang to my eyes as my pride finally permitted me to press against her bosom. "Kester," I heard her say gently, "you mustn't mind, pet. Just because I had another life before I married Daddy doesn't mean I love you and Daddy any less. But this meeting with Declan can't help but remind me of that other life which I thought had gone forever—it's as if the past's coming alive again to comfort me just when I most need it, and you mustn't begrudge me a little comfort, darling, not when I've been through such a terrible time."

I said nothing. I was too ashamed of myself for doubting her love yet para-doxically this reassurance that she loved me only made her absorption in her unknown past more objectionable. I felt that if she loved me, Declan and Rory should be superfluous; I felt that if she had loved my father she should have no desire to revive her memories of a man who had been fifteen years in his grave. To me Conor Kinsella was like my father's illness—an ugly blot on the golden landscape of my parents' romantic fairy tale, but I was a child and unable to articulate such complex feelings. I merely said, "I want you, you're mine" and flung my arms around her neck as if I could stake sole claim to her and beat back my Kinsella rivals, living and dead.

"Poor little pet!" My mother knew quite well what was going on but was uncertain how I could best be soothed. "Would you like to come to Ireland with us?" she said at last, hugging me. "I thought you'd much prefer to be with Bronwen and the babies at Penhale Manor, but perhaps I was wrong—yes, I can see I was—I was wrong and now you feel left out. Very well, we'll all go to Ireland! Think how thrilling it'll be for you to meet another brother—and a sister-in-law—and a nephew! Heavens, imagine having a nephew when you're only eight years old! Won't Harry be jealous when he hears!"

She was patronizing me. I pulled together the shreds of my dignity and stood up straight. "I'm not going to meet a wicked villain who fought against our brave soldiers in that horrid Ireland," I declared. "As far as I'm concerned he's no brother of mine."

"Oh, Lord, don't take him to Dublin, Ma!" begged Rory. "Declan'll murder him and the reunion'll be wrecked!"

"Shut up, Rory!" said my mother fiercely. Turning back to me she said in her calmest voice, "Very well, Kester. If that's your opinion you're perfectly entitled to it; but let me know if you change your mind."

I left for Penhale Manor the next day, but although I tried hard to be brave, I did shed a tear as soon as my mother's car disappeared down the drive. Fortunately Harry had returned to his prep school for the summer term so there was no one there to hiss "Sissy!" in my ear, but Uncle John sighed as if he were wondering how on earth he was going to make a perfect Godwin out of me, and as he took my hand comfortingly in his, he could not resist running true to form by pointing out the absolute necessity of maintaining a stiff upper lip no matter how adverse the circumstances.

"Oh, don't be so English, Johnny!" scolded his wonderful Welsh mistress, and suddenly Uncle John laughed and kissed her and became human. I was still too young to have read about Dr. Jekyll and Mr. Hyde, but it did occur to me then that Uncle John had two distinct personalities. Without Bronwen he was stuffy, solemn and encased in a dreary Victorian worthiness, but with her he sparkled and exuded charm without insincerity, compassion without condescension, courage without histrionics and decency without priggishness. It was then that he really did become my heroic Uncle John, someone to emulate and admire, someone with far more power to influence me than my intimidating father who had been so divided from me by his illness and by his inability to communicate with children.

"We've been so looking forward to having you to stay, Kester," said Uncle John with his most engaging spontaneity, his hand tightening on mine as he slipped his free arm around Bronwen's waist. "I'm very glad you wanted to come to us." And when I saw he *was* glad, this moved me very much. Secretly I was often frightened that he despised me and found me a terrible cross to bear, so each spontaneous gesture of affection from him was doubly precious to me.

Although I had regularly visited Penhale Manor ever since I could remember, I had never stayed there before and so had never had an opportunity to observe how Uncle John lived when he was not roaming around sporting his Old Harrovian tie and discoursing on the virtues of a stiff upper lip. I noticed he spoke a lot of Welsh and laughed a great deal and displayed eccentric habits such as dressing up in blue dungarees and tinkering with the engine of his motorcar. He went out every day on business connected with the Home Farm, and when he returned home he would spend much time pottering around the house mending things that had gone wrong. Unlike Oxmoon Penhale Manor now had electricity, a subject that Uncle John had mastered in his spare time, and when anything went wrong—as things often did—he would appear with his toolbox and put matters right. He seemed to enjoy these diversions (most curious ones for a gentleman)

471

almost as much as he enjoyed the conventional hobby of reading. Since I was a reader myself I was intrigued by his reading habits which I found very peculiar. He always seemed to be halfway through at least half a dozen books at once, but although he tried everything—detective stories, novels, works of moral philosophy and religion, history, biography, tomes on politics and economics, tracts on Welsh nationalism—detective stories seemed to be the only books he could be guaranteed to finish. It was as if none of the more intellectual writings ever satisfied him, although he never gave up hope of finding out what he wanted to know.

Bronwen read too, but like my mother she only seemed to enjoy love stories.

"All the stories I read have happy endings," she said. "I like that."

"You mean the hero marries the heroine and they live happily ever after."

"Yes."

I knew, of course, that she and Uncle John were not married. I knew they "lived in sin," and although I had no idea what "living in sin" meant, I couldn't help feeling every time I visited Penhale Manor that it must be a very happy state of affairs indeed. I could not remember my Aunt Blanche, Uncle John's first wife, who had died before my second birthday, and I had only the dimmest memory of his second wife, my Aunt Constance (I was sick at the wedding), so my knowledge of Uncle John's family life centered inevitably around Bronwen. I was four when she and my uncle had first begun to live together at the Manor, and she had quickly established herself as a heroine in my eyes when she stopped the children from bullying me during my regular visits to tea. In addition to Harry, who took as much pleasure as Robin in beating me up, my cousin Marian was not above a pinch or two, and I discovered there were two most unpleasant individuals with Welsh accents called Rhiannon and Dafydd who enjoyed following the example set by my cousins and tormenting me as much as possible. I was surprised when I eventually learned that Rhiannon and Dafydd were Bronwen's children. Neither of them reminded me of her in any way.

Bronwen was freckled and had beautiful white teeth (I was enrapt to discover that she had never been to a dentist), and she talked in a down-to-earth sensible way in a gruff foreign voice (it took me years to realize how sexy that voice was). Her voice sounded foreign to me not only because the local Gower accent was more reminiscent of Devon than of Wales but because Welsh was Bronwen's first language and she had not been brought up in a bilingual area like Swansea where English predominated. I spoke no Welsh although of course I knew I *was* Welsh; although I had been born in England I could not remember my early life there, and anyway all the Godwins were Welsh. However, meeting someone like Bronwen always underlined to me how un-Welsh I was. At an early age I found the subject of nationality confusing, and I used to discuss it with Bronwen, who on this point was far more understanding than my mother. When I said to my mother, "If England and Wales went to war with each other, which side would I be on?" she just said, "Don't be ridiculous, pet, England and Wales got over all that sort of nonsense hundreds of years ago and we're all British now." But Bronwen said to me, "You belong in the land where you feel most at home and that needn't necessarily be the land where you were born or even the land where you were educated. It's the place to which you're tied by a magic rope, and the magic rope always tries to tug you back if you go too far away."

That settled that. I was tied to Gower with a magic rope and my birth in London was irrelevant.

One of the nicest things about Bronwen was that she was always so interested in what one was saying even though one was only a child. Most adults have a tiresome habit of treating children as mental defectives, and even my tutor Simon Maxwell, whom I liked, was occasionally guilty of this attitude, particularly when I made a mess of conjugating my Latin verbs. I was five when Simon arrived at Little Oxmoon, and soon afterwards, to my horror, Harry began to visit us daily in order to share my lessons, but Simon managed the situation cleverly, keeping all competition to a minimum to reduce the possibility of open hostilities. In the end our hours in the schoolroom passed placidly enough, but I was always sorry if I was sent to tea at the Manor later on. To escape Harry's company I formed the habit of sticking close to Bronwen and the baby, Evan, whom I soon realized Harry disliked.

"I think Evan's very nice," I said to Bronwen as we played with him in the garden. "It must be exciting to be a girl and to be able to order a baby whenever you want one.... Bronwen, I'm very worried about my future. You see, when I grow up I'd like to have two boys and two girls, but I know boys can't have babies and I'm so anxious in case I can't find a girl who likes me enough to have babies on my behalf. Do you think I could grow a baby in a test tube? You know all Harry's test tubes.... I sort of wondered... hoped..."

"You funny little boy!" said my heroine laughing. "What a lovely idea but Kester, I don't think the baby would be happy in a test tube. It wouldn't be warm or dark enough for him."

"Do babies really grow in tummies, Bronwen? Mummy said they did but Nanny says the stork brings them."

"No, babies grow in wombs which are different from tummies—they're like little balloons which the baby blows up bigger and bigger in order to make room for himself."

"Gosh!" I said, picturing infantile lips blowing hard to inflate the womb. "How clever!"

"Yes, isn't it?" said Bronwen pleased. Then she added, patting herself in front. "It's happening to me at the moment—oh, I'm so excited!"

"You're having another baby?"

"Yes, yes, yes!" Bronwen hugged me. "Isn't it wonderful!"

"Wonderful!" I agreed, deeply impressed. "How clever of you!" I added admiringly, and when I returned to Little Oxmoon that evening I immediately told Nanny the good news.

Nanny went bright red and said in a strangled voice, "We won't talk of that, dear."

"Why not?" I was astounded.

"You'll have to ask your mother. It's not for me to say."

So going straight to my mother I asked her why Nanny had looked about to burst when I told her the thrilling news that Bronwen's next baby was busy blowing up the womb.

"Busy doing *what?*" said my mother, and added, aghast: "For God's sake, what baby?"

"Bronwen's having another baby—she said so!"

"Ye gods and little fishes!" exclaimed my mother, and rushed to my father's room (it was eighteen months before his death). Eavesdropping shamelessly at the door I heard her say, "God, Robert, that girl's pregnant again!"

"Can't be true. John couldn't be such a fool."

John? I pressed my ear harder against the panels and wondered whether I had misheard. As far as I could see Uncle John was quite irrelevant.

"Kester says Bronwen's just told him. Heavens, Robert, what will they do? Another baby would absolutely put the lid on any attempt to pay lip service to the conventions!"

Lip service? Conventions? The unfamiliar words struck my brain and bounced off again. I held my breath in order to hear better.

"She'll have to have an abortion."

"Don't be absurd, Robert, she's not the type—she's mad about John and probably wants to have as many of his babies as possible."

His? I forgot the word "abortion" and let it bounce off my brain along with "lip service" and "conventions." I was too busy struggling with the image of Uncle John ordering the baby (where from?) and somehow (how?) maneuvering it into the right position to blow up the womb.

"Even if that girl's bent on being a Celtic fertility symbol, Ginette, I can't believe John's mad enough to make a career of fathering bastards. I shall ask him outright if he's had difficulty acquiring a supply of French letters."

We were now apparently in the realms of foreign literature but as far as I was concerned they might have been talking Chinese. I crept away and tried to sort out the conversation but it was beyond me. I could not confide in Nanny; I knew she would only go bright red again and talk as if she were being strangled. Yet I felt I had to confide in someone. I was feeling too upset by all the appalled disapproval which contrasted so sharply with Bronwen's joy, and in the end I sought out my mother, burst into tears and begged her not to be angry with Bronwen who was always so kind to me.

"... and why shouldn't she have the baby anyway?" I sobbed.

"Oh Lord," said my mother. As usual she was exasperated by my tears. "Oh, stop that crying, for heaven's sake—it does so get on my nerves! That's better.... Well, you see, Kester, Uncle John and Bronwen aren't married, as you know, and people who aren't married shouldn't go around producing babies. Later when you're older—"

"You mean it's not the done thing?"

"Not exactly, no. I mean, no, it isn't."

"You mean *Uncle John's not doing the done thing?*"

"Living in sin's hardly the done thing either, darling!"

"But I thought it must be if Uncle John was doing it!"

"Oh Lord," said my mother again. "What do I say, let me think..." She closed her eyes for inspiration, opened them again and took a deep breath. "No," she said firmly, "living in sin's not the done thing and having babies when you're not married isn't the done thing either, but we have to be kind, we have to be charitable and we can't condemn people just because they get in a mess."

"But why's Uncle John in this mess?"

"Well, he married this simply too dreary American girl, pet, and it was an awful mistake and he should have married Bronwen and he now wants to marry Bronwen but he can't get a divorce and get unmarried from Constance because Constance wants to stay married to him. So Uncle John's in this ghastly mess, which goes to prove that even the best people can get into ghastly messes, even heroes like John, and that's why we must never judge other people too harshly because although they can make awful mistakes they can still be very nice people. Making mistakes doesn't mean that you're a villain, you see, it simply means that you're human. We all make mistakes, all of us, it's human nature."

"Yes, I do see that, but Mum, I still don't understand about this baby. How did Uncle John place the order and get it into the womb?"

"Oh *Lord!*" said my mother, and added in a rhetorical aside: "Can I cope with this? I suppose I'll have to." She took another vast breath. "Well, Kester, when two people are madly in love they share a double bed and do something called copulation which you'll understand better when you're older and I certainly don't intend to go into the quite splendid and blissful details now except to say that it's kissing and hugging and much more besides and it's absolute heaven and most people are wild about it. Then sometimes after copulation the woman finds she's having a baby and it's as much the man's baby as hers because they've been copulating together. Now run along to the nursery, there's a pet, and see if Nanny's ready with your bread-and-milk."

After pondering on this information I tried without success to find "copulation" in the dictionary. (I was spelling COPPERLAYSHUN.) Further mediation followed on Uncle John's situation, and presently I broached the subject with Cousin Harry during one of our midmorning breaks.

"A bit tricky about this baby Bronwen's having, isn't it?" I said as we munched our currant buns. "I mean, everyone knows it's not the done thing to have a baby without being married—it's not playing the game at all."

Harry parked his bun and stood up. "Papa and Bronwen love each other," he said violently. "If you love each other you have babies—and *that's* the done thing, marriage or no marriage."

"But my mother says—"

"Shut up!" Harry shouted at me. "My father says it's all right so it's all right, and if you say it isn't I'll beat you till your teeth rattle!"

"Oh, how you do drone on!" I said, affecting a yawn as I edged nimbly away around the table. "Why are you so upset? Are you afraid in case Uncle John likes the new baby better than he likes you?"

"You mean-minded, lily-livered, sick-making little sissy—" As he came at me with flailing fists I screamed for help and the next moment Simon arrived to ensure that the incident followed a predictable course. We were each set a grueling exercise in the subject we hated most; that kept us quiet for a while, but as I struggled with my multiplication sums I saw that a tear had blotted the sentence Harry had just written in his English-grammar book. I was amazed. In fact I was so amazed that I did not at first hear Simon ask me to fetch him a glass of water.

Realizing I was being dispatched on the flimsiest of excuses I naturally paused at the door to eavesdrop.

"What's the matter, Harry?"

"Nothing."

"Is there anything I can do to help? Anything you'd like to tell me?"

"No, thank you. Everything's top-hole."

Perfect Cousin Harry had his upper lip well starched again after his extraordinary lapse. In disappointment I padded away to fetch the unwanted glass of water.

I would have thought no more about the incident but to my surprise Harry revived the subject the next day.

"Sorry I was so ratty with you yesterday, old chap," he said as we again sank our teeth into our midmorning currant buns, "but the truth is I can't stand anyone being rude about my father. As I'm his favorite it's my moral duty to defend him at all times."

"Ah." Deciding I had no desire for another fight I took a second bite of my bun and kept quiet.

"Of course I'll always be Papa's favorite," said Cousin Harry, "not just because I'm the best but because he and my mother were married."

"Ah," I said tactfully again.

"Well, it's simply no good if your parents aren't married, old chap. Rhiannon told Marian. She heard it at her school. If your parents aren't married you're called a bastard and it's a pretty dreadful thing to be, even worse than being working-class."

"Gosh!" I said horrified. "Poor Evan!"

"Yes, poor Evan," said Cousin Harry benignly. "I really feel quite sorry for him sometimes."

I still wondered if he would feel equally benign towards the new arrival, but he behaved graciously enough after Gerry was born and Bronwen was very pleased.

"What an adorable baby!" said my mother to Bronwen as soon as she saw Gerry, but later to my father she said, "Yes, it's a dear little thing, but my God, you should hear what's being said in the village! There's bad feeling against Johnny now, as well as Bronwen—it's interesting, isn't it, that nobody thinks twice about a gentleman discreetly keeping a mistress but once he starts living openly with a working-class woman and treating her as his wife, everyone, even the working classes themselves, takes his behavior as a personal affront."

"Especially the working classes, I'd say. What's the point of having an upper class which doesn't even make a nominal attempt to justify its privileged position by setting an example the *hoi polloi* can respect? One might as well guillotine the lot and be done with them."

"Well, Johnny had better look out for the tumbrils, that's all I can say. . . . What's that scrabbling noise at the door? Is that you, Kester? Naughty boy, how often have I told you not to listen at keyholes!"

In fact my habit of eavesdropping, which I readily admit is detestable, was essential for a child brought up in secluded circumstances, and later it seemed to become more vital than ever; I felt I had to do all I could to keep up with my worldly Cousin Harry when he returned home from his prep school for the holidays.

"Copulation, old chap? Oh gosh, yes, everyone knows about that. No, it's no good me telling you about it now because you're much too infantile to understand, but believe me, when one goes away to boarding school one learns simply everything there is to know."

Despite this glowing recommendation I was most mightily relieved when my mother decided after my father died that I was unsuited to boarding school. I had no interest whatsoever in being deprived of all privacy and martyred on the games field in all weathers, but as soon as Uncle John heard that I was not to be packed off to prep school in the autumn of 1928, he came steaming over to Little Oxmoon to make a first-class scene.

It was July when my mother dropped this bombshell on him. My father had been dead for three months. My mother had paid her visit to nasty Darling-Declan in Dublin and had returned with innumerable photographs of a cross-eyed infant who, so I was told, was my nephew. I was also shown photographs first of a very pretty Irish girl who turned out to be my sister-in-law with the unspellable name (my mother pronounced it Sh-*vawn*) and second of a tall dark individual, running rather to fat as Rory was but with a sharp alert look and a subtle sinister smile. "He looks a rotter," I said at once, and then remembered that in books I always liked the rotters.

"Did he ask lots of questions about me?" I said later to Rory when my mother was out of the room.

"Now, what would he want to do that for? He wouldn't be interested in any son of Robert's," said Rory brutally, and I screamed back, "Good! I'm not interested in any son of..." but I couldn't think what to call Conor Kinsella. "Mr. Kinsella" seemed too respectful and "Conor" much too friendly. Confused, I rushed out of the room and slammed the door while Rory's unkind laughter rang in my ears.

I had just recovered from this renewed brush with my mother's Kinsella past when Uncle John made his big scene. Harry was due to return from school for the summer holidays, and because his arrival was imminent I suppose it was only natural that Uncle John should have remembered me and inquired of my mother— purely as a formality—whether my entry to Briarwood had been confirmed for the autumn term.

"Well actually, darling," said my mother into the telephone as she lolled on the sofa and plucked a chocolate from the box on her lap, "I've decided not to send Kester away to school."

Several indignant squeaks from the telephone made her jump. I dashed across to the sofa just in time to save the box of chocolates as it slid towards the floor.

"But Johnny—thank you, Kester pet—Johnny, listen—"

An incensed click terminated the conversation.

"Oh Lord!" said my mother, hanging up. "Now we're for it, darling. Here—help yourself to a chocolate, and then find me a nice gooey one with a soft center to cheer me up. Your heroic Uncle John is just about to make an all-out effort to save you from being ruined by your naughty old mother. My dear, I feel weak with fright!"

"Gosh, Mum, what are you going to do?"

"Oh, I shall be heroic too—two can play at that game. Pet, take these chocolates away before I eat the lot, and wherever you take them to, stay there. I think I must have a teensy-weensy little pink gin."

I pattered outside with the chocolate box and took up a comfortable position behind the lavender bushes beneath the open drawing-room windows. Then I ate an orange cream, a Turkish delight and a caramel as I waited for Uncle John to launch himself on his crusade.

He arrived ten minutes later.

"Johnny, how divine to see you! Have a pink gin!"

"No, thanks, not before six." Uncle John, shorn of Bronwen, was at his stuffiest and most English. I could imagine the exact pattern of his Savile Row suit and felt certain he would be wearing his Old Harrovian tie. "Ginevra, I won't beat about the bush. Am I to understand that you don't intend to send that boy to prep school at all?"

"That's right, darling. No boarding school."

"But—"

"I'm not opposed to boarding school," pursued my mother. "I'd have been keen for Robin to go because I know he'd have enjoyed boarding-school life as much as Harry does, but Kester's not Robin and he's not Harry and he'd hate it. He's a sensitive, solitary child—"

"Very much too sensitive," said Uncle John nastily, "and very much too solitary—and that's exactly why he should be sent away to school! He must be toughened up, he must be put in the company of other boys, he must be made to play games so that he can learn about leadership and team spirit—"

"Johnny, that's all simply lovely and absolutely the spirit that built the Empire, but it's got nothing to do with reality. The truth is Kester would be bullied to pieces, and I'm sorry but I'm not going to let my child be tortured like that!"

"My dear Ginevra, I've never heard such melodramatic exaggeration in all my life! The truth is that you're a woman and you've no idea what goes on in boys' schools—you've heard a few horrific stories and so you assume the places are all dens of sadism—"

"And aren't they?" said my mother.

"Certainly not! Briarwood's a splendid school—I'll have a talk with the headmaster about Kester to make sure the boy gets exactly the care he needs, and then you can rest assured that he'll be well looked after from his first day to his last—and what's more, he'll enjoy his school days and be grateful for them! You simply can't keep him at home, Ginevra! A fatherless boy needs—"

"I'll be the judge," said my mother, "of what my son needs."

"But what would Robert have said? I can't believe he would have approved of the boy being tied to your apron strings like this!"

"Some apron strings!" said my mother with a little throaty laugh. I could imagine her knocking back the pink gin, and sure enough a second later I heard the gurgle of the bottle as she mixed herself another drink. "Sure you won't join me, Johnny?"

"No. Oh, all right, yes—thanks. Ginevra, I'm quite sure Robert would have wanted Kester to be toughened up in a masculine atmosphere. I mean . . . well, for God's sake, do you want your son to be a man or don't you?"

"Yes, I do," said my mother, "but I happen to believe there's more to being a man than wearing an Old School tie, knowing one end of a cricket bat from another and indulging in that homosexual horseplay known as rugby football!"

The word "homosexual" bounced aimlessly off my brain but none of the other words did. I nearly expired with ecstasy. Clutching the lavender bush to steady myself I wondered if I dared peep over the windowsill but my nerve failed me as Uncle John said from somewhere close at hand, "I give up."

"Thank God," said my mother. "Look—here's your pink gin—let's drink and be friends. You know how much I rely on you and how marvelous I think you are!"

Uncle John heaved such an exasperated sigh of resignation that I could picture the stream of air rushing through the open window above my head. Finally he said, "I've certainly no wish for a quarrel. But I just can't tell you how wrong I think you're being—in fact I think your decision is bound to mean that you'll have trouble with Kester one day."

"Do you?" purred my mother in her richest, most dangerous voice. "How interesting! I rather think you're going to have trouble with Harry. You see, my domestic situation is so boringly straightforward that Kester can only yawn and feel secure. But your domestic situation, romantic and thrilling as it is, isn't quite so restful as mine, is it? In fact sometimes I think I can hear a time bomb ticking, but if any bomb goes off in the Gower Peninsula it won't be here at Little Oxmoon. It'll be at Penhale Manor."

There was a silence before Uncle John said evenly, "Perhaps your domestic arrangements won't be so dull now that Robert's dead. I can see that Kester's best hope lies in acquiring a sensible stepfather."

"Oh my dear, no—no, no and again no! I've had marriage, thanks very much, absolutely *had* it."

"I thought perhaps—"

"Yes, I daresay you did, but there's going to be no third marriage. Twice was quite sufficient."

"But. . ." Uncle John seemed to find this baffling. I couldn't think why. It seemed eminently sensible to me and I was delighted. The last thing I wanted was a stepfather; it was bad enough trying to survive a bossy uncle. "You mean to go on as you are?" he said confused at last.

"Why not? The present situation suits me very well—although I must say, I do wonder if it'll remain unaltered now Robert's dead. It's as if the journey's over and one must inevitably drift apart from some if not all of one's traveling companions."

"If things do change, might you return to London?"

"Perhaps, but I'm not going to do anything in a rush. I've spent quite enough of my life jumping out of the frying pan into the fire, and now I intend to stay where I am until Robert's been dead a year."

"That seems sensible, I agree, but all the same...how very unorthodox you are, Ginevra!"

"That makes two of us, doesn't it, darling? But where we differ is that when I practice my unorthodoxy Kester knows nothing about it—and neither does anyone else."

Uncle John left soon after this, and as soon as his new Rover had roared off down the drive I rushed back to the drawing room.

"You were marvelous, Mum!" I said hugging her. "As good as Boadicea!"

"Naughty little boy, I hope you didn't leave the chocolate box among the lavender bushes—oh yes, you did! Go and fetch it at once before I spank you. How many times have I told you not to eavesdrop?" said my mother, but she was smiling at me indulgently, and after I had retrieved the chocolate box I rushed upstairs to the schoolroom and tried to look up UNAUTHORDOCKS in the dictionary.

IV

"Unorthodox, old chap," said Cousin Harry some time later, "means not doing the done thing. You're unorthodox, not going to school. Honestly, how feeble! No wonder your father's dead—I bet he died of shame!"

This time I was the one who started the fight but before I had the chance to relieve my feelings Bronwen entered the nursery with Gerry, blue-eyed and chubby, in her arms. As Harry and I at once recoiled from each other Bronwen said simply, "Fighting's wrong." She made it sound so obvious that I had an absurd urge to kick myself for not having come to this conclusion before. "Evan!" she called over her shoulder. "Kester's arrived for tea! Harry, just hold the high chair steady for me, would you, please—I need both hands to carry the baby at the moment because I mustn't strain myself."

That was when I noticed Bronwen was changing her shape again. I had not seen her for some time, because my mother and I had been visiting Aunt Daphne in Scotland.

"Are you having another baby, Bronwen?" I said with interest, just to make sure.

"Yes," she said with a brief smile, and busied herself with tucking Gerry into his high chair.

My visit to the Manor progressed in predictable fashion until six o'clock when my mother arrived to collect me. Uncle John was at a board meeting in Swansea. Dafydd, who spent most of his time nowadays with cousins in Cardiff, was absent but Rhiannon appeared from the Home Farm, where she lived with her aunt, and stayed to tea. Ghastly Cousin Marian flounced around saying how bored she was and how divine it would be to return to school next week. Harry withdrew to his room to conduct a tadpole experiment. I played with Gerry—an exhausting occupation since he had reached the age when he wanted to destroy everything in sight—but eventually settled down to a more peaceful task, helping Evan to paint pictures. After tea we designed a landscape showing a gorgeous crimson sun setting over Rhossili Bay, while on the far side of the room Marian, Harry and Rhiannon played Monopoly to the accompaniment of remarks like "You cheat!" "I'm not cheating!" "You pig!" "That's mine!" "Oh no it isn't!" and "Oh yes it is!" I have always loathed Monopoly and consider it quite one of the most pointless games ever invented.

As the cuckoo clock in the nursery whooped six my mother streamed into the room. "Hullo, pet," she said to me. "Hullo, everyone. Evan, what a lovely picture! Oh, isn't that clever of Evan, Bronwen! Bronwen... are you all right?"

Bronwen said in a muffled voice that she was.

"Come and sit down—no, not in here—God, what a noise all these children make! Let's go into the night nursery for a moment."

"Paint another flower just here, Evan," I suggested casually, pointing to a blank spot on our masterpiece, and drifted to the playpen to retrieve a brick which Gerry had just thrown beyond the bars. As I stooped to pick it up I found the hinges of the open night-nursery door were a foot from my left ear.

"When is it due?"

"February."

"Is... is it perhaps not quite what you want?"

"It's not what Johnny wants." A stifled sob. "It was an accident."

Gerry roared for his brick but I ignored him. The hinges of the door were too alluring.

"And you?" my mother was saying.

"I don't know. I don't know anything anymore. Oh, if only Constance could see what she's doing to us—"

"If this were a detective story," said my mother, "somebody would murder that woman."

But nobody did murder Aunt Constance, and nobody was able to change her mind either on the subject of divorce. Bronwen gave birth to her third illegitimate son early in February, but I barely noticed because at that moment, even before all the gossiping tongues could sink into an exhausted silence, the great miracle happened, my grandfather dropped dead and at nine years old I became master of Oxmoon.

2

I

TO SAY that my grandfather dropped dead is perhaps a slight exaggeration, as he did live for several hours after the stroke, but the hours were passed in a coma and he never regained consciousness.

"What a merciful release!" said my mother to Uncle John when he brought the news, and added: "Too bad it didn't happen immediately after Margaret died."

My mother's experiences had left her outspoken on the subject of death. "Death's all right," she said with shattering directness to my uncle. "It's dying that's the nightmare. When I pop off I hope to God it's quick. Keel over—bang—out. That's what I want. No fuss, no mess and lashings of pink gin for everyone after the funeral. You will remember that, won't you, Johnny darling? As I'm twelve years older than you I'll probably pop off first."

But my uncle looked as if he thought these remarks were in bad taste and said stuffily that she should put her wishes concerning her funeral in writing and attach the document to her will so that there would be no risk of a misunderstanding among her heirs.

The gossips declared that Mrs. Straker had stolen even the ring off my grandfather's finger as he lay dying, but everyone hated her so much that people would willingly have believed a story that she grew horns and vanished in a puff of smoke. It was true that the Godwin family signet ring was missing, but poor old Grandfather was so dotty that he could easily have thrown it away in a fit of absentmindedness. The stroke overtook him when he was in bed, a fact which both my mother and Uncle John thought implied the presence of Mrs. Straker, but although my mother was convinced Mrs. Straker had stolen the ring Uncle John believed in her innocence.

"That woman could twist any man around her little finger," said my mother darkly, a remark that conjured up the most extraordinary pictures in my nine-year-old mind, but Uncle John said, "At least she left him tidy and dignified and removed any humiliating evidence."

"You mean she delayed calling Gavin, packed her bags and skipped off at first light! I think it's absolutely disgusting that she walked out immediately like that . . ."

As they argued irrelevantly about Mrs. Straker I edged closer and closer to my mother until finally I could tug at her sleeve.

". . . so my dear, you'll simply have to give him a lavish funeral, no choice. . . . Yes, what is it, Kester?"

"Am I... now that Grandfather's dead..."

"That's right, pet, we'll go and live at Oxmoon now. Johnny, there's absolutely no need to have a ghastly formal lunch afterwards—throw open the ballroom for a champagne reception and even Aunt Ethel will be lost in the stampede!"

Uncle John groaned at the thought of Aunt Ethel, who was a family legend and synonymous with complete awfulness. She was my grandmother's sister, and I had long pictured her as a snake-headed Medusa who lived in a pottery kiln in Staffordshire. She was fond of my Uncle Thomas (by far the most awful member of the Godwin family) and sent him a pair of hand-knitted socks every Christmas.

"... and anyway," my mother was saying, "with any luck the Staffordshire crowd will refuse the invitation. Yes, what *is* it, Kester? Don't tug at my sleeve like that!"

"Am I very rich now?"

"No. You'll go on having your sixpence-a-week pocket money and that'll be that. How's the mortgage, Johnny?"

"Not so bad. We'll have the estate back in good order by the time Kester's eighteen."

"What happens when I'm eighteen?" I said.

"That's when you come into your inheritance," said Uncle John. "Your grandfather became legally responsible for Oxmoon when he was eighteen, even though he didn't gain control of it till he was twenty. He always treated eighteen, not twenty-one, as the time we all came of age."

"But do you mean Oxmoon won't really be mine for another nine whole years?"

"Of course it'll be yours, silly-billy," said my mother exasperated, "but you'll have to have people looking after it for you while you're growing up. What did you think was going to happen? Did you see yourself sitting on a throne in the hall and issuing orders to your servants?"

This was in fact exactly what I had visualized. I tried not to look mortified. As usual, reality was proving a very poor second to my fantasies.

"You and I are the trustees, aren't we, Johnny? Thank God Bobby didn't include Thomas—my nerves wouldn't have stood it. ... No, Kester, I'm not answering any more questions—run off and ask Nanny to take you for a walk."

I retired in great humiliation. The master of Oxmoon was to ask his nanny to take him for a walk! And no increase in pocket money! As I went for a walk by myself, trudging drearily through the March drizzle, I saw all my dreams of grandeur dissolve one by one. I wouldn't have the leading role among the mourners at the funeral. I wouldn't have Uncle Thomas fawning at my feet in the dining room, and as there was to be no formal lunch I would have no chance to sit in my grandfather's great carved chair at the head of the table. Instead I would be wholly overlooked during the reception in the ballroom, trampled underfoot and suffocated by the reek of pink gin. Tears came to my eyes. I cried.

My mother, seeing me return red-eyed from my walk, became crosser than ever. "*Now* what's the matter, for goodness' sake! I thought Grandfather meant no more to you than half a crown occasionally!"

"I feel sad for *me*."

"*You!* Good God, you've just inherited Oxmoon—you're the luckiest little boy in all England and Wales! How dare you be sad! There's your heroic Uncle John, keeping a stiff upper lip and being simply wonderful as usual, and here am I, grappling with all kinds of upsetting memories of poor Bobby but trying my best to be calm and sensible, and *you have the nerve to stand there and be sad!* Oh, I could slap you!"

It was an Anglo-Saxon tradition in our family that children below the age of puberty did not attend funerals, but as my grandfather's heir I naturally had to be present, and as soon as he heard that I would be there Cousin Harry, not to be outdone, said he wanted to be there too.

"You're just trying to impress your father," I said scornfully on the day before the funeral.

"Not at all, old chap," said urbane Cousin Harry. "I'm going because it's the done thing. After all, I'm the eldest grandson, aren't I? *And*," said Cousin Harry very nastily, "I was the favorite grandson too."

"A fat lot of good that's done you!" I said wittily. "I'm the one who's inherited Oxmoon!" And I skipped out of his way feeling in very high spirits indeed. In fact, soon my tears were quite forgotten because I heard that Uncle John had decided to give a formal luncheon after all; he had been helped to this decision by the news that dreaded Aunt Ethel and her cohorts had decided not to attend the funeral, and as soon as I heard that the reception in the ballroom had been cancelled, I began to dream urgently again of taking my seat in Grandfather's great carved chair.

The family began to assemble at Oxmoon where Mrs. Wells, Uncle John's housekeeper, had once again temporarily replaced the wicked Mrs. Straker. The first guests to arrive were Uncle Edmund and Aunt Teddy with their two little boys Richard and Geoffrey. Uncle Edmund was subdued, maundering on and on about how guilty he felt because he hadn't visited his father more often, but Aunt Teddy did her best to cheer him up. Aunt Teddy was bright and bouncy, like a rubber ball, and looked as if she were constantly on the verge of dancing the Charleston. But I noticed she was very cool to Uncle John, never speaking to him if she could avoid it, and I remembered that she and Aunt Constance, who so badly needed to be murdered, were sisters.

My brother Rory, who was between jobs as usual, turned up in his red two-seater and surprised me by saying sentimentally what a wonderful man my grandfather had been. "Bobby was very good to Rory and Declan when they were boys," my mother explained, seeing my astonished expression, and added with a sigh to Rory: "It's sad Kester has no memory of Bobby as he used to be." This struck me as an interesting remark, but before I could ponder on it further my Aunt Celia arrived from Heidelberg with her daughter Erika and I was faced with the ordeal of being sociable to an unknown cousin who spoke no English. Erika was eight, blond, blue-eyed and very, very fat. We gazed at each other in mutual horror before I escaped to my room to try on my new black suit.

I half-wondered if Declan would come from Ireland, but he merely wrote a letter of sympathy to Uncle John and asked my mother to send a wreath in his name; however I read the letter. Uncle John showed it to my mother and left it carelessly on the hall table as he went off to drink pink gin with her, so it was easy for me to take a quick peep. *Dear Mr. Godwin,* I read. *Please allow me to express my sympathy to you in your bereavement. Your father was a fine man and treated my brother and myself with a kindness and generosity which perhaps we took too much for granted during those happy days we spent at Oxmoon long ago. My wife and I send our good wishes to you and your family. Yours sincerely,* DECLAN KINSELLA.

What surprised me about this letter was its Englishness. My picture of Declan as an illiterate Irish barbarian underwent a significant revision.

The day of the funeral dawned and in great excitement I dressed in my new suit. "I think I look well in black," I said to Nanny, "but I wish I could have long trousers."

"Not before you're twelve," said Nanny. "Only common boys wear long trousers before they're twelve."

I wondered who had invented that rule. Who in fact *had* invented all these rules which set out the differences between doing the done thing and behaving like a savage? It was all most mysterious, but as I prepared for the funeral that morning I knew very well that I was approaching an occasion on which the need to do the done thing was absolutely paramount. Proper behavior at a funeral could mean the difference between universal approval and eternal damnation by the People Who Mattered (Uncle John). Clutching my prayer book, I thought what a good thing it was that Grandfather had meant so little to me; thanks to my emotional apathy I felt sure I could be a perfect Godwin, sustaining a stiff upper lip for the duration of the funeral.

But at the church I remembered my mother's remark "It's sad Kester has no memory of Bobby as he used to be," and then in my mind I heard her say, "I do wish you could remember Daddy before he became ill," and suddenly I felt not only bereaved but deprived twice over, shortchanged by a fate which had cut me off from the two men in my life who should have been of such importance to me. Tears filled my eyes. I bit my lip, but it trembled inexorably. Panic filled me. I snuffled, choked, sniveled in my pew.

Nudging me sharply, my mother hissed, "Stop it!" but that only made me worse. Luckily we were in the front pew so nobody could turn around to observe my humiliation, and certainly no one behind us could see I was awash with tears, but I shuddered at the thought of Uncle John, who was standing next to me. As my mother furiously thrust her black lace handkerchief into my hands I prayed for him not to look aside from his hymnbook, and in praying I diverted myself so successfully that I forgot all about poor little me, shortchanged by fate. My tears stopped but then—horror of horrors—we all withdrew to the churchyard, and when I saw the open grave, the silent crowds and the clergyman looking like death personified, I was struck by the inescapable reality of my grandfather's nonexistence. I felt that everyone was looking at me. Terrified of breaking down I tried to hide behind my mother's ample black coat.

485

"Kester! Don't be such a little ninny!" My mother was furious again. "Stand up straight this instant!"

The earth looked dark and wet. The sky was gray, the wind was cold and I thought how awful it was that we should all have this hideous fate awaiting us in the future. Tears streamed down my face as I dwelled on the tragic destiny of mankind.

"God, look at that little pansy!" muttered bestial Uncle Thomas.

"Shut up, you brute!" snapped my mother at him.

"Ginevra—Thomas . . ." It was Uncle John. He was stooping over me, but although I braced myself for his anger it did not come. His arm slipped around me. His voice was quiet and infinitely kind. "Kester, don't think of your grandfather. Think of Oxmoon and show all these people here that you're a young man to be reckoned with."

I gulped, gripped his hand tightly and dashed away my shameful tears as I thought of Oxmoon and my new eminence. But then . . .

"Ashes to ashes . . . dust to dust . . ."

Tears streamed down my face again. It seemed so terrible that anyone, even dotty old Grandfather, should be reduced to dust and ashes, and suddenly I thought, *Poor* Grandfather; how beastly I've been! And I was deeply ashamed. After all Grandfather had left me Oxmoon, a magnificent gesture which must surely have meant that he cared about me in some vague peculiar way, but what had I ever done when he was alive to express my gratitude? Grumbled that he gave me only half a crown occasionally! Wailed that I didn't want to be bothered to go and see him! How loathsome I was! Hating myself, I wept in utter desolation.

My mother then administered the *coup de grâce*. Bending over me she whispered savagely, "Look at Harry! And pull yourself together at once!"

I looked at perfect Cousin Harry, tearless at his father's side. He looked back pityingly and lowered his bone-dry lashes over his velvet-brown eyes in an expression of utter contempt.

I stopped loathing myself and loathed him instead. My tears of grief were now tears of rage. I could hardly wait to beat him up and sure enough, as soon as we reached Oxmoon, the opportunity quickly presented itself.

All the family were assembled in the drawing room and drinking champagne, both in memory of my grandfather and in the hope of staging a rapid mass recovery from the unspeakable ordeal at Penhale Church. Canapés were being circulated by Lowell, the butler who had replaced the Venerable Bayliss (died a martyr after suffering many years of Mrs. Straker's tyranny), and by a strong silent parlormaid called Caradoc (promoted by Mrs. Straker on account of her ability to hold her tongue). Harry and I, the only children present, had been provided with our own little dish of sausage rolls and were drinking lemonade.

"A bit weepy, weren't you, old chap?" he said, snatching the largest sausage roll before I could grab it. "I suppose that's because your mother keeps you at home and lets you get soft."

"If you had a mother like my mother," I spat, inwardly burning with humiliation, "and if you had a home like Oxmoon, you'd jolly well want to stay at home too. But all you've got is a rotten old manor house which no one ever visits and a father who *lives in sin!*"

He hit me. I hit him back. We fell writhing to the floor amidst a shower of sausage rolls.

"Kester! Harry! Stop that at once! Oh God, where's John? Thomas, stop them, for goodness' sake!"

"Why bother? Let them beat each other up! Do the little pansy good!"

"Thomas, next time you call my son a pansy, I'll—"

"Now, you listen to me, Thomas Godwin!" bellowed Rory, who had been drinking steadily since breakfast. "Next time you insult my mother by calling that little nitwit a pansy I'll smash your face in!"

"My, look at that dustup! Edmund honey, your nephews are trying to kill each other!"

"I say, chaps, we can't have this," said Uncle Edmund. I was dimly aware of his hand wavering above us before clutching ineffectually at Harry's collar.

I took advantage of Harry's loss of concentration to land a perfect right to the jaw.

Harry yelped, wrenched himself free and spun round on Uncle Edmund in a rage. "Leave me alone, you stupid old fool, and get out of my way!"

Everyone gasped and suddenly I saw that Uncle John had returned to the room. I immediately felt sick. Scrambling to our feet Harry and I stood trembling before him.

At first he had eyes only for his son. "How dare you behave like this and disgrace me!"

Urbane worldly Cousin Harry was suddenly a stammering little boy of ten. "I'm very sorry, Papa."

"Apologize at once to your Uncle Edmund."

"I'm very sorry, Uncle Edmund."

"That's all right, old boy," said Uncle Edmund awkwardly. "Upsetting things, funerals."

"Go out into the garden," said Uncle John to Harry, "and wait there till I send for you."

"Yes, sir," said Harry, and stumbled away.

"Kester," said Uncle John, abruptly terminating my enjoyment of Harry's discomfort, "you'll come with me to the library."

I glanced automatically at my mother to make sure she would be there to protect me, but my mother, champagne glass in hand, regarded me with a bleak eye and made no move to accompany us.

"Come along, Kester," said Uncle John, seeing my hesitation and perfectly understanding it.

I shot my mother a reproachful glance and tramped miserably out of the room.

"So much for the new master of Oxmoon," said vile Uncle Thomas as the door closed.

I was still boiling with rage and shame as I entered the library. "I'm sorry, Uncle John," I burst out, "but Harry was beastly to me, and—"

487

"No," said Uncle John. "No telling tales, please. No sneaking. If that mother of yours would only see sense and send you to school, you'd soon discover there are some things one simply doesn't do."

"But Harry—"

"Never mind Harry. Harry at least had some excuse for behaving like a jealous child, but you had none—and at least Harry conducted himself decently at the funeral! But you! You made no effort at all to behave properly. You humiliated your mother and you appalled me. All those tears were quite unnecessary. It was sheer histrionic self-indulgence, an unpardonable display of emotion."

I knew this was true, and as the shame overwhelmed me I found to my horror that I wanted to cry again.

"Women," said Uncle John, "are permitted a certain amount of latitude in exhibiting grief; they're the weaker sex and allowances must be made for them, but men are expected to behave like men and that means controlling your emotions and behaving in a manner that won't be a source of embarrassment to everyone around you. Women look to men to display strength and men look to their leaders to provide an example for them to follow. When you're grown up you'll be the first man in this parish and everyone in Penhale will look to you for leadership. You're going to have to provide that and you're going to start learning how to provide it today. Now we'll have no more tears, if you please, and you'll come out with me into the garden to make your peace with Harry."

Rage once more annihilated the desire to cry. "I think Harry should make his peace with *me*, sir!" I said stubbornly. I was careful not to sound rude, merely burning with the desire for justice. "It was he who spoke the first insult," I said, ruthlessly casting aside any puerile convention against sneaking, "and it was he who struck the first blow, and I'm jolly well going to stand up for myself by making that clear."

I think Uncle John was startled by this show of strength. Perhaps he had expected me to collapse meekly into an abject heap after his stern reproofs, and when I remained defiantly upright he fell silent. At once I was terrified. Supposing he decided to beat me? I knew Harry was never beaten but then Harry was perfect. In contrast I was a long way from perfection, and I thought Uncle John would be sure to approve of corporal punishment.

I began to stammer an apology but he interrupted me.

"Kester," he said, "you can afford to be generous to Harry today. Just do as you're told, make your peace with him and stop arguing."

Something in his tone cut deep into my consciousness. He sounded so very bleak and cold, and suddenly I was aware of all my secret fears that he despised me and found me a terrible cross to bear.

"You're wishing it was Harry who had Oxmoon," said a small high unsteady voice which I dimly realized was mine. "You hate me and wish I was dead like Robin."

"Oh my God!" said Uncle John, and heaved one of his vast sighs. Then, most unexpectedly, he laughed. "I've never before known a child," he said, "who plays every scene in his life as if it were the final act of a Victorian melodrama! My dear Kester, if you really want to cast me in the role of the wicked uncle there's nothing I can do to stop you, but I do assure you that the performance is all entirely in your mind."

He slumped down in one of the old leather armchairs by the fireplace and drew me to him. Then he smiled. Instinctively I leaned against him for comfort, anxious for any gesture which would negate my nightmarish suspicion that I was despised, and as if he knew exactly what I needed, he put his arm around my shoulders.

"If I'd wanted Oxmoon for Harry," he said gently, "I could have got it. I was my father's favorite at the end and he would have given me anything I asked. But it would have been wrong, Kester. It would have meant cheating your father, my favorite brother. It would have meant making your mother unhappy. It would have meant depriving you of something which by tradition was rightfully yours. How could I ever have wanted something which would have involved me in so much wrongdoing? One can't go through life grabbing everything without regard for the consequences, you know. That's the road to hell, and the people who wind up in hell are the people who don't know when to stay 'Stop!' and draw the line."

I was entranced. A picture flashed into my mind of a broad golden line with a black pit marked HELL on one side of it and a pastoral vista marked HEAVEN on the other. "Gosh!" I said, my fondness for melodrama well satisfied, and leaned a little closer to him. I was greatly enjoying my first lesson in metaphysics.

"Terrible things happen," said Uncle John, "to people who fail to draw the line."

"Is that why we all have to stick to the rules and play the game and do the done thing?"

I was proving an apt pupil. He smiled at me again, patted my head and stood up. "Yes. Now let's go into the garden and find Harry."

I clasped his hand and decided I would impress him by being thoroughly magnanimous to poor old Cousin Harry, whom Uncle John had so delightfully described at the start of our conversation as a jealous child. Obviously it would be the done thing to be magnanimous. I began to feel much better.

"You do like me a little in spite of everything, don't you, Uncle John?"

"My dear Kester, what an idiotic question!" said Uncle John, sounding as irritated as my mother undoubtedly would have been in the circumstances. "You know perfectly well I think of you as my own son now your father's dead."

My last trace of insecurity dissolved. I looked up at him mistily and thought he was wonderful.

In the garden we saw Harry huddled on the bench by the tennis court, but when we appeared he stood up and trudged slowly towards us. He had stuffed his hands into his pockets, and as I watched I saw him pause more than once to dig his heel fiercely into the ground. His black hair fell forward across his forehead to shadow his face, and it was not until he was close to us that I noticed his eyes had a faint pink rim.

Uncle John, who was holding my right hand in his left, held out his own right hand to his son and Harry grabbed it, a small pin hurling itself thankfully at an all-powerful magnet. Uncle John smiled, and when I saw Harry lean against him I knew that he too was feeling relief after a nightmarish moment of insecurity.

"Well, boys," said Uncle John as we all paused by the tennis court and looked back at the house, "you've both behaved badly but I've made it clear what I think of such conduct so now we'll consider the incident closed. However, there's to be no more fighting. It's quite wrong and I'll no longer tolerate it. I draw the line."

We gazed up at him solemnly but he did not see us. He was looking at the bedraggled walls of his old home.

"We all know what happens to a house that's divided against itself," said Uncle John. He spoke idly and almost to himself as if neither Harry nor I were present. He might have been making some prosaic remark such as "Dear me, I must get an estimate to have the roof repaired." Then he remembered us and tightened his clasp on our hands. "Oxmoon belongs to all of us," he said easily, "although Kester's the one who has the responsibility of looking after it and passing it on to the next generation. That's a very heavy responsibility so we have to do all we can to help Kester, don't we, Harry? I'm sure you understand that we all have to work together and be friends."

"Yes, Papa," said Harry.

"And you understand that too, don't you, Kester?"

"Oh yes, Uncle John," I said, and added (rather craftily, I thought): "It's the done thing."

"Very well. Now shake hands, both of you, and be friends."

Harry and I shook hands, two small boys hypnotized by that powerful complex adult personality which even in later life I often wondered if I had ever truly understood.

"Sorry I bashed you just now, Harry."

"That's all right, old chap. Sorry I ragged you about not going to school."

"Of course you can come and play at Oxmoon whenever you want."

"Jolly decent of you. Thanks."

There was an awkward little pause. And that was when I looked at Harry and Harry looked at me and we both knew that no matter how often Uncle John talked of the perils of a house divided against itself, we were all heading for some very complicated long-division sums indeeds.

II

When we arrived back at the house the gong was sounding for lunch, and the family, all shrieking and laughing with the slackening of nervous tension which follows a surfeit of champagne, were milling around in the hall and declaring what a splendid funeral it had turned out to be.

"Poor Bobby, missing this!" shouted my mother, who was tight, to Uncle John. "How he'd have loved it!"

Uncle John, who was stone-cold sober, merely raised an eyebrow and moved to muzzle Uncle Thomas who, having abandoned champagne in favor of whisky, was telling an enthralled Rory some story involving chains and pillowcases. (The idiotic things grown-ups talked about!) Trailing along at the end of the crowd towards the dining room, I glumly wondered how long my new friendship with Harry would last.

The dining room was built on a corner of the main block of the house, next to the passage that led past the green baize door to the servants' quarters. Huge bad paintings of hunting scenes blazed from the walls, the pink coats of the huntsmen clashing with the dark red wallpaper. The long ravishing rosewood dining table, an eighteenth-century treasure which had somehow been allowed to coexist with all the Victorian junk so beloved by my grandparents, lay like a dream of elegance in the middle of the threadbare Indian carpet and was lovingly adorned with the renowned Godwin silver epergnes and the monogrammed Godwin cutlery (generously spared by the acquisitive Mrs. Straker). The dinner service was Doulton, a little chipped and cracked in places, just like Oxmoon, but by no means a mere ghost of past splendor. By the sideboard lurked Lowell with a couple of attendant minions, and beyond the servants I noticed that the champagne bottles were lined up like skittles. I wondered if anyone would offer me a little sip and propose a toast in my honor, but thought both events highly unlikely.

My mother was squabbling with Uncle Thomas. "John must sit at the head of the table," she was saying, murdering my best daydream with one ruthless sentence, "but I'm going to sit opposite him in Margaret's chair—no, you can't have it! Go and sit next to John—he might be able to keep you in some sort of order!"

"God, what a bitchy old cow you are sometimes, Ginevra!"

"Thomas!" said Uncle Edmund, very pink.

"Whoops!" said Aunt Teddy. "Hold on to your horses, everyone, we're off for a thundering gallop!"

"Everyone—*please!*" begged Aunt Celia, a tall angular spinsterish-looking woman with a permanently horrified expression. "Let's all show a little respect for darling Papa's memory!"

"I absolutely agree," said Uncle Edmund. "Harry, come and sit with me and tell me more about school."

"Say, that's odd," said Aunt Teddy. "There aren't enough places—or have I counted wrong?"

"Well, I'm sitting here on John's right," said Uncle Thomas, plonking himself down in his chosen chair, "so whoever ends up standing won't be me."

"I can't think why Mrs. Wells should have got it wrong," said my mother. "I gave her the correct numbers as soon as Daphne phoned to say she couldn't come. Lowell, why aren't there place cards?"

"Well, madam, I was waiting for your instructions—"

"Why didn't you *tell* me you were waiting for instructions? I thought Mrs. Wells said—"

"What are we going to eat?" said Rory, sitting down next to my mother. "I rather fancy some caviar."

"Christ!" said Uncle Thomas. "Look at all that champagne!"

"Really, Thomas!" exploded Aunt Celia. "Your language, your irreverence, your general demeanor—"

"Ah, here comes Mrs. Wells. Mrs. Wells, there are nine people and only eight places—"

"I'm so sorry, madam, I do apologize," said Mrs. Wells. "I didn't realize Master Harry was going to be present—I thought Master Kester was going to be the only grandchild to attend the funeral. I'll arrange for an extra setting straightaway."

Everyone was now sitting down except me and Uncle John. Uncle John was standing beside my grandfather's carved chair which had figured so pathetically in my futile dreams of grandeur. In a moment he would sit down in it and I would be left standing, embarrassed and humiliated, the master of Oxmoon who was just a joke, the little boy whom everyone forgot.

"Well, go on, John," said Uncle Thomas, "sit down—you make me nervous when you tower over me like this!"

"Kester," said my mother, belatedly noticing that I had nowhere to sit, "come down here by me—Rory, move up to make room for the extra place."

I trudged drearily down the room.

"Kester," said Uncle John.

I turned. I had just reached my mother at one end of the long table and he was still standing at the other. At first I thought I had done something wrong, for his voice was abrupt, but then I saw he was smiling at me.

He gestured towards the great carved chair.

I stared.

The room unexpectedly fell silent as if everyone was as stunned as I was.

"Come along, Kester," said Uncle John. "This is your place now."

I thought: I mustn't cry. *I mustn't.*

It was so quiet that I could hear my new shoes squeak. Not daring to look either to right or to left I walked towards him. Twelve steps to glory, twelve steps to ecstasy, twelve steps to the start of the fairy tale where all my dreams came true.

When I reached the chair I gripped one of the arms and looked back at my family. I expected to see scorn mingled with indulgent amusement, but no one laughed and no one looked scornful. On the contrary, far from showing any expression the family looked blank, as if they had suddenly been presented with a reality which they found as stunning as I did.

The fairy tale had come true and suddenly, magically, I was indeed master of Oxmoon, scrambling up into the chair to take my place at the head of the table.

"That's it," said Uncle John casually. "Good boy. Now up you get, Thomas, and I'll have your place on Kester's right. Ah, Mrs. Wells, set the extra place next to Mrs. Edmund, please—Rory, just move a little closer to Ginevra, would you?"

Thomas stood up without a word, dispossessed and defeated. I wanted to shout "Hurrah!" at the top of my voice but of course I said nothing and kept my face expressionless. Uncle John had waved his magic wand and I had become the perfect Godwin, effortlessly doing the done thing at all times.

"Lowell," said Uncle John, "half a glass of champagne each, please, for Master Kester and Master Harry."

The parlormaids were distributing the smoked salmon.

"Why, Kester, how cute you look in that lovely old chair!" said nice kind bouncy Aunt Teddy.

"Papa simply adored that chair," said dreary Aunt Celia. "Mama bought it in a jumble sale for his twenty-first birthday and it cost her thirteen and six. Of course they were terribly poor in those days and hardly had a farthing between them. Do you remember, Ginevra..." And she droned on as the maids completed serving the salmon and Lowell arrived with the two half-glasses of champagne.

Uncle John stood up. Aunt Celia's reminiscences stopped as if someone had mercifully turned off a dripping tap.

"Well," said Uncle John, matchlessly at ease. "I think we've had enough prayers in church this morning so I won't say grace. And I think we would all wish to grieve in our different ways for my father so I see no point in giving a eulogy. It's enough that we know he was a fine man with a tragic past which made him old before his time. Let it rest at that. And now I suggest we should be grateful for the present and hopeful for the future. Kester's an intelligent boy, he's full of promise and above all he's Robert's son. Let's think of Robert, who was without doubt the most brilliant Godwin of his generation, and let's all now join in wishing Kester well."

He raised his glass until it caught the light. I have an unforgettable memory of him standing there, straight-backed, perfectly poised, setting the example for all the family to follow.

"To Kester!" said my heroic Uncle John, and as I looked up at him with shining eyes, I thought, If this is what happens when people do the done thing, then I'm all in favor of people doing the done thing.

But then I looked down the table at Harry, white-faced, stiff-lipped Cousin Harry, and I thought he might not be enjoying the spectacle of Uncle John doing the done thing half as much as I was—and in fact might well not be enjoying it at all.

III

It says a great deal about the way Uncle John handled his private life that I took for granted Bronwen's absence from both my grandfather's funeral and the family luncheon afterwards. Officially she was his children's nanny; she took no part in his social life, and when Uncle John dined or lunched with us he came alone. It was only when he came to tea with the children that Bronwen would accompany him (I came to realize that tea was the only meal to which socially inadequate people could be invited). Uncle John seldom entertained his friends at Penhale Manor, but when he did my mother would be present to act as his hostess and Bronwen would keep out of sight upstairs. It was always stressed to me that far from minding being left out of his social life, she was only too relieved to be excused from it.

"God only knows what will happen if they ever marry and he has to present her to his friends," my mother said once. "I don't think she could cope at all, poor darling."

In making this remark my mother was not being cattily snobbish but was merely facing the facts of class as she faced the facts of death—with shattering directness. Accordingly, as I took my cue from her, it never occurred to me to look down on Bronwen; I went on loving her just the same, but I knew she was different and must often suffer for being different so I felt increasingly sorry for her, particularly when she had to miss a grand occasion like my grandfather's funeral. I wished she could have seen me taking my place in the carved chair.

By the time I inherited Oxmoon I had overheard much speculation on the subject of Uncle John's relationship with Bronwen, and I was aware that although everyone professed to understand it, no one could agree what was causing it to persist. (People tended to speak of it as if it were an unusually bad case of measles.) In other words, no one really understood it at all. My mother glibly wrote it off as a Grand Passion, but this diagnosis much irritated my father who thought that believing in romance was as futile as believing in God but very much sillier.

"I'm not denying grand passions exist," I could remember him saying, "but in my unromantic opinion they exist in order to fill a vacuum in an unsatisfactory life—they're the product of disturbed minds which yearn for an escape from insoluble problems."

"What rubbish!" said my mother. "That takes no account of factors like the irresistible chemistry of sexual attraction and the breathtaking thrill of a meeting of the minds!"

"That's the sort of remark," said my father, "which confirms my belief that women really are the stupider sex," and the conversation had then deteriorated into one of their furious rows.

I was interested to note that this phrase of my mother's, "sexual attraction" (not quoted in the dictionary, I discovered to my chagrin), recurred frequently in any discussion of Bronwen and Uncle John, but as time passed people began to agree that this mysterious force could not provide the Whole Answer.

"It's bloody sex, that's all," said sordid Uncle Thomas. "Do you think either of them would have looked twice at the other if they'd been ugly as sin?"

"Well, as a matter of fact," said my mother, "yes. After all this time there's got to be more to it than mere sexual attraction."

On the evening before my grandfather's funeral Aunt Celia confided to my mother: "I'm terribly distressed that John's situation is still going on. I really did think he might have recovered by now."

I was accustomed to hearing Uncle John spoken of as if he were critically ill, but Aunt Celia made it sound as if he were on the point of death. I stopped thinking how cold I was in my pajamas (I had left my bed to tell my mother I was too excited to sleep) and tiptoed noiselessly closer to the drawing-room door.

"It's a much more complicated relationship than you think it is, Celia. John's a very complicated man."

"Then what can he possibly see in a simple uneducated working-class Welsh girl?"

"Just that: simplicity. Although actually I don't think Bronwen's all that simple either—I think she's the most unusual and intelligent girl, but whatever she is, Celia, there's no doubt she has some vital message for Johnny which the rest of us just can't read."

"Of course she's very pretty—"

"It's not just sex."

"But my dear, surely sex must play a large part—think of those three illegitimate children! *Three!*"

"I know." My mother was uncharacteristically reticent.

"I think it's the height of irresponsibility, I really do—and what an example to set Marian and Harry! I'm sorry Daphne couldn't come to the funeral—she wrote to me last Christmas and said how worried she was about Marian—"

"I know," said my mother again, but still she refused to utter one word criticizing Uncle John.

"What's the latest arrival going to be called? I was too embarrassed to ask John when I saw him today."

"Lance. Short for Lancelot."

"Most unsuitable!" said Aunt Celia coldly. "But I suppose they think they're being romantic."

"Oh, yes, I daresay," said my mother, suddenly unable to keep her tongue in check a moment longer. "No doubt the next ones will be called Arthur and Guinevere, and then all we'll need is Tennyson to come back from the dead and rewrite *Idylls of the King.*"

"But my dear, surely there won't be any more!"

"Nothing," said my mother bleakly, "would surprise me now."

And sure enough by the time Lance was eighteen months old Uncle John told us Bronwen was having another baby.

"How nice," said my mother as if someone had handed her a bouquet of dead flowers, and there was a small tense pause.

"Bronwen's been so depressed," said my uncle rapidly, examining a speck of dust on one of his cuffs, "and having babies is the one thing that cheers her up."

"Quite," said my mother, and began to talk about estate matters.

By that time we were living at Oxmoon; the fairy-tale years had begun.

After my grandfather's funeral we remained at Little Oxmoon for four months while my mother organized certain alterations to my new home. There was little money to spare at that time for the massive improvements needed, but the roof was mended, electricity was installed and my grandparents' bedroom was completely renovated—"although I suspect it should really be exorcised," said my mother darkly, "in order to purge the atmosphere of That Woman."

495

However Mrs. Straker's presence, far from lingering on the air like the Cheshire Cat's smile, was purged as soon as my mother commanded in a moment of unbridled femininity that the room should be decorated in pink and white. (Mrs. Straker had definitely not been a pink-and-white person.) My mother's taste usually veered to bold exotic colors but she said that as this was the one bedroom in her life where nothing naughty was ever going to happen, the atmosphere must be virginal. A plump white single bed was installed and adorned with white flounces and frills. A modern white dressing table matched the modern white wardrobes; white bedside tables and white chests-of-drawers completed this pristine triumph over a murky past but the room was saved from snowy austerity by the sensuous shade of the matching dusty-pink carpet. My mother thought it was all "rather heaven" but decided a little treasure or two from Christie's would enhance it so off we went to London to haunt the auction rooms. By a superhuman display of willpower my mother somehow avoided spending thousands and bought two cheap paintings of nudes in the pre-Raphaelite style and a small bronze Edwardian statue of a naked man which, when converted into an ashtray by a local craftsman, she kept by her bed—"as an antidote to the virginal atmosphere!" she remarked gaily to Aunt Julie. My mother was in very high spirits by that time and kept saying what fun life was.

I agreed with her. Although I had passed through London on various visits to Aunt Daphne in Scotland I had not stayed for any length of time in the city since my infancy, and so now it was as if I were visiting the capital for the first time. I was enrapt. I loved Swansea, but Swansea's magic was different; Swansea is a large ugly industrial port in a position of such superb natural beauty that the ugliness is transformed into glamour; Swansea, as my mother once said, was like a plain woman with "It." But London was like a handsome hero. London reminded me of Ruritania, full of soldiers in ceremonial uniforms and fabulous palaces and beautiful parks and grand houses and glittering shops and vast noble monuments commemorating Courage, Valor and Our Glorious Dead which all helped to prove (to the British) that Great Britain represented the pinnacle of human achievement. How fortunate, I thought with relief, that Edward the First had conquered the Welsh! Otherwise I might have grown up excluded from this Land of Hope and Glory.

Naturally I wanted to go everywhere and do everything, but my mother said we had to be selective in order to avoid wearing ourselves out. So we went to Divine Harrods, which had a very good toy department, and after my mother had bought me some smart clothes we went to a bookshop called Hatchard's, which I thought was even more divine than Harrods, and as soon as my mother had bought me three books by Jeffrey Farnol, we were whisked in a thrilling taxi ride around Piccadilly Circus and Trafalgar Square to the Savoy where we had a sumptuous banquet with my mother's best friend Aunt Julie.

"I think I could become quite partial to this sort of life," I remarked as my mother let me have a spoonful of her caviar, and Aunt Julie laughed and offered me a sip of her champagne.

More glamour was to follow. We went to the theater twice, the Royal Academy once and the National Gallery three times. I fell in love with Titian, Leonardo da Vinci, Bellini, Constable, Turner, Renoir and a host of other artistic giants. Then came the thrill of the auction at Christie's. I nearly expired with excitement. Here I fell in love with Benvenuto Cellini and three Faience cats and wanted my mother to buy a swag of fruit carved by Grinling Gibbons.

After that Art was always spelled with a capital A in my mind alongside Beauty and Truth.

"Are you going to have a flat in town now, Ginevra?" said Aunt Julie during our lunch at the Savoy, and I exclaimed at once, "What a topping idea!" but my mother said firmly, "No, I want the estate to be free of encumbrances when Kester inherits at eighteen, and you know how naughty I can be about money, Julie— if I had a flat in town I'd just be naughty from dawn till dusk."

"What fun!" said Aunt Julie, and they giggled together like schoolgirls.

"Incidentally," added Aunt Julie in that peculiar way grown-ups have of skipping from subject to subject without any apparent connecting link, "how's Gavin?"

"My dear, he's getting married!"

"No! Do you approve?"

"Well, I can understand him wanting a more stable life now that he's nearer fifty than forty."

"What's she like?"

"Worthy and well-upholstered. She's the widow of a conchie."

"What's that?" I said, becoming interested. I had long since been bored to tears by all Penhale's devoted interest in Dr. Warburton's plans to remarry, but this was an item of information which I hadn't heard before.

"A conscientious objector, darling—someone who refused to fight in the war. Although actually," she added to Aunt Julie, "I believe he drove an ambulance for the Red Cross and died a hero."

"I think all conchies are heroes," said Aunt Julie.

"Tell me more, darling," said my mother indulgently, and they began to prattle away about men while I ate my roast beef and gazed dreamily out of the window at the river.

Once Aunt Julie said, "Heavens, should I be saying all this in front of Kester?" and I woke up from my reverie but my mother said, "Oh, it's all right, that sort of thing just passes straight over his head at the moment, and anyway I don't believe in treating children like little hothouse plants. Little hothouse plants have a nasty habit of withering at the first frost, and I want to bring my child up to be tough and durable."

"Very sensible, darling," said Aunt Julie. "Would you like to write the Motherhood Column in A Woman's Place?"

They gurgled away again, helpless with laughter. A lot of champagne had been consumed by that time.

"No, I'm giving up all my literary hobbies now that I'm mistress of Oxmoon," gasped my mother when she could speak. "No more unpublished masterpieces in the style of Elinor Glyn!"

"Your big mistake was not writing in the style of Ginevra Godwin! I told you that over and over again!"

"But my dear, it would have been pornography!"

"What's that?" I said.

"Naughty stories or pictures, darling, all about sex."

"Oh." I crammed my mouth full of luscious Yorkshire pudding.

"I think you should keep writing," said Aunt Julie.

"But I've no time! I'm playing Cleopatra to Oxmoon's Egypt and it's simply thrilling, I can't tell you how much I'm enjoying myself! I'm running the house, peeping over John's shoulder when he deals with the estate, giving audiences to lawyers, accountants and bank managers, making dozens of vital decisions, and—wait for it, Julie—I've even got *two different checkbooks!*"

This time they shrieked so loudly with mirth that people at nearby tables turned to stare. All Aunt Julie said afterwards as she wiped away a tear was a heartfelt "Poor Robert!" which once again illustrated to me my theory that adults littered their conversation with the most absurd non sequiturs.

"I'm forty-nine years old," exclaimed my mother in a burst of *joie de vivre*, "and a gorgeous new life is about to begin for me!"

"God knows you deserve it," said Aunt Julie. "No more terrors about getting in a mess unless you have a strong man to protect you?"

"Oh, my dear, when you've been to hell and back, the odd trivial mess or two no longer has the power to terrify."

"Darling Ginevra," said Aunt Julie, who was very fond of my mother, "I'm so happy for you—and before you leave London you simply must start your new life by meeting this divine friend of my favorite conchie..."

She did. We went to drinks at Aunt Julie's flat, which was very smart and sleek and modern, and Aunt Julie wore trousers and smoked a cigarette in a very long holder and looked very smart and sleek and modern herself, like a villainess in a John Buchan novel or perhaps an elderly version of Irma in *Bulldog Drummond*. The male guests wore peculiar ties and the female guests wore very bright lipstick and everyone chatted about D. H. Lawrence and Five-Year Plans and What Was Wrong With England and International Pacifism and Psychoanalysis and how the BBC was perpetuating Middle-Class Myths. I drank about a gallon of lemonade and ate a sinful chocolate cake and listened. My mother, very curvacious in a skimpy floral frock which seemed to finish in all the wrong places, smoked like a chimney and swilled pink gin and had the time of her life. Her eyelashes seemed to be about six inches long and perpetually fluttering.

The divine friend of Aunt Julie's favorite conchie was so entranced that he invited her out to a nightclub on the following evening. I was aghast but Aunt Julie sat at once, "What heaven! That means Kester can come out with me!" and I was so cheered that I forgot to sulk. Aunt Julie even invited me to spend the night at her flat, and this was thrilling as I had never before stayed away from home without either my mother or a nanny to supervise me. At the appointed hour Aunt Julie collected me from our hotel near Kensington Gardens, and after a sumptuous dinner we went to a picture palace where we saw a revival of a film called *The Gold Rush*. I laughed so much that my sides ached, but the climax of the evening came when Aunt Julie told the taxi driver to take us back to her Bloomsbury flat via Piccadilly Circus so that I could see the lights. At that point I felt so faint with sophistication that I could hardly wait to return to Gower in order to brag about my experiences to my new friend, provincial Cousin Harry.

However this glamorous expedition to London was only the prelude to my fairy-tale years. In the July of 1929 we finally moved to Oxmoon, and soon afterwards Uncle John took me to each of the farms on the estate and to all the tied cottages in Penhale so that I could be formally presented to every man, woman and child connected with my inheritance. At first I was shy but soon I loved all the fuss that was made of me and listened incredulously as my tenants made remarks like "Such a well-mannered young gentleman!" and "How pleased his poor father would have been!" I blossomed rapidly. By the time I was taken to visit the retired family retainers in the almshouses, I was well accustomed to drinking tea and looking wise as Uncle John chatted about the astonishing good weather and the excellent harvest.

I was in a way a stranger to Oxmoon. Unlike my father and grandfather, I had not spent my earliest years there, and although Little Oxmoon was built on land that had once formed part of the Oxmoon estate, the estate itself was not deeply familiar to me. Also although Uncle John was probably as successful as any gentleman farmer he had, as I realized later, the kind of executive mind which interests itself in planning and profit, not in the aesthetics and romance of agricultural life; in other words, Uncle John's attitude to farming was not one which I found easy to assimilate. I looked at the dear little piglets in Uncle Thomas's piggery and thought what beautiful curly tails they had. Uncle John looked at them and saw profit or loss and a line of figures in an account book. Uncle John made conscientious efforts to interest me in the estate and I made conscientious efforts to be interested, but somehow our minds continually failed to meet so that the mechanics of Oxmoon, the anatomy beyond the glamorous facade, remained a mystery which I was well content not to unravel.

But the glamorous facade I adored.

Oxmoon was like a kingdom. In the old days it had been self-supporting, and even now, despite the agricultural depression and the changes of the twentieth century, it retained the trappings of independence. The Home Farm provided nearly all the food, and in the farmyard which lay near the house beyond the stable yard I could see all my agricultural employees going about their daily work. Fewer horses were now used on the estate and the coach house had become a garage but the stables were still impressive. They were linked to the main house by the kitchens, which included the bakehouse, the still room, the wet laundry, the dry laundry and sundry pantries and larders. Various daily women came in from the village to help the resident staff run this rabbit warren of domesticity.

Below the farmyard and the stable yard there stood a slaughterhouse, a sawmill, a disused forge (the blacksmith at Penhale now worked for us at his own forge), a joiners' shop, the old kennels (disused since the disbandment of the West Gower Hunt), the timber-wagon shed and the Garden House, which overlooked the large walled beautiful kitchen garden. Next to this stood a ravishing orangerie, a temple to the great god Citrus, and inside were all sorts of peculiar bushes and straggling vines. Little grapes the size of peas occasionally appeared and almost instantly withered. No one had ever seen an orange there. Making a camp in the back I planted a Union Jack and pretended I was colonizing the jungle.

Beyond the orangerie lay the eighteenth-century pleasure garden, part of which during the long reign of my grandfather had been turned into a tennis court and a croquet lawn. On the edge of this vast sward at the point where the pleasure garden dissolved into the woods lay the most captivating summerhouse, which had been built at the instigation of my great-grandfather Robert Godwin the Drunkard. One of my first acts as master of Oxmoon was to take it over as my own special house. I would sit in a wicker chair and stuff myself with fruit purloined from the kitchen garden and gloat as I gazed across the lawn to my inheritance.

Oxmoon!

I would gaze and sigh and gaze again. Here I was, a fairy-tale prince, and there, facing me, was the palace where all my dreams were going to come true.

My nine-year-old eyes saw a great gorgeous colossus of a house, bold, broad and brilliant. The lack of paint, the patched roof, the bedraggled look were of no consequence. That was just reality, but as usual I saw beyond boring dreary old reality to Beauty, Truth and Art. I also, as I sat munching apples in that idyllic summerhouse and gazed across the dazzling sward towards Beauty, Truth and Art, knew Peace. Peace, I discovered, was pure contentment, an acute awareness of perfection, a oneness with Nature, a glimpse of God.

I looked at Oxmoon and thought, Beauty! Truth! Art! Peace! And Oxmoon seemed to look back with its dark seductive windows and Oxmoon seemed to say to me, At last! The master I've been waiting for! And I flung out my arms as if I could embrace it.

"Well, Kester," said Uncle John, arriving an hour later, "what have you been doing with yourself?"

I could hardly tell him I had been lolling in a wicker chair, crying, "Beauty, Truth, Art and Peace!" and mentally embracing my magic house with tears in my eyes.

"Well..."

"Time you had another try at learning to ride."

"Oh, do I have to?"

But apparently I did. All masters of Oxmoon had to be able to ride a horse. It was the done thing. (But why bother in the age of the motorcar? I didn't know and didn't dare ask.) To my father's disgust I had hated riding during my first attempt to be an equestrian, but now Uncle John found a pony for me, possibly the most docile pony that had ever been bred in the Gower Peninsula, and when he instructed me himself I was so worried about not doing the done thing that sheer fright alone drove me to master a few elementary skills. I did not fall off. Gradually I became almost fond of my pony and took pictures of him with my new box camera. Uncle John was delighted not only by my riding but also by my aptitude for Welsh (masters of Oxmoon had to be able to understand Welsh;

that too was the done thing), and I lived in terror that he might try to improve my cricket, but luckily cricketing skills were not judged essential for a master of Oxmoon so I was spared any torture involving a bat and ball.

Uncle John did not teach me Welsh himself but he engaged a tutor who came to Oxmoon twice a week from Swansea. Gower, of course, is English-speaking apart from the odd family like the Llewellyns who make a fetish of their Welshness, so it was quite unnecessary for me to learn the language, but it was much more fun than a dead language like Latin and I liked hearing about Welsh history as well. Simon, who was English, had always behaved as if Welsh history didn't exist. I rather savored the thought that I was learning things Simon didn't know.

As I luxuriated in my new home and basked in Uncle John's favor by doing the done thing with such aplomb, I became aware to my delight that my status had been vastly enhanced in the eyes of the world. Everyone, from the servants to the gentry, fawned on me. After Lady Appleby died there were no longer Applebys at All-Hallows Court (Sir Timothy, a butterfly specialist in Rhodesia, sold it to Dr. Warburton), but the Stourhams, the Bryn-Davieses, the Mowbrays and all the other well-known Gower families dined at Oxmoon and paid my mother lavish compliments about my size, my manners and any other virtue they could dredge up or invent. Fortunately they had no children of my age who could be foisted on me as companions, so to my relief I continued in splendid isolation from my contemporaries. It was true Oswald Stourham's daughter Belinda was only a year younger than I was, but she was so backward that she could hardly be considered seriously as a playmate. Uncle John tried to interest me in Dr. Warburton's new stepsons at All-Hallows, but I told him frankly that I considered these children a great bore. Who wanted to play Cowboys and Indians when he could be reading about Richard Hannay and Bulldog Drummond? In my opinion most children simply wasted their childhood on inanities.

However although I continued to regard my contemporaries with antipathy, their attitude to me became increasingly benign. Marian, who had always been beastly to me, told our cousin Elizabeth, who was visiting Oxmoon with Aunt Daphne: "Yes, he's much improved—I suppose good breeding always tells in the end," and shortly after this gracious judgment had been delivered, Harry expressed interest in my stamp collection and invited me to Penhale Manor to see his own album.

"Marian was right for once," he said finally after we had made some mutually satisfactory swaps. "You've improved. I suppose Papa's managed to teach you how to be a boy."

"I *am* a boy," I said coldly. "Uncle John's simply teaching me how to be master of Oxmoon."

My improvement, as it was described so snootily by my cousins, was no doubt real enough and probably sprang from a massive increase in self-confidence. Now that everyone treated me with respect I began to respect myself, and with Uncle John behaving as if nothing could stop me from becoming a true Godwin, I could at last dare to believe that I might be destined for a successful life. My academic reports from Simon became glowing, Uncle John started slipping me the occa-

501

sional five shillings and my mother even began to boast about me to Rory. Rory and I were equally staggered, and Rory stopped referring to me as a nitwit.

I even wondered if Declan might begin to curry favor but no word ever reached me from Ireland.

"However," I said to Bronwen, "of all my relations—except Mum—I like you the best, because you liked me *before* I was rich and famous."

"You funny little love!" said Bronwen hugging me, and when Evan wanted to follow her example and hug me too I said to him, "And you liked me then as well, didn't you? You're my favorite cousin!"

Evan beamed up at me but when I turned to Bronwen I saw that her eyes shone with tears.

"Bronwen—"

"It's all right, Kester. It's just that Evan's so lonely with no one to play with and it means so much when someone's nice to him."

"But I'd love to play with him!" I exclaimed, and soon after that conversation I had the chance to practice what I preached because Evan began to come daily to Oxmoon to share my tutor.

By that time Evan was six years old and very shy, but I understood all about shyness and ignored it. I read to him. We played dominoes together. I took him on expeditions into the woods by the ruined tower. Soon I saw hero worship glowing in his eyes, and I was touched. I had never been hero-worshiped before and found it a most gratifying experience.

So as I basked in everyone's unstinted love and admiration, I would gaze at my fairy-tale palace and think: Kester plus Oxmoon equals bliss but Kester minus Oxmoon equals misery. It was an equation I knew I would never forget, and that was when I knew too that we were bound together, Oxmoon and I, united forever as if married by God—"and those whom God hath joined together," I said to myself more than once with the most pleasurable romantic fanaticism, "let no man put asunder."

IV

"Is Thomas always like this?" said Aunt Julie when she came to visit us later. "How do you stand it?"

"I live in the hope," said my mother, "that he may one day show me his heart of gold. John swears he's got one."

"How deep do you have to sink the mineshaft to get to it?"

"I'm still sinking. However to give credit where credit is due—what a loathsome exercise that always is!—I have to admit that Thomas does have his good points. He's got a flair for farming, particularly animal husbandry, he's businesslike, he's efficient and John's convinced he has the makings of a first-class estate manager. John's training him to manage the Oxmoon farms during Kester's minority."

"Why can't John do that himself? I should have thought it would be rather up his street."

"Oh, John doesn't want to be too involved with Oxmoon," said my mother, lighting a cigarette. "He's too busy accumulating all sorts of business interests in Swansea. As far as I can make out he has only to play a round of golf and another directorship drops into his lap."

"That's because he's got boardroom as well as bedroom looks!" said Aunt Julie, and they started gurgling together in their usual fashion over the pink gins.

I sipped my fizzy lemonade (which I now always drank out of a champagne glass) and meditated on the new blot on my sunlit horizon, the new ugly reality which was marring the Truth and Beauty of my fairy tale: Thomas the Tyrant, monster *par excellence*.

Thomas was much too unpleasant a character for me to feel sorry for him, but when I was older I could see that his position, when my grandfather died, was an awkward one. He was then twenty-two—old enough to resent that he had no money except the salary Uncle John paid him for his work on the Penhale estate, and no home of his own beyond the hospitality that always awaited him at the Manor. He had tried to move back to Oxmoon after my grandfather's death because he had thought my mother would retire with me to London, and my mother's decision to be an active mistress of Oxmoon during my minority had infuriated him. In fact he stormed, sulked, ranted and raved to such an extent that Uncle John had been obliged to make a noble gesture in order to appease him; Uncle John not only suggested that Thomas should be trained to run the Oxmoon estate but he also offered Thomas Little Oxmoon as a home and said he could receive the rents from the sheep farm of Martinscombe which was let to tenants. Uncle John was able to do this because of a surprise twist in my father's will. Instead of leaving Martinscombe Farm and Little Oxmoon to my mother, as everyone had anticipated, my father had left them to Uncle John with the proviso that my mother should be allowed to remain at Little Oxmoon until my grandfather died and I inherited the estate. My father declared in his will that he wanted Uncle John to have his property "as a small token of my respect, admiration and profound gratitude," and my mother, who had an income of her own as well as various moneys my father had saved, said that no one deserved such a tribute more.

Uncle John, complex as ever, first of all said he couldn't possibly accept such a bequest. Then he said maybe acceptance was the easiest way out. Finally he said the whole thing was a great muddle and really, lawyers were the end when they started messing around in their own affairs, and although he was grateful to Robert, it was all most peculiar and embarrassing and he couldn't think what the right thing to do was. He continued in this vein for some time while my mother and I listened in amazement, but eventually Bronwen sorted him out in her usual down-to-earth fashion by saying, "Johnny, fate's put Martinscombe and Little Oxmoon into your hands. Don't worry about how they got there. What's done's done. Just look around and see if you can do any good with them." Bronwen had a genius for seeing the wood from the trees while Uncle John was hopelessly lost in some impenetrable thicket. After she had given her sensible advice Uncle John at once said thunderstruck: "Thomas! I'll give him a nominal lease just as soon as the bungalow falls vacant!" and that solved the problem of a home for his brother.

It was reported that Thomas and his cronies did a great deal of hard drinking to celebrate his arrival there, and it was even rumored that girls from Swansea had danced naked on the dining-room table, though since Thomas never had any girlfriends, this mild attempt at debauchery was probably no more than a drunken hallucination. Certainly the drinking was real enough. There was something very old-fashioned about Thomas, whose only ambition was to follow in the footsteps of his forefathers and live a country life in Gower. I often felt he should have been a brutish squire in the days when people daily drank themselves senseless out of sheer boredom, and if anyone ever writes the Godwin family history, I've no doubt they'll turn up one or two eighteenth-century ancestors just like him.

He had always been hostile to me, but in my new glorious role of master of Oxmoon, with my mother and Uncle John guarding me like twin watchdogs, not even Thomas could afford to display churlishness. He began to say "Hullo!" cheerfully whenever we had the misfortune to meet, and occasionally he would make some oafish remark that could be ranked as a pleasantry. On my thirteenth birthday he even said I could drop the prefix "Uncle" when I addressed him. I was astonished by this concession, but Thomas had by that time fallen in love with Eleanor Stourham and no doubt the prospect of a rich wife had made him mellow. Eleanor was the much older half-sister of my contemporary Belinda, who was the baby of the family at Stourham Hall.

Bronwen too had a baby girl by this time. She was born at the end of 1931 and named Sian, which I knew was Welsh for Jane. Since Lance was only two, Gerry four and Evan, my admiring acolyte, seven, Bronwen was kept very busy— in fact I often wondered if she was kept too busy, for she looked pale and tired and I heard Uncle John say he was worried about her. There had been a new series of anonymous letters after Sian was born and more nasty messages daubed on the Manor walls. Bronwen was again too afraid to leave the house on her own, but Uncle John used to drive her and the children to Oxmoon so that they could take the baby for walks in the safety of the grounds.

"You mustn't worry about it," I said to Evan, wanting to cheer him up. "The fuss will soon die down and then everything will go on as before."

But Evan looked up at me with grave green eyes and said nothing. Evan's view of the future was already less sanguine than mine.

Later he began to look forward to going away to school. Harry had spoken to him enthusiastically about Briarwood, and even Bronwen, who had confessed to my mother that she had mixed feelings about boarding schools, had said it would be lovely for him to meet other boys of his own age.

"Kester," said Evan once, "why don't you go to school like Harry?"

"Well, actually I'm so busy learning how to be master of Oxmoon that I just don't have the time," I said airily, but Uncle John had never given up hope of packing me off to school, and as soon as I was twelve in the November of 1931 he began his campaign to persuade my mother to send me to Harrow in the autumn of 1932. By some great mismanagement on my part I failed to eavesdrop on the vital scene (no doubt Uncle John, knowing me all too well by this time, took care to stage it when I was out of the house) but he was so often at Oxmoon in those days that I had no way of distinguishing his vital visits from the trivial ones.

The truth was that Uncle John was now using Oxmoon as his formal home in order to circumvent the difficulties of the situation at Penhale Manor. After Lance's birth he decided he could no longer expect people to accept his invitations to the Manor, but since my mother loved to entertain she was able to come to his rescue. Nobody ever refused an invitation to Oxmoon. My mother gave dinner parties, cocktail parties, garden parties—even a dance in the ballroom—and always Uncle John was there to act as host, immaculate in his impeccable clothes and looking, as Aunt Julie once remarked to my mother, the very last man in the world to harbor a socially unacceptable mistress and numerous illegitimate children.

"Uncle John was here this afternoon, pet," said my mother soon after my twelfth birthday in 1931.

Since this was such an unremarkable occurrence I merely grunted and turned a page in my book.

"He was talking again of toughening you up at school."

This horrific news made even the exploits of Ivanhoe fade into mere printed words on a page. "Oh no!" I said aghast. "I thought he'd got over that!"

"My dear, such a bore but we can't tell him to mind his own business (a) because he'd be upset and I can't bear the thought of upsetting him and (b) because it really is his business, and he's been so marvelous with you since Daddy died that the least we can do in return is consider his piont of view."

"Mum! You're wavering!"

"Well, not exactly—I'd never force you to school against your wishes, but would school really be such a disaster now you're older? Not everyone there would be like Harry—you might make some friends, and that wouldn't be such a bad thing either. You're a bit solitary, darling."

"Only because other children seem so boring! I'm mad about grown-ups!"

"Yes, but I can see why Johnny worries about you. . . . Listen, pet, if you did go to school I wouldn't send you to Harrow. I'd send you to a modern enlightened school where they'd encourage all your artistic interests—"

"Would they allow me at least three hours a day to write?"

"Well . . ."

"I'd cut my throat if I couldn't write for three hours a day."

"But darling, I can't tell Johnny I'm keeping you at home so that you can scribble in your room! Scribbling's just not the done thing!"

"What about Shakespeare, Jane Austen and Emily Brontë?"

"They weren't masters of Oxmoon."

We argued a little longer. Eventually I became so cross that I accused her of wanting to wreck the idyllic life that was absolutely due to me after all my awful early years when no one had cared whether I had lived or died.

505

"Well, we won't talk of that," said my mother, shifting guiltily in her chair. "That's over now."

"It's all very well for you to brush it aside in that fashion, but I was miserable and neglected then and I shall be miserable and neglected again if you condemn me to school! And when you're having a wonderful time at all your sumptuous dinner parties, how will you be able to bear thinking of poor little me, crying night after night into my pillow, bullied, tortured, brutalized—"

"Oh God," said my mother.

I scented victory. "I might even die," I said, much moved to think of it. "The eldest Brontë sister died at school. And when I die and you're standing at my grave—"

"Oh, do shut up, pet, you've made your point. But listen, you really do need to be with men—"

"I *am* with men—constantly! Uncle John practically lives here and Simon does live here—"

"That's true," said my mother. She puffed furiously at her cigarette. "Actually I've always thought you didn't need to go to school in order to grow up masculine."

"I may look sissyish," I said defiantly. "I suppose I must do since all my most-hated people say so, but I'm very masculine inside my head, I know I am, and when I grow up I shall marry the girl of my dreams and have four children and I'll be the best master Oxmoon's ever had."

"Darling!" said my mother, folding me in her arms. "I don't think you look sissyish at all—and no, of course I can't wreck your happiness by sending you away; you're such a good boy and you don't deserve any more misery and I'm going to keep you at home."

Uncle John was livid. There were quarrels which took place behind the closed door of the library; I eavesdropped valiantly but could hear next to nothing. An interval followed during which Uncle John stayed away from Oxmoon, but eventually he sued for peace. By Christmas he and my mother were kissing under the mistletoe and all the trouble was over—at least, all *my* trouble was over.

Uncle John's trouble was just about to begin.

V

Six months later in the summer of 1932 Uncle John heard from the headmaster of Briarwood that Evan could not be accepted as a pupil. I heard the news from Evan himself who arrived at Oxmoon as usual for his lessons and cried as he told us what had happened.

Simon and I were both horrified.

"But that's monstrous!" said Simon, understanding at once. "The headmaster must have a grudge against John!"

I was used to vandals throwing stones but the idea that the headmaster of a preparatory school might have his own stone to throw on the subject of illegitimacy did not immediately occur to me.

"But Evan, why?" I said baffled.

"He doesn't have children whose parents aren't married. Dad didn't tell him but someone else did. Dad thinks he was cross at not being told. Anyway he said if he accepted me the parents who were married would be upset." More tears. "I did so want to go."

"Evan," said Simon, "if that's the attitude of the headmaster, then you're better off not going there. It must be a very poor sort of place."

"But what's to happen to me?" said Evan, trying to wipe away his tears. "I said to Mum, 'Is it always going to be like this?' and she said no, not if she could help it. Then Dad said he'd find another school, but Mum said, 'And is he going to go on being shut up here every holidays? Or are you going to board him out like Dafydd?' And then I cried, I couldn't help it, because I don't want to be boarded out like Dafydd, but Dad said no, I wouldn't be boarded out, and then Mum said, 'Well, what sort of life is he going to have here?' and then she cried too and I cried all the more because she was crying—"

"Kester," said Simon, "run and ask Cook to make some cocoa and send it up to the schoolroom with some biscuits. We won't start lessons just yet."

On my way back from the kitchens I met my mother, and when I told her what had happened she came with me to the schoolroom.

"Evan—my poor little darling, what a cruel disappointment for you..." I saw the glances she exchanged with Simon and suddenly I felt cold.

"Dad says he'll find another school where the headmaster doesn't know, but supposing he finds out! Would I be expelled? Would the boys throw stones at me?" He broke down again, sobbing against my mother's large comfortable bosom where I had sobbed so often myself in the past, but my mother for once seemed to have no words of comfort to offer. Finally she said, "Evan, I'm going to telephone Bronwen and ask your father to take you home. I think you're too upset for lessons today."

"Dad's not there." He raised his tearstained little face to hers. "After he dropped me here he went on to Swansea. Mum told him to go away and leave her alone."

There was a dead silence.

"I see," said my mother. "Well, never mind, I'll take you home myself and have a word with your mother. Perhaps there's something I can do to help."

I had just finished my morning lessons when my mother arrived back at Ox-moon. Running down the stairs, I found her pulling off her gloves in the hall.

"Mum, what did Bronwen say? Is Evan all right?"

My mother hesitated before replying: "He was a little better by the time I left." She dropped her gloves on the hall table and moved towards the drawing room.

"Mum..." I followed, nearly treading on her heels. "Mum, what are you thinking? Tell me, *tell* me—"

"Oh, stop pestering me like that! God, how you irritate me sometimes!" said my mother crossly, and began to mix herself a large pink gin. However when she saw my expression she added abruptly: "Sorry, pet, I know you're worried but the truth is I'm worried too. Bronwen's very unhappy."

"Do you think Uncle John might take them all away to live somewhere else?"

"Oh darling, that would be no solution because the truth would inevitably catch up with them. Johnny's situation is widely known now, and wherever he went he'd be quite unable to lead an obscure secluded life. He'd join another golf club and be offered half a dozen new directorships and eventually he'd be certain to meet someone who knew of his past and then the whole trouble would begin all over again."

I was relieved to learn that no imminent departure was planned, but it was soon after this crisis that the changes began to take place at Penhale Manor. First Rhiannon left Gower directly after her seventeenth birthday and went to London with Dafydd; she found a clerical job in a bank and Dafydd went to work in a garage. After Rhiannon left Bronwen was ill for a while and had to lie in a darkened room. I took her flowers but she was seeing no visitors. My mother explained that she was suffering from migraine.

Then I noticed that Uncle John had become thinner and more careworn. He stopped coming to my mother's parties. My mother offered to have all the children to stay while he and Bronwen had a holiday on their own in Cornwall, and Uncle John was keen on the idea but nothing came of it. Bronwen refused to go.

"I'd spend my whole time worrying in case something happened to the children," she said to my mother.

"But my dear, nothing would happen to them at Oxmoon!"

"Your servants would look down on them—pass cruel remarks—I couldn't bear Evan to suffer any more—"

"Leave us, Kester, please," said my mother, and by the tone of her voice I knew I was absolutely forbidden to eavesdrop. All I heard as I left the room was Bronwen weeping: "I didn't mind when it was just myself. But I can't bear the children suffering, it's destroying me."

In the new year I noticed that whenever I visited the Manor Bronwen seemed to be sorting things out. The toy cupboards were purged. Piles of clothes were set aside for Mrs. Wells to take to the jumble sale. The nursery assumed an uncluttered, almost eerie appearance.

"Bronwen's beginning her spring cleaning early this year," I said to my mother.

Once I saw a letter lying on the hall chest. It was addressed to Bronwen and bore a Canadian stamp.

"Who do you know in Canada?" I said to Evan.

"Mum has cousins in Vancouver. We're going to visit them in the spring."

"Gosh, what fun! I wish I could go too!" I said, and when I returned to Oxmoon I remarked to my mother: "Uncle John's taking everyone to Canada for a holiday in the spring."

"No," said my mother. "Uncle John won't be going."

"Well, I suppose it would be inconvenient for him to be away for such a long time when he's so busy," I conceded, and retired to look up Vancouver in my atlas.

At Easter the Canadian visit seemed to come closer when six new trunks were delivered to the Manor to be packed and sent on in advance.

"Heavens!" I said to Bronwen. "How long are you going for?"

"I don't want the children to get homesick," she said, "so I'm taking as much as I can with me, all their favorite toys and games."

The departure was fixed for the sixteenth of May, and on the Sunday before that date my mother invited all the children to tea at Oxmoon. Bronwen did not come; she had another migraine and we did not see her when we collected the children from the Manor.

I enjoyed playing with the younger ones. Sian was very pretty; I spent some time amusing both her and Lance who had a mild shy equable temperament. In contrast Gerry was far too noisy for me to tolerate for long, but my mother gave me a rest by taking him for a walk in the woods. Later he and Evan and I played croquet, but Gerry soon tired of that and demanded a cricket bat.

"Another perfect Godwin in the making!" I groaned to my mother, but she didn't smile. All she said was "It's very sad."

Two days later they all departed, Uncle John driving them down to Southampton, and that evening, just as I had finished my homework and was on my way to my room for a quiet read before dinner, I glanced out of the landing window and saw Uncle John's Rover speeding up the drive.

I paused. The car was going much too fast. I knew, even before it screeched to a halt, that something was very wrong. When Uncle John jumped out I saw that his face was a grayish white. Pushing back his disheveled hair, he wiped his forehead with the back of his hand and stumbled up the steps to the front door.

I hared down the corridor, plunged into my room and found that the housemaid, thank God, had left the window wide open. Below me on the terrace my mother was sipping her first pink gin of the evening and browsing through her latest copy of *Glamorous Romances*. As Uncle John blundered out onto the terrace, I sank to my knees beside the window seat.

"Johnny—my dear—did you—was it—oh God, I've been thinking of you so much..."

Without hesitating, I jumped up to look down at the scene below me. They were embracing. My mother was even stroking his hair, and then as I watched in stupefaction he drew back from her to pull out a sodden handkerchief, and I had my first glimpse of his overpowering grief and despair.

3

I

I FELT as if I were witnessing the end of the world—or at least the end of civilization as I knew it. To see Uncle John—my heroic Uncle John—reduced to tears was shattering enough, but when I realized that the tears must indicate some unparalleled disaster I was terrified. Kneeling on the window seat, I trembled from head to toe.

"I can't bear to think I'll never see her again," said my uncle, making a futile attempt to wipe away the tears that were streaming down his face. "I can't bear to think of my children growing up without me. And I can't bear to go back to that house—it'll be worse than it was after Blanche died—I can never live in that house again—"

"No, of course you can't. Stay here for a while. I thought you might feel like this and I've had your old bedroom prepared for you. Sit down, my dear, and I'll get you some brandy."

My mother steered him to the wrought-iron chair next to hers and disappeared into the drawing room. As Uncle John sat down and buried his face in his hands, I noticed for the first time that his hair was graying at the temples. He was forty-one.

"I don't know what I'm going to do without them," he said as my mother returned with the brandy. "I just can't think what I'm going to do."

He wasn't the only one. By this time I had realized that Bronwen had left him, and I was feeling sick. How could I bear to lose Bronwen and Evan, the two best members of my family apart from my mother? Evan—my acolyte—my hero-worshiping almost-brother . . . I felt as bereaved as if he were dead.

"I've made such a mess of my life," said Uncle John in between mouthfuls of brandy. "I'm such a failure."

"But my dear Johnny—"

"Never call me that again! *She* called me that. If you go on calling me Johnny you'll simply remind me—"

"Yes, of course, I'm sorry. But John, you're not a failure, you've just been terribly unlucky—that wretched woman in London—"

"I've lost everything that made life meaningful. That's failure."

"Rubbish," said my mother, and suddenly I saw her as someone who knew what tragedy was all about, someone—perhaps the only person—who could help my uncle at this darkest time of his life. "You must think of the children that you still have," she said. "Think of Harry and Marian. And at least Bronwen's children aren't dead—like Robin. They'll just be absent for a few years—as Declan was. They'll come back to you in the end, just as Declan came back to me."

"Yes . . . I daresay you're right. . . . I'm sorry, I know it's unforgivable, breaking down like this—"

"Oh, what rot, it's healthy! God knows if you bottled up your troubles as Bobby did you'd soon be mad as a hatter!"

"I feel mad now, I feel demented—oh God, maybe if I were to go after them— give everything up—"

"John, listen. I know we've been over all this a dozen times, but let me go over it once more so that you've got the truth firmly nailed up in front of your eyes. Bronwen's being immensely brave and emigrating to Canada so that those four children can have the chance of a normal life. If you go crashing after them now you'll mess everything up, make a mockery of Bronwen's courage and ruin their lives all over again."

"I know but—"

"Remember what she said to you: 'If you love us you'll let us go.' Now, you told me she said that, didn't you, and you also told me you thought she was right—"

"If only she hadn't said no letters, money by bankers' order but no letters—I know I could bear it better if only I had their letters to look forward to—"

"But my dear, I thought it was you who said it must be a clean break because anything else would be too difficult and too painful?"

"Maybe they'll come back. Maybe it won't work out. Maybe if I were to go after them later I'd find—"

"John, *you must let those children grow up in peace.* Think how poor little Evan's suffered!"

"Oh Christ—"

"I'll get you some more brandy." She disappeared with his glass. Uncle John blew his nose on the sodden handkerchief and wiped his eyes on his sleeve and pushed back his hair distractedly again. When she returned he said in despair, "I don't know how I'm going to tell Harry and Marian."

"Well, personally, my dear, I think they should both have been told last holidays and I think those four little ones should have been told too."

"But we couldn't face it—how could we have explained—so much pain—all the agony—the misery—"

"I know, I know, and don't think I don't sympathize, but I do so strongly believe it's better to be honest with children, John, no matter how difficult it may seem at the time. . . . I assume you'll be going to Harrow to tell Harry?"

"But I can't upset him now! He has his exams soon—and several very important cricket matches—"

"My dear," said my mother, "some things in life really are more important than cricket, and this is one of them. Harry can barely remember Blanche. Constance doesn't count. Bronwen's the only mother he's ever known. You simply must see him as soon as possible to explain."

"I can't!" cried my uncle, obviously in a dreadful muddle and still too beside himself with grief to think clearly. "He'll blame the whole disaster on me—he'll feel I've let him down, he'll be so disillusioned—"

"Well, he's fourteen years old—it's about time he realized parents are flesh-and-blood people, not angels with halos!"

"But what can I say? How can I possibly explain?"

"Just tell him the truth, for God's sake! Tell him you and Bronwen are acting for the sake of the children. Damn it, go the whole hog and say Bronwen got so upset that she didn't want to go to bed with you anymore!"

"Oh, I couldn't possibly tell him that."

"Why not?"

"Well, we just don't talk about that sort of thing."

"But he must have asked you about sex by this time!"

"Oh no, he never asks anything like that. Anyway I'm sure he's picked up the facts at school. I mean, if not why hasn't he asked?"

"Perhaps he was waiting for you to say something. Perhaps he was embarrassed by the knowledge that you and Bronwen weren't married. Perhaps—oh John, do go to Harrow and talk to him!"

"Very well. All right," said my uncle, appearing to sink even deeper into despair. "But if I tell Harry I'll have to stop afterwards in London to talk to Marian, and Marian will want to know—"

"—if you intend to go back to Constance. Yes, of course she will—now that Marian's come out a stepmother like Constance would be very useful to her, but just declare your intentions firmly so that she doesn't cherish any false hopes. Unless... heavens, John, you wouldn't go back to Constance, would you?"

"Ginevra," said my uncle, all despair at once annihilated by his rage, "I swear to you I shall never, *never*, NEVER, so long as I live, go back to that woman!"

He went back to her six months later.

II

"No!" I said appalled when my mother broke the news.

"My dear, yes!" My mother was equally shattered.

"But that's impossible!"

"Quite impossible, yes. But he's done it." My mother adjusted her spectacles and began to read Uncle John's letter again as if she feared she was suffering from a hallucination.

I had gone to her room to share her early-morning tea, and so I had been present when the parlormaid came upstairs with the post. It was November; outside it was drizzling and I was enjoying the coziness of the room's thick carpet, sensuous paintings and energetic little fire roaring gamely in the grate. My mother, propped up on mounds of snowy pillows with her thick hair cascading around her shoulders and her reading spectacles perched on the end of her nose, looked like a Roman empress examining a communication from a particularly recalcitrant Christian who was insisting on being thrown to the lions.

"But why's he done it?" I demanded.

"Well, pet, he *says*..." She consulted the letter again. "'I have decided to do this so that Harry and Marian can have a normal home at last and also, of course, to make amends to Francesca for all the years I've been away.'" After reading the words in a wooden voice, she refolded the letter, removed her spectacles and reached without comment for her tea.

"But you don't believe that, do you, Mum?" I said, watching every line of her face for clues.

"Oh yes," said my mother, "I believe it. But I don't think this is the whole story—in my opinion it would take an earthquake to send John back to that woman, and I don't think this decision can conceivably be explained away by saying he was overwhelmed by the desire to do the done thing."

"But what do you think's happened?"

"I don't know," said my mother, "but if John doesn't intend to confide in me, I shan't pry." Then she made a remark which I was to remember long afterwards in very different circumstances. "We know so little," she said, "about even those who are closest to us. We know so little of what really goes on in other people's lives."

Since Bronwen had departed the previous May Uncle John had been living a secluded life at Oxmoon, and his one diversion had been the estate, which he had proceeded to overhaul. Thomas remained the salaried manager but while Uncle John was concerning himself with Oxmoon Thomas was temporarily dispatched to run the estate at Penhale Manor, and in October Uncle John installed him in the Manor itself as a caretaker. Uncle John had at first decided to sell the house but in the end could not bring himself to do it. Then he had decided to let it but couldn't bring himself to do that either. It was accordingly a relief to him when Thomas offered to look after the place, and as a consequence it was Little Oxmoon, not Penhale Manor, that eventually fell vacant in 1933. Martinscombe Farm was already let to tenants and now Uncle John decided to let the bungalow as well once it had been spruced up after Thomas's four-year occupation.

While these changes were taking place I found I had to endure eight weeks of the school summer holidays in the company of Cousin Harry, who joined his father at Oxmoon in July. Fortunately Marian, who had been staying with her great-aunt Charlotte in London during her first season, now retired to Scotland with Aunt Daphne and Elizabeth, so I was at least spared her pea-brained presence but Harry threatened to ruin my entire summer. I even wondered in despair if he and I were to be condemned to live under the same roof indefinitely. My mother said Uncle John would find another home of his own as soon as he had decided what to do with himself, but I was beginning to think Uncle John rather enjoyed living at Oxmoon.

However when one expects the worst one is often pleasantly surprised when the worst is better than one has dared hope, and as it turned out Cousin Harry spent most of his holidays keeping out of my way. He used to disappear every day on solitary expeditions to the Downs, and in the evenings he would shut himself in his room with his wireless set and listen to music. I was delighted. Nothing could have pleased me more. Prompted by my mother I made an effort to talk to him occasionally but when he showed no interest in being sociable I gave up. Once I did ask him if he minded that Bronwen and the little ones had gone for good, but he was very offhand and gave the impression that he couldn't have cared less.

"Well, it was the done thing, wasn't it, old chap?" he said. "Of course Bronwen had to think of the children so obviously emigrating to Canada was the right thing—indeed the only thing—to do."

Callous brute. Tears still came to my eyes whenever I thought of Bronwen and my lost acolyte.

In the following year at Easter my mother decided to hold a huge family reunion at Oxmoon, not exactly to celebrate Uncle John's return to Aunt Constance but to celebrate the end of the schism that had rent the family when Uncle John left her for Bronwen. The ballroom was cleaned in anticipation of evenings spent dancing to the gramophone; all the spare bedrooms were made habitable; extra help was engaged from the village, and on the Wednesday preceding Good Friday the guests began to arrive.

I had not seen Uncle John since the previous November. After his reconciliation with Aunt Constance he had briefly returned to Oxmoon to pack up his possessions and commit the estate once more into Thomas's hands, but as soon as that was done he had vanished into Belgravia. Harry and Marian had spent Christmas with him and Aunt Constance in London. Marian wrote sketchily to my mother that everything was "too divine," but in the new year she went to stay with Aunt Daphne again, and after Harry returned to Harrow, Uncle John took Aunt Constance and Francesca to the Riviera for the remainder of the winter. It was March before they returned to England, and as Easter approached I found myself wondering if I would find him greatly changed when I saw him again. I pictured him white-haired, bent double with the burden of doing the done thing and shuffling along with the aid of a stick. I was fourteen by this time but my imagination, far from being dimmed by the passing years, was burgeoning to new heights of prurient speculation.

"Will they both sleep in one bed, Mum?"

"In the absence of any hint to the contrary," said my mother drily, "I can only suppose that they will."

Beds were rather in the news at the time because Rory had just telephoned to ask if he could have a spare room with a double bed so that he could bring his mistress. My mother was livid and said certainly not; if he did bring his mistress they would have to have separate bedrooms to preserve the proprieties and anyway since the mistress hadn't been invited he was on no account to bring her.

"What you do in London's your own affair," she said to Rory after he arrived alone in his sports car. "But here I have my standards and here I draw the line."

"No offense meant, Ma," said Rory cheerfully. "I just thought it was worth a try in case you were getting soft in your old age."

"Old age!" said my mother incensed. "What's that?" And when Rory had finished laughing, she said, "Darling, do behave yourself this weekend—this reunion's quite tricky enough without you playing Casanova with passing house-maids. Oh, how I do wish you'd settle down and be respectable like Darling Declan!"

"But Ma, I'm only thirty-three!"

"Yes," said my mother brutally, "and crashing with the most undignified speed towards a premature middle age!"

Rory laughed again to give the impression that he didn't give a damn what his dear old mother thought, but I suspected she had made him uncomfortable. I was beginning to realize that Rory was devoted to my mother with that childlike naivety common in stupid men, and that her good opinion was very important to him. Ever since Declan had reentered her life, Rory had been making con-spicuous efforts to please her, staying in jobs longer than a year, living (occa-sionally) within his income and being faithful to one mistress whom no one could possibly have mistaken for a tart. I think Rory found it unsettling to be compared with Declan and found wanting. He was as devoted to Declan as he was to my mother, but I've no doubt he found my mother's rhapsodies about Darling Declan as tiresome as I did.

I half-wondered if Declan would come over for the great family reunion. I knew my mother had invited him, but as usual he made some excuse and stayed away.

"I don't think he wants to meet me," I said, "but that's all right because I don't want to meet him."

My mother smiled but said nothing. Perhaps she was consoling herself for Declan's absence by thinking of the guests who had accepted her invitation. By that time Uncle Edmund and Aunt Teddy had arrived with Richard and Geoffrey (both perfect Godwins born with cricket bats in their hands), Aunt Daphne had arrived with Elizabeth and now—sensation of sensations—Aunt Celia was due to arrive from Germany with my cousin Erika; her husband had run off with a Hungarian ballet dancer and had last been seen heading for Vienna.

After this drama had unfolded further at Oxmoon (Aunt Celia weeping buckets, my mother rashly offering her unlimited hospitality, Erika showing me her pictures of Hitler), Uncle John's arrival with Aunt Constance was almost an anticlimax. However so anxious was I to escape from Cousin Erika extolling the virtues of Heidelberg in fractured English that I at once rushed outside to welcome them.

They arrived in two chauffeur-driven Rolls-Royces followed by a Swansea taxi containing Uncle John's valet and Aunt Constance's maid, who had left London by train. Uncle John, Aunt Constance and Marian traveled in the first Rolls, and Harry, Francesca and Francesca's nanny traveled in the second. Luggage over-flowed from both boots. Uncle John wore a dark gray suit and his Old Harrovian tie and looked distinguished enough to have an open invitation to Buckingham Palace. Aunt Constance wore a sleek mustard-colored ensemble with a mink stole and one or two discreet diamonds. Together they looked as if they were advertising some lavish product (the Rolls-Royces?) in the glossy pages of *Country Life*.

My mother glided past me. "Dear Constance," she said smoothly, "welcome back to Oxmoon."

"Thank you, Ginevra," said Aunt Constance, effortlessly participating in this charade of friendship but unable to resist a small triumphant smile, and offered her immaculate magnolia-colored cheek to be kissed. I saw her sharp dark eyes sizing up the reception committee who were now calling greetings as they streamed through the open front door.

My mother somehow managed to perform the chilling ritual of the kiss of peace and then turned with relief to Uncle John. I noticed that during their quick fierce embrace not a single word was spoken on either side.

A dear little creature with dark hair and blue eyes skipped over to them and turned a happy shining face up to my mother. Small loving fingers slipped into my uncle's hand and clasped it tightly. Tiny feet clad in dainty shoes jumped up and down with excitement.

"Francesca?" said my mother. "Oh, how pretty you are! Kester, come and meet your new cousin!"

I saw the likeness to Gerry and Sian and could hardly speak. I didn't dare look at my uncle in case my eyes were unacceptably moist.

"Why, Kester," said Aunt Constance, "how you've grown! I declare you're as tall as Harry!" And to my horror, the magnolia-colored cheek was gently but mercilessly inclined in my direction.

I kissed it. It was soft and velvety like a newly cleaned curtain, but instead of smelling of cleaning fluid it exuded an indefinable and no doubt very exclusive scent. The memory of Bronwen made all speech impossible; I could only think how monstrous it was that I should have to kiss this repellent female, and as I stood there, gawky and tongue-tied like some caricature of adolescence, tall dark handsome Cousin Harry, never at a loss for words, sauntered up to me with his hand outstretched.

"Hullo, old chap. Nice to be back at the old shack again." He did not wait for a reply but after we had shaken hands limply he turned to flash a brilliant smile at my mother. "Hullo, Aunt Ginevra—how nice to see you after all this time!"

"Harry darling—how are you?" My mother kissed him, I was aggrieved to note, with unprecedented warmth and concern, but Harry assured her suavely that everything was absolutely first-class.

"Aunt Ginevra, what heaven to see you!" It was Marian, horribly sophisticated and dripping with nasty little fox furs. At eighteen she was exactly the kind of girl I most disliked, affected, catty, thoroughly useless and man-mad. I often wondered how her bosom friend our cousin Elizabeth put up with her. Elizabeth was useless and man-mad too but she was redeemed by a splendid sense of humor. She was said to resemble her father, my dead Uncle Lion, but I always thought she looked more like Aunt Daphne. They were both plump and pink-cheeked with a slight double chin. Later in life I suspected that Marian thought Elizabeth's plainness was the perfect foil for her own stone-cold good looks.

"I rather fancy Maid Marian," said Rory, who no longer attended debutante dances and had not seen Marian for some time. "What a tempting little prize for anyone who wants to play Robin Hood!"

"Well, this isn't Sherwood Forest," said my mother, very tough, "so we'll have no stolen kisses behind the bushes, if you please."

"Just one little kiss behind one little bush!" pleaded Rory, teasing her, and added idly as if the thought had only just occurred to him: "How much money does she have when she's twenty-one?"

"Ask John," said my mother, knowing he wouldn't dare, and kept a close eye on Marian, who was more than willing to be the center of attention.

"Things are so much better now," I heard her confide frankly to my mother. "Darling Aunt Ginevra, I can't tell you what a relief it is to have a *lady* in charge of the household at last! Of course Bronwen was sweet and I adored her, but really... well, I'm sure it's all for the best. Rhiannon? Oh, heavens no, we've quite lost touch! She's living with Dafydd at some ghastly place like Hammersmith where one simply wouldn't be seen dead—I mean I'm absolutely the last person to be snobbish and I was terribly fond of both of them, but... well, when all's said and done one really does have more to say, doesn't one, to people of one's own class..."

"Mum," I said later as the result of this conversation, "how could Uncle John have produced such a ghastly daughter?"

My mother made no attempt either to deny Marian's ghastliness or to explain it. She just said, "What beats me is how Daphne can stand her but Daphne's got rather ghastly herself lately—that affair with Lord Thingamajig, or whatever his name was, went straight to her head. I keep thinking how horrified Lion would have been to see her becoming so snobbish and pompous."

"This is going to be a very snobbish pompous weekend, Mum. Did you hear Aunt Constance saying to Aunt Teddy that she couldn't imagine why Uncle Edmund preferred a Bentley to a Rolls-Royce?"

"That woman'll be murdered yet! But what a lovely little girl Francesca is— she must be a great consolation to poor John..."

Francesca was not yet ten so she did not stay up for dinner but before I went to my room to change I looked in at the nurseries to say good night to her.

"Nanny's gone to fetch Mummy and Daddy," she confided, sitting up in bed with an air of eager expectancy. "They always come together to say good night to me."

There was something touching about her excitement. She made them sound such very important visitors.

"You must be glad your father's come back to live with you," I said kindly.

"Oh yes!" said dear little Francesca. "It was just like a miracle! Ever since I can remember I prayed every night: 'Please God, make Daddy come home again,' and then one morning I woke up and went into Mummy's room and he was there, having breakfast with her by the window! I was so happy I cried."

I was just thinking of Evan, sobbing at Oxmoon, when Uncle John himself entered the room with Aunt Constance.

"It's a little cold in here," Aunt Constance was remarking. "I can never understand why the British can't heat their homes properly. All it takes is a good engineer." When she saw me she added with a diplomatic smile: "Maybe you'll install a first-class heating system here one day, Kester, and set your compatriots a good example!"

I looked at Uncle John but he was inscrutable. I was to come to know that inscrutable look very well in the years that followed. Ignoring both me and his wife he stooped over his daughter.

"Daddy, Daddy, Daddy..." She hugged him tightly.

"That's enough, Francesca," said Aunt Constance. "John, don't overexcite her. Now, Francesca, let's hear your prayers, please."

I saw then her supreme talent for turning joy into dreariness. I slipped out of the room, and Uncle John slipped after me. Across the passage in the other night nursery, Uncle Edmund and Aunt Teddy were saying a noisy good night to their exuberant boys.

"Francesca's lovely, Uncle John," I said impulsively, feeling that even the most mundane compliment might alleviate the dreariness, but he merely said "Thank you, Kester" and gave me a polite smile.

Thomas and his fiancée joined us at dinner. Thomas had become engaged to Eleanor Stourham soon after he had moved from Little Oxmoon to Penhale Manor, and they planned to marry in July.

"Imagine being married to Thomas!" my new friend Ricky Mowbray had said after the engagement had been announced. "That really would be a fate worse than death!"

But I couldn't imagine being married to Thomas. I couldn't even imagine being married to Eleanor. She was thirty-two, five years older than her fiancé, and had a horsy, weatherbeaten face, cropped hair and a muscular frame which looked well in her customary land girl's outfit of trousers and shirt. It was odd to see her that night in evening dress, but she wore her conventional black gown with an air of defiance as if daring anyone to comment on her unusual appearance. No one did. Like Thomas, she had the reputation for being outspoken, but that night, surrounded by Godwins, she was uncharacteristically subdued, and I wondered if her bold masculine appearance might not disguise a secret feminine inclination to be shy. Everyone agreed that like her father Oswald Stourham she was "a good sort," but nevertheless no one seemed to like her much except Thomas who treated her as if she were a favorite drinking companion he had met by chance at the pub. She in her turn treated him with a benign optimism as if he were an endearing puppy who showed signs of growing into a splendid dog. My mother said they were obviously in bliss, although how she arrived at this deduction I had no idea. However after dinner when we were all in the ballroom I saw she was right as usual for the two of them retreated to a far corner and began to chew each other's faces.

I shuddered and turned away.

Meanwhile Aunt Constance, languid in her mink stole, was droning on again about central heating, this time to Aunt Celia, who said how efficiently the

Germans heated their homes. I was just thinking how boring the subject was when Cousin Erika took me by surprise and asked me if I liked Beethoven. I looked at her with new eyes. Could there be a sensitive musical soul lurking beneath those sleekly coiled blond plaits? It seemed unlikely but there was no harm in hoping; I conceded I was a passionate admirer of Beethoven's genius.

"I can play the *Moonlight Sonata* on the piano," announced Cousin Erika, for once mastering English syntax and getting the sentence in the right order.

"Good for you," I said tactfully, wondering why foreigners didn't know it wasn't the done thing to boast, and added to put her in her place: "So can Harry. In fact Harry can play anything on the piano, anything at all."

As if to prove my point Cousin Harry abandoned the group who were arguing over which record to play on the gramophone, sat down at the grand piano and began to play "The Blue Danube."

"The chandeliers look less romantic now they've been electrified," mused Uncle Edmund, a few feet away on my right. "John, do you remember how Ifor had to light all the candles with wax tapers?"

But Uncle John wasn't listening. He was watching Harry play "The Blue Danube."

"Bayliss supervised, of course," said Uncle Edmund, who could ramble on happily without encouragement. "It was a tremendous task. Ginevra, what was the name of that kitchen maid whom Ifor eloped with in the end?"

But my mother wasn't listening either. She was standing by Uncle John, and she too was watching Harry play "The Blue Danube."

Uncle Edmund would have been happy to go on reminiscing by himself, but at that moment Aunt Teddy swept up to him and cried, "Dance with me, darling!" and whirled him off around the ballroom floor.

"Oh God, no more of that old-fashioned rubbish!" shouted Thomas, emerging from his corner. "Play 'The Black Bottom' and let's have some fun!"

The gramophone began to blare "Yes, Sir, That's My Baby."

"A Charleston—how divine!" shrieked Marian, and boldly grabbed Rory's hand.

"Whoopee!" shouted Rory, who needed no encouragement, and began to kick up his heels.

"Kester," muttered my mother, "ask Erika to dance."

"Must I?"

"No, it's all right, Harry's just asked her."

I sourly watched Harry doing the done thing. Of course he danced perfectly. I disliked modern dancing and thought it a low stupid activity riddled with nasty innuendos.

When the Charleston ended Rory put on a slow fox-trot, and Uncle Edmund and Aunt Teddy immediately slid into a hot embrace.

"Torrid!" said my mother, blowing smoke rings at the chandeliers.

Thomas and Eleanor started chewing each other's faces again.

"I wouldn't mind some of that myself!" said my mother, who was rather tight. "But not with Thomas, of course."

Finding all this kissing tedious as well as disturbing, I edged away to the dark

519

corner where Thomas and Eleanor had earlier been demonstrating their prenuptial bliss and stared gloomily out of the window. The moon had risen. The garden was bathed in a mystical light. I pictured myself walking there chastely one evening in the remote future with the Princess of My Dreams while a full-scale orchestra in evening dress played Rachmaninoff's *Second Piano Concerto* beneath the glittering chandeliers of the ballroom.

"Hullo, old chap," said Cousin Harry, slinking up behind me and destroying this romantic vision instantly. "Not much of a party, is it? I've decided I'm not quite desperate enough to kiss Erika but almost desperate enough to masturbate in the nearest lavatory. What are you up to, mooning around here like a half-baked poet? Are you in love with anyone yet?"

"Certainly not!" I said outraged. "Don't be so revolting!" Because of my secluded life I had never heard the word "masturbate" before, but I had reached the age when I felt I could guess all too easily what it meant.

"What's wrong with being in love?" said Harry, giving me a pitying look as if I had expressed the wish to be a vestal virgin. "Or are you in love with that pansy Warwick Mowbray? God, he's so wet you could wring him out six times and still have enough water left to fill a rain barrel!"

"What a filthy disgusting swinish slander!" I shouted. "How dare you say things like that about Ricky Mowbray!"

"Oh, sorry, old chap, I had no idea you were so absolutely passionate about him."

"I am *not* passionate about—"

"—about sex? Well, obviously! Tell me, are you going to have false balls fitted to replace the ones you were born without?"

I swung back my fist to smash it into his jaw but he was ready for me. He slipped aside, I swiveled in pursuit—and we both found ourselves confronting my mother who, anticipating trouble, had crept up on us unawares.

When my mother was moderately angry she became fiery and histrionic, but when she was beside herself with fury she was glacial. She was glacial now; her voice was colder than permafrost in the tundra.

"I think you forget yourself, Harry," she said. "This isn't the lavatory of your school. If I ever hear you talking like that in this house again, I'll go straight to your father and tell him not to bring you back here until you can behave like a decent civilized young man."

Harry flushed. "I'm sorry, Aunt Ginevra." Swallowing hard he added in a low urgent voice: "Please don't tell my father."

"I've no intention of spoiling John's evening, no. But just remember what I've said. Now come along, both of you, remember your manners and ask the girls to dance. Harry, you can dance with your sister. I think she's had quite enough dances with Rory. And Kester, I'm sorry but you really must dance with Erika. Poor Aunt Celia's in such a state that the least you can do is be nice to her daughter."

We slunk back onto the ballroom floor to do the done thing, but all the while I was trying not to tread on Cousin Erika's toes I was thinking with shame and anxiety how much I loathed the whole bizarre subject of copulation.

<h1 style="text-align:center">III</h1>

No one had ever given me a comprehensive catalogue of the facts of copulation, although my mother had once said that Uncle John would talk to me on the subject "later." This threat had horrified me so much that I had never sought further information from her for fear she would refer me to him, and I had lived in dread that "later" might finally arrive. I did not in the least mind my mother referring in her frank, casual way to double beds and mistresses, but I balked at the thought of Uncle John revealing exactly what he did to his own mistress in his own double bed. Uncle John was a hero, and heroes, as I well knew from my reading, never discussed sex; they acted as if their genitals behaved immaculately at all times.

However although as I plowed into puberty I became prepared to believe a hero might possibly consider it his moral duty to talk about sex to a boy for whom he was responsible, I remained convinced that I never wanted to hear about copulation from Uncle John. This puzzled me, for I realized Uncle John could be considered an expert on the subject, but looking back now I can see what was beyond my grasp at the time: Uncle John's private life was so saturated with public disapproval that even the most innocuous question about sex, I felt sure, would put him in an awkward position. When I overheard him say to my mother on the terrace after Bronwen's departure that Harry had never asked him about sex I immediately thought: Yes, I'm not surprised.

However Harry, being a schoolboy, was in a better position than I was to acquire information on this vital subject and when we were twelve I tricked him into revealing a few gory details. (The technique of pretending to know more than I did in order to glean information was one which like eavesdropping I had long since perfected to supplement my formal education.) Moodily I watched animals copulating on my estate. Intelligently I pieced together the garbled information Harry had given me, and with an effort of my fertile imagination I had little trouble persuading two and two to make a very horrid four. The sum seemed like the vagary of a sick mind. How *could* any member of the human race perform such antics? I remembered that Rupert of Hentzau, dashing villain of *The Prisoner of Zenda*, had broken his mother's heart by having too many girlfriends; did this mean he had actually *copulated* with any of these fortunate and immensely privileged women? Surely he had just kissed them over a glass of champagne and gone swashbuckling on through Ruritania! The prospect of my romantic vision being cut to ribbons by such a sordid reality was so much more than I could bear that I had shut the subject from my mind, but now Harry's crude remarks about Ricky Mowbray had opened up a new vista of horrors. Could men go to bed with men? Surely it couldn't be the done thing! I was nauseated. Tossing restlessly in my bed I fell asleep exhausted in the early hours of the morning but woke in a frenzy at six. What was I to do? Could I ask Simon to explain? No, absolutely not. Simon's fiancée had jilted him during the war, and he disliked talking even about normal sexual occupations such as getting married.

I felt in despair, but as soon as I acknowledged this I felt better. In despair I always had one person I could turn to. She wasn't a man, and I was sure it wasn't the done thing for a boy to discuss sex with his mother, but I couldn't help that. I was too desperate to care.

I found her drinking her early-morning tea in bed as usual and reading a novel called *Love's Passionate Flower* by someone called Cynthia Digby-Rawlinson.

"Hullo, pet," she said. "Just a minute, I've got to find out if she can get him to kiss her." She read on and then shut the book with a bang. "Hopeless. The poor girl has no idea. Well, what are you up to? Do you want to cadge some tea?"

"No, thanks." I settled myself on the edge of the bed and sighed gustily. "I say, Mum, I'm jolly worried about all this sex business."

"Quite right, darling," said my mother, never batting an eyelid. She added an extra lump of sugar to her tea. "I've very glad you're taking it seriously and not sniggering over it like Harry."

"Well, yes, talking of Harry... Mum, he implied men can copulate with men but gosh, surely that can't be true! Or can it?"

"Oh yes, occasionally. Women can copulate with women too. After all, God made everyone different, so why should everyone be sexually the same? But quite frankly, darling, I've never been able to understand why anyone should want to copulate with their own sex. Think how dull it must be to make love to someone who looks just like oneself! There'd be no surprises, would there? However live and let live. *Chacun à son goût.*"

"Well, I think it's absolutely beastly to want to copulate with one's own sex, even beastlier than wanting to copulate with the opposite sex—oh Mum, how can one reconcile the beauty of True Love with all the sordid ghastliness of pounding away on a double bed and chewing each other's faces?"

"One of the most interesting things about sex," said my mother cozily, "is that although it can be awful it can also be sublime. After all, if it were always awful no one would bother to do it, would they, but most people do it and wind up panting for more."

"But I simply can't imagine—"

"My dear," said my mother, "trust me. Start with an attractive girl who you think is wonderful. Proceed with roses and champagne in accordance with the best romantic tradition. Then the pounding away on the double bed will follow as naturally as night follows day, *and*—listen to this, please—the pounding will be just as romantic as the roses and champagne. Divine romance and thrilling realism will then be inextricably intertwined in one glorious shattering whole."

"Gosh!" I said.

"Any other questions?" said my mother, casually sipping her tea.

"No. Well, yes. Mum, do you think I'll be all right? I mean, I'm a bit odd, aren't I? Supposing—"

"You'll do," said my mother.

"Truthfully? You're not just saying that because—"

"My dear, I'm fifty-four years old and I haven't spent all my life in a convent. *I know*," said my mother, and as I sagged in relief she added briskly: "Don't worry if you feel more drawn to men at the moment. That's normal. Of course you'd rather discuss Shakespeare with Ricky than seduce scullery maids—good God, darling, you're only fourteen! If you were rushing around copulating now I'd have a fit. Sex is an adult pastime," said my mother, suddenly very grave, "and no one under the age of eighteen should indulge in it. Children can get very hurt if they're drawn into grown-up games before their time."

I felt as if an enormous weight had rolled off my shoulders. Three and half years of blissful chastity stretched ahead of me to my eighteenth birthday.

"What a relief!" I said. "I'm sure you're right and falling in love's stunning, but actually I don't think I really feel like doing it just yet."

Within the year I had fallen passionately in love with Anna.

IV

I was sitting in the Blue Rabbit tea shop in Swansea after a visit to the dentist. It was mid-December and my mother and I had spent the morning Christmas-shopping before lunching at the Claremont. At three o'clock she had departed for the hairdresser's salon while I had kept my appointment with the dreaded Chair. We had arranged to meet again at the Claremont at five.

"Fizzy lemonade, please," I said to the waitress.

The tea shop, situated in an alley near the Market, was warm and cozy and three-quarters full of gossiping old women. I found it restful. During my visits to Swansea I always went there if I had time to kill because I knew I would be able to think in peace. Places like the Claremont Hotel were always riddled with people who knew my mother or Uncle John.

I was thinking about my new novel. I may have implied earlier that writing was the central activity of my life; let me now state unequivocally that I consider writing the entire justification for my existence and without doubt the only reason why God could have seen fit to purloin Robin and leave me alive to enjoy a considerable private income which I didn't deserve. I knew it was most unlikely that I would write a masterpiece before I was thirty, but that didn't matter. I wrote for fun. It was simply the most satisfying way I knew of passing the time. My mother sympathized with this eccentricity because she had always enjoyed writing herself; I often wished I could have read her novels, written in the manner of

Elinor Glyn, but much to my horror she had burned the lot. I was determined to destroy nothing, and each minimum *opus* was consigned on completion to a locked trunk in the attics.

Naturally I never bothered a publisher with my handwritten rubbish. I was quite intelligent enough to know that my stories would be despised by grown-ups. Besides, supposing a publisher accepted one of my efforts? (I did have my vain moments occasionally.) How on earth could I have explained such a deviation to my family? Perfect Godwins don't write books—or if they do, they pretend writing's just an amusing little whim which tickles their fancy occasionally, like playing croquet on a Sunday afternoon.

Anyway, there I was, sipping my lemonade through a straw and wondering how illegitimate Rodrigo could get himself legitimized in order to marry ravishing Lucasta, the princess of his dreams, when someone came into the tea shop and sat down at the table next to mine. I did vaguely notice that this person was female, but the details of her appearance were lost to me because I was immediately transfixed by the sight of the book in her hands.

It was *The Prisoner of Zenda.*

"Yes, miss?" said the waitress.

"Fizzy lemonade, please," said the girl, "and a currant bun." She spoke in a rich somber contralto with a tragic foreign accent and sounded like Greta Garbo.

I nearly bit clean through my straw.

The girl, I now saw, was young, perhaps a little younger than I was. She had dark hair, rather lank, a sallow skin and a nose that was large, like mine. Her dark eyes were set wide apart in a heart-shaped face. Opening the book with a sigh of content she settled down to read.

I knew just where she was. I recognized the width of the pages before and after her place and managed to read a few of the words upside down. The hero Rudolph Rassendyll had just clashed finally but inconclusively with the villain Rupert of Hentzau, and Rupert was riding off into the blue. "Thus he vanished," said the voice in my memory, "reckless and wary, graceful and graceless, handsome, debonair, vile and unconquered."

"Oh!" said the girl involuntarily, devastated to think she wouldn't meet Rupert again. Her eyes filled with tears, just as mine once had. I knew she was enjoying herself hugely.

"I say," I said before I could stop myself, "don't worry—there's a sequel."

"*Is there?*" I had made her day.

"Yes, it's called *Rupert of Hentzau.*"

She almost fainted with delight.

"I read both books when I was eight," I said, "but I was much too young then, and although I was fascinated I only understood about one word in twenty. However I reread them when I was twelve and I've been rereading them ever since. I'm mad about Ruritania."

"So am I!" said the girl.

This was so promising that I couldn't resist saying: "You sound as if you come from Ruritania yourself! Do you live in Strelsau?"

"No—Zenda!"

We laughed uproariously. Life was suddenly gay, vivid, thrilling.

"Actually," said the girl, "I come from Berlin. We left last year after Hitler came to power. My father's a doctor and my name's Anna Steinberg." She looked down into her lemonade as if she were shy. "I'm Jewish."

"Gosh, how exciting!" I said. "I've never met anyone Jewish before. My name's Kester Godwin. Kester's short for Christopher and it's spelled K-E-S-T-E-R. I'm fifteen years and one month old and I live out in Gower, near Penhale. I like reading and my favorite Shakespeare play is *Antony and Cleopatra* and I admire Tennyson, Wordsworth and Elizabeth Barrett Browning—but not to excess, of course. I'm wild about the entire history of art, and I like music too—my favorite composers are Beethoven, Schubert, Tchaikovsky and Johann Strauss the Younger—oh, and Rachmaninoff; I've worn out two sets of records of his *Second Piano Concerto* and I hope to get a third set for Christmas. I'm quite interested in God too, and philosophy and all that sort of thing, and I like to meditate on Nature, like Wordsworth—I love watching the sea crashing on the rocks at the Worm's Head and swirling across the sands of Rhossili Bay. In short I believe in Beauty, Truth, Art and Peace, and if there's ever another war, which God forbid, I shall be a conchie because I don't believe war can ever be justified. I think that's all. Oh, I do write a bit, I have to tell you that, but you needn't worry because I'll never talk about it. Could you come to tea tomorrow?"

She gazed at me. Then she closed *The Prisoner of Zenda* with a bang, took a deep breath and said, "How do I get there?"

V

"Mum!" I cried triumphantly, surging into the Claremont Hotel ten minutes later. "I've just met the Princess of my Dreams!"

"Darling," said my mother, "I never for one moment doubted that you would!" Her bosom rose with maternal pride. "Sit down, pet, and tell me all about her."

My mother looked a little anxious when I reported that Anna was Jewish, but said quickly that she had met many charming Jewish people when she had been living in New York. As I rattled on I could almost hear her purring with pleasure.

"Wait till I tell John!" was her final comment. "This proves a boy can be educated at home and still be normal!"

"Oh, but this has nothing to do with sex," I said hastily. "I like this girl so much that I'd like her even if she were a boy. It's a meeting of the minds—bodies just don't come into it."

"Quite right too at your age," said my mother. "I wholeheartedly approve."

So did Dr. and Mrs. Steinberg, who must have raised their eyebrows when informed by their daughter that she had been picked up in a tea shop by the master of Oxmoon. After Mrs. Steinberg and my mother had cautiously ratified my invitation by telephone, all three Steinbergs arrived at Oxmoon in their Armstrong-Siddeley; no doubt Dr. and Mrs. Steinberg wanted to make quite sure that Anna was in no danger of being whisked into white slavery. My mother insisted that they all stayed to tea and the obligatory tour of the house and grounds followed, but finally Anna and I managed to snatch quarter of an hour alone together in the music room, where I played her as many sides as possible of Rachmaninoff's *Second Piano Concerto*. Every time I turned over the record we paused to discuss how tragic life was. I was in bliss.

My bliss was then terminated by Anna's departure, but was resumed a week later when I went to tea at the Steinbergs' modest but comfortable new house high up on one of the hills above the city. ("One of the nicer new middle-class areas," said my mother to arch-snob Aunt Celia.) Anna said that from upstairs there was a view of Swansea Bay but as I never went upstairs I never saw it. I heard that in these forbidden quarters there were three bedrooms, a maid's room, a box room and a bathroom. Downstairs there was a long room which ran from the front of the house to the back and was called a "lounge"; drawing-room furniture was arranged at one end of the room and dining-room furniture was kept at the other, while sliding doors divided the room into two whenever necessary. (Mrs. Steinberg always insisted that the doors should be kept open six inches if Anna and I retreated to talk on our own.) The rest of the ground floor consisted of a kitchen, a cloakroom under the stairs and Dr. Steinberg's study; his surgery was built on at the side of the house and had a separate entrance by the garage. There was a tiny garden which Mrs. Steinberg had made pretty. I thought Anna had a splendid little home and decided that contrary to what I had always heard from my family it must be great fun to belong to the middle classes.

"But oh, how I love Oxmoon!" said Anna. "I think it's better than any castle at Zenda!"

"Well, Mum and I have improved it a bit," I said, "but when I come of age I'm going to make it a monument to Beauty, Truth, Art and Peace."

We had long since agreed that Beauty, Truth, Art and Peace were the only things that mattered in the world. In fact we agreed on everything, and having found the perfect friend I was in such ecstasy that I even survived the ghastly Godwin Christmas reunion without feeling emotionally flattened. In the new year Anna came to lunch at Oxmoon and we had an enthralling debate on God as we walked over Harding's Down. By the time we returned home we had agreed that God definitely existed and that the proof of this lay in the finest forms of art which represented man's struggle to reach upwards to an immortal perfection.

"In other words," said Anna, "through Beauty, Truth, Art and Peace it's possible to know God."

"Well...glimpse Him, perhaps. Actually the Christian mystics were divided on whether it was possible to know God at all."

"Who were the Christian mystics?"

"Well, there was a wonderful down-to-earth motherly woman called Julian of Norwich, and there was the author of the book called *The Cloud of Unknowing*, which I think is the most marvelous title..."

We began to discuss marvelous titles. Of course there was no question of interrupting these earnest intellectual conversations in order to hold hands.

The following week I had lunch with her at her home, but then the moment came when I had to say goodbye to her for eleven weeks. Anna attended boarding school at Eastbourne. The spring term was about to begin.

I wrote long, long letters twice, sometimes three times a week. So did she. Somehow we survived until the end of March and suddenly it was spring, Anna was arriving on the Swansea bus and we were walking down the road to Oxmoon, a large red umbrella sheltering us from the romantically misty drizzle. More visits were exchanged, and at the end of the holidays I summoned all my courage to ask Mrs. Steinberg if I could take Anna to the cinema.

"A matinée, of course," said Mrs. Steinberg.

"Oh yes!" I said, horrified that I could have been suspected of favoring anything so sinister as an evening performance.

Permission was granted. We went to the Plaza, and armed with a box of chocolates we settled down in the front row of the dress circle to enjoy *Clive of India*.

Halfway through the breathtaking Battle of Plassey, Anna whispered to me, "Isn't it exciting?"

"Thrilling!"

She sighed, I sighed and overwhelmed by the sheer drama of our mutual enjoyment I grabbed her hand. It was the most breathtaking moment in all my fifteen and a half years. Her fingers gripped mine shyly—that may sound like a contradiction in terms, but her initial warm response was at once followed by a slackening of pressure, as if she feared she was being too forward—and for one fleeting moment, as my body became locked into the most extraordinary chain of physical reactions, I had a glimpse of a future which embraced rather more than matinées at the cinema and theological ruminations on Harding's Down. I dropped her hand as if it were a hot cake but then decided I liked hot cakes. God knows what the rest of the film was about. I was too delirious to care.

The abominable summer term began soon afterwards and lasted twelve weeks, each week seeming as long as a decade. One day in Swansea after a visit to the Library I was passing a jeweler's shop off Wind Street on my way to the Blue Rabbit when I saw a little locket displayed. It was Victorian but I was prepared to overlook that because the silver heart was engraved romantically with roses. I counted my pocket money, an idle exercise since I knew I could afford the purchase, but Uncle John was forever lecturing me about the evils of extravagance and if I counted my money carefully before each rash expenditure it gave me the illusion that I was being prudent.

In fact I was becoming rather tired of Uncle John lecturing me about money. Someone who glides around in a chauffeur-driven Rolls-Royce should keep his thoughts on financial extravagance to himself, and besides, I was aggrieved because I considered my allowance was too small. Refusing to raise it Uncle John had pronounced that I should learn to manage money by finding out how I could best husband my resources, but I thought this was mean and was constantly

527

yearning for the glorious financial independence of my eighteenth birthday.

I gave Anna the locket and afterwards she wore it always. Everyone thought this was very touching, particularly my mother who was behaving well about Anna even though she couldn't resist referring a little too often to "Kester's girl-friend" during conversations with the family.

"Well, personally, Ginevra," said Aunt Celia, "I don't see why you should be quite so smug about such an unsuitable friendship. I shouldn't care at all for Erika making friends with someone Jewish."

"Don't worry, Celia darling," said my mother. "I'm sure anyone Jewish would think twice before they tried to make friends with Erika."

My mother was very tired of Aunt Celia by that time. She had finally managed to ease Aunt Celia from Oxmoon to Little Oxmoon (vacant since Thomas's promotion to Penhale Manor), but Aunt Celia, whose favorite occupation was talking of trivialities, was always turning up at Oxmoon for a gossip. This greatly irritated my mother, who was a busy woman, but some spark of compassion for poor old Aunt Celia gave her superhuman patience, and she usually managed to keep her temper.

Meanwhile Erika was improving. Her English was better, her figure was slimmer and in a formal awkward way we tolerated each other's company. She became more tolerable after Anna and I had launched a Be Nice to Erika campaign. Anna said it must have been horrid for Erika to have had to leave her home in Germany, and even more horrid to have a father who had run off with a Hungarian.

"And imagine having a mother like Aunt Celia!" I added, still seething that my friendship with Anna should have been dismissed so waspishly as "unsuitable."

Erika was fourteen and had two years to fill in before she could go to finishing school, but Aunt Celia had dithered about her education, hiring a governess but dismissing her, sending Erika to a private school in Swansea but then removing her because Erika disliked it. Finally Aunt Celia asked Simon to tutor Erika in English literature and history, and Simon, driven on by my mother, found he had no choice but to agree. His reluctance arose because he already had his hands full in the schoolroom; not only did he have to prepare me for the school-certificate examinations, but he also had to coach Ricky for Oxford.

"Warwick Mowbray's an eligible young man," said Aunt Celia, who spent most of her time sizing up young men as potential husbands for Erika. I think she had even sized me up before I had been so "louche" as to acquire a Jewish girlfriend.

"Christ!" said anti-Semitic, fascist Thomas halfway through the summer hol-idays. "Is Kester still seeing that German Jewess?"

At first I thought Thomas and Aunt Celia were the only people who could possibly disapprove of my friendship with Anna, but as the summer passed I realized there were other people who looked askance at my situation.

"Write to me at Oxford," said Ricky, "but do try not to mention Anna more than ten times per letter, there's a good chap. I hate to say it, but I'm becoming simply flagellated by *ennui* as soon as I hear the hallowed name."

"You mustn't let Anna put you off your work," said Simon when we resumed lessons in September. "Perhaps we could have fewer letters to Eastbourne and more time spent in study?"

Finally in December shortly before Anna was due home, Uncle John said to me, "You're a little young to single out one special girl for attention, Kester. Perhaps you should try seeing other girls as well."

"Oh, let him be, John!" said my mother good-naturedly. "They're not getting up to any mischief! It's just an innocent romantic friendship and I think it's splendid!"

Uncle John merely looked at her as if he could not believe she could be quite so foolish. I was becoming very tired now of this stuffy Uncle John who had emerged, like some malign butterfly from a tainted chrysalis, after his reconciliation with Aunt Constance. Fortunately he seldom came to Oxmoon, but when he did he always made me ride out with him to visit my tenants and he always gave me boring lectures about how it was my moral duty to take an interest in their welfare. This annoyed me. I was fully prepared to take an interest, but not when it was so unappetizingly described as my moral duty. In fact when the tenants united that November to protest against a rise in rents I coped so well, riding out to meet them and promising that all their demands would be met, that my mother proudly declared I had proved myself a true chip off the Godwin block, but Uncle John said I had no business making rash promises and that the tenants' demands should be the subject of a prolonged negotiation. He then proceeded to wreck my liberal and humane *tour de force* by revising the settlement in a most conservative and autocratic manner.

I was now sixteen years old, quite old enough to resent having my authority undermined in such a fashion, although not quite bold enough to tell him so to his face. For Uncle John, grave intimidating Uncle John, was no longer the man who had laughed and joked with Bronwen. Proud, dignified and impeccably correct, he would demolish my self-confidence merely by raising an eyebrow; in his presence I became a little boy again, and I hated it. By this time I was six feet tall and still growing. I had irregular but thrilling encounters with a razor. My voice had finished breaking and, by one of those curious quirks of heredity, was now as deep as Uncle John's. (Harry was a tenor.) In short I was almost grown up, and every time Uncle John glided down to Oxmoon in his Rolls-Royce to treat me like a child, I was livid.

I was particularly maddened when he suggested I should stage some form of retreat from Anna because by that time I was working myself into a frenzy as I planned my first kiss. Anna was coming to lunch on Christmas Eve, and the only problem was where to hang the vital mistletoe. I tried out half a dozen places before settling for the doorway of the music room, where the gramophone was kept, and then I shaved, dressed in my best suit and tried not to chew my fingernails while I waited. Eternity passed. The Steinbergs arrived. Detaching Anna, I hustled her down the corridor to the music room.

"Gosh, look at the mistletoe!" said Anna, forestalling my carefully prepared remark about the stunning relevance to modern life of ancient pagan customs. "How pretty!"

529

I muttered some wild inanity like "Got to kiss—no choice," and for one infinitely precious second my lips touched her cheek before I sprang aside and headed dazed for the gramophone. My euphoria was so overpowering that the "Ode to Joy" section of Beethoven's *Ninth* nearly wound up smashed on the floor.

"My mother thinks I'm seeing too much of you," said Anna at the end of the Easter holidays.

"Has she been talking to Uncle John?"

"Heavens, no, she wouldn't dare! She thinks he's sure to disapprove of us."

"Well, he might, but if Uncle John was anti-Semitic he'd never, never show it. It wouldn't be the done thing."

"I wasn't just referring to us being Jewish. I meant that he'd disapprove of us for being foreign and middle-class and having only one live-in maid and not enough lawn for a tennis court."

"But that's ludicrous! Who's going to choose their friends according to the size of their lawns?"

"Mutti thinks *you* will in the end. She says it'll all end in tears and you'll fall in love with some smart aristocratic English girl who's been presented at court—"

"Like Cousin Marian. God, what an awful fate!"

"—and anyway, she thinks I ought to start being nice to Lester Feinstein."

"Lester who? Oh, you mean that wet rag I met at your house the other day!"

"Yes, but he's Jewish and I'm supposed to like him—it's the done thing, as you'd say—"

"This is exactly the sort of adult madness which makes one wonder if it really is worth growing up. As far as I'm concerned all men are equal—Christians and Jews, the County families and the middle classes, the aristocrats and the workers— and if they're not equal they ought to be!"

"Yes, I know and I do so agree, but meanwhile, what am I going to say to my mother about Lester Feinstein?"

We resolved to placate all these demented adults by behaving even more immaculately than before, and for some time after that we slaved away at being spotless. I took trouble with Mrs. Steinberg and gave her flowers on her birthday. (That was the end of her preference for Lester Feinstein.) I invited the Steinbergs to dine at Oxmoon with the more rational members of my family (Uncle Edmund, who would cheerfully have dined with cannibals if the claret was good, and Aunt Teddy, who always radiated a splendid American tolerance). Apart from her parents Anna had no relatives in Wales, but I did meet some of the Steinbergs' friends and tried hard to give a good impression.

This behavior was all very admirable and our critics were duly soothed but being spotless is a very boring occupation and to console ourselves we fell into clandestine habits which we confided to no one. That summer I wrote to her every day, although I told everyone I was still writing only twice a week. I sent her sonnets, books, sweets and cuttings from *The New Statesman*. She sent back inspiring excerpts from *The Oxford Dictionary of Quotations* and pressed wild flowers which she had gathered during walks on Beachy Head. When the holidays eventually came, we fell into the habit of organizing secret trysts so that no one would guess we met almost every day. Gallons of fizzy lemonade were consumed in countless tea shops. We haunted the Market; we languished beneath the castle walls, we wandered along Wind Street, we meandered up and down Kilvey Hill, we met in the Library, the Royal Institution, outside the Grand Theatre, at the conservatory in Victoria Park. When we had more time to spare we took the Mumbles Railway around the curve of Swansea Bay or the bus to Rhossili where we could walk hand in hand along the romantic lonely beach. Once we even clambered across the Shipway to the Worm's Head, and as we gazed dreamily into the beautiful rock pools I told her how my great-grandmother's lover, Owain Bryn-Davies, had met his tragic fate more than fifty years before when the Worm's Head had been almost unknown and the Gower Peninsula had been a mere secret wilderness beyond Swansea.

"A grand passion!" said Anna. "How thrilling!"

That seemed a good moment to kiss her so I did. I only kissed her very occasionally, however, because I was nervous of displaying some gross physical reaction which would have alarmed Anna and marred the perfection of our friendship.

Before she went back to school I gave her a red rose and told her I loved her. We were in the summerhouse at Oxmoon, and when Anna blushed I thought it was the most romantic place, a haven which might have been specially designed for two people who had to hide their love from a tiresome and thoroughly un-sympathetic world.

Two months later I was seventeen, and it was soon after this, when Anna returned for the Christmas holidays, that I began to talk casually of marriage.

First of all I made remarks like "Later when we're married we can go to London every month," and when she gave no hint that marriage was unthinkable to her, I became bolder and began to speculate whether we could have two weddings, one in a church and one in a synagogue. This was heady stuff indeed, and driven on by the urge to bring our dreams closer to reality, I borrowed some money from my mother to buy Anna an antique garnet ring for Christmas. She said she would wear it secretly until we made our engagement public, and at that point we began to wonder when we dared make the announcement. We knew everyone would say we were too young, and although I did not tell her, I trembled at the thought of Uncle John.

"It seems to me," I said at last, "that the best plan is to wait another ten months until I'm eighteen. Then I inherit Oxmoon, and if I'm old enough to do that then by God, I'm old enough to get engaged! Who knows?" I added, carried away by this stirring vision of independence. "If our parents consent to the engagement we might even be married immediately! I know Mum will be on our side—she adores romance. In fact I suspect she can hardly wait for us to get married and live happily ever after!"

Never in all my life had I been quite so catastrophically mistaken.

VI

"...so I think Anna and I will get engaged next November," I announced, "and then we can be married as soon as possible afterwards!"

I had just arrived home after seeing Anna onto the Swansea bus and had found my mother enjoying her first pink gin of the evening. The drawing room, still swathed with the Christmas holly and paper chains, was alluringly warm but the warmth seemed to fade as my mother gave me a long cool look. Then she knocked back the remainder of her pink gin and rose to mix herself another.

"Sit down, please, Kester."

"Why, what's the matter?"

"*Sit down!*"

I sat down.

"Now," said my mother, "let me say this: I like Anna enormously. I'm delighted you've had this girlfriend for two years. But of course there can be no question of getting engaged or—God forbid!—married when you're only eighteen."

"But Mum!" I said shattered. "You said marrying at eighteen was all right!"

"I said sex at eighteen was all right," said my mother. "Or rather, to be accurate, I said that no one younger than eighteen should indulge in sex—by which I meant that in certain circumstances sex can be acceptable after one's eighteenth birthday." She poured a generous helping of gin into her glass. "But I never," she said, "*never* either said or implied that marriage would be acceptable at that age. You should wait till you're at least twenty-five."

"*Twenty-five?*" I shouted.

"Twenty-five," said my mother implacably, saturating the gin with bitters.

"But look here!" I said, outraged. "You can't sanction sex and not marriage! That's all the wrong way round! You can't expect me to have sex with Anna without being married to her! Good heavens, what sort of a villain do you think I am?"

"Of course I don't think you're a villain, darling! You're just a nice young man who's led such a secluded life that he has no idea what goes on in the world."

"Another insult! Now listen to me, Mum. Anna's the love of my life. I knew as soon as I first looked into her eyes at the Blue Rabbit—"

"Kester, this is real life. You're not in Ruritania now."

"I *know* it's real life. But this sort of situation isn't confined to Ruritania! What about my father?"

Silence. No reply. My mother was suddenly very still.

"Well, he fell in love with you when he was about my age, didn't he?" I pursued triumphantly. "And didn't he love you till the day he died? And didn't you always tell me that this was a grand passion and just like a fairy tale? You've certainly always given me the impression that you would have lived happily ever after if that illness hadn't plunged you both into hell!"

My mother tried to speak, made a mess of it, halted, drank some pink gin and fumbled for a cigarette. She was unable to look at me.

"I'm sorry," I said at once. "I know it must be so painful for you to be reminded how your glorious romance was ruined by that tragedy, and you know I'd never do it unless I was desperate, but—"

"Kester," said my mother unevenly, "your father didn't marry at eighteen. Nor did he spend his twenties yearning for me chastely. He had affairs with other women—and that was as it should be. All men need a love affair or two to help them grow up into mature people who can master the challenge marriage presents, and believe me, darling, your father would be the very first person to tell you that if he were alive today."

"Very well, I concede he married when he was a mature man of thirty-one. But he obviously felt exactly the same at thirty-one as he did at seventeen, and so shall I, because this is no adolescent dream, Mum, this is grand passion, and if you refuse to acknowledge that then you just don't understand the situation at all!"

"Oh yes I do!" said my mother, speedily recovering her equilibrium. "I understand all too well! We leave for London tomorrow, pet. I think it's time you had a good long sensible talk with your Uncle John."

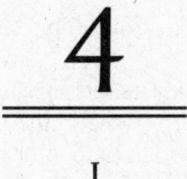

4

I

UNCLE JOHN had been having a trying time with his family during the three and a half years that had elapsed since Bronwen's departure, and accordingly my passion for Anna must have seemed to him to resemble the straw that broke the camel's back. The first family crisis had arisen less than a year after his reconciliation with Aunt Constance when Marian and Rory had decided to get married. (This was the direct result of the grand Easter Reunion at Oxmoon when they had danced the Charleston together and Rory, mindful that my mother wanted him to settle down like Darling Declan, had inquired furtively about Marian's fortune.) From my mother's point of view, there was in theory nothing wrong with this match—quite the reverse, since she must have despaired of Rory ever marrying a rich man's daughter—but in practice she was horrified. She disliked Marian and realized that the marriage could only lead to awkwardness between herself and Uncle John who was naturally appalled that his daughter wanted to marry a penniless rake like Rory.

"Darling, marry anyone but John's daughter!" she begged him, and added distractedly: "Surely you can't love her!"

"I most certainly do!" said Rory with indignation, and indeed I think he was fairly keen. It would take a man of Rory's stupidity to find a girl like Marian attractive.

But my mother remained torn between her desire to see her shady offspring well settled and her terror of Uncle John.

"Darling, what about your religion?" (My mother was now really scraping the barrel of excuses.) "I know you never go to Mass but once a Catholic always a Catholic, and—"

"Marian's going to turn," said Rory proudly, "and she's agreed—"

"*My God, what's John going to say when he hears!*"

"—and Marian's agreed," repeated Rory, raising his voice to drown her panic, "that the baby'll be brought up Catholic, so that little difficulty's quite resolved."

"What baby?" said my mother.

The bombshell exploded. Marian was pregnant. My mother nearly had apoplexy.

"*You fool!*" she shouted at Rory.

"Hold on, Ma, no need to be hysterical, I'm going to marry her, aren't I, and put everything right!"

"Shut up! How could you," said my mother, running true to form by becoming glacial as her rage deepened, "how *could* you be so asinine as to seduce *John's daughter*—"

"Well, she seduced me actually," said Rory, "and anyway she wasn't a virgin, so what the hell?"

"Kester, leave us, please," said my mother, belatedly remembering my presence. (I had been attempting invisibility in the farthest corner of the room.) Outside the door I put my ear to the panels in time to hear her repeat in a stage whisper: "You fool! Are you sure the child's even yours?"

"Oh yes, Ma! I mean . . . well, Christ, Marian wouldn't do a thing like that—"

"Why else should a snobbish girl like Marian settle for a man like you when she could do so much better for herself?"

"God, Ma, you do hit below the belt!"

"*Answer me!*"

"Well, for Christ's sake, Marian loves me, I know she does, and of course the baby's mine, I know it is, just as I know Marian can't wait to marry me and escape from that soul-destroying house in Belgravia!"

There was a long silence. Then my mother said without expression, "Poor Marian" and began to ask a series of practical questions about the wedding.

The marriage took place three weeks later by special license at the Roman Catholic church in Farm Street, and Uncle John, immaculate in morning dress, gave the bride away as if Rory were the best son-in-law he could have wished for, as if he were delighted that Marian had chosen to become a Catholic and as if all prospect of grandchildren were at least a year away. Aunt Constance drafted the notice for the papers, but made a hash of it by using the word "quietly"—a horrible hint, as my mother said in exasperation, that the circumstances had been abnormal. However worse was to follow for when Marian gave birth to a daughter Aunt Constance inserted the word "premature" in the birth announcement.

534

"Doesn't that stupid woman realize that nobody puts that word in unless they're trying to fight a rumor of premarital sex?" shouted my mother, but Aunt Constance, so humorless that she was unable to anticipate any cynical amusement, no doubt thought she was only doing the done thing.

Uncle John gave the couple a house in Kensington as a wedding present, found Rory a job in Armstrong Investments and professed delight when his first grandchild entered the world, but what he really thought of the disaster no one knew.

"John's very silent these days," remarked Aunt Daphne during an earlier visit to Oxmoon with Elizabeth. "What's going on there, do you think, Ginevra? Does he ever talk about—"

"No," said my mother. "We're all absolutely forbidden to mention her name."

"But do you think he's happy with Constance?"

"No idea," said my mother shortly. She would never be drawn into gossiping about Uncle John.

That visit by Aunt Daphne to Oxmoon was the prelude to yet another family crisis which was to try Uncle John's patience. My cousin Elizabeth, perhaps annoyed that Marian had beaten her to the altar, decided to fall madly in love with the next man who interested himself in her, and by chance, during her visit to Gower, this turned out to be Owen Bryn-Davies, who was nine years her senior and a director of Suez Petro-Chemicals in Swansea. He had spent some time working for the company in the Middle East, but now he had returned home and was clearly anxious to settle down with a nice jolly girl who had a first-class social background and some useful Gower connections. There was plenty of money in the Bryn-Davies family for his father, Alun, was chairman of the board of the Madog Collieries, none of which had been closed during the slump; but Aunt Daphne, who had long since set her heart on Elizabeth marrying into the peerage, was most upset by her daughter's plans and appealed to Uncle John for help.

"What's wrong with Owen Bryn-Davies?" I said mystified to my mother. Good-looking, Harrow-educated, wealthy, successful Owen seemed to me to be a good catch.

"Nothing," said my mother, "except that by Daphne's standards he's not out of the top drawer. She keeps blustering that Elizabeth could do so much better for herself—but where and with whom? No, I think Daphne's being very silly, and my sympathies are entirely with Elizabeth and Owen."

Uncle John agreed with her when he arrived at Oxmoon. "Daphne," he said, "there are worse fates for a girl than marrying an untitled man with a Welsh surname."

"Well, we all know that, don't we?" said Aunt Daphne before she could stop herself. Marian had just formally announced her pregnancy.

Uncle John was silent, looking inscrutable as usual, but my mother at once rushed to his defense. "Let's be honest, darling," she said to Aunt Daphne. "You married an untitled Welshman yourself, didn't you? What are you making such a fuss about?"

"At least Lion was a Godwin of Oxmoon!" said Aunt Daphne vigorously. "And at least the Godwins are listed in *Burke's Landed Gentry!* I don't ask the moon for Elizabeth, but if she could only follow my example—"

"If Elizabeth were to follow your example," said my mother, maddened past endurance, "she'd end up with a titled ex-lover and no husband at all!"

A family row ensued, much to my delight. Aunt Daphne tried to walk out in a rage but Elizabeth refused to accompany her and Owen Bryn-Davies, who had been summoned by telephone, was now obliged to take part in the battle. Uncle Lion's name was repeatedly invoked but in vain until finally Aunt Daphne had hysterics, a most interesting phenomenon which I decided to use in my next novel. Uncle John then began to exert the full force of his powerful personality until Aunt Daphne ended up consenting to the marriage and weeping in his arms; between sobs she confessed that she had never got over Uncle Lion's death and that although they all thought she was just a silly society woman she wasn't, she longed to get married again but no one ever measured up to Lion and she was so miserable which was why she couldn't bear the thought of Elizabeth getting married to Owen because once Elizabeth had gone to live in Wales, she—Daphne—would be so lonely and her life would have ended at the age of thirty-nine.

A baroque family reconciliation followed, during which my fingers itched to take notes. My mother kissed Aunt Daphne on both cheeks and invited her to stay at Oxmoon for as long as she liked. (My mother was always issuing these rash invitations under stress and living to regret them.) Elizabeth wept that of course darling Mummy could come and live with her after the wedding. (Owen looked horrified.) Aunt Celia, who had somehow managed to get in on the act, said there were all kinds of compensations for not being married and had Daphne ever considered becoming a regular churchgoer. Finally Owen put everything right by kissing his future mother-in-law and suggesting that he took her and Elizabeth into Swansea to dine at the Claremont. Aunt Daphne said, "How *very* kind, especially after that ghastly scene I've just made," and when she looked up at him gratefully I knew he had been forgiven for not coming out of the top drawer.

After the engagement was formally announced no one could talk of anything but the fact that Owen's great-grandfather had been Elizabeth's great-grandmother's lover, and everyone turned to the older generation for a full account of what had happened. But information was curiously lacking. Uncle Edmund said, "Oh, yes, it was an appalling scandal," but he didn't seem to know much about it. Thomas said, "My father used to talk about it when he was gaga—Milly and I thought him an awful bore." Uncle John looked inscrutable and when he said he didn't think a past tragedy was a fit subject for idle gossip, Alun Bryn-Davies, Owen's father, instantly said, "I quite agree!" (It occurred to me then that these modern respectable Bryn-Davieses were very keen to draw a veil over their sheep-farming ancestor who had slept his way into money that didn't belong to him.) So finally it was left to my mother to enshrine the family myth for future generations. After her third glass of champagne at the engagement party she said richly, "Darlings, the truth was it was a divine romance with a heavenly tragic ending. The poor girl had this alcoholic husband who was just the teensiest bit

536

difficult and then when she was out on the moors one day—I mean the Downs, but it's always the moors in books, isn't it?—she met this handsome virile passionate sheep farmer who at once fell madly in love with her, and my dears, it was all simply too *Wuthering Heights*, but alas! Later he drowned in the most ghastly accident right before her eyes, poor darling, and she went mad with grief but Bobby and Margaret were simply sweet to her and insisted on treating her like a queen when she came home for her Christmas visit. They kept her portrait in the attics and every year they brought it down and hung it in the dining room and it was all so touching and poor old Aunt Gwyneth was so moved by all the fuss that she could hardly speak but of course we all adored her and she adored us—"

At this point my mother was interrupted because everyone was stampeding to the attics to gaze with inebriated fascination at my great-grandmother's portrait.

"No wonder he fell for her!" said Owen Bryn-Davies at last, and as he voiced the admiration which his great-grandfather had undoubtedly shared, everyone was still. It was as if the past were echoing in our ears, not the past of my mother's synthetic fantasies but a past where madness and death had stalked a crude violent sinister landscape.

"What a story!" said I, the writer, and added, groping instinctively for the story's lost dimensions: "And I bet we know no more than half of it." That seemed like a challenge to me. I wondered if I could write the story and fill in the gaps, but just as I was speculating on this delicious prospect Uncle John covered his grandmother's portrait again with its dust sheet and announced coldly: "I can't help feeling that all this prurient interest is in exceedingly bad taste."

What a sober old killjoy he was! However I was now well accustomed to Uncle John's deplorable stuffiness, and his condition certainly showed no improvement during the months that followed. By the time I was seventeen—and about to present Uncle John with his third family crisis on the subject of marriage—I thought him a huge bore to be avoided as often as possible, and when my mother insisted on taking me to see him in the January of 1937 I was very cross indeed.

"But why can't *you* have this sensible talk with me, Mum?" I objected. "You did it so well when I was fourteen!"

"I hope," said my mother, "that when you were an anxious child of fourteen I was able to give you a reassuring glimpse of the perfect love affair. Everything I said then still stands. But you've got to learn how to look after yourself while you're traveling this road to perfection, and that's the sort of knowledge you'll find easier to accept from another man."

I gave up and resigned myself to my ordeal.

II

Aunt Constance's father the American millionaire had died three years before his daughter's reconciliation with her husband, so there had been no obstacle to prevent Uncle John gliding back to work in the Armstrong empire. As Aunt Celia once remarked to my mother, Uncle John always seemed to fall on his feet financially. Aunt Constance saw that he was put in charge of the charitable trusts and given a seat on the board of Armstrong Investments, and presently Uncle John was busy launching a new educational trust which was aimed at giving working-class children a better education. Having resigned his Swansea director-ships he soon found himself offered new ones in London, and it was generally assumed he made plenty of money in addition to his private income from his Herefordshire estate. Aunt Constance, as everyone knew, was rich as Croesus in her own right, thanks to the Armstrong fortune, and so there was certainly no shortage of material comfort in Uncle John's new life. In fact it would have seemed to any casual observer that he had everything a man could want.

Unlike Uncle Edmund and Aunt Teddy, who rattled around in a slapdash way between their house in London and their estate in Kent, Uncle John and Aunt Constance adhered to a meticulously planned schedule. Every May Aunt Constance would take Francesca and the governess to Boston to see her American friends and relations. Uncle John refused to cross the Atlantic, as if he feared he might start heading for Vancouver as soon as his feet touched North American soil, but he always took Aunt Constance on her own to the Riviera for two weeks every winter as if to compensate her for this spring absence from his side. The family holiday with Francesca took place in August, when they visited Aunt Daphne in Scotland for the grouse shooting. For the rest of the year they occupied themselves by dining with the right people and visiting the right country houses at weekends. Aunt Constance was good at this. In fact Aunt Constance led the model life of a rich married woman in London. She interested herself in the right charities, patronized the right arts, entertained the right guests and even attended, with Francesca, the right church every Sunday. Uncle John, who otherwise did the done thing as religiously as his wife did, never accompanied them.

The Armstrong mansion, inherited by Aunt Constance from her father, was a massive cream-colored monstrosity which in Victorian times had been inhabited by an obscure member of Disraeli's cabinet. Behind the opulent facade the house was a monument to dreariness. Nothing was vulgar; Aunt Constance had weeded out every one of her father's *nouveau-riche* excesses, but her scrupulous refur-bishings, all technically correct, were somehow, mysteriously, disastrous. Uncle John didn't care and even if he had he lacked the aesthetic taste which would have stopped that mansion evolving from a vulgar museum into a lifeless stately home. Formal arrangements of flowers were placed to emphasize carefully hung, meticulously lit paintings. *Objets d'art* were painstakingly grouped according to age and nationality; modern wall-to-wall carpets in dull beige screamed ANACHRONISM to overwhelmed groups of antiques. Some of the paintings were good; there was an excellent portrait by Sargent of Aunt Constance and Aunt Teddy as girls, but there were too many English landscapes featuring cows looking glumly over hedges. My mother thought the entire place was as cheerful as a morgue and often speculated how Uncle John managed to survive there without cutting his throat.

However Uncle John's throat showed no sign of damage when he and Aunt Constance received us in the drawing room on that January evening, and there with them we found dear little Francesca who danced up to give me a hug and declared I had to meet her new kitten. My mother had spent some time speculating whether Aunt Constance would produce another child to celebrate her triumphant recapture of Uncle John, but no child had appeared. Aunt Constance was rumored to be disappointed by this, but what Uncle John thought, of course, no one knew.

At first time slipped by very pleasantly as I chatted to Francesca about her Persian kitten, but at length Francesca's governess arrived to spirit her away and my temporary reprieve was terminated. A butler resembling an undertaker announced that dinner was served. We descended to the dining room (elephantine banqueting table, grossly overdecorated Gothic sideboard, cows on every wall and a horrified Chippendale mirror reflecting the lot). Valiantly we toiled through mulligatawny soup, poached trout and roast duck while Aunt Constance discussed the financial appreciation of fine art and my mother talked (fruitlessly) of aesthetic values. Finding no common ground here, and no longer able to retreat into a discussion of the Abdication crisis which had been so sadly resolved the previous month, they sought refuge in a consideration of their one mutual passion: Harrods. Uncle John listened politely with half an ear and then, smothering a yawn, embarked with me on a discussion of the Oxmoon estate.

By the time we had finished pudding (heavy apple charlotte sunk deep in the gloom of a flagellated cream), I had been forced to reveal a woeful ignorance and Uncle John was trying to restrain himself from uttering a criticism that would have soured the remainder of the evening. In the end he merely said, "You really should take more interest, Kester. What I can't understand is what you do with yourself when you're at leisure. I know you're a conscientious student, but surely you must still have a great deal of spare time?"

"Well..." This was dangerous ground indeed.

"I'm certain you could find the time to take more interest in the estate.... You're not still painting pictures, are you?"

"Oh no, Uncle John!" I said with relief. "I gave up painting years ago!"

"Good—and does that mean you've also stopped scribbling stories?"

"Uh...well, more or less....Very occasionally I do pen the odd line or two—"

"Kester, now you're seventeen you should put all such childish pursuits behind you and find a more constructive use for your spare time. Let me have a word with Thomas. I really do think you should start having some lessons in estate management."

"Uncle John," I said, blushing as I always did when I tried to oppose him, "I'm sorry but I couldn't take large doses of Thomas on a regular basis."

Uncle John did not ridicule this statement. Now that I was older I was dimly beginning to realize that his power over me was increased because he was capable of being nice. If he had always been thoroughly nasty I could have loathed him without guilt, but unfortunately for me, although I moaned and groaned about him and privately called him a stuffy old bore, I knew I was being ungrateful and hated myself accordingly. The kinder and more understanding he was, the more I hated myself. He could reduce me to pulp merely by a smile and a sympathetic comment. He reduced me to pulp now.

"I do realize," he said, "that Thomas isn't the easiest of men. Very well, I'll see if I can come up with a better idea."

I thought how utterly beastly I was, being so difficult when I had this wonderful uncle who only wanted to be helpful to me. Then I hated him for making me hate myself. In short I was already in a chaotic emotional state even before my true ordeal had begun.

Meanwhile the women were declining dessert and cheese. Aunt Constance said, "Ginevra, shall we leave the men to their port? I'm just dying to show you the new pearls John gave me for Christmas..." and the next moment the two of them had disappeared in a flurry of silk and satin.

Uncle John passed me the port decanter as the servants withdrew. "My father never permitted his sons to drink port until they were eighteen," he said, "but if we're to talk as if you're already eighteen perhaps I should now treat you as an eighteen-year-old. Have you ever drunk port before?"

"No, sir." I took a sip and hated it.

He gave a short eloquent lecture on port as he lit a cigar. I found myself taking another sip out of sheer nervousness. Then I decided port wasn't so bad after all. Declining the cigar he offered me I clutched the stem of my glass and tried to repress the urge to rush upstairs to the drawing room to listen to Aunt Constance discussing the financial appreciation of pearls.

Uncle John began by talking most kindly and with genuine interest about Anna. We agreed that Hitler's policy towards Jews was absolutely wrong, we agreed that Jewish people were often charming and cultivated, we agreed that England would be a poorer place without its small Jewish population. We agreed that Anna was a thoroughly nice girl who would undoubtedly make an excellent wife and mother one day. We agreed on everything. By that time I was so nervous that I had finished all my port and was pouring myself a second glass.

"Your mother tells me you're anxious to marry Anna when you're eighteen," said Uncle John at last, casually tapping aside the ash from his cigar. "You have of course considered the difficulties of marrying out of your religion, your culture and—most vital of all—your class?"

"Anna and I are above those divisions, sir," I said boldly. "They don't seem important to us."

"Then may I suggest that they should? Marriage is very, very difficult, Kester, and the divisions I've just mentioned can only exacerbate those difficulties. Indeed I think if you were to marry at eighteen they would present an intolerable burden to you—and to Anna too. And you wouldn't want that, would you, Kester? I'm sure you care enough about her to want to put her welfare above your own."

I drank some more port and tried to stop my hand shaking as I replaced the glass on the table.

"You mustn't think I'm unsympathetic," said Uncle John, each kind word a nail in the coffin of my composure. "You make a mistake if you forget that I'm no stranger to powerful emotions—don't think for one moment that I can't understand what you're going through. You're in love and when one's in love one loses touch with time. Everything seems eternal yet everything is now, everything is present. I think that's the most dangerous delusion passion can provide because one can't conceive of time making any changes; the future is literally unimaginable—yet that doesn't stop the future from existing, and that doesn't mean time doesn't go on ticking away, slowly making changes all the while you believe so passionately that nothing will ever alter."

He paused. Out of the corner of my eye I saw him tap the ash from his cigar again. Then he said, "No relationship is immutable. You're seventeen and in love and time is meaningless to you. But you'll grow older. You'll see more of the world. Time will change you almost without you being aware of it, and when you're thirty years old will you really be the same person as the young man I see before me now? And will your love for Anna have survived these inevitable changes? I think not."

"My love for Anna," I said, "will survive till the end of the world." The port was warm and fiery now, giving me the courage I so badly needed. I drank a little more.

"I expressed similar sentiments myself," said Uncle John, "when I married my first wife. However the truth was I didn't know what I was talking about. I did genuinely care for Blanche and to this day I remember her with affection and respect, but I was emotionally immature and quite unfit for marriage—as I believe you are at this moment."

"But Anna's the Bronwen of my life, not the Blanche!" I exclaimed passionately, and then realized I had uttered the name forbidden in his presence. Blushing with horror I poured myself a third glass of port and drank half of it straight off. "I'm sorry," I stammered; "I didn't mean—"

"If Anna's the Bronwen of your life," said Uncle John steadily, "I feel sorry for you. You'll have noticed that my relationship with Bronwen hasn't survived the ravages of time."

"But that was only because Aunt Constance wouldn't—"

"We're not here to discuss my past. We're here to discuss your future. As you'll have guessed by now, I think it would be a disaster for you to marry someone from an utterly dissimilar background—and a disaster too if you married without previous sexual experience. You've never been to bed with anyone, have you?"

I shook my head.

"Yet obviously you feel tempted to go to bed with Anna or you wouldn't be talking of marriage. Come into the library for a minute. I think you've had enough port."

Draining my glass I stumbled after him into the hall.

541

III

The library was the best room in the house because Uncle John had exterminated all trace of the Armstrong dreariness by installing his favorite possessions from Penhale Manor. Beyond the large oak desk the matching pair of eighteenth-century bookcases displayed not the leather-bound editions that had once been ordered *en masse* by Harley Armstrong (they were now serving as wallpaper in a distant morning room) but Uncle John's own books, which ranged from fishing to Froissart and from *Beowulf* to John Buchan. This wildly eclectic, curiously unfocused literary taste had recently struck me as being odd. I felt it suggested a spiritual as well as an intellectual restlessness, a ceaseless quest for escape by a disturbed mind from a reality which was inescapable, and perhaps it was then that I became dimly aware for the first time of his extreme complexity. An image took shape in my mind of a man who lived one life but longed for another, a man who said one thing yet did something else, a man who outwardly worshiped order yet inwardly grappled with chaos. But the next moment the impression had vanished; I was still too young to attempt to understand him, and anyway at that moment I had enough complex problems of my own.

I glanced feverishly around the room in an effort to calm myself. On the shelf above the chimneypiece Victorian *bric-à-brac* jostled with golf trophies and old family snapshots of my grandparents, my father and Uncle Lion, while on the desk a studio portrait of Harry, looking impossibly handsome, reminded me that at least I had been spared his presence that evening; he was away visiting a friend in Norfolk and was not due home until the last week of the holidays.

Turning my back on the photograph of perfect Cousin Harry, who was doubtless conducting his private life with matchless efficiency while I bucketed bruised from one hostile relative to the next, I dredged up the strength to resume my battle for independence.

"Excuse me, Uncle John," I blurted out, "but I think there's some sort of misunderstanding here. I don't want to marry Anna just because I've started to feel I'd like to go to bed with her; in fact I don't particularly want to go to bed with her at all. I want to marry her because we're soulmates who believe in Beauty, Truth, Art and Peace." I was by this time, of course, thoroughly drunk.

"If you don't want to go to bed with her," said Uncle John, putting me in the position that I was damned if I did but equally damned if I didn't, "it would be the height of cruelty to marry her. I think I'd better come down to Swansea to talk to her parents. It's quite obvious that you two children should be protected from each other."

"I didn't mean—of course I *would* like to go to bed with her—but that would be the result of being married and not the reason for it—"

"Sit down, Kester."

I sank down on the armchair by the fireplace but Uncle John, clever Uncle John who was well experienced in the art of wielding power, chose to remain standing.

"Now—" I was very conscious of him towering above me as he rested his hand lightly on the mantelshelf. "—let's find out what that romantic and emotional mother of yours has told you about the realities of life. Before we go any further we must make sure you know what going to bed with a woman really means."

A horrible conversation ensued in which the basic facts of copulation were established beyond dispute. An even more horrible conversation followed when Uncle John proceeded to divide the female half of the human race into categories. Females, I was told, consisted of nice girls, fast girls, married women, kept women, sluts, tarts and the dregs. The last three categories existed only for the dubious benefit of degenerates and/or the working classes who were so desperate to alleviate their boredom and misery that they were incapable of taste and discrimination. However for a young gentleman nice girls were for marriage, fast girls were for flirting with and married women were for seduction. (Kept women were the preserve of older men with money to burn and tedious wives to tolerate.)

I was warned to be especially careful of fast girls, who could include anyone from an amoral debutante to a foolish housemaid, because they had a disastrous habit of getting pregnant. (There was an embarrassing moment here as we both tried to pretend Cousin Marian couldn't have been further from our minds.) I was also advised to be wary of married women with bad reputations, because unfortunately venereal disease wasn't confined to the working classes, and indeed even the purest of married women could contract it from a straying husband. Therefore it was essential that a young man should look after himself at all times, but luckily an item could be purchased which guarded against not only disease but fatherhood as well.

"A perfect example of how to kill two birds with one stone," said Uncle John with a humor which for one brief, poignant moment reminded me of the lost hero who had laughed with Bronwen, and added as an afterthought: "I assume you've heard of venereal disease?"

"Oh yes, sir," I said, lying to preserve my dignity, but I had already realized that this was obviously one of the few subjects which had eluded my genius for eavesdropping. I wished I hadn't drunk my third glass of port.

"Do you know what the symptoms are?"

"Well, actually... no. Not really."

Uncle John began to talk of syphilis and gonorrhea. I lasted exactly thirty seconds. Then I stood up, lurched to the fireplace and vomited all over the grate. How I failed to put out the fire I'll never know.

To make matters infinitely worse Uncle John was so nice to me. If he had lost his temper and roared that I was a squeamish idiot I could somehow have made a dignified recovery, but to my horror he was kindness personified.

"My dear Kester, forgive me—please believe I meant well and only wanted to help—"

I recoiled from him. I felt as if my nose were being rubbed in the mud. I wanted my dignity, I wanted my independence, I wanted to behave like a man and yet here I was, crying in front of him like a child, utterly humiliated, thoroughly sickened and feeling absolutely defiled by everything that had been said.

I wanted to think of Anna to steady myself but I was too afraid of contaminating our perfect love by my new sordid insight into the sheer frightfulness of the adult world.

"Oh my God!" said Uncle John as I sobbed harder than ever, and I loathed myself for reducing him to despair. I felt murderous, suicidal, demented. Huge emotions, black and poisoned, billowed out of my subconscious to blight my entire mind. I was in hell.

"I'll call your mother," said Uncle John.

Perhaps he expected my mother to clasp me to her bosom and croon soothing endearments, but if he did he had miscalculated. The full blast of her fury hit me as soon as she entered the room. Walking straight up to me, she slapped me across the mouth and shouted, "How dare you disgrace me like this!"

But this approach I could cope with. This straightforward rage knifed through all my tortuous emotions and gave me no chance to hate myself for my inadequacy. She was doing the hating for me, so all I had to do in return was to pull myself together.

However I at once realized that this reaction was quite beyond Uncle John's comprehension, because he too was battling with feelings of inadequacy and he too was busy hating himself for what he nobly considered to be his failure. I heard him say—and every word struck me like a dagger because he was being so heroic, taking all the blame on himself—"I'm sorry, Ginevra, obviously I've made a complete hash of this. I can see now he's still too young to master the advice I was trying to give him."

"Rubbish!" thundered my mother, at once in a towering rage with him as well. "If he's old enough to talk of marriage he's old enough to hear what you had to say! It's about time he started facing facts instead of drifting around in a cloud of adolescent nonsense which bears no relation to reality! Very well, Kester, we'll go back to the hotel. I'm absolutely disgusted by your weak childish behavior. I didn't think any son of mine could be quite so feeble."

That did the trick. I stiffened my backbone and looked her straight in the eyes. "There's no need for us to leave so early," I said in a firm dignified voice. "I was sick because I'd drunk too much port and I cried because I couldn't hold my drink like a man. It had nothing to do with what Uncle John and I were talking about and now, if you'll excuse me, I'd like to resume my conversation with him."

There was a pause before my mother said tersely, "That's more like it" and walked out. The door banged behind her. We stood listening as her footsteps click-clacked away across the hall.

"Kester... if you'd prefer not to hear any more—"

I wanted to yell and scream and fling myself on the floor and drum my heels with exasperation, but all I said was a crisp "My mother was right. If I'm old enough to talk of marriage I'm old enough to hear what you have to say. Please go on."

But poor Uncle John was so demoralized that he could barely bring himself to show me a French letter and give me a few succinct tips about its use. This hardly mattered, as I was determined not to listen to a single word he said, but I kept an attentive expression on my face and remembered to nod occasionally.

"... so I think that's about all," he concluded, sounding weak with relief. "Are there any questions you'd like to ask?"

"No, thank you, sir," I said. "I'm very glad to have the information and I'm most grateful to you for taking so much trouble. I do apologize for making such a disgusting mess of your fireplace."

I was behaving like a perfect Godwin at last. As we both sighed with relief I glanced again at the picture on his desk and thought of worldly Cousin Harry, taking the lecture in his stride and running off to outwit unmarried fatherhood and venereal disease with consummate skill. No vomiting into fireplaces for Cousin Harry, no grinding awkwardness, no sheer unadulterated hell of humiliation and shame. He would walk out into that foul polluted adult world with a smile and take his place in it without a backward glance.

But I wasn't like Cousin Harry and I wasn't going to live in his world. No contraception, no disease, no married women, no fast girls, no filth, no obscenity, no degradation—not for me, never for me, never, *never*, NEVER. I was going to marry the Princess of My Dreams and live happily ever after at Oxmoon.

A dream? Yes, of course it was a dream, but what was wrong with that? If no one ever dreamed of perfection, reality would always be nothing but unalleviated ghastliness, but sometimes a man could make his dream reality—and sometimes, very occasionally, reality was no longer sordid but dazzling, a vision of all that was finest in human nature, a view of the absolute truth, a glimpse of God.

An idealist? Yes, of course I was an idealist, and what was more I was proud of it. It's idealism that separates us from swine. Everyone should try to be an idealist. It would make for a better world than the mire in which we're all currently submerged.

The next day I telephoned Anna and said I wanted to elope with her just as soon as I had celebrated my eighteenth birthday.

IV

"Two fizzy lemonades and two cream buns, please," I said to the waitress in the Blue Rabbit. It was well before eleven in the morning and we were the only occupants of the restaurant apart from three elderly women who were drinking tea and exchanging medical histories.

"So you see," I said to Anna after the waitress had padded away on flat feet, "since Uncle John's made such a song-and-dance about sex I just have to find out how you feel on the subject. Now, I've never done any copulation so unfortunately it's impossible for me to give you a reasonable estimate of how often I might want to do it, but I have to be honest and tell you I *would* like to do it occasionally, and not just because I want children. I sort of feel . . . well, it might be rather fun every now and then—"

"I don't know much about it," said Anna anxiously, "but I've heard some extraordinary rumors at school."

"They're probably true, but don't worry. Mum says sex can be absolutely stunning."

A hush fell over the tea shop as the three old tabbies abandoned their discussion of gallstones to eavesdrop.

"Two cream buns, two fizzy lemonades," said the waitress, plonking down plates and glasses in front of us.

We bit deep into our buns to hide our confusion.

"Heavens, Kester!" whispered Anna as the old tabbies abandoned their eavesdropping and began to prattle about gallstones again. "Do you really talk about sex to your mother?"

"Yes, of course. Don't you talk about it to yours?"

"Never! In fact I always thought talking about sex wasn't the done thing!"

"Well, it often isn't. But it's always the done thing to be mad about it."

"Goodness, how worrying it all is," said Anna, forsaking her cream bun.

"Don't worry," I said soothingly again. "Doing the done thing, I've discovered, has very little to do with what people actually think. Of course not everyone's mad about sex, but everyone has to pretend to be mad about it because they're frightened of being different."

"It *is* frightening to be different," said Anna. "It's easier and more comfortable to conform."

"But that's wrong—it must be wrong! One should hold fast and stand firm, as Uncle John would put it—one should stick to one's principles and never compromise them just to do the done thing!"

"I agree," said Anna, "but older people would laugh at us, wouldn't they? Older people wouldn't understand."

"Older people," I said, "are too busy living a lie and calling it their moral duty," and at that point I thought of Uncle John, incarcerated apparently of his own free will in that soul-destroying house in Eaton Walk.

V

Uncle John fulfilled his threat to conspire with the Steinbergs to ruin our happiness in order to "protect" us from each other, but because they were clever people who realized their greatest mistake would be to forbid us to see each other, our separation was achieved by more subtle means. First of all the Steinbergs made Anna promise that she would on no account marry before her eighteenth birthday which was then still over a year away. That gave them the necessary time to combine with Uncle John to wage their war of attrition. The Steinbergs had no objection to me in principle; they had long since reconciled themselves to the fact that I wasn't Jewish, and in social terms I was undeniably a good catch for Anna, but they were as fervent as Uncle John in believing that we shouldn't marry too young.

"Never mind, we'll simply elope later than we originally planned," I said to Anna, but I was privately annoyed that the Steinbergs had played on her filial feelings with such skill, and it was hard to control my anger with the older generation as we settled down to survive the war of attrition.

Anna returned to school soon after that. I saw her once in the Easter holidays, but then my mother whisked me away to the Continent for a month to "broaden my mind" (a repulsive euphemism, I considered, for detaching me from Anna). I began my tour of Europe by sulking beneath the Eiffel Tower but presently I fell in love with Versailles, and to my reluctance I began to enjoy myself. We wandered on via ravishing Switzerland to mesmerizing Italy. Naturally I sent Anna a postcard every day, but by the time I reached Florence I found I wanted to do more than write postcards. I began to jot down notes for a new novel, and despite missing Anna intensely I grew steadily happier in that unique, utterly satisfying way which can come only from putting pen to paper and exercising one's imagination. Meanwhile my mother was promising to take me to Venice and generally treating me with the deference due from one adult to another. She made me order the meals in restaurants, instruct taxi drivers and distribute all the necessary tips. I began to feel about thirty, and it was not unpleasant. It was far better than feeling, as I always did in Uncle John's presence, like a recalcitrant child doomed to perpetual immaturity.

"So you see you don't have to get married to achieve independence, darling," said my mother as we traveled back to England.

I gave her an appalled look but kept my mouth shut. Did she really imagine I wanted to marry simply to demonstrate my independence? I did not need to make a demonstration. When I came into my inheritance the following November the facts would speak for themselves, and later my marriage would be a celebration, not a demonstration, of my status as master of Oxmoon.

However my eighteenth birthday was still some months away, and as soon as I returned home I was plunged into the final revisions necessary before I took my Higher Certificate examinations. Simon was worried because I had been neglecting my studies during the furor over Anna, but I was sure a little hard cramming would see me through, and besides...I didn't want Uncle John to know that I had fallen behind in my work.

Cramming meant I had no time to write more than a few words to Anna each day, but she was working hard too so our formerly voluminous correspondence degenerated into cryptic notes. I realized sourly that my mother was pleased by this so as soon as the exams were over I took care to write screeds again.

The summer holidays arrived but we only had time for a quick meeting at the Blue Rabbit before my mother took charge of my life once more; we visited Uncle Edmund's estate in Kent before whirling up to Aunt Daphne's place in Scotland where a large house party was in progress. Cousin Harry, who had also taken his

Higher Certificate exams, was there with Uncle John, Aunt Constance and Francesca, and after talking to him I realized what a hash I had made of my Latin paper. Cousin Harry was planning to go up to Oxford in the autumn to read Greats. I was still too young for Oxford and would have a year to fill in first, but Uncle John said he could think of plenty of things for me to do while I waited.

I shuddered, but the sheer awfulness of Aunt Daphne's house party prevented me from dwelling on his threat for long. I yearned to write; I was lusting to develop the notes that I had jotted down in Florence, but time and privacy were in short supply at Aunt Daphne's that August and I found myself becoming more and more frustrated. Finally, locking myself in my room away from the mindless girls who bored me and the kindly married women whom I now—thanks to Uncle John—found extremely sinister, I scribbled myself into a state of exhaustion until Uncle John said I was being rude. After that I did try to participate in all the stupid social activities, but to compensate myself I got up at four in the morning and put in five hours before breakfast. I didn't mind doing this but by the time evening came I was wilting and once I even dozed off at the dinner table.

"Honestly, darling," said my mother, who knew quite well what was going on, "can't the masterpiece wait till you get back to Oxmoon?"

"No," I said. When I'm obsessed I'm unstoppable, and as I saw my mother give me a very strange look indeed I sensed she was recognizing this secret side of my personality which had been stealthily developing as I grew older. "Darling," she said uneasily, "you must be wary of obsessions, you know. Writing's a delightful hobby but you mustn't let it take over your life. That would be an escape from reality—that would be running away."

"Rubbish!" I said without a second's hesitation. "It's this idiotic house party which is the escape from reality! What you're pleased to call my obsession is the only thing that's real here!"

My mother went white. I thought she was angry and at once I began to stammer an apology for my frankness which I now realized must have sounded abominably rude, but I broke off when I realized she wasn't listening. She had moved to the window. Beyond her across the loch I could see the towering slopes of Ben Nevis shimmering in the summer sun.

"I have been here before," said my mother, and pressed the palms of her hands against her cheeks as if deeply disturbed.

I suddenly realized this conversation had become like no conversation I had ever had with her. I was so accustomed to being in tune with my mother that I had come to take our harmony for granted, yet now all I could hear was the discord. For a brief vile moment I felt wholly cut off from her, as if a door had been closed between us.

"Mum—"

"Kester, you must stop being so obsessive," she said, letting her hands fall as she turned to face me. She spoke in a low rapid emotional voice which I found both embarrassing and alarming. "I can't bear these obsessions."

"What do you mean?" I was stupefied.

"Oh, your obsession with that girl, your obsession with writing, your obsession

548

with Oxmoon—it's just so—so alien to me, I've never brought you up to be like that, how can you be like that when you're like me, everyone says you're like me, everyone." She got a grip on herself, and not a moment too soon. To my horror I realized she was on the verge of tears. "I'm sorry," she whispered. "I'm sorry. I'll be all right in a minute."

After a pause I said, "I just don't understand why you should be so upset."

"No. Well, your father had his obsessions too, Kester, and they didn't make him very happy."

"But—"

"One day," she said, staring out of the window, her eyes still bright with tears, "I'm going to have to talk to you about him."

"The very last thing I want," I said at once, "is for you to upset yourself by thinking you're under some repellent maternal duty to rake over the painful past. I know you and Daddy were miserable when I was growing up, I know he could be an absolute bastard—but that doesn't matter now, none of it matters, because I'm old enough to see beyond the results of that ghastly illness to the Truth, and the Truth, the beautiful romantic Truth which must always triumph over vile reality—is that my father wasn't a bastard at all, he was a hero who fought tooth and nail to get me Oxmoon and who had this dazzling romance with you, and *that's* Beauty and *that's* Truth and *that* cancels out all the awfulness that came later."

My mother began to cry quietly to herself. This was so unlike her usual passionate exhibitions of emotion that I felt frightened.

"And anyway," I said, my fear making me sound rude and defiant, "what exactly were these obsessions of his which made him unhappy?"

But my mother merely wept without replying.

"I don't believe they made him unhappy at all," I said. "I think if he was unhappy it was because other people called them obsessions and told him they weren't the done thing."

My mother broke down utterly.

I couldn't bear to see her so upset. It was easier to pretend she was being very silly and deserved to be left alone.

I walked out.

VI

"Mum, I'm sorry I walked out on you but I was rattled because you were being so unlike yourself. Why don't you tell me now about Daddy? Then maybe you'll feel better."

"Oh no," said my mother. "Not now. I can't."

"But why not? You always tell me everything! You've always been so truthful and honest!"

Tears welled in her eyes again.

"Oh, for God's sake, Mum!"

"Yes, I will tell you," she said rapidly, "I'll tell you everything one day, but you must let me choose my moment. I told Declan everything when we were reconciled, and he understood, he accepted everything and forgave me—it was terrible for Declan, terrible, when I married Robert—"

"I don't want to discuss Declan." I turned away.

"Kester, the day you can discuss Declan is the day when you'll be old enough to understand my two marriages and hear what I have to say."

"I have no interest whatsoever in hearing anything about your first marriage. That's got nothing to do with me. *I just don't want to know.*"

She bowed her head in silence.

"Now for the last time, Mum, what were these obsessions of my father's?"

The silence lengthened.

I went away.

VII

"Are you sure you want me to be honest with you?" said Aunt Julie a week later.

"You've got to be. Mum can't. She can't bear to think that the great love of her life ended in tragedy, and every time she tries to speak of my father the tragic memories overwhelm her."

It was September. My mother and I had at last retreated from Scotland to London so that she could raid Harrods and assault the auction rooms, but before she could get into her stride we had bumped into an old American friend of hers who had immediately invited her to a nightclub. This was not an unusual occurrence; my mother often met old friends who took her to nightclubs, but this man was much younger than she was and looked like a vulgar version of Clark Gable, and I at once decided such an outing would be most improper.

"You ought to think of your reputation, Mum," I said severely later as we returned to the hotel. "I mean, *I* understand that you wouldn't do anything vile, but other people might think—" I stopped. It had occurred to me for the first time that other people might be right. To my horror, I realized that my mother fell into the Uncle John category of Married Women (subdivision Merry Widows) and—bearing in mind her self-confessed enthusiasm for copulation—might well be capable of considerable iniquity.

Misery overwhelmed me. The world suddenly seemed quite unbearable. "I want to go back to Oxmoon," I said.

"Oh pet, do buck up and stop being such a blight on the landscape! I know— I'll ring Julie. Perhaps she can take you out to dinner and cheer you up."

I protested with dignity that I was perfectly capable of spending the evening on my own, but I was secretly pleased. After all, Aunt Julie was a real person, not just a cipher in one of Uncle John's revolting categories, and that meant I didn't have to shy away from her for fear she might have some sinister purpose in view. She also happened to understand all about the importance of Beauty, Truth, Art and Peace, although this for the moment seemed barely relevant; for me now the most vital fact about Aunt Julie was that she had known my father in the days before he became ill.

"Be honest with me, Aunt Julie."

"Very well. But that means I must start by saying I didn't like him."

"Why not?"

"He didn't like women. Don't misunderstand; he was sexually normal—your mother would hardly have been attracted to him if he wasn't—but I always thought he loved her not because she was a woman but in spite of it."

This was so alarming that I said the first thing that came into my head. "But he did love her, didn't he?"

"Yes," said Aunt Julie. "He did. And they had the most extraordinary and remarkable relationship."

I relaxed. This was exactly what I wanted to hear. "All right, now tell me about these obsessions of his."

"Well, my dear, I hardly knew him well enough to provide a comprehensive catalogue, but I could see he had an obsession-prone personality. It was as if life were just one long endless competition in which he always had to win and emerge as top dog. He was an extremely successful man, as you know, but I don't think his success meant all that much to him. It was merely an exercise in *amour-propre*."

"How peculiar." I was much intrigued. "So what you're saying is—"

"I'm saying his obsessions were all tied up with his desire to be top dog. He couldn't go to Oxford without wanting a double first. He couldn't take up politics without wanting to be Prime Minister. He couldn't take up mountaineering without wanting to climb Mount Everest. And of course, he couldn't fall in love with your mother without wanting both a grand passion *and* a fairy tale."

"But this is wonderful!" I exclaimed, suddenly seeing my father's glittering life from an angle that I could completely understand. "He dreamed of perfection and made his dreams reality! He was an idealist—a romantic!"

Aunt Julie stared at me. "How very perceptive of you," she said at last. "People thought he was so cold and cynical—but of course there's no one so cold and cynical as a romantic idealist who's been deprived of his romantic dreams."

"Yes, I can see now just how awful the illness must have been for him. It makes the tragedy more vile than ever."

Aunt Julie hesitated. I was aware of her hesitating, and in that moment some sixth sense told me I was within sight of dangerous waters. But before I could turn my back on them Aunt Julie said casually, "The illness was certainly a tragedy, Kester, but it's not impossible that your father may have seen it as imposing a solution on problems he couldn't solve."

551

"But surely he had no problems before the illness," I said. "All his dreams came true."

"Not quite all," said Aunt Julie.

There was a pause. Then I said, "Which ones—"

"Oh, your mother would know about that better than I do," said Aunt Julie. "But I could see he was a troubled man, and I suspect that this was why he staged his massive retreat into mountaineering."

"Massive retreat? Wait a minute, I knew he liked climbing but I thought that was just a hobby!"

"Hardly. He wanted to abandon both his career and his London life in order to devote himself entirely to climbing."

"Good God!" I stared at her. I was deeply, powerfully interested. "But that wouldn't have been the done thing at all!"

"That wouldn't have bothered him. He was like a man in the grip of a mystical vision."

"How absolutely magnificent!" I now had my back to the dangerous waters and had returned to comfortingly familiar territory. I polished off the rest of my wine. "Well," I said, "what a hero!" And then a thought occurred to me, just a little thought, not a thought that one would worry about but just a little idea that one might possibly want to cogitate upon at some time in the very remote future, and I heard myself say, "But Mum wouldn't have liked that at all."

"No," said Aunt Julie. "I'm afraid she didn't."

"Well, never mind," I said at once. "Despite everything they had this remarkable relationship which cancelled out all the unhappiness, and oh God, how wonderful Beauty and Truth are, redeeming the ghastliness of life and bringing one closer to God—to the divine—to heaven...Lord, I must be drunk! I *am* sorry! I've recently discovered that I get drunk far too easily."

Aunt Julie patted my hand and signaled to the waiter for the bill. "I'll take you back to your hotel."

Halfway to Kensington Gardens in Aunt Julie's little Austin I said suddenly, "Does Mum have affairs with these beastly men who keep taking her to nightclubs?"

"Why don't you ask her?" said Aunt Julie. "I'm sure she'd be truthful."

"That's what I'm afraid of," I said.

We drew up at the hotel but before I could thank Aunt Julie for her considerable kindness to me that evening, she said abruptly, "Your mother's had a tough life in some ways, Kester. Her first husband was shot before her eyes; her second took nine years to die; for a long time she never saw Declan; Robin died in that ghastly accident. When you think of all that, does the occasional visit to a nightclub really seem so important?"

It didn't. I knew that but could not find the words to tell her so.

Aunt Julie patted my hand again before adding: "Guard against jealousy—that was a great failing of your father's. Guard against all those strong violent feelings which gave him so much trouble, and be patient with your mother. I think in the end she'll be glad you're like him as well as her—she'll eventually see it as romantic, and then perhaps the past pain will die a little and it'll be easier for her to talk to you about him."

I kissed her, swore to be patient and tottered away into the hotel to sleep off the unfortunate effects of too much Nuits St. Georges.

VIII

"I've decided I've been very naughty and very silly," said my mother the next morning as we breakfasted in her room, "and I want to tell you everything about your father."

"Oh no," I said at once. "That's not necessary."

She stared at me. "Not necessary?"

"No. I know everything I need to know, thank you, so we can consider the matter closed."

There was a long, long silence. Presently she lit a cigarette, I poured myself some more tea and we went on sitting there together, watching the rain fall over Kensington Gardens.

In the end my mother said, "Last night outside the nightclub there was an old busker playing a Strauss waltz, and as I watched him I thought how odd it was that most people hear only the gaiety in Viennese music. But I think Strauss wrote about sadness, and if you listen hard you can hear the melancholy beyond that romantic facade."

"I can't hear it," I said, "and what's more, I don't want to. It's the romance that's important, not the melancholy."

She smiled suddenly, her dark eyes brilliant with an emotion I could not read. "I'd like to believe that," she said, "and maybe, despite all the awful things that have happened to me, I still do. That would be a triumph, wouldn't it? What a victory over disillusionment and despair!"

"I don't want to talk about vile things like disillusionment and despair."

"No, it's all right, pet, I understand. We'll turn it into just another bridge that has to be crossed later, and then for the moment at least we won't have to bother about it anymore."

IX

It was soon after we returned from London that I began to find my circumstances intolerable. It turned out I'd made a hash of my Higher Certificate; I had done well in English Literature, but I had barely scraped a pass in History and in Latin I had failed altogether. Uncle John said I should have followed Harry's example by waiting till I was eighteen before taking the examination—and Harry, needless to say, had achieved three superb passes and won an open scholarship to Oxford.

I loathed him.

"Well, Kester," said Uncle John, "you must spend the next year concentrating on your studies—we'll have to postpone those lessons in estate management, but never mind, I hardly expected you to run Oxmoon single-handed as soon as you turned eighteen."

I loathed him too. My magic birthday was fast being reduced to just another day in the schoolroom.

"But I can have a checkbook, can't I," I said, "as soon as I'm eighteen?"

Uncle John gave me a cool look and said stuffily, "I'm sure some suitable arrangement can be made to reflect both your majority and your apparent inability to live within your allowance. I understand you owe your mother twenty-three pounds seven and six."

I had been betrayed. My mother joined the list of the loathed.

"Damn it, Uncle John, why shouldn't I owe my mother a few pounds if she's willing to lend them to me! After all, I *am* master of Oxmoon!"

"All the more reason why you shouldn't get into debt."

I immediately wanted to go out and spend thousands.

My eighteenth birthday was eventually celebrated in ghastly Godwin style by a dinner party for my relatives and various old friends of the family. The one redeeming feature was that Cousin Harry was absent. He was doing so well at Oxford that it was quite impossible for him to tear himself away.

I was beginning to have very serious reservations about going up to Oxford. Uncle John would use the fact that I was a student to keep me in leading strings for another three years, and besides the last thing I wanted was to be in a place where I would be continually outdazzled by Cousin Harry. Could I go to Cambridge instead? No, because Uncle John would want to know why I refused to go to Oxford and might indeed even humiliate me by guessing the truth. I decided to forgo a university education altogether, even though it might have been fun to live with Anna among "the dreaming spires." After all, what was university? Just an extended version of school, and Ricky Mowbray had told me that Oxford was full of public-school louts who should have been exterminated on the playing fields of Eton.

"I hear that pansy Ricky Mowbray got sent down from Oxford," remarked Thomas to my mother. "What was the trouble? Buggery in the quadrangles?"

"You'd better be careful, Thomas," said my mother coldly. "You could be sued for spreading that kind of slander. Ricky came down from Oxford of his own free will, and there's never been any hint that he misbehaved in the way you suggest."

But I knew Ricky better than she did. I was sixteen when Ricky came down from Oxford and confessed to me.

"The truth was I just couldn't stand being away from you, Kes. . . . I was so miserable . . . missed you so much . . . I can't help it, I'm terribly in love with you."

A nightmare. I panicked, retreated into brutality. "Gosh, Ricky, if I were going to be in love with a man I'd certainly be in love with you, but I never get physically excited unless I think about Anna."

Embarrassment. Agony on both sides. Shame.

"Don't betray me, Kes. Promise. I'll never bother you again, I swear it."

"Oh, don't be so stupid, Ricky! Of course I'd never betray a friend!"

"Can I still be your friend?"

"Why on earth not?" I said, feeling desperately sorry for him, but I was relieved when he went away to France for a year to study at the University of Grenoble, and even more relieved when he returned home apparently quite recovered from his humiliating aberration.

"I *am* sorry I was such a certifiable oaf, Kes—I honestly think Oxford sent me right round the bend! However all that's over now and I've developed a penchant for blue-eyed blondes. How's your cousin Erika?"

Erika, who had been taking a cookery course in London, was back in Gower and nearly dying of boredom. I wished Ricky luck, but was somewhat less than forthcoming when he inquired about Anna. I had decided to tell no one, not even my closest friend, about my unbroken determination to elope as soon as Anna was eighteen.

She was now seventeen and a half. Six months to go.

June came. I sat for my Higher Certificate again, but this time I found the papers easy and knew I'd done well. Uncle John began to talk of Oxford but I merely listened politely; I was determined to give no hint that I was about to slash myself free of my leading strings in one grand glorious romantic gesture and celebrate my long-awaited independence in the biggest possible way.

In July Anna arrived home after her final term at school, and we met the next day at the Blue Rabbit to draw up our final plans.

She spent her birthday with her parents. We thought that was only fair to them, but on the morning of the twenty-fifth of July we caught the train to London and headed north to Gretna Green.

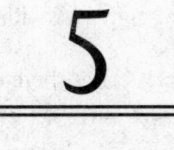

5

I

BEFORE I left Oxmoon, I wrote a note which read: *Dear Mum, I've gone off to marry Anna. Don't be too livid. I'm the sort of man who only falls in love once and this is it. Sorry I can't wait till I'm twenty-five, but I think my father would have married you when he was eighteen too if you hadn't run off with Mr. Kinsella in order to escape from that engagement to Sir Timothy Appleby. I doubt if he was really all that keen on any of those mistresses you mentioned. I certainly wouldn't have been. Anyway, remember him and forgive me. Back in six weeks. Much love,* KESTER.

Gretna Green turned out to be a humdrum town, despite its romantic fame as a center of clandestine marriages, but I had plenty of money (my bank manager Mr. Lloyd-Thomas had been most accommodating, such a refreshing change from Uncle John), so at least we were able to entertain ourselves in style as we established our Scottish residency. I hired a motor; every day we explored the pretty countryside, while every evening we would linger over a substantial dinner before drifting upstairs for the night. (Of course we had separate bedrooms.)

We were just thinking that marriage must surely be an anticlimax after such perfect bliss when we returned from our afternoon picnic to find a familiar M.G. parked in the forecourt.

"Oh God!" I said in horror as Rory emerged from the hotel with a triumphant expression on his face.

"What shall we do?" said Anna, panicking.

"Hold fast! Stand firm!" I said, resorting to Uncle John's favorite Imperialist war cry, but I was quailing at the thought of my family conspiring to save me from myself. Halting the car I got out. Rory blazed over to me. "You little fool!" he shouted. "I've come to bring you home! You've broken your mother's heart!"

"Dear me," I said, "just like Rupert of Hentzau!" And when I heard Anna laugh I felt my courage return.

"Now look here, my lad—"

"Oh, shut up, Rory—go back to sponging off your rich wife and leave me alone!"

Rory stared at me as if I'd grown horns and a tail. I was in ecstasy. I suddenly had a vision of a future in which I would say exactly what I liked to all the members of my family who had so irked me in the past.

"Will you excuse us, please?" said Rory to Anna. "I'd better talk to my brother on his own."

"As far as I'm concerned you're not my brother," I said. "If Mum hadn't gone off her head and married an Irish gangster you wouldn't even exist!"

"Christ!" said Rory, scarlet with rage. "My father was ten times the man Robert ever was—"

"Oh, go and spin your fairy tales somewhere else!"

"You're the one who's spinning a fairy tale if you think your father made our mother happy!"

I knocked him down.

Anna gasped.

Rory was too stunned to speak. He sat on the ground and shook his head rapidly as if to clear his vision. Across the forecourt by the hotel entrance I saw the porter scurry inside to broadcast news of a crisis.

"Go to hell," I said to Rory, "and bloody well leave us alone."

Rory growled in rage to conceal his humiliation, shouted, "You silly little bugger, I'm going to take you home even if I have to do it by force!" and staggered

556

to his feet to attempt to carry out his threat. He was shorter than I was but broader and heavier. However too much drinking had made him flabby, and I had the youth and agility he lacked. We fought furiously together. Anna jumped out of the car and begged us to stop, but we took no notice and in the end we were separated only by the combined efforts of the hotel manager, both porters and the boot boy.

The police arrived.

Hours of tedium followed. Rory and I were charged with a breach of the peace and spent the night in separate cells at the police station. Rory was allowed a telephone call, and after an all-night drive in the chauffeur-driven Rolls-Royce Uncle John arrived at Gretna Green just ahead of a gang of journalists who had realized that a junior member of *Burke's Landed Gentry* was trying—futilely— to elope with style and good taste.

More tedious hours passed. Uncle John's *aides-de-camp* handled the press. Uncle John's solicitor handled the police. Eventually the charges were dropped, and back at the hotel Uncle John himself prepared to mop up the rest of the mess.

"I'd be obliged if you'd return to London, Rory," he said in a voice that made his son-in-law cringe. "I've no wish for you to prolong your disastrous presence here."

Rory slunk away. If I hadn't been so consumed with nervousness on my own account I might even have felt sorry for him.

The moment had now come. It was without doubt the most crucial moment of my life so far. Did I assert my independence or did I allow Uncle John to reduce me once more to the level of a recalcitrant child? I was beside myself with fright as we confronted each other, but beyond all my terror I was aware of an iron determination not to give way.

"Well, Kester," said Uncle John, his glance flickering around my little bedroom with such distaste that it instantly became as drab and sordid as the current state of my elopement, "this is a very unfortunate situation."

"It was all right," I said, "before everyone tried to interfere." To my horror my voice shook.

"I'm sorry—I was under the impression that my interference at least was essential; after all I've just extracted you from a police cell and saved you from a great deal of unpleasantness. However, that's of no consequence. If the price I have to pay for saving you is your anger and resentment, then I've no alternative but to pay it. Now—" He paused to draw together the shreds of his patience. "—I must tell you that as Rory's pleas have had no effect, your mother wants to prevent the marriage by making you a ward of court, but I would strongly urge you to come home with me so that this step is rendered unnecessary."

"I'm not going home till I'm married."

"I don't think you quite understand. Once you're a ward of court you can be jailed for contempt if you disobey the court's order forbidding you to marry."

"Then I'll go to jail. But I'm getting married and no one's going to stop me."

"I'm sure that if you come home quietly now your mother will agree to a formal engagement—"

"No. I've waited long enough. I'm waiting no longer."

"But—"

"That's my decision and I'm sticking to it."

"—if only I could convince you to—"

"No."

"—postpone your plans for a while—"

"Never!"

I faced him. We were the same height. I looked him straight in the eyes and finally he said, "I wish your father were alive to talk to you. Robert found the reality of marrying his childhood sweetheart rather different, I think, from the romantic dreams of his adolescence."

"This is no mere romantic dream," I said. "I'm marrying for friendship, and personally I think that's extremely realistic and practical. It's certainly a lot less foolish and misguided than to marry for sex and social position as so many people seem to do."

Uncle John said nothing.

"Personally," I said, looking him up and down, "I think the real obscenity is to marry for money. If Anna were an heiress and I were pretending to love her in order to further my ambition, that would be so despicable that you'd have every right to interfere."

Uncle John remained silent. But he was very white.

"Friendship lasts longer than sex," I said. "Everyone says so. And friendship, real friendship, is something money and social position can't buy. Anyway, I *love* Anna—I love her without illusion, without pretense and without deceit—and how many men could say that on the eve of a trip to the altar? Could you, in fact, have said as much before you married either Aunt Blanche or Aunt Constance?"

Absolute silence.

"And don't you try and fling my parents' marriage in my face," I said, "because I don't believe you know anything about it. Maybe I don't know so much about it either, but one fact I do know and that's the one fact you can't deny: they were old friends who loved each other and she stuck by him to the end. So don't tell me not to marry for friendship. And don't tell me my father would ever have stood in my way."

Uncle John turned aside. He had now been silent for a very, very long time. I stared at his profile but of course, as always in moments of complex emotion, it was inscrutable. I went on watching him, I went on listening to my heart hammering in my chest and slowly, very slowly I began to realize that I had won.

At last he said without looking at me, "Very well. I'll tell your mother not to make you a ward of court," and he moved towards the door.

I tried to thank him but he cut me off. "I wish you well," he said, finally managing to look at me. "I hope you'll be happy. I've nothing else to say."

The door opened. The door closed. I sank down on the bed. I covered my face with my hands. I cried. So might William the Conqueror have wept after Hastings.

Then feeling about seven feet tall and fit to conquer the rest of the world I dashed away my tears, surged to my feet on a tidal wave of euphoria and raced off to find Anna and order champagne.

II

As soon as our three weeks' residency had been completed we rushed to be married, I in a plain dark suit, Anna in a short white dress, and as I slipped the ring onto her finger I thought: *I won!* I was in ecstasy, so was she, and immediately the deed was done we jumped into our hired car and headed north. Anna wanted to take the Road to the Isles because it sounded so romantic, and that night after a breathtaking journey west through the mountains we arrived at Mallaig where I had reserved a room in the little hotel that faced across the harbor to Skye.

I wrote *Mr. and Mrs. Christopher Godwin* in the register and stood gazing at the words in disbelief. Anna sighed and revolved her new ring as if to make sure it hadn't faded away. Meanwhile the receptionist, who had at first leaped to the conclusion that we were unmarried, decided we were so obviously newlyweds that there was no point in her continuing to look tight-lipped. We were advised kindly that dinner was at eight and a wish was expressed that our stay would be a happy one. Since unhappiness was inconceivable we beamed at her but made no comment. The porter showed us to our room. After his departure we stood hand in hand by the window and gazed at the sea, bathed in the golden light of evening, and at the purple-shadowed shores of Skye across the water.

Later we tried to eat dinner but lost interest after one course. We attempted a stroll along the harbor but soon lost interest in that too. Back in our room we sat on the bed and stared at each other.

"Shall we do it or not?" I said anxiously. I was terrified of ruining her happiness.

Anna considered the question carefully and said with her usual good sense, "Let's have a go. If we don't—"

"—it'll be hanging over us like the sword of Damocles. All right, let's do it," I said, resigned. "I expect it's really quite easy. Think of all the fools who have made it a lifelong occupation."

We took it in turns to undress and visit the bathroom, and by the time I returned from an absentminded encounter with my toothbrush, Anna was in bed. She was wearing a plain blue sleeveless nightgown with a high neck and looked about twelve. Glancing in the glass I saw an awkward, profoundly unattractive youth who looked as if he were about to go to the dentist.

"God, I'm white with fright!" I said, appalled.

"So am I!"

We saw the humorous side of the situation at exactly the same moment and we both began to laugh.

"Oh, Lord, Anna!" I gasped at last. "I must keep a straight face or else I'll never be able to drum up the necessary passion!"

"Heavens, do you have to beat a drum?"

Laughter overwhelmed us again as we visualized some ancient tom-tom secreted in my pajama trousers, but finally I managed to say, "Oh, Anna, I do love you!"

"And I love you," she said, hugging me, "and quite honestly I don't mind if you beat the drum or not because it's just so wonderful to laugh and be happy with you."

That settled it. The drum immediately began to thunder in my ears, and as all laughter was set aside at last, I knew, with an absolute certainty, that everything was going to be all right.

III

"In retrospect," I said as we lay dreamily in bed the next morning, "what did you think of it?"

"Very peculiar," said Anna, "but I can see it has possibilities. In fact once I'd got over thinking I was going to die I enjoyed feeling so close to you."

I sighed. As usual we were in complete agreement. "I thought it was jolly nice," I said. "Mum was right as usual." Yawning pleasurably I sat up and stretched myself. "Oh well, that's that—I'm glad we've got it over with. Now we can relax and start enjoying ourselves."

A mail boat sailed from Mallaig to the Inner Hebrides, and one day we set out on the ten-hour voyage which took us past Skye to the most beautiful islands I had ever seen. The weather was extraordinarily changeable; one moment the boat would be drenched by gusts of rain and the next the sun would be shining from a clear northern sky. It rained at the port of Kyleakin across the water, but as we left the Isle of Skye the weather cleared and by the time we reached the Isle of Eigg I was on deck in my shirt sleeves. We anchored off Kildonan as a small boat drew out to relieve us of the mail and supplies, but soon we were off again, sailing around the coast, swaying up and down on that dark and splendid sea.

"Isn't this wonderful?" I shouted to Anna above the wind as the boat inched past the great Sgurr of Eigg which rose from the beach towards the clouds.

"*Wonderful!*"

We watched the view for a little longer before Anna said, "I'll just see what's happening on the other side," and crossed the deck to the opposite rail. Her reaction was dramatic. "Oh Kester, look—*look!*"

I ran to join her, and there ahead of me I saw the grandest seascape I had ever seen. Huge mountains rose sheer from the white foam, their summits wreathed in shifting clouds, their slopes glittering in the sun, and as I stared, struck dumb with awe, a squall hit the water ahead of us and the next moment a double rainbow stretched unbroken from the Sgurr of Eigg to crown those mystical peaks which lay ahead of us across the sea.

I grabbed the nearest deckhand to ask him the name of the mountains and he replied in his soft Highland voice, "Ah, those are the Coolins of Rhum."

I knew I was in the presence of perfection, and at once all the pain and horror of the world faded into insignificance. Physically I was still standing on the deck of that mail boat, but spiritually I was in the presence of eternal truths beside which all worldly preoccupations were futile.

"I want to feel like this when I look at Oxmoon," I said to Anna. "I want to make it so beautiful and so perfect that long after I'm dead people will gaze at it and catch a glimpse of eternity."

Anna's hand slipped into mine. The boat plunged on to the rainbow's end where Kinloch Castle, the celebrated stately home of Rhum, overlooked a sheltered bay.

"At last—Zenda!" said Anna, laughing, and that was when I knew I was in Ruritania with my princess, just as I had always longed to be; that was when I knew I had the power to make all my dreams come true.

I remember thinking: Making one's dreams come true is simply an attitude of mind.

IV

We spent two glorious weeks wandering all over the Inner and Outer Hebrides, but eventually we drove south, returned our hired motor and caught the train to London. As we had been living so simply I thought we could afford a touch of extravagance so I wired my kind, sympathetic bank manager Mr. Lloyd-Thomas for extra money and we settled down in a suite at the Savoy. It made an engaging change to sip champagne and nibble caviar in a room liberally decorated with red roses.

"It's so romantic!" sighed Anna as we held hands and watched the dusk fall over the Thames, and I agreed with her. I even wondered if it would be too much of an anticlimax to propose the possibility of sex, but the sumptuous triple bed suggested to me that the atmosphere of romance could be sustained without trouble, and as it turned out I was not deceived.

"Wonderful!" breathed Anna, and immediately my mind was at work to form a new equation to supplement the basic equation of my life (Kester plus Oxmoon equals bliss; Kester minus Oxmoon equals misery). This time I thought: Caviar plus champagne plus red roses plus the Savoy equals marvelous sex equals Anna thinking I'm wonderful equals me feeling more heroic than any Godwin who's ever lived. I tried to abbreviate this by amending it to Lavish spending equals Anna in bliss equals me in ecstasy, but that sounded too mercenary, so I told myself instead: Being master of Oxmoon (that, after all, enabled me to spend

561

lavishly) plus having Anna (without whom no sex or romance would be possible) equals Success (whether or not I ever published a novel). After enduring many years in the company of people who thought me a freak doomed to failure, I now decided I was rather partial to being a huge success in life.

"I say, Anna . . . shall we do it again?"

"Oh yes! At least . . . is it possible?"

"Apparently."

"Gosh, you must be superhuman!"

I modestly disclaimed superhuman powers but was secretly thrilled. I only wished I'd had the nerve to ask Uncle John how many times it was possible to copulate in a single night. I felt in the mood for breaking records.

"No wonder those grown-ups used to worry about us, Kester. If we'd known sex could be like this—"

"Exactly. We'll have to forgive them for being so awful," I agreed, and the next day, full of benign concern for our parents, we sent them telegrams to announce our imminent return to Wales.

Dr. and Mrs. Steinberg were waiting to meet us at the station when we arrived in Swansea the next day. Mrs. Steinberg was so overcome with emotion that she had forgotten all her English and I found myself being embraced amidst torrents of German. Anna wept happily. Mrs. Steinberg wept happily. Dr. Steinberg said, "Jolly good," which seemed to be the only English phrase he could remember, and then he wept happily too.

I thought of Uncle John lecturing me about the virtues of a stiff upper lip and thanked God I had married into a Jewish family.

"What's the news from Oxmoon?" I inquired when we had all recovered sufficiently to conduct a normal conversation.

"I shall drive us there now," said my new father-in-law. "Your mother has been most charming and friendly. We're invited to drinks to celebrate your return."

This sounded promising. I was glad my mother had recovered from the paroxysm of rage that had driven her to threaten me with a wardship of court.

We drove out of Swansea, and because of my prolonged absence I seemed to see Gower with new eyes. What struck me most, after the vast stark ravishing wastes of Scotland, was how diverse beautiful little Gower was, sixteen slender miles of infinite variety set in a changeless yet ever-changing sea. Gower had everything, cliffs, sands, tidal causeways, estuaries, moors, miniature mountains, woods, fields, farms, villages, churches, megalithic monuments, Norman castles, eighteenth-century mansions, medieval manors, a romantic history and even, as its gateway, glorious Swansea, the plain woman with "It," lounging on her *chaise longue* of hills above the Neapolitan curve of Swansea Bay. As Rhossili Downs became visible in the distance I squeezed Anna's hand and whispered with pride as well as joy, "Nearly home."

"Home," said Anna. "Home." She sounded as if she could hardly believe her good fortune, and greatly touched I leaned over to give her a kiss. In the front seat Mrs. Steinberg saw us and wiped away another tear.

Dr. Steinberg hooted the horn three times as we passed through the gates of

Oxmoon. "Your mother's instructions!" he called, smiling at us in the mirror, and glancing up the drive I saw all the servants trooping out of the front door. As Lowell chivied them into line, my mother, massive in purple like some neo-Roman empress, stood framed formidably in the doorway.

"What's happening?" whispered Anna in wonder.

"Good God, Mum's turned up trumps! It's the royal reception, darling—Mum's acknowledging us as master and mistress of Oxmoon!"

Dr. Steinberg managed to halt the car but he was in such a state that he stalled the engine. We lurched forward, startling Lowell who had been about to open the passenger door.

"Good afternoon, sir," he said when I had recovered sufficiently to scramble out. "Good afternoon, madam. On behalf of all the servants I would like to welcome you home to Oxmoon and express the hope that you'll be very happy here. Sir, may we offer you our best wishes for the future and our sincerest congratulations."

"Thank you, Lowell," I said. "That's very decent of you." I piloted Anna past the row of servants who all bowed or curtsied. Anna was nervous, but when Cook's small daughter presented her with a bouquet of flowers she smiled with genuine pleasure, and I knew all was well.

I took up a masterful position on the porch steps.

"Thank you all for your splendid welcome," I said in Welsh, trying hard to get the accent right, and added in English: "My wife's much looking forward to living here, and we plan to make Oxmoon the finest house in Wales!"

Everyone looked thrilled. Smiling radiantly I took Anna's hand in mine and steered her up the steps to my mother.

"Hullo, Mum!" I said. "The prodigal returns!"

"Darling!" said my mother richly. "As you can guess, I decided to kill the fatted calf!"

We embraced. I was aware of a gust of perfume, a flutter of long lashes against my cheek and her almost tangible air of satisfaction as she perceived my happiness.

"Oh, I'm wild about fatted calf!" I said. "I hope it's dressed up as a bottle of champagne!"

We laughed. My mother turned to my wife.

"Anna . . . my dear . . ." There was an emotional embrace. "Dear child!" said my mother, releasing her. "At least I can't complain you're a stranger to me!"

I gave her an extra kiss to show her how grateful I was for her determination to let bygones by bygones, and to my surprise she swayed, almost losing her balance.

"Mum! Are you all right?"

"Yes—sorry, darling. No, don't worry, I'm not tight! I've had a couple of dizzy spells this weeks—old age and too much pink gin catching up with me at last, I fear!" said my mother laughing and turned to welcome the Steinbergs as I moved past her into the house.

In the drawing room I found Rory standing sheepishly by the fireplace.

"Now then, you two!" said my mother, much as Mae West, playing the owner of a Wild West bordello, might have addressed two rebellious cowboys. "Shake hands and be friends—no more fights! It doesn't matter who your fathers were—all that matters is that I'm your mother and don't you forget it!"

"She's right, you know," Rory said as we shook hands.

"Of course. She always is."

We looked at her as proudly as if we had created her unaided.

"Open the magnum, Lowell!" purred my mother.

The magnum opened with a well-bred explosion, and a pale gold liquid was soon frothing in six of the best Godwin glasses. As Lowell withdrew, we all stood in a circle and waited for my mother to propose the toast.

"To Kester and Anna—may you live happily ever after!" said my mother conventionally enough, but then exclaimed as if she were a pagan priestess flinging a defiant challenge at the gods: "Long live romance!" and drained her glass to the dregs.

It was a wonderful moment. I can see her now, cancelling out her past tragedies by that last indomitable toast. What a finale! What a triumph! And what a note on which to end.

"Romance!" we all cried in admiration, but even before we could raise our glasses to our lips she had gasped, staggered sideways and collapsed unconscious upon the floor.

God might have dealt my mother a rough hand more than once in her life, but at least at the end He was kind.

V

She was fifty-eight, glamorous to the last in her purple tea gown, but afterwards I thought not of the end of her life, when she had played her final triumphant performance as mistress of Oxmoon, but of the other days which stretched far back into my memory. I saw her in the library with Uncle John, a cigarette dangling from the corner of her mouth as they examined the estate books together; I saw her relaxing on the terrace with a romantic magazine in one hand and a pink gin in the other; I saw her greeting guests, marshaling servants, coping with tenants, sparring with Thomas, receiving fawning bank managers, lawyers and accountants. At an age when most women would have chosen to live quietly on their past memories, my mother had surged into a dynamic new life of hardworking independence. Aunt Julie had been right. The visits to the nightclubs had been of no importance. In the end my mother had been no one's mistress but her own.

I accepted her death yet could not quite believe I would never talk to her again, and the tears which had always sprung to my eyes with such humiliating ease now refused to come.

"The best mother a man ever had..." That was Rory, being emotional just like me, except that my emotions refused to be released. As he wept I found it possible to believe for the first time, without boggling, that we had shared the same mother.

"Kester darling, too tragic—I *am* sorry..." That was Marian, not caring, merely embarrassed by her husband's failure to keep a stiff upper lip. Even Thomas was more sincere than she was. "Ginevra was a bit of a bitch," he said subdued, "but I was fond of the old girl in my way."

A crowd of people arrived from London. Once more the drive was clogged with Bentleys and Rolls-Royces.

"Oxmoon will never be the same again," whispered Uncle Edmund, and Aunt Teddy exclaimed, touching me with her spontaneity, "What a gal! I can't believe she's gone."

"We all wish to express our most heartfelt condolences," droned Aunt Constance, but I never heard the end of her set speech because the next moment I was confronted by Uncle John.

Here was someone who grieved. Here was someone who looked at me and saw far back into the remote past long before I was born. He said one word, my name, and that was all. There was no need for him to say more for no words could have expressed the bereavement reflected in his face and no words could have told me more clearly than the clasp of his hand how absolutely we were connected by our loss.

Everyone was amazed by my composure as with Anna's help I arranged the funeral. Of course I had known at once that my mother had to be buried with my father, her childhood sweetheart, in order that romance could finally triumph over all the ghastly realities she had had to endure, and because of this the burial had become immensely important to me. Although my father had been cremated in Swansea his ashes had been interred in the churchyard at Penhale, and I wanted my mother to be buried beneath the stone that commemorated him.

The telephone started to ring.

I remember that telephone ringing. It was like the bell heralding the final act of a familiar play. But this time, when the curtain went up, I was to find that someone had rewritten the ending.

Lowell took the call in the hall just as I emerged from the library. Rory was already running down the stairs and I knew what that meant. He was expecting a call from Declan.

Declan had left Ireland. Declan had been due to arrive in Swansea that day. Declan was probably now telephoning from the Claremont Hotel, where he had arranged to stay, to confirm that his journey had gone according to plan. He had neither written nor spoken to me and I had neither written nor spoken to him. I had thankfully left all communication to Rory. I knew Declan would have to attend the funeral but I could hardly wait until he had retreated to Ireland and I could shovel him out of my life once and for all.

"Be reasonable!" Rory was saying urgently into the phone. "How the hell can I possibly pave the way for you by breaking the news?" He looked guiltily over his shoulder, saw me, jumped and looked guiltier than ever.

"What's the matter?" I said. My stomach felt as if I had just stepped off a cliff. "What's going on?"

Rory thrust the receiver into my hand. "You talk to him. He's got something to tell you."

I thrust it back. "I don't want to talk to him! What *is* all this?"

Rory said panic-stricken into the receiver: "He's here but he won't speak to you. What shall I do, what shall I—" He stopped. The line had gone dead. "Bloody hell!" said Rory. He replaced the receiver and turned to face me. "He's on his way over here. He says he has to speak to you without delay."

"What about?"

"Well I... Jesus, I... well, I'm damned if I know how to put this, but—"

I gripped him by the shoulders and started shaking him. "What does he want to talk to me about?" I shouted.

"The funeral. It's got to be cancelled. Ma wanted to be buried with my father in Ireland."

VI

So in the end it was not I who went looking for the truth but the truth which came looking for me. I knew, of course, by that time that there was some profound truth lying around which I had not quite grasped, but somehow it had always seemed so much more comfortable not to identify it. Now it had seized me by the scruff of the neck and I was terrified. I felt as if all the myths that had sustained me during my growing up were being wiped out, and in my terror, I panicked. Blundering into the drawing room where my family were assembled I shouted: "Declan wants my mother to be buried in Ireland with Conor Kinsella but I want to announce to you all that this is absolutely not going to happen under any circumstances and if necessary I'll go to law to prevent it!"

Everyone stared at me in appalled silence. I ran up to my room, locked myself in and broke down. I kept saying aloud between sobs, "My poor father, my poor father," as if I had somehow assumed the burden of his past suffering.

"My mother lied to me," I said to Anna, who eventually came tapping at the door to offer comfort. "She never loved him. It was all a romantic myth."

"Oh, but Kester—"

"If she'd loved him," I said fiercely, "she wouldn't have wanted to be buried with Kinsella. This request means she loved Kinsella best. It means... oh, it was all lies, all of it, there was no romance with my father, no grand passion, just a bloody unhappy marriage with nothing, *nothing* to redeem it, and vile reality's triumphed, vile reality's made even those last words of hers a hideous mockery, vile reality's laid waste my beautiful dream and I can't bear it, I feel absolutely destroyed and defiled and contaminated—"

"Darling—"

"All that rubbish about how she fell in love when she was dancing beneath the chandeliers at Oxmoon while the orchestra played 'The Blue Danube'—all lies, all false—'It was the most romantic moment of my life,' she used to say, but that wasn't true, that couldn't have been true because all the time she never loved him, she loved that vile vicious vulgar adventurer who everyone agrees was an absolute bastard—"

"It can't be true, Kester. Your mother wasn't like that."

"I feel as if I never knew her," I said, and suddenly I heard her voice saying years before, when Uncle John had so inexplicably returned to Aunt Constance: "We know so little about even those who are closest to us. We know so little of what really goes on in other people's lives."

Far away in the hall Rory called my name.

"Oh my God," I said, "Declan's here." I peered at my reflection in the looking glass. My eyes were red. "I can't see him, can't face him, I can't, I can't—"

"I'll see him and say you're not well," said Anna at once, and marched bravely to the door with her head held high.

When I looked again in the glass I saw a despicable coward cringing behind his wife because he wasn't man enough to face facts he couldn't alter. A line of much-loved poetry instantly flashed through my mind and gave me courage. I thought of Emily Brontë writing: "No coward soul is mine," and the words linked me again with my father who had chosen the poem for his funeral service.

"Wait," I said to Anna. I went to the basin, dashed some cold water over my face, combed my hair and adjusted my tie. "I must face him," I said, "and I shall. If he can represent his father, then the least I can do is represent mine."

We left the room and crossed the landing. Everyone seemed to be milling in the hall but I did not look down immediately. I descended the steps to the half-landing before pausing at the turn of the stairs to survey the scene below.

"...and I'm only sorry that we meet again under such sad circumstances," Uncle John was saying courteously.

The stranger at his side looked up and saw me. A hush fell upon the hall.

I saw a tall powerfully built man in his late thirties. He wore a well-cut black suit and exuded a subtle aura of self-confidence. His dark hair was glossy, his features heavy but regular. I searched for some resemblance to my mother but could find none.

I began to descend the remaining stairs and as I did so I knew that he too was searching for resemblances, although his face betrayed nothing. His soft dark eyes were sinister in their expressionlessness.

"Ah, here's Kester," said Uncle John, clearly deciding that the best way to handle the situation was to pretend that everything was normal.

I descended the last stair and stood upon the hall floor. I drew myself up to my full height. I looked the stranger straight in the eyes. I took a deep breath. And I spoke. I said, "My mother is being buried tomorrow in Penhale churchyard, and I refuse to alter that arrangement merely on the strength of your unsupported hearsay evidence that she wished to be buried elsewhere."

Declan said nothing. But very very slowly his hand moved to the inside pocket of his jacket, and very very slowly he extracted an envelope. He held it out to me. To my horror I saw my mother's monogram on the flap.

Anna suddenly slipped between us. "How do you do," she said, offering Declan her hand. "I'm Anna. I'm sorry this is all so difficult. Will you excuse Kester for a moment, please? He always likes to read his letters in private. Uncle John—"

"Yes," said Uncle John, rushing to the rescue, "come into the drawing room, Declan. How was the journey from Ireland?"

The next thing I knew I was alone in the library and trying to open the envelope. My fingers were as mobile as lead. When I tore the letter in my efforts to rip aside the flap I nearly succumbed to the impulse to destroy it altogether, but of course that was impossible. I had to read it. I had to see how my mother had attempted to justify her request.

The date suggested that the letter could barely have reached Declan before Rory had telephoned with the news of her death. So this was no old whim which she might have outgrown. This was her final wish.

Darling Kester...A band seemed to be tightening around my chest. It was a moment before I could go on....*I hope it'll be simply aeons before you read this, but since your wedding I've been making all sorts of plans for the future and thought I simply must sort out my death—John told me once I should leave clear instructions if I wanted to avoid any misunderstanding among my heirs, and so I've decided to leave this letter for you with Declan. He'll be able to cope if by some ghastly chance I waft up to heaven on a cloud of pink gin before I can explain everything to you. Poor darling Rory couldn't cope at all.*

Kester, when I die I don't want everyone I love keeping a stiff upper lip, doing the done thing and generally crucifying themselves in traditional English fashion. I want a gorgeous Irish funeral with everyone weeping all over the place and not a British stiff upper lip in sight. I've always loved the Irish, and during my recent visits to Ireland to see Declan and Siobhan and the children I've always felt so at home there. It brings me closer, I know, to that other life I had long ago before you were born, and closer too to the man whom you never knew but whom I've never been able to forget.

I want to be buried with Conor. When I look back on my life I can see so clearly that I really only had one husband. Robert and I had the most unique relationship but it had nothing to do with marriage, and to be quite frank our marriage was a disaster. Robert was my friend, not my husband. But Conor was my first love and my last, and so it's Conor I must be with at the end.

Darling, I'm not going to apologize to you because I think once you've recovered from the shock you'll realize that no apology is necessary. You see, this is romance triumphing over ghastly old reality—this is an affirmation of everything you and I have always longed to believe. Talk to Declan. He understands and he'll explain. I would have explained it all to you myself but you signaled so clearly that you weren't ready and I knew I had to wait until you were.

All my love, darling, and never forget how precious you are to me, my living reminder not only of Robert, who was the finest friend anyone could wish to have, but of that lost paradise which he and I once shared at Oxmoon, your Oxmoon, that magic house which you'll have always in memory of us.

A long time passed. Then when I was sure I had myself absolutely in control I rang the bell and sent for Declan.

VII

"She was a wonderful woman," said Declan, lighting a cigarette, "but naughty. Very naughty. I'm not surprised you're well-nigh destroyed with shock because I was well-nigh destroyed myself when I first found out how naughty she was—oh yes, I've been where you are now and I've stood in your shoes! She brought me up to believe my father was the love of her life and then before he was cold in his grave she was sleeping with Robert. How do you think I felt when I found that out? No, you don't have to answer. You know how I felt. I felt the way you're feeling now—bloody awful, bitter, betrayed. Murderous, even. I'm only surprised I was never certified. It took me years to get over it all."

Declan spoke with a spurious public-school accent laced with Irish mannerisms. I learned later that his accent varied greatly, depending on his surroundings, and could range from a New York twang to a stage-Irish brogue. He had a smooth, silky baritone voice which wrapped itself winningly around his words, and a powerful charm of manner which radiated a rapier-sharp intelligence. He was obviously quite unlike any Godwin I had ever met. I was mesmerized.

"So there's no denying her naughtiness," he was saying comfortably, idly waving his cigarette at the ashtray, "but oh, what a wonderful woman she was with all that passion and melodrama slopping around inside her head! Jesus, living with her in New York was like living in a grand opera; someone was always shrieking with rage or roaring with laughter or threatening to commit suicide. And my father was just as bad as she was—oh, just imagine the two of them together, both so naughty and both so wonderful, Rory and I had such an exciting life, a little too exciting sometimes, but whenever Ma saw our hair standing on end she'd say, 'Darlings, this is grand passion! Isn't it thrilling!' and we knew she was as happy as a lark even when she was screeching at my father that she'd like to bloody castrate him for running after other women and gambling away all her money. Christ, what an opera it was! Covent Garden's never seen anything like.

"Anyway..." He shed ash carelessly into the tray again with another casual flick of the wrist. "...the curtain came down on the grand opera and she went demented; she couldn't stand the silence. Result: panic. Then she remembered Robert and thought: He'll sort me out. Famous last words, but at the time it seemed to her like a brain wave because she thought she could get her grand opera running again with a different cast. 'Romance conquers all!' sings Ma, thinking herself back in business—but she'd made one fatal mistake. Your father didn't like grand opera. To put it in English terms, it wasn't his cup of tea at all.

"Well now, I know what you're thinking—no, don't say a word! There's no

569

need. You're thinking the moral of this story is to hell with bloody romance. I used to think that. Ma confessed she thought so herself every now and then, but she fought against it, she refused to accept defeat, she battled on like a bloody tank—God, what a woman she was—oh, the nerve of it! The courage! She was outrageous! You couldn't help but admire her, and I never admired her more than when she came on her last visit to Dublin and confessed to me that she wanted to tack a new ending onto her favorite grand opera. 'I want to be buried with him!' she says, eyes bright, cheeks pink, happy as a lark again. 'It'll be my final grand romantic gesture!' Oh, you should have seen her! We'd gone to visit my father's grave and there we were, standing by his tombstone, and the sun was setting in that unreal way it does in Ireland and the whole scene was just like an opera set. I had to laugh. And then she added: 'In death I want to celebrate life by commemorating my great romance!' and she began to talk about my father.

"Well, you know what old people are like once they get going on the past. The same old stories get trotted out and you have to pretend you haven't heard them all before, but on that occasion it wasn't so hard to pretend. I think it was because I admired her so much for her guts—she was such a survivor, and *that* was romantic, yes, it was, I have to admit it although I'm not much of a one for romance myself, not after seeing my parents go through all those shenanigans. So I didn't interrupt her as she talked on and on, and finally she said: 'It was the most romantic moment of my life. I was dancing beneath the chandeliers at Oxmoon while the orchestra played "The Blue Danube" and I saw Conor in the doorway—he'd come back at last to claim me, and at that moment I knew all my dreams were going to come true.' And when she said that I forgot all about the awful scenes in New York when she and my father had screamed and fought and damned-near killed each other—I forgot all the horrors that came later. That was all wiped out as if it had never been and all I could hear was 'The Blue Danube.'

"So later, when she asked me to make sure she was buried in Ireland, I felt I'd be the blackest villain imaginable if I didn't make the promise and keep it. That request represents her final triumph over the tragedies of her life, doesn't it? And once we make her last grand romantic gesture a reality we won't hear the sadness of that bloody waltz anymore; all we'll hear is the joy as we celebrate her courage and give thanks for her life."

I tried to speak but of course it was quite beyond me. He had crushed out his cigarette and as we both rose to our feet he held out his hands. His clasp was firm, and amidst all my grief I knew comfort.

"You mustn't worry," I heard him say. "All we've got to do now is to give her the happy ending she always longed for—only the real happy ending, as you'll have guessed by now, has nothing to do with romantic burials; the real ending lies between you and me. After all, a grave's just a grave, isn't it? But a brother should be far more than a stranger and blood far thicker than water—which reminds me, would you have a little whisper of whisky in this wonderful house of yours? I think I must get discreetly drunk before I can face all your terrible relations."

"What a marvelous idea!" I said, shoving the last tears from my eyes, and without more ado we settled down to drain the decanter.

VIII

"How do you get on with all those Godwins, Christopher?"

"Not very well, Declan, to tell you the truth."

"Ah, I knew you were a young man of taste and discrimination. What a crowd! The only one I ever liked was old Bobby, and of course he wasn't English, he was a Welshman who'd never been Anglicized. I'll bet he picked you out because he could see you were different from the rest!"

"Honestly, Declan, at the end of his life he was too senile to tell."

"Made you his heir, though, didn't he?"

"That was due to my father, gunning on my behalf."

"Trust Robert to wheel on the big guns. You lucky little sod! It's not often the youngest of four sons hits the jackpot in the biggest possible way. Christ, I bet those other Godwins are livid!"

"Well, I don't suppose they exactly cheered, but Uncle John's been simply heroic—"

"Uh-huh. That's a cool customer, if you want my opinion. What goes on in that Welsh-speaking mind behind that well-oiled English handshake? Jesus, I'll never forgive myself for not being around to protect you from the lot of them while you were growing up but I couldn't stand the idea of you, thought you'd be a replica of Robert. What was Robin like?"

"Awful."

"Well, there you are. (God rest his poor little soul.) It was just as well I stayed away; I might have murdered you both in a fit of pique. Have some more whisky."

"Rather. Thanks. Oh Declan, I can't tell you what a strain it's been, struggling to be a perfect Godwin—"

"Thank God you failed. Never mind, you're your own master now and you can do just as you damn well please."

"Well, it's not actually quite as simple as that, Declan. You see, Uncle John—"

"Ah, bugger Uncle John!" said Declan. It occurred to me then that he was exactly like his own description of our mother: wonderful but naughty. As I gazed at him in admiration I realized he was just the kind of brother I had always longed for and he was saying just the kind of things I had always yearned to hear. "You stand up for yourself, Christopher!" he was urging. "You crack the whip and make 'em all shit bricks!"

The thought of anyone, let alone Uncle John, shitting bricks was enough to make me boggle. I started to laugh.

"I'm a villain, aren't I?" said Declan, laughing with me. He had the most charming smile.

"Yes, it's wonderful—you're even better than Rupert of Hentzau!" I said emotionally as he topped up my glass of whisky for the fourth time. "Oh Declan, how I wish I'd met you years ago!"

"To be sure it was a tragedy you didn't, but we'll soon make up for lost time, don't you worry, and now that we've finally met you can be certain I'll stand by you to the grave and beyond."

"Do you really mean that, Declan, or are you just speaking out of a sense of moral duty?"

"I don't have a sense of moral duty."

"You mean you really do like me?"

"Why, you poor, poor little bastard!" He gave me a look of astonished compassion. "Has no one ever liked you much before? Those bloody Godwins! I'd like to machine-gun the lot of them! Now listen to me, little Christopher. If ever you need any help in the future, don't you go anywhere near a shady character like John Godwin who lurks like a shark in murky waters all the time he's pretending he's as harmless as a goldfish. You come straight to me and I'll look after you as you ought to be looked after because the truth is, as I can so plainly see, you're a rebel after my own heart and nothing could ever induce me now to wash my hands of you unless you went completely off the rails and became a perfect Godwin."

We embraced, swore eternal friendship and ended up shedding an emotional tear or two over the empty whisky decanter.

Uncle John would have been absolutely horrified.

But I was in bliss.

IX

There was a memorial service instead of a funeral in Penhale Church the next day but that same afternoon Anna and I set out for Ireland with Rory and Declan. Uncle John had offered to accompany us, but I knew he was only anxious to do the done thing so I told him not to bother; in my opinion his attendance at the memorial service excused him from any moral obligation to cross the Irish Sea.

My mother had often mentioned that Ireland was beautiful but I had never listened, just as I had never listened when she had tried to talk to me about Declan, so I was amazed when I first saw the Wicklow Mountains rising above the great curve of Dublin Bay. I found myself remembering the Coolins of Rhum, and in that special peace which I always knew in the presence of great beauty my mind became calmer at last. The cemetery seemed very foreign, but when I saw Conor

Kinsella's florid grave, I sensed in its unabashed sentiment a touch of the melodrama which had struck such a chord in my mother's heart.

"But Mum wasn't Catholic," I said troubled to Declan. "Is she entitled to a Catholic funeral?"

"To be sure she would have turned Catholic in the end in order to be buried with Pa," said Declan soothingly, "so that would put her in a notional state of grace, to my way of thinking, and I was able to tell the priest with a clear conscience that she'd received the Last Rites. I'm sure God will perfectly understand."

All Declan's Irish relatives and a large number of his friends came to the funeral. I had had no idea my mother had known so many people in Ireland. I had never asked her any questions about her regular visits to Dublin and she in turn had offered no information, but now I learned that she had talked of retiring from Oxmoon and settling near Dublin in a cottage by the sea.

"She said that once you were married she didn't want to hang around Oxmoon like some kind of bossy Queen Mother," explained Declan. "'Time to sever the apron strings!' she said to me. 'Time to begin another wonderful new life!'"

I became amazed by how imperfectly I had known her, and as I stood by her grave later in the soft Irish rain, I found there was so much I would like to have asked. Why, for instance, had she never become a Roman Catholic? I thought it would have suited her emotionally; but perhaps she had clung to the memory of her Protestant childhood because it was part of what she had described as the lost paradise of Oxmoon. And how could she ever have thought of severing herself from Oxmoon, which had for so long played Egypt to her Cleopatra? But perhaps not all her memories of Oxmoon had been happy ones. Perhaps my marriage had at last set her free to find a final peace which was unavailable to her there; perhaps it had even come as a relief to know she could retreat forever from her Godwin past and turn, as she had turned once before, to embrace the world of Conor Kinsella.

I wished too that I could have asked her about him—and of course I wished above all that we could have had that honest conversation about my father; I wished I could have heard her explain in her own words the enigma of that relationship which had somehow kept her at his side.

"I never thought she'd stick it," Declan said earlier.

"Why did she, do you think?"

"God knows. I never really got to the bottom of that relationship with Robert."

"Did she ever try to explain it to you?"

"Yes, but she couldn't. She just wound up talking crap about lost paradises."

"But Declan, if you had to put forward a theory—"

He saw how much I longed to understand. "Oh, some very powerful emotion was generated at an early age, there's no doubt about that, and I'd think it was generated by Robert, who had the kind of single-track mind which converts emotion into a sawn-off shotgun. The true mystery is why he fixed all his emotion on her like that when he was a little kid, but he didn't like his sister Celia, did he, and apparently when he was small he didn't get on with that old battle-ax of a mother of his, so Ma wound up being his nearest sympathetic female with the result that he gave her all the devotion he couldn't unload elsewhere."

"But how do you explain Mum's devotion to him?"

"Well, she might have been merely mesmerized by his strong personality but I think the explanation has to go deeper than that, and I suspect the clue lies in all that crap she talked about lost paradises. When does the past always seem bathed in a golden light?"

"The moment anything frightful happens in the present."

"Right. I've often wondered if something terrible happened to Ma when she was young, something which made the extreme past seem perpetually desirable— and Robert symbolized that extreme past to her."

"But what on earth could have happened?"

"Ah well, the standard disaster for a nubile young girl is seduction or rape, isn't it, but the only trouble with that theory is that there's no one here who fits the picture of the wicked seducer. It wasn't my father, because she rushed into his arms as soon as she could, and it wasn't yours because he symbolized Eden before the Fall, and it certainly couldn't have been old Bobby, who was one of the nicest guys I've ever met. I ought to have asked Ma straight out when she was telling me her life story, but I never did and now we'll never know. Ah, people are such a mystery, aren't they? And perhaps one's own parents are the greatest mystery of all..."

But I thought of my mother writing in her final letter of my father: *He was my friend*, and of Conor Kinsella: *He was my first love and my last.* What did the background mysteries matter when the basic truth was as absolute as that? I found then that I was resigned to the fact that I would never now hear the whole story from my mother's lips, and with my resignation came acceptance so that the past was unable to hurt me anymore. I saw her buried with her first husband and thought as Declan had thought before me: Yes, it was romantic. The romance was not as I had imagined it to be, but it was there nonetheless, allowing me to preserve all my idealism, allowing me to remember my mother as I wanted to remember her, and as I stood there in the soft Irish rain in that foreign cemetery so far from home I saw again in the glittering grass the chandeliers at Oxmoon and heard once more in my imagination the orchestra that had played "The Blue Danube."

6

I

AFTER THIS emotional Irish interlude my arrival home was very much a return to the cold hard Anglo-Saxon facts of life. With my mother dead I found myself abruptly brought face to face with a subject I had never troubled to master: the administration of Oxmoon. In the library I opened one of the estate books, but it might have been written in Etruscan, and I was just closing it with a bang when the door opened and in walked bestial Thomas.

"Oh hullo," he said. "What are you doing here buggering around with the estate books?"

My library and I'm asked what I'm doing here. *My* estate, run by someone I detest.

I looked at him narrowly and said nothing.

"How was bloody old Ireland?" said Thomas casually, flicking through some correspondence. "God, what a dump that country is!"

I knew he had never been there. I went on watching him narrowly and still I said nothing.

"Oh, by the way," said Thomas who was much too insensitive to find my silence suspicious and probably only thought I was being deferential, "John rang up yesterday. He's coming down tomorrow to discuss the future with you. He said he'd stay three days."

My house and my uninvited guests coolly tell me how long they intend to stay.

"Oh yes?" I said without expression, and walked out.

I felt like wiring Declan to come with a machine gun.

II

When I was on my honeymoon I had written a long letter to Uncle John. Of course I had been consumed by guilt that I had not thanked him properly for rushing to Scotland to extract me from jail. How could I have been so hostile and brutal to him when he had been so heroic? Grinding my teeth I penned the required letter of gratitude. Then it occurred to me that since he was already horrified by my un-Godwin-like behavior he could hardly be more horrified if I displayed some new heresy, so I broke the news to him that I had decided not to go up to Oxford. My mother's death had effectively precluded us from discussing this decision, but before I departed for Ireland he had expressed the wish that we could meet as soon as I returned.

The thought of another battle with Uncle John sickened me. The thought of Thomas downstairs in the library sickened me. In the privacy of my room I lay on my bed and groaned with nausea and rage.

"Uncle John won't force you to go up to Oxford against your wishes," said my wonderful Anna, who had been such a tower of strength to me during my recent ordeals, "and who knows? Perhaps he'll be only too delighted that you want to run the estate yourself."

This was certainly possible, but she had overlooked the core of my dilemma. "Uncle John will never allow me to get rid of Thomas. He'll say I can't cope, and the awful thing is he'd be right."

"Nonsense!" said Anna roundly. "I'm sure you could learn how to cope in no time—you're twice as clever as Thomas!"

"Only twice?" I said, cheering up. Her confidence did indeed put me in better spirits, but that night I lay awake quailing at the thought of Uncle John gliding to my rescue once more in his formidable and repellent Rolls-Royce.

III

The next morning, unable to resist the temptation, I unlocked the drawer of the bureau in my old bedroom and took a look at the manuscript which had been untouched since the week before my elopement. I at once felt much calmer. Seduced long since by the works of Miss Christie and Miss Sayers, I was now specializing in the country-house detective story and luxuriating in complicated plots involving corpses galore, alibis by the dozen and an interminable dénouement in the library. My detective, modeled on Lord Peter Wimsey, was passionately in love with an adventuress who was fast becoming much too sexy.

I wished I could let them go to bed together but I knew that wasn't the done thing in a detective story, not even when the heroine was an adventuress. It was true that Lord Peter had gone to bed with Harriet, but not until they were husband and wife. Could I marry off my Honorable Jonathan? But then the dramatic suspense of his private life would be destroyed, because he would have to live forever after in uxorious bliss; detective stories never allowed their married heroes any other fate.

I thought idly: It would be much more interesting if they did; the stories would be more true to life. But I was obliged to put this heretical thought aside when I suddenly realized that Lady Sybil's alibi was no good. She would never have had the chance to get hold of the arsenic so therefore she wouldn't need an alibi. I had to engineer a chance for her, but since Professor Metz was keeping the arsenic in a locked briefcase... but he was her ex-husband so... I futilely toyed with the idea of a seduction in the conservatory.

Time floated by in a golden haze. I scribbled away, rewriting Chapter Eight, but although I lured the professor into the rose garden, I suddenly realized Lady Sybil still had no chance to acquire the arsenic. (Professor Metz would hardly have taken his briefcase among the roses.)

"Damn," I said, and tearing up what I had written, I left my room and wandered out into the garden for inspiration. I had no idea what the time was but I was dimly aware it was day and not night. Round and round the orangerie I went, and round and round the kitchen garden. I was just moodily eating a blackberry when I suddenly saw how Lady Sybil could have had access to a lethal poison without involving the professor (who would now, of course, make a brilliant red herring).

I ran hell-for-leather out of the kitchen garden and pounded across the croquet lawn to the terrace. A flash of blue beyond the garden door told me that Anna was in the drawing room.

I burst in. "There was arsenic in the rose spray!" I shouted. "And the rose spray had been left in the rose garden!"

Anna's face told me exactly what I didn't want to know. We were not alone.

With a gasp I whipped around to face my amazed guests. My face felt as if it were in flames.

"Good morning, Kester," said Uncle John.

"Hullo, old chap," said Cousin Harry.

"Christ, Kester," said Thomas, completing this most unholy of trinities. "Have you gone completely crazy? We all know there's no rose garden at Oxmoon!"

IV

I had been caught acting like a lunatic. That was bad enough but what was worse was that Uncle John, who knew all my un-Godwin-like traits so well that they must have been engraved on his heart, immediately realized I had been writing. When I tried to welcome him in a conventional fashion I could only stammer. I felt about fourteen and getting younger every second.

Anna said composed, "Uncle John and Harry have only just arrived, Kester. Perhaps I should show them to their rooms."

"Wait a minute," I said. I forgot my humiliation. I was now grappling with the enormity of Cousin Harry's presence. "What the devil are you doing here?" I demanded fiercely.

"Maybe he can help me run Oxmoon," said Thomas, "while you run around hallucinating about rose gardens."

"That'll do, Thomas," said Uncle John abruptly, and turned to my wife. "Anna, before we go to our rooms would it be possible for us to have some coffee? We drove down without stopping, which is always such a mistake."

"Yes, of course, Uncle John."

"Wait a minute," I said again. "*Wait a minute.*"

They all stared at me.

"I'm not sure I want you all loafing around swilling coffee in my drawing room," I said. "Wouldn't it be more tactful, Uncle John—more the done thing—if you consulted *me* before bringing your son to this house and ordering my wife around as if she were a parlormaid?"

Dead silence. Thomas's jaw sagged. Cousin Harry's eyes widened. Uncle John was too stunned to speak.

Anna said rapidly, "I think I will organize some coffee all the same...excuse me." And she made her escape.

As the door closed behind her, Uncle John said with exquisite courtesy, "You're quite right, Kester, and I do apologize. I'm very much aware, I assure you, that you're master here now."

"Well, you've got a funny way of showing it."

"Why, you bloody-minded little—"

"Be quiet, Thomas," said Uncle John steadily without raising his voice. "Let me apologize again, Kester, if I've given you offense, but in fact I do have a good reason for bringing Harry with me. You see, I accept your decision not to go up to Oxford; I think it's a pity, but you're your own master now and you must do as you think fit. But of course this decision of yours makes it imperative that you now receive instruction in estate management, and I thought it would be more...acceptable to you if you didn't receive instruction from Thomas on your own. That's why Harry's here. He wants to learn about estate management too."

"He *what?*"

"Fact is, old chap," said Cousin Harry, very debonair, "I've decided to come down from Oxford and follow in Grandfather's footsteps as a farmer. Father's going to lease me Penhale Manor, and as I know as much about estate management as you do we thought it might be amusing if awful old Thomas here tries to flog the facts of farming life into two pupils instead of one. I think between the two of us we might just be able to keep him in order."

Thomas guffawed, delighted by the implication that he was an insufferable tyrant, but I barely heard him. My mind was reeling with horror. I had shunned Oxford specifically to avoid Cousin Harry, but now, by the most malign twist of fate, we were to be locked up together in the parish of Penhale. I knew at once that he would run the Penhale Manor estate brilliantly. Rage and despair met, merged and massacred my self-control.

"How dare you!" I shouted to Uncle John. "How dare you attempt to impose your will on me like this!"

"My dear Kester, I—"

"I think he wants to murder us all with the nearest rose spray," said Thomas.

"Be quiet!" snapped Uncle John, making him jump. "If you think this is a joking matter—"

"It's no joke and I'm not amused!" I shouted.

"And neither am I!" shouted Cousin Harry with that lightning descent into violence which marked those rare occasions when he lost his temper and emerged from behind his public-school mask. "Look here, Kester, I don't see why you should behave like a maniac when my poor long-suffering father's one aim in life is to treat you more decently than you deserve—"

"My God, that's the understatement of the century," said Thomas.

"*Enough!*" blazed Uncle John. The room instantly fell silent. He looked at each one of us in turn. Then he said, "I draw the line."

Nobody spoke. What was there to say? When Uncle John drew the line that was that. All one could do afterwards was simmer in silence and let the unacceptable emotions fester at leisure.

Harry, Thomas and I simmered and our emotions festered but we kept our mouths shut and our faces expressionless. That, after all, was the done thing, and having been brought up by Uncle John, we all knew that the most important task in life was to play the game and stick to the rules.

"Harry—Thomas—leave us, please," said Uncle John. "Obviously Kester and I must have a private talk together."

"Oh no we don't!" I said. "Never again!"

They stared at me. I saw them realize that they were impotent and that I was all-powerful. It was the most thrilling moment of my life, and suddenly I was abandoning the game, I was ignoring the done thing, I was flaunting my true feelings in defiance of the rules.

"I've had more than enough of all of you!" I shouted, wallowing in the luxury of naked rage. "I'm sick of you all thinking I'm some hopeless freak who has to be tolerated in the name of family loyalty! I'm sick of your sneers and your snide remarks and your patronizing condescension, I'm sick of you treating my house as if it were yours, I'm sick of your boring uncultivated conversations, I'm sick of pretending we all like each other—*I'm sick of all this bloody hypocrisy!* I put up with it while my mother was alive, but now she's dead and if you think I'm just going to carry on where she left off you'd better think again! In future you'll all wait till you're invited before you turn up at Oxmoon—and in future you'll all keep your hands off my estate! Now," I said, having worked myself up to my peroration, "get out, stay out and bloody well leave me alone to do as I please!"

No one attempted a reply and indeed I gave none of them a chance to do so, for the next moment I had walked out and slammed the door with a violence that must have shaken Oxmoon to its foundations.

The new reign had begun.

V

I took the stairs two at a time and sped across the landing to the window that overlooked the drive. Thomas's car was parked outside but all three men, when they emerged from the house, paused beside the Rolls and I realized they must be waiting for the chauffeur who was probably enjoying a cup of tea in the kitchens. Thomas was talking and Uncle John was letting him talk. Uncle John looked tired and drawn in contrast to Thomas who was obviously in fine fettle. Thomas thrived on rage and I could imagine the crude obscenities that would now be flowing happily—though for me, thank God, inaudibly—from his thick flabby lips.

Since guilt prevented me from watching Uncle John and repulsion made me recoil from Thomas, I turned my attention to the third member of the trio. Cousin Harry, evidently bored by Thomas's ravings, had wandered away until he was standing in the center of the gravel sweep before the porch, and as I watched, taking care to shelter behind the curtain, he paused to light a cigarette. Then he started to look at the house. He looked and looked and looked until at last I suspected he was not seeing the house at all but was sunk in some profound reverie which I could not begin to imagine. This awareness that his mind was a closed book to me I found both novel and intriguing. What went on behind that polished facade? Harry had always been such a myth of perfection to me, but I had seen some very long-standing myths exploded in recent weeks, and I was no longer prepared to accept a myth without questioning it.

What, I now asked myself, was really happening in Cousin Harry's life? What were his secret fears, miseries, obsessions and loathings? I had no idea, but I did know that it was very, very odd that he should have come down from Oxford after only one year. This was in stark contrast to Harry's image of unflawed perfection and most definitely not the done thing at all. Could he conceivably have been sent down? No. Not possible. His open scholarship made the chance of academic failure nonexistent, and of course he would be much too clever to get into trouble of any other kind. No, I had to accept that he had come down voluntarily, but nevertheless... what a disappointment for Uncle John! But Uncle John, running true to form, was glossing over the incident by keeping a stiff upper lip and standing by Harry just as he had earlier stood by Marian. Or was this just wishful thinking on my part? Perhaps Uncle John had been delighted by Harry's decision to cast aside the irrelevant study of Latin and Greek and adopt the life of a gentleman farmer. After all, as Harry himself had pointed out, such a life was exactly in my grandfather's tradition. In fact now that I really thought about his decision I could see it was absolutely the done thing after all.

I might have known Harry would never put a foot wrong. His was the one myth I'd never be able to crack, and now this paragon, this monster of virtue, this truly insufferable hero was about to move into my life lock, stock and barrel to form a mirror image, a reflection in which I would always find myself wanting.

That was not only a vile thought. It was a sinister one. I shuddered and tried to pull myself together. I would still be the first man in the parish. Oxmoon was bigger and better than Penhale Manor. All I had to do was run Oxmoon to perfection and then I would easily outshine Cousin Harry—in fact, once I started making Oxmoon a shrine to Beauty, Truth, Art and Peace I would soon be, to coin that most peculiar phrase, the cynosure of all eyes. Very well, I thought, let him come back to Gower! I'd make him writhe with jealousy until in the end, unable to stand the sight of me flourishing so sumptuously at Oxmoon, he'd gnash his teeth and slink away to try his luck elsewhere—in Northumberland, perhaps, or East Anglia. I supposed it was too much to hope that he would emigrate.

I laughed, and as I turned away from the window at last I saw my wife running up the stairs to meet me.

"Kester, what on earth's going on?"

"Ah, Anna—I won, I won!" I whirled her in a dervishlike dance all the way across the landing into the largest guest room which we were using until my mother's room could be refurbished, and amidst gales of laughter we collapsed upon the bed.

"Tell me everything!" she gasped.

"Later!" I was so excited that I couldn't undo my trouser buttons, and in a paroxysm of joy I gave up and ripped open the flies. "Whoopee!" I shouted.

"Heavens, what will the tailor think when he does the repairs?" said Anna, and as we almost passed out with laughter she pulled me into her arms to celebrate my mighty victory.

VI

After this triumphant severance of my leading strings, I received two letters. The first, a surprisingly neat missive in a bold upright handwriting, read: *Kester, you're a bloody fool and what Oxmoon's done to deserve you I'll never know, but when you get in a hole (and you will—a deep one) you'd better tell me so that I can dig you out. This isn't my idea of having a good time, but John says you've got to know there'll always be someone nearby who's prepared to help in an emergency, and as far as I'm concerned John's the boss of this family and will be till he drops dead (and God help us all when he does). So I'm obliged to obey orders.* THOMAS.

I made no reply to this childish effusion, but the second letter I received was far less easy to forget. Uncle John wrote with exquisite politeness that it grieved him I was so bitter towards my family, and that he personally had taken my attitude very hard as he had always tried to do his best for me; he begged me to remember that he and my father had been the most devoted of brothers, and added that whatever happened I would always have a special place in his affections.

This made me feel very mean. Furious with him for crucifying me with guilt and furious with myself for permitting the crucifixion I wrote in an effort to crush these chaotic emotions: *My dear Uncle John, Thank you for your letter. I know it was more civil than I deserved. I'm sorry about the row but I must lead my own life now and it seemed impossible to convince you of this without resorting to plain speaking—which, as I now realize, obliged me to treat you with an unkindness you've never merited. Of course I'm aware how much I owe you and I've no wish to appear ungrateful, but when we meet in the future (as of course I hope we shall) it must be on my terms. I remain now and always your very affectionate nephew,* KESTER.

This fawning effort to assuage my conscience by appeasing him seemed so nauseous that I could hardly bear to reread it, but I did feel better afterwards and Uncle John evidently felt better too. He replied by return: *My dear Kester, I was very pleased to receive your letter and of course I understand and forgive your natural desire to attain the independence which is yours by right. I wish you well, and I hope that if ever you need help or advice in the future you'll remember that you can always come straight to me. Your devoted uncle,* J.G.

In other words, to paraphrase the letter with a crudeness which diplomatic Uncle John would always have eschewed, he too suspected I was going to make a cock-up of my independence, but he was prepared, for lack of a better alternative, to sanction my efforts to go my own way. So much for Uncle John—and so much for bestial Thomas. I was determined to prove myself, but meanwhile I had to try to work out what on earth I was going to do without them.

VII

My first concern was for Anna. She had to have a housekeeper. My mother, unorthodox as always, had run her various establishments herself with the aid of a succession of henchmen who had each in turn been referred to as "My Devoted Factotum," but when we left Little Oxmoon, her current Devoted Factotum (the parlormaid Watson) had stayed on there to keep house for Thomas. However my mother had never let my father's nurse Bennett slip through her fingers, and after my father's death she had retained him as a butler, a position he had filled in London before my father became ill. When she moved to Oxmoon Bennett came too as the new Devoted Factotum which meant that he and my mother between them had assumed the household duties formerly undertaken by Mrs. Straker.

However shortly after my elopement Lowell the butler and Bennett had had "words" and Bennett, a Cockney, had decided the time had finally come when he had to move back to the sound of Bow Bells. My mother, who would willingly have sacrificed Lowell, bribed, bullied and cajoled but to no avail. Bennett departed. Probably he had only stayed on in the hope of playing gentleman's gentleman one day to the master of Oxmoon; but having been brought up in more modest surroundings than my father and belonging to a postwar, not a prewar generation I considered a valet would have represented an intolerable intrusion on my privacy.

My mother had been interviewing candidates for the role of Devoted Factotum before I returned from my honeymoon, but fortunately no one suitable had been found. I knew that a Devoted Factotum, who liked to live a life of vicarious glamour in the service of a flamboyant personality, was no answer for Anna; she needed a quite ladylike conventional housekeeper like Mrs. Wells, who had been Uncle John's housekeeper at Penhale Manor before Bronwen's departure, and if Mrs. Wells had still been in the neighborhood I would have offered her the job but she had taken a new position and disappeared into the Home Counties. How did one find a similar paragon? I wrote the word *Housekeeper* on my note pad and sat looking at it anxiously for some time.

Eventually it occurred to me that I might consult Cousin Elizabeth who employed a housekeeper herself and was bound to be full of useful advice. I had become fond of nice cheerful down-to-earth Cousin Elizabeth since she had become a neighbor in Swansea, and although Owen was an awful bore, besotted with *The Financial Times* and rugby football, he was always civil and good-natured to me. In fact if I had to have relations living nearby I could hardly have asked for more agreeable ones than the Bryn-Davieses, who treated me with friendly respect, never turned up at Oxmoon without a prior invitation and telephoned once every three months as a courtesy to check that I was still alive. If more relations were like that I was sure there wouldn't be nearly so many unhappy families in the world.

Having considered the problem of finding a housekeeper I then considered the far more crucial problem of finding a first-class estate manager to replace Thomas. Although I was sure I could learn enough to supervise the administration of my property eventually I was hardly competent to do so at that moment, and besides I had to write. I couldn't spend all my time going to market with my foremen or plotting the substance of next year's ley (I wasn't even sure what a ley was). How did I find the ideal estate manager who would relieve me of such time-consuming matters?

I decided to seek the advice of my solicitor Mr. Fairfax, the senior partner in the firm of Fairfax, Walters and Wyn-Williams. Uncle John had fired both Mr. Fairfax and my charming bank manager Mr. Lloyd-Thomas when my grandfather had had a bout of being completely incompetent, but my grandfather had later reinstated them, and Uncle John, who could so easily have quashed this sentimental decision by a flick of his power of attorney, had raised no objection. Uncle John had always been exceptionally kind to this pathetic old parent of his, and besides he probably thought it was sufficient that he had frightened Fairfax and Lloyd-Thomas out of their wits by temporarily depriving them of the Oxmoon estate. After their reinstatement they had never failed to grovel to him at all times.

As I thought of Mr. Fairfax I remembered that he had told me (creepily) that I should make a will, and although I still recoiled from this macabre suggestion I knew that as a married man in sole control of a large estate I now had what Uncle John would have described as an absolute moral duty to live up to my responsibilities. I wrote on my note pad, *Estate manager—ask Fairfax*; but as I wrote I was thinking of my will. Who, out of all my ghastly relations, was worthy to inherit Oxmoon? The obvious answer was Christopher Godwin Junior but he hadn't arrived yet and until he did I was obliged to look elsewhere. I thought with affection of Declan but I really couldn't leave Oxmoon to a British-hating Irish patriot. One had to draw the line somewhere.

I surveyed the next generation, or in other words the babies of my acquaintance. I eliminated Thomas's small son Bobby; he was automatically damned by his parentage. Then I ruled out Declan's offspring, attractive and delightful though they were, because they were certain to grow up into British-hating Irish patriots like their father, and I ruled out Rory's two daughters who showed signs of growing up like Cousin Marian. Anyway Godwin girls didn't inherit; it wasn't the done thing (although why not? Actually I'm all for girls inheriting everything in sight, think of those hugely successful estate managers Queens Cleopatra, Elizabeth and Victoria). However any daughter of Cousin Marian's was bound to fall far short of these shining examples of womanhood so that left me face to face with the last baby who had Godwin blood, Cousin Elizabeth's son little Owen, who was now a year old. But could I really leave Oxmoon to someone called Owen Bryn-Davies? What a laugh! Uncle John would have apoplexy. I couldn't resist it, and anyway it would be only a temporary measure until I had a son of my own. But I had to take that temporary measure because whatever happened I had to avoid dying intestate and leaving Oxmoon in the lurch.

I wrote on my notepad, *Little Owen—see Fairfax*, and as I wrote I thought idly: What *would* happen to Oxmoon if I were to die intestate? I wasn't sure of the answer but I thought it likely that Uncle John might tell himself it was his moral duty to buy it, and after Uncle John was dead...

Cousin Harry.

Never.

I shuddered, drew a highly symbolic line on my note pad and went downstairs to telephone Mr. Fairfax.

"You couldn't possibly be pregnant already, could you, darling?" I said to Anna that night. "After all, we've been married for several weeks now and we haven't exactly stinted on the copulation. Heavens, in novels a nice girl has only to lose her virginity and she instantly sets out on the road to motherhood!"

"I expect it's a little different in real life," said Anna with a sigh.

It was. If I could have written my life instead of being obliged to live it, I would have mastered the estate in a week and run it single-handed while I tossed off best-selling novels in my spare time and prepared for imminent fatherhood. In real life fatherhood was still a dream, my last novel was once again returned with a rejection slip and Mr. Fairfax told me he didn't know of any first-class estate manager except Thomas Godwin. I recognized this as a criticism and almost fired him, but decided my life was quite complicated enough already without dismissing the family solicitor.

By this time I had taken another peek at the estate books. How I now regretted my inattention during Uncle John's past lecture on the subject! Groaning audibly

I made a new effort to comprehend the incomprehensible.

In each book, as I already knew, there were twelve columns. These were headed PARISHES, TENEMENTS, TENANTS, QUANTITIES, TENURES, ARREARS OF RENT, RENT, TOTAL, ALLOWANCES, RECEIVED, ARREARS DUE and OBSERVATIONS. The first column was explained by the fact that Oxmoon was not entirely confined to the parish of Penhale, and the rest by the fact that in addition to the major farms on the estate there were numerous cottages and small holdings all of which had to be accounted for. So far so good. But the trouble was that although Thomas's entries were neatly inscribed, they meant nothing to me. I had no idea whether the figures were good, bad or indifferent, and as soon as I got to the OBSERVATIONS column I was plunged into mystery again because Thomas had used cryptic abbreviations such as *No cow. Month allowed,* or *6 acres oats* N.G. I looked at the heading QUANTITIES, which was divided into two columns. One column was headed £.s.d., so that constituted no problem; even I knew that £.s.d. meant pounds, shillings and pence. But what was A.R.P., the heading of the second column? Obviously Uncle John had once told me, and obviously the translation was very simple, but I couldn't for the life of me imagine what it was.

Pushing the books aside in exasperation I turned to the correspondence, but here too I was quickly at sea. There were letters from various seed merchants, a variety of bills and receipts, a peculiar communication from a large dairy in Swansea and a convoluted government memorandum about the tuberculin testing of cows. In addition to all these communications which meant nothing to me there were numerous *billets-doux* from tenants, including one from a man who whined that I owed him money for a cart horse. (Why did one still use cart horses in these days of mechanized transport? Perhaps the man was drunk or unstable.) As I toiled on, aware of a sinking feeling which I unerringly identified as boredom, the telephone kept ringing and I realized that all kinds of tedious people were trying to see me. What was I to do? This was obviously the sort of job which not only consumed one's time completely but reduced one to a nervous wreck within twenty-four hours unless, like Thomas, one had the hide of an elephant and a lust for the trivial.

I began to feel persecuted and frantic.

"I've got to write," I said to Anna, "or I'll go mad, but how can I abandon Oxmoon until I'm sure it's in safe hands?" And I added in despair to Ricky when he dropped in later for a drink: "I don't just need an estate manager, I need a Devoted Factotum—and not merely someone like Simon, whose limit is answering the begging letters and dealing with the vicar. I need someone clever and personable, diplomatic and efficient, someone who gets on well with Simon and Anna, someone I like and trust—" I broke off and stared at him. "Oh God, Ricky—"

"Well, go on! What are you waiting for?"

"Would you—could you—will you—"

"Of course! My dear Kes, I thought you were never going to ask..."

VIII

Enter Warwick Mowbray.

Apart from mentioning that he had passed through a homosexual phase when I was at an age to find such behavior acutely embarrassing, I can see now that I've given no clear impression of Ricky. Yet our friendship was so strong that it survived even his horrific declaration of passion and his prolonged absence afterwards at the University of Grenoble. The credit for the survival had undoubtedly been his; he had worked so hard to eradicate his mistake that by the time I married Anna I could meet him without embarrassment, and in the midst of my troubles he seemed the ideal person to give me a helping hand.

The Mowbrays were an old Gower family who lived in a pretty Queen Anne house above Oxwich Bay, near Porteynon. They owned no more than five acres of land but there had been one or two useful marriages in the nineteenth century, and since then they had lived comfortably. "A sad anticlimax to the bad old days!" Ricky would comment, and indeed the Mowbrays' long descent into respectability after a typical Gower history in which they had dabbled in many professions but excelled at smuggling did contain a note of elegiac sadness. Ricky said he was sick of his immediate ancestors who had cared for nothing but horseflesh, and he vowed he was going to inject a shot of glamour into the family tree.

I recognized a kindred spirit.

Ricky and I were alike—yet not alike. His father had been killed in the war, so as in my own case, the paternal influence on his life had been shadowy. But frivolous shallow little Esther Mowbray was very different from my mother, and Ricky's Uncle Adam, who corresponded in theory to my Uncle John, had taken only a nominal interest in his upbringing. Adam Mowbray, a solicitor in Swansea, was a man who exploded the myth that the legal profession tends to mummify the human spirit. Good-looking, twice divorced and a frequent visitor to the racetrack, he cut a very dashing figure in his snow-white Lagonda. It was reputed he paid his alimony bills by putting the family eye for horseflesh to a profitable account.

"Oh God, don't let's bother about that awful old bore Freddy Fairfax, Kes," said Ricky once he became my Devoted Factotum. "So unglamorous! Let's rope in Adam to help with your affairs."

I hadn't forgotten how Fairfax had offered me only veiled criticism when I had asked him for help in seeking a new estate manager. I decided that once again the ax should fall on the firm of Fairfax, Walters and Wyn-Williams.

"My dear Kester," said Adam after he had thanked me charmingly for appointing him the solicitor for the Oxmoon estate, "I must confess I think you're wise to dispense with old Fairfax—he's a bit over the hill these days, I'm afraid. . . . An estate manager? Oh yes, nothing easier. I know just the man who'd suit you."

This was all most gratifying and the huge burden of my anxiety finally began to dissolve. I kept thinking how lucky I was to have a friend like Ricky who could show me how to solve all my problems.

Like me Ricky had not gone away to school; Esther had been unable to bear the thought of being deprived of his company. But unlike me he had been badly taught by a succession of inept tutors before Simon had prepared him for Oxford, and he had resented his poor education. This resentment colored his attitude to his mother whom he blamed for what he considered to be the inadequacies of his upbringing. Although professing to adore her he often told me what a tiresome woman she was and expressed the opinion that all women were little better than certified lunatics. Since my mother was supervising Oxmoon with such success I could hardly agree with him, but I did see that Esther Mowbray's talents were limited to the occasional scatty game of bridge. Ricky despised such pastimes, judged them "fatally lacking in glamour" and spent much time wishing he could have grown up in the Eighteen Nineties. He once confided to me that he occasionally burned incense in his room while he reread *The Yellow Book*.

Five years his junior I found this behavior far more interesting than playing cricket and doing the done thing, and when we were young I hero-worshiped him spiritedly. My admiration was welcome. I can see now that he was lonely and enjoyed having me as an acolyte, just as I myself had once enjoyed Evan's company. Certainly I brought out the best in Ricky; beneath his brittle catty manner which I found so thrillingly sophisticated he was both kind and sensitive. He wrote poetry. I admired his poems and even Simon, a stern critic, thought they showed promise. But as I grew older it was not this serious side of Ricky which captivated me but his lighthearted irreverence. Life was always more fun when Ricky was around. Life had glamour.

The Gower Peninsula might be a quiet country backwater, but not when Ricky Mowbray was drinking gin-and-lime on the terrace at Oxmoon and quoting the *mots justes* of Oscar Wilde. "'We're all in the gutter,' said Oscar, 'but some of us are looking at the stars.' You and I, my dear Kes, have our glances riveted implacably on the divine glamour of the Milky Way. Your cousin Harry, on the other hand, and your feral porcine uncle Thomas are face down in the mud and peering through the drain at the sewer."

But Ricky could keep his catty tongue well in control. He was charming to my mother, who liked him. He was deferential to Aunt Celia, who doted on him. And he was busy playing Prince Charming to Cousin Erika, who had confessed to Anna that she loved him. Ricky had been thinking of marrying her ever since he had returned from Grenoble a year ago in the summer of '37.

At first I thought this was a splendid idea. Not only did I believe with profound relief that it proved Ricky's sexual normality, but I felt glad for Erika who in her bovine way was more than worthy of a decent husband. It also occurred to me gradually, so gradually that for a long time the thought was merely an unformulated intuition in my mind, that four was a more comfortable number in the circumstances than three. I was unable to analyze this opinion, but after I was married I found I felt more at ease when Ricky, Anna and Erika were all present than when Ricky and Anna were my only companions. Since the discomfort was so nebulous I said nothing to Anna, not because I wished to hide it from her but because I thought it was unimportant, and I only started to worry actively about the situation when Ricky, after a couple of gin-and-limes, made a remark that I found quite unacceptable.

It was a warm October evening not long after the dramatic severance of my leading strings, and Ricky and Erika had been invited to dinner to celebrate his appointment as my Devoted Factotum. Erika for some reason was late; Anna was still upstairs changing; Ricky and I were alone together on the terrace.

We were discussing the international situation which at that time was gilded in a rosy pacifist glow, and I had just remarked that thrilled though I was by Mr. Chamberlain's *tour de force* at Munich I couldn't help thinking the long-term outlook was sinister in the extreme.

"I agree," said Ricky. "That's why I think it could be useful to have a German wife. It would be the only hope of ensuring glamour under an army of occupation."

There was so much wrong with this statement that at first I could only boggle at him but finally I said, "Well, I'm a pacifist, but the last thing I'd ever do would be to fraternize with the army of occupation, particularly if they'd requisitioned my home and taken my wife off to a concentration camp."

"But my dear Kes, one has to survive!"

"Without Anna and Oxmoon I'd rather be dead. Ricky, you don't just want to marry Erika because she's got a German passport, do you?"

"Don't be absurd! I want to marry her for her divine blond hair—and for her divinely dreary Teutonic mind!"

I boggled again. "Ricky," I said, "you shouldn't be catty about your almost-fiancée, you know. Are you quite sure you want to propose?"

"Of course I'm sure! I'm going to pop the question tonight when I take her home! I'll halt the car and we'll gaze up at the star-spangled Welsh night and—"

"Ricky, be serious." I was by now most perturbed. "If you're not in love with Erika, then why the devil are you marrying her?"

Ricky flushed. This was unusual. He prided himself on being debonair at all times. "For Christ's sake, Kes, I *am* in love with her! What's the matter with you?"

When I saw he was sincere I felt more baffled than ever because I could see now with perfect clarity that he wasn't the least in love, no matter how much he yearned to believe that he was. I was still only eighteen but suddenly it was as if he were my age and I were the one who was twenty-three. My recent experiences had helped me to grow up; my writer's obsession with character was steadily honing my perception of others; I looked at Ricky then and recognized a man in a muddle who hid all manner of problems behind a pseudo-sophisticated mask.

That evening as soon as the guests were gone I confided in Anna.

"How very peculiar," she said baffled, but added thoughtfully: "I wonder if he feels that four would be a more comfortable number than three."

We stared at each other. Then I said, "This gets more bizarre than ever. I certainly feel that. But why?"

"I've noticed," said Anna, "that when the three of us are alone together, he's the odd one out and although he's always very nice about it perhaps he minds more than we think. Yet when Erika's here I naturally spend a lot of time chatting to her and then Ricky has you to himself and doesn't feel so left out anymore."

"Oh God," I said, my fertile imagination combining with my new maturity to form an exceptionally unpalatable vision. "Anna, this is all much more bizarre than we think it is, and particularly since I'm convinced Ricky isn't acting deliberately." But before I could explain this judgment I had to tell her about his homosexual declaration when I was sixteen. I would have told her before but a confused compassion mingled with an acute embarrassment had kept me silent; it was simply an incident on which I preferred not to dwell. ". . . so although he thinks he's got over these homosexual inclinations," I concluded rapidly, summing up the present situation, "perhaps he hasn't, perhaps they're still there, perhaps his marriage to Erika is all bound up with his feelings for me."

"Heavens!" said Anna, who had barely heard of homosexuality and could be excused for reacting with amazement to this most convoluted example I was offering her. "But darling, are you sure? You know how often you get carried away by your wonderful imagination—"

"I know I'm right." And now I saw Ricky not with the eye of friendship but with the eye of a writer bent on detached analysis, the eye that was learning how to strip a man's character to the bone in an attempt to pry into the mystery of his personality.

"Well, if you really are right," said Anna, who despite her love of romance had a practical streak which often reminded me of my mother, "I think we ought to stop worrying about Ricky and start worrying about Erika."

I knew she was right but this only deepened my dilemma.

"I can't betray him," I said, "and neither can you, because I've told you in confidence. I concede Erika ought to know but it's up to her to find out."

"But darling, how could she? In fact do you think she's even heard of homosexuality? The truth is that unless one moves in Bohemian circles it's just not talked about, is it?"

"True, but it would be impossible to be a friend of Ricky's for long without hearing all about Oscar Wilde."

We decided to drop a hint, and the next time we saw Erika on her own (she was engaged by that time—Ricky had taken advantage of the star-spangled night), Anna said brightly after I had initiated a discussion of *The Importance of Being Earnest*, "I expect poor Mr. Wilde was *very* unhappily married as he was a homosexual!"

"Heavens, yes!" I agreed fervently. "It must have been such a tricky situation for his wife!" And we both turned to gaze at Cousin Erika for a reaction.

There was none. Round-faced and placid, a blond plait coiled neatly over each ear, she merely waited politely for the conversation to continue.

"We can't hint harder than that without betraying Ricky," I said afterwards to Anna, "and frankly I think she's lucky to get him. I wouldn't have her."

"Poor Erika!" said Anna. "If only she wasn't so—"

"Lugubrious."

"Exactly!" It was rare for Anna to be at a loss for a word. Unlike Erika, who pronounced her words faultlessly yet always managed to sound stilted, Anna had a heavy accent but a perfect command of colloquial English.

"I don't see what more we can do," I said, and added to ease my conscience: "Maybe it'll be all right. After all, if Ricky sincerely wants to be a heterosexual, oughtn't we to do all we can to encourage him?"

"But is one's sexuality simply an attitude of mind?"

I didn't know, and it occurred to me then that sex was a far more complicated subject than most people thought.

"Anna, be honest—do you object to my friendship with Ricky?"

"No, I like him. He's fun. I'd only object if I thought you loved him better than you loved me, but you don't, do you?"

"No, that would be a mental, physical and emotional impossibility."

"Then I can't see that either of us has anything to worry about. There may be trouble between Ricky and Erika, but when all's said and done it can't affect our happiness."

She was wrong. The trouble began after the wedding when Ricky asked if he and Erika could live at Oxmoon.

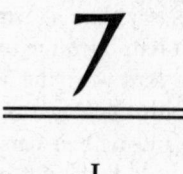

I

I KNEW at once I had to take a tough line, the kind of tough line I had taken with Uncle John over my elopement. Ricky, like most people, had never seen me at my toughest. I shocked him to the core.

"So that's why you married into the Godwin family," I said. "You saw I'd never invite you to live here while you were a factotum with a home of your own, but you thought I wouldn't turn you down if you were my cousin's husband and conveniently found yourself homeless."

Ricky turned a deep painful red. "That's a bloody thing to say!"

"Well, what am I to think? You come here and trot out this story about your mother not getting on with Erika and how you can't evict your mother because she has a life interest in the house under your father's will, but all this must have been obvious to you before your wedding—you're no fool. Now, look here, Ricky. You're my best friend. You're being invaluable to me as my factotum and I'm deeply grateful to you, but I can't have you living here. It wouldn't suit. Sorry."

"But Kes—" He was frantic, his poise shattered, his mask of sophistication falling apart before my eyes, but I did not dare feel sorry for him; the situation was too dangerous. "—why wouldn't it suit? Why? All four of us get on so well!"

"Two's company and three or four is quite definitely a crowd. Ricky, our friendship means a great deal to me and I don't in the least want to see it go down the drain, but down the drain it'll go in double-quick time if you can't accept my decision. I won't have you at Oxmoon and that's that." I then terminated the conversation by adding: "I draw the line." Not for nothing had I endured years of being brought up by Uncle John.

Ricky covered his face with his hands, and suddenly he was so pathetic in his futile unreciprocated love that I could no longer check my feelings. I felt desperately sorry for him, and beyond the pity lay guilt that I should be the cause of so much genuine misery.

"But what am I to do?" he whispered in despair. "I'm in an awful hole, Kes. I couldn't possibly raise the money to buy Erika the sort of home she ought to have. I'm in debt as it is, and now that my mother's being so difficult I can't ask her for money. You see, I've been so absolutely relying on our friendship—"

"Of course. Why not? Just because you can't live at Oxmoon you needn't think you can't rely on me to give you whatever financial help you need," I said compassionately, seizing the chance to alleviate my guilt, and that was how I came to take yet another fatal step along the road to my great disaster.

II

What was my most fatal step? Sacking Thomas? Sacking Fairfax? Engaging Ricky? Engaging Adam? No, this lethal reshuffling of personnel merely set the stage so that I could embark on my great dream; my most fatal step was beginning the long-awaited glorification of Oxmoon.

Yet this need not have been such a catastrophe. My mother and Uncle John, bent on restoring the family fortune at a time when the postwar economic climate was beggaring so many members of the Anglo-Welsh gentry, had brought me up to be very conscious of the evils of extravagance, and I did realize I had no business behaving as if I were the Duke of Westminster with the title deeds of half London in my pocket. So what drove me over the cliff into the abyss?

Looking back I can see a number of sinister facts lurking around my situation like a bunch of death's-heads at the feast. I was very young; in the September of 1938 when I severed my leading strings I was still two months short of my nineteenth birthday. Also for ten years I had been guarded by my twin watchdogs, my mother and Uncle John, and now suddenly they were both gone with the result that I was exposed not only to obvious temptations like extravagance but to subtle psychological pressures which at the time I hadn't the experience to understand.

The truth was that my mother, while tolerating my eccentricities in her own splendidly unorthodox fashion, had always made it clear to me that I should model myself on Uncle John, and Uncle John had always made it clear to me that if one could not be the perfect Godwin, keeping a stiff upper lip, doing the done thing and drawing noble lines left, right and center, one was inevitably doomed to some unspeakable fate. "Terrible things happen," thundered Uncle John, chilling my childish blood, "when people fail to stick to the rules."

Quite so. But the result of this puritanical Victorian tub-thumping was that I wound up terrified of falling short of Uncle John's heroic standards and therefore being automatically damned for all eternity by my failure not just to stick to the rules but to live up to them. While my mother had been alive she had boosted my confidence by behaving as if she thought I was guaranteed of a successful life, but with my mother gone I found that my self-confidence, never strong, was now shaky in the extreme. Consequently, I tended to embrace any course of action that boosted my confidence and gave me the impression I was being a huge success.

Oxmoon boosted my confidence. Anna boosted my confidence. And on my honeymoon I had discovered that spending money boosted my confidence. So whenever I felt a little inadequate, whenever a situation seemed rather more than I could master, I instinctively turned either to Oxmoon or to Anna or to my bank account in order to make myself feel more secure.

Ricky made me feel inadequate. After my showdown with him in the January of 1939 he represented to me not only an insoluble problem but a problem I was secretly terrified I couldn't control. A normal friendship is hard to sustain when the normality is all on one side, and although Ricky's behavior was immaculate I was aware increasingly of tensions, of uneasy crosscurrents of emotion, and Anna was aware of them too. I began to wonder where we were all going to end but I found I was too nervous to visualize the answer; perhaps what I feared was some catastrophic outburst from Ricky which would end our friendship, wreck his marriage and taint my relationship with Anna. The obvious solution, as I told Anna more than once, was to get rid of him before any catastrophe occurred, but I just couldn't do it. I felt so responsible for him. I felt so guilty. I felt I had to do all I could to make amends for my sexual indifference which I sensed was still hurting him so deeply.

"Kester, you're being very silly," said Anna severely. "Here you are, paying Ricky a salary, providing him with interesting work, even paying the mortgage on his new house—and he still sees you every day! Why should you feel guilty about him? I think he's very lucky and I don't feel sorry for him at all!"

This made me realize that the situation with Ricky was quite beyond me, and terrified that she might think me weak I said rapidly, "I know, I'm being idiotic. Let's run up to London for the weekend and stay at the Savoy and have lashings of caviar and champagne!"

We did, and once I'd started spending money I felt so much better that I was reluctant to stop. We descended like locusts on Christie's and Sotheby's, and as I bid for a pair of ravishing Chinese jade horses which I knew had been destined by God for the hall at Oxmoon I suddenly realized that the hour had come for the Great Glorification which I had been promising myself since childhood.

I might fall far short of being a perfect Godwin but at least I could make Oxmoon the most perfect house in Wales.

"I want only the best for Oxmoon," I said to my new friend Toby James. "Nothing but the best."

"Dear boy," said Toby, quickly deciding I was a young man of unparalleled good sense, "you shall have it."

I heard of Toby through Aunt Julie, who had met him at some party in Chelsea. He was a well-known interior decorator, and I knew as soon as he saw Oxmoon that I wanted to employ him.

"But it's a marvelous place!" he exclaimed as he stood in the hall and gazed with his sharp clever eyes at the sweep of the staircase. "A little gem of civilization in an enchanting rustic backwater! Imagine how stunning it must have been in the eighteenth century—imagine battling out from Swansea through miles of mud and hordes of astounded sheep and then suddenly—Beauty! Refinement! Luxury! Grace! Dear boy, it must have seemed like a vision of heaven!"

"Exactly!" I said excited. "And I want to recapture that vision of heaven—I want to make it live again!"

"How deliciously heroic!" said Toby. "What a splendid young man you are!"

Those were exactly the words I wanted to hear. I engaged him. The components of the disaster were now all slipping smoothly into place, and at my side as always stood Ricky, the catalyst, unconsciously luring me on to prove my manhood with each lavish check I rushed to sign.

III

By this time it was the February of 1939 and Ricky and Erika had been married for two months. They hadn't been the only couple in the neighborhood to walk down the aisle before Christmas. A month before their wedding, all four of us had been electrified by the news that Cousin Harry was engaged to Belinda Stourham and was proposing to stampede with her to the altar as soon as the banns had been called.

"That's quite impossible," was my immediate reaction.

Cousin Harry had been flourishing at Penhale Manor since September, although we had not met since the severance of my leading strings. I had heard Thomas had been helping him with the estate and presently word had reached me that in the opinion of the local rustics Harry was hardworking, enthusiastic and "a born farmer just like his grandfather." Bad news travels fast.

I had also heard he had been seeing Belinda since his return to Gower, but I had thought it necessary merely to raise a quizzical eyebrow and remark, "Some men are easily pleased." Nasty little Belinda Stourham, who had just turned eighteen, was Gestapo Thomas's sister-in-law, and now that old Oswald was dead I had no doubt that Thomas and Eleanor were anxious to marry her off so that they could have Stourham Hall to themselves. (The maiden aunt, Miss Angela Stourham, had also recently died, probably from exhaustion resulting from years of looking after her invalid brother and bringing up his ghastly offspring.) The bulk of the land attached to Stourham Hall had been sold off years ago to the Llewellyns, but Thomas and Eleanor had decided to expand their pig farm there when I fired Thomas from Oxmoon.

"Why is Harry's engagement so incomprehensible to you?" demanded Ricky amused when the news reached us. "There's usually only one reason for a hasty trip to the altar!"

"Certainly," agreed Erika, stilted as ever despite her animation at the prospect of a family scandal. "It is beyond doubt that she is pregnant."

"Imagine Harry not doing the done thing!" Anna was as amazed as I was.

"Well, that's just it," I said. "It's not possible. I can't imagine why they're getting married but I do know Belinda can't possibly be pregnant."

Ricky laughed. "Surely even Harry must be subject to accidents occasionally!"

"No, you miss the point. There couldn't have been an accident because he would never have slept with her. Harry wouldn't seduce anyone who could be ranked as a 'nice girl.' That wouldn't be playing the game."

"Bet you five pounds he becomes a father in seven months' time!" said Ricky, still not taking me seriously, and was astonished when I said, "Done."

"But Kester," said Anna, "if she's not pregnant, why's Harry marrying like this when he's only nineteen? Surely Uncle John can't possibly approve!"

But I was ready for this. My fertile imagination had by this time had several seconds to visualize a plausible explanation.

"Belinda must have come into money when old Oswald died," I said. "I know her mother was a platinum-blond tart, but Belinda's a Stourham and her father was one of my grandfather's best friends. So socially and financially this marriage would make sense to Uncle John—he might have hoped Harry would do better for himself, but he's not going to object if Harry's dead keen—as he obviously must be. Of course Uncle John would inevitably think nineteen's too young, but Harry will be twenty soon and he's no doubt seduced battalions of married women so at least Uncle John doesn't have to worry that he's inexperienced, and he probably feels Harry's worldly enough to reach a wise decision. In fact now that I really think about it I can see it's rather a brilliant match," I said, realizing with horror that Harry had outshone me as usual. I knew Uncle John would consider a Stourham of Llangennith a far better matrimonial prospect than a Steinberg of Berlin.

"But Kes," objected Ricky, "how could any man be madly in love with a girl who looks like Donald Duck?"

"I don't think she looks like Donald Duck," I said. "I think she looks like Mae West playing Snow White." Although I had always thought Belinda plain I suspected that Harry would never have looked twice at any woman who couldn't be ranked as a sex goddess, so I was obliged to make a hasty revision of my past judgment.

The wedding at Llangennith was not large but all the family were there so I felt there was a cast of thousands. At the reception Uncle John very kindly came up to me and inquired how I was getting on. I told him everything was absolutely

594

wonderful, and smiled radiantly. Uncle John said nothing could please him more. After that I realized I had drunk too much champagne and retired to the cloakroom to be sick. We left early.

A week later, just as I was congratulating myself that I had fully recovered from this ordeal, Harry and Belinda returned from their brief honeymoon in the Wye Valley and sent us a Christmas card.

"Oh God," I said. "We'll have to send them one."

"Should we invite them over for a Christmas drink?"

"Yes. But we're not going to."

The telephone rang. It was Cousin Harry, very charmingly inviting us to have a Christmas drink at Penhale Manor. I might have known he would outshine me as usual by doing the done thing no matter how adverse the circumstances.

"Thanks, Harry," I said, wishing Christmas could be abolished. "We'd love to come."

We arrived at six thirty and stayed exactly one hour in the drawing room, which was shabby and untidy but otherwise much as it had been when Bronwen had lived at the Manor with Uncle John. The main addition to the room was an expensive radiogram which I immediately coveted. Harry was a wireless addict and apparently unable to face life without continual concerts on the airwaves.

Despite the hour neither of them had bothered to change into evening clothes. Harry, wearing baggy gray trousers, a crisp white shirt and an old tweed jacket with leather patches at the elbows, looked very much the country squire who was pretending to be short of money, while Belinda, wearing a skirt which looked as if it had been made out of a tablecloth and a somewhat shrunken pullover which emphasized her Mae West bosom, looked like nothing on earth. Anna and I, discreetly clad in the products of Harrods and Savile Row, could only feel grossly overdressed. We all eyed each other very watchfully indeed.

"One gin-and-French, one gin-and-It!" said Harry, flashing Anna a smile as he handed us our glasses. "Now, Bella, what are you going to have?"

I was still digesting this unlikely Victorian sobriquet when Belinda gave him such an erotic look from her hot brown eyes that I nearly had an erection. Perhaps Harry did have one, but he had his back to me so it was impossible to be sure.

"Oh, just give me some of the usual jungle juice, darling," said my new cousin Belinda, confirming my suspicion that she was the last word in rampant sex appeal. (Why had I never noticed this before Harry had picked her out? I supposed I had been too busy dismissing her as an imbecile.)

"Well!" I said to Anna as we escaped on the dot of half-past seven. "No prizes for guessing what *they* do in their spare time! What do you think was going on underneath that tablecloth she was wearing?"

"Nothing," said Anna. "You're going to win that bet with Ricky."

"How can you be so sure?"

"Pregnant girls drink milk and look as if they want to redesign the nursery. They don't drink jungle juice and look as if all they can think of is copulation."

She was right. I won my bet. Seven months later Belinda was without doubt pregnant but it was plain too that she was nowhere near giving birth and the baby was eventually born a respectable ten months after the wedding.

Meanwhile there was still no sign of little Christopher on the horizon. His absence had become a constant monthly disappointment to us, and although Anna begged me not to worry I felt my demons were pursuing me again, the demon of inadequacy, the demon of problems I feared I had no power to solve, and so as time passed I flung myself more wholeheartedly than ever into the glorification of Oxmoon—until in its growing beauty I saw my power redeemed.

IV

Oxmoon!

My myth, my dream, my magic house—and I'm the magician waving my magic wand, I'm the rich man writing endless checks, and every time I sign my name another dream comes true.

I'm close to Robert Godwin, eighteenth-century Robert Godwin, the dreamer who met Robert Adam and saw a vision in Welsh stone and slate. His architect's plans are still in the library and so are his own drawings and his letters, the estimates and the bills. I've seen his dream as clearly as I've read his writing; it's as if he were walking again through the house that he created, and now I'm walking to meet him in the palace of our dreams. He's been dead for a hundred and forty years but we've beaten time, we've beaten death and in my mind he lives again.

Can you hear me, Robert Godwin, can you see me as I see you? Then rest in peace, your dream's reborn, your vision was not in vain.

That rat-infested Victorian mansion, that casual Edwardian country house, that shabby postwar ghost of a past splendor—they're all fading, all dissolving as I wave my magic wand. And in their end is your beginning, and in your beginning is my inspiration and in my inspiration lies the resurrection of that brilliant house beyond compare.

V

My first ambition was to go back to the eighteenth century and re-create the house as it had been originally but soon I realized that my own tastes were too powerful and too urgent to allow me to recapture with perfect fidelity the Oxmoon of Robert Godwin the Renovator. However what I did do, with Toby's help, was to create a strong eighteenth-century atmosphere to act as a magnificent showcase for all the beautiful things that I loved. Meissen, Worcester, Chelsea, Derby, Ch'ien Lung, K'ang Hsi—ravishing pieces surfaced in the salesroom, I waved my magic wand and then they all came to Oxmoon, radiant ravishing Oxmoon, to take their part in the mighty Resurrection of 1939.

The pictures came too, not only the Gainsborough which Robert Godwin might have known but the romantic landscapes of Sawrey Gilpin and the vistas of Welsh mountains by John Varley and the portraits of beautiful women by Lawrence and Millais. I toyed with the idea of buying more modern paintings but for the most part I left them alone; modern painting interests me but it seldom speaks to me and the only novelty I purchased in this style was a blue mess called *Woman with a Cornflower* by that Spaniard Picasso. The only trouble was that it looked out of place in the eighteenth-century ambience, so in the end I hung it in the lavatory where it looked wonderfully cheerful and made even the dreariest routine of life an aesthetic experience.

Meanwhile Toby and I had turned our attention to furniture. Out went all the ghastly Victorian whatnots and overstuffed armchairs. Down from the attics came Robert Godwin the Renovator's eighteenth-century walnut chairs with matching settees which had originally been upholstered in caffoy (cut wool velvet—ravishing and rare). Unfortunately the caffoy had perished, but Toby suggested new fabrics based on eighteenth-century designs and soon the drawing room was transformed. Gilt gesso girandoles and side tables added luminous finishing touches. The Gainsborough, my pride and joy, hung above the newly-imported Adam fireplace. It was a touching portrait of a young girl not unlike Anna with a sensitive mouth and misty romantic dark eyes.

Toby continued to pursue our policy which could loosely be described as Chippendale and civilization, but gradually, as time went on, our passion for Chippendale was exhausted and only Civilization, now spelled with a capital C, remained.

"Dear boy, I've found this heavenly Axminster carpet for the drawing room..."

I sanctioned the heavenly Axminster carpet.

"...and perhaps *Italian* marble for the hall..."

I sanctioned the Italian marble.

"...and dear boy, I've found these two divine swags of fruit carved in the manner of Grinling Gibbons—not the master himself, I'm sorry to say, but a really first-class eighteenth-century effort—I thought the pair of them would look so well in the dining room now we've decided on the eighteenth-century oak paneling..."

I sanctioned the two divine swags of carved fruit.

"...and I was at this auction the other day, dear boy, and I heard a whisper about this simply celestial chandelier coming up for sale next week—I know it would transform the hall into an absolutely major masterpiece..."

I sanctioned the celestial chandelier.

"...not too much change in the ballroom, I think, dear boy—it's all so *fragrant* in there, as dear Noël would say.... Some of the mirrors need resilvering and the floor needs attention but apart from that I recommend only decoration in white and gold—oh and dear boy, I've just had the most godlike inspiration: how about a white-and-gold grand piano to match?"

I sanctioned the white-and-gold grand piano. I sanctioned everything. I was in heaven.

However unfortunately heaven can be uncomfortable when invaded by an army of builders and decorators, so presently I decided to whisk Anna off to London for a few weeks. After all, why not? I had dear old Simon to attend to my minor correspondence whenever he wasn't recataloguing the library (Simon's health was failing, but he still loved to feel he was useful), and I had Ricky, my Devoted Factotum, to supervise my house and estate. Adam Mowbray was always available to attend to any boring legal or financial problems that cropped up, and although my bank manager Mr. Lloyd-Thomas had been surly of late, that never worried me because I knew Adam could handle him. Adam also dealt directly with the estate manager Stanley Bland (rechristened Champagne Sasha by Ricky after a particularly amusing party we gave to welcome him to Oxmoon). Sasha was twenty-four and had only recently qualified as an estate agent, but he certainly seemed to know all the answers. He was Adam's first wife's sister's nephew (or something), and Adam thought very highly of him. Meanwhile, Adam himself had exchanged his white Lagonda for a sleek black Daimler, and everyone said how well he must be doing at the racetrack.

Anyway, there I was in London with Anna and of course we stayed at the Savoy but then I had a marvelous idea and took a lease of a flat that overlooked Hyde Park. Anna thought it was wonderful, and when she returned from her fittings for the new wardrobe of clothes which I was giving her, she said she felt so like Cinderella that she had almost ordered a pair of glass slippers. That made me very happy. I sent her two dozen red roses every day and we drank champagne every night and we saw all the best plays and films in town and life was glorious, vivid, thrilling. We bought more treasures for Oxmoon too, some very rare Chelsea chocolate cups and a Ming vase which looked spiritual in the moonlight. Then I had an inspiration and remembered the Oxmoon library which was crammed with Victorian sermons and almost crying out to be restocked with dozens of leather-bound editions of our favorite books.

"We'll order the entire works of Anthony Hope!" I exclaimed, nostalgically recalling our first meeting over *The Prisoner of Zenda,* and we settled down to draw up a very long list of books that we deemed essential to our survival.

When the books had been ordered we thought it was time to see what was going on at Oxmoon, so we drove back to Wales in my new Daimler (inspired by Adam Mowbray's last acquisition). The house was still in chaos but I didn't mind because that was just dreary old reality and I could see the Beauty, the Truth, the Art and the Peace evolving steadily behind it.

Dreary old reality, however, was by this time increasingly trying to impinge on my golden vision.

"All kinds of people are panting to see you, Kes," said Ricky.

"Oh, you deal with them—I want to write." My detective story *Lady Sybil's Alibi* had just been rejected by yet another undiscerning publisher, and I knew the only way to obliterate my searing sense of failure was to begin another novel without delay.

"But who's going to sign the checks? Do you want to give me a power of attorney?"

"Well..." I was reluctant to hurt him by displaying a lack of trust but I knew it would be unwise to give access to my bank account to a man who always seemed to be short of money. I was just thinking in panic that I couldn't cope when I had a brain wave, a plausible excuse which I knew he would accept. "Ricky, don't be hurt," I said cleverly, taking the bull by the horns, "but I really think I ought to give the power of attorney to Simon. Dear old Simon, you know how much it means to him to be useful and how he hates to feel as if he's living on my charity."

Ricky knew how I felt about Simon and believed me. The crisis was averted, and telling everyone I had to have absolute seclusion I embarked on yet another detective story featuring the Honorable Jonathan Courtney-Sherringham and the woman he loved, the adventuress Penelope Michaelis. This time I was determined they should go to bed without being married and to hell with the conventions of detective fiction.

Within half an hour even Robert Godwin's eighteenth-century vision had vanished from my mind.

"I say, Kes—"

"Oh God, Ricky, what is it now?"

"Adam and I had rather a dustup with Lloyd-Thomas this morning in Swansea and Adam says you'd better put the brakes on the spending spree. The most ghastly people are starting to call here for money."

"How awful," I said, but I wasn't really listening. The beautiful Penelope, who had just donned a purple tea gown, was busy spraying an erotic perfume above her Mae West décolletage.

VI

Writing!

I was nineteen years old and writing junk. Most people do at that age. So how can I explain how mesmerizing my junk was to me as it emerged from my brain to form little black lines and curves on virgin sheets of paper? A mature writer is under an obligation to be enthralled by the creation of a masterpiece; any layman can accept that. But what laymen so often fail to understand is that it's *the act of creation itself* which generates this powerful excitement. Thus the writer at work on junk is as vulnerable to ecstasy as the writer at work on a masterpiece. They both know they're experiencing the most exquisite pleasure the human soul can know.

A majority of people, of course, think the most exquisite pleasure is sex. Poor things! I feel so sorry for them sometimes. Of course sex is great fun, but when all's said and done it's just a sport, isn't it? There's nothing wrong with sport; it's a pleasant way of filling in time if you've nothing better to do, and plenty of charming and intelligent people are dead keen on it, but... well, you don't worry about filling in time if you're a writer. When you're a writer at work, there *is* no time, only eternity, because writing's forever. Even if you tear up everything you ever do, every word you've ever written will still go towards making you a better writer and the better you become the more powerful the magic at your disposal, the magic that can triumph over time.

I'm a magician again. I'm waving my magic wand. I'm anyone anywhere. The ordinary rules of time and space no longer apply. The ink flows from my pen, the keys clack on my typewriter and little hieroglyphics emerge to reflect a vision which only I can see but which perhaps one day countless people can share.

Robert Godwin the Renovator dreamed in stone and glass. I dream in words. Dreams are all that really matter in life. To dream is to be immortal, to dream is to see eternity, to dream is—

"Kester?"

"Oh darling, I'm sorry I'm so far away from you at the moment but I'll make it up to you later..."

Had Anna ever realized I could be like this? No, of course not. She was probably asking herself why she had never guessed I could be quite so peculiar.

I knew I ought to make love to her because there was still no little Christopher on the horizon, but I was emotionally spent. I could do no more than kiss her good night. I thought: When I wake up tomorrow I'll have the energy. And I was right. I had the energy, but all I did was rush straight back to my typewriter.

Then one morning I was writing the word OBSESSION and I felt my father walk into my mind. Had he felt guilty when he rushed back to his mountains? Yes. How awful he must have felt, abandoning my mother mentally, emotionally and—as I now knew—sexually, but of course he would have been quite unable to stop himself. He'd had a dream, and beside that dream all else had become futile and insignificant.

Can you hear me, Robert Godwin, can you see me as I see you? My father, more than ten years dead, but I know you now better, far better, than I ever did when you were alive. I know you better than you ever dreamed was possible; you never thought when you looked at me that I'd come to know you through and through. Ah yes, I can see it all, I see how miserable you must have been in London with your glittering career—what do glittering careers matter when you're cut off from the breath of life? And I see for the first time how lonely you must have been with my mother, my gorgeous, stormy, emotionally exhausting mother who talked so much of passion yet knew no passion but sex. I see you unable to bear your abstinence any longer, I see you looking at those mountains, I see you coming alive again while all your weeping wife can do is talk so meaninglessly of obsessions.

You shouldn't have willed yourself to die like that. You could still have been alive, and then think how happy I could have made you, think what interesting conversations we could have had, think how glad you would have been to find that at last there was someone who understood you...

But you died.

Or did you? Yes, but I'm resurrecting you, and now once again the miracle's happening because I've beaten time, I've beaten death and in my mind you live again. . . .

VII

"Sorry to disturb you again, Kes—"

"Oh Christ!"

"—but Lloyd-Thomas is downstairs. He's looking exactly as Pontius Pilate must have looked after deciding that Christ really did have to be crucified."

"Well, tell him to wash his hands and go away."

I was with my people. I saw them all and heard their voices, and they were far more real to me than dim mythical figures like Mr. Lloyd-Thomas the bank manager. Inside my head, like a strip of Technicolor film, their lives evolved before my eyes.

"Kester . . ."

I opened my mouth to shout, *"For Christ's sake don't interrupt me when I'm writing!"* but then I saw it was Simon, loyal, faithful Simon who was still so anxious to help me even though he was so badly crippled and so prematurely aged. I could not shout at someone who had been such a good friend to me— and to my father. I was so close to my father now, so close, he was at my side all the time. Can you hear me, Robert Godwin, can you see me as I see you—

"Kester, I'm signing the most amazing checks. I think you should look at them before they go out."

I flicked through the checks, but I never saw them. I was with my father as he pulled on his climbing boots. I was with my eighteenth-century ancestor as he shook hands with Robert Adam. I was in my old bedroom at Oxmoon and I was in the middle of the most riveting scene I had ever written.

"Yes, it's all right, Simon," I said. "Don't worry. I've got everything under control."

VIII

"Adam's muzzled Lloyd-Thomas, Kes. All you have to do is sign this bit of paper here."

"What is it?"

"A contract with some moneylenders. Adam says they're really an awfully decent crowd."

601

"All right." I signed.

"And Kes—"

"No more, Ricky, not now." I had a double bed waiting for my hero and heroine, and I was already hearing the latest lines of Noël Coward–style dialogue. (I like my passion laced with wit.) What could possibly be more irrelevant than Ricky blathering about outstanding bills?

"But Vaughan is breathing fire..."

Vaughan was the tenant of Daxworth farm.

"...some sort of muddle with Sasha..."

"Send him to Adam."

"Adam's at the races."

"Then send him to the races."

My plan for a detective story had got lost somewhere in Chapter Four. I no longer cared who had murdered the Count in the locked gun room with an African spear impregnated with curare. All I cared about was my two lovers who had turned out to be doomed. Penelope eventually committed suicide. My hero boarded a boat for Argentina. I was in such agony for him in his bereavement that I could hardly type THE END after the final line.

Wandering dazed through the house some unknown time later I found that work had been completed in the ballroom. It was a mirrored paradise of white and gold, and tears came to my eyes because it was so beautiful. Then because I knew Robert Godwin the Renovator was beside me I said to him, "You never saw the ballroom, did you, because it was built by your grandson Robert Godwin the Regency Rake, but look how wonderful it is, how glorious, how perfect..."

A hand touched my arm. I had not been speaking aloud but I had been so absorbed in my conversation with Robert that I hadn't noticed Toby fluttering into the room at a brisk pace. When he touched me I jumped. Then I felt extraordinarily confused, because I knew I was in two centuries at once. I glanced out of the window and saw it was summer—but which summer? I had become so accustomed to traveling in other dimensions that it was hard for me to pin myself to an exact point in time and space.

"Dear boy, *lovely* to see you again! Someone tells me you're about to produce a new masterpiece of English literature—God knows one was long overdue—but I wonder if we could have just the tiniest word about some payment on account?"

"What?" I said.

Ricky appeared at my elbow. "Kes, bad news. Lloyd-Thomas is on his way over here—I tried to put him off, but he hung up."

It was the summer of 1939. Hitler was at his zenith and Europe was on the brink, but of course I had no idea. I hadn't opened a newspaper for weeks. The remote myths of Nazi Germany had seemed irrelevant and only Jonathan and Penelope's disastrous romance had been real.

"Excuse me, sir," said Lowell, "but a deputation of your tenants headed by Mr. Emlyn Vaughan is in the drive and Mr. Vaughan is asking to see you."

"Kester," said Simon, "Adam Mowbray's on the telephone."

If I'd been Robert Godwin the Renovator any Mowbray I talked to would have been a smuggler and probably a pirate as well.

I went to the twentieth-century telephone.

"Kester," said the pirate, "I'm afraid you can't go on ignoring the writ from that London property company about the nonpayment of rent on your Park Lane flat. However, it just so happens that I've found another firm of moneylenders who'll give you credit..."

Did they shoot pirates? Or did they hang them?

"Kester? Kester, are you there?"

I somehow slotted myself back into the summer of '39. "Adam, Lloyd-Thomas is about to arrive and all the tenants are on the warpath—please, *please* drop everything and come to the rescue!"

The pirate never even paused for breath. He had sailed dangerously close to the wind and now he had to run before the storm. "Terribly sorry, old man, but I've got a vital appointment with a titled client and it's absolutely impossible for me to break it."

Half an hour later Mr. Lloyd-Thomas was telling me in no uncertain terms that there was only one man in the world who could now save me from ruin and that man was my Uncle John.

8

I

I WOKE UP. At first I could not remember where I was or what was happening. Then I saw the sweep of headlights beyond the uncurtained library windows and remembered that after my third brandy I had switched out the light because my eyes were hurting so much. I stood up, moved to the window and saw the black shadow of the Rolls-Royce drawing to a halt in the moonlight. Then I remembered everything. Eighteenth-century Robert Godwin was dead. My father was dead. Jonathan and Penelope were just secret patterns I had made with my typewriter's keys. I was broke, humiliated and shamed, just another unstable youth of nineteen who had gone off the rails, and only Oxmoon, ravishing Oxmoon, remained to bear witness to my brief moment of glory when I had conquered time and seen eternity.

I went out into the hall. I had sent Anna to bed because I knew there would be things said which I preferred her not to hear, and after giving me a brief but loving kiss she had faded away into the shadows upstairs, my little Cinderella slipping back into her rags after her fabled evening at the ball.

I opened the front door. I was thinking how quiet it was now that all the worlds in my head had come to a stop. And how flat real life was, devoid of those extra dimensions of the imagination, how narrow, how profoundly unattractive. I felt stifled too by the straitjacket of a single personality. When one has been many people for a long time and particularly when one has been roaming casually among the centuries, the torture of reinhabiting one's own personality at a fixed point in time resembles being shut up in a small box.

And what a box. I was Kester Godwin on July the twelfth, 1939, and I was walking out into the porch to meet a man who, unlike my father, was absolutely incapable of understanding me. This man was like my mother. The only passion he recognized was sex.

He was speaking to his chauffeur as he got out of the car: "Leave it here, Bridges, for tonight. Just bring my bag in, put it in the hall and go to the servants' quarters." Turning to me, he said abruptly without any preliminary greeting, "I assume arrangements have been made for my chauffeur?"

I had forgotten to remind Lowell. That was bad. Not the done thing. One always had to think of the servants. I swallowed and said, "I'm sure Lowell's remembered."

Uncle John said to his chauffeur, "If there's no one waiting up for you, Bridges, come back to me. I'll be in the drawing room."

"Yes, sir. Thank you, sir," said the chauffeur.

Uncle John walked past me up the steps without a word and reached the threshold of the hall. Now, I thought, *now* he would see the vision which justified my folly. The marble floor glowed richly before my eyes. The jade Chinese horses reared ravishingly atop a wafer-thin Sheraton side table. Romantic pictures, mostly of beautiful women, adorned the walls, and at the half-landing on the stairs, radiant in the light from Toby's celestial chandelier, shimmered the portrait of the most beautiful woman of all, a Welsh woman, romance personified, my doomed great-grandmother Gwyneth Llewellyn restored at last to a place of glory in the house where she had once been mistress.

Uncle John said nothing but he seemed to turn a shade paler. He walked on across the hall, entered the drawing room and paused again to survey the transformation. I saw him glance at the Gainsborough but it meant nothing to him. He looked at the exquisite walnut chairs and settees but they meant nothing to him either; no doubt he merely thought they looked uncomfortable. Still refusing to speak he moved to the marble-topped table by the window, removed the stopper from the Waterford decanter and poured some whisky into one of the heavy cut-glass tumblers. In helping himself to a drink without my permission he assumed the reins of power by little more than a flick of the wrist.

I thought: If he tries to take Oxmoon away from me I'll kill him.

But that was a mad thought which showed how deep I was in misery. Anna would have said it was wrong. Wonderful Anna, keeping me sane by loving me so that in her love I could see myself reflected as the man I longed to be, the greatest master Oxmoon had ever known. Anna and Oxmoon were the twin pillars of my sanity, and so long as I had them I could survive even the cruelest humiliation at the hands of a man who would never understand what I had done.

He turned to face me. His blue eyes had never seemed emptier, and in their emptiness I glimpsed the dark side of his personality which he had always concealed from me and sensed a hard, powerful man, disillusioned, embittered, enraged. In that second I saw beyond the myth of "my heroic Uncle John," and just as my mother's final request had shattered for me the myth of her second marriage, so this glimpse of a hitherto unimagined reality seemed to wipe out all the fixed points of reference that represented stability in my life. I felt all was anarchy and chaos. It was as if there were no rules, no morals, nothing. I was looking into a bottomless pit. It was a vision of hell.

But then I saw him draw the line to shut it out. He looked away as if he knew his eyes were betraying him, and as I saw him pull down the shutters over the dark side of his personality I saw just how strong he was, disciplining the violent emotions, clamping down on the unacceptable thoughts, harnessing the power which in a lesser man could so easily have harnessed him. Then I saw he *was* heroic, not because he was a born hero but because he wasn't; he was heroic because although he was human enough to hate me he was still determined to do what he believed to be right. So the myth survived—but what a myth! I thought it would crush me utterly. I didn't see how I could survive his hatred and stay sane.

But as he stood there, tall, gray-haired, effortlessly distinguished, I remembered all his many kindnesses to me, all the gestures of affection, all the times he had proved how much he did care, and then I saw that he loved me as well as hated me—I saw that he felt towards me exactly as I felt towards him, and I recognized that love loaded with ambivalence, that genuine devotion laced with resentment, that true affection riddled with antipathy. Why does no one ever admit that hatred and love can exist side by side, each emotion genuine but only one ever acknowledged as real? Uncle John and I were locked up in a padded cell hating each other, but there was no escape because our love bound us together. There was only one retreat and that was into misery, guilt and despair.

"Uncle John—"

He held up his hand to cut me off. "Spare me the craven apologies," he said brutally. "Simply start at the beginning and go all the way through to the end. No lies, no omissions. I want the truth, the whole truth and nothing but the truth, and by God I intend to have it."

Sick with humiliation, my throat tight with grief, my whole body feeling as if it were being lacerated with shame I somehow managed to conquer my tears and start talking in a calm level dignified voice.

II

"You were *writing*? Writs were being served on you, your servants' wages were unpaid, your tenants were being subjected to the grossest extortion and you were *writing*?"

"Well, when I'm writing... nothing else seems to matter—"

"Then I suggest you either give up writing or give up Oxmoon! Oxmoon can't afford a master who lives in a pathetic fantasy world!"

"I'll never give up Oxmoon!" I shouted. "Never!"

There was a silence. Then Uncle John turned his back on me and poured himself some more whisky.

I blundered forward impulsively. "If you could only understand what I've done—"

"I see exactly what you've done! You've damned near ruined yourself all within the space of a year! How could you have behaved with such criminal irresponsibility? Give me one simple sentence of explanation!"

I could not talk of visions of perfection or glimpses of eternity. Nor could I talk of the secret fears which signing checks annulled. I groped in my mind for a concept he could understand. "I wanted to pay my debt to Oxmoon. Oxmoon made me. Before I had Oxmoon I was nothing—people despised me, thought I was stupid and pathetic—"

"Well, God knows what they'll think of you now," said Uncle John.

Tears filled my eyes. I couldn't help it. I put up my hands to hide them.

"Stop that! Pull yourself together! My God, are you really so incapable of behaving like a man?"

Black violent emotions erupted in my consciousness, annihilating my self-control. "Damn you, I *am* a man!" I shouted. "I've got this wonderful wife who loves me and I've created this great—this magnificent—this *mighty vision* of a house, and I've got guts, I've got courage, I've got more guts and courage than you'll ever know. You think I'm weak because I'm a writer, but how the bloody hell do you think it feels when a manuscript comes back from the publishers? I feel suicidal, I feel murderous, I feel absolutely crushed and wrecked, but do I give up? No, I bloody well don't! I've been rejected over and over again, but I don't stop sending out my manuscripts, I keep on trying, I live all the time with the most shattering sense of failure, but I won't give in, I'm a fanatic, I've got a will of iron, and if you think I'm weak all I can say is you don't know, you can't know and you'll never know just how bloody strong I really am!"

"Rubbish. You're deceiving yourself. The truth is you've been too weak to face reality—you scribbled fairy tales while Oxmoon went to the wall, and that's not behaving like a man! That's behaving like an immature child!" I tried to interrupt him but he outshouted me. "Be quiet! The tragedy's all the more intolerable to me because I really thought before Ginevra died that you were developing into a young man of considerable promise. But now! Consorting with queers, dressing up Oxmoon like some vulgar Hollywood film set, abandoning your responsibilities to that insolent young devil Mowbray, palming off your tenants on an inexperienced agent who was often so drunk he could hardly ride—"

"Sasha's qualified—Adam Mowbray recommended—"

"Adam Mowbray! That gambler! That crook! My God, I'll see he's struck off the rolls for what he's done to you!"

"But Uncle John, I'm sure he's done nothing wrong—"

"He set you up with the moneylenders, didn't he? And of course he's arranged with them to take a percentage on the deal! And what sort of bills has he been sending in while you've been too busy writing to care?"

"I—"

"If Lloyd-Thomas hadn't pursued the interest on the bank loans so vigorously this mess could have gone on for much longer, but fortunately Lloyd-Thomas decided to allow you no latitude—oh, he's had trouble before with an incompetent master of Oxmoon, and he resolved he wasn't going to turn the same blind eye to you as he turned to my father! Thank God my rough treatment of him back in '28 taught him a lesson which has now proved to be your salvation, but Christ, how I wish I hadn't been foolish enough to humor you when you told me to keep out of your affairs! However there's no point in further recriminations. Now just you listen to me. I'll stand by you. I'll pay your debts. I swore to my brother that so long as I lived I'd see you were master of Oxmoon, but if you want me to save you now you'll damned well have to consent to being master on whatever terms I see fit to lay down."

This was it. Not death but emasculation. I hung my head, clenched my fists behind my back and tried not to shudder with pain.

"You must surrender control of the estate to trustees. You may continue to live in the house but you're not to have a bank account. I'll bring down my own lawyers and accountants to sort out the mess once I've taken a look at it myself, and I'll supervise the reconstruction, but unfortunately it's quite impossible for me to spend more than the minimum amount of time here. I'm a busy man. I could only take over Oxmoon," said Uncle John, pouring himself another whisky, "if you wished to abandon it altogether but since that's not going to happen we must adopt some other arrangement. The first thing I intend to do is to reinstate Fairfax as the Oxmoon solicitor. He can be a trustee with me—and perhaps Edmund can be a trustee too because I think the more members of the family we involve here the better. It's obvious you need the support and stability which only a loyal family can provide."

"Uncle John—"

"And that brings me to Thomas. He must, of course, be the estate manager again."

"No," I whispered. "Not Thomas. No."

"I'm sorry, but I insist. He's not only a Godwin who'll help you out of family loyalty, but he's the best manager I know."

"But he hates me! It would be unbearable!"

"Nonsense! As you won't be running your affairs you'll barely see him—he'll report directly to Fairfax. And if for some reason he fails to behave as he should, your remedy's simple—pick up the phone and let me know." He abandoned his glass of whisky and headed for the door. "I'm very tired—I must get some sleep. Which room have you put me in?"

"The blue room—at least, it's not blue anymore—"

"Lion's old room. Yes. Very well." He walked out into the glory of the hall.

"Uncle John—" I stumbled after him.

"No more, Kester. Both my strength and my patience are exhausted. Good night." And picking up the bag which his chauffeur had deposited by the front door, he ascended the stairs without a backward glance.

I waited till I was sure he was in his room before I tiptoed after him to the floor above.

Anna was lying awake in the dark and later to comfort us both, I tried to make love to her.

But I was impotent.

III

The barbarians were at the gates, poised to rape the city and defile everything they touched.

"Christ," said Thomas, "I told you you'd get yourself in a bloody mess, didn't I? Of course I'm not one bit surprised." He swaggered over the threshold and boggled at the hall. "My God, look at this! Look at it!"

Cousin Harry, sleek in a dark suit, reached the porch.

"Sorry about all the trouble, old chap," he said charmingly, shooting me a glance of utter contempt, "but of course when Father suggested I might lend a temporary hand in the emergency, I dropped everything straightaway. Got to stick together, haven't we? Family solidarity and all that—"

"Here—Harry! Look at these bloody awful changes he's made!"

Cousin Harry looked into the hall and stopped dead.

"Did you ever see anything like it?" shouted Thomas. "He's tarted it up like a bloody gin palace!"

But Cousin Harry never heard him. Cousin Harry was gazing at the Italian marble. Cousin Harry was gazing at Toby's celestial chandelier. And Cousin Harry, my mirror image, was reflecting me, my other self.

Our glances met and in a split second of inexplicable horror we each saw a macabre enigma which had no name.

Harry spoke and at once the horror vanished, but I never forgot that sinister moment in the hall at Oxmoon when Harry and I formed a single personality and he saw my vision as his own.

"Rather amusing, old chap," said my double, slipping back behind the mask that made him my opposite. "Nice to see the old shack get a face lift. Makes a change."

He drifted idly past me. I saw his feet pause on the marble floor as he gazed upwards at the chandelier. He was obviously spellbound again, but the next moment Uncle John was descending the stairs and the spell was broken. He called a greeting; Harry jumped; I moved forward just as Thomas emerged from the drawing room.

"God, John, you look awful! What's he done upstairs? No, don't tell me, I don't want to know. Did you ever see such a load of pansyish rubbish in all your life?"

"This is a business meeting, Thomas, not a discussion of aesthetics. Kindly bear that in mind, would you, please?" said Uncle John, effortlessly exerting his power, and as he crossed the hall to the library Harry turned automatically to follow him and Thomas, the savage aging puppy, trotted in obedience at his master's heels.

Following them into the library I closed the door. It was nine o'clock in the morning and Uncle John had arranged that we should all meet for a preliminary discussion before Fairfax and Lloyd-Thomas arrived at ten.

As we sat down, Uncle John ignored the changes in the room; Thomas never noticed them; but Cousin Harry caressed the retooled leather of the writing table with his long, slim musician's fingers, Cousin Harry stole a quick glance at the rows of new books bound in calf, Cousin Harry had seen the dreaming Welsh landscape over the fireplace and the Persian carpet which glorified the floor.

"Now," said Uncle John, "we'll wait for Fairfax and Lloyd-Thomas before we begin a general discussion of the disaster, but there are certain urgent problems which must be discussed without delay. One: the unpaid servants. We must get the cash to them at once. Lloyd-Thomas will, of course, honor my check but we still have the problem of collecting the money from the bank and it must be done today. Two: the tenants. We must reassure them immediately that the past extortions will be put right and that there's a new regime beginning. Someone will have to ride out to Daxworth for a meeting with that rabid socialist Emlyn Vaughan before he starts advocating the mass extermination of the landed gentry. Three: Kester's associates. We must decide who—if anyone—should be retained."

"Sack the lot of them," said Thomas. "You tackle Adam Mowbray, John, and then at least we'll have the satisfaction of knowing he'll be shitting with fright, even if in the end he does manage to get off scot-free—I hate to say it, but there's no one so clever at escaping justice as a crooked lawyer who knows the law. But I'll make mincemeat of that bloody nephew of his—Christ, why Celia let Erika marry that bugger I'll never know, but Celia probably thinks sodomy's just a place in Palestine. Bloody queers! I'd like to castrate the lot of them! In fact if I had my way—"

"Yes, we all know what you think of sodomy, Thomas. Stick to the point."

"This *is* the point, John! Kester's mixed up with this bloody queer—Christ, Kester's even paying his mortgage for him!"

"Yes, that, of course, must be stopped."

"The whole friendship must be stopped! I think Kester should give us an undertaking he'll never see Ricky again!"

"That could be awkward. Because of Erika."

"Oh, that's no problem!" said Thomas in contempt. "That's one marriage that won't last! I doubt if he's even fucked her—Christ, that sort of queer's a bloody menace and I'm only surprised Anna put up with him continually running after her husband. Why, if I'd been Anna—"

"—you'd have castrated him. Quite. Now come along, Thomas, pull yourself together. I agree with you that young Mowbray should be sacked and I certainly agree that Kester should give an undertaking not to give the boy financial assistance again, but I think we should leave the friendship to resolve itself—as I'm sure it now will—"

"I think you should smash the friendship. Honestly, John, aren't you being a bit soft about this? After all, there's that bloody pansy, egging Kester on, leading him astray left, right and center..."

I was back in London suddenly, back in that soulless house on Eaton Walk when Uncle John had talked of venereal disease and I had had my first untrammeled glimpse of the absolute foulness of the world. I felt now as if I were drowning in that same foulness. I tried to speak to defend my poor pathetic friend who had tried so hard to suppress his love for me to a level I could accept, but speech was beyond me. No man in that room could have understood my friendship with Ricky, and if I made the attempt to defend him I would only damn myself further in their eyes.

"...all right, John, let's leave Ricky and turn to Sasha Bland. I'll shovel him out of the way, no difficulty there, and then I'll arrange for the burial of all those empty champagne bottles which I hear are stacked up in the backyard of that tied cottage of his—and who paid for all *those*, I'd like to know! Christ, I bet the little bugger's not even qualified—I bet Adam just picked him up off some muckheap, dusted him down and then spun Kester some yarn about qualifications which only a baby in nappies would believe. I think Adam was hoping to filch money through Sasha in a way which would leave Sasha taking the blame if anything went wrong. Damn it, prison's too good for that arch-shit Adam Mowbray! If I had my way he'd be—"

"—hung, drawn and quartered. Yes, I must confess I agree with you. Now let me see, is there anyone else who should be eliminated?"

"Yes," said Thomas at once. "Don't forget that crippled old bugger who wanders around here looking like an advertisement for euthanasia—the one who was in love with Robert up at Oxford and had his balls blown off in the trenches—"

I spewed out the filth that was choking me. I was trembling from head to toe but I rose to my feet to take my stand.

"Not Simon," I said. "Adam, Ricky, Sasha—yes, I know they'll all have to go. But not Simon, not my old tutor who's been with me since I was five. He's sick and dependent on me and I want him to stay at Oxmoon till he dies."

"What a lot of bloody sentimental rubbish!" said Thomas furiously. "Who signed all those checks for you? Who signed away money you didn't have? Who stood by and did nothing to save you while you went on buggering your way into this fucking awful mess?"

I looked past Thomas to the man at the head of the table. "Uncle John," I said. "Please—I'll promise never to see Ricky again, I'll promise whatever you like, but let me keep Simon. Please, please let him stay."

Uncle John looked at me without emotion, and when I saw the emptiness in those blue eyes again I knew he had seen a way to punish me for the mistakes he couldn't forgive.

"It must be Thomas's decision," he said flatly. "He's the one who's going to be answerable for the estate to the trustees."

"It's my decision and I've made it," said Thomas. "The old boy goes and that's that."

I blundered away, knocking over my chair, and wrenched open the door. "Anna!" I shouted, and the vibration of my voice mingled with the rush of air from the opening door so that all the crystals shivered in the mighty chandelier. "Anna!" I tripped, righted myself, tripped again, sprawled across the stairs. I could no longer see, but my fingers found the banisters, and I clawed myself to my feet.

She came running, a neat little figure in dark blue, and I stumbled into her outstretched arms.

"Anna, I can't bear it, they want to sack Simon—I can't bear it, they're so brutal, so cruel—my beautiful library choked with their filth—my beautiful home defiled by their mockery—they've stripped me of all pride and dignity and now they're even stripping me of everyone I love—"

"Darling, I'm still here. I'll always be here—and so will Simon." She moved past me across the hall.

"But they say he's got to go—they're implacable—"

"I'll talk to them."

"No, Anna, no—they'll defile you too—"

"But I can't let this pass," said Anna. "I can't let them do this to you." And she walked on towards the library.

"Anna, wait!" I shouted, but she was already entering the room, her head held high, the little silver locket I had given her long ago shining at her throat as it caught the light.

The three men all rose automatically to their feet.

"Good morning," I heard her say composed in her low sweet voice. "Forgive me for interrupting, but who is it who wants Simon dismissed?"

I saw them all realize that the scene which had been running so smoothly for them had suddenly veered quite out of control. Uncle John went a shade whiter; Harry was still as a statue; even Thomas shifted uneasily on his feet, and when they all remained silent with embarrassment I heard myself say violently from the doorway, "It's Thomas. He's the one. And it's he who has the final word."

Anna walked up to Thomas and stood in front of him. "Please," she said, "don't dismiss Simon. It would be cruel. You may not wish to listen to Kester but do, I beseech you, listen to me. Please—let Simon stay."

Uncle John covered his face briefly with his hands but still he said nothing. He was the only man who could have prevented the atrocity, but he stood by and looked the other way.

In contrast Harry was watching avidly. My agony must have been so clearly written on my face, and I knew with a terrible certainty as our glances met that he was enjoying this savage new twist to my humiliation.

But despite this, I was now full of hope, so full of hope that I no longer minded about Harry and Uncle John. I was full of hope because I didn't see how Thomas could refuse her. Surely right must win and good must triumph—surely they couldn't smash my idealism as well as my pride and my happiness—

"Oh, for Christ's sake!" exploded Thomas, losing his temper to wipe out his uneasiness. "What do you think this is—a Jewish holy war? And why do you bloody Jews always have to turn up where you're not wanted and make a bloody nuisance of yourselves? For God's sake run off and mind your own damned business!"

Horror poured into the room, filling every nook and cranny and thickening the air so that no one could move.

I wanted to kill him. I would have killed him but the horror was as thick as cement, entombing me. Violent emotions overwhelmed my battered mind, and as they surged through the open wounds to take root deep in my soul I knew Thomas had corrupted me, brutalized her, damned every one of us who had witnessed his barbarism. His action was catastrophic, smashing my world to pieces. I stood there, and as I stared at him I saw the future go spiraling downwards into the dark.

I knew I'd never forgive him but I knew too that he was merely the mouthpiece of a hatred they all shared. For one brief moment I faced them across the ruins of their hypocrisy, and as I looked upon the wasteland of the truth I saw beyond it to scenes I could not yet imagine. All I knew was that one day, when this catastrophe was no more than a faint echo in their minds, I'd still be remembering it in unforgiving detail. And one day, clever accomplished writer that I was sure to become, I'd rewrite the ending and take my revenge.

PART
FIVE

HARRY
1939-1952

And last of all, once you have bowed your neck beneath her yoke, you ought to bear with equanimity whatever happens on Fortune's playground. If after freely choosing her as the mistress to rule your life you want to draw up a law to control her coming and going, you will be acting without any justification and your very impatience will only worsen a lot which you cannot alter.... If you were a farmer who entrusts his seed to the fields, you would balance the bad years against the good. So now you have committed yourself to the rule of Fortune, you must acquiesce in her ways. If you are trying to stop her wheel from turning, you of all men are the most obtuse....

— Boethius
The Consolation of Philosophy

1

I

POOR OLD KESTER, poor old sod. What a mess! Very sad.

I'd always felt sorry for Kester—poor old Kester, poor old sod—because I'd found out long ago that if you pity someone you can't be jealous of him, and I knew I couldn't be jealous of Kester. I couldn't be jealous of anyone. My father who was the best man in the world had always made it very clear that jealousy's not the done thing at all.

Well, there we all were on July the thirteenth, 1939, with Europe on the brink and Oxmoon in the lurch and Kester—poor old Kester, poor old sod—quite clearly round the bend, not in touch with reality at all, a first-class example of what bloody Constance would call a neurotic misfit—and what happens? That bastard Thomas has a touch of the Hitlers and treats that nice little Anna as if she were ripe for extermination and poor old Kester, poor old sod, has hysterics.

My God, as if my father hadn't enough problems!

However on this occasion my father had only himself to blame for the disaster because it was crystal-clear that he had deliberately let Thomas run wild. I knew that and the next moment I realized Kester knew it too because he included my father in his big melodramatic threat. Naturally he included me; the poor sod had always quivered with loathing as soon as I came within fifty paces of him, but this must have been the first occasion on which my long-suffering father had been lined up alongside me and Thomas and threatened with eternal hatred.

Poor old Kester was addicted to melodrama. He ought to have been born a woman like that bitch Aunt Ginevra. Then he would have had some excuse for behaving like a hysterical female. But on the other hand, what else can one expect from a man who'd been so coddled by his mother that he hadn't been sent away to school? Poor old Kester, it was a shame. I felt genuinely sorry for him, I really did. Very sad.

"Remember this date!" he screamed after Anna had left the room. He sounded as if he expected us to whip out our diaries and make a note of it. "Remember July the thirteenth, 1939! One day you're all going to look back on this scene and wish you'd never been born!"

Quite. Poor old sod, I was so embarrassed I hardly knew where to look. I was sorry enough for him to make at least a token effort to look grave, but how the hell could one take him seriously? If any man had treated my wife as Thomas had just treated Anna, I'd have knocked him down and smashed him to bloody pulp. But Kester was an artist, that was the trouble, not a man of action as I was. All he could do was have hysterics and talk crap.

Eventually, thank God, the hysterics ceased. He burst into tears, ran sobbing from the room and slammed the door. Pathetic. However before I could spend any more time mourning his lost sanity I was treated to a rare and hair-raising spectacle: my father lost his temper. It wasn't the done thing to lose it. But it wouldn't have been the done thing to let Thomas escape unscathed from his touch of the Hitlers. As a rule my father never used bad language, even when there were no women present; his generation was far more fussy about such vulgarity than mine and besides, unlike Uncle Edmund, who had served in the trenches, my father had never experienced a way of life in which bad language was the normal method of communication. Nevertheless my father was a born linguist, and he now decided to speak to Thomas in the only language that bastard ever understood.

Thomas sulked. When he finally got the chance to speak he was bright red. All he said was "You've got a fucking nerve, talking to me like that in front of your son."

"I want my son to see that I absolutely draw the line when it comes to your fucking awful behavior. Now, do you fucking want to run the fucking estate or don't you?"

"All right!" yelled Thomas. "For Christ's sake, I've said I'll apologize to the girl, haven't I? My God, anyone would think I'd bloody raped her!"

All this before ten o'clock in the morning. What a life! I wondered if I could open my mouth without triggering another holocaust. I had in fact been wanting to speak for some time.

"Father... does this mean you'll let poor old Simon stay?"

"Good God, no; I can't possibly undercut Thomas's authority now. If I do then Kester's always going to be running to me in future whenever there's a clash of wills, and Thomas's position will soon be untenable."

Thomas looked mollified. "Well, thank you, John. I must say—"

"Shut up. You've put me in an intolerable position."

"Father, about Simon—"

"Oh yes, I'll look after him, pay for a place in an old people's home, do whatever's necessary. You needn't worry."

I was relieved. Simon had been my tutor once as well as Kester's. He could have treated me casually and lavished his attention on his employer's son, but he had always been scrupulously fair. He was a good man. Not someone who deserved to be turned out into the street just because an ex-pupil had gone berserk. My God, that bloody Kester had a lot to answer for.

"Now listen to me, both of you," said my father abruptly. "Before Fairfax and Lloyd-Thomas arrive to curtail this family conference, let me spell out exactly what we can and can't do in this thoroughly dangerous situation. What we can't do is antagonize Kester irrevocably. What we can and must do is to give him our unstinted support in helping him over this crisis, because if we don't this kind of mess is going to happen over and over again."

"You can't make a silk purse out of a sow's ear, John," said Thomas. "That boy's always going to wind up in a mess."

"Once we accept that we may as well cut our throats in the knowledge that Oxmoon will end up on the auction block in double-quick time. But I don't accept it, and I don't think you two should either. That boy's got brains. He's got determination. And in his own peculiar way he's got courage. The truth is that he could well turn into a man of considerable consequence, but at present he's crippled by his immaturity—we're now paying the price, you see, for Ginevra's thoroughly misguided decision not to send him to school to help him develop the self-confidence he so profoundly needs. If a boy, however normal, is brought up by his mother in the depths of the country with only misfits like young Mowbray for company, he's inevitably going to be riddled with secret fears that he might be inferior to the average boy who must seem so frighteningly different to him."

I looked at Thomas. "Poor old Kester," I said, signaling that I had no intention of arguing. "Poor old sod. Very sad." The words "brains," "determination" and "courage" were still drilling holes in my consciousness.

"Well, John," said Thomas, "if you say we have to give Kester our unstinted support, then of course I'll obey orders, but now that he's down and out couldn't you insist that he turns poor old Oxmoon over to us? As I see it, that's the only real solution to the problem."

"It would certainly be a solution," said my father, "but it's not available to us. Kester will never voluntarily surrender Oxmoon."

"Yes, but John, you're paying his debts. You could force him to—"

"No, I couldn't—and not just because that would break my promise to Robert. I couldn't do it because it would be the most idiotic thing I could possibly do. The only self-confidence Kester has derives from the fact that he's master of Oxmoon. If we take that away from him God alone knows what would happen, but whatever did happen I wouldn't like to feel I was responsible for it. My God, haven't we got enough trouble on our hands without looking for more? No, Kester stays master and we have to do everything in our power to build up his confidence in himself until he's mature enough to conquer his problems. It's the right thing— indeed the only thing—to do."

Thomas and I looked at each other again, and again I thought how bizarre it was that I should feel so deeply connected to this bastard I couldn't stand. But connected we were. There was no man on earth we respected more than my father, and we both knew it was useless to argue with him once he started drawing lines and doing the done thing.

The only trouble was that as far as I could see the done thing invariably turned out to be a disaster.

II

I spent the rest of that day making myself useful in a number of minor ways. After Lloyd-Thomas arrived I was authorized to go to his bank in Swansea to cash my father's check for the Oxmoon servants' wages, and by the time I had done this and distributed the money beyond the green baize door it was almost one o'clock. I retraced my steps to the hall. No one was in sight. Behind the library door my father and Thomas were still deep in their postmortem with Lloyd-Thomas and Fairfax. For one long moment I gazed upwards at the vast chandelier which had transformed the commonplace entrance hall into a palatial foyer. Then I skimmed down the corridor past the music room and eased open the ballroom doors for a quick peep.

My God.

I was transfixed. I walked in, jaw sagging, legs going through the motions of walking like a couple of addled pendulums. The mirrors had been cleaned, and as I paused I saw myself reflected with a dazzling clarity: tall, dark, poised and radiating brains, charm, muscular Christianity—I had only to imagine a virtue and I immediately shimmered with it. But then I moved closer. I walked right up to the nearest mirror, and a youth of twenty walked to meet me, a white-faced shattered young man with black eyes bright with tears.

Steady on, Harry. Take it easy, old chap. Poor old Kester, poor old sod, is the only one in this family who goes crashing around in an artistic trance and behaving like a pre-Raphaelite poet at full throttle. But the room was so beautiful. Oxmoon, as we all know, is just a plain quirky little house with character, a Welshman's pie-eyed attempt at eighteenth-century classicism, but now suddenly it was unique, it was ravishing, it was—

My God, look at that piano.

It was a white-and-gold Steinway grand. It was the kind of piano I had imagined my mother playing when I was very young and believed she'd gone to heaven. Of course I could clearly see this was a very stupid, pansyish, tarted-up piece of nonsense, and of course I knew I wouldn't be seen dead playing it, but all the same...

I raised the lid. The keys seemed to be yearning to lose their virginity. They lost it. I was playing a Chopin polonaise but it was too beautiful, too beautiful to bear, and after a moment my hands were still.

Groping for equanimity I reminded myself what a tragedy Kester's demented extravagance was. Poor old Kester, poor old sod, had wandered around in some half-baked dream and squandered his money on a little Welsh country house in the back of beyond. What could be more pathetic?

But what a house. And what a dream.

It was very quiet. I sat listening to the silence, and as I listened I heard the truth I couldn't afford to hear. For nine months Kester, risking ridicule and ruin, had defied convention and lived the life he wanted to live. Kester—poor weak feeble Kester whom I had always taken such scrupulous care to pity and despise— had somehow discovered the courage that I'd never been able to find. Walking to the nearest mirror again I no longer saw a youthful hero radiating all the traditional virtues. I saw a coward, a failure and a fool.

I blundered out of the ballroom.

In the hall a passing maid told me that "the other gentlemen" had gone into the dining room for lunch but the thought of food was repulsive to me, so I retreated to the cloakroom until I'd pulled myself together. It took me less than two minutes before I could start thinking Poor old Kester, poor old sod, again but when I emerged I still couldn't face the dining room so I took another peek at the library. Most of the new books, I now discovered, turned out to be novels. I don't read novels. I do read, but only for information. When I want to escape from how bloody awful life really is I don't open a book; I play the piano.

My glance roamed along the shelves. Jane Austen, Dickens, Thackeray, the Brontës. All very orthodox stuff. Hadn't these people been in the library before? Maybe not. Robert Godwin the Renovator had stocked the place with the usual junk in Latin and Greek as well as numerous tomes of philosophy; the son who had predeceased him had left in the library no mark which anyone had been able to discover; Robert Godwin the Regency Rake had added bound sermons after his religious conversion; Robert Godwin the Drunkard had apparently read only Ruskin, and Robert Godwin the Survivor, otherwise known as Grandfather Bobby, hadn't read at all; so it had been left to Kester to import fiction on the grand scale. I saw yards of Trollope, acres of the Waverley novels, a wasteland of Meredith and a morass of George Eliot. Then came the poetry—Tennyson, both Brownings and a pre-Raphaelite poets, all on cue. Typical. The shelves were awash with morbid romance. But what was this? *The Prisoner of Zenda* bound in calf! Now I'd seen everything! Yet I rather liked the old *Prisoner of Zenda*. It was one of the few novels which I'd read without having been forced to do so by a schoolmaster. Seeing that I was at a loose end at Oxmoon after Bronwen left, Aunt Ginevra had told Kester to lend me a couple of his Anthony Hope novels to cheer me up and I'd read both *The Prisoner of Zenda* and its sequel *Rupert of Hentzau*.

I took the book off the shelf and began to flick through the pages.

Ah yes. Ruritania. An imaginary kingdom but somehow very real. I remembered the story now; it was all coming back to me. There was this English hero, Rudolph Rassendyll, who was handsome and charming, radiating all the traditional virtues, and he took the place of the King of Ruritania—for the purest possible reasons, of course. He and the King were doubles, interchangeable. The King was weak, though, and Rudolph was so much more suited to rule Ruritania that he almost yielded to temptation and stayed on to make his temporary impersonation a permanent one. But he didn't. He drew the line and did the done thing and rode away into obscurity—except that the author couldn't bear that and brought him back for another round in the sequel. It all ended in tragedy—I couldn't quite remember how. One got the impression that Anthony Hope respected the conventions but was too much of a realist to believe any hero could follow them to the letter, but of course heroes, literary heroes, just don't go around grabbing kingdoms that don't belong to them, so poor old Rudolph had to go.

Well, there we are. We all have to do the done thing, even Rudolph Rassendyll, or else we go to hell in double-quick time. Stale news. I knew all about going to hell in double-quick time. Shoving the book back onto the shelf, I set off for the dining room in order to do the done thing by eating lunch.

The dining room was magnificent, ablaze with rich paneling, and on either side of the new fireplace huge swags of carved fruit and flowers cascaded down the walls like a Renaissance man's vision of Eden. It took me a greater effort than usual to behave like a twentieth-century philistine and give the splendor no more than a passing glance, but I managed it somehow. I'd had twenty years of hard practice, and where there's a will there's a way.

Poor old Kester was absent, probably still sobbing in his room, and Anna was absent too but my four fellow saviors of Oxmoon were all chatting away briskly over the lamb cutlets about agricultural economics. The international situation was by that time so grave that it was considered a breach of taste to make more than a casual remark about it.

I hid my cutlet under a cabbage leaf and wished I could ask for a double whisky. Lloyd-Thomas and Fairfax were drinking claret but my father never touched alcohol before six so Thomas and I felt morally obliged to share his jug of water. Thomas, normally a hard drinker, never missed the chance to demonstrate to my father how well he had his drinking in control.

After lunch Lloyd-Thomas and Fairfax retired to Swansea, and it was time for the pacification of Emlyn Vaughan, the leader of the Oxmoon tenants who had been soaked by the Mowbray cabal. Leaving his Rolls-Royce at Oxmoon in deference to Vaughan's sensitive socialist soul, my father rode off on horseback to Daxworth but still managed to look like an aristocratic survivor of some proletarian guillotine.

Once we were alone Thomas and I retired to the library, where Thomas embarked on the task of decoding the chaotic estate books and I began to make a list of Kester's personal expenditures during the past year. We toiled away for some time, Thomas cursing under his breath as he made notes in his surprisingly neat handwriting, I suppressing gasps of disbelief at the sight of so many astronomical bills. Each time I came across a new monster I felt as if I'd been hit on the head with a hammer.

At half-past three Thomas said, "Christ, this would drive a saint to drink," and rang for the whisky decanter. When it arrived he generously inclined it in my direction. "Want some, Harry?"

"No, thanks, old chap." I was panting for it, but I was afraid he might tell my father. Drinking whisky at half-past three in the afternoon wasn't the done thing at all.

"Of course I don't usually drink in the afternoon," said Thomas, swigging away, "but my God, what a day this has been! How are you getting on?"

"Well, if anyone died of sheer amazement I'd be six feet under by now. Thomas, just what is Kester's annual income?"

"That's a question only John can answer, old boy. Only John knows the scope of the private income in addition to the estate."

"But you must have an approximate idea!"

"Well, I'd guess about ten thousand."

"*Ten thousand a year?*"

"Must be, old boy. At least. It would be still more if Kester managed all the farms himself, as my father used to do, and didn't waste money on agents and lettings. Now, if Oxmoon belonged to me—"

"But I thought Grandfather frittered away most of his private income on Milly Straker!"

"He certainly tried to but luckily he went mad before he could complete the job and after that clever old John beavered away for over ten years to recoup the losses. You've only got to give John a stock and a share and they immediately mate and multiply."

"But even so . . . Grandfather must have had much more capital than I thought!"

"Well, the capital didn't all come from the little flutters on the stock exchange. It came from my mother's share of the bloody pottery works in Staffordshire. Aunt Ethel got the works, but under the terms of her father's will she had to pay my mother off. Good old Ethel, what a character she was! She used to send me hand-knitted socks every Christmas with a pound note tucked in each toe."

But I had no interest in Aunt Ethel, the family gorgon. I was much too interested in Kester. "So in spite of all this lavish spending the old sod's probably still nowhere near bankrupt?"

"No, but he'd reached the point where he would have had to start selling land to meet his bills, and of course that would have been the writing on the wall. Once you start selling off land in a place like Oxmoon you get yourself locked in a downward spiral of diminishing returns."

"Poor old Kester," I said, "poor old sod, what a catastrophic balls-up! Very sad." And as I was speaking I thought, Ten bloody thousand a year. *At least.* I didn't dare think of my own bank balance in case I started to remember I didn't have one.

"What do you make of all this, Harry? Of course John's doing the right thing, we both know that, but do you really think that bloody idiotic little pansy's ever going to add up to much?"

"No idea, old chap. Anyone's guess."

"What do you think he got up to with Ricky?"

"Damn all. Too busy being mad about Anna."

"Can't think why. Can you?"

I thought of brave loyal little Anna chatting happily away with such unaffected intelligence about Rachmaninoff's *Second Piano Concerto.* "No idea, old chap. No idea at all."

"Personally I can't imagine Kester ever having a good fuck. The whole thing's a complete mystery. Maybe he just waves his cock around and pretends, and the girl's too innocent to know nothing's happening."

"God knows, old chap. Personally I'm too busy waving my own cock around to care."

Thomas broke into loud guffaws of laughter and said I was a man after his own heart and that he could see we absolutely understood each other. I was just wondering how much longer I could stand his company when he added: "By the way, what do you think of the way Oxmoon's been buggered up? If you want my opinion—"

"Yes, it's terrible, old chap, absolute rape. Never seen such a lot of pansyish rubbish in my life—there's even a white-and-gold piano lying around in the ballroom."

Thomas thought that was the last word in effete taste. Telling him I had to go to the lavatory, I left him still swilling his whisky and staggered outside for an essential breath of fresh air.

III

At six my father returned after seeing the leading tenants and asked if we wanted to continue working. Both Thomas and I, anxious to impress him, expressed a longing to continue so after a quick drink we all retired to the library where my father could survey our progress. I had by this time reached the estimates for Oxmoon's renovation.

"Is all the work contracted for, Harry?"

"Looks like it, yes."

"Damn, that means endless negotiations with the decorator while we try to get out of what hasn't yet been done."

The three of us dined alone, a circumstance which made Thomas suggest that perhaps Kester and Anna had committed suicide, but this wishful thinking was terminated by my father who had seen them upstairs before dinner was served. Thomas and I had already telephoned our wives to warn them we would be returning late but my father made no effort to phone Constance. She was the one who telephoned when she realized he wasn't going to call.

"Oh hullo, darling," we heard him say pleasantly as he took the call in the hall.

"The old girl's checking up on him!" whispered Thomas. "She doesn't trust him an inch!"

I said nothing.

"Christ, it's odd about John," muttered Thomas who had by this time had a large amount to drink. "What the devil made him go back to that bloody cunt, Harry? Any idea?"

"Not a clue, old boy. Absolutely none."

"Of course I can see him telling himself it was the right thing to do but even so . . . Anyway John doesn't do the right thing with women, does he? That's the whole bloody point. Where women are concerned he does what he likes and I'm all for it, I hate to think of him being bogged down in Belgravia with that bitch. . . . How many mistresses does he keep? Or does he just sleep with anyone who happens to be convenient?"

"Why ask me? He doesn't send me a telegram every time he has sex."

"Thought he might have confided in you—"

"Good God, no."

"—because after all, you're very close to each other, aren't you? Never knew a father and son get on as well as you two do, it's bloody marvelous, I take my hat off to you both."

". . . yes, all right, darling," my father was saying casually. "No, I'll be back by then. . . . What? . . . No, he hasn't installed central heating. I doubt if the aesthetics of plumbing would interest him. . . . I said I doubt if—oh, never mind. Look, darling, I'm afraid I really must ring off now. . . . Yes, I will. Yes. . . . Yes, of course. Yes, I'll ring you tomorrow. All right, darling, love to Francesca—and to you. . . . Yes. . . . 'Bye." He finally managed to sever the connection, and when he returned to the library he was glancing at his watch. "Well," he said abruptly, not bothering to comment on the call, "I think we've done all we can do today. Thomas—" He took care to smile at his brother to disguise the fact that he was getting rid of him. "—I can't thank you enough for all your hard work and loyal support—I don't know what I'd have done without you. You'll be back at nine tomorrow?"

"On the dot," said Thomas, greatly pleased by these obligatory words of praise, and turned, beaming with good humor, to me. "Can I give you a lift, Harry?"

I declined, saying I fancied some exercise after sitting down all day, and he departed. As the front door closed, my father and I eyed each other in exhaustion.

"My God, Father," I said at last when I could dredge up the energy to speak, "are you sure you know what you're doing, giving that bastard free rein at Oxmoon?"

"Come into the drawing room, Harry," said my father. "I want to talk to you."

IV

"What I can't understand," mused my father as we lit cigarettes, "is why you and Kester both seem to regard Thomas as a modern Frankenstein. It's extraordinary. I realize, of course, that Thomas can be difficult and that his bombastic manners aren't to everyone's taste, but if you look beyond his idiosyncrasies you must surely see he's a thoroughly good chap."

"I concede he's good at his job."

"It's not just that. He's honest, trustworthy, loyal—and he leads, when all's said and done, a very decent sort of life. Oh, I know he drinks a bit but he has it in control and God knows I don't expect everyone to be perfect. He's happily married—Eleanor thinks the world of him—and he's really the most devoted father to little Bobby—"

"He's always on his best behavior for you, Father." My God, aren't we all.

"Well, I daresay, but if he shows me his good side at least that proves there's a good side to show. I can't understand the problem here. Dislike—yes. I could understand it if you and Kester merely disliked Thomas and found him boorish. But this rabid irrational hatred—"

"I don't hate Thomas, Father. He's just someone I'd be happy never to see again."

My father, who had never quite lost his sense of humor despite the years with Constance, gave an exasperated laugh and moved away down the room in search of an ashtray. I waited for him to sit down but he didn't. He seemed restless, troubled. God knows he had plenty to be troubled about but instinct, finely honed by my past experience, whispered that he was at present disturbed not by Kester but by me.

"What was it you wanted to talk to me about, Father?" I said, nervous enough to take the bull by the horns. As always when I scented a confrontation with him, the dread was sinking like lead to the pit of my stomach.

My father took his time in replying but at last he looked me straight in the eyes and said flatly, "I'm disturbed by your apparent dislike of the idea that Thomas should be given a free rein at Oxmoon. I hope you're not implying that you should be appointed in his place."

"Me! *Me?* My dear Father—"

"No, don't bother to remind me you haven't the experience to run Oxmoon. A young man with your brains and ambition would find it all too easy to learn."

"I...Father, I think I must be imagining this conversation. Do you seriously think I'm dreaming of some fantastic *coup d'état?*"

"God knows what you're dreaming of, Harry, but let me make it clear once and for all that I don't want you involving yourself in Oxmoon's affairs. I'm grateful to you for helping out today, but I don't want this to set any kind of precedent."

"But Father, I assure you I have absolutely no intention of—"

"Just get this into your head, Harry: Kester will never, never give this place up. And if you continue to regard Penhale Manor as a stepping-stone to Oxmoon you'll be making a very big mistake."

"I regard the Manor as my home," I said. "*My home!*" Steady on, Harry. Voice level. Upper lip ramrod-straight. Kester's the only one in this family who's allowed to shout in a shaking voice. "I'm sorry, Father, but you've got completely the wrong end of the stick here—"

"I've come to the conclusion I'd be happier if you left Gower now, Harry, instead of waiting for the expiration of your lease on the Manor. You've had your basic training in estate management and now I'd like to put you in charge of your mother's lands in Herefordshire—it would be best not only for you but for Kester. You give that boy what Constance would be pleased to call an inferiority complex. How do you think he'll feel now if you continue to flourish—as you inevitably will—on his doorstep? Can't you see it'll only add to his current humiliation?"

"But damn it, Father, why *should* I be dispossessed just because bloody Kester can't stand the sight of me flourishing at his gates? It's bloody well not fair!"

"I assure you I have only your welfare in mind—"

"All right, turn me out, go on, turn me out, I know damn well I'm only living there on your charity! Just you go ahead and deprive me of my home all over again and wreck my happiness a second time!"

There was a deep painful silence. I was appalled, and not only by what I'd said; I was stricken by the expression on his face. We stood there in that beautiful room but for a moment it was as if we were both standing in hell.

"Father—oh God, forgive me, I didn't mean it—"

"Harry, if you only knew what I've gone through in order to ensure your happiness—"

"I do know, I do—oh, Christ—"

"Believe me, all I want is for you to be happy—"

"Then let me stay at the Manor. Please, Father, please let me stay."

"But I'm just so afraid that it'll lead to a disastrous situation—"

"All I want is to live there peacefully without causing trouble. I've no sinister motive, I swear I haven't. Let Kester keep bloody Oxmoon. I don't care."

There was another silence. My father stubbed out his cigarette. His face was in shadow.

When I could bear the silence no longer I blurted out, "You're angry because I'm defying you—not doing the done thing—"

"Angry but not surprised," said my father. "After all, I'm well accustomed, aren't I, to your failures in that direction. Very well—stay at the Manor. But if ever I hear you're not making every effort to get on with Kester, I'm terminating your lease. Remember that." And bidding me a curt good night he walked out of the room and left me damned nearly obliterated by the weight of my guilt and my shame.

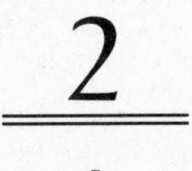

I

I WALKED back to Penhale Manor through the country night. At first the lane was bounded by dry-stone walls, but later the hedges began, hawthorn and beech mingling with blackberry, elderberry and honeysuckle. In the fields yellow wild irises were still blooming amidst the buttercups. The occasional tree was bent sideways like the hedgerows, sculpted by the prevailing sea wind, but there was no wind that night, only a stillness broken periodically by a hooting owl. The sky was a mass of stars.

I loved the country. As far as I was concerned London's only redeeming feature was the Queen's Hall.

But I loved music even more than I loved the country. I had no formal musical training but I loved music better than anything else on earth.

God, or what passed for him, had like an erratic tennis player lobbed me into this incredible family who thought famous sobriquets like *The Eroica* or *The Pastoral* referred to tours of the Bavarian Alps. How had my mother stood it? A glance at the titles in her collection of sheet music had told me that she had had a talent which had apparently brought even the most difficult pieces within her range. I knew they were difficult because when I tried to play by ear the ones I had heard on the wireless, I found myself improvising all the time, making up the notes which I couldn't hear clearly in my mind.

What could it have been like for my mother to be married to a man whose one supreme musical achievement lay in recognizing "The Blue Danube"? Well, I knew what it was like. Bella's musical limit was Jack Buchanan. Obviously one can still live happily ever after even if one's spouse doesn't share one's most important interest, but nevertheless I wondered what my parents had found to talk about. Maybe they had talked very happily without saying anything. I knew all about those conversations with my father when words were dutifully and affectionately batted back and forth but no communication whatsoever took place.

"Of course I don't want piano lessons, Papa. I wouldn't be so sissyish."

"I'm glad you're being so sensible, old chap."

"But. . . if I had lessons at school I'd have access to a piano there. Of course I'd rather be playing cricket, but—"

"Yes, I'm delighted by your progress at cricket! Nothing could please me more!"

And so on and so on. My father listened to me but he couldn't hear what I was saying. Would my mother have heard? Perhaps, but perhaps not. We tend to idealize the dead. But at least my mother would have understood how much I longed to play the piano.

I could not quite remember her. I could see a dark graceful figure seated at the piano in the drawing room but I couldn't see her face; I could only hear the Chopin polonaise that she was playing. But so absolutely did I connect her with music that when my father told me we were going back to Penhale Manor after three years in London I had said at once, "Is there still a piano in the drawing room?" Of course I'd known there was; we stayed at the Manor every time we returned to Gower to visit my grandfather, but what I had really meant was "Is Mama there? Has she come back?" I had been two when she died, and although my sister had said no one who died ever came back I had not entirely believed her. Even when I was five the disbelief had lingered, and I had returned to the Manor convinced I was going to find my mother again.

And so I had, in a way.

I so clearly remember going back. My father, who had just left Constance, looked wrecked. My sister Marian, puffy-eyed with weeping after being severed from Aunt Daphne, Elizabeth, Nanny and the governess, was at her most obnoxious. I didn't know what was happening but whatever it was I wanted it to stop—I remember misbehaving in protest until my father lost his temper with me. After that I cried, which was just about the most debasing thing I could do, and sucked my thumb, a gesture that was even beyond debasement. My father looked so miserable that I was scared to death. Marian whined on. What a journey. My father must have thought it would never end.

But it did end. The car drew up outside Penhale Manor, the front door opened and a magic lady came out.

I knew straightaway she was magic. She was slim and pale and had fiery hair that floated over her shoulders, and green eyes which read thoughts before they could be spoken. She said, "Harry, how lovely to see you again!" and when I heard that word "again" I knew I had always known her; I knew she was my mother, looking different from the photographs but still my mother, and after that I no longer minded losing Nanny and leaving Aunt Daphne. In the end even Marian was appeased. Marian had developed a morbid cult of mother worship, but gradually all the photographs but one were put away and Marian said, "Mama liked Bronwen. I can remember."

Penhale Manor began to shimmer with happiness. Bronwen, as Kester once put it, waved her magic wand and suddenly my father, who had always been so serious, was laughing and joking, a different man altogether. After living a dreary well-regulated existence with Nanny and Constance I suddenly found myself tossed into a joyous family life. Bronwen had three children of her own. Marian giggled with Rhiannon. Dafydd and I went on expeditions together. Only the baby was left out, but as he grew up I appointed him my serf. He passed me my tools as I serviced my bike. He assisted in my test-tube experiments in the potting shed. He scoured the grounds for the best conkers for me every autumn. He even braved the hostility of the village shop to spend his pocket money on a birthday present for me. I remembered to pat his head occasionally to let him know what a nice little serf he was. It was a good life.

When did the magic start to fade? Probably after Gerry was born in 1927. I was eight and my father's favorite; idiotic Marian could hardly rival me, and although I'd heard talk that Evan was my father's son I didn't believe it. Evan had been there at the Manor before we arrived so in my eyes he was just someone my father had taken over along with Rhiannon and Dafydd. My father did say with perfect clarity, "This is your brother," but I at once assumed he meant stepbrother. Marian told me later that I had been present at a big scene when she had told Nanny my father and Bronwen had produced a baby without being married, but I had no memory of this drama; at five years old I had been more interested in my toy train and more willing to accept Nanny's reported declaration that babies never arrived unless a marriage had taken place.

Then Gerry was born. Within hours it became clear to me that Nanny had told a fib. Gerry was my father's son. So was Evan. Then it occurred to me that my father was much too delighted with the new baby and very much too fond of Evan. In other words, I realized I had two rivals. Fortunately Marian explained to me that they were bastards and could therefore never be as good as we were— poor old Evan and Gerry, poor little sods—but I had some unpleasant moments before I decided with sickening relief that my position was unimpaired. All things considered I was almost anxious to go away to prep school to recover.

But I didn't like being sent away from my magic lady and my happy home. And I didn't like school either. Couldn't say so, of course. Not the done thing. And I had to do the done thing or else my father would have been disappointed in me, and if he were disappointed in me he might have started overlooking the fact that Evan and Gerry were bastards and making them his favorites instead. I decided I had to be so perfect that they would never outshine me.

As a matter of fact I rather enjoyed trying to be perfect, and once I was used to school I soon realized that the most painless way to survive it was to excel at everything. Luckily I was born athletic with a first-class memory. One can get a long way on athleticism and a first-class memory, and by God I traveled far. My father was thrilled by my progress. By the time Lance and Sian were born I was so secure in my position as the apple of my father's eye that I even deigned to shake the babies' rattles for them occasionally.

I was twelve when Sian was born. Two more magic years to go but the magic was fading fast now, slipping through our fingers, and the darkness was closing in. I knew about the trouble, we all did, but I thought it could never affect me. I was legitimate and a gentleman. Dafydd might have to be boarded out in Cardiff and Rhiannon might choose to live with her aunt at the Home Farm and Evan might have difficulty in finding a school that would take him, but no one was ever going to be hostile to me just because my father lived openly with his mistress. My father said his action was right because he and Bronwen loved each other, but he needn't have bothered to explain. I knew it was right. I could see it, feel it. It wasn't my father's fault that he couldn't marry Bronwen and do the done thing. That was the fault of Constance, the wicked witch I could barely remember. I thought that my magic lady would always be able to ward off the witch's spells, but this was no fairy tale and I saw her waste away, become thin and tired, pale and unhappy. I knew the end was near when Rhiannon and Dafydd went away to London because they said they couldn't stand living any longer among people who regarded their mother as a whore. But I tried not to see the end coming. I couldn't bear to see it. I looked the other way.

I was at Harrow when Evan was rejected by the headmaster of Briarwood and Bronwen made her decision to leave. I hated Harrow. Couldn't say so, of course. Not the done thing. Everyone went to Harrow in my family and everyone liked it, so that was that. I did try to tell my father that the only thing I enjoyed there was messing around in a laboratory, but he didn't hear me. He just said yes, science was fun, but how glad he was that I was obviously a born classicist like Uncle Robert.

I wanted to confide in Bronwen but by that time she always seemed to be either having a migraine or turning out the nursery. I almost confided in my friends at school, but I had realized that science wasn't quite the done thing and I was afraid that if I confessed how very much I liked it people would think I was different. Terrible things happened to people who were different, not only to little Evan, scurrying home in tears from the village shop, but to the misfits at Harrow who wouldn't or couldn't play the Great English Public School Game. I was a survivor and I knew what I had to do to survive. Survival was cricket and rugger, Latin and Greek, keeping a stiff upper lip and doing the done thing. So I kept my mouth shut, battened down the hatches over my emotions and survived.

"And how's everything going, Harry?" said my father when I was fourteen. "No problems?"

"Oh no, sir, none at all."

Did I know I was lying? No. The truth is we're all mesmerized by our upbringing, and although I knew that the life I was living bore no relation to my secret inclinations I absolutely accepted that there was nothing I could do about it. Rebellion would have been inconceivable and I was too young for self-analysis. Children, blinkered by the vision that's been foisted on them, always are. It's the adults who are supposed to see when something's going wrong but the adults in my world were far too busy with their own problems to pay any attention to mine.

Bronwen began to talk of visiting cousins in Vancouver.

"Is Bronwen all right, Father?"

"Oh yes, she's fine."

How could he say that when she so obviously wasn't?

"Father, how long will Bronwen be in Canada?"

"Oh, not long."

I wanted to say "They will come back, won't they?" But I couldn't. I wanted to say "Please tell me what's going on!" But I couldn't. I wanted to say "Is it because she doesn't love you anymore?" But I couldn't. I couldn't talk to him and he couldn't talk to me.

"Good luck, Harry," said my father as I left home to begin the summer term of 1933. "I do hope the cricket goes well."

Bronwen just hugged me and was silent.

I was silent too. Or at least I did say something but it had no meaning. I said, "Have a wonderful holiday in Canada."

Bronwen nodded and stooped over Sian who was tugging at her skirt. I knew then she wasn't coming back, but I shut my mind against the knowledge. I decided that if I didn't think about it, it wouldn't happen.

Three weeks later my father arrived at school to take me out to lunch. We drove to an inn in the rural country north of the Middlesex border. I remember we talked continuously about cricket, both my own efforts in the second eleven and the past winter's test matches with Australia. We were still discussing Larwood's body-line bowling as we sat down at our table. My father ordered us half a pint of beer apiece and two portions of jugged hare.

I never ate jugged hare again.

Of course I knew why he had come to see me, but when I realized that he was unable to speak of what had happened—the jugged hare was in front of us by that time—I said, "They're not coming back, are they?"

He shook his head. I thought he was still incapable of speech but at last he did say, not looking at me, "It was the right thing—the only thing—to do."

He went on talking, saying there had to be a new life for the sake of the children, but I barely heard him. As far as I was concerned everything had been said. The line had been drawn and everyone had done the done thing and sunk behind it without trace.

"She left a letter for you."

He was holding out an envelope.

"Thank you." I stowed it out of sight in my jacket.

"If you want to read it—"

"Not at the moment, thank you, Father." I suddenly couldn't stand to see him so upset, *couldn't stand it*. Fear of a mutual breakdown gripped me. I almost hated him for exposing us both to such a terrible danger. Pushing the jugged hare round and round my plate I began to talk again about cricket.

Later, back at school, I found a quiet corner in a remote passage by a linen cupboard and opened Bronwen's letter.

My dearest Harry, it breaks my heart to go but I can't bear to see the little ones suffer, your father will explain, don't blame your father, he's a good kind decent man, it's not his fault, I'll always love him and I'll always love you too just as if you were my own. I'd like to beg you to write but it would make things worse, drawing out the suffering, so better not. Stand by your father, he'll need you so much, he's so proud of you and in the midst of all this misery it's such a comfort to him to know you're happy at school and doing so well. Know that I'll look back often as we move farther apart in time, but remember too that time is a circle and that one day we may look not back but forward and see each other face to face again. Always your loving and devoted friend, BRONWEN.

I tore the letter into tiny pieces, flushed it down the nearest lavatory and went out to the cricket nets.

Couldn't let anyone see something was wrong.

Because of some minor fever my father was unable to return to Harrow at half-term to take me out, but Marian and my mother's aunt Charlotte motored down from London. Aunt Charlotte had recently presented Marian at court and was now acting as her chaperone, although Marian spent most of her time trying to escape to Aunt Daphne who was far more modern in her outlook.

"My dear," said Marian to me as we all motored into the West End to have lunch at the Ritz, "isn't it simply too tragic about Bronwen? But of course"—this was for Aunt Charlotte—"it's all for the best. The situation really was quite impossible."

We could say nothing more at lunch but afterwards when Aunt Charlotte retired to the ladies' cloakroom we had the chance for a word on our own.

"Did she write to you?" I said.

"Yes. It was rather sweet." Marian's eyes filled with tears but she added violently: "But really, the situation *was* impossible. The other day I heard someone say in the chaperone's corner at one of the dances, 'Oh, there's Marian Godwin—her father has the most extraordinary *ménage* in Wales, my dear, and the poor girl's been brought up by a Welsh peasant!' And it was just the same at St. Astrith's. 'Oh, Marian Godwin can't ask anyone home, my dear, because her situation's so peculiar!' I mean, really... *really*... it was beyond everything. And I've tried so hard to be ordinary, acting as if the only people I ever met were ladies and gentlemen, behaving as if the working classes were all quite beneath me—heavens, I think some people have even thought I was a snob!—but it was all for nothing, people always knew, people always found out, and oh, how I hated being different and everyone thinking I was so peculiar—"

"So you're glad she's gone."

"Yes, I am!" said Marian, but she was crying. "It wasn't her fault," she whispered. "She was sweet. But it shouldn't have gone on so long, it should have been stopped—"

"Well, you can't say Constance didn't do her best." A second later a horrifying thought occurred to me. "My God, Marian, you don't suppose—"

"No, it's all right, he swore to me he'd never go back to her."

I didn't care much for Marian, who was brainless and unmusical and altogether a highly expendable member of the female race, but a sister's a sister and after that conversation I detected a remote note of harmony between us. It was good to know I wasn't alone in feeling rotten about Bronwen and sagging with relief that there was no possibility of a return to the witch in Belgravia.

But there were other possibilities almost as bad. When I arrived back in Gower for the summer holidays I found that my father was staying at Oxmoon because he couldn't face Penhale Manor. To make matters worse, he was still emotionally in pieces and had no idea what he was going to do with himself. The whole situation was a nightmare.

I had been assigned a bedroom that had once belonged to my uncle Lion but I made no attempt to open the packing cases there which contained my possessions. I just sat on the bed and longed futilely for home. Later I went back to Penhale Manor but it was all shut up. Only the door of the potting shed was open. I went in and remembered my little serf, helping me with my experiments. Behind the flowerpots I found a smashed test tube. That was when the full magnitude of the disaster reached me; that was the moment when I had no choice but to acknowledge what had happened. I was dispossessed. My happy home had been smashed up. I'd lost my magic lady. I cried all the way to Oxmoon, a great big lout of fourteen sobbing like a baby in nappies. Disgusting. My eyes were so red that I knew I couldn't go down to lunch. Despicable. I hated myself for being so weak.

Eventually when I didn't turn up in the dining room Aunt Ginevra came to see if I was all right, but I had bathed my eyes by that time and looked pale but passable.

"Is something wrong, Harry?"

"Oh no, Aunt Ginevra. Everything's fine."

She gave me one of her shrewd but not unfriendly stares. "You surprise me," she said drily. "If I were you I'd be feeling wretched. Why don't we talk it over? I liked Bronwen, you know. I was very fond of her."

Something terrible was happening to my throat. Damn the woman, get her out.

"Oh, I quite accept all that, Aunt Ginevra. Nothing more I want to say about it, thank you."

She wavered but then Kester called her and she seized the chance to wash her hands of me. "All right, Harry, but do say something, won't you, if you're feeling awful? I know John's not much use at the moment."

I hated her. "My father's absolutely all right!" How I got the words out I didn't know. My throat felt as if it were housing a lump the size of a cricket ball.

"Mu-um!" sang out Kester, poor old Kester, poor old sod, who had this utterly miserable life being pampered to death in his palatial mansion by everyone in sight. "I've got something terribly funny to tell you! Honestly, I laughed so much I nearly split my sides!"

Seconds later they were convulsed with mirth in the corridor. I listened, tears streaming down my cheeks, but finally I pulled myself together and went in search of my father.

I found him drinking whisky in the library as he pretended to write a letter.

"Father, I was just wondering whether to open those packing cases in my room but then I thought I wouldn't bother if we're not going to be here much longer."

"Ah." There was a pause while he drank some whisky.

"Father... are we likely to be here much longer?"

"I don't know."

Another pause. I didn't know what to say. I just stood there and waited for him to help me, although what form the help should take I had no idea.

"You're all right, aren't you, Harry?"

"Oh yes, Father. Fine."

I saw now with a terrible clarity that I'd lost him as well as Bronwen. My bright cheerful affectionate father had been wiped out by this battered stranger who could do no more than drink whisky and attempt a fragmented parody of a conversation. Once I realized this I knew there was no point in waiting for help so I slipped away.

I stood in the hall and wondered what to do but my mind was blank. In the end I wandered outside. I crossed the croquet lawn to the woods, and when I reached the summerhouse I paused to look back. Then I remembered that this wasn't the first time in my life that I'd been dispossessed. I remembered my grandfather patting me on the head, slipping me five shillings and saying to my father, "He's got Blanche's coloring but there's a look of you there too, John," and I knew he was pleased. "Tell me the story of how you saved Oxmoon, Grandfather," I would say to him again and again, and he would tell me how he had found the vital information he needed by throwing a book at a rat in the library.

"And I made Oxmoon a great house," he said, holding my hand as we strolled together through the woods to the ruined tower of Humphrey de Mohun, "a great house, and they all came to Oxmoon, everyone came, and we decked the ballroom with red roses and we drank champagne and we danced to 'The Blue Danube.'"

"I can play 'The Blue Danube,'" I said, so we went to the ballroom and I played it for him on the untuned broken-down old piano there. It was near the end of my grandfather's life by that time and Oxmoon was sunk deep in decay.

"What a clever little fellow you are!" said my grandfather smiling at me, and when he gave me another five shillings I knew I was his favorite.

"I'd like to make Oxmoon a great house too, Grandfather, just as you did."

He gave me his brilliant smile. He had bright blue eyes, just like my father's. He said nothing.

"I'd like to live at Oxmoon one day and be just like you."

My grandfather looked away. His mouth trembled, and suddenly he seemed very old and very careworn. All he said in the end was "I'd like that too, Harry."

So of course I thought I'd inherit Oxmoon. Then Kester started boasting that he was to inherit. Naturally I didn't believe him, but my father explained that Kester had to inherit because he was the son of the eldest son and eldest sons always came first; it was the done thing.

So that was that.

Afterwards whenever I looked at Oxmoon I thought, Silly old house. I don't care.

But I did.

I cared now. I looked back across the lawn to Oxmoon and thought, Dispossessed. I had compensated myself for the loss of Oxmoon by becoming fiercely devoted to Penhale Manor, but now that the Manor too had been stripped from me I found myself face to face with Oxmoon again. I looked at it and saw clearly how much more alluring it was than pretty, charming but commonplace little Penhale Manor. Little manor houses are two a penny throughout the length and breadth of the British Isles, but there could only be one Oxmoon, only one Georgian mansion slumbering in its grounds like a lost Welsh lion and waiting for the master who would comb its bedraggled mane.

My sense of deprivation was suddenly so strong that I couldn't bear to look at the house for a moment longer. I ran off into the woods to the ruined tower but even the jackdaws in the tangled ivy there seemed to scream at me, "Dispossessed!"—which was a very stupid and improbable illusion, because the noises jackdaws make sound nothing like "dispossessed" at all. I went on through the woods. On the far side of the grounds there was a door in the wall, and letting myself out I ran down the footpath, crossed the road and set off across the moors which rose steadily to the summit of Rhossili Downs in the distance.

The sky was bright blue and the bracken was growing tall. A warm wind blew into my face from the sea and ruffled the manes of the wild ponies as they grazed by the megalithic stones known as Sweyn's Houses. It was an ancient burial chamber reputed to be the tomb of Sweyn, founder of Sweyn's-Ey, as Swansea had once been called. Vikings, Celts, Normans, Saxons—they'd all come to Gower in the old days to leave their mark upon the landscape.

"And they all came to Oxmoon," my grandfather had said, referring to his guests of long ago. "Everyone came to Oxmoon."

How could I stand living there a day longer when I knew it could never be mine? Never. What a terrible word that was. Never, never, never. Oxmoon would *never* be mine.

And why was it never going to be mine? Because my grandfather had done the done thing by leaving it to the heir of his eldest son. And why had Bronwen gone to Canada? Because, as my father had said, it was the right thing, the only thing to do. And why was I being deprived of piano lessons? Because it wasn't the done thing for a boy to waste time pursuing artistic ambitions. I was being sacrificed on the altar of The Done Thing, that was the truth of it, and oh God, how I *hated* the done thing. But of course I could never have said so. That wouldn't have been the done thing at all.

I paused, debating whether to go on or turn back, but I knew that if I went back I would be guaranteed to feel miserable so I went on—I could have stopped, but I went on. That, I was to discover later, was the story of my life, but I was only fourteen then and my life had hardly begun.

I reached the summit of the ridge. The view was so stupendous that for a few precious moments I was jolted out of my slough of despair. Below me the Downs fell away abruptly to the three golden miles of Rhossili Beach, and beyond the sands the long lines of the breakers creamed languidly on the edge of a glittering sea. Far away to my left the little village of Rhossili was perched on top of the high cliffs that formed one arm of the bay, while far away to my right the sand burrows of Llangennith, huge grass-flecked dunes, swirled towards the lesser arm of the bay and the Loughor Estuary beyond Llanmadoc Hill. Looking back inland I could see the blue gleam of the river, and beyond Harding's Down I glimpsed the village of Reynoldston shimmering in the heat haze atop the spine of Cefn Bryn. All was pastoral peace, like a landscape in a dream, and when I turned to the glittering sea I saw it as if from a great distance, as if it were a vision of happiness far beyond my reach. I noticed that the Worm's Head, the tidal peninsula beyond Rhossili, was about to be cut off; I could see the white foam as the waters roared over the Shipway.

There were a few holidaymakers below me on the sands but the beach was not easy of access and was always sparsely populated. Certainly I assumed I was alone on top of the Downs. That was why, when someone called my name a moment later, I nearly jumped out of my skin with surprise.

"Harry! Oy! Come over here a minute!"

Peering around I saw a girl lying on a rock in the distance. Who was she? No idea. Unable to think how I could escape from such an unwelcome encounter, I muttered a curse under my breath and trudged off along the track towards her. I kept my eyes on the ground and frowned heavily to convey that I was feeling unsociable.

"Thank goodness you turned up," said the girl as soon as I was within earshot. "I'm trying to raise the Devil and I need a Druid. Do you by any chance know how to fuck?"

I jumped as if I'd been shot, and looked up.

The girl was stark naked.

I recognized Belinda Stourham.

II

"Well, don't just stand there goggling at me like a lost bullfrog," she said crossly. "What's the matter? Haven't you ever seen a girl naked before?"

"Well, actually... no. No, I can't say I have."

"Doesn't your father keep picture books of ladies with no clothes on? Mine does. Well, never mind, don't let's waste any more time—do you know how to fuck or don't you? I thought it just meant making a rude noise, but I must have misunderstood the stableboys when I heard them talking about it because although I've done everything Annie-May said I haven't managed to raise the Devil. But on the other hand Annie-May did mention a Druid. So if you could play the Druid—"

"Who's Annie-May?"

"Our housemaid. Look, don't waste time, I haven't got all day. If you're not interested in being obliging—"

"Of course I am. But I don't quite see—"

"Annie-May says that in the old days people used to dance around a fallen-down standing stone—you know, one of the upright rocks from an old burial chamber—and then the most beautiful girl would take off all her clothes and lie on the fallen-down standing stone and fuck. So would the Druid, and while he was fucking he'd say a spell and the Devil would appear in a cloud of sulfur and brimstone. Well, I thought it sounded rather fun, so I decided to have a go. No one's breathing down my neck at the moment because my stupid old governess is on her summer holiday and stupid old Aunt Angela's in bed with a liver chill, and it seemed a good opportunity to go off and hunt for a suitable rock—and look how lovely this one is, almost flat and with the best view in the world. I know it's not from a burial chamber, but I'm sure the Devil wouldn't mind if only I could raise him... I say, I do wish you'd stop looking so odd. What's the matter?"

"Nothing exactly. But Belinda—"

"I'm called Bella now. Daddy's gone crackers and cries whenever anyone says my mother's name. I wanted to be called Linda but Aunt Angela said that was a common name, you know, not the done thing, so I have to be Bella instead."

"Not the done thing. I see. Yes. Actually, Bella, you wouldn't know this because you're too young, but fucking's not the done thing either, not unless you're grown up and married. So—"

"Oh rubbish, Annie-May does it all the time and she's not married, she's only fifteen! Anyway, who cares? I don't want to do the done thing like boring old Aunt. I want to be mad and bad like Eleanor who wears trousers and drinks whisky and says 'What the hell'—in fact I hope I'll be much madder and badder than she is by the time *I'm* thirty-one; but meanwhile I'm thirteen, and I'm going to start my mad bad career by raising the Devil. After all, one's got to start somewhere. Now, for the last time, are you going to be useful or aren't you? Because if you're not..."

I took a quick look around but there was no one in sight along the summit of the Downs as far as the eye could see. Far below us the waves streamed languidly over the sands and the sea faded into a blue horizon. It was the landscape of myth. The girl was part of the myth too, a naked siren upon a rock, and when I stepped into the myth to join her, I found that reality, unbearable reality, was suddenly a million light-years away.

"Gosh, what a peculiar shape boys are! How do you squeeze it all into your trousers? Or does it fold up small like a telescope?"

The waves went on streaming over the beach but I no longer saw them. The sun beat down on my naked back. Sweat got in my eyes. The rock on which she was lying was gray-green with unlikely flecks of pink in it. As my heart slammed like a sledgehammer all the colors ran together into a waving chaotic blob. I thought I was going to pass out.

"I say, Harry, have you ever done this before?"

"Shut up."

"Sorry. Just wondered if you knew what you were doing."

"Of course I know what I'm doing."

"Seems jolly odd to me."

Pain racked us both and terminated speech. I panicked, floundered, then suddenly realized the pain wasn't pain at all but the most excruciating ecstasy. I said incoherently, "Don't stop me, don't," because I thought she was bound to try to fight her way free but she grabbed me so tightly that her fingernails bit into my shoulder blades. Then one of us said "Oh God," and a sea gull screamed overhead, and the next moment the pink flecks were all flying back into place in the rock.

"Goodness, my back's killing me," said the girl. "I never knew a rock could be so hard.... Rather fun, wasn't it? But what a fibber Annie-May was, talking of the Devil appearing in a cloud of sulfur! Unless...oh yes, we never said the spell, I knew there was something we'd forgotten. Never mind, we can't try again now because I simply must go home for tea. We'll try again tomorrow." She paused, her head bent suspiciously over her private parts. "Oh gosh, what's all this mess? No, don't look, I'm all right. It's just something girls get. Or is it? No, it can't be. Gosh, this *is* peculiar! I'll have to ask Eleanor about it."

I nearly had a fit. "Good God, no, you mustn't do that! You mustn't tell anyone—anyone at all!"

"Oh, all right, all right! No need to get in such a flap! But I say, Harry...is it really very much not the done thing?"

"Very much, yes."

"Oh good. But how could something so nice be wrong? How idiotic grown-up rules are!"

"Idiotic, yes. And vile." I pulled on my trousers and stood up. Far away at the Rhossili end of the bay, the Shipway had sunk below the sea and the Worm's Head had become an island. The waves were no longer streaming dreamily over the beach; greedy white breakers were roaring up the sands, and beyond the surf the horizon was knife-sharp and the sea was a restless violent blue.

Everything was quite changed.

When I turned to look at the girl I saw her as if for the first time. I tried to remember the last occasion we'd met and thought it had been at a birthday party at the vicarage over a year ago. Little Belinda Stourham had worn a pink dress with a white sash and had sulked in a corner. I had paid no attention to her.

Now I noticed that she had shining, mouse-colored hair, not very long, and brown eyes, green-flecked, not very dark. Her nose tilted upward. Her wide mouth curved upward too as she smiled. Her pink-and-white skin looked very smooth, very fresh. She had no spots.

We stood there in silence, neither of us sure how the ritual of parting could be best observed, but at last Bella said suddenly, "I like you."

"I like you too."

"Even if we can't make the Devil appear tomorrow, could we still be friends?"

"All right. I mean, yes. Of course. I don't have any special friend here at the moment."

"I've never had a friend," said Bella. She held out her hand. "'Bye. See you tomorrow. Same time?"

"Same time."

We shook hands and parted.

Stumbling down from the ridge I ran all the way to Sweyn's Houses where I collapsed in a heap to sort out my thoughts. The wild ponies eyed me strangely but went on browsing without moving away. To them I was no doubt just another mad human, nothing to be excited about, just another crazy boy who'd gone completely round the bend.

But although I thought I would feel guilty I was in fact aware only of relief. The pain had eased. So had my utter despair. I thought, I shan't mind anything now; I'll just shut it out and forget.

Walking back to Oxmoon dry-eyed I even faced damned Kester with a smile. I was going to survive.

III

We used to meet on Rhossili Downs or, if the weather was unpromising, we'd bicycle to Penhale Manor and meet at the potting shed. After we'd made love we'd drink fizzy lemonade and eat biscuits and talk all about our awful families and how rotten life was. I even told her I hated Harrow.

"... and all I really want to do is play the piano."

"All I really want to do is fuck."

Bella's governess returned but lessons took place only in the mornings and in the afternoons Bella was allowed to go off on her own. The governess was obviously only too pleased to be rid of her and naturally never dreamed that a thirteen-year-old girl might go astray in such a tranquil rural backwater. On the fine days we would meet at the "fuck rock," as Bella called it, and scramble down to the beach to explore the sands. If it was warm enough we bathed, and afterwards among the sand burrows we'd make love and talk and make love again.

Once she said, "Why are you so dark when the rest of your family are fair?" and I told her about my mother.

"I feel angry with her for dying," I said. "Because she died there's no one who understands how I feel about the piano."

"But she couldn't help dying! My mother walked out on me when I was three months old and disappeared into the blue with an American sailor, and she jolly well could help it! How do you think I feel about that?"

"About a hundred times angrier than I ever do. What about your father? Is he nice to you?"

"Oh, he's gaga, poor old thing, can't speak since his last stroke. What about your father? Is he much good?"

"Wonderful. Best father in the world."

"You're jolly lucky. I've only got Eleanor and beastly old Aunt."

Back at Oxmoon my appetite returned. I unpacked my possessions and sorted them out. I even found it easy to make the correct responses when people talked to me.

"Now, Harry, we must get down to this ghastly business of packing your school trunk! I expect you're looking forward to going back, aren't you?"

"Oh yes, Aunt Ginevra! Can't wait!"

I was dreading it.

"I'll write, of course," I said to Bella at our last meeting. "But will your aunt try to read your letters?"

"Don't worry, Annie-May's walking out with the postman. I'll arrange something with them. When will you be back?"

"December the sixteenth."

"It'll be chilly in the potting shed! Maybe I could lock my governess in the lavatory, drug Aunt's tea and smuggle you up to my room!"

We both laughed at the thought of Miss Stourham lying in a drugged stupor as the incarcerated governess screamed for help.

"Oh Harry, it's been such fun! I'll miss you. I'll write too, of course, but I'm not good at writing so don't expect too much."

I expected far too much but I wasn't disappointed. Every word she wrote, no matter how illiterate, was precious to me. I used to carry her letters around inside my vest next to my skin, no mean feat when one considers the amount of time one spends at school changing into and out of games clothes. I kept each letter till the next one arrived but I didn't dare hold on to them indefinitely; I was too afraid some sadist might discover them and tell the world I was being peculiar by having a correspondence with a girl. That would have been the last straw.

Dear Harry, said one of Bella's letters, *how are you, I'm all right but bored, bored, bored, Miss Frensham says my work is terrible and Aunt says I'm impossible but who cares. Oh, here's some news, Eleanor's fallen in love with your uncle Thomas, she says she hasn't but she's had her hair permed and she's stopped wearing trousers and she says maybe some men aren't so bad after all, so what are we to think? How did all this happen, you'll ask, well, Farmer Llewellyn had a pig to sell and Eleanor and Thomas both wanted it and they bid and bid against each other and got very fierce but Eleanor gives way and Thomas is pleased and so he buys her a drink and they suddenly find they've got a lot in common and who knows, maybe they'll get married, after all they're pretty old and they might as well. Thomas looks at me as if I'm a pig that definitely ought to go to market but he says he knows what hell it is being the youngest of a grown-up family, so perhaps he's not so bad. But you're a hundred times better. I miss you I miss you I miss you, lots of love,* BELLA.

This sort of letter arrived every week until the beginning of December, when I received a short note which read: *Dear Harry, I'm ill with flu, can't write, doctor about to arrive, love B.*

This alarmed me. People could die of flu. I grabbed a pen and wrote: *Dear Bella, I was very sorry to hear you're ill. Please write the instant you're better— or if you're too weak just tell Annie-May to put "Still alive" on a postcard and send it to me. I shall worry about you all the time until I hear from you again.*

But I heard nothing. Anxiety gnawed me but before I could begin to be seriously worried, my housemaster sent for me to say that my father was coming to Harrow to take me out to lunch. By that time the end of the term was only a week away.

I immediately forgot Bella. I was beside myself with hope and joy. There could be only one reason why my father was making a special journey to Harrow when the end of the term was so near. Bronwen was coming back. He wanted to tell me the good news in person.

Outwardly calm but inwardly seething with excitement, I ran to meet him as he arrived in his car.

He didn't bother to get out. He just said, "Hullo—jump in," as if the extraordinary visit were the height of normality, so taking my cue from him I feigned nonchalance and slid briskly into the passenger seat. I thought, He's saving the news up as a surprise! And I marveled at his superhuman self-control.

I hazarded a remark or two about rugger, but when he replied in monosyllables I realized he was uninterested in sustaining a conversation. I supposed his excitement was too great. I was just wondering if jugged hare would be on the menu again at the inn when the car swerved abruptly off the country lane, turned through an open gateway and came to a jerky halt in a field. I was so startled that I never even gasped. I just stared at my father in disbelief and wondered what on earth was going on.

He switched off the engine and turned to face me. His striking eyes were expressionless yet when I looked at them I turned cold.

"Harry," said my father in the calmest voice he could manage, "I've come to talk to you about Belinda Stourham."

IV

How did I survive? I don't know. How did he survive? I don't know that either.

I remember that beyond a wire fence which divided the field six cows stood chewing cud. The December sky was gray; the nearby hedgerow was a mass of black spikes; the field was streaked with mud. And there were six cows. One, two, three, four, five, six. I counted them over and over again.

The inevitable disaster had happened. Dr. Warburton had arrived at Stourham Hall to treat Bella for flu and had become suspicious. Bella hadn't realized, or hadn't wanted to realize, that a pregnancy existed; perhaps she had hoped it would go away.

Six cows in a field. One—two—three—four—

"No, don't trouble to deny you've had carnal knowledge of her," said my father, terminating my mechanical arithmetic. "I can see from your face that you have."

Carnal knowledge. What an extraordinary phrase. Victorian. Puritan. Peculiar. And this was a man who had kept a working-class mistress and fathered four illegitimate children. I had a sudden terrifying glimpse into a divided personality, of a complex stranger who existed secretly beyond the shining mask of the hero I loved. Fear paralyzed me. I couldn't speak.

"How often did this happen?"

Six cows in a field. One—two—

"Harry, answer me. I must know when and how often. You see, perhaps there was someone else. Perhaps this has nothing to do with you after all. When did it first happen?"

I somehow managed to answer, "Three days after I came back home from school for the holidays."

"And after that?"

"Oh, every day till I went back."

Silence. I couldn't look my father in the face but I saw his knuckles whiten as he gripped the wheel. At last he said, "And during all that time there was no sign of menstruation?"

"What's that?"

"Oh my God," said my father. "Oh my God." He put both hands on the wheel and buried his face in his forearms.

We sat there together in the field with the six cows. I felt very ill. A long time passed before my father was able to whisper: "Didn't you realize this might happen?"

Didn't I realize this might happen. Had to answer that. He seemed to expect an answer.

"No, sir." I swallowed, made a great effort. "I thought girls couldn't have babies till they were grown up. I don't really know how girls work, sir. In fact I'm not too sure how boys work either. Of course I sort of knew what to do—all the jokes at school—but . . . well, no one ever told me, you see. No one ever explained."

My father said with great difficulty: "You didn't feel . . . it never occurred to you . . . that you could ask me to explain things to you?"

"Oh no, sir. I thought you might be upset."

"But what the devil do you think I am now?"

I couldn't stay in the car a moment longer. Scrambling out I took great gulps of the cold harsh country air and began to count the cows again.

"How could you behave like this, *how could you?*" The door slammed as he too left the car. "I still can't believe—can't accept—can't imagine how this could have happened. . . . Give me one good reason why you felt driven to behave in such a way!"

640

There was only one answer to that. "It seemed the right thing—the only thing—to do," I said, and leaning against the side of the car I broke down and began to cry.

V

"Oh God Almighty," said my father, "oh Jesus Christ, what a bloody nightmare, oh God, what am I going to do."

"Papa . . ." It was six years since I had called him by that outmoded Victorian name. The boys at prep school had laughed at me for calling him that, so I had quietly scrubbed it from my vocabulary and called him Father instead. But now I was a child again, the lost little boy who had misbehaved in the railway carriage, and this time there was no magic lady waiting to save me at my journey's end. "Papa, don't hate me, I couldn't bear it, you're all I've got, everyone else has been wiped out, if you turn against me I'd want to kill myself, I'd want to die—"

Awful neurotic melodrama spewed out of me like the blood of a terminal hemorrhage. I don't know which of us was more shocked. Kester was the only one who was ever allowed to be so disgustingly histrionic; one black sheep's enough for any family.

"Be quiet. Stop that at once. Pull yourself together."

I choked, gasped for air but still felt as if I were suffocating. "Help me," I sobbed. "Help me—"

He gripped my shoulders and gave me a shake. "Hold fast. Stand firm. I can't help you if you're hysterical. I'm here, I'll help you but you must be calm."

I tried to be calm. I watched the cows, who were placidly chewing their cud, but I couldn't count them, not anymore. It was beyond me. The numbers wouldn't come.

My father said it was cold and he made me sit in the car again. When he was back behind the steering wheel he waited until he was sure he was in control of himself and then said, "No one knows about this except Gavin Warburton, Angela Stourham and me. And no one's going to know about it. I'll see if we can arrange an abortion."

"What's that?"

"The baby's removed in an operation."

"Would it be alive afterwards?"

"No." My father paused. "If it's too late for an abortion," he said, "I'll have to pay for Angela to take the girl abroad for a few months. However, there are two dangers. First, the governess—she'll have to be dismissed and it'll be up to Angela to think of a plausible excuse. Second, Eleanor—she'll want to go with them. Or will she? No, there's just a chance she won't. If she's in love with Thomas . . ." He let that thought trail off before concluding: "All we can do is hope for the best. Then after the baby's born it can be adopted and that'll be that. Of course you must never see the girl again."

I didn't dare look at him. I didn't dare speak. But tears filled my eyes as I mourned my lost friend.

"You've done a terrible thing to that child, Harry. The experience will almost certainly scar her for life. I hope you realize now just what a dreadful thing you've done."

I nodded. No point in trying to speak. I went on crying soundlessly.

"But of course," said my father, "you're not really responsible. You're just an ignorant child. The true responsibility for the disaster must lie elsewhere."

I looked at him dumbly.

"I'm the one who's to blame," said my father, trying to light a cigarette, and then to my horror I saw he couldn't go on.

"No," I said at once in a trembling voice, "you're not to blame, you're not. You're the best father in the whole world."

"If that were true, we wouldn't be here. Harry... I must try and understand exactly what's happened, and you must try to help me. So be truthful—I promise I won't be angry. Why did you do this? Even though you were unaware of the possible consequences, you must have known that what you were doing was wrong."

"But it made me feel less unhappy." The words, long suppressed, streamed out of my mouth before I could censor them. "I've been so unhappy, Father, so bloody miserable, I just didn't know how I was ever going to bear such misery, but Bella made it bearable—and now even Bella's been taken away from me, oh, how can I bear it, I want it all back, I want a home, a real home with a mother in it, I can't bear living at Oxmoon where everyone hates me, I can't bear having no home—oh, Father, go to Canada, bring Bronwen back, please, Father, please, please, please..."

My father put his arm around me. He said simply, "I want to but I can't. It would be cruel to Bronwen to wreck her life all over again, but don't worry, Harry, because I'm going to put things right. I'll get you that home you so badly need, I swear I will, no matter how high the price I have to pay."

VI

He went back to his estranged wife.

At first I thought he did it just because I'd said I wanted a home with a mother in it, but later I suspected my disaster had so shattered him that he had conceived of the return to Constance as a form of atonement. Blaming himself as he did he took the obvious action—not simply because he wanted to suffer, but because it provided the only alleviation of a guilt that had become unendurable. Years later he confessed to me that he had been riddled with guilt about Francesca, my little half-sister, and although he had resented Constance to the point of hatred, he had at heart felt guilty about her too for the way he had abandoned their marriage. He felt guilty about Bronwen, guilty about his four illegitimate children and now finally he felt guilty about me. He was overloaded with guilt, and perhaps he even thought he would break down unless he took a radical step to lighten his burden. He went back.

How he did it I don't know. He never spoke of what he must have gone through, but when term ended a week later he fetched me himself from Harrow and said, "We're not going back to Oxmoon. You've got a nice big room in a new home, and there's a piano in the drawing room." I was touched when he mentioned the piano. I suppose he thought that if I had any doubts this would convince me that he was doing the right thing.

When he was first married to Constance we had lived in a house in Chester Square, but she had moved after her father's death to his mansion on Eaton Walk. I had been there a few times but could not remember it in any detail so I was astonished by its size and grandeur.

My room was, as my father had promised, very nice. All my possessions had been scooped out of Oxmoon, whisked to London in double-quick time and arranged on various shelves. My father gave me my Christmas present early; it was a new gramophone, and Constance, having meticulously examined my record collection and analyzed my taste, gave me some new records, all chamber music by Bach and Vivaldi. I found I even had a new little serf, nine-year-old Francesca, who spent much time gazing up at me with shining eyes. Constance said she intended to take us both to a performance of *The Messiah* at the Albert Hall, and would I like to go to Covent Garden? I asked warily what opera she had in mind. Just because I'm musical doesn't mean I'm not discriminating. Quite the reverse.

What surprised me most about Constance, whom I could hardly remember, was that she was so young. Over the years I had built up this picture of a mean old hag, ugly as sin, who never opened her mouth except to say "no" to a divorce, so it was a considerable shock to me when I now found she was a woman barely thirty, very smart, good-looking, cultured and poised. She took everything with lethal seriousness—the arts, her daughter, international politics, her social obligations, her marriage, her charities, the Prince of Wales, the Marx Brothers—everything. When presented with a new subject she would study it, master it and file it away in her mind for future reference, and as I was a new subject, as far as Constance was concerned, I presently became aware that I was being studied with a sympathetic but chillingly earnest interest.

This maddened me, although I took care to be polite to her. After all, my father had made this great sacrifice in order that I should be happy, so now I had to be happy. No choice. But I didn't like being observed as if I were some guinea pig in a laboratory. I didn't like those gray dirty noisy London streets. And after a while I knew I didn't like that house on Eaton Walk, even though it contained everything a right-minded boy could want. It was so cold and formal, so quiet and lifeless. I was used to noise and mess and people laughing as they all relaxed together. No one laughed much at Eaton Walk except Francesca, living her well-ordered little life with her nanny and governess, but she was kept out of sight most of the time in the nurseries. Marian floated in and out saying how simply wonderful everything was, and Constance, mastering the subject of Marian with typical skill, chatted to her kindly about men and clothes and the social calendar.

But in the new year before I returned to school I paid a nocturnal visit to Marian's bedroom and demanded to know what she really thought of our new home. I was in such a muddle myself by that time, not understanding how everything could be so right yet so wrong, that even my vacuous sister seemed a desirable confidante.

"Thank God," said Marian. "I thought you were happy as a lark and I was beginning to wonder if I was going mad."

"But what is it, Marian? Why is it so ghastly here?"

"My dear, it's her, of course. That woman was born to be the patron saint of tedium."

"But I thought you liked her!"

"Of course I like her—I've got to, haven't I? What choice do I have now that Papa's been so divinely noble and unselfish in order to give me an aristocratic home and a socially acceptable stepmother?"

"What are you going to do?"

"Go down on my knees and thank God as soon as they leave for the Côte d'Azur. Then I can go to Aunt Daphne."

"What about when they come back?"

"I'll simply have to get married before the men in white coats arrive to remove me to a padded cell."

It was at Easter when she met Rory Kinsella again. Aunt Ginevra organized a huge family reunion to mark my father's return to his wife, and we all dutifully turned up at Oxmoon to do the done thing.

Kester was flouncing around as usual playing master of the house and host to all his adoring family. It was stupid of me but I couldn't resist needling him with a sex joke, and the silly old sod blanched as if sex scared him stiff. Aunt Ginevra overheard and was livid with me. Silly old bitch. I was in a great state of misery at the time because going back to Gower reminded me of Bella and I wanted so much to see her. But Bella wasn't at Stourham Hall. She and her aunt had gone to Geneva directly after Christmas and were not due to return till June. Everyone said to Eleanor that they did hope her Aunt Angela would finally find a cure for her asthma, and what a wonderful experience a few months abroad would be for Belinda.

I tried to shut out my misery by playing "The Blue Danube" in the ballroom in memory of my grandfather, but that bloody Thomas shouted for "The Black Bottom" and someone put a Charleston on the gramophone, so I gave up. Marian danced a lot with Rory and later told me how much she liked him. Typical. It would take an idiotic girl like Marian to fall for a layabout like Rory Kinsella. He worked in the City and called himself a broker, but I don't believe he was ever more than a clerk. Marian said she thought he was sexy. Typical again. He was a heavily built redhead who prided himself on his questionable Irish charm.

"But he's such fun!" sighed Marian. "And the lovely thing is that he's one of the family so I don't have to *explain* anything—he's grown up with Papa's peculiar situation and takes it for granted. Heavens, he even thinks it's all rather amusing!"

It would take an oaf like Rory to find stark tragedy amusing. However mutual adversity had made me fond of Marian so I kept my opinions to myself, but in fact I kept all my opinions to myself at that time; there was no one in whom I was willing to confide.

In June at half-term my father told me Bella was back at Stourham Hall. The baby, a girl, had lived only a few hours but Bella had made a complete recovery.

"Thomas and Eleanor are getting married next month," said my father, "but luckily it's the day before school breaks up so we won't have to invent an excuse for you not to attend. Now, Harry, I want you to give me your word not to communicate with that child. I'm sure all she wants is to forget how much she's suffered, so you're under an absolute moral duty to leave her well alone."

That settled that. One couldn't argue with an absolute moral duty. I gave him my word and tried not to let him see how miserable I was.

By this time my father had talked to me—or tried to talk to me—about sex. I suppose he thought better late than never, but he got into such an agonizing muddle that in the end I cried out in despair, "It doesn't matter, I don't want to do it anymore." This was true; the horrific consequences of my sexual experience now made the thought of sex repugnant to me, and this truth very fortunately proved to be the saving of us both because it enabled my father to pull himself together.

My father's problem was that he was terrified I would now want to seduce every girl in sight so he felt obliged to lecture me on morality. But of course he was deeply and painfully aware that he was the last person entitled to lecture anyone about sexual morality. However once he had grasped that I didn't want to turn into a juvenile Don Juan, he was liberated from the compulsion to moralize and could focus on the remote future when I would be just another man who needed to know how to live a sensible private life.

This he could cope with. He said practically enough, "You won't feel repelled forever," and for a time he conquered his Victorian streak sufficiently to talk about medical facts and contraception. I was profoundly grateful to him. I was also profoundly relieved to discover he was quite capable of being down-to-earth about sex when he wasn't flagellating himself for the poor example he had set me. But then to my despair his Victorian streak reasserted itself and he got bogged down in morality again. I suppose he thought closing a discussion of sex without any reference to morality wouldn't be the done thing, but it was hopeless. He floundered around talking about sin like some mid-nineteenth-century evangelical fanatic until in the end, not being unintelligent, I forgot about being embarrassed and became intrigued instead. It occurred to me for the first time that the idea of sin—not merely sexual sin but wrongdoing of any kind—frightened my father very much, far more than it frightened any other adult I knew. In fact I couldn't think of another adult who was actually frightened of sin. Most people seemed content to leave the definition of sin to clergymen while they themselves tranquilly led their law-abiding daily lives. But not my father. He seemed to be obsessed by a vision in which absolutely anyone was capable of absolutely anything while the road to hell yawned perpetually and inexorably on the far side of his famous line. I was fifteen by then, young enough to be deeply impressed by his sincerity but old enough to think he was being most peculiar.

"But Father, why are you getting in such a sweat over this? I know you're not exactly a saint but you're a good man and I know very well you'd never dream of doing anything really wrong."

"Ah, but temptation's everywhere," said my father, "and anyone can make a mistake and yield. I've seen a good man destroyed by a past evil he couldn't endure, and terrible things happen, as I well know, to people who fail to recognize evil and reject it—to people who fail to draw the line."

Off he went on his damned line again. Most odd. I listened respectfully but try as I would I still couldn't see why he was getting into such a flap. After all, surely anyone with a reasonable upbringing could spot evil—what an emotional Victorian word!—a mile off and then either take evasive action or walk out to embrace it with outstretched arms.

I thought a great deal about this eccentric and disturbed side of my father's personality, but all I could conclude was that although he was not religious he was profoundly superstitious. I saw for the first time then how Bronwen's mystical streak would have appealed to him; although he seemed in so many ways to be a typically rational Englishman he was at rock bottom a Welsh romantic, and as soon as I realized this I wondered how on earth he was surviving with Constance. But I couldn't allow myself to dwell on that, not at first. I was too busy thinking about Bella.

I was finding that instead of receding from my mind as time passed the thought of her ordeal was preying on me more than ever. I wanted to write and say sorry, sorry, sorry, I didn't mean it, I liked you so much, I'd have done anything rather than hurt you. But of course I couldn't write because I had an absolute moral duty not to communicate with her. So I started to long for another of her illiterate letters. I could see it so clearly in my mind. *Dear Harry, how are you, I am well now, what an awful business but don't worry, I don't blame you at all...*

What a fantasy. I knew my father was right and that she would never want to see me again but still I went on longing irrationally for the absolution which only she could give.

Presently the nightmares started. I dreamed a nurse handed me a bloodstained lump of flesh and told me to bury it. I placed it in an old shoe box and buried it in the potting shed but when the earth was replaced I heard little fists beating on the lid and demanding to be let out. I scraped the earth away again and ripped off the lid but the box was empty. Yet as soon as I reburied it the fists started to beat again for release.

Crazy. Had to pull myself together before Constance guessed something was wrong.

"Father, you didn't tell Constance, did you?"

"Good God, no!" said my father, unintentionally speaking volumes about his marriage. "I never tell her anything."

That was the last honest conversation I had with him before I messed myself up again. Certainly I never dared ask him what he really thought when Marian messed herself up with Rory Kinsella and had to rush to the altar in double-quick time.

"But why shouldn't I go to bed with Rory if I love him?" screamed Marian at my father in front of us all when she was obliged to confess the news of her imminent wedding. "Bronwen went to bed with you!"

My father said with great politeness, "Constance—Harry—excuse us, if you please," and we withdrew. But he was never the same after that. I saw him become remote, detached, enigmatic. He absorbed himself in his work, and as his reputation as a businessman increased, so he seemed to withdraw behind the facade of his wealth and success. He might have been living behind bulletproof glass, and all the while I sensed he was acting, just as I was, pretending to be happy because the alternative was too terrible to contemplate.

Eventually I began to pray he might leave Constance again. I became convinced that if only we could return to Penhale Manor the bulletproof glass would shatter and I would rediscover the unpretentious hero in blue dungarees who had laughed and joked with Bronwen, but we stayed on in London, and my father remained the quiet serious stranger whom it was virtually impossible to know.

I became so desperate that in the end I tried to analyze his marriage. Was it likely to collapse or wasn't it? What the hell was going on? I wasn't sure, but once I started studying the two of them I began to get some bizarre ideas. I could see that Constance loved him but at the same time I sensed her simmering anger. No doubt she felt, as I did, that despite his physical presence at her side he had staged some massive mental retreat. They seemed to find conversation difficult and I thought that angered her too. After all, there she was, mastering all those interesting subjects in order to provide him with fascinating conversation, and my father obviously didn't give a damn.

Yet he wasn't indifferent to her. I could see she often bored him so much that he snapped at her, but he always made amends by giving her a kiss, and when I saw how much she liked those kisses—perhaps even went out of her way to needle him into giving them—I saw to my horror that he liked them too. There was no sign that he begrudged them; he could have been evasive but he chose not to be, and gradually it occurred to me that the dreary surface of their marriage might be concealing a mutually satisfactory sexual relationship. I could well imagine Constance being obsessive about sex. I could picture her studying it, mastering it and serving it up with poker-faced skill in her latest Parisian negligée.

And my father? It took me some time to work out what was going on there, but one day in the holidays the penny finally dropped. I was playing a Beethoven sonata in the drawing room and when I reached the end I thought what a miracle it was that whenever I played the piano I could so absolutely forget what I didn't want to remember. Then I realized with an intuitive leap of the imagination that this was the only possible reason for my father's continuing sexual relationship with his wife. He used sex as I used the piano: to forget, to escape, to enjoy himself in the way he liked best. The fact that she was Constance was probably irrelevant. Just as I could play on any piano, so he could no doubt gratify himself with any female, but naturally it was useful to him that his own wife could provide him with whatever quality and quantity of sex he needed. It saved him from the bore of looking elsewhere.

I had often wondered if he had mistresses but now I saw that he probably wouldn't consider extramarital sex worth the effort. I doubted that my father was by nature promiscuous. Indeed everything I knew about him suggested he would fight hard against a very natural inclination to sleep with every woman he fancied. If he had a relationship with his wife that allowed him to exercise his sexuality without constraint I could quite see him thankfully drawing the line against any immoral activity and settling down to do God-only-knew-what with Constance whenever the bedroom door was closed.

What a picture that conjured up! By this time sheer biology was conquering my revulsion towards sex which had followed the disaster with Bella, and I spent a lot of time thinking of nothing but intercourse. In a paroxysm of guilt I had promised my father I wouldn't go near a woman until I had left school at eighteen but now, reduced to pornographic visions and endless masturbation, I regretted having to live like a monk. I wouldn't have minded supplementing my piano playing with a little sex now and then to ease the dreariness of that Belgravia jail, but of course I couldn't have broken my promise to my father. That wouldn't have been the done thing at all.

My liberation finally came when I was eighteen and won an open scholarship to Oxford. To make amends to my father I had slaved at Harrow, giving up all thought of specializing in the sciences and dedicating myself to mastering the classics. I mastered them. My father was thrilled and for a short precious time set aside the bulletproof glass to give me a glimpse of the man in blue dungarees who had laughed with Bronwen. Naturally I was just as thrilled as he was that I was finally turning out to be the son he wanted me to be, and it was not until I began my studies up at Oxford that I realized just what a terrible mistake I'd made.

The truth was that I had no genuine inclination towards classical scholarship, and a logical mind, a scientific preoccupation with accuracy and that old friend my trusty memory were no longer enough now to guarantee my success. I became bored with my studies. I tried to whip up interest but found there was no interest left to whip up. Unable to cope with this lassitude and its inevitable implications, unable to face the fact that I was intellectually incapable of pursuing knowledge in a discipline that did not appeal to me, I cut lectures, drank too much, started fooling around with women. My tutor spoke to me. I did try to pull myself together but I knew I was hopelessly adrift, and in the May of 1938, after taking an exam I knew I had no chance of passing, I was caught with a girl in my room, and soon after that my father received the letter which told him I was being sent down.

VII

No six cows in a field this time. Just the drawing room at Eaton Walk, a wasteland of beige carpet studded with arid groups of antiques. Outside it was raining as it can only rain in London, dirty water dripping drearily from drab skies. It had been raining ever since I'd left Oxford. Despite the stuffiness of the room I felt dank and cold.

"I don't understand, Harry."

"Wrong subject. Sorry. Should have specialized in the sciences at school and then read engineering."

"But why didn't you tell me?"

"Thought engineering wasn't the done thing."

"But my dear Harry—"

"I knew I didn't have your gift for modern languages but I thought I could make it up to you by being a classical scholar like Uncle Robert."

"But for Christ's sake..."

We stammered away, groping for the truth, both of us damned nearly speechless with pain, until finally my father managed to say, "You'll please me best by being the son you are, not the son you think I want you to be. If you want to be an engineer—"

"I don't. Not really. All I've ever wanted to be is a pianist."

"But my dear Harry, there's no money or future in that!"

"Yes, I know, silly of me, doesn't matter, too late now anyway, concert pianists have to start young and train for years and years...But never mind, I'll be an engineer."

"I thought you just told me you didn't want to be an engineer! Harry, what is it you really want to do?"

"I want to go home."

"But this is your home!"

Silence. More ghastly truths surfaced. My father shoved back his hair awkwardly and turned aside as if he could not bear to look at me any longer.

"I want to go back to Penhale Manor," I said.

"To farm?" He was still struggling for composure.

I had had no thought beyond returning home, but now I saw not only a life I could tolerate but a life that my father would find acceptable.

"Yes," I said, "to farm. I want to follow in Grandfather's footsteps and manage an estate."

He thought about this for a moment. "Are you sure that's what you really want?"

"Yes."

"Well, I suppose Penhale Manor would provide you with a satisfactory training ground, and then later you can move on to a more challenging situation."

I thought it wiser not to say that once I got back to Gower no one on earth was ever going to dig me out of it again. I kept quiet.

"Farm management could certainly provide you with an interesting career," said my father, warming to the idea. "I often fancied it myself in the past and I'd have taken a more active interest in your mother's Herefordshire lands if I hadn't been so reluctant to leave Bronwen on her own at the Manor." He fell silent, although whether this was because he had jolted himself by mentioning Bronwen's name or because he was remembering how much he had fancied estate management in the past, it was impossible to tell. "Very well," he said rousing himself, "I'll give you a five-year nominal lease on the Manor on the assumption that at the end of that time, when you're trained and experienced, you move to Here-fordshire to manage your mother's farms there. I think that would be a very tolerable solution to your problems."

After I had finished thanking him I put my hand impulsively on his arm. "Father... I know you're not happy here. Come back with me to Penhale."

He stared. For a moment he was too astonished to speak. Then he shook off my arm, said crisply, "What an extraordinary suggestion" and walked away.

Now it was my turn to stare. "You mean you're determined to stay here?"

"Of course." He reached the window and stood watching the rain outside.

"But why? *Why?*"

"Oh, I could never leave Constance and Francesca a second time," said my father. "I draw the line."

It took me a moment to control myself because every instinct I had was scream-ing against such a decision. "But Father, never mind Constance and Francesca— what about *you?* What about *your* life? What about *your* happiness?"

"My life wouldn't be worth living if I left them—I'd never survive the guilt. And as for my happiness, how could I be happy in the hell my guilt would create for me? Anyway, I'm not unhappy at the moment—I'm just leading a life in which happiness isn't particularly important. A satisfactory life isn't dependent on sheer happiness alone, thank God. I'm doing valuable work for the Armstrong charities. I'm looking after my wife and child who depend on me emotionally. I'm leading a civilized, reasonably interesting, not unrewarding life, and consid-ering all the suffering I've caused in the past I think that's more than I have a right to expect."

I saw that locked up in his nineteenth-century metaphysical illusions he was unapproachable. If his peculiar fear of sin and guilt was driving him into mar-tyrdom I was powerless to intervene.

"I see," I said politely.

"Well, I should bloody well hope you do," said my father, "since what we're really talking about here is the difference between right and wrong."

"Of course," I said at once. "Don't worry, Father, I do understand. You're staying on here because it's the right thing—indeed, the only thing—to do."

But what a catastrophe.

VIII

At that time, the summer of '38, Penhale Manor itself was vacant, a fact that had no doubt stimulated my old longing to go home. The vacancy was the result of Oswald Stourham's death that spring; he had left Stourham Hall to Eleanor, who had been living at Penhale Manor with Thomas since their marriage in 1934, and for Thomas this bequest represented his elevation to the landed gentry after his years as a younger son living in houses provided by his indulgent brother. In fact there was little land at Stourham Hall but Thomas was hardly idle; in addition to supervising his pig farm, which he transferred from Penhale Manor, he was still in charge of running the Godwin estates in Gower, and even if I were to whip away my father's lands the likelihood remained that Thomas would be running Oxmoon indefinitely. Of course no one seriously thought poor old Kester would ever be able to manage his property himself.

My father had two farms in Gower, the Home Farm of Penhale Manor and the Martinscombe sheep farm beneath Penhale Down. Both farmhouses were assigned to foremen who reported to Thomas. Bronwen's brother-in-law Huw Meredith had moved north to the Lleyn Peninsula after her departure, and so the foreman at the Home Farm was a stranger to me. So was the foreman at Martinscombe, but that didn't concern me since my father declared that the Penhale Manor estate would be quite enough for me to cope with at the start of my new career. The bungalow Little Oxmoon, which stood on the Martinscombe lands, also belonged to my father but had been allotted to Aunt Celia back in 1934 after her husband ran off with a Hungarian.

I prepared to return to Penhale.

Did I think of Bella while I was making my preparations? Yes. I thought I would at last have the chance to assuage my guilt by telling her how sorry I was for what had happened. Did the thought of Bella influence me in my decision to return to Gower? No. It was now five years since our pathetic childhood love affair, and I had quite accepted that she belonged entirely to the past. I had had other girls by that time; I had other sexual memories to recall. It was true no memory could match the poignancy of those summer days in 1933, but that was beside the point. Nostalgia would get me nowhere. I had to look ahead, not back. I had to move on.

I wanted to move to the Manor immediately but my father refused to allow it. In his Victorian mind a young man couldn't expect to escape unpunished after being sent down from Oxford, so he cut off my allowance for three months, a gesture that was the equivalent of jailing me at Eaton Walk. However when he suspected I might be enjoying myself playing the piano for hours while he was out, he found me a clerical job at the headquarters of Armstrong Investments and I had to waste endless sunny days addressing envelopes for circulars appealing for money on behalf of the Armstrong charities.

Meanwhile, as I toiled away at my office desk in secret and sordid disgrace, poor old Kester, poor old sod, who I had always assumed was incapable of a wet dream, was staging a glorious elopement well worthy of Hollywood at its sloppiest. I could almost hear the soaring violins as he walked away into the golden sunset with that nice intelligent little girlfriend of his who was so very much too good for him. The one redeeming feature of the situation was that at least someone other than me would now receive the full blast of my father's disapproval, and this comforting prospect enabled me to go on addressing envelopes with tranquillity while I waited for my father to annihilate him.

But the annihiliation never happened. Poor feeble old Kester had somehow trounced my formidable father and gone walking on into the golden sunset. What was more, my father even came back impressed from the confrontation at Gretna

Green. I couldn't believe it. Then when I did believe it, I didn't like it. In fact, to be frank, I hated it.

"I've underestimated that boy," said my father. "I think he may well turn out to be the most remarkable young man. How well he argued his case! He even reminded me of Robert."

Uncle Robert was the family hero. With his story enshrined in myth and his memory bathed in a perpetual glowing light, his name was synonymous with colossal success in life and superhuman courage in adversity. To say that Kester recalled a memory of Robert was the highest compliment my father could ever pay his nephew. I felt as if a knife were revolving in my gut; somehow I managed to say casually, "Good for Kester—I hope he lives happily ever after," but it was no good. I couldn't resist adding: "Of course I wouldn't be seen dead at the altar before I was twenty-five."

Famous last words.

Six weeks later Aunt Ginevra died at Oxmoon and we all gathered for her memorial service at Penhale. The church was full. I was with the rest of the family in the front pews, but as we all stood for the first hymn I looked over my shoulder at the pews across the aisle and the next moment I saw Bella, sullen and luscious, looking back.

IX

She at once buried her nose in her hymnbook and looked more sullen than ever. I realized then that the child I had known and perhaps loved in my own childish way had gone forever and was never going to come back. All the women I had loved had gone away and never come back: my mother, my old nanny, Bronwen—and now Bella, replaced by this unknown young woman of eighteen who was obviously determined not to acknowledge my existence.

As the clergyman droned on I felt my anger towards women surfacing, the anger that had prompted me to play around at Oxford without caring whom I hurt. I had had no affairs, just a string of incidents. To have affairs was impossible because I knew I had to leave a woman before she could leave me. The alternative was to risk suffering a pain I was no longer prepared to endure.

So I turned my back on Bella, who was clearly so determined to abandon me, and told myself that even if she had shown interest I would have rejected her. But the rest of the service still passed in a haze of misery.

There was to be a family lunch afterwards at Oxmoon before Kester departed for Ireland with his brothers, but outside the church I heard Eleanor say to Anna, "I'm afraid Bella's feeling frightful—will you excuse her if she goes straight home?"

I tried to slip past but directly ahead of me Thomas had paused beside his wife. I turned aside—and there I was, face to face with Bella again, and my father no more than a pace behind me with Constance.

Speech was impossible. I tried to say hullo, but nothing happened. Bella stared furiously at the nearest tombstone. Around us, people chatted in muted voices of inanities.

"Hullo, Bella," said my father politely.

She didn't answer but tugged her brother-in-law's hand. "Thomas, take me home."

"All right, old girl," said Thomas kindly enough, and they moved away together through the crowd.

"What a very rude unattractive girl," said Constance disapprovingly. "I feel sorry for Thomas and Eleanor having to give her a home."

We all went to Oxmoon for lunch. Damned Kester sat in our grandfather's great carved chair and gave a gala performance as master of Oxmoon—dry eyes, stiff upper lip, the lot. In fact, he was positively glittering in his role of the perfect Godwin, sole surviving son of the most perfect Godwin of all time. Why had I never realized that Kester looked like Uncle Robert? He had those same pale clever eyes and that fine-drawn jawline which somehow, by a trick of the bone structure, gave an impression not of delicacy but of strength. Of course he was still plain as a pikestaff with that large nose and womanish hair, but all the same... plain people can be striking. I felt too dark, as saturnine as a stage villain, and profoundly unattractive. When we all stood up at the end of the meal I was very conscious that he had wound up taller than I was. I'm five feet eleven. Of course I tell everyone I'm six feet. Kester *was* six feet. He might even have been six feet one. In fact that day I even wondered if he could be six feet two.

I couldn't stand it. I got out of the house, cut across the lawn and plunged into the woods. The jackdaws in the ruined tower were still saying "caw-caw," and I still knew that what they were really saying was "dispossessed, dispossessed." I thought: I have been here before—miserable, alone and in retreat.

I walked on. I could have stopped, but I went on. I left the grounds by the door in the wall, crossed the road and set off across the heather to Sweyn's Houses. There were no wild ponies browsing nearby this time, but the sky was just as blue and the light wind still had that faint tang of salt from the sea.

I reached the summit of the ridge and there on top of Rhossili Downs I saw the dazzling view exactly as it had been five years before, the waves streaming languidly over the golden sands, the sea a glittering hypnotic blue, the Shipway about to sink beneath a wide arc of white foam.

I looked along the ridge but there was no one in sight; history never really repeats itself. Finding the fuck rock I stood looking at it. I smiled as I remembered how we had shaken hands politely after our first encounter, not knowing how else to confirm our new friendship, and suddenly I was touched by our extreme innocence. I sat down on the rock as if I could no longer remain upright beneath the weight of my memories, and it was directly after this, as I looked once more along the ridge, that I saw her running towards me from Llangennith.

I leaped to my feet. She never stopped but she waved. I ran and ran and she ran and ran too; she ran all the way into my outstretched arms.

"You came back," she said, tears streaming down her face. "You went away—but you came back."

I took her in my arms and promised her I'd never go away again.

653

"Oh Harry, it was so awful, I was so unhappy and so frightened, I can't tell you how frightened I was, and Aunt was beastly, *beastly*—"

"Shhh. Don't think about it. Just don't think."

"I can't help it. I have nightmares—"

"So do I. What was the baby like?"

"I never saw her. That was awful too. In fact that was the most awful thing of all. They gave me an injection because I was screaming so much, and when I came round it was over and she'd been taken away. I wanted to see her but they said in the circumstances it was better not and anyway she was ill and then she died and I still wanted to see her but they said no, it would only upset me more. I asked, I begged, I screamed, I wept, but they said I might get emotionally disturbed, it was better not, and now I get these nightmares when I'm looking and looking for her and digging up cemeteries—"

"We'll have another baby. We'll get married and have another. I'll put everything right."

Shoving aside her cigarette, she stubbed it out in the earth beneath the short grass and burrowed blindly into my arms. A muffled childlike voice said, "You don't have to. I don't want you to do it just to make it up to me."

"I want to."

We were sitting on the fuck rock. Below us the holidaymakers, scattered dots on the vast beach, were enjoying the rarity of a perfect summer day. Away to our right a party of people on horseback were moving towards us along the top of the Downs, and beyond them we could see hikers and a child flying a kite. The sea gulls soared in the wind currents. The surf murmured in our ears, and beyond the cliffs at Rhossili the Worm's Head was cut off once more by the white water as the Shipway went under.

"I want to make love to you," I said.

"Fuck, you mean?" she said doubtfully, and at once she became the child of thirteen again to whom fuck was just another four-letter word like skip or jump without any offensive connotations. "Oh, Harry, I couldn't, not without being married. I'd be too afraid of it all happening again."

"That's exactly why I said 'I want to' instead of 'I'm going to.'" I had a quick think. I had brought no sheaths with me to Gower; one hardly sets off for one's aunt's memorial service armed to the teeth with contraceptives. There was now a chemist in Penhale, but if I went there to buy what I needed the whole village would know in less than an hour that Harry Godwin was up to no good. I wondered wildly if my father used contraceptives but thought it unlikely. A family rumor had long been in circulation that Constance was anxious for another child.

I groaned in frustration. Bella looked anxious. I explained the problem to her.

"Maybe Thomas has some!" was her bright response. "Bobby's nearly two now and Eleanor hasn't got pregnant again."

That settled that. I jumped up. "Come on, we're off to Stourham Hall!"

We dashed off hand in hand along the path, both of us laughing, and suddenly the world seemed dazzling to me and I knew what it was to be happy. Stourham Hall lay about a mile away where the Downs sloped to the sand burrows. We sneaked into the house by a side door. Thomas and Eleanor might still be out but there was always the danger of a wandering servant.

"Supposing Thomas and Eleanor come back?"

"No, I'd say we have at least two hours—they'll wait to see off Kester and Co. who are leaving for Ireland. I heard Thomas mention that to my father this morning."

We invaded the marital chamber. It was a plain, no-nonsense room large enough to swallow up several vast pieces of Victorian furniture. There was a good view of the sea beyond the burrows.

"Lord, I hope we're right about this!" I muttered. "It'd be just our luck if he went in for *coitus interruptus* instead."

"What's that? If it's awful I bet he'd do it. He's so peculiar."

I was too busy hunting to give this remark the attention it deserved. The drawer of the bedside table was empty. I ransacked Eleanor's dressing table. Bella looked under the mattress. We were giggling all the time.

"Oh heavens, Harry, supposing we don't find any? I'll burst with frustration—I'm wild for it!"

"Wild? I'm berserk." I ripped open the door of the wardrobe and saw a dressing gown. There was a bulge in the pocket. "Eureka!" I shouted.

"Oh, thank God!"

We rushed to her bedroom, locked the door and hurtled into each other's arms.

XI

"I called the baby Melody," said Bella, "because I knew you were so fond of music. But beastly old Aunt said it wasn't Christian and she told them to put Jane on the birth certificate. There had to be a birth certificate because the baby did live a few hours. Aunt had your name put on it as the father. She said she did it to relieve her feelings but it wouldn't matter because no one we knew was ever going to go hunting in the birth records at Geneva. Oh, Aunt was cruel to me, so cruel and hard and cold—"

"Shhh." I began to make love to her again to blot out all the terrible memories. Vaguely I wondered what Thomas would think when he found not one but two of his sheaths were missing, but perhaps he wasn't the kind of man who always knew how many he had in reserve. All I could do was wish him a touch of amnesia.

Bella was only approximately the same shape as she had been at thirteen because now there was more of her, and the additional weight was so strikingly distributed that within seconds of ejaculation, or so it seemed, I was once more in a state of chronic sexual excitement. She had long lissom legs, slim hips, a narrow waist and a bosom that had to be seen to be believed. I saw it and still didn't believe it. With perfect truth I told her she was the sexiest girl I had ever seen in my life.

"How many have you seen?" she said jealously at once.

I saw no point in lying about this. "Well, of course I had a few girls up at Oxford—I thought I was never going to see you again. But they didn't mean anything. They were just good for a quick fuck."

"Lucky old you. I wouldn't have minded some quick fucks, but I was too frightened, and anyway there was no one to fuck. Aunt watched me like a jailer too. Oh, the relief when Daddy died! He left me money, you know, so I thought I'd be able to get away at last, but the money's all tied up till I'm twenty-five so here I am, still stuck with Eleanor and Thomas—and oh God, he's so *peculiar!*"

This time I took notice. "In what way?"

"He gives me peculiar looks."

I sat bolt upright in bed. "My God, are you trying to tell me—"

"Oh no, he's crazy about Eleanor; in fact he's keener on her than she is on him. It was the other way around before they were married, but—"

"Then what are you trying to say?"

"I think he amuses himself by imagining all sorts of peculiar things he'd like to do to me—only of course he never would because he's so mad about Eleanor."

I sagged back appalled on the pillows. "When did all this begin?"

"Oh, about a month after they started living here this spring. I couldn't sleep one night so I set off for the kitchens to make myself some tea, and I was just passing their bedroom door when I heard them snorting around like a couple of pigs so I stopped to listen, I don't know why, maybe because I've never been able to imagine Eleanor doing it. Anyway, suddenly a mouse ran over my foot and I screamed and a moment later Thomas came charging out and yelled that if ever I listened at the door again he'd beat me—well, he just said that, he didn't mean it, it was just a way of letting off steam, and then suddenly he looked at me as if he were thinking, 'Hullo, that's an interesting idea—'"

"I could kill him."

"Oh, it was all right! He just went bright red, returned to the bedroom and slammed the door in my face. And of course he's never done anything since. But whenever he and I are alone together now I sort of feel he's thinking what fun it would be to spank me—"

"I'm getting you out of this house. We'll get married at once."

"Oh yes, let's get married as soon as possible, but don't worry, Harry. He loves Eleanor, I know he does—"

"Yes, but you've got something Eleanor doesn't have. Maybe he has trouble getting it up with her. Maybe whenever he sees you he has an erection hard enough to bore through a steel plate. Maybe—"

But Bella was now rocking with mirth. "Imagine Thomas drilling through a steel plate with his—"

"God knows I could drill through a steel girder with mine," I said, grabbing her, and reached for the last sheath. Thomas was really going to be caught short. I pictured him casting around for a thieving housemaid with a passion for contraceptives.

"Oh God, that was heaven!" gasped Bella afterwards. "How soon did you say we could be married?"

"I don't know but I'll get a special license," I said, and then remembered I hadn't a penny in the world. The thought was the equivalent of a dozen cold showers. I felt very young suddenly, very nervous. I was still some months short of my twentieth birthday.

"I'll talk to my father as soon as I get back," I said casually, sweating with dread at the prospect, and ten minutes later I set off for Oxmoon.

XII

"I absolutely forbid it!" said my father, white with rage. No six cows in a field this time and no dead antiques on a beige carpet either. I was being granted a private audience in the morning room at Oxmoon, a little-used corner of the house which still bore witness to my grandparents' forty-year love affair with junk shops. In my grandfather's day every square inch of the mantelshelf had been crammed with bric-à-brac, but Aunt Ginevra had managed to reduce this to an Edwardian coronation mug flanked by a pair of handsome brass candlesticks.

Keeping my eyes steadily fixed on the coronation mug I said steadily, "Kester's ten months younger than I am. If he can get married, why can't I?" My heart was slamming around like a demented hammer. Icy sweat welded my shirt to my spine.

"Kester can afford a wife!" shouted my father. "He's master of Oxmoon!"

"Yes!" I shouted back. "He's master of Oxmoon! He's master because you were too bloody busy doing the done thing to think what that would mean to me!" I had never consciously formed that thought in my mind before, and once the words were spoken I was horrified. I stammered, "I—I didn't mean that—I—" but the next moment my attempt at an apology was brutally terminated as he struck me hard across the mouth.

I reeled backwards, tripped against the sofa and on my way to the floor bashed into a little sewing table which at once disintegrated. My mind was paralyzed with shock. My father had very occasionally given me a reluctant whack on the bottom when I'd been at my naughtiest as a small child, but he had never struck me like that before.

"Get up."

I crawled to my feet. But I couldn't raise my eyes to his face. I couldn't even look at the coronation mug. I looked at the brass fender around the fireplace but saw only six cows standing in a field.

"Now just you listen to me. There were reasons, good reasons, why my father felt obliged to leave Oxmoon to Kester and reasons, good reasons, why I chose not to interfere. My father did what he felt he had to do. Robert did what he felt he had to do. And I did what I felt I had to do. So what you've got to understand and accept is that this situation *could not have been otherwise*. It's ridiculous to suggest I acted out of some heroic and self-sacrificing desire to do the done thing.

I'm no hero. I acted under compulsion. I acted because I felt it would destroy me if I acted in any other way. Now stop behaving like some overgrown spoiled child and never let me hear you refer to the subject again."

"I'm sorry, I'm sorry, I'm sorry—"

"I know you've always been jealous of Kester. But it's about time you grew up, Harry. You seem to think you can get away with anything just because you've always been my favorite, but my patience is now wearing very thin and I suggest you start to do some very hard thinking. You're not the only pebble on the beach, you know. I do have three sons in Canada."

I wondered where my next breath was coming from. All the air seemed to have been permanently removed from my lungs. Three sons in Canada, he had said. I got my lungs working again, God knows how, but I found I could breathe only in shallow gasps. Three sons in Canada. I licked my lips. There was blood on them from his blow on the mouth. I tried to speak but nothing happened.

"You come here to me," said my father, still in a towering rage, "when you know perfectly well I'm shocked and grieved by Ginevra's death, and you have the supreme insolence to demand I should finance a marriage which no father in his right mind could possibly approve of—"

"I'm sorry, sir, of course I can see now that I've approached this in quite the wrong way." What an understatement. Why on earth had I made that catastrophic remark about Oxmoon? I'd behaved like a lunatic. "Sir, if you'd just let me explain how I feel about Bella—"

"Explain! I'm not interested in the puerile explanations dreamed up by an immature adolescent in order to excuse a ludicrous fantasy! You want to marry her out of guilt! What could be more obvious?"

"No, there's more to it than that, sir—I really do love her, I swear it—"

"*Love!* What do you know about love? You stand there, nineteen years old, and think that just because you seized the opportunity to misbehave at Oxford you know bloody well all there is to know—"

"Well, at least I'm not a virgin as Kester obviously was when he got married!" There I went again. Certifiable. Oh God, how on earth was I going to get out of this scene in one piece—

"You should try and take a leaf out of Kester's book instead of mocking him the whole damn time!" said my father furiously. "He's known Anna for three years. I still disapprove of him marrying when he's so young, but at least I think he's got a better chance of happiness than most people who are deluded enough to marry in their teens. But you! You see that girl today for the first time in five years and on the strength of one meeting you have the colossal nerve to start talking of marriage—"

"Well, it was quite a meeting!" I was now too demented to care what I said.

"Oh, no doubt!" shouted my father. "She's got no brains, no manners, no charm, no intellectual interests, nothing which could make her worthy to be the wife of a young man of your potential, but one thing she does have and that's the one thing you'll be tired of in six months! My dear Harry, if you think that guilt and sex are any foundation whatsoever for a successful marriage, you're being even more foolish than I thought!"

"Well, what about your marriage?" I yelled at him. "Are you trying to tell me that's not based on sex and guilt? You've no right to preach to me!" And sinking down on the sofa before he could hit me again I covered my face with my hands.

There was a long silence but when I dared look at him I saw his anger had been spent. He was leaning against the mantelshelf as if he hardly knew how to remain upright, and at once I struggled to my feet; I could endure his rage but not his despair.

"Father, it's not as you think, I really do love her, if it was just sex and guilt I wouldn't want to marry her but I do want to marry her, I must, we want to have another baby and so of course we must get married, I mean, it's just no good, is it, having babies without being married—"

He held up his hand and I was silent. Very slowly he sat down. He moved as if all his joints ached. He was gray with exhaustion. All he said in the end was "How glad I am that I don't believe in a life after death. I couldn't bear to believe Blanche knew what a mess I've made of bringing up her children."

"I—"

"Shut up. There's no comment you can make to that statement. Let me think for a moment." He went on sitting in the chair, his elbows on his knees, his eyes watching his clasped hands, but at length he straightened his back and stood up. "If I refuse my consent now," he said, "I'll only have to give way later. You'll get her pregnant again—deliberately this time—because you know I'd never let a grandchild be born illegitimate. Then we'd have all the scandal of a child arriving seven months after the wedding, and I couldn't take that again, not after what I went through with Marian." He paused to consider further. He was calm now, detached. It was as if he were viewing the situation from a great distance.

"Very well," he said finally. "I will consent. But you must compromise with me. I can't have you marrying immediately by special license. I must insist for your own sake that you wait until Christmas, and I also insist that you don't announce your engagement for another two months. That means that if you do change your mind you'll find it easier to get out of this mess—and I'm sorry, but I'm afraid I do think it's a mess. However perhaps you'll do better the next time. Naturally this marriage is bound to end in divorce. I give it five years at the most, no more. In fact," said my father, suddenly becoming angry again, "I can't stress too strongly that I think this decision of yours is absolutely wrong from start to finish."

But I knew that on the contrary, it was the right thing—indeed the only thing— to do.

3

I

TEN MONTHS after this major row with my father I was walking back in the dark from Oxmoon to Penhale and thinking what a relief it was that poor old Kester, poor old sod, had messed up his relationship with my father as thoroughly as I had messed up mine. Those bills! Incredible. But at least he still had his fairy-tale palace of a house. And what did I have? Damn all.

I'd have liked to turn Penhale Manor into the perfect house but I had no money. When I took over the estate my father had worked out how much capital expenditure the farm would require during the next twelve months and had added an extra thousand pounds to launch me on my married life. Every single penny of this sum was to be deducted from the twenty thousand pounds of my mother's money that I was due to inherit at twenty-one. My mother had left no will, and all her disposable fortune had wound up in my father's hands during her lifetime, but under the terms of her marriage settlement a portion had been kept in trust for her children.

My father refused to advance me the whole amount of my portion. "It won't do you any harm," he said, exercising his Victorian streak, "to struggle for a few months." This was bad news. I was quite prepared to slave at the estate, but the fact was that I was not only a novice at farming, which requires a high degree of experience and flair, but a novice at running my own life. One moment I was little more than a schoolboy living on my father's charity and the next I had an estate to run, a wife to keep, a new baby on the way and all manner of expenses which I hadn't anticipated. I knew moments of panic when I felt my life had slipped out of control, but all I could do was beat them back and struggle on.

Somehow I stomached the necessary instruction from Thomas and somehow I maintained a humble respectful attitude towards him so that I could always go to him for help whenever I was desperate. I was desperate very often, particularly in the early days of my new career. I didn't get on with the foreman at the Home Farm who clearly thought I was just a spoiled rich brat taking up farming for fun. He respected Thomas, who had put the fear of God into him from the start, but I knew I was too young and too inexperienced ever to win his approval. He'd have to go, I realized that, but how would I manage when he left? Besides, Thomas would probably write me off as a headstrong fool if I immediately sacked my foreman, and I had to keep on the good side of Thomas because my survival depended on it.

God, what a nightmare it was. People talk a lot of romantic bilge about what a wonderful life farming is and how living on the land is the only truly satisfying existence for human beings, but farming's bloody hard work and not one bit glamorous. It was all right for someone like my father, who simply rode around on horseback and made executive decisions—which I now realized probably weren't all that brilliant—but I wasn't yet on that level. I had a living to earn. I had to be much more deeply involved in order to work out what I could and couldn't do. I couldn't afford to make mistakes and pay for them. Also, although my father was a successful businessman, farming tends to defy a conventional business approach because one's dealing not with other businessmen but with God, thinly disguised as the weather. God tends to play havoc with the accounts, as my father had often complained, but to my mind my father wasn't a farmer like Thomas or my grandfather. You can't seriously call yourself a farmer until you've proved to your men that you too can shovel manure and do the bloody hoeing and get up at four in the morning to milk a cow.

Anyway there I was, sweating along, having nightmares about winding up hopelessly in the red and having to crawl to my father to confess my abject failure, trying to learn all I could, struggling to keep on the right side of Thomas—and that was all *before* I was married. After I was married everything was just the same but worse because I was even more worried about money. I did wonder if I could borrow against my expectations but found that even though I was married the terms of the settlement made borrowing difficult before I was twenty-one. Then I inquired about borrowing against Bella's expectations, but this was even more difficult. I began to feel hemmed in, oppressed. Picturesque Penhale Manor was easy on the eye but old houses are expensive to run. Bella was easy on the eye too, but wives aren't cheap and pregnant wives aren't cheap at all. God only knew how much the baby would cost. I did a few estimates involving prams, cots and clothes but gave up in horror. The thought of public-school fees in the remote future was quite beyond contemplation.

To make matters worse it soon became clear that Bella had no idea how to run a house, and what was worse still it soon became clear that she was never going to be able to learn. This needn't necessarily have been a disaster; Bronwen had never managed the house either but my rich father had been able to afford a first-class housekeeper. The most I could afford was a cook, a parlormaid and a daily woman from the village, none of whom seemed to do more than drink endless cups of tea. I tried firing them but the replacements went to pieces in the same way. It was because Bella didn't care about anything except the new baby that was on the way. She never seemed to notice the chaos and the dirt and the rotten cooking. I didn't mind a bit of muddle in my home; a bit of muddle's natural, indicative of a flourishing family life, but I found this chronic disorganization was very depressing.

However fortunately the human brain can cope with only so many worries at a time, and I quickly decided I couldn't afford to get in a state about the house. My prime concern was my father. I had to impress him. I had to prove I had done the right thing by choosing a career in agriculture. I had to make a success of that farm.

II

I've no intention of describing the secret struggles for power that ensued between me and my foreman, the endless debates about the pros and cons of arable farming in stock-breeding country, my growing determination to grow oats in Standing-Stone Field, my rows with Jasper Llewellyn over his bloody sheep, the recalcitrant engine of my tractor, my decision to do more dairying now that there was a good supply of piped water, the horror of cows with split udders, the nightmare of bovine infertility, the cowman who went off the rails, the dairymaid who went on strike when the cows developed lice, the cat that ate the chickens and all the other incidents which formed the backbone of my rollicking bucolic life. Suffice it to say that I had a farm of some two hundred and eighty acres which I thought would drive me crazy.

At first I decided it should be primarily arable; the rest of the country might have gone back to grass but the mild climate of Gower encouraged me to sustain an interest in crops. However I was lured into flirting with dairying (a) because it can be very profitable if everything goes right and (b) because I had some juicy water meadows which might have been designed by God as a paradise for lactating herbivores. But dairying is soul-destroying work. Those bloody cows need attention all the time and if you haven't got a saint for a cowman you may as well cut your throat. I didn't have a saint. I had a drunk who split udders during a hangover. God, what a nightmare. The vet's bills nearly prostrated me. Thomas got me a new cowman but even so I did much of the work myself. I got to the point where I never wanted to see an udder again but luckily the men respected me for proving I could work as hard as anyone I employed and even my foreman was becoming mellow, so I went on slogging away and resisting the temptation to exterminate everything in sight—men, beasts, the lot. Farming romantic? Don't make me laugh.

All the same, in its own peculiar way it was rewarding. When I saw my crops waving in the breeze just before the harvest, I did experience that unique sense of accomplishment which can come only when a job's been done well, and I realized that although I was being trained in a hard school it was going to be worth it because I was going to end up as successful as my grandfather, a farmer who'd worked his way up the ladder until he could combine astute estate management with living a relaxed gentleman's life. Of course I'd never live at Oxmoon so I couldn't follow exactly in his footsteps, but all the same...

I saw myself living a pleasant life at Penhale Manor after my father had died (which God forbid) and left me most of his money. I'd have the farms in Herefordshire to run and the Penhale Home Farm mastered and perhaps I could even buy some more land somewhere to add to my empire...Idly I tried to calculate Oxmoon's current market value, but gave up. There was no point, I told myself severely, in indulging in futile fantasies, so instead I trudged off through the farmyard sludge to supervise the mixing of the cattle feed. Kester was probably at that moment drinking champagne at Oxmoon in his Savile Row suit while he listened languidly to that sick-making *Second Piano Concerto* by Rachmaninoff.

Poor old Kester, poor old sod...

Ugh! How I hated him.

III

The one redeeming feature of this stark postwedding landscape was that Bella and I were very happy together whenever I wasn't being driven mad by the estate or the servants or the chaotic state of the house. I certainly didn't regret my marriage. What I most regretted was the estrangement from my father but as the months passed and he saw how hard I was trying to master my new life, he became kinder and I thought he would bury the hatchet once his new grandchild arrived. He treated Bella gently always, as if she were a mental defective who needed compassion. She wasn't mentally defective, of course. She just wasn't bright enough to care about learning anything but most people aren't, are they? Highly educated people like my father think anyone who never opens a book is an imbecile, but the majority of the human race have no interest in reading, and no one could argue that this huge segment of humanity is entirely lacking in brains.

It was true that all Bella liked to do was eat, drink, make love, chat and thumb her way through trashy fashion magazines, but I found I rather liked this magnificent mindlessness. It made me feel protective towards her. She was always nice-natured too, and this I found constantly endearing; the other women who had briefly appeared in my life hadn't been nice-natured at all. Also I knew she loved me; she was much too ingenuous to be deceitful, and this made me feel blessedly secure. In fact her strong childlike devotion meant even more to me than her talent for sex, although a talent for sex isn't to be sniffed at. Far from it. I like sex. In fact apart from playing the piano I can't think of anything I enjoy more.

My father was relieved to see that Bella and I were happy, and this too mellowed his attitude towards us so that by the time Kester went round the bend in the July of 1939 I regarded my father and myself as wholly reconciled. Because of this improvement in our relationship it came as a particularly rude shock to me when he resurrected the specter of the Herefordshire farms that night at Oxmoon and tried to boot me out of Gower. I knew that he had always regarded my occupancy of the Manor as a temporary measure, but I did think I had at least five years, the length of my lease, before he attempted to push me into exile. No wonder I was horrified when he suggested I should leave Penhale so soon! And as for all that rubbish about how I was lurking at the Manor in order to pounce on Oxmoon...

My father was really very odd sometimes. Most peculiar. Of course I occasionally thought how nice it would be if Kester dropped dead and the Oxmoon title deeds floated within reach of my father's checkbook; but we all have our little pipe dreams, and no one but a certifiable lunatic goes around believing every little pipe dream has a hope of coming true. By this time I had absolutely accepted that Oxmoon would never be mine. I was a hardheaded realistic man of action— the diametric opposite of poor feeble dream-ridden old Kester.

Or was I?

I thought of the eerie moment that morning at Oxmoon when I had crossed the threshold and seen his glittering dream for the first time.

I had heard of the renovations but no one had described them coherently to me because the only news I had received from Oxmoon for some time had been in the form of village gossip. So I had had no true idea what the place would look like. Perhaps I had visualized another version of Eaton Walk, groups of dead antiques littered on beige wall-to-wall carpets, but how wrong I was. When I saw the transfigured hall I heard in my head not the "Dead March" from *Saul*, as I so often did at Eaton Walk, but one of the most rampantly emotional and exuberant pieces a British ear can ever hear: Elgar's march "Pomp and Circumstance Number One." It nearly deafened me. I came in at the point where the orchestra, having darted around like a horde of lost bumblebees, finally gathers itself together and goes crashing up the scale towards that overpoweringly banal melody line "Land of Hope and Glory." Fortunately, I pulled myself together just in time to terminate the performance, but that bloody crescendo had obviously opened the emotional floodgates because the next moment I was floating into the chorus of the Hebrew slaves from Verdi's *Nabucco*. How could I have been so florid? But what a powerful nostalgic beautiful tune Verdi wrote, and what a powerful nostalgic beautiful sight lay now before my eyes.

I just stood there, listening to the chorus of the Hebrew slaves, and for a moment I knew reality, the only kind of reality that truly mattered, and that reality was all the music I had never learned and all the beauty which had been denied me and all the days of that other life which I had never been allowed to lead.

Then I turned to face Kester, my cousin Kester, and I saw not my opposite but my double—my mirror image, my other self. It was an extraordinary moment. What I shall never forget is the horror but the horror defied analysis. It had no name. I felt I had seen something quite outside the range of normal human experience—but of course this was just a neurotic illusion, for I hadn't seen my double at all; I'd just seen Kester through the distorted glass of my jealousy.

I had conformed to my father's standards and now I felt mutilated. Kester had defied them and known liberation. He, the fantasist, had lived in the truth. I, the realist, had been living a lie. I wanted his fantasy, I wanted his life, I wanted my true self, and the symbol of all my longings was Oxmoon, shining radiant Oxmoon, my dream as well as Kester's, my fairy tale which could never come true.

Well, I thought hours afterwards as I walked back through the night to Penhale, so much for that. It was time to get the world—the real world—back into focus.

664

In the real world I was slowly but surely making a success of my life while Kester was now a failure on a colossal scale. Poor old Kester, I did feel genuinely sorry for him this time, I really did.

At the gates of the Manor I paused to stare at the long, low line of the house. Its tall Elizabethan chimneys were black against the night sky. Very nice. I loved my home. I was content. No more hankering after the world of might-have-been.

I went into the house. The drawing room, which needed a coat of paint, a good clean and new loose covers on the chairs, suddenly seemed unspeakably drab so to divert myself I instinctively headed for my mother's piano and began to play the chorus of the Hebrew slaves from *Nabucco*.

Pitter-patter, pitter-patter, Bella scampered in looking like a Mabel Lucie Attwell drawing, all pink-and-white complexion, shining hair and wholesome chubbiness.

"Harry, why don't you come straight up to bed? What are you doing playing the stupid old piano at this hour of the night?"

I reluctantly allowed myself to be led upstairs.

"Was it an awful bore at Oxmoon?" said Bella.

"Awful, yes."

"What happened?"

"Oh, nothing much."

"What's he done to the house?"

"Tarted it up a bit." I began to hear the Hebrew slaves again but she wiped them out by chattering about her latest visit to Dr. Warburton.

"...and so I said I wanted a girl to replace Melody. Oh, it's so nice that Dr. Warburton *knows* and I can talk to him about her!"

"Hm."

"You want a girl too, don't you, Harry?"

"I keep telling you, Bella—I don't mind what it is so long as it's healthy and you're all right." God, as if I hadn't enough problems without worrying about the baby's sex! I gave up trying to hear the music and mechanically shed my clothes.

"Oh Harry, how are we going to manage without sex for weeks and weeks before and after the birth?"

"How are we going to manage when the war comes and I go off to fight?" I snapped, suddenly fed up with her constant preoccupation with sex.

"Oh, there won't really be a war, will there? I thought Mr. Chamberlain and Hitler got on so well at Munich."

Hopeless. Of course she never read a paper. We got into bed and started to fuck. After a while I was able to tell myself her ignorance was really rather sweet. She reached a climax. Thank God. I finished and presently she fell asleep. Thank God again. Lying on my back in the dark I listened once more to Verdi and tried hard not to think of the approaching war.

The last thing I wanted was to go away and fight. What I really wanted to do was stay at home and be a pacifist like bloody Kester.

But of course that wouldn't have been the done thing at all.

IV

Inevitably I messed myself up in the war by doing the done thing and becoming a hero, but for once this was entirely my fault and my father was in no way to blame. During one of his regular visits to Oxmoon to supervise the mopping-up operations, my father made his views crystal-clear to me.

"You must follow your conscience, Harry, and do not what you think *I* believe to be right but what *you* believe to be right. I got myself in an awful muddle over the last war when I didn't fight although now when I look back I'm strongly inclined to think Robert was right when he urged me to stay at the Foreign Office. A war is fought on many fronts. Ideally one should contribute in the way in which one is best suited, so if you honestly feel you'd serve your country better by trying to stay out of uniform, for God's sake don't think I'd disapprove."

That was very fair and very kind. It made me feel close to him again, but the trouble was that this speech did nothing to sort out my confusion. In fact my confusion was so extreme that I would almost have been glad if he had said "Fight for your country or never darken my door again." Then at least I would have had no choice and my agonizing debates with myself would have been terminated.

This conversation took place in the October of 1939. Some months before I had joined a territorial unit to convince myself I had every intention of fighting the war as a soldier, but I was still waiting to be siphoned into the war machine and meanwhile I could do nothing but wrestle with my ambivalence. It would have been much easier if I could have told myself I honestly subscribed to pacifism but I couldn't. I believed we'd been right to declare war. I wanted to serve my country by fighting for it. But I hated the thought of leaving my home, *hated* it. I was being dispossessed again, this time by Hitler. I could have disemboweled him.

Again and again I toyed with the idea of applying for an exemption from the services so that I could devote myself to reorganizing my land to produce the maximum amount of food, and if I'd been Thomas, who was thirty-two, I might have got away with it. But I was twenty and prime material for cannon fodder. I didn't think I'd get away with it, and whether I did or not everyone was certain to look at me askance and I couldn't stand the thought of collecting enough white feathers to stuff a pillow. Pacifists like Kester were in a different boat. They had the excuse of their moral principles. I had no excuse except a juvenile and selfish desire to stay at home. No, I had to fight, no choice, but Christ, what a nightmare it was. Meanwhile Thomas, whom everyone expected to join the Home Guard and stay on the land, was lusting to enlist in the army and go overseas. Typical. What an irony.

I was diverted from this tortuous and morbid state of mind by the arrival of my son at the end of October. By a miracle everything was ready in time for him—nursery, nappies, nanny, the lot. My father, who was becoming almost softhearted, had given me the money to employ a nanny instead of a mere nursemaid because he said he didn't think Bella realized how tiring newborn babies could be.

There spoke the voice of experience. My father had begotten seven children—eight if one counted my brother John who had died at birth in 1917—and the memory of Bronwen sweating away in the nurseries at Penhale was no doubt permanently engraved on his mind. If he said newborn babies could be tiring even for an enthusiastic mother like Bella, I had no doubt he was right.

This one was tiring. It was pink, bald and aggressive with powerful lungs. Bella soon got over her disappointment that the baby wasn't a girl and within hours was telling me joyfully that it was really much better that we started off with a son and heir. I agreed. I had found this hankering to replace Melody both morbid and embarrassing, so I was delighted to have a baby who couldn't merely be written off as a replacement. In fact I was so delighted with this tangible evidence of my successful relationship with my wife that I spent much time drinking champagne and distributing largesse among the servants.

Bella said he had to be called Henry after me, and fancying the idea of a namesake I agreed. But I loathe the name Henry. I'm not keen on Harry either, but at least it's livelier. "Henry Godwin" sounds like an antiquarian bachelor who keeps cats. At least "Harry Godwin" sounds like a man capable of satisfying the sexiest girl in Gower.

"But we can't call him Harry!" said Bella. "It would be much too confusing. I know, let's call him Hal! He's so tough that he deserves a tough name to match."

What extraordinary ideas women have. I looked down at this human scrap less than two feet long and wondered if I had ever seen anything so weak and helpless in all my life. However I liked the idea of little Hal. I liked the idea that I would leave a replica behind me in case I—but no, I really couldn't start thinking about getting killed. That would be the last word in neurotic cowardice.

Two weeks later I was summoned to my training camp in North Wales. I embraced Bella, took Hal's little hand for a moment between my thumb and forefinger and then set out along the road to bloody heroism.

What an escape from a full range of problems I had no idea how to solve!

What a life . . . and what a mess.

V

The massive upheaval caused by the war resulted in a realignment of the Godwin family. It was as if someone had shaken a giant kaleidoscope to form a new pattern, and the first innovation came when Uncle Edmund, egged on by my father, left London accompanied by Aunt Teddy with the intention of spending the war in the Gower Peninsula. Naturally they would have preferred to withdraw to their estate in Kent, but this was soon requisitioned by the government because of its useful proximity to London, and once my father realized Teddy was determined to leave the capital before the bombing started, he suggested they lived at Oxmoon. Kester liked them; my father thought Edmund could dole out paternal sympathy while acting as a buffer state between his nephew and Thomas who at that time was unsure if he could batter his way into the army.

Everyone thought this plan was an excellent idea but then it occurred to my father that my need was greater than Kester's. I was soon due to leave; Thomas had agreed to look after the estate for me, but his future in Gower was uncertain; Bella couldn't cope with anything except pregnancy and her trashy fashion magazines. All this meant that Penhale Manor was ripe for an invasion by a man like Edmund, who had once supervised the estate for my father, and a woman like Teddy, who could supervise anything within reach.

They arrived on my doorstep. I was relieved but also uneasy; Edmund was not a man I knew well. Since he was married to Constance's sister I had seen almost nothing of him while my father had been living with Bronwen, and even later I had seldom had the chance of conversing with him on his own. He seemed to be one of those sunny-natured fools so prevalent among the English upper classes, but I was aware that my father thought Edmund could keep a conscientious eye on my estate so I was prepared to believe he had more brain than was apparent.

I was even more cautious about Teddy. I could remember her being very cold to my father when he had lived apart from Constance, and I was inclined to take her artificial manner at face value. Both she and Constance were much younger than my father and Edmund, who were in their mid-forties. Teddy was thirty-four, smart, loquacious and foreign. Unlike Constance, who had acquired a painstaking English accent over the years, Teddy had carefully preserved her Americanisms and even exaggerated them so that she often sounded more American than the Americans. I think she believed the English found this "cute." Or maybe she just found it easier to live in England as a foreigner; the English tend to be benign towards English-speaking foreigners and more willing to excuse any un-English behavior.

Edmund and Teddy had two boys but they were now both at Harrow and away for most of the year. Richard was fifteen, Geoffrey two years younger. They were both good at games and thought Harrow was wonderful. I suspected that Geoffrey was shrewd although he never said much. No opportunity. Whenever Teddy wasn't chatting away that great oaf Richard, who had the brains of a flea, was talking rubbish and roaring with laughter. He was so ingenuous that it was impossible to dislike him but I did find him very tiring.

However Richard was hardly my problem at that time, and meanwhile his parents were busy being my salvation. Teddy took one look at the house, one look at Bella, one look at the newly arrived baby and said, "Okay, honey, leave this to me." I left it, but not before Teddy had added: "Harry darling, I keep getting these checks that I don't know what to do with now that I'm not in London—why don't Bella and I have a wonderful time while you're away and spruce up this heavenly old home of yours?"

"Well, that's most kind of you, Teddy, but—"

"Now, don't go all British on me!" said Teddy masterfully. "Edmund and I are about to take over your home so the least we can do is spend money on it. Why not? Hell, we may all be dead soon anyway so why not spend a little money before we go?"

I began to realize that this was a woman with a strong warm generous personality.

It also occurred to me that if she wanted to offer strength, warmth and generosity on a gargantuan scale, I'd be a fool to refuse.

"I'm such a villain, Teddy, that I'm not going to argue with you—thank you very much."

Teddy beamed up at me. "Why, it takes a real man to accept a gift gracefully like that—honey, I just couldn't admire you more!"

Dimly I began to understand why Edmund, kept for years by this rich strong-willed wife, had remained so thoroughly happy and normal.

"Teddy's wonderful!" sighed Bella, just before my departure. "She's the nicest woman I've ever met!"

This represented another victory for Teddy. Bella hated new acquaintances. I knew her well enough now to realize that this was because she thought people believed her to be ugly and stupid, but I had never succeeded in convincing her she should have a better opinion of herself. It was Teddy who finally managed to boost her self-esteem.

"Teddy says what a marvelous figure I have," Bella said when I came home on leave. "Teddy says I could stop the entire German army dead in its tracks."

"Let's hope you'll never have to," I said, but she hardly heard me. She was bursting to tell me more about her heroine.

"Teddy asked me about my mother, and when I said all I really knew about her was that she was a platinum blonde Teddy said, 'A platinum blonde? Whew! What a gal she must have been!' and it was so wonderful when she said that because everyone's always behaved as if having platinum-blond hair was the last word in awfulness. And do you know what Teddy said next? She said that maybe my mother was acting in my best interests when she left me behind at Stourham Hall. She said perhaps it was a great big noble unselfish gesture to ensure that I was brought up in a wealthy comfortable home, and suddenly everything seemed quite different to me, I was able to think perhaps my mother had loved me after all. . . . Teddy said that if *she'd* had a daughter she'd have done anything to ensure her happiness—it's sad, isn't it that Teddy doesn't have a daughter, but she couldn't have more children after Geoffrey was born. I feel so sorry for her."

But I didn't feel sorry for Teddy. I clearly saw she'd found that daughter she wanted after all.

"Bella, for God's sake don't tell her about Melody."

"Oh, of course not! How could I tell her that I was so wicked when I was only thirteen? She might turn against me and not like me anymore. . . . Oh, Harry, Teddy says I'm a wonderful mother because I like to spend so much time with Hal. . . . Can we have another baby straightaway?"

"Why not?" I was so pleased to see her enjoying life, and besides I had decided it would be sensible to keep her occupied when I was away for weeks on end. I knew she loved me but when a man has a sexy wife it pays him to be thoroughly realistic.

We conceived Charles who was born in the November of 1940.

"Teddy says I'm a success!" said Bella starry-eyed when she told me Charles was on the way. "She says I'm glamorous and I've got this sexy husband and a beautiful baby and another baby due before the end of the year—and all before I'm twenty-one! She says many women spend their whole lives never getting that far!"

I did occasionally wonder where all this was going to end but came to the conclusion that I could see nothing but good in the situation. My house, refurbished with exquisite taste, was neat as a pin and ran like clockwork. Bella, more luscious than ever, looked like a Hollywood actress on the brink of stardom while in the nursery a little boy with blond hair and a pink-and-white skin and black eyes smiled at me and uttered a couple of syllables which Bella assured me were "Daddy." I decided fatherhood was definitely a desirable occupation. After years of private failures I savored my public success in reproducing myself to perfection.

Meanwhile up at Oxmoon poor old Kester, poor old sod, hadn't managed to father anything. Very sad. I went out of my way to be especially kind to him at the christenings.

"Oh, do let's have another baby, Harry!" said Bella when Charles was a few months old. "After two boys we're bound to have a girl next time!"

We conceived Jack who was born in the December of 1941.

Three sons in rapid succession. Not bad. In fact I could almost hear Kester gnashing his teeth, although he always wrote the most charming letters congratulating me. However there was no doubt Kester was having a frustrating time. He had wanted to drive an ambulance for the Red Cross—typical Kester, pining to dramatize his pacifism by picking one of the most heroic jobs available—but he had been told to stay at home. At first there was talk of Oxmoon being requisitioned but just as Kester and Anna were preparing to withdraw to Little Oxmoon, which had fallen vacant after Aunt Celia's recent death, the government changed its mind and decided that it would be more rational to keep Kester in his own home with his nose to the grindstone; he was told that it was his patriotic duty as a certified pacifist to buckle down to the job of running his estate himself with the aid of government advisers who drew up plans for food production. Edmund also found himself in the hands of these agricultural experts with the result that he and Kester, pooling their resources, gave each other both practical and moral support. That took care of the Godwin estates in Gower. As for Thomas, he finally blitzed himself into the army and was exported to Northern Ireland to be trained. Eleanor ran the Stourham Hall pig farm single-handed in his absence.

"It's ironic how things turn out," said my father later when he expressed his restored confidence in his nephew by authorizing the winding up of the trust that had been supervising Oxmoon's affairs since the debacle of 1939, "but I think war may well be the making of Kester. He needed a powerful incentive like this to set his writing aside and apply himself to the estate. I wouldn't be surprised if he did very well—and I must say I do admire him for having the courage to stand up for those pacifist principles of his."

So Kester was going to wind up a hero after all. Meanwhile I'd spent many months sitting on my bottom in various military dumps waiting for an invasion which never came. It was too much. My patience, like Hitler's, was exhausted, and shortly after that conversation with my father I made up my mind to volunteer for the commandos.

VI

My war was divided into two parts. The first part, which lasted until the September of 1942, was spent in excruciating boredom but complete safety. The second part was spent in circumstances where words like "boredom" and "safety" described unimaginable states of mind in a lost civilization. Of course I did realize, as I was yawning my way through the first half of the war, that I was very lucky. I avoided being killed in Norway, France, Italy or Greece. I was also able to see my wife to ensure that she was constantly pregnant. I spent most of my time stationed along the south coast of England, and although I was never near Gower I was always less than an hour from London and the main line to Swansea.

Meanwhile the family kaleidoscope kept shifting. After Aunt Celia died in 1940, her daughter Erika left her husband and disappeared. Long after the war we found she had been recruited as a British spy but had switched sides as soon as she had been parachuted into France. After all, Germany was her native land and she had always been partial to Hitler. Personally I thought her recruitment was a typical British balls-up, but at least it got Erika back to Germany, where she wound up making bullets in a munitions factory. Her husband Ricky Mowbray tried to evade the services but his pacifism was only a synonym for cowardice, and he was eventually drafted into the Pay Corps and lost at sea in the Mediterranean. Erika married a German after the war.

With both Aunt Celia and Erika wiped off the Gower map, Little Oxmoon became a billet for Canadian soldiers who did their best to wreck everything in sight. Bloody barbarians. Someone once tried to tell me that colonial soldiers were homesick and shouldn't be judged too harshly. Homesick! How feeble! We British don't believe in wrecking everything in sight just because we're homesick. Quite the reverse. We build a little Britain wherever we go and then we never have any problems. No wonder we conquered the earth. We deserved to.

I'm not usually a rabid patriot but rabid patriotism was a form of survival in those days while Churchill breathed fire over the wireless and Hitler breathed brimstone across the Channel so I soon wound up hating all foreigners except Teddy. As far as I was concerned Teddy was the heroine of Penhale and deserved to be canonized.

She had recently had a great success in establishing a friendship between Bella and Anna. I was most surprised for they had no interests in common, but they were the same age and I suppose they enjoyed gossiping about trivialities just as all women do. I was used to Bella saying she didn't like Anna, but I knew that was only because Anna was well read and intelligent and Bella as usual was afraid of being judged stupid. However one day I came back on leave and found Bella saying that Anna was "nice" and "sweet" and "rather fun after all."

"This friendship will be very good for both those girls," pronounced Teddy. "Now, Harry dear, while I'm straightening out this family, why don't I do something about you and Kester? There you are, both bright intelligent personable guys, and what happens? Whenever you meet you behave as if you're enduring the worst form of mental torture! Edmund honey, do you understand why your two nephews act like this?"

"Not in the least, darling. Both jolly nice chaps. Mystery."

Since I could refuse Teddy nothing I eventually found myself in the library at Oxmoon with Kester while we drank whisky and wondered what the hell to say to each other. Making a supreme effort we discussed politics and music but then, God help us, we made the mistake of turning to religion. Kester said he and Anna were attending Quaker meetings. I said that was nice. Seconds later Teddy, returning with the girls from a walk in the grounds, found us sunk deep in an exhausted silence.

"I just don't understand it!" she said aggrieved. "You two should be such friends!"

I looked at Kester, and as he looked at me we each saw the double image and the horror that had no name. Teddy continued her efforts to bring us together but it was useless; we both knew our relationship lay far beyond the range of Teddy's innocent American optimism.

"Good luck, Harry," said Kester much later when I left to go overseas, and as he spoke I pictured him safe at home in Gower, spending the war on the home front, once again leading the life I longed for but which seemed always to be beyond my reach.

"Thanks, old chap," I said. "I'll need all the luck I can get. God, I can't wait to go! Sitting around on my arse in absolute safety isn't my idea of fun at all!"

What a gibe. Talk about tempting fate. Oh, I deserved what was coming to me, no doubt about that, and no doubt Kester thought I deserved it too.

VII

Before I was dispatched overseas I went to Scotland for special training and there I learned how to survive in very adverse circumstances. I was even taught how to strangle a man as quickly and quietly as possible. That was when I knew the world had gone quite mad and that I was certifiable to have got myself involved in such lunacy. However because I didn't want my father to worry about me I wrote and said I was having a wonderful time.

The one advantage of my rigorous training was that I emerged in tip-top physical condition for my final seventy-two-hour leave in Gower, and I was determined to break all kinds of sexual records in order to stop myself thinking about the future. Certainly when I arrived at the station in Swansea and saw Bella waiting for me I started thinking about fucking instead of fighting and that had to rank as an improvement.

By that time Swansea was wrecked. Swansea was an awful old place, a seaside settlement ruined by the industrial revolution, but in its own tough, bizarrely romantic way it had a vitality which against all the odds rendered it alluring. Perhaps the key to its seductiveness lay in the fact that beyond the seaminess of the industrial port lay the intellectual capital of South Wales. Swansea was a Welsh powerhouse, not just a city of Mammon but a city of the mind. Some of my most cherished early memories consisted of being taken to concerts there by Kester's tutor and discovering the Welsh passion for music. I might have inherited my musical gifts from an Englishwoman but I was a Welshman, and for me Swansea *was* Wales with all its virtues and vices, beauty and blemishes, so that whenever I saw Swansea I felt that I'd come home.

But Swansea had been destroyed, raped by a full-scale blitz in 1941, and now so many landmarks existed only in my memory and there was no singing, only the sea gulls screaming over the ruins. It made me want to kill every German in sight; in fact it was when I saw ruined Swansea that I didn't regret having been insane enough to volunteer for special duties.

It was now the September of 1942. My car had been laid up on wooden blocks for some time but Kester and Edmund were allowed petrol for the estate and Teddy had black-market contacts, so I wasn't surprised to find that Bella had turned up to meet me in Edmund's Bentley. The weather was warm. She was looking fresh as a daisy in a linen dress with plenty of cleavage, but no daisy had ever looked half so sultry. To my great relief she told me she had brought the inflatable mattress, so all we had to do was get clear of the city.

"For God's sake drive like the wind," I said, "before I melt all the buttons on my uniform."

We found a useful cart track. Being in perfect physical condition I blew up the mattress and launched myself into action without even pausing for breath. I felt very much the all-conquering soldier for a change, and as I slammed away I idly pictured my remote ancestor Godwin of Hartland pursuing the same pastime during his career in the retinue of that Norman gangster Humphrey de Mohun. "Let's call the next one Humphrey," I said to Bella afterwards when our cigarettes were alight. "I rather like it."

"But the next one's going to be a girl," said Bella. "I'm going to get my little Melody back at last."

It was odd how she went on and on about that dead baby. I never gave it a second thought nowadays.

"How's everyone at Penhale?" I said to divert her.

"Fine. Your father brought Francesca down to Oxmoon last weekend and she's all set to be a land girl, but what she really wants to do is join the air force..."

Francesca, now nearly eighteen, had left school that summer and both her parents were anxious for her not to remain in London. I had often wondered if they too would leave but they seemed determined to stick it out. Constance was heavily involved with the Red Cross while my father, who had offered his services to the government at the start of the war, was leading some sort of cloak-and-dagger existence in high finance. On account of his linguistic and financial skills he had been assigned to help the Free French in London pay their bills—a somewhat sordid aspect of *La Gloire* and one that needed diplomatic talents of the highest order. Some indication of how important this liaison work was could be gleaned from the fact that he still ran his Rolls-Royce. A fawning government granted him an apparently endless supply of petrol.

". . . and Francesca would look so sexy in a WAAF's uniform," Bella was saying.

"Hm." Francesca was not my idea of a rampantly sexy girl but she was vivacious and pretty and I knew many men would find her attractive. It was one of the miracles of genetics that she had escaped Constance's dreariness and bore more than a passing resemblance to her aunt Teddy.

". . . and I did ask her to stay at the Manor," Bella was saying, "but of course I knew she'd prefer to be at Oxmoon. She confessed she simply adores Kester."

"What! Since when?"

"Since she was little, she said. But I'm not surprised, because Kester's got such a flair for children. In fact, Teddy was saying only the other day—"

"Darling, stop talking about bloody Kester and let's have another fuck."

We had another fuck.

"You're more gorgeous than ever!" sighed Bella later. "War suits you!"

"Of course it does. War brings out the best in men, as Machiavelli pointed out."

"Who?"

"Some old bugger who ought to have been certified."

We drove on to Penhale Manor. Edmund and Teddy were waiting to greet me and so was Hal who had been allowed to stay up late for the big occasion of the paternal visit. He was almost three. His blond hair had faded to Bella's mouse-brown. Black lashes fanned pink-and-white cheeks as he stared bashfully at his toes.

"Come on, silly-billy!" said Bella to him. "It's Daddy!"

"Don't be shy, honey!" Teddy cooed.

Hal looked as if he were about to expire with embarrassment.

"That's funny!" mused Edmund. "He's not usually shy. In fact the other day when Kester was here he was chattering away nineteen to the dozen."

"What's for dinner?" I said abruptly, patting Hal's head before I turned away. "I'm damned hungry."

We ate some rabbit stew, which was very passable when accompanied by a prewar claret filched by Edmund from Oxmoon, and sat around talking for a while but everyone went to bed early. I took a look at Hal, Charles and Jack, all asleep and all looking as if they'd never had a naughty thought in their lives, and told myself I was on no account going to brood on Kester simply because my sister adored him and Hal chatted to him without constraint. After all I had more important things to do during my leave.

Having passed a strenuous night I fell asleep at dawn, and would have slept till noon if our offspring hadn't decided to wreck our peace at seven. Hal had overcome his shyness. Charles obviously had no idea what the word meant. They howled into the room followed by Jack, who was crawling along like a miniature buffalo, and jumped all over the bed. Outside in the corridor Babs the Welsh nursemaid who needed looking after almost as much as the boys did was futilely begging her charges to return to her. The original nanny had long since given notice in despair and Bella had always refused to engage a qualified replacement who would have made her feel inferior.

Stark-naked and bleary-eyed I sat bolt upright in bed. "*Out!*" I shouted, making everyone jump. "I want my sleep!"

"God, how awful you are in the mornings!" said Bella, annoyed. "All right, come along, my angels—Daddy's cross."

Charles and Jack were both screaming but Hal was telling them to shut up. At least someone was on my side. Muttering "Good boy" I disappeared beneath the bedclothes but when the room was at last quiet I surfaced. Dark eyes just like mine watched gravely as I peered over the sheet. Hal and I faced each other across a mound of pillows.

"Are they always like that in the mornings?"

"Yes."

"Good God." I stared morosely at the ceiling as it occurred to me that fatherhood was not all drinking champagne, sending proud notices to *The Times* and patting an appropriate head occasionally. I glanced at Hal to cheer myself up and found he was still gazing solemnly at me. Nice little Hal. But why wasn't he talking to me nineteen to the dozen? I tried to start a conversation with him. But I couldn't think of anything to say.

In the end I got up and began to shave. Little footsteps pattered behind me. A small pajamaed figure scrambled onto the window seat for a grandstand view of the basin. I scraped away at my jaw but finally, unnerved by this enrapt attention, I paused to look at him and something about his solemn little face amused me. I smiled.

He beamed back in delight and then blushing in an agony of self-consciousness, he turned to peer out of the window.

Nice little boy. His silence in my presence suggested brains and tact. Or did it? No. More likely an inquiring mind overawed by novelty, but never mind that. The point was he wasn't wrecking my peace. Good intelligent child. I returned to my shaving feeling pleased.

"Soldier," said Hal suddenly.

"Hm?" Stepping to one side of the basin I glanced through the window and saw a uniformed figure pausing by the gates at the other end of the drive. Why should a soldier be snooping in the gateway of my home at seven in the morning? I decided he was a newcomer who had arrived in Swansea on some dawn train and was now hunting for his billet at Little Oxmoon. The uniform was Canadian.

"Damned foreigners," I said automatically, finishing my shave.

"Daddy, look—he's coming to see us!"

I returned to the window. The young soldier, carrying his kit bag, was wandering dreamily up the drive. He made no effort to hurry, and every few seconds he would pause to gaze at his surroundings.

"The fool thinks he's at Little Oxmoon," I said, exasperated, and with Hal scampering at my heels I ran downstairs to open the front door.

675

"You've got the wrong address!" I shouted at the soldier in what I hoped was a not entirely unfriendly voice. "If you're looking for the Canadian billet..."

I stopped. I'd seen his green eyes. He stopped too. He stood there, tall and slim in his Canadian uniform, and although we were silent, holding our breath, I heard time shifting its gears and driving the past into the present like a battering ram. The present splintered, fell apart. Evan said, "Harry, how wonderful to see you again!" and as he spoke I lived once more in my most cherished memories and heard my magic lady using those same words to welcome me home.

VIII

My little serf had found his way home. He had no connection with the Canadian billet at Little Oxmoon. He was based in Surrey. This was his first forty-eight-hour leave since his arrival in England, and after catching a night train from London he had snatched a couple of hours' sleep on a bench at the station, walked off into the Gower Peninsula and thumbed a lift to Penhale on a passing farm cart.

He knew nothing. I had never been sure whether to believe my father when he had told me he had no communication with his family in Canada, and his threat to me about his three sons there had made me suspect that some form of contact was being maintained but now I found out that the contact was only financial, money transferred through banks, just as my father had said. Evan had thought my father was still living at Penhale Manor. He had had no idea that my father had resumed his marriage, and I could see that the news was a bad shock to him. His sensitive serious face acquired a bleached look. He said, "In that case he won't want to see me, will he."

"Nonsense!" I said, feeling sorry for him; I had really been very fond indeed of my little serf. But as I spoke it occurred to me that my father might well be anxious to avoid a drama in which Evan turned up on Constance's doorstep and gave a star performance of the Prodigal Son.

"Sit down and relax, Evan," I said. We were in the drawing room and I had dispatched Hal to the kitchens to find Bella. Evan was now in a state of shock. He stared around with a glazed expression in his eyes while I tried to tell him I had married old Oswald Stourham's daughter, but at last he managed to say, "I'm sorry, it's that piano...I remember you sitting there and playing 'The Blue Danube' and teasing Dad because it was the only tune he ever recognized.... Oh God, I'm sorry, I'm in pieces, I can't get a hold of myself at all.... Who did you say's living here now?"

"My wife and I, my three sons, Uncle Edmund and Aunt Teddy. Richard and Geoffrey are away at Harrow."

Evan nearly passed out. "Teddy? That's the sister, isn't it? I must go at once." He leaped to his feet. "I'll go to Oxmoon. I know Aunt Ginevra wouldn't mind if I turned up."

I grabbed him. "Steady, Evan, she's dead."

"Dead!"

"Yes, Kester's living there now with his wife."

"Wife? Kester's married too? Gee, didn't you both marry young! Is she nice? I guess she must be if Kester married her. Oh, I can't wait to see Kester again! Kester was the great hero of my childhood—he used to call me his acolyte—"

"*What?* Here, wait a minute—*I* was the great hero of your childhood! You helped me with my experiments in the potting shed—you collected all those conkers for me every autumn—"

"Oh sure—but you were away at school most of the year and anyway you didn't really want me around, you just put up with me. But Kester spent hours and hours playing with me, even though I was so much younger than he was—"

The door opened. In walked Teddy, gorgeously clad in a scarlet kimono and attended by Bella, Hal, Charles and Jack. Edmund, a notoriously late riser, was no doubt still snoozing upstairs.

"Hi, fellas," said Teddy. "What's all this about a Prodigal Son?" Intelligent little Hal had obviously repeated my message verbatim: Tell Mummy my brother Evan's turned up from Canada.

What a scene! Evan's bleached look returned and he was too paralyzed with embarrassment to speak. Bella's eyes were as round as saucers. God knows what I looked like but I felt wary to say the least. Teddy had told my father after his return to Constance that she was willing enough to let bygones be bygones, but I thought a bygone was rather more than a bygone when it turned up in a Canadian uniform hoping to find its father.

"This is my brother Evan, Teddy," I said for lack of anything better to say. "Evan, this is Mrs. Edmund Godwin."

"Right," said Teddy, thriving on the opportunity to "fix" a problem that would have defeated anyone born without American dynamism. "Now, before we all have the vapors and start passing out right, left and center, let me call a spade a spade so that we can relax and say What the hell. Okay, young man, you know who I am, your father made me very angry once, but that's all over now, he went back to my sister and he's still with her and that's that. Finish. Now, you look like a nice clean-cut well-mannered boy to me, and you're Harry's brother which must definitely rank as a big plus, so maybe you and I could get along. Why not? I get along with most people, don't I, Bella honey?"

"You're wonderful, Teddy!"

"See? She says I'm wonderful. Okay, I'm going to be wonderful. We'll get Kester and Anna to come over with all the champagne they've still got and then we'll have the time of our lives killing the fatted calf. Harry, go call John and tell him to get the hell down here at once in that god-awful Rolls-Royce."

So that was that. Leaving Evan looking utterly shattered, I went to the telephone in the hall and placed the call to London.

IX

"Good God!" said my father, but he wasn't as surprised as I'd anticipated. He added: "I wondered if something like this would happen one day."

"Teddy's being wonderful," I said. "She's almost adopted him."

"Ah yes," said my father, and revealing the antipathy towards Teddy which he usually managed to conceal he added cynically: "Another Armstrong exercise in power."

"It was she who suggested you should come down at once!" I protested, automatically defending her against the slur of insincerity.

"Of course. Power's no fun unless you can maneuver people all over the board. All right, thank you, Harry. Put the boy on the line, would you? I assume he's there beside you."

"No," I said, but then I found that he was. Passing over the receiver I retired to the far end of the hall but somehow I couldn't quite persuade myself to step out of earshot. I was thinking of Evan being Kester's acolyte. An *acolyte!* What a nasty pansyish word, redolent of emotional melodrama. Typical Kester. And I didn't like the way he was encroaching on my family, purloining the odd member here and there whenever my back was turned. My little serf—an acolyte! I felt as outraged as a conservative historian who had seen his subject rewritten by a Marxist.

"Yes, she said I must be sure to look you up, but I was too nervous to make a phone call or write a letter—I thought it would be better if I just turned up.... Well, I guess I was scared you mightn't want to see me, but I thought that if I stopped by without warning at least I'd see you..."

Pathetic. Poor old Evan, poor old sod... Three sons in Canada. Maybe they were all Kester's acolytes. How would I know?

"...yes, she's very well, thank you.... Yes, we're all well.... Oh, that would be wonderful—I don't want to cause any awkwardness but of course I'd love to see you..."

Poor little devil, he was so pleased. In fact it was really rather touching, if one was prone to be touched by that sort of thing.

"Okay. 'Bye," said Evan, and hung up. He turned to me, his face transformed with happiness. "He's coming," he said as if he hardly dared believe it. "He's coming right away."

"That's absolutely marvelous, old chap," I said warmly. "I couldn't be more pleased!" But although I knew that the muscles of my face never betrayed me, I felt the knife of jealousy revolve below my heart.

X

The grand reunion began. The only blot on the sentimental landscape was Francesca, who flatly refused to meet Evan and said she would stay secluded at Oxmoon until he had left the neighborhood.

"Best let her be," said Teddy soothingly, but Kester was most upset and said he did hope Francesca would change her mind.

Kester had arrived directly after breakfast.

"Kester!"

"My acolyte!"

Damn it, they even embraced. I can't stand to see grown men embracing. Disgusting.

"Evan, you look so like Bronwen now you're grown up! It's the cheekbones!" said Kester, fawning over the boy as if he were a pet dog.

"Oh Kester, I've thought so much about those wonderful times you gave me at Oxmoon—I'll never forget how you used to call it Magic Oxmoon and talk about Beauty, Truth, Art and Peace..."

More embraces. The conversation continued in this sick-making vein for some time before Kester said, wallowing in emotion as usual, "Now, Evan, you've got to tell us all about Bronwen—I'm sure Harry's already asked you, but I can't help that, you'll just have to repeat yourself all over again."

But I hadn't asked. I'd wanted to but couldn't. It was easier to think of her as dead. It was the best way to bear the pain of her absence.

"Ah, I did love Bronwen... I cried when she left..."

That was Kester speaking. Not me. Kester. And as I again looked at him and saw my double image, I suddenly had a vision of our lives running side by side in time. That made my blood run cold, although why I didn't know. There's nothing sinister about parallel lines—unless they defy the laws of geometry and graze against each other. Maybe I was going mad. I certainly felt mentally disordered. It was as if the world I knew had slipped out of focus and was about to disintegrate before my eyes.

"I've got a photograph," said Evan, and produced a picture of a smart attractive housewife who looked as if she might advertise soap powder in magazines. I knew then how right I was not to want to know about Bronwen. My magic lady had died and a transatlantic robot had taken her place.

"What's happened to Rhiannon and Dafydd, Evan?" I said abruptly, trying to turn the conversation into more bearable channels.

"They both joined the navy. Rhiannon's at Malta, but Dafydd was taken prisoner by the Japanese at the fall of Singapore."

A cold shadow fell across the room as we thought of the Japanese. Kester said rapidly, "Tell us about Canada, Evan—every detail."

"Well, we've got this pretty five-bedroom home in a nice suburb of Vancouver, and..."

Evan's mild Canadian voice droned on and on as he described the house, the garden, the furniture, the car, the dog and the cat. I tried not to listen to him.

For a time I managed to tune in to the *Third Brandenburg Concerto* in my head but Evan kept interrupting the flow of notes.

"But Bronwen—tell us about Bronwen!" begged Kester.

"Well...she's pretty busy. As soon as we were all in school she took some courses in English literature and history and then she took a course in stenography but she didn't like that so she gave it up and did nothing for a while—at least, she did plenty, bringing us up, joining the Ladies' Guild, making loads of friends—"

I thought of my sad solitary magic lady imprisoned in Penhale Manor.

"—but in the end she got restless so she enrolled in college part time—well, she's still at it, she wants to be a librarian, we think it's great, we're so proud of her. We all help run the house so that she can have time to study, but she still does the cooking because she likes that. There's a lot of cooking to do too because we're always bringing our pals home but she never minds, she just says the more the merrier, so we're pretty sociable...hey, Kester, are you okay?"

"Sorry, yes. I was just thinking...Oh Harry, isn't it wonderful that everything worked out so well for them?"

I agreed it was wonderful but knew nothing had changed. Bronwen was still lost and would never come back.

Late in the afternoon my father arrived and when Edmund reported that the Rolls-Royce had been sighted in the drive I immediately hurried to open the front door. It would never do to let my father think I was sulking in a corner.

"Hullo!" I called cheerfully as he jumped out of the car. "Welcome to the grand reunion!"

Evan stepped past me. I went on looking at my father, and as I watched I saw the serious formidable Englishman dissolve into the man in blue dungarees who had joked in Welsh with Bronwen.

I thought: So the dead do come back sometimes. My father had died but now he was alive again, smiling joyously and stretching out his arms.

But not to me.

The Prodigal Son stumbled down the steps. "Dad—oh Dad—"

"Evan—"

I turned away.

XI

They spent some time on their own in my study, but eventually they joined the rest of the family for tea. Everyone chatted and laughed and talked at the top of their voices. The air was heavy with nostalgia. After gnawing a cucumber sandwich I declined a slice of the new sugarless butterless cake which represented Cook's latest wartime triumph and concentrated on making the occasional appropriate remarks.

"Harry," said Evan shyly at last, "will you play the piano for us? I had this dream of sitting here with Dad while you played 'The Blue Danube' for him, just like in the old days."

I dutifully played "The Blue Danube." It's tempting to dismiss that piece as hackneyed rubbish but in fact Johann Strauss the Younger was a most accomplished composer, and although I wouldn't go so far as to say that "The Blue Danube" is worthy of a concert hall I do think it deserves to be played in the finest ballroom in the world. Instantly I remembered the white-and-gold piano at Oxmoon. One day, if Kester ever invited me to his home for more than a strained whisky-and-soda, I was going to play that tune, complete with all the codas, in the ballroom—and this time I'd make sure bloody Thomas wasn't around to interrupt me by yelling for "The Black Bottom."

After I'd finished playing my father smiled at me and said, "You remind me of your mother."

That was a curious remark to make when we all had Bronwen on the brain, but before I could wonder what was going on in my father's mind Kester exclaimed, "Heavens, that tune reminds me of *my* mother! I say, isn't it time we opened some of that champagne I've lugged over from Oxmoon?"

I settled down to get discreetly drunk. Everyone kept saying it was a simply wonderful evening.

XII

Evan and I both had to leave for London the next day, so my father took us up to town in his Rolls-Royce. None of us talked much. We were all too aware of the war, all too conscious that we might never meet again. The partings at the Manor had been harrowing. Bella had tried to be brave but had dissolved into floods of tears, and Hal had cried too, probably to see her upset. He was too young to realize I could go away and never come back, but I told myself I knew I was going to see him again. I had to tell myself that. Had to. Only line to take. But God, what hell it all was.

We left Evan at Waterloo to catch his train to Surrey, and as my father got out of the car to shake hands with him I didn't hear what was said at the end. Afterwards we traveled to Belgravia in silence. I was due to spend the night at Eaton Walk before reporting for duty the next day.

"I didn't tell Constance about Evan," my father said at last as the car halted outside the house. "I just said Edmund needed my advice urgently, but don't worry, I'm not asking you to lie for me. I'm sure Francesca's been busy creating havoc in the name of honesty. I didn't realize she'd be quite so intractable."

"That's a charitable word for being bloody-minded!"

"Damaged children need charity," said my father.

The car halted. We got out. Without waiting for the butler to open the front door my father used his own key, and as he entered the hall Constance came sobbing down the stairs. She had obviously forgotten that I would be accompanying my father, and she was so distressed that she never saw me in the shadow of the porch. I hesitated embarrassed but my father just said to me with resignation, "Wait in the library, would you please, Harry?" so I withdrew thankfully to his sanctum nearby. As I helped myself to a whisky-and-soda I tried without success to imagine their dialogue. Would he be obliged to take her to bed to shut her up? What an ordeal after a two-hundred-mile drive and a parting from a Prodigal Son! I wondered how on earth he would get an erection.

Half an hour passed. Eventually he appeared looking haggard and I saw that the man in blue dungarees had died again to allow the unhappy Englishman to take his place. Pouring himself a double scotch he drank it neat. Then he poured himself a second double, added soda and sank down in the chair opposite mine.

"Sorry," he said. "I'll be better in a minute. Poor Constance, she's so insecure. I've just been trying to convince her I'm not on the brink of using my government influence to get a passage to Vancouver."

"Too bad Francesca can't see the results of her phone call." I was thinking that tough, obstinate little Francesca was far more like her mother than I had ever realized.

"No sense in being bitter," said my father. "Bitterness can drive a man—" But he could not say the word "mad." "—to drink," he said, looking down at the glass in his hand. Madness always frightened him but as he was normally an abstemious man, he could regard alcohol without fear. "The trouble is that Constance is incapable of a rational conversation on the subject of my past with Bronwen so it proved quite impossible to explain my true feelings about Evan's reappearance to her. But perhaps I can explain them to you. Perhaps you secretly feel exactly the same as I do. Perhaps you too are wishing that he'd stayed away."

I was transfixed. All I could do was clutch my glass. God knows why it didn't shatter in my hand.

"I don't want to think of Bronwen alive in Canada," whispered my father. "I can only bear it if I think of her as dead. That boy...that photograph...I just...couldn't...bear it." And he covered his face with his hands in despair.

I was on my knees beside him. I put my arm around his shoulders and my free hand on his nearest forearm. Naturally I said nothing. Nothing to say. Words are useless in that sort of situation, any Englishman knows that, even two Welshmen who are only English by education.

"I was glad you played 'The Blue Danube,'" said my father after a while. "It was such a relief to remember Blanche, such an escape." More time passed. Then he said suddenly, "I was so fond of Blanche. She was a very...sensitive person. She would have understood at once about Evan if she'd been in Constance's shoes—but then of course she would never have put herself in Constance's shoes. She'd have given me a divorce."

He stopped speaking. Nothing happened. But a voice in my head said: Wait a minute. This is my mother you're talking about. *My mother.*

A multitude of muddled emotions assaulted me but as I thought of those old photographs of the laughing exquisite girl whom I couldn't quite remember, I was suddenly glad she had died when she did.

Pain loosened my tongue. I said, "Was Bronwen your mistress before—"

And he said "No" without letting me finish.

"How soon after Mama's death did you start the affair with Bronwen?"

My father finished his drink and stared down into his empty glass. "Blanche was dead. That was all that mattered."

I thought: So he didn't wait long. Whatever the done thing was he didn't do it. He bucketed around, messed up two women at once and finally walked out on his pregnant wife to live in sin with his mistress. What a bastard. Incredible. Why hadn't he drawn his famous line? Because it hadn't suited him to draw it. He had temporarily lost the chalk that drew the lines. What a hypocrite. And how typically Victorian.

But of course I couldn't think thoughts like those, not just because they weren't the done thing but because I loved my father, the hero of my childhood, and I wanted to forgive him everything, even the divorce from my mother which had never happened. But all the same...

"I loved Bronwen so much," said my father. "I used to get in such muddles but she always saw things clearly. She was the way, the truth, the life I longed to lead."

Quite. Here was the Welsh romantic spouting sentiments which the cynical English side of him would undoubtedly have described as rubbish. But what a mess! What a tragedy! And of course the moral of the whole story was to avoid grand passions like the plague.

"I'm sorry you've been so unhappy, Father," I said, suddenly finding I could forgive him by making Grand Passion the scapegoat. I decided it had driven him out of his mind after my mother's death and rendered him not responsible for his actions.

"I'm all right now," he said. "I can keep on an even keel by leading a useful life, but sometimes I can't bear the thought of more unhappiness. Harry..."

I knew intuitively that he was telling me not to get killed. In fact what he was saying was that he really did feel God should draw the line somewhere and not make him suffer too much for his past wrongs. I agreed with him. I didn't see the world through his Victorian eyes but I did think it was about time retribution took a back seat in his life.

"If Kester survives," I said, "I'll survive. We're plowing parallel furrows in time."

My father stared at me. "What an extraordinary thing to say."

He was right. I had voiced the sort of wild, crazy, highly peculiar thought which should never have been allowed to escape from my brain. I was so horrified that I even felt myself blushing in embarrassment.

However my father, still indulging the Welsh romantic side of his personality, was fortunately in a mood to take my eccentricity in his stride. "You've been reading Dunne!" he said with a smile.

"Who the hell's he?"

My father smiled again but all he said was "I hope that when the war's over you'll want to plow your furrow in a different field from Kester's."

"I daresay I will," I said, wanting only to leave him in a happy frame of mind, but instinct told me that if I survived the war I was going to come back to Cousin Kester. And once I'd come back I suspected I'd have a hard time busting apart the parallel lines of our mirrored lives.

XIII

I'll never know how I survived.

I was sent to Kabrit in North Africa where Colonel David Stirling had recently been told by the Middle East Commander-in-Chief General Alexander to expand his S.A.S. detachment into a full regiment of the British Army. S.A.S. stood for Special Air Service, but that name had been invented to deceive the Germans; the S.A.S. had nothing to do with the air although they did spend much time blowing up planes on the ground. In fact they blew up damned nearly everything in sight in order to be a thorn in the enemy's side, and apart from a recent disaster at Benghazi they'd been highly successful. However Montgomery regarded Stirling with a jaundiced eye, so when Stirling set about building his regiment up to full strength he wasn't allowed to annex any of Montgomery's men. Consequently he was driven to cast his net elsewhere, and thanks to a meeting with his brother Bill in London I wound up as a new recruit. Arriving in North Africa I found Stirling in charge of a motley assortment of fanatics which included the remnants of Middle East Commando, and at once I realized that hair-raising times lay ahead.

Well, we dynamited our way along the coast of North Africa and prowled around behind the enemy lines, often with disastrous results, and somehow I managed to escape being killed or captured, God knows how. Hitler had given orders that saboteurs like us were to be shot on sight but that nice chap Erwin Rommel took no notice, so when Stirling was eventually captured by the Italians he lived to tell the tale after the war. After his capture I secretly hoped life might become a little less crazy, but the S.A.S. merely continued undaunted with their preposterous heroics. I only pretended to be heroic, but that was all right because I was used to pretending to be something I wasn't. I'd survived Harrow by pretending I was a public-school success story, and now I was only playing a madder version of the Great English Public School Game.

I pined for the clean cool air and fine lines of Gower. Couldn't say so, of course. I had to act as if war were a huge adventure, but to my mind my activities only proved how bestial human beings can be when they're running around killing each other. War brings out the best in men? Don't make me laugh, Machiavelli.

I used to dream that I was playing the piano at Oxmoon and all the windows of the ballroom were open so I could smell the freshly cut grass on the lawns. Everywhere was sunlit and serene. Magic Oxmoon someone had called it once, and now more than ever it was the symbol of a life which lay utterly beyond my reach. It was the symbol of Peace—Peace with a capital P—Peace, Beauty, Art, Truth... No, I hadn't got that quite right. Beauty, Truth, Art and Peace—yes, that was it. Someone had waffled about all that a long time ago in another world and I had thought such abstractions formed a nauseous quartet, but now I knew that on the contrary they represented the way, the truth, the life I longed to lead.... Someone else in that other world had talked about ways and truth and longed-for lives, but I could no longer remember who it was. The other world was so far away, and I was on a different planet, my whole being concentrated upon staying alive. But although I was now just a Machiavellian stereotype I knew that after the war I'd go home and Oxmoon would redeem me. It lay there at the end of a hellish rainbow to compensate me for the horrors of war.

I didn't get back to base often but when I did there were always several letters waiting for me. It was odd to hear news of the other world, as odd as receiving proof that heaven really did exist, complete with celestial choirs all singing Bach's *B Minor Mass.*

Darling Harry, all well here, how are you I am well, quite recovered from the birth now, I think Humphrey's going to be dark like you, Hal and Charles are still fighting all the time, God I do have my hands full but I do so wish they were full of you . . .

. . . so everything's in order here now—I was a bit worried about the hoeing, such an awful job, but those two land girls work like Trojans so I'm sure we'll manage. Teddy says she'll write soon but you know what Americans are like—the telephone ruined them. Your very affectionate uncle, EDMUND.

. . . and anyway, honey, don't have nightmares that Bella's running around with those god-awful Canadians at Little Oxmoon because with four boys under five all she can do is put her feet up whenever she gets the chance . . .

. . . and Constance sends her love. She's just improved our air-raid shelter with matchless American efficiency—this has stopped her from worrying about Francesca who looks much too attractive in her WAAF uniform. I've no news of your other sister since she and Rory parted—she's still at Swansea with the Bryn-Davieses. Must stop now, no more room. May God, however unimaginable He is, be with you. Your devoted father, J.G.

My dear Harry, don't faint. It's me. I don't know whether you read letters from pacifists but on the chance that you don't immediately consign this to the nearest oubliette I thought I'd send a cousinly line to congratulate you on your latest medal. I expect war's all enormous fun really, just as Machiavelli says it is, although I must say I still blanch when I remember he modeled his hero on Cesare Borgia! And now from the Borgias to the Godwins (a thought-provoking transition!). Visited Uncle J in London last week—you should see Aunt C's air-raid shelter! Fit for a ten-year siege—Priam's six-gated city pales in comparison. Francesca's in love with three men, reported blissful. Marian has a new lover. Also reported blissful. Teddy and Edmund still Darby and Joan, Anna and I ditto, Bella and boys flourishing but missing you, I'm running out of space, yours, KESTER.

Dear Harry: I'm in Cairo. No chance of meeting, I guess? EVAN.

There was no chance. I was being dispatched to Italy for new horrors in another arena. Even today, if I see a picture of Italy, I want to vomit. Those cruel southern nights. Those arid mountain slopes. The ruined vineyards. The burned-out churches. The women screaming. The stinking corpses. The heat, the horror, the hell.

"You've nerves of steel," said my commanding officer to me approvingly.

That's me. Nerves-of-steel Godwin, plowing through the war without a scratch. But I have scars no one can see. I didn't see them myself at first. It took me some time before I realized I was bleeding in my mind.

"I've got this rash, doctor."

"Been with any women lately?"

But no, it wasn't syphilis. I lived in terror of it, thanks to the army's anti-V.D. propaganda, but I never missed a sheath. Had to have sex, though, had to. It was the only way I knew of staying sane.

The rash was all over my back although it was barely visible. There were no spots, only patches of angry red skin which flared in white weals when I scratched them.

"Nerves," said the doctor at last. "I'll give you some pills."

I couldn't tell anyone this humiliating diagnosis and presently I found I couldn't take the pills either. I didn't dare. They made me sleepy, and my life depended on being wide awake. The rash dragged on like a slow burn. I scratched away, complained of lice, bedbugs, fleas, anything except the truth—that I'd become allergic to war.

Finally the rash began to suppurate and I was packed off to a military hospital. This saved me from taking part in D-Day and being killed on a Normandy beach. I languished in hospital until some unusually clever doctor said, "Pump him full of dope and let him sleep for a week." After that I felt much better and I felt better still when I heard that the S.A.S. didn't want to know me once they heard the diagnosis of nervous exhaustion. I was then left for some weeks in a bureaucratic limbo, but eventually I was raked into the Eighth Army in time to witness the fall of Florence. I told everyone that a bad bout of dysentery had temporarily forced me into more mundane military channels, and in the August of 1944, after the Allied triumph I found myself sitting in a Florentine café drinking Chianti and once more perusing my mail.

Darling Harry, I'm nearly berserk with living like a nun, are you faithful, do you love me, oh yes I know you are and you do but two years is such a long time . . .

DEAR DADDY THE CAT SAT ON THE MAT LOVE HAL.

My dear Harry, it's your cousin again—I just thought I'd send you a formal line about Aunt C. No doubt you've heard the news from Uncle J . . .

Wait. What was this? What news? A formal line . . . What the devil was Kester saying?

Rummaging through my pile of letters I found the one I'd been saving till last, the envelope addressed in my father's handwriting.

My dear Harry, the house at Eaton Walk was destroyed by a direct hit last night. If Constance had been in the shelter I suppose she might have survived but the indications are that she took no notice of the air-raid warning. She often didn't bother if she was on her own. She wanted the shelter primarily for Francesca when she visited us. I had spent the weekend at Oxmoon and on my return I found the firemen at work. As your time for letter writing is so limited, write to Francesca, not to me. I don't want sympathy. I wish the marriage could have ended in a divorce court instead of like this, although in an odd way I came to respect her for those principles she refused to abandon. I didn't make her happy, but at least she knew I tried. I remain as always your devoted father...

As soon as I could put pen to paper I wrote to Evan: *My stepmother's been killed in an air raid. If by some terrible chance Bronwen's thinking of remarrying, for God's sake write and tell her not to. Yours ever,* H.G.

XIV

In a fairy tale my father and Bronwen would now marry, but the trouble was we were all a thousand light-years from any fairy tale. Over six thousand miles and eleven years apart, cut off from each other by the war, the two of them were hardly ideal candidates for the leading roles in the traditional love story complete with happy ending. I thought of the photograph of Bronwen and shuddered. I was sure my father would go to Vancouver to see her after the war, but I thought it likely that the grand passion would have fizzled into a limp affection. Still there was no harm in hoping and I hoped. We all need our little pipe dreams, and never more so than when we're living in a brutish sordid world laid waste by war.

"Did you say your name was Godwin?"

I was drinking again at the same café and two soldiers had stopped at my table. I agreed my name was Godwin.

"Any relation to Bugger-God Godwin—or Goddamn Godwin, as the Yanks call him?"

"Not as far as I know."

"Oh, you mean Pigshit Godwin!" called a man at a nearby table. "Escaped from a patrol by hiding in the undergrowth and grunting like a pig!"

"We're related," I said with reluctance, and learned to my horror that Thomas was swaggering the streets of Florence. I bumped into him soon after that and we got drunk in some hole stiff with soldiers and whores. I remember noticing that there were torn posters of the Italian lakes adorning the walls, a spoiled vision of unattainable beauty.

"Wonderful thing, war," said Thomas. "Only life for a man, of course. I can say that to you, Harry, because I've heard you're a hell of a success, bloody hero, all that sort of thing, and you'll know what I mean."

"Quite," I said.

"God, I can't begin to tell you what a wonderful time I've had..."

He told me his war experiences. They weren't particularly interesting. The

687

incident in which he had escaped from the enemy by grunting like a pig was clearly apocryphal.

"... and so there we are. Christ, it's good to see you again, Harry—let's have another bottle of this filthy stuff—yes, I always felt you and I had a lot in common. Brought up by the same man, marrying sisters, living side by side in Gower—more like brothers than uncle and nephew—here, grab that cunt and let's get some more wine—that's right. *More Chianti!*—have to shout at these bloody foreigners to make them understand... where was I? Oh yes, like brothers, both of us real men, not fucking artistic pansies like Kester—if he can fuck at all, which I doubt. Look at him—six years married and can't produce one daughter. Look at you—six years married and four fine sons! Christ, Eleanor says you only have to look at Bella to get her pregnant! Sexy girl that, by the way," added Thomas meditatively as the new bottle of wine arrived. "I've wondered once or twice if I married the wrong one, but no, I'm bloody fond of Eleanor—she's a decent old girl, and you couldn't find a woman cleverer at managing a pig."

He spoke quite without irony. I somehow managed to keep a straight face. God, he was a stupid man.

"I'd like some more sons myself," said Thomas, "but Eleanor's not too keen. Wish I could have two wives, one for friendship and one for reproduction."

"How enthralling that would be for the neighbors."

"Neighbors! Don't talk to me of neighbors, don't remind me of bloody Kester! God, I could murder him!"

"Not in the Gower Peninsula, old chap. Not the done thing. I know we've all been murdering away happily for months out here but one must draw the line somewhere."

"Oh, of course—good God, Harry, I wasn't serious! But I feel bitter about Oxmoon. It should have gone to John and if John hadn't wanted it then it should have come to me. I mean, am I my father's son or aren't I? I was damned fond of the old bugger—hell, I even called my son after him. Poor old sod, what a mess he got himself into, all those pillowcases John and I had to bury—"

"What pillowcases?"

"My father's little bits of nonsense, old boy. John and I buried the lot after Milly ran off back in '28. Wonderful chap, John. Just like a father to me. Well, he *was* a father to me after the old bugger broke down—"

"Tell me more about these pillowcases."

We talked and talked and got drunker and drunker. Finally Thomas said, "So there we are. My father fucked himself to death with that cunt Milly Straker. Bloody sex. Revolting. Hate it. Ought to be abolished." And he keeled forward, upsetting his glass, and laid his face on the table amidst a small pool of wine. I was just wondering how I was going to get him home when he raised his head and said, "Can't say that about sex, though. Not the done thing. Have another drink."

I somehow steered him back to the hotel where he was billeted. Luckily he was shipped out of Florence soon after that so I didn't have to see him again.

The surrender of Italy improved my life for I was never in danger again during the remainder of the war, but the lessening of tension failed to terminate my medical problems. After I'd stopped thanking God I was still alive a reaction set in. I felt depressed, had nightmares, couldn't eat, drank too much. My rash began to suppurate again and once more I was confined to hospital. This time there was no intelligent doctor to make a correct diagnosis and I certainly wasn't going to confess that my nerves were in shreds, so I was kept under observation for a time while everyone wondered which foul disease I'd picked up. Then I made the mistake of trying to seduce a nurse and the doctor at once decided I was well enough to be turned out. I rejoined my unit. The next day I was on my way to liberate a prisoner-of-war camp in the Italian Alps. Nerves-of-steel Godwin, or what remained of him, was once more on the warpath.

Peace came in May. Now all I had to do was wait for repatriation. I waited and waited, slept around and got drunk. I was tormented by the fear that I'd die in an accident before I could reach home. I became afraid to cross streets. In the end I even became afraid to go out. Another doctor said I had agoraphobia and told me to pull myself together. I was terrified, thought it might be some sort of V.D., but he said it was just a fear of open spaces.

"Can I have some pills for my rash?"

"What rash?"

Away we went again. This doctor turned out to be one of the clever ones.

"Hm. Eczema. Nasty. You're obviously a nervous, sensitive type."

I laughed, told him I'd been in the S.A.S., bragged of the nerves of steel. He looked polite, said: "The best medicine you could get is being demobbed. I'll see if I can speed up your repatriation."

I thought I would go mad before I ever saw England again but at last I was dispatched westward, shunted across Europe on a packed train which stopped at every station. I started to get claustrophobia, just for a change. Everything was itching, arms, legs, hands, feet. I even itched between my toes.

On went the train. People at the stations began to talk French. We were eventually disgorged at a Channel port—it was Dieppe but it might have been Timbuktu for all I cared—and crammed into a transport ship. More hell followed. I was seasick into a foul lavatory. I was afraid the ship would sink. But it didn't and at last I was at Newhaven, standing on British soil, and the autumn light was shining on the long green rolling lines of the Sussex Downs.

But I was afraid to give them more than a brief glance in case agoraphobia overwhelmed me again. Meanwhile I was once more deep in panic. Supposing the train crashed on the way to London? All through the journey I thought I'd break down, and when we reached Victoria Station I did—I fell out of the train, blundered around in a daze, couldn't see where I was going. Tears were streaming down my face. I kept saying, "I did it, I did it" until I started to shudder and had to lean against the nearest wall. The station was swarming with people in uniform. The cavernous echoing station reeked of fumes. People were talking English. I wasn't quite in paradise, not yet, but I was definitely on the first rung of the ladder.

A timid little hand touched my arm.

A plump frightened young woman gazed at me speechlessly. I saw light brown eyes shining with tears and some carefully set mouse-brown hair beneath a little navy hat.

"Bella?"

"Harry...oh my God..."

We embraced. We wept. I started to shudder again.

"Oh darling, how wonderful to have you back—and I'm so proud of you—all those medals—"

"Oh, that was nothing, all rather a lark, had the time of my life."

I hardly knew what I said. I just knew I couldn't talk about the war. I couldn't even bear to think of it.

"Harry! Darling—what's all this?"

We were in a little hotel half an hour later.

"Oh, it's not catching, just an allergy. It'll go away now I'm home."

"Oh my poor darling..."

What was I doing in this strange bed with this strange woman who called me darling?

"Harry, you still love me, don't you?"

"Don't be idiotic—of course I do!" But did I? No idea. I was like a robot catapulted to an unfamiliar planet. Couldn't think clearly at all. Perhaps now I really had gone insane.

We had sex. Without a sheath. And suddenly my mind clicked into focus. I saw the view behind her on the summit of Rhossili Downs; I saw the arching spine of the Worm rising from the sea as the Shipway sank beneath a mass of roaring foam.

"Remember the fuck rock?"

"Oh Harry, *yes*! And the burrows at Llangennith—"

"And the potting shed—"

"And our bedroom at the Manor—"

The Manor. Penhale. Oxmoon. I moved up another rung on the ladder and saw paradise.

Hugging her to me again I buried my face against her breasts and whispered fiercely, "Take me home, take me home, take me home..."

XV

We caught the train the next morning, a dirty but uncrowded train which stopped only once before Bristol. Holding Bella's hand I gazed speechlessly at the drab wintry English countryside as it floated past the window. My agoraphobia had vanished. I knew now I was going to get home. The family would be waiting for me at the Manor and my father alone would be in Swansea to meet our train.

"We've got a surprise for you!" added Bella after imparting this information.

I tried to look interested but the idea of a celebration party left me cold. I wanted to go to bed and listen to all my gramophone records nonstop for a week.

When I saw my father at the station I found him looking wonderfully well, so slim and smart and bright-eyed that he could have passed for forty. I was touched to see how my homecoming had rejuvenated him, and we embraced as emotionally as decency permitted.

"Harry—welcome back!" His shining eyes were a deep brilliant blue. In fact he looked not just rejuvenated but reborn altogether. I wasn't reborn yet, but I thought I might be heading for it. The dreamlike quality of the journey was fading and I was able to believe I really was with him again in Wales.

Leaving ruined Swansea we drove into Gower.

The fields were pastel-colored beneath the pale sun. Every turn of the road was precious to me. Oxwich Bay began to flash through the trees to the left. Cefn Bryn flickered on the right. And finally in the distance I saw Rhossili Downs.

Immediately I forgot Italy. I forgot North Africa. I was clambering up the last rungs of the ladder to paradise, and unlike Orpheus I had no intention of looking back into the hell I'd left behind.

The car swept past Oxmoon. I had a split-second glimpse of unmarred perfection beyond the gates, and the next moment as I thought of the white piano in the ballroom the music began in my head. It was Mahler's mighty *Symphony of a Thousand*. I listened. We drove on to Penhale, and Mahler evolved into Elgar. I was back with "Pomp and Circumstance" again, and on cue at the top of the crescendo I heard the chorus of the Hebrew slaves from *Nabucco*.

The car turned through the gates of the Manor.

"Welcome home, darling, welcome home..." Bella was kissing me lavishly but I was unable to respond. I was still listening to Verdi and it was only when I got out of the car that the music stopped.

A great silence fell. I paused, struck by its intensity, and as I listened I heard time shifting its gears again; I saw the present splintering to dust before the battering ram of the past, and suddenly as the circle completed itself I knew that my most treasured memory lay not behind me but in front of me once more.

I stood waiting in the drive. I knew it was going to happen but I still didn't dare believe it. And then as my father shouted cheerfully, "Where's the reception committee?" the miracle happened, the front door opened and my magic lady came out to welcome me home.

4

I

HE MARRIED her six weeks later and they lived happily ever after—more or less. Well, it does happen sometimes. Kester hit the nail on the head when he said even the cynics have to admit romance does occasionally triumph; to say no one lives happily ever after is as much at odds with reality as saying that everyone does.

Wonderful. I was ready for a fairy tale. I wanted it all—champagne, golden sunsets, true love, eternal bliss and the theme from *Gone with the Wind* playing endlessly in the background. It was the perfect antidote to drinking, whoring, murdering and going out of my mind.

"Whenever I heard a piano playing the tunes you liked to play," said Bronwen, "I'd look across the circle and I'd hear your echo in time."

Quite. Bronwen was above all a resilient practical woman; nobody brings up four children in a foreign country merely by listening to the music of the spheres. But she had this trick of treating fantasies as concrete facts and concrete facts as fantasies. To her it was natural to be a magic lady; she would have described her magic as common sense. It wasn't, but for Bronwen magic was as normal as common sense, something to be recognized without surprise and even taken for granted.

Perhaps the prosaic explanation of her magic was that she saw farther than most people did. She was always careful to disclaim any psychic powers but she combined her extreme clarity of vision with unusually keen powers of observation. This enabled her to pick up details other people would miss with the result that she often saw a broader spectrum of reality—and this meant that she could talk in concrete terms of matters which other people couldn't see and therefore assumed to be myths.

Unable to speak I embraced her, and all the time I was thinking: She went away—but she came back. And I knew my long bereavement was at last at an end.

Some unknown time later I found myself sitting beside her on the sofa in the drawing room while other people, all strangers in their teens, filtered into the room and made remarks like "Hi—welcome back!" and "Hi—bet you don't remember me!" Dimly I realized these were my lost siblings. But before I could digest this astonishing fact, an army of small boys pounded in waving Union Jacks and shouting "Daddy! Daddy!"

I heard Bella say, "They were meant to be in the drive but they locked themselves in the lavatory and couldn't get out." I gazed at them. What had happened to all those bundles in rompers? I found myself confronted by a bunch of savage midgets who yelled with a force that would have demolished the walls of Jericho more quickly than the legendary trumpet. I winced at the noise.

"Shhh, boys—be gentle with Daddy!" begged Bella nervously, but they only fell silent when Bronwen leaned forward and put her finger to her lips. Then she beckoned the smallest thug with a smile. "Come along, Humphrey—this is your special moment."

The son I had never seen presented himself proudly for inspection. He looked like the old photographs of myself at the age of two. I was too amazed to speak but when I patted him to make sure he was real he beamed in delight.

"Daddy, Daddy—"

I mixed up Charles and Jack who were the same height, but while they were elbowing each other out of the way and trampling Humphrey underfoot, Hal slid past them and sat down beside me on the sofa.

"Hullo, Hal—no trouble recognizing *you!*" I said, but I was too exhausted to say more. Vaguely I looked around for Edmund and Teddy, and it was some seconds before I remembered my father telling me they were busy reopening their house in London.

"Gerry," said Bronwen to one of the strangers, "could you organize another cricket match?"

Various people disappeared and the room became blessedly quiet. I was alone with my father and Bronwen at last, and my father was talking rapidly with great animation.

"... so I wrote to her directly after Constance died—"

"I wrote back by return," said Bronwen, speaking to me but smiling at him.

"—and after that we corresponded. We agreed to meet after the war, but of course even when the war ended transport for civilians was so difficult. However I did have my government contacts—"

"—so when I said I'd bring the children over for a visit—"

"—I was able to arrange the journey. Of course I wanted to tell her to sell everything up there and then—"

"—and I wanted to sell everything up too, but I was so afraid—"

"—we were both so afraid—"

"—that we'd find we were strangers with nothing to say to each other!"

They laughed in delight at this absurd possibility.

"Anyway," said my father, "I said yes, come for a visit. But when I met the ship at Southampton—"

"—as soon as I saw him—"

"—as soon as I saw her—"

They laughed again, more delighted than ever by their ridiculously romantic story.

"So I soon asked her to marry me and she said yes—"

"No, no, you said, 'How soon can you marry me?' and I said, 'Well, I'm not doing anything tomorrow . . .'"

They laughed helplessly, delirious with happiness. Rousing myself at last I assumed the role of the kind useful child and refilled their glasses with champagne. Some time later when I could get a word in edgeways I said to my father, "I assume Teddy decided it was a situation she could fix?"

"Oh God, yes, that woman's power-mad. She couldn't resist the chance to wield the power to forgive and forget, but if she really means well she'll do something about Francesca. That child's threatening to cancel the big wedding I've arranged for her next month—she says she'd rather marry in a registry office without me if I continue, as she describes it, to insult her mother's memory."

"Poor little Francesca," said Bronwen.

But I'd had just about enough of Francesca posing as the wronged heroine, and I decided it was time someone shook her till her teeth rattled. With reluctance I realized that my father was right to be suspicious of Teddy; she wasn't going to interfere while Francesca voiced feelings which perhaps, deep down beneath all the layers of kindness and generosity, Teddy secretly shared. Teddy was probably willing for Edmund's sake to display goodwill towards my father and Bronwen now that Constance had been dead for over a year, but her deepest feelings were unlikely to be benign.

It so happened that I had the chance to intervene on my father's behalf because three days later Francesca and her fiancé arrived for a weekend at Oxmoon. She had been engaged for six months to a colonel in the United States Air Force called William Q. Coton who belonged to one of the wealthy Eastern Seaboard families in Massachusetts. Francesca had first met him before the war during visits to America with her mother, and after a flirtatious career as a WAAF she probably found his familiarity as attractive as his respectability. He was thirty-two but born to be fifty, and when I met him he wore a worried expression which I hoped meant he realized his fiancée was behaving idiotically about her father's imminent marriage. Certainly when I asked for a private word with Francesca he guessed what was happening and smiled gratefully at me before bolting from the room.

Francesca was twenty-one, dark, slim and neat like Constance but with my father's blue eyes. Before assuming the role of the wronged heroine she had played the vivacious ingenue with great success for many years, and accepting her at face value I'd made no effort to know her better. However now my real acquaintance with my sister was finally about to begin.

"If you've come to speak to me about Daddy and That Woman—"

"Oh, shut up! For Christ's sake stop playing Elektra and come down off that stage!"

Francesca was appalled. No one had ever spoken to her like that before. She was the golden girl, Mummy's adored only daughter, forever petted by a horde of doting relatives who all thought, according to their nationality, that she was either "cute" or "sweet."

"Harry!"

"Look, Sunshine. Do you love your father or don't you?"

"Why, I adore him but—"

"Then prove it by welcoming this marriage. Now listen to me, my girl. For the past twelve years that man's made endless sacrifices in order to be a good father to you and yet all you do to repay him is yap like a rabid Pekingese just because he's at last managed to find some genuine happiness for a change! Well, I think your behavior's disgraceful and it's about time someone told you what a bloody unkind ungrateful daughter you're being!"

Floods of tears. Disconnected phrases hinted at dark fissures in that outwardly sunlit well-ordered childhood of hers. "I knew Mummy was unhappy...and all because of *her*...I couldn't blame darling Daddy, he was so wonderful, so perfect..."

I saw the problem. It had taken me too a long time to realize that my father had many dimensions to his character and by no means all of them were heroic.

"He's no saint, Francesca. He treated your mother very badly after they were married, and what's more, if my mother had lived he'd have treated her badly too."

But she couldn't accept that. She just sobbed and shook her head and said "No" over and over again.

Taking her in my arms I said, "He was a victim. He was fond of my mother and respected yours, but what use are fondness and respect when there's a grand passion sizzling in the wings? And grand passions aren't as they are in the storybooks, Francesca. They put good people through hell."

Francesca rubbed her eyes with the back of her hand and whispered, "Mummy was certainly put through hell."

"They all were, all of them, but it's over now, it's finished. Our mothers are dead—they're out of it and nothing can hurt them anymore. But Father's still alive and he's finally got the chance to have a little happiness and if you really love him you won't be angry, you'll just be sick with relief that his suffering's finally at an end."

Some minutes passed. Finally she was able to say, "I do see. All victims. I do see. But even so...I don't know how I can meet her after all I've said...I shall feel so embarrassed—"

"All you need say is hullo and she'll do the rest."

I mopped her up and took her home. My magic lady was in the garden, but as soon as we emerged from the house she waved and came towards us across the lawn. Moving briskly, like some busy housewife anxious to welcome an unexpected guest to her coffee party, she looked as if her greatest worry was whether there'd be enough biscuits to go around.

"Francesca thought she'd drop in to see Father," I called as soon as Bronwen was within earshot.

"Oh good, he'll be back in a minute—he's just gone to the village for cigarettes." She smiled at Francesca. Those razor-sharp powers of observation missed nothing. The smile set all embarrassment firmly aside as irrelevant. Bronwen's magic was at its most formidable.

"Have you brought your fiancé?" she said kindly before Francesca could open her mouth. "I hear he's at Oxmoon with you this weekend."

By the time my father returned from the village we were all having coffee in the drawing room. Innumerable photographs of William Q. Coton covered the table, and Francesca, miraculously restored to the role of vivacious ingenue, was telling Bronwen the story of her engagement. Bronwen, to her eternal credit, looked enthralled.

So much for Francesca. She married her fiancé three weeks later at St. Margaret's Westminster and sailed away into the sunset to America to live happily ever after.

Maybe.

Bronwen didn't go to the wedding. She said to Francesca: "Of course it's best if I'm just with you in spirit but you needn't think the children and I won't be drinking your health and wishing you well." She then retired with my Canadian siblings to the Lleyn Peninsula to spend a week with her sister Myfanwy who was still her only relative in Wales. Dafydd hadn't yet returned from the Far East and Rhiannon had been killed during the bombing of Malta.

When the time came for her to leave her wedding reception at Claridges, Francesca said to my father: "I hope you have a lovely wedding, Daddy—I'm sorry I can only be with you in spirit but you needn't think I won't be drinking your health and wishing you well." That was when I knew what a deep impression Bronwen had made.

My father kissed her, thanked her and said yes, he was looking forward to his wedding very much. That must have been the understatement of his life. By that time the whole family could hardly wait for the great romantic wallow of the year, of the decade and possibly of the entire century. We were all agog with excitement.

In the end they were married, like Francesca, at St. Margaret's Westminster. Penhale Church would have been suitable from a nostalgic point of view, but the thought of the entire Gower Peninsula turning up to boggle at the sight of John Godwin marrying his mistress was too intimidating. Clearly only London could offer them the quiet wedding they wanted so finally my father said, "Oh hell, I know the ropes at St. Margaret's at the moment—why don't we do it there?" and the rector kindly arranged to slip them in between two gross Society weddings.

On the morning of December the fifteenth, 1945, the family gathered with bated breath at Westminster.

Bronwen had grown her hair longer since her arrival in England and on her wedding day she wore it up beneath a fashionable saucerlike hat. Her hair was paler than it had once been but still bright enough for the exposed strands to glow in the dim light. She was plumper too but unhappiness had made her too thin in the past and I thought the new curviness suited her. She still had freckles across the bridge of her nose and very white teeth. She was forty-seven. My father was fifty-three. In their extreme happiness they looked as if they had discovered the secret of eternal youth. Everyone kept whispering, "Don't they look *young!*" and Teddy, seeing Bronwen in her Canadian silver-fox furs, added to me with an admiration which I knew was genuine: "My, that gal's got class!"

What an irony! But it was true. Teddy was using the word in its American sense, but I suddenly saw that this "class" which Bronwen had acquired in Canada had made her by English standards classless. The shy secluded uneducated Welsh nursemaid had gone forever, replaced by a well-dressed self-confident cultured woman whom the English could rank as an acceptable foreigner, someone who had a right to exist beyond the confines of the English class system. Bronwen's Welsh accent and her inner self had remained unchanged but a more egalitarian society than England had left its mark on her, and the Canadian gloss on her personality was now her passport to freedom.

I saw then how much easier it would be for my father to join her in creating a new life which bore no outward resemblance to the old. I had been amazed by the changes he had already made but now I realized they were not only desirable but inevitable. He had sold the Rolls-Royce, severed his business links with London and bought a house in a wealthy but undeniably middle-class area of Swansea. When I had last spoken to him on the subject he had even been planning with delight to take up gardening.

"How handsome your father looks," whispered Bella as we waited for the service to begin, but I barely heard her. I was listening to Bach's *Wachet Auf*, which had begun to stream through my head in defiance of the fool who was trying to play some drivel by Mendelssohn on the organ. However at last the clergyman embarked on his rigmarole and I was sufficiently diverted to glance around at the rest of the family. All the women were dewy-eyed and all the men were grinning foolishly. I was just hastily straightening out my own mouth when Gerry caught my eye and winked. I gave him a cool look. When one is eighteen years old and in the unique position of seeing one's parents married, one should know better than to wink as if the entire affair were a huge joke. I was relieved to see that my other Canadian siblings were behaving with the solemnity of anthropologists watching an esoteric tribal rite. I eyed them meditatively. I supposed I would have to make the effort to know them better, but the thought was not attractive to me.

I woke up to the fact that my father was finally putting the ring on Bronwen's finger. Better late than never. Nearly a quarter of a century after their first meeting at the Penhale Home Farm, twenty-two years after Evan had been conceived, twelve years after Bronwen had gone to Canada and three months after her return to Europe, the deed was finally done.

Afterwards outside the church Teddy, more American than the Americans as usual, brandished her expensive camera, but my father and Bronwen at first ignored her command to pose for photographs. They were too busy locking themselves in a passionate embrace.

"Christ!" said Thomas, goggling at them. "Maybe romance isn't just a load of old balls after all!"

I felt as if I had heard a lifelong atheist declare his belief in God.

My father and Bronwen, separating with reluctance, turned to smile radiantly at the camera.

"Sweet, aren't they?" said Marian idly, exercising her talent for turning the

697

sublime to the banal. "Darling Bronwen—she looks such a lady in those furs!"

Kester and I wheeled around on her, snapped "Shut up!" and promptly laughed at our identical reaction. Dear old Kester—how could I ever have thought of him in sinister terms? Absurd! I could see clearly now that he was just a harmless eccentric who was as delighted by my father's marriage as I was.

"Well, really, darlings!" said Marian, startled by our vehemence. "What are you both getting in such a state about? I'm mad about Bronwen, always have been."

"Let's have a group!" yelled Teddy, interrupting us.

Groups formed and re-formed. Finally I had the chance to embrace Bronwen and say, "Well done." Then I shook my father's hand and said, "Congratulations." I felt so happy I hardly knew how to contain myself. In my head Toscanini was conducting the final movement from Beethoven's *Seventh*.

"One last picture of John and Bronwen on their own!" shrieked Teddy.

We stepped aside and as my father slipped his arm around his wife in front of the church door we all fell silent. Beyond the railing the traffic droned around Parliament Square but within seconds even that noise seemed to fade. Westminster Abbey overshadowed us; the Houses of Parliament slumbered in the winter light. Then I heard Bronwen say softly to my father, "It reminds me of that other church, Johnny, in that other time, long ago."

He smiled down at her, she smiled up at him, and beyond them, far beyond them on the skyline, Big Ben began to blast out the hour.

II

When the wedding was over, when my father and Bronwen had streamed away into the golden sunset of a Cornish honeymoon with a hundred violins sawing away in my head at the theme from *Gone with the Wind*, I finally had time to wake up and realize that my own marriage was on the rocks. So much for romance. The cold hard facts of my life were that I was heading for the biggest possible mess—again.

Sex and guilt, as my father had noted with such chilling accuracy, had driven me into marriage, but neither he nor I had understood then the exact nature of that guilt which yoked me to Bella. The bond of sex at least had weakened; in that respect she was now just a pleasant convenience instead of a heart-stopping erotic adventure. However the bond of guilt remained, and the more I realized the impossibility of communicating with Bella on any level but the horizontal the more I realized how absolutely we were still yoked together by that summer of '33.

I could only compare my relationship with her to the bizarre comradeship that can develop between men in wartime. When two people go through hell together this comradeship automatically springs into existence; it has little or nothing to do with whether they normally like each other or not. So it was with Bella and me. We had gone through hell together when we were children and Melody, our secret which we had to share for the rest of our lives, had created this indestructible bond which existed independently of our marriage. The marriage I now found shallow, exasperating and profoundly unsatisfactory, but how could I leave her? She depended on me utterly. She relied on me not only to redeem the past—I'd already done that by marrying her and giving her four more children—but to keep on redeeming it by loving her forever, and if I did leave her I had no doubt I would only complete the destruction of her life which I had begun at fourteen. Could I ever be happy if I had to live in the knowledge that I had destroyed her? No. I had to stay.

Having accepted that I saw that my task was to try to remake our marriage in a more satisfactory mold, and if Bella had grown up, as I had, there might have been some hope of achieving this. But Bella had remained little changed from the child I had loved in 1933. It was not only impossible to conduct painful but constructive conversations about our marriage with her. It was impossible to discuss any subject in depth. She didn't understand, lost interest, started to talk of something else.

I could see she was relieved that I didn't want to talk about my war experiences. As far as she was concerned I'd come back and that was that. It would never have occurred to her that I was suffering from such a tortuous reaction from the war that I wondered if I'd ever recover. It would never have occurred to her, as I struggled to focus my attention on the estate, that I lived in terror of breaking down and being unable to cope. I worried about everything but I couldn't talk about my worries to her. I did try to talk about money but she just said, "What does it matter since your father's a rich man?" and I couldn't find the words to paint a picture of my father's Victorian streak, my horror of having to crawl to him to confess further failures and—my biggest nightmare of all—the prospect of one of those Canadian boys turning into a dazzling success and outshining me over and over again.

I wasn't worried about Evan. My ex-serf was talking of becoming a clergyman and my father had roused Bronwen's fury by exclaiming, "But there's no money or future in the Church!" My poor father! It was hardly possible for him to slough off the effects of that chauffeur-driven Rolls-Royce overnight, and although he had hastily retracted his remark I suspected he was still disappointed in Evan's decision.

Lance was a quiet studious boy who wanted to be an engineer. No problem there. My father would always think engineering came low on the list of desirable professions.

That left Gerry, and Gerry, I was beginning to realize with sickening clarity, was all set to play the role of Wonder Boy and transform my normally rational father into a besotted parent. Gerry was handsome. He was personable. He was athletic. He was clever. And most sinister of all, he was ambitious. He had decided to attend a London crammers in the hope of winning a scholarship to Oxford to read law. Naturally my father was as pleased as Punch. In fact he even started talking about Uncle Robert.

The hackles rose on the back of my neck.

I began to have a most unpleasant vision of a future in which I would be compared with Wonder Boy and found wanting. But I didn't tell Bella that. I didn't tell anyone that. I merely tucked it away among my private fears and decided not to think about it, but the trouble was I had so many private fears by that time that it was hard to find the space for a new arrival. My rash began to bother me again. I felt demented. I started to drink too much.

"Tricky thing, peace," said Edmund. "Worse than war in some ways."

It's odd how often, when one's in great trouble, help comes from the quarter you least expect it. I'd always written Edmund off as a benign old fool, but in the end when I was on the verge of breakdown it was not my father but my underestimated uncle who was there at the brink to step between me and the abyss.

Edmund had not only survived the four years of the First War. He had survived the shell-shocked years of peace afterwards. "Don't worry about the nightmares," he said when I finally poured out my heart to him about the men I'd killed and the sights I'd seen and my constant terror that I'd go out of my mind. "You've wrapped your memories up in a parcel and the nightmares just mean you can't resist undoing the parcel and having a peep inside every now and then. But eventually the desire to peep will fade away and you can treat the parcel as lost property. You'll never actually lose it, but it'll turn into a bundle you don't care to redeem from the Lost Property Office, and then it won't matter anymore."

"It'll always matter."

"No, no," said Edmund placidly. "Not so. In fact the great truth of life is that the things most people think are important aren't really important at all. Look at John. After years and years he's finally realized this. Why drive a Rolls-Royce when you can be happier on a bicycle?"

"But Edmund, about the war—"

"The only important thing about the war is that you survived it. Don't try and make sense of what happened because the world is very far from being sensible and personally I think one gets in far less of a muddle if one simply says to oneself: 'Yes, the world's chaotic and ghastly beyond belief—how do I survive it?' Then you're more likely to do the right thing for the wrong reasons than the wrong thing for the right reasons."

We began to talk about survival. I told him all my current problems.

On the subject of money Edmund said, "Stop worrying about the done thing and go to John. He can't eat you."

"No, but he could write me off as his favorite son."

"What of it, old chap? I was never anyone's favorite but look at me, I'm happy as a lark!"

"Yes, but—"

"My dear Harry, crucifying yourself in order to remain John's favorite is not the way to survive with your sanity intact. Take crucifixion firmly off your list of desirable activities."

"Yes, I'm sure you're right, but... Edmund, I'm not just afraid of being demoted as favorite. I'm afraid that if I ask for money Father will use my penury to boot me out of Penhale to the estate in Herefordshire."

"Well, what's wrong with that, old chap? Nice county, Herefordshire. Of course I know how sentimental you feel about this house, but if your financial problems are so acute—"

"Edmund, I couldn't cope. At least, I could but Bella couldn't. Here at Penhale she has Anna as a friend and Eleanor to visit now and then, but if we moved to Herefordshire she'd know no one, she'd be utterly dependent on me and quite honestly I just couldn't stand it, I'd crack, go mad, kill her in a moment of frenzy, wind up on the gallows and oh Christ what would my father say then—"

"I'll tell you exactly what he'd say," said Edmund, not batting an eyelid as all this appalling neurotic rubbish spewed out of me. "He'd say, 'This is all my fault for forcing that boy to Herefordshire when any intelligent father could see it would drive him round the bend.' Harry, isn't it about time you saw your father as he really is? He's not a heathen god who has to be constantly appeased. He's a clever man with a broad experience of life and he also happens to be devoted to you. He'll want to offer help, not mete out punishment!"

"Yes, but what do I say, how do I explain—"

"Just tell him the truth. You have a difficult marriage and a move to Herefordshire would create more problems than it would solve. . . . Have you considered a divorce?"

"Couldn't. Not possible."

"I hope you're not saying that because you're afraid of what John would think."

"No. I just couldn't leave her. Couldn't."

"All right." Edmund paused for a moment. "I won't say any more because I know Teddy wants to talk to you about her. Teddy's determined to move back to London, I'm afraid, now that our house is open again."

"I'm only grateful to you both for staying so long."

"Well, I'd stay on longer but Teddy's right, we've got to leave the two of you on your own eventually and it may as well be sooner rather than later. Teddy's wonderful at making tough decisions like that, but then Teddy's wonderful at everything. Amazing woman. Don't know what I'd do without her."

I felt so close to him by that time that I was able to say, "Isn't it a bit difficult living with someone so powerful?"

"Not at all, old chap. She deals with the things that bore me to tears, like money, and I'm set free to do what I think is really important—growing roses, for instance, or going fishing with my boys. Quite frankly, Harry, so long as I'm the boss in the bedroom I don't give a hang what goes on outside. Happiness is all a question of getting one's interests in the right order, isn't it?"

A remarkable man. A survivor. And in his own modest way a hero. I resolved to take his advice—but not just at that moment.

I couldn't face my father. Not quite. Not then. Later.

III

"Now, don't worry, honey," said Teddy the next day. "I wouldn't dream of leaving you until we've got this problem fixed."

First of all I thought how typical it was of Teddy to assume that the problem could be fixed, but then I realized she had no idea what the real problem was. No outsider can ever know the full story of any marriage.

Teddy was primarily concerned about the survival of the household once she departed. She advised me to retain the first-class but expensive housekeeper and engage a properly qualified nanny in addition to the Welsh nursemaids who appeared and disappeared with bewildering regularity.

"I know Bella wants to keep those boys all to herself," said Teddy, "but children can't live on adoration alone, Harry—it's like living on a diet of cream cakes. Now those kids behave when I'm around, but once I'm gone there'll be anarchy and I just don't think that's fair on you."

"Yes. It's really a question of money, Teddy—"

"Sure, and don't think I don't realize you're going to pass out when I show you my estimates for the future. But to my mind it's money that has to be spent if you and Bella are to have a chance of happiness, and you should make that crystal-clear to John."

Our glances met. I saw then how much she disliked him but she said at once with all her warmth and charm: "Don't take any notice of me, honey; I don't pretend to understand that father of yours, never have. But since he married money—two times out of three—I don't see why the hell he can't spread it around where it's needed."

I said nothing. She kissed me affectionately. "Never mind, dear, there's a silver lining to every cloud, and although Bella's short on housekeeping skills she's long on love. She just adores you, Harry—you'll never have to worry about her looking at anyone else!"

That was the problem.

IV

"I'm longing for another baby, Harry—I hoped I'd get pregnant as soon as you came home but I didn't and then you started using those awful sheaths again so I couldn't, and now it's three whole years since Humphrey was born and I feel so horribly out of practice—"

"I think we'd better wait, Bella," I said but I knew I didn't want another child. It was bad enough having four little ruffians running wild and wrecking everything in sight. They'd even broken my piano. That disaster had made me so angry that I'd lost my temper, yelling at her for spoiling the boys to death and making no attempt to discipline them, but when she had only cried pathetically in response I'd felt so helpless because *she* was so helpless—helpless and hopeless, not able to cope as other women coped, just playing with the children or thumbing through her mindless magazines or wanting sex whenever she could think of nothing else to do.

"But why do we have to wait, Harry?"

"I've got to talk to my father about money," I said, unable to tell her I couldn't face a fifth child and knowing this excuse would enable me to postpone the problem. By this time my father had gone on a visit to Canada with Bronwen and the two younger children in order to wind up their North American life. In surburban Swansea the six-bedroomed house with the acre of garden had been left in the hands of the decorators, while in London Gerry and Evan were sharing my father's flat as they waited to begin their new careers. Evan had applied to read theology at King's and was filling in time by working for one of the Armstrong charities. Wonder Boy was at the crammers preparing for Oxford.

"But your father's bound to give you money so why can't we start the baby now? I don't understand."

"No," I said, "you wouldn't, would you? You're too damned stupid."

A ghastly scene ensued in which she accused me of having changed, of not loving her anymore, of hating the boys, of no longer caring about poor little Melody who would have been twelve years old if she'd lived—

"Shut up, shut up, *shut up!*" I shouted. "I never want to hear that bloody silly name again!"

That was the stupidest thing I could have said. She hit me and burst into tears— oh, God, I felt so sorry for her, and oh God, how I hated myself for being so cruel.

"I didn't mean it, Bella, it was a lovely name—"

"I want a little girl—I want my little Melody back again . . ."

What could I say? I promised to see my father as soon as he returned from Canada.

V

No six cows in a field, no dead antiques on a beige carpet, no Edwardian coronation mug on the mantelshelf of the morning room at Oxmoon. Just my father's brand-new home where the kitchen was full of gleaming machines and the reception rooms oozed modern Canadian comfort. My father must have found the place a liberation after his years in that lifeless museum on Eaton Walk.

When I arrived he was wandering around in a pair of dungarees and carrying a pail of whitewash. Sian and Lance were busy with tape measures on the lawn.

"Hullo!" called my father brightly. "You're just in time to help us mark out the tennis court!"

He was enjoying himself so much that he didn't realize I wasn't paying a social call. Fortunately Bronwen then emerged from the house, took one look at me and said, "Johnny, leave the lawn and have a cup of tea with Harry."

That move took us to his study. He had managed to salvage the comfortable armchairs from the library at Eaton Walk and I also recognized various items of *bric-à-brac*, including a detestable photograph of me taken when I had been in my last year at Harrow; I looked like a successful matador who sold shares in the Kingdom of Heaven in his spare time. In contrast next to my photograph was a picture of my four Canadian siblings all looking clean, virtuous and aseptically attractive. Wonder Boy's teeth, inherited from Bronwen, were formidably white and even.

"Sorry to bother you like this, Father, but I'm afraid I'm in rather a jam again . . ."

And so on and so on. My father, who had been looking like an artisan in his dungarees and checked shirt, slowly began to emanate a miasma which suggested that the dungarees were an illusion of my anxiety-ridden mind and that he was in reality wearing a Savile Row suit and his Old Harrovian tie. I could almost hear the Rolls-Royce purring in the background.

"Well, Harry," he said abruptly when I had explained my dilemma with as much dignity as possible, "this is really a most unsatisfactory situation."

"Yes, sir. I'm afraid it is."

"A rich man," said my father, "is under a moral obligation—"

My heart sank. I had to make a great effort not to let my respectful expression slip.

"—not to allow his children to think they can always come running to him if they get into financial difficulties. I refuse to be treated as a blank check. I draw the line."

"Yes, sir." I was sunk so deep in despair that I couldn't even summon the energy to lose my temper.

"However," said my father, suddenly becoming human once he had relieved his feelings by behaving like a Victorian monster, "of course I must help you solve this dilemma of yours. You needn't think I won't bend over backwards to help you but unfortunately"—he sighed—"I don't think the answer lies in increasing your unearned income. The tax on that can only go up now that the socialists are in power."

He began to pace up and down the room. I maintained an abject silence and waited for him to try to kick me to Herefordshire.

"It would be better to expand the Penhale Manor estate," said my father suddenly, taking me by surprise. "If we do that we kill two birds with one stone. With more land you make the estate a better economic proposition and at the same time you create more deductions for yourself so that you wind up paying the minimum amount of tax. I'll let you have Martinscombe and Little Oxmoon at a nominal rent. The farm's surprisingly profitable; the sheep do well on Penhale Down. And as for Little Oxmoon, you can let it—the rent should help to pay the wages of the nanny and housekeeper which otherwise you wouldn't be able to afford."

I thanked him as effusively as decency permitted but he wasn't finished. No doubt he thought it was his moral duty not to let me escape too lightly.

"I can't let this conversation close," he said coolly, "without saying how much

I disapprove of you wasting your very considerable abilities on a small estate which can only become increasingly unworthy of you."

I explained why I felt unable to move to Herefordshire.

My father listened without expression. When I stopped he said, "I see," but made no further comment.

The silence yawned between us. When I felt my face becoming hot I said rapidly, "I admit Bella and I have our difficulties, but there's absolutely no question of a divorce."

My father said nothing.

"I love her and I'm going to stand by her," I said. By this time I was frantic for a word of approval. "It's the right thing—the only thing—to do."

"Of course," said my father politely, and after that the conversation closed.

There was just nothing left to say.

VI

"Oh Harry, *please*—once I have Melody back I'll never ask for anything else, I swear I won't..."

Poor Bella. I didn't have the heart to remind her that we could so easily wind up with a fifth boy. I just looked at her, saw the tearstained pink-and-white cheeks, the heavy bosom sagging beneath a coffee-stained blouse, the once-slim hips straining the seams of the shabby trousers I detested. I knew her disordered appearance reflected the inner disorders of her personality and that she was bleeding in her mind just as I had bled in mine during the war.

"The experience will almost certainly scar her for life," my father had said long ago in the field with the six cows. "I hope you now realize what a terrible thing you've done."

I realized. And I realized too that the knowledge had become unendurable. I could bear it no longer and could see only one escape from the pain.

I said: "I want Melody back too. I want the guilt to finish." So I stopped using contraceptives and she got pregnant straightaway.

As soon as the pregnancy was confirmed I regretted it but Bella was radiant, started eating sensibly, going to the hairdresser again, taking an interest in clothes. She couldn't understand my emotional withdrawal which too often manifested itself in bad temper, and she was angry when she finally realized I wasn't as delighted as she was.

"What's the matter with you?" she said. "Why don't you want to fuck anymore?"

"Oh, stop using that sort of language! I'm fed up with my wife talking like a bloody tart!"

"My God, anyone would think you wanted me to be some kind of bloody virgin!"

"I want you to be some kind of bloody wife, not an old bag who sits around getting fat and lets those bloody kids murder my piano!"

Slaps. More slaps. Screams. Tears. Christ, what hell marriage can be.

It all rubbed off on the children. I could see they didn't like me, but I wanted peace and order, not affection. That was why when I caught Hal banging at the piano in defiance of my orders I lost my temper and beat him.

"I hate you!" he screamed when I'd finished. "I wish you'd got killed in the war!"

That horrified me. I hated myself, tried to comfort him, but he pushed me away. Failure slugged me with the force of a sledgehammer and later the skin broke open on my back as my rash returned.

I couldn't face my father to confess another child was on the way so I told Bronwen instead. Bronwen was very sympathetic. I realized then that she knew about Melody, but I wasn't surprised because it was obvious my father would have no secrets from her.

"Oh, you mustn't think your father won't understand," she said quickly when I confessed my mixed feelings about the pregnancy. "He knows all about fathering children for the wrong reasons." And when I boggled she explained: "He wanted me to be happy—he was afraid I'd leave him."

This was horrific. "And eventually you did leave him—because of the children!"

"True. But," said Bronwen, trying to cheer me up, "think what a lot of pleasure the children give us now!"

I couldn't imagine getting any pleasure from my children, and such was my trust in Bronwen that I was even able to say so.

"A little girl will be quite a different matter," said Bronwen.

I tried to believe her.

My father eventually offered some suitable comment on Bella's pregnancy but I was sure he was thinking: More irresponsible behavior—that boy'll never make a success of his life. And I felt more bitter than ever.

Meanwhile up at Oxmoon, poor old Kester, poor old sod, was recovering very nicely from his prewar debacle as he luxuriated with his charming, intelligent, well-educated wife in his beautiful home where no little ruffians broke pianos, wrecked furniture and trailed dirty fingers all over the walls. I rarely went to Oxmoon, but Bella was always popping in and out to bore Anna to tears. She reported that Kester was haunting the salesrooms again although this time he was more careful how he spent his money. Since the war he had employed an agent to run the estate so that he could return to his writing, but although I expected my father to be disappointed he turned out to be merely resigned. Kester could now be dismissed as too old to change his ways. My father had done his best to turn Kester into a perfect Godwin but he had failed. Poor old Father, poor old Kester. Very sad.

Thomas said the agent was making a balls-up of everything in sight, but then Thomas would. He was having a hard time adjusting to civilian life and had more than once asked my father to push for his reappointment as the Oxmoon estate manager. My father had tried but Kester had procrastinated. My father said gloomily that Kester was probably in the middle of a novel and not in the mood to consider the real world.

I slogged on in that real world and wished to hell that I too could escape and spend all my working hours listening to music or playing the piano, but it was as much as I could do to get half an hour a day to myself. I was worried about the estate as usual. Growing potatoes had nearly driven me mad, so I'd cut that out and concentrated on the cows. I was now obsessed with silage and was determined that it should solve the winter feed problem. No more bloody mangolds, no more time-consuming uneconomical hoeing. But silage can go wrong. I heard terrible stories. I was nervous. And as if these Home Farm worries weren't enough I had to take on the problems of Martinscombe which wasn't quite the paradise for sheep that my father had thought it was. As far as I could gather the sheep were half-starved in winter and all the methods for rearing them were fifty years out of date. Those sheep needed scientific feeding and new hygienic farm buildings, but I couldn't afford such expenditure. I was already reeling from the builders' estimates for putting Little Oxmoon in order after the Canadian occupation. More worries. Then to cap it all my car broke down. I knew why. It was because Bella didn't drive it properly. She wore out the clutch by not using the foot break and striking a balance instead between the clutch and the accelerator. I kept telling her not to do it but she never remembered, and when the car broke down we had a row—not a big row but certainly a brisk run-of-the-mill shouting match.

The big rows nowadays were about sex. She wanted it all the time and I liked it three or four times a week—and when I did it, I did it properly. I tried to explain to her that there was more to sex than just slamming away mindlessly every night, but she just said all right, if I preferred gala performances to mindless slamming, why not do the gala performance every night. I tried to explain that the whole point of a gala performance is that it doesn't happen every night, but it was no good. She hadn't the brains to be imaginative about sex; she was too childish to see the full possibilities of an adult game.

In the end I thought, Oh hell, anything for a quiet life, and slammed away every night, but that bored me. If you're trapped with a woman you dislike your only hope of avoiding tedium is to make an intelligent use of your sexual opportunities, and even then it tends to be an uphill struggle. I wondered how long it had taken my father to exhaust Constance's possibilities. I was sure now he couldn't have remained faithful to her, although I was equally sure he would have been gentleman enough to continue sleeping with her as a courtesy.

"Mummy was so unhappy," Francesca had wept, and I now knew the unhappiness hadn't ended with my father's return. She'd got what she wanted but what a Pyrrhic victory it must have been! All the sex in the world can't make someone love you. Love can't be made to order. I wanted to love Bella but I couldn't, not anymore. All I could do, like my father, was fuck and try to be kind.

In August I finally succeeded in letting Little Oxmoon to respectable tenants, and this cheered me up almost as much as Bella's new habit of going into Swansea once a week with Anna. After my car had cost a fortune to mend I'd forbidden Bella to drive for three months, and it was after this that Anna had generously offered to be her *chauffeuse* every Thursday in Kester's Daimler. They would set off after breakfast, have their hair done, lunch at the Claremont and do some shopping in the afternoon before returning home. That got rid of Bella for the whole day and meant I could lunch in peace at the piano.

The crucial Thursday dawned in early September. There were no premonitions, no portents. I spent the morning at Martinscombe where the vet was advising me about a parasite problem. Anna drove Bella to Swansea for their weekly spree. When I arrived home for lunch I read my *Daily Telegraph* in peace, told myself how awful the socialist government was and settled down to play the piano. It was such a treat to play when Bella wasn't around to interrupt me with her inane conversation. Having had no formal musical education I need unbroken concentration when I play because I have to hear each note clearly in my head before I can strike the right keys.

I enjoyed myself so much that day that I played until half-past two, far longer than I should have done. Then I left for the Home Farm. The rest of the afternoon passed in a flash, and it was after six by the time I returned to the house and found the boys playing Cowboys and Indians all over the drawing room. Nanny, who was obviously on the verge of giving notice, had gone to bed with a migraine and Bella had apparently disappeared.

"Where's my wife?" I said to the latest ineffectual nursemaid after I'd lined up the boys and threatened to wallop the first one who opened his mouth.

"She's not back from Swansea, sir."

I dispatched the bunch to the nurseries and phoned Oxmoon, but Kester had heard nothing from Anna. "I suppose the car's broken down," he said worried. "Thank God I've rejoined the A.A."

I refrained from saying how nice it was that he could afford the subscription. We hung up to continue waiting, and because my unexpected solitude came as a bonus I postponed my bath and sat down at the piano in my work clothes. I was just playing a Mozart rondo when the telephone rang.

I had had the telephone transferred from the hall to the drawing room so the bell immediately interrupted me. Leaving the piano I grabbed the receiver. "Hullo?"

"Would this be Mr. Henry Godwin?"

"Yes." I didn't recognize the voice. "Who—"

"This is the police in Swansea, Mr. Godwin. I'm afraid I'm calling to report a serious accident."

At once I saw it all—the coffin, the clergyman, the crowds in black at Penhale Church—I even, in a moment of unforgivable emotional extravagance, saw my children crying at the graveside.

Shock swept the strength from me so that I had to sink down on the nearest chair. To my horror I realized my prime emotion was relief.

"An accident?" repeated my voice.

"Yes, sir. A lorry was coming down the hill and its brakes failed. It caught the car just as the car came round the corner. The car didn't stand a chance. I'm so sorry, sir, the ambulance came straightaway but—"

"She's dead."

"Yes, sir. Killed instantly. But the other young lady, the passenger—"

"*What?*"

"—she's going to be all right. She's in hospital now and the doctors say—"

He went on talking and the world went on turning, that messy cruel chaotic world where people died who shouldn't die and Acts of God bludgeoned those who least deserved them. My unwanted wife had lived. Kester's cherished wife had died. That was the kind of horror that could drive a man mad.

Little Anna. Not sexy, not my type, but so bright and intelligent, always so full of interesting conversation, always so kind to Bella who must have bored her to tears, always so friendly to me although I'd made no more than a perfunctory response to her warmth. I thought of her courage. I remembered her walking up to Thomas to plead for Simon Maxwell; I remembered her showing no trace of nerves as she greeted Kester's guests in an environment that must often have seemed alien and intimidating to her. There'd been no question of Anna not being able to cope with her married life, no question of Anna not understanding her husband or failing to give him the love and support he needed. I thought how the family had looked down on her because she was plain and Jewish and middle-class. I thought how she'd put us all to shame.

Before I left for the hospital I drank some brandy, phoned Bronwen to relay the news to my father and told my housekeeper I'd been called out on business. Then I drove to Swansea. In the emergency ward I found Bella in a drugged sleep. She had a broken arm and pelvis. Something had ruptured or perforated, I forgot which. Of course the fetus had been wiped out.

I hung around making a nuisance of myself until someone was able to tell me that the lost baby had been female. Another little Melody gone to waste. I knew then that I wasn't meant to have a daughter.

There was no point in staying at the hospital since Bella was out of danger and certain to sleep for many hours, so after two more double brandies at the nearest pub I drove to my father's house. The only person I found there was Lance. Gerry was out being wonderful somewhere, Sian was at the pictures and Evan, my father and Bronwen had gone to Oxmoon to be with Kester. No doubt they had rightly judged his need to be greater than mine.

"Would you like some tea?" inquired Lance diffidently.

"Tea? For Christ's sake, bring me some whisky!"

As he scuttled away to fetch it I thought of Evan running errands for me long ago. "Good little serf," I said as Lance returned. I was by this time feeling light-headed with shock and drink. "But aren't you going to drink with me?"

"No thanks, I promised Mom I wouldn't touch liquor till I was eighteen."

A serious virtuous little serf—and not so little either. At seventeen he was almost as tall as I was, a thin angular young man, his fairish hair neatly cut and parted, his green eyes respectful behind his glasses. My father and Bronwen had had rows about his education because my father had wanted him to go to Harrow while Bronwen had said that as an unathletic foreigner he would be better off at the local grammar. He was. Having won a place there he already liked it so much that my father had been forced to acknowledge that the world hadn't ended just because a son of John Godwin's had gone to grammar school instead of Holy Harrow. Meanwhile the rows about Sian's education were still going on. I suppose even the happiest marriages have blind spots where the partners have trouble seeing eye to eye.

"Can I make you a sandwich, Harry?"

I was touched by this earnest sensitive concern for me and presently found myself confronted by half a chicken stuffed between two slabs of bread adorned with mayonnaise, lettuce and tomatoes. I was touched again.

"Thanks, Lance. You're a good chap. Best of the bunch. Not too keen on the others, quite frankly." That was when I realized I was in a dangerous and indiscreet condition. I bit deep into the sandwich to shut myself up.

"I wonder what's happening at Oxmoon," said Lance at last. I suppose he felt he had to make conversation.

"Yes. Poor old Kester, poor old sod. Very sad," I said dutifully, but then I thought of little Anna again and suddenly I had to abandon my sandwich. I drank some more whisky instead. "I'd have liked a wife like that," I said, and thought: Steady. Watch it. But all the while I was thinking Steady and Watch it my voice was saying: "He had what I really wanted. Same old story. Bloody hell."

My new serf was giving me a concerned look. I could see clearly now that he was the child who was like Bronwen. Evan's resemblance was only skin-deep.

"Harry, pardon me, but are you sure you wouldn't like some black coffee?"

"No, Lance. You're a good serf and who knows, you may even be magic too, but not even a magic serf can stand between me and my moral duty." I levered myself to my feet. "I've got to go to Oxmoon and tell Kester how sorry I am she's dead."

Lance looked most alarmed. "But Harry—"

"No!" I shouted. "Don't stop me! Must do the done thing. Offer condolences. Imperative." I poured myself one for the road. "Kester's grief is my grief," I said, "because he and I are one person—my cousin Kester, my double image, my other self—and I'm him and he's me and that's why I'm grieving now just as he is." Knocking back the rest of the whisky I headed for the hall.

"Hold it, Harry," said Lance urgently behind me. "Let me call Oxmoon and find out if anyone's there. For all we know they may be heading for a Swansea funeral parlor by this time—don't Jewish people have to be buried within twenty-four hours?"

I had no idea but I recognized that this was a sensible, intelligent serf. How lucky I was to have him. "All right, go ahead and phone." I sat down on the stairs and muttered: "Have to make sure Kester doesn't turn you into an acolyte."

"I'll use the extension in Dad's study," said Lance gently, but after he had disappeared some sixth sense, finely honed by my years of playing the part of Nerves-of-steel Godwin, told me my new serf was about to stab me in the back. Creeping to the study door I opened it a crack and listened.

"...gone? Oh God! Gee, listen, Evan, I've got Harry here drunk out of his mind and talking of invading Oxmoon to sob on Kester's shirtfront. When did Mom and Dad leave? If I can somehow keep him talking here till they get back..."

Traitor. Siding with Evan, another traitorous serf who had switched his allegiance to Kester. I was betrayed. Everyone was against me. Off with their heads.

710

I glided away. Lance ran out of the house as I roared off in my car but he was too late.

I drove to Oxmoon.

5

I

OXMOON LAY WAITING for me beneath the stars, those same stars which had apparently conspired to ordain that it would never be mine. Not just the world but the whole universe was against me. Bloody hell. Halting the car I hauled myself out, swayed and steadied myself. I knew I was drunk but I knew too that it didn't matter because I was benign. I wanted to show poor old Kester that I was a nice chap, just as he was, not merely bloody Cousin Harry who didn't give a shit. Kester had this coy trick, acquired from his favorite Victorian novelists, of never dropping a family title, and although he called me "Harry" to my face I knew he referred to me sardonically as "Cousin Harry" behind my back.

The light was on in the hall. Taking a deep breath to clear my head I walked up the steps but before I could ring the bell the front door opened six inches and my ex-serf looked out.

"Harry, it's good of you to come, but frankly—"

"Out of my way." I was definitely not in the mood to be crossed.

"Look, he just wants to be alone. He didn't even want Mom with him. I'm only here because Dad thought he shouldn't be entirely on his own."

"Fuck off and let me in."

"Harry—"

"Let me in or by Christ I'll bust the door down!"

"For God's sake! You're not in the commandos now! You can't force your way into a house that doesn't belong to you!"

I kicked open the door and forced my way in. "Kester!" I shouted as Evan was flung back against the wall.

"Harry—" Evan recovered himself sufficiently to grab my arm. "—you can't do this, you just can't do it—"

"I've done it."

"But—"

"I'm justified. I've got to tell that poor sod—"

"*Get out of here!*" screamed a maniac's voice from the half-landing of the staircase.

Both Evan and I jumped and spun to face him.

711

My first reaction was an automatic Poor old Kester, deep in melodrama as usual, but as soon as I saw him I realized he was round the bend, and the instant I realized this I understood that this scene was no synthetic melodrama hammered up by actors in their appointed roles but real melodrama, spewed out by real people whose feelings were so violent that they could barely be expressed in words. The effect still smacked of the footlights but everyone seemed curiously under-rehearsed. Real life is inevitably so much messier and less aesthetically pleasing than good art.

"How dare you come here!" stammered Kester. He was grayish-white, sweating like a pig, his pale eyes stark mad. "How dare you charge into my house as if you owned it!"

I was still drunk but not so drunk that I failed to realize I'd made a big mistake. I tried to put matters right. "Sorry, old chap, I know I'm pissed but it's because I'm so bloody upset. I actually came here to—"

"You came to crow over me! You came to gloat because my wife's dead and yours is still alive!"

I was so horrified I couldn't speak. I just gaped at him as Evan charged past me up the stairs and tried to take control of the situation.

"It's okay, Kester, leave him to me—"

"Out of my way."

"Kester—"

"I'm going to kill him."

"Get out, Harry!" shouted Evan. "Get out!" He was already struggling with Kester on the stairs.

"For Christ's sake, Kester," I said stupefied, "I liked your wife, I admired her, I envied you—"

"You despised me for not marrying a bloody nymphomaniac and breeding like a rabbit, you despised me for not fighting in the war, you despised me for getting in such a mess in '39, but I'm not tolerating your contempt anymore, I'm going to wipe you out, I'm going to kill you..."

I suddenly realized he meant what he said.

I backed away. Then I began to run. Of course I could have knocked Kester out if I'd allowed him a fight, but one really can't go around knocking bereaved men senseless. That's not the done thing at all.

Would the car start first go? It did. I drove away just as Kester burst out of the front door in pursuit, but my escape was so narrow that when I reached the Manor I was sick into the nearest bush. After that, feeling very very shocked and very very sober, I made myself some black coffee and I was still slumped at the kitchen table an hour later when my father arrived from Swansea.

"But you must have realized you'd be the last person he'd want to see!"

"But I was benign. I was benign but he couldn't see it. He just looked at me and saw horrors."

"But my dear Harry—"

"Father, he's crazy. He's stark staring mad. He wants to kill me."

"Well, obviously he was thoroughly overwrought and didn't mean what he said—"

"Wrong. He meant it. He's mad as a hatter."

"Oh, for Christ's sake pull yourself together!" shouted my father who was never at his best when the subject of insanity came up for discussion. "The boy's merely distracted by shock and grief! Of course he's not mad!"

"I'm sorry, but I've had a shock, I mean an awful shock, absolutely bloody—"

"I know, I know, but you must pull yourself together and stop making these absurd statements!"

"Father, you just haven't the slightest idea what's going on here—"

"Well, whatever's going on I refuse to admit it's insanity!" cried my father who sounded manic enough himself by that time. "I won't have it! I draw the line!"

So that was that. No insanity. Any possibility of such dangerously unorthodox behavior had been terminated and we were now all officially in a state of *compos mentis*.

"What's going on here," said my father, somehow managing to speak in a formidably rational voice, "is that there's been an appalling tragedy and that both you and Kester are in a state of shock. Let me telephone Oxmoon and find out if Gavin Warburton's still there—it's obvious that Kester's not the only man in the parish of Penhale who needs a sedative tonight."

"Nonsense, I've nerves of steel, I'm tough as old boots. Now, look here, Father, I don't want to go on and on about this but I don't think you should turn a blind eye to Kester's behavior just because you find the subject of insanity distressing. The plain truth is that I'm locked up in the Gower Peninsula with a maniac who wants to kill me, and—"

"*Will you for God's sake stop talking like a lunatic!*"

"But Father—"

"All right!" said my father fiercely, somehow getting himself under control again. "All right! You're locked up in the Gower Peninsula with Kester—but you don't have to be locked up with him, do you? You know damned well that I've got the key that sets you free—what about those lands in Herefordshire!"

I felt as if I'd just fallen through a trapdoor. Was I now—after all I'd gone through—meekly going to submit to being dispossessed just because Kester had turned himself from a jealous neurotic into a raving lunatic? Not bloody likely! I wasn't going to let my life be ruined by that sodding freak! Not a chance.

"I'm so sorry," I said glibly to my father, "I do apologize for being so melodramatic and emotional—" Just like Kester. Christ! Have to snap out of that one and snap out of it fast. Time to play the Great English Public School Game again.

Stiff upper lip. A casual, nonchalant manner. The Done Thing glorified. Every unbreakable rule not only unbroken but buffed to a high luster.

"Of course you're quite right," I said, continuing to speak in a very calm, very soothing voice. "Kester and I are just suffering from shock, that's all, and actually the truth is I feel desperately sorry for him. What a tragedy! Can't see how he's ever going to recover."

That was an interesting thought. What happened to estates where the owner went permanently round the bend?

Oh no, I wasn't going to be evicted to Herefordshire! Absolutely not! I was going to stick around in Gower to see what happened next. After all, if poor old Kester, poor old sod, wound up certified, all the family would have to rally round to save Oxmoon, and how could I do my bit to help if I were bogged down miles away in Herefordshire? I mean, I had to stay, didn't I? It was almost my moral duty. In fact, it *was* my moral duty, I could see that clearly now. It was the right thing—indeed the only thing—to do. . . .

Typical, wasn't it? The story of my life.

I could have stopped—but I went on.

III

The next thing I knew I was toying with the fascinating notion that Kester might commit suicide.

It was the funeral which gave me that idea. Despite Anna's Quaker leanings she was buried according to the rites of the Jewish faith, and of course Kester couldn't let the ceremony pass without seizing the opportunity to create awful scenes. I'd never before realized what a bore Hamlet must have been when they tried to bury Ophelia. Naturally I didn't attend the funeral, but hair-raising reports filtered back to me not from my father, who preserved a humane silence, but from my cousin Elizabeth Bryn-Davies.

After the funeral the melodrama continued unabated when Kester burned the Oxmoon summerhouse to the ground. I heard later—again from Elizabeth who liked to gossip—that he had made love to Anna there in the back room on the day before her death and he just couldn't stand to be reminded of this last happy memory of her. I automatically thought, Poor old Kester, poor old sod, but my chief interest in the story lay in the fact that he could get it up. I even wondered for the first time if the marriage had been childless because of some deficiency in Anna.

The main result of Kester's arson was that he allowed his brother Declan to lead him away to Dublin where he had a complete nervous breakdown and was confined to a mental hospital. My father got the power of attorney; Thomas got his heart's desire, reinstatement as the estate's manager, and I got nothing—as usual—despite my loyal offer to help in the name of family solidarity, but having managed to convince my father that I was now sanity personified I didn't dare let a single word of complaint pass my lips. I didn't even dare ask for a prognosis of the future but fortunately on this occasion Thomas was far less overpowered by my father's personality than I was.

"Supposing Kester never comes back, John?" he said hopefully. "Supposing he has to stay in the loony bin?"

"I should think that's most unlikely," said my father, "and personally I have no doubt that he'll recover. He's as resilient as Ginevra, and look at the tragedies she survived! Besides, with Anna dead Oxmoon will be doubly important to him and he'll be very anxious to return."

This struck me as a shrewd observation. I could just see Kester turning Oxmoon into a shrine to Anna.

"No chance of him committing suicide?" said Thomas, refusing to abandon hope. I had a sneaking admiration for his monstrous honesty.

"According to Declan," said my father, "suicide's never been mentioned. Declan suspects Kester has too many books he wants to write before he's willing to contemplate death."

"Hell, I thought writers cut their throats all the time!"

"Perhaps they have to run out of inspiration first."

Kester wouldn't run out of inspiration. I foresaw years of teeming creativity ahead.

"And anyway," said my father, deciding he had permitted Thomas to be outrageous for long enough, "I can't think why you're so keen for Kester to depart for the next world because the truth is that if he dies we'll both be excluded from the estate. He's made a will in favor of little Owen Bryn-Davies, and I'm not among the trustees."

Thomas nearly had apoplexy. I kept my mouth shut and tried not to explode with bitterness. My cousin Elizabeth's son was a fat child of nine whose sole interest in life appeared to be ice cream. I thought of Hal who was tall, straight, slim, athletic, clever and handsome, and experienced one of those rare moments when I realized what parenthood was all about. I forgot he was ill behaved, noisy and tiresome. All I could think was that Oxmoon was barely good enough for him.

However before I could settle into this unlikely role of doting father, Bella returned from hospital and lapsed into the deepest depression. As the result of her injuries she had been advised to have no more children, and in a private conference with me the gynecologist advised that she should be sterilized once she had fully recovered from her ordeal.

Meanwhile the ordeal dragged on. Melody wasn't going to come back. Bella lost interest in sex. What was the point, she said listlessly, when nothing could come of it? The boys ran wild, the house was a mess, Nanny and the housekeeper gave notice. In desperation I sent an S.O.S. to Teddy, and delighted to have another serious problem to fix she rushed down to sort us out.

After twenty-four hours she presented her report to me. We were in the drawing room after dinner. The boys were in bed. Bella was crying somewhere as usual. Teddy and I were drinking whisky and chain smoking.

"Forget the sterilization," she said bluntly. "She couldn't take the fact that she'd

715

never get pregnant again, and then she'd go nuts—really nuts, I mean, much worse than she is now."

"But what's the alternative?"

"Go on as you are. I've pointed out to her that no contraception is ever one hundred percent effective. After a while that fact's bound to sink in, she'll start to hope and then she'll feel sexy again."

"Seems inconceivable."

Teddy gave me a shrewd look and said, "Let me talk to Gavin Warburton. I'll ask him to recommend a psychiatrist."

"She'd never see one."

"Oh, you British are so dumb about psychiatrists! But they really do help people—why, look at Kester! He's out of hospital now and able to live quietly with Declan."

But Bella shied away from all thought of a psychiatrist and in the end Teddy had to get her back on her feet single-handed. I kept on slogging away, working so hard that I didn't have time to dwell on the fact that I was getting no sex, and every time I wanted to go into Swansea for a quick fuck I got drunk to stop myself. The war had left me with a profound distaste for quick fucks. I wouldn't have minded a quiet affair with some saint who would have died rather than give me a moment's anxiety, but there was no time. I was either out on the land or looking after Bella or yelling at all those noisy little brutes I'd fathered in a fit of mental aberration. The dust began to settle on the piano.

Slowly Teddy coaxed Bella to take an interest in her appearance again, and slowly Teddy managed to convey to her that husbands couldn't be expected to behave like dedicated monks forever. It took Bella some while to realize she wasn't the only one who was having a rough time but when the penny finally dropped she fell into a fever of insecurity. I suddenly found myself offered sex morning, noon and night by a wife who was busy dieting herself back into all her smartest clothes.

"I'll have to use something."

"It's all right. I've accepted that now. Sorry I've been so stupid."

Teddy slipped back to London. Bella and I toiled on.

"Oh Harry, you do love me, don't you? Harry, do you still want me? Do you still think I'm sexy? Oh, say you love me, say it..."

I said it. I would have said anything just to put an end to all those bloody questions. But I was so glad to have sex regularly again that I didn't even mind the tedium of using sheaths.

"Harry, I know those things are an awful bore for you and I don't want to keep making you use them, you're bound to get tired of me if I do, so I've decided to get a Dutch cap. Everyone has Dutch caps nowadays and I've asked Eleanor and she says they're easy. Thomas can't feel it—he doesn't even know she's got one. So if I did get a cap...well, it would be much nicer, wouldn't it?"

This was unarguable but I went with her to the gynecologist to make sure everything was all right. The gynecologist said yes, jolly good idea to have a cap, why not. While the thing was fitted I sat in the waiting room and read an elderly edition of *Country Life*.

Bella emerged looking pale but swore all our problems were solved. There was a nice little shelf inside and the cap just slotted in. Easy. A bit messy and tedious, but once it was in you could forget all about it.

I said to the gynecologist, "Are you sure she understands everything?"

He was sure. He had given her the printed instructions he gave to all his patients who adopted this form of contraception, so even if she forgot what he had said she could always refresh her memory.

Bella and I went to the nearest pub and had a gin-and-French apiece.

"Bella, are you quite, quite sure you can cope with this? Because if there's any doubt in your mind—any doubt whatsoever—we'll go on as before."

"Oh no, Harry," she said earnestly. "I've no doubts—I'm happy as a lark and absolutely confident!"

She got pregnant straightaway.

IV

By that time it was the March of 1947 and we were emerging from one of the worst winters in living memory. Many of my sheep had died. The milk yield had dropped. All the pipes had burst in the dairy. In the fuel shortage we had run out of coal. In short, life was a frozen hell and when Bella told me her pregnancy had been confirmed the news seemed like the last straw.

"I might have known you'd never be able to cope!"

"I couldn't help it, I couldn't help it—"

"No? Can you swear to me you used the damned thing every single time?"

She swore but I knew she was lying. That was when I lost my temper and she broke down utterly.

"Sometimes I didn't like to ask you to wait until I'd put in—I was afraid you'd get impatient—go to another woman—"

"I wish to hell I had. Anything rather than this."

Hysterics. Misery. Rage. Despair.

That demon contraception. That devil reproduction. Wrecking marriages, ruining lives, causing untold agony and suffering.

She refused to go back to the gynecologist, because she was afraid he'd think her a fool. But I somehow got her back to Dr. Warburton. The great advantage of Warburton, who was the best kind of family doctor even though he was getting long in the tooth, was that he knew about Melody. I'd realized by this time that no one who didn't know about Melody had a hope of understanding what was going on.

"Bella, I do understand, I promise you I do..." Warburton was lean and grizzled, like an elderly greyhound; he had a gentle insistent voice and kind persuasive dark eyes. "...but for your own sake I must advise you not to continue with this pregnancy."

"I can't kill Melody. I can't do it, I can't."

I put my arm around her and tried to sound as gentle and insistent as Warburton. "Bella," I said, "this baby isn't Melody. Melody's dead. Even if this baby's a girl it won't be Melody. It's no good risking your life to achieve the unachievable."

"I'll be all right. But I must have her."

This sort of talk continued for some time before Warburton said, "The risk's too great, Bella, and it's not fair on the living to take it. Think of Harry and your boys. You don't want them to suffer, do you?"

Bella began to weep. "I'm not going back to that hospital. I'm not going back to that horrid gynecologist."

This looked like the thin end of the wedge. Warburton and I exchanged glances.

"Look, Bella"—Warburton spoke with great care—"I think I can arrange this with a doctor I know who's in charge of a private nursing home in Swansea. I expect you've heard of it. It used to be called the Home of the Assumption, but it's called Assumption House now and it's not run by nuns anymore. I don't think you'd find it such an ordeal to be there for a few days and of course no one need know why you're there—you can just tell your friends that I'd advised you to take a rest."

"For my sake, Bella," I said. "Please. I don't want to end up a widower like Kester."

As soon as the words were out of my mouth I knew she was going to die. I felt the color drain from my face. "Christ, Bella—*please!* You can't die, you've got to live, I couldn't stand it if you died—"

How would I ever live with the guilt? I'd been criminally irresponsible, assuming she could cope with the burden of contraception, and it was my fault she was pregnant. If she died in childbirth I would have killed her, but I didn't want Bella dead—it was our marriage, not her life, that I wanted to terminate. I somehow had to keep her alive for the divorce court.

"Bella, I love you—please, please do as Dr. Warburton says—"

"Do you really love me, Harry?" Tears were streaming down her face.

"I love you."

"Then I'll do it. You mean more to me than anyone, Harry, more even than Melody."

I wondered if anyone had ever died from pure guilt before. I felt as if I were fatally ill.

Later I said to Warburton, "She'll be all right, won't she?"

"Oh yes, it's actually a very simple operation."

But not so simple when your reproductive organs have been messed around by a car smash. Warburton did write a warning letter but after a preliminary examination the doctor at Assumption House decided that the old boy was huffing and puffing about nothing. One does occasionally hear of these young doctors who fancy a spot of surgery and think they're God. But this one was due for a particularly vile disillusionment because Bella's case turned into an abortionist's nightmare. The operation began but the recent wounds ruptured and while the doctor and the nurses all fought to save her she bled steadily to death on the operating table.

V

Warburton was appalled to hear there had been no blood on hand for a transfusion. He said he'd never have let Bella go there if he'd known. The poor old fellow was beside himself with distress. I felt sorry for him.

"It wasn't your fault," I said. "She was fated. I knew she was going to die no matter what we did. I knew it."

I had sunk into that sodden form of shock which resembles an alcoholic stupor. I was resigned, untalkative, barely aware of my surroundings. Warburton had gone with me to Assumption House. I hadn't yet got around to thinking I could sue everyone in sight for negligence, but in fact I never did go to law in revenge. There seemed no point. Bella was dead and nothing could bring her back.

Eventually I was taken to see her. No pink-and-white skin anymore. It was an ashen color. But the shining mouse-brown hair was the same. I stroked it. Then I held her hand for a moment but my mind was empty. I was reminded of how I had felt during the war when a comrade had died. The anger and grief came later but at first all one saw was the void.

I was in the void and I had forgotten how bleak it was, with all emotion absent and nothing in my mind except an absolute awareness of the end.

When I left the nursing home the only person I wanted to see was Bronwen so I asked Warburton to drive me to my father's house. Warburton was worried about me but I said I was used to death, I could manage, I certainly wasn't going to have a nervous breakdown like bloody Kester. I didn't say "bloody Kester," of course. I kept it dignified and said "my cousin."

Looking more worried than ever Warburton drove away and I was left to find my magic lady.

No one seemed to be at home. Presently I gave up ringing the doorbell and reviewed the list of possible occupants. Evan was away in London reading theology at King's, Gerry was up at Oxford—naturally he'd won his bloody scholarship—and Sian was away at her new school, Bedales, which represented her parents' attempt to compromise between a socially acceptable girls' public school and a progressive coeducational environment. That left Lance, but it was early in the afternoon and he was almost certainly not home yet from the grammar. My father would be out either playing golf or adorning his latest boardroom. That left Bronwen except that it didn't because she wasn't there. I sat down on the doorstep to wait, and after five minutes she returned with some dry cleaning.

Some unknown time later I was sitting at the kitchen table in front of my third cup of tea and saying, "I want to grieve. If I grieve it'll mean I loved her and then I won't have to feel so guilty. I want to grieve but nothing happens."

And Bronwen said, "There is no timetable for grief. Grief isn't a train which you catch at the station..."

She went on talking, and the heavily accented English words sank softly deep into my consciousness like feathers falling from a great height. I couldn't take in what she said but I liked to listen to the rhythms of her speech because they were so soothing. Then I realized I was understanding more than I thought I was because I could discern the shape of her meaning. I could see the circle of time, and in the middle of the circle a piano was playing, the piano of memory, sending notes ricocheting from one side of the circle to the other.

"...and you'll hear her echo in time."

But I was already hearing it. I saw the child who had talked of raising the Devil on Rhossili Downs. I saw us running along the beach and laughing in the dunes and drinking lemonade in the potting shed.

"I suppose I'd have been driven to divorce her in the end," I said, "but perhaps I could only have faced it if I'd met someone else I wanted to marry... but I never did, did I, and now I daresay I never shall."

"Why do you say that?"

"Oh, I'm not very clever with women, Bronwen, not really. I can never work out what to do with them outside the bedroom, I can't talk to them at all."

"You're talking to me."

"You're different. You're magic. I suppose the truth is that I want to marry someone just like you, but how am I ever going to find a second magic lady? I can't believe she exists." I was dimly aware that I was talking like a Freudian casebook, since I regarded Bronwen as my mother, but luckily Bronwen never bothered with people like Freud; she was much too busy being sensible.

"I'm not magic, Harry!"

"Oh yes, you are. You're magic because you know what all this means while I'm floundering around in a black fog and catching occasional glimpses of something unspeakable."

"You're circle's clouded," said Bronwen in her best matter-of-fact voice, "but that's normal after a tragedy."

"Perhaps... But Bronwen, I'm haunted by the thought that Bella was fated, that there was nothing anyone could have done to save her, and that's a terrible thought, isn't it, because it implies a preordained and inescapable future."

Bronwen said without hesitation, "I agree Bella was fated, but not in the way you fear. In our lives there are choices which have to be made, and our freedom to choose means we have at least some control over our fate. Bella chose, either consciously or unconsciously, to become pregnant again, and that was *her* choice, not the choice of some cruel god in charge of a preordained future."

"But she had no real freedom to choose! She made the choice as the result of what happened to her when she was thirteen!"

"Yes, but don't you see, she didn't have to live the rest of her life in the shadow of what happened to her when she was thirteen! She could have chosen to live her life differently but the truth was she just didn't have the will to ring the changes—as I did, for instance, when I went to Canada and escaped from a situation that was destroying me."

"You mean—what you're saying is—"

"I'm saying that the circle of time is full of little circles and those little circles can be prisons, people can be locked up in them without the will to force their way out. That's what happened to Bella. She was locked up in this circle with you, just as you were locked up in it with her. You knew that if she stayed there she'd die but your will alone wasn't sufficient to save her and so she was fated, fated to remain strapped to the wheel of her fortune and spun on to the death she couldn't avoid."

I was mesmerized. This was it. This was my magic lady working at full steam. She spoke in the brisk sensible voice of someone who describes an absolute reality, and even the most hardened cynic would have found it impossible to sneer.

I took another deep breath. "Bronwen, there's something else I must talk to you about. Bella's isn't the only circle I've been sharing. I'm sharing another one that's far, far more sinister."

"So I've noticed," said Bronwen, "but sharing a circle needn't be sinister and it needn't be unusual either, far from it—people live their lives and other people weave in and out and make patterns there. That's normal."

"This isn't normal, not by a long chalk. In fact sometimes it scares me though I'm not sure why it should."

She looked steadily at me. "You're talking about the circle you share with Kester."

"Yes. He doesn't just weave in and out. He's there all the time. His circle's my circle. We're...how did you put it just now—"

"You're both strapped to the same wheel of fortune."

"Yes, it's as if..." But I couldn't say it was as if we were one person. That really did sound too neurotic.

"...as if you were one person," said Bronwen, treating this as a perfectly rational statement. "But no, that's almost certainly an illusion caused by the fact that you feel the circle's not big enough to contain you both."

"But what do I do to expand it?"

"I don't know, Harry. I'm not a fortune teller. Nor would I dream of telling you how to run your life. The choice is yours."

We were silent for a time.

"I could go to Herefordshire now," I said at last. "Now Bella's dead I could leave Gower and start afresh in a new circle."

Bronwen said nothing.

"I think I'll have to give that very serious consideration," I said. "Yes, very serious consideration indeed. And so I will. But not just at the moment. Later."

And there I went again.

I could have stopped. But I went on.

VI

Bronwen came home with me to help with the children, but she said I had to tell them the news myself. I panicked, said I couldn't, but she was stern with me and said the one thing I could still do for Bella was to look after her children and try to be a good father.

That trapped me. I felt myself being locked up in yet another circle, this time with those four wretched little boys, and this time I knew I was never going to have the will to get out. Guilt is an all-powerful jailer.

Well, we got back and I told Nanny who looked appalled and tried to offer me some conventional words of sympathy but I couldn't stand that so I got rid of her, rounded up the boys in the nursery and tried to say what Bronwen had told me to say but I got in a muddle and made a mess of it and wound up saying, "Christ, I'm so sorry," which certainly wasn't in Bronwen's script. What a hopeless father I was! In fact I knew now that I'd had no business becoming a father at all. I'd only done it to keep Bella occupied—and to show certain people how successful I was at reproduction.

Four bright-eyed, pink-cheeked, noisy boys became as quiet as little white mice. Then after a long interval someone gave a sob, and the next moment they were all bawling at the top of their voices. Poor little devils, I was so sorry for them but what did I do next? In despair I shouted for Bronwen, and once she had come to my rescue I retreated at last to the piano to put myself beyond the reach of my pain.

VII

The funeral went off without a hitch. I'm good at funerals. My father told me once that Uncle Robert used to survive them by privately reciting classical verbs, and I had always found this a most useful trick for keeping the horrors of ritualized death under control.

I embarked on the Latin conjugations.

No point in thinking of Bella dying in her twenties as the indirect result of our childhood tragedy, no sense in thinking of my part in putting her in that bloody coffin burdened with stinking flowers. Better just to say she was fated and recite *amo, amas, amat* or—more efficacious still since they required deeper concentration—all the tenses of *fero, ferre, tuli, latum*. Once I started remembering how I'd abdicated the responsibility of birth control I might as well have booked myself into the nearest lunatic asylum and asked for its best padded cell.

Except for Kester all the family dutifully turned up at Penhale Church and admired my performance as the model widower. Kester, who was still living quietly with Declan in Dublin, sent a telegram. It read: LETTER FOLLOWS PLEASE DON'T DESTROY IT UNREAD GENUINELY SORRY KESTER.

I was too busy ordering a coffin to give more than a passing shudder at this threat to communicate with me, but after the funeral a chunky envelope arrived bearing an Irish stamp and addressed to me in Kester's flowery handwriting. I couldn't face opening the letter immediately, but after I had collected a prescription from Warburton and after I had taken two of the new soothing pills doled out by the chemist, I summoned my shredded nerves of steel and ripped open the envelope. Inside was a single sheet of large white typewriting paper. I pondered on its significance. Was it indicative of a fantasy, like his novels, or merely of a businesslike approach? I didn't know but I shuddered irrationally.

My dear Harry . . .

Odd how we all addressed each other as "dear" on paper. Sinister.

. . . I'm sorry about Bella. Please accept my sincere sympathy and believe me when I say I'm not using the word "sincere" as a formality. I know better than anyone what it means to lose one's wife as the result of a tragedy—and this leads me, of course, to apologize for those terrible things I said to you after Anna's death. The shock and grief had driven me mad, but I'm better now and certainly well enough to hope that you can forgive me. How curious it is that we should lead such parallel lives . . .

I dropped the letter and headed for the whisky decanter. Then I remembered that Warburton had told me not to drink when I had taken the pills. Bloody hell. Scrabbling on the floor, I retrieved the letter.

. . . parallel lives, both born in the same year, both with older brothers who died young, both marrying before we were twenty-one, both becoming widowers within months of each other. I suppose these coincidences have no deep significance but I can't help feeling they should draw us together, not drive us apart. Looking back I fear the gulf between us has been largely my fault; I've been very unjust to various members of my family in the past, but I shall never forget how kind everyone was after Anna's death. Even you wanted to be kind, I can see that now. In short I think it's time I abandoned my paranoia, turned over a new leaf and gave my poor long-suffering family a respite!

Anyway, it's because my attitude to the family has changed that I shall now venture to hope that we may become more at ease with each other in future. Bosom friendship is of course too much to hope for (the very idea no doubt sends identical shivers down our spines) but why can't we be casual acquaintances who can smile and say hullo to each other without having apoplexy? Let's dispose of the ghastly charade Aunt Teddy invented in which we meet for a drink and end up talking idiotically about religion in a muck sweat of panic! Let's instead just accept each other's presence in the parish of Penhale and talk about how frightful the weather is if ever we bump into each other. I think we could get along very well on that basis; it would certainly take the melodrama out of our peculiar Doppelgänger situation . . ."

Doppelgänger. The double. The mirror image. No reader hypnotized by a master novelist ever turned the page so quickly as I turned over Kester's letter to find out what he had written on the other side.

. . . and besides, I'd like to be on speaking terms with you so that I can see your boys now and then. Don't worry, I've got over my jealousy that you've got four sons and I've got none. Curiously enough it was Anna's death that helped me to

723

come to terms with this problem, because once I knew I had no wife—and of course I'll never remarry—I realized it followed as a corollary that I'll have no children. However I do like children so much, and if you could spare Hal for the odd hour or two occasionally I really would be very pleased.

I'll be returning to Oxmoon in time for Easter. I don't think I'm quite strong enough yet to face a full-scale Godwin reunion, but if you want to drop in with Hal and say hullo I think I can just about manage to say hullo back. You needn't have a drink if you don't want to. We don't even have to talk. We can just exchange greetings and run in opposite directions.

This letter comes with best wishes for a happier future from your reformed (!!!) cousin KESTER.

My prime reaction was relief. I had been expecting hysterical effusions but instead I had received this calm, sensible, amusing and eminently rational letter. Incredible. Those psychiatrists in Dublin had evidently administered some sort of mental enema so maybe Teddy was right and psychiatrists weren't just a bunch of quacks. Paranoia. That was an arresting word. Obviously the medical term for a persecution complex. I made a mental note to look it up in the dictionary.

I liked the idea of him taking an interest in Hal. Well, why not? Of course Kester was never going to leave Oxmoon to any son of mine, but... Or would he? Maybe if I made an all-out effort... I was so carried away by the idea of Hal inheriting Oxmoon that I seriously contemplated bosom friendship with my re-formed cousin Kester.

This fantasy lasted some hours, and the rash on my back quietened to such an extent that I took no more pills and was able to pour myself a drink before dinner. I was just adding soda to my glass when I heard Thomas's Hillman careering up the drive.

I had become very, very tired of Thomas. Since his reinstatement as manager of Oxmoon he had formed the tedious habit of dropping in at Penhale Manor regularly to drink me out of house and home as he conducted a monologue on estate management. I was continually tempted to tell him frankly that I couldn't afford to pay for his alcoholic excesses, but I didn't want a row. That would have meant trouble with my father, and trouble with my father was always a disaster which had to be avoided at all costs.

On the salver the water jug was empty, and filling it with whisky I hid it behind the curtain. That left the decanter one-fifth full and I could say it contained all the whisky I had in the house.

"Harry!" Thomas came bursting into the hall as I opened the front door. "Christ, old boy, what do you think's happened?" He was already heading for my study and the inevitable offer of a drink. "You'll never guess, never in a thousand years!"

Preparing for some story of a sow who had produced two dozen piglets in one litter, I showed a clean glass the decanter and reached for the soda siphon to conceal my sleight of hand.

"Make it a double," said Thomas, perhaps dimly aware that I had formed the habit of shortchanging him. "My God, I need a double after the shock I had this morning!"

"What happened?"

"I had a letter from Kester."

I nearly dropped the glass. I gaped. And somewhere, far away in the distance, the warning bell rang to tell that indefatigable survivor Nerves-of-steel Godwin that something unpleasant lay lurking below the horizon.

I said abruptly, "Why on earth should he write to you?"

Thomas at once produced a sheet of typewriting paper covered in flowery handwriting. "Read it," he offered, and added benignly: "Poor old Kester, perhaps I was a bit too hard on the sod in the past."

This was the equivalent of Hitler saying Churchill was a nice old chap when you got to know him. Too stunned to speak I read: *My dear Thomas, I feel that now I've recovered I should formally express my sincere thanks to you for looking after the estate in my absence. Uncle John informs me you've done your usual first-class job and I wouldn't like you to think that I'm not deeply grateful.*

My experiences since Anna's death last summer have made me realize how lucky I am to have such a loyal devoted family, and consequently I can't help but see I've done you much less than justice in the past. However perhaps we might meet on more friendly terms in the future because I can now frankly acknowledge that we're in a position where we can do each other a favor. You want to continue running the estate; I want to live in peace without having to worry about Oxmoon. So will you be awfully decent, bury the hatchet and agree to stay on permanently as manager after my return at Easter? I can see so clearly that my only hope of a tranquil life in future lies in giving you carte blanche *with the running of the estate.*

Of course you must have an increase in salary, that goes without saying, and if you feel you can accept my proposal I'll ask Uncle John to act as a mediator in negotiating a new figure. Meanwhile I send my best wishes and look forward to seeing you again soon. Yours, KESTER.

Looking up I found Thomas beaming at me with such childlike naivety that he seemed more like a schoolboy of fourteen than a hard-drinking thug past thirty-nine.

"Isn't that incredible?" he said sunnily as I handed the letter back to him.

"Incredible." Unlike him I spoke literally. I was thinking: One fattens pigs before sending them to the slaughter. But I checked that thought before it could blossom into paranoia. It would never do if *I* fell victim to persecution mania.

Nasty word, paranoia.

"Of course he's mad as a hatter," said Thomas, unaware of my neurotic thoughts, "but what the hell? So long as I'm running the place I don't even care if he ends up as gaga as my father—although of course Kester, being a secret queer, couldn't get up to all the tricks my father got up to. Did I ever tell you what John and I found in his bedroom after Milly ran off in '28?"

"Yes. Three times. But you usually wait till you're drunk before you trot it out."

"Christ, do I? I must be getting senile myself! Poor old Papa, I was damn fond

725

of the old bugger... hey, what's this? I asked for neat whisky, not neat pissing soda water!"

I somehow got rid of him but before I could meditate further on the situation I was diverted by the boys. It was their bedtime and Bronwen had suggested that I read them a story every night to prove I was still there even if Bella wasn't. This was something I could do. I couldn't sustain a nursery-level conversation but I could read. I sat on a bed, Humphrey on one knee, Jack on the other, Charles glued to my left side, Hal glued to my right. Everyone except me sucked his thumb, and I was almost tempted to suck mine too, just for old times' sake, to see if it had a soothing effect on me.

That night, the bedtime story concluded, I dined alone as usual and retired to the drawing room. Then I put my feet up, listened to Stravinsky and tried to work out what the devil my reformed cousin Kester was up to.

I knew that Thomas's letter was rubbish from start to finish. Kester, clever Kester, had judged his reader to a nicety and fed him no sentiment he couldn't swallow whole, but I wasn't Thomas and that taradiddle stuck in my gullet. In fact the very thought of Kester in his new role of family saint made me want to puke. *How lucky I am to have such a loyal devoted family!* he had scribbled with such winsome hypocrisy, and *I can't help but see I've done you much less than justice in the past,* he had added, fawning on the uncle I knew he would always despise.

So what was going on? Thomas might have no trouble dismissing Kester as an addled eccentric but I was beginning to see him as a very clever, highly unstable man, unstable enough to have abnormal thoughts and clever enough to conceal them. He was up to something, I had no doubt of that, and I was just wondering in incredulity how Thomas could have accepted his letter at face value when I suddenly realized that every one of the sentiments Kester had expressed there had been expressed—though much more subtly—in his letter to me.

Hurrying to my study, I grabbed the letter from my desk. Yes, here we were— the fond reference to the family, the humble plea for a new friendly relationship— but served up this time with the good-humored honesty which had so readily annulled my suspicions. The letter now struck me as being immensely clever. I told myself: "Never forget that this man's a writer." Like the rest of the family I had never taken Kester's scribbles seriously but perhaps we'd all made a big mistake. He was twenty-seven, twenty-eight in November, and he'd been scribbling away since he could hold a pen. Even if his stories were rubbish the likelihood was that by this time he would have acquired certain technical skills which enabled him to use words much as a ballet dancer uses music.

I remembered going to the ballet at Sadler's Wells. I remembered the sweeping leaps and bounds which had caught my eye, but in between these set pieces, as Constance had pointed out, lay the footwork so intricate that the audience was aware of little but a graceful flowing movement. Yet it was this subtle footwork which made the big leaps possible.

I took a look at Kester's footwork. I noticed the spare expression of condolences which floated effortlessly into the apology for our quarrel. I noticed how this apology, immaculately phrased with not a single misplaced word that might have upset me, blended seamlessly into the remarks on our parallel lives which he knew would lure me on into his further apology for our past estrangement. Liquidly, with an almost sensuous ease, the apology melted into an amusing paragraph in which he expressed the hope that we could re-form our relationship. How cunning! No mawkish talk, no rich sentimentality which he knew would alienate me. The whole paragraph was immaculate in its emotional discipline, and then at the end came the mention of the *Doppelgänger* to send me rushing over the page into the most mysterious paragraph of all—the lines in which he led me to believe, without actually promising anything, that he wanted to take a significant interest in Hal. After that he had tossed off a witticism or two in the penultimate paragraph in order to restore the good-humored tone which he knew I would find irresistible, and then produced another seamless blending, this time into a final farewell.

A masterpiece. But what did it mean? What in fact could it mean? Even if it meant he had some mad purpose in mind the doctors would hardly have let him out of the mental hospital if they had thought he was dangerous.

All the same...

A clever but unstable man. A neurotic.

Not to be trifled with under any circumstances.

Then I thought: Who am I talking about?

And when I glanced in the mirror at my reflection for one split second I saw Kester looking back.

Mad as a bloody hatter. I took two pills, drank two brandies, went to bed and passed out.

VIII

Kester arrived home a week later. I gave him two days to settle in and then I called at Oxmoon to say hullo, just as he'd suggested. Naturally I no longer believed he had any sinister purpose in mind—that was just me being neurotic— but I felt I had to see him to reassure myself that he was benign.

I took Hal with me, not merely because Kester had asked to see him but because Bronwen had said he needed special attention. He had been ill, vomiting and running a high fever. Warburton had said it was gastric flu but Bronwen had said it was grief and Bronwen was the one I believed.

I wondered what it could be like to be ill with grief at the age of seven. It was bad enough being ill with guilt at the age of twenty-eight. Despite the pills my rash was giving me hell again, and although I knew sex would soothe my nerves I shied away from it for fear it would make me feel guiltier than ever. One really can't go sleeping with other women directly after one's wife's funeral. Only a hopeless degenerate could be capable of such behavior.

As we arrived at Oxmoon I asked Hal how he was feeling but he assured me he was all right. Poor little devil. Ill with grief. I glanced at the shining mouse-colored hair and the fresh-looking skin he had inherited from Bella but it was at that moment, as concern drove me to examine his face intently, that I realized how unlike her he was. Bella had had a round chubby face with blunt heavy sensual features. Hal's face was thin, fine-drawn, and although he had my dark eyes his bone structure was different from mine. There was something about his jaw which reminded me of someone. Couldn't think who. Curious, those old likenesses which run through families like recurring trademarks. I knew I looked like my mother, but Hal was more like my father, more of a Godwin.

There had been no butler at Oxmoon since Lowell's death during the war, but a bossy parlormaid admitted us as though she regarded our call as an intolerable intrusion on her time and we were shown into the morning room. With a shudder I noticed that the Edward VII coronation mug had been placed in the most exquisite eighteenth-century curio cabinet. Perhaps the mug was Doulton or Worcester. Kester would hardly have retained it if it had been junk.

It was cold in the room and I was just starting to worry about the possibility of Hal developing pneumonia when Kester walked in. He looked well. His curious face with its lean masculine bones and soft feminine mouth was relaxed, and not for the first time I found myself thinking that with a better nose he would have been good-looking. There was something about that jaw inherited from Uncle Robert . . .

That jaw. Christ Almighty—

"Hullo, Harry! How are you?"

Had to pull myself together.

"Absolutely splendid, old chap. How are you?"

A strong, well-made but much too well-kept hand was being offered to me, and I saw the writer's callus on his middle finger, the emblem of the soft life I'd been brought up to despise.

"I'm feeling marvelous!" said Kester as we shook hands. "Couldn't be better!" Then he laughed and said with great charm, "Whew! Thank God we've got that over—now we can start talking about how awful life really is!" He stooped over my son. "Hal, I was so sorry to hear about your mum—I did feel for you so much because I could remember how frightful I felt when my own mum died. I cried and cried—imagine! And I was eighteen years old!—but I was glad I did because afterwards I felt better."

I expected Hal to find this speech as nauseating as I did but no, Hal was smiling painfully, and there was a grateful expression in his eyes.

"I felt better too after I'd cried," he confided, "but then I started being sick and I felt awful again."

"But you're well enough now for a treat, aren't you? My brother Declan has American friends who send him luscious chocolate biscuits, and I've brought some home with me."

"Real chocolate?"

"Real chocolate. One day, Hal, probably when you're quite old, rationing will end and you'll be able to buy as many sweets as you like and the shops will be full of fascinating things like pineapples and bananas—"

"Yes, I've heard of them. Is the chocolate milk chocolate or plain chocolate?"

We adjourned to the drawing room where to my relief I found a fire blazing. Kester and Hal were deep in a discussion about whether it was more stimulating to lick the chocolate off the biscuits first or whether the biscuits should be crunched up without being stripped. I could now see just how smoothly my serf must have been purloined in the past, and I had to tell myself very firmly not to feel jealous because poor old Kester, poor childless old sod, could talk to my son better than I could. Of course I could see by this time that I'd imagined the resemblance in the jawline. That was just me being neurotic again.

"Gin-and-French, Harry?"

I couldn't tell Kester that I was temporarily on the wagon because of my neurotic skin troubles. I had given up the pills but Warburton had told me that alcohol, heating the skin, could only act as an irritant, even though the immediate effect was to soothe the nerves.

"Wouldn't mind a quick one, old chap," I said. "Thanks."

"Not at all. Now Hal, what would you like to do while I have a chat with your father? Read? Write? Draw? I don't mind, it's up to you."

But Hal just sighed in bliss, his left hand clutching his glass of orange squash, his right hand already oozing chocolate, and said with a yearning I had never once anticipated, "Is there still a piano in the ballroom?"

IX

So he was like me after all, never mind the jawline and never mind damned Kester standing by to transform him into an acolyte. I at once resolved that he should have piano lessons at school. Why hadn't I thought of it before? It had never occurred to me. I'd just thought he banged the piano to give me hell, whereas all the time... I pictured endless discussions on the subject of Bach. I saw us at the Albert Hall, Sadler's Wells and Covent Garden. I envisioned myself as a battered bedridden old man with Hal being the perfect son and making sense of all that hell I'd gone through with Bella. In my head an emotional contralto accompanied by the full orchestra of the Royal Opera House was singing some richly sentimental piece of nonsense—"Softly Awakes My Heart" from *Samson and Delilah* perhaps, or else an aria from some horror by Puccini.

"Here's your gin-and-French," said Kester, recalling me to reality as Hal rushed off to the ballroom.

"Thanks." Still dazed at the thought of what a musical son might mean to me I forgot where I was and sniffed the glass, just as I had sniffed drinks in Italy during the war. Some of that Italian wine would have taken the paint off cars.

"It's all right," said Kester amused. "I've run out of cyanide so murder's not on the agenda today."

"Oh, don't be so bloody ridiculous!" I snapped, and then realized I'd sounded just as uncomfortable as if I really had suspected him of a poison attempt. I tried a lighthearted laugh but only sounded sheepish.

"Sorry!" said Kester breezily. "I didn't mean to drown you in facetiousness! Let's change the subject. Well, I'm all agog—what did you think of my letter?"

"Brilliant. So was your letter to Thomas."

Kester looked startled. "I didn't realize Thomas rushed to show you his correspondence!"

"No, I didn't think you'd anticipated that. Never mind, you've got us both eating out of your hand and thinking, Good old Kester, not such a bad old sod after all. But what happens next? Or aren't I supposed to ask?"

Kester laughed. "With any luck nothing will happen at all—I've got to write and that means I must have absolute peace. Hence the white flag waving feverishly on all fronts. I simply can't waste any more time being upset and unable to write just because I'm in a state about my family."

This was a very simple, thoroughly plausible explanation. I could feel myself relax.

"Couldn't you write in Ireland?"

"No. I tried but I felt mutilated, cut off from my roots . . . and from Oxmoon. I'm no good without Oxmoon. So I decided to come back, and as soon as I made that decision I knew I was better. A good nervous breakdown's very therapeutic, you know. I feel better now than I've felt for a long time."

"Good."

"Of course you probably think I'm mad as a hatter. Well, I was, after Anna died—madder than a hatter, in fact. Imagine burning down that summerhouse! Incredible! Oh, and by the way, I'm so sorry I said I wanted to kill you when you burst into Oxmoon that night. Awfully florid of me, wasn't it! And it wouldn't have been chic at all if I'd wound up hanged for murder—or would I have been 'detained during His Majesty's pleasure' at Broadmoor? Interesting point. Anyway you needn't worry—I did want to kill you at the time but that time's past, thank God, and I didn't kill you anyway so what the hell, have another gin. I seem to have absolutely wolfed mine."

We had another gin-and-French apiece. Kester started chatting about how awful funerals were and we wound up talking of Bella.

"My God, she was sexy," said Kester—I think we were on our third gin-and-French by that time—"and I can quite understand why you married her. I bet Thomas often thought he'd picked the wrong sister—Christ, poor old Thomas, no wonder he drinks, do you think he ever gets an erection? I'll bet he's too sodden most of the time, but if he ever does I wouldn't be surprised if he ejaculated neat whisky! Have another drink."

"Uh . . . well . . ."

"You're not really chums with Thomas, are you, Harry? You're such opposites—he's all talk and no action while you're all action and no talk! Poor old Thomas, he's pathetic, isn't he? I really feel quite sorry for him sometimes."

I tried to picture the size of the apoplectic fit Thomas would have thrown if he had heard this judgment but my imagination failed me. I accepted a fourth gin-and-French. I was beginning to be most entertained by this salty, good-humored stranger who was now my reformed cousin Kester. Who would have thought the old sod was capable of behaving like one of the boys? Wonders would never cease. I could see now that the nervous breakdown had done him a power of good.

"Of course I'm not chums with Thomas," I said. "I can't stand the damned sod. He invades my home, drinks my whisky and drives me up the wall. But Christ, if he ejaculates neat whisky I'd like to know about it, I'd follow him around with a bowl, it's about time I got some of my own back—although yes, I bet you're right, I bet he's usually too pissed to get it up. Ah, to hell with him; I wish he'd drop dead!"

"Couldn't agree with you more, old chap," said Kester, thoroughly sympathetic. "However at least he saves me the bore of looking for an agent. One must be thankful for small mercies, even if the mercy does come in the form of a shit with a pickled cock."

We laughed and laughed. It's amazing what extraordinary things seem amusing after four hefty slugs of gin gingered up with four hefty slugs of French dry vermouth.

But later when I was sober I thought, *Was* that Kester talking? And I just couldn't believe it. There was something odd going on, I knew there was, and I wasn't just being neurotic either.

Or was I?

I dragged out the medical dictionary which I had recently acquired out of a desire to find out more about my skin troubles, and eventually after much thumbing of macabre pages I found the entry PARANOIA. I read it. Naturally I had all the symptoms, but I always did, no matter which entry I read, so this meant nothing.

A common manifestation of paranoia was that you thought someone was trying to kill you. Well, I'd got over that one. I didn't seriously think Kester was trying to kill me.

But just what the hell was he up to?

No idea.

6

I

OVER THE following months various clues surfaced, but none of them were obvious and all might have escaped the attention of anyone save a certified paranoiac. My suspicions were also lulled by the fact that having shot off his two sinister epistolary masterpieces Kester appeared to sink into a blameless existence.

Scribbling made him reclusive and although he managed to face an occasional family gathering, only two cousins turned up at Oxmoon with any regularity. One was my ex-serf Evan, whose idealism Kester found appealing, and the other was Edmund's son Richard, now twenty-three, a brainless boisterous hulk who held some nominal position in Armstrong Investments. Kester told me that Richard made him laugh. Personally I find buffoonery tiresome but Richard had an indestructibly sunny outlook and I supposed that Kester in his more melancholy moments found this bouncy optimism attractive.

The only other people who saw Kester regularly consisted of a group of children whom he invited to tea during the school holidays. This group varied in size and composition but Hal was a founding member and so was little Owen Bryn-Davies. Kester also included the eldest Llewellyn child, probably out of sentimentality because she happened to be called Gwyneth. Kester had long been intrigued by the story of our great-grandmother Gwyneth Godwin, *née* Llewellyn, and after his return to Gower he announced his intention of turning this hoary old family myth into a novel.

My father was livid. I had long since realized that he was peculiar on the subject of his grandmother, and when Kester now tried to get to the bottom of this peculiarity during one of the rare family gatherings at Oxmoon I found myself listening with bated breath.

"I have absolutely nothing to say on the subject," said my father tight-lipped.

"Why not?" said Kester. "What have you got to hide?"—which was exactly the question I had never had the nerve to ask.

My father went white, said he had loved his grandmother and was determined to protect her memory from any vulgar inquiries from someone bent on a cheap tasteless exploitation of ruined lives. Kester's response was to say blandly: "But why should her memory need protecting? What did she do that was so awful— apart from taking a lover and compensating herself for a homosexual drunk of a husband?"

That rocked the entire family. A gasp rippled around the drawing room and I gasped just as loudly as anyone else because although Great-Grandfather Robert Godwin's homosexuality was known to us all it was by tradition never referred to. He was Robert Godwin the Drunkard, not Robert Godwin the Pervert, in the family folklore.

When my father could speak he said, "Let them all rest in peace. It's no good you trying to turn it into a conventional story with heroes and villains. You'll simply distort the truth."

"And what was the truth?" said Kester. I suddenly realized that where his writing was concerned he was like a tank. Short of blowing him up, no one could stop his inexorable progress towards his goal.

"The truth about my grandmother and Owain Bryn-Davies," said my father, "is that they were just two ordinary people who failed to draw the line."

"Fascinating," said Kester, and wrote something in his notebook.

My father lost his temper. Bronwen and Evan rushed to pour oil on the turbulent waters. The family gathering ended in chaos.

As the result of this scene Kester said soothingly to my father that he had shelved his novel on Great-Grandmother Gwyneth and had returned to work on another story with which he'd been toying for some time. This novel was never described and personally I didn't believe it existed. I thought Kester was probably still burrowing away at Great-Grandmother's legend.

Well, this was all very normal and even the row could be written off as an overheated example of family bickering, so I was gradually tempted to regard Kester as a harmless eccentric who had a penchant for rattling the skeletons in the family closet. It was only later that I came to recognize the pattern of his behavior; the horrors were always preceded by periods of deceptive normality.

However as usual I was diverted from Kester by my worries over the estate, although 1947 was a good summer and the Penhale Home Farm did well. But I couldn't get those bloody sheep right at Martinscombe. I had to buy new stock to replace the animals who had failed to survive the terrible winter but after I had bought the best sheep available to avoid bringing problems into the flock, the dry summer favored the blowflies with the result that although I dipped and dipped the poor sheep several of them died from infestation. And this was only one aspect of my problems. Prices were rising. So was taxation. The cost of my sons' education was raising its ghastly head as I made arrangements for Hal to go to prep school in the autumn. I wasn't exactly wondering where the next penny was coming from but I did spend much time plotting how I could squeeze more money out of my estate by cutting down labor costs—always the most expensive item in farm accounts.

Then in the summer of '47 I had a lucky break. Dafydd Morgan, Bronwen's son by her first marriage, turned up. After being rescued from his Japanese prison camp he had had to spend some months in a Singapore hospital, but eventually he was shipped home and wound up on Bronwen's doorstep. This was awkward. Dafydd had hated my father ever since Bronwen had become the scarlet woman of Penhale in the Twenties, and it was soon obvious that the two of them couldn't coexist peacefully under one roof. In an effort to ease Bronwen's distress I then offered Dafydd free room and board at the Manor in return for his help around the house and garden, and rather to my surprise, he accepted. Perhaps he thought he had made my father uncomfortable enough; or perhaps he was too fond of his mother to want to upset her further; or perhaps after his years as a prisoner Penhale Manor seemed overwhelmingly attractive to him despite its unhappy memories. I had no idea, but he was an extra pair of hands going cheap and so I decided his motives were unimportant to me.

He was two years older than I was and as small children we had been friends before class and education had raised insuperable barriers between us. He had become surly and solitary and once he was boarded out with his father's relatives in Cardiff I had seen little of him. But now I discovered his chief virtue: he was a trained mechanic and understood my new tractor far better than I did. Soon I found him so indispensable that I felt obliged to suggest I paid him a salary, but he said for God's sake no, he might lose some of his state benefits, so that was all right. I assigned him a large room in the attics and he kept himself to himself in the evenings. As time passed I realized he was one of the very few people who never got on my nerves, and considering the state my nerves had been in since the war this was no mean achievement.

However my nerves did improve later in 1947 when I had my second lucky break of the year and found a club in Swansea where I could meet a steady stream of ex-servicewomen who were all bored with civilian life and longing for a diversion. I diverted them. Probably the less said about this side of my life the better, but I did slowly begin to feel more normal. I had no intention of marrying again until I could find a woman who could communicate with me on levels other than the horizontal but since I myself was apparently unable to do anything with women except fuck them this paragon of womanhood proved to be as elusive as ever.

I was intelligent enough to know the fault was mine but not brilliant enough to know how I could change myself. Bronwen said all I needed was a little love and understanding. Wonderful. Don't we all. Meanwhile, as I waited to be loved and understood by some magic lady who didn't exist, I was grabbing all the sex I could get and becoming so tired of the limited possibilities afforded by the back seat of my car that I began to look around for some simple accommodation. When Dafydd told me a dilapidated cottage in Rhossili was up for sale, I scraped up two hundred pounds from my bank manager and bought it. I thought it would be a good investment for the future, for Gower was becoming increasingly popular with holidaymakers, and having put Dafydd in charge of the renovations I found the result was so successful that I only wished I had the money to invest in similar properties. However as I could now have sex in a decent bed again I was hardly in the mood to grumble just because I was too poor to become a property millionaire.

Meanwhile, languishing in celibate luxury at Oxmoon, poor old Kester, poor old sod, continued to entertain his little protégés and scribble away at his unpublished masterpieces while Thomas, that first-class manager, did all his hard work for him. But I was trying to swallow my jealousy of his ideal life because Hal, bright intelligent Hal who was doing so well at his piano lessons, was obviously far more congenial to Kester than little Owen Bryn-Davies. I still couldn't quite believe Kester would make Hal his heir but there seemed no harm in hoping.

I hoped.

Well, there we all were, jogging along happily enough, when suddenly at the Godwin family Christmas of 1947 Kester gave me the biggest fright I'd had since the war. He had invited me to his study to hear excerpts from his new record set of *The Messiah*, and as he changed the needle on the gramophone he asked me if Bella had been fond of music.

"No, Vera Lynn was her limit."

"Ah well, I'm fond of Vera myself—doesn't do to be a musical snob! Oh, and that reminds me, Harry...talking of Bella..." He paused to pick up a record. "...there's something that's been puzzling me for a long time. Did you and she ever have a daughter?"

A few seconds slid away. He was now looking me straight in the eyes. I looked straight back. Then I raised my eyebrows and did a double take. "What an extraordinary question, old chap! A *daughter?*"

"Yes, I realize it sounds mad. After all, if you'd had a daughter you'd hardly have kept quiet about it, would you? Not unless the circumstances were very peculiar." He casually put the record on the turntable.

"But what on earth gave you the idea that Bella and I—"

"It was something Bella said on the phone on the day Anna died—she rang up early to confirm the time that Anna was going to collect her in the car, and as Anna took the call in bed where we were having breakfast I was able to hear both sides of the conversation. Bella said that after their lunch that day she intended to use all her coupons to buy a completely new set of clothes for the coming baby, and when Anna suggested she might use at least some of Humphrey's old baby frocks again, Bella said, 'No, they're all blue and since I'm determined to have another girl the clothes have got to be pink.'"

He paused. At last I said, "Yes?"

"Well, it was the word 'another.' Anna and I both noticed it. She said she'd ask Bella about it later but then . . . she died. And I forgot all about it until the other day when I saw Humphrey in that blue siren suit he still wears. Then I thought, Yes, that *was* odd, and since my writer's curiosity had most definitely been aroused I thought I'd ask you about it. I'm sure," concluded Kester blandly, "there's a very simple explanation."

"Of course. Either you and Anna misheard, which seems unlikely, or Bella made a slip of the tongue." Some slip. "We never had a daughter." I tried to look as if I were losing interest in the subject.

"Well, no," agreed Kester, "I don't see how you could have done—and that, of course, was what I found so fascinating. If you'd had a daughter she must have been born before you were married yet I remember Bella saying clearly that before you returned to Gower in 1938 she hadn't seen you since she was thirteen."

"That's right, old chap. Some hellish children's party at the vicarage. Bella wore a pink dress with a white sash and spent her whole time sulking in a corner."

Kester had been about to set the turntable in motion but now he turned to look at me. "Oh, I remember that party," he said, "but Bella must have been younger than thirteen then—I was only twelve myself. When she was thirteen it would have been 1933, that awful year when Bronwen went to Canada."

"Awful's the word, old chap. Well, maybe I bumped into Bella then but I don't remember, I've blotted that whole bloody time out of my mind. . . . Now—what are we going to hear first? Spare me the 'Hallelujah Chorus'!"

We listened to "Comfort Ye My People." Or at least Kester listened. I just went through the motions.

When the record ended, I said musingly, "You know, that remark of Bella's was really very odd. The only explanation I can offer is that she used to pretend she had a daughter—it was a game we used to play, one of those stupid private jokes married couples so often share, and I suppose it helped to alleviate her increasing disappointment when she had boy after boy. She even had a name for this imaginary daughter. She called it Melody—if you can believe it!—because I was so fond of music."

It's wonderful how an injection of truth makes even the most preposterous story sound convincing. Kester's expression indicated that he felt the mystery was now entirely solved. "Ah, I see!" he said, turning over the record. "Well, there you are—I was sure there was some very simple explanation. It was stupid of me to get obsessive about the conversation just because it belonged to Anna's last hours—do forgive me."

I assured him he was forgiven, but as I turned away from him to light a cigarette I was hardly surprised to find my hand was shaking.

It had been a close call.

II

That incident was certainly unpleasant but it never occurred to me that it should rank as a warning sign. Yet after this conversation the unpleasant incidents, apparently disconnected, began to occur with increasing frequency.

It was now the spring of 1948. Thanks to the advent of my new adult serf Dafydd I was beginning to feel I had my life marginally in control, and the only outstanding cloud on my horizon was Thomas who was once again invading my home too often no matter how hard I tried to discourage him.

We finally had our long-delayed row over his consumption of my whisky and for a short blissful interlude he disappeared from my life; but my father, doing the done thing with lethal results as usual, was determined to reconcile us. Thomas turned up on my doorstep with a bottle of whisky and an apology. I felt morally obliged to be friends with him again but needless to say the friendship didn't last. To my surprise he accused me of influencing Kester against his son Bobby in order that Hal should be the perpetual guest of honor at Oxmoon. This was laughable. There was nothing wrong with Bobby, who was a pleasant unremarkable boy of twelve with a good eye for a cricket ball, but the truth was that Kester had never favored sporting philistines, and I could quite see why he found my son more interesting. I told Thomas to go away and spin his fantasies elsewhere.

More sulks followed and this time no bottle of whisky was put forward as a peace offering. Then I heard he was saying my dairy herd, which I had built up from scratch with great expense and care, had fallen victim to the dairy farmer's nightmare, contagious abortion. This was clearly untrue, since there had been no deterioration in the farm's milk yield, but nevertheless when I sent some heifers to market I could see the farmers shying away from them. I had to spend so much time and money engaging the vet to examine every single one of my herd to testify that they were free of infection that I told Thomas I'd sue him if he repeated the slander but Thomas was indignant, declared he'd never said a word against my bloody cows, he hated cows anyway, always had, in his opinion no cow could ever be half so absorbing as a piglet, a hog, a boar, a gilt or a sow. Equally enraged we hung up and I thought I'd heard the last of him but a week later he accused me of starting a rumor that his large whites were suffering from virus pneumonia—a hazard in pig farming which can have almost as dire consequences as contagious abortion in a dairy herd.

"Oh, for God's sake!" I said exasperated. "Why would I want to circulate stories that are obviously untrue?"

"You're out for revenge. You thought I'd started that rumor about your cows. I hadn't, of course—"

"I'm out for nothing but a quiet life, Thomas," I said, and slammed down the telephone receiver.

But it seemed that fate—or what was masquerading as fate—was determined to keep us at loggerheads. A month later I returned to the Manor from Martinscombe to find Thomas lying in wait for me in the drive. He was seething. He looked as if he'd had at least three whiskies. My heart sank.

"All right, let's have it," I said resigned, getting out of my car. "What's the new rumor I'm supposed to have started?"

He tried to hit me. That was stupid. I knocked him out. Then I remembered my father and realized with reluctance that I had to make an effort to reestablish the peace. Fetching a tumbler of whisky, I revived the sod, steered him inside the house to my study and dumped him into the nearest armchair.

"Now, look here, Thomas—"

"You bastard, how dare you say I'm always too pissed to get it up!"

One can't conduct a rational argument with someone in that state. I just said mildly, "Who did I say it to?"

"Bloody everyone! Richard says he heard it in Penhale!"

"So that oaf's back at Oxmoon playing the court jester again! Doesn't he ever do any work in that London job of his?"

"Don't try and change the subject! Richard went into the pub for a drink and he heard you'd said that Eleanor was divorcing me for impotence!"

"Impotence isn't a ground for divorce. Either Richard's practicing some particularly tasteless piece of buffoonery, which is quite possible, or else he's passing on someone else's lies."

"But—"

"Thomas, this may amaze you, but I'm just not interested in your sex life. And I'm not interested in gossiping either. I've got better things to do with my time."

"You bloody liar," said Thomas automatically, but the words lacked conviction. To cover his uncertainty he demanded, "Give me some more whisky."

I refueled him, remembered my father again and groped feverishly for a suitable olive branch of peace. "Look, old chap," I said, "of course I don't think you're impotent—in fact if you're free tomorrow night, why don't you come into Swansea with me? I'm taking a girl out to dinner but she's bound to know another girl who could make up a quartet, and then after dinner we can all go out to my Rhossili cottage and enjoy ourselves."

Thomas goggled at me. "So that's why you bought that cottage!" he exclaimed with touching naivety, and added, worried: "But what can I say to Eleanor?"

737

"Say you're having dinner with me in Swansea to celebrate the start of a new friendship between us."

He brightened. "That's an idea. Bloody decent of you, Harry, thanks a lot. As a matter of fact... well, Eleanor's not too keen on that sort of thing nowadays so I'm up the creek. I did think of looking around but... not so easy, is it? I'm very discriminating, you know—can't stand tarts or shady ladies. ... My God, Harry, your girl's not a tart, is she?"

"Of course not. Why pay for a cow when you can get milk through the fence?"

Thomas was so overcome by this proposition that I was again amazed by his lack of sophistication. I even wondered not only whether he'd been faithful to Eleanor despite his prolonged absence in the war but whether he'd been a virgin when he married. I poured myself some more whisky. It was hard work coping with an adolescent of forty-one.

"Suppose you do this sort of thing all the time," said Thomas wistfully, and then realizing he was giving himself away he moved to set the record straight. "Of course I used to as well before I was married. Do you remember Mrs. Wells?"

I remembered her very well. She had been the loyal housekeeper at Penhale Manor when my father had lived there with Bronwen. "I used to sleep with her now and then," said Thomas with an elegiac sigh.

"*With Mrs. Wells?* She must have been old enough to be your mother!"

"Yes, but she was a good sort."

"Oh, the best, I agree, but—"

"We were at Oxmoon alone together for a few weeks—it was after my father went crazy and Milly walked out. Then later when I was living at Little Oxmoon Mabel—Mrs. Wells—used to visit me on her day off." He sighed heavily again. "I wonder what happened to her. She went east, you know, after John and Bronwen parted, and she wrote a couple of times but I never wrote back. Poor old girl. Suppose she's probably dead by now."

"Probably. Thomas, talking of housekeepers... what happened to Milly Straker?"

"God knows, but you can bet *she's* alive and well somewhere—probably enjoying herself as a Mayfair madam touting the best tarts in town! Did I ever tell you... oh yes, I did. All that bloody perverted stuff John and I turned up. Disgusting."

I steered him away from the subject of my grandfather's sexual tastes which he evidently found so enthralling, and when I eventually managed to get rid of him we parted bosom friends. He said he could hardly wait for his night out. I began to wonder what on earth I'd let myself in for.

To cut a long story short we had a wild evening, although by that time I wasn't in favor of wild evenings and would have much preferred some sophisticated hours à deux; the difficulties of finding adequate privacy during the war had left me with a profound distaste for any sexual entertainment that could remotely be described as gregarious. However I didn't want to spoil anyone else's fun, so after the necessary formality of a quick dinner at a cheap Indian restaurant I drove us all to my cottage and dispatched Thomas and his new girlfriend upstairs to the double bed.

Unfortunately the second bedroom was still unfurnished but Dorothy and I put

738

the living-room sofa to good use, and in fact we were barely halfway through our entertainment when Thomas and his girl, who I think was called Irene, came clattering drunkenly downstairs to watch. I tried to go on strike to get some privacy but the two wretched girls, both of them stark naked, jumped on me and said they refused to let me be a spoilsport, so what was I to do? Of course we were all as tight as owls. Thomas, damn him, applauded occasionally but made no effort to join in. I thought his behavior went a long way to confirming the rumors of his impotence although the next day when I stripped the bed I discovered he hadn't been entirely idle; later he even told me he'd had the time of his life so presumably he at least didn't feel he'd wasted his opportunities.

Well, as I've said, I hadn't much time for that kind of frolic, so when Thomas suggested we repeated the session I turned him down. However since he was obviously dead keen to pursue Irene I did agree to lend him the cottage for an evening.

The next thing I knew I had Richard, Kester's jester, on my doorstep to ask if he too could borrow the famous double bed at Rhossili.

"No, you bloody can't!" I said much annoyed. "And how the hell did you hear about it anyway?"

"My dear Harry, it's the talk of Gower! The preacher at Penhale Chapel even called at Oxmoon yesterday and told Kester he had a moral duty as master of Oxmoon to stop his family's debauched goings-on!"

I guessed what had happened. I myself was always discreet, pulling all the curtains, shutting the necessary windows and never staying later than midnight. But Thomas, galloping around like an addled teen-ager, had probably had sex in a well-lit uncurtained room and made enough noise to wake the dead in the nearby churchyard.

I wasn't exactly my uncle's keeper but since I'd lent Thomas the cottage I did feel in some degree responsible for the uproar he had caused, so I phoned Kester to apologize.

"Don't give it another thought, old chap!" said Kester kindly. "I thought the minister was great fun."

I was only too anxious not to give the incident another thought but unfortunately Thomas had other ideas. Three days later I once more returned from work to find him lurking whisky-sodden in the drive.

"You..." Abuse flowed freely. I sighed and prayed for patience.

"Thomas, I think we've played this scene before. Let me forestall you by saying I haven't gossiped about your sex life to a single soul."

"Then how did Eleanor find out?"

"Oh God..." I sighed and prayed again. "For Christ's sake, Thomas, all Rhossili knows! What the hell you got up to I can't imagine, but—"

"You were angry that I'd left the cottage in a mess so you told Eleanor in order to pay me back!"

"I agree the mess was frightful but that was my fault. I should have laid down strict rules for you, but how was I to know you'd wreck the lavatory and upset the hip bath all over the kitchen floor?"

"You've destroyed my marriage! And if Eleanor divorces me I'll have no home and my whole life will be wrecked!"

"She won't divorce you—she's probably only too relieved you've got off your arse and gone elsewhere for sex!"

"Relieved! Christ, you should have heard some of the things she said!"

"Well, of course she had to make a fuss! Allow her some dignity, can't you? God, you're a stupid man!"

"You bloody swine!" He took a swipe at me and missed. "I'll get my revenge on you one day, just you wait and see!" he roared as my housekeeper watched the scene beyond the open front door. "No man wrecks my life and gets away with it!" And he drove off erratically in his Hillman leaving a trail of whisky fumes in his wake.

My father was saddened by this new quarrel but I did succeed in convincing him that this time Thomas was entirely to blame. However I could see that my father took a jaundiced view of my cottage at Rhossili.

"I'm entirely in favor of you abstaining from remarriage until you're ready for it," he said drily, "but surely you can organize your private life with more discretion? I'm afraid you're getting the most unfortunate reputation."

He didn't openly compare me with Kester, who was still living the life of a model widower, but I knew he had Kester in mind. I felt angry, and finally it occurred to me to wonder just who these village gossips were, alienating me persistently from Thomas so that I wound up in my father's bad books. Yet even then I had no inkling of the truth. I was distracted by the knowledge that villages like Penhale are always hotbeds of gossip, and besides, I knew I had been indiscreet, picking a cottage at Rhossili for my activities when I should have chosen a more anonymous base in Swansea.

I tried to turn over a new leaf. I prolonged an affair with a woman who ran an employment agency and who, wedded to her career, appeared to be uninterested in marriage. She had a flat overlooking the Mumbles lighthouse, and twice a week I used to trek to Swansea to put my private life on a discreet footing. Yet I didn't want to get too serious with anyone who wasn't a magic lady. In fact the very thought of getting serious made me want to run a mile in the opposite direction, and several times whenever I felt that Norah was becoming too affectionate I slept with someone else in order to reassure myself that I wasn't getting involved. That condemned me to the back seat of my car again because I had foolishly decided that using Norah's flat enabled me to make money by letting the Rhossili cottage, but so frightened was I by my increasing liking for Norah that the back seat of a car seemed a small price to pay for soothing my ruffled nerves.

Meanwhile as I muddled on in this neurotic and abortive quest for my mythical magic lady, Thomas and I had remained estranged, much to my relief, and his marriage had remained intact, much to his. But I began to wonder if his days as the Oxmoon manager were numbered. Kester struck me as being discontented. I saw little of him, but whenever we met in Penhale he never missed an opportunity to grumble about Thomas and I, sympathetic audience that I was, always allowed myself time to listen. It occurred to me that Kester might well relieve his feelings by swinging a hatchet in Thomas's direction, and that was why, when Kester at last showed his hand, all my paranoia came rushing back into my mind.

Kester invited me to an all-male family luncheon party at Oxmoon to celebrate the conclusion of Evan and Gerry's university careers, and the date he had picked was July the thirteenth, 1949.

The warning bell rang once more; the date set the famous nerves of steel jangling and without a second's hesitation I telephoned my father.

III

By that time my father had succeeded in shaking off the lingering aftereffects of his life with Constance and was sunk deep in the bliss of his third marriage. Naturally I could understand him being happy with Bronwen but what I found harder to understand was how he fitted so tranquilly into his casual, noisy and, to put it brutally, middle-class surroundings among all those peculiar Canadians he had fathered in a lost era.

The Canadians ebbed and flowed into the house according to the university vacations, and when they were at home they seemed to spend their time laughing, shouting, eating and playing Frank Sinatra records too loudly on the radiogram. I couldn't have stood it but my father said it was wonderful to be surrounded by young people who were enjoying life so much. He and Bronwen led a busy life. My father was on several civic committees concerned with the reconstruction of Swansea and had acquired the usual number of directorships which always fell into his lap whenever he moved to a new place. Bronwen was an active member of the Women's Institute and had a part-time job in the library of the Red Cross. Both she and my father knew hordes of people. Dinner parties abounded. I never visited their house without thinking how different their new life was from their past in Penhale, and whenever I saw my father's happiness, inexplicable though it was in part, I recognized the lack in my own life and felt lonely.

When I arrived to see my father that evening in July I found Bronwen making two large treacle tarts, Lance raiding the larder, Gerry chatting to his latest girl-friend on the telephone, Evan separating the dog and cat, who were having one of their fights, and my father mending the television set. Sian was still completing her final term at Bedales. When I entered the drawing room my father, who had discarded both jacket and waistcoat to tackle the television and was looking dashingly *déclassé* in his braces, glanced up at me with a smile.

I saw then what an impossible task I had set myself. The atmosphere of happiness in the house, the absolute normality, the peace—of a kind—now divided my father from me. I knew instinctively that he would disbelieve every word I said.

"Could I have a word with you alone, please, Father?"

That move took us to his study. My father mixed drinks for us and told me some interminable golfing story while I tried to work out what I could say without sounding hopelessly melodramatic.

741

I spoke. Within ten seconds my father was looking at me as if I'd gone round the bend. My heart sank.

"Just a minute," said my father, making the humane decision that I should be treated gently. "Let me make sure I've got this straight. You think there's some sinister purpose behind this luncheon party because it's being given on the tenth anniversary of that appalling scene at Oxmoon when Kester got himself into such a mess."

"Yes." I felt close to despair.

"But what in God's name do you think he's going to do?"

"I think he'll fire Thomas in such a way that Thomas is as humiliated before all the family as Kester himself was once humiliated before us. Honestly, Father, I think you should warn Thomas, I really do. I'd warn him myself, but as we're not on speaking terms I know he wouldn't listen to me."

"Yes, knowing the state of your relationship with Thomas, may I ask why you should care whether he's fired or not?"

"Because I think Kester's going to use me as a scapegoat, Father, and once Thomas goes berserk—as he inevitably will—his rage will be directed primarily against me and not against Kester. I think Kester's been at the bottom of my rift with Thomas all along—I think he's been fermenting trouble between us to set me up for the kill—"

"The kill?"

"Well, of course I'm not speaking literally—"

"No, you're talking rubbish." He opened the door into the hall. Gerry the Wonder Boy had finished his phone call but was sticking a stamp on a letter. I immediately suspected him of eavesdropping.

"Gerry, tell Evan I want to speak to him, will you?"

"Right, Dad." Wonder Boy sped off with a click of his winged heels.

Sensing that I was opposed to this summons my father said to me, "Evan sees more of Kester than you do. If Kester's really so unbalanced that he would bear a grudge for ten years and then serve it up without warning at a friendly family gathering, then Evan should be able to back up this preposterous theory of yours."

"Christ, Father, do you think Kester doesn't have the brains to deceive an idealistic young fool like Evan?"

Bad mistake. I was making a hash of this. My father looked very cool.

In walked Evan radiating honesty, sanity, decency and credibility. His reaction was so predictable that I barely bothered to listen.

"Harry, you're nuts."

"Don't you talk to me like that, you—" I bit back the word "bastard" but the effect was exactly as if I had spoken it aloud. Evan blanched. My father looked furious. With an effort I achieved a colorless apology.

"That's all, Evan—thank you," said my father, dismissing him. "Of course I don't have to ask you not to repeat a word of this conversation to Kester."

"Of course not, Dad. Don't worry, I wouldn't dream of worrying him with Harry's paranoid suspicions."

"Why, you—"

"Be quiet, both of you!" said my father so fiercely that we fell silent. Evan left the room. As the door closed I had a brief glimpse of Wonder Boy still lurking in the hall.

I made one final attempt. "Father, I beg you—give me the benefit of the doubt. You can remember that threat Kester made on July the thirteenth, 1939. You must know in your heart that Kester's very mixed up about his family, particularly about me and Thomas. Wouldn't playing safe be the prudent thing to do here? Tell Thomas. It can't do any harm and it may avoid some appalling fiasco. Please—tell him."

"No," said my father. "I'm not going to tell him. You are. It's your yarn. Spin it."

"But he won't listen to me!"

"I'll come with you to see that he does—and that, I'm afraid, Harry, is just about as far as I'm prepared to go."

IV

"I've never heard such a load of old balls in my life," said Thomas, but his rudeness was no more than an automatic reflex. I saw at once with relief that his hatred of Kester was now going to work in my favor. He had a much lower opinion of Kester than my father had and so found it much easier to believe him capable of bizarre behavior. He turned to his brother. "What's your opinion of this rigmarole, John?"

"I don't know. But I thought it worthwhile to play safe by informing you."

"Bloody glad you did. On second thoughts I wouldn't put it past that pansy to try to stab me in the back." He thought for a moment. I watched him as his brain ticked over briskly. Because of his emotional naivety it was tempting to dismiss Thomas as a complete fool but I knew very well he had a certain crude intelligence. It takes more flair than brains to run a large estate well, but flair alone won't balance the books or run an orderly office as he did.

"I won't go to this lunch," he said at last. "I'll ring up at the last moment and say I'm ill. If Kester's going to sack me he'll sack me, but at least I can stop him doing it in a big scene in front of the family."

"Good for you, Thomas," I said fervently.

"Wait a minute," said Thomas. "I'm not finished. Hasn't it occurred to either of you that if this theory's right I won't be the only one Kester'll be gunning for?"

My father was too stunned to speak but I said sharply, "Yes, that did occur to me but so long as I defuse his plan against you I'm safe. There's nothing else he can do to touch me."

"Are you trying to say—" began my father horrified.

"Wake up, John," said Thomas. "All three of us were there in the library at Oxmoon on July the thirteenth, 1939. If Kester's bent on revenge he's not going to stop with humiliating me—you and Harry will be on the agenda too."

"No," I said at once while my father was again reduced to an appalled silence, "he'd never move directly against Father, I'm sure of it. He'll consider it enough if Father's merely embarrassed by your humiliation."

"That makes sense," agreed Thomas. "But Harry, wouldn't that embarrassment be doubled if you were humiliated too? Think again. Are you sure—absolutely bloody positive—that there's nothing that sod can do to touch you?"

And that was the moment when I finally remembered little Melody and my hair-raising interview with Kester to the accompaniment of Handel's *Messiah*.

V

I said nothing to my father. By that time he was seriously worried in case I was right about Kester's plans for Thomas, and I saw no point in distressing him further. But I could now clearly visualize Kester's plan. First he would crucify Thomas by saying he drew the line at employing an agent who took part in drunken orgies, and then he would turn to me and announce to his enthralled family: "But wait—the real culprit's sitting here! He's the one who's led Thomas astray, he's the one who's been seducing every girl in sight since the age of fourteen!" Gasps. Sensation. The family would be lapping up every word he uttered and he wouldn't even have to invent the lurid details; he'd merely reel off the results of his investigations. Once he'd convinced himself that Melody had existed he would have realized that she could only have been conceived in the summer of '33 when I had spent the school holidays at Oxmoon, and once he'd scoured his memory for clues he would have been sure to remember Bella's absence in Switzerland for the first six months of 1934. After that he would have needed only to dispatch a private detective to Geneva. I remembered Bella telling me that Miss Stourham had included my name on the birth certificate. An open-and-shut case. With that birth certificate in his hand Kester could hang, draw and quarter me and drag my father through a bottomless mire of shame. What a revenge! Or so he thought. But think again, Cousin Kester.

On the morning of the lunch party I telephoned Oxmoon and left a message with the bossy parlormaid that my prize bull was at death's door. Thomas had already pleaded a touch of bronchitis and I thought it would sound more plausible if I had an urgent appointment with the vet. Then leaving the Manor I retreated to the Home Farm, found Dafydd busy repairing the roof and crawled up the ladder to join him.

"Thought you were lunching at Oxmoon?"

"Couldn't face it. Aquarius is sick, if anyone asks."

"Okay."

Dafydd made no further comment and again I was aware of how restful I found him. He bore no outward resemblance to Bronwen; he was dark and thickset, with a skin pitted from acne, but there was something in his manner that reminded me of her. I sensed not only an inner strength but a profound capacity for understanding.

"Have a cigarette," said Dafydd presently. "If you don't calm down you'll fall off the bloody roof."

"I can't think why I haven't fallen off already."

Another curious feature of my relationship with Dafydd was that I felt no compulsion to put on an act for him. I couldn't saunter around playing the ex-public-school boy and calling him "old chap" because that would have taken an intolerable advantage of the difference in our backgrounds. Neither could I saunter around playing the war hero. Dafydd never spoke of the war but anyone who had survived a Japanese prison camp knew exactly what hell war could be, and this automatically stopped me from pretending I'd enjoyed every minute of my time in the S.A.S.

"What's the bloody lunch in aid of?" said Dafydd in between fixing slates, and when I explained why Evan and Gerry were to be the guests of honor, he commented: "Typical. I don't get invited, do I, even though I'm just as much those bastards' brother as you are. I suppose bloody Kester thinks I can't hold a knife and fork."

"God knows what bloody Kester's thinking." Without mentioning Melody I gave vent to my suspicions.

"Well, either he's off his rocker or you are" was Dafydd's succinct response.

"Who's your favorite in the sanity stakes?"

"You. You're a survivor. That means you have a nose for danger. If your instinct's now telling you he's off his rocker I'd trust your instinct."

That was reassuring.

Dafydd suddenly turned to face me. He had small muddy-brown eyes with creases at the corners. "Do you think he's dangerous?"

"Dangerous? Hardly—no guts!" I said laughing, but my laughter was uneasy. "No," I said to reassure myself. "He's not the violent type. And I don't think he's really mad, Dafydd. Just unstable."

"Once people start going off their rockers," said Dafydd, "anything can happen." He picked up another slate.

After a moment I said, "Kester would draw the line at violence."

"What makes you so sure?"

"Well, I'd draw it. In peacetime."

"Maybe Kester thinks he has a war on his hands."

"God knows what he's thinking," I said again, and it occurred to me that not knowing what to believe was far more of a strain on the nerves than holding a firm, if terrifying, opinion.

We returned to the Manor together for lunch and afterwards I wound up hovering by the phone. I was in such a state of tension that when it rang I nearly jumped out of my skin.

"Heard anything yet?" said Thomas after I'd grabbed the receiver.

"No—get off the line." I hung up.

I was just on the point of defying convention by pouring myself a double whisky at three o'clock in the afternoon when my father's Rover purred up the drive. He was at the wheel. Evan was sitting beside him and Lance and Gerry were in the back. They all looked chillingly normal.

"We won't stop!" called my father cheerfully, not bothering to switch off the engine. "But I just thought I must let you know that it was a delightful lunch and Kester was at his most charming and hospitable."

"How's your sick bull?" said Evan in a tone of voice that made me want to punch him on the nose.

I ignored him. I just said to my father, "I'm glad all went well."

"Never mind," said my father kindly. "In the circumstances I could quite understand you being a little nervous. Kester mentioned the date, oddly enough. In his postluncheon speech he said, 'Ten years ago on this day I was cursing my family and vowing revenge, but now I'm entertaining them to lunch and enjoying their company!' He was really most amusing about it! And then he proposed a toast to family solidarity and said what a pity it was that you and Thomas couldn't be there."

"My God," I said before I could stop myself, "he's bloody clever."

"Harry," said Evan, "have you ever thought of seeing a psychiatrist?"

"Be quiet, Evan!" snapped my father. "That was quite uncalled for. Well, Harry—"

"Dad," said Wonder Boy urgently from the back seat, "could you hold it for a moment? I've got to go to the bathroom or I'll never make it back to Swansea. Harry, would you mind if..."

I gave him permission to use my lavatory. Then I returned to my study and once more reached for the decanter.

I was interrupted by a mouselike tap on the door.

Slamming down the decanter I flung the door wide and revealed Wonder Boy, dark hair very glossy, blue eyes very bright, tall lean figure smartly clad in a charcoal-gray suit.

"What the hell do you want?"

Wonder Boy saw he had to talk fast. "Harry, I think you're right. About Kester. I overheard that conversation you had the other day with Dad and Evan so I was on the watch today, just as they were, but I saw something they didn't see."

I stared at him. "Go on."

"I was in the hall when the maid gave him the message you couldn't come, and he looked like an ancient Roman who'd just heard the circus had been cancelled. He was planning something, Harry, I'm sure of it, and that means Evan's wrong and you're not nuts after all. Not that I ever thought you were, I've always been on your side because as far as I'm concerned you're the only sane member of this peculiar family I seem to be mixed up in. I know you're not crazy about me, and hell, I wasn't crazy about you at first either, but—"

I held up my hand. "Stop."

He stopped. We gazed at each other. Like finally spoke to like.

"Well, I'll be buggered," I said. I made a quick decision. "I'll ring you up later. We'll meet."

My father's family seemed to be dividing into separate camps. Ignoring the whisky decanter I slumped down in the nearest armchair and wondered—not for the first time—just where Kester's mad schemes were leading us.

VI

Gerry's information was as reassuring as Dafydd's confidence in my sanity. It was still possible that we were all wrong but I felt the odds that I was making some gigantic mistake had been considerably reduced.

This set me free to worry about the future.

The truth was nothing had been solved because Thomas and I had merely postponed the problem of Kester. Did I seriously think he'd now quietly abandon his plans for revenge? No, I did not. Maddened that we'd eluded him he'd be sure to redouble his efforts, and the very thought of his taking another swipe at us was enough to reduce my steel nerves to pulp. When Thomas turned up for a conference his first comment was "You look awful."

We drank for a while, two enemies forced into an alliance in an attempt to survive. I was reminded vaguely of the war.

"The worst part," I said, "is that there's nothing we can do. We just have to wait till he makes the next move."

"No chance of you being mistaken, I suppose, old boy? John went on and on about how charming and delightful Kester was."

"Father's in blinkers. He can't bear to do anything but hope for the best."

"Well, I see his point—it's a lot more fun than waiting for the worst." He finished the whisky, added: "Let me know if you think Kester's getting ready to swing the hatchet again" and drove away in his Hillman with an air of determined optimism.

To his horror I phoned him a week later to announce that Kester had been in touch. "He's invited me to Oxmoon for a drink, Thomas. I'm just about to leave."

"Christ! What do you think he's up to this time?"

"That's what I have to find out. I'll report back to you later," I said, and hung up. I felt as if I were going out on a raid, and beneath my skin the adrenaline was beginning to burn.

I drove to Oxmoon.

VII

"You wouldn't like some champagne, by any chance, would you?" said Kester casually after greeting me in the hall. "I ordered too much for the family lunch and I'm still trying to lap up the surplus."

"I'll stick to scotch, old chap, if you don't mind."

"Oh good. I'm awfully bored with champagne myself but people always expect it when they come to Oxmoon to be entertained, so what am I to do?"

We drifted from the hall into the drawing room. We were both trying so hard to be nonchalant that it was a wonder we were able to carry on a conversation at all.

Kester handed me a whisky-and-soda and began mixing himself a gin-and-French.

"I hear the family lunch was a great success, old chap," I said. "Too bad I missed it."

"Never mind!" said Kester, giving me his most charming smile. "I'm sure there'll be other equally enjoyable occasions awaiting you in the future!"

I laughed lightly to indicate gratified agreement. My back was itching. I was sweating from head to toe.

"The future!" said Kester, and drank to it.

"The future!" I echoed, and wondered what the devil was coming next.

I soon found out. Wiping the merry expression off his face Kester said urgently, "Look, Harry, I won't beat about the bush. I'm in a jam and I need your help."

This was certainly a novel approach. "What's the matter?"

"It's bloody Thomas. You guessed what I was up to, didn't you, and tipped him off. Well, all right, perhaps it was just as well, perhaps it was rather a mad idea but I couldn't resist the notion of a grand execution in front of all the family; I thought it was the least I could do to repay him for that scene in '39. However—" Kester paused to toss back some gin; I was too riveted to speak. "—the scheme failed and that's that. So the question is what do I do next?"

"What indeed, old chap."

"Of course he'll have to go. I only kept him on in order to set him up for the grand execution, and now that the grand execution's failed... well, it's obviously best if I eliminate him as quickly and cleanly as possible, but the trouble is I don't see how I can do it without triggering the most ferocious scene. You know what he's like when he's drunk. I'm honestly afraid that if I sack him he may try and beat me up."

His fear seemed justifiable. I thought of Thomas taking a swipe at me when he was under the influence. "What do you want me to do?"

"Can you be here with me while I fire him? After all there you are, the war hero, the expert in unarmed combat. I'd feel much safer if—"

"Sorry, old chap. I'd rather not be involved." I tried to imagine the size of Thomas's wrath if he found out I'd sided with Kester. "Get my father to umpire the proceedings."

"But Harry, I can't go dragging Uncle John into this! You know how soft he is about Thomas—he'd try to persuade me to retain him and we'd end up quarreling and I just can't face any more quarrels with Uncle John, I really can't."

I knew the feeling. "Don't think I don't sympathize, old chap, but I'm sitting on the fence and I intend to stay there."

"In that case I suppose I'll have to rope in Freddy Fairfax and his myrmidons to keep the peace—having a gaggle of solicitors in attendance is rather more the done thing, I daresay, than roping in an ex-commando sporting bared fists, but all the same it's a pity."

I said I thought this was a much better idea, and we chatted in a desultory way for some time. I finished my drink. Then I couldn't resist saying, "Thomas wasn't intended to be the only victim of your grand execution, was he, old chap?"

Kester raised an eyebrow and looked sardonic. "Steady on, Harry! It's only in an Agatha Christie novel that the villain slips cyanide into the champagne!"

"I somehow got the impression you had a pile of mud waiting and Thomas and I were both due to have our noses rubbed in it."

"If I didn't know you better I'd say you were suffering from persecution mania! Have another drink."

"No, thanks. So there was no mud waiting for me?"

"No, but how intriguing! What frightful secret do you have locked up in your pristine past? Obviously you can't be nervous without cause!"

"I thought you might have found out that I was sent down from Oxford for lechery, drunkenness and general academic failure."

"No!" said Kester, genuinely astonished. "Were you? Well, I'll be damned!"

I set down my glass. "Well, now that we've got all that straightened out—"

"Oh, don't rush off. I've got another favor to ask you—a very minor favor this time, you'll be relieved to hear. You play golf, don't you?"

"Not since I was up at Oxford. No time. Why?"

"But you do at least know one club from another which is more than I do."

I conceded a familiarity with golf clubs.

"Good. I'll tell you the problem: Owen Bryn-Davies—little Owen—is taking the game up and Elizabeth asked me what had happened to Uncle Lion's clubs. Well, I eventually excavated them from the attics, but I suspect some of the clubs are missing, and I was wondering if the remainder would be of any use to a twelve-year-old boy. Would you mind taking a look? The clubs are in the billiard room."

This seemed a refreshingly harmless request. I consented.

In the billiard room the table was covered with a dust sheet and the blinds were drawn, but when Kester switched on the lights I saw the battered old golf bag standing by the fireplace. As I moved over to it I automatically kept Kester in my field of vision although when I realized what I was doing I was unnerved. What a neurotic reaction! It was almost as if I expected him to carve me up with a club! Had to pull myself together.

"He'll need five clubs to start with," I said briskly as Kester drifted away from me to draw up one of the blinds. "I suggest a spoon, a mid-iron, a mashie, a mashie-niblick and a putter. Now, let's take a look at what we've got here. . . . Ah, I see a mashie he could use." I adopted a golfer's stance with my back to the fireplace and tried a practice swing. "That's odd," I said surprised. I tried another. "Wait a minute, are these ordinary clubs? They seem abnormally long. Uncle Lion was a tall man, wasn't he?"

"Vast. In the family photos he's even taller than my father, and my father was six feet two."

"I suspect these clubs were specially made for him. Tell Elizabeth to take them to the professional at Father's golf club and ask his advice. It's possible they may be of no use to Owen at all."

"What a bore—all right, I will. Thanks, Harry."

Abandoning the clubs we strolled languidly back to the hall. I had to will myself not to hurry.

"Thanks for the drink, old chap. Sorry I can't help you with Terrible Thomas. Wish you the best of luck there."

"Thanks—my God, I'll need it."

Was it significant that he didn't attempt to shake hands? I didn't know. I was preoccupied with the knowledge that I was about to turn my back on him in order to run down the steps to my car.

I turned my back and ran. Nothing happened. But what on earth had I expected? A knife in the back? I was going crazy—off my rocker, as Dafydd would have said so succinctly.

I started the engine, stalled it, restarted it and let out the clutch too fast. The car lurched forward and almost stalled again. Yes, there was no doubt about it, my nerves were shot to pieces, but why? No idea.

I drove back to Penhale, and all the time I was aware of the vibrations of violence pulsing subtly across the surface of my mind. I thought: I picked up something there, something most people would have missed. And I shuddered. Then I thought of Dafydd saying, "You have a nose for danger," and I shuddered more convulsively than ever. But I went on driving to Llangennith. I thought Thomas deserved a warning that he was about to be fired, and I certainly wasn't going to stop him if he immediately roared over to Oxmoon before Kester had had the chance to summon the guard of solicitors.

I reached Stourham Hall. I told Thomas. And that, of course, as I realized later, was exactly what Kester had wanted me to do.

VIII

"I'll kill the swine," said Thomas.

"Don't be a bloody fool. Eleanor, help me convince him it's not worth going to jail for assault."

"Harry's right, Tom," said Eleanor. "Go over to Oxmoon and make a scene by all means, but for God's sake don't start bashing him to pulp. Think how thrilled he'd be if you ended up in jail with your life wrecked."

"Bloody hell!" yelled Thomas, but he saw the logic. In frustration he said to me, "Let's go and get drunk."

But I got out of that one. My girlfriend Norah, the incumbent of the useful flat overlooking the Mumbles lighthouse, was coming to dinner at the Manor for the first time. She had said more than once how much she wanted to meet the boys.

"Watch out," said Eleanor, temporarily diverted from her husband's problems by this disclosure. "Once she's met the boys and told you what darling little cherubs they are she'll expect you to propose on the spot."

"Oh no, she's a career girl, she's not interested in marriage," I said but panic assailed me again. Danger seemed to be lurking everywhere that day.

Leaving Thomas still fulminating against Kester I retired to the Manor but I was late and when I arrived I saw Norah's car was already parked in the drive.

Hastening to the drawing room I found her holding her own well against the united curiosity of the four boys.

"Norah, I'm so sorry, I was unavoidably detained. . . ." I kissed her more to soothe my nerves than to demonstrate affection but at once saw Hal looking at me with hostile dark eyes as his sharp little brain made two and two equal a disloyal-to-Mummy four. Fortunately Charles and Jack were too ingenuous to notice and Humphrey was too young to understand, but even so I was rattled. I spilled the gin.

"Darling, relax! Why are you in such a state?"

Silly woman. I decided I was tired of her. But I'd miss her flat. I'd become very fond of that view of the Mumbles lighthouse.

"Is anything wrong, darling?" she persisted after the children had been dispatched and we were dining alone.

"It's nothing. Just the usual old family problems."

I saw then that I couldn't talk to her. Despite my irritation I was fond of her. In a vague way I even liked her. But when all was said and done I was unable to do anything with her except fuck. I tried to cheer myself up by reflecting that this was a very sizable exception, but I was depressed beyond measure and lonely beyond belief.

"You don't mind if we don't use my bedroom, do you?" I said later as I locked the door of the drawing room. "Everyone's upstairs now, so it's safer down here."

"Darling, I'd do it with you in the kitchen sink if you felt so inclined!"

I suddenly realized that even my liking for her had become past history. How was I ever going to get an erection? But I could and did. Extraordinary. Obviously stupid women were an infallible guarantee of sexual success, and no doubt if I ever went to bed with a really clever woman I'd be impotent, but I'd never been to bed with a really clever woman, never fancied it, never dared go to bed with any woman I might respect. I might have ended up liking her too much, I might have ended up loving her, I might even have wound up the victim of a grand passion, and my God, think of all the misery and suffering *that* would inevitably have caused—

"Darling, what's this simply heavenly music on the wireless?"

"Vivaldi." I knew she didn't give a damn.

"Oh, it's so—"

"Shut up. Do you want to come or not?"

The telephone rang. I cursed, determined not to answer it, but it went on and on, ruining the Vivaldi which was just reaching its best bars.

"*Hell!*" I finished in a fury, pulled out, staggered across the room and grabbed the receiver. "Yes, who's this?"

A shuddering voice whispered: "It's me."

"Kester!" I could have murdered him. "For Christ's sake, what is it now?"

"Harry, this is an emergency. It's Thomas. You've got to come, *got to*—"

"Oh my God—"

"Harry, *please*—"

"But—"

751

"Please!" shouted Kester hysterically, and hung up.

I was so shocked that I just stood there with the receiver in my hand until the postmistress came on the line. "Are you waiting to speak to me, Mr. Godwin?" she asked curiously, and I answered without thinking, "No." But as soon as I said that I changed my mind. "I mean yes. Dial Oxmoon for me, could you please, Mrs. Williams?"

The line clicked and whirred. Kester answered in the middle of the first ring. "Harry?"

"Yes." I listened but the postmistress was evidently holding her breath with the consummate skill of a practiced eavesdropper. "All right," I said, "tell Thomas I'm coming. That should calm him down." I hung up and turned to Norah. "I'm sorry but something frightful's going on at Oxmoon—Thomas is drunk as usual—and I'll have to rush up there before he murders Kester."

"Darling," said Norah, whom I had regaled in the past with stories of my feuding relations, *"what* a family!"

I seized the chance to get rid of her by adding: "I hate to say it but I see no point in you waiting here for me because God only knows how long this'll take."

That successfully terminated our evening together. I rushed to Oxmoon.

It was dark when I drove raggedly up the drive, and when Kester opened the front door the light was behind him so that at first I couldn't see his face. But when I did see it I felt as if I'd dropped six floors in a broken lift.

"What the devil—"

"Oh, thank God," he sobbed. "Thank God you've come." Tears streamed down his face and his eyes were bloodshot.

"Where is he?"

"In the billiard room—we had a fight—oh, *God*—"

I was running. I ran across the hall down the passage to the billiard room and Kester stumbled after me, poor old Kester, poor old sod, sniveling, sobbing, steeped in melodramatic emotion. But I felt I could deal with this. We seemed to have fallen back into our oldest roles: poor old Kester had got into a mess as usual and now Cousin Harry, that elderly version of Wonder Boy, was going to sweep along like the war hero he was and clean everything up.

If I'd stopped to think I'd have seen the script flowing effortlessly from Kester's fertile pen, but I didn't stop to think. I rushed headlong into the billiard room and there was Thomas, not just temporarily knocked out, as I'd anticipated, but lying full length in front of the fireplace with his head bashed in.

I saw at once he was dead as a doornail.

IX

"I didn't mean to do it—it was self-defense—I was running away from him, I ran in here and tried to shut the door but he was too quick, he burst in but he slipped and fell—he was roaring drunk, and then I don't know, I hit him on the head but I didn't mean mean to kill him, I just wanted to knock him out—"

"Shut up."

Silence fell. Without his voice ranting in my ears I could finally hear myself think. But the trouble was that I couldn't think clearly. I was too shocked. I found myself functioning automatically, every move made with a view to survival. I kept Kester in my field of vision. I knelt by the body. I made myself examine the wound on the head. I was acting on instinct, almost suffocated by the danger which had grazed my nerves so searingly during my earlier visit to Oxmoon.

Then I saw it. Beyond the shattered head, lying in the fireplace, was Kester's weapon. It was the golf club I had handled that morning.

Comprehension exploded in my brain. My fingerprints were on that blood-stained mashie. No matter what Kester told the police—and he might even try to protect poor old Cousin Harry by repeating his story that he'd killed in self-defense—he'd be safe because of course he'd used gloves to kill Thomas and only my fingerprints would be on that club. I saw at once how the situation would appear to the police. For nearly two years there had been bad blood between me and Thomas; Kester had manipulated us both into such a state of public antagonism that all Penhale would testify that we'd been sworn enemies, and once the police found out I was a trained killer their minds could leap to only one deduction.

But I had an alibi. Of course I had an alibi. Or did I? No, I didn't. I could be killing Thomas this very minute—that was why Kester had lured me to Oxmoon, and that was why he had been so careful not to say on the phone that Thomas was dead. "Tell Thomas I'm coming," I'd said, giving the eavesdropping post-mistress the clear impression that he was still alive. "Thomas is drunk as usual," I'd said to Norah. Two witnesses would testify that Thomas had been alive when I left the Manor, and the medical evidence, as always, wouldn't prove the exact moment of death. There would be at least half an hour's uncertainty and that would finish me, that and the fingerprints on the bloodstained club.

"Oh God, Harry," sobbed Kester, descending skillfully towards hysteria again. "We'd better call the police, hadn't we? No choice. We must call the police, do the done thing . . ."

My whole life was on the line. I didn't hesitate. Looking up at him I waited till he had the guts to look back at me and then I said to him between my teeth: "Fuck the done thing."

7

I

THAT WAS the turning point in our lives.

He stared, shocked to the core as I sliced his neat writer's plot to ribbons, the tears of genuine horror flowing down his cheeks as he discovered the difference between his attractive hygienic fantasies and this messy grisly reality. In the end all he could do was stammer, "But you can't do that!" as if I were under some moral obligation not to deviate from his script.

"Oh yes I can," I said. Taking out my handkerchief I wiped my prints from the club.

"But surely . . ." He gulped. "Surely we'll have to tell the police—Christ, we've got to draw the line somewhere—"

"Why, yes, of course. I'm all for drawing lines. But I draw the line a little later than most people," I said, standing up, my fingers still masked by my handkerchief as I held out the club to him. "Here—take this."

He shied away. "No!"

"*Take it!* Or by God I'll use it to smash you to bloody pulp!"

He took the club. It was a reflex action of mindless fright but he took the club in his bare hands and I instinctively moved out of his reach in case he developed any wild ideas. But he didn't. He'd realized the time for wildness had come and gone. With his fingerprints alone now on the club he had just as much at stake as I had in clearing up the mess.

"That's better," I said. "Now just you listen to me. I'm still not involved in this. No one saw me arrive here. I could drive away now, stage a breakdown in the village and no one could prove I'd ever been at Oxmoon tonight. My fingerprints have been removed from that club. I've put myself absolutely beyond your reach."

Kester tried to speak and failed.

"That club," I said, "now has your fingerprints on it. Even if you wipe them off, Eleanor and I both know Thomas wanted to beat you up for sacking him. I think a leading K.C. would get you acquitted of murder but I doubt if he could get you off a manslaughter charge, and one thing I want to make absolutely clear is that you can't fob this crime off on me. Not only can you never prove I was here—you can't prove I had any real motive. My father can testify I've been on reasonable terms with Thomas since the invitation to your lunch party arrived."

For a second Kester's eyes were expressionless and I knew there was something

I'd missed. Then I realized he was certain to have provided me with a first-class motive. The mutual hostility had been a mere useful preliminary. The real motive lay elsewhere.

"Well?" I said swiftly, not wanting to reveal I'd guessed the worst. "What do you say? Are you going to cooperate with me in clearing up this mess?"

That confused him. I could see him trying to comprehend my *volte-face*, asking himself why I should be washing my hands of the crime at one moment and then offering to clear it up at the next. "If you're so confident you can sever all connection with this," he stammered at last, "why should you want to help me?"

"Family solidarity, old chap," I said. "What else?"

He stared at me. Horrific vistas opened up into the future. He stared at Thomas's corpse. Another horrific vista. He stared down at the club in his hands. No escape from the horror. It was everywhere. I leaned lightly forward on the balls of my feet in case he panicked and took a swipe at me against his better judgment, but his will to survive had gained the upper hand and he finally brought his panic under control.

"Wait," he said feverishly. "I've got to think."

"No, old chap. You've got to act. All right, forget the horseshit about family solidarity. The truth is I don't trust you to clean this up without making some bloody awful mess and dragging me into it from a different angle. I'm not leaving until we've disposed of the body in such a way that neither of us can be blamed for the killing."

There was a pause.

"Come on, Kester, wake up and face reality."

He woke up and faced it. "All right," he said, taking a deep breath. "What do we do?"

"I need some gloves immediately. You'll need some later. Where do we find them?"

He took me to the cloakroom.

"All right, leave your pair on the hall table. Now—the servants. You did check, of course—"

"Yes, they're all in their rooms."

"Good. I suggest an immediate raid on the scullery."

We assembled a bucket of hot water, a scrubbing brush, two floor cloths and a cake of carbolic soap. Back in the billiard room I sent him off to the farthest corner and told him to keep his mouth shut.

"But can't I do anything to help?"

"No." I didn't trust him to clean up properly. He hadn't been to public school. I'd once been beaten because I'd made a poor job of cleaning out a fireplace, and that was the kind of lesson one didn't forget in a hurry.

"Luckily," I said, kneeling down again beside the smashed head, "he hasn't bled on the carpet, only on the marble of the fireplace. That's our first lucky break, and let's hope to God it won't be our last." I stole a quick look at Kester to make sure he wasn't watching me, but he had slumped onto a chair and was leaning forward with his head in his hands. Nimbly my fingers worked their way through Thomas's pockets. Melody's Swiss birth certificate was in the inside pocket of the jacket.

Very neat. According to Kester's script Thomas was blackmailing me and that was the fundamental cause of the bad blood between us; when I had arrived at Oxmoon to help poor terrified Kester defend himself against his wicked drunken uncle I just hadn't been able to resist the chance to dispose of my blackmailer—or so Kester would have confessed to the police after making a touching effort to save me in the name of family solidarity. The plot had a certain stylized insouciance which at a less dangerous time I might have paused to admire, but as it was I merely noted that the murder had been meticulously planned and despite the novelettish trappings might well have proved fatal to me. Pocketing the birth certificate I picked up the scrubbing brush.

"Are you sure I can't do anything, Harry?"

"You can get the whisky decanter. We don't want the housemaid coming in here tomorrow and wondering why the fireplace reeks of carbolic."

I set to work. I had to be very careful moving Thomas. One false drip could be fatal. The blood on my hands bore a startling resemblance to strawberry jam and it occurred to me that it would have looked more realistic in a film or on the stage. Idly I pictured a Saturday matinée with all the old tabbies in the audience clanking their tea trays with excitement.

"Here's the decanter, Harry."

"All right, put it on the table. Now let's plan our story. I think I can just about face it."

"Well, you see, what I intended was—"

"No, spare me the elaborate complexities of your master plan. Just tell me exactly what happened this evening so that we can work out how far the truth can be adapted for the police. If we stick to the truth as far as possible we run less risk of being caught out in a lie."

"Yes, of course. All right, where shall I start?"

"What time did Thomas arrive?"

"Nine thirty-two. I'd been watching the clock all evening because I was certain he'd roar up here in a rage once he was drunk enough to face me. I knew you'd tell him he was going to be sacked."

"How drunk was he?"

"At his most belligerent. He'd been all evening at the pub."

"Good. That means there'll be plenty of witnesses to swear he was breathing fire, and your phone call to me for help will sound thoroughly plausible. We'll have to incorporate that phone call into our story, no choice; I had my girlfriend with me at the time and Mrs. Williams was waggling her ears as usual at the switchboard. So what we both have to insist is that Thomas was alive when you phoned and alive when I arrived here." I wrung out the cloth and watched the water turn red. "All right," I said. "Back to the details. Thomas arrived at about half-past nine. You were on the lookout so presumably you let him in. What happened next?"

"Is this the truth or is this what we say to the police?"

"The truth. It could also be what we say to the police, of course, but let's hear it first."

"I made an attempt to pacify him by taking him into the drawing room and offering him a whisky, but after that..." He fell silent.

"All right," I said again. "The short answer to my question is that you took him to the drawing room, and as far as the police are concerned that's going to be where you both stayed. Our story's going to be that he was never in the billiard room at all. You came here earlier in the day to show me Uncle Lion's clubs and I clumsily spilled whisky all over this nice clean fireplace, but that's irrelevant. Now..." I started to polish the fireplace with a dry floor cloth. "...this is what happened. Thomas accepts your whisky but it only makes him more belligerent. Finally in desperation you suggest summoning me to act as a mediator—I'm not your ideal choice but I'm the nearest member of the family and I'm better than nothing. Thomas agrees. He's being pigheaded as usual and refusing to leave here till you've promised he can keep his job. You both wait. I arrive. We argue interminably. In the end I give up and mutter to you that you'll never get Thomas out of the house unless you promise not to sack him. You promise—it's the only thing to do. You're still determined to sack him, you understand, but you realize it's got to be done in my father's presence with your solicitors acting as bodyguards." I sat back on my heels. "Does all that ring true?"

"Yes. Very plausible. Everyone acting in character."

"Very well. We see Thomas to the front door and watch him drive away in drunken triumph. Then...what would we do next? Talk for a few minutes?"

"Have a brandy to recover," said Kester promptly.

"Yes, that's right, of course we would." I paused to consider this. "Better arrange it now. Go to the drawing room, pour out two doubles, tip them down the cloakroom basin and return the glasses to the drawing room for the servants to find tomorrow morning—oh no, bring my glass in here to me so that I can put my fingerprints on it."

"Can I drink my brandy?"

"No, better not. I want you in full possession of your faculties when we stage the car accident."

Kester blanched but slipped away without further comment to obey orders.

We plowed on. I found I needed running water to clean the gore from the golf club so we withdrew to the scullery again. The pail was sluiced out, the scrubbing brush rinsed, the floor cloths hung out to dry on the wooden rack, the carbolic soap replaced. Eventually we returned to the billiard room.

I stared at the golf bag. "I'm trying to remember if I handled any other club except the mashie, but I didn't. That's all right, though, because I handled the bag."

"I don't follow."

"If the police inquire about my earlier visit to Oxmoon I'll have to say I came to this room to examine Uncle Lion's clubs, and it'll look odd if there are no fingerprints on the clubs to back up my story. But it'll be all right because I can just say I took the bag, realized at a glance that the clubs were abnormally long and decided without more ado that they'd be of no use to Owen."

"But if our story's going to be that the billiard room is irrelevant to Thomas's visit, why should the police start fingerprinting the clubs?"

"I agree that with luck it'll never occur to them to do such a thing, but if something goes wrong and the police don't believe us, they're going to fingerprint everything in sight. Kester, think hard. Did Thomas touch anything when he came into this room? If the police do put the whole ground floor of Oxmoon under a microscope, this is the last place where they must find a trace of him."

Kester took his time. Then he said, "He opened the door when he came into the room."

I could just see it: Kester pretending to lose his nerve, Thomas crashing after him. Kester would merely have had to wait behind the door of the billiard room with the club in his hand. Thomas would have suspected nothing as he charged in like an ox to the slaughter.

Pulling on my gloves I wiped the door handle with my handkerchief. "Now put your prints there," I said. "We can't leave the handle wiped clean."

He did as he was told. Again I paused to think. Then Kester said, "The smell of carbolic—" and I said, "Christ, the bloody whisky," and the omission was rectified. As a generous helping of whisky was spilled in the fireplace the smell of carbolic died instantly.

Replacing the decanter in the drawing room we prepared to face the next phase of the operation.

"We can't be too careful about this part," I said. "Let's go to the stable block and make sure the lights are all out in the servants' bedrooms. Then we'll move round to the drive to prepare the Hillman—oh, and bring your gloves. Your prints mustn't be found in Thomas's car."

We padded around outside in the dark for some time. When we were back in the hall I said, "Turn off all the lights. What can we use to prop open the front door?"

Kester found a jade statuette. It was dark with the lights out. A quarter-moon gleamed palely over the black mass of the woods.

"Can't see a thing," muttered Kester.

"You will. Let's wait till our eyes get adjusted."

We waited, then found our way back to the body.

"Now, this is going to be very difficult. I want his head to go forward onto his chest. You can take the legs but we must be close together so that I can keep the head steady. He's no longer bleeding but he could drip."

"*Christ*. Oh God, I think I'm going to be—"

"No, save being sick for later. Vomiting's a luxury. When you murder someone your first priority is to make your stomach obey orders."

"I think that's the most terrifying thing you've ever said to me."

"Shut up and take his legs."

"How many men did you kill in the war?"

"*Shut up!*"

He shut up. We began to move the corpse.

"Take it slowly. No hurry. No accidents."

We edged our way along. I had never before realized what a long way it was from the billiard room to the front door.

"Pause here a moment. Let's just make sure there's no stray thief tiptoeing up the drive."

There wasn't. Slowly we began to descend the steps. We had already opened the door of the Hillman's front passenger seat.

"Swing his legs in . . . that's right . . . now get in the back seat and hold him by the shoulders. I don't want him slopping around and leaving blood in the wrong places."

"Where are you going?"

"I want to make sure he hasn't dripped. Then I'll close the front door. Have you got a key?"

"Yes." But he checked to make sure.

Slipping back into the house, I switched on the lights with my gloved hand and took a look. No blood. A faint scent of whisky hung on the air in the pristine billiard room. Flicking off the lights again I left the house, closed the front door softly and slid behind the driving wheel of the Hillman.

"All okay, as the Yanks say. Let's go."

The keys were in the ignition. Starting the engine I drove carefully through the gateway and turned right onto the road to Penhale, but after a quarter of a mile I halted at the top of a slope. A hundred yards ahead beyond a sharp bend a dry-stone wall marked the border of a field.

"Thomas is roaring drunk," I said, "and driving like a bat out of hell. He'd misjudge that corner, wouldn't he?"

"Entirely."

"Right. Remember that Thomas left Oxmoon five minutes before this after our protracted family wrangle. Now . . . we've got to get him into the driver's seat. Keep holding his head steady and move sideways as I drag him over. Oh, and pray no cars come while we're at it."

Our prayers were answered. Somehow we got Thomas wedged behind the wheel.

"That'll do. Now go down to the bend and make dead sure nothing's coming up the road from Penhale. If the coast's clear strike a match, count to five and blow the match out. Then start running."

"I haven't got a match."

I passed him my cigarette lighter and he ran off, a shadowy figure moving in and out of the patches of moonlight. Winding down the driver's window, I checked that the car was in neutral and restarted the engine. It died. The accelerator needed to be jiggled. I opened the door, slid my foot over the pedal and tried again. This time the engine ticked over just as my lighter flared in the distance.

I released the hand brake. I slammed the door. I jumped onto the running board. My right hand was grasping the steering wheel through the open window, and the car, still in neutral, began to pick up speed as I steered straight for the stone wall.

759

At the last moment I jumped clear, flung myself face down on the verge and covered my head with my hands. An almighty crash tore the night apart but a sinister silence sewed it together again. And then, just as I was cursing the fact that I'd apparently run the engine to no avail, the petrol tank obliged me by blowing up, the force of the explosion seared my cheek and looking back I saw a ball of fire eliminating all trace of Kester's highly successful murder.

I got to my knees. Then I leaned over, retching, on all fours, and finally succeeded in vomiting over the pretty wild flowers that were growing at the side of the road.

II

Kester had run the other way, towards Penhale, and it was some minutes before he cut back across the nearby field to join me. He tried to apologize for the delay but I stopped him. I knew he'd been vomiting too.

We walked in silence to Oxmoon and paused by my car in the drive.

"Don't forget," I said, "that since Thomas left we've been drinking those double brandies in the drawing room." I peeled off the gloves and handed them to him; he gave me back my lighter. "All right, here's what happens next: I drive to Penhale, I see the burning car, I call the police as soon as I get home. Then I naturally phone you to say that Thomas has had a terrible accident." I paused. Then I said, "We'll meet later, preferably when all the fuss is dying down. Now don't panic when the police come, just stick to the story and for God's sake don't try to be too clever and add fancy touches. Save that for your novels. And if ever you're in doubt over the correct attitude to take... what was that writer's phrase you used earlier? Oh yes—act in character."

"I understand. Thanks. Good luck."

We parted.

I managed to drive back to the Manor but the reaction was hitting me, and when I arrived it was some time before I could force myself out of the car. I noticed that there was a light in Dafydd's room. Like me he suffered from insomnia.

Eventually I dragged myself inside and made the necessary telephone calls to the village constable and to Kester. I knew I should phone Eleanor but I couldn't face it. I couldn't face anything. Sinking down on the sofa I buried my face in my hands.

I heard a quiet footfall and looked up. It was Dafydd.

"Saw you stagger into the house," he said. "You all right?"

"No, I've had a bloody shock." That at least was true.

He didn't ask what had happened but took me beyond the green baize door, sat me down at the kitchen table and brewed me some tea. He sat beside me while I drank it. His restful presence, the soothing quality of our silence and the fortifying influence of the tea eventually combined to ease my shock. I gave him a dress rehearsal of the story I planned to give to the police and was relieved when

I sounded so convincing. Then I told him about the burning car and I sounded rather more than convincing. I put my head in my hands again.

"I stopped my own car," I heard myself say, "to make sure I hadn't made a mistake, but the Hillman's number plate was still legible and suddenly the shock hit me, it was—it was—"

"The smell."

I felt fiercely grateful to him for understanding.

He took my hand and held it. It was the sort of gesture Bronwen would have made. I felt better.

"He was an awful old sod really," I said at last, "but it was a terrible end."

"Would he have known much about it?"

The answer was no, but the most I could say was, "Probably not." I had to conform to my story.

"Then I can think of worse ends," said Dafydd.

So could I. We went on sitting in silence but I was recovering fast, and by the time the police arrived to question me I was ready for them.

I was going to survive.

III

The coroner's jury brought in a verdict of accidental death and added a rider that there should be more attempts to keep drunken drivers off the roads. I attended the funeral, which took the form of a cremation of the remnants, but Kester, acting in character, stayed away and no one was surprised. Afterwards I was touched that Eleanor turned for comfort not to my father, the family's traditional Rock of Gibraltar, but to me, her brother-in-law. After the service she asked me to take her to a pub and we spent the lunch hour drinking together. My father took care of Bobby for the afternoon.

"I know you had your troubles with Tom," said Eleanor, "but I don't suppose that was all your fault—I know how difficult the old boy could be." Tears streamed down her weather-beaten cheeks again. "It's that damned Kester who's responsible for Tom's death!" she said fiercely with more truth than she realized. "If he hadn't been so vilely ungrateful... after all Tom's loyalty and hard work... oh, I'll never forgive him, never!"

I said it was bloody awful and gave her my handkerchief. It was a mere conventional gesture but to my surprise Eleanor said unsteadily how kind I was and how she'd always liked me and how I'd been a much better husband than Bella deserved.

"My dear Eleanor..." Really, it's extraordinary how different people can view a given situation in entirely different ways.

After the cremation Kester waited twenty-four hours and then invited me to Oxmoon for a drink. I accepted. The moment had come when I could no longer postpone the horror of hearing the details of his plot, but I was so cynical by that time that I wondered if he'd already rewritten it.

Taut with dread I drove to Oxmoon.

IV

"Harry, I just can't thank you enough for—"

"Spare me the gratitude. Give me the truth."

At my suggestion we were sitting on the bench by the tennis court, a spot that precluded all possibility of our conversation being overheard. The parlormaid had brought out a tray of drinks, and we were sipping gin-and-lime in tall glasses garnished, in acknowledgment of the heat of the summer evening, with ice cubes.

"Well, I know you must want to kill me but I felt I just had to say how grateful I was to you for—"

"No, old chap, I don't want to kill you. I want to listen. Contrary to what you may suppose, murder isn't on my list of favorite pastimes. Now cut out all this idiotic chatter and tell me just what the hell was really going on."

"All right. Well, here goes... I didn't mean to kill him."

"Balls. This was a premeditated crime."

"Well, it was and it wasn't. I never thought I'd actually go through with it."

I stared at him. "Are you trying to tell me this was some sort of game which got out of control?"

"Not a game. Therapy."

"*Therapy?*"

"Yes, my psychiatrist in Dublin kept saying to me, 'Act out your grief. Don't just sit around saying life's finished because that's a purely negative response. Take positive action and you'll feel better.'"

"My God, these psychiatrists have a lot to answer for!"

"No wait—let me explain." Kester paused, but it was the pause of someone trying to phrase the truth accurately, not the pause of a storyteller wondering what fable to invent next. "After Anna died," he said at last, "I became utterly obsessed by that scene in '39. I'd vowed at the time to avenge her but then the war came and we all went our separate ways, and after the war all I wanted was to get back to my writing. And then... Anna died. And the guilt absolutely overwhelmed me. I felt I'd failed her. I felt... diminished because I'd made no attempt to repay those gross insults to my wife. That was why my grief for Anna was so all-consuming. My guilt was such that I just didn't know how I was going to live with myself." He looked directly at me. "Can you understand that?"

"All too clearly." I thought of Bella.

Kester looked relieved. "Well," he said, finding himself able to continue more fluently, "the psychiatrist helped, and finally I saw a way I could exorcise this guilt. I wasn't primarily interested in revenge by this time, you understand—after all, no revenge could bring Anna back. All I wanted was to alleviate the guilt. And I thought: I'll write about it. I'll write about this hero who takes an elaborate and masterly revenge on the uncles and cousin who have tormented him for so long."

"My God—"

"Yes, I know it sounds mad but as soon as I'd made that decision I felt much better. I came back here, held out the olive branch of peace to you and Thomas so that I could have absolute peace, and began. Scribble, scribble. I tossed off a first draft in three months and felt euphoric but that sort of euphoria, the writer's ecstasy, isn't to be trusted, and I put the manuscript away for six months so that I could view it with detachment. I didn't want to make any mistakes in the plotting. Then to pass the time I began another book—the novel about our great-grand-parents and Owain Bryn-Davies."

"I'm beginning to believe the *roman à clef* should be banned by law. All right, go on. How did the manuscript look six months later?"

"Poor. The characterization was all wrong and I knew why. It's hard to explain to a layman, but to get a character on paper you have to turn off your own personality and turn on the personality of the character you're trying to capture— it's a trick of mental projection, and my problem here was that I hadn't projected myself properly; I'd remained Kester Godwin seeing Cousin Harry as a two-dimensional villain. What I had to do to make you convincing was to put myself in your head and work out what was going on in your life—and of course as soon as I did that, I came up against that incredible fact which defied explanation: your marriage to Bella."

"I see," I said, and I did. Kester had played the psychological detective, refusing to abandon the trail until the mystery had been unraveled. "You constructed a theory based on Bella's remark about 'another daughter' and proved it by digging up that birth certificate. And then I suppose you saw how you could incorporate the facts into your story."

"Exactly. I sat down, tossed off two more drafts, improved the characterization and reworked the plot."

"Where had the plot got to by this time?"

"Well, Thomas was to be the victim, that was obvious from the start, but my real problem was that I couldn't think what to do with you. I came to the conclusion that what I really wanted was to give you the devil of a fright and at the same time scare poor old Uncle John out of his wits. I didn't want to go further than that (a) because I'm fond of Uncle John and (b) because artistically speaking it would have been too melodramatic if I'd had you hanged for a crime you didn't commit. All you'd done in '39 was gloat, and that was awful but hardly worthy of a hangman's noose. So what I planned was a murder which *looked* as if it had been committed by you but which in fact I could turn inside out in the last chapter with the result that all charges against you would have to be dropped."

"But how on earth could you have achieved that? You'd set me up as the perfect suspect! I had no alibi, and the birth certificate in Thomas's pocket gave me a splendid motive—"

"Wrong. That certainly suggested a great deal, but there was no real evidence of blackmail, was there?"

"My God! Yes, I see but . . . wait a minute—my fingerprints were on that club! How did you get me out of that one?"

"Thomas wasn't killed with the club."

"*What!*"

"I used a poker," said Kester serenely, unable to stop himself looking pleased with his inventive powers. "Then I smeared the club and left it as a red herring."

I was speechless.

"The police are very clever nowadays," said Kester. "They'd assume at first that the club was the weapon but later they'd make tests and find that the club face didn't match the wound. Then I'd call their attention to the poker, and the whole point of the poker, you see, was that you couldn't possibly have used it. It came from my bedroom upstairs, as any of the housemaids would testify."

"But..." I could barely speak. "You could only clear me by incriminating yourself!"

"Yes, but I'd have got off. I'd have confessed to manslaughter and who was going to disbelieve me when I swore I'd struck a violent drunken man in self-defense? I thought the odds were I'd be convicted but discharged without a sentence—or at the most given six months in jail, and that would have been no more than I deserved for failing to avenge Anna while she was alive."

"But how would you have explained your failure to confess your guilt straight-away?"

"Sheer nervous panic. I thought that would be quite in character. But as soon as I saw you were heading for the gallows I'd do the done thing and own up. That would have been in character too."

There was a pause. I finished my drink in a single gulp and stood up to mix myself another.

"However, that was just what I planned for the novel," said Kester. "In real life I never planned to go that far, but in the end—"

"You found you had to make your dream a reality."

"—I found I couldn't resist the temptation to see how well the plot worked. The crucial scene was the sacking of Thomas—I was sorry when that lunch party didn't come off. But later... it was really rather exciting when Thomas came roaring up the drive that night, but then—" He stopped with a shudder.

"Fantasy ended and reality began."

"Yes. It was very much more than I'd bargained for. He wasn't just violent. He was *bloody* violent. And I wasn't just frightened. I was *bloody* frightened. I ran to the billiard room because the weapon was there—I'd acted out the book by getting everything ready beforehand—but right up to the last moment I never meant to do more than knock him out. And then... and then—"

"You found you couldn't stop."

"I meant to stop, I meant to, but then—oh God, Harry, I never knew it could be like that. I suddenly found that once I'd set my plot in motion there was no way back; it—it was as if I'd crossed some final crucial line which couldn't be recrossed. I'd never thought I'd actually commit murder, but once that die was cast I'd *crossed that line*, and then I could only move forward to destruction—"

"Shut up. I can't stand that kind of melodramatic talk. Save it for your next book."

He tried to check the emotion, and when I finally realized it was genuine I added more gin to his glass.

"Two questions," I said when the glass was empty. "One: did you destroy the manuscript of this masterpiece?"

"Yes."

"Thank God. Two: where's the poker? I want to make sure you haven't spun me the biggest fairy tale of all time."

Abandoning his glass he led the way past the patch of uneven turf that covered the foundations of the old summerhouse, and the next moment we were entering the woods. Kester counted ten trees back and stopped. At that point we both glanced at the house far away across the lawn but we were in shadow among the trees and I knew we would have been invisible to any distant observer indoors.

Kester scuffled around amidst last autumn's leaves, burrowed into the earth and produced the poker wrapped in newspaper. Thomas's gore, dried and crusty, was well preserved at one end.

"All right. Bury it again. It's as safe there as anywhere else."

He reburied it. Slowly we returned to our bench by the tennis court. In front of us Oxmoon basked peacefully in the hot evening light but as we drew nearer I saw the sunset reflected in the western windows. The sky looked as though it had been massacred.

We drank for a while in silence but suddenly I said, "I'll tell you something, old chap. You'd have been hanged." As I turned to face him I saw his stunned expression. "Yes," I said, "you made a mistake—all in accordance with the best traditions of detective fiction. Isn't the fictional murderer always supposed to make one fatal mistake?"

"But my God—what was it?"

"The poker. You said it came from your bedroom—'as any of the housemaids would testify,' you added just now. But how do you reconcile that poker with your story that you killed accidentally in self-defense? If you took the poker from your bedroom and put it in the billiard room beforehand, that implies the crime had been premeditated."

"Christ!" He nearly fainted with horror. Then he tried to drum up an explanation. "The billiard room has no set of fire irons. I brought the poker down because I wanted to burn some papers in the fireplace."

"Very implausible. Why pick the billiard room? Why not pick a room that has a set of fire irons? Why not burn the stuff in your bedroom, where the poker belonged?"

Kester began to shiver. I poured him some more gin.

"But how *could* I have overlooked that, how could I—I worked everything out so carefully—"

"Even a genius can have a blind spot when constructing a supposedly infallible theory, and you're no genius, Kester. Stick to writing books. Editors are much kinder than the police when they spot an error and a rejection slip is so much more acceptable than the gallows."

Kester drank all his gin straight off. Eventually he managed to say: "So I owe you my life." He couldn't have sounded more horrified.

We sat there, staring at the house. The sun had sunk a little lower, and all the windows looked like the floor of a slaughterhouse.

"I suppose it would sound too melodramatic," said Kester at last, "if I said I don't know how I can ever repay you."

"Oh, don't worry about that, old chap," I said. "The last thing I'd ever want from you is repayment. I might wind up as the corpse in your next novel."

Silence. We both went on sitting there side by side, both went on watching that sinister sunset.

"However," I said idly after a while, "if you press me, I daresay I could think of a good turn or two you might do."

Another silence.

"Purely to assuage your conscience, of course," I added, voice still immaculately idle, "and to help you to live with your guilt."

It took Kester twenty-four seconds to reply. I was counting. Probably we were both counting. Twenty-four seconds is a very long time to be sitting in silence with a murderer while the clouds appear to be committing mayhem in a crimson sky overhead.

At last he whispered: "What do you want?"

"Oh, just a little favor, old chap. Just an unmistakable clarification that Hal's your favorite nephew."

Kester swallowed. "You mean—"

I terminated the delicate sparring match and prepared to slug it out. "Look. If we want to survive this disaster we've got to find a way we can live with each other without going berserk, and Hal's that way, Kester. If you change your will and make Hal your heir I swear I'll never move against you. Then you can relax— and once you relax I can relax and we'll be at peace."

"But you can't move against me," said Kester. "You daren't. You're in this with me up to the neck."

"True. But that still leaves my head above water, and you'll never be able to convince yourself that there's really nothing I can do to you. But if you make my son your heir—"

"You'll kill me and move in here with Hal!"

"Don't be ridiculous, if I did that I'd wind up on the gallows because the police would immediately find out I was a trained killer with a motive the size of an elephant. Now pull yourself together, Kester, and think. *Think*. I'm offering you the only available olive branch of peace. For Christ's sake grab it before the men in the white coats arrive to lock us both up in the nearest asylum."

Kester chose that moment to go to pieces. He shuddered with dry sobs and whispered, "Oh God, oh Christ, what have I done."

"Shut up." I shook him. "It's the future not the past that matters now." One of my father's well-worn catchphrases slipped into my mind. "How fast!" I urged, and Kester, in an eerie echo of the upbringing we had shared, automatically responded: "Stand firm. Soldier on."

This sort of talk eventually doused the hysterics. He mopped himself up and said, "Very well, I'll do as you say. I'm fond of Hal. But if I die before he's twenty-one, don't expect my will to appoint you to be a trustee. I'm going to make very sure you never get your hands on my Oxmoon."

"Your privilege, old chap. Suit yourself."

We sat there hating each other, two men locked up in a steadily shrinking cell, and the next moment we again saw the double image and sensed the terror that had no name.

"Erika told me once," said Kester in a shaking voice, "that the Germans have a peculiarly vile legend about *Doppelgängers*. They say—"

"Shut up. I don't want to know." I stood up. "We're not *Doppelgängers*," I said. "I absolutely refuse to sink to your overemotional melodramatic level. The plain truth of the matter is that we're just two cousins with a fatal amount in common." I began to walk away from him. "Send me a copy of your new will," I said over my shoulder, "and send it soon. My reserves of patience are very far from endless, I assure you, and I feel I now need a prompt gesture of good faith to soothe my nerves."

"I'll see Fairfax tomorrow."

We said nothing else. He remained slumped on the bench, I went on walking away across the lawn, and seconds later I was driving erratically back to Penhale.

Did I really think our mutual interest in Hal would keep the peace between us? No. But at least I'd bought myself a little time so that I could work out how to lock Kester up in the nearest madhouse.

Of course he was a certifiable lunatic.

V

I was now in the most unenviable position because although I knew Kester was crazy I couldn't prove it without disclosing my own role in Thomas's murder. I was not only an accessory after the fact. I was guilty of that offense which I believe is called "misprision of a felony,' the concealment of a serious crime. There was also the possibility that if I openly accused Kester of murder he would deny it and cook up a new plot in which I'd killed Thomas with the golf club and threatened to kill Kester as well unless he helped me cover up the crime. And in addition to all these hair-raising dilemmas, at least one member of my family thought I was paranoid about Kester and would be certain to believe Kester's story in preference to mine. To use a cricketing metaphor, I was on the stickiest of sticky wickets and no matter how hard I tried to hook my way out of trouble I ran a heavy risk of being clean-bowled.

There was only one person who would believe me, but how could I ever explain to my father why I hadn't drawn the line immediately I found Thomas's body and summoned the police no matter what the possible consequences to myself? Useless to say that I thought I was being framed for a murder I hadn't committed. He would reply that the police would have sorted out the muddle—as indeed they would have done, once they had uncovered Kester's mistake with the poker. Then I would have been proved innocent and Kester certifiable and that would have been that. But as it was . . . I was in my usual big mess. And what was worse, I couldn't see my way out; I couldn't see how the mess could be terminated. Every instinct suggested that Kester would take another swipe at me in the future; I knew too damned much for his peace of mind so I had to get him locked up, had to, but how? *How?*

Obviously it would help if I convinced my family that I was a sane rational man instead of a paranoid neurotic, but this exercise in public relations would take time, and meanwhile Kester might murder me. I wasted many hours picturing my own murder, but at last I pulled myself together sufficiently to perceive two important and reassuring truths. The first was that I suspected Kester had frightened himself so much by his bizarre behavior that it would be some time before he had the nerve to start plotting his next novel. And the second was that I sensed he would be reluctant to move against me while my father was alive. He might want to, but I thought sheer terror of being exposed to my father as my murderer if anything went wrong would be a powerful deterrent to him. If Kester grew desperate I knew he'd say "To hell with Uncle John!" and take a swipe at me. But if I handled him with kid gloves and kept desperation at bay I thought my father's powerful influence might prevail for a long time.

So the immediate problem was How did I handle Kester with kid gloves? I'd made a good start by behaving as if all saintly Cousin Harry wanted in compensation was Oxmoon for his son, but the trouble was that Kester was going to have difficulty in believing indefinitely in the myth of saintly Cousin Harry. He knew very well that I wanted his money, his house, his way of life—the whole damn lot. I knew he knew. I certainly knew *I* knew. We might periodically make valiant efforts to cover up the truth by talking of mirror images and *Doppelgängers*, but this retreat into metaphysical claptrap was prompted by our secret knowledge that we were locked up in a situation which was so absolutely not the done thing that there was no way we could refer to it except by elaborate circumlocution. But if one thrust the metaphysical claptrap aside the stark truth was that I wanted his life, always had, and he was prepared to kill me to keep it.

For years this potential holocaust had been kept in control because neither Kester nor I had been able to conceive of a situation in which I could legally take over his life. (My father's presence of course made all thought of an illegal takeover out of the question.) But I'd never given up hope, had I? How clear my past actions now seemed in retrospect! I'd come back to Penhale. I'd stayed on at the Manor. I'd invented all those plausible half-true excuses for refusing to leave. And all the time the unacknowledged truth was that Oxmoon had been pulling me like a magnet, glittering Oxmoon, the symbol of the life of which I'd been deprived; the unacknowledged truth was that I had felt compelled to stay close to Oxmoon, my Oxmoon, in the hope that one day, dispossessed exile that I was, I'd have the chance to go home.

And now, against all the odds, my chance could be coming. If Kester were locked up, certified insane, the court would have to appoint someone to run the estate, and what better candidate could be found than that hardworking farmer Harry Godwin whose son was Kester's heir? Who could be more suitable?

And it would all be perfectly legal. I wouldn't even have to bump Kester off—not, of course, that I'd ever be stupid enough to kill the sod, but one does occasionally have these idiotic thoughts when one's under stress. If I could get Kester locked up, Oxmoon was mine. But that truth brought me back to Square One again. How the devil could I get him locked up without ruining myself, causing a first-class scandal and killing my father with grief and shame?

I couldn't, that was the short answer. All I could do was wait for Kester to go round the bend again to provide my family with incontrovertible proof of his insanity.

In other words I had to play a waiting game, but unfortunately my nerves—those rusting nerves of steel—decided they couldn't tolerate waiting games, and I became ill. Up at Oxmoon Kester, demonstrating the splendid recuperative powers he had inherited from Aunt Ginevra, was soon in the pink of health once more, hiring a passable new agent, continuing to hold his eccentric children's tea parties and entertaining his family in the Godwin tradition every Christmas and Easter. Kester, as Teddy put it, was doing just fine—and why not? He'd committed murder and got away with it. What a triumph! Having avenged Anna in the most positive way imaginable, he had annihilated the burden of his guilt and was now clearly set to embark on the prime of life by giving a matchless performance of the sane law-abiding landowner thoroughly devoted to his loving and loyal family.

Meanwhile down at shabby old Penhale Manor, poor old Harry, poor old sod, was racked with insomnia and plagued with eczema as he was obliged to admire his cousin's splendid recovery and watch Oxmoon receding once more into the distance. I felt fate had dealt me the roughest hand I'd yet encountered, and in my anger and frustration my eczema grew worse. Finally it became so bad that I felt obliged to have sex fully dressed, and that was the end; I asked Warburton if he could refer me to a skin specialist.

The skin specialist said the trouble was nervous in origin. Stale news. He then stupefied me by suggesting that I saw a psychiatrist.

"Never!" I was incensed.

"Very well." He was unperturbed. "I'll give you some drugs but they won't cure you; they'll just alleviate the symptoms. If you want a cure you must look elsewhere."

I didn't believe him. Then to my horror I found that the drugs had little effect. Meanwhile I was still having sex with my clothes on. Swallowing my pride I crawled back to him and agreed to be dispatched to a psychiatrist.

By this time it was early in 1951 and I was still recovering from the great family Christmas of 1950. The very sight of Kester sitting at the head of the table in my grandfather's chair and beaming at everyone in sight had made all the sores break open on my back. Thomas had now been dead for seventeen months, and Kester was as far from a lunatic asylum as the King at Buckingham Palace.

So much for my daydreams of taking over Oxmoon. So much for all those longings which could never be fulfilled. I was so angry that I didn't get a wink of sleep for two nights, and by the time I arrived at Dr. Mallinson's house in

Swansea for my appointment I was so thoroughly depressed that I didn't even feel humiliated that I'd wound up in psychiatric hands.

A receptionist took my name and showed me into a waiting room where I stared like a zombie at *Punch* but after five minutes a woman in a white coat looked in and said, "Mr. Godwin? Would you come this way, please?" and I followed her into a light austere room which contained a sparse arrangement of modern furniture. There was a couch which I instantly decided to ignore. Heading for the easy chair by the desk I glanced around expectantly. "Where's Dr. Mallinson?" I said to the woman in the white coat.

She said, "I'm Dr. Mallinson. Do sit down, Mr. Godwin."

It was the last straw. I was outraged. I stared at her. She was very thin and flat-chested and she had dust-colored hair tightly permed and she might have been any age between thirty-five and fifty. She gave me a cool look from eyes the color of iron bars.

I said furiously, "I'm not talking to a woman!"

"Very well," she said tranquilly without much interest. "We'll just sit in silence."

"If I'd known you were a woman I'd never have come! I don't need a psychiatrist anyway, and I certainly don't need a woman psychiatrist!"

"Really." She had a well-bred, thoroughly English accent and looked as if she ought to be living in Surrey among the pearls-and-twin-set brigade. As I shook with rage she sat down behind her desk and idly began to sharpen a pencil.

"As far as I'm concerned women are good for one thing and one thing only!" I shouted, maddened by this intolerable calm. "All they're fit for is lying on their backs with their legs apart!"

"I see," said Dr. Mallinson, and made a neat hieroglyphic on her note pad with her newly sharpened pencil.

I suddenly realized I was behaving like a lunatic. My God, suppose *I* was the one who ended up in an asylum! My blood ran cold.

"I'm so sorry," I said in a rush. "I do apologize. I must be going crazy."

"Well, if you are," said Dr. Mallinson with a deadpan humor, "you've come to the right place."

I gave a nervous laugh. She smiled serenely. The next thing I knew was that I had subsided into the easy chair and was facing her across her immaculate desk.

"If I were to tell you," I said, "that someone wants to kill me and that the strain's driving me round the bend, would you certify me?"

"Not today," said Dr. Mallinson kindly.

"Don't I look sufficiently wild-eyed?"

"You do look a little anxious, certainly. But mainly you just look tired. Have you been having trouble sleeping?"

I found this perception thoroughly unnerving. "Well..."

"When did you last have a holiday?"

"I don't have holidays. Don't believe in them. I'd rather stay at home."

"Because you were away for a long time in the war?"

This time I was so unnerved by her perception that I could only stare at her speechlessly.

"Well, in that case," she said, taking my silence as an assent, "it's quite natural that you should want to stay at home, but nevertheless why don't you at least try taking a rest by going away for a few days? It may do no good at all, of course, but I can't see any harm in giving it a try."

I said feebly, "I don't want to go anywhere."

"Not even to London? There's always something to do there, and you look as if you might be an artistic type. You could go to galleries . . . and the theater . . . and I believe there are some simply splendid concerts coming on at the Albert Hall."

I opened my mouth and shut it again. I gazed at her. Then I tried to say, "Artistic type? Nonsense, I'm a man of action!" but the words that came out were "I love music."

"Ah. Yes, I can imagine you playing the piano . . . you do play the piano, don't you?"

I nodded. By this time I could clearly see that she was magic—not Celtic magic like Bronwen, but Anglo-Saxon magic, the kind of magic which invades the jungle, tames the savages, builds an outpost of the Empire and produces tea parties below a flying Union Jack all within the space of six months. I looked at this cool clinical competent woman who was not one scrap sexy and who was almost certainly years older than I was, and I thought: This is it. I've found my magic lady. And my relief was so enormous that I'd finally found someone who would sort me out and show me how to be happy that I nearly broke down and wept. However I held myself together, as befitted someone who didn't need a psychiatrist, and said casually, "Are you married?"

"Yes. My husband's a neurosurgeon."

Bloody hell. Why did I never, never have any luck? I knew I hadn't a chance of competing with a neurosurgeon.

"Any children?" I said, trying to pretend this was just a polite social conversation.

"No."

"Oh." A woman who was probably either sterile or else childless by choice! I sighed. Then I realized I was behaving like a lunatic again so I said briskly as I rose to my feet, "Well, perhaps I will go to London for a few days. Thank you. Of course I shan't need to see you again, but if I do—"

"My secretary would be delighted to make an appointment," said Dr. Mallinson inscrutably.

"Uh . . . could I make it now? Before I leave?"

Dr. Mallinson gave a small, *Mona Lisa*–like smile and looked professionally satisfied.

For some hours after this extraordinary interview I indulged in daydreams that the neurosurgeon would drop dead with the result that Dr. Mallinson would be free to iron out my life, but then sanity returned and it slowly dawned on me that I had stumbled into the well-known farcical situation of the patient who falls in love with his psychiatrist. How mad could one get? I at once decided to be sane—much too sane to see Dr. Mallinson again—so I cancelled my next appointment, but I did take her advice to go to London for a week.

This did me so much good that at the end of the week I bought a postcard of the Albert Hall and wrote on it: *Your cure worked, chalk me up on your list of successes, many thanks,* H. C. GODWIN. But this sounded too dull so I bought a second postcard of the Albert Hall and wrote: *I'm a new man, thanks to you. I must see you again but does it have to be in that damned consulting room?* HARRY GODWIN. But I decided I really couldn't send this so I bought a third postcard and wrote: *I shan't see you again but I'll never forget how you helped me. With gratitude,* H. GODWIN. Then I made an awful mistake—or was it a Freudian slip?—and posted the wrong one, so in the end I sent them all, just to give her something to think about, and resolutely made up my mind to forget her. Like Oxmoon she apparently wasn't in my stars.

Bloody stars, I hated them all.

VI

The most important result of my visit to London was that I was at last able to see my problems in perspective. No doubt this was just what Dr. Mallinson had hoped would happen. I'd been in a hellish position which had been made even more hellish because I had become too bogged down in Penhale to see it clearly, but once I had struggled out of the bog to London clarity of vision soon returned.

Having posted my mad postcards to Dr. Mallinson I walked away from the Albert Hall into Kensington Gardens and eventually sat down by the Round Pond where, long ago, my nanny had boasted to the other nannies that my mother had been one of the Beauties of the Season back in 1914. The weather was uninviting; it was a chilly day in January, but I sat down on a bench and gazed over the tranquil water. I wanted to be sane. Where lay the road to sanity? Herefordshire. Timbuktu. The North Pole. Anywhere, in fact, except Kester's doorstep. If I wanted to keep myself out of a straitjacket and away from a padded cell, I had to escape from Cousin Kester once and for all, and escaping from Cousin Kester meant giving up all hope that Oxmoon would drop into my lap.

Which was more important, Oxmoon or my sanity? My sanity. The truth which I now had to face after thirty-two years in the world was that I wasn't going to get Oxmoon either now or in the future, and it was quite pointless to hang around Penhale on a second-rate estate waiting for something that was never going to happen. My father had always known this, of course. No wonder he had been worried about me! He had had good cause. But never mind, I'd woken up now, I'd faced the unpalatable facts squarely and I'd made up my mind to reorganize my life along more rational lines.

I allowed myself to brood for one last time on those unpalatable facts but I knew I was powerless to alter them. The truth was that there was nothing I could do about Kester—short of murdering him (ha ha)—and I'd be a fool to continue to crucify myself with frustrated rage just because he'd got away with murder while I, hoist with the petard of my own assistance, had been unable to lock him up. If we'd been characters in one of Kester's novels, retribution would be waiting in the wings to remove Kester from the scene; murderers never escaped unpunished in novels, but this was messy real life and as far as I could see there was no ghost of retribution on the horizon. Kester wasn't going to drop dead. Nor was he going to go mad again, I could see that clearly now. He'd obviously been mad when he'd killed Thomas, but with his guilt towards Anna assuaged he'd made a complete recovery, and the odds were he'd live another fifty years in perfect mental health. Probably, now that he was no longer feeling guilty about Anna, he'd even remarry and produce sons.

Very well. So much for him. Lucky old Kester, lucky old sod, but before I died of jealousy I had to get the hell out of his life.

I went back to my hotel and telephoned my father.

VII

"I draw the line," I said.

So I was my father's son after all, and here we were, right in the middle of this supremely edifying scene which would have warmed the cockles of any Victorian heart and served as an illustration for a story entitled "The Reconciliation"—or perhaps, in true Victorian style, "The Repentance." If we had belonged to any race on earth but the British we might have shed a pardonable tear or two, but there we were, two Welshmen strangled at birth by the Anglo-Saxon culture, so of course all we could do was grunt dry-eyed at each other and keep a stiff upper lip as we bust our guts to do the done thing.

"I draw the line, Father."

"Finally?"

"Finally."

"Thank God."

"Yes. Behaved like a lunatic. Sorry."

"No need to apologize. Tricky situation."

"Bloody."

"Hm."

Silence.

We were sitting working-class style at the table in Bronwen's kitchen. I had returned home a day early from London to convey my great decision to my father, and was staying the night at his house. Humphrey was already there. I had given Nanny a week's holiday to coincide with my own and she wasn't back yet. The three elder boys were all away at school.

My father and I were alone in the kitchen. After tea Bronwen had lured Humphrey into the drawing room to play Ludo, and all my siblings were absent. Evan was working in a slum parish in Cardiff; Gerry, articled to a Swansea solicitor, and Lance, employed at an engineering works at Port Talbot, were still out at work, while Sian was away in London where she was attending one of the famous secretarial colleges. She was staying with Marian, who for some extraordinary reason beyond my comprehension had resumed her marriage to Rory Kinsella.

My father and Humphrey had met me at the station. I was very fond of

Humphrey, who looked just like me, and I secretly regarded him as my favorite. Charles and Jack were too like the Stourhams, while Hal... But I didn't understand Hal. I'd thought the music would make a bond between us, but it hadn't. Whenever I tried to talk to him the right words always eluded me.

"Daddy, Daddy..." Humphrey chattered all the way from the station to my father's house, and I listened and smiled and thought what an attractive little beggar he was. But Humphrey wasn't musical. He seemed to be like me but he had no ear for music, and in my sadder moments I knew that that meant he wasn't really like me at all.

However before I could start to feel depressed about the gulf which existed between me and my sons, we arrived at my father's house and my magic lady came out to meet me. She at once said how much better I looked. Then she turned to my father and asked him if he was all right. My father said, "Yes, yes, yes" impatiently and tried not to walk like an old man. Apparently he had played thirty-six holes of golf in the rain the day before and was now feeling stiff in the legs.

In the kitchen the kettle was on the boil, my favorite cake was on the table and we settled down to relax. I was so happy I ate like a horse. So did Humphrey, and when he looked afterwards as if he regretted his third slice of cake Bronwen suggested the game of Ludo to divert him.

"Are you sure you're all right, Johnny?" she said over her shoulder as she left the room. My father had drunk two cups of tea but had eaten nothing.

"Stop nagging me!" said my father crossly.

Bronwen made an acid-sounding comment in Welsh and withdrew.

"If I want to play thirty-six holes in the rain I'll damn well play thirty-six holes in the rain!" shouted my father after her in English.

The door banged.

I allowed him a couple of minutes to recover from this little exhibition of marital normality but finally launched myself upon a monologue declaring my intention to reorganize my life. I confessed my neurotic preoccupation with Oxmoon. I confessed my mind-destroying jealousy of Kester. I confessed that I'd reached the end of an exceptionally disastrous road. My father listened and listened and sagged deeper and deeper in his chair with relief. When I finally reached the point where I could utter his famous phrase I knew quite well there was a lump in his throat. There was certainly a lump in mine. How we both managed to sustain a few more seconds of fractured conversation I have no idea.

After the inevitable silence while we both took the necessary time to restarch our upper lips, I managed to say: "I'll be all right now."

"Yes. I know you will. But all the same..." My father leaned forward with his forearms on the table and clasped his hands. Then he said violently, taking me by surprise: "How I resent you being driven into exile like this! I feel..." He stopped to choose his words. "I feel," he said slowly, "as if there's some terrible injustice here somewhere but I can't quite work out what it is."

That shook me. I said nothing. My one unbreakable resolution was that he should never know the truth about Thomas's death.

774

"It was justice that Oxmoon went to Kester," said my father. "Your grandfather... But no, let his memory rest in peace. That's all over now... my poor father, I was so fond of him. But although it was justice that Oxmoon went to Kester, justice somehow seems to have gone adrift here... Why should you have to suffer like this? I suppose it must somehow be my fault because—"

But I couldn't have him blaming himself for anything, not when he was entering old age and entitled to an unflawed happy ending.

"No, this isn't your fault, Father! Absolutely not!"

"But I allowed you to grow up feeling shortchanged about Oxmoon—I never gave you the real explanation of my father's motives for passing you over. I wanted to protect my father, protect myself from all those painful memories.... You see, it was all to do with my grandmother—my grandmother and Owain Bryn-Davies—"

"Father, that's past. It's irrelevant."

"No, that's where you make your big mistake. My grandmother's tragedy made my father the man he was—and if my father hadn't been the man he was he wouldn't have put himself in a position where he was so guilty about Robert that he allowed Robert to dictate to him about his will—"

I couldn't cope. "Father, I'm sorry but if I start dwelling on chains of causality I'll go round the bend with rage and frustration. I've got to concentrate on the future now if I want to stay sane."

"I don't want to think of the past either, but I do. Where did I go wrong with you two boys? What did I do? I made rather a success of bringing up Thomas— with his appalling home background in early adolescence he could well have turned out to be completely delinquent, but he did well for himself, settled down happily, excelled at his job... until it all ended in tragedy. Harry, talking of Thomas—"

"Father if you start blaming yourself because Thomas smashed himself up while drunk I swear I'll have a complete nervous breakdown. For Christ's sake—"

"I sometimes wonder," said my father, not looking at me, "whether the whole story of Thomas's death was ever known."

Batten down the hatches. Lock up the truth.

"Father, I was there at Oxmoon. I watched him weave drunkenly away in his Hillman. Why would I lie? What possible motive could I have for suppressing any facts?"

My father judged this question to be unanswerable and sagged with relief again. "I'm sorry, I know I'm being irrational, but sometimes I lie awake at night—"

"Well, don't. Stop it. Pull yourself together." It's a bizarre fact of life that after a certain span of time the parent–child relationship slowly reverses itself and the child begins to assume the parental role.

My father smiled as if he were glad to see me assuming his role so ably, but then he pressed his hand against his forehead in pain.

"Father—"

"Yes, it's a bloody nuisance, but I'm going to have to give in—obviously I've got a chill. In fact I think I may even have a temperature."

"I'll call Bronwen."

"No, wait," he said. "Wait." I shall always remember his tone of voice when he said that. It was one of extreme disbelief. "Harry, can you come and help me? Something seems to have happened to my legs."

They were paralyzed.

He had polio.

He died four days later.

VIII

He died in hospital, and although only Bronwen was in his room at the end all his children except Francesca were waiting nearby for the recovery that never came. Marian and I, Evan, Gerry, Lance and Sian were bunched together in the corridor like a group of dazed sheep, and with us was Kester whom my father had treated as a son. Kester said, soft mouth trembling, "He was more of a father to me than my own father was," and tears ran down his cheeks. Disgusting. Evan had to mop him up. No one had to mop *me* up, thank God, although the tenses of the Latin verbs became tangled in my head when everyone went to pieces around me, everyone except Bronwen who said calmly that she would grieve later. Fine. At least there was one member of the family who was behaving sensibly, and by God I was going to be another. I herded my flock of dazed sheep into the bleak white room where my father lay dead. After all, we had to say goodbye, didn't we, each of us in his own way. That was the right thing to do—except as usual I couldn't do it. I was too afraid of breaking down and all I could think was what hell it is for the survivors when death slams into life without warning and smashes every fixed point on the emotional map. It makes one realize how fragile human beings are, how absolutely at the mercy of that fate they can postpone but never escape.

Morbid thoughts. Doesn't do to think about death. But what else can one think about when one's in a room with a corpse? I wondered if I'd contracted polio myself. Maybe within a month I too would be dead. That would solve all Kester's problems neatly. . . .

Kester.

He was facing me across the bed, facing me across all the horrors of the past and the horrors still to come, and suddenly I knew with a terrible certainty that I wasn't going to be able to escape after all from our shared circle of time. Wherever I now went, wherever I ran to, he'd follow and try to kill me because I was the living reminder of his madness, the living witness of his crime. I represented the side of his personality he couldn't bear to live with and he had to cut me out of his life in order to stay sane. I was his nemesis, his evil genius; I was his double image, his other self. In the tragedy our minds had merged to become as interchangeable as our personalities, and now it was as if our two bodies had at last been united in a single indivisible soul.

Outside the hospital he even said to me, "This has united us, hasn't it?" and

I said, "Yes, it has," but none of the others realized what we meant. They all thought we were acknowledging a new bond of amity, but Kester and I were moving deeper into our metaphysical nightmare and the new bond was the old horror that had no name.

We looked at each other and knew we were finally alone in our circle. My father was dead—and that, for Kester and me, could have only one meaning: it meant there was no one left to stand between us. It meant there was no one left to draw the line.

8

I

WELL, I GOT over all that—of course the shock of my father's death had temporarily unhinged me—but it was not until I saw Kester at the funeral that I realized just how paranoid I'd been. Kester was only poor old Kester, poor old sod, sniveling away because he'd lost his father figure. Out to kill me? Ridiculous! I began to fear seriously that I was unbalanced on the subject. In fact there was no doubt I had to pull myself together very firmly, and the sooner I left Gower and settled in Herefordshire the better.

However first of all I had to organize my father's funeral, and that was difficult because as soon as I got home from the hospital I went to pieces. Awful. Less said the better. God knows what I would have done without Dafydd. He sat up with me all night while I wept and drank myself into a stupor and said what a rotten son I'd been and how I'd failed to live up to my father's standards and didn't know how I was going to live with my guilt. How Dafydd stood such disgraceful emotional self-indulgence I don't know, but he listened and chain-smoked and occasionally held my hand and at the end of it all he just said, "But you put everything right, didn't you? You told him you'd drawn the line."

That made me feel better but the next moment my grief had veered from guilt to rage and I was shouting how bloody unfair it was that he had died before he was even sixty and what had he ever done to deserve it and what did it all mean anyway and how could people think there was a God who allowed such unfairness—and Dafydd nodded and made me some tea and went on listening patiently as I ranted and raved like a lunatic.

"All that bloody business of doing the done thing, and where did it get him? To a middle-class house in Swansea, the local golf club and a bunch of civic-committee meetings—oh, and five years at the end with Bronwen, *five years only!* He should have had fifty years with her and died master of Oxmoon—oh, bugger the done thing, fuck it all, wipe it off the map! My father wasted his life, wasted it, and *what does it all mean?*"

"Nothing," said Dafydd. "Life's meaningless. Accept that and you'll feel better."

I couldn't. I didn't. I raged on and on and on, but the rage died at the funeral. It was as if someone were slowly turning off a tap in my mind. I left my father's house with Bronwen for the long drive to Penhale, and as we drove deeper into Gower I noticed that we were one of many cars all traveling in one direction. In fact beyond Oxmoon the road became so choked with traffic that it took us some time to reach the village, and I was relieved when I found that Dafydd had saved a space for our car by the church. The green was packed with silent crowds. So was the churchyard. A bell was tolling quietly in the tower.

Then I began to realize that people had come from all over the world to pay their last respects to him—Francesca and her husband from America, Declan Kinsella and his wife from Ireland, even my lost cousin Erika had emerged from Germany—and beyond the family were the people from London, from Scotland, from Wales itself—all those whose lives he had touched, rich and poor, young and old, everyone who believed his life had meant something special to them. And when I saw those crowds I realized how wrong I had been to judge his life a failure when his success had been greater than I had ever imagined. What had Oxmoon mattered in the end to my father? For him it had become merely another symbol, like the house at Eaton Walk, of the worldly success which had made him so unhappy. How meaningless it was to judge a life by its outward affluence or by its length! It was the quality of life that counted. Five years with Bronwen at the end—fifty years—it was all the same. The point was that he had achieved more happiness with her than most people achieve in a lifetime, and his fifty-nine years in the world represented a more powerful statement than many lives lived far longer than his.

I groped for a Latin verb. No good. I tried Greek. A blank. All I could remember was that extremely morbid quote from Shakespeare "Bid me not remember mine end." *Henry the Fourth Part Something-or-other.* I could remember quoting it in some far-off exam. Glancing around feverishly to divert myself I became aware of Marian, sitting next to me and weeping soundlessly into a dainty black lace handkerchief. Poor Marian, she had her guilty memories, just as I did. I took her hand in mine.

Well, I got through all that but even then the ordeal wasn't over because an endless stream of people came up to me after the service to shake my hand and tell me what a great man my father had been. Splendid. I was delighted. But I could barely hear what they were saying, all the words seemed to blend into a single repetitive monologue, and I didn't dare to listen too closely in case I began to grieve.

I was frightened of grieving, frightened of breaking down, frightened of not living up to my father's standards. Awful. A nightmare. How I survived that funeral I'll never know but I did and later, much later at Penhale Manor, I encountered Edmund, the lone survivor of his generation, a balding stout elderly man with clouded blue eyes. He and Teddy were staying at Oxmoon with their sons but all the family had gathered at the Manor after the funeral; as the eldest son I had felt obliged to offer the necessary hospitality and save Bronwen from yet another harrowing ordeal.

Evan had taken Bronwen back to Swansea immediately after the service. She had wanted only to be alone.

I wanted to be alone too so when I saw Edmund in the rose garden my first instinct was to avoid him. But I couldn't. I went up to him and touched his arm.

"Edmund."

"Oh hullo, Harry, I was just thinking how I replanted part of the rose garden when I lived here after your mother died. John couldn't stand those white roses and wanted another sort put in. Funny how clear it all is in my mind, exactly as if it had happened yesterday . . . but that's what happens when you're old, isn't it? The past seems clearer and closer than the present. My father lived a lot in the past but in the worst possible way—John was always afraid, you know, that he'd end up like him but he didn't, I knew he wouldn't, I always knew John was much tougher than my father was."

He paused as if meditating on this toughness. Then he said, "Yes, there's a tough streak in our family and it came from my mother who was tough as old boots—my God, you should have heard *her* on the subject of doing the done thing! But then you've got to be tough to do the done thing the whole damn time, haven't you, tough, ruthless and a bit of a bastard . . . like John—yes, I'm rather horrified that everyone's trying to canonize John now he's dead, he wouldn't have liked that at all. *He* knew his own faults better than anyone and *he* knew he wasn't a saint, far from it, he was human, he was real, he was my brother John. . . . And now there's no one left," said Edmund, looking past me down the garden, "who remembers the old days at Oxmoon as I do, the summer days long ago in another century when we had tea on the lawn and my mother presided over the silver teapot and my father played tennis with Robert and Celia showed me her pressed wild flowers and Lion and John talked of what they would do when they grew up and Thomas was still unborn. . . . And then later I can see Thomas spilling milk over Glendower and Ginevra crossing the lawn with Robert— that was when she came home after her first husband was killed—and we all thought how gorgeous she was, how ravishing, how beautiful . . . and now she's dead and they're all dead except me and suddenly it seems—"

"Unbearable."

"No. I can bear it. Have to, don't I? No choice. But it's sad all the same . . . and lonely," said Edmund, "very lonely to have a past no one else can share."

After that I got drunk, and some unknown time later I wound up saying to Teddy: "I've met this wonderful woman and she's a psychiatrist and she practices Anglo-Saxon magic and I send her postcards of the Albert Hall . . ."

Teddy somehow steered me upstairs.

". . . and her name's Dr. P. Mallinson and she has a husband and a flat chest and eyes the color of battleships."

"Well, that's not the usual description of a sexy woman, honey," said Teddy, helping me take off my jacket, "but hell, why should you follow the crowd?"

"Next time I marry," I said, slumping onto the bed, "I'm going to marry a robot with a high I.Q. I want someone utterly different from—from—"

"Poor Bella," said Teddy. "But she could be such a sweet little girl."

I cried. But not for my father. I cried for Bella. They were the first tears I'd shed for her since her death.

"There is no timetable for grief. Grief isn't a train which you catch at the station. . . ." Was that me talking? No, that was Bronwen talking in the past but the next moment I was beyond both past and present. Kissing Teddy I closed my eyes and finally succeeded in escaping into oblivion.

II

I could feel Kester meditating about me but I didn't meditate about him. My mistake. But the trouble was that even with the funeral behind me I remained thoroughly preoccupied with the aftermath of my father's death.

The main problem was the will.

It was a complex document but that was only to be expected; my father had been a complex man with a complex family situation. What no one had expected, however, was his paranoid distrust of his beneficiaries, but I believe men who are clever with money often feel their heirs are bound to make a balls-up of their inheritance unless the testator takes firm steps to prevent it. My father had no doubt told himself he had an absolute moral duty to save his children from self-inflicted penury. The result was a disaster.

With a few exceptions, everything was tied up on trust. The main exception was a disgracefully large hunk of the Armstrong fortune that was willed, in a faultless Victorian gesture, to charity. Even Francesca, who had a rich husband, was piqued, and as for Rory Kinsella, who had obviously returned to Marian in the belief that he could look forward to a luxurious old age, he was so livid when he discovered he couldn't get his hands on her legacy that he stormed off again to live with his latest mistress. Marian was livid too—not because of Rory's desertion but because my father had treated her like a mental defective who couldn't defend her own bank account. In fact my father succeeded in infuriating just about everyone. The chorus of complaint increased. I felt sorry for us all—and in particular I felt sorry for myself. I received the freeholds of Penhale Manor, Martinscombe and Little Oxmoon, just as my father had promised, and as this represented a generous inheritance I was duly grateful, but the trouble was I didn't get what I needed most; I didn't get those vital lands in Herefordshire.

My future immediately became very murky indeed.

Of course my father would have changed his will if he'd lived but that was beside the point. The point was that he had ordered that the lands should be sold and the proceeds invested for the benefit of my four sons and Marian's two daughters. There was still nothing to stop me selling my Gower properties and moving elsewhere, but if I did I would be reduced to buying an estate of a similar size, and to be frank I now wanted more from life than a career as a working gentleman farmer. I had been content to sweat away at a second-rate estate while I had cherished the illusion that Oxmoon might miraculously drop into my lap, but with that myth exploded I was no longer content to be a big fish in a small pond.

The more I thought about my dilemma the more intractable it seemed to become. I was still keen to move. At the same time common sense cautioned me against it. Farming requires capital and if I moved to an unknown area I would inevitably incur considerable capital outlay. Moreover one bad mistake could land me promptly in a financial quagmire from which extraction might prove both painful and difficult. I wouldn't have the capital to set myself straight. Besides, on a small estate it's tougher to recoup one's losses. Repeating to myself the maxim "Better the devil you know than the devil you don't," I found myself strongly tempted to remain in Penhale.

These thoughts alone were sufficient to distract me from meditating on Kester, but I continued to be distracted by the other reverberations from the will. My father had possessed three fortunes to devise. The Armstrong fortune, as already mentioned, went to charity and to Francesca (on trust); it also obligingly paid the death duties on the whole estate. The Lankester fortune went not only to my mother's grandchildren but also to Marian (on trust) in order to bring her legacy vaguely in line with mine. That left my father's personal fortune. I received the Gower lands but not the money accumulated by my father during his notable career as a boardroom ornament and a gambler on the stock exchange; this money was left to Bronwen (on trust) for life with the remainder to my Canadian siblings. Bronwen was fifty-three and could well expect to live another twenty years. Meanwhile those children got nothing and she couldn't touch the capital in order to give them a helping hand. I felt very sorry for them and particularly sorry for Gerry who earned no salary as an articled clerk. It was true he would eventually qualify as a solicitor and earn a substantial income, but he was long past the age when he could easily accept being financially dependent on his mother and a sizable legacy would have been invaluable to him.

The trouble was, as I pointed out to Gerry, that although my father must have known that his will should reflect his current situation, he had nonetheless refused to consider the possibility that he might die while his third family were all struggling at the start of their careers. For a hardheaded businessman his attitude had hardly been the last word in unsentimental common sense.

So much for the will. It was small wonder that a great deal of my time after my father's death was occupied in discussing this testamentary disaster with my fellow victims, but as a first-class hypochondriac I still found the odd moment or two to wonder if I might be about to die of polio. I didn't. The incubation period passed and I found I'd survived. I decided that that had to rank as some sort of triumph but once I stopped worrying that I might die of polio I started worrying that I might be murdered by Kester. I tried to convince myself I was being neurotic but I didn't succeed. I tried to convince myself that for my own good I still had to leave Gower but I didn't succeed in believing that either. What was I to do? I dithered. I couldn't make up my mind.

Yet perhaps all the time I knew that Kester was going to make up my mind for me. Kester had no idea that I'd told my father I wanted to move. Kester still thought he had me on his doorstep forever, and soon after the funeral his nerve snapped, all my worst fears proved justified and he took a swipe at me.

That sealed our fate. My patience was exhausted. At once I found myself fanatically determined that he shouldn't get away with any further iniquity, and abandoning all thought of retreat I settled down to swipe at him in return.

III

He stole my land. Not Penhale Manor. He had no claim on that, but he grabbed Martinscombe and Little Oxmoon and without the income those two properties represented to me I was financially ruined. It would have been quite impossible, as he well knew, for me to remain at Penhale Manor. I would have had to move to much humbler surroundings elsewhere.

I was having breakfast with Humphrey when the charlady stumped in with the morning's post. It was March but the other boys hadn't yet returned for the holidays. Humphrey was talking about how he wanted to be a spaceman.

"...and I shall go to Mercury, Mars, Venus..."

Discarding the bills and circulars I opened the typed envelope from Swansea. It was from my father's solicitors.

"Dear Mr. Godwin—" That gave me a jolt. Old Freddy Fairfax had called me Harry since I'd been Humphrey's age. Checking the signature I found that my correspondent was a new partner, a certain P. D. St. J. Carmichael.

"Daddy, you're not listening to me!"

"Just a moment, Humphrey."

"I write on behalf of our client Mr. Christopher Godwin," wrote P. D. St. J. Carmichael, "about a matter relating to the will of your late father, Mr. John Godwin, the news of whose recent decease I received with profound regret. May I, in passing, offer you my sincere condolences on your bereavement."

This Carmichael sounded like a smooth bugger. I read on with increasing alarm.

It has been drawn to your cousin's attention that under the terms of your father's will you inherit the property known as Martinscombe Farm which incorporates the dwelling known as Little Oxmoon. On behalf of your cousin I respectfully beg to inform you that this bequest unfortunately cannot be valid since your father had no legal title to this land. Your father believed he had inherited the property from his brother Robert, but this belief was in fact erroneous as Mr. Robert Godwin himself had no legal title to devise by will.

According to the papers which are in our keeping there is no evidence that your grandfather, Mr. Robert Godwin senior, ever donated the land to his eldest son by a formal deed of gift. Nor did your uncle, the younger Mr.

Robert Godwin, live long enough to acquire the property under the Statute of Limitations. Consequently it must be construed that your grandfather still owned the Martinscombe property when he died in 1929, and therefore the land, including both farm and bungalow, automatically devolved at that time to Mr. Christopher Godwin, his heir.

Our client desires to inform you that he now wishes to reclaim this property . . .

I stopped reading. The letter was shaking in my hand. "My God!"

Humphrey jumped. He'd been trying to hide scrambled egg under his plate and he thought my anger was directed against him.

"No, it's all right, Humphrey." As I spoke, the Llewellyns' car came up the drive and he ran off to get his satchel. I thanked God it wasn't my week for driving the children to school. I was so angry I might have rammed the car into the nearest wall.

"Calm down" was Dafydd's advice when I collared him five minutes later. "He's pulling a fast one. Don't let the sod drive you off your rocker."

I did calm down sufficiently to drive to Swansea without having an accident, but then I unleashed my fury and stormed the offices of Fairfax, Walters and Wyn-Williams. Poor old Freddy Fairfax, trembling behind his mustaches, started to babble how sorry he was.

"Sorry!" I shouted, making him cringe. Then I remembered Dafydd's advice not to go off my rocker and I managed to say in a level voice, "Before I wash my hands of your firm I'd like some information. When did my uncle Robert Godwin acquire control of the Martinscombe lands?"

The poor old boy was too senile to remember. He feverishly pressed a button on the intercom and the next moment in glided P. D. St. J. Carmichael, a smooth individual of about forty wearing an Old Wykehamist tie. That was bad news. Winchester schoolboys were famous for their brains.

"According to our client Mr. Kester Godwin," said Carmichael, "Little Oxmoon was completed in 1920 but obviously it took some months to build and I would assume your grandfather's decision to allow his son the use of the Martinscombe land was taken in 1919. But there's nothing to indicate that a formal deed of gift was ever made."

"Did your firm act for the Oxmoon estate then, Mr. Fairfax?"

"No, the Oxmoon solicitors were Owens, Wood for many years but after the war—the First War—old Owens died and young Owens approached us with the idea of a merger—"

"You took over the firm."

"Yes. In 1922. And that was when I became your grandfather's solicitor."

"Is this chap young Owens still alive?"

"No, he was killed in the war—the Second War."

"Could there be any clerks still alive who might remember what the hell went on at Oxmoon in 1919?"

"Young Owens did have a clerk, of course," said Fairfax. "But he was well over sixty in 1922. I think he died in—"

"The point is," said Carmichael, terminating these meanderings, "that we have the Oxmoon papers, all the deeds relating to the estate, and there's no record of a deed of gift among them."

"That proves nothing. The copy could be lost, the original could be lodged with some unknown solicitor—"

"I would most strongly advise you," said Carmichael, "to take independent legal advice."

I gave him some strong advice of my own and walked out. I then telephoned Gerry, who was articled to another leading firm of Swansea solicitors, and ordered him to meet me at the Claremont Hotel.

I had become fond of Gerry since he had revealed himself as my supporter two years before. Periodically he would consult me about his problems, which were usually female, and a picture had slowly emerged of a lonely insecure young man, unable to talk frankly to either of his parents and not sure what he wanted to do with his life. He didn't care much for his legal studies but he saw the law as the gateway to Big Opportunities which would satisfy his burning ambition to Be Accepted. Gerry talked a great deal about Being Accepted and Getting On and Finding the Right Role to Play. After playing the Canadian at Oxford he had decided that no one Got On unless he was an English gentleman, so he was now busy trying to acquire a BBC accent. He told me pathetically that he never missed the nine-o'clock news.

That day at the Claremont I bought him a three-course lunch which he could never have afforded, and then having demonstrated what a kind generous brother I was I described Kester's bombshell and asked for some free advice.

Gerry was much intrigued. "There's something shady going on there, Harry—they're not telling you the whole story."

"Why do you say that?"

"Well, to start with there's got to be some sort of deed in existence. There must be. How else could Uncle Robert have transferred the property to Dad?"

"But Freddy Fairfax isn't a crook—if there is a deed he must obviously think it's invalid."

"What I'd like to know is why this problem's suddenly surfaced. When did Uncle Robert die?"

"'28. But it's no mystery, Gerry. Kester has a genius for excavating skeletons in the family closet. Once he'd decided to force me out of Gower he'd naturally attack my bank account, and once he started calculating how he could halve my income it was inevitable that he should start thinking about my property and thumbing his way through the family deeds."

"But you can't let him get away with this!"

"Why do you think we're here? I want you to beat your brains out and drum up the script of what must have happened back in the Twenties. I can't fight Kester while I'm in the dark."

Gerry obediently put his legally trained brains to work. Finally he said,

"Let's assume they're right and there was no deed of gift in 1919. Let's remember that Uncle Robert was a lawyer who knew he was dying. Let's not forget that Grandfather was senile in the late Twenties and probably legally incompetent. I think Uncle Robert must have figured out a way to pull a fast one—probably for the best possible motives. Leaving Martinscombe and Little Oxmoon to Dad was his way of saying Thank you, wasn't it?"

"I'm quite sure Father wouldn't have connived at anything illegal."

"True, but he hero-worshiped Uncle Robert, didn't he? And if Uncle Robert had told him he had an absolute moral duty to help him out—"

"Of course." I was remembering my father's deep and inexplicable embarrassment when he discovered he had inherited the property under the terms of Uncle Robert's will. Kester had even remarked on it to me at the time. "Uncle Robert probably told him he wanted to make sure Aunt Ginevra inherited a good title to the property," I said. "I can just see Father thinking it was his moral duty to help regularize the position. . . . But how do we know Father was involved?"

"If this happened near the end of Robert's life when he was too paralyzed to write—"

"Yes, he'd have needed help. . . . All right, how did Robert pull the fast one?"

"I'm just trying to think. 1928. Land Registration was in force. If I were him I'd have tried to register the property—in fact he must have registered it, I can't see how else he could have passed it on to Dad, but how the hell did he register it without Grandfather's consent?"

"Maybe Grandfather did consent."

"If that was so, then Fairfax would have a record of it. Did Dad have a power of attorney for Grandfather?"

"Yes, but not until Uncle Robert was at death's door and surely Robert would have wanted to regularize the position earlier than that."

"That's true. But how the devil did Robert do it?"

We went on beating our brains out. I ordered some brandy to help us along.

"Well, never mind that for now," I said at last. "Let's just assume Robert pulled a fast one. Where does that leave me?"

"Up the creek."

"I was afraid you'd say that. So Kester's on a good wicket?"

"Not necessarily. You might be able to prove Robert's fast one was legal after all, I don't know, we don't have sufficient information. But the point is, Harry, that this case would be a lawyers' playground. You could take years going around this particular mulberry bush and it could cost you a fortune. You might win in the end, but—"

"I'd be ruined. A Pyrrhic victory." I was so angry that I flagged down the nearest waiter and demanded a second brandy. "That damned Kester, I could bloody kill him!"

"Take it easy. Come back to the office and consult Roland Davison, the partner I work for. You need a qualified prognosis, not just the opinion of an articled clerk."

This was sensible enough. "I could at least engage him to track down some facts for me," I conceded and added as an afterthought: "If Robert did register the land,

785

I suppose this would be on record at the Land Registry?"

"Of course. And once we establish that the land was registered in Robert's name—"

The same thought struck us both at the same moment.

"Oh my God," I said, "they had the same name—Robert Charles Godwin. Kester'll claim the Robert Charles Godwin on the deed is Grandfather and I won't be able to prove that he's wrong."

"But by law," said Gerry, "not only the name and address but a description of the owner must appear on the Land Registry records in order to differentiate between—"

"Yes, but can't you see? Robert would have picked a description that would apply to both of them—he probably described himself by some meaningless term like 'gentleman' which applies equally to a landowner like Grandfather and to a barrister prematurely retired through ill health like himself! I'll bet you any money you like that the land is simply registered in the name of Robert Charles Godwin, gentleman, of Oxmoon in the parish of Penhale!"

"But Robert didn't live at Oxmoon!"

"Yes, he did. At the time of registration he could claim with perfect truth that he lived on the Oxmoon estate. Gerry, this must have been how Robert did it, it must have been—"

"Okay, but you realize what this means, don't you? It means he registered the land legally in the name of the true owner but then fooled his solicitors into thinking he was the Robert Charles Godwin in the Land Registry records."

My heart sank at this brutal summing up of Robert's machinations. "I suppose that has to be fraud."

"Of course. Harry, Kester's got you by the balls."

"*Christ.*"

"Look, get someone to negotiate between you—Uncle Edmund, for instance—"

"Edmund couldn't even negotiate between us if we had a dispute at Ping-Pong."

"Well, maybe Evan—after all, he's a clergyman—"

"Let's keep God out of this."

"Hell, if only we could get the Statute of Limitations to work in your favor, but it won't—Robert didn't occupy the land continuously for the right amount of time and anyway if fraud was involved—"

"Fuck the Statute of Limitations. Now, look here, Gerry, let's call a spade a spade. That property may be legally Kester's. I don't know and damn it, I don't care. The point is that it ought to be mine—I'm sure Grandfather meant to give it to Robert and I'm sure Robert would never have stooped to fraud unless he believed he was morally justified and I'm sure Father would never have got involved if he hadn't believed he was merely regularizing a situation that already existed."

"Yes, but—"

"I'm not letting that bastard get away with this, Gerry. I'm just not going to let him ruin me."

"Well, I'm with you all the way, Harry, but for God's sake calm down and don't do anything crazy...."

I calmed down and allowed him to lead me to his boss. I already knew Davison slightly; he was a golfing crony of my father's and an influential man in Swansea. When I explained my dilemma he was sympathetic but I had a layman's distrust of a clever lawyer who scents a gold mine so I merely instructed him to make the preliminary inquiries that would prove or disprove the theories Gerry and I had constructed. Once the facts were established I could then start praying for the miracle which could preserve me from disaster.

Still seething with rage I returned to Penhale, and as I drove up to the Manor Dafydd came out to meet me. One glance at his face told me something was wrong.

"Christ, what's happened now?"

"Bloody Kester's men have rounded up your sheep from Penhale Down and dumped them at the Home Farm."

"My God! How dare that sod clear my land before he's proved his title to it! I'll get an injunction, I'll—no damn it, I'll bloody well go straight over to Oxmoon and shake him till his teeth rattle!"

"Steady, Harry, don't go off your rocker!"

I suddenly remembered what had happened to Thomas, the last person who had roared off to Oxmoon to shake Kester till his teeth rattled.

"You're coming with me," I said to Dafydd. "Go on—get in the car. I want a witness in case that bastard tries to kill me."

"Harry—"

"*Get in!*" I shouted in a frenzy, and the next moment we were heading at breakneck speed for Oxmoon and the most crucial scene of my life.

IV

It was a cold March day, more like midwinter than spring, and the rain whipped sporadically across Rhossili Downs from the sea. Oxmoon looked bleak. Some of the blinds were drawn on the ground-floor windows, as if to suggest that the house was closed while its owner enjoyed a warmer climate elsewhere. The whole place appeared to be waiting patiently for something. Or for someone.

No one answered the front doorbell yet I felt sure we were being watched. Retreating to the car again I stared at the upstairs windows but there was no one in sight.

"Not all the servants can have the day off," muttered Dafydd. "Why doesn't someone come to the door?"

"He's obviously given instructions that I'm not to be admitted. He wants me to bust my way in as I did after Anna died—and then he can use violence to eject me."

"What do we do?"

"Flush him out." I swung back to face the house, and this time I thought I saw the curtain move on the upstairs-landing window. "Kester!" I shouted. "I'm staying here till you show yourself!"

We waited but nothing happened.

"He's trying to egg you into losing your temper," said Dafydd.

"If he thinks I'll ever give him the chance to kill me in self-defense he'll have to think again."

We went on waiting but the deadlock persisted. Finally I had an idea.

"Dafydd, take yourself out of his range of vision and let's see what happens when he thinks I'm on my own. Go and stand over there by the wall of the ballroom."

Dafydd took himself off. That did the trick. Kester wanted to know what he was up to. Above the porch the curtain twitched and the next moment the window was flung up.

Kester leaned over the sill. When he had satisfied himself that Dafydd was up to no mischief he called out abruptly to me: "All right, what do you want?"

The question was so incredible that it took me a moment to reply. He had grabbed my land, threatened me with ruin and now he was asking why I wanted to see him! How I maintained my self-control I've no idea.

But I did maintain it. I stood there, fists clenched, and shouted up at him: "I've come for what's mine!"

Mine, mine, mine...

The word echoed in my mind. I'd come for what was mine. It had taken me thirty-two years but I'd got there in the end. I'd come for what was mine—not just the Martinscombe lands but the life that might have been and the inheritance I should have had. I'd come for my true self, the self that had been denied me. I'd come for Oxmoon.

"You'd better negotiate through your solicitors," called Kester unperturbed. "In the eyes of the law—"

"Fuck the law!"

That rattled him. "Oh, don't be so childish, Harry! There's nothing you can do here and you know it!"

"Wrong!"

"What do you mean?"

"I'll see you sodding hanged for that murder I know you committed!"

Silence. Utter silence. Then a cold wind blew in from the Downs and moaned softly in the woods. Out of the corner of my eye I could see the beech trees shivering.

"That's a bluff," said Kester. He was leaning forward to check that Dafydd was out of earshot. "You know it's a bluff."

"Then call it!"

But he couldn't. Of course he couldn't. We went on standing where we were, he upstairs looking down, I in the drive looking up, but I felt the balance of power shift between us and suddenly I knew I had the whip hand.

"Wait," said Kester reluctantly. "I'm coming down."

Closing the window he disappeared.

Dafydd rejoined me. "What do I do?"

"Go back and stand where you were. It doesn't matter if you can't hear. I just want a witness in case he tries to kill me—no, don't say I'm off my rocker. This man's more dangerous than anyone's begun to believe."

Dafydd looked startled but withdrew without further comment and after a long interval Kester emerged from the house. He was wearing a coat and muffler; his hands were buried deep in his pockets and he shivered as another gust of wind blew in from the sea.

I kept the car between us and we faced each other across the bonnet.

"The land's mine," said Kester. "Sorry and all that, but it is. I've been conducting some investigations—"

"I'll bet you have. You remembered Father's extraordinary embarrassment when he found he'd inherited the property from Uncle Robert."

"Well, it *was* odd, wasn't it? And if Uncle John was acting in character something was clearly involved which wasn't the done thing. So I got hold of old Fairfax—"

"—and I suppose the two of you began to ransack all the Oxmoon deed boxes for the record of the deed of gift in 1919."

"Yes, poor old Freddy was in an awful state. You see, his firm weren't the Oxmoon solicitors in 1919 but he'd made the classic mistake of taking the word of a gentleman when my father swore to him there'd been a deed of gift. By doing this my father got hold of the Martinscombe deeds which he needed in order to register the title—poor old Freddy just assumed that the deeds had been left among the Oxmoon papers by an oversight of the previous solicitors Owens, Wood after the deed of gift had been executed."

"Poor old Freddy ought to be bloody shot. Why didn't he check then and there that the deed of gift existed?"

"Because it never occurred to him that my father was behaving like a villain. And there are an enormous number of documents relating to the Oxmoon estate and no inventory—"

"Okay, Fairfax made the fatal error of trusting your father and no record of a deed of gift turned up. But what makes you so sure—"

"Well, as soon as we established there was no evidence of a deed of gift we turned to your father's papers—this was just after his death and poor old Freddy had custody of them all. And there we found the Martinscombe deeds—all with a Land Registry endorsement to show they'd been registered, and of course Freddy at once saw what had happened. Then he got in touch with my father's former solicitors in Lincoln's Inn—"

"And the whole mess started to unravel. Christ! What the bloody hell drove Robert to such machinations?"

"I gather the problem was Milly Straker. Grandfather was absolutely under her thumb and unwilling to cooperate with his sons on any matter concerning the estate."

"But for Robert to stoop to fraud—"

"Would he have seen it as fraud? I suspect the world looks very different when one's near death, and probably he saw his act merely as a necessity, a step that had to be taken to protect his wife and child from Straker's acquisitive streak."

"I still don't see how he got away with it. Surely as soon as Grandfather heard about Robert's will—"

"But don't you see, he would never have heard exactly what was in it! My father used different solicitors; my grandfather wasn't a beneficiary; Uncle John, who was, thought the best thing to do was to keep quiet and my mother certainly wasn't talking. Obviously she and Uncle John discussed it—in fact I can remember them doing so—but equally obviously they never discussed it with anyone who would have relayed the news to Grandfather who by that time was living in seclusion anyway and wasn't on close terms with his family. And don't forget that the property was left to Uncle John with the proviso that my mother and I should remain at Little Oxmoon until I came into my inheritance, so there was no change in the status quo while Grandfather was alive, nothing that would have openly indicated what my father had done. The fact is his move was primarily a defensive measure; it would have been revealed in Grandfather's lifetime only if Grandfather had become mad enough to give Milly Straker *carte blanche* with the estate—in which case the fraud could have provided my mother with a valuable shield because in those circumstances Grandfather would almost certainly have been judged too incompetent to give evidence in court about what had really happened back in 1919. However that nightmare never actually surfaced so Grandfather went to his grave in ignorance and the fraud was never put to the test."

"But why the hell didn't my father draw the line?"

"Obviously my father manipulated Uncle John with consummate skill. Uncle John thought he was safeguarding me and my mother against the wicked predator Milly Straker. What could be more heroic?"

I groaned. Kester laughed and looked compassionate. I wanted to smash him to pulp.

"So you see, Harry, you really don't have a leg to stand on, do you? Now, look—let's try and be sensible about this. Don't you honestly feel that it would be better for both our sakes if you left Gower? I know this move of mine will put you in a financial jam, but if you now agree to leave I'm prepared to give you financial assistance to help you start again elsewhere—"

"You don't want to give me financial assistance. You want to kill me. I know too much."

"Well, of course you do, but you can't prove any of it, can you, so I'm safe. All the same, we've wound up in an unbearable position so if you could see sense and take yourself off—"

"You can't be serious."

"But Harry—"

"You snatch my land—yes, *my* land, it's morally if not legally mine—you force me out of my home, you boot me into bloody exile—and do you really think I'm going to smile, turn the other cheek like a saint and go meekly off into the blue so that you can live happily ever after? You must be mad!"

"I realize it's tough for you, but—"

"Tough? *Tough!* It's bloody unjust and I'm not standing for it! I've had just about enough of you getting away with murder! I think it's time you started to pay!"

Kester turned a shade paler. "Don't be idiotic! If I pay you pay—you were an accessory after the fact, you helped conceal the crime—"

"Oh, I shan't go to the police! I shall go to the family! I shall tell them exactly how you murdered Thomas and once they realize you ought to be locked up they'll back me when I get a committal order to shove you into a bloody asylum!"

"They'll never believe you," said Kester calmly.

"Oh yes, they will—you're going to corroborate my story!"

"I bloody well will not!"

"All right, I *will* go to the police if you don't confess to the family! Damn it, I'll even go to jail if I have to in order to put you behind bars for good!"

"Don't make me laugh! How are you going to convince the police? You haven't a shred of evidence!"

"Oh yes I have!"

"You're bluffing—I don't believe you—"

"I dug up the poker."

Dead silence. It was very cold. The house had a bleached frozen look.

"The poker that only you could have used," I said. "The poker that has Thomas's blood on it. The poker that can send you to Broadmoor."

Kester slid his tongue quickly around his lips. He was very pale.

"All right," I said when no reply was forthcoming. "Let's approach this problem from a new angle. I won't go to the police and I won't go to the family either—but only if you do exactly as I say. If you don't I won't rest till I see you hanged or committed for life. It's as simple as that. I don't care if I ruin myself to do it, but I'm absolutely determined that you're going to pay."

Another long silence. Kester took his hands out of his pockets and rested them lightly on the bonnet of the car. Obviously he was trying to drum up a fresh plot, but panic was overwhelming the creative genius. When he looked at me at last I saw the fear in his eyes.

"What do you want?"

"What do you think?"

His nerve snapped. He became hysterical. "I'll never give it up, never, never, never—"

"Right," I said, opening the door of the car as if I intended to leave him. "I'm summoning the family and if they don't believe me I'm off to the police."

"Wait!" he screamed at me.

I waited but he was speechless with terror and rage.

"Go and live in Dublin with Declan," I said. "We'll tell the family the estate was too much for you as usual and that you're having another nervous breakdown. That would ring true enough, wouldn't it? In the words of that favorite phrase of yours, you'd appear to be acting in character."

I thought he was going to pass out but he didn't. He just leaned forward, the palms of his hands flat on the bonnet, and closed his eyes. At last he opened them and said, "You'd never dare do this if Uncle John were alive."

"And you'd never have dared steal my land. But he's dead, isn't he? He's dead and the rules of the game have changed and by God, I'm going to have what's always been owing to me. You've forfeited it. It's mine."

"Never!"

"Suit yourself. Enjoy Broadmoor." I again pretended I was about to leave.

The conversation continued in this fashion for about five minutes but of course he gave way in the end. He had to. He was now wholly convinced I'd stop at nothing to put him behind bars.

"All right," he whispered at last. "All right." He forced himself to look at me again. His eyes were a very pale clear blue. "Perhaps..." It was hard for him to get his words out but he managed in the end. "Perhaps I can turn this disaster to my advantage. I'd certainly have more time to write if I... if I gave up..." But he couldn't say the word "Oxmoon." "... if I went away, and as you know, writing's all I really care about. And so long as Hal gets everything in the end... I suppose you wouldn't consider—"

"No. You're not going to give Oxmoon directly to Hal. You're going to give it to me. You're going to instruct Fairfax to draw up the deed of gift and you're going to do it straightaway."

More hysterics followed. We sparred away for a little longer but it was just postponing the inevitable and finally he said, "All right, I'll sign the deed, stage a nervous breakdown and go off to Dublin. But you mark my words, you're the one who's going to end up in an asylum. You're violent, dangerous and thoroughly unstable."

"Speak for yourself!"

We stared, each man seeing himself in the other, and at once the air thickened with horror—the horror that had no name. Kester's pallor assumed a waxen tinge, and all the while I watched his color fade I knew I saw myself in the glass darkly and I felt the distortions rippling across my mind.

We shuddered. For one long moment we remained paralyzed with revulsion but at last he turned his back on me, bolted inside the house and slammed the door. As Dafydd came running I slumped against the car.

"Are you okay?"

"Fit as a fiddle." I nearly passed out. God knows how I got myself together. "Here, take the wheel, would you, I'm shot to pieces."

"Where are we going?"

"Back to the main road. Park the car by the bridle path that leads up onto Penhale Down. I want to go into the grounds through the back entrance."

"What the hell are we up to now?"

"We're going to dig up a poker."

V

All Dafydd said when I had the poker in my hands was "Thomas?"

We stood there beneath the trees. The light was yellowish, indicative of extreme winter weather. In Humphrey de Mohun's ruined tower all the jackdaws were silent.

"So you guessed," I said.

"Yes, but I got it wrong."

"What do you mean?"

"I thought you were the one who'd killed him. And all the time it was bloody Kester, wasn't it?"

When I'd recovered I said incredulously, "You thought I was a murderer and yet you stood by me and kept your mouth shut?"

"Of course," said Dafydd surprised. "You've been more of a brother to me than any of those little bastards my mother produced for your father, and besides . . . in the war, in that camp . . . one got used to the ordinary rules not applying."

We stood there, brothers yet not brothers, related yet not related, and I knew we both felt as if we'd been born of the same parents.

"I won't forget this, Dafydd."

"See that you don't—because I'd do anything for you, Harry, remember that. Anything at all."

VI

"So you see," I declared to my family in the language my father had made famous to us all, "it was the right thing—indeed the only thing—to do." And as I sat down at the head of the table in the dining room at Oxmoon, I gripped the arms of my grandfather's great carved chair to reassure myself that justice had finally prevailed.

I was presiding at a conference. The deed of gift had been signed. Kester had withdrawn to Dublin. Oxmoon was mine, but this was the exact moment when I couldn't afford any celebration. I had to be sober and subdued, hardworking Harry Godwin who had come to his poor sickly cousin's rescue and was now entirely preoccupied with doing the done thing. Accordingly I had decided that I should entertain my family at Easter in my future home and explain to them what was going on—or what I wanted them to think was going on. I needed to keep them informed. I needed them to believe I was an honest, truthful, thoroughly decent chap. It was imperative that everyone should think my actions had been justified.

I hadn't yet moved my belongings from Penhale Manor because I thought haste would be a gesture of bad taste in the circumstances, so Oxmoon was exactly as Kester had left it. It had even occurred to me that it was like living in a shrine to his memory. But of course I'd make plenty of changes later when the family had settled down and my takeover had been accepted.

The family had assembled in response to my invitation; the lawyers on both sides had agreed to attend the conference to bear witness to the legality of my occupation; everything in fact had been going meticulously according to plan when after breakfast on the day of the conference my seedy brother-in-law Rory Kinsella had sidled up to me and announced that his brother Declan had crossed the Irish Sea to represent Kester's interests and would be arriving at Oxmoon in half an hour.

I manifested courteous delight and cornered Gerry. "That crook Declan Kinsella's about to turn up. We're in for a rough ride."

"I don't see why," said Gerry mildly. "Kester signed that deed of gift of his own free will while of sound mind. What can Declan do?"

Naturally I hadn't revealed to my lawyers that Kester's free will had been tempered by my friendly persuasion. Only Dafydd knew that. I had decided that if Dafydd could keep quiet about murder he could keep quiet about anything so I had confided in him.

Abandoning Gerry I headed for the telephone. "Dafydd?" I said when my housekeeper had summoned him from the garden of the Manor. "Get over here. Trouble's brewing." And when he arrived ten minutes later on his motorbike I told him of Declan's imminent arrival. "That gangster's capable of anything," I said. "I think he'll try and blast me right out of the water."

"But how can he? Who's going to believe Irish scum like that?"

This was true. I began to feel better. But not much better. I grabbed his arm. "I want you with me at this conference. You don't have to say anything, just be there."

"What, me? With all those gentlemen? I'm not even wearing a tie!"

"Fuck the tie. I want all the allies I can get."

At this point Kester's lawyers arrived, old Freddy Fairfax looking as if he should be in a Bath chair, and that smooth Wykehamist Carmichael. They were both effusive towards me; no doubt they believed that if they licked my boots hard enough their firm would retain the business generated by the Oxmoon estate. What a hope.

I had just shown them into the dining room where my own solicitor Roland Davison was waiting with the male members of the family, when the parlormaid told me Declan had arrived, and assuming my most charming smile I returned to the hall to welcome him.

I had only met him twice, once after Aunt Ginevra's death and once at my father's funeral, but on both occasions he had struck me as being quite the most sinister man I'd ever met. He was now in his early fifties, a tall fat man with receding gray hair and soft dark eyes which looked as if they could watch a mass execution without blinking. He spoke with a bizarre English accent, like someone who had learned a foreign language long ago but was unaware how much it had changed. This peculiar trait should have made him sound absurd but it didn't; it merely made him sound more sinister than ever.

"Hullo, Declan—what a delightful surprise! How's Kester?"

But Declan had the politician's trick of ignoring the questions he had no wish to answer. He gave me a small subtle smile, murmured, "Hullo, old fellow. Terrible weather, what?" and cruised casually past my outstretched hand towards the sound of voices in the dining room.

My back started to itch. I spent five futile seconds listening to my heart throbbing and then I followed him across the hall.

The maids were serving coffee as I reentered the dining room. Various members of the family asked after Kester and Declan said with a sigh that poor Kester was deeply, deeply depressed. Everyone looked sad and worried and no one looked sadder and more worried than I did, but fortunately Gerry came to my rescue by asking Declan what he thought of the British political situation. Declan said he supposed Attlee would soon be disemboweled by either Bevan on the left or Churchill on the right and this might or might not be a bad thing. After this masterpiece of political noncommitment had been delivered, I put the cigarette box in circulation and suggested that we all sat down. Declan ignored the box and lit a very large cigar. Perhaps he thought he was being British. He looked like a comrade of Al Capone.

"Well, gentlemen..." I had remained on my feet, and once everyone was settled I willed myself to ignore Declan and embark on my carefully prepared speech. I felt less nervous once I'd started. By the time I reached the point where I declared Kester had welcomed the opportunity to solve his problems once and for all by leaving Oxmoon in safe hands, I even believed wholeheartedly in what I was saying.

"...and so you see," I said, reaching my peroration, "it was the right thing—indeed the only thing—to do."

I paused. Nobody spoke. When I was seated again I glanced around the table. I had Edmund on my right and beyond him were his two sons, Richard, who'd been Kester's jester, and Geoffrey, who worked in a London publishing house and presumably knew everything there was to know about unstable writers. I sensed that Geoffrey was more of an Armstrong than a Godwin; he always seemed to keep to the edge of the family circle as if he were perpetually trying to escape, and I decided I could rely on him to remain neutral.

My glance traveled on down the table, flicked past the Kinsella brothers, ignored Kester's lawyers and alighted on Owen Bryn-Davies whom I'd invited in deference to Elizabeth. I thought Owen would be aggrieved to hear Kester had disinherited his son in favor of Hal. Or did he suspect I'd forced Kester's hand? Hard to tell. He was looking inscrutable. I glanced on past Roland Davison to my three half-brothers. Gerry I could count on. Evan, looking insufferably virtuous in his clerical collar, would be for Kester but I didn't think he'd have the guts to make trouble. Lance, mild as always, merely looked as if he wished he were a hundred miles away. No trouble in that quarter. Next to Lance and on my immediate left was Dafydd, surly in his work clothes; all the gentlemen around the table were busy pretending he was invisible.

"So that's the situation," I said. "I don't know if anyone wishes to comment, but I wanted you all to know that I'm more than willing to discuss this tragic change in Kester's fortunes in an honest and straightforward way... Edmund—

795

you're the senior member of the family now. Would you care to give us your views?"

Edmund sighed. "Yes, well, it's all very sad, certainly, because we know how much Oxmoon meant to Kester, but if he can't cope and Harry can...and since Hal's going to be the heir...well, there we are, aren't we, I daresay it's all for the best."

"Richard," I said before anyone could comment, "let's hear from you."

"Oh, I agree," said Richard glumly. "It's a rotten shame, poor old Kester, but I did see him before he left for Ireland and there's no doubt the poor chap's at the end of his tether. I've never seen him so low."

"Geoffrey?" I said, anxious to keep the ball rolling at a brisk pace.

"Oh, you take it on, Harry, give Kester a bit of peace. Besides, I should think the place is a white elephant nowadays, isn't it? I'm only surprised it's survived the Labour government."

"Ah, it's still a nice little nook, believe me," said Rory, "for the cuckoo that's looking for a nest."

Everyone shifted uneasily. I instantly decided to try and gloss over the Kinsella brothers.

"Gerry!" I said, drumming up my next ally. "Your turn."

"I'm with Harry all the way," said Gerry firmly to the rest of the table. "Since Kester—on his own admission—can no longer cope this is quite clearly the best possible solution."

"Thank you, Gerry," I said. "Well, I daresay Evan and Lance would agree with that. Now, what I'd like to do next is to report on the condition of the estate and outline my plans for the future. I haven't yet had the time to conduct a comprehensive investigation, but—" I stopped.

Evan was on his feet.

"Yes?" I said abruptly. "Did you want to say something?"

"I want to give my opinion on what you've done."

"Fine," I said, heart sinking. "Let's hear it."

Evan took a deep breath, glanced around the table and said, "This is wrong."

Out of the corner of my eye I saw Declan give his small subtle smile.

I kept calm. "Go on. The whole purpose of this meeting is for us to have a free and frank discussion."

"This is wrong," repeated Evan, not looking at me, "and I can't condone it. I draw the line."

As if I hadn't enough problems. Declan Kinsella sits shrouded in cigar smoke like the demon king in a pantomime. Owen Bryn-Davies is looking as if he wished he had a hatchet to swing. Rory's been drinking brandy since breakfast and looks as if he's about to wreck everything in sight. And to cap it all my bastard half-brother starts drawing lines.

"I'm not questioning that Kester's voluntarily given you Oxmoon," Evan said, finally nerving himself to look at me. "What I'm questioning is the morality of your act of acceptance. If Kester can't cope then I think we should set up a family trust to run the estate for him so that he can remain master here. Oxmoon belongs to Kester. You've no right to it while he's still alive, Harry, and if you're as well intentioned as you're trying to make us all believe you are, you'll give Oxmoon back to Kester and work with us all to achieve a more satisfactory solution."

"Hear, hear!" shouted Rory, but Declan still said nothing. I knew then that he was preparing to make a big entrance. With consummate skill he was waiting for the right moment when he could move in to take control of the scene.

"Look, Evan," I said, straining every nerve I possessed to keep my voice calm and reasonable, "the plain truth is that I'm the only one who's qualified to run this place and I'm the one, no matter how we arrange the legal side, who's going to end up running it. Now, because he realized this, Kester made this purely voluntary decision—"

"You shouldn't have let him," said Evan.

"Oh, for God's sake!" said Gerry. "Can't a man dispose of his property as he pleases?"

"He was insane with grief!" shouted Rory.

"Not legally speaking," said my solicitor.

"I agree," said the sycophant Carmichael, anxious to show me how willing he was to turn traitor.

"But he was certainly very disturbed," said that old idiot Fairfax, "and I must say I did wonder if—"

We were getting into deep waters. I had to haul us out at once. "Gentlemen," I said, "let me put an end to any suggestion that I might have taken advantage of Kester while the balance of his mind was disturbed. I acted in good faith. I took Oxmoon because I honestly and sincerely believed that that was what Kester wanted. But if I'm wrong of course I'll give it back to him. All he has to do is ask."

A second after I'd finished speaking I realized I'd made the biggest possible mistake. To those who suspected me of extortion I had just confirmed that I had such a hold over Kester that he would never dare seek Oxmoon's return.

I broke out in a cold sweat but before anyone could comment on the disaster Geoffrey said unexpectedly, "What I can't understand is why we're wrangling like this—or indeed why we're here at all. It's good of Harry to explain what's going on, but why argue about whether or not he should own Oxmoon? After all, legally speaking the ownership's a *fait accompli.*"

"Not quite," said Declan Kinsella, and rose to his feet to annihilate me.

VII

"Gentlemen," said Declan, and when he was sure he had everyone's attention he pointed his finger at me. "This *thief*—this *traitor*—"

Had to stop him, had to. No choice. A nightmare. "Oh, come off it, Declan— you're not in the Dail now!"

"—this *rogue*—this *villain*—"

How did I stop him? For Christ's sake, what the bloody hell did I do? "Cut the melodrama and get to the point!" Had to keep calm. Had to keep very, very reasonable. Sanity personified. Hold fast, stand firm—I took a deep breath. "I suppose Kester's been saying—"

"Kester's not said one word to me; not one word has he said," said Declan, discarding his English accent and sliding with sinister speed into an Irish-American rasp. "But can't I see with my own eyes that he's destroyed with grief, shattered beyond description, with his life wrecked and his world in ruins? Ah no, there's no need for him to speak! I know my brother Kester, through and through I know him, and if there's one thing I know about my brother Kester, gentlemen"— Declan flung out his arms in a gesture which riveted everyone's appalled attention—"it's that he would never—never in a million years—*never*, I tell you gentlemen!—surrender Oxmoon voluntarily."

"I swear—"

"Keep your oaths, Harry Godwin! You've told enough lies today!"

I somehow got to my feet. "I absolutely insist," I said, "that Kester surrendered Oxmoon of his own free will."

"And *I* absolutely insist," said Declan to the family, "that this thief stole it from him—and I don't just call you a thief, Harry Godwin! I call you a blackmailer and an extortionist! I call you a liar, a cheat and a fraud!"

I turned at once to Davison. "That statement must be actionable. I want a writ issued for slander."

Declan laughed. "Oh, you'd never sue me!" he said. "Never! You'd be too afraid of what truths might come out in the witness box!"

All the lawyers made an attempt to intervene. Amidst the babble of voices I heard Edmund quaver, "That's enough, Declan. That's enough. No more."

I had only one retreat which offered a hope of dignity and that retreat was into the role of an English gentleman. "I must ask you to oblige me," I said to Declan, "by removing yourself immediately from my house."

"It'll never be your house!" said Declan. "Oxmoon belongs to Kester and it'll be Kester's till the day he dies!"

He walked out with Rory at his heels. It was a magnificent exit. Turning away I managed to wipe the sweat from my forehead by pretending I had something in my eye. "Well, really!" I said, affecting nonchalance. "What a performance!" I sank down in my chair again and finished my coffee. "Lance, ring the bell, would you? I feel we all need a shot of brandy to recover—there's nothing so exhausting, is there, as a well-acted Irish farce!"

The lawyers tittered obediently but only Richard was brainless enough to laugh with genuine amusement. Owen Bryn-Davies was looking more like a hatchet man than ever. Lance was white. Evan was ashen. Edmund was again mumbling horrified at my side.

"Terrible behavior . . . terrible things he said . . . terrible, terrible . . . If John were alive—"

"If my father were alive," said Evan, "we wouldn't be here." He walked straight up to me. "I don't know if there's any truth in what Declan said. I don't even want to know. But I think you should give Oxmoon back to Kester."

"Quite. Now can you either keep quiet or run off and be a clergyman somewhere else? I'm finding your halo a bit tiresome."

Another bad mistake. I was betraying how rattled I was. Well, not just rattled. Shattered. I was scratching my neck, scratching my face, every inch of skin was throbbing, and when the parlormaid wheeled in the drinks trolley I poured myself a triple brandy.

Somehow I pulled myself together sufficiently to outline my plans for the future of the estate, and somehow everyone contrived to listen with a show of politeness. But I couldn't decide whether to close the meeting without referring to Declan's accusations or whether I should make another attempt to laugh them off. Which course would look less guilty? I didn't know, couldn't decide. Whatever I did I felt my guilt would be declaimed.

Then I thought of Kester murdering Thomas. *There* was the villain. All I had to do was behave like the innocent man I was.

"... and I can't let this meeting close," I heard myself say, "without stressing that from start to finish I've only tried to do what's right. I absolutely deny every one of Declan's hysterical accusations."

My audience muttered soothing platitudes but God alone knew what each man was thinking. I wound up the meeting. The lawyers then left, Gerry accompanying them to the front door, while Edmund and his sons wandered away to the drawing room to join the women. Owen suddenly remembered a vital phone call he had to make. Within seconds I found myself alone with Evan, Lance and Dafydd.

"I must be on my way," said Evan.

"Far be it from me to stop you." I turned my back on him and confronted Lance. "You're making a big success of keeping your mouth shut! What's going on in that head of yours?"

Lance looked at me with Bronwen's green eyes, said politely, "I thought it was a vile scene. Excuse me, please" and followed Evan into the hall.

"Tough," muttered Dafydd. "Surprising."

"Under Evan's thumb." I made sure the door was shut before demanding: "What's your verdict on that bloody assassin Declan Kinsella?"

"If he knew Kester had killed Thomas he'd have kept his big mouth shut. You're okay, Harry. He knows nothing."

"I suppose Kester revealed that Oxmoon had been extorted from him but refused to say how it was done."

"And he never will. Kester won't want to confess to anyone, least of all to the brother who's sentimental about him, that he's nothing but a bloody murderer."

"Yes, but what are the odds on a man like Declan making a shrewd guess or two? My God, how he rocked them just now!"

"So what? Nothing was proved, was it? And nothing can ever be proved. It's just his word against yours and in the end you're the one people will want to believe because it'll be more comfortable to believe you than to believe him. Keep calm. Brazen it out. He can't touch you."

"No, of course he can't," I said.

But I was on the rack.

VIII

A week later Bronwen came to see me. She was wearing black and I noticed how that drained the color from her, emphasizing the faded red of her hair and the transparent quality of her skin. She looked ethereal, remote, like someone who had traveled a long, long way to see me from another world which no one could describe. Kissing her I said, "I'm very glad to see you." I had seen little of her since my father's death. She had spent day after day in seclusion, and her children had thought it best to leave her undisturbed.

We sat down. I tried making small talk but she didn't respond so at last I fell silent and the silence wrapped us together until I felt her mind entwining itself with mine.

At last I said, "Evan's been worrying you about me, hasn't he?"

"Oh, I see far beyond Evan."

I thought of those razor-sharp powers of observation grasping realities no one else could perceive.

"I'm all right, Bronwen. And so's Kester." I groped for the words to answer her unspoken questions. "This is our way of living with each other," I said at last. "We've finally resolved the problem."

She was silent again. Eventually I put my arm around her. "Tell me," I said. "Come on, you didn't come all the way to Oxmoon to say nothing."

"I came to remind you of your promise to Johnny."

Now it was my turn to be silent.

"You said you'd go away, start afresh."

"I would have done. But Kester's done it instead, so all's well."

She shook her head. "I'm no fortune-teller," she said. "I've always told you that. But when one knows two people very well one senses instinctively how they'll behave in a certain situation, and I'm sure—I'm just so sure—"

"Yes?"

"Kester's going to come back for Oxmoon, Harry. Your final clash with him is still to come."

Couldn't tell her this was impossible. Couldn't explain how I had the whip hand. "It'll be all right, Bronwen, I promise you. I know everything's going to be all right."

But did I know? *Did I?*

Neurotic question. Of course I knew. I beat back the paranoia. Kester might well try to cook up some plot with Declan but the truth was that any plot would be doomed to failure. He couldn't declare he'd relinquished Oxmoon under duress unless he disclosed he was a murderer, and unless he could prove he had handed over Oxmoon under duress he could never recapture it.

So I was safe—safe yet subtly divided from Bronwen, who believed I was doing the wrong thing. But she didn't know Kester was a murderer, did she? She didn't realize I'd had to move against him to protect myself from his aggression. She didn't understand that it had been more or less my moral duty to act as I had— damn it, it *had* been my moral duty, no "more or less" about it. One really can't let unconvicted murderers go running around persecuting innocent people; only the most naive would claim that retribution should be left entirely to God, and besides . . . isn't God supposed to help those who help themselves?

I'd never been quite sure whether I believed in God. When I was being a man of action I didn't. When I was being a musician I did. On the whole I thought there was probably something out there somewhere, but whatever it was, I felt sure it could do with a human hand helping it along occasionally—for the best possible motives, of course. I'd given God a helping hand in assigning this retribution to Kester, although I had to be careful how I phrased that interpretation of my conduct because everyone knew about the maniacs who walked around and claimed to be God's instrument all the while they murdered everyone in sight. Well, I wasn't murdering everyone in sight. I'd simply put right a wrong, and my conscience was absolutely clear—although I did wish Bronwen hadn't reminded me of my promise to my father.

"I draw the line."

Yes. Well, I knew I'd left it a little late, but I really would draw the line now. No more trouble with Kester. I was going to settle down at Oxmoon and live a decent hardworking life.

If he'd let me.

I shuddered, and to calm myself I wandered through the house, *my* house, through all those beautiful rooms which I now knew I could never change. I had to keep Oxmoon exactly as it was, just as if I'd been Kester; but of course I *was* Kester, I'd taken over his life as well as his house, and now he was me, dispossessed and in exile; it was as if some transference of the personality had taken place, although that was a mad thought which I couldn't possibly believe so I had to think of something else. I walked on through the beautiful rooms and tried to meditate on Beauty, Truth, Art and Peace—but I couldn't because I wasn't at peace, not yet. But I would be. In time.

I reached the ballroom and as I sat down at the white-and-gold piano I remembered how often I had dreamed of being alone there to play "The Blue Danube." I played it. Another dream had come true, and as I stroked the hackneyed tune in that beautiful room the melody became fresh again, reborn and renewed, a symbol of a perfection that could never die.

I felt better. I went on feeling better until I was passing through the hall again and noticed the jade statuette which Kester had used to prop open the front door on the night of Thomas's murder. That little memento would have to go. In sudden distaste I picked it up but I hadn't anticipated its weight and it slid through my fingers to crash back upon the side table. I tried to catch it. My hand knocked one of the Chinese vases nearby. The vase toppled. I grabbed at it. I missed. It smashed. I winced.

A pity.

Never mind, it was just a vase. Of course if I were really neurotic I'd tell myself the smash was an omen.

I told myself the smash was an omen.

Rubbish!

Or was it?

To my horror I found I didn't know.

IX

By the time my three eldest boys returned home for the summer holidays their new rooms were ready for them and their possessions had been moved to Oxmoon from the Manor. Lucky little sods, growing up at Oxmoon! I thought of my soul-destroying years at the mausoleum on Eaton Walk.

I wasn't yet sure what to do with the Manor but I thought I might let the house and grounds while merging the Home Farm with the Oxmoon estate. I had now been studying Oxmoon's affairs for some weeks, and there was no doubt I needed all the land I could get if I were to live comfortably without the aid of Bobby Godwin's depleted but useful personal fortune. Kester still had access to that little nest egg. However, provided the estate was well run—and provided the Labour government was slung out at the next election—and provided I beat my brains out to gyp the Inland Revenue legally whenever I could—and provided there were no disastrous Acts of God such as floods or blizzards—I thought I could do well enough. It was certainly a challenge. No longer could I complain of an unsatisfied ambition and recurring boredom. I'd got what I wanted and now all I had to do was put my nose to the grindstone and work like a Trojan until the estate was running with maximum efficiency.

I'd been working so hard that I hadn't visited the boys as I usually did once a term, and because I'd had no opportunity to see them I hadn't told them of the move from the Manor. During the spring holidays I'd merely said I was looking after Oxmoon for a time while Kester was ill, and even after Kester had signed the deed of gift I'd had a superstitious dread of saying I was master of Oxmoon until I was actually living in the house. But now I was glad of my reticence. I thought it would make a wonderful surprise for the boys when I revealed they had a new home, and I had promised Humphrey that he could be the one to tell them the good news.

We met them at the station in Swansea. The trunks traveled separately, and the boys were carrying only their overnight bags as they raced down the platform to the ticket barrier. They all seemed larger and noisier than ever. Hal was going to be twelve that October. He had grown again and was much thinner than Charles and Jack who were shorter, squarer and heavier than he was.

"We've got a secret!" piped Humphrey after the initial clamor had died down. Clinging to my hand he jumped up and down with excitement.

"Wait till we get to the car," I ordered, so we headed out of the station and Humphrey somehow managed to hold his tongue.

"Is Kester back yet?" said Hal. "He wrote to me from Ireland but he didn't say when he'd be returning."

I immediately felt persecuted. "What did he say?"

"Oh, just that he was better and having a nice holiday. I wrote back and asked when he'd be coming home but I haven't had a reply. Perhaps there's a letter waiting at the Manor."

I was horrified. I'd had no idea that Kester was in the habit of writing to Hal at school. If I'd known I'd have stopped it. I'd had just about enough of Kester trying to turn my son into an acolyte.

"Can I tell them now, can I tell them?" sang Humphrey, still bobbing up and down like a cork, and I suddenly realized we had reached the car. A couple of fiends had parked too close to me at the front and back; I was going to have a diabolical time getting out.

"Well..." Still contemplating my parking problem I wasn't at my quickest.

Interpreting "Well" as "Yes," Humphrey shouted to his brothers: "Kester's gone away for good and Daddy's the master now and we're all going to live at Oxmoon forever!"

Uproar. Charles and Jack cheered and flung their caps in the air. Hal looked pale and shocked.

"Into the car," I said, "before we're all arrested for breach of the peace."

According to tradition the three youngest crammed themselves into the back and Hal claimed the privileged position on the front seat. As soon as the doors were slammed he turned to me.

"Daddy, I don't understand. Kester would never abandon Oxmoon forever— it's his shrine to Anna, it's his monument to Beauty, Truth, Art and—"

"Quite," I said, starting the engine, "but unfortunately, Hal, Kester's health can no longer stand the strain and he now has to live very quietly." I turned to glance out of the back window as I put the car into reverse.

"Are we rich now?" said Charles exuberantly. "Can I have my own gramophone?"

"Can we keep Kester's television?" said Jack wildly.

"Over my dead body." I could have kicked myself for not dumping the set before the holidays began. Those boys made quite enough noise without adding a television to the cacophony.

Changing gears I wrestled with the wheel again.

"Daddy..." Hal was trying to talk to me, and as I glanced at him I saw that his pallor had assumed a greenish tinge. "Daddy, is Kester dying? I'm sure he wouldn't give up Oxmoon unless he was! Has he got that awful disease, the one his father died of? Cook told me the disease was so terrible that no one knew what it was called, and I used to have nightmares in case it ran in the family and we all died of it one by one—"

Very neurotic. Had to slap that one down straightaway. "What nonsense! Of course the disease had a name! It was called multiple sclerosis and not everyone dies of it within ten years as Uncle Robert did—some people have it for three times as long and even lead normal lives. It's not catching and it's not hereditary and by the time you've grown up they'll probably have found a cure for it." I slammed the car into reverse again.

"Daddy, do you promise me he's not dying?"

"Oh, stop being so idiotic, Hal! Of course he's not dying! He's just having a nervous breakdown!"

"Then he'll come back," said Hal. "When he's better he'll come back to Oxmoon."

I stalled the car. Swearing under my breath, I restarted the engine. "Hal, he's not coming back. He's given Oxmoon to me. We're there for good."

"But Daddy—"

"Oh, for Christ's sake, Hal, stop pestering me and let me get out of this bloody space!"

That was bad. Although I did swear before the children, I restricted my language to a mild "Damn" or "Blast." In panic I realized I was mishandling the scene, and once more I was overwhelmed by my failure to be an adequate parent.

"I'm sorry, Hal," I said as by some miracle of willpower I got the car away from the curb and drove off. "I realize this is all rather a surprise for you, but—"

"I'll see him again, won't I?"

I didn't know what to say. Why hadn't I anticipated that he'd be so upset? What a rotten father I was. "Oh yes, of course you'll see him again," I said glibly, and thought: But not if I can help it.

"Can I ring him up in Ireland?"

Who would have thought he'd be so tenacious? He was going on and on at me like a miniature battering ram. "Well, we'll talk about that later, Hal," I said, and called to the boys in the back: "How did Sports Day go?"

We drove on to Oxmoon, Charles and Jack chattering happily, Humphrey tossing in a question now and then and Hal sitting quiet as a ghost in the front seat. When we arrived Charles and Jack scampered everywhere yelling with delight but Hal disappeared. I found him later in the den, once known as "Aunt Celia's music room," where Kester kept his television set. It was the one twentieth-century room on the ground floor. Demented abstracts adorned the walls and were reflected in a distorted fashion by the curve of the magnifier on the television screen. Hal was sitting on the window seat, and as soon as I entered the room I saw that he had been crying.

I didn't know what to say. I was such a hopeless father and I didn't know what to say. All I could offer him was the futile question "Is everything all right, Hal?"

"Oh yes, Daddy," he said. "Wizard."

But I had been here before. I had been where Hal was and now I was standing in my father's shoes. In mounting panic I realized that something was going very, very wrong.

"Hal, I . . . it was stupid of me not to realize you'd be so upset—"

"We were going to do *The Tempest* in the ballroom, Kester was going to adapt the play specially for us, I was so looking forward to it, I just took it for granted he'd be home by the time I got back for the holidays . . ."

I'd forgotten the Oxmoon tea-party set.

"I'm sorry, Hal, I really am."

"It's all right," said Hal, making a great effort to respond to a sympathy he sensed was genuine. "You weren't to know."

I wasn't to know. Why not? Why hadn't he told me? Why had he never talked about it? My fault, of course. I'd done something wrong. *But what was it?* My God, what a torture parenthood was, what a bloody crucifixion. . . .

"I think I'll write to Kester," said Hal, standing up. "I'll feel better then."

My scalp prickled. "Well, to tell you the truth, Hal," I said, "I'd rather you didn't write to him. In fact to be honest, I'd rather you didn't have any further communication with him at all."

"Why?" His dark eyes were suddenly bright with anger.

"Well, you see, Kester and I aren't exactly the best of friends, and I just feel that in the circumstances—"

"Oh, I know you hate each other," said Hal flatly. "That's no news to me."

"Did he tell you that?"

"No. He never says a word against you. But everyone knows, don't they? It's an open secret." I saw his fists clench at his sides. "And now," he said, his voice shaking, "you're trying to turn me against him."

"Not at all. I'm simply saying that it's time Kester stopped treating you as his page boy. He's got no right to you anyway. You're my son, not his."

"More's the pity," said Hal.

Silence. Black eyes regarded me with implacable bitterness. That fine-drawn jaw was suddenly sculpted in iron.

"Would you say that again, please?" I said. I felt as if I'd sustained some horrifying injury.

"No," said Hal, "I won't. You'll beat me."

"That's right, I will. And if you ever, ever say such a thing again after all the bloody trouble I've taken to bring you up—"

"If I was nothing but a bloody trouble, why didn't you turn me over to Kester altogether? I was never a bloody trouble to Kester!"

"That's because he has no idea what parenthood's really like!"

"Well, if you hate it so much, why did you do it? Why did you go on and on making Mummy have babies till she died of it?"

"I—"

"You killed her! You took her away from me! And now you're taking Kester away from me too! I hate you, I hate you, *I hate you!*" screamed Hal, trying to run out of the room, but I slammed him back against the wall.

"I didn't kill your mother!" I shouted, stumbling over my words. "I tried to save her, I did everything I could, I—"

He spat at me.

Well, I really couldn't let that pass. I mean, I couldn't, could I? One can't let children think they can spit at their parents and get away with it.

I twisted his arm, shoved him forward and bent his little spine so that from the waist up he was lying flat along the back of the sofa. Then I hit him six times with my belt.

He was pathetically brave and only whimpered at the end. I hated myself. I hated him for making me hate myself. In fact I was so upset I could hardly bring myself to speak but I did manage to close the incident by saying, "Now, let that be an end to all talk of Kester and let that be an end to your intolerable behavior towards me."

He rushed away, blundering against the doorframe, and disappeared.

After a while I found myself in the ballroom nearby, but I saw it through a haze of pain and felt that its beauty was far beyond my reach. Instinctively I headed for the piano. I knew that everything would be well again once I started playing "The Blue Danube," so I sat down on the stool and raised my hands above the keys. But no notes sounded in my head. I could remember the tune but I couldn't hear the notes in that special way I had to hear them in order to play by ear.

My gift was gone. I was musically deaf. I couldn't play.

X

The gift came back. Of course it came back. I'd given myself a fright but within twenty-four hours I was playing again and once I could play I felt better. Meanwhile Hal had calmed down and was treating me politely, so I told myself I must put the wretched incident aside and refuse to dwell on it. Later I even told myself that Hal was probably grateful to me for taking a firm line. Children like to know just how much they can get away with; I'd no time for the modern theories which declared parents should let children do what they like. What a recipe for anarchy.

The rest of the holidays passed smoothly but I saw little of the boys because I was so preoccupied with the estate. Taking control of unfamiliar farms is a nerve-racking experience, but the deeper I dug into the unfamiliarity the uneasier I became. There was no doubt that those farms were undermechanized. Over-mechanization may be the more serious trap for the twentieth-century farmer to fall into, and I had long since learned for myself the hazards of tying up capital in a machine that was used for only two weeks of the year, but undermechanization meant higher labor costs and labor costs since the war had been rocketing out of sight. Also the laborers were getting Bolshie and wanted their cottages to have indoor lavatories. A nineteenth-century crusader like Rider Haggard would no doubt have cheered them on, but I wasn't a nineteenth-century crusader and I had to pay the plumbing bills. No doubt they'd all be demanding free television sets in the end. No wonder the country was going to the dogs.

However I was more worried about Oxmoon going to the dogs than Britannia sinking beneath the waves so I curbed the desire to think like a conservative reactionary and tried to work out how I could drum up the capital to make a substantial investment in mechanization. The short answer was that I couldn't—not without selling off the Penhale Manor estate. My first instinct, born of sentimentality, was to say "Never!" but I got over that. Oxmoon was now my first priority and only if I sold the Manor could I shore up my new estate effectively against the ravages of the mid–twentieth century.

I sold the Manor.

It was a wrench but once I'd done it I felt better. I paid off my debts, straightened out my income tax and plowed the money into Oxmoon. I was still sorry I wasn't able to incorporate the Penhale Manor Home Farm in the Oxmoon estate, but it was better to have a smaller estate running at maximum efficiency than a larger estate gobbling profits as the result of undermechanization.

Having straightened out my financial affairs so successfully I was able to enjoy the great family Christmas of 1951 when I took care to continue the tradition of lavish hospitality at Oxmoon. I even spent rather more on champagne than I should have done because I didn't want my family thinking I was less generous than Kester, but fortunately nobody seemed to be thinking of Kester at all.

I thought of him continually. He was still staying in Dublin with Declan and I wasn't in touch with him, but news filtered through to me from Marian, whose rocky marriage to Rory never quite ended in the divorce court. According to Rory Kester was trying to write again. That sent a predictable shudder down my spine but I told myself not to be neurotic. Kester was a writer. Let him write. Nothing, I said to Marian, could please me more than to hear he was taking advantage of his new freedom to do exactly as he pleased.

I had written to Kester to ask him not to communicate with Hal, and although I'd received no reply I realized he had honored my request; the headmaster reported that no letters from Ireland arrived for Hal at Briarwood, and certainly none arrived at Oxmoon. Poor little Hal. But in fact he'd soon recovered, and in retrospect I couldn't think why I'd allowed myself to get into such a state about him.

Humphrey went off to Briarwood in the September of '51 but I was slaving so hard trying to pull Oxmoon together that I barely had the chance to savor my childless bliss. Of course I never met a woman who wasn't eager for a guided tour of Oxmoon, but all the same I couldn't stage guided tours morning, noon and night. Oxmoon didn't give me the time. In fact I began to see Oxmoon as a highly demanding mistress, beautiful, extravagant, rewarding, inspiring—and exhausting. I spent most of my time feeling satisfied but worn out.

In the new year it turned out I wasn't the only one with a demanding mistress, because Gerry asked me if he could borrow the fabled cottage at Rhossili. Although I now let it to holidaymakers every summer it stood empty in the winter and I was willing enough to let Gerry use it when he pleased. In fact I was so sorry for him still being obliged to live at home that I even offered him the cottage on a permanent basis. Flats were scarce in Swansea, and although he was due to qualify as a solicitor that summer, I suspected that even when he was earning he would have trouble finding a place that suited him.

However Gerry at once rejected my offer by saying he couldn't possibly give Acceptable Parties for the People Who Mattered if he was reduced to living in a hovel in the back of beyond, and I was so annoyed that my generous gesture had been so peremptorily refused that when Marian called to see me a week later I said to her, "That Gerry's got ideas above his station. In fact that boy," I concluded after I had told her what had happened, "has a very cheap vulgar streak in his nature. All he can think of is social climbing."

"Well, darling, what can you expect? Bad breeding always tells." Marian, who looked rather ill bred herself after her latest reconciliation with Rory, knocked back her pink gin and glanced at her watch. Having taken a week off to recuperate from the strain of renewing her married life, she was staying with the Bryn-Davieses in Swansea. "I say!" she exclaimed impulsively as she rose to her feet. "What's this cottage like? Maybe I'll take it over next time I leave Rory! Does it have a lavatory or is there just a nasty hole in the garden?"

The upshot of this somewhat banal conversation was that Marian told Rory I didn't know what to do with the cottage, Rory told Declan, Declan told Kester and Kester, poor old Kester, poor pathetic exiled old sod, wrote me a rueful charming letter saying how he just couldn't write in Ireland and he was longing, absolutely longing for a little cottage by the sea in Gower where he could live quietly, getting in no one's way and being as good as gold at all times. Would I be very, very kind and let him have my Rhossili cottage? Of course he would pay me rent. He did hope I wouldn't object because it would mean so much to him and he was sure all the family would understand his request and sympathize with it.

I knew a threat when I saw one. I went straight to Dafydd. "If I don't let him have the cottage, he'll go whining to the family that he's been victimized—and I can't afford that, not when I've finally got them eating out of my hand. I'll have to agree. But what the hell do you think he wants?"

"A quiet life."

"Don't be ridiculous! He's had a quiet life in Ireland and now he's ready for action again!"

"You're off your rocker."

"You're off yours if you think he doesn't mean trouble!"

We stared at each other. Finally Dafydd said, "Okay, so he's on the warpath again after cooking up some plot with bloody Declan—he's dreamed up a scheme where he can crucify you without crucifying himself. But what is it? You tell me that. Just what the hell can he do?"

"God knows."

"Exactly. You're imagining this, Harry. It's all in your mind. Kester's finished. Beaten. Washed up."

"Yes. That's right. Of course."

"So you don't have to worry."

"No. I don't have to worry."

I went away telling myself I wasn't worried, not a bit of it, hadn't a care in the world.

But my God, *what the bloody hell was Kester going to do next?*

9

I

I COULDN'T REST. I couldn't sleep. I was afraid to consent to Kester's request but equally afraid to turn it down. Finally I summoned Gerry. I decided it was time Wonder Boy stopped beating his brains out to be Accepted and started beating his brains out on my behalf once more.

"Don't just say he can't touch me," I said as we conferred in the library. "Try and think of a legal way he could get Oxmoon back."

Gerry obligingly began to check off the possibilities. "One: he could claim there was some technical defect in the deed—but I'd say it was impossible that Roland and I, Fairfax and Carmichael were all blind to some huge howler."

"Go on."

"Two: he could claim he was insane when he signed the deed."

"Possible?"

"Most unlikely. Insanity's a very sticky legal wicket and he's never been certified—in fact he hasn't even been in a mental hospital this time around. I know he's claiming he's had another breakdown, but as far as hard evidence is concerned—"

"All right, forget insanity. What have we got left?"

"Well..." Gerry examined a fingernail. "Of course there's that hoary old chestnut duress but we don't really believe Declan Kinsella's Irish fairy tale, do we?"

"Certainly not. But if Kester could prove duress—"

"Oh, he could get Oxmoon back."

I got up and began to pace around the room.

"But Harry, why should you be so sure Kester's on the warpath? If he was, wouldn't he communicate with you through his lawyers? Why go through this charade of pretending all he wants is to hole up at Rhossili and write a new masterpiece?"

"Okay, I'm crazy." I went on pacing around the room.

We were silent for a moment before Gerry said with impressive delicacy, "Harry...I know there was no duress involved, but couldn't there...maybe...have been a little wholly insignificant persuasion?"

I made a quick calculation. Qualified or not, he was in the position of a lawyer who had to respect a confidence. I had no wish to confide in anyone but I felt I had to find out where I stood.

"He could claim duress," I said abruptly, "but the fact is he daren't. He committed a crime and I knew of it. Moreover I've got the evidence that convicts him."

Gerry blanched. I could see him instantly trying to work out how he could steer himself clear of this mess which was so very far from being Acceptable.

"I didn't hear that," he said.

"No," I said. "You wouldn't, would you?"

"Harry, don't think I don't want to help you. Look, maybe I could negotiate with Kester on your behalf—fix some kind of deal in which he got the house back but you went on running the estate—"

"Don't be a bloody fool. I've sold my home. I've sunk all my money in Oxmoon."

"Oh, some kind of financial reparation would of course be made," said Gerry glibly to help us skate past this vista of an unthinkable future. "Rather a tricky situation, old chap"—Gerry's BBC accent was really much improved—"but perhaps it's better not to dwell upon it further at this stage. We'll have to wait till Kester shows his hand—if he's got a hand to show—and meanwhile you ought to stop this crazy talk about crimes and so on, I mean, I don't take you seriously, I know there's nothing in it, but other people might think—"

"Quite." I got rid of him and went in search of my henchman. "Dafydd, I think the worst's going to happen and Kester's going to call my bluff."

Dafydd stared at me. "He can't. Daren't. Remember the poker."

"I know. But Dafydd, supposing he just says sod the poker. What's a poker with a bit of blood on it? Even if the forensic scientists prove Thomas's blood group was the same as the group of blood on the poker, that still doesn't prove conclusively that the blood's his."

"Yes, but—"

"Dafydd, if I accuse Kester of murdering Thomas he'll deny it. If I start waving the poker around he'll just say it's nothing to do with him. Furthermore, it'll look as if I'm a certifiable paranoiac—or, as you would say, off my bloody rocker. And in the end—" I drew a deep breath as the nightmare unfolded in my mind. "—Kester could even turn the whole story around and cast me as the villain from start to finish. He'd say I was unbalanced by the the war. He'd say I first killed Thomas and then threatened to kill him too unless he kept quiet. He'd say that was why he left Oxmoon—because he was too bloody frightened to stay any longer!"

"Wait. Don't forget you couldn't have used the poker. It came from his bedroom, he said—"

"Oh, what the hell, he'll say I killed Thomas with the golf club, he'll say I took the poker in an attempt to incriminate him, he'll say bloody anything! The poker's meaningless, Dafydd! Declan probably saw that at once as soon as he'd coaxed Kester to confess. Outsiders often see a horrific situation more clearly than people who are in it up to the neck."

"Well, if I was a murderer like bloody Kester, look you," said Dafydd calmly, "I wouldn't take the risk of calling your bluff. Too dangerous. Keep your head,

Harry. Don't play into his hands by doing anything stupid. Call *his* bluff and say he's welcome to have the cottage rent-free for as long as he wants—act as if your conscience was as clear as bloody crystal."

This struck me as good advice. Certainly no other advice was on offer so I sent the note agreeing to Kester's proposal and he wrote back by return. I left the breakfast table and retired to the cloakroom as soon as I saw the flowery writing on the envelope. It seemed an elementary precaution against queasiness.

With the cloakroom door locked and the basin within retching distance I opened the envelope and read: *My dear Harry, many thanks! I can't wait to see that wonderful view of Rhossili Bay—now I know I shall be able to write a masterpiece! I'm planning to arrive on May 5th—let me know if this isn't convenient. Could you leave the keys at the hotel at Rhossili so that we don't have to meet? True Doppelgängers should never meet face to face, you know. Ever your enthralled mirror image,* C.G.

I didn't vomit but my bowels felt as though they'd been sliced to ribbons so it was some time before I unlocked the cloakroom door. Scared shitless. Literally. Hadn't had that happen since the war.

"Dafydd, take a look at this."

He took a look. "Off his rocker. You've got nothing to worry about."

"Look at the signature—'C.G.'"

"Well, Christ, that's his name, isn't it? Christopher Godwin!"

"But don't you see? He's not just poor old Kester, poor old sod anymore. He's Christopher, my formidable cousin Christopher—clever, cunning, powerful, violent—"

"Oh, fuck off, Harry, for Christ's sake—this is just a crazy bugger who likes writing stories!"

I got a grip on myself. But then the sores began to break open on my back. I felt as if I were ripe for the padded cell—or at the very least a hospital bed and a shot of morphine, but I couldn't break down, there was no time. We were behind with the spring sowing, some fool had buggered up the bloody tractor at Daxworth and I was having rows with everyone in sight. Thank God I got the boys off my hands at the end of April, but I'd only just finished soothing the housekeeper, who was threatening to give notice after packing four school trunks, when another old nightmare surfaced. Dafydd reported that a little note in childish handwriting had been slipped under the door of the cottage to await Kester's arrival.

Steaming open the envelope I read: *Dear Kester, we're all so thrilled you're coming home to Gower. Gwyneth and I can't wait. She wears Anna's locket every day in memory of you. I've read* Wuthering Heights *now and you're right, it's wonderful, much better than* The Prisoner of Zenda! *I can't wait to talk to you about it. I've wanted to talk to you about so many things and I wish I could have written to you although I knew you were right in that last letter you sent when you said I had to obey my father like in the Ten Commandments, but what I want to know is, does one always have to obey orders? Can't one be excused if one knows*

811

the order's wrong? Please could you explain all this to me when we meet next holidays. With love from your friend HAL.

I read this letter slowly and painfully. Had I known that Hal had read *Wuthering Heights*? No. I hadn't even known he'd read *The Prisoner of Zenda*. And had Hal obeyed me by having no communication with Kester over the last year? No, he had obeyed Kester who had seen how our conflict was disturbing Hal and had moved to defuse it by citing the Ten Commandments. Kester emerged from the mess as an unselfish hero, I as a boorish maladjusted parent. Bloody hell. I was in misery again. How was I going to stop Hal visiting Kester whenever my back was turned? I couldn't. He'd be rushing off to Rhossili to play the acolyte as soon as he returned from school for the summer holidays.

I wanted to tear the letter up but I stopped myself. That would have made me a worse parent than ever and alienated me from Hal for good. So I resealed the envelope and told Dafydd to replace it in the cottage. But my rash now started to suppurate.

May came.

So did Kester.

Naturally I wasn't at the docks to meet the ferry, but Richard the court jester was loafing around at the Bryn-Daviesès' house and he bounced along to give Kester a hero's welcome. If Richard hadn't been so patently ingenuous I'd have thought him a slippery customer, supporting my takeover of Oxmoon at one moment and rushing off to fawn over Kester the next, but his extreme lack of brain made it impossible for me to be angry with him. He gave Kester a lift to Rhossili where I'd left the keys at the hotel, just as Kester had requested. Dafydd had prepared the cottage and everything was in order except for one of the kitchen taps which had started to drip. Richard reported it when he bounded over to Oxmoon to tell me that Kester was safely installed and happy as a lark.

"Let it drip," I said morosely to Dafydd afterwards. "It might rank as a form of Chinese water torture."

"I'll get a new washer on Thursday when I go into Swansea—or do you want me to get it earlier?"

"Oh, for God's sake don't make a special trip!"

Odd how so much depended in the end on that dripping tap. Like that nightmarish nursery rhyme about the lost nail from the horse's shoe which resulted in the loss of a kingdom. That kind of causality can make strong men weep and drive sane men mad.

"Why are you going into Swansea on Thursday?" I asked Dafydd as an afterthought.

"It's my day for seeing my mother."

In fact Bronwen came out to Gower to see Kester before then but we didn't find that out till later. Evan also called on Kester and unlike Bronwen he visited Oxmoon afterwards to tell me how happy Kester was now that he was able to devote himself single-mindedly to his writing.

"He even said," Evan added, "that relinquishing Oxmoon was turning out to be one of the best moves he had ever made! So all's well that ends well, and I hope we can be friends again, Harry."

Hm. Very edifying. But did I really believe we were all destined to live happily ever after in a glowing aura of brotherly love? I was quite willing to consider such a fantastic possibility, but at that moment I happened to be distracted by two problems. The first was that the Inland Revenue were trying to tell me that I had cut a couple of my past corners too fine and that I still owed them a considerable amount of money. What a bloody jungle income tax is! It's a wonder we don't all go on strike and refuse to pay.

My second problem turned up three days after Kester's arrival when my mistress wrote to say I'd become absolutely impossible and she'd had enough, thanks very much, and she'd got a new man in her life now and was I sure my skin trouble wasn't catching.

I stormed over to the guesthouse she kept on Oxwich Bay and made a scene. I wasn't crazy about the woman but she was very convenient and I just couldn't stand the prospect of trying to find someone new at that particular moment. I spent much time nowadays wishing I had that unsurpassably convenient sexual accessory, a wife, but I never found anyone who measured up to the magic Dr. Mallinson who was still living with her neurosurgeon. Every time a new telephone directory was printed I checked to see if he was still alive, but he always was. Often I thought it ironic that a man such as I, accustomed to having any woman he fancied, should be afraid to pursue a woman because she had brains and a husband, but I was afraid she would at once reject me as an undesirable womanizer, and I couldn't bear the thought of how much I'd mind. Better to love her hopelessly from a distance than to involve myself in an affair which might tear me to shreds.

Meanwhile my current mistress was trying to tear me to shreds but I put a stop to that by having sex with her—which was a bad idea because by the time I arrived home in the middle of the afternoon I was so exhausted that I fell asleep on the drawing-room sofa. That meant I would find it impossible to sleep that night, and when my housekeeper woke me by bringing in tea and the afternoon post, my first reaction was to slip into a disgruntled mood.

But the next moment I had forgotten about being disgruntled. I had discovered that the afternoon post consisted of two bills and another familiar white envelope addressed to me in flowery handwriting.

Dropping all the letters on the floor I headed at once for the decanter and poured myself a double brandy.

II

My dear Harry, Kester had written, *I can't tell you how much I'm enjoying the cottage and the view is so stimulating to my fevered imagination, but alas! I've come to the conclusion that it wouldn't be at all comfortable here in winter when the gales start to blow, so I think, if you don't mind, I'd like Oxmoon back. I hope this won't be too inconvenient for you but Declan did tell me how you'd promised the family that if I wanted Oxmoon back all I had to do was ask—jolly decent of you, old chap, I always knew you were a nice fellow despite our little differences of opinion! Anyway, why don't you drop in and see me soon so that we can talk the matter over? I feel in the mood for a sociable, benevolent, eminently rational chat! Yours ever, C.G.*

I crumpled the letter, stuffed it into my pocket and knocked back a second brandy. I was quite calm. I had wanted Kester to show his hand and now, thank God, he'd shown it and put an end to all my agonizing uncertainty. He wanted Oxmoon back. Right. Well, at least I now knew where I stood. And where was that? In the biggest mess of all time.

I panicked. I wanted my henchman but it was Thursday and he was in Swansea with Bronwen. He paid this visit once a month so I knew what the form was: they would go to the cinema together and afterwards she would cook him a high tea. No Dafydd, not for several hours yet. I felt vulnerable without him, vulnerable and lonely. One grows lonely when one has secrets no one else can share; I'd found that out long ago and no doubt Kester had discovered it too.

Kester.

I had to think what I was going to do about Kester but I was in such a state that rational thought was beyond me. All I could think of was that Kester was going to crucify me. He'd call my bluff, accuse me of murdering Thomas, claim that I'd terrorized him into relinquishing Oxmoon, and our horrified family would flock to his side. The charge of murder might remain non-proven but that charge of duress was sure to stick, and that would be my final curtain. I'd have no home and no money—unless Kester decided to be generous with me, and did I seriously think Kester was going to be generous? No. Kester was going to hang, draw and quarter me—the traditional death for a traitor, and yes, that was how I'd look to my family, a traitor to my father's principles, a traitor to the Godwin honor and good name.

But it wasn't true, was it? I'd just been trying to right a wrong, avenge Thomas's murder and protect myself from my dangerous cousin. I was the hero of this story but Kester had cast me as the villain in his brilliant script and now I was going to wind up thoroughly damned, the usurper who had earned his annihilating retribution.

"Justice seems to have gone adrift," my father had said just before his death.

My God, if my father could see me now...

But he couldn't. Or at least I hoped he couldn't. Had to believe he couldn't. Had to.

To calm myself I began to walk around Oxmoon, my Oxmoon, the inheritance that would have been mine if only... what had my father said? Something about Uncle Robert and Grandfather, something about my great-grandmother and Owain Bryn-Davies... Mad. What the hell could he have meant? Should have asked him. Why hadn't I asked him? Because all I'd been able to think about at that particular moment had been the future, the future when I was going to draw the line and retire to Herefordshire, the future that might have been, the future that was now lost beyond recall.

I should have drawn the line.

Never mind, I'd draw it now. Better late than never. The best way out of my mess was undoubtedly to kill Kester, but of course I'd never do it. Thank God there was at least one line left to draw! All right, no murder today, thank you, but what's the alternative? Damn all. No, think. *Think.* Have to compromise. Try to bargain with him. I'll have to give up Oxmoon, of course, that goes without saying, but I must find a way to stop Kester disemboweling me. If I were to offer him something of my very own which I know he wants...

Hal.

Well, it was a chance, wasn't it? Better than nothing. If I let him adopt Hal he might—for Hal's sake—be lenient with me. Hal wouldn't mind being adopted by Kester, of course. In fact he'd be delighted. In Hal's opinion I was just a dead loss.

Tears burned my eyes. Shameful. Disgusting. Had to put a stop to that sort of behavior at once. Dashing the tears aside I went out to the stable block to my car—Kester's car, the shining black Daimler which he had bought just before I'd forced him to Ireland. I'd enjoyed driving that Daimler. Didn't want to give it up. Didn't want to give anything up, that was the trouble—the Daimler, Oxmoon, Hal... No, I couldn't give Hal up, couldn't. Strange how for years I'd made Humphrey my favorite as if favorites could be chosen by a mere exercise of the will. But one doesn't choose favorites. They choose you. That sort of powerful emotional connection has nothing to do with the will at all. No, Hal was my real favorite, not Humphrey, I knew that now, just as I knew I was going to have to give him up. Losing Hal was to be the price I had to pay for my extortion; losing Hal was to be the penalty for my cheating and my lies.

More tears. Disgraceful. I was getting just like Kester, weeping at the drop of a hat, but of course I *was* Kester, I'd become him, and now there was just this other stranger who wrote me debonair notes and who sounded just like *me*, using that bloody awful public-school phrase "old chap" and being so cool and suave the whole damned time. Yes, I was Kester now and he was me, he was the other side of my personality, the artist I'd always suppressed, and now as he tried to eliminate me I had to kill him to stay sane. . . .

No. Steady, as Dafydd would say, don't go off your rocker. Negotiate with Kester and get the whole hellish dilemma resolved peaceably as soon as possible.

I drove to Rhossili. It was early on a brilliant May evening and I drove out to Rhossili to confront my double image, my other self.

Several times I thought: I'll go back. But each time I kept going. Well, I always did, didn't I? Story of my life.

I could have stopped—but I went on.

III

I reached Rhossili. The bay was a dazzling azure blue and long white waves creamed languidly upon the miles of empty sands far below. In the clear evening light the Downs seemed deceptively close and I felt I could almost reach out to touch the old Rectory as it basked in its sunlit isolation far away at the head of the beach.

By the little green a lane led down to my cottage and when I arrived I parked the car in the barn which Dafydd had converted into a garage. The lane was too narrow to permit a car to be parked outside the cottage, and there was no verge by the dry-stone wall nearby.

Instinct told me Kester was out. I paused. I could hear the sea. It was very faint and far away like a dream of happiness. I glanced across the fields towards Rhossili but the tourist season had barely begun and there was no one about. I remember noticing the stunted steeple of the church silhouetted against the brilliant sky.

The front door was locked but he hadn't bothered to bolt the back door so I walked in. "Kester!" I called in the front room at the foot of the stairs, but there was no reply. I took a quick look around and noticed that in one corner he had parked his sophisticated wireless which Evan had evidently returned to him on his recent visit. The wireless had been one of the few possessions that Kester hadn't left at Oxmoon and he had given the set to Evan for safekeeping before leaving for Ireland.

The dial was tuned to the Third Programme, just as my wireless always was. Perhaps we listened to the same music; perhaps his musical taste was now exactly the same as mine. In revulsion I glanced around for evidence of the main difference between us, but there was no sign of any manuscript and the typewriter stood covered on the table.

Shuddering irrationally I wondered what to do next. Obviously he had gone for a walk before dinner. I looked at my watch. Five past six. Various choices lay before me. I could go back to Oxmoon but no, I couldn't, I had to see him and get the scene over with or I'd lie awake all night in a cold sweat—in fact I might well go mad with tension. I could wait where I was in the quiet living room but I thought that might well send me mad with tension too. Or I could go looking for him. There were no trees on the headland at Rhossili, and if I went past the Coastguard station I thought there was a good chance I could track him down.

I decided to walk out to the tip of the headland. Any activity seemed better than none, and so although I could have remained where I was I didn't.

I could have stopped—but I went on.

By the church a farmer drove past me in his tractor and the normality of his cheerful wave was soothing to me. Moving on down the street I passed the hotel at the road's end and headed down the track past the car park and the Coastguard's cottages. Automatically, responding to a lifetime's experience of Gower, I checked the board where the Coastguard set out information about the state of the tides and saw that the Shipway was safe for another hour and fifty minutes. I was hardly planning an expedition to the Worm, but I thought it possible that Kester might be pottering around down on the rocks if the tide was favorable. I could remember him gazing into a pool there when we were children and declaring how ravishing the seaweed was. I'd been collecting dead starfish at the time.

With my mind still deep in the ragbag of the past, I drifted on past the Coastguard's cottages before veering to the edge of the cliff to check the beach below. But there was no one down there who looked like Kester. I did wonder if he might be hiding in a cave but I could think of no plausible reason why he should be.

I went on.

The most likely solution to the mystery of his disappearance was that he had strolled to the end of the headland and then veered south along the top of the cliffs. It was a reasonably level walk and not too arduous. I couldn't quite see Kester trekking down to sea level and back after a busy day, but when I approached the end of the headland and glanced along the cliffs to Porteynon there was no sign of him and when I finally reached the point where I could look down upon the Shipway I saw him immediately.

He was loafing around a rock pool not far from the bottom of the cliffs.

Surprising but not, as far as I could see, either extraordinary or bizarre. I stood watching him and for a moment I thought he'd looked up but he hadn't, he was just pushing the hair out of his eyes as he straightened his back. It would have been useless to call out. The clear evening light was creating the optical illusion that he was close to me but the cliffs were high, the sea was droning away and we were probably at least ten minutes apart in time. I hesitated, not sure what to do. I glanced at my watch. Half-past six. The Shipway would remain exposed for well over an hour and even though Kester was bound to come back eventually up the cliff path to the summit where I was now lying in wait for him, it was possible that he could be mooning around gazing soulfully into rock pools for some time. Could my nerves stand the wait? No. Better to go down and confront him.

I set off down the path.

The path zigzagged and I wasn't watching him all the time, but before I was halfway to the bottom of the cliff I noticed that he was on the move. I stopped to stare at him. He was heading out across the Shipway. At first I thought I might be mistaken because the Shipway is such a jumble of rocks that no one who traverses it can travel in a straight line, but as I watched I knew I was right. He wasn't hurrying; he was moving casually, but he was keeping up a steady pace and he was no longer pausing to look at the rock pools.

Now, this *was* bizarre. I glanced at my watch again. I even listened to it to make sure it hadn't stopped but it was ticking away normally enough, and as I'd set it right by the one-o'clock news I knew it couldn't possibly be more than a minute slow. Could Kester be making some sort of balls-up? No, he was Gower-bred, just as I was, and he too would have looked at the Coastguard's notice on his way out. So that meant he knew what he was doing, but what the hell was it?

If he was going out to the Worm he was mad—not suicidal; he had plenty of time to get there and back before the tide turned nasty; but just plain mad. Crossing the Shipway was a hard slog. It took half an hour to get from the foot of the cliffs to the Inner Head, the first of the Worm's three humps, and the terrain was terrible nearly all the way. No one in his right mind would battle across the Shipway at the end of the day in order to twiddle his thumbs for a few minutes before being obliged to start the journey back.

I went on, driven by curiosity, and by the time I reached the grassy bank at the bottom of the cliffs he was a long way ahead. In fact he was halfway across. He was standing on that little shingle beach in the middle of the great tilting C formed by the Shipway, and gazing out across Rhossili Bay. It was hard to judge distances in that seascape of optical illusion, but if he was on that beach I calculated we had to be at least a quarter of an hour apart; I had dithered on the cliff while he had been striding out so he had gained a few minutes on me. Was he aware of my presence behind him? He gave no indication of it. I had half-wondered if he had seen me and was running away, but he showed no sign that he was unnerved—rather the reverse. He looked like a disciple of Wordsworth absorbed in the wonders of nature.

Most odd.

So what did I do? I decided to stay where I was because at any minute now he was sure to turn back; I just couldn't believe he'd slog on across the Shipway. But he did. He stopped gazing across the bay and went on.

Extraordinary. What did it mean? I glanced at my watch again. Plenty of time. No danger. He could get to the Worm and he could certainly get back, no problem about that, but what the hell was he up to? I had no idea, but if he was mad enough to trek across the Shipway for no reason on a fine spring evening I supposed I could be mad enough too. At least a trek over rough terrain was better than sitting on the bank beneath the cliff and going crazy wondering what the hell he was doing.

I went on.

As I scrambled down the bank onto the rocks I met two holidaymakers, a man and a woman, who were just completing the ordeal of the return journey, and we all said good evening to each other. The man added some jovial warning to me about the rising tide, and to reassure myself I glanced at my watch. Nearly a quarter to seven. An hour and fifteen minutes of perfect safety—and probably longer. The Coastguard, all too aware of how often people underestimated the time it took to cross the Shipway, was sure to make allowances in its calculations for the misguided and the foolhardy.

I began to slog across the Shipway. I couldn't see Kester all the time because the taller rocks often hid him from view, but as time went on it gradually occurred to me how odd it was that he never once looked back. One often had to pause on the Shipway to calculate the best route and it would have been natural to glance back during these routine surveys, but whenever I did catch sight of Kester he was either gazing out to sea or else resolutely confronting the Inner Head.

Why didn't he look back?

But on the other hand, why should he? It wouldn't do to start being neurotic, although it was hard not to be neurotic in the face of his peculiar behavior. I decided that for my own peace of mind I needed to know what he was doing and why. Could he be luring me on in order to kill me? If I was going to give way to paranoia I might as well give way entirely, but no, the whole point of our situation was that Kester didn't have to kill me to get what he wanted. I was the one who had to kill him except that I wasn't going to. That took care of that particular theory but I was still no closer to guessing what the devil he was up to.

I reached the middle of the Shipway and stood on the little shingle beach where Kester himself had stood a quarter of an hour before. The water of the bay nearby was tranquil but I could hear the surf booming on the other side of the isthmus as the tide swept up from the south. As I paused for breath I glanced ahead at Kester again and at that moment he reached the Inner Head and scrambled up from the rocks onto the grassy bank. Now, I thought, *now* he'll look back. One always did when one had finally conquered the Shipway. One looked back not only to see the dazzling view but to pat oneself mentally on the back for crawling the full distance over that nightmarish terrain of jumbled rocks and pools.

I stood stock-still and waited to be discovered. But discovery never came. He didn't look back. He drifted on down the path that led away from the Shipway, and soon he had disappeared from sight along the southern flank of the Inner Head.

Incredible behavior. Could he be quite mad, so mad that he wanted to kill me just for the hell of it even though my murder was unnecessary? I decided that I could believe that—just—but what I couldn't believe was that Kester would try to kill me by luring me out to the Worm's Head and tossing me (how?) into the sea. After all, *I* was the expert in unarmed combat. That would be a great way for me to kill Kester but hardly a great way for Kester to kill me—strychnine in the scotch would be more in his line and a nice grave waiting in the woods, although if the police searched the grounds they'd be bound to discover any newly made grave... No, on second thoughts Kester would favor a murder that could look like an accidental drowning, but hell, it was all quite irrelevant because I hadn't a shred of evidence that Kester had murder on his mind.

I just had it on mine. But no, it would be crazy to kill him, those holidaymakers would testify that I'd been chasing Kester out to the Worm and even a policeman with the brains of a louse could see that I had a gargantuan motive for wanting Kester dead. And I wasn't going to kill him anyway. So that was that.

Maybe my wisest course was simply to turn back and wait for him on the mainland, but no, I really had to stop being so paranoid and pull myself together—

I had to stop picturing either Kester or myself as a drowned corpse, because if there was one certainty about our present situation it was that no one was going to wind up killed on an expedition to the Worm's Head like—

My God, yes, like Owain Bryn-Davies back in the Eighteen Eighties.

I'd never really understood that story. Apparently Bryn-Davies had gone to look at the Penrice flock which was kept on the Worm in those days, but he was a North Gower man from The Welshery and he hadn't understood about the tides. Why not? He obviously wasn't a fool. He must have consulted the tide tables— or asked someone to consult them for him. So what had happened? God only knew, but anyway the net result had been that the usurper at Oxmoon had been neatly eliminated and my grandfather Bobby Godwin, the rightful heir, had wound up the undisputed master of his stolen inheritance.

The usurper had been neatly...

I swallowed some air in a moment of complete panic, floundered in among the rocks again and clawed my way up onto the spine of the Shipway so that I could see what was happening on the other side, but no, I was still thoroughly safe; the tide, though looking snappish, was still thundering at a distance but as I watched it I knew as absolutely as if I'd seen the family history printed in black-and-white that my grandfather had trapped Bryn-Davies, trapped him and drowned him on the Shipway, because he had seen no other way of removing the usurper from his home.

Kester wasn't Bobby Godwin and I wasn't Owain Bryn-Davies. History never exactly repeats itself. But it reverberates, and as I stood there listening on the Shipway I was nearly overwhelmed by those echoes in time.

I checked my watch. Could Kester have altered the Coastguard's notice? Of course not. Impossible. However I came to the conclusion that I really wasn't very happy right in the middle of the Shipway with the tide coming in, so the big question once again was Did I go back or did I stagger on to the Inner Head to find out exactly what Kester was doing with himself?

I dithered away and the minutes ticked on. At this rate I'd be drowned through sheer indecision and it wouldn't even be Kester's fault. I had to act, and in an effort to marshal my thoughts I found myself again looking at my watch.

It was five minutes past seven. In less than an hour's time, at eight o'clock, the Shipway would begin to go under and both Kester and I, unless we were certifiable lunatics, would be back on the mainland because if we weren't we'd be marooned together on the Worm until the early hours of the morning. That was a hideous thought so the sensible thing for me to do now was go back and wait for him beneath the cliff.

But on the other hand...

I considered the other hand. I could go on, confront him and still be back on the mainland before the Shipway went under. The advantage of that was that it would put me in a strong psychological position when it came to striking a bargain with him. Obviously he didn't know he was being followed; that crap about him luring me on was just me being paranoid. If he now found himself alone in an isolated spot with a trained killer who had a huge motive for wanting him dead, he'd be so unnerved that he'd agree to whatever I suggested and the odds were I'd get a much more favorable compromise. He might even let me keep Hal.

That settled it.

I went on.

V

I felt as if I were crossing lines, line after line after line, but that was all right because I knew there was always the final line that I'd never cross. Kester had talked of lines when he had told me how he'd killed Thomas; I could remember him gabbling how he'd crossed the last line without being aware of it and then found there was no way back. "Once that die was cast, I'd *crossed that line*, and then I could only move forward to destruction..." Typical Kester, melodramatic and emotional as always, very stupid. He'd been hysterical, that was the trouble, too hysterical even to see a line, let alone draw one. No one in his right mind, as I was, could cross a crucial line without being aware of it. Impossible. The very idea was ridiculous.

I reached the Inner Head. The Worm's three humps all rose high above the sea. The Inner Head was connected to the Middle Head by a rough stretch of rocks not unlike the Shipway but set above the high-water mark, and the Middle Head was connected to the Outer Head by a natural arch known romantically as the Devil's Bridge. The entire Worm was a mile long and provided endless dazzling panoramas of sea, cliffs and sky, but I was hardly in the mood for sight-seeing that evening so when I reached the Inner Head I didn't linger to dwell upon the view. I did glance back across the Shipway as usual, but I made the glance a brief one; I was too nervous that Kester might sneak up and tap me playfully on the shoulder when my back was turned, but of course he didn't and when I swung around to examine the steep treeless flank of the Head I could see no sign of him.

I paused to consider my position. I now had ten minutes—ten minutes to confront Kester, ten minutes to bargain with him, ten minutes to salvage my future—and then I had to turn back with him to the mainland if we were to avoid Bryn-Davies's fate on the Shipway. The discussion could be continued on the return journey, of course, but the crucial foundations of our agreement had to be laid during those initial minutes when he would be frightened and pliable. Was I setting myself an impossible task by trying to shake him to the core in such a limited time? Not necessarily. It depended on how limited the time was—and that in turn depended on where Kester was now but I thought it almost certain that he was relaxing just beyond the bend in the path which lay some way ahead of me. I couldn't believe he'd be heading for the Outer Head and a night in splendid isolation beneath the stars. No, he'd be pausing to rest and then—within the next few minutes—he'd be coming back to the Shipway to begin the return journey.

Rather than pursue him farther I decided my best course of action was now to conserve my energy, drum up all my courage and wait. Fine. This was where I drew the line and behaved like a rational human being. I'd wait for Kester, give him the shock of his life and then launch myself on some forceful but nonviolent bargaining. Dead simple. What could be easier? What course of action could be safer or more sensible? I'd be all right. He'd be all right. We might experience some nasty moments but we were both going to battle through the meeting without destroying each other.

I drew the line.

I waited.

Nothing happened. No Kester. The sun went on shining, the tide went on rising but Kester didn't come back.

I was just looking at my watch for the umpteenth time when such a horrifying thought occurred to me that I nearly passed out.

Supposing I had, finally, gone off my rocker. Supposing I'd hallucinated and had only imagined that I'd seen Kester ahead of me. My whole pursuit of him had had such a dreamlike quality, a mysterious quest in a setting so beautiful that it might have been a landscape of myth, and Kester had moved as a wraith in my imagination, traveling so steadily, not once looking back, never showing me his face.

I thought: It's no good, I've got to go on.

Well, I mean, I really did have to go on, didn't I? I had to know he was real and not some nightmarish projection of my disordered mind. I couldn't have stopped myself, not at that stage. I couldn't possibly have stayed where I was.

So I took a step forward—and as I did so the die was cast, *I'd crossed that line*, I could only move forward to destruction. . . .

PART
SIX

HAL
1966 AND AFTERWARDS

Not today, O Lord,
O, not today, think not upon the fault
My father made in compassing the crown!
I Richard's body have interred anew,
And on it have bestowed more contrite tears
Than from it issued forced drops of blood...
　　　　　　　—William Shakespeare
　　　　　　　Henry V

I

Oxmoon was destroyed, the Oxmoon of my childhood, Kester's shrine to Anna, his monument to beauty and peace. The mid–twentieth century was brutal to houses like Oxmoon. Racked by fiscal assaults and hammered by financial disasters, the estate broke up and the house drifted on towards extinction.

I went back in the summer of '66. It was two years since I'd last been there. I'd been trying to escape from the past but escape had proved impossible. I'd realized in the end that I was wasting my time, and when I reassessed my life after my friends died I saw how hung up I was. Yet now I was beyond mere fashionable phraseology. I was determined that there should be no more excuses that I was "hung up" and that Oxmoon was "irrelevant," no more escaping from reality by bucketing around in a psychedelic minibus on a tidal wave of cheap wine and sweet smoke, no more pretending that the past could no longer touch me. If I was to have any kind of worthwhile future I now had to take time out from the present to exorcise the ghosts that haunted me.

To my surviving friends I merely said, "I quit."

But to myself I said, I'm going home.

II

The iron gates were rusted, padlocked against vandals. The wall looked as if it had been freshly crowned with broken glass, but when I left the road and followed the footpath uphill towards Penhale Down I found the wall untouched by the new defenses. The door into the grounds was bolted. I climbed the nearest tree,

825

swung along a branch and dropped down on the far side of the wall without breaking a leg. Picking up my duffel bag I moved on. Brambles tore at my leather jacket. The wet undergrowth drenched my jeans. The path was so overgrown that it was barely visible and above my head the dense foliage of the trees dimmed the light of the gray summer afternoon.

It was very quiet. When I came to the ruined tower I found that more of the upper walls had collapsed, tearing the heavy creeper apart. I paused to look upon its corpse and suddenly I was so conscious of death that I found it hard to believe I was still alive. I moved swiftly on but at the edge of the woods a dead wilderness stretched before me. The tennis court was a memory, the netting rotted beside the posts. The lawn was ravaged by weeds and littered with rusted croquet hoops. And beyond the lawn was the house, another corpse, its shuttered windows blind to the light, its derelict walls waiting for their inevitable demolition.

I said one word, an obscenity, and moved on.

Skirting the terrace, where weeds were growing, I walked around the house to the side door. The frame was rotted. One hard shove broke the lock. I went in. I held my breath and the silence came to meet me, the silence of death and disintegration, the silence of my jail, the past. I had to find a way of living with that silence, but how does one live with death and how does one bear the un-bearable?

I was standing in the passage by the television room, the passage which con-nected the ballroom to the main part of the house. Turning aside I walked down the corridor to the hall.

The light was gloomy because of the fastened shutters but I could see a hundred spiders' webs, intricate and beautiful, linking the posts of the banisters on the staircase. The vast chandelier was caked in dust. I stared up at it and then as I stepped forward impulsively the silence was broken by the echo of my footfall on the marble floor.

"Ah!" I said, although why I spoke I didn't know. Echoes vibrated in my mind but when I again paused to listen they fell silent. I walked into the dining room. Little puffs of dust rose from the carpet as I crossed it. The long table and all the chairs were swathed in dust sheets, but the paneling was as ageless as the marble floor of the hall, and on either side of the fireplace the carved swags of fruit and flowers seemed to glow uncannily in the dim light.

The house was dead but Kester's treasures were still alive, waiting for the inevitable day when they would be auctioned to pay the death duties, and mean-while they too were locked up in the past, entombed in that atmosphere of decay.

Yet when I looked at the carvings again they seemed to pulse with life, and suddenly I heard the echo again, a little louder, a little closer to me in time.

I went into the drawing room. The eighteenth-century furniture was invisible beneath the dust sheets, but the great Gainsborough painting shone in the twilight and on the mantelshelf the four china cherubs were still holding aloft the dial of time. I found the key. It was still in the vase nearby. I wound the clock. The pendulum needed a nudge, no more, and then the silence was broken at last as time began to run again for Oxmoon, not time present but time past, the golden past which I had thought lost beyond recall.

I wound up the clock in the morning room. I was winding time on yet winding time back, and as I turned the key I remembered Bronwen telling me long ago after my mother's death that time was a circle and that the past could not only coexist with the present but even lie ahead of the present in the future.

Tick-tock, tick-tock, thudded the grandfather clock in the hall, and as I turned away, I saw the dusty chandelier glitter in my mind. I ran back into the drawing room. I ripped aside the dust sheets. The room blazed with blue and gold.

"Beauty..."

I was in the dining room again. The dust sheets were swirling to the floor and I saw the great carved chair as I had seen it in my childhood, a chair for heroes, the magic throne of my magician.

"Truth..."

I flung wide the library door. The books were all there, just as I remembered. I began to wind the clock.

"Art..."

Tick-tock, tick-tock, sang the clock as my fingers closed on *Wuthering Heights*. Tick-tock, tick-tock, shouted the clock as I pulled out *The Prisoner of Zenda*.

"Peace..."

I was in the ballroom. I saw myself reflected in the clouded mirrors. Sitting down at the piano, I tried to play "Walk Right Back" but the notes were out of tune so I stopped playing and sang instead as the lyric played itself back in my memory. "'I want you to tell me why you walked out on me...'" I had sung the lyric so often at one-nighters up and down the country but I had never until that moment connected that song with my past at Oxmoon. "'I want you to know that since you walked out on me, nothing seems to be the same old way...'" I broke off and moved to the doors but although I stopped singing, the song went on playing in my mind. "Walk right back to me this minute..." But there could be no walking back.

Or could there?

Fourteen years ago he had walked out on me by committing suicide but now I had finally willed myself to face his memory and against all the odds he was walking right back after all into my life.

And what did I feel? Rage that he had abandoned me? Contempt that he had taken a coward's way out? Bitterness that he had proved himself a weak man instead of the hero I'd believed him to be? Yes, but beyond all these familiar emotions I was aware this time of something else. I was aware of a deep-rooted and ineradicable bewilderment, and I knew then that there was an unsolved mystery here that no one, least of all myself, had ever begun to unravel.

Kester was dead. But by some magician's trick he was still alive. My father was still alive. Yet it was as if my father were the one who had died.

I walked back through the house, retrieved my duffel bag and went out through the side door. It had begun to rain but I made no effort to hurry as I walked on past the ruined orangerie and the shambles of the kitchen garden. I felt hot and muddled, and the melody of "Walk Right Back" was reverberating endlessly in my head.

When I reached the stable block I stopped to stare for there in the far corner, just as Humphrey had reported, lay a new oasis of extreme neatness. Part of the stables had been converted into a chic little mews house. Painted a pristine white which was alleviated only by the black front door, it was adorned with window boxes in which geraniums flourished with military precision. Voile curtains gave the windows a hostile glare. The brass of the door gleamed fiercely. To complete the impression of a siege mentality at work a new car stood in the yard; it was an aggressive red mini which displayed its radiator like a watchdog baring its teeth.

I had reached my journey's end. Here in fortified seclusion, separated from his family, alienated from those who had once supported him, racked by ill health and tortured by a personality that was deeply and incurably neurotic, lived the present and as far as I could see the final master of Oxmoon.

Taking a deep breath I walked up to the front door and rang the bell.

III

My stepmother opened the door. She always paid meticulous attention to her appearance to disguise the fact that she was older than my father, and today was no exception; she was fifty but looked forty. Her narrow figure heightened the illusion of youth but as always I found her physically repellent. Her slate-gray eyes saw too far. In her presence one felt perpetually encircled by a powerful mind and placed ruthlessly in deep analysis.

"Oh, it's you," she said. "I thought you'd turn up eventually. How handsome you look now you've cut your hair." She made this statement in such a deadpan voice that it became a mere clinical observation. "Come in."

I stepped past her into the living area. The architect had employed an open-plan design. I saw a galley kitchen along the far wall and a pine-paneled alcove where four pine chairs were tucked into a pine dining table. The kitchen cupboards matched the furniture. Electrical appliances were lined up by the sink. Everywhere was immaculate, hygienic, sanitized. Nearby a small sofa and two armchairs were grouped around a large television set. On the wall a bookcase displayed bound medical journals and books on psychiatry.

"Very nice," I said to my stepmother.

"Don't worry, I don't expect you to like it."

The sound of music drifted towards us through an open doorway. I recognized Sibelius's *First Symphony*.

"How's Father?"

"Not too bad. I got him out yesterday. We went for a walk on Penhale Down."

"Quite an achievement." My father suffered periodically from agoraphobia. "Will he see me?"

"I can't think why not." She made it sound as if it were normal for a father and son to greet each other nonchalantly after a two-year estrangement. "Sit down and I'll tell him you're here."

She disappeared through the doorway towards Sibelius's *First Symphony* and I sat down in front of the blank television screen. I was remembering Humphrey's information about this new home of my father's. There were two spare rooms and a bathroom upstairs, but my father and stepmother lived on the ground floor where in the larger of the two bedrooms my father listened to his radio and conducted his long love affair with his record player. The smaller bedroom, like the living area, reflected only my stepmother's taste in interior decoration. Humphrey had described the predominating color as iceberg-blue.

Sibelius's *First Symphony* stopped. My stepmother's high heels came tapping back down the passage.

"He'll see you," she said, very much the efficient doctor deciding that the patient was strong enough to submit to stress. "Second door on the right."

I walked past her into a short corridor. On my left an open pine staircase rose to the floor above. On my right the iceberg-blue bedroom reflected the accuracy of Humphrey's descriptive powers. I shuddered and glanced on past the stairs to the open door of a bathroom. Opposite this another door stood ajar and without knocking I walked in.

In sharp contrast to the rest of the house this room was chaotic and disorganized. I guessed my stepmother was allowed in once a week to dust, hoover and change the bed linen. The single bed, very disheveled, lay along one wall in silent testimony to my father's chronic insomnia, and beside the bed a table bore the burden of my father's pillboxes and ointment jars. Records and books lined the walls. I saw a transistor radio but knew this would be used only for listening to the news. The VHF radio in the corner was tuned permanently to the Third Programme. His record player was the most expensive money could buy and large speakers hung on either side of the curtains. There was no piano. My father never played now. He'd had a gift for playing by ear but he'd lost it when Kester died. Or so he said. The loss existed entirely in his mind but that, as my stepmother pointed out, didn't make the loss less real. It was her opinion that the gift would come back if he experienced a sufficient improvement in his mental health, but the improvement never came and my father never played. At some stage, after the first nervous breakdown or the second, I forget which, he'd taught himself to read music so that he could follow the notes while he listened to his records, and as I now entered the room I wasn't surprised to see the score of the Sibelius symphony lying open on the table by the window.

My father was standing nearby. He wore a creased open-necked blue shirt, faded with age, and a pair of baggy gray flannel trousers which sagged at the waist. He deliberately wore clothes which were too big for him because his skin was so sensitive to pressure. Since he had had warning of my arrival he had had time to button his shirt and pull down his sleeves to hide the eczema that plagued him. Some years ago when a daily shave had become too much of an ordeal he had grown a beard, and although a small patch of eczema was visible on his face it was partially obscured by his heavy sideburns. He wore his hair long at the back, no doubt to conceal other sores, and this hirsute appearance gave him a curiously modern look. In the King's Road in so-called Swinging London no one would have thrown him a second glance.

His black hair was streaked with gray; his dark eyes were tense with suspicion. As I approached he stood stock-still, difficulty personified, a perfect example of paranoid parenthood.

"Hullo, Father, how are you?"

"What do you want?"

After a pause during which I successfully kept my temper I said, "Can't we sit down and exchange a few routine social pleasantries before I tell you why I've come?"

"If you want money—"

"I don't. I have plenty."

"My God, that's a comment on our sick society! A young man only has to pick up a guitar, learn a few chords and sing a cheap vulgar song and immediately he has more money than he knows what to do with! How you can prostitute your musical talent by earning a living in a business like that—"

"I've left the music business." I put my hand on the nearest chair. "May I sit down?"

"Left the music business? Why? What for? Are you in trouble? What's happened?" My father was immediately in such a panic that it was impossible not to feel sorry for him.

I tried to put him out of his misery. "I'm not in trouble, Father," I said, but he wasn't listening.

"Is it drink, is it drugs, is it women, is it—"

"I've given up drink, drugs and sex."

"Given up? *Given up?* But my God, why? What do you mean? What's going on?"

"Father, either we sit down and have a rational conversation or I leave. Which is it going to be?"

We sat down facing each other across the table and my father lit a cigarette with unsteady hands.

"I'm sorry, Hal. I just worry about you so much. I worry and worry and worry—"

"Then now's the time to stop. I've made up my mind to live very differently. No, I won't have a cigarette. I've given that up too."

"But Hal, for God's sake, what's happened?"

"My drummer killed himself with an accidental overdose of heroin and his girl committed suicide. My friends died," I said, "but I lived. It made me stop and ask myself what I was doing with my life."

"You mean . . . are you trying to say you nearly killed yourself too?"

"I've never touched heroin, but that's beside the point. The point is that I'd locked myself up in a self-destructive situation—and not for the first time either. I've been locking myself up in self-destructive situations for fourteen years now."

"I don't understand. Are you saying—"

"I'm saying I'm sick of bucketing down the road to nowhere in a psychedelic minibus, sick of the groupies and the grass and the endless string of cheap hotels. A week before my friends died I wound up in a VD clinic in Brighton getting penicillin shots for clap. People laugh about VD now, think nothing of it, but I didn't laugh. I started wondering what I was doing. Then came the heroin disaster and I saw the light—and it was no ordinary light either, it was a red warning light, in fact it was a bloody beacon. And at once it seemed crystal-clear to me that I had a choice: I could stop—or I could go on. So I've stopped. I've turned aside towards another life. I've..." I hesitated before using the one cliché that I knew would reach him, and at once he knew what I was going to say. His eyes filled with tears. Like most neurotics my father cried easily and used tears in cheap bids for sympathy. "... I've drawn the line," I said abruptly, and stood up so that I could turn my back on him. I had no patience with his emotional histrionics.

"But Hal, this other life—the new life—"

"It's no good asking me about that, because I can't tell you anything. I don't know what I'm going to do ultimately. All I know at the moment is that I've got to be at Oxmoon for a while to sort myself out, and I want your permission to camp out in the kitchens of the main house—no, don't worry, I'm not going to found a commune. I want to be alone. I want to think. I want to work out what's gone wrong."

"Perhaps a psychiatrist—"

"Good God, no! I don't share your touching faith in psychiatrists, I'm afraid, Father. In my opinion competent self-analysis is purely an attitude of mind." I knew we were irritating each other. Obviously the interview had to be brought to a speedy conclusion. "May I have your permission to camp out in the main house?"

"Yes, of course, but—"

"Thank you. I'll see you later."

"Wait!" shouted my father.

I waited.

"You can't just come back here after two years and walk out after two minutes, it's not fair, it's bloody selfish, it's downright cruel...."

Being an atheist I was unable to pray for patience. I shored up my strength with a monumental effort of my will and sat down opposite him again. "Try and understand that I don't want to quarrel with you, Father, and that everything I do, no matter how selfish and cruel it may seem to you, is done with that simple aim in mind. I've had enough of our quarrels. That's another example of self-destructive behavior which has to be terminated."

"Are you suggesting—"

"Yes, I am. And don't tell me that you, a fanatical devotee of psychiatry, haven't an inkling of what's going on here. Why did I get myself expelled from Harrow? Why did I flunk my O-levels the first time around? And when I finally made up for all that at the crammers and won a place at university, why did I drop out after a year and go bumming around Europe until I damned nearly ended up in a Turkish jail for smuggling hash?"

"I don't understand," said my father, but he did. His eyes were panic-stricken.

"Okay, I admit I turned over a new leaf after that and did my best to help you with Oxmoon, but why did I walk out two years ago and wind up in the music business which is probably the most destructive business, short of motor racing and boxing, that I could have chosen? Do you really think I did all this for my own pleasure? Okay, yes, I did—I did it for my own pleasure, the pleasure of giving you hell. And why did I want to give you hell? Because—"

"I don't want to hear any more," said my father. He groped his way to his feet and stumbled across the room.

"I blamed you for Kester's suicide," I said. "I haven't been able to think rationally about Kester before, but now that I'm determined to face his memory, I can see very clearly that what I've got to do is bury his corpse—he's lying around here like an unexorcised ghost; it's exactly as if he's still alive—"

"Pam!" shouted my father. "*Pam!*"

"—and so I'm going to bury that corpse, Father. I'm going to prove he didn't commit suicide because once that's proved I don't have to blame you any more for what happened—"

My father blundered out of the room. I followed him, but not quickly enough. The bathroom door slammed in my face and the key turned in the lock just as my stepmother arrived to reduce our chaos to order.

I began to hammer on the panels. "Father, for Christ's sake, I'm on your side! I want to absolve you from all responsibility for Kester's death!"

My father pulled the plug of the lavatory to drown the sound of my voice.

"*Father!*" I yelled, but it was useless. I stopped battering the panels, gave the door a kick and turned aside.

"Come and have some coffee, Hal," said Pam briskly. "Or would you prefer tea?"

"Fuck off."

We retreated to the kitchen. On the counter a jug of coffee had just finished percolating. A delicious aroma filled the room.

"I'll have it black," I said before I could stop myself, and slumped down at the table.

Pam produced cups and saucers without comment and poured out the coffee. After that we sat without speaking for a while. Psychiatrists are skilled in the art of silence. Pam spent twenty seconds contemplating one of her fingernails. Then she gazed meditatively out of the window. She gave the impression that conversation couldn't have mattered less and that she hadn't the slightest curiosity to find out more about the disastrous scene she had interrupted.

"Okay," I said at last, unable to stand her professional silence any longer. "You tell me. Where did I go wrong? A conversation that is terminated by one of the participants locking himself in the lavatory can hardly be rated as a triumph of communication!"

"Why do you think your father locked himself in the lavatory?"

"Well, of course I upset him! I didn't mean to—quite the reverse—but obviously he just can't talk about Kester."

832

"The most interesting thing about that remark," said Pam, "is that it isn't true. Your father's quite capable of talking about Kester—but not to you. And why do you think that is?"

"Well, because...look, what the hell are you getting at?"

"He sees that the subject upsets you, Hal. It's not your father who gets distressed when he talks of Kester. It's you."

Silence fell again. I drank some coffee. When I had myself sufficiently in control I said, "Things have changed. I'm now going to talk about him rationally and unemotionally in an attempt to prove he didn't commit suicide."

"That sounds like an interesting project. How long have you been skeptical of the suicide theory?"

"The doubts began recently, after my friends died and I tried to work out what was going on in my life. I got as far as realizing I was trying to pay Father back, and then it occurred to me that I might be blaming him for a suicide which might never have happened. After all, I was just a child when Kester died and I was so shocked that I accepted the suicide theory without questioning it—and then later it was too painful to think of it at all. But if I can now drum up the nerve to play Sherlock Holmes—"

"Hm."

"What's that supposed to mean?"

"Nothing in particular. It could be a good idea of yours, it could be a bad one. We'll have to see."

"I thought psychiatrists were all in favor of people confronting the truth and straightening out their hang-ups?"

"That depends on the truth. And it depends on the hang-ups. Very few people are actually strong enough to look unpleasant truths straight in the face."

"What makes you think this particular truth's bound to be unpleasant?"

"What makes you think it won't be? Someone you loved very much died, and he didn't die a natural death. That's a situation impregnated with a grief which apparently you've always found hard to handle, and discovering the truth isn't a guarantee you'll find the problem any easier."

"I disagree. If I can prove the death was an accident—"

"But suppose you wind up proving it was a suicide?"

"I'm certain now that Kester didn't kill himself. A short while ago I was in the main house and remembering him talking of Beauty, Truth, Art and Peace. He would have seen suicide as a negation, an ugliness."

"Yet your father, who knew Kester very much better than you did, finds the suicide theory utterly convincing."

"Knowing Kester well is obviously no guarantee of infallibility here. After all, look at Declan Kinsella. He thought Kester was murdered."

"True."

"Oh, of course that was all balls; the inquest proved conclusively that Father wasn't a murderer and Declan's opinion was laughed out of court later in the Bryn-Davies lawsuit—I know quite well that no murder was involved. But if I could prove Kester's death was an accident—"

833

"Well, have a go," said Pam. "Why not? If you feel so strongly it would be wrong to oppose you. . . . Heavens, look at the time! I must put the potatoes on. I presume you're staying at least one night with us?"

"If Father can stand it. Otherwise I'll go to the pub." I was curt because I sensed I was being handled with kid gloves and I disliked being treated like a psychiatric patient.

"Harry can certainly stand it and he'd be mortified if you went to the pub. Now, give me the dirty washing in that duffel bag and I'll run it through the machine while I peel the potatoes."

I turned over the dirty washing in sullen silence and thought how I detested bossy, managing, overefficient women.

"Why don't you choose one of the bedrooms upstairs?" she was saying. "All the beds are made up and the water's hot if you want a bath."

"Maybe I'll stay at the pub after all."

"Seriously?" said Pam, turning to look me straight in the eyes. "You surprise me. I thought you'd decided to stop running away from your problems."

Wishing all psychiatrists could be instantly exterminated I tramped upstairs, invaded the nearest bedroom and loudly slammed the door.

IV

Sitting down on the bed I wondered what Pam really thought of my determination to play the detective. I suspected she was horrified even though she saw no alternative but to acquiesce; Pam would always want to protect my father, and my father's mental health was too delicate for him to welcome prolonged inquiries into a past that was painful to him.

After my father married her Pam had gone to great trouble to explain his problems to his children with the result that instead of reacting to him like delinquents we had merely said instead, "Poor old Father, poor old sod" and accepted that he was a cross which we had no alternative but to bear with patience. According to Pam, my father blamed himself for Kester's suicide, and this fact, combined with a rough war and years of nervous strain during the subsequent peace, had represented the straw which had broken the camel's back. Realizing Kester was behaving oddly on the night of his death, my father had followed him out to the Worm's Head, but had then turned back in order to avoid being cut off by the tide. If he had gone on he would have caught up with Kester and saved him. Kester would hardly have committed suicide in his presence.

Pam had then explained that although my father and Kester had long been enemies they were at the same time deeply connected emotionally, as deeply connected as twin brothers, and as soon as Kester was dead my father had been so overwhelmed that he had been unable to adjust to his loss. I would have laughed at this but it had chimed with Bronwen's view of my father's breakdown, and my trust in Bronwen had been absolute. She too had insisted to me that my father had been deeply bereaved.

Kester had never talked to me in detail about my father, but he had been loyal to him. Once I had made a disparaging remark but he had said at once, "I'm your father's stand-in whenever you come to Oxmoon, Hal, so if you abuse him you abuse me." And naturally I had never abused my father in his presence again.

I could remember being alone with the two of them at Oxmoon after my mother died. They had been charming to each other, friendliness personified, but with a child's special sensitivity I had felt the loathing crackle between them, and I had escaped as soon as possible to play the piano in the ballroom. Yet Kester had said to me later as if he sensed that I'd been disturbed, "You mustn't worry— Harry and I understand each other. That's why we can share you with never a cross word," and that uneasy peace had lasted until Kester gave up Oxmoon. But once my father had become the master we had all rocketed to hell in double-quick time.

Moving to the window I looked out across the stable yard to the kitchen wing of the house.

"I put the magic back into Oxmoon," said Kester's voice in my memory, and suddenly I was there again, back in the lost Oxmoon of my childhood, and Gwyneth Llewellyn and I were racing down the path in the kitchen garden to raid the strawberry beds.

I wondered what had happened to Gwyneth Llewellyn.

I went to the bathroom. It was still a luxury to be able to urinate without taking ten minutes and two shots of scotch to face the pain, and as I relieved myself I wondered how long it would be before I felt obliged to acquire another girlfriend. However one of the unexpected results of that one-night stand when a passing groupie had given me so very much more than I'd bargained for was that it had come as a relief to abstain from sex. I had even had the heretical thought that I'd been promiscuous merely to follow the crowd. Mindless hedonism had been the done thing and I hadn't had the courage to do the right thing and be different. Kester would have been ashamed of me. "Hold fast! Stand firm!" he would have said if he could have seen me floundering around in the quicksands of immorality like a demented satyr. The truth was that cheap thrills were just that: cheap. I supposed I could make the effort to develop more expensive tastes but the emotional extravagance of romance held no appeal for me. I had only ever been in love once but that had all ended at sixteen when Gwyneth had turned me down.

"I don't want any of your boys messing around with my daughters!" Jasper Llewellyn had shouted at my father. Jasper had never liked my father but he had admired Kester, saying that Kester had been a true Welshman, devoted to the arts, a talented remarkable man. My father, who unlike Kester spoke no Welsh, had been too successful a farmer, too pushy and ambitious, to give Jasper, a successful farmer himself, much peace of mind. Their lands had bordered each other, and there had always been quarrels over rights-of-way, straying sheep and first-class laborers poached by the lure of higher wages.

After Jasper complained about me my father had summoned all his sons and delivered one of his fevered lectures about how no one should indulge in sex before the age of eighteen. My father was fanatical on the subject of morality. "You have to know where to draw the line!" he would thunder, and we would all look at each other in despair. Kester too had talked of drawing lines, but unlike my father Kester hadn't been guilty of hypocrisy. Kester had lived a good decent life, loyal to the memory of the wife he had adored. My father had been a notorious womanizer. I thought he was peculiarly ill suited to give us such straitlaced lectures on morality but since the breakdown of his health my father had read nothing but books on philosophy and religion and he had become more rigid in his outlook than any clergyman. Naturally he had made rakes of us all at an early age and we had spent our adolescence trying to keep him in ignorance of our adventures.

In fact lies and disillusionment, rage and estrangement had been the standard fare of our family life until Pam had arrived to sort us out. Ruthlessly she had pulled us one by one from the mire of misery my father had created at Oxmoon, and once extracted we had been dusted down, sanitized and reduced to order. Pam had made order attractive. We had soon seen that if we played our cards right we could live comfortably in pleasant surroundings; all we had had to do was avoid upsetting our father, and so long as we observed this basic rule Pam had made sure we were comfortable. Good behavior had suddenly seemed worth the effort. Family life had improved, and Pam had been hailed on all sides as the miracle worker who had civilized a hopeless neurotic and four hooligans.

She had come to know my father well when she attended him during his first nervous breakdown after Kester's death, but they had met some time before that while her first husband was still alive. However he had conveniently died a month before Kester in the spring of '52, and as soon as my father met Pam again he had proposed to her. Pam had refused to marry him until he had been well for six months, a move that gave my father a powerful incentive to recover, and he had somehow stayed well for the required amount of time. During his second nervous breakdown which had followed the Bryn-Davies lawsuit he had been obliged to see other psychiatrists, but they had never done him any good and eventually in defiance of medical etiquette his wife had taken over his case again. At once he had become well enough to leave hospital, but this time he had never made a full recovery and had only been able to lead a quiet existence at home. Pam had again coaxed him to see other psychiatrists and again they had done no good. After making the decision to abandon the main house, sell off the remaining farmland and retire to a corner of the stable block on what remained of his fixed income, he had lived like a recluse, seeing no one except the immediate family.

The real mystery, as I had said once to my brothers, was not why he had married Pam; obviously he had to live with a psychiatrist in order to stay on the rails. The real mystery was why she had married him. It had been very inconvenient for her. She had had to give up her full-time work and turn to part-time consultations. She had had to cope with the disintegration of Oxmoon, my father's increasing incapacity and four respectful but privately hostile stepsons. Various explanations for her decision had been put forward, ranging from wealth and social position to my father's notorious appeal to the opposite sex, but Pam was no ordinary woman and I doubted that her motives for marriage had been ordinary either. I had come to the conclusion that she had fallen in love with my father because she found him of absorbing psychiatric interest. Certainly she was devoted to him. He was devoted to her. My brothers and I had spent much time saying how bizarre their devotion was, but we had nevertheless dimly realized that she was the best thing to have happened to my father for a long time. Without her he'd probably have killed himself. In his worst depressions he was always suicidal.

He had been very different once. He had been strong, striking, physically fit. But that had been before he took over Oxmoon.

Oxmoon had killed him, that was the truth of it. Oxmoon the monster, not Kester's Magic Oxmoon anymore but Malevolent Oxmoon, draining my father of money and strength, beating him to his knees. Oxmoon was like a dog who had loyally served a much-loved master and had turned vicious after his master's death. Oxmoon belonged to Kester and my father had never mastered it. And Oxmoon, as I'd realized in the house that afternoon, was Kester's still.

I opened the window and as I did so I saw my reflection in the swinging glass. The reflection was transposed upon the house beyond, and in that moment I realized that Oxmoon was just the mirror in which I saw myself reflected. *I* was the dog who had turned vicious when deprived of his much-loved master. It was *I* who had belonged to Kester and whom my father had never mastered. And as I looked back across the past to the magician of my childhood I knew I was Kester's still.

I leaned out over the sill. Downstairs my father was playing Verdi's *Requiem*. At the other end of the yard a black cat was walking elegantly across the cobbles with a mouse in his mouth. Below me in the window boxes the geraniums were nodding gently in the summer breeze.

To Kester I said: "I'm going to bring you back."

And to myself I said: I'm going to win.

V

I survived dinner by eating so steadily that my mouth was always too full to argue. The food was first-class. Pam had taken to cooking late in life but had mastered it with typical skill. I ate my way through two large helpings of lamb stew, new potatoes and fresh peas while my father pushed a chunk of meat around his plate and talked incessantly of his worries. He apparently had no intention of referring to our previous conversation.

He started by grumbling about his health. This was standard behavior, although curiously he never spoke of his eczema, the one complaint that merited sympathy; perhaps that was because his skin troubles genuinely frightened him. Instead he grumbled about various pains in his legs and the fatigue arising from insomnia. I acknowledged these complaints by grunting at intervals. Pam looked thoughtful but could have been meditating on anything from tomorrow's shopping list to my father's new tranquilizers.

After he could find no more to say about his health my father complained about the state of the world, the state of the nation and the Youth of Today and judged them all diabolical. However this led to a grudging tribute to my brothers Charles and Jack who wore white shirts, kept their hair short and held steady jobs in London. Charles worked in the Current Affairs Department of the BBC, and Jack was an agent in some import-export firm based at Heathrow Airport. Humphrey, the only brother I had kept in touch with during my two years on the road as a singer, was racketing around as a medical student but since he was my father's favorite he was referred to as "ambitious" and allowed to be mildly eccentric. Nevertheless even Humphrey had to be careful, cutting his hair before his visits to Gower and leaving his striped shirts behind in London, but no doubt he considered these sacrifices a small price to pay for maintaining his position as the favorite.

I didn't like my brothers but adverse circumstances had bound us together. When I was very young I had been annoyed with my mother for refusing to concede that I was the best of the bunch. "But I love you all equally, darling!" she had protested. Later that had struck me as unnatural. Parents always have favorites. I was the cleverest and the best. Why wasn't I the favorite? I'd become cross with her for being too stupid to see how first-rate I was. My father had been too busy treating me as a nuisance for breaking his piano so I'd known I'd never get preferential treatment from him and besides it had been plain he was soft about Humphrey. Humphrey had looked just like him. I hadn't looked like anyone. I'd felt a changeling, misunderstood and unappreciated. And then Kester had taken me by the hand, my magician had waved his magic wand, and suddenly I'd been special, I'd been privileged, I'd come into my own at last.

"First is best, isn't it, Kester?" I had said to him once, forgetting he had been the youngest of four sons, and Kester had said, smiling at me, "Sometimes—but not always!"

"...Hal?"

I jumped. "Sorry, Pam, I wasn't listening."

"More apple pie?"

"Yes, please."

"I must say," said my father, concluding his grudging tribute to my brothers as he lit a cigarette, "it's a great relief to me that three out of my four sons are doing well. It makes up for the way you've steadily wasted your opportunities. However if you want to turn over a new leaf we'll say no more about that."

I sank my teeth into my apple pie to ensure that I kept quiet.

"It'll be uncomfortable for you to camp out in the kitchens," said my father, "but of course I know it's no good asking you to stay here. I expect you're having a hard time hiding your contempt that I'm obliged to live in a corner of the stables like this."

"Some corner," said Pam. "Coffee, Hal?"

Not trusting myself to speak I nodded.

"Anyway," said my father, "I don't care if you want to camp out like a hippy; suit yourself, it's none of my business. And I don't care either if you want to reexamine the past. Pam says everyone needs to pause and take stock of their lives every now and then. That's healthy, she says. Well, all right, if you want to talk about, well, about Kester, go ahead, why not, ask whatever questions you like and I'll tell you anything you want to know. Pam says that's fine, we should have talked it all out long since, she says. Well, of course I would have if you'd asked but you didn't ask, did you? You never said anything about Kester before, never mentioned his name, so how was I to know what you were thinking?"

"Don't forget your Vivaldi concert, darling," said Pam. "Would you like coffee in your room? You know how you hate to miss the opening bars."

My father ignored her. "I don't want you to think I'm hostile," he said to me. "As a matter of fact I'm very touched that you want to disprove the suicide theory and exonerate me from responsibility. When you said that earlier I...well, I couldn't take it, could I, but that was only because it all seemed so sad and I felt I couldn't bear it, I couldn't bear to think of you being tortured as well as me—"

"That's the point, isn't it? It's time the torture stopped. Thank you, Father, it's very good of you to say you'll cooperate with me, we'll talk later. Don't feel you have to miss your concert."

"What upsets me," said my father, "is that I can't tell you what you want to hear. Kester was very unstable. Everything had gone wrong for him. I'm quite sure he came back to Gower with the intention of dying in the place he loved best. That would have been acting in character."

"I can think of nothing more out of character than Kester committing suicide."

"But you never really knew him, did you?"

Pam decided this was the right psychological moment to intervene. "This is the real question you have to answer, Hal," she said. "What was Kester really like?"

"You must realize," said my father, "that he had great problems. I mean, I'd never have taken over Oxmoon unless I'd honestly felt he couldn't cope—although now when I look back I can see this must have aggravated his sense of failure and driven him further along the road to suicide. I shouldn't have allowed him to give Oxmoon to me—Christ, if only you knew how guilty I feel about that now—"

"Yes." I drank my coffee. "It's okay, I understand."

"I mean, you do believe, don't you, that Kester gave me Oxmoon of his own free will? I know Declan said—"

"I'm not interested in Irish fairy tales." I went on sipping my coffee.

There was a silence. Then my father sighed, rubbed the raw patch of skin above the line of his beard and leaned back in his chair for a moment before he remembered his concert. "Do you want to come and listen?" he asked me as he rose to his feet.

"I'll join you later."

My father withdrew, coffee mug in hand, and presently we heard the faint strains of chamber music in his room. Pam began to load the dishwasher. I was busy finishing my coffee and repressing the craving for a cigarette.

"Can I give you some advice?" said Pam presently. "Don't let your discussions with your father degenerate into arguments. Try listening and making neutral comments. You'll learn more."

"Thanks for the tip."

"I'm quite serious."

"So am I. I need all the tips I can get."

Pam gave me one of her thin smiles of approval and closed the dishwasher. Then she said abruptly: "What do you really think about Declan Kinsella's evidence during the Bryn-Davies lawsuit?"

"The accusation of murder?"

"No, the accusation of extortion."

"Ridiculous."

"That's interesting," said Pam, sitting down opposite me again. "I can understand why you found the accusation of murder preposterous—in view of the findings of the inquest everyone did. But the extortion's rather a different kettle of fish, isn't it? I think many people secretly believe your father extorted Oxmoon from Kester, and bearing in mind your attitude to both those men I wouldn't be in the least surprised if you told me you believed that too."

I saw her point. "I still say extortion's impossible. If you argue that Father obtained Oxmoon by duress what you're really saying is that he blackmailed Kester, and once you say he blackmailed Kester you imply that Kester had done something that would render him liable to blackmail. And that's out of the question."

"Ah, I see."

"I suppose that ranks as a neutral comment."

She smiled. "Perhaps!"

"I know just what you're thinking," I said. "You think I'm blinded by hero worship where Kester's concerned."

"You don't see him as a hero?"

"No, of course not. Heroes only exist in myths."

"Then how would you describe him?"

This was easy. "He was a magician," I said. "He waved his magic wand and fantasy became reality. Oxmoon was a fairy-tale palace. Home was crude and noisy and boring, all those damned brothers getting under my feet and my father shouting at me, but whenever I went up to Oxmoon Kester led me through the looking glass into another world. He encouraged me to play the piano in the ballroom, he talked to me about books and art and films and the theater. I'd go up to Oxmoon and suddenly life wasn't boring anymore, life was glittering, and there at the center of it all was my magician, talking of all the values that made life worth living. Of course he was an idealist, but what made him so different from the usual crackpot was that he was strong and brave and he had the guts to stand up for what he believed in, he didn't compromise his principles just to follow the crowd. There was a line from Byron he used to quote: 'Yet Freedom! yet thy banner, torn, but flying, streams like a thunderstorm *against* the wind.' I often remember that line when I think of Kester because he wasn't afraid to go against the wind. He knew freedom. He kept faith with himself. He was a hero."

I stopped. Pam said nothing. Presently I managed to say: "Okay, very clever, I congratulate you, you caught me out. I said I didn't see him as a hero and here I am, describing him as just that. But all I can say is that Kester was one of those rare men who deserve such a description because now I'm grown up I know it's not easy to maintain one's idealism, as he did, in a corrupt cynical world. You have to be very strong to go against the wind. I've found that out for myself."

Pam waited a moment before saying: "Don't think I can't accept what you say. Obviously Kester was able to show you children who visited him regularly at Oxmoon a very special side of himself, but what kind of a magician was he, Hal? What kind of spell was he really weaving, and for what reasons?"

"Well, you're the psychiatrist who knows all the answers. You tell me."

"The day I start believing I know all the answers is the day I need to be certified, but this situation does strongly suggest to me that Kester used you children as an emotional outlet and that the more his fortunes waned the more necessary it became to him that he should have a bunch of little supporters who all loyally regarded him as a hero. In other words I suspect he was on rather a dubious ego trip and his motives were far more clouded than you've ever been able to acknowledge."

"Yes, but—"

"You're being much too simple about this, Hal, much too ready to see everything in black-and-white. This is a complex case which embraces all the colors of the emotional spectrum. Be careful about rushing to judgment."

In the pause that followed I was aware of Vivaldi's music far away, very pure, very precise, a soothingly clear-cut translation of black notes on white paper.

"You don't want me to get involved in all this, do you?" I said at last.

"No, but I accept that I can't stop you."

"Why don't you want me to get involved?"

"Because I don't think this quest will help you. Obviously you've reached the point where you have to come to terms with Kester's death before you can go on with your life, but what worries me is that this solution which you've invented for yourself will create more problems than it solves."

"Go on."

"You seem to think," said Pam, "that if only you can uncover the truth—THE TRUTH, in capital letters—everything will automatically be resolved but in fact this is most unlikely to happen. For a start it's almost certain that THE TRUTH, whatever that is, can never now be established beyond all reasonable doubt. In other words, you'll get nowhere, Hal, and that won't solve your problem—quite the reverse. It'll simply make you as obsessive about Kester as your father is. The real truth—as opposed to THE TRUTH in capital letters—is that there's only one way to come to terms with Kester's death, and that's to acknowledge that his absence is something you can't change. How he died doesn't matter. All that matters is that he loved you but he's gone."

"But I have to prove he didn't choose to go."

"You mean you have to prove he loved you and didn't abandon you voluntarily. You have to prove that his heroism wasn't a fraud."

"If you like. It's all one." I got up and began to move restlessly around the room. Finally I swung to face her. "What do *you* believe?" I demanded. "Don't try and tell me you haven't worked out what happened!"

"The suicide theory can certainly be made to look convincing."

"But suppose I were to tell you that after he died both Gwyneth Llewellyn and I were convinced he would never have left us like that?"

"I'm afraid I'd reply that this is the classic reaction of a suicide's bereaved relatives. The terrible truth is that a suicide can and does leave those he loves, and in fact often feels he's doing them a favor."

"Give me one good reason why Kester would have thought he was doing us a favor by killing himself!"

"I'd prefer not to at this stage. I don't think you could handle it."

"I think that's the most infuriating thing you've ever said to me. If you're trying to protect me from—"

"I'm trying to save my breath. If I told you my theory you'd ridicule it."

"How do you know?"

"Because it's not consistent with your picture of Kester." She too rose to her feet and moved closer to me. "Hal, let me give you one last tip. Be very careful. If you've been spellbound by a magician you could be more vulnerable than you realize. You're like someone on a trip. You could have a hard time coming down."

It always startled me when Pam used hip phrases but she picked them up during her part-time work at Assumptionsville, the trendy new clinic for drug addicts on the outskirts of Swansea.

"If I'm on a trip," I said, "it's got nothing to do with Kester's spells. I'm not mainlining on magic. I'm mainlining on truth."

"Then fasten your seat belt," said Pam, wryly misquoting the immortal line from *All About Eve*, "because I think you're in for a bumpy ride."

2

I

THE NEXT MORNING I hitched a ride to Swansea, hired a car and found a shop that sold camping supplies. I had told my father the truth when I'd said I wasn't short of money. I'd long since blown my legacy from my grandfather, but I had three thousand pounds in a bank in London, not a large sum compared with the fortune the Beatles must have been amassing, but a useful one. It was certainly enough to enable me to live like a hermit at Oxmoon while I sorted myself out.

I chose my supplies, collected some miscellaneous items from Woolworth's and stopped at a suburban supermarket. When I arrived home the gates were unlocked. I guessed this meant my father had a visitor, possibly the local doctor, so I avoided the mews house and went directly to the old kitchens. I had collected the key of the back door from Pam after breakfast.

I had decided to camp out in the scullery not for its aesthetic beauty but because it offered certain practical advantages. There was water available. There was an outside lavatory near the back door. There were cupboards with shelves where I could stash my supplies. There was even an old wooden table with two broken chairs which Pam had thought too decrepit to donate to charity. After unloading my gear I fixed the chairs with glue and a screwdriver, set a couple of mousetraps and assembled the Primus stove so that I could brew myself some coffee. Then I discovered the water had been turned off. This was no big surprise but I was annoyed when I failed to find the wheel that would turn on the supply, and it was at that point that I glanced out of the window and saw two men standing by the front door of the mews house at the other end of the yard. One was my father. The other was obviously the owner of the white Ford parked nearby, but it wasn't the local doctor. It was my father's stepbrother Dafydd Morgan.

I crossed the yard to join them and as I drew nearer they fell silent. They made an odd couple, my father heavily bearded like some middle-aged dropout, Dafydd as morose as a hit man in a modern movie. My father had once said he found Dafydd restful but that was the last word I should ever have used to describe Dafydd Morgan. I found him sinister. It occurred to me to wonder for the first time what Pam thought of their unlikely but profound friendship. It crossed all the normal barriers of class which hamstrung men of their age. They appeared to have nothing in common. But my father, recluse though he was, couldn't bear to be parted for long from Dafydd while Dafydd, turning up regularly for a cigarette and a cup of tea, apparently couldn't bear to be parted for long from him.

"Hi," I called when I was within earshot.

Dafydd grunted an acknowledgment. His sharp little eyes looked me up and down. All he said was "Your father was telling me you were back." He had an odd accent which wasn't entirely Welsh. Having spent some years at the village school in Penhale he had more than a hint of the old Gower inflections which were becoming obsolete. In the old days the men of the Gower Englishry had felt closer to Devon than to Wales.

"How's business?"

"Good."

He owned a building firm which specialized in converting cottages into holiday homes, and he had supervised the conversion of the mews. Remembering his legendary talent as a handyman I found myself saying to him automatically: "I wonder if you could give me a hand for a moment? I can't see how to turn on the bloody water."

Despite his morose air he set off with me willingly enough, but my father remained by the house. It was probably one of his days when he was afraid to cross the courtyard. When I reached the scullery I looked back at him but he hadn't moved and his extreme stillness hinted at his tension.

"Could the wheel be in the cellar?" I said to Dafydd.

"No, it's in the old wet laundry." He led me straight there and tried to turn the wheel himself but his wrists weren't strong enough. His years as a prisoner of war had impaired his strength and the wheel was stiff with disuse.

"I'll do it." I used some muscle and presently we had water running in the main sink.

"Want me to check the toilet for you?"

"Thanks."

We withdrew to the lavatory. He stood on the seat to examine the tank but it was filling. Giving a grunt of satisfaction he stepped down. "We'll flush it in a minute to make sure the cistern's okay," he said, so we stood there waiting for the tank to fill.

"I hear you're giving your father a hard time as usual," he said suddenly.

"Not at all. I'm trying to make things easier for us both."

"Bloody funny way of doing it." He stared bleakly at the stained lavatory bowl.

"I'm glad you find it amusing."

He didn't like that but although he gave me a surly look he kept quiet.

"I suppose you share Father's view that Kester committed suicide."

"I don't give a shit how he died. He's dead, thank God, and that's all that matters." The water stopped running. He reached up, grasped the chain and pulled it. Water cascaded through the bowl.

"Why did you hate Kester?"

"He ruined Harry, didn't he? It was as if he murdered him. You remember the way your father was and look at the way he is now." He stood on the seat again, peered into the tank and was satisfied. Stepping down he dusted his hands on his trousers and moved outside. "Let it be, Hal; let it rest. Christ, hasn't that sod caused enough trouble?"

"He's not a sod to me."

"Well, he fucking ought to be." He looked me up and down again. "He stole you," he said suddenly. "He stole you and turned you against your father. He knew you were the apple of Harry's eye and he stole you to give Harry hell."

"Bullshit. I was never the apple of Father's eye. Besides Kester made a point of not turning me against him."

"Well, if he didn't turn you against Harry, why have you been nothing but trouble to Harry ever since Kester died? You answer me that!"

"I was mixed up."

"Damn right you were—and who the hell do you think did the mixing?" shouted Dafydd, and stumped away across the yard without looking back.

II

Back in the scullery I brewed myself some coffee, ate an apple in lieu of lunch and sat down at the table in front of the notebook I had bought at Woolworth's. Then I drank two mugs of coffee and thought for a long time.

How was I to approach my investigation? Eventually I decided that my first task was to set down on paper the story as I knew it in order to clarify my mind and separate hard facts from mere speculation. Then with my thoughts in meticulous order I would be better able to work out my future moves.

Pulling my notebook towards me I uncapped my pen and began to write on the waiting page.

III

INVESTIGATION INTO KESTER'S DEATH: SUMMARY OF THE FACTS:

Kester died on May 8th, 1952. He had returned to Gower from Ireland three days previously (May 5th) and had gone straight to my father's cottage at Rhossili.

My father and Kester didn't meet. Richard, who was staying with the Bryn-Davieses at the time, met Kester off the ferry and drove him to Rhossili. I was away at school. During the three days before he died Kester saw the following people in addition to Richard: (1) Evan (2) Bronwen and (3) Gwyneth. Richard, Evan and Bronwen were all interviewed afterwards by the police although only Richard and Evan were called at the inquest. Gwyneth never told anyone but me that she'd seen Kester and at her request I kept quiet about it too. Apparently her parents had begun to be worried about the rumors of his instability and they'd forbidden Gwyneth to see him. She disobeyed. Hence her desire to keep the visit a secret. She didn't want to get into trouble.

NOTE: I must reread the detailed account of the inquest. I mustn't rely on my memory because it's over ten years since I looked up the report.

On the afternoon of May 8th my father received a note from Kester asking him to drop in for a drink at some time. My father decided to go over straightaway but Kester was out. It was a fine evening. My father then took a stroll to see if he could intercept Kester. He eventually saw him on the Shipway and realized to his astonishment that Kester was on his way out to the Worm. This was bizarre behavior because the tides were wrong; there was time to get across the Shipway and back but hardly any time to enjoy the Worm on arrival. My father was baffled and became alarmed enough to follow him.

NOTE: So far my father's testimony can be verified by independent witnesses. Two tourists returning from the Worm testified that Kester and my father were a quarter of an hour apart on the Shipway.

When my father reached the Inner Head he waited, thinking Kester was bound to come back into view at any moment to begin the return journey, but Kester didn't show up and after a minute my father, unable to stand the suspense, went on down the path and around the bend onto the southern flank of the Inner Head. He then realized that Kester had planned to be cut off by the tide because although Kester was visible he was far away by the Middle Head. My father was then faced with a dilemma. If he went on he'd be marooned on the Worm overnight. If he went back he'd be leaving Kester in what might well have been a thoroughly disturbed state of mind. My father, not unnaturally, was reluctant to be marooned. Telling himself that Kester was being eccentric but not necessarily demented, my father then made the decision to go back.

NOTE: This is my father's testimony as I remember it in the report. My father and I have never discussed this privately. The testimony is unsupported by witnesses but supported by his cast-iron alibi which proved conclusively that he did turn back and recross the Shipway.

My father reached the headland shortly after eight that night and the Shipway had begun to go under. Kester was thus left marooned on the Worm. My father returned to the cottage, and when he arrived he found Dafydd replacing a defective washer on one of the kitchen taps; they talked together for a while.

NOTE: This alibi sounds as if it could have been cooked, but the fact that no one queried it at the time seems to suggest that it's far too solid to be easily dismissed.

After Dafydd had gone my father decided to wait at the cottage till Kester was able to recross the Shipway at dawn. My father had started to worry again and wonder if he'd been right to abandon him.

Kester didn't return. Later a search party was organized but there was no one at the Worm. Kester's body was washed up a week later.

The coroner's jury brought in a verdict of accidental death, but the general consensus of opinion was that Kester had committed suicide while the balance of his mind was disturbed. (It was felt the jury wanted to spare the family the unpleasantness of a suicide verdict.) The possibility of murder was eliminated when the coroner stressed the fact that was clearly brought out in the testimony: that my father couldn't have caught up with Kester and still got back across the Shipway before the tide rose that evening. As far as I know everyone completely accepted this, and even if the Kinsella brothers didn't they kept their mouths shut. It wasn't until the Bryn-Davies lawsuit two years later that Declan stood up in the witness box and called my father a liar, a killer and an extortionist.

COMMENT: Sooner or later I'm going to have to face up to the evidence of that bloody shit Declan Kinsella.

WARNING: I must keep my cool.

VERDICT: Soldier on.

IV

Uncapping a bottle of Coke in an attempt to kill my longing for a cigarette, I reread what I'd written and was satisfied that my words formed the authorized version of the truth. Perhaps this version was indeed the truth. But I knew I shouldn't forget that the real truth about this particular truth was that no one knew for certain what the real truth was. The coroner's jury had declared an accidental death, the public at large had diagnosed a suicide, the Kinsella brothers had talked of a murder, but the proven truth had eluded everyone, slipping through the concrete facts like an illusion manipulated by a magician. But in fact was this situation so very unusual? How far was it ever possible to know the whole truth? Human perception was so limited; in a moment of depression I remembered that there were even some philosophers who believed it was impossible for the human mind to grasp reality at all, a belief which would mean that my quest for the real truth would be doomed to sink in a sea of illusion.

Then I pulled myself together. I was a rational man who believed in the reality of hard facts, and I refused to be depressed by philosophical idiocies. As far as I was concerned, establishing the truth by stripping reality of distortion was purely a matter of willpower and determination; all it needed was the right attitude of mind.

Picking up my pen again I once more turned to face the past.

V

KESTER'S DEATH: POSSIBLE EXPLANATIONS.

There are four possible explanations for Kester's death: (1) natural causes (2) accident (3) suicide and (4) murder.

Let's dispose of natural causes: the autopsy revealed that death was by drowning. There was no evidence of heart attack or stroke.

Now let's take murder, the least likely of the remaining possibilities. If I accept the alibi, then my father could have killed Kester only if Kester had been waiting for him on the Inner Head. This doesn't seem to have occurred to the coroner, who apparently had no trouble accepting my father's evidence that he and Kester had remained a quarter of an hour apart. Or perhaps it did occur to the coroner but he discounted it.

My inclination is to discount it too. After all, why should Kester loll around on the Inner Head and wait for my father to murder him? If I were being followed by a trained killer who hated my guts, I'd keep going in the hope that he'd turn back. Also, why should my father want to murder Kester anyway when all Kester wanted to do was to write in peace at Rhossili? And finally, even if my father did want to murder him why do it after two witnesses had seen him chasing Kester to the Worm? If my father did kill Kester—and I can think of no sane reason why he should—then the real mystery here is not how Kester died but why.

VERDICT ON THE MURDER THEORY: *No motive. And almost certainly no opportunity. Murder highly unlikely if not downright impossible.*

So we're left with accident or suicide. I have to admit that suicide's the most plausible explanation. He'd been mentally disturbed, he'd lost everything that made life meaningful to him, he'd continued to fail as a writer. What I really have to do here, to disprove the suicide theory, is to prove Kester had a powerful motive for staying alive.

VERDICT ON THE SUICIDE THEORY: *It's possible. But it's a possibility that I could still explode.*

Finally, how likely is it that Kester died by accident? The main argument against it is that Kester was no athlete and therefore he would have taken no physical risks. However there is a chance he could have been whipped away by a freak wave. In any other setting this would be almost too unlikely to consider seriously, but on a tidal causeway like the Shipway such a disaster wouldn't be improbable at all. Kester might well have tried to recross the Shipway before it was entirely safe—in which case the danger of a freak wave would have been very real.

VERDICT ON THE ACCIDENT THEORY: *I think this must have been how Kester met his death but I must keep an open mind until I've exploded the suicide theory. This is because there's no way I can prove he died by accident except by proving he couldn't have died in any other way.*

VI

I uncapped another Coke and again read through what I'd written. So far so good. I had stated the puzzle in its orthodox version and listed the rational explanations. But now my task became more difficult because I had to consider the alternative to the orthodox version, the facts that didn't tally with this somewhat fragile reality, and here waiting for me, as I knew very well, was the ghost of Declan Kinsella.

Declan had died a year ago of a coronary. In a television news item he had been described as a notable patriot and statesman. Kester's most powerful champion and the star witness of the Bryn-Davies lawsuit was now permanently beyond my reach.

So was his brother Rory. He'd died of drink back in the Fifties.

Yet I couldn't ignore the Kinsella brothers. I couldn't ignore anyone who had called the authorized version a pack of lies. The Kinsella brothers were a dimension of reality and I couldn't merely dismiss them as a myth, no matter how absurd or unlikely their evidence seemed to be. Declan in particular wove in and out of this saga like a recurring nightmare. The temptation was to diagnose him as a grief-crazed Irishman who was prepared to say anything to avenge his brother's death, but was it really possible or likely or credible that this "notable patriot and statesman" had told a pack of lies in the witness box in pursuance of what the judge had described as "a peculiarly sordid family feud"?

And that brought me to the horror of the Bryn-Davies lawsuit, the catastrophe which had locked my father into a downward financial spiral and driven him for the second time beyond the edge of sanity into a nervous breakdown. Pam had said to me at the time: "I expect you're a bit bothered by Declan's evidence, aren't you? It would be only natural if you were. Would you like to talk it over?" But I had refused to talk it over. It was easier to refuse to think about it; easier, much easier just to tell myself that Declan Kinsella was a shit and his testimony was a lie.

I drank my Coke and remembered Pam saying to me the night before: "Very few people are strong enough to look unpleasant truths straight in the face."

But I was now going to be strong enough. The Bryn-Davies lawsuit was an unpleasant fact but it had to be confronted, and picking up my pen again I began to will myself into a cold analytical state of mind by writing down the facts as I remembered them.

VII

KESTER'S DEATH: THE CONSEQUENCES: THE BRYN-DAVIES LAWSUIT. *The Bryn-Davies lawsuit was engineered by Declan Kinsella in order to give himself a public platform from which he could attack my father. His silence at the inquest is probably explained by the fact that he was unable to prove his suspicions of murder and merely wanted to listen to the evidence so that he could take full advantage of it later. Could he have foreseen the lawsuit as early as that? Yes, because the odds were he knew what was in Kester's last will. Kester had made this will after he had given Oxmoon to my father, and in the circumstances it's more than likely that he discussed his will with Declan when he discussed the loss of Oxmoon.*

The will gave Declan the chance to initiate a lawsuit, and he used Owen Bryn-Davies Senior as a cat's-paw in his plan. The will represented Kester's attempt to strike an equitable balance between his protégés, in view of the fact that I was now sure to inherit Oxmoon from my father. After the loss of Oxmoon Kester's fortune consisted of money invested in various stocks and shares but in addition there was a pied-à-terre in London, a fact of considerable importance because it meant that Kester's will still spoke of real and personal property, even though the bulk of his real property had been ceded to my father. With the exception of a few legacies this personal fortune of Kester's was devised and bequeathed to my contemporary Owen Bryn-Davies Junior. I received a hundred pounds, all the books in the library at Oxmoon and all Kester's unpublished manuscripts.

As soon as probate had been granted, Declan swung into action. He convinced Owen Bryn-Davies Senior that my father had obtained Oxmoon by extortion—

and this meant that Kester's deed of gift was invalid and that Oxmoon now passed to Owen Junior as the heir to Kester's real property. Owen Senior decided to go to law on behalf of his son, but when the case got to court it wasn't the will that was on trial; it was my father.

Declan's story—which was laughed out of court—was that Kester had accidentally killed Uncle Thomas in a brawl and had then panicked, summoned my father and with his help covered up the crime by faking the car smash. Later, according to Declan, my father had turned around and used his knowledge of the crime to blackmail Kester. In this way he had extorted Oxmoon.

That covered the extortion theory. Then Declan elaborated his theory of murder. He said that Kester had eventually become so determined to recover Oxmoon that he had been prepared to go to the police and risk winding up in jail for a spell rather than continue to submit to my father's blackmail. Declan said Kester had returned to Gower to reclaim Oxmoon from my father and my father, facing ruin, had killed him to keep him quiet.

At this point the judge lost patience, mourned the absence of proof and said the case should never have been allowed to come to court. He dismissed the case without awarding costs and told the parties to resume their sordid family feud elsewhere. The press had a field day. My father was generally acknowledged to have been exonerated but a lot of mud had been flung at him and some of the mud inevitably stuck.

The Director of Public Prosecutions considered whether the investigations into the deaths of Kester and Thomas should be reopened, but decided against it on the grounds of insufficient evidence. This meant that my father was technically innocent because no one had proved him guilty, but the gossip was rampant and it was then that my father embarked on his career as a recluse. Footing his legal costs also started him on the downward path to financial ruin. So Declan achieved his object. He wanted to crucify my father and he crucified him. Not only that, but my father's still on the cross and no psychiatrist, not even Pam, can apparently succeed in cutting him down.

So much for the facts of the Bryn-Davies lawsuit. But what do I make of Declan's evidence?

There are three possibilities here: either it was fact; or it was fiction; or it was a mixture of the two. Whichever possibility is correct, the fact remains that Declan, who knew his brother very well, believed that my father was morally responsible for Kester's death. Declan may not in fact have believed Kester had been murdered; he may just have propagated that story out of sheer revenge, but if he didn't believe in murder he must surely have believed my father had driven Kester to suicide. If he thought Kester had died by accident Declan wouldn't have gone to such lengths to make my father pay.

All this means that if I'm to prove Kester died an accidental death I've somehow got to prove that Declan was dead wrong in his interpretation of the tragedy. However, there's at least one way of explaining why Declan wound up dead wrong: he could have been blinded by rage and grief, unable to reason effectively with the result that he drew a series of false deductions from the facts. I think I might be prepared to concede he spoke sincerely but sincerity is no guarantee that what he spoke was the truth.

Can I forget the preposterous theory of extortion and write it off as an Irish fairy tale? I only wish I could. But I can't because Declan based his belief that Kester was murdered on the theory that my father extorted Oxmoon from Kester and was then obliged to kill Kester to keep it. In other words, the extortion gives my father a motive for murder. If there had been no extortion then the deed of gift would have been perfectly valid and my father would have been secure in the knowledge that Kester could never get the property back. Murder would have been quite unnecessary. So the way to explode any theory of murder is to explode the theory of extortion, and I don't see how I can avoid including the subject in my inquiries.

Had Kester done something that would lay him open to blackmail and if he had, what was it? It's very hard to believe Declan's story. For instance, if Kester had accidentally killed Thomas, why had he panicked? He'd have been much more likely to hold fast, stand firm, do the right thing and call the police. It wouldn't have been pleasant but he probably wouldn't have wound up in jail. And if he had panicked, why call in my father, the one member of the family he couldn't stand and didn't trust? And why would my father have lifted a finger to help him stage a car smash? The story just doesn't stand up at all.

So what does this mean? It means that either Declan invented the whole story to support his extortion accusation or else for reasons of his own he was putting a gloss on some true facts. Maybe there was a crime and maybe it did concern Thomas, but whatever happened didn't happen the way Declan said it did.

Yet Pam says many people secretly believe in the extortion theory. Does this mean they also secretly believe my father was a murderer? What in fact do all the witnesses who gave evidence at the inquest truly believe? They may have told the truth as far as possible in the witness box but how close to the real truth is that truth? I shall have to question everyone again and form my own opinion.

One further thought occurs to me. I still can't believe there was any extortion, but if there was it actually presents a powerful argument against a theory of suicide. If Kester had been forced to surrender Oxmoon he'd never have rested until he'd got it back. He'd have fought to the last ditch. He'd have kept himself alive for Oxmoon, and the last thing he'd ever have done would be give up and throw himself despairingly into the sea.

So I must pursue this issue of extortion. There's no way I can kid myself it's irrelevant to my inquiries.

VIII

It was midafternoon, but I wasn't finished. I still had to make a list of the witnesses I needed to interview but I felt exhausted. Taking a hard look at unpalatable facts is an exhausting occupation, and after eating a bar of chocolate I brewed myself some more coffee before I turned to a fresh page of my notebook.

At once I was faced with the fact that the Kinsella brothers weren't the only crucial witnesses whom I was now unable to interview. There was another witness too who was permanently beyond my reach, the one witness who had loved both Kester and my father, the only witness who could have had sufficient intuition to grasp exactly what had been going on. Bronwen had only survived my grandfather by four years. Sian had said to me with resignation after her mother died: "She did try to survive but it was too difficult without him. She said the wheel was wrecked beyond repair."

I thought of Bronwen talking of the Wheel of Fortune.

After Kester's death she had said to me: "It was fated. He was strapped to a wheel of fortune from which he hadn't the will to escape," and when I was grieving that I would never see him again she had said to me: "But you will see him again—and again—and again. You'll look across the circle and you'll hear his echo in time."

But I'd felt I couldn't bear to hear that echo so I had closed my ears against it and I hadn't mentioned Kester to Bronwen again. She was the one who had spoken of him in the end. I'd just been expelled from Harrow and I'd gone to visit her in the hospital where she was dying. She had said: "You're making such a mistake, Hal, by trying to punish your father. He's suffering enough as it is." But I'd been only fifteen and I'd no idea what she meant. I was too young then to connect my performance at Harrow with my rage at Kester's death.

"Forgive him," Bronwen had said. "Forgive them both. Don't let them draw you into their shared circle, don't let them destroy you as they've destroyed each other."

"What circle?"

"The wheel of their fortune, the circle of their lives.... The wheel must be reshaped, the circle redeemed, such a burden to pass to you, you must be very strong, very brave."

"I don't understand, Bronwen. I don't understand a single word you're saying."

"Be loyal to your father." Those had been her last words to me. "Be loyal to your father," she had said, so I had turned over a new leaf, working hard at the crammers, gaining a place at Bristol University to read classics, trying to help my father as he floundered deeper into debt and despair after the catastrophe of the Bryn-Davies lawsuit.

But my father had been impossible to please. Even Gerry, his favorite brother, had quarreled with him in the end.

"You want to destroy yourself, Harry. You're not basically interested in survival. You just want to open the floodgates and let disaster pour in."

Gerry had quit. I'd quit. That was when I'd bummed around Europe and nearly wound up in a Turkish jail. I'd arrived home full of new plans to reform and had found that my father wanted to give Oxmoon to the National Trust in order to preserve it for posterity. He had been too ill to see the Trust's officials himself, but he had asked me to negotiate with them.

The Trust had been interested but had pointed out that all houses which came to them had to be endowed with a capital sum that would ensure their maintenance. They had wanted four hundred thousand pounds to restore the house and grounds and establish a fund for the future upkeep, but when my father had offered to sell the art collection to raise the money the Trust had recoiled in horror. The officials had said that the art collection was the only reason why they would wish to acquire Oxmoon; as the house was of no great architectural merit, it could be justifiably preserved only as a showcase for Kester's unique collection of paintings, furniture and *objets d'art*.

Although greatly disappointed, my father had also been relieved that he hadn't been obliged to sell Kester's treasures. Some psychological bar had always prevented him from sending even the smallest item to the auction rooms despite Gerry's frantic advice to sell antiques and not land to ease his financial troubles. It was all part of his mental disturbance.

"If I sell any of Kester's possessions then he'll never forgive me and then my gift for playing the piano by ear will never come back," he had said more than once in the past, and Gerry had commented to me: "Mad as a bloody hatter."

When Gerry and I realized that all our efforts to help were futile, Gerry had told my father to find another solicitor while I had escaped through the Chelsea coffee bars into the music business. Later I had heard from Humphrey that my father was hoping that I'd make the fortune required for Oxmoon's endowment. If this hope hadn't been so pathetic I would have laughed. I'd been making good money but nothing on the scale of four hundred thousand pounds. Only the very lucky and the very talented hit the real big time in the music business, and my luck and talent had been merely moderate.

Oxmoon was doomed, that was the truth of it, as ruined and ravaged as my father and just as utterly beyond redemption.

"The wheel must be reshaped, the circle redeemed..." I could hear Bronwen's voice again, but this time, although her words were still an enigma they seemed to connect in some inexplicable way with my present situation. "Such a burden to pass to you, you must be very strong, very brave," she had said, and suddenly I could feel the weight of the burden she had seen so clearly. I could not identify it, I could only dimly perceive its dimensions, but I knew beyond doubt it was there.

I thought: Suppose redemption's not just a word, not just a matter of semantics, not just a philosophical concept which has no true existence in reality. Suppose redemption's a tangible burden, a profound psychological ordeal, a reshaping of the past achieved only by pain and suffering.

I shuddered with revulsion and then it occurred to me that the real question which lay unanswered—the challenge beyond the challenge and the mystery beyond the mystery—was not whether I could solve the riddle of Kester's death but whether I would be strong enough to shoulder the tragedy I had inherited and re-form the circle which had been destroyed.

I shuddered again but Kester's voice urged in my memory: "Hold fast! Stand firm!"—and then at last, as I looked across the circle, I was nearly deafened by his echo in time.

IX

I suddenly realized that I was still facing a blank page of my notebook, and at once I pulled myself together. It was most unlike me to give way to metaphysical meanderings and superstitious speculation, and I could only conclude that remembering Bronwen had catapulted me down mental avenues which had no place in my rational world of hard facts and cool analyses. Writing WITNESSES TO BE INTERVIEWED at the top of the page, I turned aside from the dead, as represented by the Kinsellas and Bronwen, and embarked on a survey of the living.

I began by noting the names of Evan and Richard, both of whom had seen Kester in those three days before his death. Evan was a clergyman in Cardiff. Richard was a jet-setter; after Uncle Edmund's death Aunt Teddy had moved back to Boston, Richard's brother Geoffrey had emigrated to New York and Richard himself spent much time bouncing backwards and forwards across the Atlantic in the company of Beautiful People. There had never been any shortage of money in that branch of the family, although since Aunt Teddy's inheritance was locked up on trust, no large capital sum was available to help my father.

I was unable to add Bronwen's name to the list of people who had seen Kester before he died, but I did add Sian's. Sian and her mother had been close, the only two women in a family of men, and I thought it likely that Sian could provide me with some hearsay evidence as well as some interesting opinions of her own. In the hope of hearing more interesting opinions I added the names of her brothers. Evan was already on the list but I wrote down Gerry and Lance.

Then casting my net wider I noted Aunt Marian's name, not because she'd been close to Kester but because she'd been married to Rory and might be another source of hearsay evidence. I thought of Siobhan Kinsella, Declan's widow, but I'd never met her and I decided that I should start my investigations by interviewing the people I knew. I added my Aunt Eleanor's name. She'd been married to Thomas and was bound to have a relevant opinion on the subject of Declan's evidence.

But the most important name was still missing. I wrote down FATHER and sat looking at it.

A liar, an extortionist, a murderer? An innocent victim, a helpless neurotic, a good man crucified by ill luck?

Who was my father? I didn't know. To me he was just a source of pain labeled

PARENT. I considered him a hopeless father and I knew very well he had been a bad husband to my mother. I could remember how he had shouted at her and made her cry. I knew it was wrong to believe he'd killed her; Bronwen had told me not to believe that so I hadn't, but I had to blame someone for her death and who else was there to blame but him? Even if he'd done everything he could to save her—and Bronwen had sworn that he had—the fact remained that he'd set in motion the chain of events which had led to her death. She couldn't have got pregnant without his help and obviously he'd been criminally irresponsible. That indicated selfishness and callousness on a large scale but I didn't think that was incompatible with what I knew of my father. I saw him as selfish and callous. He'd always acted as if his children were millstones around his neck. That sort of man shouldn't be allowed to father four children. Such things should be banned by law.

I remembered Dafydd saying I was the apple of my father's eye. Dafydd wasn't usually given to flights of fancy, and suddenly I found myself remembering that alibi he had given my father, the alibi which was apparently tough enough not to crack under pressure. Dafydd was so uncommunicative that I felt an interview with him would be useless but I wrote on my list: *Dafydd—check his evidence with maximum care when I reread the inquest report.*

The word FATHER continued to hold my attention. "Be loyal to your father," Bronwen had said. Of course. One had to be loyal to one's father. That was the right thing to do as well as the done thing. But who was really my father here?

"Sometimes I feel I've got two fathers, Kester."

"Then make the best of both of us!"

My magician.

"This is the real question you have to answer, Hal," Pam had said to me. "What was Kester really like?"

I tried to see Kester but all I could see was his magic wand and then suddenly, miraculously, I was back again at Oxmoon, the lost Oxmoon of my childhood, and Gwyneth was moving to meet me once more in the fairy-tale palace of our dreams.

My last crucial witness. I'd nearly forgotten her. I wrote down GWYNETH LLEWELLYN, and as I sat staring at the name of the cousin who had been my childhood friend a voice in my head said: Take me back to Oxmoon, the Oxmoon of our childhood. Take me back to Oxmoon and make it live again.

3

I

IT WAS half-past four. Driving into Penhale I shut myself in the call box by the church hall and phoned my three uncles. Gerry I arranged to meet at the Claremont Hotel that evening at six. I forgot to ask him for Lance's number at work but when I called Lance's house his wife Jean obligingly invited me to dinner. She also gave me Evan's new number in Cardiff but he was out; I told his wife I'd call back later.

When I emerged from the booth I saw the Swansea bus draw into the village and as it halted by the green, four girls dismounted. They were dressed in the uniform of the Swansea Grammar. Gwyneth, I knew, had won a place at the grammar school and I thought it likely that her younger sister had followed in her footsteps. I accosted the nearest uniformed figure.

"Excuse me—was Caitlin Llewellyn with you on that bus?"

"She's just going up the lane," said the girl, pointing over her shoulder, and as she stared at me in amazement I knew I'd been recognized. Television is death to anonymity.

"Thanks." I broke into a run. "Caitlin!" I shouted, and sprinting across the green I caught up with her by the wall of the churchyard. When she turned to face me I recognized her as the child I had known some years before. She must have been about seventeen. She bore no resemblance to Gwyneth; she was taller, slimmer, prettier, probably much less intelligent, and as she too recognized me I realized I had seen girls like her in a hundred audiences. They had shining hair and screamed in all the right places. There was nothing to set her apart from the crowd.

"Wow!" she said. "It's Hal Godwin!" She went bright pink.

"Hi, how are you," I said with a routine smile, and added without pausing for her reply: "I want to get in touch with Gwyneth but as you probably know, I'm not one of your father's favorite people. Can you tell me where she is?"

The child made a supreme effort to compose herself. "She's got a flat in Swansea. She's teaching at Abbeybrook. I can't remember her phone number offhand, but—"

"That's okay, I'll get in touch with her through the school. Thanks." I turned to go.

"But Hal—she's coming out here tomorrow for the weekend. Aunt Dilys is visiting us from Bettws-y-Coed and Mum's staging a family reunion."

"Great. Tell Gwyneth I want to see her and that it's very urgent. I'll be in the churchyard tomorrow evening at eight."

"Okay, I'll tell her."

I gave her the smile I kept for autograph hunters and wound up the interview with a formal "Many thanks—I really appreciate that!" She looked dazzled. I added the empty words "So long, good luck" and walked away. It was a bleak moment. I had waved my magic wand by projecting my public image, and this had called forth a response that had no relation to reality. Her adulation was not for me; it was for someone who didn't exist, and beyond the myth I remained my troubled self, a private person who hid behind glittering images in an attempt to escape from truths too hard to face.

I thought of Kester, perhaps another private person who hid behind glittering images, and remembered Pam implying that he had fed his ego with the adulation of children in order to keep his inadequacy at bay.

"We know so little about even those who are closest to us," Kester had said to me once. "We know so little of what really goes on in other people's lives." He had been talking about a project of his, a novel based on the story of my great-great-grandmother Gwyneth Godwin and her lover Owain Bryn-Davies, and trying to explain how difficult it was to perceive the whole truth about any situation, past or present. I could hear him saying, "I suspect all we know now about those two is little better than a distorted myth. Time has transformed their story into a golden romance with a beginning, a middle and an end, but I'm more inclined to believe their affair was a cataclysmic event with repercussions we're still experiencing." And he had talked of a stone breaking the surface of still water and sending ever-widening ripples flowing outwards to the remotest banks of the pool.

I stood on my remote bank and looked across the pool to my great-great-grandmother, but I was unable to see how I could have been affected by her tragedy. And then it struck me that I was about to begin interviewing her descendants in an attempt to solve the enigma of yet another catastrophe in time. Who was to say where the rhythms of causality ended? I felt as if I were about to weave the final strand in some immensely complicated pattern, but of course that was irrational rubbish and I had to curb any desire to be fanciful. My job was to nail reality, not nurture myth.

Returning to my car I drove to Swansea to interrogate my first witness.

II

Gerry was waiting for me in the bar of the Claremont. He was wearing a well-cut gray suit with a striped blue shirt and a plain blue tie that toned with the stripes. To conform with current fashion he had grown a pair of sleek sideburns, but this was a mistake; they made him look more like a car salesman than a solicitor. The Americans have a word for men like Gerry. He was a wheeler-dealer. Floating acquisitively in the upper reaches of the Swansea business world he had accumulated various interests in property and had slithered onto the boards of various companies which operated under the Bryn-Davies flag. He was thirty-nine, twelve years my senior.

"So how are you, old chap?" he was saying as he snapped shut his silver cigarette lighter and glanced around the bar to see if there was anyone of importance who ought to be acknowledged. His carefully cultivated public-school accent always managed to sound phony, but nowadays when most public-school boys were doing their best to sink into a midatlantic twang his phoniness only made him fashionable. "Wonderful to see you again! By the way, my girlfriend's rather a fan of yours—buys all your records and watches you on television . . ." Gerry was famous for the beautiful girls he escorted, kept for a time and then casually dusted out of his life. He was always saying he would marry one day but I doubted he would ever find a woman who didn't bore him after six months. I sensed he wasn't fundamentally interested in women. Gerry was an egoist. The only person he was interested in was himself.

"Gerry, I need to talk to you about Kester," I said after playing the good listener for some minutes. Then after explaining that I wanted to straighten out the past by gathering the frank opinions of those who had been closely connected with the tragedy, I said abruptly: "Okay, let's have it—how do you really think Kester met his death?"

And Gerry said without a second's hesitation: "Oh, it was an open-and-shut case, old chap. There's absolutely no doubt in my mind whatsoever that he committed suicide."

III

"This is the way it was," said Gerry. "Poor pathetic old Kester was just a burnt-out case, very sad, I really did feel bloody sorry for him. Well, I mean, it was obvious he couldn't cope with Oxmoon, it was literally driving him round the bend, and because he loved the old place so much he made up his mind to do the noble thing and pass it on to someone who could cope better than he could—he did it for Oxmoon's sake, you see. I know he didn't like Harry, but let's face it, Harry was the best man for the job and damn it, you were the heir anyway. It all made perfect sense to me, and if Declan Kinsella had kept his big mouth shut it would have made perfect sense to everyone else too, but of course once that smooth bastard started spinning his Irish fairy tales everyone got flustered. All a lethal rumor needs to take off, mate and multiply is one whopping big lie from a polished crook like Declan Kinsella. . . .

"Extortion? Don't make me laugh! Old chap, my sense of self-preservation was, believe me, very keenly developed even back in the early Fifties and if I'd known Harry had committed a criminal act I'd have run a mile in the opposite direction.

Of course he didn't cover up a crime and of course Kester didn't commit one! The whole idea's ludicrous. Kester gave Oxmoon away of his own free will and was afterwards relieved and delighted that he'd done so—well, talk to Evan if you don't believe me! Kester told Evan just before he died that he felt liberated without Oxmoon and had taken on a new lease of life. . . .

"Okay, yes, so he terminated the lease unexpectedly. I agree that looks like an inconsistency, but you see, it was a manic mood swing, old chap, very common in cases of depression. The rock-bottom truth was that Kester was a failure, couldn't get published, couldn't cope with Oxmoon, couldn't even face life itself. Hell, even Harry felt sorry for him! Although to tell the truth, Harry was the one *I* always felt sorry for. Wish we could patch up that estrangement. I'm very fond of Harry. . . .

"Oh, I know you never liked him, I know you were one of Kester's fans, but the truth, Hal—the real honest-to-God truth—is that your father's the hero of this story and he's had the bloodiest luck imaginable. Mind you, I haven't always thought of him as a hero. I didn't like him much when I came home from Canada, thought he was a bit of a cold-blooded snob, standing on his Old School tie and his legitimacy and all that crap—well, of course I was more insecure then than I am now, I was mixed up about a lot of things and there was no one I could talk to, not really, I didn't get on with my father too well, he was a tricky kind of guy—chap, I mean—stuffy, you know? All hung up on morality, and Christ, what had he got to be so stuffy about, treating my mother like a tart, wrecking her life and then, my God, walking back in a cloud of romance after playing dead for twelve years and having the nerve to think he could pick up where he left off! I couldn't believe it, I just couldn't believe she'd take him back, but of course she was useless, too besotted with him to think straight, Christ, women are bloody odd sometimes! Well, I didn't get on well with my mother either, to be honest—it's all very well Harry talking sentimentally about magic ladies, but damn it, she was tough as old boots and *she* was all hung up on morality as well except that she dressed it up in that way-out Celtic mysticism—my God, it was impossible to have a straight talk with either of those two. . . .

"Yes, they were an odd pair all right—people talked so much romantic drivel about my parents' marriage when it finally happened, but what the hell do you think it was like trying to live with a middle-aged couple who were so taken up with each other that they weren't plugged into reality at all? Grand passion isn't designed to incorporate a bunch of kids, that's the unromantic truth—Christ, the rows over our education! However, my parents have nothing to do with Harry and Kester, have they, although as a matter of fact I often wonder, looking back, what effect my parents' catastrophic mess of a love affair had on those two—I think that grand passion affected more people adversely than my parents could ever bring themselves to admit. . . . But that's life, isn't it? Unless you live like a hermit, you can't help affecting other people in some way or other, and hell, I was very fond of my parents really, they just drove me up the wall, that's all, but most people feel that way about their parents, don't they? I know you feel that way about Harry. . . .

859

"Ah, yes, Harry—I was going to tell you how good Harry was to me when I was a kid. Yes, *he* talked to me, *he* held out a helping hand when I was lonely and insecure and just plain bloody miserable, he was a good brother to me, he listened, he cared, he was there when I needed him. He was a fine man, Hal, the best. And yet all the time up at Oxmoon, living in the house Harry should have had, living the kind of life Harry deserved to lead was this creep, this phony, this bloody hypocrite talking about beauty, truth, art and peace—my God, all that crap about pacifism! Kester was no pacifist! He was as tough and aggressive as they come. He had it in for Harry; he went after him with no holds barred— do you remember how Kester grabbed Little Oxmoon and Martinscombe? That was a naked act of aggression if ever I saw one. Okay, maybe Kester did have a case for annexing them—God knows what the legal position was on that land— but the point was that Kester wanted to ruin Harry and drive him out of Gower. He was ruthless and unscrupulous, he stopped at nothing—

"What was that, old chap? How do I reconcile that picture of Kester with Kester the pathetic old has-been who jumped off the Worm and drowned himself? Okay, good question, but it's not so hard to answer. Kester was nuts, that's all—nuts enough to want to destroy Harry and nuts enough to want to destroy himself later. Just because he could be tough doesn't mean he was incapable of cracking up. After all, look at your father. He was the toughest guy in Gower and look at the way he cracked up! But Harry was a good decent guy who had lousy luck and went to pieces whereas Kester was in pieces to start with, and every time he put himself together he was mayhem on wheels. That's the truth, Hal. That's the way it really was. He was a nut case who suicided. What else can I possibly say?"

IV

Notes on Gerry: *He could give no concrete reason why Kester should have committed suicide. Did Kester in fact suffer from a clinical depression which could have given rise to manic mood swings? It's a convenient theory for explaining the suicide but it rings false. However this may be because Gerry's personality is so synthetic that nearly everything he says does ring false. He was sincere when he talked about Father, though, and I think he was sincere when he talked of Kester as being ruthless and unscrupulous.*

What do I make of his story that Kester grabbed the Martinscombe lands in order to drive my father out of Gower? That bears little relation to the story Kester told me in one of the last letters he wrote to me at school before Father stopped the correspondence. Kester said he'd found out that legally the lands belonged to him and that he'd reluctantly decided to reclaim them as he needed every extra penny he could get in order to cope with rising costs and taxation. This seemed reasonable enough—a tough break for my father, of course, but Kester was only claiming what was his by right.

But now think again. Kester tries to grab the Martinscombe lands—and what happens directly afterwards? My father gets Oxmoon, all of it, the lot, including the disputed property. Was it given or did he grab it? If Kester's trying to grab lands at one moment why should he give the whole lot away the next? Can this merely be explained away by saying he was a crackpot at the mercy of manic mood swings? No, extortion's the answer—and Declan's evidence begins to seem just a little more than an Irish fairy tale.

Gerry denied the extortion theory, but he would, wouldn't he? If extortion existed and he, as my father's lawyer, knew of it, of course he'd have to lie to the back teeth to say it never existed—and of course he'd have to back up my father over the suicide theory. Never forget that if extortion exists it gives my father a motive for murder.

VERDICT: Not to be trusted, but his picture of Kester as a tough man who cracked up is intriguing. He made Kester and my father seem like mirror images of each other, although that's ridiculous because I know they were radically dissimilar. Or do I? I'm tempted to wonder if I know anything at all, but I mustn't get discouraged just because Gerry proved a slippery unsatisfactory witness.

Soldier on.

V

Lance lived in the comfortable Swansea house which had once belonged to my grandfather and which Lance had inherited after Bronwen's death. Evan hadn't needed it; Gerry, who preferred plush modern apartments, hadn't wanted it; Sian had already been married with a home of her own. Like Vershinin in *The Three Sisters*, Lance had a wife and two little girls. Probably he hoped to have more children in time. The large house suited him.

His little girls were long since in bed and his wife had tactfully retired to the living room to watch television, but Lance and I were lingering over our coffee at the kitchen table. The kitchen was as warm and friendly as it had been when Bronwen was alive, and although at first I had attributed this impression to Jean's good cooking and the relaxed nature of the company, I was beginning to sense that Lance was reminding me of his mother, mysteriously re-creating that atmosphere of intuitive sympathy which I could remember from my visits to the house as a child.

Lance was only ten years my senior, tall and thin, lanky and bespectacled, casual and nonchalant, an engineer who dabbled with inventions. He struck me as being a profoundly contented man, and despite his vagueness it occurred to me that evening that he was a much better-balanced personality than Gerry, kind, sensitive and unselfish. I remember thinking as I embarked on my set speech that he would be a better witness too, more perspicacious, more truthful and possible more detached. He hadn't been close to either Kester or my father.

"...so that's the position, Lance. Now tell me honestly: what do you think was going on?"

"God only knows, Hal," said Lance, shattering my assumption that he would have a clear-cut opinion to offer. "I could never make up my mind."

VI

"There was something weird going on," said Lance, "that's for sure. But I don't know exactly what it was. In retrospect I think the weirdest feature of the story is that as soon as my father died those two men went straight to pieces. That seems to prove they were so neurotic about each other that without a strong man keeping the peace between them their paranoia at once rocketed out of control.... No, I'm not exaggerating. They really were paranoid about each other. For instance, after Anna died Harry bust his way into Oxmoon to offer condolences and Kester wanted to kill him because he thought Harry had come to gloat. How paranoid can you get! And then there was a bizarre scene in 1949 when Harry and Thomas both thought Kester meant to humiliate them before the family and they refused to turn up at a big Oxmoon lunch party. Nothing happened, of course—Harry was imagining the whole thing, but even my father was in a hell of a sweat at the thought of Kester creating some thoroughly unpleasant scene.... You didn't hear about any of this? Well, of course you were pretty young then. But there was a long sequence of hostilities between Kester and Harry, although in the end it was Thomas who came to be the real problem to both those two. Harry couldn't stand him and Kester couldn't stand him either—apparently Thomas had insulted Anna back in 1939 and Kester never forgot.... No, I wasn't surprised when Kester tried to fire Thomas on the night of the car smash—nor was I surprised to learn that Thomas had got roaring drunk and crashed up to Oxmoon to make a scene. Given the people involved, anyone could have anticipated that particular script. But afterwards...

"Well, this is where we get to Declan Kinsella, isn't it? I know his story seems implausible but the truth is it's not impossible—Kester could well have killed Thomas in a drunken brawl, and if Harry had been there and was perhaps involved in some way which we don't know about, it's not beyond belief that he could have taken part in a cover-up. I know in retrospect we can say it would have been an idiotic thing to do, but people do do idiotic things in the heat of the moment when they're under stress... yes, I can see why Declan thought he could capitalize on that story. I don't suppose it happened just as he said it did, but I certainly wouldn't be surprised if his story had a factual basis—the real five-star liars of this world always use the truth as far as they possibly can.... Declan a five-star liar? Oh no, that wasn't what I meant at all. After all, it wasn't Declan's story, was it? It was Kester's.

"You see, Hal, there's only one way you can satisfactorily explain the evidence of Declan Kinsella, and that's to say he was a front for Kester's paranoia. Declan was in his own way a distinguished man. I don't believe he'd have deliberately perjured himself in the witness box; I think he believed in the truth of every word he was saying, but where did his facts come from? Well, he had only one source, didn't he: Kester. And Kester was a writer. He'd spent years and years perfecting the art of storytelling and only a practiced storyteller could have hoped to deceive a cynical politician like Declan.

"What makes me think Declan got the extortion story straight from the horse's mouth? Oh God, Hal, we all knew that for a fact! Has no one ever told you about the great scene at Oxmoon when Harry called a family council to explain his takeover and Declan gave a dress rehearsal of his performance in the Bryn-Davies lawsuit? Well, no, on second thoughts perhaps that's not so surprising—it was such a vile scene that I think we all tacitly agreed not to talk about it afterwards, least of all to the child you were at the time. But Declan accused Harry of extortion, and as Kester was at that time alive in Dublin, the inference was that Declan had been briefed by him. And yet...

"And yet that doesn't actually prove anything, does it? Not when you remember that Kester was a neurotic, paranoid about Harry. Kester might well have felt so ashamed that he'd given Oxmoon away because he couldn't cope that he invented the story of extortion in order to present himself to his brother in a less humiliating light....

"No, I'm not trying to protect you. I'm just telling you I don't know whether Declan was speaking Kester's truth or Kester's lies; I'm just telling you I don't know how or why Kester died; I'm just telling you I don't know whether Harry extorted Oxmoon or not but even if he did that still doesn't prove he murdered Kester. In fact I don't think you can prove anything here, Hal—I don't think we'll ever know what really happened, no matter how hard you play the private eye.... And by the way, aren't you being rather romantic, acting the crusader on the white horse in pursuit of the Holy Grail of Truth? And aren't you being just a little dishonest? This cold dispassionate inquisitorial air is an act. You care about those two men. If you didn't care you wouldn't be here, asking all these questions. Don't deceive yourself, Hal, or you'll wind up crucifying yourself over this....

"Okay, so you've been on the cross and now you're trying to cut yourself down by working out who's the hero and who's the villain of this story, but that's another false trail, because it's just not that kind of story. If you want a really way-out opinion, I'd say they were both mad. I think they were in the grip of some peculiar psychiatric condition—perhaps even an occult condition—for which there's no name. I think their relationship was sinister in the extreme and so lethal that it resulted in the destruction of their personalities. Stay away from it, Hal, let it be. I'm sorry I can't help you, I've done my best, but I really have nothing more to say..."

VII

NOTES ON LANCE:

I'm tempted to regard the interview as a failure since Lance when pressed for a verdict could only serve up a whimsical piece of mysticism reminiscent of Bronwen on an off day, but in fact despite his refusal to commit himself to any rational opinion he did let fall some interesting information.

(1) He revealed that my father and Kester had been at loggerheads for far longer than I realized. And more important, he confirmed that even my grandfather believed, on the occasion of this 1949 lunch party, that Kester was capable of thoroughly unpleasant behavior. This backs up Gerry's opinion.

(2) Lance confirmed something I thought was non-proven: that Declan was talking of extortion while Kester was still alive. It wasn't just a story he invented for the Bryn-Davies lawsuit after Kester's death. Lance rightly pointed out that this still doesn't make the story true but it does mean I must stop protecting myself by writing it off as an Irish fairy tale.

(3) Lance stated that Thomas's death, which is at the heart of the extortion mystery, followed an extended sequence of hostilities between Kester and my father. I didn't know this before. Nor did I know that Thomas joined them in forming a triangle of men all hostile to one another. This is unquestionably sinister and makes the possibility of a lethal termination of the triangle much more plausible.

VERDICT: This interview enabled me to see various random events of the past in an interesting and suggestive perspective. Lance said he couldn't help me, but in fact I feel I'm further on. I certainly don't believe his wild assertion of double insanity, but now I can see a nightmare taking shape, the nightmare of mutual loathing periodically swinging out of control. And when two people loathe each other to such a neurotic extent, then surely anything becomes possible—blackmail, land grabbing, the lot.

The past is getting murkier. If I were neurotic myself I'd feel that at any moment the lights were about to go out, the ghosts were about to walk and the horrors were about to begin. But I'm not neurotic and I'm not afraid of ghosts. I don't believe in them.

Soldier on.

VIII

Before leaving Lance and making the short journey east to Cardiff I phoned Evan to make sure he was at home and on arrival I found him alone in the vast kitchen of his Victorian rectory. His wife was out counseling at the social-services center. Evan was brewing tea, listening to the radio and jotting down notes for a sermon. Six books ranging from an Agatha Christie novel to a critique on Descartes lay open on the table to aid his quest for inspiration.

Evan was forty-two, thin and scanty-haired like Lance, but without Lance's air of tranquillity. He had a much more forceful personality, and the impression of force was heightened by the clergyman's tricks he had acquired since his ordination, the clarity of speech, the firmness in expressing his opinions, the unobtrusive skill in handling people who could be awkward, demanding or just plain dull. However despite his stylish clerical manners he always seemed to me to be an unlikely clergyman. He was the kind of restless idealist who could hardly be content indefinitely with the same theological surroundings, and he fancied himself an expert on the more esoteric reaches of the Christian faith. He had performed a notorious exorcism which had landed him in trouble with his bishop. He had dabbled in the laying on of hands. His routine experiments with ecumenism had turned into radical flirtations with Rome. As I grew older I saw him not just as a rebel but as a complex man trying not altogether successfully to submerge his complexity within the confines of orthodox religion, and I had occasionally wondered if later he might drop out, perhaps run for Parliament, start a business, become a television personality. He had that unfocused dynamism which could have made him a success in any field that gave him the chance to project his personality. Although he resembled Lance physically in some ways it was easier to believe he was Gerry's brother. He had Gerry's charm without Gerry's vulgarity, Gerry's drive without Gerry's shady amoral streak.

"I know what you said at the inquest," I said to him when I had explained the purpose of my visit. "But I want to make quite sure that you were saying what you really thought."

"Certainly I was!" said Evan at once and added firmly: "It was an accident, Hal. I have no doubt in my mind whatsoever that Kester would never have commited suicide."

IX

"You want me to recap the evidence I gave at the inquest?" said Evan. "No, of course I don't mind, why should I, I'm only glad you want to talk it over frankly. It always worried me that you never felt able to discuss it before. . . .

"Okay, here goes. I saw Kester on the day before he died when I took over to Rhossili his extremely sophisticated radio which I'd been guarding and enjoying while he'd been in Ireland. When I arrived at the cottage I found Kester in magnificent spirits. He said giving up Oxmoon was the smartest thing he'd ever done and that because he'd been relieved of the burden of looking after it he was now enjoying a period of unprecedented creativity. Mark you, I'm not sure whether he'd actually started this new novel—I never asked Kester about his work unless he volunteered information—but I definitely got the impression that if he hadn't started a masterpiece he was just about to begin one. His whole attitude, you understand, was quite incompatible with suicide. He was buoyant, excited and radiant.

"Now, the coroner asked me if I felt Kester's mood could have been some form of manic mood swing compatible with a serious depressive illness. I'm not a doctor so my opinion is of only minimal value, as Harry pointed out to me later with perfect truth, but in my opinion it wasn't a manic mood swing. The suicide school of thought, of course, says that it was. However at least I gave the jury their opportunity to file their verdict of accident.

"Here's what I think happened: I believe Kester drowned on the Shipway. From Harry's evidence it was obvious to me that Kester was wandering around in a haze of creative euphoria, and in those circumstances I think it's highly possible that he got mixed up about the tides—for instance, perhaps his watch stopped and having lost all track of time he misjudged the state of the Shipway. After all, the Shipway's deceptive, isn't it? It's not easy to tell when it's about to go under. It doesn't sink uniformly. It's quite possible for a man to start out thinking he's quite safe and then realize in the middle that he's made a fatal mistake—why, think of Owain Bryn-Davies back in the Eighteen Eighties.

"Okay, so much for Kester; if one bears in mind that he was on the brink of a new novel this stroll out to the Worm in a creative haze, though eccentric, would have been entirely in character. But the real mystery, Hal, isn't Kester's behavior that evening; it's your father's. Why did he follow Kester out there? Obviously he wanted to talk to him and I'm afraid I don't for one moment believe that Kester had invited him to the cottage earlier for a drink. They just weren't on those terms, not by that time. Besides, if Kester had really invited him for a drink, why issue the invitation in a note that afterwards conveniently couldn't be found? Why not ring up? I realize the cottage had no phone but there was a call box close at hand in the village.

"I think Harry invented that note. The postman and the parlormaid could only recall that there were several letters which arrived by the afternoon post, so their testimony doesn't help, but it strikes me that Harry had to invent that note to explain why he went to Rhossili that evening—it would be the only way of explaining the inexplicable. There was no logical reason why either of them should have wanted to see the other at that particular time. Kester was happy, sunk deep in a creative stupor. Why should he have wanted to upset himself by inviting Harry to see him? And why should Harry have put himself on the rack by paying him a visit?

"Yes, that's certainly a mystery, and the plot thickens, doesn't it, when you remember that Harry didn't just sit waiting for Kester at the cottage. He went out to look for him and when he found him he staggered all the way after him across the Shipway. It was the most extraordinary thing to do. I admit Harry explained it all very convincingly at the inquest by talking of his anxiety and concern, but I still think the whole thing was bloody odd. Harry was a brilliant witness, of course. He had the coroner eating out of his hand and certainly I believed him at the time, but... well, that's what being a brilliant witness is all about, isn't it?

Everyone believes you at the time and it's only afterwards that people start to wonder. And talking of witnesses...

"Yes, I knew you'd want to ask me about Declan. Well, as far as the murder theory goes, I think that just has to be nonsense. Harry might well have been capable of killing Kester, but I'm quite sure he didn't do it. I think if he was going to kill Kester he would have done it more efficiently—after all he was a trained killer. I can see him bashing Kester over the head and then disposing of the body in such a way that it would never be discovered, but I have great trouble seeing him pushing Kester into the sea after pursuing him out to the Worm's Head in view of two independent witnesses.

"So I'd dismiss the charge of murder, but the charge of extortion is certainly much more plausible. I have no trouble at all in thinking Harry capable of taking Oxmoon by extortion but I do have trouble seeing how he did it. I don't believe all that rubbish about Thomas. Kester was a man of peace. He wouldn't have taken part in a drunken brawl, so how could he have killed Thomas by accident? And even if he had, he certainly wouldn't have been fool enough to ask Harry to help him cover up a crime. Harry may well have extorted Oxmoon, but if he did we'll never know how it was done.

"The biggest argument against extortion is that I can't see Kester ever sitting back and accepting it. But on the other hand one could argue that he'd found life without Oxmoon unexpectedly carefree and that he was prepared to let matters ride until he'd finished his new book. I'm quite sure in my own mind, Hal, that Kester returned to Rhossili purely and simply to write. But if extortion did exist and Harry had a guilty conscience it's quite possible he might have put a different construction on Kester's behavior and that, of course, would explain why Harry was so determined to see Kester that night: sheer paranoia would have induced him to think Kester had returned to Gower to reclaim Oxmoon and Harry would have felt driven to seek a showdown. No wonder Kester kept going once he reached the Inner Head that evening! Yes, I know Harry said at the inquest that Kester was apparently unaware that he was being followed, but what Harry was really saying was that he never saw Kester look back. But of course Kester must have looked back and of course he must have seen Harry—and that was why he kept going.... No, this needn't necessarily mean he was frightened of Harry. The most likely explanation is that he just didn't want an interview with anyone, least of all his paranoid cousin, when all his characters were trekking through his head in glorious Technicolor.

"So we come back to my theory of an accident. I don't really believe Kester planned to be marooned on the Worm that night, no matter how deep he was in his creative haze. Nor do I believe that he would have toiled all the way out to the Worm if he'd known he had so little time to enjoy the view on the other side of the Shipway. I'm sure something was wrong with his watch and he was misled about the time. My theory is that he kept going along the Worm to avoid Harry but when Harry turned back he turned back too. They were visible to each other, remember, when Harry came round the bend onto the southern flank of the Inner Head and saw Kester far away by the Devil's Bridge; if Harry saw Kester, then Kester could have seen him.

"So what happens? Harry turns back and recrosses the Shipway but by the time he reaches the mainland again the Shipway's about to go under. He looks back and sees to his horror that Kester, in a muddle about the tides, is leaving the Inner Head and setting out across the Shipway. Then Harry does nothing. There are no witnesses. He doesn't call the Coastguard. He just watches Kester drown—and then he panics. He knows there are witnesses who saw him going out to the Worm earlier. He knows his hatred of Kester is notorious. He knows the police are bound to look at him askance once they realize Kester died in mysterious circumstances. So he rushes off and cooks up an alibi with Dafydd—the one person in the world who'd do anything for him—and it works. He's exonerated at the inquest. But then his guilt—the guilt that he did nothing to save Kester—eventually surfaces and crucifies him. Harry's mental collapse is really only explicable, isn't it, if he'd either killed Kester or else believed he'd failed to save him from death, and that is the one theory of accident which covers this point—indeed, I'd go so far as to say that my theory is the only possible explanation of the tragedy, the only explanation that fits all the facts. So there you are, Hal. Take my advice, call it an accident—and for your own sake, let the matter rest..."

X

As he stopped talking I rose to my feet and we stood facing each other in that shadowy room.

"Is that what you want?" I said. "You want me to let the case rest?"

"Yes. It would be better. Let it be."

I sat down again abruptly. "Okay," I said. "Cards on the table. Now, just what the hell do you really think was going on?"

There was a long, long silence. Then Evan too sat down again and said, "You're bound to think I'm some sort of mystic crackpot."

"Try me."

"I think you should refrain from investigating forces which even today we don't really understand."

"Come again."

"I'm talking about evil. It was present between those two men. Individually I believe they were no worse than anyone else, but they were a catalyst to each other, and whenever they met evil was generated."

"Uh-huh."

"As I say, such things are very imperfectly understood even today—perhaps especially today when people have this touching faith that everything can be explained in scientific terms. But in my opinion, what we have here is a spiritual malaise which can't be explained scientifically; I believe Harry and Kester were locked together in a metaphysical nightmare which ended in their deaths—physical death for Kester, spiritual death for Harry. They were like two sides of a schizophrenic personality. It was as if they shared a common soul."

"Fine. What does all that ultimately mean?"

"It means that how Kester died doesn't matter. It means that you should stop right here and go no further. There are worlds existing which any sane man should be afraid to enter, and the world which your father shared with Kester was one of them."

"Let's try and translate that into basic rational English. Are you trying to say that the solution to this mystery is so unnerving that I'm bound to go mad myself if I find out?"

"I'm saying that both those men staked a claim to you in the past. I'm saying that they could still tear you apart. I'm saying that unless you stop now you could wind up right in the middle of their metaphysical nightmare."

"And how would you, a clergyman, deal with a metaphysical nightmare?"

"I would pray for an act of redemption."

I got up, wanting to terminate the conversation not only because I was unnerved that the word "redemption" had surfaced again but because I was having a hard time deciding what to say next. I respected him as a man and believed that the world of the spirit was as real to him as the world of the mind was to Pam, but I felt I was temperamentally unsuited to both theology and psychology and I believed I should be interested only in concrete facts. Yet here was this highly intelligent man propounding a thesis to which I somehow had to find a courteous reply.

Finally I said, "You've got a lot of courage to say that to me when my skepticism must have been so very obvious. I admire your guts. Thank you for being honest." I moved to the door.

"I haven't reached you, have I?"

"Oh yes, you have, but not quite in the way you intended. I'm now more determined than ever to get to the bottom of all this."

"Then all I can do is pray for you."

"Sure. Do anything that'll stop you worrying about me. But I don't believe in metaphysical nightmares, Evan, and I don't believe there's anything here which can't be explained rationally. I'm going on."

XI

Notes on Evan:

His accident theory is flawless but the only problem is that there isn't a shred of proof to support it. I was particularly interested in his somewhat cynical attitude to my father's alibi. It's quite true that Dafydd would do anything for my father. The way to prove Evan's theory would be to bust that alibi because if my father stayed to watch Kester drown he'd have arrived back at the cottage much later than he said he did and the odds are he would have missed Dafydd altogether. It wouldn't have taken Dafydd long to change the washer on that tap.

NOTE: Why did this alibi prove so unbustable? Was there an independent witness who could swear Dafydd was at the cottage when he said he was? I can't remember so it's more vital than ever that I recheck his evidence in the inquest report.

The suicide theory would appear to be in shreds, although ideally I'd like another witness to confirm that Kester was euphoric only hours before he died. But if he was on a big creative high I can't believe he'd abort it by jumping into the sea.

The extortion is still a puzzle, and before I really start believing Declan's story I'd like another piece of evidence that would link Thomas's death squarely with some form of neurotic or peculiar behavior on Kester's part. This is because I agree with Evan that Kester was a man of peace, and if he was indeed driven to commit a crime and cover it up, then the circumstances must have been very bizarre indeed.

And talking of the bizarre brings me to Evan's metaphysical bullshit. I want to dismiss it, but there does appear to be a weird dimension to this story and that dimension keeps on surfacing. From Gerry I got the impression that my father and Kester were like mirror images—and that's certainly weird since I know they were utterly dissimilar. Then Lance said they were both mad in an occult sense which he was too fey to define further, and now Evan says they were possessed by something which he doesn't quite have the nerve to call the Devil. I don't believe any of this, of course, but nevertheless it's hard not to form the opinion that my father and Kester were on some very way-out trip indeed. But what were they tripping out on? Mutual paranoia would certainly be a more rational explanation than evil spirits, but why should the paranoia have existed? Probably only someone like Pam could dream up an answer to that one; but I don't want to get involved with psychiatry any more than I want to get involved with religion.

VERDICT: Evan was helpful and—before he degenerated into mysticism—very credible, but ultimately he was baffling. Did I really get to the bottom of what he believed? Two sides, he said, of a schizophrenic personality. Weird. But I don't believe in that kind of claptrap. I'm a rationalist.

Soldier on.

XII

When I reached home it was after midnight but as I drove into the stable yard I saw there was a light still burning in my father's room. I switched off the engine. I thought I saw the curtain shift but I was some yards away and it was impossible to be sure. As I watched the light went out.

I wondered what he was thinking.

Waking at seven I brewed some coffee and reread my notes. I had lost the habit of eating breakfast; my years on the road as a singer had meant that morning was a dead time for me, and I had grown used to combining breakfast and lunch in a noontime meal.

When the coffee was finished I drew up a shopping list which included more mousetraps. The mouse population of Oxmoon was spirited. Small wonder that Pam's cat was looking so sleek. I toyed with the idea of borrowing it for a night or two.

The shops opened at nine and after collecting the items I needed in Penhale I drove on to Llangennith to see my mother's half-sister Eleanor.

Stourham Hall had been converted into holiday flats which supplemented Eleanor's income during the summer months. Probably it needed little supplementing as the pig farm was prosperous and my grandfather Oswald Stourham had left money to both his daughters, but Eleanor was a businesswoman and never let an opportunity to make money pass her by. At this time she was in her sixties, gray-haired and heavily lined, but I still found her much as she had always been. I looked at her and saw the Nineteen Thirties, a vanished world where people said "Jolly good!" and asked "Who's for tennis?" and played huge black discs of Noël Coward songs on something they called a gramophone.

"How simply splendid!" said Eleanor, ushering me into the living room of her flat on the ground floor of the Hall. "I wondered when you'd turn up—I saw Pam at the W.I. meeting last night and she said you'd come to Oxmoon to meditate. Glad you've cut your hair. Your father must be thrilled. How *is* the poor old stick? Pam said he was a bit better but of course one can't believe a word these psychiatrists say."

I knew Eleanor was fond of me; her own son had emigrated to Australia, and after that she had taken a deeper interest in her four nephews, so in deference to her affection I took time to chat with her over a cup of coffee. Twenty minutes elapsed before I allowed myself to broach the purpose of my visit.

"Aunt Eleanor, would you mind talking of the past?"

But old people love talking of the past. I had noticed by this time that when people reach the end of their lives they automatically turn back to the beginning as often as possible as if the present had become unimportant and only the past was real.

I embarked on my set speech. "I've been doing a lot of thinking about Kester—"

But no explanations were needed. Eleanor at once launched herself into her reminiscences.

"Ghastly Kester!" she exclaimed. "Oh sorry, old boy, he was rather a chum of yours, wasn't he, but honestly! What a creature! Of course, you were too young, poor little chap, to understand a *thing*, but if you want my opinion—"

"Yes, I do. Very much. Do you think he committed suicide?"

"God knows, my dear; I was too glad he was dead to care. Oh yes! *There's* someone who got what was coming to him, no doubt about that! No doubt about it at all. ..."

XIV

"Kester was morally responsible for Tom's death," said Eleanor fiercely. "Tom slaved for years to run that estate for a ridiculously small salary, and yet Kester sacked him for no good reason and without a word of thanks! No wonder Tom got drunk and smashed himself up in his car! Too bad he didn't smash up Kester! Of course I implored him not to at the time because I didn't want him ending up in jail, but if I could have foreseen how that day would end...

"Yes, old boy, it really did end with Tom crashing his car. Of course Declan Kinsella's allegations later were absolutely riveting, but there wasn't a word of truth in them, unfortunately. Why am I so certain? Heavens above, I should have thought it was obvious the story was a complete fairy tale! In fact it would take an ex-terrorist like Declan to dream up a story of a faked car crash. God knows what goes on in Ireland but two Welshmen brought up to be English gentlemen just don't stoop to that kind of uncivilized behavior—and even if they did, the story's still incredible because if Kester had somehow killed Tom, why would he have appealed to Harry for help and why on earth would Harry have helped him? You answer me that! Well, you can't, of course, those two questions are unanswerable. No, Declan invented that story to put your father on the rack, no doubt about that at all; but let me tell you this, old boy: if Kester *had* killed Tom, it wouldn't have been by accident! He'd have murdered him!

"Oh yes, I know Kester liked to pretend he was a pacifist and I know a lot of people thought he was soft, but that was all stuff and nonsense! The truth was he was as tough as they come, just like his mother—and *there* was a game old war-horse if ever there was one. ...

"No, I certainly shed no tears for Kester when he died and I certainly didn't waste time wondering about how it had happened, but for what it's worth I don't think he committed suicide. If he was the suicidal type I think he would have killed himself after Anna died, but he didn't, did he, and if he could survive that then I'd say he could survive just about anything. I suppose his death was an accident. Accidents do happen, don't they, and he wouldn't be the first person who'd drowned on an expedition to the Worm. But one thing I know for certain, old boy, and I was so glad it was clearly proved at the inquest: Harry didn't kill him. No matter how much you may be worrying about Kester, at least you don't have to start worrying about *that*. ..."

She offered me more coffee and there was a pause while she refilled my cup. Then as I reached for the sugar bowl she began talking again.

"Your father had a rough time," she said. "I felt sorry for him. I'm very fond of your father, Hal. There are plenty of people who can't stand him, but I think he's a good man. He was a loyal husband to Bella, and... well, you're grown up now and I can admit to you that his marriage couldn't have been easy."

There was a silence. I was stirring my coffee but my hand halted. I glanced up.

"Yes," said Eleanor reflectively, not looking at me, "he must have had a hard time. Bella... well, I was fond of your mother, Hal; she was a sweet child in many ways but she wasn't very good at being grown-up. I don't mean she was mentally defective. Mentally she was all there—just—but emotionally she never grew much older than thirteen. And that's a burden for a man, you know—well, of course you'd know. You're a man yourself and you can imagine now what it must have been like for your father to come home from the war when he was your age and find he had four little sons, money worries and a wife who couldn't cope with any of them. Poor Bella! She needed looking after almost as much as you children did."

There was another silence. The spoon was still stationary in my cup.

"But your father stuck by her," said Eleanor. "In the end he failed to cope with this awful obsession she had to be pregnant the whole time, but my God, at least no one could say he didn't try. Heavens, I even remember him going with her to the gynecologist because she insisted on taking over the birth-control problem and he wanted to make quite sure she could manage! Of course she got pregnant straightaway but that was what she wanted, wasn't it? Poor Harry, he was absolutely frantic. I felt so sorry for him. What a mess! But it wasn't his fault."

The coffee had long since stopped swirling. I removed my spoon and laid it in my saucer.

"But he stuck by her," repeated Eleanor, "and after she died he stuck by you four boys. To be honest I never thought he would. I thought he'd palm you off on his father and Bronwen and make a fresh start with another woman as soon as it was decently possible, but no, he stayed with you at the Manor and he struggled on alone. I suppose you probably took it all for granted and grumbled about him behind his back—children are such insensitive little brutes!—but I admired him. Parenthood's a hard grind. It's all very easy for childless men like Kester to give little tea parties and play at being a father, but when all's said and done that's got very little to do, has it, with what parenthood's really all about."

She stopped. I had become aware of a tap dripping in the nearby kitchen. It dripped on and on and on.

"Of course we all know Harry was a war hero," said Eleanor, "but I think his heroism really began when the war was over. I'll never believe that Harry was the villain of the Oxmoon saga, Hal. I think the real villain was your cousin Kester."

XVI

NOTES ON AUNT ELEANOR:
Her views on Kester ought to be valueless because of her rampant prejudice against him, yet her opinion chimes with Gerry's so I can't dismiss it out of hand. This vision of a dangerous aggressive Kester I find very disturbing. It's so contrary to all the memories I have of him.
VERDICT: *From the point of view of my investigation it was disappointing. I found out nothing new about Thomas's death and merely got another vote for the accident theory. Yet from a strictly personal point of view I can hardly write the interview off as a waste of time. The truth surfaced here all right, but it wasn't the truth about Kester and Thomas. It was the truth about my parents' marriage.*

XVII

I closed my notebook. I was alone in the living room as Eleanor had had to leave to see her pig man, but she had given me permission to use her phone. I was sitting by the phone but had so far been unable to begin my calls. I was too busy imagining myself with four children, constant money worries and a wife with an emotional age of thirteen.

Eventually I opened my notebook again and found my list of witnesses. Lance had given me Sian's London number. I sat looking at it for a while and then finally I pulled myself together, lifted the receiver and began to dial the number of that trendy flat in the heart of Knightsbridge.

Sian was only eight years my senior. Having made an astonishing marriage some years ago to a viscount who had been at school with her at Bedales, she had somehow managed to keep her head in a chaotic peripatetic world. Her husband was a rock fan who had just launched his own record label and they spent their time commuting between New York, Nashville, London, Juan-les-Pins and, occasionally, the Bahamas. The viscount was energetic but naive. I gave him two years in the music business, no more, and sensed Sian would be greatly relieved when it was all over.

After the opening pleasantries I kept my explanations minimal but Sian had no trouble understanding them.

"Of course it's important to get the past straight," she said. "I had quite a past to straighten out myself, what with being born a bastard and having to adjust to Dad glissading back into our lives and smothering us all with moonlight and roses and doing the done thing. Poor Dad, he was sweet but he did cause an awful lot of trouble—just like Kester. He was sweet too but just look at all the trouble he caused."

"Do you think he committed suicide?"

"No."

"Then how do you think he drowned accidentally?"

"I don't think he did drown accidentally."

"You mean—"

"I think he was murdered," said Sian, "and I think Harry killed him."

XVIII

"Sorry," said Sian. "I've never said that to you before because after all Harry's your father, and even though you do detest him you might at rock bottom be fond of him as well. But if you're trying to straighten out the past I won't help you by lying, will I?

"Yes, I'm sure Kester was murdered, although the stupid thing is that my judgment is based purely on feminine intuition and I haven't any real evidence to support it. I'll tell you what happened: On the day before Kester died my mother went over to Rhossili to see him and I went too, acting as her *chauffeuse*. I was at home because I'd had a bust-up with David in London—it was before we were married and he wanted me to sleep with him—as if I would after what had happened to my mother! Anyway I was miserable as hell and finding driving therapeutic—all very Freudian, of course—so as I was making love to the steering wheel the whole damn time Mum asked me to give her a ride to Rhossili. When we arrived it was early evening and Evan had just left after delivering Kester's radio. Kester himself was in very good spirits. I wouldn't go so far as Evan does and say he was euphoric but he was definitely cheerful. However my mother was worried about him for some reason and I could see they wanted to be alone together, so I went out for a mini-stroll to the church and back. I didn't exactly eavesdrop on my return but as I passed the open window of the living room I heard Kester say, 'Of course Harry might murder me if I do this but I don't think he'd be quite such a fool.'

"Well, when I heard he was dead—after being followed by Harry to the Worm— of course I asked my mother what he had said to her but she wouldn't speak of it. In fact she never would speak of it to any of us and I'm positive she didn't tell the police. Neither did I. Harry and I weren't close but he was my brother and I didn't want him winding up on the gallows.

"But I did unburden myself to Evan and after we'd discussed Kester's remark at some length, I came to the conclusion that the only explanation was that Kester wanted Oxmoon back. Why else would Kester think Harry might try to murder him? However, Evan said my theory didn't jibe with Kester's story that the loss of Oxmoon had liberated him—Evan just thought that Kester had been talking facetiously to my mother and that I'd heard the remark out of context. You know how sometimes one says 'Heavens, so-and-so will *murder* me if I do this!'

"I could see Evan's point of view, but I still wasn't wholly convinced. I just couldn't get over the sinister fact that Kester had talked of being murdered by Harry and twenty-four hours later he was dead after Harry had followed him to the Worm. The more I thought of it, the more intuitively convinced I became that Harry had indeed killed him, although paradoxically the moment I tried to sit down and work out a rational theory nothing seemed to make sense. For instance, if I was right and Kester really had wanted Oxmoon back, why not stay in Dublin and negotiate with Harry through his lawyers? Of if he had no legal case for demanding Oxmoon's return, why not involve the family, who would almost certainly have been kind and sympathetic, and approach Harry through someone like Uncle Edmund? Why come back to Gower and enter into some sort of macabre sparring match? And then, of course, one gets into the mystery of what really did happen at the Worm that evening. If Kester was alive to the possibility that Harry might murder him, he wouldn't have loafed around on the Inner Head that night and waited for Harry to catch him up. Yet unless Kester was waiting on the Inner Head, Harry couldn't have caught him up, killed him and still got back across the Shipway in time to beat the tide. And we know Harry did beat that tide because he had that genuine alibi—oh yes, that alibi was real enough, no question about it. Mum and I could both testify that it wasn't something Harry and Dafydd invented later to cover Harry's tracks.

"Dafydd was visiting Mum that day. We all went to the cinema and then directly after the matinée Dafydd said he had to run off and buy a washer before the shops closed. He did. Then later, after supper, I volunteered to drive him home—he didn't have a car in those days. He said, 'Okay, but don't take me home, take me out to Rhossili so I can fix the bloody tap—I should have done it three days ago and I'm feeling guilty.' So I actually drove him to Kester's cottage. I offered to wait while he changed the washer but he said no, he'd prefer to walk home, so off I went back to Swansea again.

"You see the point I'm making, don't you? There was no way they could have cooked that alibi after Harry received Kester's note that afternoon, the note inviting Harry to call on him. If Harry had then phoned Dafydd and said, 'Look, I'm going off to Rhossili to murder the sod—do me a favor and give me an alibi,' Mum and I would have known about the call—and so would the village of Penhale, since all calls in those days went through the village switchboard.

"The only way you can argue that the alibi was faked is to say that Harry and Dafydd arranged it well in advance, but then you get into the problem of explaining how Harry knew Kester was going out to the Worm that night. In fact unless he was clairvoyant there was no way he could have foreseen that it was going to be of crucial importance to him that Dafydd turned up at the cottage at around eight thirty that evening to change the washer. No, that alibi's genuine, Hal—the police couldn't crack it and the coroner accepted it without a murmur. So that means Harry couldn't have murdered Kester. Logically, rationally, I know I've got to accept that. And yet... and yet... well, it's stupid, isn't it, but I still have this awful feeling that he killed him...."

XIX

NOTES ON SIAN:
Her evidence is certainly odd. It's tempting to take Evan's view that she got the wrong end of the stick during her brief moment of eavesdropping, but she doesn't believe she did, and her firsthand impression should count for more than Evan's secondhand deduction. So what does this mean? It means that Sian's raised questions not about my father but about Kester. What on earth was he up to? If he was really after Oxmoon, why tell Evan he was liberated without it and then tell Bronwen he wanted it back? And assuming Sian's right that he wanted to reclaim Oxmoon, how good a chance did he have of succeeding?

I wouldn't rate it high. To get the deed of gift declared invalid he would have had to plead he had signed it under duress—but Declan was laughed out of court when he tried to spin the extortion yarn. Would Kester have been more credible than Declan? Almost certainly not, as he was a neurotic subject to nervous breakdowns. He'd also have to bear in mind that he'd be battling against a man who at that time had a dazzling reputation as a war hero and who according to Evan was a brilliant witness. Kester would have been batting on a very sticky wicket, and if I'd been my father in those circumstances I certainly wouldn't have murdered Kester. I'd have sat tight and waited.

VERDICT: *Sian's intuition was interesting, but basically she underlined the two big objections to any theory of murder: (1) The rising tide and the cast-iron alibi give my father no opportunity, and (2) my father had no real motive. So once again I'm left asking myself: If he did do it, how was it done and why?*

But I've never believed he did it and despite Sian's intuition I don't believe it now. As Kester himself apparently said to Bronwen: not such a fool.

Soldier on.

XX

"Well, darling," said Aunt Marian far away in Kent where she was enjoying her recent second marriage to a stockbroker, "of course Kester committed suicide. Could anything be more typical? He simply adored melodrama, my dear, always did, and I can quite see him striding out along the Worm into the golden sunset and diving into the sea—I mean, as Harry said, it was all so absolutely in character, wasn't it, but my God, *what* a trauma we all went through afterwards! It simply broke up my marriage to Rory. Well, let's face it, the marriage spent most of its time on the rocks anyway but at least Kester's death gave me the push I needed to walk out for good. 'I'm sorry,' I said to Rory, 'I know Harry and I aren't close but he's my only brother—' Well, of course, Hal darling, I know I do have other brothers and they're all simply adorable, but somehow I've always found it just a *little* difficult to remember I'm related to them—although I was devoted to darling Bronwen of course, always was... Where was I? Oh yes. 'Harry's my only brother,' I said to Rory, 'and no man, not even my husband, calls him a murderer in my presence. This is the end, darling,' I said, and started to pack a suitcase. 'It's the truth!' he yells—of course he's simply pie-eyed with whisky—'Declan and I have proved it! Harry killed Kester!' so I said, 'Good—it's about time someone killed him,' and then Rory started crashing around trying to hit me and frankly, darling, violence is *not* my scene so I drew the line, as darling Papa would have said, and wound up in the divorce court. I only wish I'd done it long before but I had the children to think of and then Rory was always rather heaven in bed—I can say that to you now you're grown up, can't I? So *super* to have a nephew who's a pop singer! I'm the envy of all my friends....

"Yes, that's right, darling—no, you didn't mishear. Rory did say he and Declan had proved Harry murdered Kester, but of course that was just exaggeration and you can be sure they proved no such thing. Harry might certainly have *felt* like murdering Kester now and then but he would never have done it, never, and anyway he couldn't have done it, could he, because of that ghastly tide. 'What about the tide?' I screamed at Rory when he was making his awful accusations. 'Fuck the tide!' he screamed back and tried to rape me. God, *what* a marriage it was, how *did* I stand it....

"Well, yes, darling, actually Rory did say a little more than that. He said Harry could have killed Kester and still got back across the Shipway to beat the tide. He said obviously Kester was waiting for Harry on the Inner Head and Harry lied when he said Kester had kept going. So I said, 'The coroner didn't think Harry lied!' But Rory said that was because the coroner had been at Harrow with darling Papa and was constitutionally incapable of believing an Old Harrovian like Harry would either commit murder or tell lies in the witness box....

"Oh, of course I was at the inquest! I remember I wore this simply stunning hat... What? Oh darling, *of course* Harry was telling the truth! He was quite wonderful, so calm, so rational, so... well, there's only one phrase for it, Hal: he was *such a gentleman*. It was simply impossible to believe he wouldn't do the done thing at all times. Well, I know Declan and Rory didn't believe him but then they were hopelessly prejudiced, weren't they? I remember I said to Rory when he and Declan came back from the Worm's Head—oh yes, they went out there after the inquest, didn't you know? They actually knew the Worm quite well because before Aunt Ginevra married Uncle Robert Declan and Rory spent some time at Oxmoon and my grandfather often took them on expeditions to the coast, but after all that was a long time ago and I suppose they wanted to refresh their memories about what it was like out there. Rory even had the nerve to call it reconstructing the crime—honestly! I could have murdered him...although actually the Worm nearly murdered them both instead, and serve them right too. Well, you can imagine it, can't you, two overweight men, both past fifty, toiling to and fro across the Shipway! They took all day over it, came back wrecked and killed a bottle of whisky between them. God knows why they didn't drop dead from coronaries then and there....

"Oh darling, you can't take them seriously, you really can't! When all was said and done they were just two hard-drinking Irishmen trying to avenge their brother's death by scraping up some mud to fling at poor darling Harry—by the way, how *is* poor darling Harry? I must send him a little something from Fortnum's when I'm next up in town. I suppose Pam's still being a saint—such a funny woman, I can't make her out at all, but I'm sure she's charming when you get to know her. After all, she must have *something* to attract Harry, mustn't she, and there really isn't much else. If my bosom were that flat I'd have silicone injections...Listen, Hal darling, I simply must rush now because I've got six people coming to lunch and I haven't even stuffed the avocados, but it was too sweet of you to phone and yes, of course Kester committed suicide, I know he did—in fact ever since Anna died I'd always felt he was willing himself, my dear, absolutely *willing* himself towards the most sensational tragic ending..."

XXI

Notes on Aunt Marian:
Back comes Declan Kinsella, the recurring nightmare.

What am I going to do with him? He's not going to go away. He won't conveniently drop out of this story. Rory might have been a fool but Declan wasn't, far from it, and if he went out to the Worm and came back convinced my father could have killed Kester I've got to take him seriously, even though I've just convinced myself that murder's more or less out of the question.

How did Declan think it had been done? Presumably he visualized some sort of fight taking place on the southern flank of the Inner Head, out of sight of the mainland. My father admitted he had gone round the bend onto the southern flank before turning back. If Kester was waiting there, I suppose my father did just have time to kill him, toss the body into the sea and rush back to beat the tide, but it would have been a close call and is it really very likely? It seems more probable to me that if my father had killed Kester in a fight he would have been so shattered that he would have been unable to nerve himself to make a rapid retreat across the Shipway in the face of the rising tide.

But the real problem with Declan's theory is that I can't see why Kester would wait for my father to catch him up. It's hard to disagree with Evan's opinion that Kester would have had every reason to keep going.

VERDICT: *Any theory that my father killed Kester, whether accidentally or on purpose, gets bogged down in implausibilities, and I don't believe Declan could have solved the basic mystery of how and why the killing could have happened.*

Soldier on.

(Why do I keep writing that?)

XXII

I flicked back through my notes. They were a model of detachment, the conversations on the subject of my investigation reported with my own dialogue filleted from the record, my notes reflecting no emotion as they commented on the meaning of each interview. I had recorded reality and offered a gloss on that reality—and yet all the time another reality had been running parallel to this controlled careful record, the reality of an increasing involvement and mounting anxiety. "This cold inquisitorial air of yours is an act," Lance had said, and I knew now that he was right. The reality of what was going on in my mind lay not in the neat well-ordered handwriting in front of me but in the muscles which ached with tension and the knuckles which shone white as I gripped the phone.

From now on my interviews could no longer be recorded coldly as monologues. My detachment was slipping away from me and as I realized I could no longer play the neutral investigator, I felt as if I were being drawn inexorably into the black mouth of a tunnel in pursuit of two men who formed an enigma which menaced me.

However that was an absurd thought, irrational and neurotic, so I had to wipe it from my mind.

I did. I believed in the power of the will, so naturally I wiped the thought from my mind and applied myself to the task of calling my next witness.

But my knuckles still gleamed white as I gripped the phone.

"Wowee, man—great to hear you!" crowed my cousin Richard in his best midatlantic accent, and again I was amazed that so many men in early middle age were struggling to climb aboard the fashionable bandwagon of youth. Richard was nearly forty-two. He had been married twice with dire results and was now bounding around with shoulder-length blond curls, flowered shirts and flared trousers. Cushioned by the Armstrong money he had long ago decided not to waste his time earning a living, but always told inquiring strangers that he was "in investments." Con men regularly tried to fleece him but with mixed results. Although he was foolish he had a keen sense of self-preservation and had developed a certain low cunning over the years. I knew, for instance, that he kept off hard liquor and used only soft drugs.

"... and it's all happening!" he was saying breezily. "I'm just off to Paris for lunch!"

"Seems a long way to go for a hamburger. Listen, Richard, before you dive into the private jet, can I send you on a trip into the past? Like back to 1952?"

"Nineteen—my God, that's not history, that's prehistory! *Was* there a 1952?"

"You were flourishing at Oxmoon as Kester's jester."

"Not in 1952. That was when Kester died. And I only went to Oxmoon once or twice after Harry took over. There was this incredible family powwow when Declan Kinsella blew his mind—"

"Yes, I've heard about that but I want to ask you about the other guy who apparently blew his mind. Do you think Kester committed suicide?"

"Yes, in the sense that Depression was his middle name and no, in the sense that he had the plot of a terrific new book in his head and I was surprised he took the ultimate trip before committing the inspiration to paper."

Here we went with the corroboration of Evan's evidence.

"You're sure about the book, Richard?"

"Sure I'm sure! When I met him off the ferry three days before he died I saw straightaway he was sunbathing on Cloud Nine!"

"And he actually mentioned the book?"

"Yep—said he had a great new plot brewing and he hadn't felt so creative since before Thomas died."

I felt as if a routine piano sonata had been interrupted by the clash of the cymbals. I remembered writing in my notes that before I could start believing wholeheartedly in Declan's story of extortion I needed another piece of evidence that would link Thomas's death squarely with some form of neurotic or peculiar behavior on Kester's part, and this unexpected reference to Thomas's death seemed to give me a lead I couldn't ignore.

"Kester mentioned Thomas's death in the context of his work? But what a curious thing to do!"

"What's so curious? I remember all too well what dear old Kester was like in the months before Thomas died—scribble, scribble, scribble—wow, how high he got on creativity! And how we used to laugh together in the evenings once he'd finished work! He'd have me in stitches by inventing crazy plots. 'Let's play murder!' he'd say, and off we'd go with bodies in the library and Miss Snooks shooting the butler with an arrow dipped in curare—you know those fantastic Agatha Christie–type plots which everyone thinks are so cute nowadays. Kester was great at it—way out—boy, what an imagination! Jesus, the plots he dreamed up—they were fantastic, they really were!"

I felt sure this was important although at that moment there wasn't time to work out why. But instinct pushed me to pursue this line on Kester's work.

"Richard, when you met him off the ferry did he say what this new book was going to be about?"

"No, but that wasn't unusual because he never discussed his work in detail. All he did say was that he couldn't write it anywhere except at Rhossili."

This again struck me as a curious remark—and again Richard seemed to find it unremarkable. Reminding myself that he had known Kester better than I had I tried to dig a little deeper for the rational explanation.

"Wait a minute, Richard, let me recheck that statement. Did Kester actually say to you: 'I can't write this book anywhere except at Rhossili'?"

"Right on. No. Wait. Cancel that. He said something more like 'I've been inspired by the Worm's Head and I can't start to write till I get back there.'"

"Did he normally have to write in the place where he'd set his story?"

"Well, put like that it sounds crazy, but I knew what old Kester meant. He liked to write in a beautiful setting and he thought the Worm and Rhossili beach would be guaranteed to turn on the creativity taps. Poor old Kester—Lord, how I miss him! It's god-awful to think he suicided when he was so happy, but I gather that's not uncommon with depression. I had a friend like that once—one evening he was being the life and soul of the party and the next moment he'd jumped off the Eiffel Tower."

"Did Kester in fact suffer so heavily from depression?"

"Oh sure. It was because he couldn't get published. I asked Geoffrey to help him but Geoffrey just said Kester had to submit his manuscripts in the orthodox way. I think Geoffrey found it embarrassing to work for publishers and have a struggling writer in the family. . . . Incidentally, Hal, what happened to Kester's manuscripts? He left them to you in his will, didn't he?"

"Yes, but they weren't in the attics, so he must have taken them to Ireland when he left Oxmoon. My father never bothered to recall them for me—typical!—but now Declan's dead I must get in touch with Siobhan Kinsella and arrange for their return. They're probably stashed away in her own attic and she doesn't realize she has them."

"How come you yourself never bothered to recall them?"

"I couldn't face any contact with Declan."

"Well, I'm not surprised, considering how he wowed them in the High Court, but actually I always flipped over Declan Kinsella. He was a real groovy guy. . . . Hey, look, Hal, I'd better go and grab that plane, but give me a call when you're next in town and we'll freak out together, okay?"

"Richard, I've given up drugs and booze and I'm hooked on chastity. But thanks for the offer—I'll see you around," I said, and hung up as he began to bellow in horror for an explanation.

XXIV

NOTES ON RICHARD:

The suicide theory's in shreds. Kester would never have killed himself if he was on a big creative high, and I have two witnesses testifying that he was. Even if he'd suffered a manic mood swing he'd have beaten it back merely by sitting down at the typewriter.

What do I make of Richard's spontaneous linking of Thomas's death with Kester's previous period of exceptional creativity? Logically nothing. Or is there in fact some kind of logical progression going on there? Kester enjoys a period of exceptional creativity in 1949—and Thomas dies. Kester hits another period of exceptional creativity in 1952—and another death follows. But all that has to be just a coincidence. How can it be anything else? But the word "murder" keeps cropping up. Richard says Kester invented murder plots as some kind of bizarre parlor game.

Supposing...No. Not possible. Kester couldn't have dreamed up a plot to kill Thomas during a creative high—I must be going nuts even to think of such a thing. It's one thing to plot murder as a parlor game; it's quite another to plot murder and act out the plot. If Kester behaved like that he'd be a certifiable lunatic; but he wasn't.

Yet just what the hell was Kester up to? And who was Kester anyway? An artist, a man of peace? A killer, a man of violence? A hero, a villain, a lunatic? A saint, a magician, a fraud?

Stop. I'm getting irrational and—worse still—emotional. I must believe only what is proven and avoid this sort of melodramatic speculation like the plague.

Soldier—No, not "soldier on." I can't flog myself along with that phrase any longer, not now, I must pause, I must rest. I've gone a little too far, a little too fast, and it's time to fall back and retrench.

VERDICT: *Richard provided my most disturbing interview yet. But what does his evidence really mean? There was some sort of revelation going on there, but was the revelation truth or fantasy? And Kester's slipped right out of focus. I can't see him clearly at all.*

XXV

I left some money to pay for the phone calls but I rejected the idea of relaxing for an hour at the nearby beach to soothe my nerves. I drove back to Oxmoon because it was lunchtime and although I wasn't hungry I thought eggs and bacon would have a beneficial effect on my psyche. Protein was good for the brain.

Parking the car in the stable yard I walked into the scullery and picked up the matches to light the Primus but then I paused. The tap was dripping in the main sink and suddenly I remembered the tap dripping at Aunt Eleanor's flat when she had talked of my parents.

Four small boys, constant money worries and a wife who couldn't cope with any of them.

I went on standing there with the matches in my hand, and gradually I knew I'd never be able to eat. I was too distressed. I thought of my father struggling in the dark, I saw Kester coruscating in the light and for the first time in my life my magician seemed sinister to me.

The truth shifted focus, reality altered its course and the cherished certainties of childhood began to disintegrate. A dark unnamable emotion gnawed at my consciousness, and as I saw the rack of my ordeal defined at last I knew it could tear me apart. Kester was on one side of the rack, my father was on the other and I was impaled between them.

I tried to wipe my mind clean again by the usual exercise of my will, but this time nothing happened and I was still struggling with the image of that rack when I heard the knock on the door.

Immediately I guessed that Pam had come to invite me to lunch but Pam was the last person I wanted to see at that moment. I didn't want to be placed in deep analysis as soon as my distress became obvious to her. I tried to drum up an excuse for escape.

The knock sounded again on the door.

Gritting my teeth I got up and flung the door wide, but the moment I did so I realized that Pam wasn't after all the last person on earth I wanted to see. The very last person I wanted to see now stood revealed on the threshold and I knew at once that no escape was possible.

"Forgive me for interrupting you," said my father, "but I just wanted to make sure you were all right."

4

I

"I'M FINE," I said to my father. I abandoned the Primus, picked up the saucepan and moved to the sink. That gave me time to compose myself. "And you?"

"Oh, I'm all right." His eyes were red-rimmed with tiredness. Above the beard his face was grayish-white, and suddenly I had a picture of myself, equally pale, equally tense, partnering him in this dialogue of noncommunication. I searched for the words to pull the scene together but before I could find them he added, trying to be cheerful: "No problem crossing the yard today" and glanced back at the open space which so often frightened him.

"Well, now that you've crossed it," I said, trying not to imagine the state of mind that had driven him to conquer his phobia, "have some coffee." I somehow got the Primus alight.

"No, thanks. I was really just wondering how you were getting on."

"Not too badly."

"Ah."

There was a pause. I looked at him and for the first time saw the wall between us, the cruel wall conjured up by my magician.

I grabbed the words to smash it. "Tell me about her."

"*Her*? Who?"

"My mother."

"Your mother? But what's that got to do with Kester?"

"Absolutely nothing. But I don't want to talk about Kester, not now, not at this particular moment. I want to talk about my mother. We've never talked about her either, have we? We never talk about anything. What was she like to be married to?"

He stared. Then he pushed back his hair, scratched his neck and groped for a cigarette. At last he said carefully, "She loved me. I was lucky to have her."

"No, no, I'm not interested in sentimental platitudes. Tell me what it was like for you, an intelligent cultivated man, to be married to a girl who never opened a book, couldn't tell Mozart from Beethoven and had an emotional age of thirteen."

"Who says your mother had an emotional age of thirteen?"

"Eleanor. Isn't it true?"

"I'm not saying one word against your mother."

"Why? Because you're afraid of upsetting me?"

"Because to me she meant something very special."

"What was it? Come on, for Christ's sake, wake up, look at me, I'm grown up, I'm not a child anymore and I've got a bloody right to know how I came to be in the world. Why did you marry her?"

"Sex."

"That all?"

"More or less."

"How much more and how much less?"

"My God, what an inquisitor you are!" cried my father, rubbing his forehead fiercely with his hand. "You're like a bloody tank!"

"I need to be a bloody tank to get through to you. Now sit down and tell me what was going on. Why did my mother have this obsession with reproduction? My mother had four sons who all loved her, so why wasn't she satisfied with us? What went wrong?"

"She wanted a daughter."

"Yes, but—"

"We had a daughter but it died."

In the pause that followed I turned off the Primus and emptied the saucepan of water into the sink. Then I moved back to the table.

"When?"

"Long before we were married. It was all hushed up. Bella was neglected; no one really cared about her. I was very unhappy because Bronwen had left. It was... well, I suppose it was a tragedy, although tragedy's such an overworked word it hardly seems worth using, but whatever it was we never got over it. We were both haunted by a compulsion to put right what had gone wrong. I found I had to marry her. She found she had to bring Melody back."

"Melody?"

"The baby. Bella called her Melody because she knew I was so fond of music."

I thought of my mother. I could just picture her saying ingenuously to my father: "I called her Melody because I knew you were so fond of music." I suddenly found I had to sit down.

"She did love you boys," said my father, "but she idealized that dead child. My God, if only you knew how I came to hate that pathetic banal name—even today, if I listen to a talk on music and hear the word 'melody,' I find myself cringing with horror—"

"But this must have been a nightmare."

"Yes. It was. I'm afraid we didn't make each other very happy, and afterwards, when she died, I thought I'd go mad with guilt. However at least I could try to do my best for you children. That made me feel better. Of course I made a complete hash of fatherhood, but—"

"You never thought of walking out?"

My father looked shocked. "Oh, I couldn't possibly have done that. You were all so young, you depended on me. Fathers can't go around palming off their children on someone else and disappearing into the blue."

"But they can," I said. "They can and they do. They do it every day."

We stared at each other.

"Well, I suppose that's true," said my father at last. He sounded confused. "But I never considered that such an option was open to me."

I thought of him sticking it out when he could have walked out. I thought of him doing his best when he could have done his worst. No child had the right to ask more of a parent than that.

"I wonder what I would have done if I'd been in your shoes," I said, "but on second thoughts I'd prefer not to think. I've spent so much time running away from my problems. Probably I'd have run away from that one too." I got up. "I must be off. I've planned to spend the afternoon in Swansea."

"Doing what?" called my father sharply as I opened the door.

"Rereading the report of the inquest," I said, and escaped into the yard to my car.

II

Notes on my father:

So Eleanor was right. My father was the war hero whose heroism really began when he came home from the war. So was Eleanor also right about Kester? Not necessarily. The point about Eleanor is probably not that she was a hundred percent right but that she was a hundred percent certain which side she was on.

However, competent investigators don't take sides. They stick to the facts and don't get emotionally involved.

But the most important fact to me at the moment is that some people suspect my father of murder, and I'm involved enough to know I have to acquit him once and for all.

III

I drove out of the car park among the sand burrows of Llangennith where I had been scribbling my disjointed note, and headed finally for Swansea. I spent the drive thinking of my mother. I could remember her hugging us, playing with us, giggling with us, spoiling us. Yet all the time she had been yearning for that dead child. "But I love you all just the same, darling!" Of course. We were all the same to her because her favorite was the child who had been lost.

That knowledge didn't destroy the past; I knew I would continue to love the mother I remembered. But it put the past in a radically different focus. I could see my mother now as a troubled woman, someone who had made my father unhappy, and in his unhappiness I saw the genesis of the bleak home which had driven me to my magician.

Just as Kester had slipped out of focus, so I could now see my father with unprecedented clarity. Memories flickered through my mind in kaleidoscopic patterns. I saw my father in uniform, in work clothes, in evening dress, in lounge suits, sportswear and pajamas; I saw him shouting, smiling, cursing, laughing, sane and insane, calm and hysterical, whole and destroyed; I saw the stranger I had never cared to know.

I thought of him seated at the piano. I was musical but my talent was a mere shadow of my father's. My father was an artist. I could remember him saying to me after playing the piano in the ballroom at Oxmoon: "I love to play the piano here and think of Beauty, Truth, Art and Peace. . . ."

But now my memory was playing tricks. My father had never spoken Kester's famous slogan. Or had he? How hard it was to be sure. The two of them seemed to be merging in my mind, and suddenly as I remembered Evan talking of metaphysical phenomena I felt the darkness which had no name. It was very heavy and it was bunched on my back. I could feel the weight on my spine. It was making me breathless. I had to stop the car. I was on the outskirts of the city by that time and as I drew the car into a parking area, I found myself beside a promenade of suburban shops. Women wandered around with shopping bags and pushchairs. Children screamed. A dog was running around lifting his leg against every lamppost. I saw normality but I was outside it and at once I knew I had to get in.

I went into the nearby newsagent's shop and bought some chewing gum. That made me feel better. I was back inside a normal world again, chewing gum and checking the gauge on the dashboard to see if the car needed petrol. So what was the explanation of that moment of horror I had just experienced? Diagnosing a bout of irrational panic I told myself severely: "Nerves. Stress. Pull yourself together at once." And closing my mind resolutely against the incident, I drove on to the city center and headed for the newspaper files in the library.

IV

CORONER: I assume the deceased had been in touch with you, Mr. Morgan, about the kitchen tap which needed a new washer.

MORGAN: No, sir. Mr. Richard Godwin reported the dripping tap to my stepbrother. Mr. Richard had met Mr. Kester off the ferry and taken him to the cottage in Rhossili.

CORONER: But you were responsible for the maintenance of the cottage—why did you let three days elapse before you attended to the problem?

MORGAN: I didn't have a washer among my supplies and I knew I'd have to go to Swansea to get one. I was going there later that week to see my mother so Harry said it would be okay if I waited till then. The problem wasn't urgent.

CORONER: I see. So you did the job directly after your visit to your mother. Did you warn the deceased that you'd be coming out to the cottage that evening?

MORGAN: No, sir. The cottage has no phone.

CORONER: Might it not have been more convenient for the deceased if you'd waited till morning before arriving unannounced?

MORGAN: Oh no, sir. Mr. Kester would be working at his writing in the mornings. I knew the evening would be the best time.

CORONER: Very well. Now, you had a lift, I understand, from your mother's house to the cottage. What time did you arrive?

MORGAN: Around eight twenty. Maybe eight twenty-five.

CORONER: And what exactly did you do on arrival?

MORGAN: I got my toolbox out of the garage, went into the kitchen and set to work.

CORONER: And what time did your stepbrother come in?

MORGAN: Soon afterwards. Perhaps five minutes later.

CORONER: Now, Mr. Morgan, can you tell us, please, what happened when your stepbrother arrived?

MORGAN: He said to me that Mr. Kester had marooned himself on the Worm. I could see he was worried. Mr. Kester's health wasn't good and Harry was afraid that this latest behavior might mean Mr. Kester was off his rocker again.

CORONER: What was the story as you understood it?

MORGAN: Harry had seen Mr. Kester crossing the Shipway. Harry knew from the Coastguard's board that the tide was on the rise and he thought that going out to the Worm at that time was the oddest thing to do. So he decided to go after him and make sure he was all right. But he never caught him up and finally he had to turn back to beat the tide.

CORONER: And what was your opinion of the deceased's behavior, Mr. Morgan?

MORGAN: Off his rocker, sir. He'd just spent the past few months having another of his nervous breakdowns, and it was well known he acted peculiar at times.

CORONER: All right. Now, what happened after your stepbrother told you what had been going on?

MORGAN: I finished changing the washer. Then Harry and I sat talking for a while in the living room. I was trying to reassure him, but he decided to stay on at the cottage to make sure Mr. Kester returned safely at dawn. I saw that this was the best way to put his mind at rest so I didn't argue. At around nine I packed up my tools, put them back in the garage and left.

CORONER: And after that?

MORGAN: Harry came back to Oxmoon at dawn, woke me up and said there was still no sign of Mr. Kester. I went back with him to Rhossili and when we found the cottage was still empty we went to the Coastguard.

CORONER: Thank you, Mr. Morgan.

V

NOTES ON DAFYDD:

The story's very convincing, right down to the explanation of why he called to do the job in the evening and not the morning. Small wonder that Declan thought he'd never be able to crack the alibi and decided instead to incorporate it in his theory.

How does one bust an alibi that's as unbustable as that? Of course, it's possible that Dafydd's visit to the cottage was just my father's lucky break, but how does one prove that my father was never there when Dafydd says he was? One turns up a witness who saw my father stagger back at dawn the next morning—but obviously the police failed to do this, so that's a dead end. Or alternatively one turns up some other detail which shows that my father was never at the cottage that night, but how does one ever do that? That has to be a dead end too.

VERDICT: *Dafydd's evidence means I'm driven to follow in Declan's footsteps: I can't get around that alibi, since there's no indication whatsoever that it was faked, so I now have to see if there's any evidence to support Declan's theory that my father killed Kester, beat the tide and got back to the cottage in time to meet Dafydd. This means that once again I have to ask myself, just as Declan must have done: What really did happen when my father reached the Inner Head that night?*

VI

CORONER: Very well, Mr. Godwin, there you were on the Inner Head. What happened next?

GODWIN: I paused for about a minute, not only to recover my breath—that Shipway's a terrible haul—but because I was convinced that Kester would be coming into view at any moment to begin the journey back to the mainland. I just couldn't believe he'd want to be cut off. However when there was no sign of him returning I couldn't stand the suspense so I took the path around the bend onto the southern flank of the Inner Head. The time was running out but I still had a few minutes to try and discover what on earth he was doing.

CORONER: May I direct the jury to look at their Ordnance Survey maps of the Worm's Head. Thank you. Yes, Mr. Godwin.

GODWIN: I came round the bend onto the southern flank. At that point the ground rises, but when you reach the top of the slope you can see a long way. The Worm isn't straight and there were parts which remained hidden but I could see down to the Devil's Bridge in the distance and beyond it to the Outer Head.

CORONER: Did you see your cousin?

GODWIN: Yes, and as soon as I saw him I realized I'd misjudged the situation because quite obviously he wanted to be cut off by the tide. He was on the Middle Head, not far from the Devil's Bridge. It was difficult to estimate distances in that empty landscape but he seemed even farther away from me than before.

CORONER: Why was this, do you think?

GODWIN: I'd dithered on the Shipway. Several times I'd stopped to debate with myself whether to go on or not.

CORONER: I see. Very well, he was a long way away and clearly it was going to be impossible for you to catch him up. What was your reaction when you realized this?

GODWIN: I dithered again. I was extremely worried about him but at the same time my heart sank at the prospect of spending the night on the Worm. It was a mild evening but temperatures can fall rapidly on a spring night and the pullover I was wearing was a thin one.

CORONER: I see. So—

GODWIN: So with considerable reluctance I turned back. Later, of course, I wished I'd gone on, but at the time it seemed the sensible thing to do.

CORONER: I'm sure we all know how easy it is to be wise after the event. Now, Mr. Godwin, there's one aspect of your evidence which I'd be grateful if you would clarify for me. You say you were worried about the deceased and certainly your behavior would indicate grave anxiety. But were you actually on close terms with your cousin? There seems to be some sort of discrepancy here.

GODWIN: I'm glad you've brought that up, sir, because I was hoping I'd have the chance to set the record straight and explain exactly what was going on in my mind. My cousin and I were not close. In fact our mutual dislike was notorious. But that was precisely why I became so concerned when I witnessed his bizarre behavior and started wondering if he was planning suicide. I knew that if Kester died in obscure circumstances there were people who'd say I'd killed him, and I foresaw a scandal of catastrophic dimensions. In those circumstances I felt I couldn't rest until I knew he was safely home again and that was why, when I returned to the cottage, I felt driven to stay there to wait for him.

CORONER: But after your return to the cottage, you would have realized surely that Mr. Morgan was in a position to give you an alibi.

GODWIN: Oh yes, I knew the police would work everything out correctly but I wasn't worried about the police—I was worried about my enemies who would fasten on the fact that Kester and I went out to the Worm together and only one of us came back. Let me explain further by saying I've always had a horror of virulent gossip. When I was a child, my father was the center of a scandal—a scandal of quite a different nature, I admit; but I knew what it was to suffer daily as the result of gossip and I didn't want my children going through what I went through.

891

CORONER: I understand. Yes, that certainly clarifies your state of mind. Thank you, Mr. Godwin. Very well, let's proceed. You returned across the Shipway—

GODWIN: Yes, and by the time I reached the mainland the Shipway was beginning to go under. I was feeling done in, but I didn't rest—I decided to push on back to the cottage where I knew Kester had something to drink. When I arrived I found my stepbrother Dafydd Morgan changing the washer in the kitchen. I told him what had happened. We sat in the living room for a while as I drank some scotch. He suggested I come back with him to Oxmoon but I felt I couldn't. He left. I didn't notice the time. Then I sat up hour after hour in the living room. I did doze around two but I woke at dawn and resumed the wait. He never came. Finally I was so concerned that I went back to Oxmoon to consult Dafydd and together we went to the Coastguard.

CORONER: Yes. Now, Mr. Godwin, when you were waiting all those hours, did you stumble across any clue about why your cousin had asked to see you?

GODWIN: No, sir, I didn't.

CORONER: What then is your final explanation of that note he wrote you? It seems to me very odd that he should ask you over for a drink when you weren't on good terms.

GODWIN: Oh, not at all, sir, not a bit of it. Kester was doing the done thing, I understood that at once. We might have been on bad terms but of course we considered we had a duty to maintain a reasonably civilized standard of behavior towards each other. After all, we were both gentlemen.

CORONER: Of course, of course, but nevertheless—

GODWIN: I'd lent Kester my cottage, sir. I'd done him a favor and so of course I knew he'd feel obliged to offer me the courtesy of a drink in return.

CORONER: Yes, but did he actually ask you to visit him that evening?

GODWIN: No, it was just a casual invitation but I knew I'd have to accept it so I thought I'd go and get it over as soon as possible.

CORONER: So it was entirely a courtesy—there was no specific business he wanted to discuss?

GODWIN: As far as I know, sir, that's true. But since we never met it's impossible for me to be entirely certain.

CORONER: Quite. Now just one last question on this point: why did you throw away your cousin's note?

GODWIN: It never occurred to me not to. It was just a casual line of invitation. I read it and chucked it into the wastepaper basket, just as I would a circular. My desk was much too cluttered with important correspondence to encourage me to keep trivialities.

CORONER: Yes, of course. But how do you explain the fact that the note didn't turn up when the police sifted the Oxmoon rubbish?

GODWIN: Obviously one of the servants tipped the wastepaper from that basket into the kitchen range instead of putting it out into the paper-salvage dustbin, and afterwards whoever it was didn't like to own up. I'd given innumerable lectures to my servants, sir, on the subject of our patriotic duty not to waste paper.

CORONER: Yes, I must confess I've had similar problems with my own servants about that in the past. . . . Now, Mr. Godwin, we'll turn back, if we may, to your journey out across the Shipway from the mainland to the Inner Head, because there's one point I'd like to get absolutely clear. Are you quite sure that your cousin was unaware you were following him?

GODWIN: I'd swear he never looked back.

CORONER: You never wondered, for example, if he might be under the impression you were chasing him?

GODWIN: That did occur to me, of course—when I was racking my brains to make sense of his behavior I did ask myself if he was simply running away, but all I can tell you is that he gave no sign of panicking. He made no attempt, for instance, to quicken his pace and I'm quite positive he never looked back over his shoulder.

CORONER: What did you make of this?

GODWIN: I was wholly puzzled. That was one of the reasons why I kept following him. He was moving like a man in a dream. It was all most bizarre.

CORONER: Bearing in mind the extremely spectacular nature of the scenery, isn't it very unlikely that he never paused to look around him?

GODWIN: Very unlikely, yes, but I was watching him very closely and although the lie of the rocks on the Shipway occasionally prevented me from seeing him, I never once saw him look back when he was within my field of vision.

CORONER: Most bizarre, yes; very strange behavior indeed. I can quite see why you were perturbed. Very well, Mr. Godwin—thank you, you've been most helpful.

VII

NOTES ON MY FATHER'S EVIDENCE AT THE INQUEST: *It seems even more of a tour de force than I remembered. I suppose now I'm older I can better understand how brilliantly plausible he must have been, talking of doing the done thing and adopting a martyred air about his servants. This was 1952 and despite the war, class and privilege were still capable of dazzling everyone in sight.*

He certainly had an answer for everything, and what answers they were! Each one fitted so smoothly into his story and sounded so rational, so right. Is there any part of his evidence that could be a lie? Yes, of course, but how does one start to separate fact from fiction when they're woven together with such skill as that? Lance said that the really consummate liars of this world always use the truth as far as they possibly can, but he was talking about Kester, spinning yarns for Declan. It seems unfair to suspect my father of being a consummate liar just because he was so brilliantly plausible in the witness box, but I know why that thought's crossing my mind—and not just crossing my mind; it's scaring me shitless. Now that I'm seeing my father as the hero of this story the ultimate nightmare would be if I proved that my father was the one telling lies while Declan was the one telling the truth. I'm a long way now from those days when I could dismiss Declan's stories out of hand and refuse to think about them. I now see more clearly than ever that if I'm to have any peace of mind I've got to explode his murder theory—but to explode it I must first understand why he reached his conclusions.

And this is where my father's evidence is unexpectedly helpful. I'd forgotten how positive he was that Kester had never looked back, but of course in the light of that testimony I can now see why Declan became so convinced that my father could have beaten the tide by achieving a quick murder on the Inner Head. If Kester really didn't know my father was behind him then he might well have sat down and enjoyed the scenery once he reached that southern flank. It was a clear evening. Perhaps North Devon and Lundy Island would have been visible. In fact I can easily see Kester sitting down to recover from the Shipway, enjoy the sunset and savor the stupendous view. If he thought he was quite alone this would be the natural thing do do.

I still think my father would have been hard-pressed to kill him and get back over the Shipway in time, but I have to concede it's technically possible. I'll have to go out to the Worm, there's no getting away from it. I'll have to stage a reconstruction just as Declan and Rory did.

Bearing Declan's theory in mind, the big question now becomes this: Is it really possible that Kester never looked back? I remember Evan thinking this was so unlikely that he had no trouble constructing his own theory on the premise that my father had been mistaken. And Evan's not alone here; the coroner thought it was unlikely; my father thought it was unlikely; I think it's unlikely. But why on earth should my father lie on this point? In fact it would help his story more if he said Kester was looking back repeatedly and behaving like a man on the run—then my father could have said, "It became obvious that I hadn't a hope of catching him up," and his decision to turn back would have seemed more logical than ever.

If my father was mixing fact and fiction, this seems to have been one of the occasions when he thought to himself: "The truth here can't hurt me; it supports my story that Kester was behaving oddly, so why not sling it in and give the jury food for thought?"

But if my father is indeed telling the truth about this, what does it mean? Why did Kester never look back? Can one really explain his behavior, as Evan did, by saying he was on a creative high?

VERDICT: The coroner was right. My father was right. The entire incident's very bizarre.

VIII

It was five o'clock. Since I'd skipped lunch, I knew I should eat so I found a café by Victoria Station and ordered baked beans on toast and a glass of milk. It was quarter to six when I left the city and quarter to seven when I reached the car park on top of the cliffs at Rhossili. The rush-hour traffic had been heavy and the journey had taken longer than usual.

Rhossili Bay lay ahead of me, a vast arc of sand below the cliffs and the unspoiled Downs. The sea, reflecting the sky, had a grayish cast. Leaving the car park, I walked past the hotel to the end of the road and moved down the track to the three cottages that belonged to the Coastguard.

One of the coastguards was pottering around his garden. In answer to my inquiry he told me that low water would be around twelve thirty in the afternoon on the following day, and the Shipway would be passable at ten.

I walked out to the tip of the headland and twenty minutes later I was standing on the edge of the cliffs that faced the Worm. The Shipway was a whirlpool of waves shot with angry flecks of foam. The three humps of the Inner, Middle and Outer Heads, ringed with white water, rose from the sea like a monster; I could clearly see how the Worm had earned its name which had once meant "the Dragon," and as I stood there, Saint George on a cliff top, I felt as if I were contemplating the ordeal that would make me a legend. All I needed now to complete the myth was the maiden and in less than an hour's time Gwyneth Llewellyn was due to keep her appointment with me in Penhale churchyard.

Not even Saint George could have asked for more.

I retraced my steps to the car.

IX

The lych-gate creaked beneath my hand. I walked up the path to the church. Here was old, old age indeed, weathered stones, ancient glass, enduring slate—all representing a profound peace which mocked the vapid transience of twentieth-century values. This church had seen many fashions come and go and had outlived all of them. The ideology it represented was a closed book to me but I respected its permanence.

Glancing up at the tower I remembered how Kester had donated the money to have the clock restored. He had arranged for a new chime, melodious and discreet, and the villagers, who for decades had been battered by the clanking of the old chimes, had been well pleased.

It was almost eight o'clock. I looked in the porch. There was no sign of her but when I moved around the tower I saw her at once by the Godwin graves. She was sitting by Kester's tombstone and tugging at the grass with abrupt restless movements of her fingers. Her long brown hair, dead straight, fell like a curtain so that I could barely see her profile but as I moved towards her she looked up.

I saw the face I remembered. She sprang to her feet but I came to a halt, and above us, far above us in the belfry, the church clock began to whisper the hour.

X

"Hi."

"Hi."

"Do we shake hands or just smile at each other?"

"Neither," she said in a voice I didn't remember. Three years up at Oxford had eliminated all trace of her Welsh accent. "I see no point in formality and I'm not in the mood for simpering. What a very arrogant message you sent me! I suppose you're used to women rushing to meet you whenever you toss out a summons!"

"I wanted to see you and I thought you'd want to see me—and here you are so I was right. How come you're so uptight? I'm not interested in making it with you—I got over all that when I was sixteen."

"Super," she said drily. "Well done."

We moved past Kester's grave to the iron bench beneath the ancient yew tree.

"Are the flowers from you?"

She shook her head. "No, but there are often flowers on his grave nowadays— he seems to have become rather a cult figure. The older people regard him as a symbol of the good old days when everyone kept their hair short and went to church on Sunday, and the younger people think of him as a real cool guy who did his own thing."

"Kester would have been tickled pink!"

"My God, yes, I believe he would!" she said, and the next moment we were both laughing.

Then we paused and took a long look at each other. I saw a woman of twenty-six, very much shorter than I was. I'm six feet two. She was no more than five feet three. She had a rich heavy curving body which she had penned up in a prim navy-blue dress with a starched white collar. Her lower lip was full but the thin line of her upper lip held it resolutely in a straight uncompromising line. She had a square pugnacious chin and a high wide intelligent forehead below the center parting of her hair. Her eyes were bright blue, just like my grandfather's, and this eerie resemblance to one of my own relatives reminded me of the nineteenth-century connection between the Llewellyns and the Godwins. My great-great-grandfather had married her great-great-great-aunt. Kester had drawn up an elaborate family tree to show that we were fourth cousins.

It was a long time since we had last met.

After Kester died various circumstances had combined to drive us gradually apart. I was away for most of the year at school; we were both on the verge of adolescence with all its accompanying constraints; perhaps most important of all we each reminded the other of Kester and as time passed we came to shun the pain of remembering him.

Then when I was fifteen and she was a few months younger we had met by chance in Swansea. I had recently been expelled from Harrow, and my father had found a tutor in Swansea who was trying to prepare me for my O-levels. I used to meet Gwyneth in a coffee bar every afternoon when she finished school.

When we discovered how much we were still haunted by Kester we had decided to look up the report of the inquest in an attempt to face the facts of his death squarely. Singly we had never been able to drum up the courage to do this, but together we had given each other the strength.

Because of its sensational nature the inquest had been reported with exceptional fullness in the local press and we read every word we could find. By this time, three years after Kester's death, the public had almost forgotten the tactful verdict of the coroner's jury that Kester had died by accident and it was the firm opinion not only of the majority of my family but of hers that Kester had committed suicide. Consequently neither Gwyneth nor I seriously queried that he had killed himself. We regarded it as unarguable, and although we noted Evan's evidence of euphoria we discarded it. Gwyneth thought Kester had been happy because he had come back to Gower in order to die in surroundings of great beauty and peace. I just thought he had been putting on an act so that Evan wouldn't worry about him. Neither of us believed that Kester had been on the brink of beginning a new book. "He never mentioned it to me," said Gwyneth, who had seen him on the morning of his death. "Obviously it was just something he invented to make sure everyone thought he was normal." We both assumed that the loss of Oxmoon had been responsible for his suicide. We told each other that without Oxmoon and Anna he would have been unable to write or to see any purpose in continuing to live.

This resurrection of our mutual grief drew us still closer together, and I began to see her at weekends. Not being a virgin I was soon sure what I wanted. Being a virgin she wasn't so sure as I was. In the end, as we were struggling together in a time-honored fashion in the nearest haystack, she lost her temper and screamed, "Leave me alone—you'll never measure up to Kester!" and that was that. Jasper Llewellyn arrived on the scene seconds later but by that time it was all over.

Later she wrote: *I'd like to be friends with you but you make it impossible. Why can't you be more like Kester? He was sensible about sex—he just regarded it as something married people do and I'm quite sure he would never have let it spoil a perfect friendship. If you can measure up to Kester, then I want to know you. If you can't I'd rather we didn't meet again.*

I never wrote back. We never met again.

She did well at school and won a place at Oxford to read English. Kester would have been proud of her. When she had her degree she spent a year acquiring a teacher's diploma, and that was the last I heard of her before little Caitlin told me of the job in the big private girls' school in Swansea.

"I hear you're a huge success," she said as we sat down together on the bench beneath the yew tree. "I can't stand that kind of music myself, but I'm glad you're doing well."

"I'm not doing well. And I'm not a success. But things are going to change," I said, and I began to talk of my past and my present.

She kept a sizable space between us on the bench as she listened, her legs firmly crossed, her hands folded primly in her lap. Here indeed was the maiden of myth, a virgin bound to the stake of chastity and guarded by the magic dragon of the past.

The urge to play Saint George stole over me again. To combat it I too crossed one leg over the other and folded my hands primly in my lap. My jeans began to feel as close-fitting as a second skin.

"...and so there it is," I heard myself say at last. "I've quit on drugs, booze and sex and I'm living like a hermit at Oxmoon while pursuing a career as Sherlock Holmes."

"Wonderful," she said. "Women go mad over reformed rakes. You'll soon be besieged—probably much to your relief."

"Well, at least I don't have to worry about you, do I? Or are you making it with six different guys on the grand scale?"

"Mind your own business." She got up and wandered towards Kester's grave. That meant no. I followed her. "Gwyneth—"

"Oh Hal," she said, suddenly dropping her defenses as she swung to face me, "how I wish I could help you!"

"What do you mean? Why do you say it like that?"

We stood by his grave and stared at each other.

"Do you think I haven't tried to prove to myself it was an accident?" she said. "Do you think I haven't been where you are now?" Tears suddenly sprang to her eyes.

"You mean—"

"It was suicide," she said. "He really did kill himself. I know he did. I know it."

XI

"It all began," said Gwyneth, "when I went up to Oxford and met this man who said I was hung up on sex. I wasn't sure he was right, but because I liked him very much I found myself being forced to think hard again about Kester, and that was the first time I'd made a serious adult attempt to analyze my feelings for him. I knew I loved him very much but since I was nineteen by that time and not stupid I had to acknowledge that my feelings were very far from unambivalent. I felt he'd betrayed me by committing suicide, and as soon as I'd faced up to the anger I felt I wondered if I'd been subconsciously venting my resentment on all the men I'd met since his death.

"Well, this amateur psychology was all very well, but just sitting around thinking wasn't going to cure me and I knew I had to do something constructive. That was when I made up my mind to prove that Kester hadn't committed suicide; like you I felt that once I'd proved he'd died by accident I wouldn't have to be so angry with him anymore.

"So the next time I came home to Gower I roped in my brother Trevor and we went off to the Worm together. What I wanted to prove was that it was possible for Kester to have fallen into the sea by accident, but Hal, we spent the whole five hours between tides crawling over that bloody peninsula and we both agreed afterwards that the possibility just didn't exist. Kester wasn't athletic. He wouldn't have taken any risks. There are only three places where an accident of that kind might have happened: first there's that rough stretch between the Inner and Middle Heads, but I'm sure he would have kept clear of the edge that falls sheer to the sea; second there's the Devil's Bridge, and third there's the blowhole on the Outer Head, but I can't see him falling down the blowhole which is such a famous hazard. In fact I can't see him ever getting as far as the Outer Head because I can't see him making the effort to cross the Devil's Bridge.

"You know the Bridge. There's basically nothing dangerous about it—it's wider than it looks from a distance—but it's a nightmare to anyone who's afraid of vertigo and Kester wasn't keen on heights. I know he did cross the Bridge on our expeditions to the Worm, but it was an effort he made to show us we didn't need to be afraid, and I think if he'd been on his own he wouldn't have bothered. And even if he had bothered I can't see him suffering such an attack of vertigo that he reeled into the abyss. As a matter of fact, I don't think he'd ever actually had an attack of vertigo. His dislike of heights was debilitating but not disabling."

She stopped talking. A few yards away the flowers on Kester's grave trembled in the faint breeze.

I thought of Evan's theory which I had found so plausible but all I said was "And the Shipway?"

She looked at me in surprise. "Oh, but we know he couldn't have drowned there! Why, I don't believe I ever raised the possibility with you when we read the inquest report—I just assumed we both knew a disaster on the Shipway was quite out of the question!"

I could feel the palms of my hands sweating as I clenched my fists. "But is it?"

"Of course! Hal, Kester would never, never have made a mistake about the Shipway. For God's sake, don't you remember? He crossed it, recrossed it, photographed it, mapped it and watched it sink over and over again when he was writing that novel about Gwyneth Godwin and Owain Bryn-Davies. Kester was the world's expert on the Shipway. He could have seen at a glance exactly when it was due to go under."

XII

There was a silence. Then I said, "Well, I suppose all investigators have their blind spots and that was certainly mine." I groped for my notebook, found a clean page and wrote: NO ACCIDENT. While I was writing my voice said, "But of course you can't rule out the possibility of a freak wave."

"That's true. But I'm afraid I'm not very good at believing in freak waves, especially as Kester would never have risked crossing the Shipway until it was quite safe."

"I'm not very good at believing in suicide. Listen, Gwyneth. Both Evan and Richard are certain that Kester either had begun or was about to begin a brand-new book. Now, can you honestly see Kester committing suicide when he was on a big creative high?"

She was silent, and as I realized there was something she wasn't telling me I felt the dread tighten my muscles once more. Her striking face with its powerful sensual mouth was in shadow. She looked away.

"Tell me again," I said at last, "exactly what happened when you called at the cottage on the morning of his death."

Still she was silent. Then she made an effort and turned to face me.

"I thought I could wait till the weekend to see him but I couldn't. I cut school and cycled over to Rhossili. I wondered if he'd be working but he wasn't—he was about to go out for a walk. He seemed pleased to see me, but at the same time he was preoccupied and finally he tried to leave. I wanted to go with him on the walk but he said as nicely as possible that he had a lot on his mind and he wanted to be alone to think. I got a bit upset... stupid of me... I suppose I was in rather an emotional state; it was just so wonderful to see him again and I couldn't bear it when he seemed to be brushing me off.... Then he—well, he was nice. He stayed a little longer after all and when I was better he gave me some chocolate and told me to come back at the weekend with Trevor.

"I asked him if he'd be working in the morning and he said, 'Oh no, there's no question of that,' and that was when I got the impression he had no literary plans at that time. I remember noticing he hadn't taken the cover off his typewriter.

"Then I asked him if I could come alone without Trevor but he said, 'I think a group's more fun, don't you?' and so I had to tell him that I didn't think Trevor would come as my parents didn't want us to see him—Kester—anymore. He was very upset by that. It was awful. He said, 'Why? What are they getting at?' and then I became upset again too because of course I couldn't tell him they thought he was mentally unstable. But I flung my arms around him and I kissed him and I said, 'I trust you and I love you,' and I showed him the locket he'd given me, Anna's locket, and I said, 'I wear this every day in memory of you,' and then..." She stopped.

Nothing happened. The churchyard was still. I didn't move. She didn't move. I didn't breathe. She didn't breathe. Time was suspended for a long moment before she said rapidly: "It was frightful. He pushed me away from him and burst into tears."

I breathed again. So did she. To beat back the nausea I concentrated on saying: "You never told me that before."

"No. Well, it's not really the sort of thing one reveals easily, is it? Kester was our hero. Heroes don't burst into tears when little girls of twelve declare their undying love."

"Right. What happened next?"

"He pulled himself together, apologized, had a shot of scotch and said he was under great strain but he'd be better soon. Then he said he really did want to go for his walk and so we parted. By that time I was glad to escape. He'd rather frightened me."

We went on sitting there. I tried to imagine the note I was going to have to write but my mind went blank.

"He was a good decent man," said Gwyneth at last. "It was all right. But—"

"Yes?"

"—but I think he was a bit unbalanced. Now that I'm an adult I can see that. He lived in a fantasy world, didn't he, writing his books, playing with us children ... and who's to say where fantasy ended and reality began? Did he say he had a new book to write? Maybe that was just to impress people. Did he act as if he were on a big creative high? Maybe he was just striking a bold pose. I saw no high and heard about no book. All I remember now are the tears." She swallowed. It took her a moment to go on but finally she said: "I think he'd reached the end of the road and somehow I was the last straw. You know we said to each other that we couldn't think of one good reason why he would have left us? Well, I can think of a good reason now why he might have chosen to leave me. I think he loved me and was terrified he might do something wrong. I think he killed himself to protect me. It was suicide, Hal, I just know it was suicide ..." And she broke down and began to cry.

XIII

"I don't believe it," I said, but I remembered Pam talking of the suicidal motive which she had refused to divulge. I put my arm around Gwyneth. She stiffened. I withdrew. I didn't have a handkerchief to offer her so I just sat there helplessly while she wiped her eyes with the back of her hand.

"I just don't believe it," I said, "and you mustn't believe it either."

"Oh, if only you could persuade me—"

"Okay, let me try." I was appalled to think she had been secretly blaming herself for years for Kester's death. I saw clearly now that she was shackled by guilt to his memory and I knew I had to do everything in my power to smash those shackles and set her free. "Gwyneth, Kester had sides to his personality that we never saw.

Your theory rests on the premise that he was a burnt-out case but the impression I've got after talking to all the people who knew him best was that he was a strong man, much stronger than we ever realized, and not only very durable but very determined. Now, he may have been abnormally fond of you. Lewis Carroll was abnormally fond of his Alice, but I've read about Carroll and there's no doubt nothing unsavory ever happened between them—he just wanted to marry her when she was grown up. Maybe Kester wanted to marry you too when you were grown up. After all, he fell in love with Anna when she was only fourteen. Obviously he always liked very young girls."

"Yes, but—"

"Wait, hear me out. The point about Kester is that he would have had the strength and determination to wait. He proved it. He waited over three years for Anna, and I think he'd have waited even longer for you. It seems to me sex wasn't particularly important to him—no one's ever suggested he had mistresses, so presumably he found he could live without them, and if you add all this up the inference would be that he could keep any abnormal affection for you well in control. I know the way he burst into tears suggests his control was weakening, but in fact all that those tears prove is that he was feeling overwrought—and not necessarily about you. It must have been very touching when you declared your faith in him like that. If he was strung up about something else that sort of moving declaration could well have triggered him into tears, and don't forget he was notorious for being emotional. This scene may have been off-key but I don't think it was sinister and I certainly don't think it was a prelude to a suicide for which you can be held responsible."

She thought over what I had said. When I finally had the nerve to take her hand in mine she whispered, "Thanks. I feel better," and we drifted down the path away from the grave. "All right," I heard her say evenly, "perhaps he didn't commit suicide because of me. Your argument's certainly convincing. Perhaps after all it was because without Anna and Oxmoon he couldn't write and felt he had nothing left to live for."

"I'm absolutely one hundred percent certain you're wrong about that. He'd adjusted to Anna's loss. He had a new book to write. And there's even the possibility, I've discovered, that he thought he could get Oxmoon back. No, I still think he had everything to live for."

"Yes, but—" She stopped dead in the shadow of the tower. "—Hal, if he didn't die by accident and he didn't commit suicide, what's left? The inquest made it clear he wasn't murdered."

"Maybe he's still alive." We looked back at the grave. Then I laughed and said, "No, this isn't *The Third Man* and Kester isn't Harry Lime. He's dead all right."

"Not for me," she said. "Never for me."

I looked at her. I was still Saint George but I knew I was in retreat before the dragon and the maiden was still shackled to her stake.

"You don't have to feel guilty about him anymore, Gwyneth, can't you see?" I said, but even as I spoke I was realizing I could hardly expect her to slough off an entrenched emotional attitude instantly. My words of reassurance would take time—perhaps a long time—to bite deep into her mind, and even then she would probably need someone like Pam to set her squarely on the road to freedom. "Come on," I said abruptly. "Let's forget him. I'll drive you home."

Halfway up the lane to the Llewellyns' farm she said, "You're driving like a maniac. For God's sake slow down."

"You really did love him, didn't you?" I had just begun to realize I was vilely upset. I was suffering some sort of annihilating reaction to her disclosures in the churchyard, and although I knew rationally that I couldn't expect her to abandon Kester at once I was so overcome with chaotic feelings that rational thoughts no longer had any power over me.

"Of course I really loved him," she said, "and I still do."

"So all that bloody do-it-yourself psychology got you bloody nowhere! You're still a virgin, aren't you?"

"What the bloody hell's that got to do with you?"

"Just about bloody everything. I want you, I've always wanted you, I've never been able to get you out of my mind, I've lost count of the girls I've had but no one's ever measured up to you, no one's ever recaptured the magic of all our wonderful days at Oxmoon—"

"Did you pop some pills when I wasn't looking? You sound stoned out of your mind! Look, if you don't slow down I'll bloody well pull up the hand brake—"

I slowed down. The open gates of the farmhouse drive lay ahead in the dusk. I almost sheared the wall as I swung the car into the yard.

"Meet me again. Name the time, name the place, name anything you bloody like—"

"I thought you'd given up sex! That little vagary didn't last long, did it?"

"Marry me."

"Don't be ridiculous."

I slammed on the brakes. The car screeched to a halt and skidded on the manure. Gwyneth got out. I got out. The doors slammed.

"That bastard Kester—"

"*Shut up!* Don't you dare talk of him like that!"

"He was a magician! He dazzled you! You're in love with a magic myth!"

"Let me go—you're hurting me—"

The back door opened and little Caitlin rushed out, seventeen years old, shining-eyed and innocent, my latest record album in her arms.

"Okay, turn on the sexy smile," said Gwyneth to me as she wrenched herself free, "and let's see how the great star handles his loyal fans."

Caitlin skimmed across the yard. She wore a short cotton dress and flimsy sandals. Her hair looked as if it had just been ironed.

"Oh, Hal—sorry to interrupt—please excuse me—I just wondered if—well, could you possibly..."

Reaching for the album, I found my pen and uncapped it. "Gwyneth—"

"I'm sorry, Hal, I do wish you all the best with your investigations and I'm glad we did meet again, but—"

"Give me your telephone number."

"No."

"Ah, come on!" I was writing on the album's sleeve: *Kiss me, Cait! Lots of luck*—HAL GODWIN.

"If you're not interested in platonic friendship then I'm not interested in handing out my phone number."

"Okay, forget it. I've got enough hang-ups of my own without taking on yours as well."

She walked away with a shrug and as I watched her disappear into the house I realized I was still holding the album. The child was no longer shining-eyed. She was looking after Gwyneth despondently and as I realized how tough it was for her to have such a sexy sister, I suddenly saw how I could be kind.

"Caitlin."

She jumped as if she'd been shot. "Yes?"

"Can you help me?"

"Oh, *yes!*"

"I'm working on a project and tomorrow I'll need someone to help me. Can you make some excuse to your family and get away for the day?"

"Oh yes, easily!"

The back door crashed open again as Jasper Llewellyn emerged like some neo-Victorian *paterfamilias*. All he needed was a horsewhip.

"Caitlin!" he bellowed before shouting something in the Welsh I couldn't understand.

"Coming!" shouted Caitlin in English. To me she whispered: "Where and when?"

"Penhale churchyard. Nine thirty."

"I'll be there."

"Wear gym shoes. We're going to the Worm."

"Right."

"Don't tell your parents."

"Never!" She looked astonished that I should think her capable of such an idiocy and skimmed away again with my album tucked lovingly against her breast.

I got into my car and drove away.

XIV

NOTES ON GWYNETH:
Of course I don't think he ever actually did anything to her. Of course I don't. But it's as if he did.

BLOODY HELL.
Keep your cool. Draw a nice line of pretty asterisks. And start again.

* * *

NOTES ON GWYNETH:

Gwyneth convinced me that the possibility of an accident was nil. I convinced her that the possibility of suicide was nil. So there we are. Except that we're not. I can't think straight about this. But I must. Keep trying.

Kester was strung up when Gwyneth saw him but that was probably because by that time he had sent the note to my father and was psyching himself up for a grueling interview. If Sian's right, he could well have been about to demand Oxmoon's return. And obviously he hadn't started his new novel because he was too strung up. That all hangs together. But where do I go from there?

No accident. No suicide.

Right. Time for another line of asterisks.

* * *

VERDICT: *Of course it must have been an accident, and tomorrow at the Worm I'm sure to see the solution Gwyneth and Trevor missed. Maybe I can even manage to believe in the freak wave. After all, freak waves are well-documented phenomena. They do happen.*

But not to the world's expert on the Shipway in calm spring weather.

XV

I stopped writing because it was too dark to see properly and my eyes were hurting. I was parked on the village green at Penhale and around me I could see the lighted windows of the cottages and hear the sound of rock music vibrating in the parish hall. The new vicar had the reputation for being trendy. The youth club was evidently in full swing.

I drove back to Oxmoon. It was a very dark night. I felt on the brink of something I knew instinctively would be dangerous to analyze, but I told myself everything would be all right so long as I just stuck to the facts. I felt strung tight as a trip wire.

When I reached the stable yard I halted the car, switched off the lights and sat watching the bright window of my father's room. I was reminded of a poem by Emily Brontë. Kester had been a great admirer of hers and had often read her poems aloud to us. I tried to remember the one about the candle burning in the window for the traveler, but all I could recall was a fragment of her final and perhaps most moving poem.

"No coward soul is mine. . ."

But I couldn't remember how it went on. I could only remember that she'd been facing a great ordeal and drumming up her courage.

I got out of the car and paused in the dark. The curtain of my father's window moved slightly and was still. He was waiting for me. And I was coming. I walked steadily across the yard and just as I was raising my hand to ring the bell the door opened and my father asked me to come in.

XVI

"I heard the car," he said. "Come into my room and tell me how you've been getting on."

"Okay. Is Pam out?"

"No, in the bath. If you want to cross-examine me without my watchdog in attendance this is your golden opportunity."

"I'm not interested in being hostile. But I'd certainly be grateful if you could clarify one or two minor points."

"Of course. As I said before, I want to do all I can to help you."

That conversation took us to his room which as usual was in a state of chronic disorganization. The air was heavy with cigarette smoke, and as soon as the door was closed my father poured himself some scotch into a tooth mug.

"Are you supposed to drink, Father? For God's sake don't overdose on alcohol and barbiturates."

"I haven't had any pills today. I thought alcohol would be more fun."

"What about your skin?"

"What the hell, it could hardly get much worse." After a mouthful of scotch he swung to face me. "Well? What did you make of the inquest report?"

"I thought you were a brilliant witness. But you were lucky with the coroner, weren't you? He seemed to look very benignly at your Old Harrovian tie."

My father laughed and embarked on the ritual of lighting a cigarette. His hands were quite steady. I wondered how long he had been drinking. "The coroner was no problem, I admit," he said, snapping shut the lighter and reaching for the tooth mug again. "But don't forget Declan was sitting in court. I didn't realize he was saving his fire for the Bryn-Davies lawsuit and I kept expecting him to interrupt at any minute to stage some lethal scene."

"In that case your performance was even more remarkable than I thought it was. Father—"

"Yes?" He responded so fast to my hesitation that I knew I wasn't the only one in that room who was strung tight as a trip wire.

"—I hesitate to ask this, but did you lie? Not about the main facts—I'm quite prepared to accept that your evidence was basically true, but was there any point at all, even the smallest point, which you omitted or distorted—perhaps in order to simplify matters for the jury?"

"Oh yes," said my father without a moment's hesitation. "We all knew the importance of saving paper in those days but I never actually gave the servants lectures on the subject. I just slipped that statement in for good effect."

"Ah yes—I did wonder about that. A bit tricky about that note not turning up, wasn't it?"

"Very," said my father. He picked up a stray record that was lying on the table and casually examined the sleeve.

"Father, I can't help being curious about that note. Can you remember it word for word?"

"No, but I can certainly remember the gist. It was rather facetious in tone—very typical of Kester. He said how pleased he was with the cottage even though he thought it might be hair-raising in winter when the gales started to blow. Then he said he had a good bottle of scotch and why didn't I drop in sometime for a drink."

"I see. He never mentioned Oxmoon?"

"No," said my father, "but that was hardly surprising. Oxmoon was a delicate subject and it was obvious to me that he wanted to keep the peace."

"You're sure of that? You don't think he might have returned to Gower in order to renegotiate the ownership?"

"No."

"Why? I must tell you that it's been suggested to me that that was what he was really after."

"There are several things wrong with that theory," said my father with the ease of someone responding to a well-worn question. "One: he had no case for demanding its return. Two: if he had, the sensible thing to do would have been to negotiate with me through a third party. Three: he never mentioned such a possibility to me in his correspondence. And four: Evan and Richard were sure he'd returned to Gower primarily to write."

"Ah yes," I said, "his writing. Richard especially was very interesting about that. He said Kester hadn't been on such a creative high since before Thomas died."

Bull's-eye.

Dead silence.

My father very, very slowly turned to face me again. "Richard said that?"

"No, Kester said it. Richard was repeating Kester verbatim."

"Ah." My father put down the record album and stood staring at it.

"Father, if you really want to help me, you'll tell me exactly what happened when Thomas died."

Another silence.

At last my father said, "You mustn't believe Declan."

"I don't. His story doesn't pan out. But I think his fiction had a factual basis. I think there was something weird about Thomas's death and I want to know what it was."

"No," said my father. "You're wrong there."

"I know why you say that," I said at once. "It's because you've always denied Declan's testimony and you're afraid that if you now admit that even part of it is true I'll start suspecting it's all true. But look here, Father. I don't care whether or not you extorted Oxmoon. If you did it was the stupidest thing you could have done, and my God, you've paid for it. All I'm interested in right now is the relevance of Thomas to my present inquiry. I've got this hunch that his death has some sort of significance here."

"I'm afraid you're inventing a red herring for yourself, Hal. Sorry, but Thomas really did die in that car crash."

"Okay, let's try another tack. Kester was on a big creative high—what kind of story was he creating?"

"No idea. Evan and Richard said he didn't go into detail."

"Yes, but Father, you owned that cottage—I know you sold it later to Llewellyn but after the police unsealed it you presumably were the one who had to sort the place out. What happened to Kester's final manuscript?"

"There wasn't one. Obviously he hadn't begun it."

"Okay, what about his notes?"

"There weren't any."

I walked right up to him. "Father," I said, "you've got to trust me. I'm on your side, I'm not out to crucify you, but I've got to get to the bottom of this. Now, let's try again. It's inconceivable that Kester, bursting to begin a new novel, hadn't made copious notes. I know how he worked and he always made notes beforehand. So what happened to them?"

My father was very shaken. He helped himself clumsily to some more scotch. "I don't know how I can convince you of this," he said, "but I absolutely swear, Hal, that there were no notes."

I stared. I was almost sure he was speaking the truth. Not only did he look truthful and sound truthful; I could think of no good reason why he should lie.

"But that's incredible," I said. I sat down abruptly on the bed. "This whole episode gets more and more bizarre."

"It *was* bizarre," said my father. He drew up a chair and sat down beside me. "Hal, listen. I'm quite sure in my own mind that Kester was mad. You've just read the inquest report. You'll know that the coroner found Kester's behavior that evening as baffling as I did—"

"Did Kester really never look back?"

"Never, I swear it, never—"

"But that's fantastic—that's just so unlikely—Christ, I don't understand anything here—"

My father made his decision. I saw him make it. The expression in his eyes became confidential. "Okay," he said suddenly. "I'll come clean with you." And leaning forward he looked me straight in the eyes and said with unflawed sincerity: "I didn't want to tell you because I knew how fond you were of Kester, but now I see I've no choice. I've got to tell you the truth. It's the right thing—indeed, the only thing—to do. . . ."

XVII

"You were right about Thomas," said my father. "Kester killed him but he killed him in such a way that I was to take the blame for the crime. Fortunately I saw I was being framed and I forced him to help me out of it by assisting me to stage the car crash. When Kester had his great burst of creativity beforehand he was dreaming up this fantastic murder plot which he later put into operation."

He waited for me to speak but when it became obvious I was beyond speech he added rapidly: "That was why our relationship deteriorated so disastrously. That was why we became so paranoid. He thought I knew too much and I thought he might kill me to keep me quiet."

I finally found my tongue. "Are you trying to say—"

"Our nerve eventually snapped. He tried to grab my land and I paid him back by extorting Oxmoon."

"But does this mean—"

"Wait. Let me finish. I'll tell you what it means. Now, Hal, although I did extort Oxmoon, *there was no way Kester could prove that* without putting his own neck on the block, and *he'd never have dared challenge me.* He knew I was capable of being a first-class witness—he'd seen me in action at Thomas's inquest—and he knew that if it were a question of my word against his, my word would be sure to win. So in the end, when he came back to Gower, I was relaxed because I was wholly convinced he couldn't touch me. There was no question of him getting Oxmoon back. It just wasn't on the cards at all. And that meant I had no reason to kill him."

"But in that case—"

"Wait. Just listen. Kester realized his cause was hopeless. He knew he'd never get Oxmoon back. He also knew he couldn't write anywhere except in Gower, and do you really think he'd have been content to live humbly at that cottage for the rest of his life while I lorded it in his home? No, of course not. He had nothing left to live for, Hal, but he was determined that if he was going to commit suicide he'd take me with him. So in a new fantastic burst of creativity he dreamed up this plot in which he committed suicide but I took the rap for his murder."

"*Jesus Christ—*"

"He invited me over to the cottage for a drink that evening but of course I burned that note and of course I lied to the coroner—if I admitted that Kester had set up a specific appointment, the jury might well have assumed he had something specific to discuss and the last thing I wanted was for them to get involved in speculation about the ownership of Oxmoon, the last thing I wanted was to stimulate them into thinking I might have a good motive for murder. But Kester wanted to lure me to Rhossili and so he knew he had to issue a specific invitation—if he'd kept it casual, why would I have bothered to take him up on it? I had no reason to go—I knew there was no risk of me being ousted from Oxmoon. I was calm, I was relaxed, I was confident, and when Kester issued this specific invitation I merely thought the most likely explanation was that he wanted to discuss how often I would allow you to visit him.

"Anyway I arrived at Rhossili, just as I said I did, and found he was out. As we had an appointment, I was sure he couldn't be far away and that was why I strolled back up the lane to intercept him; that was why, when I found he was nowhere to be seen, I became baffled enough to embark on a search.

"After that everything happened exactly as I said at the inquest—although I can go further to you now and confess that I soon began to wonder if he was luring me on. It was the only explanation that made sense. Not only did it explain why he'd broken our appointment—he knew I'd be sufficiently irritated and on edge to go out and look for him—but it explained that mysterious and eerie fact that he never looked back. You see, he had to pretend that he didn't know I was behind him because he wanted me to think I could catch him up. If he'd been constantly looking over his shoulder and obviously running away then I wouldn't have chased him across the Shipway. Why bother? I'd have given up right at the start. But as it was I felt sure he'd be loafing around on the Inner Head and so I was tempted to go on. My behavior will seem more comprehensible to you when I confess that I was extremely worried about your relationship with Kester and I thought I could drive a better bargain with him if I were conducting the negotiations in an intimidatingly isolated spot. I thought that if I put the fear of God into him with sufficient skill he might stay away from you out of sheer terror.

"All right. So I deduced he was luring me on—but for what purpose? In my paranoia I immediately suspected him of wanting to murder me, but that was nonsense. I'd have got the better of him in any fight. Then I thought of suicide and suddenly it all began to make sense. If he lured me on so that we were both cut off and if he subsequently never came back I'd have the hell of a time proving I hadn't murdered him. It was true I had no real motive, but that didn't matter— I knew Declan could drum up a motive with ease; I knew what Declan could do even then—my God, that scene at Oxmoon when he gave us all a dress rehearsal of his performance during the Bryn-Davies lawsuit! Yes, I knew I was in bad trouble. Two independent witnesses had seen me go out after Kester that evening, and I knew their evidence would mean a hard time for me with the police. Obviously I had to counterattack but how the hell was I going to do it?

"Well, I had no choice, did I? I just had to go on, catch him up and drag us both back alive.

"So on I went. And then . . . oh God, I'm tempted to lie to you here but I won't because I'm determined that this account is going to be absolutely truthful all the way down to the last detail. I got to the Inner Head, I went round the corner and up the slope onto the southern flank—and there he was, yes, he was there, I lied when I said at the inquest that he was far away on the Middle Head, but I only lied to clarify the issue to the jury, to make them understand that I couldn't possibly have caught him up."

"But surely if he was waiting on the Inner Head—"

"He was waiting, but *he wasn't nearby*. He was at least a hundred yards beyond that rise in the footpath. There's a spur of rock running out from the path to the edge of the sea and he was sitting on it—obviously he wanted to make quite sure I was following him, but at the same time he wanted to make sure I wasn't in a position to grab him as soon as I came around the bend. He was still luring me on, you see, and he thought he'd let me catch up a little to give me encouragement—he wanted to make certain I was marooned with him.

"But of course by that time I'd realized just what he was up to, and when he hared away immediately towards the Middle Head I didn't automatically hare after him. I knew then that I'd never catch him up and still beat the tide, and once I'd acknowledged that, I knew I'd be done for unless I got back over the Shipway and tried to establish some kind of alibi. If I were marooned with Kester

I'd never be able to prove my innocence, but back on the mainland I'd at least have a fighting chance.

"So I went back—and when I reached the cottage I had this most colossal stroke of luck because Dafydd was there changing the washer. Of course I would have tried to rig an alibi with him to safeguard myself, but as it turned out I didn't have to do any rigging and that proved to be my salvation. The police had their suspicions of me, of course they did, but there was no way they could break that alibi.

"I was hoping all the time that once Kester realized he'd failed to frame me he would have second thoughts about suicide, but I'm afraid I was being too optimistic. He killed himself—and as soon as I knew he'd done it, I couldn't bear it, I felt so responsible for him, I felt I should have gone on and tried to save him. . . . You see, he was mad, unquestionably insane, but *I felt I'd driven him mad* by always outshining him and being the successful man of action he'd always secretly wanted to be. We had such a very strange relationship and one day I'll have to tell you more about it, but meanwhile . . . well, there's nothing more I can add. He killed himself, and I'm afraid you must accept that, Hal. He killed himself and tried to have me hanged for his murder."

XVIII

There was a long silence. He poured himself some more scotch and drank it. Finally I heard him say, "I'm sorry. I wanted so much to protect you."

The silence continued. Then he said awkwardly: "What can I do? Do you want to go on talking about it? Is there anything else you'd like to ask?"

I shook my head, rose to my feet and began to pace slowly around the disordered room.

Eventually he said in desperation: "Would you like to hear some music?" Music for him was the great panacea which soothed all ills.

"No thanks." To pretend I was calm I took out my notebook and began to flip through the pages. At once Declan's name seemed to hit me between the eyes.

"How much do you think Declan knew?" I heard myself say, and although my eyes were on my notebook I was aware of my father relaxing as if he felt he had surmounted the most difficult interview of his life.

"I suspect Declan didn't know as much as I originally thought he did," he said readily. "One can argue, I think, that Kester would have shied away from confessing to his idolized elder brother that he had murdered Thomas during a period of insanity—and I also think one can argue that Kester wouldn't have revealed his last crazy plot either. If Declan had realized Kester was insane again and contemplating suicide, I'm quite sure he'd have stopped Kester leaving Dublin."

"Yes, Declan never believed in the suicide theory, did he? He thought you murdered Kester on the Inner Head."

"Declan was bound to want to believe that when he found he couldn't break my alibi, but you go out there, Hal. You look for that spur of rock and you'll realize that once Kester started to run from there I could never have caught him up and dragged us both back in time to beat the tide."

"And if he didn't run?"

My father was ashen. "Don't you believe me?"

"Well, as a matter of fact I do. I can't see Kester sitting around and meekly waiting for you to be aggressive—I'm sure that as soon as he saw you on the Inner Head his first instinct would have been to run, and that would have been true whether or not he knew you were behind him. So that means Declan's story is a lot less plausible than yours is." I flicked through my notebook again. This time the words that hit me between the eyes were BRILLIANTLY PLAUSIBLE.

"Excuse me, Father. Back in a minute."

I got to the bathroom, locked myself in and leaned back against the panels. I was in that most unpleasant condition where one wants to be sick but knows that vomiting is impossible. The bathroom was overpoweringly hot and the air reeked of heavily-scented talcum powder. Pam could only have departed seconds earlier.

I got the window open, leaned out over the sill, took several deep breaths and realized with a vague, curiously unemotional horror that I was going to have to go back into that room where my father was waiting. And not only that: I was going to have to have a few minutes of casual conversation with him in order to soothe his nerves. The one thing I couldn't do was to betray my own shattered nerves by rushing off instantly to my scullery.

I thought: "No coward soul is mine." And somehow I got myself out of the bathroom.

"Are you all right?" said my father immediately as I reentered his room.

"Yes. Well, no, to be honest I'm in pieces, but that's okay, don't worry about it, I'll put myself together again soon enough."

"I know my story must have been the most appalling shock to you—"

"Yes, it was. But don't think I haven't had my suspicions of Kester's sanity. Father, I want to thank you for being honest with me. I know it was a great ordeal, but I really am very grateful." While I spoke I sat on the bed and stooped to retie my shoelace. I was trying to think what to say next. All subjects of casual conversation were eluding me.

"I'm glad I was able to help," said my father. "Yes, it was an ordeal, but in a curious way it was good to talk of it—talking can come as a relief. . . . My God, what I went through that night! I never slept a wink, of course—I told the jury I did but that was just to make them think I wasn't feeling too guilty. In fact I was awake all night. I thought of the past, all of it, my father with his various families, Uncle Robert and Aunt Ginevra, my grandfather—my God, I even thought of my great-grandmother and Owain Bryn-Davies!—I thought of everything that had gone into producing Kester and me and making us the men we were—"

I saw a banal topic of conversation and seized it. "Didn't you manage to find some nice soothing music on the radio?"

"What?"

"I said: Didn't you manage to find some nice soothing music on the radio?" I was surreptitiously glancing at my watch and wondering how soon I dared escape.

"Well, no," said my father after a pause, "I didn't. As a matter of fact I didn't turn on the wireless."

"Why not? Was it broken or something? I can't imagine you being in a room for hours on end without trying to find some music on the radio!"

"That's quite true," said my father, pouring himself some more scotch. "But of course I was very upset."

"All the more reason for you to want some music."

"That's true too. How strange! Let me think for a moment. Why didn't I turn on the wireless? I'm sure there was some very good reason, but for the life of me I can't remember what it was."

"Well, never mind, it doesn't matter." I stood up. "And now if you'll excuse me, Father—"

"But this is really very puzzling," insisted my father, becoming so intrigued that he ignored my attempt to depart. "Naturally I wouldn't have acted out of character! I was just trying to recall that room . . . yes, I don't remember the wireless at all; in fact I could swear it wasn't there. Yet it must have been there because Evan had delivered it the day before—maybe Kester took it up to the bedroom?"

"That figures," I said, moving to the door. I was so anxious to escape by that time that I hardly knew what I was saying. "Kester liked absolute quiet while he worked. Well, Father—"

"Hal, are you quite certain you'll be all right?"

"Yes, sure, no problem; I just want to go to sleep now and forget the whole bloody business but tomorrow I'll be okay, I know I will; no doubt in my mind whatsoever."

"If there's anything more I can do, anything at all—"

It was painful how much he cared. I felt as if the weight of his caring were opening up deep cracks in my mind but I managed to say in a calm reassuring voice: "Don't worry about me—I'll be all right, I promise." And then at long last I was able to escape.

XIX

FURTHER NOTES ON MY FATHER:
It's a brilliant story. But there's just one thing that worries me: is it true?
VERDICT: *Reserve judgment till my investigations at the Worm are completed tomorrow.*

XX

I lay awake in the dark.

At two o'clock in the morning I lit a candle and walked into the main part of the house. It was quiet but not still. I could hear the pitter-patter of mice in the wainscoting.

The great chandelier gleamed beneath the dust and as I crossed the marble floor of the hall my footsteps sounded curiously muffled by the darkness. The library door creaked as if in parody of a ghost story, but this was no ghost story; I'd made up my mind about that from the start. When all was said and done everything depended not upon my imagination but upon my logic, my courage and my will.

Did I go on? Or did I say "Mystery solved" and turn aside? I didn't have to go out to the Worm tomorrow. I could take my father's word.

But I couldn't. Not quite. I wanted to believe him. I did believe him. But I had to be one hundred percent certain that this brilliant witness hadn't just delivered the most creative testimony of his exceptionally creative career.

Yet I was afraid to go on. I could see I was afraid. My hand shook as I found the well-remembered book and opened it at the page Kester had so often read.

"No coward soul is mine," Emily Brontë had written, "No trembler in the world's storm-troubled sphere: I see Heaven's glories shine, And faith shines equal, arming me from fear."

I read the last line again. I had no faith in God, but I now had faith in my father. I thought of Eleanor saying, "I'll never believe your father was the villain of the Oxmoon saga, Hal. I think the real villain was your cousin Kester."

Right. All I had to do now to eradicate my fear, safeguard my sanity and terminate the nightmare that encircled me was to prove Eleanor was right.

Returning to the kitchen I printed in my notebook: NO COWARD SOUL IS MINE. Then I went back to bed and slept.

I was going on.

5

I

THE SHIPWAY curved in a jagged arc beneath a hot cloudless sky. It was a Saturday, and tourist hordes unknown fourteen years before when Kester had died were swarming around the top of the cliffs. The car park was packed. Yet the sands of Rhossili beach remained almost empty, for only a minority of the lazy visitors bothered to clamber down the long steep path to the beach and only the hardiest marched across the headland to tackle the Shipway. Ahead of us a party of hikers were starting out across the rocks. A pack of Cub Scouts was yelling behind us. A courting couple had halted dreamily on our left. It was a very different scene from the sight that would have met my father's eyes in the May of '52, but the Shipway at least was unchanged, a huge sweep of wet rocks exposed by the tide, a wilderness of little pools where stranded fish waited for the tide that would liberate them, a lunar landscape baking beneath the June sun.

"Time for you to receive your briefing," I said to Caitlin. She was sensibly dressed in jeans, a blue blouse and gym shoes. Her long hair which was finer and darker than her sister's was scraped back from her face into a ponytail. As I spoke, she looked up at me with obedient intelligent eyes. She had already apologized for seeking my autograph, as if Gwyneth had mercilessly upbraided her for such ingenuous behavior, and I felt sorry for the girl who was undoubtedly a nice child, clean, bright and not unattractive but obviously suffering from the loneliness of adolescence. I hoped she would soon find a steady boyfriend, marry young and have two point three children or whatever the average girl produced nowadays, the kind of girl who was uninterested in winning a place at Oxford, indulging in do-it-yourself psychology and treating men like horseshit. I made an additional resolution to be kind.

"What I want to do," I said to her, "is to reconstruct my cousin Kester's last hours. Never mind why for the moment. I expect you know roughly what happened, don't you? He came out here and my father followed him. Okay—you're going to be Kester and I'm going to be my father."

She nodded. The Cub Scouts streamed past us and howled around the rocks.

"Two independent witnesses," I said, "supported my father's claim that he and Kester were quarter of an hour apart on the Shipway, so you're going to start out and I'm going to follow you after fifteen minutes. How's your knowledge of the Shipway? I advise you to keep to the inside of the curve until you reach the little shingle beach and then flounder on as best you can."

She nodded again. "I'll manage. Do I hurry?"

That struck me as an intelligent question. "No, this isn't a race. My father said Kester moved like a man in a dream. Just keep going steadily."

"Okay."

"When you get to the Inner Head don't stop. Go on along the path until you're out of my sight and continue until you see a spur of rock that runs from the path towards the sea. Once you get there, sit down and wait for me. All clear?"

"Yes."

"One thing more: don't turn around to see how far I am behind you, but at the same time try and glance back surreptitiously to see where I am. In other words, keep an eye on me without me being aware of it."

"Okay."

"Now repeat your instructions."

She repeated them. I wished her luck. She set off, and sitting down on the grassy bank at the foot of the headland I wrote in my notebook: *10:16. Caitlin starts out across the Shipway.*

II

I had forgotten what a large area the Shipway covered, and I had forgotten how sinister it was once one had been swallowed up in it. The hikers were ahead of me but taking a different route far over to the left. The Cub Scouts and the courting couple were lost among the rock pools. There were other people behind me but keeping a steady pace I soon outdistanced them and within minutes I was alone among the tall rocks, my shoes slipping on the seaweed, the barnacles scraping my hands as I scrambled past each hazard. It was like mountaineering on the horizontal.

After a while I became aware of the special quality of the silence. The water of the bay on my right seemed motionless as the tide fell steadily toward low water, and far away on the other side of the Shipway the surf from the Bristol Channel was receding so that the muffled boom of the waves became steadily fainter. I began to feel as if I were journeying through a graveyard packed so densely with tombstones that normal walking was impossible. There was the same forlorn atmosphere of abandonment yet the same eerie air of expectancy; the Shipway was waiting for high tide just as a graveyard waits for Halloween, a time when life returns and the horrors begin. I tried to picture the water running many feet over the rocks that towered over me but the vision seemed preposterous. Yet it happened. It happened twice a day. It was unbelievable but it was true.

In an effort to divert myself from things that were unbelievable but true I began to sing. I had made my name in the music business by picking hits from the American country-music charts and converting them into popular songs which the English public could digest. I thought of it as translation work, moving a song from one culture to another. I liked country music. I did sing rock, but that was just an exercise to warm up the audience. Once the tension was humming I could slip from rock to country-rock with an early Presley number and from country-rock into pop-country and a Jim Reeves song. Having softened up my listeners I could then achieve my goal, a song by the master of country music, Hank Williams. I did write and record my own songs; there was more money in that than in rerecording masterpieces but I was enough of a purist to find my work imitative and unsatisfactory.

While I was singing it occurred to me what a ragbag of culture the twentieth-century mind was, and as I meditated on my unlikely journey from Emily Brontë to Hank Williams I found myself wondering whether Kester would have liked American country music. He hadn't been a musical snob and he would have been romantic enough to enjoy all the endless tales of lost love.

Kester had never talked of sex, only of romance. "My parents had this fairy-tale love story," I could remember him saying. "They fell passionately in love with each other as they danced beneath the chandeliers at Oxmoon while the orchestra played 'The Blue Danube.'"

That sounded like a tall story. I was just mentally chalking it up as one of Kester's fictions when I reached the shingle beach, and pulling out my notebook I paused to jot down the time. Ahead of me Caitlin had almost reached the Inner Head. I could see her blue shirt and jeans bobbing up and down among the last rocks while her ponytail fluttered in the breeze.

She never looked back.

I toiled on.

Caitlin reached the Inner Head, scrambled up the bank, brushed down her jeans and moved on. Within minutes she was disappearing around the curving path, and although I watched her closely I could have sworn she never once looked back.

I looked back. I glanced around at the dazzling views of sky and sea, sands and cliffs which stretched away from me on all sides into the heat haze. Anyone communing with nature or sunk deep in a creative dream would surely have stopped to absorb the sights that now met my eyes. To ignore such scenery would have been unthinkable to someone who had elevated the concept of Beauty into a slogan for the Good Life.

I slithered into a rock pool, cursed, clambered out, trod on a starfish, winced and thanked God I hadn't broken an ankle. I tried to quicken my pace but the terrain was brutal. I started cursing again.

A quarter of an hour later, hot, breathless and exasperated by my struggles, I reached the Inner Head and crawled up onto the shallow bank where the springy turf was carpeted with little pink wild flowers. In my notebook I wrote: *11:03. I reach the Inner Head.* The view was so extraordinary that I felt I could classify it as hypnotic. I could have gazed at it for far longer than the ten seconds I allowed myself but I hadn't toiled across that Shipway just to enjoy the view. Snapping my notebook shut I stowed it away and moved on.

I saw her soon after I had reached the southern flank. She had found the rocky spur and was perched at one end of it overlooking the sea. She was still a small figure many yards away but there was no mistaking her. Her clothes made a splash of color among the browns and greens of that treeless landscape.

I shouted: "Kester, what the bloody hell do you think you're doing?" but she didn't move. Several seconds elapsed before she turned her head and saw me. I waved, and after noting the time again I walked briskly down the path towards her.

"Hullo!" she said as soon as I was in earshot. "Was I all right?"

"Did you hear me just now?"

"Hear you? No."

"And while you were staring out to sea you didn't see me. So if you hadn't been expecting me you wouldn't have been aware of my approach even if I'd called out when I first saw you. . . . Okay. Now for the big question: Did you look back?"

"Oh yes, constantly. I kept a close watch on you all the way."

III

NOTES ON THE SHIPWAY:

The truth is that quarter of an hour apart is a long way and although the big gestures are visible the smaller ones are not. I'm now certain that Kester knew he was being followed, and this explodes the premise on which Declan based his theory. Whatever experiments Declan and Rory conducted here after the inquest, they obviously didn't bother to keep themselves quarter of an hour apart on the Shipway. This brings us back to Evan who was sure that Kester would have kept going if he knew my father was behind him—but of course Evan was assuming that Kester was innocent of any hostile intentions towards my father. Kester would surely only hang about on the Inner Head if he were masterminding an elaborate plot—and this brings me to my father's testimony. So far it pans out. I'm now very tempted to believe my father when he says Kester was waiting for him on this spur of rock— that was the point when my father had to make his crucial decision about whether to go on or turn back, and Kester would have made an extra effort to lure him on by allowing him to catch up a little.

VERDICT: *So far so good. But what in God's name happened next?*

IV

"What do we do now, Hal?" said Caitlin as I closed my notebook.

"Just stay there for a minute."

I walked down the spur and looked at the sea. There were no cliffs at this point. The land sloped to the rocks at the water's edge. I was thinking of Declan again and trying to work out the conclusions he had drawn. It now seemed clear that he had visualized Kester lost in thought, gazing out to sea and utterly oblivious of my father's approach, and bearing that picture in mind I had no trouble imagining Declan's script: my father had come into view, seen Kester, called out but received no response; at that point he'd suddenly realized he had an opportunity to dispose of his neurotic cousin once and for all, and driven on by a paranoid impulse he had forgotten the witnesses on the Shipway earlier, crept up behind Kester, stunned him with a karate chop and shoved him into the sea.

I decided that up to this point the script was credible—just—but it then occurred to me to wonder how Declan had visualized the disposal of the body. The tide now was still falling to low-water but back on that evening in '52 the tide had been on the rise. I knew that the currents around the Worm were fierce but so was the tide crashing up the Bristol Channel, and I thought a body ditched on the southern flank would have been almost immediately washed up again. I wondered how Declan had talked his way out of that one.

I decided that Declan's theory couldn't be made to work even if, against all the odds, Kester really had remained unaware of my father's presence. And that meant I had now disposed once and for all of the evidence of Declan Kinsella.

"Okay," I said to Caitlin as I rejoined her. "Now we're going to play a rerun of the scene where I come into view, but this time as soon as you see me you get up and start to run."

"Is it a race now?"

"Yes, but for God's sake don't break your neck on the rough stretch that connects the Inner and the Middle Heads—in fact don't take any risks at all. Kester would have shunned acrobatics."

"Okay, but Hal, this never happened, did it?"

"No, my father turned back. But what I want to establish is what Kester thought might happen if my father chased him."

Again she showed intelligence. "How can we be sure we're moving at their pace?"

"We can't. But I still think we can arrive at a similar result. Kester had longer legs than you but you're more athletic. I'm younger than my father was then but he was probably in first-class physical condition. Let's try the experiment and see what happens."

I retreated from her sight. Then I entered the time in my notebook, nerved myself for action and once more headed towards that spur of rock.

I saw Caitlin. Caitlin saw me. She hared away, and within seconds she was out of sight, following the curve of the path away from the flank to the end of the Inner Head.

I was my father. I counted to ten to give him time to make up his mind, took a deep breath and began to run.

I was horrified by how out of training I was. I got a stitch before I reached the end of the flank and I had to bend double for a cure. My father would have done better than that. On recovering I sprinted off again, turned the corner and saw Caitlin still far ahead of me as the path led onto the connecting link between the Inner and the Middle Heads. This was a minor version of the Shipway, but set above the high-water mark. By the time I reached it, Caitlin was nearer but already halfway across.

This stretch of rough terrain was more puzzling to traverse than the Shipway although it looked easier. I made a false start and had to go back. My father, following Kester the expert, would have done better, but Caitlin was no expert and I guessed she had made a false start too.

We sweated on. Caitlin finally reached the Middle Head and hared off again along the path. She was obviously in prime condition, much fitter than Kester would have been. With a great effort of will I raised my speed to put me level with my father, and when I too reached the other side of the rocks I raced headlong down the path to reduce Caitlin's lead.

I saw the Devil's Bridge.

Caitlin was there, skimming across the slender arch of rock that spanned the abyss between the Middle and the Outer Heads. But she was ahead of Kester. Kester was still in the middle of the Bridge and Kester in my mind's eye was turning to face me. I rushed on. The ground fell away on either side of the path. I was there. I was on the Bridge. I looked down. The abyss was deep, the rock face sheer, and far below the sea was a mass of roaring foam.

I stopped, and as I remained motionless I saw my world go black. The impossible had become the possible, the inconceivable had become the conceivable and there was darkness at noon.

I covered my face with my hands to shut out the horror of that brilliant morning, and then very slowly I sank to my knees, let my hands fall and once more looked over the abyss into the hell which lay churning below.

V

She thought I had vertigo. She sped back to me. Her strong sunburned little hand gripped my wrist. "It's all right, Hal, it's all right—*you can't fall.* No one could possibly fall off here unless someone gave them a terrific shove—"

No coward soul is mine.

"Oh my God, my God—"

"Take my hand, Hal, hold my hand."

I held it. I got myself together. I did it by thinking of Emily Brontë, facing death at thirty and writing her courageous poem. Struggling to my feet I walked back off the Bridge, sat down on the nearest rock, glanced at my watch and made a careful note of the time.

Of course my father had never got back across the Shipway that night. Never. Impossible.

"Hal, are you all right?"

"Uh-huh. Sorry. Stupid of me." My pen was still poised in my hand. I began an elaborate doodle in the margin of my notebook. Nothing much happened for a time. We sat listening to the water beneath the Bridge. The sun was hot, the view idyllic. The beauty bludgeoned me. I had never before realized that beauty could be so cruel.

"I'm on a very bad trip," I said suddenly to Caitlin. "Talk to me."

"Oh gosh. What shall I talk about?"

"You."

"Me? But I'm so ordinary!"

"Exactly. I want to hear someone ordinary talking about ordinary things. Tell me the story of your life. Go on. Begin: 'I was born at the farm—'"

"But I was born in Swansea. Mum had to go into hospital for a Caesar. I was christened Caitlin because Mum liked it, and Dilys after Aunt Dilys in Bettws-y-Coed, who's my godmother, but I don't like either of those names; I'd like to be called Tracy..."

She talked on. It must have been an effort for her as she was shy but she had sensed my distress and was making a heroic effort to help. She talked about growing up at the farm as the little afterthought of the family, ignored by Gwyneth and Trevor but indulged by her parents. I heard about Aunt Dilys in Bettws-y-Coed and Aunt Olwen in Llandaff and Uncle Dai in Cardiff and her Welsh Nationalist cousins in the Rhondda Valley and her cousin Kelly-Jean in California who knew someone who knew someone else who had been in the army in Germany with Elvis Presley, and all the time I was watching the sea and thinking of Emily Brontë and trying to drum up the courage to acknowledge a truth I couldn't face.

"...and I'm not going to university, I'm not brilliant like Gwyneth. I'll do a secretarial course and then perhaps a course in farm administration—I'd like to run a farm with my husband and do all the paperwork for him, like Mum does for Dad. I don't suppose I'll find a boy with his own farm, though—that's just a dream. I don't have a boyfriend at the moment. I had one last year but he took up with someone else because I wouldn't sleep with him. I wondered if I was silly not to but I don't know, supposing I got into trouble, and anyway I didn't want to, it all seemed too much, I just wanted someone to go to the pictures with or maybe go dancing on Saturday night; how hard life seems sometimes, how difficult it is to know what to do, although I don't suppose you find that, do you, I expect once one's as old as you are one knows all the answers and you're probably thinking I'm very peculiar, not having a boyfriend and not having been to bed with anyone."

"Rubbish. Girls like you may be an endangered species but you needn't think there aren't plenty of men still around who want to practice conservation." I stood up. I could hardly go on sitting in a stupor by the Devil's Bridge. It occurred to me then what an idiotic name that was. Was it traditional or had it been invented by some coy guidebook? I didn't know. "Well," I said, turning my back on the Outer Head, "that's one place I'll never revisit. Let's go."

Halfway along the southern flank of the Inner Head, she said, "Is there anything I can do to help you?"

"No. Yes. Stick up for what you believe in and don't go to bed with anyone just to follow the crowd. My cousin Kester used to say..."

Silence.

"Yes?" said Caitlin.

"He used to say: 'Hold fast, stand firm. Don't just do the done thing, do the right thing.'"

"That's great," said Caitlin. "That's cool. I wish I'd known him."

I was walking ahead of her so she couldn't see my face. I was remembering my lost hero in the golden myth which reality had blackened beyond recall, but although grief nearly overwhelmed me I beat it back. I told myself that maintaining my self-control merely required the right attitude of mind, and the right attitude of mind now consisted in refusing to grieve for Kester and refusing to remember my father.

I managed to sustain that defense until we reached the mainland. Then although I was still too afraid to think of my father a voice in my head began to repeat fiercely: Not true, not true, not true.

On the bank below the cliff we sank down on the grass to rest and I immediately pulled out my notebook. "If you'll excuse me for a moment, Caitlin—"

"Oh, of course."

I uncapped my pen and began to write.

VI

NOTES ON MY RECONSTRUCTION AT THE WORM'S HEAD:

All that I've really done this morning is explode Declan's theory. What I haven't done is disprove a single word of my father's testimony, and the episode at the Devil's Bridge shows the danger of letting one's imagination run riot at the expense of one's reason and intelligence. All I actually proved at this point was that the Devil's Bridge would be the ideal spot to kill someone by administering a hefty shove. What I didn't prove was that my father had done the shoving—in fact I haven't even proved he got as far as the Devil's Bridge. The only way I can prove that is to prove he missed the tide, and the only way I can prove he missed the tide is to bust that unbustable alibi of his.

VERDICT: *I can't convict him of murder unless I turn up some piece of evidence that proves he never returned to the cottage that night.*

VII

I snapped shut my notebook. I felt much better. The darkness had faded. The sea of Rhossili Bay was a limpid Pacific blue.

"I'm all right now," I said to Caitlin. "Thanks for the helping hand."

"That's okay." She smiled, suddenly shy again, and then added impulsively: "I don't remember your cousin Kester, but I remember going to the cottage just after his death when my father decided to try and buy the place. Dafydd Morgan lent him the key. He thought your dad might be willing to sell."

"Holiday homes must be a gold mine these days—my father shouldn't have sold. . . . What were you doing inspecting cottages with your father?"

"I was very little and hadn't started school, so when Mum went with Dad to see the cottage she had to take me along. Looking back I suppose it was a bit spooky. Everything must have been just as your cousin left it, because the police had only unsealed the place the day before. I remember—"

"Caitlin—"

"Yes?"

"No, I'm sorry; there's no reason why I should want to stop you. Go on."

"I was only going to say I remember the typewriter standing on the table by the window. I'd never seen one before and I wanted to know what it was."

"Ah yes. The typewriter." We went on watching the sea and the beauty no longer seemed cruel. Everything was so peaceful, so perfect, but it was beyond low-water now and I knew that all the time the tide was thudding closer, every wave building up to that terrifying moment when the first channel in the rocks would disappear beneath the surf and the Shipway would begin to sink in a roar of flying foam.

"Tell me, Caitlin," I said as we sat idly in the hot sunlight, "what else do you remember about that living room at the cottage? Describe it to me."

"Oh gosh, I couldn't, I was so little and it was such a long time ago! In fact, there are only two things I really remember—one was the typewriter and the other—"

"Yes? The other?"

"—the other was this really fabulous radio—in fact it was the radio, not the typewriter, that was the first thing I saw as I ran into the room. . . ."

I had caught my father out in his one fatal lie.

The alibi exploded in my hands, the case cracked wide apart and my last hope sank like the Shipway beneath the roaring waters of the truth.

VIII

I didn't give up. I didn't dare. Kester and my father had drawn me deep into their dark tunnel and now they were behind me, blocking the way back to the light. My only hope of survival was to go on.

I was now sure that my father had killed Kester, so my next task was to exonerate him. This proved well within my capabilities. After I had returned Caitlin to the farm I drove on to Llangennith, parked the car among the sand burrows and went for a long walk on Rhossili beach. There were people around but the beach was so vast that it still seemed empty. I walked on and on and all the time the tide was coming in, the surf hissing over the hot sand and driving me back to the foot of the Downs.

When I reached the burrows again I sat down out of the wind and wrote the note acquitting my father of murder. I had by this time worked out how I could both acquit him and forgive him. Problem solved. Ordeal conquered. Happy ending.

On my way back to the car I felt dizzy, and diagnosing the trouble as lack of sustenance I stopped in Llangennith to buy a bar of chocolate and a couple of bottles of Coke. Back in the car I refueled myself and drove on.

But halfway to Penhale I realized I hadn't the nerve to go on to Oxmoon. I needed more time. I had to make quite sure I had myself in control so I drove around Gower, in and out of the winding country lanes which were all radiant with wild flowers, and as the day drifted into evening I wound up on the summit of Cefn Bryn and watched the sun sink in a brilliant sky shot with red and gold. I went on watching the sky until I could see the stars. Then with my nerve strengthened, my courage repaired and my will at maximum strength I finally returned to Oxmoon.

IX

My nerve shattered on arrival. As I drove into the yard the front door of the mews house opened and I saw my father silhouetted against the light. My courage dissolved, my will snapped in two and I knew I couldn't face him. I got out of the car. "Hi!" I called cheerfully, slamming the door. Then I blundered into the scullery before he could reply. Once the door was closed it was pitch-dark. I stood there leaning back against the panels and listening to my heart beating. The room was silent as the grave.

I struck a match. It went out. I struck another, and as I struggled with my shaking fingers I knew I'd made a bad psychological mistake by not even pausing for the briefest of conversations. I got the candle alight and tried yet again to get a grip on myself but my will was tiring. I had a fleeting image of a strong swimmer who finds to his horror that he has underestimated the strength of the sea.

There was a tap on the door.

I opened my mouth to say: "Come in!" but nothing happened. I tried to think: No coward soul is mine. But I was in terror. I just stood there by the table in the candlelight and as I watched the door it began to open.

He looked in. There was a long silence. Of course he had only to glance at me to realize that I knew.

Eventually he crossed the threshold, closed the door and said, "You look very ill. Let me take you over to the house," but all I said was "You shouldn't have lied to me about the radio."

A few more seconds slipped away. He joined me at the table. Pulling out a chair for himself he suggested that we should sit down.

We sat down.

"Exactly what's been happening?" said my father.

"I've been reconstructing your crime."

We faced each other across the table with the candle burning steadily between us. We must have looked like figures in a painting of a Dutch interior, an exquisitely balanced composition gilded by a glowing light.

"I was with Caitlin Llewellyn," I said. "She remembers the cottage as it was shortly after Kester died. She remembers that radio in the living room. If you'd been waiting at the cottage that evening, you'd have turned on the radio—you admitted as much yourself. In fact you knew it would have been so out of character for you to wait for hours in a room without trying to find a musical broadcast that you knew you had to lie and say the radio wasn't there; you couldn't lie and invent some concert because of course all broadcasts can be checked. No, you weren't at the cottage that night, were you? You spent the night cut off on the Worm and when you finally staggered back at dawn there would have been no music to hear on the radio—the BBC would have closed down hours before, and besides it was hardly the time, was it, to listen to music. You probably had some whisky, just as you said you did, but then you went out to your car—"

"You should have a drink yourself," said my father. "You should have brandy."

"—and finally you drove back to Oxmoon. You were frantic. You knew you had to cook an alibi but then you had your lucky break, the break all lucky criminals get, because it turned out that Dafydd was in a position to give you a grade-A alibi. No problem there. The big problem was to work out what the hell to tell the police but you did that brilliantly, mixing fact and fiction with such skill that it was impossible to know where the truth ended and the lies began. But let me tell you now what I think happened—no, don't interrupt. I've spent the whole afternoon working on this story, and I think I've finally got it right and at long last I can see the way things really were."

I got up. I retrieved a Coke from the larder, uncapped the bottle and drank. Then I sat down again and said, "This was a conjuring trick, a grand illusion, a master plot dreamed up by a master magician. You admitted as much to me earlier when you were handing me yet another brilliant embroidery on the true facts. But Kester had no intention of committing suicide, did he? Not Kester.

Kester wasn't a suicide, he was a murderer. I think he planned to kill you and get away with it."

I paused but my father just said simply, "Go on."

I drank some more Coke. "The point about this case," I said, "is that everyone got hung up on the survivor. Everyone focused on whether *you* had had the motive for murder and whether *you* had engineered a crime. But that was all wrong, wasn't it? It was Kester who had the motive and Kester who engineered the crime, and once I'd cast Kester in the role of the villain who was crazy everything started to make sense.

"If you'd disappeared that night at the Worm, what could have been pinned on Kester? Damn all. He wouldn't have reported you missing, of course. His line would have been that he'd never seen you that night, and besides it might well have been hard to pinpoint the exact time of your disappearance—it might even have been hard to prove you had been in Rhossili at all that evening, and even if the police turned up witnesses who had seen you there, no one could say they'd seen you with Kester—quite the reverse. Kester had kept himself a quarter of an hour ahead of you and the tides were unfavorable. He had the excuse of his eccentricity to explain why he had chosen to be marooned on the Worm that night, but there was no reason why you should have wanted to be cut off—again, quite the reverse. The inference would have been that you'd somehow drowned on the Shipway—if indeed anyone had seen you in the area at all—but why should Kester have known anything about that? He'd be on the Outer Head by that time, communing with nature and thinking about this brilliant new novel of his which was actually, as we now know, just the plot for your murder. His line would have been complete innocence and it would have been a line very difficult, if not downright impossible, to disprove.

"In fact it seems to me Kester had only two serious problems with this master plot. One was your car. Ideally no one was going to know exactly when you went missing, but if you had driven over from Oxmoon and left the car in his garage to avoid blocking the lane, the police were bound to ask him later why he didn't wonder where you were. But in fact it was his car, wasn't it? He could always have said he'd reclaimed it from you, just as he'd reclaimed his radio from Evan— he could always have said he found the car had been returned while he was out and he assumed you hadn't bothered to wait for him. But the second problem was more serious and that was the note he wrote to lure you to Rhossili.

"He didn't make a specific appointment to see you, did he? He didn't dare. He couldn't bank on you destroying that note before you went off to be killed, and that meant he had to write it on the assumption that it might wind up in the hands of the police. So he could write nothing that might tie him to the mystery of your disappearence. He had to keep that note dead-casual yet at the same time he had to write something that would guarantee you'd immediately drop everything and rush to Rhossili.

"He mentioned Oxmoon, didn't he? He knew the way your paranoia worked, but I'll bet he kept the tone so benign and facetious that any outsider reading the note would think he was offering you infinite room for negotiation. That way you'd know he was on the warpath but the police would think he was pacifism personified.

"I suppose you believed at the time that he was on a good wicket for getting Oxmoon back, but that was just your guilt and paranoia making you irrational, wasn't it? As you yourself said when you spun me that fake explanation last night, the truth was Kester hadn't a hope of making a legal move to get Oxmoon back— and that was precisely why he had to murder you; if he'd killed Thomas, he'd never have dared raise the issue of extortion. He could arrange for Declan to give you a hard time before the family but that was as far as he dared go.

"But once you were dead, the scene would have been very different. I was the heir—and I was also his hero-worshiping slave. He could simply have moved back into Oxmoon to look after me. What could have been more suitable? I can just see the whole family clapping their hands in delight and exclaiming, 'Happy ending!'"

I finished my Coke and set down the bottle. "How am I doing?"

My father said, "So far so good. But I can't imagine how you can sustain—"

"Watch me. Okay, so Kester had set himself up very carefully, and apparently with one exception no one guessed what he was up to. Almost everyone who saw him during those final three days believed him to be cheerful and bursting with creativity—liberated, as Evan put it, from the burden of Oxmoon. Obviously Kester wanted to give the impression he was reconciled to Oxmoon's loss, but the truth was that given Kester's character and past that was just about the most unlikely thing which could have happened, and I think that Bronwen, who had this trick of seeing farther than anyone else, saw that his story was a fraud and asked him straight out what the hell he was up to. Well, I'm sure Kester didn't tell her the truth but I'd guess he said to fob her off that he hoped to get Oxmoon back and was planning to negotiate with you for its return. Perhaps he asked her to keep quiet about it until he'd broached the subject with you, I don't know, but the fact remains that she never spoke of that interview before he was dead and I suppose that after he was dead she realized what had happened and kept silent to protect you."

My father said, "I loved Bronwen" and shaded his eyes with his hand. He sounded like an old, old man talking of someone who had existed a long, long time ago.

"And so we come to the disaster itself," I said, rising to my feet and beginning to pace around the room. "Kester's biggest advantage was that he knew exactly how you'd react to the situation he set up for you. He knew you'd respond instantly to that note. He knew you'd never sit around waiting for him at the cottage. He knew you'd never be able to resist following him across the Shipway—and of course when you came he knew you were there. Caitlin and I proved conclusively today that he could have kept you under observation without you being aware of it.

"Kester was luring you on, just as you said he was. He wanted to make you think you could catch him up in that isolated spot and intimidate him in a round of tough negotiation about the future of Oxmoon."

"I only wanted to negotiate with him," said my father. "Only to negotiate."

"Yes, I can believe that because Kester clearly thought that was all you'd be prepared to do—he didn't think you'd be such a fool as to kill him and get yourself into what could only be a big mess. He'd hardly have lured you out to the Worm if he'd seriously believed there was a possibility you might kill him there. He knew you so well, didn't he? Your mind would have been an open book to him."

"He was my double image," said my father. "He was my other self, and we'd finally reached the point where our lives merged and we became identical. The Germans have a terrible legend about *Doppelgängers*. They say that when you see your double you die. It was as if Kester and I both died that night. It was as if neither of us came back alive."

"I'm not interested in folklore, just in hard facts. Now, here's what I think happened: you reached the southern flank and you saw him on that spur of rock, just as you said you did last night. I've no doubt at all that he'd picked that spot very carefully—he wanted to offer you a chase that would end by you catching him up at the Devil's Bridge, and you found you couldn't refuse this offer. You didn't turn back—you went on, and by the time he reached the Bridge and stopped in the middle you were only a few yards behind.

"Then comes the climax. Then this magician, this consummate actor stages what turns out to be his final scene. Heights don't in fact disable him but he's seen how he can make use of his dislike of them, and suddenly, there in the middle of the Bridge, he stages an attack of vertigo. He moans, he shouts, he calls to you for help, he gives a bravura performance of a coward in terror. Poor old Kester, you think—round the bend as usual. And you step forward to give him a helping hand.

"But this is the one spot where Kester, who's not a trained fighter, can get the advantage of an expert in unarmed combat. All he'd need to do would be to give you a hefty shove when you were off guard, and Kester was more than capable of a hefty shove. So he grabs you. But you're a fraction too quick for him—in the end he underestimated those commando reflexes—and you fight for your life so that in the end it's Kester, not you, who goes over the edge into the sea."

I stopped. My father said nothing. I looked at his white dead face and his black dead eyes and the candle began to flicker between us. We were both breathing rapidly and in a moment of panic I heard myself stammer, "It's all right. You can't prove it to me, but you don't have to. I *know* it was an accident. I *know* you killed in self-defense."

Nothing. No reply. Nothing.

"It wasn't murder," I said. "It's all right, I'll never believe it was. I acquit you."

My father leaned forward on the table and slowly buried his face in his forearms.

"Father..." I stumbled over to him, dragged up my chair, sat down at his side. "Forgive me, he was a magician, he dazzled me—I didn't understand what I was doing to you but I understand everything now, I can see the past in its entirety, I can see that Kester was the villain and you were the hero and I was fool enough to get everything mixed up—"

"But Hal," whispered my father, "there were no heroes and no villains in this

928

story. There were just two ordinary people who failed to draw the line."

He stopped speaking. Neither of us moved but as we stared at each other something happened to the silence in that room. It was no longer empty. It was heavy with the vibrations of a powerful personality as if some great actor had walked onstage to begin his final terrifying performance. I looked around but there was nothing to see. I looked over my shoulder but there was no one there. I looked back at my father and suddenly I realized that he was the source of the terror which was being generated in that room.

"My life merged with Kester's," said my father. "It's as if we're one now and that's why you mustn't call him a villain. If you condemn him you condemn me."

I tried to push my chair backwards away from him. I tried to speak but the air was so thick that I choked on it. I tried not to listen anymore but my father was saying rapidly in a low uneven voice: "It's no good; I can't keep silent. God help me, but I've got to tell you the truth, Hal—I've got to tell you the truth you don't want to hear."

X

There was no escape. I was paralyzed with fear. I had to listen.

"You guessed so much correctly," said my father. "You even guessed the vertigo at the end. But Hal, I knew Kester better than any other man on earth and I'd seen what he'd done to Thomas. Do you honestly think that in the end I didn't guess what was going on?

"When Kester collapsed in the middle of the Devil's Bridge and gave his bravura performance of a man suffering from vertigo, I didn't think, Poor old Kester, poor old sod. I saw straight through that act so I just stood at the beginning of the Bridge and waited. Finally he realized his plan had failed—he realized he was cut off in one of the most dangerous spots in Gower with a killer who wanted him dead. His nerve cracked. He went to pieces.

"He started crying—tears always came easily to Kester—and then he stumbled back towards me and begged me to forgive him. He confessed he'd planned to kill me but he said he now realized he'd never again delude himself that he could go through with it. I didn't believe him. I just asked him why he had wanted to kill me—at that stage I still believed he didn't need to kill me to get Oxmoon back—and then he began to say the most horrifying things . . . terrible truths . . . I could see quite plainly that he was mad but I knew I was mad too because I believed them. Everything he said made sense.

"He said he had to kill me because I was the violent distorted side of his personality, the man of action who throughout history had been the enemy of the man of peace. He said he had to kill me before he could live at Oxmoon again, just as war always had to be eliminated before peace could prevail. Then he said—he was still crying—he said he could see now that he could never go through with it because this theory had been based on an illusion. 'You're not really like that,' he said. 'You're just the man I might have been if my creative leanings had been stamped out, and I'm the man you might have been if you'd had the courage to live your life a little differently.'

"And as soon as he said that he became intolerable to me.

"'I can't kill you,' he said, 'because if I kill you I kill myself,' but although I heard him say that I took no notice. All I could think was that he was the man I'd never been allowed to be—I looked at him and I knew I'd wasted my life and I couldn't endure it. I just couldn't look at him and stay sane.

"Moreover I didn't believe he wouldn't try and kill me again. I didn't see how he could look at me and stay sane either. I stood between him and Oxmoon which symbolized all that was finest in his nature. It was as if I'd deprived him of his true self and he had to kill me to get his true self back.

"He walked the last few steps towards me and I held out my hand as if in friendship. But when he reached to take it I caught him with a hook to the jaw. He wasn't badly hurt. I reckoned he'd be unconscious for no more than two minutes—two minutes I had to work out the best way to murder him.

"I nearly tossed him straight over the side but I thought, No, the cold water could bring him round and who knows what's down the bottom there; he might be able to swim to the side and climb out. Then I decided to strangle him but just in time I realized that a postmortem had to reveal water in the lungs so I knew I had to throw him over while he was still alive. I took a look over the edge but I was reassured. He couldn't have survived down there. The tide was rising fast and the water was roaring through the channel below and I knew he'd be smashed to death at once on the rocks.

"But I didn't want him to know anything about that. Before I pushed him over I gave him another blow to make sure he stayed unconscious. Then I did it. I murdered him in cold blood. And even before he hit the water I realized the full horror of what I'd done.

"I'd done what Kester himself had realized he couldn't do. I'd killed my other self—and my other self was the finer side of my nature, the artistic, creative side, the side that longed for peace. Then I saw my future, I saw it all; I saw Oxmoon turning to dust in my hands as I won every battle but lost all the way along the line—I even saw myself sitting at that piano in the ballroom and being unable to play anymore. Later I tried to kill myself to escape the nightmare but I wasn't even allowed to die. I met Pam again and then I lost my nerve for killing myself because I loved her too much to prefer death to life. So my punishment wasn't to die; it was to live. I had to live with Kester's memory. I had to live on with the knowledge of what I'd done.

"I never wanted you to know. Pam always said you ought to be told, but I couldn't, couldn't... In fact I thought right up till now that I'd never be able to do it; but somehow... when you acquitted me like that... I couldn't have lived with that acquittal, I couldn't have stood by and known I'd destroyed your faith in what Kester represented to you, I couldn't have permitted our reconciliation to take place at his expense. It wouldn't have been fair to him, and he was such a remarkable man, Hal, there was so much that was fine about him—you mustn't think of him as an evil magician, you must remember him as the cousin who loved you—"

"No." I was shaking my head. I shook it violently. The room seemed to be revolving. I heard the scrape of my chair as I struggled to my feet.

"But Hal, you can't forgive me and not forgive him—"

"I must." I could feel my mind begin to split in two. "I can only forgive you if I think of him as the villain."

"But can't you see—"

"You're trying to divide me," I said, "but I can't be divided. You both want me but you can't both have me. *I'll die if I'm divided.*" I somehow got to the sink and started to retch. All that came up was the Coke. I retched again and again and again.

I was aware of him crossing the room to me. Or at least I was aware of someone crossing the room. Of course I knew there were more than two of us present but I didn't dare look back to see which one was coming to claim me. The air was like lead. I could hardly breathe. My mind kept trying to split and I was only just able to hold it together.

"It's all right, Hal. I'm here."

But I didn't know which one he was. He was right behind me. I lost my nerve. "Go away!"

"Hal..." That was my father. I was almost sure it was my father but I still didn't dare turn around.

"Stay away from me!" I shouted, and the next moment Kester's voice shot back: "Hold fast! Stand firm!"

I blew my mind.

XI

"*Kester!*"

"Hal, no—"

"*Kester, Kester—*"

"Hal, it's your father—*your father—*"

"Oh no, oh my God—*Kester—*"

"Kester's dead, Hal—he's dead, he's dead, I killed him—"

I shouted in terror. I was in a frenzy. I tried to fight him but then the miracle happened and he pulled one of his commando tricks on me. That was how I knew he really was my father. He tripped me, flung me against the table and doubled my arm behind my back to keep me there. I was reminded of the time long ago when he had beaten me for spitting at him and shouting that I wished I were Kester's son.

"Help me, Father, help me—"

"Yes, but you must be calm. I can't help you unless you're calm."

I tried to think of Emily Brontë. There were no words but I remembered her courage and her faith. My breath was coming in sobbing gasps but I tried to breathe more evenly. The air still felt like lead. I kept my eyes squeezed shut because I knew that if I opened them I'd see Kester watching us.

My father's grip slackened. "That's better. All right, up you come."

He helped me stand upright. As soon as my hands were released I pressed them to my eyes.

"Come along," said my father. "This way." And although my hands covered my closed eyes I heard his quick breath as he blew out the candle and plunged us into darkness. At once I was in terror again but his voice said levelly, "It's all right. Keep your eyes shut and hold on to me," and his arm was around my shoulders to prevent me splitting into pieces.

He led me outside. We crossed the yard. When we reached the mews house the front door must have been on the latch because he never paused to find a key or ring the bell. Opening my eyes a fraction I peered through my fingers. Pam was there. I saw her crossing the kitchen towards us and for the first time in my life I was glad to see her because I knew she could cope with me without turning a hair. In fact to Pam I'd be just another run-of-the-mill case, nothing to get excited about, just another mind that needed vacuuming, sanitizing and stitching together again with her usual professional skill.

The tears were streaming down my face. I said: "Please help me, I've gone mad," and then I stumbled forward into her outstretched arms.

XII

"Harry, bring down the electric blanket—it's in the small spare room. It's all right, Hal, you're suffering from shock, this is perfectly normal, nothing to worry about, just do exactly as I say."

But I couldn't. I was too frightened. "Don't give me any drugs. I can't lose consciousness. If I lose my grip on my mind I'll never get it back together again."

"Yes, of course," said Pam as if I'd made a rational statement. "I quite understand, don't worry about it."

Some unknown time passed. They remade the bed in my father's room. My father undressed me and stuffed me into a pair of his pajamas. I tried to help him but I had to give up because I had to concentrate fully on holding my mind together. The bed was hot. The electric blanket was at full blast. Pam brought me some disgusting sweet tea.

"Shall I put on some music?" said my father, trying to help.

"Oh, no, nothing must distract me. Nothing. Don't even talk. I've got to stop my mind splitting."

My father looked appalled but Pam said, "Of course," sat down in a chair nearby and took some pink knitting out of a faded carpet bag. Then she said to my father, "It's all right, I'll sit with him for a while. You go in the other room."

A long time passed in a silence broken only by the click of Pam's needles. I kept a watch on the room to make sure Kester didn't come back but we remained undisturbed and slowly I started to relax. But that frightened me. I was afraid I might fall asleep.

"I'm not going to sleep tonight, Pam."

"All right." Click-click-click went the needles. "One night without sleep never did anyone any harm."

"But I've got the rest of my life to live through! Pam, stop that bloody knitting and listen a minute. How mad am I? I want to know."

Pam stopped knitting and regarded me sympathetically. "What makes you so sure you're mad?"

"I blew my mind."

"Uh-huh. How? Or would you rather not talk about it?"

But words streamed out of me as I discovered that by talking I could keep my mind together. Pam listened and made what I recognized as neutral comments except that they didn't seem neutral anymore. I had never realized that words like "I see" and noises like "Hm" could exude such infinite understanding.

". . . and so as I heard the voice of a dead man," I concluded at last, "that must mean I'm crazy."

"Hm. Tell me . . . why are you so convinced it was Kester's voice?"

"Oh, there was no question about it. He had a deeper voice than my father's— he sounded just like my grandfather."

"Then why couldn't it have been your grandfather speaking? What made you so sure you were hearing Kester?"

"He used the words 'Hold fast, stand firm.' That was a great catchphrase of Kester's."

"But Kester hardly had the monopoly of it—I've heard Harry trot out those words more than once, and perhaps your grandfather trotted them out too."

"Well, I . . . yes, as a matter of fact I think he did. But do you mean to say—"

"You still haven't explained why you were so sure it was Kester speaking."

"Well, I . . . well, he . . . Pam, *he was there*, I know he was, he was in the room, I could feel him, the air was like lead, it was weighted with his presence. And then he seemed to emanate from my father. I looked at my father and saw Kester— not physically; physically they were dissimilar, but Kester's spirit was there. My father made this remark about how his life had merged with Kester's, and then of course I saw at once—"

"Of course. You were in a highly disturbed and emotional state. All you needed was a suggestion."

"But Pam, it was more than that, I swear it! Kester was *in that room*, I'm absolutely convinced he was—"

"Okay," said Pam laconically. "He was there. So what?"

I stared at her. She'd hooked me. I was so stunned by the question that all terror was wiped from my mind.

"What do you mean, for God's sake?"

"Well," said Pam reasonably, "if he was there, surely he would have been benign to you? He loved you; you were like a son to him. Why should he have wanted to frighten you out of your mind? Or to put it another way, what made you think that he'd be so angry with you? Why were you so terrified of seeing him?"

"But don't you see," I said unsteadily, the words tumbling from my mouth, "I'd turned against him, I'd been disloyal, I'd called him the villain of the story— Kester who loved me..." But I couldn't go on. Tears were streaming down my face again. That was when I knew how mad I was. I wasn't mad just because I was crying in front of a woman. I was mad because I didn't care that I was crying in front of a woman. I felt tears were the only conceivable release from an intolerable grief. I wondered dimly how I was going to stop. I didn't want to stop but I had to hear what Pam was going to say next and I knew she wouldn't speak till I was quiet. Curiosity won. I stopped crying and waited.

Eventually she said without emphasis: "Yes. You were feeling guilty. You sat there with your father and the two of you generated this colossal miasma of guilt. No wonder the air seemed like lead! That sort of atmosphere would make any lungs function abnormally."

I was conscious of being on the brink of a huge relief, but I couldn't quite believe it. I whispered: "What you're really saying is that I hallucinated."

"That's a very emotional word, and like all emotional words it can be very misleading. It's so often used to describe reactions that have little to do with its clinical definition."

"But I heard his voice! Don't people who hallucinate hear voices?"

"Well, if you'd heard the voice of Napoleon or Queen Victoria I confess I'd be slightly perturbed, but I think Kester's voice seems natural enough for you to hear in the circumstances. Your father used a phrase that reminded you of him. Well, why not? They were cousins, brought up by the same man who you tell me also used that phrase. They probably had a lot of tricks of speech in common, and perhaps at that crucial moment when he was under great stress your father's voice was lower than usual with emotion; we don't always speak in exactly the same timbre. Also don't forget that you yourself were under great stress and in your guilty terror you were highly suggestible. Quite honestly, Hal, I think this is all very normal and I don't see the need to resort to emotional explanations."

When I could speak I said, "I want so much to believe you. But Pam, how do you explain this... this metaphysical nightmare, this... this terrifying relationship between my father and Kester?"

"Oh that," said Pam, picking up her knitting again. "Oh, that's all very simple, no problem there. I could give you a rational explanation of their relationship without batting an eyelid."

All I could say was "Christ Almighty." I gazed at her with the most profound admiration. "You don't believe in paranormal phenomena?" I said cautiously at last.

"I wouldn't say that. I believe there are different ways of looking at a given situation and none of those ways need necessarily be invalid. But I do think the classification 'paranormal' should be reserved for those situations which can't be explained rationally, and in my opinion this case just doesn't fall into that category."

I sat up in bed, punched the pillows into a better shape behind me and said, "Explain."

"Certainly. You can dress this case up to the nines in occult language and make it out to be quite a ghost story, but in fact all that's really going on here is an extreme case of sibling rivalry aggravated by some very malign coincidences."

I saw salvation. "Okay, I'll buy it. Let's have your professional analysis."

She smiled at me. Then she put aside her knitting again, settled herself more comfortably in her chair and said: "Very well. This, as a modern Chaucer might say, is The Psychiatrist's Tale. . . ."

XIII

"This is the story," said Pam, eminently rational, utterly sane, "of two boys, not overpoweringly alike but with three vital things in common: an artistic inclination, the background of Oxmoon and your grandfather John Godwin—and let me say straightaway that *there's* the man I'd like to put in deep analysis! A classic example of someone who says Do as I say but don't do as I do. 'Do the done thing!' he says as he lives openly with his mistress! No wonder those boys got mixed up.

"Now, what are we to make of John? In some ways he cuts an attractive figure, and certainly in these days of sexual revolution and blurred class distinctions we're not going to faint with horror at his private life. But the point about John is that he had hang-ups which this unorthodox private life underlined and even exaggerated; if he'd merely spent fifty years living with your grandmother Blanche I doubt if those hang-ups would have stood out like a bunch of sore thumbs, but as it was, the deeper he waded into immorality the more obsessed he became with his two favorite psychological occupations: doing the done thing and drawing the line.

"Now, normal people like you and me don't agonize much over this sort of thing—we just go out and do what we instinctively feel is right or wrong and that's that. But for John Godwin, life is apparently not so simple. Here you have a divided man, a man who comes on strong as a conservative moralist but who spends years of his adult life behaving like a freewheeling radical. Both roles seem equally right to him but at the same time he can argue that both, for various reasons, are equally wrong. Now, this is the sort of moral conflict which can drive people not necessarily round the bend but certainly into a disturbed emotional state, and according to Harry the one subject that was taboo in his father's presence was insanity.

"Was Bronwen the cause of this troubled state of mind? I doubt it. I see Bronwen as the catalyst, splitting open deep fissures that already existed in his personality. I haven't sufficient information so it's impossible to explain John comprehensively to you, but I should very much like to know more about his relationship with his parents and with that grandmother in the asylum—and indeed more about his whole childhood at Oxmoon. The impression is of a man obsessed with keeping himself in check—a man irrationally frightened of losing control of his mind. Thus 'doing the done thing' and 'drawing the line'—or trying to—was his way of feeling safe, of staying sane. Mind you, I'm not saying he wasn't basically a good man but what I am saying is that he wasn't a simple one.

"Anyway he was the vital father figure in those two boys' lives and they picked up all his off-key vibrations with the result that they too became obsessed with the need to do the done thing and cut a conventional figure as an English gentleman—a pattern of behavior which in fact had very little to do with their highly individual personalities. So you wind up with two boys facing the same problem: how do they fit themselves into this artificial but apparently highly desirable mold?

"Well, Kester appears to wriggle out of the dilemma. He has the advantage that John's his uncle, not his father, and he has this mother who backs him up. It's hard for me to form much of an impression of Kester's parents, but the father seems a shadowy figure, no doubt prevented by his illness from being much involved with his son. However the mother's a strong personality and she's not afraid to be unconventional. Kester's very much influenced by his mother—and contrary to twentieth-century folklore this need not necessarily be a disaster; it all depends on the mother, of course, and even from this distance Ginevra comes across as well integrated, someone capable of living her own life and not being too emotionally wrapped up in her son. No, Kester's problem wasn't his mother. It was his uncle John.

"The more Kester, encouraged by his mother, wriggled away from John's straitjacket, the more guilty and the more inadequate he felt. John was a powerful figure. Kester was no doubt made to understand that he should emulate him—and he couldn't. Now, there's a problem situation if ever there was one, but it's all made a hundred times worse because there at Penhale Manor, being—apparently—the model son whom John adores, is this paragon, Cousin Harry.

"All right, Kester looks as if he's escaped from his fix but in fact, as we can see, that's an illusion, and he's locked up inwardly if not outwardly in this fatal straitjacket. Harry, on the other hand, appears to be wearing his straitjacket as if it were tailor-made for him but the truth is it's pinching at every seam. Harry's not allowed to be his real self—a scientist, a musician, a gifted unusual boy. He's packed off to boarding school to do the done thing and subconsciously he resents it. Now, that would be bad enough but the situation is made a hundred times worse—again—because there at Oxmoon, living the life Harry longs to lead and doing as he pleases in apparently unclouded bliss, is this fairy-tale prince, Cousin Kester.

"So by adolescence they're already locked in this bitter sibling rivalry for John's approbation and the jealousy's doubling with each twist of the screw. Oxmoon's the symbol of their relationship by this time—for Harry it represents the life he longs to lead but that is always denied him, and for Kester it represents his vital edge over his cousin and the ultimate justification of his failure to cut a conventional figure; he may not be a perfect Godwin but he's going to be the best master Oxmoon's ever had.

"And then the malign coincidences start to happen.

"They marry at about the same time and they marry radically different women. This should have helped but I suspect they found it disturbing. I'm not suggesting that they wanted each other's wives, but I know Harry admired Anna's intellect and—forgive me—perhaps she underlined that your mother was a little unsatisfactory to him in some respects. Then perhaps Kester admired your mother's sexiness which would have underlined to him that his own wife, though clever and charming, wasn't attractive in that way. In other words I think these marriages subtly exacerbated the jealousy which already existed, and this in its turn perhaps showed up the weak spots in both marriages and led to discontent.

"We don't actually know much about Kester's marriage. Kester's gilded it with a glowing romantic light but we never get to hear Anna's side of the story, do we? I'm quite prepared to believe it was a happy marriage, but I just wonder if it was as unflawed as Kester would have us all believe it was. In any marriage there are areas of stress and here, for instance, I can see at least two potential problems: one, it was childless, though they longed for children, and two, Kester was a writer and writers are notoriously difficult to live with. However as far as Harry was concerned Kester had the perfect marriage with this intelligent delightful wife in childless peace, and as far as Kester was concerned Harry was married to this sexy girl who was as good as a fertility goddess and produced four sons in four years. More jealousy, more discontent, more fatal twists of the screw.

"I don't need to elaborate on the war, do I? Kester the pacifist, Harry the war hero, each of them envying the other and feeling inadequate. Harry was quite unsuited to the S.A.S., of course, but as Kester was making a success on the home front Harry felt compelled to go out and do the done thing as glamorously as possible. What a disaster—but not quite such a disaster as the second malign coincidence which occurred when their wives died within months of each other.

"Kester gives the classic performance of the bereaved widower complete with nervous breakdown and Harry pretends to be contemptuous but he's not. He'd like to have a nervous breakdown too—he's riddled with guilt about your mother—but of course it's not the done thing so he can't. More repressed emotion. It never occurs to him that Kester might also be feeling guilty—not only about Anna but about his breakdown. I'm sure he envied Harry's stiff upper lip and apparently effortless adjustment to the single life—although the truth is that Harry's made a most unsatisfactory adjustment; he's just seducing every woman in sight in an attempt to stave off a breakdown.

937

"However Kester can't see that. Perhaps he's thinking that he too would like some kind of sex life, but Anna's the only woman he's ever had and maybe he secretly lacks confidence in himself. After all, he must have thought, how could he ever match that glittering Casanova, Cousin Harry? Safer not to compete at all.

"Nevertheless Kester longs for affection so it's quite natural for him to turn to children and particularly to little Gwyneth Llewellyn who even at an early age promises to be a miraculous fusion of Bella and Anna—clever, charming *and* sexy. An attraction to a child is a sign of sexual insecurity; a child is less of a threat than an adult. However Kester's not a willing pedophile; he's quite prepared to wait till Gwyneth's grown up before he makes any sexual move but at the same time he's intelligent enough to know that this could be a dangerous relationship for him, so although he invites her to Oxmoon he always has her chaperoned by other children.

"So the children's tea parties have their dark underside, but Harry never sees that. All he sees is that Kester's captured you, and now Harry's the one who's feeling inadequate again, seeing himself as a complete failure while Kester exhibits this undeniable talent for children . . . and so it goes on.

"Then finally—into this deeply disturbed and thoroughly unstable relationship between these two deeply disturbed and thoroughly unstable men—comes the catalyst, Thomas, which sets them on the road to tragedy.

"Now, to me, the outsider, the figure of Thomas is at this point almost as intriguing as the figure of John. For what have we here? We have a third man who regards John as a father figure. And if you look beyond Thomas's bombastic manners you finally see the man who fits the mold John's held up to those boys as ideal. Thomas conforms. He's very, very conventional. He works successfully on the land, just like his father before him, he's made a good marriage, he has a son to whom he's devoted, he did well in the war and thoroughly enjoyed being a soldier. He may be and probably is a far more mixed-up person than he seems, but the point is that he's projecting an approved image and although his hard drinking would indicate this isn't entirely easy for him, Harry and Kester aren't aware of any conflicts that would help them identify with him. Harry and Kester look at Thomas and they can't stand what they see—he's intolerable to them. Yet a lot of people seem to have been rather fond of old Thomas. That nice woman your Aunt Eleanor, for instance, still speaks warmly of him even now after all these years.

"But for Harry and Kester, who have both in their minds failed John, Thomas is anathema. Most of the time Harry's in a position to conceal this because he too is outwardly conforming to the right image, but no such pretense is available to Kester. Kester loathes him—and what he loathes, of course, isn't Thomas himself but what Thomas represents. Thomas's success in wearing the Godwin straitjacket underlines Kester's failure. Kester may appear to revel triumphantly in his unconventional life, but in his mind he always feels guilty that he's never managed to conform as his powerful—and probably much-loved—father figure wanted and expected him to do.

938

"In other words Thomas stimulated Kester's neurotic conflict just as Harry did, but because Thomas was a much more abrasive personality it was he and not Harry who finally lit the fuse to the keg of dynamite. If Anna had survived I think she could have put out the fire before the explosion; she would have had the intelligence to spot any abnormality before it got out of control and persuade Kester to seek help. But Anna was dead and so Kester was alone in this unbalanced state which inexorably deteriorated to the danger point.

"Kester believed he was avenging Anna when he went after Thomas, but I'm certain there was much more going on in his mind than that. I'm sure Thomas was indeed monstrously rude to Anna in 1939 and I'm sure Kester did want to avenge her, but I think in the end this was just the excuse he used to justify his behavior to himself. In my opinion what Kester really wanted to do was to kill this living reminder of his guilt and his inadequacy. In the disturbed mental state that followed his bereavement he found he could no longer live with this walking symbol of his failure to achieve what he believed to be a successful manhood.

"So he killed Thomas—and by killing him he locked himself up with your father in the downward spiral that led them both to the Worm's Head on that May night in 1952.

"You should ask your father to tell you the whole story of Thomas's murder. It would do him good to talk about it and I think it would be best for you now to know all the facts. That's a story where Kester really was the villain and your father just an innocent bystander. And yet . . .

"It's not so simple as that, is it? Words like 'villain' and 'hero' are so overworked that they have no meaning, and the truth is they explain nothing here. The explanation of this story lies in the past, perhaps even in the remote past, in the vast complicated web of personal relationships and interrelating circumstances that made those two men what they were. Your father, mirroring John, sums it up by saying, 'We were just two ordinary people who failed to draw the line.' Well, let him see it that way. Why not? It's an interesting point of view. But to my mind those two men weren't ordinary. They were two severely maladjusted people who failed to avert tragedy by resolving their neurotic conflicts. I'm a psychiatrist so naturally that's the way I see it, but what we have to do now is to work out how *you're* going to see those two men. We have to work out a way you can live with all this and go on to lead a normal life—no, I don't think we should start now. You're too tired and you won't be thinking clearly. We'll talk again tomorrow. Do you think you can sleep now? Or are you still reluctant to relax your grip on your mind?"

I said, "I'm going to be okay," and she kissed me and said gently, "Yes, you are." Then she took out her knitting and started clicking her needles again.

Ten minutes later I was asleep.

XIV

He came to me in my dreams, not the glittering hero of my childhood but a bedraggled magician with a broken wand in his hands. "Help me," he said. "Help me." But although I knew I had to perform an act of magic, I couldn't see how to mend his broken wand.

Then I remembered I was Saint George so I realized I had to find the dragon and kill it. The dragon, I now saw clearly, was the villain of the story and my father and Kester were its innocent victims. Drawing out my sword I rode my white horse across the Shipway but time and space were so fluid that when I reached the Inner Head I found myself at the gates of Oxmoon.

Then I saw it. I saw the dragon. It was the house. It was that brutal decayed monster with the shuttered sightless windows. Vile Oxmoon, not fit to live, destroying those I loved.

I made a Molotov cocktail and tossing it through the open front door I watched the house burn to the ground. But later as I walked through the charred ruins I found my father grieving with Kester and beyond them a man in an eighteenth-century wig said to me, "Look what you've done to my dream."

Then Evan said, "Let us pray for an act of redemption," and as I sank to my knees I was a medieval knight again and a church clock was thundering the hour. It struck twelve. I looked up. The sun was pouring down on me from a brilliant sky and as I rose to my feet my soldier's sword shone in my hand. I stared at the blade, and suddenly I realized it wasn't a sword at all but Kester's magic wand, restored and renewed.

I turned to face ruined Oxmoon. The earth was moving, the skies were rolling back, and at last in that electrifying moment of revelation my strength returned to me, I raised my sword above my head and *I waved his magic wand*. . . .

XV

"I had this dream," I said to Pam, "but I'm not going to tell you about it because I always vowed I'd never sink low enough to tell my dreams to a psychiatrist."

Pam laughed. "I'm glad to see you exhibiting characteristic behavior! I can see that unlike your father you really do have nerves of steel."

We were sitting in the dining area over the remains of breakfast. My father had reclaimed his room and was listening to chamber music. I had drunk three cups of coffee and eaten an egg I didn't want. My untouched toast lay on a nearby plate.

"I'm all right," I said to Pam. "I was all right as soon as I knew that everything could be explained rationally. They were just two guys in need of a shrink, that's all, and I don't have to condemn them, you don't condemn the mentally ill, you just say 'That's tough' and feel sorry for them. So that's okay, isn't it, I don't have to be divided after all, I can just say 'That's tough' and be compassionate—to both of them. It's a kind of forgiving and I have to forgive, don't I, because if I go on trying to decide which one to blame I'll go nuts. Okay, fair enough, I forgive them. And now I can get on with my life and think about the future."

"Uh-huh," said Pam.

We were silent for a time. She was idly finishing a cigarette. I began to fidget with my cold toast. First I broke the bread up and then I tried to reduce the fragments to crumbs. Finally my voice said, "But they did such terrible things," and the next moment I was breaking down again.

This time I did mind crying. I minded it very much. I stumbled outside into the yard but it was raining. I ran across to shelter in my scullery but when I reached the back door I couldn't face opening it so I ran back. On reentering the mews house I found Pam was still sitting at the kitchen table.

I sat down and said, "I've got to put it right. It's as if they've passed me the burden of their guilt and I have to find some way of setting that burden aside. I can't live with the situation as it is; I've got to put right what went wrong." And I told her about my dream.

"I see them as crucified," I said, "and Oxmoon—today's ruined Oxmoon—reflects that crucifixion. And the only way to wipe out a crucifixion is to stage a resurrection, so that's what I've now got to do. I've got to wave the magic wand and restore what's been destroyed, because only then, when Oxmoon's been redeemed, can I live in peace with what they've done."

Pam said simply, "How are you going to do it?"

"I don't know." I crumbled some more toast. Then I said irritated: "Aren't you going to analyze my dream?"

"You seem to have done that rather ably yourself. What you have to do now is to find the magic wand—your instrument of redemption."

"I suppose you find redemption a very emotional word loaded with religious overtones."

"Oh, I'm not hung up on religion," said Pam mildly. "To me it's just another way of looking at a given situation. I could say you're looking for a satisfactory adjustment to an unpalatable set of facts, but why bother? Redemption's a good word. It means to buy back, doesn't it, and you want to buy back the past so that you can reshape it in a way that'll fit your present. That all seems very reasonable to me."

"But how do I find my magic wand?"

"Ah. Well . . . Where did you get the idea of a magic wand from?"

"From Kester. My magician."

"And what was *his* magic wand?"

"I suppose you'd say it was a phallic symbol."

"I could certainly argue that it had phallic overtones for Kester, but we're not concerned with symbolism at the moment, only with reality. What was the wand that Kester waved day after day with the most unquenchable determination?"

I saw the light. "His pen." I hit the table with my fist. "That's it—his novels!"

941

I leaped to my feet. "I'm going to sell his novels and raise the money for the endowment the National Trust needs to take over Oxmoon!" I kissed her. "You're a genius! Thank God I've got a psychiatrist for a stepmother!"

"Hm," said Pam. Of course she knew a manic mood swing when she saw one.

"Novels make millions nowadays! Think of Geoffrey's publishing stories! I'll take the novels to New York, enlist Geoffrey's help, make a fortune and resurrect Oxmoon from the grave!" I was shouting in my ecstasy. After hours of appalling pain I had finally achieved a miraculous relief. I was going to put the magic back into Oxmoon, I was going to recapture the lost paradise of my childhood, I was going to wipe out all the tragedy and ruin, I was going to make my two fathers live again.

"Sit down, Hal," said Pam gently. "There's something I have to tell you."

I humored her. I was already planning my drive to Swansea to collect the inevitable bottle of champagne.

"I had to lead you through all that," said Pam, "because I knew you'd eventually work out the full meaning of your dream for yourself and I thought it was better if you did so in my presence. Hal, it's a lovely idea, and certainly the perfect answer to your desire for redemption, but very unfortunately it's not an option that's available to you."

I stared at her. "Why the hell not?"

"Now, don't worry—I'm sure we can find another way of coming to terms with this problem—"

"Pam, for Christ's sake tell me what the hell you're getting at!"

Pam sighed. Then she said with extreme reluctance: "Kester's manuscripts no longer exist. Your father burned the lot."

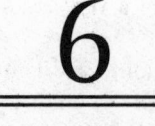

I

THAT WAS the moment when I ceased to be a rationalist. If behaving in a rational manner and thinking rational thoughts couldn't redeem Oxmoon I was no longer interested in behaving like a rational man. It was time for fanaticism, time for belief when all logical hope was gone, time to put iron in the will and granite in the soul.

"I can't accept that," I said to Pam. "To accept that would be to admit defeat— and I'm not interested in losing." I felt like some general leading his men into battle against fearful odds and haranguing them to victory. "I'm going to win," I said. "I'm going to win."

For the first time in my life I saw Pam look rattled. She kept calm; no doubt this was a reflex developed by years of experience, but her characteristic nonchalance hardened into an expressionless immobility. She said nothing.

I said to her: "Why did my father burn those manuscripts?" but I already knew. I asked the question to force a conversation and compel her to communicate with me.

"It was Kester's passion for the *roman à clef*. Your father couldn't be certain that Kester hadn't based his final master plot on a previous novel."

"So Kester never took those manuscripts to Ireland. He left them at Oxmoon. Is that what you're saying?"

"That's right. Of course it was a relief to your father when you deduced the manuscripts were in Ireland but shied away from contacting Declan."

"You seriously expect me to believe that Kester would have left his manuscripts—which were like children to him—at Oxmoon for my father to burn?"

"But he did, Hal. They were in two trunks in the attics."

"Then those must have been the manuscripts that Kester was content to have destroyed. I'm sure he would have taken his most precious work to Ireland."

"Harry spoke to Siobhan Kinsella on your behalf after Kester's will was granted probate—after all, Kester wanted you to have his work and Declan would hardly have refused to let you have any manuscripts that were in his possession. But there was nothing in Ireland, Hal. Nothing."

"But this is insane. I just can't believe—"

"You're looking back with the wisdom of hindsight. Try and see the situation in its context. When Kester left Oxmoon he had no reason to think his manuscripts were in any danger. Harry doesn't normally behave like a book-burning fascist and how could Kester have foreseen a situation in which Harry would feel driven to destroy those manuscripts for fear they might provide the police with clues? Harry, as a talented man himself, respected the talent in Kester. Normally he wouldn't have dreamed of destroying Kester's work, and if Kester had feared such a destruction when he left Oxmoon in '51 he would have been acting irrationally."

"But that's the point, isn't it?" I said. "Those two men were irrational about each other. That's the one thing that's been proved beyond all reasonable doubt! No, I'm sorry, Pam, but I think Kester would have taken every precaution that his most precious work didn't fall into my father's hands, and if the manuscripts aren't in Ireland then they must be hidden here at Oxmoon."

There was a pause while Pam tried to figure out the best way to handle me. In the end she fell back on the most neutral question available. "So?"

"So," I said, "I'm going to find those manuscripts. I'm going to find them even if it's the very last thing I ever do."

I went to interrogate my father.

At one point he tried to apologize for burning the manuscripts but I cut him off.

"I don't want your apologies, I want your help. Now, think, Father, and think hard. Where's the one place at Oxmoon where you'd never look for a manuscript?"

My father made an effort to compose himself but I could see he found me very intimidating. "The attics," he said. "Two trunks were easy enough to find, but searching for a stray manuscript in those rooms full of junk would be like searching for a needle in a haystack."

"Yes, but you'd be guaranteed to search there—it's the obvious place. Try and think of some place where you'd never look."

My father racked his brains. "Well, I suppose Kester could have taken up a floorboard somewhere—"

"Not Kester. The only thing he could do with his hands was hold a pen. How about the furniture? Do any of the cabinets have false sides?"

"The bureau in the morning room has a secret drawer but it's not big enough to hold more than a pocket diary. Why don't you have a look at the detailed inventory Kester drew up after the war? It's in the library among my 1963 correspondence with the National Trust. I sent them a copy to whet their appetite."

I withdrew to the library, and as soon as I entered the room I had such an inspired idea that I nearly swung all the way into a manic euphoria again. The one place at Oxmoon where Kester could safely have left his manuscripts was on a shelf in the fiction bays of the library. My father never read novels. In fact he had once told me he hadn't opened a novel since he had been forced to do so at school.

I combed the fiction bays. The shelves began immediately on the right of the door and extended some way down the room. Kester had been a great fiction reader and although his preference had been for nineteenth-century novels, the authors of the twentieth century were well represented.

But there were no unpublished manuscripts there.

I tried again. I checked behind each row of books to make sure there was no cache hidden beyond the leather-bound facade. Then pulling each book forward a couple of inches I checked that it was real and not a cardboard dummy containing the missing treasure.

That all took some time.

When I had drawn another blank I sat down at the library table and contemplated the room. I still thought Kester would have favored the library. A couple of manuscripts could have been slipped in among the bays of family papers at the far end of the room and they would be impossible to spot at a glance. I decided to make a comprehensive search but first, to satisfy myself that the furniture in the house could be excluded from my attentions, I found the inventory and skimmed through it.

The morning-room bureau was the only piece with a secret drawer, and my father had known about it. Obviously I was on the wrong track there.

Replacing the inventory I rolled up my sleeves and prepared to ransack the rest of the library.

III

It took me several days to ensure I had left no stone unturned. The family papers stretched all the way back to the eighteenth century when Robert Godwin the Renovator had put his architect's drawings of the future Oxmoon on file for posterity. Many shelves were dedicated to the records of my great-grandfather Bobby Godwin's forty-six years as master, but although these papers occupied a considerable amount of space they were orderly; my task in sifting them was time-consuming but not difficult. However Kester's papers were in a more chaotic state. He hadn't been the kind of man who could be bothered with efficient filing, and in between the immaculate records which marked the period when Thomas had been in control of the estate lay an uncharted wilderness of receipts, business correspondence and personal letters, all crammed into bulging files without regard for subject matter or chronological order. The temptation was to gloss over them as soon as it was obvious that no manuscripts were concealed there, but instinct told me they might contain some kind of clue and instinct, for once, was right.

I found an invoice, dated more than a year before Kester's death, from a publisher. The publisher was a representative of the so-called "vanity press," a firm that specialized in printing books at the author's expense. The invoice recorded that three novels had been printed for Kester, and on the bottom of the page Kester had noted: *Paid 2/2/51. Spare copies to attic trunk.*

I returned to my father.

"Do you remember the privately printed copies in one of the trunks?"

"Oh God, yes, although they weren't inside either of the trunks—he'd left them in boxes on the top. They were very difficult to burn and made a terrible smell."

"Did it occur to you to check the library to see if he'd left copies on the shelves?"

"Yes, I assumed the point of the private printing had been to enable him to place his own work alongside *The Prisoner of Zenda* and his other old favorites."

"So you found the library copies and burned them too." So completely did I accept this as inevitable that I didn't even bother to inflect the statement into a question.

"Well, no," said my father, "as a matter of fact I didn't. I searched the entire library but found nothing."

"That's odd." I stared at him. "Didn't you think at the time that it was odd?"

"Yes, but what struck me as even odder was why he'd arranged for the private printing. He never distributed any of the copies—I asked both Evan and Richard but they knew nothing about it at all."

"Maybe he planned to distribute the copies later—the date he paid the bill suggests he could only just have received them before you turned him out."

"Even so," said my father, "I still think it's odd that he never mentioned the printing to the members of the family who were closest to him. If an author goes to the expense of having even a small number of copies of his work printed the inference must surely be that he intends to circulate them."

"Perhaps he got cold feet about the idea. Kester was reserved about his work—and modest. In fact this whole flirtation with the vanity press is hard to understand."

"I agree it seems out of character, but it did happen."

"Yes—and what I'd like to know," I said, "is what happened to those copies which he didn't classify on the invoice as 'spare.'"

I returned to the library and subjected the nonfiction shelves to the same intense scrutiny which I had given the bays of novels, but there was nothing my father had missed. Still puzzled I resumed my examination of the family papers.

Pam offered to help but I saw through that ruse and realized she only wanted to signal sympathy so that I shouldn't become alienated from her. No doubt, anticipating the failure of my quest, she thought I was heading for a mental crash of catastrophic dimensions and she wanted to ensure that I had an easy retreat available into psychiatric care. As I drew near the end of my search of the library she encouraged me to tackle the attics. I could see her thinking that this would occupy me for at least another week and give her more time to help me find a "satisfactory adjustment" to my problem.

Despite my father's protests I had returned to lead an independent life in the scullery, but to appease him and to show Pam that I appreciated her misguided concern for my mental health I agreed to join them for dinner each night. I also reasoned that I would function better if I were fueled at least once a day with an adequate supply of cooked food.

I abandoned the library. I began to search the attics for those printed copies of the three novels which I felt sure still existed. And in the diary I was now keeping to relieve my troubled mind I found myself once more writing, *Soldier on.*

IV

I met him on my fourth day in the attics. I had never met him before because eleven years had separated his death from my birth and I had never before seen a close-up photograph of him taken in those brilliant glamorous days before he had become ill.

I met my great-uncle Robert Godwin, Robert Godwin the Winner. I met the family hero whom Kester had glorified in myth. I could remember Kester saying, "My father was this wonderful man, brilliantly clever, classically handsome, utterly charming, hugely successful, matchlessly brave—someone who always aimed at perfection, someone who had the courage and dedication to make all his dreams come true, someone who was a romantic, an idealist, a hero in every possible respect..." Kester had laid on the praise with a shovel but then he had been talking to children who liked larger-than-life heroes. Later when I was more cynical it occurred to me that he could never have known his father well; Great-Uncle Robert had died when Kester was eight. Nonetheless he had left a powerful legend behind him and the legend hinted at a powerful personality beyond the florid phrases of Kester's hyperbole.

I had just stumbled across another trunk of Kester's and once again I thought I'd struck gold because beneath the love letters from Anna, all bound with pink ribbon, I found two books with the name GODWIN on their spines. But the author wasn't Kester; it was his father. One book was a memoir about Lloyd George and the other was an account of various murder trials in which Robert had played a starring role as counsel for the defense.

When I had recovered from my disappointment I wondered why these books hadn't been on the library shelves but then I realized that these copies, personally inscribed to Great-Aunt Ginevra, were special. They would have been so precious to Kester, admiring his father as he did, that he would have preferred to keep them alongside his other sacred mementos of the past.

On the dedication page of the Lloyd George memoir the printed inscription merely read: FOR MY WIFE, but underneath this Robert had written: *For my dearest Ginette in memory of happier days—when we danced together beneath the chandeliers at Oxmoon while the orchestra played "The Blue Danube." My love now and always, your devoted friend,* ROBERT.

My first reaction was So they really did do it. It's always a shock when a story that one has cynically regarded as apocryphal turns out to be true, and in this case I found it was also a pleasant surprise. It's not often one finds documented evidence of a fairy tale. The discovery cheered me. Since I was bent on achieving a fairy tale myself it was good to know that fairy tales occasionally did happen.

The date of publication was 1921, when Kester was only two and Robert had already fallen ill, and on rereading the inscription I was struck by the curious substitution of the word "friend" for "husband." I turned to the murder-trials anthology to see if he had been consistent and found that he had. Then flicking over the page to the photograph at the front of the book, I found myself face to face with Robert Godwin at the zenith of his legal career.

This was not the invalid in the wheelchair I remembered from my father's old photographs, and this was not the indistinct figure in any of the Edwardian family groups which my grandfather had loved. This was a formal studio portrait of a man a few years my senior. Contrary to Kester's romantic propaganda he was not classically handsome. He looked a thug, tough as nails. There was a fanatical cast to those light eyes and a brutal set to his strong straight mouth. His brown hair was ruthlessly parted and severely cut. Kester had inherited the jaw and the high broad cheekbones and the paleness, if not the hypnotic setting, of those bold unnerving eyes.

I propped the book open at the photograph and as I continued my examination of the trunk I occasionally looked at him. He looked back. After a while he began to look as if he knew all about me and after a longer while I looked back and felt I knew all about him.

I completed my search of the trunk. Then snapping the book shut I tucked it under my arm and went off to the mews house for dinner.

V

"I don't see the resemblance," said my father obstinately. He could never bear to think I was more like Kester's side of the family than like his own. Evan had remarked once on the slight physical resemblance. So had Great-Uncle Edmund.

"Look at the bone structure of the face."

"That's like your grandfather."

"No, Granddad was handsome and distinguished. This guy's just a thug with sex appeal."

"This," said Pam, abandoning her cooking, "I have to see." She took one look at the photograph and said: "An obsessive personality—almost certainly treated women as sex objects—possibly needed psychiatric help."

"You see?" I said to my father. "Just like me."

Even my father had to laugh. He took another look at the photograph. "I never knew Robert well," he said. "I just remember him as a bad-tempered bastard but of course with that illness one could hardly have expected him to be a ray of sunshine. But my father was devoted to him, absolutely devoted, and used to visit him every day."

"I can't tell you how much I wish I could have talked to John," said Pam, returning to her pan of chicken Maryland, "but all psychiatrists have their stories of the one who got away." Turning the chicken she added over her shoulder: "To me, Hal, the big mystery of the whole story is why your great-grandfather left Oxmoon to Kester when the obvious and very much fairer solution would have been to leave it to John, the family saint. If you come across any explanation during your searches, do let me know."

This riveted me. I stared at her. "My God, how different everything would have been if Kester hadn't inherited Oxmoon!"

"Exactly. Bobby had a strong motive to break with any family tradition of primogeniture. So what happened?"

"I don't see your problem," said my father. "Bobby obviously felt so sorry for Robert that he fell over backwards to grant Robert's dying request."

"I agree that the answer must lie in Bobby's relationship with Robert," said Pam, "but is Robert's illness really sufficient to explain this mystery? I wonder. The trouble is that we don't know enough about Bobby to figure out what might have been going on in his mind. All we know for sure is that he was the child

948

of an unhappy marriage and had to lock up his mother in a lunatic asylum. Now, *there's* a nice trauma for you! And to my mind that mental disorder at the end of his life was never satisfactorily diagnosed—"

"You can see why we married," my father said to me. "She was seduced by our family's unsolved psychiatric problems."

This sort of frivolous conversation successfully carried us through dinner. I was very much aware of their tact in not asking me how I was getting on with my search.

After coffee I said, "I'd better be getting back," but Pam thought it was time to prescribe some therapeutic relaxation, so she answered, "No, don't go yet—now that we're in a nostalgic mood let's get out the family albums," and I thought it wiser not to argue with her. Besides by this time I was more than willing to escape into the past.

Opening the first photograph album I was immediately transported back more than fifty years into another world. I saw THE FAMILY, headed by a good-looking cheerful *paterfamilias* who towered above a plain dumpy woman labeled MARGARET. Grouped around this ill-assorted couple were four young men, a girl of uncertain age and a sulky cherub labeled THOMAS. I read the names of the young adults from left to right: ROBERT, CELIA, LION, JOHN, EDMUND. The date was 1913.

Pam and my father had drifted into an argument over group therapy but I interrupted them by saying, "What was Lion's real name?"

"Lionel."

"Oh, I see. I thought he might have been nicknamed Lion the way some people are nicknamed Tiger." I turned the page and saw another photograph of the family but this time Celia was missing, presumably operating the camera, and her place was taken by a gorgeous piece who was batting her eyelashes at Robert. Six years before Kester's birth Great-Aunt Ginevra was already hell-bent on setting the tragedy in motion by seducing her childhood sweetheart, although Robert, looking straight ahead, was inscrutable.

". . . well, I'm absolutely opposed to group therapy—I think it's a load of rubbish."

"All right, darling, you can live here in splendid isolation forever as far as I'm concerned, but I just thought I'd mention this new group in case . . ."

I was looking at wedding photographs, pictures of Robert and Ginevra, Lion and Daphne, John and Blanche. All the couples looked as if they were thinking noble thoughts on true love. I wondered what it could have been like to marry a girl without sleeping with her first.

". . . and the last thing I want is to sit around with some neurotic middle-aged executives and listen to them whining about their sex lives—"

"Father, were your parents happy?"

"What? Yes, of course—devoted. Now, look here, Pam—"

"All right, darling, you stay in your room and listen to music twenty hours a day and never speak to a soul. If you're happy the last thing I want is to make you miserable . . ."

My grandmother Blanche was beautiful. I recognized my dark eyes in the face so different from mine and suddenly I wished I could have known her. And yet here she was in the present, just as Robert was, and in a way I was meeting her after all.

"Father, why didn't Granddad marry Bronwen straightaway after your mother died?"

"Bronwen was married to Morgan. And anyway, men of his class didn't marry women of her class in those days—it's probably hard for you to understand but back in the Twenties this country was a different planet. Marriage between the classes was practically banned by law, like marriage between blacks and whites in South Africa today."

"The culture of the classes was so different, Hal," said Pam more rationally, "that the only common ground on which their representatives could meet was in the bedroom. That's why John's first instinct would have been to keep Bronwen as his mistress—he wasn't just being selfish, he was being realistic. Marriage would have been very difficult if not downright impossible."

"Marriage is always very difficult if not downright impossible," said my father.

"Oh Harry, for God's sake forget I mentioned the group therapy! Run off and listen to a string quartet!"

I continued turning the leaves of the album. I saw Aunt Marian, pigtailed, with a shy-looking girl labeled RHIANNON. I saw Bronwen and various babies. I saw Dafydd, a chunky boy of twelve, holding up a fish on the end of a line.

"Father, why do you get on so well with Dafydd?"

"... and anyway I couldn't face the journey to Swansea, you know quite well I won't leave this house.... What, Hal? Oh, Dafydd's like Bronwen; he understands more than most people do—and he's like Pam; I can rant and rave at those two as much as I like but they never lose patience with me, God knows why. Well, Pam loves me, but as for Dafydd—"

"He loves you too," said Pam.

"Don't be absurd! Dafydd's not queer, he's just not interested in copulation. Christ, all you psychiatrists think about is sex—sex, sex, sex, sex, sex..."

Great-Uncle Edmund flitted by with Great-Aunt Teddy and a juvenile Richard and Geoffrey. There was a bright studio portrait of my aunt Francesca who lived in America, but no photographs of her mother Constance. However my grandfather reappeared again and again, aging steadily until he became as I remembered him, silver-haired and distinguished, with Bronwen still smiling at his side.

"... and Thomas used to say all queers should be castrated—"

"A highly suspicious remark," said Pam, "but I've long since added Thomas to the list of Godwins I wish I'd met."

"I know what you're thinking but for once you're dead wrong. Thomas wasn't queer. My God, when I remember him wrecking that cottage with his heterosexual horseplay—"

"Well, of course the homosexuality was repressed—"

"Balls!"

There was a photograph of Thomas with Eleanor at my parents' wedding but I barely noticed him. I had eyes only for my mother. It was the first time I had seen her since my father's revelations. I looked at the fresh-faced girl in the white dress and thought of her calling that secret baby by that childish pathetic name.

"... and anyway I think he fancied Bella although he never actually made a play for her. But then any man would have fancied Bella so I mustn't be too tough on poor old Thomas. No, Kester's sex life was more debatable than Thomas's—oh, and by the way, Hal, you won't find any photographs of Kester in that album. I chose the photos when I was in therapy at the hospital, and selecting pictures of Kester was the point where I drew the line."

I didn't answer. I had found a photograph of a blond stout baby clutching a beer bottle and looking outraged. The caption read: HAL, 1940.

I closed the book. "How strange it is," I said, more to myself than to them, "that I should be in the same album as long-extinct people like Great-Uncle Lion—how strange that I should be so absolutely connected to so many people I never met or barely knew. When I save Oxmoon it won't just be for Kester and Father. It'll be for all of them."

There was a silence. I had referred to the great unmentionable subject, my dream of redemption which was coming to a sticky end. As my father looked at Pam for help I realized that his inconsequential bickering had been his way of concealing his frantic anxiety.

The telephone rang. We all jumped. It rang four times before Pam answered it.

"Oh hullo," she said in a pleasant voice. "Yes, he's just here." She turned to me and held out the receiver. "It's Gwyneth Llewellyn."

VI

"I'm calling you as an old friend," said Gwyneth tentatively.

"Sure. In what other capacity could you possibly call?"

"Don't be hostile." It was a plea, not a reproof. "I've been thinking so much about our meeting. Have you got any further in your investigations?"

"I'm on a different tack. I'm trying to track down Kester's last manuscripts so that I can get them published."

"Great! But aren't they in Ireland?"

I turned my back on my father and Pam, who were trying to pretend they had no interest in the conversation. "The majority are lost," I said, "but he had his three favorites privately printed, and I'm sure there's a surviving copy of each one of them somewhere at Oxmoon." I paused for no more than a couple of seconds. "Why don't you come over tomorrow and join the search?"

She never even hesitated. "I couldn't make it till the evening."

"That doesn't matter, it's light till well after nine. I'll be in the attics—come in through the scullery," I said and hung up. Then I stood looking at the phone in disgust. I knew quite well it wasn't help with the search that I wanted. I wanted to divert myself from the coming failure which I hadn't the guts to face.

951

VII

Some time after lunch on the following day I found the oil painting which Kester had hung on the half-landing of the staircase but which my father had returned to its old home in the attics—probably because it reminded him of someone else who had drowned at the Worm's Head.

The painting showed a beautiful woman with the blue eyes that had become one of the family's recurring trademarks. She was wearing an elaborate evening gown but there was an earthiness about her which suggested she hadn't always spent her time lying on a chaise longue to conform with the Victorian image of desirable womanhood. I wondered what the Llewellyns had been like in those days. They could hardly have been on a social par with Anglo-Welsh gentry like the Godwins, but they must have been a cut above the usual Welsh families in Gower.

I worked on, toiling through the detritus of the nineteenth century, and as I worked those blue eyes followed me around the room.

"Hal?" It was the other Gwyneth, twentieth-century Gwyneth, recalling me to the present. As I heard her footsteps on the back stairs I glanced at my watch. The time was half-past eight.

"I'm in here!" I shouted, and listened to her footsteps echoing in the corridor. As she walked in I almost expected to see her in a Victorian evening gown but she was wearing a navy linen suit with a frilly white blouse and looked as if she were about to lecture the Upper Sixth on some tiresome corner of English literature—Lamb's *Essays*, perhaps, or Sterne's *Tristram Shandy*. I could now clearly see that the resemblance to the other Gwyneth was minimal. The only link was the color of the eyes.

"Oh look!" she exclaimed, seeing the picture. "It's the Harlot! I'd forgotten how sweet she looked, all togged up like that! Poor girl, how tough it must have been for her, marrying into another culture—and how terrible to think she became so unhappy that she went mad at the end."

"Oh, everyone goes mad at Oxmoon in the end," I said. "That's standard behavior. I'll go mad myself if I don't find these three novels." And as I brought her up to date with the details of my search my jeans once more began to feel like a straitjacket around the groin.

"How odd about the private printing," said Gwyneth, "but I bet those three novels were his trilogy. The trilogy was the one work he felt was really good."

I paused. "I do remember him mentioning a trilogy—didn't it incorporate that novel about Gwyneth Godwin and Owain Bryn-Davies?"

"Yes, it was a family saga, although I don't know how closely he stuck to the true story. But I do know why he wanted to write it. He told me once that he didn't like Galsworthy and wanted to prove he could do something better than *The Forsyte Saga*."

"I can remember him being cutting about Galsworthy. In fact he put me off so much that I never read any of the Galsworthy novels."

"Neither did I. Elizabethan literature was my specialty up at Oxford." She walked over to Robert Godwin's memoir which I had left on top of Kester's trunk of mementos. "What was your final verdict on Kester's death?" she said, glancing at the book. "Accident or suicide?"

"I came to the conclusion that it didn't matter. What matters is that he's dead, and death was a solution, whether he chose it or not, to problems which had led him into hell."

She went on turning the pages of the book.

"He did care about us," I said, "but we were only a small part of his life. I don't feel anymore that he deserted me. Or if I do still feel that, I can forgive him."

On and on she went, flicking through the pages, not looking at me, her face in shadow.

I took the book from her hands.

"Forget him," I said.

"I can't."

I had hoped her willingness to come to Oxmoon that evening had signified that she was ready to try casting off her shackles but I realized now that I had been mistaken. Unbeatable Kester, fourteen years dead, and still winning a race I seemed forever destined to lose. I knew this was the moment when I should abandon all hope of winning her from him, but the trouble was that I wasn't the kind of man who found it easy to abandon all hope. The thought of failing was intolerable to me.

"All right," I said, "then if we can't forget Kester, let's remember him." I headed for the door. "Let's take a stroll through the house and see if we can pick up some vibes."

She said surprised, "You believe in ESP?"

"No. But you talk as if you do. If Kester's ghost is alive and well for you then here's where you can best achieve a paranormal reunion."

"You shouldn't joke about such things."

"I'm not joking. I'm all for recalling Kester. I want you to compare the two of us and realize that I'm the better man."

She said nothing. That was when I realized how confused she was. As I started to hope again she put her hand impulsively to her throat and the next moment I saw Anna's silver locket glinting between her fingers.

"Come on," I said, "Let's go downstairs and meet him."

"Shut up. You're frightening me."

"A modern girl like you with a high I.Q.? Don't make me laugh!"

"Haven't you ever felt frightened when threatened with something that can't be rationally explained?"

Now it was my turn to fall silent. We descended the back stairs.

"Okay," I said as we reached the floor below. "We'll rule out a paranormal reunion. Let's just think of him and remember." And I led the way to the bedroom which by tradition had always belonged to the master of the house.

At first I thought she wasn't going to follow me but she did. She moved with extreme reluctance, as if driven by a compulsion she recognized but couldn't master. The furniture in the room was under dust sheets. The shutters were fastened. In the twilight the brass of the bedstead gleamed dully through the layers of tarnish.

Turning to face her I found she had stopped halfway across the room and when I moved back to join her she seemed lost in some memory that put me far beyond her reach. I touched her arm but she failed to respond. She was as lifeless as stone.

"Gwyneth.... Life's for living, not for mourning. He's dead. I'm alive. Live in the present, not the past."

She slowly looked up at me. "But that's what I want," she said. "I want to live again in the past." Then she cried out: "Oh Hal, take me back! Take me back, take me back, take me back—"

And then we saw the road to Oxmoon, the lost Oxmoon of our childhood, and our magician was raising his wand once more in that fairy-tale palace of our dreams.

My mouth closed on hers.

Then shoving all romantic thoughts aside I unzipped my jeans, pulled her down on the bed and embraced the rock-bottom realism of requited lust.

VIII

We never paused to remove the sheet but lay naked amidst the layers of dust. I kissed her and kissed her. The bloody locket got in the way so I wrenched it out of sight around her neck until it was lost in a mass of tangled hair. I was out of practice but it didn't seem to matter. Of all the sports sex is the only one in which the unpracticed can travel a long way on sheer desire alone. I had long since decided that one couldn't seriously describe sex as more than a pleasant pastime but I had always conceded that among pastimes it was unique.

This experience was certainly unique. And suddenly I realized that sex was capable of being rather more than just a pleasant pastime. Though physically experienced I had apparently remained an emotional virgin and now I was losing my virginity. I was conscious of a raging possessiveness. I felt I wanted to make love to her every night for the rest of my life and kill any man who tried to stand in my way. Obviously I was mad. Then I remembered that love was often defined as madness. I felt dimly horrified but was too overcome by the physical side of my condition to attempt further analysis. Analysis was the pastime of the rational and the cold. I felt like an ice cube that had just been chucked into the fire. There was no way back to the refrigerator. All I could do was dissolve mindlessly in the flames.

"Christ..." I was in such a state I hardly knew what I was doing. I seemed to be on the brink of serving as an illustration for a sex manual's chapter on premature ejaculation, but on the other hand I was in such mental chaos that I was equally afraid of subsiding into impotence as the result of a total failure of nerve. "Christ," I said again.

"It's okay," she said, thinking I was nervous about her virginity, but in fact I'd forgotten it. Now I remembered. Somehow I managed to stop myself saying "Christ!" a third time. That would have been too much.

Suddenly she whispered: "I expect I should keep my mouth shut but I've just got to tell you—"

"Forget it, I don't need flattery."

"—that I'm so happy," she said, and smiled at me through her tears.

That fixed me up. I could see she spoke straight from the heart and the next moment I'd forgotten the sex manuals and overcome my panic. I caressed her. She gave me the response I wanted. I got myself together. I went in.

The glove fitted. It was a glove like no other I had ever worn, a glove that might have been tailor-made for me by some master craftsman. But there was just one thing wrong with it. I knew straightaway it had been worn before.

Everything died. Potency, lust, love, romance—everything. The next thing I knew I was sitting bolt-upright on the edge of the bed and shuddering from head to toe.

"Hal—" She tried to take me in her arms.

"Shut up."

"But what happened?"

"We achieved that paranormal reunion after all! He seduced you, didn't he? When you went to see him at the cottage on that last morning, he didn't just burst into tears, he—"

"No! My God! For Christ's sake, have you gone mad? Of course he didn't, how could he, he wouldn't, it's unthinkable! All right, so I'm not a virgin, but do you honestly think I haven't at least tried to love someone else? Why, I told you about him—I told you about that man I liked so much up at Oxford—his name was Paul, he was reading modern languages, he came from Cheshire, he liked classical music and Lauren Bacall films and he had pictures of Simone de Beauvoir and Albert Camus on the walls of his room, oh God, what can I tell you, how can I make you believe—"

"Forgive me." I leaned forward, elbows on my knees, and covered my face with my hands. After a long time, I said: "I do believe you. Kester would never have done it. Never."

"No. He wanted to, I can see that now, but he never did, I swear it."

I turned to her and said: "I wish he had. Then I know I could get the better of him. But as it is . . ." I got up and began to pull on my clothes. "As it is," I said, "I'll never be able to beat the man who made love to you in your imagination. That's one battle I'm always going to lose."

"But Hal—"

"Sorry, but I don't like coming second. I never did and I never will."

"But surely we can give it a try!"

"No, you'd drive me mad. We'd both wind up in hell."

We dressed in silence. She took longer than I did and I went out onto the landing to wait for her because I couldn't bear to remain in that room. I felt wiped out. My mind was blank. I wanted to grieve but couldn't.

When she joined me she said, "Surely we can at least be friends?"

"Friends?" I said. "How could we ever manage that? Sexual desire has to be dead as a doornail before a man and a woman can be genuinely at peace in a platonic friendship."

"You're just running away because you're so hung up about coming first!"

"No, I'm turning aside because you're so hung up on a dead man! What a disastrous combination of hang-ups—that's a ticket for a bad trip if ever I saw one, and there's no way I'm ever going to take it. I'm not putting myself in competition with a bloody ghost!"

"I thought you didn't believe in ghosts!"

"Ghosts, unshriven souls, psychological hang-ups—they're all the same. They all exist in the mind to put people through hell—they're just different ways," I said, remembering Pam's phrase, "of looking at a given situation."

She started to cry. As usual I had no handkerchief, but when we reached the scullery I tore off a strip of paper towel and handed it to her.

"I do love you," she said when she had finally mastered her tears.

"Not enough."

"My God, what a bastard you are!"

"Shut up! I love you so bloody much more than you'll ever love me!"

"Then why the bloody hell don't you do something about it instead of shying away and making excuses?"

"Because I'm through with self-destructive behavior."

She tried to hit me, and as we struggled with each other in a paroxysm of rage and grief the last light was fading from the evening sky outside. We wound up on my camp bed. That was what she wanted. But naturally I was impotent. That was what I wanted. Afterwards we both knew it was quite over so we were able to achieve a civilized farewell.

I saw her out to her car.

"Bloody men!" said Gwyneth, trying to smile. "Sometimes I feel I hate them all."

"Your God slipped up. She should have created just one sex, women, and arranged for reproduction by cloning."

She somehow managed to laugh. As she opened the car door she said, "Let me know if you find the books."

"When," I said. "Not if."

She drove away. I went back into the scullery, slumped down on the camp bed and wished I could get stoned out of my mind. I was in such pain that I couldn't even remember my Emily Brontë poem. I just lay there in despair in that dark sordid room until at last, well over an hour later, I heard the click-clack of Pam's heels in the cobbled courtyard and knew that once more I had to nerve myself to go on.

IX

"Sorry, Hal," said Pam as I opened the back door. "I can see I'm interrupting some vital meditation, but I thought I must tell you Gwyneth's on the phone again. She says it's urgent."

That jerked me out of my inertia quickly enough, and I followed her across the yard to the mews house. The living room was empty but the faint sound of music from my father's room told me he was still up.

"Hullo?" I said into the receiver.

"Hal, sorry to be a drag but I was just undressing for bed when I realized I'd lost Anna's locket. I've searched the flat and checked the car but it's not there and I think it must be at Oxmoon—probably in the bedroom. Some of the links in the chain were thin, and perhaps when you twisted it round my shoulder—"

"I remember. Okay, don't worry, I'll go and look for it straightaway and call you back."

She gave me her number and then said, "Hal, I do appreciate this—I know I'm making an awful fuss, but you know how much that locket means to me."

"Give me ten minutes," I said and hung up. Turning to Pam I explained what had happened and asked if she had a torch I could borrow.

She had. As she gave it to me she commented, "I don't envy you hunting for a locket in a house the size of Oxmoon."

My mood was so black that I just said to her, "We had sex. She thinks the locket's in the bed. I'm sure you'll be delighted to hear that I've been behaving so normally."

"Well, never mind what I think about your behavior," said Pam. "The important question is What did you think of it?"

Cursing all psychiatrists I walked out on her and slammed the door.

X

He was waiting for me in the dark as soon as I entered the scullery. He was so distressed because of Gwyneth and he wanted to comfort me. Or, to look another way at a given situation, *I* was so distressed because of Gwyneth and *I* thought he should want to comfort me. I turned the beam of the torch around the room but naturally, there was nothing there. Walking steadily through the kitchens I listened to the echo of my footsteps and when I reached the other side of the green baize door I switched off my torch and listened again.

He was still with me. On clicked the torch as I walked down the corridor to the hall. The marble floor glowed in memory of him but although the beam of the torch swept from side to side there was still nothing to see. Then the green baize door bumped shut, making me jump, and as I stood there by the stairs the faint draft from the closing door made the crystals of the chandelier shiver above me in the shadows.

I had not told Gwyneth the entire truth when I had denied my belief in extrasensory perception. I was indeed willing to believe that a sixth sense could exist dimly in a select group of sensitive people, but what I doubted was my own receptivity to the paranormal; an unimaginative man with an obsession for hard facts is hardly a likely candidate for a mystical experience. However by that time I was so revolted by hard facts and so repulsed by the negative realities of the present that I did something I would never normally have done. I made a conscious effort to wipe my mind clean of skepticism so that it resembled a blank slate. Then I turned off my torch again and waited.

Into the silence, by some exceptionally clever trick which defied description, my magician poured his personality and wrote his monogram, no more, on the blank slate I was holding out to him.

He was there.

He was benign. Terror was absent. I felt his loving concern, just like my father's, and I knew that just like my father he was so anxious about me and so eager to help.

I kept my mouth shut. I knew that the moment I started talking to him was the moment I became certifiable; but I felt comforted. As I switched on the torch and began to mount the stairs I thought how intriguing it was that one could project one's emotions so subtly that they bounced back off the memory of someone who was dead. The wonders of the human mind impressed me. I made a note to offer the story later to Pam, complete with rational explanation, as a peace offering for my recent rudeness.

On the upstairs landing I didn't pause again but moved straight to his bedroom. I saw the locket at once. It was glinting in a fold of the dust sheet, and as I straightened my back with that precious memento in my hands I felt him struggling to write again on the clouded slate of my mind.

This time I spoke aloud—not to him but to myself, to shore up my link with reality. I heard myself say in the shadowed room as Oxmoon held its breath: "'No coward soul is mine'"—and at once I knew he was urging me on. "No coward soul is mine..." Had I really said that aloud? Or had he? Had the words been spoken at all? Or had he merely written them soundlessly in my mind?

I cleared my throat as if this would clear my confusion, and slipped the locket into the hip pocket of my jeans. Then I decided that my experiment with ESP had gone far enough. It was time to draw that famous line.

Walking out of the bedroom I crossed the landing and began to clatter down the stairs. I was just pursing my lips to whistle a Hank Williams song when I heard a sound from the library.

I stopped dead. My stomach writhed. My heart beat like a rock drummer ricocheting into top gear. I tried to tell myself I'd imagined the noise but I knew I hadn't. Then I tried to tell myself I'd heard mice, but this was no mild scampering in the wainscoting. I thought one of the candlesticks had been overturned on the library table.

I tiptoed noiselessly down the last stairs and stood holding my breath in the hall. There was definitely someone in the library. Very, very slowly I turned the beam of my torch towards the half-open door.

"Kester?" I called softly.

There was no reply but I felt him pouring his personality into the silence again and suddenly, in a moment that electrified me, I realized that he was in two places at once. I heard another sound in the library but at that exact moment he took my arm and piloted me across the hall until I stood on the library threshold. Then he put my hand firmly on the handle, he helped me fling wide the door and he steadied the beam of my torch.

ESP ended and reality began.

An enormous rat was sitting on top of the library table. He had dislodged the empty inkpot, overturned a candlestick and was busy chewing the leather blotter. As the door banged he looked up at me indignantly and bared a set of vile yellow teeth.

"Oh my God—"

My nerve snapped. The disappointment was unendurable. I was out of my mind with rage and pain, and the next moment I'd gone berserk. I turned to the bay immediately on the right of the door and ripping the books from the shelves I began to hurl them across the room. The rat scuttled away but he didn't escape. I killed him, and long after he was dead I went on throwing the books—all twentieth-century novels—in a fusillade of violence and despair.

Then amidst the jumbled works of Lawrence, Waugh, Snow, Huxley, Greene, Galsworthy, Graves, Bates, Spring and Du Maurier I sank to my knees and faced defeat.

The cover of one of the books had come off and was lying nearby. After a while I found myself staring at it. It was the cover of *The Man of Property* by John Galsworthy. Kester had owned *The Forsyte Saga* in three volumes, but as I had told Gwyneth earlier, I had never read them; Kester had looked askance at Galsworthy and even later it had never occurred to me to question my magician's judgment.

Three volumes by Galsworthy.

The penny dropped.

I gasped. Then I grabbed the book which that cover had concealed in my previous searches of the library and saw engraved on its spine not THE MAN OF PROPERTY by JOHN GALSWORTHY but THE CIRCLE OF TIME by KESTER GODWIN.

XI

Three seconds passed while I wondered whether I was hallucinating. Then all the strength drained from my fingers and I dropped the book. Immediately it hit the floor a letter fell out and as I picked it up I saw that the envelope was inscribed: *For Hal.*

He had written the letter on the eve of his departure for Ireland in 1951.

It took me a while to read it. My eyes were dim, my hands were shaking, I couldn't get my mind to concentrate. It was the shock. I had had too many shocks too recently and it was becoming so hard to whip my battered nerves into line. *My dear Hal...*

The voice from the dead. I couldn't get over it, couldn't cope. I sat there like a zombie on the floor.

Eventually I levered myself into the nearest chair and tried again.

And this time I was more successful.

XII

My dear Hal, I've just had these three novels of mine printed privately but let me hasten to reassure you that I'm not in a terminal stage of vanity. I was merely in such a rage when the manuscripts were returned from the umpteenth publisher in the most disgracefully dog-eared condition that I made up my mind to resort to radical measures of conservation (and to hell with all publishers!). Take no notice of the spare copies in the attics. I had to place a minimum order with the printers and that was the result. Bury the copies with me when I'm dead, if you like, because if you tried to circulate them the family would without doubt expire with embarrassment!

However as I don't intend to sink into the grave just yet let me now explain what I'm up to. I'm putting my affairs in order because I have to leave Oxmoon temporarily and it may be some time before I can get back. In these somewhat fraught circumstances my prime thought is to safeguard my masterpieces in case I'm run over by a bus in Dublin or perhaps die a hero's death on a sinking ferry in the Irish Sea. I don't seriously think your father will have a touch of the Nazis and start burning my books, but I'm afraid our relationship at the moment is at such an all-time low that even the most bizarre behavior can't be ruled out. I've toyed with various schemes (giving a set to Evan, taking a set with me to Ireland), but none of these possibilities puts my mind at rest (Evan's rectory might burn down, the Irish ferry might sink, etc., etc.), and I've been determined, Hal, to devise a foolproof way of passing on my work to you.

I'm now glad to report that inspiration has finally smitten me and I can see the solution. All I have to do is to leave a set of the books on the fiction shelves here

960

in the library. Not only does your father never read novels; he'd never let Oxmoon burn to the ground. Of that I'm fully confident.

A cloak-and-dagger streak in my nature has driven me to take the extra precaution of hiding my huge failures behind the covers of Galsworthy's huge successes (by the way don't bother to look for the Galsworthy novels—I've just donated them, coverless, to the Red Cross), and this ruse ensures that although your father will never find my trilogy you most certainly will. You're bound to want to meet the Forsytes in the end whereas your father till his dying day will probably assume Galsworthy is a market town in Hampshire. I can just see it, can't you? A population of five thousand and rather a fine twelfth-century church. Early-closing day would be on Wednesdays...

But now I must be serious. I have every intention of coming back to see you again, but as there's always the chance that this letter may turn out to be my farewell to you I must now set out my final request.

I absolve you from making any attempt to publish my work, but please could you preserve my trilogy here in the library in case any future member of the family ever wonders how I spent the happiest hours of my life? You may of course read the books yourself but only if you're grown up and only if you wish. But I hope you will wish to try them one day. It seems almost too much to hope that you may enjoy them, but if you do—if you enjoy one single paragraph—then I shan't have written for all these years in vain.

The one advantage of being childless is that one can choose one's children and so avoid the bizarre game of chance in which one passes one's best—or one's worst—genes to one's poor innocent offspring. I can't pass you my genes, good or bad, Hal, but that doesn't matter. All that matters is that I can pass you my work and in the end, despite this interregnum of your father's, I'm going to come back and pass you Oxmoon. Your father has no moral right to transmit your inheritance to you, and I alone can pass on not the legal deeds but the magic of my brilliant house beyond compare.

My writing is insignificant in comparison; in the long run my books are of no more importance than my genes, but look after Oxmoon, Hal. Love it and keep it in memory of me and of those before us, and when the time comes pass it on as I shall pass it on to you. Despite all the volumes written by learned men on the meaning of life the reality is very simple: all things die except life; despite death life gets handed on.

I can't sign myself "your loving father," but you'll know as you read this that I think of you as my much-loved son.

Yours now and always,
Kester.

A long time passed.

I read the letter many, many times with varying degrees of emotion but in the end one sentence stood out from the rest.

I'm going to come back and pass you Oxmoon, he had written, and he had kept his word.

With his books in my arms I said to him, "Rest in peace." And then I set out on the road to redemption.

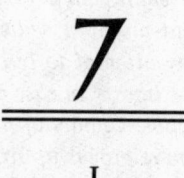

I

THEN THEY all came to Oxmoon, the agents from the National Trust, the experts from the Victoria and Albert Museum, the representatives from Sotheby's. My first task was to seek not only a new valuation of the collection but a new estimate of the endowment required by the Trust before it could accept the house as a gift.

"Ah yes," said the Trust, "the little house in Wales at the end of the road to nowhere—yet right on the tourist beat nowadays, of course! Yes, we must allow for increasing inflation but five hundred thousand pounds should see us through. That's a lot of money but we wouldn't want to skimp on the restoration—we'd want only the best for Oxmoon..."

"...so you see how remarkable it is," said the man from the V&A to his colleagues. "It's just an old country house, nothing exceptional, but it was renovated by Sir Toby James in '39 regardless of cost as a showcase for this extraordinary collection..."

"...and your cousin had no formal training in fine art, did he?" said the expert from Sotheby's. "What a remarkable man he must have been!" And turning to his subordinate he said, "Take a deep breath. I'm going to show you the Picasso in the lavatory."

Then the lawyers came to Oxmoon to discuss how the copyright of Kester's trilogy should be transferred to the Trust. At first they were patronizing towards me. It was hard for them to believe that three much-rejected novels could ever net a vast sum of money, and of course I couldn't tell them that those stories represented Kester's magic wand, restored and renewed. But I silenced their skepticism. I had had my hair cut unfashionably short and for the meeting I wore a new dark suit with my Old Harrovian tie; I had learned long ago how to project a selling image, and I was an old hand at surviving in circumstances in which the survival rate was low.

Later one of the lawyers said kindly to me, "We do wish you luck in New York—we only hope you're not disappointed." But I just answered, "I'm going to take American by storm."

My faith never wavered. Doubt and despair belonged to the past and now, as in my dream, the earth was moving, the skies were rolling back and all I had to do to save ruined Oxmoon was to wave the magic wand.

II

The novels made over two million dollars in the end. They're still selling. Kester wrote about people and since human nature doesn't change his observations hadn't dated. He also wrote a readable story. When I found myself turning the pages without trouble I was surprised as well as relieved; I'd assumed his rejections had been the result of a lack of technical competence, but Kester had written for over twenty years and his technique had been accomplished. Later I realized that he had probably been rejected because his uncompromising view of life had jarred a postwar readership which had wanted only to escape from the harsher of life's realities. To my astonishment I found that Kester, outwardly an incurable romantic, had as a writer been obsessed with presenting his characters without regard to romantic convention. It was as if in his private life he had indulged a craving for romance which his professional life refused to permit. In fact as I read the books it occurred to me that he must have suffered some profound disillusionment in the past which while not destroying his passion for the way the world should have been had made it impossible for him not to explore the way the world really was.

For the first time I sensed the tension in his personality which had driven him to persist with writing beyond the introverted years of adolescence. It was his way of trying to make sense of the world without losing faith in it. For me, a man of the Nineteen Sixties, he had a message which declared itself at once; he was urging that no matter how sordid the world one should keep one's faith because without faith one becomes as sordid as the world one lives in. The faith was in the value of idealism. A romantic faith? No, realistic. It was a survival kit. Without such a creed one could only long to get permanently stoned in order to escape the ordeal of modern life.

I thought Kester's books deserved to sell, and sell they did, but I doubt if they would have sold on such a grand scale if I hadn't marketed them with a fanaticism which he in his modesty could never have matched. I was helped by the fact that I had a salable product but in the end the victory was mine as well as Kester's. I was one of the pioneers of the American belief that novels could be marketed like soap, and I conducted one of the biggest selling campaigns the publishing world had seen. I invaded the radio stations, I laid waste the television networks, I blazed like a conqueror across America, I beat that country at its own game. Projecting my selling image, crushing audience after audience beneath the power of my will, I hypnotized, I electrified and I seduced my way from coast to coast. A cold calculating performance? Certainly. But sentimentality has never been one of my strong points. I had a job to do and it was more than a job. It was a mission.

At the end of it all they said I should rest but that was out of the question. Turning down the free holidays I was offered, I grabbed a plane to London and began my conquest of Britain.

III

Years later people said to me, "Once you found the books no doubt success was a foregone conclusion," but magic can't operate without a magician, and being a magician can beat a man to his knees. Few people realized how difficult my life became and how hard I had to struggle to endure it. People see only the glamour of success and not the isolated drudgery beneath. I loathed the life on the road, and in the fear that I might crack beneath the increasing pressures I continued to abstain from drink and drugs; that decision ensured my survival but it made life tougher and later when I was wooing Middle America and deciding that no breath of scandal should mar the clean-cut image I was projecting my life became tougher still. Was I a hypocrite? Of course. My so-called "good life" sprang from no deep moral conviction, only from a desire to win. I was a fanatic, and as with all fanatics the end justified the means.

I had to prove my fanaticism at the start of my American visit when my cousin Geoffrey, who was by this time editor-in-chief of a major publishing house, told me Kester's work was junk which he'd never touch.

This was a major setback. Geoffrey was my trump card. A major portion of my optimism had been based on my assumption that he would help me.

"Geoffrey, you just can't do this."

"Look, buster, I've got my living to earn. I can't take this rubbish on just for sentimental family reasons! What do I care about Oxmoon anyway? What's that old dump to me?"

"Oxmoon's a symbol. It's got a message for everyone."

"Not for me it hasn't! What did I ever get out of Oxmoon? Fucking all! I was a misfit in that family, I felt like a man from Mars, my American grandfather was the only guy I could ever identify with—"

"I'm not interested in your identity crisis, I'm interested in your professional judgment. How can you sit there and tell me seriously that these books are unreadable?"

"Family sagas went out with Galsworthy. Forget it. Give me a good Jewish novel any day."

"But Geoffrey—"

"Sorry. Subject closed. Excuse me, please, I have to go to a meeting."

I leaned forward with my hands on his desk and said, "I never want to speak to you again."

"You think I'm going to be beating a path to any Godwin door?"

He walked away. In the outer office his British secretary, smart status symbol of every successful New York executive, regarded me from behind a curtain of blond hair. "Hey!"

I stopped.

She smiled at me conspiratorially. "They were fabulous. I read every word."

I classified the image required: sexual charm with a touch of class. I projected that image. I glided over to her desk. "Did you tell him?"

"Uh-huh. But he's hung up. Can't bear family sagas, says wasn't it enough that he had to spend all his early life living in one."

I smiled at her. It was my special smile, the one I reserved only for the most vital occasions. "So where do I go from here?"

"My apartment? After work?"

Those were the days before I started peddling my clean-living image to Middle America.

The next day she gave me the address of one of New York's leading literary agents, and after typing a glowing letter of introduction on her employer's letterhead, she signed it on behalf of my unforgiven cousin, that traitor Geoffrey Godwin.

IV

"I'll take them on," said the agent, "and we'll see how the first one goes. I think family sagas could be coming back. The dialogue creaks a bit now and then but don't worry, there's nothing a good editor can't fix...."

I didn't worry. I was too busy savoring my victory. In a town where it was hard to be published without an agent and hard to acquire an agent without having been published I had eliminated yet another obstacle on the long painful road to success.

Another editor-in-chief, a rival of Geoffrey's, bought all three books after reading them over a weekend. Later the magazine *McCall's* published an excerpt from the first one and the Literary Guild book club made it its Main Selection for the month of publication. At that time publication was still several months away but already the financial omens were glowing with promise and when I returned to New York for the publicity tour Geoffrey was the first to phone my hotel to welcome me back to town.

"Hal, I just couldn't be more pleased—"

"Keep your pleasure," I said. "You'll need it when everyone in New York dines out on the story of how you turned down Kester Godwin." And I hung up on him without waiting for his reply.

V

And they all came to Oxmoon, the builders and the stonemasons, the carpenters, plumbers and electricians, the sewing experts who were to restore the fabrics, the metalwork craftsmen who were to repair the wrought-iron gates. The roof was replaced, the chimneys were rebuilt, the leaning outside wall of the ballroom was shored up and underpinned. After the dry rot had been removed the timbers were replaced and after the wet rot had been conquered the damp course was introduced. Rewired and replumbed, Oxmoon resembled a hospital patient, wheeled from the operating theater to the intensive-care unit where it could be nursed devotedly back to life.

My father couldn't bear the invasion of people and the constant noise of the restoration work so he retreated to a rented house on the outskirts of Swansea. Pam was pleased; she thought she might be able to coax him into group therapy once he was so much nearer the city but he stubbornly resisted, never going out, never seeing anyone, his health varying from poor to indifferent. Like many disturbed people he often gave such an impression of normality that it was hard to remember how ill he was. I often had trouble connecting the apparently rational man, who could conduct sensible conversations, with the man who was afraid to go out and had such a horror of the outside world that he refused to answer the front door. As time went on I became steadily more distressed that he couldn't talk of Oxmoon. Pam said he didn't dare believe in its resurrection for fear some disaster might occur at the last moment, but the more I tried to calm his irrational fears by talking of new alarm systems and caretakers, the more he seemed determined to believe in an inevitable catastrophe.

Yet I found it impossible to say nothing of Oxmoon's progress.

"Father, all the gardeners came today, the horticultural experts, the landscape architects, the laborers—they've all come to Oxmoon now. They're going to lay out the old pleasure garden just as it was in the eighteenth century and the orangerie's going to be rebuilt—"

"I don't want to think of it."

"But for God's sake, why not?"

"It's too painful."

"Why is it painful?"

"Because it can't help me. You think that by redeeming Oxmoon you'll redeem me but you won't. I'm beyond that sort of fairy tale."

"Well, if you want to be beyond it I can't stop you," I said exasperated, "but you've bloody well suffered and you've bloody well repented so why shouldn't you bloody well be redeemed?"

"Redemption's just a word and as I'm not a Christian it means nothing to me. If restoring Oxmoon helps you to live with what Kester and I did, then I'm glad for your sake but don't expect it to help me."

"People were talking about the cycle of birth, life, death and resurrection long before Christ hit the scene," I said, playing down the religious angle to counter his argument, but of course I came to Christianity in the end. I write "of course" because it must have seemed inevitable to the people who kept hearing me speak of redemption, but it took me some time before I realized that I was in the grip of an experience which was intractable to rational analysis. I was living not on reason but on faith. No rational man would have believed that I could save Oxmoon. But I'd done it, and in doing so I had passed through some gateway of the mind into another way of looking, as Pam would have put it, at a given situation.

No doubt reformed rakes are particularly prone to religious conversion. Evan started talking to me of Donne and Sian mentioned the poet Rochester and Humphrey said religion, any religion, was the big new trend nowadays and look at the Beatles in India.

"Do be careful, Hal," said Pam, who spent much time worrying in case my mysticism led me into murky psychiatric waters. "You've got exactly the right temperament to be a religious fanatic."

"I'll let you know when I order a hair shirt," I said, but in fact I wasn't fanatical about Christianity. I merely found it more intellectually satisfying than the occult, more positive than Buddhism, more British than Islam and less depressing than psychiatry.

"Maybe you'll wind up in a monastery," said my father gloomily, but I knew there was no possibility that I might become a monk. My feelings for Caitlin made perpetual chastity unthinkable.

I turned to Caitlin in the end, of course, and again I write "of course" because it must have seemed inevitable to those who knew me well that I would return to Caitlin just as time after time I returned to Oxmoon: to rest, to recuperate and to spend a few precious hours with my true self before continuing my crusade behind a variety of selling images. For a long time I didn't see her, but the ordeal on the Devil's Bridge linked her with me in my memory, and often, particularly when I was alone in some hotel room, I would remember her gentleness when she had thought I was in the grip of vertigo, her sensitivity in never pestering me for information and her intelligence which had told her when to stay silent as well as when to ask the right questions. As I battered my way across America her memory became increasingly precious to me until she became a symbol of someone unspoiled and of a normal world to which I prayed I might one day return.

She took her secretarial course and the diploma in farm management. We corresponded. Eventually we were reunited. One day at Rhossili beach she tried to teach me Welsh and as she spoke in that language I couldn't understand I knew that she was telling me she loved me.

"Say that in English, Cait!"

"The cat sat on the mat."

"Now teach me to say that in Welsh!"

She taught me. I said it. She blushed. We embraced. Finally I said, "I could make all manner of fine speeches but I'm too cynical about fine speeches to sound sincere."

"I don't want fine speeches."

"I'm really a very simple man—"

"That sounds like the beginning of a fine speech."

"—so all I shall say is: Will you?"

"That's too simple. In this day and age, that sort of question can mean almost anything."

After we'd picked the date for the wedding she said, "Did it take you a long time to get over Gwyneth?"

"Yes, but I'm at peace with the past now."

"She was a symbol of the past, wasn't she?"

"Yes. The past created the illusion that we were suited to each other but of course she was much too independent for me. Marriage with her would have been a disaster."

"Does that mean you expect me to be a robot with no mind of my own?"

"Certainly not. Marriage isn't about either independence or dependence—it's about interdependence. I'm not afraid of a woman who wants to be a person in her own right but Gwyneth's kind of person wasn't my kind of woman."

"Thank God."

"Thank God, yes—at least that's one self-destructive future I've managed to sidestep," I said, and once more took her in my arms.

VI

And they all came to Oxmoon, magic fabled Oxmoon, they all came to see the house that was rising from the grave.

The BBC arrived to make a television documentary, and I was interviewed on the newly mown lawn of the pleasure garden as the stonemasons worked on the repair of the terrace and the painters paused on their scaffolding with the brushes in their hands. Publicity has its disadvantages. There were always tourists at the gates now and the National Trust was finding it an increasingly strenuous task to keep the hordes of well-wishers at bay. Sometimes on a Sunday afternoon it seemed that all Gower cruised down the road to Penhale for a glimpse of the miracle, and as the waiting world hovered at its bedside Oxmoon emerged from the intensive-care unit into the recovery ward on its long journey back to health from the illness which everyone had believed to be terminal.

Then one day I came home to Gower and found the fairy-tale palace of Kester's dreams, the outer walls washed, the paint gleaming, the new roof of Welsh slate shining in the sun. The shutters were still closed for conservation purposes; the fabrics needed the minimum dose of light, but inside the house the main rooms dazzled the eye, the upholstery repaired, the furniture polished, the wallpapers cleaned, the carpets restored, every item of the collection glowing and cared for, and in the hall the cleaners were washing every crystal of Kester's famous "celestial" chandelier. Beyond the house the gardens were trim and tended again. The orangerie had been reconstructed, and in the renovated stable block the broken-down old carriages, relics of another age, had been painted and repaired for display to the public.

Even the kitchens had been transformed. The main kitchen had been restored to its original Georgian design, but the scullery, the stillroom, the laundry rooms, the larders and the pantries had been converted into a restaurant and shop. An army of cleaning ladies was cleaning up after the builders. Mops, pails and scrubbing brushes seemed to be ceaselessly on the move.

"The exterminator's paid his last call," said the land agent of the Trust. "All the rats have gone." And his colleague said, "We're almost home."

I drove straight to my father's house in Swansea.

"If you'd only come and see it, Father—you've never seen anything like it—you couldn't imagine such a resurrection!"

"I can't travel. I can't go out."

"But you must! Please! Be with me on the day of the opening!"

"I can't."

"Be patient, Hal," said Pam afterwards in private. "You're only upsetting him by haranguing him like this."

"But how can he refuse to be there at the opening? I know the Trust owns the place now but he's still the master of the house!"

"No, Hal. He was never the real master, was he? Kester passed it on to you, and this triumph is yours and yours alone."

VII

And so the great day dawned and *everyone* came to Oxmoon—or so it seemed—all Wales, all England, all the world made the pilgrimage from Swansea into Gower to that "little house on the road to nowhere." The celebrities came from London with the BBC and ITV news crews; the journalists and photographers swarmed at my heels; the tourists, the sight-seers and the well-wishers streamed through the gates and among them were the members of my family, all of them except Geoffrey whom I'd ordered to stay away. My aunt Francesca came from Boston, my unknown cousin Erika emerged from Germany, Sian came with her viscount from a holiday at Juan-les-Pins, Aunt Marian breezed along saying everything was too divine, Richard arrived in a psychedelic helicopter with a crowd of Beautiful People, Gerry came with his latest sexy mistress, Lance turned up with his wife and two little girls, Evan appeared in his clerical collar and my three brothers, trying not to look jealous, all presented themselves to me to pay their respects.

Haunted by the memory of Pam's story of sibling rivalry I made a great effort to be friendly. Charles talked rubbish about Kester's collection but I made no attempt to contradict him; Jack made idiotic remarks about the media coverage but I merely smiled kindly; Humphrey said with deceptive cheerfulness: "I suppose you must feel as if you're God, old chap—issued any trendy commandments lately?" but I reminded myself he was probably aggrieved that he had been usurped as The Favorite. I shook his hand and patted him on the back and told him how glad I was to see him, but although he returned my smile I could tell he was skeptical. My brothers were going to demand hard work on my part in the future, but I refused to regard our relationship with pessimism. If I could conquer America I could conquer my siblings; all that the conquest required was the right attitude of mind.

At that moment I was diverted from my family, for Royalty had come to Oxmoon to declare the house open to the public. Royalty was very gracious, saying all the right things, but I think Royalty was genuinely impressed by Oxmoon, so many centuries of Anglo-Welsh history encapsulated in that little house on the road to nowhere.

"...and so," said Royalty at last, addressing the television cameras, the celebrities, the Beautiful People, the sight-seers, the tourists, the natives of Gower and all the other people within range of his microphone, "it gives me the greatest pleasure..."

Oxmoon was declared open.

Royalty shook my hand and said, "Well done!"

My loyal friends at the National Trust followed suit, and after them came the rest of the world, shaking my hand until it was swollen at the joints.

"So what are you going to do now, Hal?" shouted NBC-TV's news correspondent, thrusting a microphone under my nose.

"Get married and live happily ever after."

Everyone cheered.

"And after that?"

"I'm going to write a rock opera called *The Saving of Oxmoon*," I said to shut them up, but for the first time I wondered if I might go into the Church.

VIII

Oxmoon was opened on a Saturday, and to allow both Caitlin and me time to recover the wedding had been arranged for the following weekend. The day after the opening we went to church and lunched at the farm with a crowd of Llewellyns, but eventually, longing for seclusion and impatient with the never-ending questions about our wedding plans, we withdrew to my father's house in Swansea.

"How are you, Hal?" said Pam who now lived in terror that I might crash into depression after the all-time emotional high of seeing my dream come true, but before I could reassure her my father came out of the living room with the Sunday paper in his hands.

"Have you seen the pictures of Oxmoon?"

"Uh-huh." I'd decided to be reticent on the subject in his presence so a neutral comment was all I was prepared to offer in response to his question.

But Caitlin said to him, "It's such a very lovely place—and so quiet and peaceful once the crowds have gone."

"It looks well," said my father. "Kester would have been pleased." He disappeared again into the living room.

We all looked at one another. Pam whispered to me: "Don't press him. Let him work his way round the problem by himself."

"Are you saying he might—"

"Why are you all whispering in the hall?" shouted my father furiously.

"We're not sure how far you want to discuss Oxmoon, darling," said Pam, leading the way into the living room. "It's perfectly natural that Hal should want to know."

"I can't talk about it."

"Okay." Pam turned back to us. "Do you two want to stay for supper? I've got a large shepherd's pie I can heat up."

Before we could reply my father said, "When does Oxmoon close its gates to the public?"

"Six."

We all looked at the clock above the fireplace. The time was quarter to seven.

"I'm not hungry," said my father.

"Never mind," said Pam. "The pie will keep. We don't have to eat it now."

"Are you two hungry?" said my father.

Caitlin and I denied hunger.

My father turned to Pam. "I want to get dressed. I'm tired of this bloody dressing gown."

"Fine," said Pam. "I'll find a clean shirt for you."

They disappeared. We sat down and waited. He took a long time to dress and when he came back we saw why. He was wearing his best suit, which smelled faintly of mothballs. A venerable silk tie glowed in faded splendor against his snow-white shirt. Pam had polished his shoes. He had trimmed his beard. He looked neat, ordered—but not composed. He was in such a state that I saw at once that speech was beyond him.

"You go on ahead of us," said Pam to me. "Your father's taken some medication and it needs time to work."

I drove Caitlin back to Oxmoon and while we waited I began to pray.

IX

So in the end we all came home to Oxmoon, resurrected Oxmoon, which belonged now to neither Kester nor my father nor me but to everyone who chose to turn to the symbol which the National Trust had intervened to preserve. The Sunday crowds had long since departed by the time Caitlin and I reached the stable yard, and after a word with the caretaker we savored the pleasure of having the place to ourselves.

Oxmoon basked in the summer-evening light, ravishing Oxmoon, still a fairy tale and perhaps in the late twentieth century more of a fairy tale than even Kester in his most romantic dreams could have imagined. Caitlin and I sat down to wait on the front steps and eventually Pam's mini brought my father home.

His pallor had a grayish tinge but he was better as soon as he stepped indoors. He sat down for a moment to recover from the ordeal of the journey and as we allowed him the time he needed Pam and I chatted idly about the attendance figures.

Finally he said, "I'm ready now. Let's have the guided tour," so I took him through the main rooms slowly while Pam and Caitlin followed at a distance. I noticed that Pam always made the right casual comment whenever the silence threatened to become too deep.

"Very nice," said my father awkwardly at last, but he managed to add in a more natural tone of voice: "Not what I expected."

I was surprised. "What did you expect?"

"Kester's 1939 renovations. But the Trust have gone beyond that, haven't they? Much of this is new."

"It's new yet it's old. Robert Godwin the Renovator would have recognized this as his Oxmoon."

"That's right. Eighteenth-century Robert Godwin. No one we ever knew. All quite past."

"And all quite present."

"It's like a miracle," said my father as we recrossed the hall on our way to the ballroom. "No, I'm sorry—what a stupid thing to say. It's not like a miracle, it *is* a miracle."

I opened the double doors into the ballroom and saw myself in the long mirrors, a tall lean figure in my jeans and my OXMOON LIVES! T-shirt, a man of the Nineteen Seventies, an anachronism in that room which was so very symbolic of the past. But my father in his formal dark suit looked less out of place. He stood silent, spellbound, gazing up at the chandeliers.

Pam tapped in, smart and conventional in her blue linen suit. Caitlin followed, less precise in her movements, dreamier. She was wearing flower-patterned slacks and a white blouse.

"They've been clever with this room, haven't they?" said Pam. "They haven't meddled too much. My God, look at those chandeliers! I wonder how long it took to clean them?"

My father's eyes shone with tears. He was beyond speech again; but as I watched he drifted like a man in a dream towards the piano at the end of the room.

Pam opened her mouth to make another of her casual remarks but nothing happened. It was the first time I had ever seen her at a loss for words. She seemed to be holding her breath as she watched my father, and as Caitlin halted at my side I knew we were both holding our breath too.

My father sat down at the piano, opened the lid and stared at the keys. Pam at once moved to the side of the room and pretended to examine one of the curtains, but Caitlin and I remained transfixed in the middle of the floor.

My father said suddenly: "I can hear." He rubbed his eyes with the back of his hand. "I can hear!" he called dazed. "I can hear all the notes again, every one of them. . . ." And he raised his shaking hands above the keyboard.

Pam was still unable to speak but I said laughing to Caitlin, "Shall we dance?" and Caitlin, her eyes shining, said, "Why not!"

The piano began to play but in my mind I heard the violins of the nineteenth century and saw the final gap closing in the great circle of time. Caitlin's hand touched my shoulder, my arm slipped around her waist and then we danced at last beneath the chandeliers at Oxmoon as the orchestra played "The Blue Danube."

Author's Note

The Wheel of Fortune is a re-creation in a modern dimension of a true story in which the following people played leading parts:

EDWARD OF WOODSTOCK (1330–1376), known to history as The Black Prince;

His wife and cousin, JOAN OF KENT, whom he called Jeanette;

His brother JOHN OF GAUNT;

His younger son, RICHARD OF BORDEAUX, later King Richard II;

John of Gaunt's legitimate son HENRY OF BOLINGBROKE, later King Henry IV, and

Henry of Bolingbroke's eldest son, later KING HENRY V, who restored England to her former military glory and completed the full circle of the Plantagenet family's wheel of fortune.

While paying tribute to the National Trust, which saved the Yorkes' home of Erddig in North Wales during the 1970s, I should nevertheless make it clear that Oxmoon is not Erddig—or indeed any other house in the British Isles. The Gower Peninsula does exist in South Wales beyond Swansea and any visitor can cross the Shipway to the Worm's Head, but there is no parish of Penhale and no Oxmoon in the valley between Cefn Bryn, Harding's Down and Rhossili Bay.